The Tami Hoag Omnibus

The Tami Hoag Omnibus

MAGIC
LUCKY'S LADY
CRY WOLF

TAMI HOAG

ORION

First published in Great Britain in 2001 by
Orion
An imprint of Orion Books Ltd
Orion House, 5 Upper St Martin's Lane, London WC2H 9EA

A CIP catalogue record for this book is available
from the British Library

Typeset by Deltatype Ltd, Birkenhead, Merseyside

Printed and bound in Great Britain by
Clays Ltd, St Ives plc

Contents

MAGIC   1

LUCKY'S LADY   173

CRY WOLF   399

MAGIC

Prologue

University of Notre Dame, South Bend, Indiana, spring 1977

'Okay, everybody, this is it – the final portrait of the Fearsome Foursome. Make sure your caps are on straight, ladies. I'm setting the timer now.' Bryan Hennessy hunched over the 35-millimeter camera, fussing with buttons, pausing once to push his glasses up on his straight nose.

Decked out in caps and gowns, three women stood on the damp grass near the blue expanse of St. Mary's Lake. The clean, cool air was sweet with the scents of spring flowers, new leaves, and freshly cut grass. Bird song mingled with Alice Cooper's 'School's Out' blasting from a boom box in a distant dorm.

Peering through the viewfinder, Bryan focused on his three best friends: Faith Kincaid, Alaina Montgomery, and Jayne Jordan.

It didn't seem the least bit odd to him that his three best friends were women. He happened to like women. These three were like sisters to him, surrogates for the siblings he had left behind in Chicago. He valued their company, their views, their support. He cherished their friendship. He missed them like hell and they hadn't even parted company yet. Just the idea of it made his heart ache.

He adjusted the camera lens, blurring the images before him then bringing them back into focus, willing his memory to hold their likenesses with the same sharp clarity.

Faith Kincaid, her dark eyes bright with innocence and unshed tears, adjusted the shoulders of her gown and checked her cap, poking back long spirals of burnished gold hair. With a little sigh she settled herself and her sunny smile in place, doing her best to look brave and optimistic.

Bryan had always thought of her as their Madonna figure – sweet, serene, kind, and forgiving. It frightened him a little to think of Faith going out into the real world. She was too trusting. Who was going to look out for her? Who was going to steer her clear of men who would take advantage of her innate innocence?

That was the last worry he had about Alaina, who stood to Faith's right. Tall, cool, and poised, Alaina didn't trust anybody. Bryan doubted there were many men who wouldn't back off from her 'ice princess'

3

look. But were there any who would be brave enough to look past those barriers of hers to find the lonely woman on the other side?

She seemed tense now, and Bryan realized she was dreading what was to come – the ceremony that would aggrandize their parting, the phony celebration afterward with her social butterfly mother and the latest in a string of stepfathers. Alaina might have been cynical and as practical as the short style of her dark chestnut hair, but Bryan knew that beneath the brusque exterior lay a tender heart that had adopted the other three members of their group as the only real family she had ever known. He could already feel the sharp ache of loneliness echoing inside her.

At the other end of the line stood petite Jayne Jordan, her pixie's face dominated by wide black eyes and a cloud of wild auburn hair. Jayne was the observer, taking in every detail of the scene around her and committing it to memory. She was their resident flake, a student of all things mystical. She was his soulmate in a lot of ways. Jayne understood about magic and mystery. But who would understand Jayne?

These were Bryan's three best friends in the world. They had banded together in their freshman year. Four people with nothing in common but a class in medieval sociology. Over the four years that followed, they had seen one another through finals and failures, triumphs and tragedies, and doomed romances. They were friends in the truest, deepest sense of the word.

Depression threatened to smother him like a wet woolen blanket. Bryan did his best to ignore it. He set the camera's timer and hustled around to stand behind his friends, his cap askew. Had he been able to be in two places at once, standing in line and behind the camera, he could have objectively viewed himself. He was tall and athletic with a strong, honest face, and tawny hair that tended to be a bit shaggy because he tended to forget little details like barber appointments. The girls always had to remind him about things like that – haircuts and dates and eating meals. What was he going to do without them?

'Okay. Everybody smile,' he ordered, his voice a little huskier than usual. 'It's going to go off any second now. Any second.'

They all grinned engagingly and held their collective breath.

The camera suddenly tilted downward on its tripod, pointing its lens at one of the white geese that wandered freely around St. Mary's Lake. The shutter clicked and the motor advanced the film. The goose honked an outraged protest and waddled away.

'I hope that's not an omen,' Jayne said, frowning as she nibbled at her thumbnail.

'It's a loose screw,' Bryan announced, digging a dime out of his pants pocket to repair the tripod with.

'In Jayne or the camera?' Alaina queried, her cool blue eyes sparkling with teasing mischief.

Jayne made a face at her. 'Very funny, Alaina.'

4

'I think it's a sign that Bryan needs a new tripod,' said Faith.

'That's not what Jessica Porter says,' Alaina remarked slyly.

Bryan felt a blush creep up to the roots of his hair as the girls giggled. While he had never been romantically involved with any of them, he had an active social life, something the girls teased him about unmercifully.

Not that he was a masochist, but he was going to miss that. The girls helped him keep things in perspective. He tended to fall in love at the drop of a hat. Romances came and went in his life, flaring brightly and burning out like shooting stars, but Jayne and Faith and Alaina were always there to sympathize or console . . . or make a lewd remark.

'If you want a sign, look behind you,' he said as he fussed unnecessarily with the aperture setting on the camera.

The girls turned together and immediately caught sight of the rainbow that arched gracefully across the morning sky above the golden dome of the administration building.

'Oh, how beautiful,' Faith said with a sigh.

'Symbolic,' Jayne whispered.

'It's the diffusion of light through raindrops,' Alaina said flatly, crossing her arms in front of her.

Bryan looked up from fiddling with the camera to frown at her, his strong jaw jutting forward aggressively. 'Rainbows have lots of magic in them,' he said, dead serious. 'Ask any leprechaun. It'd do you some good to believe in magic, Alaina.'

Alaina's lush mouth turned down at the corners. 'Take the picture, Hennessy.'

Bryan ignored her, his wise, warm blue eyes taking on a dreamy quality as he gazed up at the soft stripes of color that painted the sky. 'We'll be chasing our own rainbows after today. I wonder where they'll lead us.'

They each recited the stock answers they'd been giving faculty, friends, and family for months. Jayne was leaving to seek fame and fortune in Hollywood as a writer and director. Faith was heading to a managerial position in a business office in Cincinnati. Alaina was staying on at Notre Dame to attend law school. Bryan had been accepted into the graduate program of parapsychology at Purdue.

'That's where our brains are taking us,' he said, pulling his cap off to comb a hand back through his hair as he always did when he went into one of his 'deep thinking modes.' 'I wonder where our hearts will take us.'

He knew three of the answers to that question. He was the confidant the girls entrusted with their secrets. He was the only person on earth who knew Alaina's deepest wish was for emotional security. He knew Faith longed for a simple life with a husband and children. Jayne's quest was for understanding and acceptance.

'That's the question we should all be asking ourselves,' Jayne said, wagging a slender finger at her friends. 'Are we in pursuit of our true bliss, or are we merely following a course charted by the expectations of others?'

'Do we have to get philosophical?' Alaina groaned, rubbing two fingers to each throbbing temple. 'I haven't had my mandatory ten cups of coffee yet this morning.'

'Life is philosophy, honey,' Jayne explained patiently, her voice a slow Kentucky drawl that hadn't altered one iota during the four years she'd spent in northern Indiana. The expression on her delicately sculpted features was almost comically earnest. 'That's a cosmic reality.'

Alaina blinked. Finally she said, 'We don't have to worry about you. You'll fit right in in California.'

Jayne smiled. 'Why, thank you.'

Faith chuckled. 'Give up, Alaina. You can't win.'

Alaina winced and held her hands up as if to ward off the words. 'Don't say that. I *abhor* losing.'

'Anastasia,' Bryan declared loudly. He gave a decisive nod that set the tassel on his cap dancing. The word would have seemed straight out of left field to anyone who didn't know Bryan Hennessy and the workings of his unconventional mind, but he knew his compatriots would understand immediately.

Anastasia was the small town on California's rugged northern coast where the four of them had spent spring break. While watching the surf crash against the rocky shore, they had made fantasy plans to move there and pursue idealistic existences. Jayne's dream had been to have her own farm. An inn with a view of the ocean had been Faith's wish. They had somehow gotten Alaina to admit to a secret desire to paint. Bryan had wanted to play the role of local mad scientist.

'That's right,' Faith said with a misty smile. 'We'd all move to Anastasia.'

'And live happily ever after.' Alaina's tone lacked the sarcasm she had no doubt intended. She sounded wistful instead.

'Even if we never end up there. It's a nice dream,' Jayne said softly.

A nice dream. Something to hang on to, like their memories of Notre Dame and one another. Warm, golden images they could hold in a secret place in their hearts to be taken out from time to time when they were feeling lonely or blue.

Bryan set the timer on the camera once again, then jogged around to stand behind Faith. 'Who knows?' he murmured, almost to himself. 'Life is full of crossroads. You can never tell where a path might lead.'

And the camera buzzed and clicked, capturing the Fearsome Foursome – wishful smiles canting their mouths, dreams of the future and tears of parting shining in their eyes as a rainbow arched in the sky behind them – on film for all time.

1

Anastasia, California,
the present

'Great big head. Eyes of red. Don't know how long he's been dead. Has anybody seen my ghoul?' Bryan sang softly in his pleasant tenor voice as he worked. He paused as he adjusted the angle of the still camera and smiled broadly into the wide-angle lens, as if posing for a self-portrait. Then he pushed his old-fashioned gold-rimmed spectacles up on his nose, moved on to the next piece of equipment, and continued on with his song.

Ghosts. His life was filled with them. He searched for them and lived with them. Sometimes he wished he were one, he thought darkly, his enforced good mood slipping. The whole point of going back to work was to get away from depression. He was finding that returning to his former upbeat, optimistic self was as tough a job as any manual labor he'd ever done. Squaring his shoulders with determination, he double-checked his photographic equipment, the video camera on its mount above the carved oak door, the light stands set in their strategic positions around the wide foyer. He checked the still camera last.

Finally satisfied that everything was in place and in working order, he flipped off the hall light, turned, and trudged up the first short flight of stairs, his usually lithe step somewhat weary. He had been raised an athlete in a family of athletes. His brother J. J. was a former professional quarterback, his sister Marie was a world-class figure skater. Bryan himself was no slouch on a tennis court, but these days he felt every day of his thirty-six years, and then some.

With his back pressed to the mildewing wallpaper he slid down to sit on the dusty hardwood floor of the landing. He settled back into the shadows, not caring that the floor was cold or that a draft wafted down the stairwell. Those kinds of discomforts were not unusual in his line of work. He'd crouched in the damp, cramped holds of ships, waiting. He'd spent night after night in castles built long before the invention of central heat, waiting. A run-down Victorian mansion like this one was actually fairly cozy by comparison. Besides, it had been a long time since he'd paid any attention to physical discomfort. It was probably a victory of sorts that he had even noticed the draft. The girls would be proud of him.

It was funny how they had ended up there after all. The Fearsome Foursome had disbanded to chase four different rainbows, and still they had ended up in Anastasia, the place they had dreamed of and fantasized about years ago. Faith had her inn and her family. Jayne had her farm and a husband who may not have understood her precisely, but who accepted her nevertheless. And Alaina had finally found a place where she belonged, a family to love and who loved her in return.

Bryan had come to Anastasia to seek solace and sympathy, and his old friends had given it to him in ample measure . . . for a while. They had consoled him and given him a place to heal his broken heart. Then each had begun to hint in her own way that the time had come for him to start living again.

Faith had been gentle about it. That was her way, gentle, diplomatic, sympathetic, skills that had been polished to perfection by six years of motherhood. Alaina had been blunt. Jayne had been empathetic and philosophical.

It had been the girls' collective idea that he investigate Addie Lindquist's house for paranormal activity. Bryan had to smile. He had always been the one to look out for and look after them, but here they were, banding together to see to his emotional well-being. You couldn't custom-order better friends.

He knew they were right. A man couldn't go on mourning forever. Yet, there was a small measure of resentment inside him. There was a certain perverse comfort in grief. In clinging to his grief he was clinging to Serena. If he let the grief go, if he involved himself in work again and made new friends and stopped devoting all his time and energy to missing her, he would be letting her go. Her memory and the memory of the pain of losing her would dim, and a part of him didn't want that. He had loved her so deeply, even holding on to painful memories was better than nothing at all.

So, he had reached a compromise with himself. He would go back to work, ease back into the routine, but deeper involvement with people would have to wait. For the time being he just didn't have anything left to give.

Settling back more firmly into the corner, Bryan heaved a sigh. Soft gray moonlight spilled into the foyer from the narrow windows that flanked the door. All was still in the hall below. All was still inside him. He didn't sense anything in the air around him except mold. So far, Drake House wasn't exactly proving to be a hotbed of psychical activity. Of course, as out of touch as he'd been with his own gift, there might have been spiritualistic manifestations all around him, and he wouldn't have noticed.

Addie Lindquist claimed there was a ghost in this house. Addie claimed she spoke with this ghost on a regular basis. Perhaps *claimed* wasn't quite the right word. *Declared* was more like it. Addie was sixty-six, opinionated, and imperious. Of course she spoke with Wimsey, she had announced to Bryan, her blue eyes flashing with impatience. She couldn't understand why other people thought it unusual that she spoke with Wimsey. She didn't understand that she was the only one who had ever actually seen Wimsey.

Whether or not the ghost existed was the matter in question. There were people in Anastasia who vaguely remembered stories of strange goings-on at Drake House told by previous owners, but no one had firsthand experience. Addie was the only one with that, and Addie's mind was going round the bend on greased tracks, as Jayne's husband put it.

In fact, Addie's doctor had been trying for weeks to contact Rachel Lindquist, Addie's daughter, to let her know about her mother's condition. Whether or not the woman would respond was anyone's guess. No one in Anastasia had even known of her existence.

Bryan hated to think of what would happen to Addie. Not that he was getting involved in her situation, he told himself stoutly. It was just sad, that was all. It didn't sound as if Rachel Lindquist cared what happened to her mother. Addie would probably be packed off and forgotten, dead in all the ways that mattered most, the shell of her body left to the care of strangers.

'I could win a prize for being morose,' he mumbled, disgusted with himself and his morbid frame of mind.

It wasn't like him, really. He had always been an optimist, a great believer in magic and rainbows. Besides, he was supposed to be thinking about the case, about the possibility that Addie's Wimsey was in fact a psychic disturbance of some sort. He knew nothing would happen to Addie as long as he was staying in Drake House, and he had no immediate plans to leave.

Producing a playing card from inside his shirt-sleeve, he walked it between the fingers of his left hand with careless dexterity, wondering only vaguely at the sudden strong sense of anticipation that surged through him. It was a pleasant feeling, both soothing and exciting, like a promise of something good. The warmth washed through him, chasing out the chilling ache. Tension seeped from the muscles in his broad shoulders, and his eyes drifted shut as he let himself enjoy the sensation without questioning where it came from or what it meant. His glasses slipped down his nose as his head bobbed forward, and the playing card dropped from his fingers.

2

The scream could have pierced steel.

Bryan jolted awake, his body exploding out of its cramped position on the landing. His actions were purely instinctive. He had no idea who or what had issued the sound. All that registered was the buzzing of his alarm telling him that sensors indicated a presence in the downstairs hall. He was halfway down the stairs when the flash of his still camera went off, blinding him. Unable to see and unable to stop himself, he stepped out into thin air.

'Aargh!'

His cry of surprise was abruptly cut off with a grunt as he bounced the rest of the way down the steps, rolling like a human tumbleweed. Another otherworldly scream split the air as he hit the marble-tiled floor in a heap and sprawled out, groaning.

The sound had a definite ghostlike quality, he thought excitedly as he struggled to sit up. He was going to have bruises from here to Hyannis, but they would be well worth it if he had captured something on film or tape. He could already see his articles in the scientific journals. Funding for studies and documentaries would come out of the woodwork. Maybe he'd even get invited to the *Tonight Show*. At the very least he'd get a segment on *Unsolved Mysteries*.

Wincing, he hauled himself to his feet and fumbled for the light switch beside the front door. His breath hardened in his throat as the foyer was flooded with amber light from the old chandelier. He'd caught something all right, and she was beautiful.

Bryan straightened his glasses and stared, his heart beating a curious rhythm. The woman before him was quite real, vision though she seemed. The professional in him acknowledged an appropriate amount of disappointment at that, but the basic male in him could find no regret. It would have been physically impossible for a red-blooded man to have been anything but awestruck by the young woman gazing up at him.

She had the face of an angel – gently prominent cheekbones with slight hollows beneath, a chin that looked as if it were made to be cupped by the hand of a handsome lover; a slim, tip-tilted nose; and full pink lips that looked so soft and kissable, they almost made him groan aloud. Her skin was like rose-tinted cream, so tempting, he nearly reached out to touch her cheek. Instead, he pulled his hand back and splayed his fingers across his chest, as if he were having a heart attack.

The overhead light caught in the woman's halo of pale golden hair, adding to her ethereal quality. She wore it up in a loose chignon, but soft tendrils escaped all around her head, framing her feminine features. She stared at him, her periwinkle blue eyes wide and brimming with terror.

Her obvious fear struck him like a slap in the face. He cleared his throat nervously, peeled his hand off his chest, and offered it to her, attempting a genial smile.

'Bryan Hennessy.'

Rachel flinched at the sound of his voice. The silence had held her spellbound, now she was jolted out of the trance. She stared first at the big hand hovering before her, then her gaze traveled up a considerable distance to take in the rest of the man.

He was fairly tall with shoulders so wide, they seemed to block out the stairwell behind him. His hair was disheveled. The strands falling across his broad forehead were a color somewhere between blond and brown. With panic overruling her other senses, the only thing she noticed about his face was the strong jaw and the five o'clock shadow that darkened it. His clothes – worn jeans with bits of paper sticking out of one front pocket, and a chambray shirt that was tucked in on only one side – were rumpled.

All things considered, she thought, he looked dangerous, maybe even unbalanced. He certainly didn't look like anyone her mother would invite into her home. The woman she remembered wouldn't have sat next to this guy on a bus. How, then, had he come to be the one to greet her at the door? The possible answers were not reassuring.

She choked down what fear she could and called on years of vocal training to project a confident tone when she spoke. 'What have you done with my mother?'

'I don't know,' Bryan said, bemused. He was too thrown off by her remarkable beauty and by his reaction to it to think straight. He pulled his hand back and combed his fingers through his hair. 'Who is she?'

Rachel swallowed hard. She started to back away from him, wondering what her chances were of making it to her car and from there to the police station. Not good, she figured. He appeared to be in wonderful physical condition. That was probably essential when one was running from the law. As she took a step back, the man took a step forward. She held up a hand to ward him off.

'If you touch me, I'll scream,' she promised.

'You've already done that,' Bryan pointed out ruefully. 'Quite well, I might add. My ears are still ringing. Now I know the full meaning of the word *shrill*.'

'I know karate,' Rachel blurted out. She braced her feet, squared her shoulders, and raised her hand as if she were preparing to take on Bruce Lee. It was ludicrous, of course. Bryan Hennessy dwarfed her. He wasn't the stocky, no-neck, muscle-bound type, but he was big and athletic-looking; and she was all of five feet seven, a hundred and twenty pounds. She decided she would have to make up the difference with her temper.

Bryan's brows bobbed up and his face lit with genuine interest. 'Karate? Really?'

Now was not the time to be overly honest, Rachel reflected as she frantically cast her gaze about for a handy sharp-edged instrument with which she might defend herself.

She thought of her mother and a terrible pang reverberated through her. All the years they'd wasted! And for what? Now she was finally returning, hoping she and Addie could patch up their relationship. What if she were too late? Dr. Moore had told her it wasn't safe for Addie to live alone any longer, that her mother's impairment made her forget things like turning off the stove and who to allow inside her home. Had her mother let this man into the house thinking he was a friend? It was entirely possible.

On the drive to California from Nebraska, Rachel had thought about what time she would have left with her mother – the mother she knew and loved – not some vacuous stranger existing in her mother's body. And she had vowed to make the most of it. Time for them may have been snatched away. The thought filled her with a sense of almost overwhelming loss.

'Rachel,' he said abruptly.

Her eyes widened at the sound of her name. The stranger's voice was husky and warm, but the fact that he knew her name sent chills down her back.

Bryan nodded decisively. 'You're Rachel Lindquist. You're Addie's daughter. I should have recognized you right off. You look a lot like your mother.'

He stared at her hard, his straight brows drawing down low and tight over his eyes. A slight frown of disapproval turned the corners of his mouth. It wasn't triggered by Rachel Lindquist's appearance or her identity, but by his own reaction to both. This was the daughter who had not bothered to visit her mother in five years, the girl Addie herself had labeled ungrateful. This was the young woman who had run off with a folk singer, the young woman he had thought of as selfish and uncaring. And he was damned attracted to her.

It came as a very unpleasant surprise, that warm, curling sensation deep in his gut. It was something he hadn't felt in a long, long time, but he was too strongly, basically masculine not to recognize it for what it was – desire. The primitive male in him was responding to a pretty female, and he heartily resented it, resented *her* for stirring that dormant need inside him.

'So, you decided to come back after all,' he said coldly, trying to distance himself from her emotionally as well as physically.

Rachel willed herself to stand still while Bryan Hennessy's gaze bore through her. He moved back and a little to her left, and the light from the old chandelier fell more fully across his face. He looked as if he'd just awakened from a sound sleep. Behind his glasses his eyes were bleary and bloodshot, but there was nothing truly dangerous in their stare. He looked annoyed more than anything. More than anything except male. He looked very male – big and brooding and sexy with his tousled hair and beard-shadowed cheeks.

The silence between them swelled with unspoken messages, messages Rachel didn't want to hear or understand. Just the same, she felt a strange fluttering deep inside her, and she pressed a hand to her stomach as if she could push the sensation away. It was probably just hunger. Most of a day had passed since she'd eaten.

Tearing her gaze away from Bryan Hennessy, she gave herself a mental shake. She was experiencing hunger, all right, but it wasn't the kind that she could appease with a sandwich. If she had learned anything over the course of the past five years, it was to be honest with herself. The kind of hunger coursing through her had little to do with prime rib and everything to do with primal attraction.

The realization shocked her. She had lived to the ripe old age of twenty-five and had never experienced such a strong physical reaction to a man, not even to Terence, whom she had once loved. She hadn't expected ever to feel it. It simply wasn't in her nature. She certainly hadn't expected to feel it for a complete stranger, especially one who was suddenly regarding her with subtle disdain. She didn't like it, didn't want it, and she most definitely didn't need it. The reason she had come to Anastasia loomed over her like a dark cloud. There would be no time in her life now for anything but Addie.

'Where is my mother?' she asked firmly, effectively breaking the strange spell between them.

'Upstairs. Asleep, if she's lucky,' Bryan said, shouldering his way past her, 'though I'd be surprised if there's a dog in this county you didn't wake up with that shrieking.'

'Shrieking!' Rachel said indignantly. She pressed her lips into a thin line and planted her hands on her slim hips as she watched him fiddling with the array of equipment clustered in the foyer. Anger surged through her as other feelings subsided. 'Of course I was shrieking. I step into my mother's house and am virtually attacked by mechanical contraptions.

'What is all this junk?' she asked impatiently, gesturing sharply at the stuff. 'What's it doing here? What are *you* doing here? Who do you think you are anyway?'

'Most of the time I think I'm Bryan Hennessy,' Bryan said dryly. He righted a light meter that had tipped over and tapped it gently with a finger, relieved to see it was still functioning. 'I got hit in the head with a shot put once, and for about three hours afterward I thought I was Prince Charles, but that was fifteen years ago. I've pretty much gotten over it, except for a strange yen to play polo every now and again. And I was once mistaken for Pat Reilly, the actor.' He shot her a Cheshire-cat smile that made Rachel's heart flip. 'Personally, I don't think we look all that much alike, but the lady tearing my shirt off didn't agree.'

Warmth bloomed under the surface of Rachel's skin as her imagination conjured up an unusually vivid picture of this man with his shirt half off. Her image of his chest was smooth and solid with well-defined muscles, a sprinkling of tawny curls, and a tiny brown mole just above his left nipple. She could almost feel the heat of his skin against her palms, and her nostrils flared as she caught the faintest hint of his male scent. It was an altogether weird experience, one that had her fighting to get a good deep breath into her lungs.

Oblivious to Rachel's predicament, Bryan had turned back to his machinery. He checked each item thoroughly. At the moment he couldn't afford to have a piece needing repair. His finances weren't in the healthiest of states. In fact, he was more or less broke.

'This "junk," ' he said, 'is highly sensitive electronic surveillance equipment essential to my work. I'm a psychic investigator specializing in locating and defining paranormal phenomena.'

It came as a complete surprise to Rachel that a man who looked as rumpled and ratty as Bryan did was capable of speaking in more than monosyllables. She tucked her chin back and frowned as she tried to translate his explanation into garden-variety English. 'Is there a generic term for what you do?'

He flashed her a smile that revealed even white teeth worthy of a toothpaste commercial. This time his eyes twinkled with amusement, the corners crinkling attractively behind his spectacles. 'I'm a ghostbuster.'

Rachel blinked at him, certain she had heard him wrong. 'You're a what?'

'You know, a ghostbuster. When people hear things that go bump in the night, I'm the guy they hire to find out what those things are. Is it Aunt Edna coming back to get them for all those jokes they made about her pot roast, or is it just bad plumbing?' His broad shoulders lifted in a shrug. 'Is that disgusting ooze in the basement crud from hell, or do they just need a new septic tank?'

'People actually pay you money to do that?' Rachel questioned in disbelief. The idea went completely against her innate sense of practicality. 'You actually take money from people to do that?'

'A crime against humanity, isn't it?' Bryan said sardonically. He was used to dealing with skeptics. When one made his living investigating things a great many people refused to acknowledge, one learned to handle criticism in a hurry. But he made no effort to argue his case to Rachel Lindquist.

Let her think what she liked, he told himself. He was going to be much better off simply leaving her alone. Between his involuntary attraction to her and his anger over the way she'd treated her mother, there was no telling what would happen if he let himself get involved. Not that he wanted to get involved, he amended hastily. Noninvolvement was his credo these days. He was just minding his own business, looking for ghosts.

'You play on the superstitions and fears of lonely old women,' Rachel said, her anger building. He was a con man. Thank God she had arrived when she had. There was no telling how much this handsome charlatan might have bilked Addie for. 'You set up a lot of electronic gizmos, spout a bunch of scientific-sounding mumbo jumbo, and take money for it. I think that's deplorable.'

Bryan's shoulders stiffened, and his hands stilled on the light stand he had righted. He gave her a hard look, the expression in his warm blue eyes severe. 'Yes, well, we all have our own ideas as to what amounts to deplorable behavior, don't we, Ms. Lindquist?'

'Just what do you mean by that?'

'Oh, just nothing,' Bryan muttered, tearing his gaze away from her.

Dammit, how could he feel so drawn to her knowing what he did about her? Even as he stood there fuming with righteous anger, a part of him never once stopped assessing the gentle beauty, the exquisite femininity Rachel Lindquist possessed. This indiscriminating lust dawning inside him was a disconcerting new character flaw, to say the very least. With a considerable effort of will he attempted to block it from his consciousness.

Rachel could feel his disapproval of her like an icy rain, and it rankled. The man was little better than an out and out thief, and he was looking down his nose at her! What could he possibly know about her? Nothing. Unless . . . Addie had told him something. That idea irked her even more, that her mother would share family secrets with this stranger.

'I don't know what my mother may have told you, Mr. Hennessy, but she is not a well woman. She has Alzheimer's disease.'

'I'm aware of that, Ms. Lindquist,' Bryan said pointedly. 'I've been dealing with Addie on a daily basis. I dare say, I know a hell of a lot more about her condition than you do.'

The blow was on target. Rachel flinched at his words and at the burning guilt that immediately flooded through her. Still, she pulled herself together and lifted her chin. 'Dr. Moore wasn't able to contact me until just last week.'

'Oh. Pardon me for thinking you might give your mother a call every once in a while,' Bryan said dryly. 'You know, once a year or so.'

Tears stung the backs of Rachel's eyes. She had called Addie over the years. She had tried to bridge the chasm that had divided them. Addie had hung up on her every single time. Every letter she'd sent had gone unanswered. Every overture of peace had been met with bitter, stony silence. But none of that was Bryan Hennessy's business, and, despite all she had been through, Rachel had too much pride to enlighten him.

She pulled her shoulders back and gave him her haughtiest look. 'You will pack your things and leave this house, Mr. Hennessy.'

'No, I won't,' Bryan said evenly.

'I won't have you taking advantage of my mother.'

Won't have me taking advantage of her inheritance is more like it, Bryan thought. He gave her a black look that only darkened as he leaned over her and caught a whiff of her perfume, an elusive scent so delicate, he almost thought he'd imagined it, and yet it lured him closer.

Tempting fate, he bent his head so he was almost nose to nose with her – well within kissing distance. Her full, soft lips beckoned like a siren's call. It was as if their bodies were communicating on a level of their own, impervious to opinions on character. His heart thumped hard, then slowed against his breastbone, and his lungs fought every shallow breath he tried to take. It was unlike anything he had ever experienced.

'Addie and I have a deal,' he said softly, straining to concentrate on the subject at hand. 'More to the point, we have a contract. And most important to me, I gave her my word I'd find out what's going on around here. That may not mean much to you, but I stand by my promises.'

Rachel barely heard his words. They were absorbed into her brain on one level while her conscious awareness dwelled on the man. She felt overwhelmed, enveloped by his masculinity, and she felt her body responding to it. A satiny warmth unfolded through her, down her arms and legs and into her breasts, making them feel heavy and full. Her gaze fastened on his mouth. In a way she couldn't begin to explain or understand, she could almost taste his lips, could almost feel them on her own. The sensations were so vivid, they frightened her, and she took a step back from him in obvious retreat.

Bryan turned away and speared both hands back through his hair as he dragged in a deep, cleansing breath. Dammit, he swore inwardly, more shaken than angry at the moment. He'd never felt anything quite like the power that had held him in its grasp as he'd stared down at Rachel Lindquist's petal-pink lips. He shook his head to clear it.

It must have had something to do with a combination of exhaustion and celibacy. Once he might have called it magic, but he couldn't call it that now. Magic was what he had shared with Serena. All his magic had died with her. What he was feeling now – well, it was something he wanted no part of, certainly. He was there to do a job, that was all. That was all he could handle right now. That was all he wanted to handle.

'Hennessy?' an imperious voice sounded from the top of the stairs. 'What in God's name is going on down there?'

'I wish I knew,' Bryan mumbled to himself, shaking off the last of the sensation that had stunned him so. He planted his hands at his waist and looked up as Addie Lindquist descended the grand staircase.

Addie moved like a queen. She kept her thin shoulders square and her back straight. Age had shrunken her some, but she did not see that as an excuse for bad posture. Her hand skimmed the mahogany banister lightly. She held her head high. Her frazzled braid of silvery blond hair was draped over her shoulder. She looked like she should have been wearing a velvet cloak instead of a flannel nightgown.

'Who's down there with you?' she demanded, squinting. 'Is it Wimsey? The rascal. I haven't seen him all day. I can't imagine where he's taken himself off to.'

'No, it isn't Wimsey, Addie,' Bryan said, heartily wishing it were the elusive ghost of Drake House. He stepped to the left so Addie would have an unobstructed view of her visitor.

'Well, who is it, then? You'd better not be cavorting with the kitchen help again.'

'She sort of thinks I'm her butler,' Bryan whispered, tilting his head down so Rachel could hear him.

But Rachel wasn't listening. She was seeing her mother for the first time in five years. When had Addie gotten so old? The beautiful, vital woman Rachel remembered had faded like a photograph left in the sun. Her hair was paler. The vibrant glow that had always radiated from Addie had dimmed. She seemed smaller, and, while she still had a beautiful complexion – something she had always taken great pride in – her face was deeply lined. In the time they had been apart Addie had slipped from middle age to old age. Suddenly the five years that had passed seemed even more of a waste.

As Addie stared down at her, Rachel suddenly felt as she had at sixteen when she'd been caught coming home after curfew. A hundred fears and anxieties tumbled inside her. How would Addie react to her coming here? It was Dr. Moore who had contacted her, not Addie. Addie wouldn't even accept her phone calls. How would her mother receive her now that she was there in the flesh?

If you leave with that cheap musician, don't think you can ever come back here, Rachel Lindquist. If you leave here now, if you defy me, I will cease to have a daughter.

The ultimatum rang in her ears as if her mother had delivered it only yesterday.

Addie's gaze settled on the pretty young woman standing beside Hennessy in the hall below her. At first there was no spark of recognition in her mind whatsoever, but, as she moved down one step and then another, she felt her mind shift gears. A quiver of fright ran through her as she realized this was someone she should know but couldn't place. The feeling lasted only a second or two, but its intensity sapped the strength from her, and she had to pause on the landing before descending the last

17

few steps. Then the fog of confusion cleared abruptly and recognition startled her so, she nearly gasped.

'Rachel,' she said, her pale eyes round with wonder. She didn't smile or rush forward, but held still. If she moved toward this vision, there was every chance it would vanish. If she was still, she could soak it up greedily and pray that her memory would hold it.

Rachel. Lord, when had she become a woman? She was beautiful. She was dressed like a cheap Gypsy in faded jeans and a purple sweater that hung to the middle of her slender thighs, but it made no difference; she was beautiful.

Her daughter, the child she had thought lost, was there before her, a woman. Emotions ran riot inside her, joy and regret and anger swirling and tumbling around in her brain and overwhelming her. She could only stand on the landing of the grand staircase and stare and say her daughter's name. 'Rachel.'

Rachel shivered, rooted to the spot. She wanted to rush forward and embrace her mother, but that was not the way of the Lindquists. They had never been the type for hugs and kisses and 'vulgar' public displays of emotion. Instead, she tried to swallow down her fears and simply said, 'Mother.'

It was a simple word full of complex feelings. There was so much between them, such a complicated history, so many memories, so much pain. Rachel pressed a hand to her pounding heart. Since she had received Dr. Moore's call, she had thought of little besides her mother and how they would handle the situation. But now she realized that never once in all that time had she allowed herself to recognize the hope she'd harbored for this moment.

Bryan watched the exchange between mother and daughter with interest. What kind of family was this? His mother would have had him in a bear hug the instant he'd come through the door. Addie and Rachel stared at each other as if there were an invisible wall between them.

Perhaps there was.

The look in Addie's eyes was guarded, almost defensive. Rachel appeared to be more frightened than joyful. Had she caught that second of blankness in her mother's gaze when Addie had almost certainly failed to recognize her? Bryan tried to tell himself it served her right. She was the one who had left and not come back for five years. She deserved to be frightened. But he couldn't stop the rush of sympathy that welled inside him. The expression in Rachel's eyes was a little girl's, hopeful and repentant. If she had looked at him that way, he knew he would have forgiven her anything.

'Rachel,' Addie said again, stepping down from the landing. She held herself perfectly erect.

This was the daughter she had devoted her life to. This was the daughter who had chosen to throw away all their dreams to chase after a two-bit drifter who had an adequate voice and a beat-up guitar. This was the daughter who had left her. Her deteriorating mind had no trouble recalling these facts while it ignored the attempts at peacemaking. All the old hurt and bitterness boiled inside her anew, obscuring the joy and the guilt. Her mind wasn't capable of dealing with many emotions at once, and so it seized upon the strongest. Stubborn pride tilted her chin up as she stared into the face that so resembled the ghost of her own past. 'What are you doing here?'

Rachel felt disappointment crush her. She didn't try to stop the tears from springing into her eyes, but she did manage to keep the sorrow out of her voice. 'I came to help you. Dr. Moore called me and told me about your illness.' *Why didn't you? Why couldn't you put that damned pride aside long enough to tell me you needed me?*

'Broderick Moore is a Nazi and a fool. There's nothing wrong with me. I don't need your help,' Addie said coldly. She turned toward Bryan. 'I have Hennessy to help me.'

Bryan took an involuntary step backward. He already felt like a voyeur, watching the interchange between mother and daughter; now he felt like an interloper as well. Rachel glared at him, her violet-blue eyes luminous with tears, and he held his hands up in a gesture of surrender. He shot a look at Addie. 'Addie, you know I'm here only to look for Wimsey.'

'Well, I don't know why you can't find him,' she grumbled as her mind tuned out. 'He's all over the place.' She turned and started to shuffle down the hall, her green rubber garden boots scuffing against the marble floor. 'I'm going to feed Lester. I'm sure you forgot to do it. No doubt practicing your smooth lines in front of a mirror again. Big Irish rascal.'

Bryan rubbed a hand along his jaw, realizing dimly that he had forgotten to shave. He didn't know quite what to say to Rachel, who stood in the foyer looking like a piece of crystal on the verge of bursting into a million shards. It suddenly didn't matter what kind of daughter she'd been, it was obvious Addie's cold reception had hurt her, and almost certainly the decline of her mother's mental state had shocked her. He couldn't feel anything now but sympathy for her and the desire to take her in his arms and hold her.

'Dangerous thinking, Hennessy,' he mumbled to himself. 'Don't get involved. Make a note of that – don't get involved.' He patted his shirt pocket, looking for his pencil, but it was gone again. 'And don't forget to shave tomorrow.'

'What was that?' Rachel asked. If she could not function in any other way, she could at least be polite, she thought ruefully. Wasn't that one of the Lindquist rules of deportment? A hysterical little laugh threatened but never emerged from her throat.

Bryan blushed a bit. 'Nothing.'

Rachel hugged herself, trying to ward off a chill that came from within. 'I suppose I shouldn't have expected anything better than that,' she murmured to no one in particular. Her gaze followed her mother down the hall into the nether reaches of the big house. 'She never wanted me here before. Why should she want me here now?'

'You tried?' Bryan blurted out. Shame crawled around in his stomach. It hadn't occurred to him that Addie's side of the story might have been biased.

Rachel gave him a cool look, her pride returning to rally around her. 'There are lots of things you don't know, Mr. Hennessy.'

Bryan pushed his glasses up on his nose and nodded. 'Oh, yes. I readily admit there are lots of things I don't know.' He tossed her his most inane grin in an effort to lighten her mood and said, ' "A man doesn't know what he knows until he knows what he doesn't know." Thomas Carlyle. I've adopted that as my motto.'

'I see,' Rachel murmured, though she clearly didn't.

Bryan was unconcerned. The point was, Rachel's eyes had lost their tragic quality. She was no longer staring after Addie with an expression of shattered hope. She would have to deal with those feelings later, he knew, but at least the intensity of the impact had been defused.

He stuffed his hands into the front pockets of his jeans and gazed up at the chandelier, his blue eyes drowsy with thought. 'Of course, John Wooden once said, "It's what you learn after you think you know it all that counts the most." For instance, did you know that an alligator's length in feet is the distance between his eyes in inches?'

Rachel opened her mouth to comment, then closed it and simply stared at him. How had he gotten on this topic? Who in his right mind would try to measure the distance between an alligator's eyes? The man was a lunatic. A rumpled, handsome lunatic.

She shook her head, deciding she had to be a little off the beam herself to be going on this way about how sexy this strange man was. Finally she decided to ask a question that seemed more pertinent. 'Who's Lester?'

Bryan sobered and sighed. 'There is no Lester. Um . . . your mother thinks she owns a parakeet.' He shrugged apologetically. 'If she does, I haven't been able to find it.'

'Oh.'

'I keep meaning to buy her one, but I forget things. I'm sure I've written myself a note about it,' he said, pulling a fistful of paper scraps from his pants pocket. He sorted through them, frowning.

'That's all right,' Rachel said.

Addie thought she owned a parakeet. This man, who was a virtual stranger, intended to buy her one to placate her. How sweet. What a sweet, sexy, rumpled con man he was. Her heart warmed, then she caught herself and shuddered, cursing her wildly swinging emotions. She felt as if she were trying to keep her balance on the deck of a ship pitching violently in a stormy sea.

Stuffing his notes back in his pocket, Bryan watched her from under his lashes. She looked so lost. In a way it made him think of Addie at the instant her mind snapped from normal to non-functioning. But then Addie would retreat into her fantasies. Rachel didn't have that option.

Without thinking, he took a step toward her. Odd, but he felt almost as if he'd been pushed toward her. When he caught himself he had already begun to reach out to her. Stopping in his tracks, he slapped his hands together and tried to look decisive. 'You must have a suitcase or something out in your car. I'll go get it.'

He turned and let himself out, taking big gulps of the cool night air as he crossed the porch and jogged down the steps.

'Holy Mike, that was a close call, you moron,' he grumbled to himself. His sneakers crunched on the gravel drive as he headed for a beat-up little Chevette that was parked beside Addie's old Volvo wagon.

The farther he got from the house, the steadier he felt. The sea air was refreshing. Moisture from the fog that had rolled in at sunset dampened his skin. He leaned against the roof of the little car and let the sound of crashing waves wash the tension from him.

Drake House stood on a cliff overlooking the bay on the very northern edge of Anastasia. Because of the lay of the land and the size of the estate, its nearest neighbor was a quarter mile away. The house on its lonely precipice was a giant sentinel, a gaudy reminder of a bygone age.

It might have looked like a happy, magical place once with its turrets and gingerbread and gables. Now, run-down and in dire need of a coat of paint, it looked like something out of a horror movie. The land that stretched out before it had at one time been a beautifully manicured lawn. There had been gardens and even a maze. He'd seen pictures of it in *Anastasia's Architecture: A Pictorial Essay*. The gardens had long since gone to weed and the maze had become a tall, tangled mass of wild brambles.

The few people who came to visit Drake House called during daylight hours, bowing to superstitions they would never voice. Most of them came to browse through the antiques Addie had collected to sell. The kids of the town sometimes came to the end of the driveway at night. Bryan had seen them – groups of four or five kids who weren't brave enough to come any closer. They stood down at the gate, shoving each other through the portal but never farther. They were thoroughly convinced the place was haunted. They were also scared to death of Addie.

Addie. Bryan glanced up at the house and caught a glimpse of her silhouette as she passed a window. He knew she was going to all the bird cages she had collected, filling the little dishes with seed. In the morning he would clean the trays out before she got up, or she would be upset thinking there was something wrong with Lester. It never seemed to bother her that Lester wasn't in any of the cages. Unless, of course, she was seeing birds that weren't actually there. Ghost birds.

He found his pencil and a crumpled bit of paper and made a note of that, then shook his head as he tucked the scrap of paper into his hip pocket and forgot about it. Addie could be fairly lucid. At times she was sharp as a tack. Then in the blink of an eye she would be talking to people who weren't there, feeding birds she didn't own.

It was a sad situation, but it wasn't any of his business, he reminded himself. He'd dealt with his own sad situation; he didn't need to get wrapped up in another.

Rachel watched her mother go from bird cage to bird cage, panic tightening her throat. Addie couldn't be this bad already. The possibility that she was terrified Rachel. The further her mother retreated from reality, the less chance there would be for them to reconcile.

In her own mind, because she had only just learned of the problem, Rachel felt as if her mother had just developed this illness. She wanted to forget that Addie's decline had doubtless begun several years earlier, and her mother had either ignored or hidden it for a long while.

Addie had moved to Anastasia upon her retirement from teaching music in Berkeley, not long after Rachel had gone on the road with Terence. According to Dr. Moore, the people of Anastasia had labeled her erratic behavior 'eccentric,' and, by the good doctor's own admission, the town had more than its share of oddballs, so Addie hadn't really stuck out. It was only after she had backed her Volvo clear across Main Street and into the front of the movie theater that anyone had thought to alert Dr. Moore.

'Mother, it's very late,' Rachel said wearily. She leaned against the door frame of the parlor, letting it support her weight for a moment. Now was not the time to try to deal with any of this mess – the illness, the emotional baggage, Bryan Hennessy. 'You should be in bed.'

Addie set her birdseed down and turned toward her daughter, arching a brow. Resentment burned through her. She resented Rachel for leaving her, for abandoning their dreams, for trying to tell her what to do now. She resented the fact that it had taken a call from that idiot Moore to bring her daughter home. The pressure of her feelings built inside her like steam, which she vented on Rachel.

'I won't have you telling me what to do, missy,' she snapped, eyes flashing. 'I'm not some incontinent old woman who needs to be taken care of like a child.'

Rachel reined in her own ready temper, forced a sigh, and hung her head. She was so tired. She'd driven clear from North Platte, stopping to sleep only once for just a few brief hours. Before the marathon drive had been the marathon fight and subsequent end of her relationship with Terence. And before that had been the devastating news of her mother's illness. All of it weighed down on her now like the weight of the world on her shoulders. At the moment she would have given anything for someone to lean on, just for a minute or two.

The image of Bryan Hennessy drifted through her mind. For an instant she could have sworn she felt a man's arms around her. How absurd, she thought, shaking free of the strange sensation.

'What room should I take?' she asked. 'I'm going to bed.'

'Not in my house.'

Rachel's head snapped up as her heart skipped a beat. 'What?'

'I don't want you here,' Addie said bluntly. 'Go away.'

Rachel stared at her mother. She couldn't have moved if her life had depended on it. Maybe she couldn't have expected to be welcomed with open arms, but she hadn't expected a total rejection either.

Addie raised her fists suddenly and jigged around like an old-time prizefighter, her braid bouncing, a truculent light in her eyes. 'Go away! Get out of my house!'

'Mother, don't!' Rachel ordered, wincing as Addie popped her one on the arm.

'You're a traitor! I don't want you here!'

'Mother, stop it!' Rachel shouted, dodging away from another blow.

She couldn't believe this was actually happening. She had been bracing herself for a fight, but not one like this. As she backed into the hall and toward the front door, she kept thinking that any second she would wake up and discover it had all been a dream, a strange black dream. But how far back would the nightmare go, she wondered dimly. A week? A year? Five years?

'Get out! Get out!' Addie chanted. She couldn't seem to stop herself from saying the words over and over, but she couldn't bear to look at Rachel's face as she said them, so she turned her back to her daughter and went on shouting. It was as if the floodgates on her emotions had been suddenly thrown wide. Anger and hurt spewed out unchecked.

Rachel pressed her hands over her ears and squeezed her eyes shut. Abruptly it all become too much. She turned and bolted for the front door, knocking over half of Bryan Hennessy's equipment as she went. She flung the heavy door open and ran out onto the porch, where she stopped and leaned against a post, feeling dizzy and sick.

'What happened?' Bryan asked, setting her two suitcases down on the ground at the bottom of the steps.

'She threw me out,' Rachel whispered, stunned. 'She doesn't want me here. She meant it. She told me to leave and never come back, and she meant it.'

She sounded so small and lost. Bryan's heart twisted in his chest.

Rachel hugged the wooden column as if it were the only solid thing in a world suddenly turned to illusion. 'I have to help her,' she murmured to Bryan beseechingly. 'She's my mother. I have to help her. She's my responsibility now. But she doesn't want me here.'

'Look,' Bryan said, climbing the steps to the porch, 'it's late. Addie gets really irrational when she hasn't had a good night's sleep.' He wanted to tell her that everything would seem better in the morning, but the bald truth was Addie could be irrational at *any* time. There was no guarantee of her behaving any differently tomorrow.

Rachel faced him, leaning her back against the post. She wrapped her arms across her middle, fighting to hold herself together. In a matter of days her whole world had torn loose from its moorings. All the dreams she had believed in had died. The rainbow she had followed away from home hadn't ended in a pot of gold. And the home she had returned to was full of strangers. The nightmare wasn't going to end when she opened her eyes in the morning. The bad dream had just begun.

'My mother is losing her mind.' She uttered the words as if she had only just realized what they meant and what the ramifications for her own life would be.

She looked up at Bryan through a shimmering window of tears. It suddenly didn't matter that he was a stranger or that she had questioned his motives. He was someone's son. He had a family somewhere, a home he would return to one day. Maybe he would understand a little of what she was feeling, and she needed so badly to share it with someone, just for a minute or two.

As the first fat tears teetered over the barrier of her thick lashes, she said, 'What am I going to do?'

Bryan instantly forgot his vow of noninvolvement. What man could stand there and watch this lovely creature crumple like a wilting rose? He could offer her his strength if nothing else. He took her gently into his arms, as if her body were as fragile as her spirit, and pressed her cheek to his chest. Sobs tore through her, terrible, wrenching sobs. She didn't seem strong enough to cry so hard, he thought. He could feel her sobs echoing through his chest, and he had to fight down the knot in his throat.

She was hurting – not physically, but with the kind of pain that comes from confusion and broken dreams and mourning a lost future. He could understand that all too well. He could understand her need to be held. He couldn't understand his own overwhelming need to hold her, but even as his brain tried to decipher it, his arms tightened around her and his lips brushed against her temple.

'Shhh . . . you're too tired to think straight. Let's get you settled in. We'll talk about it in the morning,' he murmured, not even aware that he had included himself in her dilemma.

Even though he whispered something about going inside, he made no move to leave the porch. He simply rocked her gently back and forth as the mist swirled around them and the sea crashed in the distance. He knew a strange contentment in holding her, but he didn't question it. For the first time in a long time something was soothing the ache in his heart. He didn't dare wonder why.

3

They entered the house through a back door, passed through a corner of the large dark kitchen, and went into an old-fashioned pantry, where Bryan opened what appeared to be a tall cabinet set into the wall. Rachel followed him, mute, as they went up a dusty, unembellished servants' staircase, a place hung with cobwebs and bare light bulbs dangling from thick black cords in the ceiling.

'I'm sorry about breaking down that way,' she said, embarrassed now that the tears had dried. 'I don't ordinarily do that kind of thing.'

'That's okay. You don't ordinarily get chased out the house by your mother either,' Bryan said. 'Careful on this step. Stay to the right. Dry rot, you know. You have to watch for stuff like that in these old houses.'

Rachel glanced down at the crack in the wooden tread as she bypassed the step altogether, wondering how much of the rest of the house was rotting away. She had hoped to get by without investing much in repairs before they sold the place. What money of hers she had managed to keep out of Terence's slippery hands wasn't going to go far. Her mother had been running an antiques business for several years, and then there was the money from her father's police pension fund, but their expenses were going to run high. She had to consider Addie's medical bills, the deposit on an apartment in San Francisco, and their day-to-day living expenses. She had no idea how Addie had taken care of her money recently. If Bryan Hennessy was an example, she had been squandering it with a lavish hand.

A ghostbuster. Rachel shook her head.

They exited through a door that blended into the paneled wall of the second-story hallway.

'Here we are,' Bryan said softly. He put on a pleasant smile and slid the hidden door shut with the toe of his battered sneaker. 'Just like in the movies, huh?'

Rachel took in little of her surroundings. Her normal curiosity had been diluted by the circumstances of her visit. Maybe in a day or two she would find it interesting that the house had a secret stairway and real mahogany paneling, that the floor in the foyer below was made of imported Italian marble. Right now none of that penetrated her senses.

Nor did the musty smell of old carpets and draperies. For the moment it was all she could do to put one foot in front of the other and follow Bryan Hennessy down the hall.

'Don't read too much into your mother's reaction tonight,' he said quietly, slowing his long strides and turning to regard her with a serious expression. He carried a suitcase in each hand and his faded blue shirt was stained dark from her tears in spots across his chest. 'You took her by surprise. She doesn't handle surprises very well.'

Rachel thought of Terence and Addie's reaction to him, and she smiled sadly as she reached up to tuck a strand of hair behind her ear. 'No, she never did.'

'She'll probably be perfectly composed tomorrow.'

A weak smile was the best Rachel could manage. She hoped her mother was perfectly composed in the morning, but that wouldn't help her tonight. She felt shaken to the very foundation of her soul. If she lived to be a hundred, she would never forget the wild fury in her mother's eyes as she'd shouted at her to get out of the house. Remembering the scene now sent a shaft of pain through her so sharp, it nearly stole her breath from her lungs. She had known it would be difficult coming back, but she'd never imagined anything like the bizarre scene she'd been a part of. It didn't even help to know it was the illness that made Addie behave irrationally. There was just too much true emotion beneath the madness to easily push the outburst aside.

'You can take my room for tonight,' Bryan said, shouldering open a door and standing back in invitation for her to precede him into the room. 'It's the only spare bed with sheets on it.'

'I can't throw you out of your bed,' Rachel protested, going to stand over the heat register, hoping it would chase away some of the chill that was permeating her bones.

'A little while ago you were ready to throw me out of the house,' Bryan said with a charming smile, trying to tease an answering smile out of Rachel. He kept his gaze on her as he bent to set her suitcases down beside the dresser.

Rachel closed her eyes and sighed. She managed a wry twist of her lips, but that was all. There was no way she could handle this man on any level – teasing, arguing, anything. Aside from being tired enough to drop, her feelings toward him were completely tangled. He was a stranger, a man who was taking her dotty mother's money to hunt for ghosts. He was an antagonist who seemed to disapprove of her. He was inane one minute and serious the next. He was an attractive man, arousing needs in her that had been left unattended for too long. He was a compassionate human being, offering her comfort and support. That would have been a confusing mix for a person to handle on the best of days, and this was most certainly not the best of days.

'Get some rest,' Bryan whispered.

He didn't remember crossing the room. He didn't remember making the decision to touch Rachel Lindquist, but his finger was crooked beneath her chin and he was tilting her face up as if he had every intention of kissing her. It took a considerable effort not to do just that. Her lips were slightly parted. Her thick lashes were lowered, lying like a pair of delicate lace fans against her pale cheeks.

Desire ached all through his body, throbbing a little harder behind the suddenly close confines of his jeans. He cursed his rogue hormones. What was the matter with him – acting like some randy stallion when this poor girl was so physically and emotionally exhausted she seemed near collapse? What was he doing feeling attracted to her anyway? For all he knew she had come there to pack Addie up and hustle her off to a rest home. The only significant facts he knew about her were that she had run off five years ago and hadn't come back.

But she had tried to call . . . and she had cried on his shoulder . . . and she looked so small and sad . . .

He shook his head for the umpteenth time that night, amazed by his sudden, strange feelings. True, he had always had a soft spot in his heart for a damsel in distress, but he wasn't interested in getting involved with one just now. No. His life was falling back into order; that was all he wanted to concentrate on now. He wasn't interested in taking on the problems of a complicated mother-daughter relationship or the raft of troubles that would accompany Addie's illness. He didn't want to concentrate on Rachel Lindquist and all the pain and broken dreams he'd seen in her eyes.

She opened her eyes and stared up at him, and yet another blast of heat seared through him.

'Get some rest,' he murmured again, backing away before he lost all sense.

'Where will you sleep?'

'Don't worry about me,' he said, forcing one of his silly, sunny smiles as he moved toward the door. He had the distinct impression he wasn't going to sleep at all. 'I'm a magical being; I can sleep anywhere. Tables, chairs, stairs. I once spent the night in the trunk of a Mercedes-Benz, but that's a long story and I'm really not at liberty to divulge the details. Suffice it to say they put all the luxury features in other parts of the car.'

Rachel stared at him, amazed. She wanted to laugh. After all the horrid things that had happened in the past few days, she wanted to laugh at Bryan Hennessy because he was silly and funny in a way unlike anyone she had ever known. It amazed her that she still had a sense of humor. She felt a little warmer inside because of it.

'You're a very unusual person, Mr. Hennessy,' she said with a wry smile.

He beamed. 'Why, thank you.'

Rachel chuckled. 'It wasn't exactly a compliment.'

'It was to me. We Hennessys pride ourselves on being unique.'

'You're certainly that,' she said, trying unsuccessfully to stifle a yawn.

'The bathroom is down the hall on the right,' Bryan said over his shoulder as he started out the door. 'Watch out for the faucet in the sink, it sprays like a geyser every once in a while for no apparent reason. I think it may be possessed. Poltergeists often take up residence in the plumbing, you know. No doubt the result of faulty toilet training when they were toddlers. That's my theory anyway.'

'Mr. Hennessy,' Rachel blurted out, a part of her loath to have him leave.

'Bryan,' he corrected her, turning back and bracing a forearm against the doorjamb. He felt old enough as it was these days; he didn't need this lovely little thing calling him mister. He had to have ten years on Rachel Lindquist – at least. At the moment she didn't look a day over fifteen, and still he wanted to kiss her. That thought left him feeling like a lecher.

'Bryan,' she said hesitantly, clasping her small white hands in front of her. 'Thank you for giving me your room and . . . for . . . everything.'

She couldn't quite bring herself to say 'holding me.' She wasn't comfortable with the idea of having turned to a stranger that way, pouring her pain out to him. She couldn't remember the last time she'd cried in front of someone. Not even when her mother had told her she could never come home had she let the tears fall with a witness present. She hadn't cried in front of her mother, nor had she cried when she had gone outside and gotten in the car with Terence. Her fierce pride hadn't allowed it.

But tonight she hadn't been able to keep the tears in check. They had fallen in torrents onto Bryan Hennessy's solid chest. And he had held her as if it had been the most natural thing in the world.

Bryan stared at her for a moment from his position in the doorway. She stood beside the bed, looking vulnerable in her baggy purple sweater, her baby-fine hair framing her face in wisps. Her skin looked as soft and rich as cream. Her eyes were like pools of twilight. Longing ribboned through him. Without a word he left the room, closing the door behind him.

Immediately Rachel felt lonely. Lonely for a lunatic. How silly, she scolded herself. She was lonely for a con man just because he had a nice smile and a weird sense of humor. That was hardly like her normal, practical self.

To take her mind off her feelings, she busied herself getting ready for bed. She was so tired, it took all of her flagging concentration to accomplish that simple task. She pulled her nightgown out of one battered suitcase and changed into it quickly. It wasn't a nightgown precisely, but an extra large T-shirt with a bust of Bach silk-screened on the front above the words 'I go for baroque.' Forgoing her nightly ritual of washing her face and brushing her teeth, she removed the pins from

28

her hair and let it fall in waves past her shoulders. She pulled back the covers of the bed and slipped between them, groaning in relief as her weary body settled into the mattress.

As exhausted as she was, she couldn't sleep. She lay in the bed, staring at the ceiling for a long while, trying not to think of anything at all. But she wasn't able to blank her mind. Thoughts kept creeping in from the edge of her consciousness – thoughts of Addie, of Terence, of the past, of the future, of Bryan Hennessy.

The pillow she lay her head on carried his scent. The sheets that enveloped her body had covered his. The mattress beneath her had dipped beneath the weight of his lean, athletic body. Those thoughts seemed almost unbearably erotic to her. She moved restlessly, sexual awareness arousing all her nerve endings so that the gentle rasp of the sheets against her skin had all the impact of a caress. Her suddenly fertile imagination conjured up an image of him lying beside her, his big hands stroking her soothingly, his lips feathering kisses along her jaw. Her nipples tightened, and a dull ache coiled low in her belly.

Joining all the other emotions jumbled inside her was a vague sense of guilt and shame. She had no business thinking such thoughts about a man she hardly knew. It wasn't like her to indulge in sexual fantasies anyway. She had never been a particularly sexual person. She discounted her feelings as a reaction to stress. She was feeling overwhelmed. It was only natural to want to turn to someone, to be held, to forget.

And there was so much she would have liked to forget – the dreams she had abandoned, the ones that had drifted away, the opportunities she had squandered.

Finally giving up on the idea of falling into a peaceful sleep, Rachel turned on the ancient lamp that sat on a lace doily on the stand beside the bed. She propped her pillow against the massive carved headboard and leaned back against it.

The light cast its glow on only half the room, leaving the farther corners shrouded in shadows. There was an enormous, sinister-looking armoire standing opposite the bed with one door open and athletic socks hanging out of the top drawer as if they were trying to slither out and escape. To the right of the bed an assortment of junk lined the wall – old steamer trunks, wooden chairs, and a bird cage large enough to hold a vulture. To the left of the bed was a dressing table with a cracked mirror. There were books piled on it, and charts and notes were strewn across the top of it as if it was being used as a desk.

On the nightstand beside the bed was additional evidence that Bryan Hennessy occupied the room. There was a watch that was either running down or was set for the wrong time zone. Rachel picked it up and examined it more closely, telling herself she had a right to know who this man was her mother had invited to stay in her home. It was a nice watch, gold with a brown leather band that was curved by long use to the shape of its owner's wrist. It had an old-fashioned face – no glowing digital readout, but script numerals and delicate hands. The back was engraved WITH LOVE, MOM AND DAD. 1977.

Carefully replacing it on the table, Rachel glanced at the snapshot held in a plain gold frame. A younger Bryan Hennessy stood in a cap and gown behind three smiling young women – a blonde, a brunette, and a redhead. At least he wasn't prejudiced, Rachel thought with a strange spurt of something akin to jealousy.

Pushing the unwelcome feeling aside, she looked at the crumpled scraps of paper that had been tossed across the dusty surface of the night-stand. They were notes with odd messages like 'Jayne says to eat breakfast tomorrow,' 'Go to library – background, Drake House,' 'Dinner with Faith and Shane, seven sharp. Get a haircut!' 'Addie capable of hidden psychokinesis? That could explain object movement in grid nine.'

Was it possible Bryan Hennessy was truly a scientist of some sort? It seemed unlikely a con man would be so thorough as to leave notes like that last one on his nightstand on the off chance someone with a fully functioning mind might stumble across them. On the other hand, a ghost hunter seemed too farfetched for words.

Rachel couldn't find it in her to believe in ghosts. Reality was proving tough enough to deal with; she didn't have time to wonder about the supernatural as well. She knew she had to focus on the here and now. She had to concentrate on the grim practical aspects of her future and her mother's future. In view of what had happened in the past few years, she knew it was pointless to waste time on dreams and wishes. There was no such thing as magic or happily-ever-after. There were no such things as ghosts.

As if to mock her, the image of Terence Bretton filled her head. Handsome, smiling Terence, as he had been when she'd met him at a coffee house located just off the campus of Berkeley. She'd been a sophomore, diligently studying classical music on a scholarship, dutifully pursuing the career in opera her mother had been grooming her for for her entire life. Terence had been a breath of fresh air to a girl who had lived a sheltered, structured life of voice lessons and practice and study. Terence, with his disarming, lopsided grin and twinkling green eyes. Terence, full of big dreams but lacking the ambition to make them come true.

Only she hadn't know that at the time, Rachel reflected with a wistful smile. She had fallen for Terence's charm and his dreams and his honest, untrained voice. He had offered her love and freedom, and she had embraced both.

Her initial attraction to him had been calculated. Terence, a folk singer who led a Gypsy's life, was everything Rachel knew her mother would detest. She had loved her mother, but rebellion was a natural part of growing up. Rachel's had come later than most, she knew. She had abruptly become fed up with the control Addie had wielded over her life.

She had suddenly burned out on the hours of training, the discipline, the lack of a normal social life, the constant reminders of how hard Addie worked to secure her future. She had gone to the Coffee Mill out of defiance and had determinedly fallen for the handsome young man playing the guitar on the small stage there.

It didn't seem like five years ago. It seemed like a lifetime ago. Another lifetime down a trail of broken dreams.

Terence had never made it big, and the burden of his mediocrity had fallen on Rachel's shoulders. Terence didn't like to deal with the realities of booking gigs and balancing books. Sensible and practical, Rachel had taken on the responsibilities. Their relationship had gradually cooled from lovers to friends.

Her love for Terence Bretton had slipped away until a part of her had almost come to hate him. According to Terence, it was always someone else's fault he didn't hit the big time. According to him, there was always another golden opportunity around the corner just waiting for him.

The news about Addie had been the final straw. Terence's reaction had been no less than Rachel should have expected. Still, she had held on to the last of her hope that he would somehow redeem himself, would somehow make up for all the disappointments he had handed her over the years. All she had wanted was his friendship and his support. It hadn't seemed so much to ask. What a fool she'd been.

'Put her in a home.'

'She's my mother.'

'She disowned you.'

'She raised me by herself after Dad died. She took care of me. I should do the same for her.'

'If her mind is going, she'll never know the difference, Rachel. Put her away someplace. We've got our lives to live. We've got plans. We can't stop now. I'm going to make it big, Rachel. I need you there beside me.'

'So does my mother.'

Now Rachel sighed and hugged the spare pillow to her chest as sadness overcame her. Terence wasn't going to make it big. He didn't have plans, he had dreams, and he spent his time expecting them magically to come true with little or no effort on his part. Rachel had learned the hard way that there was no such thing as magic.

In the end her choice had been clear. In fact, there had been no choice to make. She had known the instant after Dr. Moore had told her the news that she would go to Addie.

Now she was there and Addie didn't want her.

They would get over that hurdle somehow. Beneath the hurt and the uncertainty, Rachel had bedrock determination, no doubt inherited from her indomitable mother. She would reconcile with Addie somehow. She would deal with the reality of Addie's condition somehow. As they had after Verne Lindquist had been killed, the two of them would get along

. . . somehow. It wasn't going to be fun. It wasn't going to be easy. But they would manage it. Somehow.

And what about Bryan Hennessy?

A sharp pang ran through her, and she hugged her pillow a little harder. Bryan Hennessy was a stranger. He had nothing to do with their situation. He couldn't. She had all she could handle with Addie. A relationship with a man was out of the question. Why she was even thinking about it was beyond her. She didn't know Bryan Hennessy from a goose. He might have been a con man or a killer or another Terence Bretton. Judging from all his nonsensical piffle, he was probably worse than Terence. At least Terence aspired to something. To what could a ghost hunter aspire?

She was just overreacting to him because she was exhausted and he had been gallant enough to offer her his shoulder to cry on and his bed to sleep in. He wouldn't want to get involved with her, at any rate. What fool would volunteer to take on the problems she was facing?

You have to help her.

Bryan scowled. He shifted positions in the blood-red leather wing chair. The study was located in grid nine of his chart of the first floor of Drake House. Addie had told him she'd seen things move in this room – move with the assistance of Wimsey. According to her, Wimsey had twice rearranged the furniture because 'he likes it the way he likes it.' She had moved it all around once, just out of stubbornness, but Wimsey had put it back.

Bryan had chosen this room to spend the night in because he knew damn well he wasn't going to sleep, and he was hoping against hope for a distraction – the appearance of Wimsey, a book falling off the shelf by itself, a sudden cold breeze, anything. Anything that would help get his mind off Rachel Lindquist sleeping in the same bed he had slept in, wrapping the sheets around her slender body, burrowing her angel's face into his pillow.

He groaned as his blood stirred hot in his veins. He could just imagine what she looked like sleeping: soft and tempting with her wild honey-gold hair mussed around her head. She was probably wearing a T-shirt, and the soft fabric would mold around her breasts the way his hands wanted to mold around them. The thought had him more than half turned on.

He swore under his breath. What kind of depraved creep was he turning into? There was poor Rachel, exhausted, frightened, hurt, trying to manage a few hours rest and escape from her troubles, and here he was lusting after her!

She's very pretty.

'Yes, she's pretty,' he grumbled. 'She's very pretty. And she's got a lot of problems, and I don't want to get involved.'

For the first time he wondered about the folk singer Rachel had run off with five years before. Where was he? What kind of jerk was he that he would send Rachel to deal with this crisis on her own? Clarence something. 'A common tramp' Addie had called him. Somehow, Bryan doubted Rachel would run off with a common tramp. Despite her casual style of dress, she radiated class. It was there in the way she held herself, in the way she moved, in the way she spoke.

There was obviously a lot more to the story than an 'ungrateful' daughter taking up with a 'cheap folk singer.' Bryan was a little disappointed in himself for so readily believing the worst. Especially since it had come from Addie, who was disoriented much of the time. Maybe Rachel Lindquist was rotten to the core, but it wasn't his place to make that judgment without having all the facts. On the other hand, his life would be a whole lot simpler if he believed the worst and stayed away from her.

Even as he thought it, he had the sinking realization that it wasn't going to happen. It wasn't in him to judge people harshly. It wasn't in him to stand by and watch a lady struggle with a load that was too heavy for her to carry, either.

He had always taken care of the women in his life. His sisters first, and then Faith and Alaina and Jayne. Then Serena. Now Serena was gone, and the three lovelier members of the Fearsome Foursome were being taken care of by their mates. Enter Rachel Lindquist with her big violet eyes and incredible pink mouth and stubborn pride tilting her little chin up.

Fighting an inner battle, Bryan flung himself out of the chair and paced the width of the room, head down, his hands combing back through his tawny hair again and again.

You have to help her. She needs help.

'No, not me. I can't help anybody. I can't even help myself. She can get help from the doctor. She can join a support group. Just leave me out of it.'

He paced some more, feeling the pressure in a strangely tangible way, as if it were pressing in on him from all around. It was not unlike diving deep into the black depths of the ocean, a silky nothingness pushing in on him from all sides, threatening to crush his chest. To escape it, he threw open the French doors and strode out onto the stone terrace.

As it had earlier, the cool air calmed him. He dropped onto a bench and leaned over, his elbows on his thighs, his hands rubbing the back of his neck.

He had known Serena was dying when he had married her. He had loved her, and the thought of letting her face death alone had been incomprehensible. Her decline and ultimate death had been the worst thing he could ever imagine going through. He had endured it for her, but he had vowed to himself never to go through anything like it again.

Rachel isn't facing death.

'No, but she's facing pain, and I've had enough pain to last me a lifetime.'

What about her? You could ease her pain. You could lighten her burden.

'How?' he asked his inner voice as he pulled his glasses off and rubbed the bridge of his nose with a thumb and forefinger.

Magic.

Bryan laughed at that. He wasn't sure he knew what magic was anymore. Was he supposed to believe he could pull a rabbit out of his hat, and Rachel and Addie's troubles would disappear? It wouldn't happen.

But it might help.

After settling his glasses back into place, he reached into the breast pocket of his shirt and withdrew a short black wand, not more than five inches long and as big around as a cigarette. With a flick of his wrist, it became a silken red rose with a thin stem that abruptly drooped over his hand. A smile lifted the corner of his mouth.

'If I can't dazzle her with my magic, maybe I can be a source of comic relief,' he said dryly, tucking the wilted rose back into his shirt pocket.

He hadn't been able to perform the simplest of tricks for months now. Though he kept trying, deep down he was afraid he had lost his magic forever.

He pushed himself up from the bench and wandered back into the house. His broad shoulders sagging under the twin burdens of exhaustion and stress, he picked up the glass of whiskey he had left on the leather blotter of the walnut desk. He had hoped the excellent liquor he'd found in a bottle in a desk drawer would help him sleep. The glass was nearly empty. Bryan frowned. He could have sworn he'd left a good inch in it when he'd gone outside. He didn't notice the stain near his feet on the old woolen carpet or the scent of liquor seeping up from the fabric. He noticed only that his whiskey was gone, and he didn't feel like pouring another.

Shrugging, he dismissed the question and tossed back most of what was left of the drink. Remembering things had never been his strong suit.

The study was quiet. This room was supposed to be a hotbed of paranormal activity, but not one thing out of the ordinary had happened in the few days he'd been there. Worse than that, Bryan felt nothing unusual, sensed nothing whatsoever.

As he gazed around the dark room, he wondered morosely if he was losing his touch professionally as well as with his magic. He had always had phenomenal success seeking out psychic disturbances. He had always been able to tune in to the scene and feel things others couldn't. His special sensitivity had led him to his career. Had it deserted him?

Too tired to think about it, he wandered from the room and down the hall to search for something comfortable to stretch out on.

4

Rachel awoke early from a fitful sleep. Soft gray light seeped into the room through the window. She struggled with the covers that were tangled around her, and pushed herself up in the bed so she could lean back against the headboard. She was exhausted. The mere idea of getting out of bed made her groan, and when she thought of what she would have to face, she almost crawled back under the covers. Not that it would have done her any good. She hadn't gotten a moment's rest during the night. Dreams had haunted her, one right after another, interweaving and intermingling until they couldn't be separated. Even now emotions assailed her, panic chief among them.

The main theme of the dream marathon had been Addie. How were they ever going to get through what was ahead of them if her mother wouldn't accept her help? It was one thing for Rachel to say she was going to take care of Addie. Accomplishing that task was going to be another thing altogether. Addie had never been the kind of woman who stood to the side, wringing her hands and letting other people run her life. She had always been so strong, so independent, such a dictator, running their lives like an admiral on a tight ship.

Rachel was a woman now and hardly the subservient, obedient little thing she had been in her youth. Because of Terence's lack of responsibility, she had been forced to the role of leader. She had handled the job with the same grit and determination her mother had always shown. She knew from experience how to take charge of a situation.

But she didn't know how to take care of Addie. It seemed completely unnatural to assume her mother's role as head of the family and relegate Addie to second place. And she knew with a sense of dread that was like a lump of ice in her stomach that Addie wasn't going to go down without a fight.

The first logical step was the appointment Rachel had scheduled with Dr. Moore. Perhaps he would be able to make Addie see reason. Hopefully Bryan had been right in saying Addie would be more composed in the morning, better able to understand and to cope with the changes that were inevitable.

A tiny flame of hope flared to life inside her, and it burned a little hotter as she continued to think about Bryan.

A strangely clear image of him waking up filled her imagination. His tawny hair would be tousled, his blue eyes bleary and heavy-lidded. He would rub his hand along the stubble on his strong jaw. She could almost smell his warm male scent, could almost feel his warm weight in the bed beside her. That warmth crept into her and swirled lazily through her body.

Rachel forced her eyes open wide and all but leapt from the bed.

'What are you doing, thinking that way, Rachel Lindquist?' she demanded, staring at her reflection in the cracked mirror. With her cheeks flushed and her hair a wild tangle around her head, she looked like a strumpet. A scowl turned down her pretty mouth. 'What's the matter with you? Bryan Hennessy is not now, nor will he ever be a part of your life. You are going to see to that first thing this morning.'

Whether he was a legitimate scientist or not didn't enter into it. She couldn't afford to pay him for his questionable services. She had things like doctor bills and rent to consider.

It still made her angry to think he would take money from Addie. Her mother was obviously not in full command of her faculties. This ghost business of hers was most probably some result of the Alzheimer's. Rachel had read that some victims of the dementing illness experience hallucinations. This ghost, this 'whimsy,' was probably just that – whimsy. The mother she remembered would no more believe in ghosts than she would believe in Santa Claus.

Rachel padded across the cold floor to the window for her first glimpse of the view from Drake House. Stepping over a large pair of battered loafers and around a bird cage, she peeled back one of the sheets from the glass. Fog obscured the view. She could hear the distant crash of the ocean, but she couldn't see the lawn, let alone the cliff edge or the blue water beyond.

'How symbolic of my life at the moment,' she said dryly.

She turned away from the window and set herself to the task of preparing to face the day. With an eye toward pleasing her mother, she dressed in a conservative white blouse and a hunter-green jumper, painstakingly restored order to her hair, then turned to make the bed. That was when she found the rose.

A single yellow rose, slightly mangled, was peeking out from beneath the spare pillow she had hugged and punched and tussled with throughout the night. She picked it up by the end of the stem, staring at it in shock and disbelief as a petal dropped off and drifted to the bed.

Warmth surged through her before she could check it. A rose. How lovely. How thoughtful. How sweet. Then a blush bloomed on her cheeks and indignation rose up inside her. Bryan Hennessy had snuck into her room! He'd come into her room while she had been asleep.

Of all the low, strange things to do. How long had he stood beside the bed, looking at her? A minute? Five minutes? The very idea was mortifying! She might have been talking in her sleep or snoring or drooling, while this man she barely knew watched her!

Leaving the housekeeping for later, Rachel turned on her heel and stormed purposefully from the room to go in search of her midnight caller.

Bryan woke slowly, knowing instinctively that he would be better off unconscious. All the clues were there as his mind reached cautiously up out of the depths of sleep: an ache here, the beginnings of a pain there. Still, his eyes came halfway open, and he rubbed his hand along his jaw, rasping a two-day growth of whiskers against his palm. He really did have to remember to shave later.

The light in the billiard room was dim. It was early, he guessed, early enough for him to get to the bird cages before Addie did. Groaning, he pushed himself upright on the felt-covered slate of the old billiard table and swung his long legs over the edge. His body protested in more places than he cared to count.

'Maybe I'm getting too old for this kind of thing,' he reflected as he retrieved his spectacles from the cue-stick rack and put them on. He looked at himself then in the ornate mirror that hung on the wall, taking up a space equal to that of the billiard table. Even through a couple of decades worth of dust he looked bad. He looked like a vagrant. His shirt was rumpled beyond redemption, the tails hanging out of his equally wrinkled pants. His wilted magic rose drooped over the edge of his shirt pocket.

A shower, a shave, and clean clothes were the order of the morning, he thought as he slicked his disheveled hair back with his hands. But first, the bird cages.

He went into the parlor and unearthed the coffee can filled with bird seed Addie kept stashed behind a burgundy velvet fainting couch. Also behind the couch were a dozen unopened bags of bird seed and a foot-high stack of mail. Addie was notorious for stashing things away, like a squirrel hoarding nuts for the winter. And, like a squirrel, she often forgot where she had buried her booty. She never forgot her bird seed, however. She only forgot that she didn't have a bird.

Bryan wondered what her frame of mind would be this morning. He hoped for Rachel's sake Addie would be in one of her more normal periods. The two of them had a lot to talk over, a lot to settle between them, and not much time to do it. That was the one sure thing about Addie's illness: it would progress. There would be no remission, no reprieve. What needed settling between mother and daughter needed settling as soon as possible.

'Not that I'm getting involved,' Bryan mumbled as he opened a wire cage and scraped the seed out of the little dish and into the coffee can. 'I'm just here minding my own business, doing my little job.'

To distract himself from the inner voice that was trying to tell him differently, he began to sing softly to himself. 'I got a ghoul in Kalamazoo—'

'Mr. Hennessy.' Rachel paused in the doorway of the parlor, ready to launch into her tirade, but the sight of Bryan brought her up short. He was crouched over a little bamboo bird cage – just one of dozens of bird cages in the room – digging bird seed out of the tiny dish with one large finger.

'Addie gets upset if Lester doesn't eat,' Bryan explained, his expression serious.

Rachel's heart turned over in her breast. Not many men of her acquaintance would have catered to an old lady the way this one did. But then, he was getting paid for it, she reminded herself, steeling her resolve.

She marched across the room and thrust the bedraggled flower in his face. 'Would you care to explain the meaning of this?'

Bryan rose slowly to his full height, wincing absently at his stiff muscles. His gaze moved from the flower to Rachel and back again. He took a deep breath, pondering. His eyebrows rose and fell, and he pushed his glasses up on his nose.

'It's a rose,' he said finally.

'I know it's a rose,' Rachel said irritably. 'Would you care to explain why I found it on my pillow this morning?'

She was staring up at him with fire in her violet eyes, as if finding a rose on her pillow were some horrible affront to her sensibilities. Bryan couldn't stop the soft, thick warmth that filled his chest. She was lovely. There was no denying that. She had to have just combed her honey-colored hair back and arranged it at the nape of her neck, but already wisps had pulled loose to curl around her face. She was no doubt trying her darnedest to look indignant, but her features were too soft and angelic for her to quite pull it off.

'Mr. Hennessy,' she repeated, her tone clipped. It was the tone of an irate schoolteacher. 'I'm waiting for an explanation.'

Bryan sighed a bit, dragging his gaze off the lush, kissable curve of her lower lip. He gave her a bright smile. 'Is this a riddle? I do like a good riddle.'

'It's an infringement on my privacy, and I don't like it at all,' Rachel said, thumping the bedraggled flower against his chest. 'I know I was sleeping in what is technically your room, but that doesn't give you the right to just walk in—'

'I wasn't in your room.'

'Then how did this get on my pillow?' she asked, shaking the flower for emphasis. Yellow petals floated to the floor.

Bryan's broad shoulders rose. Behind his spectacles his blue eyes sparkled. He smiled his most engaging smile. 'Magic?'

Rachel frowned in disapproval. 'I don't believe in magic, Mr. Hennessy.'

'My name is Bryan,' he corrected her soberly as he lifted the flower from her small fingers. 'Everyone should believe in magic, Rachel,' he said. He held her gaze with his as he performed a little sleight of hand, making the rose disappear and a playing card appear in its place.

His eyes went wide. The trick had worked! He had his magic back!

Trying to swallow some of his excitement, he handed the queen of hearts to Rachel.

She looked at it and went on frowning, unimpressed. 'Card tricks?'

'It's the best I could do on short notice,' he said cheerfully. 'I'm not the kind of fellow who keeps silk scarves tucked up his sleeve, you know. You must know, or you wouldn't have thought I was the one in your room last night.'

'It had to be you,' Rachel insisted. 'Who else could it have been?'

'Addie, I suppose.' He rubbed his chin in thought, and his eyes brightened suddenly. 'Or Wimsey. Did you see anything, hear anything? Did you notice any change in the air temperature?'

'I don't believe in ghosts, either,' Rachel said. 'No sensible person does. Which is another reason I've come to see you. I'm going to have to ask you to leave, Mr. Hennessy.'

'Oh, dear.' Bryan sighed. 'I thought we'd settled this. My deal was with Addie.'

'My mother isn't . . . up to . . . making decisions like that,' Rachel said, avoiding the word *competency* and its legal ramifications. 'Really, I think it's quite cruel of you to play on her illness this way. I should probably report you—'

'Whoa there, angel,' Bryan said, a thread of steel in his soft voice and the glint of it in his eyes. His jaw hardened as he stared down at her, all traces of the innocuous magician gone. 'Let's get something straight here right away. I'm not taking advantage of Addie. I'm not taking a red cent from her, and I heartily resent that you think I would.'

'But you said you have a contract—'

'That's right. Addie has agreed to let me stay here and search for the ghost.'

'There is no ghost,' Rachel said in exasperation. 'Don't you understand? Addie isn't well. This ghost is just what she calls it – whimsy.'

Bryan stared at her, solemn and sad. 'Just because you don't believe in something doesn't mean it isn't true, Rachel. Trees fall in the woods all the time, and they make plenty of noise even though you're not there to hear it.'

Rachel refused to listen. Her mind was made up. 'My mother is a lonely old woman who has invented this whimsy to keep her company. There's no reason for you to stay, Mr. Hennessy.'

'I'm going to start walking with a cane if you don't stop that mister business.' Bryan grumbled, combing his hair back with his fingers. He took a deep, cleansing breath and started in again. 'I am aware of Addie's illness. Has it occurred to you what it must be like to know your mind is slipping away a little bit at a time and realize there's nothing you can do about it? Have you considered what it must be like to have everyone in town think you're some kind of lunatic and not believe a word you say?

'You may not believe in ghosts, Rachel, that's your prerogative, but Addie believes in Wimsey, and I believe there's every chance that he's a genuine, bona fide entity. If I can prove that, I can give Addie a little bit of her dignity back. Don't you think that's worth having a nuisance like me around for a little while?'

Rachel couldn't find any words for a rebuttal. She felt ashamed of herself for the things she had accused Bryan of. Worse, she felt a strange flutter of panic in her throat. If he had been a con man, she could have gotten rid of him. If he had been a crook, she could have sent him on his way and held on to her righteous anger. But he wasn't a con man or a crook. He was a temptation. Her heart rate shifted gears at the realization.

She had wanted him gone not only to protect her mother, but to protect herself. There was something about Bryan Hennessy that attracted her beyond reason, and she couldn't allow that. She was there because of Addie. Addie would need her undivided attention. She couldn't waste her energy on an attraction to a man who made up silly songs and pulled playing cards out of thin air.

'What do you say, Rachel?' Bryan queried softly. He suddenly felt compelled – almost *pro*pelled – to step closer to her. It was too early in the day to question the wisdom of getting too near, so he gave in to the urge. He inched a little closer so she had to tilt her head back to look up at him. It would have been so simple to raise his hands and frame her face. The desire to do that and to lean down and kiss her swam through him.

His held breath burned in his lungs as he waited for her answer. Would she let him stay? Why did it matter so much? This trembling hope inside him had to do with something other than Wimsey, but he refused to think of what it could be. He told himself he needed this job right now because he needed something to focus on. It wasn't that he was interested in getting involved with Rachel. Despite the argument his inner voice had put up the night before, he wasn't convinced he could help her.

But as he looked down at her, at the uncertainty and the questions that filled her eyes, the need to have her say yes grew inside him to mountainous proportions. And the attraction both of them would rather have denied strengthened and tightened its hold.

'What do you say, Rachel?' he asked, his voice a whisper. 'Will you give me a chance?'

Rachel swallowed hard. Her heart was pounding, her knees were wobbling. There was something more in his question than permission to work in the house. She read it instinctively as she stared up into his earnest blue gaze. She felt it in her heart, and fear cut through the haze of this strange desire. How could she cope with a man who believed in magic?

In some distant part of the house a door banged and voices sounded.

She couldn't, Rachel whispered to herself. The last thing she needed was a man who believes in magic.

Bryan flinched slightly. He had heard the words spoken only in her soul, and they went straight to his heart.

Before he had a chance to wonder about it, the voices that had sounded faraway were suddenly sounding again – just outside the parlor. Then the doorway was filled with the substantial form of Deputy Skreawupp. The deputy hooked his thumbs behind the buckle of his belt, his arms framing his pot belly. He scowled, his frown reaching down his face nearly to his double chins. He bore a striking resemblance to Jonathan Winters but hadn't nearly the same sense of humor.

Bryan raised his eyebrows and stepped back from Rachel, breaking the tension that had enveloped them both. Suddenly a hand reached around from behind the deputy and a finger thrust forth.

'There she is!' Addie's voice was muffled by the deputy's bulk. 'She's the one.'

The deputy lumbered forward, his dark gaze pinned on Rachel, whose expression was the very picture of stunned surprise. 'All right, angel face, the jig's up,' he said, his voice a flat, comical monotone that could have belonged to a detective in a movie from the forties.

'I beg your pardon?' Rachel squeaked, her gaze darting from the deputy to her mother and back.

Addie gave her a cold, hard look. 'She's the one, Officer. The intruder.'

'Mother!' Rachel exclaimed, aghast. Embarrassment flamed in her cheeks.

'She looks like my daughter, but she isn't,' Addie said. 'She's an imposter. She broke in here last night and stole my dentures.'

'That's low,' the deputy said, shaking his head reproachfully. 'I've heard it all before. Desperate times and desperate measures. Makes me sick.'

'It's not true!' Rachel insisted emphatically. 'I *am* her daughter.' She turned toward Addie, her big eyes imploring. 'Mother, how could you say that?'

'You're not my daughter. My daughter left me,' Addie said flatly. She lifted her slim nose regally and gave a dismissing wave of her hand. 'Take her away, Deputy. I'm going to go have my toast. Hennessy, to the kitchen.'

With that she turned on the heel of her green rubber garden boot and marched from the room, obviously expecting Bryan to follow her. Bryan cleared his throat and smiled pleasantly at the deputy. 'I believe there's been a small misunderstanding here.'

The deputy pulled out a pocket notebook and a pencil, prepared to take Bryan's statement. 'You were here last night?'

'Yes. I slept on the billiard table. I wouldn't recommend it.'

Skreawupp halted his scribbling and pointed at Bryan with his eraser. 'Don't get cute with me, bub. I'll clip you like a wet poodle.'

Bryan looked shocked. 'Please, sir, there's a lady present!'

'Look,' the deputy growled, his droopy shoulders slumping further. He gave up on Bryan, directing his questions to Rachel. 'I am damned sick of being called out here on all kinds of wild goose chases. Are you Batty Addie's daughter, or what?'

'I am Rachel Lindquist,' Rachel said tightly, her chin rising defiantly, her eyes burning with fury at the deputy's attitude. 'Would you care to see proof of identification?'

'Skip it.' He tucked his notebook back into his breast pocket. 'I should have known this would be another waste of my valuable time. Last month she had me out here because she thought a commie sub had washed up on her beach. Before that she was being abducted by a religious cult. I don't need it.'

'Well,' Bryan said in a tone that belied the anger in his own eyes, 'we'll all kick in a little extra on our taxes next time around to compensate.' He followed the deputy into the hall and pointed the way to the front door. 'I'd show you out, but I have to go make the toast.'

'Hippie,' Skreawupp muttered, swaggering away. He turned and pointed a finger at Bryan. 'I've got my eye on you, Jack.'

Rachel pushed past them both and strode stiffly down the hall, trying to find her way through the maze of rooms to the kitchen. She found rooms packed full of dusty old furniture, one room that was crammed full of old wooden church pews stacked one on top of another like cordwood. Finally she pushed open the correct door.

The kitchen had once been sunny yellow, but the color of the walls had dulled over the years to a dingy ivory shade. It was a huge room with black and white tiles on the floor and an array of oversize appliances, one of which was an outdated wood-burning cookstove that had been left ostensibly for decorative purposes. Near the window was an oak table that had been haphazardly set with mismatched china. Addie sat at her place, her back straight, her hands folded in the lap of her flowered cotton housedress. She refused to look when Rachel entered the room.

'Mother, we have to talk,' Rachel said through clenched teeth.

'I don't want to talk to you. Where is Hennessy? I want my toast.'

Rachel pulled out the chair beside Addie's and sat down. She composed herself as best she could. She had read about the kind of behavior her mother was exhibiting, but comprehending a textbook and living the reality were proving to be two very different things. Logically, she knew Addie's behavior stemmed from her illness. Realistically, she knew her mother was probably incapable of manipulation because manipulation required a great deal of careful thought and planning, and those were abilities Addie was losing.

Emotionally, she couldn't help but feel hurt and humiliated and angry. She resented the way she'd been treated since coming to her mother's house. She felt manipulated, because Addie had been a master at it in her day. It had been Addie's machinations that had ultimately driven them apart. That was a difficult thing to forget now, when Deputy Skreawupp's squad car was rolling down the driveway.

'Mother,' Rachel said, trying to speak calmly so she wouldn't precipitate another catastrophic reaction like the one she had been greeted with the night before. 'I'm Rachel. I'm your daughter.'

Addie glanced at her, annoyance pulling her brows together above her cool blue eyes. 'Of course I know who you are.'

That was her standard reply when she wanted to cover up a lapse in memory, but this time it was the truth. She hadn't recognized Rachel earlier, when she'd seen her in the upstairs hall. Now she was ashamed of having called the police, but it was over and done with and there was nothing she could do about it. She closed her eyes and turned away.

'Mother, I know about your illness. I've come here to help.'

'I've been a little forgetful recently, that's all. I don't need help.'

'You don't need help or you don't need *my* help?' Rachel asked, her anger lapping over the edge of her control like a pot threatening to boil over. She reined it in with an effort, but the toll it took came through in her voice. 'Can't we put the past behind us and deal with this together?'

The past. Addie looked at her daughter long and hard. There were gaps in her past that grew larger by the day, but she remembered word for word the fight that had taken place before Rachel's departure from Berkeley. 'You abandoned me. You abandoned everything we'd worked so hard for.'

'You forced me out!' Rachel responded without thinking, lashed out. All the hurt, the pain, the bitterness was there just under the surface. The only difference between herself and her mother was the amount of control she exercised over those feelings.

Rachel took a shallow, shuddering breath and pushed herself up out of the chair. The bread was sitting on the counter, and she methodically undid the twist tie and reached into the bag.

'We're going to see Dr. Moore today to talk.'

Addie made a face. 'He's a Nazi. I don't want anything to do with him.'

Rachel's hands shook as she placed two slices of bread in the toaster. The urge to explode made her tremble from her emotional core outward. 'We're going.'

'You can't tell me what to do, missy,' Addie began. Her movements very deliberate, she rose from her chair and pushed it back. A flush stained the whiteness of her cheeks. Her daughter was trying to wrest her independence away from her. Well, she wouldn't take it lying down! She wouldn't take it at all! Simply because she was getting older and a little

43

forgetful didn't give Rachel the right to waltz in and take over. 'Who do you think you are, coming back here after all these years and thinking you can just walk in? Terence put you up to this, didn't he? That no-account, whining little weasel.'

'Terence is out of this, Mother,' Rachel said softly, her throat tight with a building flood of emotion.

A triumphant gleam flared in Addie's eyes. 'That's the first sensible thing you've done in years. I warned you about him. I told you—'

Suddenly, the kitchen door was flung wide open, and Bryan danced in, singing 'I've Got a Crush on You.' Seemingly oblivious to the tension in the room, he grabbed Addie and danced her around, hamming it up outrageously as he sang the song to her. Addie blushed like a bride and giggled. Almost instantly her anger was diffused.

'Hennessy, you big Irish rascal,' she said, batting a hand at him as he left her by her chair and danced away. 'You don't know the meaning of decorum.'

Bryan halted in the center of the room, cleared his throat, and began to orate: 'Decorum: conformity to the requirements of good taste or social convention; propriety in behavior, dress, et cetera; seemliness.'

'Did you catch any of that, Rachel?' Addie wondered dryly.

Rachel slammed the butter knife down on the countertop. 'Your toast is ready.'

'Hennessy makes my toast. I won't eat yours. You're probably trying to poison me.'

'The thought has crossed my mind,' Rachel muttered to herself, then was assailed with guilt, even though no one else in the room had heard her and she hadn't meant it.

'Let me handle this,' Bryan whispered, bending down near her ear as he lifted the plate of toast from the counter.

'No,' Rachel said forcefully. She grabbed the plate back out of his hand, nearly sending the bread to the floor.

The fact that Bryan, an outsider, could deal better with Addie was like salt on an open wound. And it was yet another reason she couldn't allow him to stay. She and Addie had to square things between them now, or at least establish their new roles. She was the one who was going to be taking care of her mother, not Bryan Hennessy. Lord knew, men like Bryan Hennessy opted out the minute the going got rough.

He was Terence in spades – a dreamer, a coaster, a man who ignored reality with an idiotic grin on his face. Abruptly, the comparisons overwhelmed her and coupled with her need to take care of Addie.

'No. I don't need you. *We* don't need you,' she said, glaring up at him. 'Take your stupid card tricks and your stupid roses and get out of here!'

Bryan backed away as if she'd slapped him. He really didn't need this, he told himself, echoing Deputy Skreawupp's line. He didn't need the kind of trouble Rachel Lindquist was facing, and he sure as hell didn't need to get kicked for his efforts to help.

Without a word he turned to leave the room, but the door from the kitchen to the hall wouldn't budge. He put a shoulder up against it and heaved his weight into it, but it held fast. Drawing a slow breath into his lungs, he stood back and planted his hands at the waistband of his jeans. Behind him, he could hear life going on at the Lindquist family breakfast table. Rachel was trying to give Addie her toast, and Addie was refusing to touch it, her voice rising ominously with every word.

'I have to be the world's biggest glutton for punishment,' Bryan mumbled to himself, shaking his head. He turned around, his sunniest smile firmly in place. 'Did you say you're going to town? I'll ride along; I need to go to the library.'

'I didn't invite you, Mr. Hennessy,' Rachel said. A perverse thrill raced through her at the thought that this man did not take no for an answer. He was like a human bulldozer. And that innocently pleasant face he presented the world was nothing more than a very distracting mask.

'No, you didn't,' he said affably, taking his seat at the table. 'What time do we leave?'

'Two,' she answered automatically, then halted her thinking process. Her eyes narrowed and her lush mouth thinned. She wasn't going to be bullied. She wasn't going to let Bryan Hennessy worm his way into her life. 'Be sure to pack your tooth-brush,' she said, rising and going to the stove to start a pot of coffee. 'We'll drop you off at the nearest hotel.'

'The truth is, it may already be too late, honey.' The memory of Dr. Moore's gentle, fatherly voice played through Rachel's mind as she sat behind the wheel of her decrepit Chevette.

'For all the research being done, we know very little about the disease. It progresses differently in different people, depending upon what areas of the brain are attacked. Some people lose the ability to read, while others can read but not comprehend what they've read. Some can understand a conversation in person but not over the phone. Some can remember everything that happened in their lives ten years ago, but they can't remember what happened ten minutes ago.'

'She seems to remember everything that happened five years ago,' Rachel said ruefully.

Dr. Moore, who had the wisdom of decades in medicine and in dealing with people, had reached out to take her hand, knowing that small comfort might soften the blow. 'But she may not be able to comprehend what happens today or tomorrow. I'm not saying it can't happen, sweetheart. At this point in Addie's illness, it's anyone's guess. I just want you to realize that you can't pin your hopes on a reconciliation, because it might never come about.'

Rachel rested her forehead against the steering wheel and closed her eyes against a wave of despair. A reconciliation with Addie was the one thing she had wanted, needed, to pin her hopes on. What else was there? Certainly not a cure for Alzheimer's; no one knew yet what caused the disease, let alone what would cure it.

'Are we going to sit here all day, or is there some other vile place you intend to force me to go to?' Addie asked imperiously.

'We need to stop at the drugstore,' Rachel said.

'I don't want to go to the drugstore.' The drugstore was a confusing place, aisle upon aisle of items and millions of brands from which to choose. Addie never went there if she could help it. She gave Rachel a shrewd look. 'I suppose you're going to force me to go in there nevertheless.'

'You don't have to go in. You can wait in the car if you like.'

Too distracted to notice her mother's sigh of relief, Rachel started the engine and pulled out of the clinic parking lot and into the flow of tourist traffic. The fog that had blanketed the coastal village in the early morning had long since burned off. The day was bright with a blue sky. Anastasia's quaint streets were clogged with people browsing and window-shopping and admiring the carefully restored Victorian architecture of the town. Through the open windows of the car came the sounds of the traffic, the calling of gulls, and the distant wash of the ocean against the shore.

It all seemed comforting, Rachel thought. So normal and sane. She could easily grow to love Anastasia. Unfortunately, she would never have the chance. She had a job waiting for her in San Francisco when the fall school term began. A call to a former vocal instructor who was now an administrator at the Phylliss Academy of Voice had landed her a position. As soon as she had sorted out Addie's affairs, and they had sold Drake House, they would be moving south to the city. Anastasia would be a place to visit on weekends if they were lucky.

By some small miracle of fate there was a parking spot opening up in front of Berg's Drugstore just as Rachel piloted her car across the intersection at Fourth and Kilmer. She pulled into it and cut the engine.

'I'll only be a minute,' she said as she grabbed up her purse and slipped out of the car.

Addie smiled serenely, her eye on the keys dangling from the Chevette's ignition.

'So, Addie has a daughter,' Alaina Montgomery-Harrison mused, seizing instantly upon the one significant thing Bryan had said since she'd walked outside her office with him to enjoy the sun. She leaned back against the sun-warmed side of the building that housed her law practice, her smart red Mark Eisen suit a startling contrast against the white stucco. Her cool blue eyes studied her friend intently. 'What does she look like?'

Bryan shrugged uncomfortably. He stuck his nose into one of the library books he'd borrowed on the history of the area and mumbled, 'Like a woman.'

Alaina gave him a look. 'Oh, that narrows it right down. So she falls somewhere between Christie Brinkley and Roseanne Barr?'

'Hmmm . . . ' Glancing up with bright eyes and a brighter smile, Bryan attempted to derail her from her line of questioning. 'How's my beautiful goddaughter?'

'She's perfect, of course,' Alaina said, idly checking her neatly manicured nails. 'What a lame attempt to throw me off the scent, Bryan, really. Why so secretive?'

'I'm not being secretive,' he protested. 'There's simply not that much to tell. She's Addie's daughter. She's young, she's pretty, they don't get along.' *She cried on my shoulder, and I haven't wanted to kiss a woman so badly in ages,* he added silently, turning the pages of his book without seeing them.

'That's putting it in a nutshell. You should get a job with *Reader's Digest*. Think of the money they could save on paper if they had you to condense books for them,' Alaina said. She reached out and gently closed the book Bryan was using as a prop to evade her questions. Her gaze searched his face with undisguised concern. 'Where do you fit in at Drake House?'

Bryan held his expression carefully blank. 'I'm there to find a ghost.'

'And?'

'Sometimes I really despise your keen insight,' he complained. Alaina was characteristically unmoved by the remark. He heaved a sigh. 'All right. It's a tough situation. If I can in some small way help Rachel and Addie—'

At that instant a car horn blared and a rusted orange Chevette squealed around the corner. People on the sidewalk leapt back, shrieking as a wheel jumped over the curb and a trash can went sailing. Bryan's eyes rounded in horror as he caught sight of the driver.

'Addie!' he shouted, dropping his books and taking off after the car.

The Chevette veered across the street, eliciting a chorus of horn-honking from cars in the oncoming lane, and jumped the curb into Kilmer Park. People and pigeons scattered. Addie stuck her head out the window of the car, waving and shouting for people to get out of her way.

Bryan caught up with her as she cranked the steering wheel and began driving in circles around the statue that immortalized the late William Kilmer, an obscure botanist who had grown up in Anastasia and gone on to relative anonymity. He jogged alongside the car until he managed to get the passenger door open, then he executed a neat gymnastic movement and swung himself into the moving vehicle. All he had to do then was reach over and switch the ignition off. The Chevette rolled to a halt.

Bryan heaved a huge sigh of relief. The park was full of tourists now gathering around to satisfy their morbid curiosity. Addie might have ended the earthly outing for any one of them and sent them on to a more permanent sort of trip.

'There's something wrong with the brakes,' Addie grumbled, scowling, completely unwilling to admit she had forgotten how to work them.

Rachel ran up beside the car, her face as pale as milk. Bryan climbed out, rounded the hood, and took her by the arm. He dangled the keys from his forefinger, then closed his fist gently over them as he guided Rachel a short distance away.

'Addie isn't allowed to drive,' he said softly, managing a half smile at the look on her face.

Rachel was too petrified to speak. She merely stared up at him, horrified at what had happened and what might have happened.

'It's all right,' Bryan said, easily reading her feelings. 'No one was hurt.'

Without thinking, he leaned down and pressed a soft kiss to her lips. Golden sparks of electricity burst through him, stunning him.

'I'll drive us home.' he said breathlessly, not quite certain how he had managed to speak at all. His heart was pounding like a jackhammer.

Dazed, Rachel lifted a hand to her lips. He'd kissed her. He'd kissed her and immediately the icy terror that had filled her had melted away. She knew she was supposed to tell him he wasn't coming home with them, but she couldn't begin to form the words in her head. For one of the few times in her life she was rendered completely speechless. It was amazing.

'We'll go home. You can have a nice brandy and lie down for a while,' Bryan went on as he led her back to the car. 'Dinner is at seven.' He opened the door to the backseat and helped her in, then leaned down into the open window. 'By the way, we dress for dinner at Drake House.'

'Dress?' Rachel questioned dumbly.

'Hmmm. Black tie or the closest you can come.'

'You're serious?' she said, trying to read his expression. 'You're not joking?'

Bryan smiled. 'Quite and no. At any rate,' he said, his eyes crinkling attractively at the corners, 'I'm hardly ever more serious than when I'm joking.'

He straightened then and took the ticket Deputy Skreawupp handed him without saying a word. His look warned the deputy to follow suit. Opening the driver's door, he slid into the Chevette beside Addie, saying, 'Scoot over, beautiful, and let a man handle this machine.'

Addie giggled and punched his arm. 'You big Irish rascal, you.'

He piloted the car slowly out of the park, leaning out the window, waving and smiling to the crowd as if he were driving in a parade. Addie joined in his enthusiasm and leaned out her window, throwing out old Life Savers she had found in her handbag.

And in the backseat, Rachel sat staring blankly into space, marveling over the power of a simple little kiss.

5

Rachel checked her watch and frowned. Ten of seven. She hadn't meant to fall asleep. On returning to Drake House from Anastasia she had taken Bryan's advice and modified it slightly, trading his suggestion of a brandy for a hot bath. She had shut herself in the upstairs bathroom and soaked in the deep old claw-footed tub until the tension of the day had all washed out of her. It had taken a concerted effort on her part to push it from her mind, and the effort had left her feeling drained. When she returned to her room at last, wrapped in an old terry-cloth robe, she had curled up on the creaky old bed, intending to rest for just a few minutes.

Two hours later she had awakened abruptly from a deep sleep with the distinct feeling that she was being watched. She had sat up, clutching her robe to her chest, and stared all around the bedroom she had moved into that morning. It was located in the turret on the south side of the house. The walls curved; there were no dark corners to hide in. The room had been quiet and empty, but someone had been there. It wasn't just the lingering tension that had told her. Laid out across the foot of the bed had been a dress. A dress she had never seen before.

Rachel ran her hand down the front of it now in a gesture of uncertainty. It seemed strange to be wearing it when she didn't know where it had come from or whom it belonged to, yet she hadn't quite been able to resist the urge to put it on. If Bryan had been telling the truth about dressing for dinner, then she didn't own anything suitable to wear – nothing that came close to this dress anyway. Most of her skirts and dresses were comfortable cotton fabrics in styles that leaned toward a Gypsy or prairie look. She had never had the occasion or the money to buy an evening gown during her life on the road with Terence.

The whole idea of dressing for dinner seemed absurd. It was a custom from a bygone age and a class of people she had only read about or seen on television. No doubt it was one of the little eccentricities Addie had developed since her illness. In light of all that had happened since she had arrived, Rachel thought it best to go along with the odd dictate. If it would make her mother happy, if it might somehow help Addie to open up to her, then it would be worth the effort.

She stared at her reflection in the freshly polished mirror above the vanity. The dress was burgundy silk decorated with black jet beads. The thin straps flowed into a V neckline in both the front and the back. The fully pleated skirt fell from a dropped waist to swirl about her calves. It was pure 1920s, an antique in its own right. It was the most beautiful thing she'd worn in ages. And Bryan Hennessy had brought it to her.

Her chest tightened at the thought. He must have slipped in and put it across the foot of the bed while she'd been sleeping. What if she had opened her eyes and turned to look up at him. Her robe might have fallen open, and his gaze would have lowered deliberately—

Rachel gasped in embarrassment. The woman who looked back at her from the mirror wore an expression of uncertainty. Her wide eyes were pansy-purple in the dim light of the room. Soft color rose on her cheekbones. There was a decidedly vulnerable look about her mouth. She didn't have time to put up her hair again, so she left it to fall down her back in luxurious golden waves. She wondered if Bryan would like it down.

'Oh, Lord,' she said with a groan, squeezing her eyes shut and rubbing at her temples, 'what am I going to do about Bryan?'

Somewhere a gong sounded.

'A dinner gong?' she questioned on a laugh. 'Well, I suppose I shouldn't be surprised. There isn't anything ordinary about this house or anyone in it.'

Slipping into a pair of black high-heeled shoes, she gave her reflection one last glance in the mirror and left the room.

She caught sight of Bryan as she began to descend the grand staircase, and her heart vaulted into her throat. Her hand gripping the mahogany banister, she halted on the stairs and stared down at the scene below, where Bryan stood sipping a drink and chatting with a woman Rachel had never seen before.

She had thought him attractive in a rumpled, all-American way. Big and cute with his earnest blue eyes and his tawny hair falling every which way and notes sticking up out of all his pockets. But in a tuxedo he was devastating. Handsome with a capital H. The black jacket hugged his shoulders in a way that nothing off the rack could have. The wings of his shirt collar framed his strong, freshly shaved jaw. His hair looked as if he had actually taken a comb to it. The overall effect was one of intelligence, authority, and money.

He looked completely at ease in formal attire, and that threw Rachel off balance. Would she ever get a handle on who Bryan Hennessy really was? Was he charlatan or scientist? Buffoon or bon vivant? The only thing she knew for certain was that he believed in ghosts and magic, and she would be far better off steering clear of him.

As she resumed her descent of the stairs, she forced her gaze to the woman with the wild mane of dark auburn hair. The light from the chandelier brought out the red in her tresses, surrounding her pixie face with extraordinarily rich color. She had enormous black eyes and an infectious, mischievous smile that seemed vaguely familiar. She was quite lovely despite what she was wearing – a man's white dress shirt and black necktie over a wildly flowered dirndl skirt and paddock boots.

She glanced up suddenly and grinned with pure delight. 'You must be Rachel,' she said, her voice honey-rich with the sounds of the South.

Bryan jerked his head up and stared openly at the woman on the stairs. He felt awed, paralyzed, thrilled – as if he were witnessing some kind of vision. The studs on his shirtfront strained as he tried to take in a deep breath.

Rachel stood on the landing, staring uncertainly back at him, her eyes wide, her hair spread out behind her in a fall of softest gold. The old-fashioned dress she wore bared her angular shoulders and hugged her small breasts just enough to hint at their fullness. With its straight lines and long skirt it was hardly a revealing garment, yet it emphasized her femininity and her own innate sense of class.

Jayne gave him a quick, practiced elbow to the ribs, her smile never wavering. 'Bryan Hennessy, I know your mama taught you better manners than this.'

'What?' he asked, looking confused, then he snapped out of it. 'Oh, yes. Jayne, this is Addie's daughter, Rachel Lindquist. Rachel, this is Jayne Jordan Reilly, a friend of mine from college, and a friend of Addie's as well.'

'I'm so pleased to meet you,' Jayne said, extending her hand. 'I've heard so much about you.'

'But I arrived only last night,' said Rachel, a little taken aback by the stranger's warm welcome.

Jayne shrugged, winding an arm through Rachel's and leading her away from the stairs. 'It's a small town. News travels around here at the speed of light. What a lovely dress. Wherever did you find it?'

'Laid out on my bed,' Rachel said pointedly, her gaze meeting Bryan's head on. He had the gall to look innocent. 'Things have a funny way of turning up in my room.'

'Oh, honey, I'm not at all surprised.' Jayne waved a dainty hand, her purple fingernails flashing in the light from the chandelier. She leaned close to Rachel, her expression intensely serious, as if she were about to confide an enormous secret. 'This house is haunted, you know.'

'So I'm told,' Rachel said, managing a polite smile. Her gaze darted to Bryan, flashing her disapproval his way.

'You haven't been lucky enough to see Wimsey, have you?'

'No, I haven't had the pleasure.'

Jayne frowned her disappointment. 'Too bad. Addie's the only one who's actually seen him. My theory is their consciousness coexists on a single plane of understanding, while ours is on a dual plane, which is why we never see him. What do you think?'

Rachel stared at her for a moment, not quite sure how to respond. Jayne, while undeniably sweet, was apparently just as batty as everyone else in Drake House.

'Rachel doesn't believe in ghosts,' Bryan said, handing her a glass of white wine. His eyes sparkled like sapphires. 'Rachel is practical.' He said the word as if it were the name of a strict religious order.

Jayne's dark eyes widened. She looked from Bryan to Rachel and back. 'Oh, my.'

'I'm sorry I didn't come down earlier,' Rachel said, changing the subject. 'I'm afraid I dozed off. I meant to help Mother with the meal.'

'Oh, Addie doesn't cook,' said Bryan.

Her brows pulled together as she looked at him. 'What do you mean? Mother used to work nights at a very nice restaurant when we lived in Berkeley. She's a wonderful cook.'

'Not since the infamous incident of the fish-head soup and chocolate-laxative cake,' Bryan said.

Jayne rolled her eyes in dismay at the memory. 'Reverend MacIlroy was indisposed for a week.'

Bryan sighed. 'Thankfully, the soup filled me up, and I passed on the cake.'

'You ate fish-head soup?' Rachel asked, both incredulous and nauseated at the thought.

'I prefer to think of it as a variation on bouillabaisse. It was hardly the strangest thing ever to cross my palate. A particular dinner in China comes to mind. They do things there with snakes—'

'That shouldn't be discussed before dinner,' Jayne said firmly, giving him a look of disgust. She took Rachel by the arm again and steered her toward the dining room, interrogating and commenting all the way, her conversation flowing from one topic to the next without pause. 'I think it's just wonderful that you've come back to take care of Addie. We all try to check in on her from time to time, but it's not the same. I hear you're a singer. Will you look for work here in Anastasia?'

'I have a job lined up at the Phylliss Academy of Voice in San Francisco,' Rachel said, seeing no reason to hide the fact from them. At any rate, she needed to practice saying it. She was going to have to tell Addie soon, so they could make plans to sell Drake House and move.

'San Francisco?' Jayne said it as if it were a place totally foreign to her.

Bryan merely stood silent, his expression carefully blank.

'Yes. As soon as I get my mother's affairs in order, we'll be selling the house and moving to the city.'

'Does Addie know about this?' Bryan asked, taking great care to sound more neutral than he felt.

Rachel nibbled at her lower lip. She couldn't quite meet his eyes. 'Not yet.'

At that moment Addie made her grand entrance into the dining room.

Her style of dress was even more incongruous than Jayne's. Over her flowered housedress she wore a filmy pink robe trimmed in pink ostrich feathers. On her feet, her ever-present green rubber boots. She took in the group with one regal, sweeping glance.

'Hennessy, my G and T, please.'

Rachel grabbed at Bryan's coat sleeve. He turned toward her and her concern momentarily fled. He was so close. His mouth was no more than inches from hers as he leaned down toward her. She moistened her lips nervously as the memory of his kiss came flooding back. Beneath her fingertips and the fine wool of his jacket his arm was a rock of muscle.

'Don't worry,' he whispered, easily reading her mind. 'There's almost no G in Addie's G and T. I just splash some on the ice so I'm not really fibbing when I give it to her.'

He turned toward the sideboard to mix the drink. Rachel sighed, helpless to stop the sweet warmth flooding her chest. It would be so very easy to let herself fall for him. He was handsome and charming in a rather bizarre sort of way. He was so kind and solicitous toward Addie. She watched him hand her mother the weak drink. He winked at Addie and pretended to pull a quarter out of her ear.

'You're an idiot, Hennessy. I don't know why I keep you on,' Addie blustered, shooing him away, but there was a rare twinkle in her eye and a bloom in her cheeks that hadn't been there when they'd returned home after the incident in the park.

How Rachel envied him that easy rapport with her mother. He didn't have the burden of a past full of pain and mistakes weighing down his every word. He didn't have the burden of a future full of heartache and sacrifice holding him back. He could walk away anytime he liked, and no one could ever fault him. He didn't have to deal with issues like selling Drake House. All Bryan had to worry about was pulling quarters out of people's ears.

They sat down to a meal of thick, aromatic beef stew and hot biscuits. It wasn't exactly a five-course dinner to go along with the china and silver on the polished walnut table, but it was hearty, healthy fare and required only one utensil to eat it – an important consideration for Addie, who was slowly losing her ability to deal with a full complement of flatware.

'Hennessy is quite an adequate cook,' Addie said, dipping her biscuit into the gravy on her plate and nibbling at it delicately. 'He's an impudent rascal, insisting on eating at the table with the rest of us, but I tolerate him.'

Rachel frowned. Bryan wasn't the butler, and she didn't see any reason for him to be treated like one. But when she opened her mouth to set her mother straight, Bryan caught her eye and shook his head ever so slightly.

'That's very big of you, Addie,' he said. 'Not everyone is as generous and forgiving as you are.'

Addie gave him a shrewd look. 'Remember that, young man.' She tossed back the last of her gin and tonic and thrust the glass at him for a refill. Lifting her nose slightly, she glanced askance at Rachel. 'Some people don't appreciate generosity and sacrifice, and look what happens to them.'

Rachel ground her retort between her teeth and choked it down with a piece of potato.

'Did I mention how stunning you look tonight, Addie?' Bryan said affably, handing her glass back to her filled with tonic water and a slice of lime. 'I can't think of another woman who could wear that outfit quite the way you do . . . unless it might be Jayne,' he added, grinning across the table at his friend, who stuck her tongue out at him.

Addie beamed and fluffed her ostrich feathers.

'And didn't Rachel find a beautiful dress?' Bryan said, not realizing the way his voice dropped and softened. Nor did he realize the longing that shone in his eyes.

Rachel sat directly across from him, between Addie, at the head of the table, and Jayne. A tiny smile of gratitude canted the corners of her lips.

Addie gave her daughter a hard, assessing look. 'Yes, it's very suitable. For once you don't look like some cheap, wandering Gypsy.'

The smile faded away as Rachel closed her eyes and counted to ten.

'Rachel,' Jayne said brightly as she picked around the meat in her stew. 'Tell us all about your career as a singer. My, how exciting that must be. I couldn't carry a tune in a bucket.'

'That's not much to tell,' Rachel said, bracing her shoulders. She kept her head down, her eyes trained on her plate as she tried to extricate herself from the subject as quickly as she could without being rude. 'We played a lot of clubs, managed to get on a couple of PBS folk music shows.'

'That's wonderful.' Jayne smiled. 'I just love folk music. It's very spiritual. So visual and honest in its images. Don't you agree, Addie?'

Addie's lips pinched into a white line. 'Drivel. Opera is the only pure form of vocal music.'

Jayne never missed a beat, turning back to Rachel. 'You said "we." I take it you have a partner?'

'Had,' Rachel said shortly. Her fingers tightened on her fork in anticipation of the comment her mother would surely make.

'Feckless little ferret.'

'Mother, please . . .'

'Addie, I love your hair in that style. What do you call it?' Bryan asked.

Addie scowled at him. 'A braid. Honestly, Hennessy, there are times I wonder if you aren't mentally deficient.'

'Well, the color is marvelous,' he went on, grinning as he speared vegetables with his fork.

Addie's attention shifted between Rachel and Bryan, between

unpleasantness and inanity. Bryan's wink won her over, and she turned toward him with a pleased look. 'You think so?' she asked, stroking the frazzled braid that lay over her shoulder. 'I've been thinking of dyeing it. I saw a color on television called Sable Seductress.'

'Oh, no. Blondes have more fun. Take it from me,' Bryan said, winking at her again.

Addie blushed and turned toward Jayne. 'He's such a flirt.'

'Always has been, Addie,' Jayne said. 'His whole family is that way. Why it would make you swoon to see all those men together. They look like something out of *Gentleman's Quarterly*.'

'Where is that Australian tonight?' Addie demanded, her mind already drifting from the topic of Bryan.

'Reilly's in Vancouver shooting a movie,' Jayne said, automatically glowing at the thought of her husband.

Bryan managed to steer the conversation in Jayne's direction for the remainder of the meal. He coaxed her into speaking at length about her husband's acting career and her own budding career as a director. As curious as he was to learn more about Rachel and her past, he wasn't eager to have Jayne prize the information out of her there at the dinner table, where Addie could carve it all up for ridicule.

He'd been willing to do the carving himself less than twenty-four hours earlier, he reminded himself. But that had been before he'd had the chance to observe Rachel. That had been when his only knowledge of her had come from Addie's cutting remarks and the obvious pain behind them. Now he had seen Rachel. He'd seen – and felt – the turbulent tangle of emotions she was struggling with. He'd watched her look for the slightest sign of forgiveness or approval from her mother, and he'd seen the hurt flash in her lavender eyes when her hopes had met with cold disappointment.

He had accepted his own decision to help Addie and Rachel as best he could. And with that acceptance had come a subtle shifting in his feelings toward Rachel. The beginnings of protectiveness were coming to life inside him. Every time Addie inflicted another small cut with the razor edge of her tongue, the faint urge to take Rachel in his arms washed through him. He ignored the feeling on a conscious level, on a level where he was still not ready to involve himself completely, but it was there just the same.

Finally, Jayne scraped her chair back from the table and gave everyone an apologetic look. 'I hate to say it, but I've got an important meeting tonight. I really have to be running along. Thanks so much for inviting me, Addie.'

'You invited yourself,' Bryan said, a grin teasing the corners of his mouth as he rose from his chair.

Jayne made a face at him. 'Don't get snippy. I brought the biscuits, didn't I?'

'So you did,' he conceded graciously. 'And they were delicious.'

Jayne bent, kissed the parchmentlike skin of Addie's pale cheek and bid all good night.

'Where's that Australian?' Addie asked.

'He's working,' Jayne replied patiently. She leaned down and impulsively gave Rachel a hug around her shoulders. 'It's been such fun, Rachel. You'll have to come over to the farm one day soon for a visit.'

Rachel managed a genuine smile for her new friend. It was impossible not to like Jayne immediately. 'I will. It was nice meeting you, Jayne.'

'Same here,' Jayne said sincerely. 'By the way, what's your sign?'

'Um . . . Aquarius, I think,' Rachel mumbled uncertainly, knocked off balance again by Jayne's sudden change of subject.

Jayne's dark eyes took on a considering gleam as she looked from Rachel to Bryan, a secretive smile on her lips. 'Bryan, honey, walk me out, will you?'

Leaving the Lindquists in the dining room, Bryan took Jayne's arm and strolled down the hall with her. Neither spoke until they were on the wide porch.

'She's very pretty.'

Bryan put on his blank, amicable smile and stuck his hands into his trouser pockets. 'Who?'

Jayne frowned prettily. 'Don't play that role with me, Bryan Hennessy. I know you too well to be fooled by it. Really,' she said in a huffy tone, toying with the dainty gold bracelet that circled her left wrist. 'I ought to be offended.'

'But you're too busy recapping the dinner conversation and condensing it for analysis to bother.'

'I'm sure I don't know what you mean,' she said, pouting.

Bryan grinned openly at that. He reached up and tugged playfully at the end of her necktie. 'Tell me, does this miraculous turn of events warrant a conference call or an all-hands-on-deck type meeting?'

Jayne's eyes twinkled. 'Faith has baked a cake for the occasion.'

'And what occasion is that?'

'Alaina thinks you're falling in love.'

Bryan wouldn't have been more stunned if she'd suddenly smacked him between the eyes with a hammer. He literally staggered back a step. 'That's absurd! I only just met her last night—'

'Ample time for you.'

'—and she's done nothing but try to throw me out of the house ever since. That's hardly romantic,' he argued, doing his best to tamp down the memory of holding her.

Jayne just shrugged. 'Monica Tyler hit you in the face with a peace pie, and you fell in love with her.'

'You're taking that pie thing completely out of context,' Bryan said, shaking a finger at her. 'That was an entirely different situation. I'm not in love with Rachel. You may report that to the rest of the joint chiefs of staff. I'm not in love. I'm not going to fall in love.'

'Don't say that, honey,' Jayne whispered, all teasing aside. She reached up a hand to touch his flushed cheek. 'I know how it hurts to lose someone. I also know a very wise man once told me we can't orchestrate our lives, that we have to take our happiness where we can get it.'

Bryan scowled as Jayne threw his own words up to him. 'I'd forgotten how that photographic memory got you through art history.' He heaved a sigh and stared out at the unkempt lawn and the fog that draped it all in a dreary cloak of gray. 'Yes, we have to enjoy our lives while we can. I want to help Rachel and Addie do that. But I'm not ready for anything more.' He gave a derisive half laugh. 'Besides, I'm the last man Rachel wants to get involved with.'

Jayne watched him closely. 'How do you know that?'

'Just a feeling,' he murmured absently, recalling very clearly the way he had heard Rachel's own inner voice state that fact earlier that morning.

Jayne's eyes widened slightly. She opened her mouth to comment, but thought better of it. Instead, she offered him a soft smile and rose up on her toes. 'Kiss me good-bye.'

After Bryan had complied dutifully, Jayne adjusted the strap of her enormous canvas purse on her shoulder and trotted down the steps and across the yard to her little red antique MG, whistling softly to herself all the way. Her dear friend Bryan hadn't had a 'feeling' about anyone else since Serena had died . . . until now. Until Rachel Lindquist.

'In love,' Bryan muttered in disgust as he let himself back into the house. Of course he wasn't in love. He was attracted to Rachel, yes. Any man with eyes in his head would be attracted to Rachel. He was sympathetic toward her, naturally. Any caring human being would have been. But in love with her? No. It would be a long time before he felt ready to make that kind of emotional commitment again.

He made for the dining room, intending to excuse himself for the rest of the evening. He had a lot of reading to do about the history of the area and about Drake House in particular. If Wimsey had lived here, the fact would likely be documented someplace. Wimsey was, after all, his main reason for being there – work, getting back his professional instincts, getting back on track. Falling in love was not on the agenda.

The dining room was deserted. He hadn't been on the porch for more than ten minutes, yet the table had been cleared of china and linen. The room looked as undisturbed as if dinner had never been served. He was about to count himself lucky and escape to hit the books when a sound drew his attention toward the kitchen. It was soft, muffled, like a cough or a sniffle . . . or crying.

Quietly he stole across the room and cracked open the door to the kitchen. Rachel stood near the sink, which was full of suds and dirty dishes, her arms crossed in front of her and one fist pressed to her lips. Her bare shoulders lifted stiffly as she sucked in another shaky breath and valiantly fought the urge to cry.

Bryan's heart dropped to his stomach. It took every ounce of strength he had to keep from rushing across the room and scooping her into his arms. Instead, he backed away from the door and began humming loudly. He gritted his teeth and forced his frown upward at the corners, then burst through the door into the kitchen.

'What ho! This looks like a job for the butler,' he said cheerfully.

Rachel swallowed down the last of her unshed tears and cleared her throat. She took the chance to speak but didn't turn to face him, afraid her eyes might betray the overwhelming emotions she had been struggling to keep at bay. 'We haven't got a butler.'

'I suppose I could take that as an insult, but, being such a sweet-tempered soul, I won't. At any rate, I suppose it's a matter of opinion.'

'It's a matter of money,' Rachel said firmly. 'Which is something I haven't got much of.'

'That's all right,' Bryan said, taking a position beside her and eyeing the dirty dinner dishes. 'I work cheap. Find me a ghost or two, and I'll be as happy as a clam. Where's Addie?'

Rachel gave a short, humorless laugh. 'She chose to retire to her room rather than spend another minute in my tainted company.' The tears threatened again, but she lowered her head and fought them off with a tremendous burst of will.

'I see,' Bryan said quietly. Then, coming to a decision, he waved a hand at the sink in a gesture of dismissal. 'These dishes can wait. Come along.'

Rachel started to protest as he took her by the hand and led her from the room, but the set of his jaw told her it would be pointless. For all his pleasant manner, the man had a stubborn streak a mile wide. She trailed along after him, marveling instead at how strong his hand was, and yet how gentle.

He towed her into a study, a masculine room with cherry paneling and a fireplace. After depositing her on a leather-covered camel-back love seat, he knelt on the hearth and put flame to the kindling already lying beneath the andirons. Warmth bloomed outward from the blaze as Bryan went around behind the desk, withdrew a cut glass bottle from a drawer, and poured amber liquid into two of the glasses that sat on a tarnished silver tray on one corner of the desk. He returned to her then and pressed a glass into her hand.

Rachel scooted back into one corner of the love seat as Bryan settled at the opposite end. She watched him, taken by surprise by his sudden air of authority. He was regarding her through his spectacles with serious eyes.

'Rachel,' he said with utmost gravity. 'I think it's only fair to warn you: I'm going to help you whether you like it or not.'

'Help me?' she questioned, eyeing him suspiciously. 'Help me what?'

'Deal with Addie. I get the distinct impression you're not good at accepting help.'

'Probably because I haven't had much practice recently,' she murmured candidly as she stared down into the liquid in her glass.

'Are you going to explain that rather cryptic remark, or do I get to make use of those interrogation methods I'm not supposed to talk about?'

She glanced up at him sharply, completely unable to tell whether he was joking or not. He wore a pleasant expression – the mask again, she decided.

'I know this much: you and Addie had a falling out five years ago, you left with Clarence somebody-or-other and didn't come back,' Bryan began, priming the pump for her in hopes that she would jump in with the rest of the story.

Rachel placed her drink on the low butler's table and stood up. 'I really don't think there's any need for you to know all the details of my life, Mr. Hennessy,' she said, her sense of self-preservation rushing to the fore. 'The gist of the story is this: One time in my entire life I defied my mother's authority, and she has never forgiven me.'

'You were in love with this Clarence?'

'Terence.'

Bryan noted with a certain satisfaction that she corrected him only on the name, not on the past tense he had used in regard to the relationship. 'Where is he now?'

Rachel wandered away from the heat of the fire to the cool air near the French doors that led out onto a terrace shrouded in mist. 'Chasing a rainbow,' she murmured softly. Terence Bretton seemed a lifetime away from her now, so far removed from her situation that even his memory seemed unreal.

'And what about you, Rachel?' Bryan whispered.

She jumped a bit at the sound of his voice. He had come up behind her without her realizing it, but her sudden awareness of him was acute. She could feel the heat of his body, hear the subtle sigh of fabric on fabric as he shifted position. He didn't touch her, but she realized to her shame that she wanted him to. She hadn't known the man two days, and she wanted him to take her in his arms and hold her. She wanted it so badly, she ached.

Her lashes fluttered down, and she was immediately overtaken by the imagined sensation of being held. His arms were hard and strong, but his touch was gentle . . . She felt herself leaning back, almost as if she were being pushed back, and she caught herself and fought the strange feeling off.

'What about you, Rachel?' he asked. 'Where does your rainbow end?'

'You mean this isn't Oz?' she said ruefully, an acute sadness filling her, a sadness that came through in the soft, clear tone of her voice. 'I was so sure it was. You're the Wizard and Mother . . .'

Addie was the wicked witch telling her she could never go home, telling her she was destined to be trapped in a surrealistic nightmare, that somewhere over the rainbow was a place dreamers longed for but could never find.

In the silence Bryan could feel her disillusionment as sharply as if it had been his own, and he hurt for her. Whatever she had given up to return to Addie had been better than the future she faced here.

Seemingly of its own volition, his hand rose toward the shimmering fall of Rachel's hair. It spilled down her back, a pale river of moonspun silk. He couldn't quite bring himself to resist the urge to touch it. Like a man trying to touch a dream, his fingers reached out hesitantly to brush against the curling ends. There was something incredibly sensual in the act, something strongly erotic, though he had barely grazed her. He inhaled sharply as desire streaked through him, setting all his nerve endings ablaze.

'And who are the munchkins?' he asked, trying to offset his reaction with a bit of levity. He barely recognized his own voice, it was so hoarse and low.

The absurdity of the question struck Rachel in the tattered remains of her sense of humor, and she managed a soft laugh. There was something wonderful about a man who could make her laugh on a night when her whole life seemed like a bad dream.

She turned away from the window and looked up into his eyes, so warm and caring behind his glasses. He was much too near. She had told herself to keep him at least an arm's length away at all times, but there he was, no more than a deep breath away, and, while her wary heart told her to flee, Rachel found herself rooted to the spot.

'I never thanked you for this afternoon.' She rolled her eyes and smiled wryly. 'I never dreamed Mother would try to take off with my car. Thank God no one was hurt. You saved the day.'

Bryan shrugged it off, uncomfortable with genuine praise. 'Any other magical being would have done the same. See how invaluable I'll be to have around?'

It was the perfect opportunity to tell him he couldn't stay, Rachel thought. But she couldn't bring herself to say the words or even to consider the consequences of allowing him to remain in Drake House and in her life. She couldn't bring herself to say anything at all.

She stood staring up at him as if transfixed by a spell. The light from the fire cast her face in an amber halo, glistened off the vulnerable curve of her lower lip. It caught on the black jet beads adorning the old dress she wore and set each one with a miniature starburst of light.

'Have I told you how beautiful you are in this dress?' Bryan asked softly, something vital trembling deep inside him, something that had lain dormant, like a seed beneath the snows of winter. He felt it struggling to come to life with each shallow breath.

'I think you did,' Rachel murmured.

'Oh.' His mouth quirked up on the right in sheepish self-deprecation. Again he raised his hand to touch her hair, this time letting his fingers sift through the strands of silk. 'Then, have I told you how much I want to kiss you?'

He didn't wait for a reply. He didn't wait to question himself or his vow of nonromantic involvement. He bent his head to hers and brushed his mouth gently across the satin of her lips. She tasted of sweetness and wine and need, a need that called out to her own lonely soul. His fingers threaded deeper into her hair, his hand sliding to cup the back of her head, to tilt her face to a better angle as the first kiss faded and the second began.

Just a kiss, Rachel thought. What harm could there be in a kiss? The solace and warmth and tenderness she found as she let herself melt into Bryan's arms – how could anything bad come of this? She felt so alone, and he was so sweet. She had forgotten what it was like to feel like a woman, and he was so masculine. She had been so filled with misery, and he was magic.

Her hands slid up to grip the solid strength of his arms, her fingers drinking in the feel of his tuxedo jacket as her mouth drank in the taste of him – warmth and whiskey and desire. It was a tender kiss, but not a tame one. There was a hunger in the way his lips rubbed against hers, a barely leashed demand for more. His tongue slid gently along the line of her mouth, asking for entrance, then taking it at the first hint of acquiescence.

Rachel sighed as she allowed him the intimacy. Her heart raced as her breasts molded against the planes of his chest. She lost all sense of time and place, of who and where they were. She forgot all about duty and practicality. She gave herself over to a kind of sweet, gentle bliss that could have carried her into the night . . . until a crash and a scream shattered the still air.

6

Bryan bolted for the door with Rachel right behind him. He took the grand staircase two steps at a time and ran straight for Addie's room. Addie shrieked again as he burst into the room.

'Blast you, Hennessy!' she blustered, shaking a gnarled fist at him. 'I ought to pop you one! You startled the life out of me!'

Bryan brushed the reprimand aside. 'Addie, what happened? We heard a crash. Are you all right?'

'I'm fine, no thanks to you.' She clutched a fistful of nightgown to her chest. Her knuckles were white. 'There was a ghost outside my window, trying to get in! Go out there and catch it,' she ordered, thrusting a finger at the portal. 'You're supposed to be good at that, aren't you?'

For all her effort to appear calm, she was still terribly rattled. She'd been lying in bed, trying to sleep as memories tumbled through her mind all out of order, like the colors in a kaleidoscope, when the apparition had appeared. The shock had thrown her into a mental tailspin. Now fragments of the past mingled with the present so that she couldn't distinguish one from the other. Her heart beat frantically as she tried to sort it all out.

'Mother!' Rachel gasped as she burst into the room belatedly, her shoes having hindered her progress on the stairs. 'Are you all right?'

Rachel. Addie stared at her, confused. Love ached inside her. She lifted a wrinkled hand to brush her daughter's hair back from her flushed face. 'Rachel,' she said firmly but with far more gentleness than she'd used in years. 'You ought to be in bed. You're going to ruin your voice, staying up all hours. What will Mrs. Ackerman say?'

Rachel blinked at her. She hadn't had a voice lesson with Mrs. Ackerman in ten years, but she couldn't bring herself to say that to Addie. She didn't want to do anything to ruin this single fragile moment of peace between them. Still, something had happened in this room, and they had to find out what it was.

'Mother, why did you scream?' she asked carefully.

Addie looked at her blankly.

'The ghost,' Bryan prompted. 'Was it Wimsey?'

Rachel scowled at him. Why did he persist in this ghost business? How would Addie be able to cling to any part of her sanity with Bryan encouraging her hallucinations?

'Of course it wasn't,' Addie muttered crossly as she backed up and sat down on her rumpled bed. She couldn't think for the life of her who Wimsey was. It seemed best to lay the blame elsewhere. 'It was a ghoul. It was the ugliest thing I've seen since Rowena Mortonson bought that horrid little Chinese dog. Perfectly hideous little thing. You couldn't tell if it was coming or going.'

'Who's Rowena Mortonson?' Bryan asked Rachel.

'She was our next-door neighbor in Berkeley.'

'Don't speak as if she's dead, Rachel. She's only gone to Los Angeles to visit that effeminate son of hers,' Addie muttered, playing with the fraying end of her braid. 'There's a boy who needs a can of starch in his shorts.'

'What did it look like?' Bryan questioned.

'Oh, he favored Rowena, poor homely boy – pug nose, receding chin, limp brown hair. That pretty well describes the dog too.'

'No, Addie. The ghost that was at your window. What did it look like?' Bryan asked, earning himself another glare from Rachel.

'Oooooh . . .' Addie shuddered. 'Pasty white with black eye sockets, and it made the most horrible strangled retching sound.'

'You say this ghost was trying to break in?' Bryan asked.

'The window *is* broken,' Rachel said, slightly unnerved but unwilling to admit it. She sat down on the bed beside her mother and took advantage of Addie's confused state, wrapping an arm around her frail shoulders. She wanted the physical contact, to comfort and be comforted, whether Addie was coherent or not.

'The glass was broken from the inside,' Bryan said, examining the gaping hole in the window. Shards littered the footwide ledge outside. Carefully, he raised the window and stepped out with one foot. He looked up at the gable peak and around the ledge itself, which was ornamented by a rusting wrought iron railing that had come loose on one end. There was no evidence of Addie's 'ghoul,' just a mournful howling as the wind swept around the various turrets and gables of the old house. In the distance the ocean roared.

'I threw a rock at the ugly thing,' Addie said truculently. Her eyes narrowed with anger and suspicion. 'Coming in to steal my bird cages.'

Rachel closed her eyes and sighed. She was sure there hadn't been anything at the window except a figment of Addie's imagination. She had read that paranoia was one of the more common effects of Alzheimer's. The person wasn't able to remember where she'd put something and wasn't able to reason that no one else would want it, so she was sure people were stealing from her. Seeing and hearing things that weren't there were also common nighttime occurrences for someone with Addie's affliction. Knowing that, it seemed painfully obvious to Rachel what had happened.

'Well, he's gone now,' Bryan said, climbing back inside. He had pulled a screw from the loose base of the railing and stood rubbing the clinging bits of rotted wood from the threads, a thoughtful expression on his face. 'I'll take care of this window first thing in the morning. For tonight—'

'You can sleep in my room tonight, Mother.' Rachel offered, not only eager to make her mother comfortable, but eager to score some brownie points with her as well.

Addie looked around the room with a slightly frantic widening of her eyes. This was her room. She knew where everything was – most of the time. She usually remembered how to get from this room to any other part of the house. But if she spent the night in Rachel's bed, she would be lost, and everyone would see it.

'This is my room,' she said, her chin lifting. 'I shall sleep in it if I so choose.'

'Mother,' Rachel said wearily, 'please don't be stubborn.'

'Never mind.' Bryan smiled suddenly, bending to take off his shoe. Using the heel for a hammer, he drove the tip of the rusty screw into the thick meeting rail of the window. Then he took a large, gloomy oil painting of a foundering ship off the wall and hung it so that it covered the entire lower portion of the window, blocking out the damp cool air that had flowed in through the broken glass.

'Good as new and more interesting to look at,' he said as he dug a crumpled scrap of paper out of his trouser pocket and scribbled something down.

Relieved, Addie's shoulders relaxed as she let out a breath. She slipped out of Rachel's loose embrace and went forward to pat Bryan's cheek. 'Good boy,' she said as if he were a dutiful spaniel.

'I know how fond you are of your room, Addie,' he said. He took her hand in his, but his gaze went meaningfully to Rachel. 'We don't want to uproot you if we don't have to.'

'Hennessy, you're a treasure,' Addie said.

Rachel sat on the bed, running a finger absently across her lower lip, reflecting on Bryan's actions – both there and in the study below. She could still feel his arms around her, could still taste him. He kissed wonderfully. Whether or not she should have allowed him to kiss her, she felt stronger and less alone now than she had before.

Her mother looked relaxed and was happily fussing with the painting at the window, straightening it to her satisfaction, the incident of the ghost apparently forgotten already. Rachel's thoughtful gaze slowly swept around the room with its garish red moiré silk wallpaper. A place for everything and everything in its place. Everything in the room was arranged just so. Not all the items seemed to belong there – like the weird assortment of smooth stones on the white linen dresser runner – but Addie apparently found comfort in having them there, just as she found comfort in being in the room itself.

'Good night, Addie,' Bryan said. His gaze was on Rachel as he crossed to the bed and took her by the hand. He smiled gently. 'Come along, Rachel. We don't want you to ruin your voice staying up late; what would Mrs. Ackerman say?'

She'd say you were a treasure, Hennessy, Rachel thought, a small ember of warmth glowing inside her, but she kept the words to herself as Bryan escorted her out of the room and down the hall.

'I'll have a look around outside, and I'll keep an eye on her room,' Bryan said. 'But I doubt anything more will happen tonight.'

'I doubt anything happened at all,' Rachel muttered. 'I wish you wouldn't persist in encouraging these fantasies of hers.'

'What makes you think this was a fantasy?'

Rachel gave him a look. 'An ill woman looks out her second-story window and sees a ghost she knows is trying to break in to steal her bird cages. You don't have to be Sherlock Holmes to figure this out.'

'Well,' Bryan conceded grudgingly. 'I'll admit the bird cage thing is a little farfetched.'

They stopped outside the door of Rachel's room, and Bryan leaned a shoulder against the frame. Rachel looked up at him pleadingly. 'Don't you see it, Bryan? She imagined there was something there, panicked, and threw a rock through the window.'

Bryan frowned, the corners of his handsome mouth cutting into the lean planes of his cheeks. He looked disappointed. 'You didn't see it, therefore it doesn't exist? There are lots of things in this world that can't quite be explained, Rachel. "The best and most beautiful things in the world cannot be seen or touched, but are felt in the heart." Helen Keller wrote that. She was blind and deaf. Just because she couldn't see or hear the rest of the world, do you think she gave up thinking it existed?' he asked quietly.

Rachel took a breath, preparing to argue, but it occurred to her suddenly that he had changed the subject, had subtly altered the slant of the conversation so that ghosts were only a small part of it. The man was much more clever than that innocent smile of his let on.

Holding her gaze with his, he reached up into the darkness of the hall, and when he brought his hand back down, he held a tiny white flower between his thumb and forefinger. He tickled her nose with it and gave her a sweet, lopsided smile.

'Explain that, Miss Lindquist.'

Rachel laughed and batted his hand away. 'You had that up your sleeve, you charlatan.'

'You'll never know for sure, unless you get me to take my shirt off,' he said, teasing. 'And I'm not that kind of boy,' he added, squaring his big shoulders and lifting his nose in the air.

'Don't let Mother hear you say that,' Rachel said, eyes twinkling. 'She'll think you need starch in your shorts.'

'Hardly,' Bryan muttered dryly, gritting his teeth on the surge of desire that came automatically from just looking at her. He couldn't seem to keep his gaze from wandering to the low V of her neckline. With every subtle movement she made, the silk of the old dress slid sensuously over her creamy flesh. Lord, how he envied that dress! Just the thought of touching her made his lungs hurt from lack of oxygen.

Rachel smiled up at him, unaware of his torment. It was wonderful the way he made her feel relaxed and playful in spite of all that had happened. He had a rare way with people, Bryan did. And he was a heck of a kisser.

As if he had read her mind, he leaned down and brushed his lips across hers. The kiss caught fire as quickly as dry kindling, burning hotter and hotter as Bryan's mouth slanted across Rachel's. He pinned her between the doorjamb and his own body, seeking as much contact as he could get. Rachel's arms wound around his neck, and she arched into him, swept away by a flood of physical desire that had leapt out of control before she had even had a chance to consider damming it up.

Need built inside them and around them in waves of heat. Rachel gasped at the feel of Bryan's hand skimming down her side, tracing the outer swell of her breast, following the inward curve of her waist and the flare of her hip. His fingers stroked downward to cup her bottom and lift her against him. She gasped again at the feel of his arousal, pressing hard and urgent against her belly, and succeeded in drawing his tongue deeper into her mouth.

Somewhere in the dimming regions of her mind she knew she should have been putting an end to this instead of encouraging it, but her sense of logic seemed to have little control over the situation. Her body wanted Bryan Hennessy. She'd never been one to throw herself at a man, but it felt as if her body was ready to change that trait right now.

It didn't make sense, she thought, struggling against the wanton need rampaging inside her. Why would she lose control this way with a man like Bryan, a man who believed in ghosts and magic, a man who, in the end, would only bring her more disappointment. She couldn't fall for him. It just wasn't smart.

'Good night, angel,' he whispered softly, pushing himself away from her. His chest rose and fell quickly with shallow breaths. There was a sadness in his steady gaze that made Rachel want to apologize, though she wasn't certain for what.

He slipped the tiny white flower into her hair behind her ear and backed into the hall, tucking his hands into his trouser pockets in a vain attempt to disguise his state of arousal. 'Put the flower under your pillow and you'll have sweet dreams.'

Her confusion plain on her face, Rachel waved to him as she disappeared into her room. And Bryan turned and wandered down the hall, thinking it was going to be another endless night.

In the long, sometimes illustrious life of Drake House, not once had the estate been owned by anyone named Wimsey. Nor had any of the owners had any children with the first name Wimsey. These facts Bryan had managed to discover easily enough, checking old records and browsing through the library books he had found. That left a number of possibilities. Wimsey might have been someone's nickname, or he might have been a servant of one of the families or a friend or an enemy.

Or he might have been, as Rachel had interpreted the name, a whimsy, a figment of Addie's deteriorating mind.

'No,' Bryan muttered, paging through yet another book. 'I don't believe that.'

Addie was too matter-of-fact about Wimsey. She didn't bring his name up to garner attention or to divert attention from herself. Wimsey was real to her, and Bryan wanted badly to prove her right, if for no other reason than to show Rachel that ghosts existed as surely as dreams and rainbows and magic did.

Rachel. So responsible and practical and level-headed. Rachel, who had been avoiding him like the plague for two days – ever since they'd shared that searing kiss at the door of her room. She believed she couldn't have magic in her life when it was what she needed most. He meant to give it to her.

He'd made his decision. He couldn't stop thinking about her, couldn't stop wanting her. It seemed he had no real choice in the matter. He was going to pursue a relationship with Rachel Lindquist whether either of them thought it prudent or not.

A thread of guilt drifted through him, and he sat back in the desk chair with a sigh. Elbows on the arms of the comfortable old chair, he steepled his fingers and his gaze came to rest on the small etched-gold ring he wore on his left pinky. Even in the subdued morning light of the study the ring glittered on his finger, bright and merry and pretty, just like Serena had been.

She would have wanted him to get on with his life. She wouldn't have wanted him to shut himself off from people the way he had been doing. His self-imposed isolation had closed him off from his gift and his magic. And since he had begun to open up again, he had begun to feel again.

He could feel himself standing unsteadily on a threshold with the cocoon of his grief behind him and the rest of his life before him. Already he could feel himself leaning through the portal toward whatever the future held for him. A part of him was eager and a part of him was sad because of it.

He bent his head and pressed a gentle kiss to the ring Serena had given him, the ring that encircled his finger in warmth, and tears rose up in his eyes as he said his final good-bye.

'Bryan?'

Rachel's voice preceded her into the study, giving him enough warning so he could clear his throat and squeeze his eyes shut.

'Bryan, are you – oh, here you are,' Rachel said. She stopped uncertainly as she stepped into the study. Her brows pulled together in concern. 'Are you all right?' she asked hesitantly.

'I'm . . . fine.'

He didn't look fine, Rachel thought. He looked like a man laboring under the strain of some terrible emotion. The idea caught at her heart and squeezed it tight. Bryan was always smiling – except when he was scolding her for not believing in magic. In the short time she had known him, she had seldom seen him be entirely serious. She had never seen him in pain. Until now.

'I was resting my eyes,' Bryan lied. He plucked his glasses off and rubbed at the bleary blue orbs. 'Too much reading.'

He settled his spectacles back on his nose and stared up at Rachel. She was worried about him. He could sense her concern. Warmth stirred inside him, and a soft smile tugged at one corner of his mouth.

'What are you searching for?' she asked, approaching the desk slowly, trying not to appear too curious.

She had been forcing herself to steer clear of him, but discovered she was so drawn to him that she kept dredging up excuses to seek him out. Her emotional tug-of-war was wearing her out.

'Proof of Wimsey,' he said.

'You haven't found any, have you?' It was more a statement than a question. She felt the pendulum inside her swing away from him.

'That doesn't mean there isn't any,' Bryan said with forced cheerfulness, 'only that I'm not looking in the right places.'

Rachel sighed, her shoulders drooping with resignation. 'Do you really think this whimsy is what Mother keeps seeing at night?'

There had been two more incidents involving Addie's elusive intruder. Both times she had been the only one to see anything. Rachel was no more convinced now than she had been that the apparition was real. Bryan, on the other hand, seemed as sure as ever that it was.

'She says not. She seems to think it's some other entity. Odd that she's never spoken of other ghosts before, only Wimsey,' he reflected, clearing a fat book aside so he could stare at his charts. 'And there's been almost no activity recorded in the parts of the house where these last three sightings have been.'

'So?'

'So,' he drawled, beckoning Rachel nearer still. He swept a hand across his blueprint of the house on which he had drawn a numbered grid and jotted down smaller numbers that were circled. 'Sightings are almost always concentrated in specific areas. This very room, for instance, and the foyer.' He tapped his pencil to two separate grid blocks, each of which was crowded with a cluster of little numbers.

'This looks very . . . scientific,' Rachel said, surprised. She might have decided Bryan was no con man, but that didn't mean she had decided to accept his so-called profession.

He gave her a wry look. 'Yes, they try to train us properly at Transylvania U.'

Rachel felt a blush creep into her cheeks. 'You said the other night you and Jayne went to college together.'

'Yes.' Mischief twinkled in his deep blue eyes. 'She majored in witchcraft and druid rituals. Ask her to change a man into a toad for you sometime. She's quite good at it.'

'Stop it,' Rachel commanded, narrowing her eyes at him. Laughter threatened, and a smile tugged at the corners of her mouth. 'I'm trying to extricate myself gracefully.'

Bryan winced. 'Sounds painful.'

'You're not making it any easier.'

'Sorry,' he said, utterly unrepentant. 'Jayne and I and two other friends you will no doubt meet soon attended Notre Dame. I got my master's at Purdue.' Rachel's eyes widened comically. Bryan chuckled. 'And you thought you Californians had cornered the market on weird.'

Her brows lowered ominously, and she tapped a finger to the blueprint. 'You were explaining this to me.'

'All right,' he conceded. Maybe he would be able to convince her with a logical scientific explanation. Somehow the idea didn't appeal to him as much as simply having her believe did. He took a deep breath and began. 'Many parapsychologists believe all places are "haunted" by memories of past events. Some places more strongly than others, naturally, say the scene of a violent death, for instance.'

'Why can't I see this whimsy of Mother's? I heard her talking to him in the hall this morning, but when I stepped out to look, there wasn't anybody with her.'

Bryan shrugged as he wrote himself a note to check the hall tape recorder. 'Maybe you haven't got the right kind of psychic sensitivity. You don't want to believe in him; that doesn't help. People tend not to see things they don't want to see.'

'Why doesn't he appear to you? You want to see him.'

'I don't know. I don't know why my equipment hasn't picked anything up either, but then, these things are never predictable. If they were, we wouldn't call them "paranormal," would we?'

'I'm sorry,' Rachel said, shaking her head, 'but I still don't believe in ghosts.'

'Neither do many psychic investigators. As a whole, we tend to be a very skeptical lot.'

'You seem anything but skeptical.'

He grinned at her, and Rachel felt her heart lurch. She reminded herself that this was exactly why she'd been avoiding him. He made her body react entirely against the better judgment of her mind.

'I'm one in a million,' he declared happily.

That was for sure, Rachel mused, watching him as he leaned toward her. She thought he was going to kiss her again, and her lips buzzed with the memory of the kisses they had shared. But he touched the tip of his nose to hers instead, and smiled the most devastatingly sexy smile. Heat washed through her, and she unconsciously wet her lips with the tip of her tongue.

'Did you have sweet dreams the other night, angel?' he asked in a voice so soft it was like a caress.

Rachel's cheeks bloomed red. *Sweet* was probably not quite the word to use regarding the dreams she'd had. *Erotic* was far and away the most accurate. She didn't understand it. Bryan was hardly the first good-looking man she'd ever known. And she was categorically against getting involved with him. Why then did she continue to go on feeling such a fierce attraction?

It made no sense. But then, little that had gone on in the past few days had made any sense. It was this blasted old house, she decided irrationally. The sooner she was out of it, the better for all concerned. Her life was pointed down a very narrow road. There was no room for a dreamer to tag along.

Bryan drew back, a gleam of satisfaction in his eye. She had dreamed about him. That bit of news was certainly a balm to his bruised male ego. He decided not to gloat; it wasn't his style. Instead, he produced three small red foam balls from nowhere and began to juggle.

Rachel stared at him, bewildered. That was all right, he decided. It would do her some good to be thrown off balance on a regular basis. It was too easy to picture her letting her life settle into a rut of dreary, dutiful routine. If she didn't learn to look around for magic and rainbows now, she certainly wasn't going to start in a year or two. The struggle to cope with Addie's illness would have worn her down and extinguished all belief in dreams and happiness. He just couldn't let that happen.

'Did you have a question?' he asked.

'What?'

'When you came in here, did you have a question, or dare I hope you came seeking out my pleasant company?'

Rachel gave herself a mental shake and gathered her wits. She straightened away from the desk, looking suddenly very purposeful. She was wearing a soft blue prairie-style dress with a simple shirtwaist and gathered skirt. A big turquoise pin was fastened at the throat of the stand-up collar. Her hair, which had flowed like fine champagne down her back the night they'd kissed, was up now, secured in a sensible knot at the back of her head. Wild tendrils curled around her face.

Bryan thought she looked like a schoolmarm – a very pretty, vulnerable schoolmarm.

'Perhaps you've come to discuss our relationship,' he suggested.

Rachel nearly bolted. 'We – we don't have a relationship,' she said, sounding more rattled than resolute.

'I beg to differ,' Bryan argued with a charming smile. He caught the red foam balls and clutched them to his chest, his expression turning melodramatic. 'Or were you just leading me on when you kissed my socks off?'

'I was not leading you on!' Rachel protested. He made the whole incident sound as if she had planned it.

'Well, then . . .' He shrugged innocently, implying that if she hadn't been leading him on, then she had been seducing him with a purpose.

Rachel ground her teeth and refused to rise to the bait. She wasn't getting involved with him. She wasn't even going to argue about getting involved with him.

'I was wondering if you knew where my mother keeps the books for her antiques business. I've been looking all over for them. I have to get started on them so I can find out exactly where we stand financially.'

'Did you ask Addie?' He settled back down on the desk chair.

'Do you honestly believe she'd tell me?' she questioned, unable to keep all the bitterness out of her voice. She and Addie seemed no closer to a reconciliation than they had five years before. It didn't help that Rachel had been to see her mother's lawyer to find out where they stood legally and financially. Talking about power of attorney and conservatorships did not make for ice breaking.

'Have you spoken with her about selling the house?' Bryan asked.

'No.'

'She isn't going to like it.'

'Then I'll have to deal with her anger, because there isn't any other way,' Rachel said stubbornly. The frustration of the past few days boiled up anew inside her. 'I have a good job waiting for me in the city. We need the money.'

'There's always another way, Rachel,' Bryan said, his disapproval of her plan subtle but clear.

'Oh, really?' Rachel arched a brow as her temper flared up. She crossed her arms in an effort to keep from trying to strangle him. 'What is this wonderful alternative? Maybe you could enlighten me. So far I've discovered that this house is probably worth less than Mother owes the bank because it's falling down around our ears. The electric company is threatening to discontinue service because she hasn't paid the bill in months. The doctor bills we're going to incur will wipe out my own bank account all on their own.'

'You need to have a little patience,' Bryan insisted. 'Something will turn up.'

Rachel felt as if a switch had been flipped inside her, letting anger pour forth unchecked. Something will turn up. That had always been Terence's line. He'd forever been telling her to lighten up, loosen up, that the future would take care of itself. She'd seen firsthand that wasn't the case. Nothing ever just 'turned up.' She had learned the hard way that the world had two kinds of people: People like Terence who believed in rainbows, and people like her who accepted responsibility.

It made her angry to think that Bryan belonged to the first group, the group she knew better than to get tangled up with. And deeper down it made her angry that she had to belong to the second group. Her life would have been a whole lot brighter with a rainbow in it, but she couldn't have one, and she didn't have time to go chasing it, at any rate. She had responsibilities.

She was angry with him. Bryan could feel the heat of it, he could see it burning in her eyes. He had stepped on a nerve. He opened his mouth to smooth things over, but Rachel didn't give him the chance.

'It must be nice to be able to coast through life believing everything takes care of itself,' she said bitterly. 'But I wouldn't know, because I've always been one of those people destined to pick up after dreamers and shoulder the realities they can never seem to face.'

Bryan shot up out of his chair and grabbed her by the wrist as she turned to storm out. 'Rachel, wait—'

'I can't wait, Mr. Hennessy,' she snapped, glaring at him. 'I've got work to do.' She jerked her arm from his grasp and rubbed at it as if to erase the memory of his touch. 'I'll let you get back to your juggling,' she said with a sneer.

Bryan closed his eyes and heaved a long sigh. Each click of her heels on the wooden floor made him wince until the sound faded away. He turned to stare up at the portrait that hung on the paneled wall.

'Got any bright suggestions?' he asked.

The pleasantly pudgy man in the painting was Arthur Drake III, the last Drake to own the house. He merely went on staring straight ahead, a secretive smile on his small mouth, one hand raised, palm up, as if gesturing to the viewer to behold the room around them. A badly tarnished brass plaque fastened to the bottom molding of the frame was engraved with a quote by Seneca: Gold is tried by fire, brave men by adversity.

'I guess this is adversity,' Bryan muttered. 'We'll see how acceptable I am.'

He sank slowly into the chair and swiveled around, letting his gaze take in the gracious room: the cherry paneling, the built-in bookshelves crowded with musty old leatherbound volumes, the fireplace, which had apparently been renovated at some point because the brick was newer than any other in the house.

What was he going to do about Rachel?

Kissing her seemed like a good idea.

'Right,' he murmured wryly in answer to his inner voice. 'I'll do it again next time she lets me get within a hundred yards of her.'

Rachel finally found the books for her mother's antiques business squirreled away inside an oak icebox in what was supposed to be Addie's office. It was a sunny room at the front of the house, cluttered with stacks and stacks of old newspapers, and wastebaskets full of splintered glass figurines. The desk contained hundreds of old lace doilies. One drawer was brim full of ballpoint pens. But not one scrap of relevant business information had been housed there. Inside a file cabinet she had found cigar boxes full of buttons of every description, but not until she checked the icebox and looked beneath three dozen old *Life* magazines did she find what she'd been looking for.

She realized, as she eased down into the chair behind the desk, that while she had been looking for this financial information, she had been dreading actually finding it. It had become obvious to her that Addie was in no condition to run a business with anything remotely resembling efficiency. She feared the books on Lindquist Antiques would only confirm what she already knew to be true.

Shoring up her resolve with a deep breath, she brushed the dust from the cover of the old ledger and turned it back. The first few pages of columns were written in her mother's neat, brisk hand. Sales and acquisitions were noted with proper care and detail. The columns of figures added up to the penny.

Rachel checked their accuracy with her calculator, feeling slightly inferior. Addie had always done math in her head as quickly and unerringly as any machine. She had always expected Rachel to be able to as well, and she had always seemed let down when Rachel hadn't been able to live up to that standard. Rachel recalled with a pang the nights she had sat up in her bed with her covers over her head to hide the brightness of the flashlight as she worked on her math tables, determined to make her mother proud of her.

The only thing about Rachel that had unfailingly pleased Addie had been her voice. Addie had been a demanding taskmaster, forcing her to practice, practice, practice; correcting her slightest error; critiquing every note. But when Addie had sat and listened to a performance, a look of rapturous longing had stolen over her face. Pride and love had shone in her eyes. And afterward Addie had always roused herself, as if from a dream, and said, 'You have the voice of an angel, Rachel. I am so very very proud of you.'

Rachel shook herself now from the bittersweet memory. She had fought against that pride in an attempt to gain her mother's understanding, and she had lost. It had been a foolish thing to do, but she'd been young and rebellious and longing to have her mother love her for who she was, not how she sang. She rubbed at her temples now as she thought of how it had all backfired on her, how all her pretty rainbows had melted into grayness.

Maybe if Bryan had had to deal with a harsh reality or two, he wouldn't be so quick to believe in magic either, she thought.

A relationship with Bryan Hennessy. She shuddered at the thought, though whether it was out of fear or anticipation she couldn't have honestly said. She told herself it was righteous indignation. The nerve of the man insinuating that she had been pursuing him!

Turning another page in the ledger, she noticed that the handwriting had changed subtly. It wasn't quite as neat or strong. A figure or two had been scratched out and written over. The penmanship worsened with every page, until she began to find words misspelled, letters transposed, mistakes in the math. And Rachel realized that what she was seeing was documentation of Addie's decline.

Nearly a year had passed since the last entry had been made in the book, and that final column of figures had never been tallied. The page was wrinkled and dark from a coffee stain, as if Addie had perhaps become upset with her inability and had spilled the cup in her haste to escape the written evidence of the illness that was progressively stealing her mind.

Rachel set the ledger aside and picked up the inventory book, hoping against hope that it was more up-to-date. But what she found was a repeat performance. The entries started out logical and legible, and gradually declined to the point that what little she could make out made no sense. The book was no more up-to-date than the ledger had been, and it was too much to hope that nothing had been purchased or sold in the interim. She was going to have to inventory everything in the house, then they would have to have a sale of some kind to dispose of the bulk of the merchandise.

They would be able to take only Addie's most personal possessions and a few antiques to San Francisco. Rachel knew they would not be able to afford much in the way of an apartment. There certainly wouldn't be room for the hundreds of pieces of furniture Addie had accumulated, or the bric-a-brac . . . or the bird cages.

'Oh, Mother,' she whispered, planting her elbows on the desk and rubbing her hands over her face as a wave of helplessness crashed into her. 'What are we going to do?'

Addie stood in the doorway to the office, motionless as she stared at Rachel. Spread out on the desk before her daughter were the books she had come to dread and hate. It was clear to her that Rachel had seen them. A cold knot of panic settled in her stomach.

'What are you looking for?' she asked, trying to sound commanding but sounding uncertain instead. She shuffled into the room, her garden boots scuffing on the worn rug. 'Money to give to Terence, the slimy snake?'

'I don't see Terence anymore, Mother,' Rachel explained calmly. She wondered how pleased Addie would have been to know her relationship with 'the cheap folk singer' had died long ago, that the bloom of love had faded along with her dreams.

'Good,' Addie said, taking a seat on a dusty chair that sat beside the desk. 'I never liked that boy. He wasn't good enough for you.'

Rachel didn't comment on the remark. Terence was in the past. There was no sense wasting energy thinking about the past when the future was going to take everything they had.

'Mother, we need to talk,' she said gravely. She was bracing herself for a fight, but when she looked into her mother's eyes, she didn't see the anger she had come to expect. She saw sadness. Somehow that was worse.

'I'm a little behind on those books,' Addie said.

'It's all right. We'll get them straightened out.'

'Here. Let me, Rachel. You were never good with numbers.'

For an instant there was a flash of her old efficient, businesslike self as Addie reached across the desk and picked up the ledger. She sat up straighter, her bony shoulders squared beneath the thin cotton of her housedress. Taking a pencil out of a cup on the desktop, she opened the book.

Gritting her teeth in determination, she began at the top of the page. She saw the numbers, took them into her brain, and tried to put them together, but they scattered and went off in all directions in her mind. She took a deep breath and tried again. She had always been so good at math. Now she could barely comprehend the numbers on the page before her. She tried to add two numbers together, and just before the answer became clear to her, it slipped away.

A terrible chill ran through her. She could excuse her forgetfulness. She was a busy woman with a lot on her mind. So what if she put her car in reverse instead of park once? So what if she went to the mailbox on Sunday? Busy people forgot things all the time. But this, this was something else. She couldn't discount her inability to add these simple numbers together.

She stared at the figures on the page until they seemed to leap out of their columns and spin around one another in a whirlpool of black and red ink. Panic rose up in her throat, and she slammed the ledger shut. She wanted to throw the book aside and run out of the room, but her brain suddenly couldn't separate all the intricacies of each task, and she clutched the book to her breast instead.

'Mother?' Rachel asked softly. Her own sense of panic was growing inside her, and it trembled in her voice. She had never seen her mother as anything other than strong, invincible, indomitable. And before her very eyes Addie was shrinking down on her chair, her face a mask of stricken confusion. Rachel reached out toward her, the fingers of her hand curling over the edge of the musty old ledger, 'Mother?'

'Rachel,' Addie murmured, her voice straining. She felt too fragile and frail to speak louder than a whisper. She felt as if she might shatter like the many china figurines she had broken over the last few months as the connection between her brain and her fingers had shorted out. The shield of anger and indignation that had held her up so many times was gone, vanished as suddenly as her memory could vanish.

All her life she had been strong. She had stood on her own to raise her daughter when her husband had been killed. She had never asked for help from anyone. But now she turned instinctively to her daughter, her eyes full of anguish and tears. 'Rachel, I'm so frightened.'

Rachel took her mother in her arms and held her as her mother had held her when she'd skinned her knee or had had a bad dream. And she offered what comfort she could while she shared her mother's pain and felt the pain of her own loss. She was losing her mother. Addie would never be the strong one again. It was Rachel's turn. At that moment both of them realized it.

'I'm frightened too,' she murmured through her tears. 'But we'll manage. Together, like it used to be. Just the two of us. I'll take care of you. I love you. I love you so much.'

Bryan stopped in the doorway, everything inside him going still at the sight. He had intended to barge in and sweep Rachel away from the books for a walk around the grounds. He wanted to show her that there was more to her life than worrying about money. But it looked as if she didn't need him to tell her that at the moment.

He knew he should have stepped back out into the hall and allowed Rachel and Addie absolute privacy, but it seemed important that he see Rachel this way – as a loving daughter, as a caring person, not embarrassed by her mother's illness, but heartbroken for a loss that could never be replaced.

Or perhaps what was truly important was the feeling coming to life inside himself, the feeling he had denied over and over the past few days. He was in love with Rachel Lindquist.

He did step back then, as if the realization had come in the form of a physical blow. He let himself out of the house and strode quickly toward the fence that ran along the cliff's edge, breaking into an athletic lope that ate up the distance. When he reached the rusty iron railing, he stopped, sucking in great deep gulps of sea air. In each hand he grasped a spear point that decorated the top of the wrought iron pickets, twisting at them so that the oxidizing metal flaked against his palms.

Without really seeing it, he stared out at the ocean. The gray-blue waves rolled in, one after another. Fishing boats dotted the misty horizon. Gulls keened and swooped along the rocky beach below.

How had it happened so fast, he wondered. He hardly knew anything about her. Except that she loved a mother who had shunned her for five years, and she'd had dreams broken, and she tasted of need and sweetness. And when the moon shone in her eyes, he could see how badly she needed to believe in rainbows and how afraid she was to reach out for one.

It didn't seem possible that he could have fallen in love when he had just opened up enough to offer Rachel his help. He had meant only to reach out to her, to offer her a little respite from her worries. But in opening up he had not simply given, he had received. He could feel again. Now Rachel's pain would be his pain, her fears would be his fears.

'I don't know if I'm strong enough to go through that again,' he whispered.

You are. Love makes you strong.

He thought of Rachel holding her mother, whispering assurances through her tears. Love was the most powerful thing in the world. It could endure time and turmoil, hurt and heartache, pride and pain. Love was magic.

Bryan's broad shoulders rose as he drew a deep breath, filling his lungs with cool air, and a deep, abiding calm settled inside him with the kind of acceptance that comes only from the heart. It might not have been smart or logical for him to love Rachel Lindquist, but love her he did, and if he could give her magic, he would.

7

' "I love a maiden fair with sunlight in her hair. Her beauty was so rare, but she did scorn me," ' Bryan sang as he trailed along behind Rachel and Faith Callan like a wandering troubador.

They were systematically working their way through Drake House, making an inventory. Faith, who had experience with antiques, was identifying each piece, then Rachel looked the item up in a dealer's catalog, and they tried to arrive at a fair market value. Bryan tagged along behind them, jotting down their findings in the inventory book, Addie followed them to each room, then stood in a strategic spot and glared at them as they went about their business.

She wasn't taking it well at all, he thought, stealing a surreptitious glance at the older woman. The peace mother and daughter had made the day before had already been wrecked. Addie was sulking in the corner of the room near the window, her mouth pinched into a line as she twisted the end of her braid. She dug a hand into the patch pocket of her cotton housedress, pulled out a long stalk of celery, and began to munch on it angrily.

Bryan knew Rachel had explained to her that the antiques would have to be inventoried and sold because they needed the money, and Addie had seemed to comprehend the situation, but that didn't mean she had to like it. He couldn't blame her. Her independence was being taken away from her bit by bit. A proud woman like Addie wasn't likely to accept it with a smile.

Still, Bryan thought with a sigh, he had promised to try to ease this transition for both Addie and Rachel. Drawing in a deep breath, he broke into song again.

' "She was a maiden fair with sunlight in her hair. Her name was Addie." '

Addie scowled at him and gave him a loud raspberry, spraying bits of celery out at him.

'I think she likes me.' Bryan grinned, and winked at Faith. 'What do you think?'

Faith giggled, dark eyes twinkling. The sun streaming in the window caught in her mop of burnished curls, turning them more red than gold.

She poked Bryan in the ribs with the eraser end of her pencil. 'Behave yourself, Hennessy, or we'll send you out to do some real work.'

'You could have brought along my darling godchildren,' he said with a hint of reproach. 'They would have kept an eye on me.'

'No doubt. Lindy would make you toe the line. You know how she bosses Nicholas around.'

'He's just biding his time,' Bryan said. 'In another few years he'll be towering over her. We'll see who the boss is then. I can give him some pointers on diabolical brother-type revenge.'

Rachel listened to their good-natured bantering. It was clear that Bryan and Faith were as close as brother and sister. There was a special understanding between them, evident when they smiled at each other. She envied them that. She had never felt that kind of kinship with anyone, not even with Terence.

As she was thinking it, Bryan turned and regarded her with the same warm expression, the same keen knowing in his blue eyes. There was an invitation in his gaze, an invitation for her to share that kind of special friendship with him.

Temptation pulled at her. A part of her wanted badly to accept. It would have been nice to have a friend to lean on, but another part of her flatly denied her that option. She had to take her responsibilities on her own shoulders, because she knew from experience she couldn't count on a man like Bryan to give support forever.

Not that she blamed him. She couldn't see how anyone in his right mind would want to take on the task she was facing if he didn't have to. Why would anyone ask to share that kind of pain?

The word *love* passed fleetingly through her brain, but she dismissed it. She had given up on the idea of romantic love, just as she had given up on the notion of rainbows and happy endings. She couldn't afford romantic fantasies any more than she could afford to lose sleep over the erotic dreams she'd been having lately.

Bryan Hennessy was proving to be one big distraction from the things she needed to concentrate on most. One big, handsome distraction . . .

She stared at him as he made a note in the book he cradled on his right arm. He wore faded jeans that hugged his lean male body in all the right places. A polo shirt clung to his strong shoulders. The color matched the blue of his eyes in a way that made Rachel's breath catch. Glossy strands of tawny hair fell across his broad forehead.

His glasses were slipping down his nose. Without looking up from his work, he reached up and pushed at the wire bridge with the middle finger of his left hand. It was a gesture she'd seen him perform a hundred times, and yet, for some inexplicable reason, this time she thought it was curiously sweet.

Her gaze focused on his hands, and longing rippled through her. Those big hands were strong, yet so gentle, almost as gentle as his lips had been against hers. She'd dreamed of those hands caressing her every night. It seemed like eons had passed since he'd touched her, kissed her. It had been three days. She probably could have said how many hours and minutes had passed.

It irked her that she'd spent so much time thinking about it. She had told herself she couldn't get involved with Bryan Hennessy. That should have been the end of the longing. Since their argument, she had avoided him as best she could, considering they were living in the same house. She had been as cool toward him as possible without being out and out rude.

And still he was sweet to her. The growing bouquet of roses on her dresser was testimony to that. There was one waiting for her on her pillow every night when she went up to bed. It seemed only a sweeter gesture when he denied knowledge of it.

She couldn't stop thinking about him. If she had been the fanciful sort, she might have thought he'd cast some kind of magic spell on her. Instead, she blamed it on the flowers. She had always been a sucker for roses.

'Rachel?' Faith asked for the third time.

Rachel snapped out of her musings with a start. 'I'm sorry. What?'

A gentle smile turned the corners of Faith's mouth, setting her heartshaped face aglow. 'I was just going to suggest a coffee break.'

'Oh, yes, of course,' Rachel stammered, embarrassment heating her face. She stifled the urge to rub at the spots of color blooming on her cheekbones, winding her hands more firmly around the book she clutched against the front of her baggy pink T-shirt.

Suddenly Addie stamped her booted foot. 'You're thieves, the lot of you! You're going to steal my bird cages. I won't stand for it, I tell you. I'm going to call the police!'

'Mother!' Rachel wailed, at the end of her emotional rope. She had been over this with Addie a half dozen times. It was difficult to tell herself that Addie had undoubtedly forgotten every one of those conversations, that she wasn't being difficult deliberately. 'Don't go dragging that horrid deputy out here again.'

'He'll get to the bottom of this business,' Addie said. 'He can find that ugly ghost while he's out here, too, and haul you all away together.'

'If he hauls anyone away, it'll be you, Mother. He's angry enough with you as it is.'

Addie tossed the last of her celery stalk at her daughter and stomped toward the door. Bryan headed her off.

'Hennessy, get out of my way,' Addie commanded.

'Not a chance, beautiful,' he said with an amicable grin. 'You know you have the most lovely complexion, Addie. How do you keep it that way?'

Addie blushed like a schoolgirl. She had always been vain about her flawless skin. Bryan's compliment bolstered her flagging ego and easily derailed her thoughts from calling the police.

'All the Gunther women have beautiful skin,' she said coyly, patting a hand to her pale cheek. 'It's an old family secret.'

'Ah, a secret,' Bryan said with great relish. He took her arm and tucked it in his. 'I've got one too. I'll tell you mine if you tell me yours. Then we'll dance the tango on the lawn.'

Rachel watched, bemused by the strange mix of feelings inside her as Bryan led her mother away. 'Is he ever serious about anything?'

'Oh, yes,' Faith said on a long sigh of remembrance. Heedless of the layer of dust, she settled herself on an old desk and folded her hands in the lap of her worn jeans. 'We went for a long time without seeing Bryan smile after he lost Serena.'

'Serena?'

'His wife,' Faith said gently. She paused then to let Rachel absorb the information, compassion welling inside her at the look of shock on the woman's face. 'She passed away about a year and half ago. Cancer.'

'I – I didn't know.' Rachel felt as if she'd been hit by a truck. Her knees wobbled, and she sat down on a huge square iron bird cage.

Bryan had been married. He had been in love with a woman who had died. Oh, Lord, she thought, unable to stop the tears that flooded her eyes, what a disservice she'd done him, thinking he had never had to endure pain or accept responsibility.

'So if we seem a little overindulgent of his silliness,' Faith went on, 'it's only because we missed it so much. Besides,' she added, summoning up one of her sunny smiles, 'there's a lot more to Bryan than meets the eye.'

'I'd already guessed that,' Rachel mumbled.

Dammit, she thought, she felt completely off balance. She felt utterly guilty and mean and self-centered. Anger struggled to life inside her. She didn't need this. She had enough emotional baggage to deal with. She couldn't afford to spend her energy on dealing with Bryan's as well. It was just one more reason she shouldn't get more deeply involved with him.

If they'd met at some other place and time in their lives, things might have been different. But the facts remained: she had her mother to take care of, Bryan had his own wounded heart to heal, and they wanted to deal with those issues in two completely different ways. She could see no answer other than practicality, no matter how unpleasant it might be. He chose to gloss everything over with magic and foolishness.

Rachel looked up suddenly, and in the next instant Bryan danced through the door with Addie in his arms. Her mother's cheeks were flushed, and she held a rose between her teeth. He deposited her in a high-backed chair and strode toward Rachel purposefully, stopping before her with an earnest look on his face.

'Dorothy,' he said. 'I believe the munchkins have arrived.'

'The what?' Faith asked.

Rachel, however, knew exactly what he was referring to. She had spoken of this place as Oz. But who exactly the munchkins were, she didn't know. Her eyebrows lifted in question.

Bryan glanced back over his shoulder to make sure Addie wasn't listening. She was twirling her rose by its stem and softly singing a snatch of something from *Aida*. He turned back to Rachel. 'There are two rather remarkable-looking gentlemen at the front door, asking to speak to you about purchasing Drake House.'

'But I haven't put it on the market yet,' Rachel said. 'How did they know it was for sale?'

'I wonder,' Bryan said, stroking a hand back through his sandy hair. Behind his glasses his eyes took on a faraway look. 'I wonder.'

Rachel excused herself and went out into the hall, wondering why she wasn't eager to meet these prospective buyers. She'd been worried that they would have trouble unloading the house, it was in such a sad state of disrepair. She should have been bubbling over about this turn of events, but she wasn't.

Swinging the heavy front door back, she immediately saw what Bryan had meant by 'remarkable-looking.' One of the men was about five feet tall and nearly as wide. His head was as round and bald as a bowling ball. His companion was a few inches taller, built like a rail, and had a face with sharp, sly features and deepset eyes. There was a fading blue bruise on his left cheek.

Rachel cleared her throat delicately and offered her visitors a polite smile. 'Can I help you? I'm Rachel Lindquist.'

The rotund one stuck out a dimpled hand. 'Miles Porchind, Miss Lindquist,' he said with a smile, 'and my partner. Felix Rasmussen. May we take a few moments of your time to discuss some business?'

Her immediate reaction to the men was dislike, but she reminded herself beggars couldn't be choosers, and invited the prospective buyers inside. She led the way to the study, the skin on her back prickling as she felt their gazes on her.

Once in the room, Porchind and Rasmussen looked around with hungry eyes, taking in the paneling, the old furniture, the bookshelves – particularly the bookshelves, with their dusty old tomes. Their expressions were like those of starving men who had stumbled into a bakery. Rachel half expected them to start salivating. Grimacing in distaste at the thought, she seated herself behind the desk and motioned the men to help themselves to seats. Oddly, they chose to sit side by side on the leather love seat, with Porchind taking up more than half of it.

Bryan wandered in then, juggling two apples and an orange. 'Hello again,' he said, sending the men his most innocuous grin. He caught two pieces of fruit against his chest with his right arm, caught the remaining apple in his left hand, and promptly took a bite out of it.

'We're here to discuss business with Miss Lindquist,' Porchind said with a trace of annoyance.

'So you said. Care for a piece of fruit?'

They merely stared at him, then turned to Rachel, clearly hoping she would toss Bryan out on his ear.

'It's all right,' Rachel said. 'Mr. Hennessy is the family retainer.'

She supposed she shouldn't have, but she wanted Bryan there with her, and, for once, she gave in to her desire. He shot her a wink that seemed inappropriately intimate, and immediately heat streaked through her body. She had to force her mind back to the business at hand.

'Bryan tells me you're interested in purchasing the house,' she said. 'May I ask where you heard it was for sale?'

The men glanced sharply at each other and answered simultaneously. 'In town.'

Porchind went on. 'We heard you had come back to settle your mother's affairs and close up the house. Perhaps it was nothing more than smalltown gossip.'

'Gossip, perhaps,' Rasmussen echoed.

'No, I have been considering it,' Rachel said cautiously.

'But it's nothing definite, by any means,' Bryan interrupted.

Rachel scowled up at him. 'I thought you wanted to help,' she muttered between her teeth.

'I am helping,' he said, ignoring the anger he felt rolling off her in waves. He turned back to their visitors. 'There are so many things to consider. The ghosts, for example. You must have heard by now, the house is haunted.'

The strangers exchanged another glance. 'We're not put off by ghost stories,' Porchind said.

His partner shook his head. 'Don't believe in ghosts.'

Immediately, two huge drops of water fell from the ceiling – one landing squarely on the head of each man. Before they had a chance to recover from the surprise, two more drops fell, followed by two more. Porchind looked up and caught one in the eye.

'And then there's the plumbing,' Bryan said. It was almost impossible to contain his excitement. It churned inside him as he looked up at the ceiling, which showed no evidence of a water spot. Wimsey. He knew it. He could sense it. This was his first physical sign of Addie's ghost.

'The plumbing is fine,' Rachel insisted. 'That's just humidity.'

'Humidity from hell,' Bryan said dramatically.

Porchind looked past him to Rachel. 'My partner and I are interested in the house, Miss Lindquist. Have you set a price yet?'

'No, I haven't,' Rachel said, trying to keep her anger out of her voice. She was going to skin Bryan Hennessy alive when this was over. 'I need to discuss the matter with my mother.'

'Mrs. Lindquist doesn't want to move, you see,' Bryan explained cheerfully. 'She's attached to the place. Hard to figure, isn't it? But you know how elderly people are. They get something in their heads and there's no telling them otherwise. She wants to stay here forever.'

Bryan tossed his apple core into the wastebasket beside the desk, then resumed his juggling, adding a paperweight to the apple and orange. From beneath lowered lashes he watched the two men scowl at him.

'Perhaps we should come back at a more convenient time,' Porchind said, heaving himself to his feet.

'When it's more convenient,' Rasmussen muttered, rising and trying to straighten his suit over his bony frame.

'Once you've had a chance to speak with your mother and determine a price,' the round man said as he and his partner moved toward the door. 'We only thought it prudent to let you know of our interest.'

'Interest.' Rasmussen nodded, smiling at Rachel in a way that made her skin crawl.

She managed a thank-you as she walked them to the door. When she returned to the study, she was seething. Bryan had seated himself behind the desk and was absorbed in one of his history books.

'How dare you interfere!' she snapped, releasing the pent-up anger not only over the house issue, but the anger and frustration that had been building inside her for days. She kicked a sneakered foot against the handsome walnut desk. 'How dare you! Those men may be the only people in the free world strange enough to buy this house, and you practically chased them away! And even if they do come back, I'll be lucky to get enough out of them to pay off the mortgage, thanks to you and your infernal ghost stories and your candor about the plumbing.'

'Addie isn't going to want to move,' Bryan said calmly.

'It isn't a question of whether or not Addie wants to move,' Rachel said, planting her fists on the desktop. 'It's the way it has to be. Will you face reality for once? I have a job waiting for me in San Francisco. I'm going to have to support my mother. Her medical bills alone will probably put me in debt for the rest of my life. Insurance would be a great help, but Addie doesn't have any because she lined a bird cage with her premium notice and let the policy lapse. Are you comprehending any of this, Bryan?' She snatched up a pen and pad of paper and thrust them at him. 'Maybe you should write yourself a note. I have to sell this house!'

Bryan looked up at her and sighed. 'I know it's a cliché, but you're beautiful when you're angry.'

Rachel clamped her hands to her head as if to keep the top of it from exploding off. She counted to ten and took deep breaths. Blessed, infuriating man! He could be every bit as impossible to deal with as her mother.

'I don't think you should be too hasty about selling, Rachel.'

'Bryan, this house is as expensive to keep as a herd of elephants, and there's no chance of me finding a job around here that would pay more than peanuts. You're allegedly an intelligent man – you do the math. I have to sell this house. I haven't got a choice.'

'We always have at least two choices, angel. You're just too stubborn to look for yours.'

'*I'm* stubborn?' Rachel went red in the face as a hundred scathing retorts clogged her throat and cut off her air supply.

Bryan had turned back to his book. 'I've got a bad feeling about Messieurs Porkrind and Rasputin. I think they're up to something.'

Rachel didn't like them either, but she was too angry to agree with him about anything. She regarded him with narrowed eyes. 'I suppose now you're going to tell me you're a mind reader.'

'Not precisely.' Bryan pressed his lips together to fight off the smile that threatened.

He studiously avoided looking at Rachel, concentrating instead on his book. His eyes brightened suddenly, and he tapped a finger to the page before him. 'Edmund Porchind, alias Pig Porchind, alleged bootlegger during the Prohibition era, resided in Anastasia until 1931.' He pushed his glasses up and stared across the room. 'I wonder what one of the late Mr. Pig's long-lost relatives wants with Drake House.'

'I'm sure I don't care,' Rachel said crossly. She turned to start for the door, but Bryan caught her wrist, and with one deft tug pulled her into his lap.

'Bryan!' she squealed. Her fury was instantly overrun by surprise and a giddy kind of desire that kept her from trying too hard to get away. She squirmed just enough so Bryan had to wrap his arms around her.

'Don't you know when a woman is furious with you?' she asked, fighting to maintain her scowl.

'Yes, but I also know when she's having to work at it.' A wicked grin split his features. Rachel was angry with him, but she would recover. In the span of a few short minutes he had had a bounty of clues dropped in his lap. It was as intoxicating for him as was any liquor.

'Look sharp, Watson!' he said merrily. 'The game is afoot!'

He covered her frown with an exuberant kiss. He had meant only to give her a quick smack on the lips, but as soon as he tasted her, his intentions melted away on a groan of pure male need. She tasted so sweet. Even angry she tasted sweeter than anything he'd had in his life for a long time. And beneath her initial resistance he could taste a dozen other emotions – longing, hesitancy. He could taste a woman who wanted to believe in his brand of magic but wasn't going to allow herself to.

He slanted his mouth across hers in warm invitation as his left hand slid up the supple lines of her back to tangle in her hair. Pins slipped their moorings and dropped to the floor as the mass of pale silk tumbled loose. Her lips softened beneath his, and she yielded to temptation with a moan.

She shouldn't have been giving in to him this way, Rachel thought dimly. But she didn't seem to have the will to pull away. She felt safe in Bryan's arms. She felt womanly in a way she hadn't experienced in ages. She felt her troubles drift to the back of her mind. That alone was worth the lapse in behavior. What would it hurt to let go of reality for just a moment or two, she rationalized as desire surged through her veins in a hot stream. What would it hurt to take what Bryan was offering, so long as she realized it couldn't be permanent?

His tongue gently traced the line of her lips, and she invited him inside before her brain could summon an objection. She framed his face with her hands as she took his tongue into her mouth, and reveled in the textures her heightened senses experienced – the softness of his lean, clean-shaven cheeks against her palms, the velvet rasp of his tongue against her own. She could feel his arousal press against her thigh, and an answering heat pulsed between her legs. She twisted in his embrace to press closer, flattening her breasts against the solid wall of his chest.

She slid her hands up the sides of his face, hooking her thumbs under his glasses and sliding them up out of the way, so she could kiss him even harder. At the same time, Bryan traced a line around her rib cage, down to the point of her hip. His fingers snuck under the bottom of her T-shirt and slid up to cup a small, full breast. Rachel's breath caught in her throat at the feel of his thumb rubbing back and forth across her hardened nipple.

Bryan drew back a little, planting tiny kisses along the line of Rachel's jaw, then drew back a little farther so he could look at her face. Fresh air rushed in and out of his lungs, bringing with it a measure of sanity. It seemed an eternity had passed since he'd wanted a woman this badly. His hormones were screaming for him to press his advantage and take Rachel right there and then, but as he looked into her violet eyes he saw not only desire, but vulnerability and uncertainty.

She might want him, but she wasn't clear on the reasons why, and for him it had to be something more than an act to obliterate the present and push away the specter of a lonely future. He'd been down that road himself. He wasn't willing to go down it again, even with Rachel. When they made love, it would be just that – love.

He smoothed down the hem of her soft pink shirt and gave her a gentle smile as he dropped his glasses back into place. 'For someone who doesn't believe in magic, you do a pretty good job of weaving a spell,' he said.

Rachel stared at him as if he had just materialized before her, taking in his tousled tawny hair, the gleam of residual desire in his blue eyes, the slight puffiness of his sexy lower lip. She could still feel him, rigid and ready against her thigh, and a bolt of heat shot through her.

Magic, he'd said. Illusion. That was all this was, she told herself, her heart sinking. She could lose herself to the illusion she found in Bryan's arms, but the reality of her life would still be there waiting for her when the smoke cleared.

She tried to bolt off his lap, but he held her there, his hands firm but unyielding.

'Love isn't the trick, Rachel,' he said softly, his earnest gaze holding hers, 'believing is.'

Awareness shivered through her. Almost immediately panic closed her throat. She couldn't be in love with Bryan Hennessy. She just couldn't be. Fate couldn't be that cruel to her again, to make her fall in love with a man who believed in magic. Love would make her weak when she most needed her strength. It would hand her disappointment when she already had a wagonload of it.

This time when she tried to extricate herself from Bryan's hold, he let her go. She straightened her clothes and pressed a hand to her mouth as she looked away from him. Her lips were hot and sensitive and still tasted of him, of apples and man. Longing ribboned through her again, and she squelched it, wincing as she ground out the fragile emotion.

Bryan watched her, hurting for her as he sensed her inner struggle, hurting for himself as she denied them both. But despite the mild setback, optimism brimmed to life inside him, and he smiled. Things were looking up. There was a mystery to unravel, and Rachel Lindquist had just kissed him silly. What more could a man ask for?

'We'd better get back to work,' she said, her voice remote. 'Faith will be wondering what happened to us.'

'You might be wondering that yourself,' Bryan murmured as Rachel walked away. He took one last look at the history book open on the desk, then focused his gaze on Rachel's delectable derriere as he pushed himself out of his chair and followed her into the hall.

'Faith, thanks for all your help,' Rachel said. She stood on the porch with her arms wrapped around herself as the fog bank rolled in for the evening, obliterating what was left of the sunlight. 'Are you sure you won't take anything for your time?'

'Absolutely not.' Faith shook her head, her curls bouncing. 'I was just lending a hand. That's what friends do. If you're a friend of Bryan's, you're a friend of mine. Remember that.' She skipped down the sagging steps and turned around at the bottom with a sunny smile. 'I'll expect to see you at the inn one day soon for tea.'

'All right.'

Rachel couldn't help but smile in return. It would have been nice to nurture a friendship with Faith Callan. For a moment she let herself think of what it would be like to settle there and have the kind of friends she could call simply to chat with or meet for tea. Another thing she wanted but could never have, she told herself as she watched Bryan walk his friend to her station wagon.

'Dear Miss Lindquist,' Bryan said as he ambled along with his hands in his pockets, 'you are cordially invited to an interrogation at Keepsake Inn, Anastasia-by-the-Sea. Thumbscrews optional.'

Faith frowned at him in disappointment. 'I like her, Bryan. She probably deserves better than a man who questions the motives of his dearest friends. Besides,' she added, 'Alaina and Jayne and I are only looking out for you the same way you look out for us.'

'Yes,' Bryan agreed, 'and I love you for it. But I'm a big boy, now; I can take care of myself – more or less.'

Faith didn't look the least bit convinced as she opened the door and slid behind the wheel of her car. 'You need a haircut, big boy.'

A wry grin twisted Bryan's mouth as he ran a hand back through his hair. He was going to have to write himself another note. He bent and kissed Faith's cheek through the open window, then handed her a little blue flower he had produced from thin air. Faith tucked it into a buttonhole on her white oxford shirt and looked at him with an expression as earnest as any he could have mustered.

'Please be careful with your heart, Bryan. You give it so easily. I'm not saying Rachel isn't worthy of it. I'm just afraid that maybe you're falling in love with her because she needs someone to take care of her and you've run out of people to look after.'

'That's not it,' he said evenly, though he suspected he was fibbing a bit. He did want to look after Rachel, but caring was a part of love. Besides, kissing her this morning had had little to do with her plight and everything to do with the way she felt in his arms.

Faith sighed and told him good-bye. He stood in the yard, watching as she drove down the long driveway, a pensive mood settling over him. He had a lot to think about tonight – Rachel, Porchind and Rasmussen, the possibility that Wimsey had showered those two with disapproval over their opinion of ghosts.

A mournful wail drifted to him on the cooling breeze. He snapped himself out of his musings and listened, holding his breath. The sound came again, faint but real, and he turned and jogged off across the lawn toward it, not at all sure of what he might find.

Addie wandered through the maze with no idea of where she was. All around her were high wild bushes, their branches tangled into an angry mass with leaves that rattled at her in the wind. They towered over her, casting a sinister shadow across the narrow, weed-choked path.

She had left the house because she was angry and frightened and she had thought the fresh air might clear her head, but she had promptly become lost. She had no idea how long she had been gone. It seemed like hours had passed. She had no idea of how far she had wandered. All she knew for sure was that she was cold and that Rachel was going to sell her home and make her move to a place where nothing would be familiar.

She had overheard her daughter's conversation with those strange little men and her argument with Hennessy afterward. She had thought about confronting Rachel, but fear of the future had overwhelmed her, and she had run away instead. Her forgetfulness wasn't such a terrible thing here in Anastasia, where people knew her, and in Drake House, where things were usually familiar. But to go to a place where everything would be strange, where there would be no memories at all to draw on, where she would have to learn new faces and new ways of doing things . . .

Tears welled up in her eyes and in her throat, choking her as she stumbled along the path, her garden boots catching on the rough ground. How could Rachel betray her this way? How could the daughter she had sacrificed so much for treat her so badly?

Addie stopped and looked around her, her eyes wide with fright. No matter which way she turned, everything looked the same. She pressed her bony hands to her cheeks and sobbed aloud as she sank down on a cracked stone bench.

Suddenly a man burst through the shrubbery. She looked up at him, terrified, and sobbed again.

'Addie,' he said, stopping in his tracks. He was out of breath and his hair was disheveled. 'Are you all right?'

'Who are you?' she demanded.

'It's me, Addie. Bryan Hennessy.'

'I don't know you,' she said vehemently, swatting at him as he came nearer and knelt down at her feet. 'I don't know you. Go away! Go away or I'll scream!'

'It's all right, Addie,' Bryan said in a soft voice. He never broke eye contact with her as he reached out and captured one of her frail hands in his. 'It's all right. It's me, Hennessy.'

'I don't know you!' she shouted, panic rolling through her like a tidal wave as she stared at him. She fought the horrible fog that clouded her mind, searching for a memory of this man's face. A part of her thought she should know him, which only made her more desperate to find something there that she couldn't quite grasp. Tears spilled down her cheeks, and she slumped on the bench in abject misery, mumbling, 'I don't know you. I don't know you.'

Bryan settled himself on the bench beside Addie and pulled her thin, trembling body into his arms. Cradling her against him, he stroked a big hand over her hair, and, rocking her gently back and forth, he began singing to her. It was a soft, sweet song he'd learned in Scotland about a girl named Annie Laurie, who was fair and lovely with a voice like a summer wind's sigh. His voice rose and fell with the melody, and trembled a bit as he ached with Addie's pain and confusion. But he sang on, the gentle notes coming from his heart, just as they had when he'd held Serena and sung to her.

Rachel stood at the edge of the clearing in the maze, her body shaking.

She had gone into the house, intending to speak with Addie about selling the place, but her mother had been nowhere around. She'd run out into the yard to get Bryan to help her look for Addie, and the sound of crying had drawn her to the overgrown maze.

She stood there now, unable to move or breathe. She stared at the scene before her: Bryan, his eyes closed, but a lone pair of tears escaping the outer corners, holding her mother and singing to her; and Addie rocking back and forth within the embrace of his strong arms, crying.

'It's all right, Addie,' Bryan murmured, kissing the old woman's temple. 'It's all right if you don't know me. I'll still help you.'

It struck Rachel then. As she stood there with her defenses stripped away by raw emotion, with her heart laid bare and the truth confronting her with nowhere for her to hide. She was in love with Bryan Hennessy. And it wasn't a question of whether or not he was the kind of man she needed, it was a question of whether or not she deserved to have the kind of man he was.

8

'Is Addie asleep?' Bryan asked, looking up from the papers he had spread out on the desk. A small brass lamp illuminated his work area. The only other light in the room came from the fireplace. Shadows jumped on the dark paneled walls.

'Finally,' Rachel said on a sigh. She leaned a hip against the desk and allowed her shoulders to sag beneath the weight of her worries. 'She wouldn't let me in her room, but I managed to peek inside once it got quiet. She wore her garden boots to bed. I could see them sticking up under the coverlet. I wanted to go in and take them off for her, but I'm sure she would have hit me in the head with a rock and called the police.'

Bryan frowned. 'Back to square one, eh?'

'I'd do handsprings if we were that far along,' Rachel said dryly. 'I tried to explain to her that selling the house is the only practical thing, but she didn't want to hear it.' She held up a hand as Bryan opened his mouth to speak. 'Please refrain from saying you told me so. In fact, a change of subject would be warmly welcomed.'

'You're an absolute vision in that dress.' He gave her a wicked smile and forced all thoughts of the mundane from his mind.

Rachel beamed as if his words had injected new energy into her. She was wearing the beaded burgundy gown, the same gown that had so mysteriously appeared on her bed that first night she'd had dinner at Drake House. Addie claimed it was Wimsey who insisted they dress for the evening meal, but Rachel didn't see the difference. It was Addie who became upset if she showed up underdressed, so it was Addie she dressed for – most nights.

Tonight she had chosen the burgundy dress without a thought about her mother. She had chosen it because she wanted to feel special and feminine and alluring. She had laid it out on her bed before her bath, and when she had returned, there had been a white rose lying on it.

'How did you know that was the perfect thing to say?' she murmured, settling her hip more comfortably against the desk.

'I'm psychic,' Bryan admitted with a smile. 'I'll go out on a limb and say that you're probably a vision out of that dress as well.'

His voice was dark with desire. The rich quality of it stroked her senses like the caress of the silk she wore.

'Have you been spying on me in the bathtub?' she asked, conjuring up a teasing note to cut through her own sudden rush of yearning.

'Not exactly,' Bryan mumbled cryptically. He fixed his gaze on the steaming cup she held, breathing deep of the aroma and sighing in appreciation. 'Coffee.'

'Would you like a cup? I'll go back to the kitchen—'

'Don't bother,' he said, not wanting to lose sight of her. 'Just let me have a sip of yours.'

Warmth curled inside Rachel as if he had just made a terribly erotic suggestion. She bit the inside of her lip and offered him the mug, sucking in a breath when his fingertips brushed hers. Her senses were so heightened, the slightest glance or touch from him set her nerves sizzling. She had spent her entire time in the bathtub reliving the few kisses they had shared and imagining what it would be like to make love with him, fantasizing until she had hardly been able to stand the brush of the washcloth against her skin.

She had come to a decision about Bryan, about the desire that burned inside her. She had a long, hard road ahead of her. Her future didn't look particularly bright, but for the present she had Bryan. She would have been a fool not to take what happiness she could while she had the chance.

Bryan looked up at her, his blue eyes sharp with awareness. He could sense the shift in Rachel's feelings toward him. They had been changing gradually, constantly, since they'd met, but tonight she had taken a giant step in his direction. He wasn't sure what had pushed her over the edge in his favor, but he wasn't inclined to question his good fortune either. He was a conscientious man, but he was a man first. A man with needs.

It was a cold, rainy night. The kind of night a man wanted to spend curled up in bed with the lady of his heart, making love to her until they both drifted off into exhausted sleep. He hadn't been able to get that image out of his head all evening. Nor had he been able to stop picturing her in the bathtub, sliding a bar of scented soap over her slick skin. That image still seemed particularly strong. He could see the gleam of light on her wet skin. He could smell the soap. Even now the vision played through his mind, and heat coiled in his belly.

Never taking his eyes from Rachel's, he sipped at the coffee and set the cup aside. Her eyes darkened from violet to deep purple, and a flush crept along under the surface of her fair skin.

'You must be cold,' he murmured, pushing himself up from his chair. He pulled his tuxedo jacket off and draped it around her shoulders before she could object. In a move he'd perfected as a teenager, he let one arm slide down her back and fastened his hand on the curve of her hip as he herded her toward the love seat.

Rachel gave him a look. 'That's an old trick, Hennessy.'

'I'm an old guy,' he quipped, and then winced. 'I shouldn't have mentioned that. You may not have noticed.'

'I'm not concerned. You seem able-bodied to me.'

'You don't know the half of it,' he muttered, gritting his teeth at the surge of anticipation that stirred in his loins.

'But I guess I'll find out, won't I?' Rachel said softly, lowering her gaze in genuine shyness as they settled on the love seat.

Bryan was so stunned, he felt as if he'd taken a punch to the gut. He hooked a finger beneath her chin and tilted her head up. The sight of the firelight glowing on her face nearly made him forget what it was he'd meant to ask. Holy Mike, she was lovely, and, unless he'd completely lost his ability to read women, she wanted him. After all the fighting she'd done against the attraction that pulled between them, she was admitting she wanted him. Wasn't she?

'Rachel,' he began, his voice low and hoarse, 'just what are you saying?'

She made a little face. 'I was hoping I wasn't going to have to say it. You're a perceptive man – can't you figure it out?'

'Yes, I guess what I need to know is why.'

'Does it matter?'

'Yes.'

Rachel looked toward the fire, her expression pensive. She couldn't bring herself to tell him she was in love with him. Not when she knew what they could have was only temporary. Not when she wasn't certain of his feelings for her. He had mentioned love in passing that morning, but that didn't mean anything. In her meager experience, love was a word some men tossed around too casually. And Bryan was by nature so openly giving of himself, she might have been reading too much into his attitude toward her. She suspected he had strong feelings for her. She knew he wanted her. But love . . .

Besides, it was so soon. They had known each other such a short time, he was liable to think she'd lost her mind if she told him she was falling in love with him.

But none of that seemed to matter. What was left of her mind had made itself up as she'd stood in the shadows of the maze, watching Bryan comfort her mother. It had all struck her with a force so powerful, she'd nearly fallen to her knees. She loved him. There was no future in it, but that didn't seem important now. As she'd stood there, watching her mother cry, she had realized just how suddenly tomorrow could slip away.

Over the past five years she had told herself that one day she would return and make things right between herself and Addie. One day. Tomorrow. Now tomorrow had come and it was too late, and all those days that could have been were nothing more than wishes that would never come true. She didn't need any more regrets haunting her life. She would take what Bryan could give her now, love him while she could, and deal with the consequences later.

She turned back to him with pleading in her eyes. 'Bryan, please don't—'

'Shh.' He pressed a finger to her lips as he leaned close. A soft, secretive smile curved his mouth, and his blue eyes shone like lapis lazuli. 'It's all right,' he whispered. 'It's all right.'

He lowered his mouth then, and kissed her slowly, sweetly, deeply. It was a kiss not of possession, but of sharing. It was a kiss that stirred the hunger in them both and sparked the desires banked inside them to flare into full flame. Questions and motives slipped away, were burned away by needs. He needed to love her. She needed to feel his strong arms around her.

Bryan slipped his coat from Rachel's shoulders and spread it out on the rug in front of the fire. Kneeling there, he reached a hand up to her in invitation. She smiled as she settled her hand in his and joined him on the floor.

'This is romantic,' she whispered, cuddling against him knee to knee, thigh to thigh, happy just to be close to him.

He brushed her long hair back, baring one shoulder. 'Romantic, hell,' he murmured, lowering his mouth to nibble kisses along the creamy line of flesh. The ache in his groin made him pause to grit his teeth, and he shook his head in amazement. He was as eager as an untried kid. He chuckled and nipped at her chin. 'I'm just afraid you'd change your mind on the way upstairs.'

Rachel laughed softly, marveling at this man's ability to lighten her mood. Even now, when she was trembling with nervous anticipation, Bryan was able to tease a giggle out of her. It was one of the things she loved most about him.

She raised her hands and tugged loose the bow tie that perched crookedly on the collar of his shirt. Her fingers moved down the neatly pleated shirtfront, revealing a V of hard flesh where the snowy white fabric parted and fell away from the contours of his chest. He held still as she peeled the garment back from his broad shoulders and let it fall to the floor behind him.

She paused a moment to simply look at him, to drink in the sight of his solid chest and the ridged muscles of his belly. Firelight caught in the curls scattered across his chest, turning them gold. Her breath caught as her gaze rested on the small brown mole above his left nipple. Somehow she had known it would be there, but she had no time to wonder how, because Bryan was reaching for her.

His thumbs hooked under the loose straps of her gown and drew them down over her shoulders. He traced his fingertips along the line of the bodice, gently pulling it down, slowly uncovering her. Her small, full breasts plumped themselves into his hands as the dress slipped away, her nipples tightening instantly as his thumbs brushed across them. The gown pooled at her knees in a wine-colored drift studded with sparkling black stars.

'So lovely,' he whispered, gazing at her in open admiration. 'So soft.'

He drew his hands downward, following the indentation of her slender waist and the outward slope of her hips, drawing her lace panties down as his exploration moved on to her thighs. Rachel struggled for air as his fingers traced delicate patterns on the satin-soft skin on the inside of her legs. She moaned and bit her lip as he delved into the tender warmth between them, his fingers parting the feminine petals and stroking the aching bud hidden there.

Heat flared through her hotter than the flames that lit their makeshift bed. She leaned into him, gasping at the feel of his flesh against hers, her feminine softness against the hard contours of his masculine body. It was wonderful. It was like coming back to a place she belonged. She rubbed herself against him in a sinuous caress, her hands sliding up his arms to knead the tight muscles in his shoulders and neck. She tangled her fingers in his hair, then brought her hands forward, pulling his glasses off and setting them aside on the low butler's table.

'You don't need these to see, do you?'

'That's okay,' he murmured, bending his head to kiss her ear. 'I'm good with my hands.'

Rachel's giggle turned to a sensuous purr as his big hands slid down her back to cup her buttocks, his fingers kneading her flesh in a way that made her breath flutter in her throat. 'So I noticed.'

He pulled her hard against him then, letting her feel the strength of his arousal as he took her mouth once more. This kiss was hotter and wilder than the last, hinting at the passion he was struggling to keep in check. His tongue stroked over hers, teasing, tasting, claiming possession.

Rachel pulled her mouth from his and dragged her lips down the strong column of his neck to his chest. Her tongue darted out to tease one flat brown nipple. His flesh beaded into a tight knot; Rachel impulsively took it into her mouth and sucked on it gently, excitement shooting through her when Bryan groaned in appreciation.

She had never felt so uninhibited with a man. She had expected to feel shy with Bryan; instead, she felt strong and right and so very turned on. She wanted him with an intensity she had never known. She wanted to please him in ways she had never dreamed of. The desire swept through her, overwhelming her normally practical, sensible self, and she let go of that drab cloak of responsibility like a butterfly shedding its cocoon.

Her kisses followed the faint line of downy hair that bisected Bryan's flat abdomen as her hands undid the front of his trousers. Her tongue dipped into his navel. She lowered his trousers and briefs in one motion and another hot flame of desire coursed through her as she revealed his manhood.

He was eager for her. She brushed her thumb across the velvet flesh, drawing another groan from him.

Bryan's control broke with a snap that was almost audible. In the next instant, Rachel found herself on her back, staring up at him as he peeled away the last of her clothes. He stood and shucked his pants. Notes flew from the pockets like confetti as he flung the trousers aside.

He settled himself beside her then, his gaze flowing over her with a heat that seemed scorching in its intensity, and his hand followed the path his gaze had burned along her skin. He caressed her breasts with exquisite care, teasing them to a sensitivity that was nearly unbearable. Only when she began to beg him did he lower his head and take one taut peak into his mouth. At the same instant he swept a hand down over her quivering belly to the apex of her thighs and eased a finger inside her.

Rachel's hips leapt off the floor, arching into his touch in rhythm to the tug of his mouth on her breast. She moaned, but didn't recognize the sound as her own. The sensations building inside her were incredible and overwhelming as they intensified. The coil of desire tightened in her belly with each hard pull of his mouth on her nipple, with each deep stroke of his finger. When his thumb moved to rub against her most sensitive flesh, she was certain she would explode, but still the feelings built. She tangled her fingers in his hair and tugged, frantic in a way she had never experienced.

'Bryan, please,' she said with a gasp. 'I want more. I want all of you. Please.'

He needed no more invitation than that. His own body, so long denied, was screaming for release. He knelt between her parted thighs, struggling to draw breath as he looked down at her. She was everything a man wanted in the woman he loved – open to him, eager for him, her hips arched up toward him in invitation. Grinding his teeth, he fought for some measure of control, reached for her hand, and closed it around his throbbing shaft.

'Guide me, Rachel,' he whispered.

He kissed her as she led him into her body, his tongue delving into the dark warmth of her mouth as his maleness slid into the tight warmth of her womanhood. He groaned as she took him into her measure by measure, her breath catching at each small thrust until he was fully embedded inside her.

Again Rachel felt that sense of coming home, which seemed odd considering she was on the verge of shattering into a million shards. She thought she should have been terrified, teetering on the brink of something she knew instinctively would be overwhelming, but she wasn't. With Bryan she felt safe. He would be there to catch her. He would be there to gather the pieces together again. He might not be there over the long haul, but he was there now. Oh, was he there now!

'Oh, Bryan,' she moaned in rapture, rolling her hips into his. 'You're so . . .'

'I know,' he managed to say through his teeth, gasping as her body tightened around him. 'Am I too . . . ?'

'No. It's wonderful.' Oh, so wonderful. But it was nothing compared to what she felt when he began to move.

He eased nearly out of her, then thrust deep and hard. His chest heaved like a bellows as he levered himself above her on his arms and repeated the process. Sweat beaded on his forehead and chest as he struggled with the effort to hold back. It had been so long, and he wanted her so badly. He could feel his climax rushing toward him like a freight train. He eased out of her again and reached between them as he began what he knew would be his final thrust, teasing her already sensitive flesh as he buried himself inside her.

Rachel bit her lip, fighting back the cry of completion as her hips strained upward against his and he took her over the brink. The explosion that rocked her went on and on. Her consciousness dimmed as she clutched at Bryan's back. He had collapsed against her, spent, and she hung on to him as the sensation of floating filled her with a sweet golden bliss.

This was making love. This was magic.

Magic, she mused, a tender smile curving her lips. Maybe there was such a thing after all.

Bryan rolled onto his back, holding Rachel to him so that she ended up sprawled on his chest. Their bodies were still joined, and he savored every aftershock of the shattering climax she had experienced. He ran a hand over the pale silken curtain of her hair.

'I'd break into song, but I think I'm beyond words,' he murmured.

He pressed a kiss to her temple and hugged her tight, a fierce sense of rightness surging through him. Fear came close on its heels. He felt so certain about this love growing within him for Rachel, but did Rachel feel that way about him? Had she merely given in to the feelings overwhelming her? After the day she'd had with Addie and with the prospective buyers for the house, had she simply not possessed the strength to fight the attraction? Or had she needed a chance to escape it all for a few glorious moments? Perhaps the thing that frightened him most was that he wasn't so sure he cared what her motives had been. The love he felt for her was growing so that he was ready to accept her on whatever terms she wanted.

The seed of love was there in her heart. He knew that. Or was it just what he wanted to believe?

'Rachel,' he murmured, his heart pounding. 'If you're going to regret this, tell me now.'

Rachel lifted her head, brushing her hair back behind one ear. She stared down at him, her heart aching at the vulnerability she saw in his eyes. 'No,' she whispered. 'No regrets. I have too many of them already. I don't regret making love with you, Bryan.'

She regretted that it wouldn't last. She regretted that her future wouldn't include him and his crazy magic tricks and his contagious optimism. But she wouldn't regret anything that passed between them. She would take what time she had with Bryan and make the most of it, and she would cherish the memories afterward, but she wouldn't regret a minute of it.

Bryan looked up into her dark eyes and smiled sadly. It didn't take a mind reader to see what she was thinking. He barely had to make use of his special gift, the gift that had slowly been returning to him in the time since he'd met Rachel and become a part of her life. She still didn't believe in the magic they shared, but she would. Come hell or high water, she would. He would see to it.

'What?' she asked, startled by the sudden fierceness of his expression.

'I was just thinking,' he said, willing himself to relax. He pulled Rachel's head down to his chest and stroked her hair as he might stroke a cat, rhythmically, absently, soothingly as he dredged up the courage to tell her what was in his heart.

'The first time I went to bed with a woman after my wife died I went into the bathroom afterward and threw up for half an hour. She was a nice lady, a colleague of mine, pretty. She . . . expressed an interest, and I . . . needed to.' He forced the words out, still uncomfortable with the memory. 'It seemed harmless enough. We were taking care of each other's needs. But when it was over, I felt so empty and so disgusted with myself, it literally made me sick. I told her I had the flu, but she knew better. I decided then and there that there wasn't going to be a next time until I could honestly call it making love.'

'Are you telling me I shouldn't get too comfortable?' Rachel asked with forced lightness. She pulled away from him a bit, raising her head, bracing herself.

For once Bryan didn't grin or answer with a joke. He reached up and tucked a strand of hair behind her ear. 'I'm telling you I love you, Rachel. I'm telling you I'm feeling something I didn't expect to feel again for a long, long time.' He rolled her beneath him again and stared down at her with undisguised hunger in his eyes. 'I'm telling you I want to take you upstairs and make love to you until the sun comes up. What do you have to say about that?'

Say? She was supposed to say something? With her heart in her throat and her brain suddenly numb, she was supposed to think of something to say? She swallowed hard and raised her head as his mouth descended toward hers, and whispered just before their lips met. 'I'm praying for an eclipse.'

Flowers. What a lovely dream. There were flowers everywhere. Rachel sighed and burrowed deeper into the soft mattress of the old bed, a smile curving her mouth. There were flowers of every kind and color, delicate wild blossoms with the softest, sweetest scents clinging to their petals. She could feel them against her, cool and dew-damp. They rained down on her and fluttered over every exposed inch of her skin like a hundred silken kisses. And Bryan was the magician responsible for this wonderful illusion.

She couldn't see him in her dream, but Rachel knew he was the one responsible, just as she knew he was the one who had left a rose on her pillow every night since she'd come to Drake House.

Bryan. Her smile widened and she purred in almost feline appreciation as she stretched on the bed. As he'd promised, he had made love to her all night. While the rain had fallen outside the windows of her turret bedroom and the cold wind had howled, Bryan had warmed her with kisses and caresses. He had awakened in her a woman she had scarcely realized existed, a woman of uninhibited passion. He had taken her to heights she had only imagined and set her soul free from the past and the future.

The future. A cloud scudded across the surface of her dream. Now that she knew what real love was, it hurt worse to think of a future without it, but she pushed the thought aside. She had vowed to take no regrets with her when she left for San Francisco, so she concentrated instead on her dream and the flowers.

'Rachel.' His voice came to her through the soft fog of sleep. 'Rachel.'

Stretching, she raised her eyelids to half mast and rolled onto her back. The light in the room was dim, but one thing was clear – it was snowing. She could see Bryan through the flakes falling down all around her. He was standing beside the bed, wearing his jeans, his glasses, and a wickedly sexy smile. She wondered why he didn't look cold, bare-chested in the snow.

Snow? Her drowsy brain struggled to function. They were in Drake House. It couldn't possibly be snowing, not even in this strange place.

'Bryan?' she asked, coming more fully awake. She pushed herself up in bed, looking around, puzzlement creasing a little line between her eyebrows. 'What in the . . . ? Flowers!'

She laughed out loud in delight when she realized what he was doing. He was showering her with flowers! The petals covered the bed in multi-colored drifts – pink and blue and violet and yellow and white. They clung to her skin and hair and to the ivory lace bodice of her nightgown. The cloud of fragrance rising from them was intoxicating.

Bryan dropped the last of the blooms and joined her on the bed, scooping her into his arms and rolling through the fragrant cloud, laughing as petals stuck to the lenses of his glasses. He leaned down and kissed her with enthusiasm and rising passion.

99

'Since you keep accusing me of bringing you flowers, I decided I might as well go all out,' he murmured, nuzzling her neck. 'Mmmm . . . they smell almost as good as you do.'

Rachel scooped up a handful and rubbed them down his bare back. 'Where did you get them?'

He smiled as he rose up above her, but his gaze was hot as he lowered the thin straps of her peachy-pink negligee, baring her breasts. 'Magic,' he said, his voice turning low and velvety as desire flared anew in his eyes.

As Rachel had done, he scooped up wildflowers in his hands and caressed her with them, crushing them as he cupped her breasts. He lowered his head and took one nipple into his mouth, sucking at that tender bud of flesh and the pansy petal that clung to it. His hands swept down her hips, tugging her nightgown up out of his way.

He turned onto his side and admired the view as he showered a handful of flower petals down on the bare skin of her belly and thighs. Sliding down on the bed, he blew gently across her abdomen, sending the buds skittering. With a purposeful look on his handsome face, he parted her legs and settled himself between them, planting kisses on the petals that clung to her inner thighs.

Rachel raised herself up on her elbows, her hair tumbling around her as she watched him, wrapped in sensual fascination stronger than any narcotic. With gentle fingers Bryan parted her most tender flesh and caressed her intimately with the bud of a wild rose. She gasped at the feel of velvet brushing her, cool and damp against her heat. He caressed her again, then lowered his head and tasted her, kissing her softly at first, hesitantly, increasing the pressure slowly, opening his mouth over her and stroking her with his tongue until she was sobbing at the intensity of her pleasure.

He kneeled then, and lifted her into his arms, pulling her against him and kissing her deeply. His lips trailed to her ear, where he traced the danity shell with the tip of his tongue and whispered, 'And they taste almost as good as you do too.'

Rachel purred and arched against him. A languid smile lifted one corner of her mouth as she reached between them and undid Bryan's zipper. She tugged the denim down his lean hips, scooped up two handfuls of flowers, and encased his manhood in cool soft petals, wringing a gasp from him. She stroked him with them as she planted kisses across his chest. Then it was her turn to gasp as he lifted her against him. She dropped the flowers, her hands going up automatically to his broad shoulders as he pulled her hips to his and joined their bodies once more.

The light in the room was considerably brighter when Rachel awoke for the second time. Bryan's tousled head was on her breast, one of his long, hairy legs was thrown across both of her considerably smoother ones. He was humming the Notre Dame fight song in his sleep.

'Bryan,' she murmured softly. 'Wake up.'

He grumbled and growled, finally lifting his head and pushing his glasses up on his nose. 'What time is it?'

Rachel reached to the nightstand for his wrist-watch and peered at it, shaking her head. 'Three-ten, Bryan Hennessy time. Do you ever intend to set this thing correctly?'

'Oh, sure,' Bryan said, hauling himself up to lean back against the ornately carved headboard. 'I'm sure I wrote myself a note to do it.' He scratched his kneecap through the sheet, looking puzzled. 'I wonder what became of that note.'

'It's quarter to seven,' Rachel said, consulting her travel alarm.

Time to get up and face the day, she thought. Her gaze roamed over the tangle of sheets and flower petals, and she smiled. With a night like this last one to remember, the day wasn't going to be quite so hard to face.

She yawned, stretched, and scratched her arm. Snuggling against Bryan's hard shoulder, she said coyly, 'Thank you for the flowers. I loved them.'

Bryan turned his head and kissed her temple. 'And I love you.'

Rachel's heart jumped. She couldn't get used to hearing him say that. She was afraid to say it back for fear the spell would be broken somehow, afraid she would be putting too much pressure on him, expecting too much of him.

She sifted a handful of petals through her fingers and scratched absently at her left hip. 'Making love in flowers is the most romantic thing I can think of.'

'Flowers are romantic,' Bryan agreed absently. He shoved the sheet down and stared, frowning at his belly as he scratched it. 'Ants aren't.'

'Ants?' Rachel questioned, scratching her shoulder.

'Hmmm, yes,' he said. 'It seems we have a bed full of them. They must have ridden in on the flowers,' he ventured, but his explanation was lost on Rachel, who shrieked and leapt from the bed, shaking herself like a wet dog. He watched her grab up her robe, thrust her arms into the sleeves, and bolt for the door.

'Have a nice shower!' he called, laughing, then he found a scrap of paper and a pen on the nightstand and he wrote himself a note – Beware of Ants.

9

Rachel stood outside the door to her mother's bedroom, as nervous as she had been at fifteen when she had needed to ask permission to go on her first date. She was freshly showered, debugged, and looked as presentable, in her black dirndl skirt and lavender cotton blouse, as any voice teacher she had ever encountered. Her hair was secured in its knot at the back of her head and only a few tendrils had as yet escaped to frame her face.

It occurred to her that she shouldn't have had to go to such pains to see her own mother. A mother wasn't supposed to care about appearances. A mother was supposed to be accepting of her children whether they were in rags or designer wear. But it was that line of thinking that had caused the problems between her and Addie in the first place, so Rachel stopped that train of thought before it ran out of control.

It was a new day, a day for beginnings. She felt fresh and strong, rested despite the precious little sleep she'd had. Spending the night in Bryan's arms had revitalized her, recharged her. She was brimming with energy and ready to take on whatever the day had in store for her. As she had showered the flower petals and ants from her skin, she had come to the conclusion that she would redouble her efforts to solve the problem with Addie.

Rachel raised her hand to knock at the door, but it suddenly fell open as if someone on the other side had jerked it back. Addie, however, was standing across the room in a yellow flowered house-dress, scowling into her mirror as she struggled with the task of braiding her hair. She crossed one strand over, twisted it around again, pulled another across, then swore and let go the entire mess to start again.

It was clear to Rachel that her mother had either forgotten how to braid or the message from her brain to her hands was getting lost somewhere along the way; apraxia was the term the doctors used for it. In either case, it was sad, and it reminded Rachel yet again of how their roles were being reversed. She could easily remember Addie painstakingly plaiting her long hair on her first day of kindergarten, how she had sat very still on the wire vanity stool in her mother's bedroom, staring wide-eyed into the mirror as her mother's fingers had magically tamed her wild locks.

'Mother?' she asked softly, forcing herself to step into the room before her memories could steal her courage from her. 'Can I help you with that?'

Addie stared at her daughter, wondering just how much Rachel had seen. 'Don't you know how to knock?'

'It was open.'

Addie muttered, 'Wimsey. Meddling old coot.'

Rachel ignored the odd remark. Taking a brush from the cluttered dresser, she went to stand behind her mother and began working on the hair that had once been as golden as her own, but had now paled to silver.

'I can do my own hair,' Addie said, staring at their reflections in the mirror.

'I know you can. I just want to help. Like you used to help me.'

Their gazes met in the glass, and Addie's heart lurched. She had done everything for Rachel. She had been both mother and father. She had raised her daughter without help from anyone. She had held down two jobs at a time and had never run out of energy or drive. Now that daughter was standing behind her, braiding her hair because she suddenly wasn't able to manage so simple a task herself.

'I believe I'll wear it down today,' she said, moving away from the dresser. In the mirror she could see Rachel standing with her hands still raised, the hairbrush in one, reaching out toward her. Her daughter's eyes were filled with hurt. Rachel let her arms fall to her sides as Addie moved another step out of reach.

She found a black sweater lying at the foot of the bed and put it on inside out. 'I'm going down to breakfast. Hennessy should have the toast done by now.'

Rachel stood by the dresser, twisting the hair-brush around in her hands. Every ounce of that newfound strength had drained out of her. 'Why won't you let me help you?' she asked softly, hurting in a way that is peculiar to mother-daughter relationships – a deep, sharp hurt, like a needle piercing her heart.

'I don't need any help,' Addie replied, squaring her bony shoulders with stubborn pride. 'Not from you or Wimsey or anyone. I have managed quite well on my own for some time now, as you well know.'

With that she clomped out of the room, her boots thumping on the wood floor. Rachel closed her eyes and counted to ten, wrestling her temper and her tears under control.

'No luck?'

Startled, she looked up to find Bryan standing not two feet away. She shook her head, at a loss for words. She wasn't sure she would have trusted herself to say them anyway. Her emotions were running dangerously close to the surface, muddied and churning like floodwaters. She had the strange feeling that if she let them out, they would swell up and drown her.

'You'll work it out,' Bryan said gently, taking the hairbrush from her fingers and setting it aside. He gathered her into his arms and hugged her close, pressing soft kisses to her hair. 'It'll all work out. You'll see.'

Rachel let her hands sneak inside the old cardigan he wore unbuttoned. Her arms slid around his lean waist. She nuzzled her cheek against his Chicago Cubs T-shirt, taking comfort in the solid muscle beneath the soft gray fabric. She noticed he didn't say 'give it time.' Time was not on their side. A little bit of Addie slipped away with every grain of sand in the hourglass. But he offered her his strength and his comfort, and she loved him for that.

'Here now, enough of this,' Bryan said, standing her back from him. There was a devilish twinkle in his eye. Rachel realized with a start that he was wearing a bedraggled black top hat. 'I know you can't get enough of me, but I won't spoil you – unless you beg me to,' he added with a wicked grin.

'Conceited man,' she said, fighting back a chuckle. 'I should beg you to have your head examined. Why are you wearing that ridiculous hat?'

'Ridiculous?' he questioned, highly offended. 'I'll have you know this hat was given to me by Anton Figg-Newton, master magician of England.'

He rolled the hat down his arm Fred Astaire-style and presented it to her upside down.

'Just reach in there and see what you find, girlie.'

Cautiously, Rachel leaned over and peered into the hat, narrowing her eyes in suspicion. 'There's nothing in there.'

Bryan made a great show of looking into the hat himself, turning it over, and shaking it.

'I think you got taken on that one, Merlin,' Rachel quipped.

A gleam came into Bryan's eye. 'Oh, ye of little or no faith. I merely forgot to say the magic word.'

'The magic word,' Rachel parroted flatly. She crossed her arms over her chest and tapped her foot in mock impatience.

'Marshmallows!' he intoned dramatically, and tapped the brim of the hat three times with the fingers of his left hand. This time he reached inside, and when he withdrew his hand, he was holding a brooch of intricately worked silver filigree set with a translucent stone of deep purple.

Rachel's mouth dropped open as he handed it to her. It was an exquisite thing that looked to be very old and very valuable. The stone gleamed as it caught the morning light that streamed in through the window.

'Bryan, it's beautiful,' she whispered reverently. 'Where did you find it?'

'In my hat. Jeez, Rachel, I think your memory is worse than mine.'

'Really,' she insisted, fingering the brooch lovingly. 'I've never seen anything like it. Is it an heirloom or something?'

He cleared his throat and looked uncomfortable. 'I came across it in a country that frowns on exporting such things. You're probably better off not knowing.'

She gave him a suspicious look, wondering, not for the first time, just who Bryan Hennessy really was.

'Legend has it that when a man gives this brooch to the lady of his heart, she'll love him into eternity,' he said, taking the gift from her and pinning it carefully to the throat of her prim blouse. The stone picked up and intensified the color of her eyes, making Bryan's breath catch. A crooked, self-deprecating smile tugged up one corner of his mouth. 'It's a custom also known as hedging your bets.'

'Thank you,' Rachel whispered, smiling at him. She rose up on her toes and kissed his cheek. Practically in the blink of an eye he had lifted her mood out of the doldrums. He was amazing and wonderful, and if she could tell him nothing else, she could at least tell him that. 'What an extraordinarily sweet, bizarre man you are.'

Remarkably, he blushed, and Rachel's heart swelled a little more with love for him. Grinning, she plunked his magic hat upon his head, grabbed his hand, and pulled him toward the door.

'Come on, Hennessy. Let's go get some breakfast. I'm starved.'

'What's your hurry?' Bryan asked, patting her bottom with a loving hand. 'Ants in your pants?'

'Very funny.'

They sauntered down the grand staircase together, hand in hand, smiling at each other the way only lovers do, arguing amicably over how they would spend the day. Rachel insisted there was no time for anything other than marking prices on the antiques that would be offered at the tag sale in two days. Bryan insisted there was more than enough time for a stroll along the beach. But as they neared the kitchen, he broke off in mid-rebuttal and held a finger to his lips, suddenly alert to something going on in the next room. Together they inched toward the door, listening.

'You're a meddling, bone-headed Democrat, Wimsey,' Addie said. 'Just keep that long nose of yours out of my affairs. I don't need you. I don't need anybody.'

There was silence then. Bryan held his breath as he tried to tune in, hoping for anything – a sigh, a vibration in the air, anything.

'Keep your opinions to yourself, you blithering British idiot,' Addie snapped.

The rattling of pots and pans blocked out whatever response she might have gotten, and Bryan frowned in frustration. Rachel rolled her eyes in impatience.

'She's just talking to herself,' she insisted in a harsh whisper.

Bryan ground his teeth. If only he had enough equipment to monitor every room in the blasted house. He had chosen to concentrate on the study and the foyer. Of course, Rachel wouldn't have believed Wimsey was in the kitchen if the ghost had walked up to her and kissed her on the nose.

'This is ridiculous,' Rachel muttered. 'Every sensible person knows there's no such thing as ghosts.'

As soon as the last word left her mouth, the kitchen door swung inward so quickly neither of them had a chance to brace themselves, and they both went sprawling across the cracked linoleum. On the far side of the room Addie stood staring at them, a gray cloud billowing around her.

Bryan's eyes widened at the sight. 'An apparition,' he whispered.

'Apparition nothing,' Rachel said, clambering to her feet. 'The kitchen's on fire!'

Smoke rolled out of the old cookstove, an appliance that hadn't seen action since Thomas Edison was in short pants. Rachel grabbed her mother's hand and jerked her away from the thing while Bryan, who had scrambled to his feet, grabbed the fire extinguisher and blasted the blaze with white foam.

'Hennessy! You're ruining my eggs!'

'Mother,' Rachel said between her teeth, 'you were ruining the house. That stove doesn't work.'

'Of course I know that,' Addie grumbled, but there was uncertainty in her eyes as she looked around the room as if seeing it for the first time.

'You should have waited for us to come down,' Rachel said, her temper rising like steam in a pressure cooker. Why couldn't Addie accept her help? Was she going to cling to that damned stubborn pride of hers until she burned the house down around them?

Addie bristled like a cat. 'I don't take orders from you, missy!'

She hauled back to punch Rachel on the arm, but Bryan caught her fist in his hand and pulled her into his arms.

'Come on, beautiful. Let's go dance in the fresh air while Cinderella cleans up the kitchen. Maybe we'll run into Wimsey.'

'Pompous, presumptuous pinhead,' Addie said with a snarl, though it wasn't clear whether she was referring to her invisible friend or to Bryan. She dug the heels of her rubber boots into the floor and gave him an amazed look. 'Why on earth are you wearing that ridiculous hat?'

'There's a rabbit in it,' Bryan said, coaxing her toward the door as Rachel began flinging pots off the stove in a rage. 'I thought you might want hasenpfeffer for breakfast.'

'You're an idiot, Hennessy,' Addie declared, but followed him out of the room nevertheless.

'I'll second that,' Rachel grumbled, poking at the debris inside the cookstove with a tongs. 'Ghosts. What intelligent man with degrees from two major universities believes in ghosts? What intelligent woman falls in love with a man who believes in ghosts? Ghosts. The man must have been hit over the head with something when he was young.'

She bent over to look inside the oven, and an enamel pot tipped off the cooking surface and bounced off her skull. She stared at the pot as it rolled across the floor, sure she had knocked it over during her initial burst of fury. Dismissing it, she turned her attention to the mess her mother had made.

'Oh, no . . .' she said on a long groan.

With her tongs she fished out a stack of half-burned mail. She flipped through the ruined envelopes, her heart sinking. Bills. Bills that had never been opened. Bills that had certainly never been paid. She bent over again and tugged out another long envelope, this one only slightly charred, and her heart dropped from low to the pit of her stomach, where it lay like a rock.

'Ooooh, noooo . . .'

'What is it?' Bryan asked, returning to the kitchen without his dancing partner.

In a daze, Rachel handed him the envelope. 'You know how you keep saying something will turn up? Something just did.'

Bryan took the letter out, pushed his glasses up on his nose, and began to read to himself. He paled a bit beneath his tan and handed the piece of stationery back to Rachel, muttering, 'Oh, no . . .'

Feeling as if all her bones were dissolving, Rachel sank down on a chair at the kitchen table and stared across the room in a trance. It wasn't the first time she had seen a letter like this one. It was, however, the first time she had felt dizzy because of it.

The IRS was going to audit Lindquist Antiques.

Visions of Leavenworth danced in her head.

She looked up at Bryan and forced the corners of her mouth into a parody of a smile. 'Got anything in your magic hat for this one, Mr. Hennessy?'

'I am not moving from this house.' Addie pressed her lips into a thin line and crossed her arms over her meager bosom. She leaned back into the worn red velvet of an enormous thronelike Victorian chair, settling in for the battle.

Rachel and Bryan had spent the day working their way through the huge maze of rooms that made up Drake House, tagging the antiques that would be offered at the sale. It had been a long day of building tension. Addie had trailed after them, pulling the tags off the furniture and complaining incessantly about the way Rachel was treating her. Twice she had called the police to tell them she was being robbed. Twice Rachel had had to call them back and tell them it was another false alarm. Meals had been stilted affairs seasoned with sharp remarks. Addie's mood had darkened with every hour, and Rachel's control on her temper had worn down to the last frayed threads.

Bryan watched both women with a terrible sense of foreboding. He could feel Rachel's tension, the hurt and anger that had been simmering just under her lovely surface for days. Her jaw was set at a mutinous angle and trembled with the emotion she was struggling to keep in check. And Addie, who had been on a rampage all day, showed no signs of backing down.

He pulled his glasses off and rubbed at his eyes. He was exhausted from intercepting Rachel's feelings all day and from running interference between the two Lindquist women, but it was clear there would be no rest for the weary this evening.

'Addie, you look like a queen in that chair,' he said, flashing one of his inane smiles. 'Did I ever tell you about the time I met the queen of Sweden?'

'Could she sing?' Addie asked. 'Rachel used to sing, you know. She had a voice like an angel, but she wasted it, and now we're destitute.'

'Addie, that's not fair—'

'No, she's right, Bryan,' Rachel said with a frightening smile. She threw her hands up in the air in a gesture of surrender. 'I screwed up the whole flipping world because I didn't become an opera singer. I'm sure they would have found a cure for cancer by now if only I had gone on to perform *Aida*. And anyone with a brain in her head knows, there would have been an end to world hunger long ago if I had toured with the Metropolitan Opera. Certainly, Mother and I would be wealthy beyond our wildest imagining, living in a state of bliss if only I had played Carmen.'

'Rachel, don't be flip,' Addie snapped. 'Carmen was never a role for you.'

'I'm sorry, Mother,' she said without a hint of remorse. 'How could I have been so foolish?'

'You take after your aunt Marilyn. She never had any sense of responsibility either.'

Rachel staggered back as if she'd been struck a savage blow. No sense of responsibility? She had always been responsible! She had given up much of her childhood and adolescence to her responsibilities for her singing talent. She had given up her dreams to take on the responsibility of managing Terence's career. Now she was giving up all hope of a happy future, taking on responsibility for the very person who sat in judgment of her.

'Rachel,' Bryan said softly, reaching out for her.

She could see him out of the corner of her eye, could easily read the concern in his expression. She could have gone to him for comfort, but she didn't. The pain she was feeling was too personal. It went too deep for comfort, too deep for tears. She stepped away from Bryan and nearer her mother, isolating the two of them in the aura of her pain. She stared into Addie's pale eyes and spoke softly in a voice that trembled with the strength of the emotions underlying it.

'I'm sorry, Mother. How many times do I have to say it? I'm sorry for the disappointment I caused you. I'm sorry I wanted something more in my life than training and practice and performance. And most of all, I'm sorry I wanted you to love me regardless of what I did, because obviously you weren't capable of it.'

It was Addie's turn to look stricken. Her thin, lined face turned ashen, and she pressed a hand to her chest, as if to see if her heart was still beating.

'How dare you?' she said, her voice as soft as Rachel's had been, as full of pain. 'How dare you say I didn't love you! I did everything for you.'

'You turned me away. You exiled me. That's an awfully funny way of showing love.'

Addie said nothing. She struggled to sort through her feelings. They seemed to assail her from all sides and from within – anger, guilt, resentment, regret, disappointment. The present faded, and she suddenly found herself in the past, wishing back the words that had forced Rachel to leave, wishing Rachel hadn't pushed her into saying them. They were in the little house in Berkeley, and Rachel was backing away from her, moving toward the door with a terrible look of hurt in her wide eyes. It was too late. Her daughter was leaving her. She had pushed too hard, expected too much, laid down one law too many. Her sweet Rachel was leaving her.

'This is all your fault,' Addie said bitterly, turning on Bryan. 'You good-for-nothing, god-awful folk singer!'

She pulled a man's shoe out of the patch pocket of her housedress and flung it at him. Bryan caught it and stared at it, frowning, not quite sure what to say. A cherry tomato sailed through the air and caught him unaware, bouncing off his forehead.

'Mother, stop it!' Rachel ordered. 'That's not Terence, it's Bryan.'

'Bryan—' The word caught on the end of Addie's tongue, and she bit it back, but her confusion was already apparent and she knew it. Panic left her only one option – escape.

She pushed herself up out of her throne chair and backed toward the hall. She pulled half of a cheese sandwich from her sweater pocket and held it out in front of her as if it were a gun.

'Stay back or I'll shoot!' she demanded. 'I'm going to call the police!'

'Mother!' Rachel started after her, but Bryan caught her by the arm and pulled her back.

'Let her go, honey. I unplugged the phones after the last call.'

Rachel shook her head and sighed, what little strength she had left draining out of her. This time when Bryan tried to gather her close, she let him. Bryan squeezed his eyes shut and pressed a kiss to her temple. He could think of nothing to say that would ease her pain. Words from him were not going to mend her past with Addie. All he could give her was his support and his love, and he gave them both without reserve, wrapping her in his strength and pressing her head to his heart.

They stood there for a moment in silence, letting the tension settle into the dust around them. Finally, Rachel stood back a little and scrubbed at the few tears that had managed to escape the barrier of her lashes to slide down her cheeks. She took a deep, cleansing breath, gathering herself together, dredging up a little more determination from the deep well inside her.

'I shouldn't have lost my temper,' she said evenly. 'I know it doesn't do any good. It only upsets Mother.'

'You can't always keep it all in.' Bryan reached out a hand to toy with the whisper-soft tendrils of hair that framed Rachel's face. 'Look on the bright side: In ten minutes Addie is liable to have forgotten you had this conversation.'

Rachel managed a wry smile. 'That's true. Too bad she can't forget the phone number for the police department.'

Bryan's heart welled with pride and love. She was some kind of lady, his little Rachel. Life wasn't exactly being kind to her, but she took it on the chin and came back smiling. That she managed to keep a sense of humor through all of this was a real indication of the depth of character she possessed.

He stared down at her in the gloom of the poorly lit room. All around them stood dark, dusty, neglected furniture. The striped paper on the walls was stained and buckling, the draperies, heavy with mildew and age, drooped from their hooks. It was a grim setting, and yet Rachel shone like a gem, so bright, so pretty, her amethyst eyes smiling up at him, echoing the glow of the old brooch he had given her.

'I love you,' he murmured, leaning down to kiss her.

She melted against him, all warmth and willingness. She slid back into his arms, fitting there as if she were a part of him. Rachel gave herself over to the kiss, trying to communicate the words that were locked in her heart. She couldn't bring herself to say them. Somehow she thought that if she said them aloud, it would only hurt worse when the parting came.

'I want you,' Bryan whispered, trailing his lips down the ivory column of her throat as he bent her back over his arm.

'Oh, Bryan,' she said, all the longing she felt dragging the words out on a moan of need.

His hand slid up between their bodies to cup her breast, his gentle fingers kneading her swelling flesh, his thumb brushing across her nipple, teasing it to hardness. Desire surged through her like an electric current, converging in the most feminine parts of her body and intensifying there into pools of heat. She didn't try to stop the sensations from overwhelming her. There were too many things in her life now that needed rigid control and discipline and self-sacrifice. In these few stolen moments with Bryan she was going to be selfish. She was going to take his passion, as much as he wanted to give her. She was going to revel in the strength of this desire. It was so unlike anything she had ever known, and she knew nothing would ever compare to it.

They sank down onto an old fainting couch, coughing at the cloud of dust that enveloped them but not letting it interfere in the proceedings. Rachel purred her contentment as Bryan settled himself on top of her, his manhood prodding at her from behind the snug barrier of his jeans. She loved the weight of his trim, hard body bearing down on her, loved the masculine sounds of frustration that rumbled in his throat as he tried to get closer to her. Wantonly, she arched up against him, her legs parting so he could press against her more intimately.

'Oh, Rachel,' Bryan groaned. 'Oh, Rachel.'

A scream rattled the chandeliers above them.

'Oh, hell.' He uttered the words through gritted teeth, feeling as if he might start sobbing at the agony of thwarted passion. 'Oh, hell.'

He levered himself up off Rachel and staggered to his feet, gritting his teeth at the throbbing in his groin. 'If there isn't a ghost upstairs, there will be when I'm finished.'

'If you get violent, can I help?' Rachel asked dryly as she forced herself off the couch.

'Absolutely.'

The second scream kicked them into action. They ran down the hall and bolted up the grand staircase, turning in at Addie's room only to find it empty. They found Addie at the back of the house, standing in the hall in her nightgown, her face as white as paste.

'Mother, what happened?' Rachel asked, going to her mother's side but hesitating to put an arm around her.

'It was that terrible ghoul again!' Addie said, panting. Her hair was in a wild tangle around her head. She looked as if she had stuck her finger in a light socket. 'It was standing down there at the end of the hall with this weird white mist all around.'

All three peered down the corridor, but nothing was there.

'What happened to it?' Bryan asked.

'Poof!' Addie said, flapping her arms at her sides. 'He just disappeared.'

Rachel ground her teeth as she followed Bryan to the end of the dark hall. 'People don't just disappear.'

'Ghosts do.'

'There're no such things as ghosts.'

' "Asserting a statement an infinity of times does not in itself make it true," ' Bryan quoted. 'Abel J. Jones.'

Rachel scowled at him. ' "No matter how thin you slice it, it's still baloney." Alfred Smith.'

Bryan met her look with a determined one of his own. ' "There is nothing so powerful as the truth – and often nothing so strange." Daniel Webster.'

He stopped at the spot Addie had pointed to, letting his gaze roam over the area, letting his sixth sense listen for any kind of sign. It was one of his ordinary senses, however, that picked up a clue. He held himself very still and sniffed the air like a bird dog.

'Ammonia,' he mumbled, his eyes taking on a faraway look.

'Ammonia?' Rachel questioned, making a face as the scent burned her nostrils. 'What does ammonia have to do with anything?'

'Magic,' Bryan said flatly, almost angrily.

'A ghost that does housecleaning,' Rachel mused, leaning back against the paneled wall and crossing her arms over her chest. 'I love it. Do you think we could get him to do windows? There are about ninety of them in this dump that all need a good scrubbing!'

She squealed the last of the word as the wall shifted behind her. Startled, she bounded into the middle of the hall, and then did her best to not look embarrassed, straightening her lavender blouse and smoothing her hands over her skirt as if yelping and leaping were not the least bit out of the ordinary.

Bryan was too absorbed in his inspection to notice the instinctive flame of fear that had burst to life in Rachel's eyes. Following his nose, he moved toward the wall, where he stopped and stood staring down at a smudge of dirt on the wooden floor. His heart sank a little, but he stemmed the rush of disappointment. Ghost or no ghost, there was a mystery to be solved, and solving mysteries was his forte.

With a look of grim determination on his face, he opened the door in the wall, flipped on the light, and followed the scent of ammonia down the dusty servants' stairs. The step with dry rot was cracked through, and he skipped it altogether, frowning harder. He slipped out of the cabinet in the pantry, careful not to make a sound.

The kitchen was dark, illuminated only by the reflection of moonlight on the fog that hung outside the windows, but his eyes adjusted quickly. He eased along the wall, keeping to the deepest shadows, his gaze taking inventory of every object as he moved toward the back door. Nothing moved. The only sound was the wind outside and the metallic screech and clang of the vent for the stovepipe of the old appliance Addie had set ablaze earlier in the day.

He let himself out the back door and stood on the porch with his hands on his hips. He looked out across the grounds of Drake House, solemn and silent. There was nothing to see but overgrown bushes shrouded in fog. There was nothing to hear except the roar of the wind and the sea. But there was something out there. He could feel it. He could sense it – a menace, a threat. There was something out there, and he was determined to find out who or what it was.

After locking up and thoroughly checking the downstairs for any sign of an intruder, Bryan climbed back up the servant's staircase, going slowly in hopes of picking up some sense of who their uninvited guest had been. Rachel met him at the door in the second-floor hall.

'I got Mother to go back to bed,' she said quietly, wrapping a sweater around her shoulders. 'Did you find anything?'

Bryan shook his head. 'No, but I have an idea or two.'

'Casper the Cleanly Ghost?' she suggested with an irrepressible smile.

'Very funny,' he drawled, sliding an arm around her and steering her down the hall toward her bedroom.

'Ammonia and hydrochloric acid. It's an old magic trick,' he explained. 'You soak a wad of cotton in ammonia and one in hydrochloric acid. Forcing air through the cotton produces volumes of white smoke. Very eerie-looking stuff. My dad taught me how to do it when I was ten. You can't imagine the trouble I got into in Sister Agnes's religion class when Mark Tucker and I engineered a surprise reenactment of the Ascension, using that trick.'

Rachel had a fleeting impression of the adorable little boy he must have been with his serious expression and his glasses sliding down his nose, his bag of magic tricks tucked under one arm. A little more of her heart gave itself over to him.

'So,' she said, forcing herself to stay on the topic, 'you're admitting what Mother saw wasn't a manifestation from the spirit world after all?'

'Reluctantly. I'm not saying Wimsey isn't legitimate, but I think our other visitor is a ghost of a different color.'

They stopped at the open door of Rachel's room. Bryan leaned back against one side of the jamb and Rachel leaned back against the other. He gave her a serious look. 'I think someone is trying to frighten Addie into leaving Drake House.'

An automatic shiver ran through Rachel at the thought, but she dismissed it. 'Why would anyone do that? It seems to be common knowledge that we're going to sell the place. Why would anyone bother?'

'Why, indeed,' Bryan murmured, combing a hand back through his hair. He had his theories, but they were only beginning to form. For the moment he had nothing concrete to share with Rachel, and heaven knew she had enough on her mind already.

A sexy smile curving his mouth, he pushed himself away from his side of the door frame. Bracing his hands above Rachel's head, he leaned close and brushed his lips across hers. 'I think we ought to sleep on that.'

'Really?' she whispered, heat sweeping through her. She ran her hands under his open sweater and up his sides, following the outward slope from his lean waist to his solid chest. 'I was going to suggest we sleep on the bed.'

'Were you?' He chuckled, a low, masculine sound that rumbled deep in his throat as he pinned Rachel to the door frame with his hips.

'Mmmm . . .' she sighed, forgetting all about ghosts and goblins as her body melted into his. 'Clean sheets, no ants.'

'Sounds inviting,' he said, nibbling at her ear-lobe. 'Can I make one more suggestion?'

'What?'

'Let's skip the sleep. I can think of better things to do in a bed.'

10

'Thieves! Thieves! We're being overrun by thieves!'

Addie stamped her foot on the hall floor, causing several more people to turn their heads and stare at her. She glared back at them. The gall. For all these people to simply walk into her home and steal her things! She couldn't imagine what the world was coming to. No good, that was for certain.

One of the strangers, a pudgy, middle-aged woman in a brown pants suit and a bad blond wig, emerged from the parlor, cradling a large white wire bird cage in her arms. Addie gasped in outrage, her narrow gaze boring into the woman. She recognized the culprit as being the receptionist for the intolerable Nazi doctor, Moore.

'I should have known you'd be a thief!' Addie snapped, launching herself at the woman.

She grabbed at the bird cage, her fingers threading through the wire. The startled receptionist hung on to the other side of the cage and the two women jerked each other around the hall like children fighting over a new toy.

'Mother! For heaven's sake!' Rachel exclaimed, pushing her way through the crowd of bargain hunters. She grabbed Addie by the shoulders, halting the tussle.

'She's stealing my bird cage!' Addie accused the receptionist as she gave her the evil eye.

'She's not stealing it, Mother,' Rachel explained patiently, even though her patience had pretty much worn out an hour into the tag sale. She pried her mother's fingers away from the now-bent wire cage. 'Mrs. Anderson is *buying* this bird cage. We're having a tag sale, Mother. We can't take all this furniture with us to San Francisco, so we're selling it.'

She turned to the receptionist, whose wig was askew, and mustered an apologetic smile. 'I'm sorry, Mrs. Anderson. Mother is a little . . . confused about all this.'

'It's all right, Rachel,' the woman said, composing herself like a plump pigeon whose feathers had been ruffled. 'I understand.'

'Oh, I get it,' Addie said, turning on her daughter. 'You're in on it. It's a conspiracy.'

'It's a tag sale, Mother,' Rachel said through her teeth as she bit back her temper and her feelings of guilt.

It *was* a conspiracy. There was no getting around that fact. She had conspired to usurp her mother's authority over her own property. The fact that she didn't have a choice, that what she was doing was perfectly legal, that Addie wasn't competent to handle these affairs, didn't make it any more palatable. Not even thoughts of their dwindling finances and the upcoming visit from the IRS could make her feel justified.

'I'm calling the police,' Addie said flatly.

Rachel's shoulders slumped, and she heaved a weary sigh as she watched her mother stomp away. She debated whether it would take more strength to stop her from calling or to deal with Deputy Skreawupp's ire after the fact. Suddenly Bryan bounded into the hall, blowing a party horn. His magic hat was perched on his head.

'Hennessy!' Addie said. 'What is the meaning of this?'

'It's a party, beautiful!' Bryan declared, flashing her his most brilliant smile. He removed his hat with a flourish and pulled another party horn out of it for Addie. 'Let's go dancing on the lawn.'

Addie scowled at him, uncertainty flashing in her eyes. She didn't like what was going on here. She didn't like that she seemed to have no control over it. And all the strange faces in her house frightened her. There were so many of them, she had trouble distinguishing one from the next. But Hennessy, she knew. Hennessy, she trusted.

'I love your hair that way, Addie,' he commented. 'It's very . . . carefree.'

She raised a hand to pat at the hairdo, blushing like a schoolgirl. She had hacked off her long tresses with a pinking shears because she hadn't been able to remember how to braid it. Now it fringed her face in a kind of frenetic pixie look. 'You're such a flirt, you big Irish rascal.'

Bryan tucked her arm through his and led her down the hall toward the front door, shooting a wink at Rachel as they went.

Rachel smiled her appreciation and mouthed a thank-you. Clutching her clipboard to her chest, she sighed up into the limp curls that had long ago escaped her sensible hairstyle. What would she have done without Bryan here these past few days? What would she do without him when she and Addie moved to the city?

'He's something, isn't he?'

She turned in surprise toward the voice that had suddenly sounded beside her. Alaina Montgomery-Harrison stood there, looking cool and immaculate in her Pierre Cardin ensemble of a black pleated skirt and cream-colored sweater. Tall, angular, elegant, she was just one of Bryan's many friends who had volunteered to help with the tag sale.

Rachel wondered how the woman managed to appear so unfrazzled. They had all been run ragged in the four hours the sale had been going.

She decided Alaina was just one of those few lucky women who got out of bed in the morning looking like an ad for ageless beauty.

'Bryan,' Alaina prompted with a wry smile.

'Yes.' Rachel shook her head. 'He's something.'

They were alone in the hall for the moment. Alaina fixed her with a sharp, intuitive stare that made Rachel feel as if she were suddenly under a very powerful microscope.

'May I ask what exactly he is to you?'

Rachel's eyes widened, revealing most of the information Alaina required.

'It's not that I have designs on him,' Alaina said, deliberately softening both her look and her attitude. Her translucent blue eyes glittered with warm affection. 'My husband is the only lunatic I need. It's just that Bryan is a very special friend. I don't want to see him get hurt.'

'I don't want to hurt him,' Rachel said carefully.

Alaina bit her tongue on the words *but you will if you have to*. A little worry line formed between her eyes, then her gaze came to rest on the brooch Rachel wore at the throat of her white blouse.

'Did he, by any chance, give you that?'

Rachel lifted her fingers to the heavy pin and brushed them across the smooth surface of the stone. 'Yes, he did. Why?'

A soft, knowing smile curved Alaina's mouth. 'No reason,' she said softly. Changing gears smoothly, she motioned toward the empty hall. 'There seems to be a lull in the storm. Can I buy you a cup of coffee?'

Rachel had the distinct impression she had just passed some kind of test. Relief poured over her, and she smiled at the dark-haired woman, glad, though she wasn't quite sure why. 'I'd like that.'

They walked outside, onto the porch, where Alaina's husband, Dylan, was overseeing the group of children running the refreshment stand. Dylan's son, Sam, who Rachel guessed to be about eleven, seemed to be in command of everything. He was a very serious boy with sandy hair and a mind-boggling vocabulary. His assistants included his younger sister, Cori, a dark-eyed, dark-haired charmer; and Faith Callan's daughter, Lindy, an adorable little six-year-old moppet with burnished gold curls. Lindy appeared to be in sole charge of the brownies – there was a telltale smudge of chocolate frosting on her cheek and a dot of it on her button nose. Dylan was lounging on a folding chair with his feet up on the porch railing and a chubby baby girl on his lap.

'Hardly working, as usual, I see,' Alaina said dryly, an affectionate light in her eyes as she mussed her husband's unruly chestnut hair.

Dylan flashed her a lazy smile. 'I know how to delegate authority.'

'That's one explanation.'

Alaina scooped the baby up in her arms and cuddled her, making a comically disgusted face when the baby squealed in delight and wiped chocolate frosting on her immaculate sweater. Alaina dabbed ineffectually at the stain with a napkin.

'I swear, they gave us the wrong baby in the hospital,' she said mildly. 'They gave us the dry cleaner's child; it was a plot.' She kissed her daughter's nose and grinned. 'But I won't trade you back, will I, sweetheart? No way.'

The baby squealed again and bounced in her mother's arms.

Rachel smiled and sipped at her coffee. Alaina didn't strike her as the baby-cuddling type, which made the display of affection all the more touching. Her gaze fell on her own mother, who stood with Bryan near a set of lawn furniture they were trying to sell – a wooden glider and three chairs. Addie had never been the cuddling type either. Still, they had been close once. Rachel had hoped they would be close again, before Addie's illness stole away all familiarity. But they didn't seem to be able to manage it. The past stood between them like a wall, and the present, with the conflict about the move and their changing roles, was only reinforcing that wall.

'Excuse me, Miss Lindquist.'

Rachel nearly bolted out of her skin. Her coffee sloshed over the rim of her cup, and she had to hop back to avoid getting it on her plum-colored slacks. 'Mr. Porchind. You startled me.'

To say the least, she thought as she looked down at the man. Mr. Rasmussen stepped out from behind his partner, where he had been almost completely obscured from view. The bruise had faded from the thin man's cheek, but he still looked creepy with his sunken eyes and sharp features.

For just a second Rachel tried to picture either of them as Addie's ghost, but she dismissed the idea. Bryan was being overly dramatic thinking someone was trying to get her and Addie to leave Drake House. She was convinced it was just some local kid playing a prank, if indeed anything *was* going on. The last incident, which had happened several days before, had faded enough from her memory to seem almost as unreal as Addie's whimsy.

'Mr. Rasmussen and I thought we would stop by and do a little bargain hunting.'

'Bargains,' Rasmussen echoed, steepling his hands in front of him like a preacher giving a blessing.

'Yes, well,' Rachel said with a smile that looked more pained than pleasant, 'there are plenty to be had here today. I see you've found some things already.'

Porchind held a small stack of old books in his dimpled hands, the bindings pressed back into his enormous belly. 'Indeed.' He gave a nervous little laugh. 'Have you had a chance to speak with your mother?'

'No, I haven't. No, not yet. I'm sorry.'

As if on cue, Addie, standing down on the lawn, shouted, 'I'm not leaving this house! Get that through your thick head, Hennessy! I am not leaving this house!'

Rachel felt the color drain from her face as all eyes turned toward her mother. There had to be close to thirty people on the lawn, browsing at an assortment of sale items, and another ten on the wide porch. Addie stared back at them, a truculent gleam in her eyes. She pulled her party horn out of the pocket of her sweater and blew it at them.

Jayne Reilly saved the day, bravely stepping forward to comment on the attractiveness of Addie's new hairstyle, thereby distracting her from Bryan, who had suddenly fallen out of favor.

'Well, there you have it,' Bryan said, shrugging as he mounted the steps to the porch. A particularly inane smile graced his handsome face as he regarded Porchind and Rasmussen. 'Addie's not moving. Looks like you're out of luck, gentlemen. How about a consolation prize?'

He flipped off his magic hat, reached into it, and pulled out a bouquet of red carnations. The children paused in their work at the refreshment stand to applaud. Their cheers broke abruptly into laughter as Bryan offered the flowers to Porchind and a fountain of water suddenly sprayed up out of the silk blossoms, drenching the man.

'Gee, I'm sorry about that,' Bryan said, thoroughly unrepentant. He tossed the flowers aside. 'I didn't know they were loaded.'

Rachel glared at him as she grabbed a handful of napkins. 'Bryan, must you be so *helpful*?'

'Helpful is my middle name,' he said pleasantly. He took the books from Porchind's hands and handed them back to young Sam Harrison, who wrapped them in a towel to dry them while the fat man dabbed at his eyes and his dripping double chins with cocktail napkins. 'Bryan Liam Helpful Hennessy. It's on my confirmation certificate.'

'I'm sorry, Mr. Porchind,' Rachel said sincerely, handing him more napkins. 'I hope it didn't ruin your suit.'

'Impossible,' Alaina muttered dryly.

'No, no, I'm fine, Miss Lindquist,' Porchind said, shooting Bryan a malevolent look. 'We were just leaving.'

'Oh, well, here are your books.' Bryan took the stack wrapped in white terry cloth from Sam and handed it back to Porchind. 'Keep the towel – our compliments.'

The two men nodded to Rachel, glared at Bryan, and stomped down the steps. Bryan watched them cross the yard toward an old brown Ford Galaxy that was parked among the dozens of cars on the lawn. Out of habit he memorized the license plate. He also noted with grim satisfaction that Rasmussen was limping slightly.

'That was really uncalled for,' Rachel said through her teeth when the rest of the crowd had dispersed.

'On the contrary.' Bryan regarded her with an earnest look. 'It was most necessary.'

'Here are the books, Uncle Bryan,' Sam Harrison said, handing the little stack over.

'Well done, Sam. Worthy of the Baker Street Irregulars, I'd say.'

'Thanks, gov'nor,' Sam said, using the dialect of the London street urchins who had come to the aid of Sherlock Holmes on occasion.

The conspirators grinned at each other.

'Bryan!' Rachel gasped, appalled. 'You stole those from Porchind!'

'Borrowed,' he corrected her.

'And made my son an accessory!' Alaina fixed him with a steely look, turning her body as if instinctively shielding her baby daughter from Bryan's powers of corruption.

Bryan ignored them both, totally absorbed in examining his ill-gotten booty. He singled out one small book from the others and tapped a finger against the title handwritten inside the front cover. ' "The Journal of Arthur Drake III." ' He turned to Rachel and lifted an eyebrow. 'Now, what do you suppose Porky and the Rat would want with this?'

'To read it, I imagine,' she said tightly.

'What's going on out here?' Faith Callan asked, stepping out onto the porch with her son Nicholas perched on her hip. The toddler rested his dark head on his mother's shoulder, and had his thumb firmly planted in his mouth. His eyelids were at half mast, indicating naptime was at hand.

'Just a little shell game,' Bryan said absently, stroking his godson's head.

Alaina tugged Faith aside to give her the play-by-play, and Bryan turned to Faith's husband as he came out onto the porch. Shane Callan was tall, aristocratically handsome with black hair and pale gray eyes, but most important to Bryan at the moment was the fact that Shane had spent sixteen years as a federal agent.

'Shane,' he said with a bright smile. 'You're just the man I wanted to see.'

'I'm glad Addie refused to let this thing go,' Bryan said as he and Rachel settled back against the chintz cushions of the old glider.

'Me too.'

They had moved the old swing around to the back of the house. It now stood near the fenced edge of the cliff with overgrown shrubbery on either side of it, creating a secret bower from which they could watch the sun sink into the ocean and the stars drop down into the twilight sky. A benevolent weather system had kept the fog bank from rolling in and made the evening lovely and warm. Waves washed against the shore below in a soothing rhythm. It was such a peaceful scene compared to the afternoon that Rachel took a long moment just to savor it.

Addie had gone to bed directly after supper, exhausted from the day's events. Rachel felt the same kind of freedom as a mother whose toddler had drifted off extra early for a change. She and Bryan were going to have a few extra hours all to themselves. Bliss.

She had changed into a loose-fitting purple cotton sweater and a comfortable lavender skirt. Her hair was still up, but the chignon was very loose, and the evening breeze set all the fine tendrils around her face fluttering like ribbons. She curled her bare feet beneath her on the cushion and sipped at her glass of white wine.

Bryan sat beside her, the picture of relaxed masculinity in old jeans and a faded denim work shirt. His long legs were stretched before him and crossed at the ankles. His profile was to her as he gazed out at the ocean, and Rachel studied him as an artist studies a subject to be sketched. His was a strong, handsome face with its high forehead and solid jaw. His evening beard shadowed the lean planes of his cheeks. His eyes looked tired, but intelligent, contemplative as he stared out at the sea.

A wave of love swept over Rachel, echoing the surf that surged against the shore below them. It took her a little by surprise and it frightened her deep inside. Summer was slipping away from them.

Bryan turned to her slowly, his eyes mirroring the ache she felt. He lifted a hand to cup her cheek, and his thumb brushed away a teardrop she hadn't been aware of.

'Summer's not over yet,' he whispered, and bent to press a sweet kiss against her lips.

When he sat back, he took a deep breath, almost visibly shrugging off the mantle of melancholy that had fallen over them. He smiled gently and sang a line from an old Celtic folksong about a young man who had wandered into Edwards Town unknown, unloved, and unseen, there to meet a beautiful girl he called his County Leitrim queen.

Rachel smiled. He had a lovely voice. 'Did you learn that in Ireland?' she asked, suddenly realizing how little she knew about him, about his background.

'No. My father likes to sing that one. It makes my mother furious because the girl in the song is blond and my mother's hair is black. She claims Dad sings it to remind her of one of his old girlfriends. He's allowed to sing it only when he's in the garage making his fireworks.'

'He makes fireworks for a living?'

'No. That's his hobby. He designs twelve-meter racing yachts for a living.'

'That's . . . unusual.'

'We Hennessys are an unusual bunch,' he admitted with great pride.

Rachel chuckled. 'So I gather. Tell me about them.'

Tell me about you, Bryan heard her ask, though she didn't speak the words. That gentle, knowing smile curved his mouth again as he put his arm around her shoulders and she settled against him with her head tucked beneath his chin.

He told her about growing up in the Hennessy household with his three brothers and three sisters, about how they had all been encouraged to be themselves, to pursue whatever dreams caught their fancy. He told her about Catholic school and Sister Agnes, the Iron Nun. He told her about his travels and his work. He told her about Serena. He told her about the Fearsome Foursome and how they had all ended up in Anastasia.

'They're wonderful friends,' Rachel murmured. 'You're very lucky.'

'They're your friends now too,' he said, pushing one sneakered foot against the ground to set the glider into lazy motion. 'That's the wonderful thing about having friends – you get to share them.'

Rachel said nothing. She would have loved nothing better than to stay in Anastasia and have Bryan's friends become her friends. But that wasn't the way things were going to be.

'It'll work out, Rachel,' Bryan promised. He lifted her chin and smiled down at her, his blue eyes twinkling like stars in the dusk. 'All you need is a little faith in magic.'

Rachel shook her head sadly. 'You can't pull a happy ending out of that hat of yours, Bryan. Life doesn't work that way.'

'We'll see.'

She opened her mouth to protest, but he silenced her with a kiss.

'Don't be so practical,' he said against her lips as his big hands found their way under her sweater. 'Love wasn't meant to be practical. Love is magic.'

Rachel didn't try to argue. Bryan seemed intent on showing her the truth of his statement, and she couldn't bring herself to stop him. She didn't want to stop him; she wanted to love him. She wanted to drink in his love and store it up inside her against the promise of a lonely future. She wanted to make love with him there in their secret bower with the ocean sighing below them and the last rays of twilight slipping into the sea.

'Show me,' she whispered, leaning back from him. Her fingers caught at the bottom of her sweater, and she slowly drew the garment over her head.

Desire tightened Bryan's expression as he stared at her, his intense gaze lingering on her firm, small breasts and the nipples that hardened with the kiss of the cooling breeze. She was so young and lovely, like an innocent goddess as she sat there on the swing looking up at him with fathomless violet eyes.

With deft fingers he pulled the pins from her hair and the pale tresses spilled around her like champagne in the soft light. She reached up to pull his glasses off and set them carefully aside, then her fingers fell to the task of unbuttoning his shirt. Bryan sat very still, almost as if he were afraid to move for fear of breaking the spell. He absorbed every nuance, every subtlety of feeling – Rachel's sadness, her vulnerability, the love she kept locked in her heart because she was afraid of how badly it would hurt when the end came.

But there wasn't going to be an end. He swore that to himself with a fierceness he hadn't known in years. There wasn't going to be an end to this. He loved Rachel Lindquist, and he was damn well going to have her for the rest of his life. He'd been forced to give up the woman he loved once. It wasn't going to happen again, not if he had any power over the matter.

'I love you, Rachel,' he whispered, his voice low and rough as he pulled her into his arms.

Her mouth opened beneath his as she melted against him. Her breasts were cool and soft against the searing heat of his chest. Her back arched as his hands roamed the gentle slopes and ridges. Her tongue met his in urgent play as each tried to telegraph feelings to the other.

Bryan eased her down on the cushions of the glider. His mouth trailed little sipping kisses down the column of her throat to her left breast, where he drank his fill of her, rolling the tight bud of her nipple in his mouth, sucking at it and teasing it with his teeth. He wrapped his fingers in the hem of her skirt and dragged the garment up between them, baring her silky legs to his touch. She moved restlessly beneath him as he tugged down her panties just enough so he could tease her.

'Oh, Bryan, please,' she whispered brokenly, desperation consuming her whole.

'Please, what?' he taunted, nibbling at the corner of her mouth. His fingers slid into the dark silk at the apex of her thighs again and again, only to withdraw without touching the burning core of her desire.

Driven by a deep need and an even deeper fear, he wanted her as wild for his love as he was for hers. He wanted to possess her completely, body and soul, with nothing held back, not feelings, not words.

'Show me,' he whispered darkly.

Fire leapt in his veins as her small hand guided his, showing him exactly how she wanted to be touched. He complied willingly, growling his satisfaction as Rachel squeezed her eyes shut and arched up into his caress. He stroked her to the brink of completion, then pulled away.

Rachel braced herself up on her elbows and stared at him, her swollen breasts rising and falling with her hard, shallow breaths. Bryan kneeled on the cushions of the glider with one knee planted between her bare thighs, the other foot braced against the ground. She'd never seen him look more purely male. His bare chest gleamed in the fading light with the sweat of passion restrained. The button of his jeans was undone, and his manhood strained against the blue fabric.

Sitting up, she reached out with trembling hands to lower his zipper. She leaned forward, pressing hot, open-mouthed kisses against his quivering belly as she freed him. Her hands closed around his hard, hot shaft, caressing him reverently. She wanted him with a need that went beyond desire. She needed him in a way that went straight to the heart of her, to the essence of what made her human. At that moment she would rather have died than deny herself the chance to join with this man in this elemental, mystical act.

Driven by his own desperation, Bryan forced her back down on the glider, his body arching over hers like a bow. He paused at the threshold, the tip of him nudging insistently against her sweet warmth. Bracing himself on his arms, he stared down at her. He had thought it would be enough to know that she loved him. He had thought he could go without hearing the words, but he couldn't. He needed to hear them now.

'Tell me you love me, Rachel,' he whispered hoarsely.

She looked up at him, her eyes wide and dark, stark with sorrow and pleading. She was frightened and he knew it, but he was more frightened.

'Say it,' he demanded, his whole body trembling with the tension of holding back.

'Bryan, don't—'

He tangled his fist in her hair and arched her head back as he lowered his mouth toward hers. He halted, inches from kissing her. 'Say it. Please, Rachel.'

Rachel looked up at him, her heart aching. Lord, how she loved him! It wasn't just her own heart she was trying to protect, it was his as well. She didn't want to hurt him. But as she looked up into the tortured expression in his eyes, she knew she was hurting him. Her silence was tearing him apart. He was a good man. He was a dreamer, and there was no room in her future for a dreamer. But there would always be a place in her heart for Bryan and his magic.

Tears welled up in her eyes and slid in a stream down her temples.

'I love you,' she whispered, her lips trembling as she leaned up to kiss him. 'I love you.'

Bryan clutched her to him, a storm of emotion sweeping through him as he eased his body into hers. He made love to her with everything he was feeling – passion, tenderness, anger, and pain. He held her and kissed her. When the end came, he told her again what was in his heart. And she clung to him and cried.

'Hush, sweetheart, don't cry,' he whispered, holding her close, pressing kisses into her tear-damp hair. He inched over onto his side and cuddled Rachel against him. 'It'll all work out. You'll see.'

Rachel smiled sadly against his solid chest. Don't fall in love with a dreamer, the song went. But she had. She couldn't regret it. She wouldn't have traded what she and Bryan had just shared for anything. She only regretted that the world didn't work the way people like Bryan wanted it to.

'I'm all right,' she said, dredging up a smile for him. Tenderly, she brushed his hair out of his eyes. 'You need a haircut.'

'Do I?' he mumbled, marveling at her strength.

She looked so soft and fragile, but under all that exquisite loveliness was a core of steel that would get her through whatever she had to face. It killed him to think of that hardness taking over her life, obliterating the young woman as she sacrificed her happiness and her dreams on the altar of responsibility. If only he could make her see that she didn't have to give up life's magic, that loneliness didn't have to be a part of her penance for past sins committed against Addie. If only he could make her see that his love for her wasn't going to fade away like a rainbow in the mist.

'I love a maiden fair with sunlight in her hair. Her name is Rachel,' he sang softly, toying with the tendrils of spun gold that curled around her face. 'My love for her is true. Whatever shall I do? She – aargh!'

The glider gave a sudden lurch backward. Instinctively, Bryan's arms tightened around Rachel, pulling her off the thing with him as he fell with a thud to the ground. She gave a squeal of surprise and landed on him, forcing the breath out of him.

'I've heard of the earth moving, but this is ridiculous,' he said, coughing and squinting against the pain as he tried to suck air into his lungs.

'Are you all right?' Rachel asked. She sat up and tugged her sweater on over her head.

'Nothing wounded but my pride.'

Bryan's attention was riveted on a spot behind the bench. He fumbled for his glasses and pulled them on, squinting into the darkness as his sixth sense hummed inside him.

Rachel's suddenly startled gaze followed his. 'Did you see someone?'

'No,' Bryan said evenly. It was what he hadn't seen that was important, but he knew Rachel wouldn't want to hear about it.

He stood up, straightening his clothes, then offered Rachel a hand. 'I guess that was just a sign that it's time for us to go back to the house.'

Rachel scooped up their wineglasses and they walked back across the yard arm in arm. Rounding the corner of the house, they stopped in their tracks at the sight that greeted them.

There was a woman sitting on a stack of suitcases on the front porch. She was a thin, birdlike creature with a wild nest of gray hair on her head. The tip of her cigarette glowed red in the dim light of the porch.

'Bryan!' She shouted his name and popped up off her perch like a jack-in-the-box. 'There you are! I must have rang the bell a hundred times! A hundred times!'

'It's broken,' Bryan mumbled, momentarily stunned. He mounted the stairs in a daze.

'My stars, it's good to see you, sweetheart!' The woman had a voice like sandpaper, and her cigarette bobbed up and down on her lip as she spoke. She threw her arms around Bryan in an exuberant hug which he started to return, but he quickly jumped back as she burned a hole through his shirt.

He plucked the smoldering fabric away from his skin, pain putting a brittle edge to his grin. 'Aunt Roberta! It's so good to see you!' he said with genuine affection, but his brows pulled together in confusion. 'What are you doing here?'

Roberta cackled like a crazed chicken and waved a hand at him. 'Making the rounds of my nieces and nephews. I wrote you, sweetheart. I know I wrote you.'

'You did?' Bryan searched his brain for any memory of such a letter but came up blank.

Roberta's glassy green eyes took on the same kind of absent look as she shrugged her thin shoulders. 'I meant to.'

Rachel cleared her throat discreetly, drawing both their attention. Bryan looked at her as if he had never seen her before, then jumped to introduce her.

'Rachel, this is my aunt, Roberta Palmer. Aunt Roberta, this is Rachel Lindquist.'

Roberta's eyes seemed to bore right into Rachel. 'My gosh, Bryan, she's a doll! A *doll*!' She grasped Rachel's hand in a death grip. 'You're just a doll, Raquel!'

'Rachel,' Rachel mumbled, completely thrown off by this strange woman who appeared to be drowning in a Notre Dame sweatshirt five sizes too big for her. 'Thank you.'

'My gosh,' Roberta whispered, shaking her head at some secret amazement.

They all stood staring at one another for a long moment. Finally Rachel roused the manners her mother had drilled into her. 'Why don't we all go inside? I'll make us a pot of coffee. Decaf,' she added, thinking Bryan's aunt didn't need to get any more wired than she already was.

They trooped into the hall, and Bryan dropped his aunt's luggage down on the marble floor at the foot of the grand staircase. The stuff weighed a ton and a half.

'How long will you be staying, Aunt Roberta?' he asked.

Roberta shrugged, her face alight with excitement as she set off after Rachel. 'A month or so.'

With a wry smile Bryan dug into the pocket of his jeans and pulled out a handful of notes. He sorted through them until he found the one he wanted, then he located his pencil and amended the missive.

Beware of aunts.

11

September 12, 1931
Great luck at Monte's. Mrs. R. very accommodating.

September 21, 1931
Clement sisters staying with H. Langely. Real gems.
Must call again.

September 25, 1931
Langely off to San Francisco. Golden opportunity.
Thank you, C. sisters.

Bryan shifted his back against the headboard, sighed, and turned the page. So far Arthur Drake's journal was providing him with nothing but an account of the man's rather promiscuous love life. He couldn't imagine what Porky and the Rat would have wanted with it, but he figured he had only a short time to find out. They would be back to claim the thing, of that he was certain.

Why did they want Drake House? What did Porchind's relative, the late Mr. Pig, have to do with it?

Money. That word came to him strongly, but it didn't make any sense. The condition it was in, Drake House wasn't worth anything. The property itself might have had development possibilities, but that didn't strike him as the reason. There was no adjacent development in the works. Anastasia already had its share of inns and hotels. There was some other reason, and it had to do with money and this little black book he held pressed to his bare chest.

It was nearly two A.M. They had settled Aunt Roberta in Rachel's room for the night. Rachel lay snuggled against him, sound asleep. She looked so young when she was sleeping, so pretty, so free of worry. Desire stirred in him anew. He would have liked nothing better than to rouse her with kisses and make love to her again, but she was exhausted and he had work to do.

He turned another page in the diary.

September 27, 1931
Party with A.W. at Garner's. My friend has a dangerous tongue. Worked to my advantage tonight. Caught Cecilia Jonstone unawares while Archie made a friend.

September 29, 1931
Pig getting too fat and sassy. Must roast soon.

October 10, 1931
Stuck pig. Ducky outfoxed the pig! My turn to get fat.

'Stuck pig,' Bryan mumbled. He ran a hand back through his disheveled hair. 'Stuck pig.'

'Mmmm?' Rachel mumbled in her sleep.

She turned over and snuggled closer to him still, kicking the sheet off and using his belly for a pillow. Bryan bit his lip against the groan that rose up in his throat. Her cheek was soft and cool against his skin. Her warm breath swept across his groin as she sighed. As she settled down he forced his attention back to the book.

October 12, 1931
Can't find A.W. anywhere. Worried he said the wrong thing to the wrong person.

Rachel murmured something unintelligible in her sleep and Bryan had to choke back another groan as her lips brushed against his stomach muscles. She nuzzled against him and brought her hand up his thigh to rest it in a spot that made sweat break out on his forehead. A contented smile curved her mouth as she stroked him. Molten heat seared his veins, pooling in the pit of his belly.

His body's reaction was inevitable, which seemed to please the sleeping Rachel. She mumbled something softly and the vibration of her lips against his skin just about sent Bryan over the edge. He tried to ease away from her, but her fingers closed around him and all he could do was close his eyes and whimper. She was giving him a five-star arousal and the little minx was sound asleep!

'Rachel,' he said, abandoning the journal on the cluttered nightstand. He stroked a shaking hand over her hair. 'Rachel, sweetheart.'

Rachel lifted her eyelids just enough to peer up at him. His face was flushed. His blue eyes seemed unusually bright. His expression was pained.

'Why is the light on?' she mumbled.

'The better to see you with, my dear,' he quipped, baring his teeth.

'Are you feeling all right?' she asked, concern knitting her brows.

'Wonderful,' he said sardonically. 'Can't you tell?'

The last fog of sleep drifted out of her head as she realized she was at eye level with his belly button. Her gaze snapped downward, and she gasped. Bryan was roused and ready, and her fingers looked very guilty considering where they were.

'Caught red-handed with the loaded gun, so to speak,' Bryan said. He chuckled as he took in the blush that bloomed on her cheeks. 'I've heard of sleepwalking, but sleep seducing is a new one on me. What have you got to say for yourself, Miss Lindquist?'

Her initial embarrassment evaporated in the sensual heat that was rolling off him. Beneath her cheek his stomach muscles were like rock. He smelled deliciously male and musky. Desire rippled through her. Scooting down a little farther on the bed, she turned onto her stomach and looked up at him, her hair a wild golden mane around her head and shoulders, her eyes nearly purple with passion.

'I always finish what I start,' she whispered in a languid, smoky voice.

'An admirable trait in a young woman,' Bryan said through his teeth as she lowered her head. He groaned long and with feeling.

Somewhere below them a scream split the air.

'A man could die from this kind of frustration,' Bryan complained as he threw his long legs over the edge of the bed and reached for his jeans. 'Cases have been documented. You could look it up.'

Rachel wasn't interested. She had already thrown on a robe and was rushing down the hall toward Addie's room in her bare feet.

'Mother? Mother, are you all right?'

'Rachel?' Addie burst out of her room, clutching her pink chiffon robe to her chest with one hand. In the other hand she clutched a rock. 'Someone's broken into the house! Call your father!'

Bryan dashed past them, threw one leg over the mahogany banister, and shot down the polished railing to the foyer. Lights flashed at the end of the hall. The alarm on his electronic sensor buzzed furiously. He ran for the study, adrenaline pumping through him.

'Aunt Roberta!'

Roberta stood in the center of the room, her green eyes wide, her hair literally standing on end. 'Oh, my stars, Bryan! I am so glad you're here! I can't tell you. I just can't tell you!'

Bryan flipped off the alarm, pulled off his glasses, and rubbed at the bridge of his nose, heaving a weary sigh. Aunt Roberta had always demonstrated an amazing talent for setting off his machines.

'I came down to fix myself a little snack,' Roberta said, pulling a bent cigarette and a lighter out of the pocket of her ratty blue robe. She paused to suck a gallon of smoke into her lungs. 'This place is a maze. A maze. I've never seen the like, have you, Regina?' she asked Rachel, smoke billowing out of her nostrils. She patted Bryan on the arm. 'I don't know why you'd want such a big place, honey. These old houses are a beast to heat, you know. An absolute b—'

'What happened?' Bryan asked, his normally generous patience wearing thin. He could have been upstairs in the throes of bliss if it hadn't been for his batty aunt.

'I got lost. Lost,' Roberta said, waving her cigarette at him. Ash sprinkled to the floor. 'So, I'm wandering down the hall, and I decide to ask that pale, thin fellow how to get to the kitchen.' She turned to Rachel again, shaking her head. 'I hope he's not your boyfriend, Renita. He is one ugly dude. Ugly. My gosh, he's ugly.'

Bryan perked up. 'A thin man with sunken eyes and white, white skin?'

'White as a ghost. As a ghost! All dressed in white. Pale as death. I guess I startled him. Kind of a flighty guy, isn't he? Well, I followed him in here and all hell broke loose with these crazy machines going off. Just about gave me a heart attack. A heart attack!' She shook her head and crossed herself reverently with her cigarette. 'My gosh.'

'What did the man do?' Bryan asked as he rewound the film in his camera.

'Grabbed a stack of books off the shelf and ran out that way.' She waved her cigarette in the general direction of the French doors which stood open. 'Strange time of the day to be going to the library, don't you think? Very strange.'

While Bryan went to investigate, Rachel introduced her mother to their new guest. 'Mother, this is Bryan's Aunt Roberta. Roberta, my mother, Addie Lindquist.'

Addie stared at the woman, obviously confused. 'Who is she? The maid? Of course I knew that, Rachel. You needn't introduce me to the maid.'

'A little off her rocker, eh?' Roberta whispered behind her hand to Rachel, nodding knowingly. 'That's all right, Renée. I understand.'

Rachel looked from one to the other helplessly. She honestly didn't know what to say. She felt like Alice must have in Wonderland.

'*Great* hair, Adelle,' Roberta rasped, blowing out a jet stream of smoke. She reached out to fluff Addie's pinking-shears special, taking another deep drag on her cigarette. 'Did you get it done around here? My gosh, I *really* like that. I do.'

'Well, there's no sign of him now,' Bryan said, coming back into the room. 'I suggest we all go back to bed.'

The two older women wandered off together, talking beauty secrets.

Rachel stood in the doorway, hugging her robe around her, watching as Bryan stood on a chair and carefully removed the cassette from the video camera he had mounted in the corner above the door.

'I suppose it's too much to hope for to think they might be having identical hallucinations.'

'It's unlikely,' Bryan said. He rattled the video cassette. 'Just as it's unlikely that a ghost could pull an iron railing loose or track mud into the house or step through rotted wood. I believe we'll have all the proof we need right here to show that Rat is our mystery man.'

Rachel shook her head. 'I don't understand why Rasmussen and Porchind would try to drive us out. They know I'm interested in selling the place.'

'They also know Addie doesn't want to move,' Bryan pointed out. 'In any case, they could be trying to frighten you into dropping the price, make you so desperate to leave that you'll practically give the place to them rather than put it on the market and let someone else have a chance at it.'

He went very still, staring past Rachel, his eyes clear and intense. 'Don't let anyone else have a chance at it,' he repeated. 'Yes.'

Rachel ignored his odd trance. She was getting used to such behavior, much to her surprise. 'What about Addie's whimsy? Are you finally giving up that ridiculous belief in ghosts?'

'Not at all. I haven't figured out where Wimsey fits in yet, but I will.'

Bryan smiled brightly, happy as a clam with his evidence. One mystery was well on its way to being solved. The whole thing would come to a head soon. He could sense it.

Rachel stepped out into the hall. 'I'll see you upstairs. I'm going to go make sure Mother and Roberta aren't giving each other crew cuts.'

'I'll be right up,' Bryan promised.

He reset his equipment on the off chance of a return appearance by their ghoulish visitor, then poured himself a drink from the bottle that still resided in the desk drawer. He had told Rachel he would purchase the desk himself, but he needn't have worried. For some odd reason the study had remained virtually untouched throughout the tag sale. People had avoided the room. He had a strong feeling he knew why.

Now he raised his glass to whatever presence might have lingered in the room and said, 'I don't know where you fit in yet, Wimsey, but I'm going to find out.' He took a drink, then turned and stared long and hard at the portrait of Arthur Drake. The man was gesturing out toward him with an infuriatingly enigmatic expression on his face. 'And I'm going to find out where you fit into this too, Arthur. See if I don't.'

The videotape showed the back of a man's head. That was it as far as evidence went. The rest of the show was Aunt Roberta, shouting, screaming, waving her arms. She managed to block the culprit out of the picture entirely. The film in the still camera was no better – mainly photographs of Aunt Roberta getting the bejeepers scared out of her. It was a disappointment, to say the very least.

His call to Shane didn't exactly improve Bryan's morning.

'I didn't turn up anything on either one of them,' Callan said. 'Porchind was teaching literature at some two-bit junior college in

131

Oregon until this summer. Rasmussen ran a used-book store. They haven't had so much as a parking ticket between them. Sorry.'

Bryan managed a smile. Shane apologized as if it would have been infinitely preferable to have discovered the men were notorious serial killers.

'Any clue as to what brought them to Anastasia?' Bryan asked.

'None. But Faith says you should talk to Lorraine at the Allingham Museum on Seventh Avenue. Apparently, she's lived here forever. She should be able to answer questions concerning the history of the place.'

Bryan pulled a scrap of paper out of his pocket, located his pencil behind his left ear, and jotted the message down.

'Faith also says to tell you you need a haircut.'

'Thanks,' Bryan said, scowling at his reflection in the hall mirror.

'Anytime. You know where to call if things get exciting.'

Bryan smiled as he bid his friend good-bye. Shane seemed perfectly at ease at Keepsake Inn, working on his music and his poetry. He was a wonderful father and a dutiful, doting husband to Faith, but Bryan sensed Faith hadn't domesticated the agent completely.

Stuffing his notes back into the pockets of his khaki chinos, Bryan set off in search of Rachel, his mind mulling over what little information Shane had been able to give him. He pictured Miles Porchind in an ill-fitting tweed jacket, spraying the students in the front row of his stuffy classroom with spittle as he read aloud from Chaucer. He imagined Felix Rasmussen creeping around the musty stacks of books in a dark little store on some dingy side street.

Literature. Books. Porchind had come to the tag sale for books. Their late-night visitor had snatched an armload of books on his way out. Was it possible they weren't after Drake House at all, but something in it?

'Bryan, they're driving me insane,' Rachel said, coming out of the kitchen, wringing her hands in a dishtowel.

'Who?'

Rachel stared at him as if he had completely lost his head. 'Who? Who do you think? Tweedledee and Tweedledum. My mother and your aunt.'

He waved a hand to dismiss the subject. 'They'll be fine once they get to know each other.'

'How can they get to know each other? My mother is perpetually confused, and your aunt never calls anyone by the same name twice. They're like squirrels chasing each other's tails!' She did a wickedly accurate imitation of Roberta, substituting a ballpoint pen for the ever-present cigarette. ' "My word, Rochelle, you make good eggs!" Then my mother says, who's Rochelle? "Your daughter, for heaven's sake, Amelia! Your daughter, Roxanne!" Then they start the whole thing over again! It's worse than having breakfast with Abbott and Costello!'

'Honey, relax,' Bryan said with a cheerful smile. He pulled a quarter out of her ear, handed it to her, and patted her cheek. 'Buy yourself a cup of coffee. They'll be all right. It'll all work out. You'll see.'

Rachel stared at him in exasperated disbelief as he turned and headed for the front door. 'Where do you think you're going?'

'To get a haircut!' he called, waving at her over his shoulder.

Rachel ground her teeth. Wasn't that just like him to blithely wander off on some silly errand, leaving her to deal with the problem.

No, she corrected herself as she slumped back against the wall, that was like Terence. Her stomach churned at the thought. Bryan was sweeter than Terence had ever been, and less self-absorbed, but when it came to accepting responsibility, it was looking more and more as if they were peas in a pod, smoothing the rough spots over with platitudes, leaving her to deal with reality while they chased rainbows.

When Bryan returned to Drake House several hours later, he was brimming with barely contained excitement. Unfortunately, Rachel was in neither the mood nor the position to hear his latest theories and the history behind them.

Bryan unfolded himself from behind the wheel of Rachel's Chevette, staring in stunned disbelief at the scene that greeted him. Addie was hanging out her bedroom window, flinging Rachel's clothes out onto the lawn one article at a time. Rachel stormed around the yard, gathering up undergarments, pulling her bras off bushes, digging her shoes out of the shrubbery.

'What's going on?' Bryan asked with a quality of innocence that earned him a scathing glare from Rachel.

'Mother is upset with me because I let a realtor into the house this morning.'

'Traitor!' Addie shouted, and let fly a pair of loafers.

'She's taken all my things and locked herself in her room.'

'Oh, dear.' Bryan frowned. 'Where's Aunt Roberta?'

'She went scuba-diving with someone named Brutus, an old friend of one of your brothers,' Rachel said, retrieving one of her shoes from the hood of her car. 'If you want my frank opinion, the man did not appear to be mentally balanced, but who am I to judge?' She gave a brittle laugh that managed to combine fury and hysteria.

Bryan's brows shot up in surprise at the news.

'This is all your fault.' Rachel glared at him and shook a loafer under his nose. 'You told Mother we wouldn't have to move. Naturally, she has no trouble remembering that little gem of information. Thanks a lot, Bryan,' she said, smacking him on the arm with the shoe. 'You've made my job so much easier.'

Bryan winced and rubbed his arm. 'But Rachel—'

'You keep saying you want to help me,' she ranted, running under a pair of jeans as they floated to earth. 'Then you turn around and undermine my efforts to get Mother to accept the inevitable.'

'But honey, it's not—'

They both broke off as a brown Ford Galaxy rattled up the drive. The car coughed to a halt and Porchind and Rasmussen emerged from the interior. A rock sailed down from above and ricocheted off the grille of the car with a *ping*! All heads turned to see Addie wielding a bra-turned-sling-shot.

'It's Porky and the Rat!' she shouted, loading a bra cup and letting another stone fly. 'Get away from my house!'

'Please excuse my mother, gentlemen,' Rachel said as they all took cover on the porch. 'She's been hallucinating a lot lately.'

'We've come to retrieve our books, Miss Lindquist,' Porchind said without preamble, tugging at his brown vest in a vain attempt to get the garment to cover his protruding girth.

'Books,' Rasmussen echoed. He cast a glance at Bryan, his sunken eyes gleaming with restrained temper. Bryan merely smiled at him inanely.

'Oh, yes,' Rachel said, giving Bryan her own fierce look. 'I'm so sorry about the mixup. Bryan will get them for you.'

'They're in the study,' he said, pleasantly unrepentant. Opening the door, he motioned everyone inside. Rachel stomped past him. Porchind and Rasmussen sidled by, reluctant to turn their backs on him. 'Wasn't that funny – those two stacks of books getting switched around that way?'

His only reply came in the form of three furious stares, which rolled harmlessly off his shield of innocuous enthusiasm.

'My, that old journal was certainly interesting reading,' he said brightly as they went into the study.

The two visitors turned abruptly to each other, their complexions paling from white to ashen.

'I couldn't make head or tail out of it myself,' Bryan said with a grin. He fought the urge to chuckle as Porchind and Rasmussen relaxed visibly, letting out a collective breath.

They sank down on the leather love seat, apparently weak with relief as Bryan handed the little stack of books over to them. Porchind's fingers, as stubby and round as breakfast sausages, curled greedily over the bindings as he pressed the books to his ample belly.

'I've spoken to a realtor about the house,' Rachel said abruptly, drawing startled glances all around. She leaned back against the desk, crossed her arms over her chest, and gave Bryan a mutinous look.

'We were hoping to save you the trouble, Miss Lindquist,' Porchind said with a nervous twitter.

'I had to get a fair idea of the market value,' Rachel explained.

'You're certain you're going to sell, then?'

'Yes,' she said, avoiding Bryan's intense look.

'There's still the little matter of Mrs. Lindquist,' he said pointedly. 'It is, in fact, her house.'

Rachel reined in her temper and her own feelings of guilt. She hated to have it come down to a competency hearing. She had the ominous feeling that all hope of a reconciliation with Addie would be utterly destroyed by that. But the situation was getting desperate. Their funds were dwindling, and the IRS was breathing down their necks. She could see no way out other than her original plan of selling the house and going on to her new job in San Francisco. Her emotions were only complicated by Bryan's unreasonable opposition. She felt as if he were betraying her.

'And there is the little matter of my contract with Mrs. Lindquist,' he continued. With a tremendous effort of will he ignored the fury rolling off Rachel in waves and resurrected his foolish grin. He turned to the gentlemen and began juggling a trio of red foam balls he had produced from thin air. 'I've been hired to find the ghost.'

'There are no such things as ghosts, Mr. Hennessy,' Porchind said as if he were admonishing a ten-year-old.

Immediately both he and Rasmussen gave a little squeal of surprise and leapt forward a bit on the love seat. Their heads swiveled simultaneously, looking behind them as if they expected to see daggers protruding from the back of the chair. Everyone then glared accusingly at Bryan, who went on happily juggling, ignoring their unspoken accusation that he was somehow to blame.

'Sure there is,' he said enthusiastically. 'This one's name is Archibald Wimsey. He was staying here in 1931 as a guest of Arthur Drake. Mysteriously disappeared. I'm quite convinced that his spirit inhabits Drake House to this day.'

'That's ridiculous,' Porchind said severely.

'Absurd,' Rasmussen reiterated.

Together they popped up from the love seat, their eyes and mouths round O's of surprise, their hands going to their backsides.

Rachel sent Bryan a withering glare, then stepped forward to console her guests. 'The springs must be going in that old thing. No wonder no one wanted to buy it yesterday.'

She walked the men to the front door, promising them she and her mother would come to a definite decision about the house very soon. When she returned to the study, she gave free rein to the fury that had been building inside her all day.

'Of all the childish, infantile tricks!' she shouted, standing toe to toe with Bryan. 'Booby-trapping that chair with your magic gizmos. Isn't that just like you!'

'Well, yes,' Bryan admitted grudgingly. 'But I didn't do it.'

'Oh, sure,' Rachel said with a sneer. She turned and began pacing back and forth in front of him in an effort to burn off some of her anger before she exploded. 'What do I have to do to get through to you, Bryan? I have got to sell this house.'

'No, you don't,' he said. Suddenly he was grinning again with almost boyish excitement. 'I think I've found out why Porky and the Rat want it.'

'I don't care why they want it. I don't care if they want to set up a nudist colony for the terminally strange.'

Bryan grimaced. 'There's an ugly thought.'

Rachel's eyes flashed. 'It's nothing compared to what I'm thinking about you at the moment.'

That was true. The signals he was intercepting were more than a little hostile. He cleared his throat, took a deep breath, and took the plunge.

'I think they're after gold.'

Rachel halted her pacing and stared at him in disbelief. 'What?'

'Porchind's late relative, Pig Porchind, was a big-time bootlegger back in the days of Prohibition,' he explained, visibly warming to his topic. 'According to the gossip of the time, he had a fortune in gold stashed somewhere around Anastasia.'

'What has that got to do with Drake House?' she asked impatiently.

'At that same time in history there was a notorious cat burglar on the loose around here. His targets were the homes of wealthy lumber barons and shipping magnates. There were rumors about the theft of an enormous amount of gold from old Pig. It was apparently never found. Neither was Archibald Wimsey, an old British chum of Arthur Drake's who was visiting during the summer of 1931. By coincidence, all concerned in this story were either dead or gone missing shortly after it all happened, and most everyone forgot about it.'

'That's a very entertaining story, Bryan,' Rachel said. 'Does it have a point?'

'Of course it has a point,' he said irritably. 'Wimsey is your mother's invisible friend, and Porky and the Rat think the stolen gold is stashed somewhere in Drake House.'

'That's absurd,' Rachel said. 'If there were a fortune in gold in this house, don't you think someone would have found it by now? It's been more than sixty years since Prohibition.'

'And almost that long since these rumors were in circulation. Why would anyone look for something they didn't know was there?' he asked reasonably.

'Why would anyone look for something that doesn't exist?' Rachel countered. 'Did you find any mention of this legend in that journal?'

'Uh – no,' he admitted, 'not precisely.'

Rachel rolled her eyes. 'This whole tale is so farfetched, I can't believe you're telling it to me. Who gave you all this golden information anyway?'

'Lorraine Clement Carthage, who was a debutante at the time and is mentioned – er, fondly in the diary.'

'And who is now, no doubt, as senile as my mother.'

He couldn't quite meet her eyes after that statement. Lorraine hadn't exactly been in step with the world around her, he had to admit, but to his way of thinking the evidence was all adding up very nicely. Lorraine had thought the dashing Wimsey was the thief. Apparently Pig Porchind had thought the same thing and had probably had Wimsey done away with, which explained the restless spirit. The fact that the gold had never been recovered meant it still had to be around someplace, and Drake House appeared the likely spot since attention was being focused on it by the late Pig's relative.

'Bryan, don't you see this is all a wild goose chase?' Rachel asked wearily. 'All you've got are some moldy old rumors and half-baked speculation. It would be wonderful to find a fortune in lost gold. It would be the answer to my prayers. But life doesn't work that way.'

'Not if you don't let it,' he muttered.

'What's that supposed to mean?'

'It means you have to believe a little.'

Rachel closed her eyes and counted to ten, but the anger was still there afterward, the anger and all the old bitterness. 'You think problems can be solved by magic?' she asked. 'You think all we have to do is believe in fairy tales and everything will end happily ever after? Magic is for fools and children.'

Bryan's head snapped back as if she had slapped him. His jaw tightened ominously. 'Well, it certainly isn't for martyrs, is it?' he asked darkly.

Rachel stared at him, her eyes round with hurt.

In a saner moment he would have called himself a bastard, but he had some pent-up pain of his own to vent, and he was only human.

'I think you don't want to believe there could be a painless solution to your problems because you're so damned determined to sacrifice yourself to Addie,' he said, leaning over the desk toward her, unconsciously trying to intimidate her with his size. 'You've got it all mapped out in that pragmatic head of yours how you're going to make it up to her for wanting a life of your own. You've probably got it figured out to the nth degree the exact amount of suffering you've got to do to redeem yourself.'

Silence hung between them like the blade of an ax. Bryan stood on one side of the walnut desk, his chest heaving in the aftermath of his outburst. Rachel stood on the other side, her shoulders stiff with pride, her eyes shining with tears she refused to shed.

After a long moment she said quietly, 'I'm not a masochist, Bryan. I'm a realist. In the real world people have to learn to deal with problems in a realistic way. Now, if you'll excuse me, I have to go see to mine.'

She turned and went to the door, praying she could make her getaway before the dam burst, but the study door wouldn't open. She grasped the knob with both hands, twisted it, rattled it, yanked on it, but it wouldn't budge.

'Dammit,' she swore, sniffling as she yanked on the knob and kicked the door with the toe of her sneaker simultaneously. 'Damn this stupid old house.'

Bryan watched her, his whole being aching with a ferocious attack of remorse. He'd meant every word he'd said, but he had certainly never meant to say them out loud. He would have done anything to spare Rachel hurt, yet he had just inflicted her with a verbal forty lashes because he was feeling frustrated? It would serve him right if she never spoke to him again, he thought morosely. It would serve him right if she threw him out. Or maybe he should just go . . .

Apologize, stupid.

He hesitated, but suddenly his feet were moving forward. He felt almost as if some outside force were propelling him toward Rachel, who was still struggling with the door. He stopped behind her and reached out to carefully cup her shoulders in his big hands. She jumped and stiffened as if she expected him to become violent. Bryan winced. It wasn't enough that he had to deal with his own pain for what he'd done; now he had to feel Rachel's as well. It was apt punishment, he supposed, but he couldn't help but curse his sixth sense just the same.

'I'm sorry,' he whispered, bending his head down so the fresh scent of her hair teased his nostrils. 'I'm sorry, angel. I shouldn't have said any of that. I know you're doing what you think is best. I shouldn't have lost my temper.'

Rachel tried to hold herself rigid, but she wasn't able to sustain it against the strangely physical pressure to lean back against him. The sting of his words was still bringing tears to her eyes, but she had to admit to feelings of regret herself. She'd been the first one to draw blood, bursting Bryan's bubble of enthusiasm with the pin of practicality. Maybe he wasn't realistic or responsible, but he was trying to help her in his own misguided way. And she couldn't deny the fact that she loved him, or that it hurt her to hurt him.

She sighed as the fight drained out of her and Bryan wrapped his arms around her. 'I'm sorry too.'

She was sorry for a lot of things, not the least of which was the inherent differences in their philosophies. She was sorry fate had thrown them together at such an inopportune time. She was sorry she couldn't believe in magic the way he did.

'I don't want us to fight,' she whispered, twisting around in his embrace and throwing her arms around his neck. Their time together was going to be too short as it was, she thought, her heart aching. There was no sense wasting it on senseless battles about ideology.

Bryan hugged her tight, closing his eyes against another wave of pain.

He had to find some way to show her that her life didn't have to be all sacrifice. He especially had to find a way to show her they didn't need to sacrifice their love, that it would be strong enough to withstand anything if only she would believe.

He gave her a tentative, heart-stealing smile, his blue eyes brimming with vulnerability. 'Friends again?'

Rachel nodded. She sniffed, blinked back the last of her tears, and lifted a hand to brush at the errant lock of tawny hair that fell across Bryan's forehead and into his eyes. A gentle smile curved her mouth.

'I thought you were going to get a haircut.'

His expression went comically blank, then guilty. A warm blush colored his high cheekbones. He ducked his head sheepishly. 'Um . . . I guess I forgot.'

'Come on,' Rachel said, chuckling softly. 'Maybe we can get Mother to do it for you. She's a whiz with a scissors, you know.'

They shared a smile, letting the moment heal the wounds they had inflicted, then Bryan turned the doorknob with suspicious ease and they walked out of the study together.

12

The term *fool's gold* had taken on a whole new, personal dimension for Bryan. In the three days since he'd discovered the possibility of there being a treasure hidden somewhere in or around Drake House, he had spent nearly every waking moment searching for it. He had inspected the house from its musty, cobweb-filled attic to its dank, dark cellar. He had painstakingly examined every wall and floor in search of hidden compartments. He had experienced considerable excitement upon discovering a secret vault in the basement, only to be visited by crushing disappointment hours later when he finally managed to get the thing open and found nothing inside but some old *National Geographics* and a ship in a bottle.

His search of the grounds had been no less futile. If Arthur 'Ducky' Drake had buried his booty, he had certainly left behind no clues in the lawn as to where it was. Of course, nearly sixty years had gone by. Whatever Ducky might have left behind could have been long gone by now.

Bryan heaved a sigh as he went over it all in his mind yet again. He'd spent the entire morning in the study, mostly sitting and staring. This had presumably been Arthur Drake's favorite room. It was where the man had hung his portrait. It was probably where he had written the journal Porky and Rat so coveted – the journal Bryan had photocopied in its entirety before handing it over to them.

He went over the last of the entries again, then pulled his glasses off and rubbed at his weary eyes. The nearest thing to a clue he had found in Drake's writings was mention of his pleasure boat, the *Treasure*. It was on that craft Ducky Drake had met his end on Armistice Day, 1931, when the ship had gone down with all aboard her. The last few notes Drake had made in his journal after the mention of 'sticking the pig' were about his concerns over the whereabouts of his vanished friend A.W. and a couple of vague references to having some workmen come to do minor repairs around the house – plumbing and brickwork and the like.

Maybe Arthur Drake and his gold were both now lying at the bottom of the Pacific. Maybe Lorraine Clement had been correct in her hunch that Wimsey had been the elusive gentleman bandit, in which case poring over the Drake journal was a waste of time. But if Wimsey were the thief, why wouldn't he tell Addie where the gold was? Because it wasn't there?

Maybe Rachel was right, he conceded. Maybe it was all a big wild goose chase.

'That's no way to think,' Bryan muttered to himself in disgust. Pessimism had never gotten anybody anywhere.

Pushing himself up out of the desk chair, he stretched and cast a cursory glance over his shoulder at the image of Arthur Drake that hung on the wall. He would unravel this mystery as he had unraveled dozens of others over the years. But he needed a clear head to do it.

He had run himself into the ground, spending his days searching for the gold and his nights watching out for signs of Wimsey, not to mention their other nocturnal visitor. What little time he'd spent in bed he'd spent making love to Rachel, trying his best to bind her to him in the most elemental way he could, trying to show her with his body how much he loved her. He couldn't escape the sinking feeling that his message wasn't getting through. Or maybe she was simply ignoring it.

Even though they hadn't argued again, neither had things been the same as before their fight. There was a tension straining their relationship. Bryan could sense the invisible barrier Rachel was erecting layer by thin layer between them. She might have forgiven him for his harsh words, but she couldn't forgive him for believing in things that couldn't be seen or touched. And the harder he tried to convince her that his outlook was a better one, the farther she drifted away from him.

She had been working as hard as he, slaving over the state of Addie's finances and struggling with Addie herself, fighting a futile battle to repair her relationship with her mother before it was too late.

Standing by the French doors, Bryan heaved a sigh. Outside, the morning had turned blue and beautiful. He flung open the doors and drank in the scents. The air was fresh with the tang of the sea and the sweetness of sun-warmed grass and wildflowers.

It was the kind of day meant for playing hooky. It was the kind of day meant for picnics and hand-in-hand walks, for taking leisurely drives along the shore and making love under the afternoon sun. It was the kind of day too many people let pass by, sure that another would come along at a more convenient time in their lives. Bryan knew for a fact that wasn't always true. You had to enjoy life moment to moment because tomorrow was a promise that wasn't always kept. Too many people waited until it was too late, then looked back on their lives with bitterness and regret.

He couldn't let Rachel be one of them.

Determination giving him a fresh burst of strength, he strode to the desk and picked up the telephone.

'My word, that's a lovely color on you, Abbey,' Aunt Roberta commented. 'Just lovely. And the feathers are really you. Don't you think so, Rebecca? I think they're really *her*.'

Rachel sighed wearily and raised her head, looking past the sea of bank statements, bills, and canceled checks spread out across the dining room table to where her mother sat in a pool of yellow light near the window, glowering at her.

Addie wore another of her nondescript loose housedresses and had an emerald-green feather boa draped around her neck. In her hands she clutched a pottery ashtray the size of a Frisbee, and every so often she thrust it beneath Roberta's cigarette to catch the fallout. Roberta sat in a rocker beside her, pumping the thing as if she were out to set some kind of record. Smoke billowed from her nostrils, giving the impression that her boundless nervous energy came from a combustion engine.

'For goodness' sake, Rowena, you look exhausted!'

'I've had a lot of work to do.'

'Stealing my money,' Addie muttered.

'There isn't any money to steal, Mother,' Rachel shot back. Gritting her teeth, she tamped down her temper. 'I'm trying to help you. I came back here to help you.'

Addie narrowed her eyes. Her lips thinned to a white line of disapproval. It made her so angry to see Rachel going through her business papers. It made her angry to know she couldn't have gone through them herself because they made no sense to her anymore. She certainly didn't want Rachel sifting through them looking for yet another way to humiliate her and snatch away a little more of her independence.

'She's not my daughter, you know,' she said to Roberta.

Rachel rolled her eyes.

Roberta's black brows arched up. 'She's not? I thought she was. Bryan said she was. He *told* me Ramona was your daughter.'

'Ramona who?'

'Your daughter.'

'I don't have a daughter. Pay attention here, Roberta,' Addie said crossly, smacking the woman on the arm. 'After all the sacrifices I made for my daughter so she could go on to greatness as a soprano, she ran off with a nightclub singer.'

'Oh, my gosh, Althea,' Roberta whispered in shock, crossing herself with her cigarette. 'My gosh.'

Rachel tuned out. She really didn't have the energy to deal with her mother today. She had been on the telephone half the morning with a woman from the California Health and Welfare Agency, discussing financial aid for people with Alzheimer's. The bureaucracy was incredible, the benefits negligible in relation to the expenses a chronically ill person faced. She had to consider Addie's loss of income, housing costs, medical costs, cost for in-home help or respite care, the normal costs of living, taxes, miscellaneous expenses. And somewhere down the road she would have to deal with the expense of putting Addie in a nursing home.

As badly as she wanted to care for her mother herself, Rachel realized that would eventually become impossible. Addie's condition would inevitably decline to the point where she would need constant care and supervision, and Rachel would not be able to provide that and keep a job as well.

She planted her elbows on the tabletop and rubbed her hands over her face. Already the strain was getting to her. What was she going to feel like after months, even years of this? Despair welled inside her at the prospect of a bleak, joyless future.

Bryan.

His name drifted through her mind as if someone had whispered it low and soft in her ear. Warmth cascaded through her, enticing, like forbidden fruit. It was strange, but just thinking about him relaxed her.

'Come along, angel,' Bryan said briskly.

Rachel's head snapped up. Cautiously, she turned to look at him as if she didn't quite believe he would be there. But there he stood, looking rumpled and sexy in his snug jeans and faded Notre Dame sweatshirt.

'Come along,' he said again, taking her by the hand and tugging her out of her chair.

'Where . . . ?'

He flashed her a brilliant smile. 'To play hooky.' Rachel dug her heels in. 'Bryan, I don't have time to play hooky.'

'I'm not giving you a choice.'

There was definitely something steely and predatory about his smile, reminding Rachel that there was a great deal more to this man than what so pleasingly met the eye. A shiver danced through her at the glint of determination in his deep blue gaze.

'Bryan, I would like nothing more than to take a day off, but I have responsibilities.'

'They'll still be here when we get back.'

'Bryan, honey, what are you doing with Rhonda?' Roberta asked.

'I'm abducting her, Aunt Roberta.' He let go of Rachel's hand, quickly bent and put a shoulder to her stomach, and heaved her up, wrapping his arm around her wildly flailing legs. She squealed in surprise.

'Oh, well, fine, dear.' Roberta smiled and waved her cigarette at them. 'Have a nice time!'

Addie stuck her tongue out at them.

Bryan frowned at her and turned back toward his aunt, balancing Rachel on his shoulder as if she were a sack of potatoes. He gave Roberta a meaningful look. 'You and Addie keep each other out of trouble, okay?'

'Trouble! My stars, honey!' She cackled and coughed. 'What trouble could we get into?'

'I shudder to think,' Rachel grumbled. She wriggled on Bryan's shoulder as he carried her out of the room and down the hall. 'Bryan, neither one of them should be left alone.'

'Don't be silly. Aunt Roberta is a little unique, but she's perfectly capable of being left on her own.'

'Personally, I think it's a toss-up as to which of them is loonier, but the point is: I shouldn't be leaving Mother.'

'Rachel, you can't spend every hour of every day with her. It isn't good for either one of you,' he said, toting her down the porch steps and across the lawn. 'Think about it. You're going to be taking care of Addie for a long time. Do you want to end up hating her because you shackled her to you like a ball and chain and threw away the key?'

She was silent as he deposited her in the passenger seat of her car and went around to the other side. Any retort she might have made was silenced by the knowledge that she already had feelings of resentment toward her mother. Hadn't she wondered herself how bitter she would be in the end?

'Don't worry about Aunt Roberta.' The Chevette started with a squeal of protest that settled into a pathetic whine. 'I explained to her all about Addie's illness.'

'When?' Rachel asked in surprise. She thought he hadn't done much of anything lately except search for his ridiculous buried treasure.

'When you had your nose buried in work, I imagine.'

'Better submerged in trying to solve my problems than burying my head in the sand or running off to do Lord knows what—'

'Oh, didn't I tell you?' he said as he turned the car out onto the busy coastal highway. 'We're going ballooning.'

Rachel was momentarily struck dumb. For one terrible instant her heart stopped. When she found her tongue again, she said, 'Going what?'

'Ballooning.' Bryan grinned, his handsome face lighting up with excitement. 'Up in a montgolfier.'

'Turn this car around right now,' Rachel demanded in her sternest voice, proud that none of her sudden panic came through in her tone. She thumped her index finger against the dash. 'I mean it, Bryan. Turn this thing around and take me home right this minute.'

'Sorry, angel,' he said. 'I'd rather take you to heaven.'

She could tell by the set of his jaw that he wasn't going to back down. The man could be unbearably stubborn. Well, if he thought he was going to get her into the basket of a hot air balloon, he had another think coming. Of all the silly pranks, dragging her away from work for an afternoon of absolute foolishness. The idea was completely . . . tempting.

Settling back into her seat, Rachel crossed her arms over her chest and fumed. This was precisely the reason she and Bryan didn't belong together. He wanted to dazzle her with magic and fun when there simply was no room in her life for either.

They turned off the main road and headed east over the hills. Even this narrow, winding county road was busy, clogged with tourists out for a day of gawking at the beautiful scenery. The lower slopes of the golden hills were speckled with dark fir trees, and the heavier forest worked its way up toward the incomparable blue of the summer sky. They passed sheep farms and apple orchards.

Finally, Bryan slowed the car and turned off the road onto a dirt path where a colorful wooden cutout of a balloon was tacked to a fence post. The sign read SKY DRIFTERS BALLOON RIDES. Rachel swallowed hard.

They parked near an enormous weathered gray barn, beside several cars with out-of-state plates.

Bryan turned and gave her a serious look, though his eyes were twinkling. 'Do you walk from here or do I get to carry you some more?'

'I'll walk,' Rachel replied in a cool tone, her slim nose in the air.

Still, he took her by the hand when they got out of the car, as if there were some danger of her making a break for it. A loud hissing roar sounded on the far side of the barn. It was a sound that Rachel might once have imagined coming from a mythical dragon. Of course, she didn't believe in dragons anymore, at least not the green, scaly kind.

They rounded the side of the barn, and her heart went into her throat. Some distance away, in a large open field, a balloon was tethered to the ground, its gaily striped bag swaying in the gentle breeze. Several young men in casual dress were leaning indolently against the wicker gondola, obviously having fun shooting the bull. There was another roar as one attendant sent a blast of heat from the burner into the balloon. The striped bag rippled as the air inside it expanded.

'She's all ready for you, Bry!' the slender, bearded man called as they neared the enormous contraption. He pulled his leather gloves off and slapped them against his thigh. 'Great day for it!'

'That's what I thought,' Bryan said with a grin, tugging a reluctant Rachel nearer the balloon.

Her eyes were riveted to the narrow wicker basket even as the introductions were made. The name of Bryan's bearded friend and the rest of the balloon crew went in one ear and out the other. She'd never been afraid of heights, she reflected, but then, she'd never been asked to go up in a balloon. She could feel her face going pale as Bryan nudged her closer.

'You'll love it, sweetheart,' he promised as he lifted her into the gondola.

It didn't seem as necessary to express her skepticism on that point as on the next. 'Do you really know how to fly this thing?'

'No,' he admitted with a mischievous grin. He pulled on the gloves his friend handed him and swung himself gracefully into the craft. 'But I'm pretty sure I can make it land. I managed to do it once near Berlin, and there were people shooting at me then, so this should be a piece of cake.'

Rachel stared at him in horror.

His friend took pity on her. 'Don't worry, Rachel, he knows more than he's letting on. Besides, you'll be tethered to the ground the whole time. Bryan just wanted a place where the two of you could have a nice, private picnic. Pretty romantic, huh?'

Rachel gave him a blank look, but it was too late to ask questions. Picnic? Who could think about food at a time like this, she wondered as the ground crew moved away from the gondola and the balloon above them tugged the basket up a few feet off the ground. She dug her fingernails into the dry brown wicker and watched in horrified fascination as Bryan attended the burner. Flame roared up into the fabric bag. He shot her a wink as they lifted into the air, but mainly he kept his eyes trained on the instrument panel that hung from the framework just below the burner.

He did indeed appear to know what he was doing, which left Rachel free to experience her first ascent in a montgolfier. The sensation was not unlike going up in an elevator – a wobbly elevator that swayed slightly with their movements, an elevator that had no safe, solid building around it. She braved a peek over the edge, and her stomach fluttered the same way it had on her first roller coaster ride. The crew stood on the ground below, waving happily at her, growing smaller and smaller as the balloon lifted higher and higher. Then the tether lines pulled tight, halting their flight.

'Well, what do you think?' Bryan asked.

She dragged in a deep breath, ready to tell him exactly what she thought of this irresponsible escapade of his, but the words caught in her throat as she took in the view around them. It was spectacular. She could see for miles in every direction. Golden hills, soft green pastures, dark patterns of forest. Northern California in all its rumpled wild charm lay beneath them. In the distance she could see another brightly striped balloon floating free above the countryside. To the west the ocean stretched across the horizon, a ribbon of misty blue between the coast and the fog bank. And the beauty was not only in the landscape, but in the silence – it was exquisite and absolute.

The sudden sense of peace was so startling, it brought tears to Rachel's eyes. For days now she had been feeling worn out and beaten down. Her focus had narrowed to a kind of tunnel vision that allowed her to see only what was wrong with her life. She had been ignoring all this wondrous beauty, had shut it out of her life. And Bryan had given it back to her.

She turned to him now with a tremulous smile and said, 'I think I love you.'

His wise, warm blue eyes sparkled, and he slid his arms around her and kissed her.

They stayed aloft admiring the view while enjoying a leisurely picnic lunch of fresh croissants, cheeses, grapes, and an excellent bottle of

California white wine. They talked about everything they could think of that had nothing to do with Addie or Drake House or money. They stood and enjoyed the silence and the simple pleasure of being alone together. It was a wonderful treat. A perfect way to spend part of a perfect afternoon.

Sadly, Rachel knew they would have to come down to earth, both literally and figuratively. But she held the memory of their golden afternoon in her heart as they drove home. Maybe there was some merit in the occasional burst of reckless frivolity. She felt refreshed, rejuvenated. If that wasn't magic, she didn't know what was. Somewhere up in the sky she had left behind her guilt over abandoning Addie and their troubles for a few hours, and she didn't miss it a bit. Now she felt ready to go back and face her financial troubles, ready to try again with Addie. And she had the man beside her to thank for it.

The real jolt to earth came as they turned up the coast road at the edge of Anastasia and headed north, toward Drake House. On the opposite side of the road a police car and a tow truck sat with their lights flashing. Officers and other assorted folk milled around. Traffic had slowed to a crawl, allowing all passersby a clear view of the trouble.

A rusty powder-blue Volvo station wagon had taken out a roadside vendor's cart, then mushed its nose into a stone retaining wall. There were flowers everywhere – on the road, draped across the car's hood and roof, crushed beneath the wheels of the police car. There were roses and daisies and carnations and tiger lilies, flowers of every color. It looked almost as if someone had strewn them about to make the scene of the accident look less tragic. The vendor's cart had been reduced to a pathetic pile of toothpicks, and the vendor, a huge woman in a Hawaiian muumuu and a tennis visor, stood beside it looking stunned.

Rachel's eyes widened in horror as realization dawned. 'Oh, my – oh, my – That's Mother's car!'

Bryan was already steering the Chevette to the shoulder. They abandoned the car and made their way across the road, grim and silent.

'No more gawkers!' Deputy Skreawupp commanded in his gruff monotone. He scowled at them, his jowls drooping like a truculent bulldog's. He pointed an index finger at Bryan as if it were a loaded gun. 'This is police business, bub. Now, get out of here, or I'll flatten you like pie crust, and I can do it.'

'That's my mother's car!' Rachel said, pushing her way past the deputy's pot belly.

'Humph! Batty Addie's gone and done it this time,' he said, flipping back a page in his pocket notebook. 'Driving without a license, expired tags, reckless endangerment, destruction of property—'

Rachel wasn't listening to the litany of charges. Her heart was hammering in her ears as she stumbled to the open driver's door of the Volvo, where Addie sat with her legs out, her garden boots planted on the gravel. She was as white as the waxy day lily that was stuck under the windshield wiper. 'Mother! Mother, are you all right?'

Addie looked, her eyes wide. She was still stunned from the accident, and the confusion of its aftermath had short-circuited her brain. She stared at the young woman crouching down in front of her and tried to concentrate on the girl's face. She was someone Addie was certain she should recognize.

'Rachel?' she murmured uncertainly. Fear shivered through her. She'd never felt so old or so frail . . . or frightened.

'Mother, what happened?' Rachel asked gently. She took one of Addie's thin, cold hands between hers and held it, both to comfort her mother and to reassure herself.

'I'm . . . not . . . sure,' Addie said slowly, tilting her head this way and that, as if the movement might jar loose a memory.

'I am,' Roberta said.

Bryan's aunt was still strapped into the passenger's seat. Her hair stood up around her head like an abused Brillo pad. 'She can't drive worth a damn, can she? It's a good thing we remembered our seat belts. My gosh.'

It was a good thing they had remembered their seat belts, Rachel reflected, shaking her head. Too bad neither of them had remembered Addie wasn't supposed to get behind the wheel.

Deputies came then to take the two ladies' statements and Rachel wandered away from the wrecked car. Hugging herself, she stood beside the retaining wall and stared out at Anastasia, nestled below, picture-postcard perfect with its Victorian buildings and boat-filled bay.

'Nobody was hurt,' Bryan said, coming up behind her. He refrained from mentioning that the flower vendor was threatening to sue. He would speak with Alaina about that. Rachel looked rattled enough as it was. 'I'm afraid Aunt Roberta misunderstood me when I told her Addie couldn't drive. She thought I meant the car was broken, so, when she looked under the hood and saw that the only thing wrong was that the coil wire wasn't hooked up to the distributor cap, she just fixed it,' he explained apologetically. 'She learned to be a mechanic in the army. She was a WAC.'

'*Wacky*,' Rachel muttered darkly.

'That too.'

She wheeled on him suddenly, jabbing an index finger to his sternum. 'I never should have let you talk me into leaving Mother with her! She's certifiable; any sane, responsible person can see that.'

Bryan winced. 'Rachel, I'm sorry. I should have been more thorough about disabling the car. I'll accept responsibility—'

'Since when?' she asked angrily. All the fear and fury and frustration crested at once inside her, and she unleashed it on him without hesitation. 'Since when do you accept responsibility? You're the most irresponsible person I know. You with your don't-worry-be-happy mentality.

Everything will take care of itself. Everything will turn out fine,' she said bitterly. 'If you knew anything about accepting responsibility, this never would have happened! I would have been home to keep an eye on Mother, not off in the wild blue yonder with you!'

She paced away from him, shaking her head in self-reproach.

'Don't beat yourself up with guilt, Rachel. An accident happened. Nobody was hurt. I'll take care of the rest. It'll all work out.'

He couldn't have chosen a worse phrase had he been deliberately trying to goad her. His last four words rang in her ears. She could hear Terence saying them and Bryan saying them, and she could see herself dealing with the messy reality while they blew it off because nobody had gotten hurt.

'Why can't you face reality?' she asked, her violet eyes full of pleading and pain. 'Things don't just work out, Bryan. Things don't just turn out fine. We struggle to do the best we can and we still get kicked in the teeth. *That's* reality, not buried treasure and eating Brie in a hot air balloon.'

She shook her head again, lifting her hands to cradle it as it hung down. 'I should have known better. I should have known from the start.'

I should never have gotten involved with you.

Bryan's head snapped back sharply. She didn't have to say the words; they arced between them like an electrical current that seared his nerve endings with excruciating pain. Their love meant so little to her, she was wishing it away. It was inconvenient, getting in the way of her noble self-sacrifice. His own defense mechanisms snapped into action to stem the flow of blood from his battered heart.

'Fine,' he said tightly. 'You shouldn't have any enjoyment in your life. God forbid! There's work to be done, sins to be atoned for, hair shirts to be worn.'

Rachel grabbed his arm as he started to turn away from her. 'Don't you go calling me a martyr. I'm a sensible, practical person trying to deal with a nightmare in a sensible, practical way.'

'Oh, right,' he said sarcastically. He smiled a rueful parody of a smile. 'Maybe I should have taken my cue from you and behaved in a sensible, practical way, because I sure as hell didn't need the kind of aggravation falling in love with you has been.'

It was Rachel's turn to wince. The pain wasn't entirely unexpected. She'd told herself from the start Bryan would cut his losses when the going got rough. That was what dreamers did.

'Well, don't let me stand in your way,' she said softly, opening her arms wide in a gesture of resignation. 'There's no time like the present. I'm certainly not going to try to stop you.'

Bryan stared at her long and hard, doing everything he could to hide his own hurt while he looked for some evidence of hers. She was bitter and disillusioned and had meant every word she'd said. She hadn't believed in his love from the beginning, not really, not in the way that mattered most. It was clear she was determined to carry out her plans for her penance, and he had no part in them. Or maybe in some perverse way he did. It made her sacrifice only greater if she could look back on their relationship and think of what she had given up, of what might have been.

'Fine,' he said, looking past her to the crumpled powder-blue Volvo, where Aunt Roberta was having an animated conversation with the erstwhile flower vendor. 'I'll move my aunt out to Keepsake. I'll stop by tonight for our things.'

He didn't look to Rachel for confirmation or approval. He didn't look at her at all. He simply walked away. She watched him go, thinking he looked like a stranger. There was an air of cold authority about him as he took his aunt by the arm, murmured a few curt words to her, and led her away.

Rachel wondered if she had ever really known him. But the point was moot. She was never going to have the chance to find out now. He was walking out of her life, taking all the light with him. As the fog bank rolled in around her, she thought of her future and ached at how empty it would be.

13

'Now, keep your eye on the dollar bill,' Bryan said.

He sat back on his barstool, his concentration on the trick rather than on the small group of semi-interested onlookers. He folded the bill into an intricate bow shape, squeezed it between his palms, turned his hands. When he turned his palms outward again, the bill was gone.

'Great trick,' Dylan Harrison said from behind the bar. He wiped his hands on a towel and leaned against the polished surface. 'Now make it reappear, Houdini. I want my buck back.'

Bryan sighed, took a sip of his whiskey, and performed the trick in reverse. The bill did not reappear. On three tries the best he could manage to produce was a wilted flower and a lint ball. He frowned, his broad shoulders slumping dejectedly as his audience wandered away.

Dylan reached across the bar and patted him on the shoulder. 'Don't sweat it, Bry. I'll put it on your tab.'

'I've lost it again,' Bryan mumbled. 'I've lost my magic.'

'You're having an off day, that's all.'

'There's an understatement.'

Losing Rachel put the day in the catastrophic category. He'd seen it coming, of course. It was just that his unflagging optimism had convinced him he would be able to prevent it when the time came. He'd been wrong.

After the fight to end all fights, he had taken Aunt Roberta out to Keepsake – Faith and Shane Callan's inn – dumped her there, and made a beeline for Dylan's Bar and Bait Shop, the popular waterfront establishment owned and run by Alaina's husband. He still needed to return to Drake House for Roberta's and his belongings, but he hadn't been able to face that task without a little fortification of the distilled variety. He needed something to dull his too-sensitive senses. Time, mostly, but in lieu of that a nip or two of Dylan's Irish wouldn't hurt – especially since Dylan was liberally watering the stuff when he thought Bryan wasn't looking.

That wasn't the standard practice at Dylan's. It was a neat bar that catered to tourists and locals alike. The floors were swept, the glasses clean, and the booze uncut. He was getting special treatment because he was obviously in such rough shape. Dylan was looking out for him, like any good, conscientious friend would. It made him feel a little better to think that Alaina had ended up with such a good guy. If he had to be lonely and miserable for the rest of his life, at least his best friends had found happiness.

'My, you look like hell,' Alaina said mildly, sliding onto the stool next to his.

'I know, I know.' He sighed. 'I need a haircut.'

'That too.'

She was immaculate as usual, every chestnut hair in place, not so much as a speck on her Ralph Lauren ensemble of gold slacks and a midnight-blue silk blouse. Bryan, on the other hand, knew he looked as if he'd been sleeping in an alley. His jeans were rumpled. Roberta had burned a hole in his sweatshirt, and the tail of his white T-shirt hung down beneath the hem. It might have been a style popular with the fraternity crowd, but it didn't cut the mustard with Alaina, who probably would have given up her civil rights before her Neiman-Marcus charge card.

He shot her a look, wincing at the tender sympathy and concern in her gaze. He didn't know if he was up to having Alaina feel sorry for him. She was more in the habit of giving a person a swift kick in the britches and telling them to buck up and get on with it.

'Oh, don't get nervous,' she said, extracting one of her precious, rationed cigarettes from her monogrammed case. Ignoring her husband's scowl, she lit it and took a deep, appreciative drag. As she exhaled, her shrewd gaze shifted to Bryan again. 'I'm not going to do the poor-Bryan routine. Faith tells me she already failed in the attempt.'

'Have the three of you ever considered sharing your amazing communications skills with the intelligence community?' he asked, his brows pulling together in annoyance. 'I could give you a phone number.'

Alaina ignored the remark if not its implication. 'And if it's spiritual analysis you want, Jayne will be more than willing to provide that. Practical advice is more my line of expertise.'

He cringed at the mention of the word. 'Please. I've had all the practicality I can stand for one day. I think it's giving me a rash.'

'Can we see?' Dylan asked with a bright smile. His wicked sense of humor actually managed to cut through Bryan's cloak of pain and coaxed a chuckle out of him.

Alaina rolled her eyes. 'Don't you have to go gut fish or something?'

Her husband leaned across the bar, grinning as he touched the tip of his nose to hers. 'Yeah, but I was saving that to share with you later, sweetheart. I know how you like to get slimy.'

'Beat it, Harrison,' she said without batting an eyelash. The polar ice caps would melt before Alaina Montgomery-Harrison would put her manicured hand on a dead fish.

'You don't want me around?' Dylan shrugged. 'I get it. I can take a hint.'

'Since when?' she said dryly, tilting her cheek up for his kiss.

He waved to Bryan and let himself out from behind the bar so he could help attend to the many customers who had wandered in before heading off for dinner at one of Anastasia's several fine seafood restaurants.

'You've got a good one there,' Bryan commented.

'Yes, I have. How about you?'

'Dylan? Gee, honey, I like him, but . . .'

She gave him a look that ended his nonsense in mid-sentence. 'Don't pull that act on me, Bryan. I'm sure you fool the uninitiated on a regular basis, but I am hardly that, now, am I?' She paused with typical lawyerlike drama to let her point sink in, then started her line of questioning over. 'Rachel?'

Bryan sipped his drink and stared across the bar at the crowded shelves that lined the wall. 'It's not working out,' he said shortly.

Alaina took another long pull on her cigarette. She had been afraid something like this would happen. Still, her instincts told her Rachel Lindquist really loved Bryan, and an idiot could have seen how in love Bryan was with Rachel. The man was absolutely besotted. She even knew the problems – irreconcilable differences of philosophy, and extenuating circumstances. The question was, how to reconcile the irreconcilable?

'Look,' Bryan said, hoping to avoid any more painful prodding of his feelings for one night, 'maybe it's best this way. I didn't come to Anastasia looking to get embroiled in another hopeless situation. I did what I could to help Rachel and Addie . . . It didn't work out,' he finished lamely.

Alaina chose her strategy with ruthless calm. Delivering the blows, however, was another matter. She didn't enjoy inflicting pain, especially when Bryan had suffered so much already, but it seemed the only way.

Taking a deep breath, she braced her shoulders and launched her attack. 'Yes, maybe you're right. You're really not up to this. You gave it a shot, you failed the test,' she said with an idle shrug. 'Let it slide. Heaven knows a chance at everlasting love comes along as regularly as the bus to Mendocino. You might as well wait for a woman who isn't so much trouble.'

Bryan sucked in a surprised breath, but Alaina retreated before he could voice his rebuttal.

'If you'll excuse me, sweetheart, I think I'll go help my husband gut fish.' She slid gracefully off her stool, leaned over to kiss Bryan's cheek. 'You have fun wallowing in your self-pity.'

She left him sputtering, sauntering away in a cloud of Chanel and smoke.

'Dirty player,' he muttered. He should have known better than to go against her. He probably had a note someplace reminding him of that, but he was too tired to look for it.

So he was feeling sorry for himself, he thought angrily. So what? He had a right to.

So does Rachel.

'Right?' He sneered. 'She practically makes a living at it.'

That's not fair.

'Oh, shut up,' he said to his little voice, ignoring the stares he drew from several other patrons at the bar. He wrapped his hand around his chunky tumbler of liquor and took another sip.

It was a matter of circumstances conspiring against them, he reflected. If he and Rachel had met at another time, in another place. If he had been able to prove to her Wimsey's existence. If he had found the gold.

To take his mind off his self-pity, he thought about the gold. Lorraine Clement believed Wimsey had stolen it. But if Wimsey had stolen it and Addie truly spoke to Wimsey on a regular basis, if Wimsey was indeed the force he knew was present in Drake House, then why wouldn't Wimsey have led Addie to the treasure?

No. His mind kept turning to Arthur Drake. He knew with certainty that Ducky was their man. If only the clever thief had thought to leave a clue for some worthy adversary . . .

'Adversary,' he mumbled, his brows pulling together. He pushed his glasses up on his nose. Suddenly his eyes went wide. 'Ad*versity*.'

Realization roared through him like a flood tide, leaving him awash in goose bumps. It had been there all along, right under his stupid nose!

He swiveled around on his barstool just as the front door opened and Felix Rasmussen slipped in and slinked along one wall like the rat he so resembled. Bryan fought back a grin. Maybe his luck hadn't all run out.

Helping himself to the whiskey bottle, he splashed a little more in his glass, then on his hands, and he baptized his cheeks with it as if it were aftershave lotion. He rubbed a little through his hair, took a quick swig, and gargled before swallowing. Then, with his glass in one hand and the bottle in the other, he made his way unsteadily across the room to the small table where Rat had taken a seat.

'Mister Rasmussen!' He gave the man a lopsided grin. Rasmussen's eyes darted back and forth as he searched hastily for an escape route. He found none, and his bony shoulders drooped in resignation as Bryan straddled the chair across from his.

'How ya doin'?'

'I'm – fine – Mr. Hennessy,' Rasmussen said solemnly, the way a dying man might say he was fine.

Bryan slapped a big hand down on the tabletop. 'Glad to hear it! Me, I've had better days.' He leaned back in his chair and took a gulp of his drink, letting it dribble down his chin. 'Yeah, yeah. Got tossed out of Lindquist's, you know. She gave some feeble excuse about my drinking, but . . .' He waved a hand. 'Women, huh, Felix? Women! You know how it is.'

'Women,' Rasmussen echoed. He looked as uncomfortable as a man who had accidentally sat down in something wet. 'A – yes.' He nodded, but his expression clearly said he had not the slightest idea of how it was.

Bryan gave him a shrewd sideways look. 'You'll never get that house away from them. You know that? You never will.'

Rasmussen's thin mouth tightened to the point of disappearing entirely.

'You know what I think?' Bryan asked, breathing heavily in the man's face. Rasmussen coughed and blinked. 'Do you know what I think, Felix? She said she didn't believe me, but I think she wanted it all to herself, the little—'

He paused to belch, tapping his sternum with his fist. Rasmussen was on the edge of his seat, waiting to hear the rest of the statement, but Bryan waved it away.

'Forget it. What do I care? Huh, Felix? What do I care? I don't need her with her loony mother. Rich babes are a dime a dozen.' He paused to take a swig right out of the bottle and wiped his shirtsleeve across his mouth. Leaning across the table, he pointed at Rat. 'Hey, you got a dime?'

Half the bar turned to stare as he burst into loud, obnoxious laughter, reached across the table, and thumped Rat on the arm in a gesture of male camaraderie that nearly knocked the man to the floor.

'Jeez, I kill me!' Bryan laughed. 'I'm a damn genius. Did you know that, Felix? Huh? Did you know you were up against a damn genius?'

'Genius,' Rasmussen murmured, his furtive gaze zipping nervously around the room.

'Let 'em rot in their ugly ol' house. Ha! I can get what I want. It's in the wall behind that por – hic! – trait. I can get what I want just like that.' He tried to snap his fingers and managed to overturn his drink in the process. The watered-down liquor pooled on the table and ran over the edge and onto the floor, the whole process enchanting Bryan. He smiled boyishly, leaning down close to the mess. 'I made a waterfall. Look at that, Felix.'

Dylan suddenly appeared beside the table, looking sad and sympathetic. He dropped a towel into the miniature lake and put a steadying hand on Bryan's shoulder, just saving him from falling off his chair. 'Come on, pal. I think you've had enough.'

'Says who?' Bryan demanded. His chin jutted out at an aggressive angle.

'Says me.'

'Yeah? Both of you?' He dissolved into giggles and reached across the table toward Rat, who arched back out of his way. 'Maybe they're right!'

'Come on,' Dylan said with the tolerance of long experience. 'You can sleep it off out back. There's nothing like the smell of live bait to sober a guy up.'

He helped Bryan up and led him toward the door that separated the bar from the bait shop. Rasmussen bolted for the front without hesitation. The instant he was gone, Bryan straightened and stretched and grinned at his friend.

'Well, that was fun!' he said brightly. 'Can I use your phone?'

Dylan shook himself out of his incredulous stare. 'Yeah, sure.'

Bryan was already across the room and behind the bar. He dialed the number of Keepsake from memory.

'Shane, it's getting exciting.'

Rachel went into her bedroom, barely dredging up enough energy to put one foot in front of the other. She was exhausted, done in, wrung out. She couldn't imagine being more tired without actually lapsing into unconsciousness.

After straightening out the situation at the accident, she had packed Addie into the Chevette and gone to a fast-food place for dinner. That had been a disaster in its own right, with Addie accusing the help of giving her food she hadn't ordered because they wanted to poison her. Neither of them had ended up eating very much. By the time they had returned to Drake House, her mother had insisted on going straight to bed. Rachel hadn't argued.

She had spent a couple of hours sorting out the papers she had left in neat stacks on the dining room table. They hadn't been neat upon her return. They had been shuffled into one enormous multicolored mountain. The sight had brought tears to her eyes. She supposed she was lucky Addie hadn't set the pile ablaze, but lucky was the last thing she was feeling. Finally she had given up on trying to concentrate and had dragged herself upstairs.

Maybe things wouldn't look quite so bleak in the morning.

'Now I sound like Bryan,' she muttered, pulling her Bach T-shirt out of the dresser drawer. 'A good night's sleep won't make everything better.'

But it would have been a comfort. To sleep in Bryan's arms, snuggled against his warm body, her legs tangled with his. To have him hold her and kiss her hair and sing in his sleep.

She shook her head. 'Whoever heard of anyone singing in their sleep?'

She pulled her sweater off and dragged her T-shirt on in its place. She let her jeans drop to the floor and lay there, too tired even to dream about being neat. Taking her hair down from its messy knot, she turned toward the bed.

There was a red rose lying on it, a perfect red rose lying on the bodice of another old dress. This dress was pearl-pink satin encrusted with seed pearls and trimmed in lace that had turned dark ivory with age. It was of the same era as the burgundy dress. It was beautiful.

Rachel let her fingertips brush across it as she picked up the rose. Tears flooded her eyes. Bryan. When had he put it there? She tried to sort out the answer to that question as she brushed the rosebud against her cheek, but her brain was too exhausted to function. He couldn't have had time to do it that morning, but he had to have. The only other explanation was that he had come back after . . . after and done it, but that made no sense at all. Besides, she knew his things were still there – his clothes and magic tricks and juggling balls and all the paraphernalia associated with his odd work.

He hadn't come back. He probably wouldn't come back while she was in the house. She had made it more than clear that she didn't want him around.

Sniffing back a tear, she sank to the bed and sat there clutching the rose and the satin dress. She'd never felt so empty in her life, not even when she'd left Terence in Nebraska and headed west. That was probably because she hadn't loved Terence anymore, had never loved him in that deep, soul-searing way she loved Bryan. She couldn't have felt this empty, because she hadn't lost nearly as much.

She tried to tell herself it was best they had ended it now. She'd known all along it would have to end before she and Addie left for San Francisco. But she had never wanted it to end so bitterly. She would have preferred they part as friends, that they let the passion simply fade away into sweet, gentle memories. That would have been nice, to have those memories stored away inside so she could take them out on long, lonely nights and smile at them and hold them close to her heart. Now there would always be a certain sadness attached, even to the best of them. And every time she took them out, there would be regret for the way they parted, for the things that might have been if only she had been able to believe in magic.

Closing her eyes, Rachel tried to block out the pain. It was no good having regrets for being practical. Someone had to face life's problems and deal with them in a sane, rational way. It didn't do any good wishing that someone weren't her.

Addie stood at the door to her daughter's room, peeking in, hesitant to enter. Rachel looked tired and miserable, and Addie couldn't help but wonder how much of that was her fault.

She had awakened from a deep sleep, feeling strangely calm and clearheaded, but also feeling a sense of urgency. She needed to see Rachel, to speak to her.

The accident had etched itself in her otherwise foggy memory with a clarity that made her heart clench every time she closed her eyes. She had been behind the wheel, driving toward town, when whatever knowledge she had possessed about driving went right out of her head. She had suddenly looked at the steering wheel and had no idea what to do with it. She knew the pedals on the floor served some purpose, but she hadn't been able to recall what it was. And when her brain had tried to send a message to her hands or her feet to do something, anything, the message had never arrived.

It turned her stomach to think of it. The result could have been disastrous. She might have hit someone. That strange woman who had been with her might have been injured or killed. She might have been killed herself, and then she never would have seen Rachel again.

The chill that drifted through her frail old body made her pull her robe more closely around her. She had it on inside out, but she hadn't been able to fix it, and it didn't really matter anyway. The only thing that mattered right now was Rachel.

The door drifted open a little wider, and she was suddenly stepping forward with her heart in her throat.

'Rachel?' she asked softly.

Her daughter looked up at her with luminous eyes that were brimming with tears. 'Mother? What are you doing up? Is everything all right?'

'No,' Addie murmured. 'It's not.'

She shuffled into the room and sat down on the bed, her back perfectly straight, her hands folded on her lap. They had done this before. It might have been a long, long time ago – she wasn't sure – but it seemed like yesterday. They had sat on her bed in the little house in Berkeley and made plans about Rachel's future. Now her daughter sat across from her expectantly, waiting for her to say something.

'Don't slouch, Rachel,' she admonished, tapping the girl's knee. Then sadness settled over her like a veil, and she drew her hand away. 'I've always pushed you too hard. Talent needs a firm hand directing it, but I pushed too hard. That's why you left with that guitar player, isn't it?'

'Yes,' Rachel whispered.

Addie shook her head. 'He's not good enough for you.'

Rachel smiled sadly. 'I know, Mother. I don't see him anymore.'

'Good,' she said decisively. 'You've always been a sensible girl, except for that business.'

'I wanted you to love me in spite of that. I wish you could have.'

'Love you?' Addie asked, incredulous. She stared at her daughter, certain Rachel had taken leave of her senses. 'I've always loved you. You're my life.'

'But you wouldn't forgive me.'

'I wouldn't forgive myself either. That doesn't mean I didn't love you, it means I wouldn't forgive you. They are two quite different things,' she insisted.

'Do you forgive me now?'

'You threw away all our dreams,' Addie began, but she cut herself off.

What good were those dreams going to do her now? They were gone forever. Rachel had to run her own life.

She straightened her shoulders and stared at the floor, at the green rubber garden boots she wore all the time because they were easy to get on and off. The hem of her pink robe hung above them, inside out. 'I'm not a well woman, Rachel. I know I do a good job of hiding it, but I forget things. All the time, more and more. I forgot how to drive that car today.'

'It's all right—'

'No, it isn't,' she insisted sternly. 'It isn't all right at all. It's the pits. I had a perfectly nice collection of bird cages. Do you think I have any idea where they've gone?'

'We sold them,' Rachel said carefully. 'At the tag sale.'

Addie just stared at her, drawing a blank.

'Never mind. I came back to help you, Mother. We'll manage.'

Addie mustered a smile and patted her daughter's knee. 'We'll manage. We always have. We have each other. And we have Hennessy.'

Rachel closed her eyes against the wave of pain. 'No, Mother, we don't have Hennessy.'

Addie's brows pulled together in concern. 'You sacked Hennessy?'

'He can't come with us to San Francisco. It wouldn't work out. He's not a butler.'

'Oh. Well . . .' She guessed she'd known Hennessy wasn't a butler. He had played along so well with her, she had eventually decided to believe their little game was real. She waved her hand in a regal gesture that managed to combine resignation and regret. 'He made me laugh.'

'Me too,' Rachel murmured. She bit her lip against the tears, but they fell nevertheless, down her cheeks and onto the bodice of the beaded dress.

'You mustn't cry on satin, Rachel,' Addie said in gentle reproach. 'It stains.'

She took the dress from her daughter's hands and brushed it off before hanging it over the foot of the bed. She got up then and went to the dresser to fetch the hairbrush.

'We have to move, Mother,' Rachel said, watching as Addie plied the brush to the squirrel's nest she'd made of her hair. 'Do you understand that?'

'Yes,' Addie said, staring at their reflection in the mirror above the dresser. She didn't want to talk about moving. The idea frightened her more and more. She didn't precisely understand why they had to move. Rachel would explain it to her if she asked, but what was the point? The decision was no longer hers to make. Her independence had slipped through her fingers. Fighting it only made her tired.

'One hundred strokes a night,' she said, shuffling across the floor to stand behind Rachel. Slowly, gently, she drew the brush bristles through her daughter's pale gold hair. 'You'll have to count, dear, I can't get past forty anymore. Or is it sixty?'

'That's all right, Mother,' Rachel said, smiling through her tears. 'I'll count.'

'No.' Addie brushed steadily, methodically, her ability to accomplish the simple task calming her. 'Sing for me. You have a voice like an angel. Sing the aria from *Zaïde*. Mozart was an idiot, but he made wonderful music.'

Rachel took a deep breath, swallowing down the knot in her throat, and she sang the aria from *Zaïde*, '*Ruhe sanft*' – rest quietly. It was a sweet song, the notes all purity and light and innocence. She was out of practice, but she had been blessed with a natural talent that made practice seem redundant. Her voice held an ethereal loveliness, a purity of its own that carried the song throughout the old house though she sang softly. And when she finished, the silence was absolute, as if the house itself were holding its breath in awe.

Addie put the brush aside and rested her thin, age-spotted hands on her daughter's shoulders. 'You're a good daughter, Rachel.'

Rachel smiled. This was what she had prayed for, what she had pinned her hopes on, some sign from Addie that all was forgiven. There would be no emotional reconciliation scene full of hugs and kisses and tears of joy. That wasn't the way of the Lindquists. But this, in its own way, was just as touching, just as meaningful. It was certainly every bit as precious to her. She had feared this moment would never come, that Addie would slip away from her and they would never be anything but strangers with nothing between them but bitterness.

She reached up to cover her mother's hand with her own and wished fleetingly that she could have shared this moment with Bryan. But Bryan was gone. All she had now was Addie.

'Thank you, Mother.'

Addie sighed and shuffled toward the door. 'Go tell Wimsey dinner will be ready soon. I just have to feed the bird first.'

That quickly Addie was gone. The fragile connection between reality and her mind was lost.

What a gift these last few minutes had been, Rachel thought, watching her mother shuffle away. Like magic.

Maybe there was such a thing after all.

Addie's shriek pulled Rachel from her musings and catapulted her off the bed. She pulled her jeans on and ran out in to the hall, heading in the direction of her mother's angry voice.

'I'll get you this time, you ugly thing!'

Addie stopped halfway down the hall and flung a rock at the apparition standing wreathed in smoke near the secret door. Her form would have done a major league pitcher proud. The stone sailed high and inside, catching the ghostly figure squarely on the forehead.

He grunted in pain and fell back against the partially opened door, closing it and sealing off his own escape route. His sunken eyes went wide with panic. He turned toward the two women, raising his arms and his white cape along with it.

'I am the ghost of Ebenezer Drake!' he wailed, stepping toward them, smoke rolling out from behind him accompanied by a high-pitched wheezing sound. 'I come to cast you from my – ouch!'

Addie let fly another stone, bouncing this one off his chest. Rachel grabbed her by one arm and attempted to drag her away from the advancing figure, but her mother shook her off long enough to reach into her pocket. She heaved a half-finished cheeseburger that hit her target smack in the face. Ketchup trickled down his long nose.

'Mother, come on!' Rachel insisted, pulling Addie down the hall. 'We have to get the police!'

'Leave!' the ghost wailed. 'Leave this house!'

Miles Porchind let himself into the study through the French doors. Dressed all in black in a vain effort to hide his considerable bulk, he waddled across the room with a flashlight in his hand, going directly to the portrait of Arthur Drake III that hung on the paneled wall behind the desk. He shined his light up at the man's face.

'Thought you were so clever, didn't you?'

'As a matter of fact, yes,' Bryan said, stepping out from behind the curtains. 'I think I was awfully clever, don't you?'

'You!' Porchind gasped, wheeling away from the wall. He made a dash for the door to the hall, grabbing the knob, twisting and rattling it. The door didn't budge.

'Oh, that door sticks something fierce,' Bryan said mildly, flipping on a light. 'You know how these old houses are. Actually, I like to think the ghost is holding it shut.'

'There is no ghost, you moron!' Porchind snapped, wheeling back around to face him, his florid face contorted with rage.

'No?' Bryan frowned in mock disappointment. 'I guess that means Shane might get to use his gun after all.' He shrugged as the fat man blanched. 'Well, that'll make him happy. So, Mr. Porchind, to what do we owe this not-so-unexpected visit? Doing a little after-hours art shopping?'

'I came to claim what is rightfully mine!' he declared emphatically.

Bryan looked surprised. 'Yours? Hmmm. I think the authorities might have something to say about that, seeing how you don't own this house or anything in it.'

'Drake stole that gold.'

'From a notorious criminal.'

'I will have the gold, Mr. Hennessy,' Porchind said purposefully.

Bryan raised a brow as the man produced a revolver from behind him. 'Deciding to follow in the family tradition, I see.'

'Shut up,' Porchind ordered, his breath coming in short gasps. 'Come over here and take this picture down.'

Bryan shrugged. 'If you say so.'

He sauntered across the room and easily lifted the heavy gilt frame from its hook. The wall behind it was blank.

'Where's the safe?' Porchind demanded, his chest heaving like a bellows. Sweat beaded on his bald head and ran down the sides of his face in little rivers.

'There is no safe.'

The fat man's eyes bulged as his cheeks turned crimson. 'But – but – you told Rasmussen—'

Bryan grinned engagingly. 'I lied.'

His admission met with a murderous look. 'You rotten . . .'

Porchind lifted the revolver and aimed, Bryan swung the portrait sideways, catching the man hard across the stomach with the thick frame. Porchind staggered back as his breath left him in a gust. Suddenly his feet kicked out from under him, and he fell backward with a strangled squeal. The revolver discharged as he hit the floor, the bullet exploding into the fireplace, nicking a chunk out of the brick.

The study door burst open, and Shane Callan charged into the room with a nine-millimeter Smith & Wesson in his hands. He trained the gun on Porchind and smiled a purely predatory smile, gray eyes gleaming.

'I'd drop that peashooter if I were you, sport,' he said, his voice a low, rough caress.

'Where's Rasmussen?' Bryan asked.

'Out front with Deputy Screwup.'

'Bryan!' Rachel exclaimed, rushing into the room, her face white, eyes wide. 'Are you all right? We heard a shot!'

'I'm fine,' he said coolly.

Turning away from her, he hung the portrait of Arthur Drake back in its place, brushing his fingertips across the tarnished brass plate that was affixed to the bottom molding.

'Are you all right?' he asked as they watched Shane haul Porchind to his feet and shove him out into the hall.

'I'm fine.'

'And Addie?'

'Are you kidding? The police are here,' Rachel joked, trying to muster up a laugh of her own and failing. 'She's ecstatic.'

The silence that fell between them was awkward, filled with unspoken questions. Bryan let his gaze drink in the sight of her, memorizing everything about the way she looked at that moment – young and frightened in a baggy T-shirt and jeans, her hair falling around her like a rumpled curtain of silk.

Finally, she broke the quiet, asking a question that had nothing to do with the ones in her heart. 'How did you know they would be here tonight?'

'Oh, I had a hunch. I sort of sent them.'

She gave him a puzzled look.

'I guess I just wanted to clear all this up for you before I left.'

Rachel's heart leapt into her throat. 'You're leaving? Leaving Anastasia?'

'I've been asked to go to Hungary.'

'I see.'

'I wanted to find the gold for you first,' he explained. 'After all, you and Addie deserve it more than Porky and the Rat do.'

Rachel hung her head and sighed. He'd come back here and risked his life for something that didn't exist. All for her. What was she going to do? She would love him with her last breath, but she couldn't afford to go chasing rainbows with him.

She watched as Bryan went to the fireplace and selected the poker from the stand of heavy brass fire irons. Using the handle end, which was shaped like a hammerhead, he rapped it against the brick that Porchind's bullet had struck. The thin layer of brick crumbled and fell away, revealing a surface of shiny gold.

' "Gold is tried by fire," ' he said, ' "brave men by adversity." Seneca.'

Rachel stared in stunned disbelief. She fell to her knees in front of the fireplace and lifted a trembling hand to touch the treasure that had lain hidden all these years, safe and snug behind a wall of false brick.

'Oh, my—It's real,' she said on a soft breath. 'Gold.'

'Yes,' Bryan murmured, watching her. 'A considerable fortune's worth, I'd say, though I admit I don't exactly keep abreast of the market prices. You'll want to call Dylan Harrison. He does a little investment counseling on the side. He can tell you what it's worth in dollars and cents.'

At the moment she didn't need to know what it was worth in dollars and cents. She knew what it was worth. It was the answer to all her financial woes. It meant they wouldn't have to sell Drake House. They wouldn't have to leave Anastasia. Practicality could take a flying leap right out of her life.

She closed her eyes and laughed as giddy joy flooded through her. Sighing, she pressed her cheek to the exposed bar of gold.

'It was really here,' she whispered. 'Like magic.'

'Yes,' Bryan said sadly. 'It's a good thing one of us believed in it.'

14

Bryan turned to quit the room, but the door had swung shut and refused to open when he tried it. He hung his head and let out a slow, measured breath, struggling to rein in his temper. Rachel had made it clear where he fit into her life – nowhere. He wanted only to make a graceful exit, but that privilege was being denied him. He had a feeling he knew why, but he was in no mood for interference from a sixth sense or anything else. Both his pride and his heart were still stinging from Rachel's rejection. He wanted only to leave.

Cursing under his breath, he stood back and gave the door a kick that clearly demonstrated an acquaintance with martial arts. Part of the jamb splintered away, and the door flew open. An odd thud sounded on the far side of the hall, and a vase teetered on its stand.

Rachel watched him go, her eyes wide, her heart pounding. He was leaving, leaving Anastasia, leaving her. The final barrier to their happiness had been eradicated, and he was leaving!

She scrambled to her feet and dashed out of the study and down the hall.

On the porch Deputy Skreawupp and another of Anastasia's finest were reading Porchind and Rasmussen their rights. The pair of erstwhile criminals stood glumly side by side with their hands cuffed behind their backs. Porchind's bowling-ball head was red with indignation. Rasmussen looked as if he would have been stark white even without his greasy makeup. The thin man rolled his shoulders uncomfortably against the straps of the contraption he and his cohort had devised to make the mystic smoke that had floated around him as he had 'haunted' Drake House.

'I never should have listened to you,' Porchind hissed. 'You should have known it was a trap, stupid.'

'A trap,' Rasmussen mumbled miserably, his head lolling from side to side.

'Moron,' Porchind grumbled.

'Clam up, Porky,' Skreawupp ordered, shaking a stubby pencil beneath the man's nose. 'I'll muzzle you like a fat circus bear, and I can do it.'

Shane Callan leaned indolently back against a post, watching the scene with an almost feline smile of amused satisfaction. His hands were tucked casually into the pockets of his black jeans. The butt of his pistol peeked out from under his left arm.

Addie watched the proceedings from Skreawupp's elbow with avid interest.

'I knew they were up to no good,' she said, earning herself a scowl from the sour-faced deputy. 'It took you long enough to figure it out, Deputy Dope.'

'They needed evidence, Addie,' Bryan said.

She waved a hand at him. 'Twaddle.'

'You have the right to remain silent,' the deputy said to Porchind. He shot a dark look at Addie. 'That goes for you, too, honey bun.'

She blew a loud raspberry at him and wound up to sock him one. Rachel caught her by the arm and swung her toward the door. 'Mother, why don't you go in and find a sweater . . . before the deputy decides to charge you with harassment,' she added under her breath as her mother clomped away.

'Miss Lindquist, we'd appreciate it if you'd come down to the station in the morning to make a statement,' the younger deputy said.

'And we'd *really* appreciate it if you left your mother at home,' Skreawupp added. Rachel's narrow look glanced off his double chins as he turned to his captive scoundrels and herded them down the steps. 'All right, you two scum balls, it's the slammer for you. The cooler, the can, the county condo. I've seen your kind a hundred times. You stalk the helpless on little cat feet and strike in the dark of night. Makes me sick.'

'He's one of a kind,' Shane commented mildly as the deputy's voice faded away and the doors slammed on the squad car. He lit a cigarette and sighed a stream of blue smoke into the night air. 'Thank God.'

'Thank you for helping, Mr. Callan,' Rachel said, wrapping her arms around herself in a vain attempt to ward off the damp chill of the night as it seeped through her T-shirt and into her skin.

Shane just shrugged as he pushed himself away from the post. 'That's what friends are for.' His cool gray eyes slid from Rachel to Bryan. 'I'll see you back at Keepsake?'

Bryan nodded. 'Later. Thanks for the hand.'

'You made my day,' Callan said dryly, shooting his friend a handsome grin. He trotted down the front steps and disappeared into the night.

'He's an intriguing man,' Rachel said, more to fill the uncomfortable silence than anything. Bryan was standing less than five feet from her, and yet he felt as distant as the moon – and as cool.

'I have to go pack.' He turned stiffly toward the door.

'Would you like a cup of coffee first?' she asked, stalling for time. She felt like a coward for the first time since she'd stood up to her mother five years earlier.

'No.'

The blasted man wasn't going to make this easy for her, was he? She swallowed a little more of her pride and tried again. 'I'd like to hear the whole story behind the gold and Porchind and everything.'

'Does it matter?' Bryan asked, giving her a sharp look. 'The gold is yours. I wouldn't think you'd care how it got there.'

Rachel sucked in a breath at the blow. 'That's not fair.'

Bryan steeled himself against the hurt he'd caused her. She had dealt her share of it earlier. He gave a careless shrug of his broad shoulders. 'Well, as I've been told time and again,' he said, a sardonic smile twisting his mouth, 'life isn't fair. Now, if you'll excuse me?'

'Bryan.' Rachel abandoned all pretense of subtlety or pride and grabbed at the sleeve of his sweatshirt as he started through the door. She looked up at him with pleading eyes. 'I don't want you to go.'

'That's not what you told me this afternoon,' he said, his expression carefully blank.

'Things were different this afternoon. I was upset and angry and—'

'And now you're rich?' he suggested sarcastically.

Rachel took it on the chin and plowed right ahead. 'I won't have to sell the house. I won't have to worry about the kind of care I can provide for Mother. The gold changes everything.'

He gave her a bleak look. 'Does it?'

'Bryan, I love you,' she said, the beginnings of desperation coloring her voice.

Instead of filling with joy, his earnest blue eyes only grew sad behind his glasses. 'And it took something as solid, as tangible as gold to get you to trust in that love, to get you to believe it can work and last,' he said quietly. 'I wasn't worth taking a chance on before, but now, since you're rich, what the heck? How is that supposed to make me feel, Rachel?'

She didn't answer. She knew how it made him feel. That same horrible, hollow feeling was yawning inside her. At that moment she would have given the lion's share of the gold to be able to take back everything she'd said to him that afternoon.

'Love can't be contingent on financial security,' Bryan said gently. 'It can't be contingent on anything at all. Tell me what happens when the gold runs out? Will you stop believing? Will it no longer be sensible or practical to be in love with me? The vows say for richer or poorer, Rachel. For better or worse. In sickness and in health. They don't say anything about convenience. I sat by and watched someone I loved die. Do you think that was easy or convenient or fun?'

'No,' she whispered, tears clinging to her thick golden lashes.

'No,' he echoed softly, his eyes shadowed with remembered pain. 'I won't stay here because it's suddenly become easy for you to love me, Rachel. There are lots of times when love has to subsist on nothing more than hope and a belief in magic. When you're ready to believe that . . .' His words trailed off on a tired sigh, as if he had already given up on the idea. 'I'll leave you the number of a Mr. Huntingheath in London. He knows how to find me.'

He turned then and went into the house. Rachel's hand fell to her side. Her fingers closed around the memory of touching him, and she raised her fist to press it to her mouth. She watched Bryan go up the grand staircase, but she made no effort to stop him. She wasn't sure if she had the strength or the right to. Instead, she went to the study and curled up in the corner of the leather love seat to think.

To her left, amid the dark bricks of the fireplace, the exposed bar of gold gleamed dully in the soft light. She stared at it dispassionately. It was the answer to all her prayers save two: It couldn't bring her mother's health back, and it couldn't keep Bryan from walking out on her.

What was it worth, then? Nothing. Less than nothing. It would pay her debts and secure her future, but her future would be empty without Bryan and the magic he brought to her life.

Bryan folded his shirts mechanically. Packing was a routine that had long ago become automatic to him. His hands knew what to do. His mind was free to wander.

He had no taste for a trip to Hungary. The work might prove to be a good diversion, but he could dredge up none of his usual enthusiasm. Maybe he would go home first and visit his parents or take a trip to Connecticut and spend some time with his brother J. J. and Genna and their kids.

But thoughts of family only sharpened the ache of loneliness inside him. He wanted a family of his own. He wanted a wife and children and a home he wouldn't be a visitor in. For the second time in his life he had had that kind of happiness within his reach, and again the rainbow had eluded his grasp.

It hurt. Maybe it hurt worse because he believed so strongly that wishes could come true. Maybe Rachel was right in expecting the worst from life. At least then you couldn't be disappointed when that was what you got.

Rachel. He loved her. She loved him. But she wasn't willing to believe in magic, and he wasn't willing to settle for less.

'Being a bit hard on the girl, aren't you, Hennessy?'

Bryan looked up at the sound of the cultured British voice. His gaze went to the cracked mirror above the dresser. In the reflection of the room he could see himself and a shadowy figure standing some distance behind him, near the armoire. The man was tall and slender, an elegant figure in formal attire; a pale, thin man with the insolent bearing of aristocratic breeding. His hair was combed straight back. His suit was immaculate, his bow tie just slightly imperfect – the mark of a true gentleman of his day.

'Archibald Wimsey, I presume,' Bryan said, not exhibiting the least sign of surprise. 'I was wondering when you were going to come out of hiding.'

'Hiding?' Wimsey frowned but chose not to challenge the remark. 'Work to be done, don't you know, dear fellow. Couldn't be the life of the party what with all these good deeds to do, now, could I?'

'Good deeds?'

Wimsey leaned against the armoire as if the thing could actually support his translucent form. He tucked his hands into the pockets of his trousers and scowled up at the ceiling. 'I've been stuck in this wretched house for fifty-nine years, waiting for some great humanitarian act to perform so I could go on to a more appropriate afterlife. Fifty-nine years! Rather the ultimate story of a house guest overstaying his welcome, eh?'

He dropped his gaze back to Bryan and shrugged. 'I wasn't inclined to muck up my chances by showing myself to one and all just so you could get your name into some bloody obscure pseudoscientific journal.'

'In fifty-nine years you haven't had a single opportunity to redeem yourself?' Bryan asked dubiously.

'The closest I came was setting fire to Cornelia Thayer's collection of miniskirts in 1969,' Wimsey reflected with a fond smile of remembrance that faded into a look of disgust. 'The woman possessed thighs to rival the trunks of the great redwoods, don't you know. Unfortunately, eradicating an affront to refined sartorial tastes was not deemed sufficient to get me out of my spiritual exile. To make matters worse, Cornelia took to wearing hot pants.' He shuddered in revulsion at the memory. 'Confined myself to the attic over that ghastly turn of events. Finally drove the Thayers to sell by pouring buckets of ooze down the walls of their bedroom. Don't reckon that garnered me any brownie points in the great beyond,' he added thoughtfully, rubbing his long chin.

'I don't imagine,' Bryan agreed, rolling his eyes. 'What landed you here in the first place?'

Wimsey gave him a shrewd look. 'I think you've figured that one out, chum. You tell me.'

'All right. While your pal Ducky was quietly robbing everyone blind, you let people think you were the gentleman bandit because the ladies thought it was romantic. Unfortunately, the ladies weren't the only ones who believed it. Pig Porchind believed you stole his gold and he—'

Wimsey made a face and held up an insubstantial hand to cut him off. 'Don't let's relive the truly unpleasant past.'

'You didn't know where the gold was, did you?'

'You think I'd be here now if I had?' he asked incredulously, straightening away from the armoire and hovering near the bed. Frowning darkly, he shook out one of Bryan's dress shirts and refolded it to his own satisfaction. 'I'd have bloody well told old Pig where it was and what he could do with it. Ducky had it hidden someplace until it was already too late for me, then he apparently brought the stuff in already disguised as bricks. I hadn't the vaguest idea where it was.'

He directed his frown at Bryan again. 'If I'd figured it out ahead of you and revealed the stuff to Addie or the girl, perhaps I wouldn't still be here.'

'Sorry.'

'Sorry?' Wimsey snorted. 'After fifty-nine years of dead boredom I finally get a shot at redeeming myself. You pinch it, and the best you can do is tell me you're sorry? I say, that's really frightfully inadequate.'

Bryan shrugged helplessly. 'Well, what would you have me do?'

Wimsey smiled brightly and patted Bryan's shoulder. 'Do kiss and make up with the girl. There's a good chap.'

'Rachel?'

'Of course Rachel,' he said irritably. 'Who do you think I mean? I've been playing cupid for you all along, you ungrateful swine. The least you can do is marry her.'

Bryan sighed. 'I'm afraid that's up to her.'

'Bloody hell,' the ghost murmured, crossing his arms over his chest. He shook his head. 'I'm not cut out for this humanitarian work. Never been comfortable with charitable behavior.' He waved a hand as if to ward off a denial that wasn't forthcoming. 'Oh, yes, I gave the odd quid to Oxfam in my day, but all this – this – *personal* stuff.' He shuddered again, his distaste for his task more than apparent. 'All that selflessness goes quite against my grain, I don't mind saying.'

'Probably has something to do with why you're here,' Bryan suggested dryly.

'Don't be glib, Hennessy. It's really quite irritating.'

'Sorry.'

'Don't tell me, tell Rachel,' he insisted. 'Getting the two of you together is my last hope of getting out of here. I did what I could to help her reconcile with Addie, and that didn't solve my dilemma. You've got to be the key. So stop slacking off and do your duty. I'm fed up with being subtle, holding the doors shut and shoving the two of you together. By the way, I was not amused by your little jujitsu demonstration downstairs.'

'Tae kwon do,' Bryan corrected him with a bland smile.

'Don't split hairs,' Wimsey snapped. 'This facetious manner of yours is damned annoying. ''Pon my soul, if I were alive, you'd be giving me a roaring headache. Do make up with the girl and get on with it.'

Bryan arched a brow. 'Does coercion count in the good-deeds category these days?'

Wimsey screwed up his mouth in annoyance. 'You really are too flip by half. Just wait until you get stuck in an alternate plane of existence. We'll see how amusing you are then.'

Bryan sighed and put on his most contrite look. He wasn't in the mood for jocularity. Encountering Wimsey had lifted his spirits, but the fact remained, he was losing Rachel. Their difference of philosophy was a wedge between them, and he could see no way over, under, or around it. The next move had to be hers.

'I'm truly sorry, Wimsey. I've done all I can. The rest is up to no one but Rachel.'

'That's what you think,' the ghost muttered darkly.

A knock sounded at the door. Rachel's voice floated through. 'Bryan? Can I come in?'

'Yes.' At least he would get the satisfaction of seeing her face when he introduced her to Wimsey, he thought with a wry smile. He went on folding clothes as she swung the door open and stepped inside the room.

'Who were you talking to?'

He opened his mouth to tell her as he straightened. His gaze went to Rachel's reflection in the mirror, then his own, then – Wimsey was gone. A black scowl pulled his brows together. He pushed his glasses up on his nose and grumbled, 'Myself.'

'Oh.' Rachel looked confused. 'That's funny. I thought I heard another voice.'

'I do that when I'm talking to myself,' he said irritably. 'I make up another voice. It makes the conversation seem so much more realistic.'

'That's kind of odd.'

'I'm an odd person,' he said curtly, snapping his suitcase shut and reaching for another. 'What do you expect?'

'I expect you to give me a straight answer,' Rachel said, more than a little irritated by his nasty mood. She'd come there in contrition, after all. The least he could be was polite.

'Fine,' Bryan said, abandoning his packing. 'You want a straight answer? I was talking to a ghost. I was talking to a man who was killed in this house fifty-nine years ago. Archibald Wimsey. He was here, but now you can't see him, so, as we all know, he must not really exist. He's just a figment of my overactive, irresponsible imagination.'

Rachel winced. 'I'm sorry I called you irresponsible. We have different ways of looking at things, you and I. We have different ways of dealing with problems.'

'But I do deal with them, Rachel. I don't just brush them off and expect you to clean up the mess.'

'I know,' she mumbled, head down.

'Do you?' he asked sharply.

She looked up at him, nibbling the corner of her lip. 'I'm willing to learn,' she said sincerely. 'Are you willing to show me?'

Bryan sighed wearily, his wide shoulders sagging in defeat. 'I've been trying to show you all along.'

Rachel thought back across the memories she had stored up in the past weeks, memories of Bryan intervening when things had been going badly between herself and Addie, of his silly diversionary tactics that had kept her from dwelling on her problems. She thought of the way he had come back to find the gold for her and to trap Porchind and Rasmussen. If it hadn't been for him, she probably would have sold Drake House to the pair and been glad to get what little she could for the place.

Bryan had looked out for her all along. He was simply so unorthodox in his methods, she hadn't realized what he was up to. Still, she had fallen in love with him in spite of his eccentricities, in spite of thinking he was just another hopeless dreamer. Now she loved him even more.

She put her hands on his solid forearms and looked up at him with her heart in her eyes. 'I love you, Bryan. You said you needed me to believe in magic. I believe I love you. I believed that even when I was sure you were the last thing I needed in my life. Isn't that a kind of magic – believing in something even when you think you shouldn't?'

'I guess so,' he whispered, lifting a hand to brush at the soft, wild tendrils of spun gold that curled around her face. She was so lovely, and he loved her so much, the thought of leaving her was like cutting out his own heart.

'I do need you in my life, Bryan,' she said, leaning closer. 'I need you more than all the gold in California. Please don't leave me.'

As he stared down at her, his blue eyes misty, there was a strange scraping noise in the hall. It sounded suspiciously like heavy furniture being pushed across the floor. Rachel's eyes rounded as something bumped against the closed door. She snuggled closer to Bryan, her arms sneaking around his lean waist.

'What was that?' she asked weakly.

Bryan smiled and shook his head. 'Just someone trying to make sure I don't leave you.'

She gave him a puzzled look.

'Don't worry about it,' he said, giving in to the powerful longing. 'I don't have any intention of leaving you for the next hundred years or so.'

Rachel's spirits soared. 'You mean that?'

'I do.'

'What about Hungary and Mr. Huntinglodge?'

'Neither one of them is as important to me as you are. Will you marry me, Rachel?' he asked softly.

'I will,' she whispered, tilting her face up to meet his kiss.

His lips were warm and solid against hers, masculine and welcoming, and trembling just enough to bring a lump to her throat. She melted into his arms, never questioning the sensation of coming home. This was where she belonged. This was where she was safe and warm. This was where she wanted to spend the rest of her days – in the arms of a man who brought magic to her life, who lightened every darkness and put a rainbow in her heart.

'I say, good show.'

Rachel bolted in Bryan's arms, but he held her fast. He raised his head to shoot the intruder a meaningful look. 'No show. Beat it, Wimsey.'

'Wimsey?' Rachel asked, goose bumps pebbling her flesh to the texture of sandpaper.

Bryan nodded, tilting his head in the direction of the mirror that hung above the old dresser. Rachel turned and looked. Her mouth dropped open so hard, it was a wonder it didn't put a dent in her chest.

There he stood – the figment of her mother's imagination, the whimsy Bryan had refused to give up on, the ghost she didn't believe in. His image was slightly translucent. He was handsome and smiling, decked out in formal attire. And he was holding a rose.

Her heart skipped a beat as her gaze fastened on the perfect white bud of the flower. Then her eyes went to the eyes of the man who held it. Wimsey nodded in answer to the questions she couldn't quite force into words. It had been Wimsey all along.

Now he held the rose out toward her. Rachel turned away from the mirror, twisting in Bryan's arms to face the apparition that stood by the armoire.

'Thank you,' she whispered, taking the flower by the stem.

'Thank *you*, my dear,' he murmured in return, his pale eyes shining as he handed her the rose.

Then, in a flash of brilliant white light, he was gone.

'Where did he go?' Rachel asked, never once questioning that he had been there.

'Where he belongs,' Bryan said with a soft smile. 'Where he belongs.'

'Then we're alone?'

He nodded.

With a beguiling smile, she wound her arms around his neck. 'It seems like now might be a good time for you to start teaching me all about magic.'

'Hmm, yes,' Bryan agreed, his eyes twinkling as he pulled her with him to the bed. They tumbled across the coverlet, laughing and breathless, Rachel's hair spilling around them like moonlight.

Bryan kissed her cheeks and her eyelids and the corners of her mouth.

'Why don't we start with making the earth move?' he suggested. 'That's a trick you seem to have a natural aptitude for.'

Rachel grinned and hugged him, loving him with every fiber of her being. He might have been slightly crazy, and he might have been something of a puzzle, but he was all hers, and he would fill her heart with magic every day of her life.

She threaded her fingers through his tawny hair and pulled him down for a long, slow kiss that left him with only one reverent word to say.

'Abracadabra.'

LUCKY'S LADY

'*Le coeur a ses raisons que la raison ne connaît point.*'
The heart has its reasons that reason knows nothing of.

French Proverb

1

'You want to do what, *chère?*'

Serena Sheridan took a deep breath and tried again. 'I need to hire a guide to take me into the swamp.'

Old Lawrence Gauthier laughed as if at the punch line of some grand joke. His voice rang out through the shop, drowning out the Cajun music coming from the radio on the cluttered shelf behind him as well as the noises of the all-star professional wrestling emanating from the black and white television that sat on the counter. Lawrence sat on a stool behind the counter, his slender legs crossed at the knees, slouching in a posture reminiscent of an egret on a perch – thin shoulders hunched, head low between them. His face was narrow with a prominent nose and eyes like jet beads. His skin was tanned dark and lined like old leather.

His laughter ended in a fit of coughing. He reached for his cigarette makings and shook his head. 'What for you wanna do dat, *chère?* You goin' after dem crawfish, you?' He laughed again, trying to shake his head and lick the edge of his cigarette paper at the same time.

Serena smoothed her hands down the front of the immaculate oyster-colored linen blazer she wore over a matching pencil-slim skirt. She supposed she hardly looked dressed to walk into such a place, much less make the request she had. 'No, I'm not interested in fishing.'

She looked around the store, hoping to spot someone else who might be able to help her. It was the middle of the day and Lawrence appeared to be the only person tending the dingy, dimly lit sporting goods store, though some banging noises were coming from behind him, from a room Serena knew to be an even dingier workshop where men fussed with their boats, drank beer, swapped outrageous tales, and passed girlie magazines around.

She knew because she had once snuck in there as a girl. A headstrong child, she had taken exception to being denied the chance to go in with her grandfather and had stowed away inside his bass boat under a canvas tarp. Her vocabulary had gained a number of choice words that day that their housekeeper had later attempted to wash out of her mouth with soap.

'I need to find my grandfather, Mr. Gauthier,' she said. 'Apparently he's gone out to his fish camp. I need someone to take me to him.'

177

Lawrence looked at her, narrowing his eyes. Finally he shook a gnarled finger at her. 'Hey, you dat Sheridan girl what left to be a doctor, no?'
'Yes.'
'Yeah, yeah! *Mais yeah!*' He chuckled, tickled with his powers of recollection. 'You lookin' for Big Giff.'
'Yes, but I need someone to take me. I need a guide.'
He shook his head, still smiling at her as if she were a dear but infinitely dimwitted child. '*Non, cherie*, all what fishin' guides we got 'round here is gone busy now till Monday. Lotta sports coming down to fish these days. 'Sides, ain't nobody crazy 'nough go out to Giff's. Go out there, get their head shot off, them!'
He sucked on his little cigarette, holding it between thumb and forefinger in an unconsciously European fashion. Half of it was gone before he exhaled. He reached out with his free hand and patted Serena's cheek. 'Ah, *ma jolie fille*, ain't nobody crazy 'nough to go out to Big Giff's.'
As he said it, a loud bang sounded in the shop behind him, followed by a virulent French oath. Lawrence went still with his hand halfway to a tin ashtray on the counter, an unholy light coming into his eyes, a little smile tugging at a corner of his mouth. 'Well, mebbe there's somebody. Jes' how bad you wanna go, *chère?*'
Serena swallowed the knot of apprehension in her throat, clasping her hands together in front of her like a schoolgirl. Now was not the time for a faint heart. 'It's imperative. I have to go.'
He bent his head a little to one side and gave a Gallic shrug, then shouted over his shoulder. 'Étienne! *Viens ici!*'
What Serena had braced herself for she wasn't sure, but it certainly wasn't the man who filled the doorway. The impact of his sudden presence had the same effect as being hit with the shock wave of an explosion, jolting her chest with a hollow thud and literally making her knees go weak – a phenomenon she had heretofore not believed in.
Her first impression was of raw power. Broad shoulders, bulging biceps. His chest, bare and gleaming with a sheen of sweat, was massive, wide, and thick, slabs of hard muscle beneath taut, tanned skin. The strong V of his torso narrowed to a slender waist, a stomach corrugated with muscle and dusted with black hair that disappeared beneath the low-riding waistband of faded green fatigue pants. Serena was certain she could live to be a hundred and never find a more prime example of the male animal.
She raised her eyes to his face and felt a strange shiver pass over her from head to toe, making her scalp tighten and her fingers tingle. He stared at her from under sleepy lids with large, unblinking amber eyes, eyes like a panther's. His brow was heavy and straight, his nose bold and slightly aquiline. His mouth did the most damage to her nervous system, however. It was wide, with lips so masterfully carved, so incredibly

sensuous they would have looked perfect on a high-priced call girl. The effect of that mouth on a face so masculine – all lean planes and hard angles and five-o'clock shadow – was blatantly sexual.

He regarded her with a subtle disdain that suggested he didn't much care for women other than to bed them – something he appeared to be capable of doing on a more than regular basis. Pulling a cigarette from behind his ear, he planted it in the corner of his mouth, lit it, and said something to Lawrence Gauthier in rapid Cajun French, a patois no Parisian could begin to understand. The dialect had nearly been eradicated by the Louisiana school system decades before. And although it was making a comeback of sorts due to the latest craze for all things Cajun, it was still not widely spoken. This man spoke it as if it were his primary language.

Having grown up in Louisiana's French Triangle, Serena had picked up the odd word and phrase, but he spoke too quickly for her to understand anything more than the implication. That was clear enough by Gauthier's reaction – another laughing and coughing fit and a slap on the shoulder for his barbarian friend.

Serena felt her cheeks heat with embarrassment as the man sauntered to the end of the counter and leaned a hip against it, all the while assessing her blatantly with those lazy amber eyes. She could feel his gaze like a tangible caress, drifting insolently over her breasts, the curve of her waist, the flare of her hip, the long length of her legs. She had never imagined it possible to feel so naked while dressed in a business suit.

He took a leisurely drag on his cigarette, exhaled, and delivered another line to keep Gauthier in stitches. Serena gave him her coolest glare, defending herself with hauteur. 'Excuse me, but I was raised to believe it is extremely rude to carry on conversations not all those around you can understand.'

One black brow sketched upward sardonically and the corner of that remarkable mouth curled ever so slightly. He looked like her idea of the devil on steroids. When he spoke to her his tone was a low, throaty purr that stroked her senses like velvet. 'I told him you don' look like you're sellin' it or givin' it away,' he said, the words rolling out of his mouth with an accent as rich as Cajun gumbo. 'So what could I possibly want with you? I have no interest in *américaine ladies*.'

He drawled the last word with stinging contempt. Serena tugged at the lapels of her blazer, straightening the uniform of her station. Her chin went up another notch above the prim collar of her fuchsia silk blouse. 'I can assure you I have no *interest* in you either.'

He pushed himself away from the counter and moved toward her with the arrogant grace of a born athlete. Serena stubbornly stood her ground as he stepped near enough for her to feel the heat of his big body. Her heart fluttered in her throat as he stared down at her and raised a hand to smooth it back over her hair.

'That's not what your eyes are tellin' me, *chère catin*.'

Serena dragged in a ragged breath and held it, feeling as if she were going to explode from sheer fury. She slapped his hand away and took a step back from him. 'I didn't come here to be insulted or manhandled. I came here to hire a guide, Mister—'

'Doucet,' he supplied. 'Étienne Doucet. Folks call me Lucky.'

Serena vaguely remembered a Lucky Doucet from high school. He'd been several classes ahead of her, an athlete, a loner with a reputation as a bad boy. The girls whose main interest in school had been guys had swooned at the mere mention of his name. Serena's interests had lain elsewhere.

She looked at him now and thought whatever reputation he had sown back then he had certainly cultivated since. He looked like the incarnation of the word *trouble*. She had to be half mad to even consider hiring him. But then she thought of Gifford. She had to see him, had to do what she could to find out what had made him leave Chanson du Terre, had to do her best to try to convince him to come home. As tough as Gifford Sheridan liked to pretend he was, he was still a seventy-eight-year-old man with a heart condition.

'I'm Serena Sheridan,' she said in her most businesslike tone.

Lucky Doucet blinked at her. A muscle tensed, then loosened in his jaw. 'I know who you are,' he said, an oddly defensive note in his voice. Serena dismissed it as unimportant.

'I came here to hire a guide, Mr. Doucet. Gifford Sheridan is my grandfather. I need someone to take me out to his cabin. Mr. Gauthier has informed me that all the more reputable guides are booked up for the weekend, which apparently leaves you. Are you interested in the job or not?'

Lucky moved back to lean negligently against the counter again. Behind him, Lawrence had switched off his wrestling program in favor of live entertainment. In the background Iry LeJeune sang 'La Jolie Blonde' in crackling French over the radio. *The pretty blonde.* How apropos. He took a deep pull on his cigarette, sucking the smoke into the very corners of his lungs, as if it might purge the feelings shaking loose and stirring inside him.

When he had stepped from the back room and seen her he had felt as if he'd taken a vicious blow to the solar plexus. *Shelby.* The shock had dredged up memories and emotions like mud and dead vines churning up from the bayou in the wake of an outboard motor – pain, hate, fear all swirling furiously inside him. The pain and hate were old companions. The fear was for the control he felt slipping, sliding through his grasp like a wet rope. The feelings assaulted him still, even though he told himself this wasn't the woman from his past, but her sister, someone he had never had any contact with. Nor did he want to. They were twins, after all, maybe not perfectly identical, but cut from the same cloth.

He stared at the woman before him, trying to set all personal feelings aside to concentrate on only the physical aspects of her. It shouldn't have been difficult to do; she was beautiful. From the immaculate state of her honey-colored hair in its smooth French twist to the tips of her beige pumps, she radiated class. There wasn't anything about her that shouldn't have been carved in alabaster and put in a museum. His gaze roamed over her face, an angel's face, with its delicate bone structure and liquid dark eyes – eyes that were presently flashing fire at him – and desire twisted inside him.

He swore, throwing his cigarette to the battered wood floor and grinding it out with the toe of his boot. Without looking, he reached behind the counter and pulled out a bottle of Jack Daniel's, helping himself to a generous swig. Lawrence said nothing, but frowned and glanced away, tilting his head in silent reproof. Resenting the twinge of guilt pinching him somewhere in the vicinity of where his conscience had once resided, Lucky put the bottle back.

Damn. He damned Gifford Sheridan for having granddaughters that looked like heaven on earth. He damned women in general and himself in particular. If he had a lick of sense he would send Miss Serena packing. He would go about his own business and let the Sheridans do what they would.

That was the kind of life he had chosen to live, solitary, and yet other lives kept drifting into his. He didn't want to be touched. He didn't need the trouble he knew was brewing on the Sheridan plantation, Chanson du Terre, didn't need the reminder of past pain. But Giff had dragged him into it to a certain extent already and there was too much riding on the situation for him to decline playing so slight a role in the drama.

He cursed himself for caring. He had thought himself beyond it, thought the capacity to care had been burned out of him by the acidic quality of his experiences. But it was still there, which meant he had to find the strength to deal with it. God help him.

Serena gave him one last scathing glare and turned on her slim, expensive heel, heading for the street entrance of the store. Lucky swore under his breath and went after her, catching her by the arm.

'Where you goin', sugar? I never said I wouldn't take you.'

She looked pointedly at the big dirty hand circling her upper arm, then turned that defiant gaze up to his face. 'Maybe I won't take *you*, Mr. Doucet.'

'The way I see it, you don't have much of a choice. Ain't nobody else gonna take you out to Giff's.' He laughed without humor. 'Ain't nobody else crazy enough.'

'But you are?'

He smiled like a crocodile and leaned down toward her until his mouth hovered only a few inches above the sweet temptation of her lips. 'That's right,' he whispered. 'I'm over the edge. I might do anything. Ask anyone 'round this town here. They'll all tell you the same thing – *Il n'a pas rien il va pas faire*. There's nothing he won't do. That Lucky Doucet, he's one bad crazy son, him.'

'Well, I'm a psychologist,' she said with a saccharine-sweet smile. 'So we ought to get along just peachy, shouldn't we?'

He let go of her arm as if she had just told him she had leprosy. The expression of smug male arrogance abruptly disappeared, and his face became blank and unreadable. He turned and strode for a side door that stood open and led directly onto a dock.

Serena stood a moment, trying to gather some strength, her gaze on Lucky Doucet's broad bare back as he walked away. Her limbs felt like jelly and her stomach was quivering inside. She could feel old Lawrence staring at her, but she didn't move. She'd never had such a . . . primal reaction to a man. She was a sophisticated, educated woman, a woman who prided herself on her ability to maintain control in every situation. But that foundation of control was trembling in the wake of Lucky Doucet, and she didn't like it. He was rude and arrogant and . . . The other words that came to mind were far too flattering. What difference did it make what he looked like? He was a Neanderthal.

He was also her only hope of reaching Giff. And she had to reach him. Someone had to find out what was going on. Shelby claimed she hadn't a clue as to why Gifford had suddenly deserted the plantation in favor of living out in the swamp. It might have been nothing more than a matter of Giff getting fed up with having Shelby and her family underfoot while their new house was under construction, but it might have been something more. It wasn't like him to leave during a busy time of year, simply turning the reins of the sugarcane plantation over to his manager.

Shelby had peevishly suggested Gifford was getting senile. Serena couldn't imagine her grandfather as anything other than sharp as a tack, but then, she hadn't actually seen him in a while. Her practice in Charleston kept her too busy for many visits home. She had been looking forward to this one, looking forward to simply enjoying her ancestral home in all its springtime glory. Then Shelby had greeted her at the door with news of Gifford's defection to the swamp.

He'd been out there two weeks. Two weeks with no word, and Shelby had done nothing about it except complain.

'What did you expect me to do?' she had asked. 'Go out there after him? I have two children to raise and a real estate business to manage and a husband, and I'm the chairperson of the Junior League drive for canned goods for the starving peasants of Guatemala. I have responsibilities, Serena! I can't just jump in a boat and go out there! Not that he would ever listen to a word I have to say anyway. And you can't expect Mason to go out there. You know how beastly Gifford is to him. I'm just at my wit's end trying to deal with him. You're the psychologist. You go out there and talk some sense into that hard head of his.'

182

Go out there. Into the swamp. Serena's blood had run cold at the suggestion. It ran cold now at the thought. But she was just angry enough and stubborn enough to get past her fear for the moment. She had stormed from the house to go in search of a guide without even bothering to change her clothes. She wouldn't allow herself to dwell on her fear. She had to see her grandfather and there was only one way to do that. She had to go out into the one place she thought of as hell on earth, and the only man available to take her had just walked away.

Serena rushed after Lucky Doucet, struggling to hurry in her narrow skirt and shoes that had not been intended for walking on rough planking. The midday sun was blinding as she stepped out onto the dock. The stench of dirty water and gasoline hung in the thick, still air. Lucky stood at the open door to the workshop.

'We haven't discussed your fee,' Serena said, ignoring the possibility that he had changed his mind about taking her. She struggled for an even breath as she faced his chest. Even up close he looked as if he were cast in bronze rather than flesh and bone.

He looked down his nose at her with an expression that suggested she had just insulted his mother. 'I have no need of your money,' he said contemptuously.

Serena rolled her eyes and lifted her hands in a gesture of exasperated surrender. 'Pardon me for thinking you might like an honest wage for an honest job. How bourgeois of me.'

He ignored her, bending to pick up a heavy cardboard box full of oily black motor parts. He lifted it as though it weighed no more than a kitten and set it on a workbench to sort through it. His attitude was one of dismissal and irritating in the extreme.

'Why are you making this so difficult?' Serena asked.

He turned his head and gave her a nasty, sardonic smile. 'Because I'm a difficult kind of guy. I thought you might have figured that out by now. You're an intelligent woman.'

'Frankly, I'm amazed you would credit a woman with having a brain. You strike me as the sort of man who sees women as being useful for only one purpose.'

'I said you were intelligent, not useful. I won't know how useful you are until I have you naked beneath me.'

Heat flared through Serena like a flash fire. She attributed it to anger. Certainly it had nothing to do with the sudden image of lying tangled in the sheets with this barbarian. She crossed her arms in front of her defensively and made a show of looking all around them before returning her belligerent gaze to Lucky. 'Pardon me, I was just checking to see if I had somehow been transported back into the Stone Age. Are you proposing to hit me over the head with a dinosaur bone and drag me back to your cave, Conan?'

183

He raised a warning finger, his brows drawing together ominously over glittering eyes. 'You got a mouth on you, *chère*.'

He shuffled toward her, backing her up against the door frame. Serena managed to swallow her first gasp, but couldn't help the second one as his spread thighs brushed the outsides of hers. He braced his forearms on the wood above her head and leaned down close. His breath was warm against her cheek and scented with the smoky taint of tobacco and whiskey.

'I have *never* forced a woman,' Lucky said, his voice low and soft, the molten gold of his eyes burning into Serena's. 'I never have to.'

He stared at her mouth with rapt fascination. It was rosy and soft-looking and he wanted badly to taste it, but he denied himself the luxury. She was a spoiled society bitch and he wanted nothing to do with her. He'd been burned badly enough to know better. *Dieu*, he'd learned his first lesson at the hands of her twin! To get that close again was to give in entirely to the demons of insanity.

Still, desire ribboned through him, as warm as a fever in his blood. The subtle, expensive scent of her perfume lured him closer. He dropped his head down near the curve of her shoulder and battled the urge to nuzzle the tender spot just below her ear and above the prim stand-up collar of her dark pink blouse. He could feel his sex growing warm and heavy.

'I'm hiring you as a guide,' she said through her teeth, her voice trembling with rage or desire or both. 'Not for stud service.'

Lucky mentally thanked her for breaking the spell. He stepped back, cocking one hip and hooking a thumb in the waistband of his pants. He gave her a devilish grin. 'Why not, angel? I'd give you the ride of your life.'

She glared at him in utter disgust and walked away to stand at the edge of the dock, her slender back rigid. He had no doubt irreparably offended her ladylike sensibilities, he thought. Fine. That was exactly what he wanted. The more emotional distance he put between himself and a woman like Serena Sheridan, the better. His mother would have peeled the hide off him for talking that way to a woman, but this was more than just a matter of manners, it was a matter of survival.

He scooped up the box of motor parts and started down the pier with it, calling over his shoulder as he went. 'So, you comin', *chère*, or what? I don't have all day.'

Serena turned and stared in disbelief as he headed down the worn dock. She noticed for the first time that his hair was nearly as long as hers, tied in a short queue at the back of his thick neck with a length of leather boot lace. A pirate. That was what he reminded her of – in looks *and* attitude.

'You're leaving *now*?' she said, once again rushing to catch up with him.

He didn't answer her. It was perfectly obvious he meant to leave.

Serena cursed Lucky Doucet and spike heels in the same breath as she picked up her pace. Talk about your grade-A bastards, this guy took the prize. And she wanted to be the one to personally pin the medal on him, preferably directly onto that bare boilerplate chest of his. If they were in Charleston, never in a million years would she have put up with being treated the way he was treating her. She had too much sense and self-respect to fall for that tame-the-rogue-male syndrome, no matter how overwhelmingly sexy the rogue happened to be. But they weren't in Charleston. They were in South Louisiana, at the edge of the Atchafalaya Swamp, some of the wildest, most remote swampland in the United States. And Lucky Doucet wasn't some button-down executive or construction worker she could bring to heel with a cool look. He was a breed unto himself and only marginally more civilized than the bayou country around them.

Abruptly, the heel of one of her pumps caught between planks in the dock and gave way, nearly pitching Serena headfirst off the pier and into the oily water. She swore aloud as she stumbled awkwardly, hampered by the narrow skirt around her knees, just managing to catch her balance before it was too late.

Lucky stopped and turned toward her with a look of mock affront. 'Why, Miz Serena, such language! What will the ladies at the Junior League think?'

She narrowed her eyes and snarled at him as she hopped on her ruined shoe and pulled the other one off. The instant she put her foot down, she ran a sliver into it, but she refused to cry out or even acknowledge the pain. She limped up to Lucky, struggling to maintain some semblance of dignity.

'I'm not prepared to leave just now, Mr. Doucet,' she said primly. 'I was thinking more along the lines of tomorrow morning.'

He shrugged without the least show of concern. A brilliant white grin split his features. 'Well, that's too bad, sugar, 'cause if you're leavin' with me, you're leavin' now.'

2

It was a no-win situation. If she stood her ground, she lost her ride. If she gave in, it was another blow to her pride and another peg up for Mr. Macho's overinflated ego. Serena took a slow, deep breath of air that was as dense as steam and tasted metallic and bitter. Maintaining as much of her dignity as she could, she lifted her slim nose and gave Lucky a long, cool look.

His eyes flashed as gold as doubloons behind ridiculously long paintbrush lashes. One corner of his lush mouth curled like the end of a cat's tail. 'What'sa matter, *chère?* You'd rather give orders than take them? Well, I'm not your hired boy. You want a ride, then you climb in the boat. You wanna boss somebody around, you can take a hike.'

Serena was certain she could actually feel her temper start to boil the blood in her veins. She clenched her jaw and fought a valiant battle to keep the lid on when all she wanted to do was tell Lucky Doucet to take a long walk off a short pier. Despite her name, her apparent serenity was little more than a shield, a defense mechanism, protective camouflage. All her life she'd had to struggle with strong doses of Sheridan temper and stubbornness. Now she wrestled one into submission with the other. The man was doing his best to make her angry, so she stubbornly refused to lose her temper.

'You are a remarkably obnoxious man, Mr. Doucet,' she observed in the calmest of voices, as if she were commenting on nothing more interesting than the weather.

'I always try to excel.'

'How admirable.'

'So are you comin'?' He set his box down on the dock and sat beside it, dangling his long legs off the pier.

'I'll need to stop by Chanson du Terre for a few things. You wouldn't have any objection to that, would you?'

He gave her a flat look.

Serena motioned impatiently to the suit she was wearing. 'You don't really expect me to travel out into the swamp dressed this way, do you?'

He scowled and grumbled as he lowered himself into his boat. '*Non.*

Come on, then. I been here too long already. Just look at the trouble I got myself into, havin' to haul you around.'

Serena moved to the edge of the dock and looked down. It was then that the full folly of what she was about to do hit her. Lucky's boat was no more than twelve feet in length, slender as a pea pod, and it looked about as stable as a floating leaf. Sitting in it would put her no more than an arm's length from the black water of the bayou.

Fear rose up in her throat and wedged there like a tennis ball. What was the matter with her? Had she completely lost her mind? She was about to put her life in the hands of a man she wouldn't sit next to on a bus and trust him to take her into the deep swamp in a boat that looked about as seaworthy as her broken shoe.

The swamp. Where anything could happen. Where people could get lost and never be found.

A chill raced over her flesh, settling into her arms and legs in trembling pools. She clenched her jaw and held her breath, forgetting every relaxation technique she taught her own patients. It had been too long since she'd been assaulted by this fear. The strength of it took her by surprise. It swelled and shook her, crowding at the back of her throat like a scream demanding release.

Lucky stood in the pirogue, watching her, annoyed by her dawdling. Then the color drained out of her face and his annoyance was replaced by something he refused to name. Serena Sheridan had come across as a lady who could handle herself in most situations. She had stood up to him better than most men did. Now she looked like a piece of porcelain about to crack from some fierce internal pressure. Something deep inside him responded to that, commiserated with it.

He ground his teeth, resenting the feeling and giving in to it at the same time. As hardened as he liked to think he was, he couldn't just stand there and watch her fall apart. He told himself it was because he didn't want to have to deal with a woman in hysterics. Besides, he had already decided the safest thing for him was to keep her half mad at him all the time. A man stayed wary of a snake poised to strike; it was the ones that appeared to be docile and dozing in the sun that were dangerous.

'You don' like my boat, *chère*?' he drawled, an unmistakable note of challenge in his voice.

'A – um—' Serena pulled herself out of her trance with difficulty, trying to focus not on her memory but on the boat and the man standing in it leaning indolently against a long push-pole. 'It's not exactly what I had in mind. Don't you have something a little . . . bigger?'

'Like a yacht?' he asked sarcastically. 'This ain't Saks Fifth Avenue, sugar. I don't have a selection for you to try on for size. Now, are you gonna get on down here or do I get to spend the rest of the day lookin' up your skirt?'

A welcome surge of reckless anger warmed the chill that had shaken

Serena from within. She narrowed her eyes as she pressed her knees together demurely and pulled her slim skirt tightly around them. Clutching her purse and shoe in one hand, she lowered herself awkwardly to the rough planks of the dock, dropping her legs over the edge and grimacing as she felt her pantyhose run all the way down the back of one leg.

She looked down at the pirogue bobbing gently on the oily water and a second wave of apprehension rose up to her tonsils. She hadn't gone out on the bayou in a boat of any kind in fifteen years. She doubted she would have felt safe on the *Queen Elizabeth II*, let alone this simple shell of cypress planking. Still, why couldn't he at least have had a nice big bass boat with a motor on it? Nobody used pirogues anymore . . . except Lucky Doucet.

'My pirogue is all the boat I need,' Lucky said as he reached up for her. 'What'd you think – that I'd go around in a cabin cruiser on the off chance I might have to give some belle a ride somewhere she hadn't oughta be going in the first place?'

Serena flashed him a glare. 'No. I was just hoping against hope that you weren't as uncivilized as you appear to be.'

He laughed as his big hands closed around her slender waist. Serena's eyes went wide with surprise as his thumbs slid upward and brushed the undersides of her breasts, sending sparks shooting through her. She gave a little squeal of protest as he lifted her down into the boat. The pirogue rocked beneath his spread feet and she sacrificed pride for panic, dropping her shoe and purse and grabbing on to Lucky's biceps for support.

For an instant she clung to him as if he were the only thing keeping her from falling into the gaping jaws of hell, and in that instant the hard masculine contours of his body branded hers. Every line and plane of muscle etched itself into her memory, never to be forgotten. Her breasts pressed against his upper rib cage, her belly arched into his groin as his big hands splayed across the small of her back, holding her close. His thighs were as solid as oak trees against hers. A shiver of primitive awareness shimmied down her back as she looked up at him.

He flashed her a smile that would have given the devil goose bumps. 'Oh, I'm every bit as uncivilized as I look.' His voice dropped to that throaty purr that set all her nerve endings humming like tuning forks. 'You gonna try to do somethin' 'bout that, *chère?* You gonna try to domesticate me?'

The suggestion elicited an involuntary trill of excitement inside her. It was like a starburst of sensation deep in her belly, and Serena cursed it for the foolishness she knew it was. Any woman who took on the task of domesticating Lucky Doucet was just asking for trouble. Still, she couldn't seem to quell the feeling as she looked up at him, at his hard, beard-shadowed jaw and that decadent mouth. She steeled herself against it, pushing herself back from him. He let her put an inch of space between them, but only after letting her know he could have held her there all day if he'd been of a mind to.

'Domesticate you?' Serena said derisively, arching a delicate brow. 'Couldn't I just have you neutered?'

'No need.' He gave her a little push that landed her on the plank seat of the pirogue with an unceremonious thump, and turned to get his box of motor parts. 'I wouldn't touch you with a ten-foot pole, *lady*.'

'That's the first good news I've had today,' Serena grumbled, ignoring the twinge of disappointment that nipped her feminine ego. Ignoring, too, the obvious comparison to be made between Lucky Doucet and a ten-foot pole.

She fanned herself with her hand, feeling suddenly flushed, and watched as Lucky lifted his box off the dock, back muscles bunching and sliding beneath his taut, dark skin. He settled the box in the bow of the boat, then moved gracefully toward the stern, stepping over the jig and over the seat, carelessly rocking the tippy pirogue.

Serena's fingers wrapped around the edge of the seat like C clamps, and her gaze drifted longingly down the pier to a shiny aluminum boat. It seemed huge and luxurious compared to the homemade pirogue. A fat man wearing a black New Orleans Saints cap and a plaid shirt with the sleeves cut off sat at the back of it, jerking the rope on the outboard motor.

'You might think about joining the twentieth century sometime soon,' Serena said, shooting Lucky a sweet smile. 'People use motors nowadays.'

Lucky stared at the gas and oil bleeding into the water from the outboard as the fat man yanked on the rope. He frowned, brows pulling low over his eyes as he took up his push-pole. 'Not me.'

He poled the pirogue away from the dock and let the nose turn south.

Serena jerked around, looking up at him over her shoulder with alarm. 'This isn't the way to Chanson du Terre or Gifford's fish camp. Just where do you think you're taking me, Mr. Doucet?'

Lucky scowled at her, but lifted his gaze quickly to avoid the sight of her breasts straining against the fine silk of her blouse. 'I got other things to do besides haul your pretty face up and down the bayou.'

It was apparently all the answer he was going to give her. He had set his face in an expression that declared the subject closed, and Serena decided not to push her luck. After all, he wasn't running a taxi service. She had no claim on his time. Considering his attitude, it was a wonder he had agreed to take her at all.

She faced forward and tried to concentrate on the scenery instead of the sinuous feel of the boat sliding through the dark water. They were at the south edge of town, and the only buildings along the banks of the bayou were the occasional bait shop and a couple of dilapidated tar-paper shacks on stilts with boathouses made of rusting corrugated metal.

A spindly-legged blue heron stood among the cattails near the bank, watching them pass. Serena focused on it as if it were the subject of a painting, its graceful form set against a backdrop of orange-blossomed trumpet creeper and clusters of dark green ferns. Rising in the background, hackberry trees reached their arms up to a china-blue sky and live oak dripped their tattered banners of dusty gray Spanish moss.

Their destination eventually became clear as Lucky poled toward the bank and a wharf hung with barnacle-encrusted tires to buffer its edge. The structure that rose up on stilts some distance behind it was as big as a barn, an unremarkable clapboard building with peeling white paint and a sign hanging above the gallery that spelled out MOSQUITO MOUTON's in two-foot-high red letters. Rusted tin signs advertising various brands of beer were nailed all along the side of the building above a long row of screened windows. Even though it was only the middle of the day, cars were parked on the crushed-shell lot and Zydeco music drifted out through the double screen doors in swells of sound accented by occasional shouts and laughter.

'A *bar?*' Serena questioned imperiously. She looked up at Lucky, incredulous, as he brought the boat alongside the dock. 'This is where you had to stop to delay us? A *bar?*'

'I've got some business here,' he said. 'It won't take long. You wait in the boat.'

'Wait in the——?' She broke off, watching in disbelief as he hauled himself onto the dock and headed for the bar without looking back. 'Swell.'

God only knew what his business was or how long it would take. In the meantime she could sit and rot in his stupid boat. The sun beat down on her, its heat magnified by the humidity. She could feel her linen suit wilting over her frame like an abused orchid. Not that it was going to be salvageable after today anyway, she thought, grimacing at the greasy handprint on the sleeve of her jacket.

She cursed her temper for getting her into this. If she hadn't let Shelby goad her into rushing right out to find a guide . . . If she hadn't let old feelings of inadequacy push her . . . If she had taken the time to think the situation through in a calm and rational manner, as she would have back in Charleston . . .

This was what coming home could do to a person. She had an established persona back in Charleston, an image she had fashioned for herself among acquaintances she had chosen. But this was home, and the minute she came back here, she became Gifford Sheridan's granddaughter, Shelby Sheridan's twin, the former captain of the high school debate team; old feelings and old patterns of behavior resurrected themselves like ghosts, peeling away the veneer of adulthood like a pecan husk.

It was part of the reason she stayed away. She liked who she was in Charleston – a professional woman in control of her life. Here she never felt in control. The very atmosphere wrested control away from her and left her feeling unsettled and uncertain.

This place, Mosquito Mouton's, was a perfect example. It was the most notorious place in the parish. She had been raised to believe it was frequented by hooligans and white trash, and no decent girl would come within shouting distance of it. Sitting in Lucky Doucet's pirogue, she had to quell the urge to look around for anyone who might recognize her. She felt as if she were a teenager cutting class for the first time.

Crossing her arms in front of her, she heaved a sigh, closed her eyes, and thought of her cool, pretty apartment back in Charleston. It was done in soft colors and feminine patterns and had a view of the water. There was a garden in the courtyard, and it was a long, long way from the swamp and Lucky Doucet.

The instant the screen door banged shut behind him, heads turned in Lucky's direction.

The place was about half full and would be bursting at the seams by sundown. Mouton's was the hub of trouble. There was gambling in the back and girls who might do anything for a few bucks or just for the hell of it. From here a man could find his way to a dogfight or a fistfight or a whorehouse or any number of dens of iniquity that were no longer supposed to exist in the civilized South.

It was the hangout of poachers and men whose backgrounds were filled with more shadows than the swamp. And even among them, Lucky Doucet stood out as a remarkably dangerous sort of man. The men sized him up warily, the women covetously, but no one approached him.

The bartender, a portly man with a dense, close-cropped salt-and-pepper beard, groaned and rolled his eyes like a man in pain. He brought up the rag he was wiping the bar with and patted it against his double chins like an old matron trying to ward off a fainting spell.

'Jesus, Lucky, I don' want no trouble in here,' he wailed, waddling toward Lucky's end of the bar. His little sausage fingers knotted together around the towel in a gesture of supplication. 'I just barely got the place patched up from the las' time.'

Lucky shrugged expansively, blinking innocence. 'Trouble? Me cause you trouble, Skeeter? Hell, I just came in for a drink. Give me a shot and a Jax long-neck.'

Muttering prayers, Skeeter moved to do his bidding, sweat beading on his bald spot like water on a bowling ball.

Lucky's gaze homed in on Pou Perret, a little muskrat with a pockmarked face and a thin, droopy mustache. He was sitting at the far end of the bar, deep in conversation with a local cockfight referee. Picking up his beer bottle by the neck, Lucky sauntered down to the end of the bar and tapped the referee on the shoulder. 'Hey, pal, I think I hear your mother callin'.'

The man took one look at Lucky and vacated his seat, shooting Perret a nervous glance as he moved away into the smokier regions of the bar. Sipping his beer, Lucky eased himself onto the stool and hooked the heels of his boots over the chrome rung.

'How's tricks, Pou? Where's Willis? In the back cheatin' at *bourré?* You out here keepin' watch or somethin', little weasel?'

Perret scowled at him and shrunk away to the far side of his stool like a dog afraid of getting kicked. He muttered an obscene suggestion half under his breath.

'That's anatomically impossible, *mon ami,*' Lucky said, taking another sip of his beer. 'See the things you might have learned if you'd stayed in school past the sixth grade? All this time you've probably been wearin' yourself out trying to do that very thing you suggested to me.' He chuckled at Perret's comically offended expression as he helped himself to a pack of cigarettes lying on the bar. He lit one up and took a leisurely drag. Exhaling a stream of smoke, he shrugged and grinned shrewdly. ''Course, mebbe Willis, he helps you out with that, eh?'

Perret narrowed his droopy eyes to slits. 'You bastard.'

Lucky's expression went dangerously still. His smile didn't waver, but it took on a quality that would have made even fools reconsider the wisdom of getting this close to him. 'You say that in front of my *maman,* I'll cut your tongue out, *cher,*' he said in a silky voice. 'My folks are respectable people, you know.'

'Yeah,' Perret admitted grudgingly, bobbing his head down between his bony shoulders like a vulture. He scratched his chest through his dirty black T-shirt, sniffed, and took another stab at belligerence. 'How'd they ever end up with the like of you?'

Lucky's eyes gleamed in the dim light as he looked straight into Perret's ferret face. 'I'm a changeling, don'tcha know. Straight up from hell.'

Perret shifted uneasily on his seat, superstition shining in his dark eyes like a fever. He lifted a hand to the dime he wore on a string around his neck. He snatched his cigarettes out of Lucky's reach and shook one out for himself, sliding a glance at Lucky out the corner of his eye. 'What you want, Doucet?'

Lucky took his time answering. He stood and shoved the barstool out of his way so he could lean lazily against the bar. He set his cigarette in an ashtray and took another long swallow of his beer before turning to look at Perret again.

'You been sniffin' 'round the wrong part of the swamp this last couple of weeks, louse,' he said quietly. 'Me, I think it might be better for your health if you go raidin' elsewhere.'

Perret made a face and shrugged off the warning. 'It's a free country. You don' own the swamp, Doucet.'

Lucky arched a brow. 'No? Well, I own this knife, don't I?' he said, sliding the hunting knife from its sheath. He grabbed a fistful of Perret's T-shirt and leaned over until Perret nearly fell off his stool. The wide blade gleamed just inches from the man's nose. 'And I can cut you up into 'gator bait with it, can't I?'

Conversations around them died abruptly. On the other side of the bar, Skeeter Mouton whimpered and crossed himself, sending up a prayer for the survival of his establishment. Clifton Chenier's accordion sang out from the speakers of the jukebox, sounding as raucous and out of place as a reggae band in church.

'Come on, Lucky, don' go cuttin' him up in here,' Skeeter pleaded. 'I won' never get all the blood out the floor!'

Perret turned gray and swallowed as if he were choking on a rock, his dark eyes darting from Lucky's face to the knife and back.

There was a commotion at the back of the room as a door burst open and a group of men emerged, their expressions ranging from avid interest to livid anger. At the front of the pack was Mean Gene Willis. Willis had been a rough-neck down in the Gulf and a convict in the Angola penitentiary. He was a good-sized man with fists as big as country hams and a face like a side of beef. He made a beeline for Lucky with murder in his eyes.

Lucky let go of Perret, snatched up his untouched whiskey, and flung it into Willis's face. The big man howled and lunged blindly for Lucky, who met his advance with a boot to Willis's beer gut. Perret took advantage of the distraction to grab Lucky's beer bottle and break it on the edge of the bar. As he swung it in an arch for Lucky's head, a gun went off. Women screamed. Someone kicked out the plug on the jukebox. There was an instant of deafening silence, then a man's voice rang out.

'That's enough! Y'all stop it or I swear I'll shoot somebody and call it in the line of duty.'

Perret dropped his broken bottle and slinked away like the rat he was. Willis lay groaning on the floor, holding his stomach.

Lucky stepped back casually and sheathed his knife, his gaze drifting over the uniformed agent who had hurried out of the back-room card game with Willis. He had gone to school with Perry Davis and had disliked him since kindergarten. Davis was a man of fair, baby-faced looks and an annoying air of self-importance that was only more grating in adulthood, considering the fact that he was lousy at his job.

Lucky picked up his cigarette from the ashtray on the bar and took a slow pull on it. 'Is this the kind of thing they were referring to when they named it the Department of *Wildlife* and Fisheries, Agent Davis? You playing *bourré* in a roadhouse?'

Davis gave him a cold look. 'What I'm doing here is none of your business, Doucet.'

'No? A respectable employee of the government gamblin' on taxpayer's time? That's none of my business?'

'What do you care? I doubt you pay taxes and you sure as hell aren't respectable.'

Lucky chuckled. 'That's right, *cher*, I'm not. You'd do well to remember that.'

'Are you threatening me, Doucet?'

'Who, me? I don't make threats.' His gaze took on the cold, hard look of polished brass, and his voice dropped a notch. 'I don't have to.'

A muscle worked nervously in Davis's jaw. 'I'm not afraid of you, Lucky.'

Lucky smiled. 'Well then, I guess it's not true what folks say about you, is it? You're every bit as dumb as you look.'

Davis's pale complexion turned blotchy red, but he said nothing. He holstered his gun and turned away to shoo the bar's patrons back to whatever they had been doing before the ruckus.

Willis struggled to his feet. Doubled over with an arm across his belly, he glared at Lucky. 'I'll get you, you coonass son of a bitch. You wait 'n' see.'

Lucky dropped his cigarette and ground it out on the floor with his boot. 'Yeah, I'll be losin' sleep over that, I will,' he drawled sardonically. 'Stay out of my swamp, Willis.'

He turned toward the door to make his exit and his heart jolted hard in his chest. Serena Sheridan was standing right in front of him with her little calfskin purse clutched to her chest, her eyes wide and her pretty mouth hanging open in shock. In her prim suit and slicked-back hairdo, she looked like a schoolmarm who'd just gotten her first eyeful of a naked man.

Lucky swore under his breath. He didn't need any of this. He would have been just as happy never to have to tangle with the likes of Gene Willis and Pou Perret. He sure as hell had never asked to baby-sit Serena Sheridan. This all came back to the other lives that kept insisting on crossing paths with his, and it was damned annoying.

He took Serena by the arm and ushered her toward the door. 'You've got a real knack for showing up in places you hadn't oughta be, don't you?'

Serena looked up at him but said nothing. She suddenly felt way out of her depth. Anyone with half a brain would have spotted Lucky Doucet for a tough customer, but she hadn't quite realized just how tough, just how dangerous he might be. Somehow, the fact that he knew her grandfather had diluted that sense of danger, but what she'd just witnessed had brought it all into sharp focus.

He was a poacher, a thief. He was a man who threatened people with knives and thumbed his nose at authority. He had practically laughed in the face of the game warden. God only knew what other laws he might break without compunction.

'Serena? Serena Sheridan?' Perry Davis stepped in front of them with a questioning look that clearly said he couldn't have been more surprised to see her there on the arm of a gargoyle. 'Is this man bothering you?'

Serena's gaze darted from him to Lucky. This was her chance. This was the part in the movie where everyone yelled at the screen for the heroine to cut and run. But she couldn't seem to find her voice, and then the opportunity was lost.

'Take off, Davis,' Lucky said on a growl. 'The lady is with me.'

Davis looked anything but convinced, but when Serena made no move to object, he shrugged and turned away.

'You know that guy?' Lucky asked, steering her toward the door again.

'He's a friend of the family.'

Lucky sniffed. 'You gotta choose a better class of friends, sugar.'

Serena almost burst out laughing. She shook her head and marveled at the whole scene. What the hell was she doing here? Why wasn't she taking the opportunity to get away from him? She looked at him with something like amazement, trying to see some sign, some sterling quality shining through all the rough machismo.

'I thought I told you to wait in the boat,' he grumbled irritably, dodging her gaze.

'I *was* waiting in the boat until a truckload of rough-necks pulled up. Then it became a matter of the lesser of two evils. I decided the riffraff in here was probably safer than the riffraff out there.'

'And now you're not so sure?'

He opened the door for her and she stepped out onto the gallery to a chorus of wolf whistles and crude come-on lines. Closing her eyes, she sighed a long-suffering sigh and rubbed her temples. This just wasn't her day.

The screen door banged behind her and the harassment ceased abruptly as Lucky walked up beside her and put an arm around her waist. It was a possessive gesture, a protective one, not anything sexually threatening. In fact, it was almost comforting. Serena looked up at him, surprised. He was scowling at the oil-rig workers assembled on the wide porch.

'Don' they teach you respect for ladies where you boys come from?' he asked in that silky-soft tone that raised the hair on the back of Serena's neck.

No one said anything. The men who worked the oil rigs were a rough breed. They wouldn't back down from a fight, but they didn't appear ready to pick one either. They were probably exhibiting better judgment than she was, Serena thought. Perhaps they had met Lucky and his friend Mr. Knife before. They were probably all sitting there wondering what she was doing with the most dangerous man in South Louisiana.

She lifted her chin a notch and drew together the tattered remains of her composure as Lucky guided her down the steps and across the parking lot.

'I'd like to go home now, if you don't mind,' she said. 'I can see you're a busy man, Mr. Doucet. I can make other arrangements to get to Gifford's tomorrow.'

Lucky stopped and jammed his hands at the waistband of his pants. He looked out at the bayou, squinting into the afternoon sun, and exhaled a long breath through his teeth.

This was stupid. He wanted to be rid of her, didn't he? He wanted her to think the worst of him, didn't he? He should have been happy that she was ready to give up, but he wasn't. *Dieu*, what a masochist he was! Why should he care that a woman like Serena Sheridan looked at him with wary contempt? The feeling was reciprocated a hundred and ten percent. He couldn't look at her without feeling . . .

What?

Hot. But that was just an instinctive response. He was a highly sexed man; of course he wanted her. Any man with feeling below the waist would want her. She was beautiful in the cool, ethereal way of a goddess. Of course it drove him wild. Of course he wanted to pull the pins from her hair and run his fingers through the masses of honey-colored silk. Of course he wanted to bury himself between those long, sleek legs. Of course he wanted to stroke and kiss those high, proud breasts. But he knew too well that what lay under those pretty breasts of hers could be pure evil.

Anger. That was what he really felt, he told himself. Anger. Resentment. She was her sister's twin. She was Shelby with a doctorate in psychology – *Dieu*, what a nightmare!

She was also Giff Sheridan's granddaughter. And he had made Giff a promise. The reminder made him sigh again and mutter an oath in French.

'Look,' he said quietly. 'I don't know what all you saw or heard in there, but it's got nothin' to do with takin' you out to Giff's. I promise you'll get there in one piece. I'm not gonna feed you to the 'gators or sell you to white slavers or anything like that. Giff's a friend of mine.'

Serena watched him closely, amazed. There was a flush on his high, hard cheekbones. He shuffled his boots on the crushed shell of the parking lot and refused to look at her. He actually looked contrite and embarrassed and . . . well, cute.

Lord, what was the matter with her, thinking he was cute? Puppies were cute. Boy scouts were cute. Lucky Doucet was a grown tiger. He probably had boy scouts for lunch and ate puppies for dessert and picked his teeth with prim blond psychologists who saw redeeming qualities where there were none. She shouldn't be thinking any kind thoughts about him. She should be afraid of him . . . but she wasn't.

She was obviously losing her grip on sanity. It was this place, this wild, primal place. The air was ripe with scents that invaded the brain. What common sense she had left told her not to trust this man any farther than she could throw a horse, but she couldn't bring herself to walk away from him.

'I'm amazed,' she said at last.

'What?' He gave her a narrow look. 'That I wouldn't sell you to white slavers?'

A corner of her mouth lifted in a wry smile as she started toward the dock. 'That you have a friend.'

3

Chanson du Terre. If she lived to be a hundred, Serena knew she would never tire of seeing it. It gave her a feeling of security and tradition. Sheridans had lived there since winning it in a card game in 1789. She may not have chosen to live there herself, but it was her heritage.

The house stood at the end of an *allée* of moss-draped live oak, the broad crowns of which knitted together to form a high bower above the drive. The house was an old Creole chateau, a combination of French Provincial and West Indies in style, with a sloping roof and broad galleries surrounding it on both the upper and lower levels.

At first glance the house looked the same as it always had to Serena – graceful, welcoming, impressive without being ostentatious. Then she blinked away the golden glow of her memory and saw it exactly as it was, as if seeing it for the first time ever.

The roof was in a state of disrepair, due to heavy spring rains. Shingles were missing and a bright blue tarp had been thrown over a portion near the west dormer. The columns of the upper gallery needed paint and some of the balusters were missing from the handrail, giving the house the appearance of having a wide gap-toothed grin. The brick of the ground floor and the wooden siding of the upper story were still painted yellow, but the color had faded with age to the shade of old parchment instead of the butter-yellow of her memory.

Memory was flattering, Serena reflected; reality was like seeing a beloved relative who had passed from middle age to old age between visits.

She made her way across the broad lawn at a hurried, half-lame walk, her shoes and purse cradled against her. A screen door on the upper level of the house swung wide open and her niece and nephew burst out like racehorses from the starting gate. Six-year-old Lacey ran shrieking down the wide steps, a blur of blond ringlets and pink frills, with eight-year-old John Mason right behind her, a bullfrog clutched between his hands and a maniacal grin on his face.

'John Mason, leave your sister alone!' Shelby Sheridan-Talbot shouted, bustling out onto the gallery.

She was a fraction of an inch shorter than Serena with a softer, slightly rounder figure. Her brown eyes were a bit more exotic in shape, and her mouth seemed perpetually set in a petulant frown. Beyond those slight differences they appeared very much the same physically. Shelby looked ready to address the chamber of commerce in a bright yellow suit with a fitted jacket that flared out at the hips in the current style intended to denote femininity. The emerald silk blouse beneath the jacket sported a flamboyant candy-box bow at the throat. Serena felt like a bag lady in comparison.

'Oh, my Lord, Serena!' Shelby exclaimed dramatically. She pressed perfectly manicured hands to her cheeks, displaying a diamond ring big enough to choke a cat and a large square-cut topaz. 'What on earth has happened to you? You look like you've been mugged or run over by a truck or both.'

'Gee, thanks.' Serena trudged up the steps, uncharitably wishing that she had been born an only child. Shelby's temperament was as capricious as the weather – sunny one second and stormy the next. She tended to be silly and frivolous. Her constant theatrics were tiring in the extreme, and she had a way of saying things that was at once innocent and cuttingly shrewd and that made it exhausting to endure a conversation with her.

Serena frowned at her as she limped onto the gallery and Shelby inched back, making a moue of distaste, careful not to brush up against her.

'I'm not having a great day here, Shelby, and I don't have time to go over the gory details with you,' Serena said. 'I've got to change and get going. Can you please arrange to have someone pick up my car in town? I left it down by Gauthier's.'

Shelby's expression quickly clouded over from feigned concern to childish annoyance. 'Of course, Serena. I have nothing better to do than run errands for you. My stars, you come home looking like something the cat dragged in, worrying me to a frazzle, and the first thing out of your mouth is an order. Isn't that just like you.'

Serena limped past her sister. She seriously doubted Shelby had given a single thought to her absence from the house. Shelby's most pressing concerns in life were her children, her wardrobe, and her prominence in community affairs – which she entered not with an eye to civic duty but social status. She was as pretty and shallow as a lily pond in a Japanese garden.

Serena stepped into the house and made her way down the hall, regretting the fact that she didn't have time to take in the ambience of the home she'd grown up in. Aside from one major renovation in the early 1800s and modifications since then to install plumbing and electricity, it had remained largely unchanged over its long history. It was a treasure trove filled with heirlooms and antiques that would make a museum curator's mouth water. But there was no time to appreciate the cypress-paneled walls painted a mellow gold or the faded Turkish rugs that spilled jewel-tone colors across the old wood floor. She went directly toward her old bedroom, where earlier in the day she had done nothing more than deposit her suitcases before storming off in a stubborn huff to find a guide.

'Going, did you say?' Shelby questioned suddenly, as if Serena's words had only just managed to penetrate through her sense of indignation. She rushed to catch up, plucking at the sleeve of Serena's rumpled jacket like a child trying to catch its mother's attention. 'Going where?'

'To see Gifford.'

'You can't go now!' Shelby whined in dramatic alarm, following Serena into her room. She positioned herself well within her sister's range of vision and put on her most distressed expression, wringing her hands for added effect. 'You simply can't go now! Why, you only just arrived! We haven't had a chance to chat or anything! I haven't had a chance to tell you a thing about our new house or about how well the children are doing in school or how I may very well be named Businesswoman of the Year by the chamber of commerce. You simply can't go now!'

Serena ignored the dictate and began undressing, tossing her ruined clothes into a pile on the floor. She frowned at the suitcase on the bed, knowing there was nothing in it suitable for a swamp. She might have grown up dogging Gifford's heels around the cane fields, but the woman she had become in Charleston had no call to wear jeans or rubber knee-boots.

'And Odille is making a leg of lamb for supper,' Shelby went on. She moved around the room in quick, nervous motions, flitting from place to place like a butterfly, lighting only long enough to straighten a lace doily or fuss with the arrangement of cut flowers in the china pitcher on the carved cherry dresser. 'You can't know the battle I had to wage to get her to do it. Honestly, that woman is as churlish as the day is long. She has defied me at every turn since Mason and I moved in. And she frightens the children, you know. They think she's some kind of a witch. I don't doubt but what she told them she'd put a spell on them. She's just that way. I don't understand why Gifford keeps her on.'

'He enjoys fighting with her, I imagine,' Serena said, smiling as she thought of the cantankerous Odille facing off with the equally cantankerous Gifford.

Odille Fontenot was as homely and hardworking as a mule, a tall rack of bones with the hide of a much smaller person stretched tautly over them. Her skin was as black as pitch, her eyes a fierce shade of turquoise that burned as bright as gas jets with the force of her personality. She was dour and superstitious and full of sass. She had taken over as housekeeper after Serena and Shelby had gone and Mae, the woman who had helped raise them, had retired. Odille was probably well into her sixties by now, but no one could tell by looking at her and no one dared ask.

Serena opened her suitcase and pulled out a pair of white crop-legged cotton slacks and a knit top with wide red and white stripes. A quick

200

glance in the beveled mirror above the dresser confirmed her suspicions that her hair was coming down, but there was no time to fuss with it.

'Besides,' she said, her voice muffled as she pulled her top on over her head, 'Odille's brother is Gifford's best friend.'

Shelby abruptly stopped rearranging knickknacks on the dresser and looked sharply at her sister's reflection in the mirror. 'Did you say you're going *after* Gifford? You're going out into the swamp?'

Serena zipped her slacks, meeting Shelby's gaze evenly. 'Isn't that what you told me to do?' she said with deceptive calm.

Shelby's cheeks flushed beneath her perfect makeup, and she glanced away, suddenly uncomfortable. 'I guess I didn't think you'd really do it. I mean, for heaven's sake, Serena, *you* going out into the swamp!'

'What did you think I'd do, Shelby? Nothing? Did you think I'd just ignore the problem?'

Shelby turned and faced her then, her mood changing yet again. 'Ignore it the way I have, you mean?' She narrowed her eyes and pinched her mouth into a sour knot. 'Well, I'm sorry, Serena, if I don't live up to your standards, but I have many other responsibilities. If Gifford wants to go live in the middle of some godforsaken, snake-infested swamp, I can't just drop everything and go after him.'

'Well, you won't have to,' Serena said tiredly. 'Because I'm going.'

'Yes.' Shelby flitted to the French doors that opened onto the gallery. She drew a length of sheer drape through her fingers, then twirled away, tossing her head. 'Won't Giff be tickled to see how you've overcome your fears.'

Serena gave her twin a long, level look brimming with anger and hurt, but she made no comment. She refused to. She had never once discussed with Shelby her fear of the swamp or how she had acquired it. The topic had tacitly been declared off-limits years earlier, a dangerous no-man's land that Shelby danced along the edge of when she was feeling spiteful.

Serena wasn't even certain her sister realized how potentially volatile the subject was. It wasn't that Shelby was stupid; it was just that she magnified the importance of things that pertained directly to herself and tended to minimize all else.

Stepping into a pair of red canvas espadrilles, Serena snapped her suitcase shut with a decisive click. She had no time to analyze her sister's psyche even if she had wanted to. She had a boat to catch.

'I'm leaving now,' she said softly, still struggling to control her temper. 'I don't know when I'll be back. Knowing Gifford, this could take a day or two.'

She slung the strap of her carryall over her shoulder and hefted the suitcase off the bed. Without so much as glancing in Shelby's direction, she left the room and headed for the front door.

'Serena, wait!' Shelby called, her voice ringing with contrition as she hurried down the hall.

'I can't wait. Lucky gave me ten minutes and I have no doubt he'll leave without me just to prove his point if I'm not there on time.'

'Lucky?' Shelby's step faltered as she repeated the name. 'Lucky who?'

'Lucky Doucet,' Serena said, bumping the screen door open with her hip. 'He's taking me out to Giff's.'

Shelby's face fell and paled dramatically, but Serena wasn't looking.

'Good heavens, Serena,' she said breathlessly, scurrying out onto the gallery. 'You can't go off with him. Do you have any idea what people say about him?'

'I can well imagine.'

'Mercy,' Shelby fretted, patting her bosom with one hand and fanning herself with the other, as if she might swoon like a belle of old. 'I don't know how his poor mother can hold her head up in public. And she's just the dearest woman you'd ever care to meet. The whole family is perfectly nice with college degrees and I don't know what all, but that – that – Lucky . . . Good heavens, he's nothing but trouble. He's been living like an animal out in the swamp ever since he got out of the army. Folks say he's half crazy.'

'They may be right,' Serena conceded, remembering Lucky's own words to that effect. 'But he was the only person I could find to take me.'

'Well, I don't think you should go with him. Who knows what he might do or say?'

Serena sighed heavily. 'Shelby, one of us *has* to go talk to Gifford. You're not willing and Lucky Doucet is the only person able to take me.'

Shelby pouted, plumping her lower lip out and batting her lashes. 'Well, I just don't think you should, that's all.'

'Your protest has been duly noted. Now, I'm off. Give my apologies to Odille.'

'Be careful.'

Serena paused on the last step at her sister's hesitant admonishment. It was one of the rare shows of concern from her twin that always made her do a double take. Shelby was for the most part completely self-absorbed. She could be silly and frivolous, petty and downright cruel on occasion. Then every once in a while she would suddenly come forth with a small slice of affection, concern, love, offering it like a jewel. The gestures were both touching and unsettling.

'I will be,' Serena said quietly.

She crossed the lawn at a hobbling half run once again, suitcase banging against her leg, foot throbbing from the sliver she had yet to remove. She set her sights on the landing and worked unsuccessfully to force Shelby from her mind.

All their lives people had remarked to them how special, how close they must feel being twins, what a unique bond they must share. Serena had always taken the comments with sardonic amusement. She and Shelby had never been close. Aside from their looks, they were as different as summer and winter. By Shelby's decree, they had been rivals from birth. Shelby had always seemed to resent Serena for being born at the same time, as if Serena had done so purposely to steal Shelby's glory. In her attempts to avoid rivalry, Serena had drifted further away from her sister, cultivating separate interests and separate dreams, creating an even wider gap between them.

Serena had always regretted the fact that they weren't close. Being the twin of a virtual stranger seemed much lonelier than being an only child. But they were too different, existing on separate planes that never quite seemed to intersect. They shared no telepathy. Sometimes it was almost as if they didn't even speak the same language. The only thing that seemed to bind them was blood and heritage and Chanson du Terre.

The elements of their relationship were complex. As a psychologist, Serena might have found it fascinating – had it been someone else's relationship, had she been able to look at it with cool objectivity. But she was too close to the subject; there were too many painful memories binding all the facets together like vines, and she was too afraid of what she might find if she ever did tear all the clinging creepers away, afraid the core might be as shriveled and dead as a sapling that had been smothered by the growth around it. And then what would happen? She would have to let go of the hope she still harbored in a corner of her heart. It was easier for them both to simply leave it alone.

As she neared the landing, her niece and nephew came running from the bank, screaming as if the devil were chasing them. They ran past her without slowing down, flying toward the safety of the house and their mother. Lucky stood on the dock smoking a cigarette, one hip cocked and a nasty smile tugging at a corner of his mouth. Serena scowled at him.

'Can't you go ten minutes without terrorizing someone?'

'Your ten minutes were up five minutes ago. You're just lucky I didn't leave without you.'

'That's a matter of opinion,' she grumbled. 'What did you say to them? You ought to be ashamed, trying to give little children nightmares.'

Lucky rolled his eyes and tossed the butt of his cigarette into the bayou. 'Those two *are* nightmares.'

'I wouldn't say that within Shelby's earshot if I were you.'

'There are far worse things I could say to that one,' he said, almost under his breath.

Serena gave him a curious look. His expression had gone cold and closed. He had slammed a door shut, but she felt compelled to push at it anyway. 'You know my sister?' she asked. It seemed as unlikely as . . . as herself going into the swamp with him.

Lucky didn't answer. His relationship with Shelby Sheridan had never been shared with anyone, not brother or stranger or priest. He certainly had no intention of sharing the story with Shelby's twin. It had happened in another lifetime, in another place. He preferred to leave the wound scarred over, if not healed. There was no way on earth he was going to tear it open for this woman. In addition to the sin of being Shelby's sister, she was a psychologist. The last thing he needed was some college girl digging around in his psyche.

He turned his attention to the luggage she carried and the stylish outfit she wore. 'Where do you think we're goin', *chère*? Club Med?'

Serena gave him one of her haughty ice-princess looks. 'For your information, Mr. Doucet, my wardrobe doesn't hold an extensive collection of army fatigues and waders. You may find this hard to believe, but I don't particularly care to spend my free time in the swamp.'

'Oh, I don't find that hard to believe a-tall. I'm sure you're far too busy givin' dinner parties and goin' to concerts to even think of a place such as the swamp.'

'Why should I think of it? It doesn't require anything from me. It simply is.'

Not for long. Not if your sister has anything to say about it. The thoughts passed instantly through Lucky's head, but he didn't speak them aloud. He was as involved as he intended to get, ferrying Serena out to Gifford's cabin and doing the odd reconnaissance job. It wasn't up to him to save the swamp. It couldn't be. *Dieu*, he had his hands full just trying to save himself.

What would be the point in arguing with Serena anyway? She was a slick, sophisticated city dweller who obviously had no affinity for the area she had grown up in. What would she care if Tristar Chemicals furthered the ruination of a delicate ecosystem man had been bent on destroying for years? For all he knew she was well aware of the situation and was going out to Giff's only to badger him into selling his land. She was her sister's twin, after all. How could he expect anything better of her than deceit and treachery?

He looked at her now in her prissy little designer sportswear outfit. She was a woman born to money, used to fine things. It stood to reason she would want more. That was the way of women of her class – see to the comfort and luxury of number one and to hell with the rest of the world. She wouldn't listen to him. He was just a means to an end . . . again.

'Get in the boat,' he said with a growl, his temper rising like a tide inside him.

She took another step toward him, her chin lifting to a stubborn angle. 'You know, Mr. Doucet, we would get along a whole lot better if you would stop bossing me around.'

Lucky all but closed the gap between them, leaning over her, trying to intimidate her with his size and the aura of his temper. 'I don't want to get along with you. Is that clear enough, *Miz* Sheridan?'

'Like crystal.'

She tilted her head back to meet his furious gaze, refusing to back away from him. Lucky's breath caught in his throat. *Bon Dieu*, she was beautiful! It didn't seem to matter to his eyes that she was everything he needed to stay away from. It didn't matter to his hormones that she represented more trouble than he could afford to handle. For an instant, as he leaned close and the scent of her perfume lured him closer still, desire flared hot and bright inside him and burned away all common sense.

His gaze drifted over the elegant line of her cheek and jaw, the perfect angel's-wing curve of her brows, the delicate pink bow of her mouth. He wanted nothing more at that instant than to kiss her, to taste those lips, to trace his fingertips over cheek and jaw and brush back the errant tendrils of golden hair that had escaped the bonds of style. He wanted to kiss her, taste her, plunge his tongue into her mouth. It was crazy.

Crazy.

A shudder went through him and he tore his gaze from her. He turned away from her abruptly, jerking her suitcase from her grasp and climbing down into the pirogue with it. He settled the bag on the flat floor of the boat, up in the bow with the rest of his cargo, and moved back toward the stern, taking up the push-pole. His hands were shaking.

Sweet heaven, he thought, gripping the pole and looking away as Serena eased herself into the boat; the sooner he got her to Gifford's, the better. He didn't need this kind of torment in his life. All he wanted was to be left in peace.

Peace, a derisive voice sneered inside his head, what was that? A dream. Something he was continually longing for that seemed forever beyond his reach. Something Serena Sheridan seemed to hold effortlessly, he thought, taking in the air of calm she wore like a queen's cloak as she settled herself primly on the seat of his pirogue. He couldn't help but envy her that. But if she were a cold, unfeeling bitch like her sister, why wouldn't she feel peace? Nothing would penetrate her armor of selfishness. She would be safe from caring and pain.

He heaved a sigh as he poled the boat away from the dock and steered it around, pointing the bow upstream, away from civilization and toward his home, his heartland – the cypress swamp of Bayou Noir. He focused on the wilderness that had been his salvation, never turning his head to catch the bright flash of yellow on the gallery of Chanson du Terre.

4

The first thing that always struck Serena about the swamp was the vastness of it. What land there was in this part of the state was crisscrossed by a labyrinth of waterways, some so wide they appeared bent on swallowing up everything in their path, some so narrow they were hardly more than a series of puddles cutting through the dense overhanging growth of willow and moss-draped hardwood trees. As far as the eye could see there was nothing but water and woods twisted together in combat with one another – water eating away at land, land rising up where water had been.

It was a place where one could literally spend days wandering the bayous, trying to reach a point only a few miles away. It was a place where trails twisted and turned, cut back and looped around until the traveler had no concept of direction. A place where shadows distorted the perception of time.

The area was inhabited by few people. Those who still made their living in the swamp generally preferred the comfort and convenience of civilization, buzzing into the wilderness in their aluminum boats only to return at the end of the day, leaving the bayous to such native inhabitants as snakes and alligators . . . and Lucky Doucet.

The waterway they were on branched off again and again like cracks in a windshield. It seemed to Serena that Lucky turned at random, steering the pirogue east, then west, then turning south again, then north. They weren't thirty minutes away from Chanson du Terre and already she was hopelessly lost, her fear robbing her of the ability to remember the route. She sat on the hard bench with her back straight, arms at her sides, fingers curling around the edge of the seat, bracing herself as if for a fierce blow.

'What'sa matter, darlin'? You afraid the boat's gonna sink?' Lucky punctuated the question by shifting his weight to set the pirogue rocking.

Serena felt the meager contents of her stomach rise up the back of her throat. She swallowed hard, concentrating on keeping her fear contained inside a shell of outer calm. *Don't let him know you're afraid. Don't let him know you're afraid.*

'O-of course not,' she stammered.

Lucky sniffed, offended. 'The only way this pirogue is gettin' water in it is if it rains. I built it myself. This one, she rides the dew.'

'Is that what you do for a living? You build pirogues?' Serena asked, looking at the paraphernalia in the front of the boat. There was an assortment of gunny sacks and red onion bags, wire and mesh crawfish nets, a bundle of mosquito netting. Fisherman's gear. She thought of the knife he carried and corrected herself. Poacher's gear.

'*Non,*' he said shortly.

'What do you do?' she asked, twisting around to squint up at him. He looked like a giant looming over her. She wondered if he would take the opportunity to lie to her or try to shock her by telling the truth. He did neither.

'I do as I please.'

Serena arched a brow. 'Does that pay well these days?'

Lucky tilted his head and looked away, giving her his profile. '*Pas de bêtises,*' he muttered. 'Sometimes it doesn't pay at all.'

He thrust the pole down into the muddy bottom and pushed. The boat shot ahead, nosing the edge of a floating platform of water hyacinth, delicate-looking lavender flowers shimmering above dense masses of green leaves. They turned again and the bayou grew narrower and darker. The pirogue skimmed the inky surface like a skater on ice, cutting across a sheet of green duckweed as they aimed for a narrow arbor of willow trees with streamers overhanging the water from either bank.

Serena took a slow, deep breath before they entered the tunnel of growth. Her throat constricted at the sudden absence of light. Her skin crawled as the willow wisps brushed against her like serpents' tongues.

When the boat emerged on the other side of the bower, they had an extra passenger. A thick black snake lay like a coil of discarded electrical cord on the floor of the pirogue near the toes of Serena's red shoes. Serena tried to scream, but couldn't. She bolted back on the seat, pulling her feet up and rocking the pirogue violently as she scrambled to escape, reacting on sheer instinct. She might have flung herself out of the boat if Lucky hadn't caught her.

He banded her to him with one brawny arm, bending her over backward as he reached down to snatch up the snake and fling it into the water.

'Just a little rat snake,' he said derisively as he released her.

Weak-kneed, Serena wilted down out of his embrace. A shudder passed through her as she watched the snake swim for shore, nose above the water, body undulating like a ribbon in a breeze. She didn't care if it was made of rubber and came from Woolworth's. It was a snake. Still, she didn't like the idea of this man knowing her fears, so she forced herself to recover quickly. Control was her best defense.

'Pardon me for overreacting,' she said primly.

Lucky scowled down at the back of her head. Wasn't there anything that could put a permanent wrinkle in that serene demeanor of hers? She'd come unglued at the sight of the snake, but that fast she was Miss Calm-and-Cool again, apologizing as if she had burped at the dinner table. He felt ready to explode from pulling her against him for that brief second; she sat there looking unmoved.

An irrational burst of anger shook him. How could she look so unaffected? How could he want her so much? How could he stand there looking at her, wanting her, knowing what she'd done—

What her *sister* had done . . .

Everything inside him went still as he realized what he was doing – substituting Serena for Shelby, letting an old hatred bubble up like rancid air that had been trapped in the bottom of a pond. After all these years it could still emerge, just as acrid as ever.

'*C'est ein affaire à pus finir,*' he muttered, shaking his head in an effort to clear it.

'I beg your pardon?' Serena asked, turning a questioning look up at him.

'I said, you'd better get used to seeing snakes if you think you're gonna stay out here, sugar. There are fifteen species of nonvenomous and six venomous – coral snakes, cottonmouths as long as whips, copperheads as thick as a man's wrist.'

Serena squeezed her eyes shut, as if that would somehow keep her from hearing him. Her mind took advantage of the blank screen to throw up one of her most terrible memories – muddy water swirling toward her, three dark, slender shapes writhing at the base of her perch, black heads shaped like arrows and mouths that flashed pinkish-white as they opened and came toward her . . .

What the hell had possessed her to come out here? She hated this place. It terrified her the way nothing else could. It shattered her sense of control. She looked around at the ghostly gray trunks of the huge cypress trees, the impenetrable growth beyond them, all of it shrouded in sinister shadows and hung with a tattered bunting of dirty-looking moss. It was a place of nightmares.

Tears stung Serena's eyes. She wanted to cling to her façade of calm, but she could feel her grip on it slipping. It inched away as if through sweaty hands that struggled frantically to hang on. To this point she had run on stubbornness and steam, but her anger and her singlemindedness had suddenly seemed to desert her, leaving only her fear.

Think, Serena. Think about something, anything.

This boat is too damned small.

'Hand me that canteen.'

Her heart jolted at the sound of Lucky's voice. She snapped back to reality, glad for the distraction. She picked up the canteen and handed it back to him, giving him a wry look as she turned to sit sideways.

'Please, Miss Sheridan?' she said sweetly. 'Thank you, Miss Sheridan. You're most welcome, Mr. Doucet.'

Lucky rolled his eyes. He unscrewed the top on the canteen and took a long drink, the muscles of his throat working rhythmically as he swallowed.

'What is that you're drinking?' Serena asked, trying to drag her eyes away from the thick column of his neck.

He wiped his mouth with the back of his hand. 'Water,' he lied.

Serena's gaze flicked to the canteen. Unconsciously, she drew the tip of her tongue across her bottom lip and swallowed.

Heat seared through Lucky's veins.

He thrust the canteen toward her in an ungracious offer, angry with himself for caring at all about her comfort and angrier still for not being able to control his body's response to her.

She took the canteen and sniffed dubiously at the opening.

'This isn't water, it's liquor,' she said, making a face.

Lucky scowled at her. 'It has water in it.'

Serena gave a little snort of disbelief. 'You drink it like water, which probably accounts for your foul temperament.'

'I like my temperament just fine,' he said on a growl.

'Well, you're a minority of one, from what I've seen.' She sniffed again at the canteen and grimaced.

'Are you gonna take a drink or are you afraid you might catch something drinking out of the same can as the likes of me?' Lucky asked sarcastically.

Serena narrowed her eyes at him and took a swig from the canteen, partly to prove him wrong and partly to bolster her flagging courage. The professional in her frowned on the latter reason. There wasn't anything healthy about rationalizing alcohol consumption. But she ignored the disapproving inner voice. She wasn't a professional out here; she was scared. The kind of fear that she was experiencing was terrible. She would have done just about anything to escape it. If nothing else, this experience was giving her a renewed sympathy for her patients who suffered from phobias.

As she had suspected, the brew in the canteen was nothing that had ever graced the shelves of a liquor store. It was homemade stuff so potent there probably wasn't a proof percentage high enough to categorize it. It was the kind of stuff that could double as paint thinner or battery acid in a pinch. Liquid fire seared a path down her throat and sizzled as it hit her belly, spreading warmth through her. As if she wasn't already warm enough from looking up at her guide, she thought, cursing her hormones.

Perhaps this physical attraction to him was some kind of temporary insanity, she reasoned. Perhaps Lucky Doucet with his mile-wide shoulders, his panther's eyes, and courtesan's mouth was the thing her mind wanted to focus on instead of the swamp. That was the only reason that made any sense. Aside from his looks, his list of faults was endless. He was rude, crude, chauvinistic, overbearing, arrogant, had a violent temper, and he drank. No sensible, self-respecting woman would entertain a single thought about getting involved with him on any level.

Her gaze drifted once again over his physique. Well, maybe there was *one* level . . . but of course she wasn't interested in that. She didn't involve herself in affairs that were strictly sexual. In fact, she hadn't involved herself in an affair of any kind for what suddenly seemed like ages.

She kept busy with her practice and her volunteer work at a mental health clinic in one of Charleston's poorest areas. She had friends and a nice social life, but no serious romantic entanglements. She'd been married once to a fellow psychologist, but the marriage had fizzled for lack of interest on both their parts. It had been based on friendship, mutual interests, convenience. Noticeably absent had been the kind of intense physical magnetism that often acts as an adhesive to hold the other parts of a relationship together. They had drifted apart and divorced amicably four years after taking their vows.

Since the divorce, Serena had dated sparingly, casually, never finding a man who motivated her to anything more than that. She had decided that perhaps she simply wasn't a sexual creature. She hadn't inspired that much passion in her husband, nor had he excited her to the kind of mind-numbing ecstasy she'd heard about from other women. She had decided she simply wasn't made to react that way to a man. It probably had something to do with her need for emotional control. Looking up at Lucky Doucet, she decided she might have to rethink the issue.

'Like what you see, sugar?' he drawled lazily, staring down at her with those unblinking amber eyes.

'Not particularly.' She thrust his canteen back at him in an effort to keep him from noticing the telltale blush that warmed her cheeks.

'Liar.'

It was a statement of fact more than an accusation. He took the canteen, deliberately brushing his fingertips over hers. Serena jerked her hand back, winning her an amused chuckle.

Serena lifted her chin a defiant notch. 'You have an amazingly high opinion of your own appeal, Mr. Doucet.'

'Oh, no, *chère*, I just call 'em like I see 'em.'

'Then I suggest you make an appointment with an optometrist at the earliest possible date. A good pair of glasses could save untold scores of women the unpleasantness of your company.'

Their gazes locked and warred – hers cool, his burning with intensity. She congratulated herself on defusing a potentially disastrous sexual situation. He congratulated himself on goading her temper. Both went on staring. The air around them thickened with electricity.

On the eastern bank of the bayou an alligator roused itself from a nap, plowed through a lush tangle of ferns and coffee-weed stems, and slid down into the water.

Serena jumped, jerking around to stare wide-eyed at the creature. The alligator was lying in the shallows among a stand of cattails, just a few feet away from the pirogue, its long, corrugated head breaking the surface of the murky water as it stared back at her.

Lucky gave a bark of laughter. "*Mais non, mon ange*, that 'gator's not gonna get you. Unless I throw you overboard, which I have half a mind to do.'

'I don't doubt it – that you have half a mind, that is,' Serena grumbled, snatching the canteen away from him to take another swig of false courage.

And just how much of a mind do you have, Serena, antagonizing this man? Good Lord, he was a poacher and a bootlegger and who knew what else. He gave her a nasty smile, reminding her enough of the nearby alligator to give her chills.

'No wonder Gifford's holed up out here,' he said, taking up the push-pole again and sending them forward with the strong flexing of his biceps. 'I don't see how a man could stand to be stuck in a house with two just like you.'

Serena kept one eye on the alligator and both hands firmly clamped to the edge of the seat. 'For your information, my sister and I are nothing alike.'

'I know what your sister is like.'

The cold dislike in his statement made her glance over her shoulder at him. 'How? I can't imagine the two of you run in the same social circles.'

Lucky said nothing. That mental door slammed closed again. Serena thought she could almost hear it bang shut. He looked past her, as if she had ceased to exist, his face a stony mask. His silence left her free to draw her own conclusions.

Perhaps Shelby had made some kind of public statement against poachers or places like Mosquito Mouton's. It would be like Shelby to get on a soapbox and publicly antagonize people she thought of as unsavory. Her views would be met with widespread approval among the upstanding members of the community, something that would appeal enormously to her ego. Shelby had always required a great deal of attention and praise, and had been willing to go to whatever length she needed to get those things. It wouldn't have been beyond her to pick on a man as dangerous as Lucky Doucet. She would have considered the potential for self-aggrandizement long before giving a thought to the potential for trouble.

Serena wondered if her sister had any idea she'd made an enemy of a man who carried a hunting knife the size of a scimitar.

They moved on up the bayou, the silence of the swamp as heavy and oppressive as the heat. The denser the vegetation became, the more overwhelming the stillness. It played on Serena's nerves, tightening them so that something as innocent as the 'quock' of heron set them humming.

The deeper they penetrated into the wilderness, the less it looked like man had ever intruded upon it. The most conspicuous sign of human habitation Serena saw was the occasional slip of colored plastic ribbon tied to a branch to mark the location of a crawfish trap.

Lucky pulled up beside one of these – a red ribbon tied to the branch of a willow sapling – and set about emptying the dip net set in the shallow water beneath it. The thin mesh was brimming with red crawfish. He raided four nets along the same bank, emptying their contents into the onion sacks he had stored in the bow of the pirogue, going about his task as if Serena were nothing more than an annoying piece of cargo he had to step around. She watched him with interest, not daring to ask if the traps he was harvesting were his.

'Are we nearly there?' she asked as Lucky once again began to pole the pirogue north, then east.

'Nearly. You'll know when we're just about onto Gifford's.'

'I doubt it. It's been years since I've been out here.'

'You'll know,' he said assuredly.

'How?'

'By the gunshots.'

Serena made a face. 'That's ridiculous. Old Lawrence said something about people getting shot at too. I know my grandfather can be cantankerous, but shooting at people? That's absurd. Why would he shoot at people?'

'To scare them off.'

'And why would he want to scare people off?'

'So they'll leave him alone.'

Serena shook her head impatiently. 'I don't understand any of this. In the first place, it's not like Giff to desert the plantation for so long a time, not even during crawfish season.'

'He's got his reasons,' Lucky said enigmatically.

Serena gave him a long, searching look. She didn't like the idea of this man knowing more about her family's concerns than she did. It made her feel like the outsider. It also threw a glaring spotlight on her deficiencies as a granddaughter. She didn't come home often enough, didn't keep up with the local news, didn't call as often as she should. The list of venial sins went on, adding to her feelings of guilt. Still, she couldn't keep herself from asking the sixty-four-thousand-dollar question.

'And just what do you think those reasons are, Mr. Doucet?' she queried, looking up at him.

His face remained impassive. 'Ask Gifford, if you want to know. I don't get involved in other people's lives.'

'How convenient for you. You have no one to worry about, no one to answer to except yourself.'

'That's right, sugar.'

'Then what are you doing bringing me out here when you would clearly rather have come alone?'

Lucky scowled at her, his black brows pulling together like twin thunderheads above his eyes. When he spoke his voice was soft and silky with warning. 'Don' you go tryin' to get inside my head. Dr. Sheridan.'

Serena rolled her eyes. 'God forbid. I'm sure I'd rather fall into a snake pit.'

One and the same thing, *chérie*, Lucky said to himself, but he refrained from speaking that thought, knowing it was the kind of statement a psychologist would pounce on. He was managing just fine. If everyone would just butt the hell out of his life, he would be great.

'How come you don' know Gifford's reasons for comin' out here?' he asked, going on the offensive. 'Don' you ever talk to your grandpapa on the telephone? Mebbe you don' care what goes on down here. Mebbe you don' care about this place or Chanson du Terre, eh?'

'What kind of question is that?' Serena bristled, rising to the bait like a bass to a fly. 'Of course I care about Chanson du Terre. It's my family home.'

Lucky shrugged. 'I don't see you livin' there, sugar.'

'Where I live is none of your concern.'

'That's right. Just like it's none of my concern if someone wants to come in and flatten the place with bulldozers. It's not my family what's lived and worked on that land two-hundred-some years.'

Serena stared up at him, feeling as if she'd been hit in the chest with a hammer. 'What do you mean, flatten the place? What are you talking about?'

'Chanson du Terre, angel. Your sister wants to sell it to Tristar Chemicals.'

'That's absurd!' she exclaimed, laughing at the sheer lunacy of the statement. 'Shelby wouldn't want to sell Chanson du Terre any more than Scarlett O'Hara would put Tara on the market! You obviously *don't* know my sister. It would never happen. Never.'

She went on chuckling at the idea, shaking her head, trying to ignore the terrible certainty in Lucky's eyes as he stared down at her. The look was meant to assure her of the fact that he knew many things she didn't have a clue about. A part of her rejected the notion outright, but another part of her churned with a sudden strange apprehension.

At any rate, there was no time to question or argue the issue, because as they rounded a bend in the bayou there came the sudden deafening explosion of a shotgun – firing at them.

5

Serena had no trouble managing a scream this time. She shrieked, dropping to her knees on the floor of the pirogue and covering her head with her arms as buckshot hit the bayou in front of them, spewing muddy water and bits of shredded lily pad everywhere.

Her first thought was that they were being set upon by one of the honest men Lucky had been poaching from. Perhaps even the rightful owner of the crawfish squirming in the onion sacks two feet from her nose. She expected to hear another volley of shots and wondered if Lucky had a gun tucked away someplace to defend them with. But the initial *boom* faded away. In the ensuing silence, she lifted her head a few inches and peeked out between her fingers.

Gifford stood on the bank, legs spread, the smoking gun cradled loosely in his big hands. He was a tall, well-built man who didn't look anywhere near his age except for his thick head of snow-white hair, one lock of which insisted on tumbling rakishly across his broad forehead. With his square shoulders and trim waist, he still looked fit enough to wrestle a bear and win. His bold features were set in a characteristically fierce expression – bushy white brows lowered, square chin jutting forward aggressively. His nose was large and permanently red from years spent in the fields under the relentless southern sun.

'Goddammit, Lucky!' he bellowed, his voice a booming baritone that rivaled the shotgun for volume. 'I thought you were that bastard Burke!'

'Naw,' Lucky called back calmly, poling the boat forward as if getting shot at didn't affect him in the least. 'You might wanna shoot me anyway, though, when you see what I brought you.'

Serena rose up on her knees, snapping her head around to give him the evil eye before turning back toward her grandfather. She pushed her hair out of her eyes with one hand, hanging on to the side of the pirogue with the other to steady herself. Conflicting emotions shoved together in her chest like a log jam as she looked at the man who had essentially raised her. With adrenaline still pumping through her veins and the sound of the shotgun blast still ringing in her ears, anger took precedence for the moment.

The pirogue slid in beside a weathered dock with gnarled pilings and pitted planks. Serena didn't even wait for the boat to settle. She clambered out of it, awkward in her haste as she pulled herself up onto the rickety wharf. The pirogue scooted away as she pushed off from it and she slipped and hit her shin but managed to keep from falling back into the muddy shallows. Dirty, disheveled, with blood seeping into the previously immaculate white cotton of her pant leg and her hair tumbling in disarray around her shoulders, she stormed for shore, limping.

'Dammit, Gifford, what the hell do you think you're doing? Shooting at people! My God!'

Gifford scowled at her. 'Jesus Christ. What the hell kind of language is that for a lady to use?'

'The kind I learned from you!' Serena shot back. She planted herself in front of him, her hands on her hips, staring up at him with as much defiance as she could muster.

'Well, hell,' Gifford muttered. There wasn't any way around that one. He cracked the shotgun open and extracted a shell, which he slipped into the breast pocket of his faded chambray workshirt. 'I'll bet you don't use that kind of language up in Charleston.'

'I'm not up in Charleston.'

'For once,' he said with a snort. 'What are you doing out here?' he asked, frowning down at Serena again. 'I sure as hell never expected to see you riding around the swamp in a pirogue.'

'Believe me, it's not my idea of fun,' Serena said, shooting a glare Lucky's way. 'I can think of a lot better things to do with my free time and much more pleasant company to do them with.'

'She takes exception to my temperament,' Lucky said with a sardonic smile as he approached, an onion bag of crawfish swinging from his fist.

'Among other things,' Serena muttered.

Lucky stopped beside her, dropped the bag at his feet, and lit the cigarette dangling from his lip, his eyes on Serena the whole time. She could feel his gaze burning into her as hot as the flaring tip of his cigarette. Color rose to tint her cheeks.

He tilted his head back and blew a thin stream of smoke into the air. 'Guess I'm gonna have to go back to charm school for a refresher course,' he drawled laconically.

'Don' you believe him, Miz 'Rena,' Pepper Fontenot said with a gravelly chuckle as he ambled toward them from his lawn chair. Pepper was a thin, wiry man with the same pitch-dark skin and light eyes as his sister, the formidable Odille. He had somehow managed to sustain a very merry personality despite having lived with Odille his entire life, and wore his wide smile as comfortably as he wore his faded old coveralls. He slapped Lucky on the shoulder. 'He charm the hide off a 'gator, dis one, if he be of a mind to.'

Serena arched a brow at Lucky. 'He must not have been of a mind, then.'

'Mebbe it was the company,' Lucky said through his teeth.

Quelling the juvenile urge to stick her tongue out at him, Serena turned back toward her grandfather. 'You might tell me you're glad to see me,' she said, not quite able to hide her hurt at his cool reception.

'I might say it once I find out what you're doing here.'

'What *I'm* doing here!' she exclaimed, splaying a hand across her chest. 'I'm here because you took off without a word of explanation to anybody. I come down for a visit and the first thing I'm told is that you moved yourself out here two weeks ago and haven't been heard from since. What was I supposed to do? Say, "Oh, gee, too bad I missed him" and just go on with my vacation? My God, Gifford, you could have been dead for all we knew!'

'Well, I'm not,' he snapped. 'If that's all you came to find out, you can go on home now. You aren't going to inherit for a while yet if I can help it.'

'What kind of a rotten thing is that to say?'

'It's the kind of thing a man starts saying when he's nigh onto eighty with a bum ticker and a couple of ungrateful granddaughters.'

He snapped the shotgun closed with a decisive click, turned, and walked away.

Serena stood there, dumbfounded, watching him walk up the slight incline toward the cabin. Every time she saw Gifford in the flesh she was stunned by how badly she wanted his love and approval and how badly it hurt when he didn't offer them freely. It was as if the instant she encountered him, the child in her revived itself.

She was tired and frustrated, hungry and dirty. All she wanted to do was snuggle into her grandfather's embrace and let go of the determination that had gotten her this far. She wanted to be able to tremble and have Giff soothe her fears away as he had when she'd been a little girl, but that wasn't an option. She wasn't a child anymore, and Gifford hadn't been sympathetic to her fear of the swamp for a long, long time.

When she hadn't gotten over it after what he thought was a reasonable amount of time, his understanding had metamorphosed into a subtle disapproval and disappointment that had colored their relationship ever since. He thought she was a coward. Watching him walk away, she wished he could have realized how much courage it had taken her to get this far.

'Yeah, there's just nothin' quite so heartwarmin' as a family reunion,' Lucky muttered, his eyes also on Gifford's back as the old man walked away.

Serena glared at him. 'Butt out, Doucet.' She stomped after her grandfather, her espadrilles squishing in the damp, spongy dirt that constituted the front yard.

The cabin was a simple rectangular structure covered with tan asphalt shingles. It was set up a few feet off the ground on sturdy cypress stilts to save it from the inevitable spring flooding. The roof was made of corrugated tin striped with rust. A stovepipe stuck up through it at a jaunty angle. The front door was painted a shade of aqua that hurt the eyes. There were no curtains at the two small front windows.

The cabin had never contained any amenities, certainly nothing that could have been considered 'decorating' unless one included mounted racks of antlers. Serena doubted that had changed since the last time she'd been out here. The hunting lodge was one of those male bastions where anything aesthetically pleasing was frowned on as unmanly. Gifford undoubtedly still used the same old tacky, tattered furniture that hadn't been good enough for the Salvation Army store twenty years earlier. The floor of the two-room structure was probably still covered with the same hideous gray linoleum, the kind of indestructable stuff that promises to last forever and unfortunately does.

Serena wasn't going to find out immediately. Gifford didn't go to the door of the cabin. He climbed partway up the stairs, then turned around and plunked himself down with his gun across his lap as if he meant to block the way. Serena's step faltered just long enough so that the two old blue tick hounds that had jogged out from behind the woodshed could jump up on her and add their paw prints to the front of her shirt. She groaned and shooed them away, scolding them.

'You used to love them dogs,' Gifford grumbled, scowling at her disapprovingly. 'I suppose they don't allow hounds like that up in Charleston.'

Serena shook a finger at him as she came to stand at the foot of the steps. 'Don't you start that with me, Gifford. Don't you start in on how Charleston has changed me.'

'Well, it has, goddammit.'

'That's not what I came out here to discuss with you.'

Gifford swore long and colorfully. 'A man can't get a scrap of peace these days,' he said, addressing the world at large. 'I came out here to get away from people, not to form some pansy-ass discussion group.'

Serena ignored his protest and pressed on. 'It's not like you to just take off, especially this time of year. There's too much work to be done around the plantation.'

He rolled his big shoulders and looked down at his feet. 'That's what I've got Arnaud for. He's the manager, hell, let him manage. Tired old men like me are supposed to take off and go fishing.'

'When you knew I was coming to visit?' Serena pushed the hurt away with an effort and gave an unladylike snort. 'Since when are you a tired old man?'

'Since I figured out I don't have an heir who gives a rat's ass about everything I've broke my back for.'

'Oh, for heaven's sake, Gifford!' she snapped. 'What are you talking about?'

217

'I'm talking about you living eight hundred miles away and your sister ready to sell the old place at the drop of a hat. That's what I'm talking about.'

'What is this nonsense about Shelby wanting to sell Chanson du Terre?' she demanded irritably. 'I've never heard anything more ludicrous in my life. Ever since we were little girls she's talked about growing up and getting married and living on the plantation. She wouldn't dream of selling it!'

'Well, that just shows how out of touch you are with your own family, young lady,' Gifford announced piously.

'Oh, for the love of Mike!' Serena cut herself off abruptly, not trusting herself to say anything more until she reined her temper in a notch. She clamped her mouth shut and paced back and forth along the base of the stairs, her arms banded tightly across her as if to keep herself from exploding.

'Honestly, I don't know what to think,' she muttered more to herself than to Gifford. 'People telling me Shelby's lost her senses and wants to sell Chanson du Terre. Shelby tells me she thinks you've gone senile—'

'Senile!' Gifford launched himself off his step like a rocket, shooting up to his full height. His craggy face turned an unhealthy shade of maroon. 'By God, that tears it! Is that what you've come out here for, Serena? Is this a professional visit? You out here to see if the old man's lost his marbles? Then y'all can get that candy-ass lawyer husband of Shelby's to have me declared incompetent, sell the old place, and live off the sweat of my carcass – By damn – By God – I won't have it!'

He clutched the railing with one hand and the shotgun with the other and hissed a breath in through his teeth, struggling suddenly for air.

Serena rushed up the steps, her own heart thundering in alarm. 'For God's sake, Gifford, sit down!'

He complied without argument, his knees buckling, backside hitting the old step with a thump. The tension went out of his muscles. His wide shoulders sagged and he drew in a ragged deep breath. He fished around in his shirt pocket for a pill, pulling out the shotgun slug and tossing it carelessly aside.

Serena kneeled at his feet, shaking all over. She pressed her hands against her lips and struggled not to cry, realizing for the very first time just how old he was, just how mortal. She watched him stick a little pill under his tongue and held her breath as his color faded slowly from red to pale gray. He seemed to age twenty years before her eyes, his incredible inner fire dimming like a flame that had been abruptly turned down.

'You all right, Giff?' Lucky said, his dark voice shot through with tension. Serena realized with a start he was on the step right behind her. He leaned down to get a look at Gifford's face, laying a hand on her shoulder in a manner that might have been intended as comforting.

Gifford muttered one of his more virulent oaths.

218

Pepper stuck his head in under the stair railing and flashed a smile of relief. 'He kin cuss like dat, he all right. He stops cussin', him, den you ax him if he be dead.'

'Smartass,' Gifford growled.

Pepper gave a hoarse laugh and withdrew to snatch the squirming bag of crawfish away from the inquisitive coon hounds that were sniffing and pawing at it.

Serena felt herself sag with relief. She couldn't stop herself from reaching a hand up to touch her grandfather's knee, just to reassure herself. 'You ought to go in and lie down, Giff. We can talk later.'

'I don't need to lie down,' the old man snapped. 'Just a little dizzy spell, that's all. Christ, I don't know who wouldn't be dizzy with all this going on around them. It makes me so damn mad, I can't see straight half the time. I make one remark about selling, and your sister, who couldn't sell ice water in hell, runs right out and finds a buyer. Judas H. Priest. And where are you? Off shrinking heads in Carolina, as if there aren't enough lunatics in Lou'siana to go around.'

'We can talk about it when we get home,' Serena said softly.

There were a hundred questions to be asked. Why hadn't Shelby called her when Gifford had left? Why had she denied knowing the reason Gifford had left? Why would Gifford ever have mentioned selling the plantation and why would Shelby agree to it, much less find a buyer?

Feeling a little like Alice waking up in Wonderland, Serena pushed herself to her feet and wiped the remaining tears from her eyes. The questions would have to wait. She wouldn't quiz Gifford now and run the risk of giving him another attack. It could all be sorted out once they were back home. And the sooner the better.

She turned around to look back at the dock. Gifford's bass boat was tied up on the side opposite Lucky's pirogue. 'Pepper, would you please get the boat ready?'

Pepper shook his head, smiling at her much the way Lawrence Gauthier had earlier. 'Oh, no, *chère*. Me, I kinda like bein' alive. You ax Giff 'bout it, he don' wanna go nowhere.'

Serena turned back to her grandfather. He refused to look at her. 'Gifford, please. You can't stay out here.'

'I sure as hell can.'

She turned to Lucky.

He shrugged and physically backed away from the conversation. 'It's a free country.'

'I don't believe this,' Serena said angrily, raking her hair back from her face with trembling hands. 'Dammit, Gifford, you nearly had a heart attack right before my eyes. You can't stay out here!'

'I can do whatever I damn well please, young lady,' he said, forcing himself to his feet. He swayed a bit, but gripped the rail with a white-knuckled fist and locked his knees. 'I won't have you or your sister or anybody else trying to run my life.'

Serena cast one last glance at Pepper and Lucky, looking for help but finding none. Pepper shuffled his feet and dodged her gaze, staring down at the bag of crawfish. Lucky merely stared back at her, saying nothing, offering nothing. She shook her head. 'I think you've all gone mad.'

'Well then, why don't you just go on back to Charleston, where you won't have to worry about all your crazy relatives,' Gifford said coldly. 'Outta sight, outta mind. You don't care what all goes on down here.'

Serena held up a hand to cut him off, pressing her lips together and blinking hard to ward off more tears of frustration. 'I won't discuss this with you now, Gifford. I won't.'

'Fine. Then go on and get out of here. Leave me in peace.'

'I'm not going anywhere,' she announced. 'I'm staying right here until I convince you to come home.'

'The hell you are. I won't have you,' Gifford barked. 'Lucky, you take her on back to Chanson du Terre.'

Lucky backed away another step, brows drawing together ominously low over his eyes. 'Forget it. I ain't running no goddamn ferry service. I'm not takin' her all the way back to Chanson du Terre. It's gettin' dark. I've got things to do.'

'Then she can stay with you at your place, 'cause she sure as hell ain't staying here,' Gifford declared. 'I came out here to get *away* from ungrateful women.'

'Stay with *him!*' Serena said with horror.

'Stay with *me!*' The idea nearly made Lucky choke.

They regarded each other with a kind of terror that didn't go unnoticed by Gifford. The old man raised an eyebrow.

'She's not stayin' with me,' Lucky said emphatically. 'It's out of the question. Absolutely out of the question.'

His house was his sanctuary. It was the space he had created for himself to heal in, to have some measure of peace. It was his private refuge, the last stronghold of his sanity. The last person he wanted breaching those walls was this woman, a woman he wanted beyond all reason, a woman whose face haunted his mind with memories of the pain and betrayal of another.

'*Non. Non,*' he muttered, shaking his head. '*Sa c'est de la couyonade.*'

Gifford snorted. 'So you think I'm foolish too? By God, the two of you deserve each other. You can sit around over coffee tonight and compare notes on ways to avoid your responsibilities.'

Lucky wheeled around, stomping up three steps to thrust a warning finger in Gifford's face. 'You're skatin' on thin ice, old man,' he said through his teeth. 'I don' owe you. I don' owe Chanson du Terre.'

'Oh, that's right,' Gifford drawled sarcastically. Lucky's ferocious look didn't impress him; he was too old to be frightened by the idea of his own mortality. 'You don't owe anybody anything. You're your own man. Good for you, Lucky. You can pat yourself on the back after the swamp silts up and everything dies.'

'Don' you talk to me about responsibilities, Gifford,' Lucky snapped. 'You've got your own. And where are you? Out here fishin' and takin' potshots at Tristar reps. How the hell is that gonna solve anything?'

'I've got my own way of dealing with the situation.'

'*Mais, yeah*,' Lucky said with a harsh laugh. 'By *not* dealing with it.'

Serena stepped between them. 'Excuse me. Do I get a say in this matter?'

Both men scowled at her simultaneously and answered in thunderous unison. 'No!'

She fell back a step in utter disbelief.

Lucky jumped off the stairs and started pacing again. He knew Gifford – mules had nothing on him when it came to stubbornness. If he said he wasn't letting Serena stay with him, he meant it. He'd leave her on the doorstep all night if it came to that. The idea went against Lucky's grain on a fundamental level where he'd long ago thought he'd given up all feeling.

He glanced at Serena out of the corner of his eye and mentally swore a blue streak. She was just as proud and stubborn as her grandfather. She'd stood toe to toe with the old man. She'd been on the brink of tears with worry over him. She obviously loved him. And old Giff had given her an emotional buffeting for her trouble. She looked like a hothouse flower that had been thrust outdoors during a thunderstorm – bedraggled, dirty, exhausted.

And Gifford was bent on turning her away.

Damn.

It wasn't that he *cared* about her, Lucky assured himself. It wasn't that he *wanted* to get involved. It was none of his business how Gifford treated his granddaughter. For all he knew, she deserved to be left out on the porch all night. The extenuating circumstances were what concerned him – another example of the way other people's affairs kept drifting into the path of his life. This swamp was his world. He couldn't bear the idea of seeing it destroyed.

He heaved a sigh and raked his hands through his hair. What were his options? He wanted Gifford to deal with the Tristar problem before something catastrophic happened, like Gifford shooting Len Burke or Shelby succeeding in selling the place to a company with a record as environmental rapists. That meant getting Gifford to go back to face the situation. Serena had resolved to get him to return, and heaven knew she had the determination to convince him, given enough opportunity. That meant keeping her near the old man and away from her sister's poisonous influence. And that meant . . .

Hell and damnation.

He examined the dilemma from another angle. How long could it take Serena to talk Gifford into going home? A day or two. Three at the outside. How much harping could a man take, after all? Lucky decided he wouldn't actually have to stay with her if she was in his house. He could easily spend that much time out in the swamp. He had plenty of other things to keep him occupied. Still, he didn't like the idea of being cornered into doing something.

He stopped his pacing, turning his head to glare up at Gifford. 'All right,' he said, his voice low. 'I'll keep her.'

Gifford successfully fought off a smile.

Serena's jaw dropped.

For a long second no one said anything. The tension building in the air was enough to make the coon hounds whine and trot away in search of a safe haven.

'Keep me?' Serena questioned softly, glaring at Lucky. '*Keep me!*' Her voice rose several decibels. She planted her hands on her hips and leaned over him, enjoying the height advantage for once. 'You most certainly will not keep me!' She whirled toward Gifford, her face livid. 'I will not stay with this man! I hardly know him and what I do know about him is hardly flattering. For heaven's sake, Gifford, you can't really expect me to stay with him!'

'Who knows what I might expect,' Gifford said, putting on a wounded air. 'I'm just a crazy old man waiting to die.'

'Stop it!' Serena spat out. She stared up at him in the fading afternoon light and felt a big ball of fear swell up in her chest like a balloon. He had that same look he'd had on his face when she'd been seventeen and the sheriff had brought her home after catching her and two other honor students splitting a jug of cheap wine under the bleachers at the football stadium.

Her voice softened to a whisper. 'Gifford?'

He shook his head. 'Don't you even ask me, Serena. I'm so mad right now I could spit brass tacks. You think you can just come breezing in here and fix everything up with a sentence or two because you've got a sheepskin from Duke and a fancy practice up in Charleston. You don't know what's going on here and you don't care. You just want to put all the parts back in their places and get on with your vacation.' He shook his head once more and blew out a breath. His color was heightening again, a flush creeping up from his throat into his face like mercury rising in a thermometer. 'Go on, get out of here. You'll be all right with Lucky.'

He turned and trudged up the rest of the steps, letting himself into the cabin without looking back. Serena felt stunned, as if someone had hit her between the eyes with a rock. Well, she'd gotten what she deserved, hadn't she? In his usual no-nonsense style Gifford had cut through to the heart of the matter. She *had* thought she'd come out here and simply set things straight, put her world back on track, rearrange things to her satisfaction. She had inherited that take-charge manner from Gifford. She used it to great success in her everyday life back in Charleston. But they weren't in Charleston.

Damn this place. She closed her eyes and rubbed her hands over her face, erasing what was left of her makeup.

'I'm sorry, Miz 'Rena,' Pepper said, climbing the stairs to stand beside her, his wriggling, clicking crawfish sack hanging down from his fists. 'You know old Giff. He gets in a temper, him, there's no tellin' what he say. He don' mean half.'

Serena tried without much luck to muster a smile. 'Does that mean you'll run me home after all?'

He frowned, something that looked completely foreign to his face, as if his mouth didn't quite know how to turn that way. 'Can't. Dat old boat, she's not runnin'. Lucky, he bring the part, but dat don' make her run. Take me a coupl'a days to fix.'

Serena hadn't thought it possible for her spirits to sink any lower. She'd been wrong. They seemed to fall now from their last toehold into a bottomless black pit. It must have been a painful thing to watch, because Pepper made another attempt to frown. He shuffled his feet on the worn tread of the step, working up to making a run for it.

Why, oh, why had she let her temper goad her into coming out here without thinking it through, without first finding out exactly what was going on? Now she was stuck in this god-awful place. Turned out by her own grandfather. Turned over to the care of a man who wouldn't know a scruple if it bit his handsome butt.

She turned her bleak gaze to Lucky. He stood absently scratching the head of one of the coon hounds as he watched her, his expression inscrutable. In the long, sinister shadows seeping across the ground as the sun slid away, he looked more dangerous than ever.

'Get in the boat, *chère*,' he said softly. 'Looks like we're stuck with each other for a little while longer.'

6

'Come on,' Lucky said, nodding toward the pirogue. 'I'll bring you back tomorrow and you can have all day to hound him.'

Serena followed him reluctantly to the water's edge. She looked out across the bayou and at the black forest that seemed to be looming ever larger as the light faded. Fear started to claw its way past the last wall of her resistance.

'I'll pay you anything if you just take me home.' The words were out of her mouth before she was even aware of thinking them, but she didn't try to take them back. They were true. She could have managed staying at the cabin with Gifford and Pepper, but the idea of staying with a stranger – a dangerous stranger – and having him see her fear . . . she couldn't do it. At that moment she would have given him the keys to her Mercedes if he would have agreed to take her back to civilization. She wanted a long hot bath, a meal, some aspirin, and an explanation from her sister – not necessarily in that order.

'Anything?' Lucky arched a brow and gave her a slow, wicked smile as he considered. 'That's tempting, sugar, but I just plain can't take you back tonight. I have a previous engagement.'

Serena ground her teeth and forced the word through them. 'Please.'

Lucky bent and lifted the box of motor parts out of the bow of his boat, setting it aside on the bank. 'Look, angel,' he said as he straightened, resting his hands just above the low-riding waist of his fatigue pants. 'I'm sure you think I'm gonna take you back to my place, tie you to the bed, and ravish you all night long, but I've got more important things to do. You'll just have to content yourself with fantasizing.'

Serena gave him a look of complete disgust. He ignored her, wading out and pushing the pirogue away from the shore.

'Come on, sugar, *allons*. Get in the boat, or you can spend the night with Gifford's coon hounds out in the woodshed.'

What choice did she have? Serena knew her grandfather. He was fully capable of leaving her to spend the night outside. He seemed angry enough to do it. Not even the idea of sharing a house with Lucky Doucet seemed as terrible as the idea of being out alone all night.

Dragging her tattered cloak of pride around herself once again, she lifted her nose and walked out onto the dilapidated dock to get in the boat.

They headed away from Gifford's and deeper into the wilderness. The bayou narrowed to a corridor flanked on both sides by what looked to be impenetrable woods. Cypress and tupelo trees stood in dark, silent ranks in their path like a natural slalom course. Dusk had fallen, casting everything in one last dusty glow of surrealistic light.

Serena sat, trying to keep her back straight, trying to keep from crying. Now that the confrontation with Gifford was over and the anger had subsided, pain rushed in unabated. She had come for him. Couldn't he see that? How could he accuse her of being so callous as to be thinking only of her inheritance? She had never even thought about him dying, much less what he would leave her.

Gifford dying. In her mind she relived the horror of watching him turn purple and collapse. She couldn't bear the thought of losing him. She especially couldn't bear the thought of losing him now when he seemed so angry with her, so disappointed.

Tears welled in her eyes and she blinked them back furiously. She would not cry now. She would not cry in front of Lucky Doucet and give him yet another reason to sneer at her. She couldn't let go and cry now, anyway, because she was afraid that once she started, she wouldn't be able to stop and she had too much yet to face before this day was over.

That was hardly a cheerful prospect, she thought, fighting another wave of despair. She already felt as if she'd been dragged by the hair for eight hundred miles and brutally dismembered. The person she had been just yesterday was no longer recognizable; she had been dismantled by this place and its people and the memories and emotions they evoked. She was exhausted from the ordeal, but she clung to her one last shred of strength and dignity and fought back the tears.

Lucky stood behind Serena, watching the little tremors that shook her shoulders. He could hear her catch a breath and knew she was trying valiantly not to cry. Proud, stubborn little thing. He felt something twist in his chest and did his best to ignore it.

He was having a hard time maintaining his image of her as an ice bitch. The woman who had tried to hire his services had been a professional woman, prim and cool, consummately businesslike in her designer suit, not a hair out of place. That woman had been easy for him to dislike. But that guise was long gone now, and her efforts to appear calm and in control were no longer irritating but touching – or they would have been had he been susceptible.

She hiccuped and sniffled and swatted at the mosquitoes that were rising off the water in squadrons to swarm up around her head, and Lucky clenched his jaw against the very foreign urge to feel sympathy.

'I hate this place,' Serena announced, smacking at the mosquitoes with both hands. The swarm dispersed and regrouped to mount another sortie.

She hiccuped and sniffed again, sounding perilously close to bawling. Her voice trembled with the effort to hold the tears back. 'I have *always* hated this place.'

Great. Lucky frowned. The fate of the swamp was coming to rest on the shoulders of a woman who hated it.

He eased the pirogue to a halt and secured the pole. He stepped gingerly around Serena, narrowly avoiding having her hit him in the groin as she slapped at the mosquitoes. He snatched up the wad of *baire* he kept in the front of the boat and tossed the sheer netting over her like a dust cover over an old chair.

'Now you can stop your squirming before you capsize us and serve us up to the 'gators for dinner.'

Serena shuddered at the mention of alligators, but didn't look at the water for evidence of any. 'Thank you for your concern,' she said dryly. 'Why aren't the mosquitoes after you, enormous, half-naked target that you are.'

'They like your perfume. Very uptown tastes, these skeeters have. Mebbe you'd like to take some of them back to Charleston with you, *oui?*'

'Don't you start in on me,' she warned, her voice hoarse from the big knot of emotion lodged like a rock in her throat. 'You don't know anything about it.'

'I know Giff needs you here,' he said, taking up his stance behind her once again. The pirogue slid forward. 'That is, if you care anything about your heritage. Mebbe you don't. You say you hate this place. Mebbe you'd like to see it poisoned and ruined, yes?'

'Gifford would never allow such a thing to happen.'

'Gifford won't have any say in the matter if he doesn't take charge of the situation soon. He thinks it'll just go away if he stays out here and shoots at the Tristar rep every time he comes around.'

'You make it sound like he's running away from the problem. Gifford Sheridan never ran from a fight in his life.'

'Well, he's runnin' from this one.'

'It's ridiculous,' Serena insisted. 'If he doesn't want to sell to Tristar, all he has to do is tell them no. I don't understand what the big problem is.'

'Me, I'd say there's a lotta things here you don' understand, sugar,' Lucky drawled.

Not the least of which was *him*, Serena thought, plucking at the edge of the mosquito netting. The man was a jumble of contradictions. Mean to her one minute and throwing mosquito netting over her the next; telling her in one breath he didn't involve himself in other people's affairs, then giving his commentary on the situation. She wouldn't have credited him with an abundance of compassion, but he was rescuing her from having to spend the night outside, and, barring nefarious reasons, compassion was the only motive she could see.

She wondered what kind of place he was taking her to. She didn't hold out much hope for luxurious accommodations. Her idea of a poacher's lair was just a notch above a cave with animal hides scattered over the floor. She pictured a tar-paper shack and a mud yard littered with dead electricity generators and discarded butane tanks. There would probably be a tumbledown shed full of poaching paraphernalia, racks of stolen pelts and buckets of rancid muskrat remains. Certainly it would be no better than Gifford's place. She couldn't imagine Lucky hanging curtains. He struck her as the sort of man who would pin up centerfolds from raunchy magazines on the walls and call it art.

They rounded a bend in the bayou, and a small, neat house came into view. It was set on a tiny hillock in an alcove that had been cleared of trees. Its weathered-cypress siding shimmered pale silver in the fading light. It was a house in the old Louisiana country style, an Acadian house built on masonry piers to keep it above the damp ground. Steps led onto a deep gallery that was punctuated by shuttered windows and a screen door. An exterior staircase led up from the gallery to the overhanging attic that formed the ceiling of the gallery – a classic characteristic of Cajun architecture. Slim wooden columns supporting the overhang gave the little house a gracious air.

Serena was delightfully surprised to see something so neat and civilized in the middle of such a wilderness, but nothing could have surprised her more than to hear Lucky tell her it was his.

He scowled at the look of utter shock she directed up at him through the mosquito netting. 'What'sa matter, *chère?* You were expecting some old white-trash shack with a yard full of pigs and chickens rootin' through the garbage?'

'Stop putting words in my mouth,' she grumbled, unwilling to admit her unflattering thoughts, no matter how obvious they might have been.

A corner of Lucky's mouth curled upward, and his heavy-lidded eyes focused on her lips with the intensity of lasers. 'Is there something else you want me to put there?'

Serena's heart thudded traitorously at the involuntary images that flitted through her mind. It was all she could do to keep her gaze from straying to the part of his anatomy that was at her eye level.

'You've really cornered the market on arrogance, haven't you?' she said, as disgusted with herself as she was with him.

'Me?' he said innocently, tapping a fist to his chest. '*Non.* I just know what a woman really wants, that's all.'

'I'm sure you don't have the vaguest idea what a woman really wants,' Serena said as she untangled herself from the *baire* and tossed it aside. She offered Lucky her hand as if she were a queen, and allowed him to hand her up onto the dock, giving him a smug smile as her feet settled on the solid wood. 'But if you want to go practice your theory on yourself, don't let me stop you.'

Lucky watched her walk away, perversely amused by her sass. She was limping slightly, but that didn't detract from the alluring sway of the backside that filled her snug white pants to heartshaped perfection. Desire coiled like a spring in his gut. He might not have known what Miss Sheridan really wanted, but he damn well knew what his body wanted.

It was going to be a long couple of days.

He pulled the pirogue up out of the water and left it with its cargo of suitcases and crawfish to join Serena on the gallery. He didn't like having her there. This place revealed things about him. Having her there allowed her to get too close when his defenses were demanding he keep her an emotional mile away. He might have wanted her physically, but that was as far as it went. He had learned the hard way not to let anyone inside the walls he had painstakingly built around himself. He would have been safer if she could have gone on believing he lived like an animal in some ancient rusted-out house trailer.

'It's very nice,' she said politely as he trudged up the steps onto the gallery.

'It's just a house,' he growled, jerking the screen door open. 'Go in and sit down. I'm gonna take the sliver out of that foot of yours before gangrene sets in.'

Serena bared her teeth at him in a parody of a smile. 'Such a gracious host,' she said, sauntering in ahead of him.

The interior of the house was as much of a surprise to her as the exterior had been. It consisted of two large rooms, both visible from the entrance – a kitchen and dining area, and a bedroom and living area. The place was immaculate. There was no pile of old hunting boots, no stacks of old porno magazines, no mountains of laundry, no litter of food-encrusted pots and pans. From what Serena could see on her initial reconnaissance, there wasn't as much as a dust bunny on the floor.

Lucky struck a match and lit a pair of kerosene lamps on the dining table, flooding the room with buttery-soft light, then left the room without a word. Serena pulled out a chair and sat down, still marveling. His decorating style was austere, as spare and plain as an Amish home, a style that made the house itself seem like a work of art. The walls had a wainscoting of varnished cypress paneling beneath soft white plaster. The furnishings appeared to be meticulously restored antiques – a wide-plank cypress dining table, a large French armoire that stood against the wall, oak and hickory chairs with rawhide seats. In the kitchen area mysterious bunches of plants had been hung by their stems from a wide beam to dry. Ropes of garlic and peppers adorned the window above the sink in lieu of a curtain.

Lucky appeared to approve of refrigeration and running water, but not electric lights. Another contradiction. It made Serena vaguely uncomfortable to think there was so much more to him than she had been prepared to believe. It would have been easy to dislike a man who lived in a hovel and poached for a living. This house and its contents put him in a whole other light – one he didn't particularly like to have her see him in, if the look on his face was any indication.

He emerged with first aid supplies cradled in one brawny arm from what she assumed was a bathroom. These he set on the table, then he pulled up a chair facing hers and jerked her foot up onto his lap, nearly pulling her off her seat. He tossed her shoe aside and gave her bare foot a ferocious look, lifting it to eye level and turning it to capture the best light. Serena clutched the arm of her chair with one hand and the edge of the table with the other, straining against tipping over backward. She winced as Lucky prodded at the sliver.

'Stubborn as that grandpapa of yours, walkin' around half the day with this in your foot,' he grumbled, plying the tweezers. '*Espèsces de tête dure.*'

'What does that mean? Ouch!'

'You're a hardheaded thing.'

'Ouch!' She tried to jerk her foot back.

'Be still!'

'You sadist!'

'Quit squirming!'

'Ou-ou-ouch!'

'Got it.'

She felt an instant of blessed relief as soon as the splinter was out of her foot, but it was short-lived. Serena hissed through her teeth at the first sting of the alcohol, blinking furiously at the tears that automatically rose in her eyes.

'Your bedside manner leaves a lot to be desired,' she said harshly.

Lucky raised his eyes and stared at her over her toes. The corners of his mouth turned up. 'Yeah, but my manner *in* bed won't leave anything to be desired. I can promise you that, *chère.*'

Serena met his hypnotic gaze, her heart beating a wild pulse in her throat as his long fingers gently traced the bones of her foot and ankle. All thoughts of pain vanished from her head. Desire coursed through her veins in a sudden hot stream that both excited and frightened her. She didn't react this way to men. She certainly shouldn't have been reacting this way to *this* man. What had become of her common sense? What had become of her control?

With an effort she found her voice, but it was soft and smoky and she barely recognized it when she spoke. 'That's no promise, that's a threat.'

Lucky eased her foot down and rose slowly. His fingers curled around the arms of Serena's chair and he tilted it back on its hind legs, his eyes never leaving hers as he leaned down close.

'Is it?' he said in a silken whisper, his mouth inches from hers. 'Are you afraid of me, *chère?*'

'No,' she said, the tremor in her voice making a mockery of her answer. She stared up at him, eyes wide, her breath escaping in a thin stream from between her parted lips. The molten heat in his gaze stirred an answering warmth inside her and she found herself suddenly staring at his mouth, that incredibly sensuous, beautifully carved mouth.

'You're not afraid of me?' he said, arching a brow, the words barely audible. He leaned closer still. 'Then mebbe this is what you're afraid of.'

He closed the distance between them, touching his lips to hers.

The heat was instantaneous. It burst around them and inside them, as bright and hot as the flare of the lamps on the table beside them. Serena sucked in a little gasp, drawing Lucky closer. He settled his mouth against hers, telling himself he wanted just a taste of her, nothing more, but fire swept through him, his blood scalding his veins. One taste. Just one taste . . . would never be enough.

Her mouth was like silk soaked in wine – soft, sweet, intoxicating. His tongue slipped between her parted lips to better savor the experience. He stroked and explored and Serena responded in kind, reacting on instinct. Her tongue slid sinuously against Lucky's. His plunged deeper into her mouth. The flames leapt higher.

A moan drifted up from Serena's throat, and her arms slid up around Lucky's neck. She could feel herself growing dizzy, as if her body were floating up out of the chair. Dimly she realized Lucky was rising and pulling her up with him. His arms banded around her like steel, lifting her, pulling her close. His big hands slid down to the small of her back and pressed her into him.

He was fully aroused. His erection pressed into her belly, as hard as granite, as tempting as sin. She arched against it wantonly, reacting without thought. A growl rumbled deep in his chest, and he rolled his hips against her as he changed the angle of the kiss and plunged his tongue into her mouth again and again.

He stroked a hand down over the full swell of one hip. Cupping her buttock, he lifted her to bring her feminine mound up against his hardness. She made a small, frightened sound in her throat and need surged through him like a flood. He wanted her. God, he wanted her! He wanted to take her right here, right now, on the table, on the floor. It was madness.

Madness.

Sweet heaven, what was he doing? he wondered, finally hearing the alarm bells clanging in his head. What was she doing to him? He set her away from him with a violence that made her stumble back against the chair she'd been sitting in. She stared at him, her eyes wide and dark with a seductive mix of passion and fear. Her hair tumbled around her shoulders in golden disarray. Her mouth, swollen and red from the force of his kiss, trembled. She stared at him as if he were something wild and terrifying.

Wild was exactly what he was feeling – out of control, beyond the reach of reason. His chest was heaving like a bellows as he tried to draw in enough oxygen to think straight. He speared his hands into his hair and hung his head, closing his eyes. Control. He needed control.

Control. She'd lost control – of the situation, of herself. Serena swallowed hard and pressed a hand to her bruised lips. How could this have happened? She didn't even *like* the man. But the instant his mouth had touched hers she had experienced an explosion of desire that had melted everything else. She hadn't thought of anything but his mouth on hers, the taste of him, the strength of his arms, the feel of his body. Shivers rocked through her now like the aftershocks of an earthquake. Heaven help her, she didn't know herself anymore. What had become of her calm self-discipline, her training, her ability to distance herself from a situation and examine it analytically?

You wanted him, Serena. How's that for analysis?

She shook her head a little in stunned disbelief. 'I think I would have been safer with the coon hounds,' she mumbled.

Something flashed in Lucky's eyes. His expression went cold. '*Non*. You're safe in this house, lady. I'm out of here.'

He turned and stormed into the next room. There was a banging of doors that made Serena wince. When he reappeared he was wearing a black T-shirt that hugged his chest like a coat of paint. He shrugged on a shoulder holster. The pistol it cradled looked big enough to bring down an elephant. Serena felt her eyes widen and her jaw drop.

'It's not hunting season.' She didn't realize she had spoken aloud, but Lucky turned and gave her a long, very disturbing look, his panther's eyes glowing beneath his heavy dark brows.

'It is for what I'm after,' he said in a silky voice.

He pulled the gun and checked the load. The clip slid back into place with a smooth, sinister hiss and click. Then he was gone. He slipped out the door like a shadow, without a sound.

Serena felt the hair rise up on the back of her neck. For a long moment she stood there, frozen with fear in the heat of the night. With an effort she finally forced her feet to move and went to the screen door to look out.

The night was as black as fresh tar with only a sliver of moon shining down on the bayou. The water gleamed like a sheet of glass. She thought she caught a glimpse of Lucky poling his pirogue out toward a stand of cypress, but in a blink he was gone, vanished, as if he were a creature from the darkest side of the night, able to appear and disappear at will.

'Heaven help me,' she whispered, brushing her finger-tips across her bottom lip. 'What have I gotten myself into now?'

7

The pirogue cut across the inky surface of the bayou as softly as a whisper on the wind. Mist drifted like smoke among the smooth dark trunks of the trees. The air was heavy with scents, like a courtesan's perfume, sweet, almost palpable – honeysuckle and jasmine, verbena and wisteria, all mingling with the darker metallic scent of the water and the decaying growth that lay beneath it. Intertwined with scent was sound – the chirp and trill of insects, the song of frogs, the call of an owl and the whoosh of its wings as it left its perch. In the distance an alligator roared, a nutria screamed. Night feeders had come out to hunt and be hunted.

Lucky let his boat drift toward the shelter of a massive live oak that overhung the water's edge. The bank had been eaten away to the gnarled roots of the tree and formed a tiny cove that was deep enough to keep the boat afloat. It provided natural cover with the canopy of the tree spreading out wide and low, its ragged beards of moss hanging down like a moth-eaten curtain. It was the perfect place to wait.

He dug a cigarette from the pack in his shirt pocket and lit it, taking a deep, soothing drag. The tip flared red in the gloom of the night. The match hissed as it hit the surface of the water. Tension hummed inside him like an overloaded power line. Tension for the job he was here to do, but a greater part of it was sexual frustration. He'd never wanted a woman so badly in his life. Never. Not even in his youth when his hormones had roared in perpetual high gear. Not even after he'd spent a year in a Central American prison. He had never wanted a woman more than he had wanted Serena Sheridan in that blinding flash of heat. He was still shaking with the intensity of it. He was still half hard.

Damn her. *Why* her? Of all the women on the planet, why her? How could it be possible for him to look at Serena and remember Shelby's duplicity and still want her?

She wasn't Shelby. He knew that. Shelby would never have come after Gifford. She would never have stood nose to nose with the old man and matched him temper for temper. Shelby's methods of getting what she wanted fell more into the eyelash-batting and pouting categories. No, in terms of personality, the sisters were nothing alike. Shelby was all calculated flirtation and coy charm. Serena was all business and sass. Still, he didn't want to want her. She was dangerous to his sanity, reminding him of the past and the affair that had set his life on a near-disastrous course.

He had surrendered to Shelby's charms, succumbed to her, and lost himself. He was a junior at the University of Southwestern Louisiana in Lafayette, young and hot and full of himself, caught up in the idea of taking the world by storm, determined to show everybody what he could do. The big brooding kid everyone watched with a wary eye was going to be the first Doucet to get a college education. He was going to be a biologist. Having Shelby Sheridan on his arm – and in his bed – was another feather in his cap. He had the world by the tail that spring. Then it turned around and knocked him senseless.

He was nothing but a means to an end, a tool for Shelby to get what she really wanted – John Mason Talbot IV. Talbot was balking at the idea of marriage. Shelby took up with Lucky to provoke jealousy. A simple, time-honored plan. The fact that she had gotten pregnant with his baby had been an inconvenience easily dealt with just as soon as Talbot put his ring on her finger.

Lucky could still taste the bitterness. He hadn't loved Shelby as much as he had loved the idea of her. When she dropped him, the blow to his youthful ego was terrible. When he found out about the aborted pregnancy, the cut went to his very core. Shelby had shattered his pride with careless ease and gone on with her life as if nothing had happened at all, while pain and humiliation drove him to abandon school and all his grand plans.

With youthful drama he dropped everything and joined the army, sending his life down a path that led to a gray place of shadowed existence, where there was no good or evil, only missions and objectives, a place where his soul was stripped away from him a little bit at a time.

Thirteen years passed and he could still feel the shame of having been played for a fool by a pretty dark-eyed blond belle.

And now he was being tempted by another.

He swore in French and flung the butt of his cigarette away. As if he didn't have enough trouble already, he had to go stirring up old nests of resentment. Maybe that was it. Maybe it was revenge he wanted when he looked at Serena. Or maybe he was complicating matters unnecessarily. Maybe it was just sex.

Hell, he could handle sex. It would be fabulous between them. He already knew that. The instant he'd touched his mouth to hers he'd been wild to get inside her. And she'd lost that cool control of hers and responded to him with all the fire she had previously reserved for sarcasm. Yeah, he could handle sex with Serena Sheridan. The idea of having all that cool beauty and inner heat beneath him and around him damn near made him burn up from the inside out.

It was an emotional entanglement he wanted to avoid. He was smart enough to keep that from happening. He wouldn't let Serena get that close to him. He wouldn't let anyone get that close, not even his family. He didn't have anything left to give anyone. He guarded what was left of his soul like a miser.

The distant buzz of an outboard motor broke in on his thoughts. Lucky came to attention, following the sound carefully. It wasn't too far off – over on the next bayou and nearing the fork that branched into the little no-name stream he was on. He was exactly where he needed to be. A nasty smile unfurled across his dark face. He pulled a pair of infrared goggles from his gear bag, put them on, then took up his *baire* and draped it over himself, pulled his gun, and waited.

Serena couldn't sleep. She hadn't tried. Her exhaustion went bone deep, but the fear went deeper. She was alone. It didn't seem to matter very much that she was in a house with a roof over her head. She was still in the swamp, alone. In the ordinary course of things she thought of herself as a strong, competent, self-reliant individual able to handle most anything that might come her way. This she couldn't quite handle. Even after all these years the memories were too strong. Every sight, every sound, every smell only brought them into sharper focus. She would have given her left arm for a Valium. Just one. Anything to dull the little knives that were splitting her nerve endings.

'Pull yourself together, Serena,' she muttered aloud, tightening her arms across her chest in a symbolic gesture as she paced the width of the dining room. 'If your patients could see you now, they'd pack up their neuroses and go shrink shopping.'

A skittering sound rattled across the gallery just as she passed the screen door. She shrieked and bolted sideways, banging her knee and stubbing her toe on a table leg. She swore a litany of curses under her breath and limped around the table.

In the time since Lucky had left she had done little else but pace. She had washed up in the tiny spotless bathroom, found a comb and restored some order to her hair. She'd made a sandwich with a spongy slice of Evangeline Maid white bread and peanut butter and eaten on the move, too keyed up to sit. Really, she'd been too keyed up to eat, but she knew from experience that not eating properly only magnified her paranoia. So she had walked and chewed, hiking over every inch of the first floor of Lucky's house.

There was nothing much to distract her from her fear. There was no television, no radio, no stereo. She spotted a CB radio on a shelf in the kitchen, but she had no idea how to work it. She couldn't even amuse herself by unpacking and repacking her suitcase because it was still outside.

She assumed Lucky had taken her luggage out of his pirogue. It probably wouldn't do for a poacher to be caught toting silk lingerie and a supply of makeup. Other swamp boys might get the wrong idea. But even if he had left her bags on the dock, they weren't going to do her any good because there was no way in hell she was walking out to get them. The ground was literally crawling out here at night. In her imagination she could picture herself trying to tiptoe across yards of writhing reptilian bodies.

'Stop it!' she snapped as a spasm of fear ran down her back and a wave of it rose up in her throat as thick and sour as grease.

From somewhere in the far distance beyond the front door came the *crack! crack!* of what sounded like gunfire.

Lucky.

'Oh my God,' Serena whispered. Her eyes teared up and she lifted a trembling hand to her lips. What if he were shot? What if he were killed? What if whoever did him in came looking for God knew what?

Her heart thudding like a paddle ball behind her ribs, she crept toward the door, straining her eyes to see something in the stygian blackness beyond. For a moment all she could hear was the blood roaring in her ears, then the raspy screech of frogs. Something screamed, a terrible blood-chilling sound that might have been an animal in its death throes or a woman on the brink of hysteria. The sound tore across the night like a knife ripping through silk and then it was gone, leaving an eerie stillness in its wake. Serena sucked back a sob and moved quickly away from the door and into the next room.

She resumed her pacing, picking up speed as she walked a path from the front window past the old horsehide sofa to the bed and back. The sore on the bottom of her foot had gone past the point of pain to numbness. She wished for the pain back; it would have been something else to think about besides this awful choking fear.

She tried to think about the situation at Chanson du Terre, but there were still too many pieces missing for her to make any sense of it. Thoughts of her last few moments with Lucky drifted through her head, but she shooed them away. She didn't yet want to consider the ramifications of getting that close to a man who claimed to be crazy and carried a gun.

Her toe connected with something solid hidden under his bed as she turned the corner to pace back toward the front window. Hesitantly, she turned to face the bed. It was a mahogany half-tester with delicately carved details. A thick curtain of mosquito netting was draped back from the headpiece. The coverlet was an exquisite example of Cajun weaving in soft brown cotton with narrow indigo stripes.

The idea of Lucky, pagan and barbaric, stretched out naked on this elegant bed stirred the embers of desire deep inside her. She could see him, dark skin against white sheets, his stallion's mane loose across the pillow, his golden eyes staring up at her, hot and mesmerizing.

Serena shook her head in amazement. How could she want a man who was so contrary to her idea of what a modern man should be? She knew there were women who wanted to be dominated, women who would have melted into puddles at the feet of a man like Lucky Doucet. She was not among them. She had always held to the idea of equality between the sexes. Lucky was a throwback to the heyday of male chauvinism. She didn't trust him, didn't like him, didn't respect him. How could she want him?

Her gaze roamed over the bed again, and heat unfurled like a dozen ribbons in her belly, tickling, tantalizing.

Tearing her thoughts away from sex, she dropped to her knees on the woven rug beside the bed and lifted the edge of the coverlet. There were several large cardboard boxes stashed away and she reached for one, stopping herself just as her fingertips grazed the edge. She could find something she would be better off not knowing about. Or she could find something that would give her a clue to who Lucky Doucet really was. She nibbled her lip in indecision but jerked the box toward her as another strange scratching sound drifted in through the window.

The carton was packed with books.

'God, who would have guessed he even knew how to read,' she muttered to herself.

Her fingers drifted lightly over the spines of the hardbound volumes that had been so carefully packed. They were largely college-level text books on biology. There was a collection of Shakespeare, several tomes on art history, and a set of small, very old-looking volumes with French titles in faded gold print. Serena carefully lifted out one of the science books and turned back the cover. It smelled musty and sweet and the pages stuck together as she turned to the title page and read the handwritten note in the upper righthand corner:

Étienne Doucet. USL. 1979.

College. She tried to imagine Lucky walking the hallowed halls of USL, going to class with books in his arms, but could picture him only in army fatigue pants and no shirt, climbing up into a tower with an assault rifle. But he'd been a student, and a serious one, if these books were anything to go by. Why then was he making his living by nefarious means?

'*I'm over the edge. I might do anything.*'

'*He's been living like an animal out in the swamp ever since he got out of the army. Folks say he's half crazy.*'

How did a student of science and the arts make the jump to the military and from the military to here? What had happened? What events had shaped him into the tough, sullen man he was today?

Her mind working on the question, Serena replaced the book and shoved the box back under the bed. She perched herself on the edge of the bed and sat there for a long moment, thinking, her gaze drifting around the room as she tried to make sense of the enigma that was Lucky.

The stillness crept in on her by degrees. By the time she was fully aware of it, it seemed absolute. The night that had seemed almost raucous with sound was suddenly silent. The eeriness of it felt like fingers tracing down her back.

She felt totally vulnerable. If someone outside the house were bent on coming in, the only thing to stop an intruder was a screen door. She thought she heard the scrape of a boot on the gallery floor, but the sound was gone so quickly she might have imagined it. The fear that had temporarily abated rushed back like a flood tide. There was more than snakes and alligators to be wary of in the swamp at night. The faces of the men Lucky had confronted at Mosquito Mouton's came to mind with nauseating clarity, and the big man's threat came back loud and clear – *I'll get you . . .*

Serena blew out the kerosene lamp on the nightstand, dousing the room in blackness. Grabbing a heavy brass candlestick, she crept on tiptoe toward the front wall. Lucky could fight his own fights, she was sure, but if his enemies came looking for him, she was not interested in being made a secondary target for their violence.

She pressed her back against the wall beside the window and strained to hear. Nothing . . . a faint thump . . . or was that just her heartbeat? She inched her way toward the door, breath aching in her lungs, candlestick raised in a white-knuckled fist.

A hand grabbed her arm from behind.

She didn't have time to draw breath to scream before she'd been spun around and pinned to the wall. A large hand clamped over her mouth and a heavy male body pressed into hers, his weight holding her with ridiculous ease. The candlestick dropped from her grasp and clattered to the floor.

'You lookin' to put a few dents in my head, sugar?'

Serena went limp against the wall. The tension ran out of her, leaving the trembling afterglow of fear. Lucky. He dropped his hand from her mouth and eased back from her, an amused smile twitching his lips. The smile died the instant Serena launched herself at him.

'You bastard! Of all the rotten things to do!'

He caught her by the wrists and held her off. 'Hey, cool out!'

'I will not cool out!' She aimed a kick at his shin, but he dodged it easily, which only made her angrier. 'If you had any idea how frightened I was to begin with – Damn you!' she raged, tears of terror swelling over the dam of her lashes. She kicked again and won the satisfaction of hearing him grunt as her toe made contact. 'If you had any idea . . .'

It all caught up with her then. The fear, the memories, the episode with Gifford, her exhaustion, the futility of trying to hurt Lucky all rushed up on her and hit with the strength and finesse of a freight train. She stopped struggling against him. His grip relaxed and she jerked her arms back, pulling free. She turned toward the door and pressed her hands over her face as the last brick in her wall of resolve crumbled.

She didn't want to be there. She didn't want to be frightened. She didn't want to have to deal with any family problems. She didn't want to have to deal with a man like Lucky.

Tears came very much against her will, but she didn't have the strength to stop them. They rolled like pearls down her cheeks.

Lucky watched with something akin to horror. The sound of a woman crying flipped a panic switch inside him. He could deal with her smart mouth and her cool reserve and the temper she had just unleashed on him, but tears . . . *Dieu!* And these were the real thing, not some phony whimpering designed to win her something. These were real tears, and it was plain she didn't like having him see them. She kept her back to him, her shoulders rigid as she tried in vain to fight them off. He stood there helpless, his hands jammed at his waist. The image of her standing on the pier at Gauthier's came back to him – the way the color had suddenly washed from her face as she'd looked down at his pirogue, the impression he'd had of inner fragility. It was there again, that sense that something inside her had cracked.

He couldn't help but feel empathy. He knew what it was to feel strength give way inside, to feel darkness creeping in like cold black ink. It didn't matter how many times he told himself he wouldn't get involved with her beyond the physical sense. It didn't matter how detached he told himself he was. He couldn't ignore this kind of pain.

'Hey,' he said, coming to stand directly behind her. He rested a hand on her shoulder and held on, gentle but firm, as she tried to shrug him off. 'What'sa matter, *chère?* Did I scare you that bad? I didn't mean to. I don' like comin' in the front door. It's an old habit that's saved my miserable hide more than once. Saved me from gettin' a goose egg this time,' he said, pushing at the candlestick with the toe of his boot.

'It's not that,' Serena whispered miserably. She shook her head and tried to sniff back the tears, but they still squeezed out to dribble down her face. She felt too defeated to cling to her pride. It served no purpose anyway. Why not tell him and get it over with? He probably thought the worst of her as it was, and what did it matter if he did? She didn't have to answer to him.

'It's this place. The swamp,' she said. She brushed her hair back from her face and stared out the door at the shades of darkness beyond. 'It terrifies me.'

'Is that why you never went out to get your bags?'

Serena nodded. 'I'm sure it seems completely stupid to you, but going out there in the dark is one of my worst nightmares.'

'Why is that?' Lucky asked, backing a step away from her and letting his hand drop from her shoulder. 'Why do you hate this place so? Is it too dirty for you? Too primal? It offends your sophisticated sensibilities that much?'

The bitterness in his voice touched Serena's raw nerves like acid. She jerked around to face him, glaring up at him through her tears. 'Stop it. I'm sick of your reverse snobbery. Stop putting me down because I prefer to live in a city and hold a regular job and wear a complete set of clothes. You don't know anything about me. You don't have any idea why I hate this place.'

'Then tell me.' He spoke it like a challenge, told himself he didn't care what the answer was, and waited to hear it just the same.

Serena blew a long sigh of resignation between her lips. Wrapping her arms around herself, she turned once again to face the door. 'When I was seventeen I got lost out here,' she began, relating the tale in a voice carefully devoid of emotion. 'My sister and I and some friends came out for the day in Giff's bass boat. We were just fooling around, having fun. We had packed a picnic lunch and we stopped off at a little clearing to eat. I wasn't sure where we were, but the boy driving the boat said he was, so I didn't worry about it.

'Shelby and I started getting on each other about something. I don't even remember what it was. We were always like that – bickering over little things, always taking opposite sides of an issue no matter how trivial. Anyway, when we got ready to leave, I realized I had forgotten my jacket in the clearing and went back alone to get it. Shelby talked the boy who was driving the boat into leaving me there.'

'She left you there. Alone.' Anger simmered in Lucky's gut, hot and furious. *Shelby.* 'The bitch.'

Serena made a dismissive gesture with one hand, then tucked it back against her. 'It was just a spiteful joke. She didn't mean for anything bad to happen.'

'Didn't she?' Lucky said flatly.

'No. Of course not. She was just mad at me and wanted to give me a scare. They went off in the boat, intending to come back and get me in an hour or so, but a storm blew up.

'It was one of those days. The sky was blue one minute and black the next.' She could still see it clearly in her mind's eye – the clouds rolling in across the swamp, gray and black with a strange yellow tinge, like noxious smoke boiling up out of a hundred factory chimneys. She could still taste the air, could still feel the weight of it pressing on her the moment before the storm broke. She could still hear the deafening thunder, the vicious cracks of the lightning as it ripped across the sky.

'It rained so hard it looked like ice coming down in sheets. It stormed for hours, and when the thunder and lightning finally quit, it just kept on pouring. I got scared. I knew no one would be able to come and get me with a boat the way it was raining. I thought if I got pointed in the right direction, I might be able to find my way back. I was wrong.'

She stopped there, unable to talk about what it had been like to walk on and on, following swelling streams that ran one direction and then another, turning so many times she'd had no idea whether she had been going toward home or hell. She couldn't talk about the terror of spending the night with no shelter, no supplies, no food. She couldn't put into words what it had felt like to crouch on a tree stump as that dark water swirled up toward her, driving a trio of cottonmouths up to share her perch.

The pressure building inside her as she relived the memories forced the false sense of calm from her voice. 'I don't remember a lot of what happened,' she said in a tremulous whisper. 'I blocked a lot of it out. I remember being cold and wet . . . and so afraid, I thought I'd choke on it . . . shaking so hard with fear that I almost couldn't walk. I remember the look on Gifford's face when they found me.'

'How long did it take?'

'Two days.'

Lucky swore under his breath. He had grown up on the bayous, fishing and hunting with his father and brothers, exploring just for the sheer joy of it. It was nothing for him to spend days in this wilderness. He knew every plant, every animal, every insect, every inch of mud and water. But he could imagine the kind of girl Serena had been – a soft, pretty debutante, member of the country club and cheerleading squad – and he could imagine her terror. The swamp was an unforgiving place, a place of natural beauty and natural violence. It didn't suffer fools gladly. Serena had been thrown into it completely unprepared. Considering the circumstances, that she had survived was a miracle.

And it had all been Shelby's fault.

It was Shelby's fault Serena was standing before him now, her fierce pride in tatters, trembling as if she were being given jolts of electricity at regular intervals. She had had this fear inflicted on her by her own sister, her twin. That was unthinkable to Lucky. Whatever else he might have done in his life, he had never intentionally hurt one of his own family members. But Shelby had. Shelby, who didn't care whom she hurt as long as she got what she wanted.

Anger surged through him now as he stared down at Serena. Anger and an emotion he refused to recognize as protectiveness. She stood with her back to him, but he had shifted to one side so he could see a little of her face over her shoulder. She looked impossibly young and sad standing there with her hair down around her shoulders and no makeup on her face.

'I was in the hospital for a week,' she said. 'Suffering from exposure and snakebite. As you can see, I never did quite get over it.' She gave a little laugh, but it held no humor, only pain and frustration and a sense of shame. She sniffed and shrugged. 'Now you know my disgraceful little secret: The calm, cool psychologist has a phobia she can't overcome.'

Lucky closed his eyes and folded his arms around her, holding her because he knew how badly she needed comforting. He could hear it in her voice and he couldn't keep from responding. He pulled her back against his big, solid body and marveled absently at how perfectly she fit.

Serena didn't fight his embrace. She wasn't sure what it meant, this show of caring from such a hard man, but she accepted it. She let herself lean back against his strength and soaked in the feeling of safety his arms inspired. In that moment it didn't matter how they'd fought or how different they were from each other. He was just a man offering her compassion when she needed it badly. She turned her head and pressed her cheek to his chest, listening to the solid thud of his heartbeat.

'This is why you didn't want to come out here in the pirogue, *oui?*' he asked softly, resting his cheek against the top of her head without even realizing it, certainly without recognizing the tenderness of the gesture.

'I didn't want to come out here, period.'

'Why did you?'

'Because I had to. Somebody had to.'

'That you're so afraid of the swamp – why didn't you tell me this sooner?'

'And give you another reason to sneer at me? No thank you. Frankly, I didn't think my fears would be of any interest to a man like you.'

'We've all of us got fears, *chère,*' he murmured almost to himself.

She looked up at him over her shoulder, arching a brow. 'Even big, bad Lucky Doucet?'

Lucky said nothing. It was one thing to have Serena confess to him. It would be quite something else to turn the tables. He wouldn't, couldn't, let her get that close to him. He had worked too hard to pull himself together to let some lady shrink dissect him.

'What are you afraid of, Lucky?' she whispered, her dark eyes glowing with intelligence and curiosity. There were tear tracks on her cheeks and her mouth looked soft and vulnerable.

'Nothing,' he murmured, turning her in his arms, 'nothing.' He lowered his mouth to hers.

He kissed her deeply, parting her lips expertly and sliding his tongue into her mouth in a gesture of possession. She tasted salty and sweet and so damn good his mind nearly went numb from it. He stroked his hands over the unbound silk of her hair and down her back to the subtle curves of her hips.

He hadn't stopped wanting her in the time he'd been gone. The fire had merely been banked, not put out. The flames leapt to life as her mouth moved beneath his, as her body moved against his. He had pulled away the first time, but he had no intention of pulling away now. He wanted her. It was desire, nothing deeper, nothing more complex than the basic story of a man wanting a woman, of a male needing a female.

With one hand splayed across the small of her back, he pulled her hips tighter against his. With his other hand he found the hem of her top and slipped beneath it to stroke the smooth satin of her skin. With deft fingers he un-snapped the front catch of her bra and cupped a breast. The fullness of it surprised him. The feel of her nipple hardening at the brush of his fingertips excited him.

He dragged his mouth from Serena's lips to her jaw to her ear. She shivered as he traced the delicate shell with the tip of his tongue and trembled when he whispered to her, his voice as dark and hot as the night.

'I want your breast in my mouth, *chère*. I wanna taste you. I wanna feel your nipple between my lips.'

A whimper caught in her throat.

'I wanna be inside you. I wanna feel you around me, tight and hot and wet.'

Serena's mind reeled with the seductive images he was conjuring. She could feel her temperature rising, sexual desire like a fever in her blood. It was exhilarating, intoxicating, frightening. Her body pressed against his, making its own desires known even as her mind grappled for control.

He kissed her throat, letting his teeth graze the skin. Serena caught her breath against the moan that threatened, but she couldn't stop herself from arching her neck to give him better access. He whispered a more explicit request in her ear, then sucked gently at the soft petal of her earlobe.

'No,' she barely managed to say between gasps. It sounded more like a question than an answer. 'No,' she said more forcefully.

Lucky rolled her nipple between thumb and forefinger, tugging subtly at the turgid peak. He raised his head a fraction and stared down at her, his eyes heavy-lidded and dark with passion, the thin band of amber ringing the pupils as warm as the light from the lamp on the table.

'Yes, *chère*,' he whispered.

Serena's gaze drifted to his mouth, that incredible, sensuous mouth, gleaming wet and red from their kiss. She stared at it, imagining it at her breast, tugging, sucking, his tongue laving her nipple while his fingers stroked her most sensitive flesh.

'No,' she murmured, the word barely a breath moving from her lips. 'I hardly know you.'

'You know I'm a man. I know you're a woman. What more do we need to know?'

'We don't even like each other.'

Lucky growled low in his throat as his mouth moved toward hers. 'I'm likin' you just fine right now, sugar.' He kissed a corner of her mouth, probing gently at the cleft of her lips with the tip of his tongue.

'J'aime te faire l'amour avec toi,' he breathed the words against her lips. *'Bien, ma chère, casse pas mon cœur.'*

He might have been saying anything. He might have been telling her

242

she was uglier than a mule, but the words, spoken in his smoky voice and flavored with their rich French accent, had their desired effect just the same. Serena felt her common sense further diluted by desire. A languid weakness floated through her arms and legs. She leaned heavily against Lucky and his scent filled her head – musky and warm and indisputably male.

He kissed her again, filling her mouth with his taste. His fingers left her breast to encircle the wrist of her right hand. He drew it down from where it rested flat against his chest and pressed it to the shaft of his manhood, letting her feel his length, his hardness. Serena moaned, a sound that managed to combine longing and admiration.

He moved against her hand, nuzzled her cheek, nipped her ear. 'That's all for you, angel. Let me give it to you, *chère*.'

Serena let her fingers flex hesitantly. Another wave of heat flashed through her. Oh, God, she wanted him. She wanted a man she'd only just met, a man who was a mystery to her, a man whose overwhelming masculinity frightened her on a fundamental level.

She turned her head away to draw in a deep breath, and her gaze hit the butt of the semi-automatic pistol that nestled against his ribs. Her heart skipped a beat, then rushed into double time as she looked beyond the gun to his biceps. An ugly two-inch-long gash was carved in the flesh and a line of dried blood trailed from it.

He was a dangerous man. A criminal. A man without scruples.

Shaking from the conflict that raged inside her, Serena pushed herself back from him. 'You're bleeding.'

'What?'

'Your arm. The one next to the gun,' she said pointedly. 'It's bleeding.'

'It's nothing.' Lucky reached for her.

Serena stepped back, crossing her arms in front of her, still avoiding his gaze. 'Not to me it's not.'

He reached out slowly to touch her hair, lifting a golden lock to rub it between his fingers. 'If I put a Band-Aid on it, will you go to bed with me?'

'No.'

'Why not?'

'Because I don't indulge in meaningless sexual flings with men I barely know,' she said, struggling to resurrect her façade of calm.

Lucky watched her lift her chin and straighten her shoulders and resented like hell the ease with which she seemed to throw off the need that still pounded through him. 'You mean you'll fuck a man only if you think he'll put a ring on your finger,' he said brutally.

'That's not what I said.'

'*Mais non,* but that's what you meant.'

'That isn't what I meant,' Serena argued. 'I don't believe in casual sex.

I don't go to bed with men who have no intention of investing emotionally in a relationship just because they happen to be well hung. *That's* what I meant,' she said bitingly. 'Are you going to try to tell me you're in love with me?'

Lucky forced a laugh. 'Not a chance.'

Serena clenched her jaw against the unexpected stab of hurt his words inflicted. Of course he wasn't going to say it – not now, not ever. Nor did she want him to. 'That settles it, then, doesn't it?'

'Only for tonight, sugar,' he said, hooking a finger beneath her chin and tilting her head back. He bent his head and brushed a mocking gentleman's kiss against her lips. '*Bonsoir, chérie*. Sweet dreams.'

Serena watched him saunter out the front door. She had no idea where he was going. She told herself she didn't want to know. At any rate, she was too exhausted to care. She'd been put through an emotional wringer, and every muscle and bone ached with it.

Avoiding even a glance at the bed, she curled herself into one corner of the sofa and tried not to think about Lucky, his heat, his passion . . . the way he had held her when she'd told him she was afraid. . . .

8

Serena sat in the pirogue, shading her eyes from the fierce morning sun that had come up like a ball of fire to burn off the low-lying fog. It was not yet noon and already the heat was as oppressive as a fur coat in July. She had dressed in a sleeveless white cotton blouse and khaki walking shorts, but even these summerweight garments wilted and clung to her and made her think longingly of a swim suit and a quiet day at the beach.

Adding to her discomfort was the knowledge that Lucky was standing behind her. She could feel him glowering down at her, and she straightened her back to show she wouldn't be intimidated by his evil mood.

She had gone searching for him at seven-thirty, eager to get to Gifford's – partly because she didn't quite trust herself to be alone with him. She had slept all of two hours after they had parted company the night before. And those two hours had been full of erotic dreams starring Guess Who. Just the memory was enough to make her blush. She didn't want to begin to decipher its meaning.

Lucky Doucet was trouble; he was an outlaw. The fact that he had a body to rival Adonis's couldn't enter into the argument. She couldn't get involved with him. She kept repeating that to herself like a mantra, but every time she thought she had herself convinced, her mind would sneak in the memory of the way he had held her after she'd told him about getting lost in the swamp. For that moment he had been gentle and tender and compassionate. . . .

He had been none of those things when she found him that morning. After searching the galleries back and front and finding only a trio of baby raccoons playing on the steps, she made her way up the exterior staircase to the attic.

Lucky stepped out and slammed the door shut behind him as she neared the landing, glaring at her with bleary, bloodshot eyes. His jaw was shadowed with morning beard. His hair was loose and disheveled, falling to his shoulders in unruly blue-black waves.

'What the hell are you doin' up here?' he demanded, his voice low and as rough as gravel. 'I don' want you comin' up here. You got that?'

'Why?' Serena questioned, arching a brow. 'Is this where you keep the bodies?'

'*C'est pas de ton affaire*,' he muttered. 'Never you mind what I keep up here. It's nothin' for a pretty shrink to go sniffin' through. You're a helluva lot better off not knowing.'

The mere suggestion made Serena curious. What was he hiding? Stolen goods? Illegal liquor? Drugs? Guns? It could have been any of those things, all of them, or something even worse.

'I'm sure I don't care what you keep in there, Mr. Doucet,' she said with as much cool as she could muster. 'I only came up here looking for you.'

He moved down to the step below hers, putting them nearly at eye level. Giving her a look that was at once calculatedly cruel and seductive, he lifted a hand to cup her cheek and brought his mouth down close to hers.

'Change your mind, sugar?'

'Certainly not.' Making a disgusted face and leaning back to escape his breath, she fanned the aroma away with her hand. 'You've been drinking.'

'Heavily,' Lucky said, straightening away from her. 'You oughta try it sometime. Loosen you up. From what I've seen, you could stand it.'

On that infuriating note, he turned and descended the stairs, his heavy boots barely making a sound on the wooden treads. Serena followed at a discreet distance, her mind wrestling with the conflicting facets of the man and with the conflicting emotions he aroused inside her. Her overriding thought was that the sooner she got to Gifford's, the sooner she would be free of Lucky Doucet and the strange spell he seemed to have cast over her.

While she sat at the table waiting impatiently, Lucky went through his morning ablutions without haste, shaving, showering, emerging from the bathroom barechested, wearing a pair of jeans that were nearly white with age. His wet hair was slicked back into its queue and bound with a length of leather boot lace. A scrap of red bandanna was tied around his right biceps, hiding the ugly wound he had acquired the night before.

Serena's gaze fastened on the makeshift bandage, and she felt something twist in her stomach. She told herself it was revulsion at the reminder of how this man made his living, but she knew that wasn't the whole truth. A part of that knot could be directly attributed to fear of what might have happened to him if the bullet had gone high and inside. He would have been dead and there would have been no chance left for anyone to reform him.

She shied away from the direction her thoughts were taking. That path was a dead end, a fast track to heartache.

'I suppose you'll tell me the other guy looks worse,' she said, still staring at the bandage and the massive arm it was bound to. Looking at it at least kept her eyes off his chest and the taut, hard muscles of his stomach.

Lucky looked down at the bandanna as if getting grazed with a bullet had slipped his mind. He flicked a speculative glance at Serena. '*Mais yeah*, but then, he was an ugly son of a bitch to start with.'

'Shouldn't you have a doctor look at that?'

'You're a doctor,' he said, his voice low and rough, his eyes capturing hers. He braced his hands on the arms of her chair and leaned down until his mouth hovered a breath away from hers. 'You wanna look at it?'

'No,' Serena murmured, tensing against the waves of heat rippling through her. He was much too close. His body gave off an electrical charge that shorted out her common sense and stimulated the primitive instincts buried beneath her sophisticated façade. His clean male scent filled her nostrils, and she caught herself wondering what it would be like to kiss him when he tasted like toothpaste instead of tobacco.

'No?' he questioned softly, arching one black brow. 'Is there some other part of me you'd care to examine. Dr. Sheridan?'

Her memory leapt at the opportunity to remind her of the way he had molded her hand to his erection. Serena bit back a curse, but she couldn't stop the heat from rising in her cheeks.

'Just say the word, sugar,' Lucky announced. 'Your wish is my command.'

Serena broke away from the beam of his gaze and spoke through her teeth. 'I wish you would stop wasting time on crude seduction routines and take me to Gifford's.'

He backed away from her, his expression cold and closed. 'You'll get there.'

'When?'

'When I'm damn good and ready to take you.'

He proceeded out onto the back porch, where he set down a dish of dry cat food for the baby raccoons, shooting Serena a look that dared her to comment. She stood at the back door, watching quietly as the little bandits gamboled around his big feet, vying for his attention, playing with his shoelaces. Lucky grumbled at them in French, but made no move to kick them away. He looked annoyed and embarrassed and Serena felt a most disastrous weakening in the heart she was trying to steel against him.

'It's just easier to feed them than have them in my garbage all the time, that's all,' he said defensively. 'It's not like they're pets.'

The words had barely left his mouth when one of the coons sat up on its hind legs and snickered at him, reaching up with its front paws to bat at his pant leg.

'Why not just shoot them?' Serena asked sweetly. 'You could save up all their little hides and make yourself a shirt.'

Lucky narrowed his eyes and growled at her, but the effect was ruined when another raccoon reached from its perch on the gallery railing for the shiny button on Lucky's jeans. He arched away from it, scolding it in rapid French. The little coon sat back and whinnied at him, and he reached out grudgingly to scratch it behind one triangular ear.

Serena felt her heart give a traitorous thump. The big bad poacher had a soft spot for little animals. She reminded herself that even Hitler had had a pet, and she forced herself to go back to the table to wait.

Only after a breakfast of fried catfish and a bottle of beer did Lucky give any indication of being ready to take her to Gifford's.

'I've got better things to do than play chauffeur,' he grumbled as he poled the pirogue away from the shore.

Serena shot him a look over her shoulder. 'You know, I'm sick of hearing you complain. If you didn't want to get involved in this, you could have left me at Gifford's yesterday. Why bring me here if you're too busy to take me back?'

He arched a brow above the rim of his mirrored sun-glasses with insulting lasciviousness. 'Do you really have to ask, sugar?'

She narrowed her eyes speculatively. 'You know, I think you do that on purpose.'

'What?'

'Make obnoxious sexist remarks. I think you do it to make me angry, to throw me off the topic. Why is that, Lucky? Are you afraid to have a real conversation with a woman?'

'I'm not afraid of anything,' he said too vehemently, giving the push-pole a mighty shove. 'I'm sure as hell not afraid of you.'

They traveled on in a silence that was as thick as the muggy air.

No shotgun blast greeted them this time as they rounded the bend to Gifford's cabin. Gifford sat on the steps tying fishing flies. Pepper Fontenot sat in a ratty old green and white lawn chair in the yard with a gutted outboard motor on a tarp at his feet. The clamorous sounds of a Cajun band blasted out of a portable radio on the gallery.

'Hey, Giff, what'sa matter with you? You run outta shells or somethin'?' Lucky hollered as he piloted the boat alongside the rickety dock.

Gifford pushed himself to his feet and jammed his big hands at his waist. 'Hell, I ain't wasting good buckshot on you, Doucet.'

'What about me?' Serena called. She waited for Lucky to pull the nose of the pirogue up on shore and exited from the bow, preferring to step on land rather than risk her neck on the rotted pier again.

Gifford gave her a long, hard stare as she came to stand at the foot of the steps. 'I figured you'd be on your way back to Charleston by now.'

Serena swallowed down the hurt and met his gaze head-on. 'I told you, I won't leave this swamp until you do. I want you to come back to Chanson du Terre with me.'

'And I told you, I'm not going. You're not bossing me around, little girl. I don't give a toot how many degrees you have. You can't hightail it out of Lou'siana first chance you get, then come on back and try to run things on the weekend.'

She didn't back down. Lucky watched her take it on the chin. He cursed Gifford for being so hard on her, then told himself he didn't care. He leaned a hip against the newel post and lit his fourth cigarette of the morning, sucking smoke down a throat that was already raw.

He felt like holy hell. Even in the best of circumstances he never slept more than a couple of hours at a stretch because of nightmares, but the previous night had been worse than usual. What little sleep he'd gotten had been plagued with memories of pain and betrayal. As if his conscious mind hadn't been doing the job well enough, his subconscious had seen fit to remind him that beautiful women were the cause of most of his problems. First Shelby, then Amalinda Roca, the lovely little viper whose duplicity had helped to land him in a Central American prison.

He had finally given up on the idea of sleep and had proceeded to attempt to drown his foul mood and sexual frustration with whiskey, succeeding only in giving himself a colossal hangover. Now his head banged in syncopated rhythm with the gash in his arm where Mean Gene Willis had managed to nick him.

'You look like hell,' Gifford said, his hard gaze still on Serena. His voice had lost some of its edge, betraying his true concern as he took in the dark crescents beneath her eyes. He glanced at Lucky to distract himself from his guilt. 'You both look like hell.'

'Mebbe they both been *raisin'* hell,' Pepper suggested, chuckling merrily at the dark looks his comment received from both Lucky and Serena. Gifford only raised a bushy white brow in speculation as he studied them.

Serena felt a blush rise to her cheeks at the memory of the near miss of the night before. There but for the grace of God and Smith & Wesson . . . If the sight of Lucky's gun hadn't brought her back to reality in a cold rush, she may well have had something to blush about now. Dropping her head, she made her way up the steps, past her grandfather and onto the gallery.

'I could use a cup of coffee. Pepper, do you still make it strong?'

'Black as dat bayou and strong 'nough to curl your purty blond hair, *pichouette*,' Pepper said, flashing his teeth.

'Sounds like heaven,' Serena mumbled, letting herself in the front door.

Gifford remained on the steps, staring down at Lucky. 'What have you got to say for yourself? You been fooling 'round with my little girl?'

Lucky slid his sunglasses on top of his head and gave Gifford a belligerent look. 'What would you care, old man? All you wanna do is give her the sharp side of your tongue. You're the one left her with no place to stay last night.'

'I got my reasons.'

'Like you got your reasons for holin' up out here?' Lucky shook his head and muttered an expletive. 'Cut her some slack, Giff. She came, didn't she?'

'Yeah, she came, and she'll leave again too,' Gifford drawled, nodding. 'First chance she gets. She don't give a damn about what happens here. The girl oughta have some respect for family, for tradition.'

Lucky snorted. 'You got a funny way of teachin' respect. Dump her out in the swamp to spend the night. She'd probably cut your heart out if you had one.'

The idea that Gifford had known about Serena's fear and played on it infuriated Lucky. And the rise of his protective instincts made him even angrier. He swore again, tossed his cigarette butt to the dirt, and snuffed it out viciously with the toe of his boot. 'I oughta just wash my hands of the lot of you. It's nothin' but trouble, this business.'

'Me, I hear you got 'nough trouble wit' dat Perret boy and dat big ugly son Willis,' Pepper said, rocking back on the hind legs of his lawn chair. His light eyes sparkled like aquamarines in his dark face.

Lucky scowled at him. 'Where'd you hear that?'

'Me, I heard dat wit' my ears, I did.' The old man chuckled at his little joke, not heeding Lucky's ferocious glare in the least.

'Yeah, well, you keep your ears out of it or they might just get shot off.'

The end of his warning was punctuated by the sound of the screen door slapping shut, the soft 'pop' sounding like a toy gun. Serena made her way across the small gallery, trying to concentrate on the steam rising from her coffee instead of the conversation she'd heard plainly through the screen while she'd been inside.

'Are you going to make this easier on all of us and explain to me what's going on, Gifford?' she said, lowering herself carefully to sit on the top step.

Gifford looked down at her and frowned. 'Shouldn't have to be giving you an update like some kind of goddamned foreign correspondent.'

Serena sighed heavily, feeling too exhausted to even bring her cup to her lips so she could draw on the amazing elixir that was Pepper Fontenot's coffee. 'Gifford, please. You've made your opinion of my life abundantly clear. Yes, I'm living miles away. People do that, you know. They grow up, they move on, they make their own lives.'

'You've got no sense of tradition.'

'I won't be a slave to it, if that's what you mean. I appreciate the history of Chanson du Terre, but I'm not going to become a planter to keep it going. Shelby is the one who always planned to carry on the tradition in one way or another. My career has taken me elsewhere. That doesn't mean I don't care about Chanson du Terre or you. I love you both,' she said, looking up at him with fierce earnestness in her wide dark eyes. 'Is that the confession you were looking for? Are you happy now?'

'Hardly,' the old man grumbled. Still, he backed up a step and sat down beside her. 'If you cared about the place, things would never have come to this.'

'And just what is 'this'? What's going on?'

He hesitated a long time, considering and discarding options. Serena didn't rush him, but sat patiently, sipping her coffee. Finally, he heaved a sigh and plowed a hand through his white hair, leaving short strands standing on end.

'Some hotshot political people have got it into their puddin' heads Mason Talbot is destined for political stardom. They want him to run for the legislature next year. He's just pretty enough and stupid enough to get elected too. He'll make a nice little puppet for the oil kingpins. His daddy may have lost his fortune in the bust, but he hasn't lost any of his connections. I'm sure old John Talbot would love to have a son in the governor's mansion one day.'

'Mason running for office,' Serena murmured, a troubled frown drawing her brows together. 'I can't believe Shelby didn't mention it to me.'

'Seems to me there's quite a few things Shelby didn't mention to you, *chère*,' Lucky commented darkly.

Serena shot him a look of annoyance and turned back to Gifford. 'I don't see what this has to do with Chanson du Terre.'

'Think about it, Serena. Shelby has her heart set on Mason going to Baton Rouge. They won't need the plantation. The state the place is in right now, all it is is a liability. But if I were to sell it now and advance her her inheritance, that would give Mason enough money to buy his way into any office he wanted.

'Everybody knows it's advertising wins elections nowadays. Plaster Mason's pretty face on billboards, on television, on the sides of buses, nobody's gonna care that he's got cotton for brains.'

Serena felt compelled to stick up for her absent brother-in-law. She had always liked Mason. He was too laid back for Gifford's taste and he might have been more fluff than substance, but he had a good heart. 'Mason has got more than cotton for brains. He graduated from law school fifth in his class.'

Gifford gave a snort that eloquently spoke of his regard for lawyers in general. 'Don't mean he's got a lick of sense. All it means to me is he has a nose for loopholes and technicalities. Hell, that hound over there can sniff out a coon fast as dammit, but that don't mean he's Einstein.'

It was pointless to argue with him, and they had gotten off the most important topic, so Serena steered them back with effort. 'You said yesterday you'd mentioned something to Shelby about selling. Why would you do that if you don't want to sell?'

He scowled at his boots and looked uncomfortable. When he spoke, it was as grudgingly as a schoolboy owning up to sticking gum on his teacher's chair. 'Hell, I was just makin' noise. We've been having a rough spot here – cane smut last year, too much rain this spring, production costs are up, that damned gas tax gets us coming and going. I was just grumbling is all, trying to see if I might raise a little interest in Shelby for something besides redecorating the house while she's staying in it. So I say over dinner one night, "By God, if all I'm gonna do is work myself to death on this place so some stranger can come in and take over, I might as well sell it and go to Tahiti." Faster than I could spit and whistle, she had a Tristar rep nosing around the place.'

Serena frowned as she listened. It had seemed unlikely to her that Shelby would want to sell Chanson du Terre, if not because of a sense of tradition, because it had always represented status in the community – something Shelby prized almost above all else. But if she had set her sights on an even higher plateau and saw selling the place as a means of achieving that end, that was a different story. Shelby's talent for rationalization was unsurpassed in Serena's experience.

'Why Tristar Chemical?' she asked.

Gifford shrugged wearily. 'I don't know. There's probably some connection through Mason's family. How else would she have found a buyer at all? Since the oil bust, the market down here is soft as butter. Shelby couldn't sell igloos to Eskimos to begin with. Mason only let her have that office space downtown to placate her. You know I love her, but she's a silly little thing and always has been. The only reason she went into real estate was so she could dress up, look important, and go to the chamber of commerce meetings.'

'So you don't want to sell the place,' Serena said, uncomfortable with the topic of her twin. 'Tell the Tristar people no and be done with it.'

'They don't take no for an answer,' he grumbled. 'That damned Burke is like a pit bull. I can't shake him for love or money.'

Serena fixed her grandfather with the stern look she'd learned from him. 'Gifford Sheridan, in all my life I've never known you to back down from a fight.'

He frowned at her. His square chin came up a notch. 'I'm not backing down from a fight.'

'Then what are you doing out here?' she asked, exasperated.

He raised his head another proud inch, looking as stubborn and immovable as the faces on Mount Rushmore. 'I'm dealing with it my own way.'

They were back to square one. Serena squeezed her eyes shut for a second and concentrated on the needle of pain stabbing through her head. She took a sip of coffee, hoping in vain that the caffeine would bring her energy level up. Instead, it churned like acid in her stomach and made her feel even hotter and more uncomfortable than she had been to begin with.

Of course, Gifford's obstinacy wasn't helping. Nor was having Lucky's steady gaze fastened on her. He stood at the foot of the steps, staring at her through the opaque lenses of his sunglasses, an unnerving experience in the best of circumstances. The only thing that might have made it worse was if he hadn't been wearing the glasses. She couldn't think of anything more disturbing than the heat and intensity of those amber eyes.

Pepper broke the tense silence, rising lazily from his chair. Without a word to anyone he ambled down to the edge of the bayou and stood for a moment, apparently admiring the view. When he turned to come back, he looked up at Giff and said, 'Company comin'. Me, I hears dat ol' Johnson outboard wit' the bad valve.'

Gifford swore, pushing himself to his feet and turning for the cabin. He returned with his shotgun, the twelve-gauge cracked open so he could shove slugs into it as he pounded down the steps and across the yard.

'Gifford!' Serena set her coffee cup down and ran after him. 'Gifford, for heaven's sake!'

He managed to get one shot off before she reached him. The buckshot hit the water, sending up a spray just off the port bow of the game warden's boat. Perry Davis's voice crackled at them over a bullhorn.

'Goddammit, Gifford, put the gun down!'

Gifford lowered the shotgun but wouldn't relinquish it to Serena when she tried to pull it away from him. She ground her teeth and counted to ten and tried to call on her years as a counselor to cool her temper. Nothing helped much. She was furious with Gifford and she knew she was simply too close to him to ever be completely rational and objective in dealing with him.

The engine of the game warden's boat cut and the hull bobbed on the dark water a few feet from shore. Perry Davis stood behind the wheel, looking outraged and officious, his baby face flushed. Beside him was a middle-aged man, big and raw-boned with a fleshy face and a head of slicked-back steel-gray hair. He wore navy slacks and a striped necktie that had been jerked loose and hung like a noose around the collar of his sweat-stained blue dress shirt.

'You keep shooting at people and I'm gonna have to arrest you, Gifford,' Davis threatened, switching off the bullhorn.

Lucky, who had come to stand on Serena's left, gave a derisive snort. 'You don't arrest nobody else. Why start with him?'

The game warden worked his mouth into a knot of suppressed fury. 'Maybe I'll start with you.'

Lucky pushed his sunglasses up his nose and gave Davis a long, level look, smiling ever so slightly. 'Yeah? You and what army?'

'I'll get you, Doucet. I can promise you that,' Davis said, thrusting a warning finger in Lucky's direction. 'Crazy bastard like you running around loose. Folks aren't gonna stand for that forever.'

Serena could feel the tension humming around Lucky like electrical waves. The muscles in his jaw worked. He never took his eyes off Perry

Davis and he never said another word. Yet, even from a distance of several yards, Davis felt compelled to back away; he moved to the back of the boat on the excuse of looking at the motor, trying to appear as if he had casually dismissed Lucky and their conversation. Gifford took advantage of the silence.

'Burke, you turn yourself around and get out.'

The big Texan let a phony grin split his meaty features. 'I can't do that, partner. We've got business to discuss.'

'I've got nothing to say to you that can be said in front of a lady,' Gifford retorted. 'I'm not interested in your offer. Go on back to Texas before I shoot you full of holes.'

'Gifford,' Serena said, schooling herself to at least appear calm and under control. 'Why don't you invite Mr. Burke in? I'm sure we can settle this business amicably with a little plain talk.'

Burke gave an exaggerated shrug. 'The little lady has a head on her shoulders, Gifford. I've said that all along. Isn't it about time you listened to her?'

It occurred to Serena that the Tristar rep had mistaken her for Shelby, but she didn't have the chance to correct him.

'I don't have to listen to anybody!' Gifford shouted, color rising in his face from his neck up. 'I'm not senile, by God. I can make up my own mind. And if there's gonna be any plain talk, it's gonna come from the business end of old Betsy here,' he said, raising the stock of the shotgun to his shoulder.

'Gifford!' Serena shouted, lunging toward him.

He squeezed the trigger as she knocked him off balance. The shotgun bucked as another deafening explosion rent the air. Water sprayed up against the hull of the game warden's boat, dousing Burke and Davis with a rain of mud and shredded vegetation. The two men ducked, covering their heads with their arms, then came up swearing.

Burke pointed a warning finger at Gifford. 'I've had it with you, Sheridan. You're a crazy old man. There's been plenty of witnesses to that. I can get the sheriff out here. You can't just go around shooting at people who want to do business with you.'

'Hell,' Gifford said, wading out into the water, his fierce gaze fixed on Burke. 'I said a long time ago they ought to open season on Texans. This state wouldn't be in the mess it's in if we'd 'a kept you greedy sons of bitches on the other side of the border!'

Serena eyed the muddy water with distaste, a tremor of fear snaking down her spine. Then she looked at her grandfather's back as he advanced toward the game warden's boat and forced herself to take the first step in, her shoes sinking into the muddy bottom. She grabbed Gifford by a belt loop on his jeans and tried to pull him back toward shore.

Burke had turned hot pink; his eyes bugged out of his head as if someone had suddenly pulled his tie tight enough to cut off his wind. 'Keep it up, Sheridan! Come on, say a few more lines like that one! They'll sound real good at your competency hearing!'

Gifford tried to launch himself toward the boat, but Lucky stepped in front of him and planted a hand on his chest.

'*C'est assez.* Go on up to the house, *mon ami*,' he said softly. 'Go on.'

The old man stood for a moment, grinding his teeth, his weight on his forward foot, his big hands twisting on the shotgun. The only other sound was Beausoleil playing '*J'ai Été au Zydeco*' on the portable radio with inappropriate joy.

'Gifford, please,' Serena whispered behind him, pressing her cheek to his broad back as her feet sank deeper into the goo.

'Come on, Giff,' Pepper said from the bank. 'He ain't worth the trouble.'

Gifford snarled a curse, jerked around, and waded back to shore. With Pepper whispering and gesturing animatedly beside him, he headed for the cabin.

Lucky's gaze settled on Serena. She was up to her knees in the bayou. The color was draining from her face and her eyes looked huge as she stared at him.

'*Foute ton quant d'ici*,' he murmured. 'Go on, *chère*, get away from here. I'll take care of this.'

She backed away slowly, grimacing as the mud sucked at her shoes.

Lucky turned and advanced on the boat, wading right up alongside it until he was waist-deep in the muddy water. 'This is no way to do business, M'sieu Burke,' he said, his low, rough voice just above a whisper.

Burke leaned down, bracing his hands on the side of the boat, his gaze intent on Lucky's face. 'You tell your friend to start cooperating, then, son,' the Texan said, also speaking softly, as if the weight of the subject required a tone of conspiracy. 'My company has gone to a lot of trouble to choose that site, and they mean to have it.'

'Is that supposed to be a threat?'

'It's a fact, son.'

The words hit him wrong. Burke's tone, his voice, his accent, his air of command, all conspired against him in Lucky's mind. For a split second he was back in Central America taking orders from a big Texan who had sold him down the river, a lieutenant colonel who had been using his covert operations team to make himself a bundle. Lucky had uncovered the man for the traitor he was, but not before spending a year in hell. That all came back to him in a flash, and the reins of control slipped a little through his mental fingers.

'You know, there's a lotta things I'm not too sure of,' he said to Burke, a chilling smile curving his mouth. 'But there's one thing I do know for certain.' In the blink of an eye the smile was gone. He grabbed the knot of Burke's tie and gave it a yank, pulling the man down toward him so they were nose to nose. 'I'm not your son.'

The Tristar rep was over the side of the boat and diving headfirst into the bayou before he could register a protest. He landed in the water like a whale and came up spitting mud.

'You hadn't ought to lean over the side that way, *mon ami*,' Lucky said, wading casually toward the shore. 'You might fall in. You fall in, there's no tellin' what might get you in this water.'

As if he had conjured it up by magic to illustrate his point, a water snake slid out of some reeds near the bank. Burke swore and scrambled to get back over the side of the boat. Davis helped him, grabbing him by the back of his pants and hauling him up, shouting at Lucky all the while.

'I mean it, Doucet! I've had it with you running roughshod! Your days out here are numbered.'

Lucky made a face and waved him off. Serena met him on the bank, glaring up at him. Color had come back into her cheeks, he noticed.

'Can't you show respect for anybody?' she asked sarcastically.

'Mais *yeah*,' he said flippantly. 'My *maman*, my *papa*, the Pope. Len Burke ain't the Pope, sugar. I don't think he's even a good Catholic.' He gave her an infuriating indulgent look. Behind them the motor of the game warden's boat roared to life, then faded into the distance.

'That's it,' Serena declared, stopping in her tracks. She threw her hands up in a gesture of defeat. 'I've had it. There's something about this place that drives people over the edge. I can't stand it. Gifford is going around shooting at people. You – You're—' She couldn't finish the sentence, she was so upset. She gave in to the urge to stamp her foot. It seemed she could control little or nothing out there – not the situation, not her fears or her passions or her temper, least of all her guide.

'This whole situation is just ridiculous,' she said, pacing a short stretch of bank, her arms crossed tightly against her. 'Why didn't Shelby call me? Why didn't she just explain all this to me to begin with?'

'Gee,' Lucky said with mock innocence. 'Could it be she didn't want you to know? Could it be she thought she might pull off the deal without having you know a thing about it until it was too late?'

Serena shot him a look from the corner of her eye. 'Oh, for Pete's sake, you make it sound like a big conspiracy.'

'That's because it *is* a big conspiracy, sugar,' he said, leaning back against the trunk of a massive live oak. He shook a cigarette out of the pack from his shirt pocket and dangled it from his lip without lighting it.

'Don't be ridiculous,' Serena snapped. 'You're trying to tell me Shelby is in league with the Tristar people to drive her own grandfather from his land?'

Lucky shrugged. '*C'est bien*. You got it in one. It's a sweet deal. She gets a nice fat commission on the sale and her inheritance besides. On top of that, she and the politically ambitious Mr. Talbot bring industry to a town with a depressed economy. There's nothing like a local hero in an election year, you know.'

Serena planted herself squarely in front of him, settling in for the argument. 'You're way off base. In the first place, Mason doesn't have an ambitious bone in his body. If he were any more laid back, someone would have him interred.'

'You heard your grandpapa, *chère*. The powers that be want Talbot in office. His daddy wants him in office. Shelby wants him in office. You think he's gonna tell all those people no? You think Shelby would let him?'

'You make my sister sound like Lady Macbeth. Shelby is hardly that calculating or devious.'

Lucky knew exactly how devious and calculating Shelby could be, but he didn't give voice to his own experiences.

He used Serena's instead. 'Isn't she? Are you forgetting what you told me last night? She left you out here alone. You could have been killed.'

'That was an accident, a joke that went wrong.'

'Was it?'

Serena dodged his steady gaze. He was dredging up old hurts inside her and they had no place here. Besides, no one had been more relieved than Shelby when Serena had been found after her ordeal. Her sister had wept at her hospital bedside and had begged her forgiveness . . . and she had thrown her fear of the swamp, the fear that had resulted from that incident, up in her face time and again since then.

Serena shrugged off the grain of doubt trying to insinuate itself into her mind. Her feelings toward her twin were complicated enough already; she didn't need Lucky's dark suspicions adding to the morass.

'Stop trying to turn me against my own sister,' she said irritably. 'I'm sure you have every reason to be paranoid, considering the kind of life you lead, but I refuse to fall into that kind of thinking.'

'You shrinks have a word for that too, don't you?' Lucky said, arching a brow. 'Denial?'

'Talk about denial,' Serena grumbled, changing the subject as she resumed her pacing. She threw a fuming look up at the cabin. 'I can't believe Gifford. He says he's dealing with this *his* way. He's not dealing with it at all. He's making me—'

She broke off as the realization hit her like a brick square in the forehead. Making her deal with it *was* his way of dealing with it. He wanted to force her into caring more about the plantation. He wanted her to take up the banner and fight for the cause, and in doing so revive her sense of tradition and duty. God, he had even lured her into the swamp, the place she had lived in fear of for fifteen years.

'That old fox,' she muttered, planting her hands on her hips. 'That old son of a boot.'

He had manipulated her as neatly as a chess master, and now there was no honorable way out. She was involved and she would have to do her best to resolve the situation or lose face with Gifford again. She might have run the risk of incurring his wrath, but she couldn't bear the thought of facing his disappointment in her. He had bet on that and won, the old horse thief.

'Take me back,' she said suddenly, turning toward Lucky. 'Take me back to Chanson du Terre. I have to talk with Shelby. I'll straighten this mess out as best as I can. But if Gifford thinks he can guilt me into staying here forever, he can just think again.'

9

Lucky dropped her off at his house, telling her he would be back in an hour to pick her up and return her to Chanson du Terre. Serena watched him pole away, then let herself inside. It was silent and cool. One of the baby raccoons peered in the back door at her, its long front paws pressed to the screen. When Serena moved toward it, the coon whinnied and scampered away, its claws clattering on the wooden floor of the gallery, making the exact sound that had scared her witless the night before.

She set her suitcases by the front door, then raided Lucky's small refrigerator and made herself a ham sandwich, taking great care to make certain the kitchen was as spotless when she was finished as it had been to begin with. When that small task was accomplished, she still had forty minutes to wait.

Her mind turned to the question of what she would find awaiting her at Chanson du Terre. It all seemed so unlikely. Mason running for office. Shelby plotting against Giff. The plantation's existence threatened.

Bulldozers, Lucky had said. Tristar would raze the place to make room for labs, offices, manufacturing facilities, warehouses. The possibility, as remote as it was, hit Serena in a tender spot. That old house had borne silent witness to a lot of history. It had seen the last days of French rule in Louisiana, the golden era before the war. Yankees had camped on the lawn, and the staircase still bore the marks where a drunken officer had ridden his horse up it. It had survived the Reconstruction and the Great Depression. Had it survived all that only to fall victim to greed?

No. Of course not. The current situation would be cleared up and life would go on at Chanson du Terre with Gifford ruling the roost as he had for nearly sixty years.

And when Gifford was gone and Shelby was off in Baton Rouge and Serena was back in Charleston . . . what then?

'Oh, no, you don't,' Serena muttered, pushing herself up from her place at the table. This was exactly what Gifford wanted – to rouse her sentimental streak.

Instead, she turned her mind to another puzzle – Lucky. She wandered the two rooms of his cottage, trying to discern as much as she could about him from the things she found. It was an exercise in perception and reasoning, she told herself, not simple curiosity about the man.

What she found in examining Lucky's lair was almost nothing. Utilitarian furnishings that happened to be antique. Nothing frivolous, nothing personal, nothing more revealing than a respect for his heritage and a need for order. He kept no books in sight, no magazines, no photographs, no art on the walls. But that in itself was a revelation. He was a man in hiding. His house was hidden. In his house, everything personal was hidden. He let nothing of his inner self show if he could help it at all.

Why was that? It didn't seem like a wholly natural reticence. It seemed more as if he had carefully constructed a maze of walls around himself for protection. What would a man like Lucky need protection from? He seemed so tough, so self-reliant. And yet there were the contradictions. He gave food to orphaned raccoons. He had defended her to Gifford. He had held her when she had felt miserable and afraid.

She opened the tall door of the armoire in the dining room. The shelves of the cupboard were stocked with only the kind of things one would expect to find in a dining room. Serena groaned a little in disappointment and hesitated a moment before crossing into the other room, which was, with the exception of the quality of the furnishings, barren as a monk's cell.

'Jackpot,' she whispered as she swung open the door of the large armoire that stood opposite the foot of the bed.

The closet had a column of cubbyholes along the left side, with an area for hanging clothes on the right. A set of three deep drawers created the base. She glanced over his wardrobe, which consisted of jeans, fatigue pants, T-shirts, and an army dress uniform with a chest full of decorations. The uniform interested her, but the smaller shelves on the left drew Serena's immediate attention.

They held framed photographs. The Doucet family captured at all different times of their lives. There was a sepia-toned wedding picture of his parents – a handsome, smiling couple gazing at each other with love. There was a battered black and white snapshot of his father standing with his hand on the shoulder of a gangly boy who was proudly displaying a trophy-size fish and a gap-toothed grin. Lucky, she assumed, looking much younger and lighter of heart. There were more recent photos of other members of the clan, unmistakable by their resemblance to one another, children of various ages, chubby babies in frilly baptism gowns, and grade-schoolers taking first communion in their Sunday best with their faces shining and their cowlicks slicked into submission.

Serena felt her heart melt a little as she looked at the photographs. Lucky had a family and he loved them. He wouldn't have gone to all the trouble of framing the pictures if he hadn't cared deeply. Why did he isolate himself from them? Shelby had said his parents were nice people, respectable people. Did Lucky feel unworthy of them because of the life he led? Or was there something else that made him feel separate?

She reached out to touch the photograph of Lucky and his father, brushing her fingertips over the smiling face of the boy he had been. What had happened to that boy to put shadows in his eyes? What events had turned him into the dangerous, brooding man he was today?

A yearning to know that was deeper than professional curiosity ached inside Serena. She wanted to know Lucky's secrets, wanted to reach past them to offer him something – solace, comfort. This longing wasn't wise, and it brought her no joy, but she didn't try to deny it. She just stood there, hurting for him, hurting for herself, wishing to God she had never left Charleston.

'Mom sent over a chocolate cake and some cookies and two loaves of French bread she baked today. I just set 'em on the counter.'

Serena shrieked and jumped back from the armoire as if it had suddenly come alive. She swung around with a hand over her heart to keep it from leaping out of her chest. Standing at the entrance to the room was a boy of about thirteen, beanpole-thin in jeans that were too short and a T-shirt that proclaimed Breaux Bridge to be the crawfish capital of the world. His eyes were dark and round with excitement.

'You ain't Lucky,' he blurted out. 'But Lucky sure is.'

The instant the remark registered in his brain he flushed a shade of red that rivaled the color of the baseball cap he wore backward on his head.

Serena laughed, more out of relief than anything. 'You startled me,' she said, pushing the door of the armoire closed. 'Lucky's not here right now. He should be back in about half an hour. I'm Serena Sheridan.'

'Will Guidry.' He came forward hesitantly, started to offer her his hand but stopped midway to check it for dirt. Finding it relatively clean, he stuck it out in front of him again, looking as if he fully expected contact with her to give him a painful shock.

'It's nice to meet you, Will.' Serena gave his hand a firm shake and released it. 'Would you care to wait for Lucky to come back?'

'Um – well – no – that's okay,' the youth stammered. He jammed his hands into his pants pockets and shuffled his oversize feet, staring down at them as if they were the most amazing sight he'd come across recently. 'I was just leavin' off some stuff. Mom says she knows he won't take nothing—' He grimaced and corrected himself. 'Won't take *any*thing for runnin' them poachers off our crawfish nets, but she said the least she could do was bake him somethin' nice seein' as how he lives out here all alone—' He broke off and winced again, as if some unseen etiquette monitor was smacking him with a switch every time he goofed up. 'I mean, he *did* live alone until you – But then, maybe you aren't – I mean, this could just be – Aw, hell – I mean, *heck*—'

Serena stared at him, everything inside her going still. 'What did you say?' she asked softly, ignoring the boy's red-faced embarrassment. 'Did you say "running poachers off"?'

Will shuffled his sneakers and shrugged, giving her a look that told her he suspected she might be a little odd. 'Well, yeah. That's sorta what he does.'

'But I thought—' Serena cut herself off, snapping her mouth shut with an audible click.

She had thought what Lucky had wanted her to think. She had taken one look at him and assumed he was an outlaw, and he had let her believe it, had reinforced that image every chance he'd gotten. This was certainly her day to feel like a fool.

'We been havin' some trouble, you know,' Will said somberly, scratching his bony elbow. 'My dad's gone down to the Gulf to look for work, so it's just Mom and us kids to home. Poachers figured our nets would be easy pickin'. Lucky showed 'em different.'

'Lucky,' Serena murmured. Big bad Lucky Doucet. Savior of orphaned animals. Defender of the defenseless. Not poaching, but chasing poachers away from the nets of women and children.

'He's some kind of man,' Will said happily. 'But I guess you already know that.' His gaze dropped abruptly and he turned red again. He was at the age where nearly everything struck him as a sexual innuendo, and every social blunder seemed catastrophic. He looked at Serena with horror. 'I didn't mean that you'd *know*. I meant, you know . . .'

'I know,' she said absently, still too stunned to take much pity on the poor kid.

If Lucky wasn't a poacher, then why had he let her believe he was? And why the antipathy between him and the game warden? Maybe they simply didn't like each other. Maybe Lucky didn't think Perry Davis was doing a good enough job. There could have been any number of reasons, not all of them good. Just because he wasn't a poacher didn't mean he wasn't guilty of something. There was still the matter of the illegal liquor and the room upstairs he didn't want her to see.

'Anyhow,' Will said, gulping down his embarrassment. 'I oughta be goin'.' He shuffled backward toward the door, swinging a long, bony arm in the direction of the kitchen. 'I just left the stuff on the counter.'

'Yes, thank you. I'm sure Lucky will appreciate it,' Serena said, resurrecting her manners and her smile. 'It was nice meeting you, Will.'

He blushed and shrugged, ducking his head and grinning shyly. 'Yeah, you too. See ya 'round.'

He bolted out the front door and loped across the yard to a canoe beached on the bank of the bayou. Serena wandered out onto the gallery and waved to him as he paddled away. Even from a distance she could see him blush. Adolescence. What hell. She shook her head in a combination of amusement and sympathy, and wondered what Lucky might have been like at that age.

As if she didn't have enough to figure out about the grown man. If he wasn't a poacher, then what was he? A bootlegger? A gun runner with a heart of gold?

Her gaze drifted across the porch to the stairs that led up to the overhanging *grenier*, the forbidden room.

Never you mind what I keep up here. . . . It's nothing for a pretty shrink to go sniffing through. . . . You're a helluva lot better off not knowing.

She was better off not knowing, or he was safer if she didn't know?

She was on the steps before she could tell herself not to go on. Whether it was a need to understand the man that compelled her, or a need to justify her attraction to him, she didn't try to discern. In fact, she tried not to think at all. Almost as if they belonged to someone else's body, she watched her feet ascend one step at a time, watched her hand reach for the doorknob and turn it, watched the door swing back.

Nothing could have prepared her for what she saw. Not in her wildest imagination had she suspected this. She thought she had been prepared for anything – crates of guns, bales of drugs, boxes of stolen goods – but she hadn't been at all prepared for beauty, for art.

The room was ringed with paintings. Canvases, stacked three deep, leaned back against the walls. An easel took center stage in the open, airy room. On it was propped a work in progress.

Serena wandered into the room, gazing all around her in a daze. Unlike the first floor, the attic was not divided, but was one large room with windows at either gable end and skylights punctuating the ceiling on the north side. The light that filtered in through the blinds was soft and dusty-looking, spilling onto the floor in oblong bars of gold. There was a long workbench against one wall, loaded with jars of brushes and tubes of paint, sketch pads, pencils, paint-spotted rags. A heavy sheet of canvas served as rug and dropcloth, covering a large area of the wooden floor surrounding the easel. The smell of oil paint and mineral spirits hung heavy in the air like cheap perfume.

So this was Lucky's deep dark secret. He was an artist.

Serena walked around the edge of the dropcloth, trying to take in the paintings propped against the wall. They depicted the swamp as a solitary place of trees and mist, capturing the stillness, the sense of waiting. They were beautiful, hauntingly, powerfully beautiful, filled with a dark tension and an aching sense of loneliness. They were magnificent and terrifying.

She stood before one that featured a single white egret, the great bird looking small and insignificant among the columns of gray cypress trunks and tattered banners of gray moss and smoke-gray morning mist. She stood there in the hot, stuffy room and felt as if the painting were drawing her in and swallowing her whole. She could feel the chill of the mist, could smell the swamp, could hear the distant cries of birds.

All the paintings shared that ability to draw the viewer into the center of the swamp and the center of the artist's anguish. They were extraordinary.

'Oh, Lucky,' she whispered as understanding dawned painfully inside her. She closed her eyes and pressed her hands to her face.

This was what he hadn't wanted, for her to see beyond the façade of macho bravado, not because he was ashamed of what she would find, but because it was too personal, too private. He wasn't a man who would easily share his inner self; she'd known that all along. But she had never suspected his inner self would be so tender, so full of pain and longing.

Hugging herself, she looked at a painting of a storm building over the swamp. An angry sky churned in a turmoil of gray, green, and yellow above the stillness of the bayou. Tears rose in her eyes.

He had told her more than once he didn't want her prying into his life. He was nothing more than her unwilling guide and unwilling host. But she had pushed and prodded, excusing her behavior as professional curiosity, telling herself she had a right to know just how dangerous he really was, and in doing so she had violated the most basic human right – the right to inner privacy.

She turned to leave and jumped back, sucking in a startled breath as her heart vaulted into her throat. Lucky stood at the open door, staring at her. He was perfectly still, but there was a terrible sense of raw tension vibrating in the air around him. His eyes flashed like lightning warning of a coming storm.

'I'm sorry,' Serena whispered. She realized dimly that she was trembling. 'I shouldn't have come in here.'

'No, you shouldn't have,' he said, his voice low and thrumming with fury.

He stared at her, struggling to hold himself from flying into a rage. What he did in this room he did for himself. This had been his solace, his salvation when he came back from Central America. He spent hours in this room, healing, focusing on his canvases to keep his mind together and to vent what was trying to tear him apart. These paintings were his most private feelings, the pain he couldn't escape, the fear he wouldn't acknowledge. Having someone see them was like stripping his soul bare and putting it on public display. It was unthinkable. And now it was inescapable.

'I didn't mean to pry,' Serena said stupidly.

'Of course you did,' Lucky snapped. He strode into the room and began throwing cloths over the paintings, his movements jerky with anger. 'That's what shrinks do best, isn't it? Dig into people's heads, dig out their secrets.'

'I was only trying to see if you were doing something illegal. I have a right to know who I'm staying with,' she said, the words sounding self-righteous and foolish even to her.

He wheeled around suddenly and grabbed her by the arms, jerking her up against him, bending over her so that she had to arch her back to look up at him. 'You don't have any rights out here,' he growled. 'You don't belong here. This isn't polite society, Shelby. There are no rules except my rules.'

'Serena.' Her name trembled on her lips. She stared up at him, at the wild look in his eyes, genuinely afraid of him for the first time. *I'm over the edge . . . Folks say he's half crazy . . .* 'I'm Serena, Lucky,' she said softly, her heart pounding as she watched him struggle to pull himself back from that edge.

Lucky blinked at her, his mind sliding back from the darkness and chilling as he realized what she had said. He straightened and let go of her abruptly. She stumbled against the easel, setting the canvas on it rocking.

'I know who you are,' he said bitterly. Plowing his hands through his hair, he began to pace the width of the room like a caged tiger, his head down, eyes burning bright with fury and pain and fear.

'Damn you. Damn you,' he muttered as the breath soughed in and out of his lungs in gusts. So much had been taken from him – his youth, his innocence. It seemed all he had left was his pride and his privacy, and the woman standing there staring at him with doe eyes full of fear was stripping him of both. He didn't want her interference. He didn't want the reminder of his past she brought him. He didn't want the fire she set in his blood. Damn her, *damn her!*

Serena reached out to steady the easel, steadying herself at the same time. She watched Lucky pace, watched the storm of emotions raging inside him and witnessed the awesome battle to contain those emotions within him. As she watched, her fear receded and was replaced by something stronger – the need to reach out to him.

'Lucky, I didn't mean any harm,' she said softly. 'I'm very sorry. Really, I am.'

He stopped abruptly and looked at her sideways, his eyes as bright and hot as molten gold. A savage smile cut across his dark face. 'You're sorry. You invade my life, invade my privacy, drag me into your battles, and all you have to say is that you're sorry. Use me to your own end and excuse it all with an apology. Very civilized. Very proper. *Dieu*, isn't that just like the Sheridan girls?'

The words rang in his ears like the clashing din of cymbals. If he could have reached out and grabbed them back, he would have, but they hung there. Serena met his gaze, her face filled with dawning awareness and questions.

'How well do you know Shelby?' she asked carefully, not wanting to hear the answer.

'Well enough to know better than to let her twin take me for the same ride.'

Serena was unprepared for the stab of jealousy that pierced her at the thought of Shelby and Lucky together. It didn't seem possible. She didn't want to believe it, but she didn't have much choice.

'I'm not Shelby,' she said, drawing her armor of cool poise around herself. 'I'm nothing like Shelby. I'm sorry if she hurt you, but I won't pay for her sins, Lucky.'

'Forget it,' he muttered. 'It was a lifetime ago.'

He could see she had more questions, but before she could voice them, he jerked his head around and resumed his pacing, dismissing the subject as if it hadn't been the one pivotal event that had changed his life's course.

'What did you think you would find up here, *ma petite*? Contraband? Guns? Drugs?'

'You let me think you were a poacher,' Serena said evenly. 'Why, Lucky? Why let me think you're something bad when you're not?'

To keep you away. To keep from getting hurt. He pressed the heels of his hands to his temples as if to hold the thoughts in as they swelled and throbbed behind his eyes. When he started toward her, he roared, an animal cry of impotent rage and guilt and fury. Serena jumped, but held her ground, waiting for an answer. Lucky lunged at her, pulling himself up just a hairbreadth in front of her.

'You look at me and see something bad. That's because I am,' he insisted.

'I've seen what you wanted me to see, not who you really are.'

'*Mais non, chère,*' he said bitterly. 'You've seen all there is.'

'That's a lie. What about this?' Serena raised a hand toward the half-finished canvas on the easel. 'You wouldn't have let me see this. There's nothing bad here. Your paintings are beautiful and touching, Lucky. Why wouldn't you let me see them? Do they show too much?'

Snarling an oath, he pushed past her, grabbed the canvas off the easel, and hurled it across the room like a giant Frisbee. It hit the leg of the workbench with a loud crack, the stretcher snapping in two along one side of the canvas, ruining it.

'Cloth and pigment,' Lucky spat out. 'That's all it is. I do it to pass the time. Don't read anything into it, Dr. Sheridan,' he warned, leaning over her again. 'Don't look for symbolism or metaphors. Rest assured, the only way I want to touch you is with my hands,' he said, pulling her against him with barely leashed violence.

'This is how I want to touch you, *chère*,' he whispered savagely, sweeping his hands over her hair, down her back to her hips. His fingers pressed into her flesh, stroking roughly, caressing without tenderness. 'This is the only way I want to touch you.' He brought one hand up to cup her breast through the sheer fabric of her blouse. 'This is all I have to give you, all I'll let you take.'

He lowered his mouth the rest of the way and kissed her hard.

She should have pushed him away. Common sense told Serena to push him away. Common sense told her that poacher or artist, Lucky Doucet

266

was a man with problems, a man who wouldn't share himself. He'd given her fair warning on that score. All he wanted was this, the physical, the sexual. He wanted desire and nothing more. Even that need he gave in to grudgingly, angrily. He wanted her, but he didn't like it. She wanted him and it confounded her. She was too smart a woman to fall into the trap of wanting a man who would never give of himself. She was too slick and polished to want a barbarian, too in need of control to surrender it utterly.

She should have pushed him away. But she didn't. Couldn't. She wanted his touch, his kiss. He had awakened an instinct in her that had lain dormant even through marriage. Now it roared with life, with hunger. It frightened her and thrilled her, and she surrendered without a fight because no matter how wrong her common sense told her it was, the woman in her said it was right.

The woman in her, who had never known true passion, yearned for it now, with this man, this warrior with the soul of an artist. She had held herself in check with the idea he was a criminal, but he wasn't a criminal. He was a man with hidden fears. He was a man who covered his tenderness, his inner loneliness, his goodness with a mask of toughness and danger, a man who needed love but would never reach out to take it.

Serena didn't push him away. She melted against him.

Lucky groaned helplessly as her mouth softened beneath his. He hadn't meant this to happen. He had meant to push her away, to frighten her, to repel her, to chase her so far away she wouldn't want to come within an emotional mile of him. But the instant her resistance melted, so did his anger. Need swept over him like a tidal wave. He needed to touch her, to taste her, to hold her. He wanted to lose himself in her. It was madness, he knew, but such sweet madness he couldn't resist.

He raised his head a scant inch and looked into her eyes. What he saw was a mirror of his own bewilderment, need, and wariness of that need.

'I want you,' he murmured, untangling the overwhelming knot of emotions to the root of the problem. 'I want you, Serena.'

'I know.'

Her words were little more than shadows of sound passing between her lips, lips that were swollen from his kiss. Her braid had come loose and her hair fell around her shoulders in disarray, a shaft of light from the window above turning it the color of spun gold. She was temptation personified, a temptation Lucky had no intention of resisting.

'I stopped last night,' he reminded her. 'I'm not stopping this time, chère.'

Serena could feel him, hard and urgent against her belly, and she knew he meant what he said. A primitive thrill shot through her at the thought that he meant to take her, to claim her as males had claimed their mates from the dawn of time. He lowered his mouth to hers again, sipping, tasting, testing her. Serena framed his face with her hands and pressed her lips more solidly against his, letting him know she had no intention of stopping him.

She met the thrust of his tongue eagerly as reason and logic shut down and instinct took control. He filled her mouth with the taste of him, surrounded her body with his heat and raw power. She slid her arms around his neck and gasped as her breasts flattened against the granite wall of his chest.

Lucky pulled her lower body tight against his with one hand and slid his other hand between them, seeking and finding the open throat of her blouse. He needed to touch her skin, needed to see her. The top button gave way as he curled his fingers into the fabric and pulled downward. One by one the buttons surrendered, falling to the floor.

He trailed his kiss down her jaw to her throat, stripping the blouse from her shoulders and discarding it. His thumbs hooked under the straps of her bra and he drew them down off her shoulders, peeled the cups away to reveal her breasts to his touch, his gaze, the hunger of his kiss.

Serena cried out as he took one turgid peak into his mouth and sucked strongly. She tangled her fingers in the black silk of his hair and pressed him closer as heat swept through her.

Together they sank to their knees on the rumpled canvas dropcloth. Serena leaned back, arching into the heat of Lucky's mouth. It was exquisite – the pull of his lips, the rasp of his tongue, the feel of his hand kneading her other breast. Her own hands moved restlessly over his broad shoulders, gathering the fabric of his T-shirt into her fists.

He pulled away and tore the garment off, flinging it aside, never taking his eyes from hers. His gaze was searing, hot, wild with desire. It took her breath away to look at him, at the intensity of his face and the perfection of his body. His body was a living sculpture of muscle. He looked to Serena like the consummate male animal, hungry and untamed, intent on one purpose.

She made a sound of surprise when he snatched her into his arms again, then moaned at the contact. They met flesh to flesh, soft white skin to hard, tanned muscle, woman to man. She trembled at the power of just touching him, and excitement swirled through her at the thought of being possessed by him.

He kissed her roughly, wildly, his arms banding her to him, his hands sweeping down her back, pressing her hard against his arousal, then finding their way around to the button of her shorts. The baggy khaki shorts fell to pool around her knees. She gasped into his mouth as he caught his fingertips in the waistband of her panties and jerked the scrap of silk and lace from her hips, tearing it free.

He whispered to her as he smoothed one hand over her bare hip and the delicious roundness of her buttock, kneading, squeezing, lifting her. While the fingers of his other hand slid into the nest of dark blond curls at the juncture of her thighs, seeking the heat and silken softness that lay beyond, he murmured against the shell of her ear – words of sex, words of praise, words in a language she didn't understand.

Serena tried to catch her breath to whisper his name, but couldn't. He stroked her intimately, knowingly, wringing another gasp from her as he slid a finger into her heat to test her readiness. Her hips moved against the pressure of his hand, inviting him, begging him silently.

Lucky raised his head and looked down at her. Her eyes were closed, her lips parted. Her back arched as she moved against him, thrusting her full breasts upward. With her hair tumbling around her shoulders she looked like a wanton angel. There was no sign of her infuriatingly cool control. There was no hint of polished sophistication. She was a woman who wanted a man, wanted *him*, and her body was making no secret of the fact. She moved against his hand, caught up in sensation, the soft petals of her feminine cleft dewy and warm.

Desire roared inside Lucky like an inferno, licking at his sanity, pulsing in his groin. He'd never wanted a woman like this. Never. He wanted her with every fiber of his being and she was hot and ready for him, her body begging him to take her. His nostrils flared like a stallion's scenting a mare, his head filling with a mix of expensive perfume and the subtle musk of arousal.

He pulled back from her and tore at the fastening of his jeans, fumbling with the button and struggling to get the zipper down over his erection. His manhood sprang free into Serena's waiting hands. She closed her fingers around him, measuring the length and thickness of his shaft. She stroked downward, opening her hand to cup him gently, then drew her hand slowly back up, tightening her fingers until he was throbbing. He pulled in a breath as her thumb brushed across his velvety tip.

She pressed her lips to his chest and flicked the tip of her tongue across one nipple, and Lucky lost what was left of his control. It tore away from him on a wild animal groan that started in his chest and worked its way up the back of his throat. He had to have her now. Sooner than now.

He lowered Serena onto her back and mounted her, attempting to enter her fully with a single thrust, the need to claim her as his overwhelming. She cried out and dug her fingernails into his back, her body tensing against his intrusion.

'Oh, sweet heaven,' Lucky groaned, bracing himself on his elbows above her, fighting his natural urge to bury himself in the tight wet glove of her body. 'Take it all, baby,' he pleaded. 'Please, *please*, Serena! All of me. All of me.'

'Oh, Lucky,' she gasped. 'I can't. You're too—'

'Shh . . .' he whispered, brushing his lips tenderly against her temple. 'Just relax for me, *chère*,' he went on seductively, schooling his own body to sink down against her. 'Relax. It's gonna be all right. It's gonna be so good. Just relax for me, sugar. That's it. That's right.'

She moved hesitantly beneath him, taking another inch, then

tightening around him, taking him to another level of ecstasy. Lucky checked his passion ruthlessly, reining in the urge to drive himself into her, to bury himself to his hilt. He brushed her hair back from her cheek and kissed her slowly, deeply, sinking into her a little at a time as her body relaxed beneath his.

'You're tighter than a fist,' he whispered breathlessly, his lips brushing hers. He struggled to hold himself still against the gentle rippling of her woman's body as it adjusted to accommodate him. '*Mon Dieu*, don't those men up in Charleston know what to do with a beautiful woman?'

Serena didn't answer him. She couldn't. She was beyond speaking, beyond telling him she couldn't even remember the name of the last man she'd gone to bed with because it had just been permanently erased from her mind. All she could think of was Lucky. All she could feel was Lucky, filling her, stretching her, kissing her. She stroked her hands over the sweat-slick muscles of his back, stroked a finger down the valley of his spine. Her hands cupped his taut buttocks and pulled him deeper into her as she tilted her lips to accept him fully.

His big body pressed down against her and he began moving slowly, easing in and out of her, gaining speed and strength with each thrust, until he was lifting her hips off the floor each time he drove into her. Serena arched against him, straining to meet him, straining toward something she had only guessed at before now. It was unlike anything else she had experienced, this feeling of intense excitement that grew like a bubble inside her, pushing away sanity, pushing aside her need for control. It was at once frightening and exhilarating, sweeping her away on a wave of sensation.

She clung to Lucky as if he could anchor her to the real world. She wrapped her arms around him, wrapped her legs around his lean hips. And still the wild sensation grew, hotter and brighter and more intense, swelling until it burst into a million brilliant shards.

'Lucky!'

Lucky felt her climax, heard her cry his name, then his own consciousness dimmed as he exploded inside her. He arched into her with a hoarse cry, unable to think, unable to comprehend anything except the exquisite pulsing of her body around his. The moment was so sweet, so perfect, so golden that for an instant all the darkness was banished from his soul and he felt clean and whole and at peace for the first time in a long while. He clung to the feeling, clung to Serena, holding her to him as if he might be able to absorb some of the goodness he'd found in her.

Reality returned by slow degrees, coming to him as if out of a mist. The paint-stained dropcloth. The feet of his easel. The stripes of filtered daylight falling through the blinds. The woman beneath him.

He looked down at Serena and felt something squeeze painfully in his chest. She was crying silently, her head turned to the side, the teardrops leaking out through the barrier of spiky lashes. He'd hurt her. He'd taken her like a stag in rut. He'd felt how tight she was and still he'd let his own need overwhelm him and banged the living daylights out of her. *Dieu*, what kind of an animal had he become?

As many times as he'd told himself he didn't care about anyone or anything, Lucky couldn't stomach this. He'd been raised to treat women gently and with respect. Despite the cynicism that had taken root inside him over the years, the idea of a man physically abusing a woman, overpowering her with his strength, was abhorrent to him. The idea of hurting Serena, brave, proud Serena, whose regal mask hid secret fears, cut deeper than he wanted to admit.

His hand was trembling slightly as he brushed her hair back from her temple. 'Serena? Serena, I'm sorry—'

'Don't be,' she whispered. 'I'm all right.'

'I hurt you. I was too rough. I—'

'No. That's never happened for me before,' she said, breaking in on his apology with her confession.

Lucky went still above her as comprehension dawned. 'Never?'

She turned her head and gave him a tremulous smile. 'Not like that. I didn't have any idea it could be like that. I've never been very good at sex.'

Nothing could have aroused Lucky more strongly or more immediately save having her tell him she was a virgin. Knowing he had taken her somewhere no other man ever had was the next best thing. Possessiveness surged inside him and for once he didn't try to fight it or deny it. She was his. He felt it on a fundamental, instinctive level. She was his.

Still snug in the silken pocket of Serena's womanhood, his body stirred strongly and her body tightened around him in automatic response. He stared down at her, feeling caught in the grip of a powerful emotion he couldn't name. She looked up at him, her eyes dark and liquid, her lips parting softly as her breath caught.

'Oh, *ma jolie fille*,' Lucky said, lowering his head to gently nuzzle her throat. 'That might have been your first trip to heaven, but it sure as hell won't be your last.'

10

He'd had the dream a hundred times. He was crawling through a sewer tunnel under the private prison of self-styled general and drug kingpin Juan Rafael Ramos, the fumes choking him, the screams of prisoners in the interrogation rooms coming to him through the stone walls like the eerie cries of tortured souls from another dimension.

He had planned this escape since the day he had regained consciousness after his first 'questioning' by Ramos's men. He had concentrated on the plan every time they tortured him, focusing his mind on freedom instead of the excruciating pain, had visualized it in his mind over and over through the endless hours in a dark, dank cell. Now the end of the tunnel was literally in sight. His fingers threaded through the rusted grate and pushed it out. On the other side, standing in a ball of bright light were Ramos, Amalinda Roca, and Lieutenent Colonel R. J. Lambert.

He lunged for Lambert first and killed him with a rough metal shank. Blood gushed from the body like water from a fire hydrant and pooled around him, thick and warm and shoulder-deep. He could hear a woman's laughter, and he turned toward it slowly, his movements hindered by the fluid rushing around him. Amalinda hovered above him, her long hair flowing around her like streamers in the wind.

The instant he recognized her her face contorted grotesquely into a monster's snarling countenance with fangs dripping venom. Her fingers transformed into snakes that wrapped around his throat and pulled his head under the swirling current of blood, drowning him. He could feel the pressure, the pain in his lungs, the panic rising in the back of his throat—

Lucky jerked awake, gasping for air and looking wildly for the source of the pressure on his chest. A woman lay with her cheek pressed over his heart, her hair spilling like a curtain of silvery silk over his dark skin. Shelby. No, no, he told himself, working to keep another rush of ugly memories at bay. Not Shelby. Serena.

It took him a long moment to sort reality from the nightmare, to realize who Serena was and where they were. Fragments of thought and emotions swirled like dust at the edges of his mind, and he painstakingly selected the appropriate pieces and frantically attempted to push the rest aside.

Serena. Safety. Home.

She lifted her head and blinked sleepily, looking up at him in silent question. Lucky said nothing. He eased out from under her and left the bed, padding naked to the front window.

A cold sweat filmed his skin. His hair was damp as he ran his fingers through it, slicking it back from his face. He was shaking – perhaps not visibly, but inside he was shaking violently and his heart beat like thunder. He braced his hands against the frame of the open window, trying to get a breath of fresh air, trying to hang on as fear tore at the edges of his sanity. It crawled up the back of his throat to choke him, and he coughed and gripped the window frame harder as he fought the sensation back down.

They were old companions, the nightmares and their aftermath, the shaking, the blinding fear that maybe this time he wouldn't be able to push the darkness back from the edges of his mind, the weariness, the regret. The thing he wanted most was to lie down and escape from it all with sleep, but he knew he wouldn't sleep again this night. The dreams were too terrible, too vivid, too seductive in their attempts to pull him over the edge.

He wouldn't sleep again this night because he was afraid, and because he was afraid he was ashamed. A stronger man could have slept. A better man wouldn't have been plagued by demons the like of these. Knowing Serena was there to witness it all made the shame a hundred times worse and he called on his deep reservoirs of anger and self-protection to deflect it.

Serena watched him from the bed. She couldn't see his face, but the pale moonlight spilling in through the window washed silver over his shoulders and back as he stood with his head lowered. Every muscle was tense, taut, perfectly delineated from its neighbor. His back rose and fell as he struggled for breath. She had no idea what kind of nightmare had driven him from sleep to this mental ledge he was clinging to now. All she knew was that she wanted to help. She wanted to reach out and offer him her strength as he had offered his the night before.

She found Lucky's T-shirt among the tangle of clothes on the floor beside the bed and pulled it on. It fell to the middle of her thighs as she slipped from the bed and went to him.

'What's wrong?' she asked quietly. For a long moment the only sounds that answered her came from outside – the chirrup of frogs and insects, the distant whinny of a raccoon.

'*Rien*,' he said at length, then shook his head impatiently as he realized he hadn't answered her in English. 'Nothing.'

She reached out to lay a hand on his arm. 'Lucky—'

'Nothing!' he roared, turning on her. It was a tactical error. Serena didn't back away. Instead, she looked up into his face and read it as plainly

273

as a college professor might have read a grade-school primer. Lucky turned away to stare out the window again, schooling his voice to a calmer tone. 'It's nothing to do with you. Just some leftover stuff from my stint in Central America.'

'What were you doing in Central America?'

A sardonic smile twisted his mouth. 'Well, I wasn't down there with the Maryknoll Fathers, that's for sure.'

'The army?'

'Yeah. Doin' a little job for Uncle Sam. It was nothing.'

'We don't get nightmares from nothing.'

'*Pas de bêtises,*' he muttered.

'If you want to talk about it, I might be able to help,' Serena said softly, her eyes warm with concern.

Lucky forced a laugh. 'You can't even help yourself,' he said, almost wincing at the deliberate cruelty of his words.

Serena ignored his verbal strike. He was scared and hurting; lashing out was a natural response. 'It's easier to solve other people's problems.'

'Yeah, well, forget it,' he growled.

She shrugged and crossed her arms in front of her. She looked all of nineteen standing there swallowed up in his T-shirt, her hair down, her skin smooth and flawless in the moonlight. Lucky felt a fresh stirring of desire and a dangerous tenderness. They added to the burden of all the other emotions he was shouldering at the moment, and he wondered if he would be able to shrug them off before he buckled beneath the load.

'All right,' Serena said, nodding. 'I just thought—'

'What?' Lucky snapped. 'You thought what? That just because I've spent half the night inside you that gives you the right to open up my head to see what kind of snakes are in it? Think again, angel.'

Serena wanted to argue with him. She wanted the right to ask him what haunted his dreams. She wanted to know everything about him. She wanted him to share that information with her willingly, but she knew he wouldn't any more than he would have shared his paintings with her. He would have been happier if she had gone on believing he was a criminal.

Maybe she would have been happier too. She would have stayed her distance from the man she had first believed him to be.

She turned and looked back at the bed they had shared the last few hours. Day had faded into night. Between bouts of lovemaking they had found their way down from the *grenier*, trading the hard floor of Lucky's studio for the comfort of an old-fashioned mattress stuffed with Spanish moss and fragrant dried flowers and herbs. Lucky had made love to her again slowly, tenderly, drawing out the anticipation and the climax, taking her to yet another height she had never before scaled. Her body was still alive with the sensations, her every nerve ending humming in awareness of the man standing beside her.

'Don't read anything into it,' he muttered, following her gaze. 'It's just sex.'

Serena's mouth twisted in a wry, rueful smile. 'Gee, thanks for making me feel like a cheap one-night stand.'

'It's nothing personal.'

'Oh. I see,' she said dryly. 'I'm just one in a long line of cheap one-night stands. That makes me feel a lot better. You sure know how to flatter a girl, Lucky.'

'If you wanted pretty words, you came to the wrong man. There's nothing pretty inside me.'

Serena thought of the haunting beauty of his paintings but said nothing. He hadn't appreciated her seeing them, and he wouldn't appreciate her seeing anything else that was buried beneath his tarnished armor either.

'I'm just being honest with you, *chère*. Isn't that what you shrinks always want? Honesty? The straight line?'

Serena said nothing. The awful fact of the matter was that deep down she would rather have had him lie to her tonight. She felt so raw emotionally; so much had happened in the last two days, she would have been glad to have a man hold her and tell her she meant the world to him even if it wasn't true. But she would have been a fool to think this man would do it. Lucky wouldn't let anyone that close to him, not even in a lie.

She walked away from him, moving gingerly. Unaccustomed to sex, her body ached in muscles she'd forgotten she had. She went to the screen door and looked out at the bayou. The fear that had assaulted her the night before was conspicuously absent tonight. Other things had taken precedence over it – thoughts of Gifford, Shelby, the very real and physical presence of Lucky. Lucky, her hero, her antihero, her lover.

She'd never taken a lover before. She'd never even known a man like Lucky before – hard, haunted, dark, and complex. It all seemed so unreal, being in this place with this man. She felt as if she didn't know herself anymore. She had a wild urge to look into a mirror to see if she even resembled the person she had been two days before.

'Are you all right?' Lucky asked.

He had moved to stand behind her. She could feel the heat of his body and didn't resist the urge to lean back into him. His arms folded around her automatically, offering comfort he would never voice.

Serena sniffed, a wry, weary smile tugging at one corner of her mouth. 'Sure. I have my whole life turned upside down on a regular basis. Doesn't everyone?'

'You could leave. Go back to Charleston. Make Gifford deal with this on his own.'

'No. Unlike you, I *am* obligated to other people. I may live my life apart from them, but that doesn't mean I can just shut them out. I can't walk away from this until it's over.'

Lucky listened to the mix of resignation and conviction in her voice and wondered how he could have ever confused her with her sister. The only thing they had in common was a pretty shell. Serena's hid a core of integrity and a deep well of strength she was having to draw on again and again, thanks to Shelby and Gifford. She was at once tough and fragile, a combination that touched him in a way he didn't want to admit. And it hurt him to think she was going to lose what was left of her innocence before everything was done here – hurt him in a place he hadn't believed he could be touched.

Out of a strong sense of self-preservation he denied the feelings. What he felt for Serena was desire and nothing more, he told himself. A desire that seemed insatiable. It stirred in his gut again like the glowing coals of a fire that could be banked but not extinguished.

He bent his head and brushed his mouth against her cheek and her temple. 'Can I have you until it's over?' he murmured, his hands moving restlessly upward, over her ribs and stomach to her breasts.

Serena shivered from the heat of his touch and the coldness of his words. No pretense of love or affection. Just the bald, blunt truth. She tried not to let it bruise her heart. Lucky was no man for a long-term commitment. If she wanted him at all, she would do well to take a page from his book and see it as an opportunity for great sex and nothing more. An adventure, an odyssey she could look back on later when she returned to Charleston and sanity, and marvel at the recklessness of it.

At any rate, she didn't think she had a choice. She wanted him whatever way she could get him. Her body was responding to his now as if they had been lovers for weeks instead of hours. Heat rose inside her, inflaming the tips of her breasts as his fingers rubbed them through the soft cotton of the T-shirt. It seared her core as she felt his erection press into her back and throb relentlessly in the tender flesh between her legs. He turned her in his arms, pulling the T-shirt up so she would fit against him skin to skin.

'I can't get enough of you, *chère*,' he whispered, tasting her lips with soft, ardent kisses. 'I want you again.'

Serena ducked her head against his chest. 'I don't think I can.'

Lucky hooked a finger under her chin and tipped her head back. What he saw in her face wasn't rejection but embarrassment, and he smiled softly in understanding.

'Me, I've got just the thing for that, sugar,' he said seductively, leaning down to nuzzle her cheek. 'Come on back to bed and let ol' Lucky kiss it and make it better.'

They left for Chanson du Terre while the mist still hovered over the bayou like thin wisps of cotton batting, giving the swamp its most primitive air. It looked like the dawn of time, when the earth was still cooling beneath the waters. Dinosaurs would not have appeared out of place.

It was easy for Serena to imagine they had slipped through a hole in the fabric of time and had fallen into earth's prehistory, that she and Lucky were the only woman and man on earth. It was an uncharacteristically romantic notion, but she didn't try to chase it away.

She took in the scenery silently as Lucky poled the boat. She still wasn't comfortable with the swamp – she doubted she ever would be – but her perceptions had changed subtly after having seen Lucky's paintings of this place. She glimpsed it now a bit through his eyes, and she tried to understand both the swamp and the man better.

Both were filled with secrets. Both were cloaked with an air of mystery and shrouded in isolation and loneliness. It was no wonder Lucky had taken refuge here; the swamp understood him. Serena wondered if she would ever be able to comprehend him fully, if she would ever be able to unlock his secrets or if he would remain as much a puzzle to her as the swamp.

The yearning to know more about him yawned inside her like a sudden crack in her block of knowledge that needed filling with details. She wanted to know what he'd been like as a boy, why he'd left college, what incidents had sown the seeds of cynicism in him. The questions buzzed on the tip of her tongue, but Serena didn't give them voice. It was foolish to encourage the desire to deepen their relationship. Lucky had set the bounds very clearly and concisely: they could share each other's bodies for the duration of her stay, offer the rudiments of friendship on occasion, but nothing more.

'What are you thinking?'

Serena jerked her head up in surprise, looking at Lucky with what she supposed was an unfortunately guilty expression.

'Nothing,' she mumbled. She wasn't much of a liar. The word was probably emblazoned in red across her cheeks. Lucky frowned at her and she changed the subject before he could comment. 'I'm not looking forward to dealing with this situation at Chanson du Terre. I don't feel it's my place to interfere.'

He planted the push-pole, and the pirogue slid forward. 'You said yourself, you don't have a choice.'

'I know, but I don't have to like it or feel comfortable doing it. I feel like an outsider butting in. Shelby is going to resent it in a big way.'

'There are more important things at stake here than Miz Shelby's feelings,' Lucky said acridly.

Serena twisted around on the seat of the pirogue to get a better look at him. His jaw was set, his eyes trained on some point in the middle distance. His face gave nothing away.

'Is your family close?' she asked.

Lucky flinched inwardly. Was his family close? Oh, yes, they were close, like the woven threads in homespun Cajun cloth ... with one exception – him. He had kept his distance since returning, though he knew it puzzled them and hurt them. They were good people, his parents, his brothers and sisters, too good to risk tainting them with his experiences and his problems. He visited his parents dutifully if not often, and he saw the others from time to time, but he remained the loose thread in the fabric of the Doucet clan. The one that had come unraveled, he thought with bitter humor.

'Lucky?'

'*Oui*,' he said shortly. 'They're close.'

'I've never been fortunate enough to say that about my sister and me. What's going to happen with the plantation isn't likely to help matters in that respect.'

'As I said, *chérie*, there are bigger things to consider.'

He steered the pirogue to the shore. Serena looked around them. They were in what seemed to be the heart of the swamp. There was no sign of civilization, certainly no sign of their destination. There was nothing much visible except black water and dense forest. She lifted a brow in silent question when Lucky glanced down at her.

'I need to show you something.'

He hopped out of the pirogue and pulled the nose ashore. Serena remained stubbornly in place as he offered her his hand.

'Where is this thing you need to show me?' she asked suspiciously.

'Down this path,' he said, motioning toward the woods.

Serena saw no evidence of Lucky's path. All she could focus on was the wild tangle of trees and underbrush and the knowledge of what might be under the underbrush. The old fear rose to the surface of her feelings like oil.

Lucky gently cupped her chin in his hand and turned her face up so she would look at him instead of the forest. 'Don' be afraid of this place, *chère*,' he whispered. 'You're with me. You're mine now. I won' let anything hurt you.'

Staring up into his hard face, Serena felt a strong elemental connection with him, a bond that had been forged without their knowledge or consent as they had come together in passion. She was his, Lucky Doucet's lady, bound to him in the most fundamental of ways. He would protect her as well as possess her, as males had protected their females for eons.

'You trust me, *chérie?*'

'*Yes,' she answered. With my life if not my heart.*

She trusted him. It would have been unthinkable just two days earlier. She would never have believed a man who seemed so unscrupulous, so untamed, a man who defied authority and solved his problems with violence would be trustworthy on any count, but she knew now that there was so much more to Lucky than what met the eye. He was like a diamond in the rough – hard and dark on the outside, a multitude of facets within.

She took his hand and allowed him to help her from the boat. As soon as her feet touched shore he swept her up in his arms and carried her to the place he wanted her to see. The path he followed was overgrown with ferns and thorny dewberry bushes and crowded on both sides by trees. The swamp was doing its best to eradicate the evidence of man's past intrusion. For the most part, Serena saw no trail at all, but Lucky walked on as steady and sure as if he'd been strolling down Main Street in town.

He took her to a small clearing at the edge of another stream. The clearing was framed with hackberry and magnolia trees, the magnolias scenting the air with the heavy perfume of their last few blossoms. The opposite bank of the stream was dotted with white-topped daisy fleabane and black-eyed susans. Silhouetted against the rising sun were a doe and twin fawns that had come to drink.

Lucky stood Serena down in front of him, keeping her within the shelter of his arms. He pointed to a raft of water hyacinth that stretched from bank to bank.

'That stuff can choke a bayou to death,' he said softly. 'One plant can produce sixty-five thousand others in a single season. It blocks the light from getting to the plants beneath it and they die. The phytoplankton the fish feed on goes, and so go the fish. The pond weeds the ducks feed on die and the ducks leave. Man introduced that plant here by accident.'

He turned slightly and pointed to a stand of cattails along the far bank where the head of an animal that resembled a beaver was visible between the reeds. 'There's a nut'ra. They were brought to Lou'siana in the thirties for breeding experiments. Some got away. Now there's so many down in the marshes, they're eatin' the place up. They chew the grass down to nothin' in places where the oil companies won't let trappers in. Without the grass roots to hold it together, the marsh soil breaks up and washes away, and saltwater leaches in from the Gulf and poisons everything. Man brought the nut'ra here.

'You look at this place and think it's a world away from anywhere,' he said. 'But right here are two examples of man's intrusion. The swamp might seem an unforgiving, indestructable place, but it's a delicate place of checks and balances. Man could destroy it in the blink of an eye.'

'Why are you showing me this?' Serena asked, looking up at him over her shoulder.

'I just wanted you to understand before you go back to deal with Shelby and Talbot and Tristar. It's not just Chanson du Terre ridin' on this, angel, and it's not just your relationship with your sister or Gifford. It's a whole ecosystem,' he said, staring out at the wilderness as if he felt the need to memorize every aspect of it before it was too late. 'This

279

swamp is dying already a little bit at a time. Silting up from the big channels that were built to keep the Mississippi from flooding farm land that never should have been farm land to begin with. Tristar has plans to dig their own navigation channel. That'll bring in more silt. *Le bon Dieu* only knows what they'll dump out here where nobody can see. They have a rap sheet of environmental crimes as long as your arm.'

Serena listened carefully, taking in not only his words but the sentiment behind them. This wasn't Lucky the erstwhile poacher talking, it wasn't Lucky the tough guy. This was Étienne, the student of biology, the boy who had grown up on these bayous, learning their secrets. 'You love this place, don't you?'

Lucky said nothing for a long moment. This swamp was his home, his salvation, the solitude that had helped him heal when he'd been clinging to the ragged edge of sanity. The silence grew heavy, weighed down with the importance of his answer.

'*Oui*,' he said at last. 'I know you hate it, but this place is my life.'

His admission touched Serena in the most tender corner of her heart, and she felt a dangerous rise of emotion pressing against the backs of her eyes. This was the first part of his inner self Lucky had shared with her willingly, candidly.

No matter how foolish her brain told her it was, her heart embraced this small piece of hope greedily. She turned in Lucky's arms and hugged him, wanting something she didn't dare name and feeling in that moment that she would do anything to save this place, no matter how much she feared it, just to be able to give something to Lucky that went deeper than desire.

11

'Can't you *do something*, Mason?'

Shelby paced the width of the small study her husband had taken for his own use when they had moved temporarily into Chanson du Terre. It was a dark cubbyhole of paneled walls and wood floor, filled with masculine leather furniture and shelves of musty books. Portraits of stern men from the last century stared down disapprovingly from the walls. Shelby ignored them, crossing her arms tightly beneath her breasts as she paced and listened to the click of her heels in the silence.

Mason looked up distractedly from the papers on the desk, shoving his glasses up on his nose. There was a bland, slightly vacuous look in his eyes as he took in Shelby in her new red and black suit. 'I'm not sure what it is you want me to do, darlin'.'

Shelby bore down on him, her dark eyes flaming with impatience. She braced her hands against the desk, her fingers newly manicured and decked with a garnet and diamond ring. 'You heard what Burke had to say. He thinks we should have Gifford declared incompetent.'

'Now, Shelby,' Mason said, smiling benignly. He abandoned the papers he'd been going over and folded his hands neatly on top of them. 'I have explained to you before why that won't work. In the first place, how would that look if I had my wife's grandfather declared incompetent so I might profit from the sale of his estate? That wouldn't do, sweetheart. The voters frown on that sort of thing. Secondly, Serena would never agree to it.'

'Serena.' Shelby spat out her sister's name like a curse as she pulled back from the desk to resume her pacing. 'Blast her. Why did she have to come back just when things were looking so good for us? She's going to ruin everything for me. She always does.'

Mason tut-tutted at her from behind his smile. 'Have a little faith, sugar plum. Serena may very well see reason when she hears the whole story.'

'She'll side with Gifford,' Shelby snapped, smoothing a stray hair back toward her neat French twist. 'I'm sure he's been filling her head with nonsense. And who knows what that Lucky Doucet has been telling her.'

'Why should he be telling her anything? She only hired him to take her out to Gifford's.'

'Well . . .' she stalled, dodging her husband's vaguely curious stare. 'Well . . . because he's crazy, that's why.'

Mason shook his head. 'You're getting all riled up for nothing.'

'One of us had better get riled up. If we don't raise some cash soon, we're going to be in trouble, Mason. You need funding for your campaign and we have to close on the new house soon.'

'It would help if you could get the old one sold.'

Shelby stopped in her tracks, pressing a hand to her heart and looking wounded, as if her husband's suggestion had been a stake driven into her. 'I am trying to sell the house, Mason. It isn't my fault the Loughton's financing fell through at the last minute. It isn't my fault the market is soft right now.'

'I know it isn't your fault, pet,' Mason hurried to assure her. 'Of course it's not. I was just wishing out loud, that's all.'

He did the rest of his wishing in silence as he thought of the credit card Shelby had run to its limit even before she'd bought this new ensemble. He had a terrible sinking feeling the red leather pumps were exorbitantly expensive, but he said nothing. Previous suggestions for Shelby to curb her spending habits had been met with hysteria.

'I'll tell you what I wish,' Shelby muttered, putting on her most effective pout. 'I wish I were an only child and that Gifford would come to his senses. That's what I wish.'

'You worry too much, peach,' Mason said. 'Things will work out. You'll see. They always do.'

There was a sharp rap at the door, and Odille Fontenot slipped into the room. Her bony frame was painfully erect, her light eyes and thin mouth fierce and disapproving, as always. Her hair was a distressed ball of salt-and-pepper frizz around her head. She wore a cotton housedress in a bright flowered print that was subdued somehow by her general aura of gloom. It hung shapelessly from shoulders as sharp and thin as a wire hanger.

'You ought to wait to be invited in, Odille,' Shelby said defensively, not certain what the housekeeper might have overheard. 'Your manners are atrocious. If you worked for me, I'd fire you for insolence.'

Odille sniffed indignantly. 'Me, I don' work for you. Day I work for you, day I lose my mind.'

Shelby puffed herself up like an offended pigeon. 'Of all the impertinence!'

'Was there something you needed to tell us, Odille?' Mason intervened tactfully.

Odille's narrow eyes shifted from Mason to Shelby and back. 'Miz 'Rena home,' she announced ominously, then turned and stalked out without waiting to be dismissed.

Serena appeared a moment later. She'd left her bags by the door and gone directly in search of her sister, intending to clear up a few things immediately.

'Shelby, Mason, I think we need to have a talk,' she said as she stepped into the library.

'Serena!' Shelby gushed with a great show of worry. She rushed forward, wringing her bejeweled hands. 'Are you all right? We were just worried sick about you! Anything might have happened to you out in the swamp with that madman!' Her gaze flicked over Serena's shoulder. 'Did Gifford return with you?'

'No, he didn't.'

Mason came around from behind the desk, moving with the grace of breeding, a smile of welcome beaming across his face like the sun. He was attractive in the mild, unassuming way of all the Talbots. He wore a rumpled blue oxford shirt and an air of good-natured distraction that had an immediate calming effect on Serena. She managed a smile as he reached for her.

'Serena, darlin', it's so good to see you,' he said, giving her a brotherly hug, then standing her back at arm's length to get a good look at her. 'I'm sorry I wasn't here to greet you the other day. I'm afraid my practice is a taskmaster. And then Shelby informed me you'd gone off on your own after Gifford.' He shook his head in reproach. 'I must say, you had us concerned.'

'The situation with Gifford seemed to demand immediate attention.'

'Gifford. Yes.' He nodded, arranging his features into an appropriately grave expression as he tucked his hands into the pockets of his tan chinos. 'Well, Shelby tells me she didn't get a chance to explain things adequately before you rushed off.'

'As I recall,' Serena said dryly, giving her sister a pointed look, 'Shelby made no attempt to explain.'

Shelby summoned up the same wounded look she'd bestowed on her husband earlier and directed it at her sister. 'That's simply not true, Serena! I practically begged you to stay so we could chat!'

'You told me you didn't know why Gifford had gone into the swamp.'

Mason stepped in to arbitrate like a born diplomat. 'I think what Shelby meant was that we're all a little baffled as to why Gifford left instead of staying here and dealing with the situation in his usual straightforward manner. Things are in a bit of a tangle, as you may have gathered.'

'Yes, I figured that out somewhere in between shotgun blasts,' Serena said sardonically. 'Can we sit down and discuss this from the top?' she asked, moving toward one of the big leather chairs.

Mason made an apologetic face as he consulted his watch. 'I'm afraid I can't at the moment, Serena. I've got a meeting with a client at two. I really must rush now or I'll be late.' He consulted his reflection in the glass doors of a bookcase, buttoning the collar of his shirt and pushing up the knot of his regimental tie. 'There will be ample time to go over it all tonight at dinner. Mr. Burke is coming, as well as Gifford's attorney. We thought perhaps Lamar might have some sway over Gifford in the event you weren't able to bring him back.'

Serena heaved an impatient sigh. She had wanted to tackle the problem immediately, the sooner to finish with it, but that wasn't going to be possible now. She looked at Mason and wondered if there really was a client. Her brother-in-law gave her another earnest, apologetic smile before he kissed Shelby's cheek and left, and she chided herself for hunting for conspiracy and deceit where there probably was none. Mason had never been anything but sweet to her.

'And I just have a million things to do today!' Shelby declared suddenly. She bustled around the desk, straightening papers into stacks. 'I have an open house to conduct at Harlen and Marcy Stone's. Harlen is being transferred to Scotland, of all places. Imagine that! And John Mason has a soccer game and Lacey has her piano lesson. And, of course, I'll have to oversee the dinner preparations.

'I asked Odille to fix a crown roast, but there's no telling what she might do. She's a hateful old thing. John Mason hasn't slept for two nights since she told him his room is haunted by the ghost of a boy who was brutally slain by Yankees during the war.'

Serena sank down into a chair and dropped her head back, her sister's bubbling energy making her acutely aware of her own fatigue.

Shelby stopped her fussing, turning to face her twin with a motherly look of concern. 'My stars, Serena, you look like death warmed over!' Her eyes narrowed a fraction. 'What happened to you out there?'

'Nothing.'

'Well, you look terrible. You ought to take a nice long soak and then have a nap. I'd tell Odille to slice some cucumber for those horrid black circles under your eyes, but she'd probably take after me with a knife. She's just that way. I can't imagine why Gifford keeps her on.'

'Why didn't you tell me about Mason possibly running for office?' Serena asked abruptly.

Her sister gave her a blank look. 'Why, because you never gave me a chance, that's why. You just had to run off into the swamp before I could explain a thing. And now I have to run. We'll tell you all about it over dinner.' Her face lit up beneath a layer of Elizabeth Arden's finest. 'It's the most excitin' thing! I'm just tickled!' She checked the slim diamond-studded watch on her wrist and gasped delicately. 'I'm late! We'll talk tonight.'

'We certainly will,' Serena muttered to herself as the staccato beat of her sister's heels faded down the hall.

As the quiet settled in around her, she thought longingly of Shelby's suggestion of a bath and a nap. She thought about lapsing into unconsciousness in the chair she was sitting in. But in the end she forced herself to her feet and went outside in search of James Arnaud, the plantation manager.

Chanson du Terre had once been a plantation of nearly ten thousand acres, but it had shrunk over the decades a parcel at a time to its current two thousand acres. Rice and indigo had been the original money crops. Indigo still grew wild in weedy patches here and there in ditches around the farm. There had been a brief experiment with rice in the 1800s, then sugarcane had taken over. For as long as Serena could remember, the fields had been planted half with cane, a fourth with soybeans, and a fourth allowed to lie fallow.

Growing cane was a gamble. The crop was temperamental about moisture, prone to disease, vulnerable to frost. The decision of when to harvest in the fall could be an all-or-nothing crap shoot, with the grower putting it off to the last possible day in order to reap the richest sucrose harvest, then working round the clock to bring it in. Once the freeze came, the cane in the fields would rot if not harvested immediately.

Gifford had always said sugarcane was the perfect crop for the Sheridans. They had won Chanson du Terre on a gamble; it seemed only fitting to go on gambling. But the gamble hadn't been paying off recently.

James Arnaud, found swearing prolifically at a tractor in the machine shed, informed Serena that the plantation was caught in a downward spiral that showed no promise of reversing itself any time soon. Arnaud was a short, stocky man in his forties who possessed the dark hair and eyes of his Cajun heritage and a volatile temper to match. He had been manager of the plantation for nearly a dozen years. In that time he had proven himself worthy of Gifford's trust time and again. Serena knew he would tell her the truth, she just hadn't realized how grim that truth would be.

Much of the previous season's crop had been lost to disease. Heavy spring rains had hurt the present crop's growth in several fields where drainage was an ongoing problem. As a result, there was no extra cash to replace aging equipment and they had been forced to cut back on help. All in all, Arnaud thought it was more than most seventy-eight-year-old men would care to deal with, and he said he wouldn't blame Gifford a bit if he did indeed sell the place and go to Tahiti.

What they needed, Arnaud said, was an influx of money and possibly a new cash crop to rotate with the sugarcane. But money was as scarce as hen's teeth, and Gifford was resistant to change.

Serena walked away from the conversation more depressed than she had been to begin with. Even after this business with Tristar Chemicals had been settled, the ultimate fate of the plantation would still be up in the air. She would go back to Charleston. Shelby and Mason would go off to Baton Rouge. Gifford would remain; an aging man and an aging dream left to fade away.

She walked along the crushed-shell path with her hands tucked into the pockets of her shorts, her wistful gaze roaming over the weathered buildings, looking past the pecan orchard to a field of cane. The stalks were already tall and green, reaching for the sky. In her memory she could almost smell the pungent, bittersweet scent of burning leaves at harvest time, when machines the size of dinosaurs crept through the fields and workers bustled everywhere. Harvest time was one of her favorite childhood memories. She had loved the sense of excitement and urgency after the long, slow days of summer.

It had been a good childhood, growing up here, she reflected as she climbed the steps to the old gazebo that was situated at the back of the garden behind the big house. She slid down on a weathered bench, glad for the shade, and leaned back against the railing, staring up at the house. Odille came out the back door wearing an enormous straw hat with a basket slung over her arm, and brandishing garden scissors and a ferocious scowl as she headed for a bed of spring flowers. At a corner of the house John Mason crept around a pillar, intent on scaring the living daylights out of Lacey, who was sitting on the grass playing with dolls. It was the kind of scene that brought memories to the surface – hot spring days and the unencumbered life of childhood in the shadows of Chanson du Terre.

It was the only home Serena and Shelby had ever known growing up. Their parents had settled in immediately after their wedding. An only son, Robert Sheridan, their father, had been groomed from an early age to take Gifford's place at the helm of the plantation. Serena couldn't help but think how different things would have been if he had lived. But he hadn't. He had died in a plane crash the day she and Shelby had turned fifteen.

His wife had preceded him to the grave by ten years. Serena barely remembered her mother except in random adjectives – a pretty smile, a soft voice, a loving touch. She remembered that her father had been devastated by her mother's death. She could still hear the terrible sound of his crying – wrenching, inconsolable grief confined to his bedroom while ladies from their church had placated everyone else with tuna casseroles and Jell-O. There had been no second marriage, no more children, no sons to carry on the line or take up the reins of the plantation.

What was it like to love someone that much? To love so that death meant the death of one's own heart. Serena couldn't imagine. She had never known that depth of emotion with a man, had never expected to. In her work she'd seen too many crumbled relationships to believe the other kind came along very often.

Her thoughts drifted to Lucky. She told herself it was only natural. She'd just spent a long hot night in his arms. That didn't mean she was thinking of him in permanent terms. But she couldn't help but wonder if he had ever known that kind of love. He would deny being capable of it. Of that she was certain. He didn't want anyone to know there was a heart under that carved-from-granite chest. Why? Because it had been broken, abused?

He had known Shelby, had been involved with her to some extent. Every time she thought of it, Serena felt a violent blast of disbelief and jealousy. Had they been lovers? Had they been in love? Was it Shelby who had bred that distrust of women in him? The idea brought a bitter taste to her mouth. It was yet another perfectly logical, practical reason for her not to get involved with Lucky Doucet, but she had taken that ill-advised step anyway. She had seen all the warning signs and plunged in headfirst in spite of them.

What a mess, she thought, a long sigh slipping between her lips. She picked absently at a scab of peeling paint on the railing and shook her head. She'd left Charleston with nothing on her mind but thoughts of a pleasant vacation and had fallen into a plot worthy of a Judith Krantz novel.

That was another reason she had left Chanson du Terre to begin with. In Charleston she had no complicated family relationships to deal with. She didn't have to wonder if her own sister was up to no good. She didn't have to look at her ancestral home and wonder what would become of it after two hundred years of Sheridan stewardship ended. She didn't have to worry about falling short of Gifford's expectations. She didn't have to watch him grow old. She could come back for the occasional dose of nostalgia and leave before it became necessary to deal with anything as unpleasant as past hurts and old fears.

'You can't hightail it out of Lou'siana first chance you get, then come on back and try to run things on the weekend.'

Gifford's voice still rang in her ears. The old reprobate. He had hit a nerve with that line, had scored a bull's-eye, sticking the dart right smack in the center of her guilt. And even while he'd been doing it, he had been maneuvering her so she would either have to deal with the problems or dig her guilt a deeper hole. He had her right where he wanted her, in the last place she wanted to be, dealing with questions she had never wanted to face.

'Serena, I don't believe you've met Mr. Burke from Tristar Chemical,' Mason said smoothly. He came forward, innocuous smile in place, and took her gently by the arm as she entered the front parlor.

'We haven't been formally introduced, no,' Serena said, extending her hand to the big man in the western-cut suit. 'I'm afraid you mistook me for my sister the other day out at Gifford's, Mr. Burke. I'm Serena Sheridan.'

Burke let his eyes drift down over her, taking in the subtle lines of her figure revealed by the straight cut of her toffee-colored sleeveless linen sheath. He pumped her hand and grinned. 'By golly, who'd a guessed there'd be two this pretty? It's a pleasure, *Miss* Sheridan?' His brows rose with a hope that made Serena loath to answer his implied question.

'Yes,' she murmured. She extracted her fingers from his meaty grasp and managed a twitch of the lips that passed for a smile. His gaze homed in on her breasts like radar.

'Now, what was a lovely young thing like yourself doing out in that swamp anyway?' he asked, settling a too-familiar hand on her shoulder.

Serena shrugged off his touch on the excuse of reaching up to smooth her fingers over her loosely bound hair.

'Serena is here on a visit from Charleston. She was trying to persuade Gifford to return so we might all deal with this offer in a proper manner,' Mason explained.

'And did you?'

'No, unfortunately not,' Serena replied. 'As you no doubt realize by now, Mr. Burke, my grandfather can be a very stubborn man.'

'It goes a mite beyond stubborn, if you ask me,' Burke said, baring his teeth. 'I have my doubts about his sanity.'

'Do you?' Serena arched a brow. 'Are you a psychologist, Mr. Burke?'

'No—'

'Well, I am,' she said, her tone as smooth and cool as marble. 'And I can assure you that while Gifford may be unreasonable and cantankerous, he is very much in control of his faculties.'

Burke's face turned dull red. His nostrils flared like a bull's and his chest puffed out. Mason intervened with diplomatic grace.

'Would you care for a drink, Serena?'

'Gin and tonic, please,' she said with a sweet smile, resisting the urge to lick a finger and chalk up a point for herself.

'Coming right up. And can I freshen that scotch for you, Len?'

Frowning, Burke followed him across the room to the antique sideboard that served as bar and liquor cabinet. Serena took the brief moment of solitude to survey the room. It looked exactly as it always had – taupe walls trimmed in soft white, faded Oriental carpets over a polished wood floor, heavy red brocade drapes flanking the French doors that led onto the gallery. The furniture was too formal to invite relaxation. It was a room Gifford never set foot in unless forced. He called it a place for entertaining people he didn't really like. How appropriate that they were gathering here, Serena thought as her gaze wandered over the people assembling for dinner.

Mason was already looking the part of the junior senator in a crisp shirt and tie and dark slacks, not quite as rumpled or distracted as he usually seemed. He made harmless small talk as he dug ice cubes from the bucket with tiny tongs. She had never thought about it before, but he would probably make a successful politician with his mild good looks and genteel manner.

Burke, in spite of the expensive cut of his suit, struck her as a man who wasn't afraid to get his hands dirty. He had the predatory air of a man who had clawed his way up to his present status and had no intention of going back down. He wore a gaudy diamond pinky ring and a boulder-sized chunk of turquoise on a bolo tie, flaunting the rewards of his labors like a warrior brandishing the trophies of battle.

Serena hadn't liked what she'd seen of him at Gifford's, and her instincts were telling her not to like anything about him tonight, but she tried to be objective. It wasn't a fatal character flaw for a man to be vulgar or pompous or sexist, and she had to admit he'd had a right to his temper of the day before – Gifford had been shooting at him, after all. Still, there was something about him that made her uncomfortable. Something about his narrow eyes and the set of his mouth. Gifford had said the man wouldn't take no for an answer. Serena wondered what lengths he might be willing to go to to achieve his objective.

Shelby breezed in from the hall then, resplendent in an ultrafeminine dress done in a dark English-garden print with a square ivory lace collar and a flowing skirt. Her hair was neatly confined in an old-fashioned ecru snood that perfectly completed the picture of refined southern woman-hood. The scent of Opium drifted around her in a fragrant cloud.

'Mr. Burke! How delightful to see you again!' She preened and sparkled, treating him to her most flirtatious smile as she came forward and offered him her hand.

'It's a pleasure, as always, Mrs. Talbot,' Burke said, treating her to the same once-over he had Serena. 'I've just had the chance to meet your lovely sister as well.'

Shelby's smile tightened as she shot a look at Serena. 'You're looking a little better tonight, Serena. Not quite as haggard as before.'

'Why, thank you,' Serena said, fighting a wry smile. She accepted her drink from Mason and sipped it, enjoying the bite of the gin a little more than she probably should have. This crowd was enough to drive anybody to drink. The room hummed with undercurrents.

'I've just been down to the kitchen to check on things,' Shelby said, batting her lashes at the big Texan. 'We're having a lovely ham. I do hope you like ham, Mr. Burke. Our Odille's ham gravy is simply sinful!'

'What happened to the crown roast?' Serena questioned innocently.

Shelby flashed her a dark look. 'That didn't work out as I'd hoped.'

'Pity.'

'Well, now,' Mason said expansively. 'We're just waiting on Lamar and then we can go in.'

Shelby pouted, stirring the swizzle stick of the drink her husband handed her. 'That doddering old fool. I don't understand why Gifford retains that man. It's an embarrassment that he won't let his own grandson-in-law handle his legal affairs.'

'Now, Shelby,' Mason cajoled. 'Lamar has been Gifford's attorney since God was a child. I certainly wouldn't expect him to dissolve an old loyalty like that.'

'Well, I would,' Shelby said, fussing with one pearl earring. 'What must people think? That he doesn't trust you to handle his affairs? It's disgraceful. I only hope it doesn't have an adverse affect on your campaign.'

Mason smiled at her benignly. 'I'm not concerned about it, darlin'. Don't you be.'

'I'm sure securing new jobs for the community will more than outweigh it, Mrs. Talbot,' Burke said smugly, swirling the ice in his glass. 'Bringing industry to a stagnant economy could take Mason here a long, long way.'

'Aren't you forgetting something, Mr. Burke?' Serena said mildly. 'Our grandfather has no intention of selling his property to Tristar.'

Burke flushed again, his eyes narrowing. Shelby shot daggers at her sister with her eyes. Mason flashed a big politician's smile and said, 'I do believe I hear Lamar's old Mercedes coming up the drive.'

Lamar Canfield was eighty if he was a day, a southern gentleman lawyer from the old school. He was a small, neat man with large dark eyes and thin white hair that now grew only on the sides of his head. He was dressed meticulously in a blue seersucker suit and starched white shirt with a jaunty striped bow tie at his throat and a fine Panama hat in his hands.

'Shelby! How good it is to see you again!' he said, beaming a smile as he came forward with the grace of Fred Astaire to take Serena's hand and plant a courtly kiss upon her knuckles.

'I'm Serena, Mr. Canfield,' she corrected him gently.

He pulled back, beaming a broad smile, his eyes gleaming with a sparkle that had set more than one female's heart aflutter in his day. 'Yes, of course you are, my darling,' he said without missing a beat. 'How lovely to have you home for a visit. You don't return often enough, you know,' he chided her, tilting his head in a look of reproach.

Serena couldn't help but smile at him. She had always liked Lamar. He was all flirtation and show and he had the voice of a snake-oil salesman – smooth and exaggerated, rising and falling dramatically. He displayed all the airs and mannerisms of a completely charming charlatan, all presented with a twinkle of amusement in his dark eyes that suggested he didn't take himself or anyone else too seriously.

'How doubly fortunate for us gentlemen to have the company of both our lovely Sheridan ladies,' he said, turning and bowing to Shelby, who regarded him with wary petulance, for once not swayed by a compliment. He straightened and turned his hat in his hands, directing his attention toward Serena once again.

'Are you back to stay, perchance, Serena? Heaven knows there is an abundance of warped minds in the immediate area. You could certainly keep yourself entertained.'

'No,' Serena said a bit hesitantly. 'I'm just here for a visit, I'm afraid.'

Lamar looked at her speculatively from under his lashes and clucked his tongue.

Mason stepped forward. 'Lamar, you've met Mr. Burke from Tristar, if you'll recall.'

'Yes . . . of course,' Lamar drawled, dragging the words out and letting them trail away as if they pained him. 'You're that man from Texas, aren't you?' He pronounced it *takes-us*, though whether he had done so as a deliberate slight or whether it was simply his extravagant drawl was impossible to tell.

Burke gave him a stony look, rattling the ice in his scotch.

Odille slipped into the room then and cast a baleful glare over them all as she announced dinner.

'Odille, my love!' Lamar said brightly. 'Charming as ever. Tell me what I might be able to do to entice you away from Gifford's employ.'

Odille sniffed indignantly, squeezing her light eyes into slits of disapproval. 'Nothin'.'

'Loquacious, isn't she, Shelby?' Lamar said, arching one brow as he took Serena's arm and tucked it through his.

Dinner was served in a formal dining room that had changed very little in a hundred years. They were seated at a mahogany table that had hosted planters from antebellum days. They used silver that had spent the war in a gunny-sack in the bottom of the well to keep it safe from Yankee plunder. The oil painting on the wall above the sideboard portrayed a Sheridan standing on the lawn of Chanson du Terre, holding the reins of a prized race horse; a brass plaque on the frame dated it to 1799.

'Such a lovely home,' Lamar remarked idly as he cut his ham. 'So gracious and full of history.'

'Yes,' Serena agreed. 'It would be a pity to see it destroyed.'

'There are more things to consider here than architecture,' Mason said. 'Chanson du Terre is a graceful old home, I grant you, but should it be placed ahead of the welfare of an entire community?'

'That's a good point, Mason,' said Burke. He looked across the table to Serena. 'You don't live around here, Miss Sheridan. Maybe you don't realize how hard the oil bust hit. People moved out of Lafayette by the convoy. Many of those who remained in South Louisiana were faced with unemployment. The new Tristar plant will employ two hundred fifty people to start with and eventually many more.'

'But at what cost to the environment, Mr. Burke?' Serena asked. 'I understand your company has a rather bad reputation in that area.'

Burke's eyes went cold. A muscle in his jaw twitched. 'I don't know where you get your information, but it simply isn't true. Tristar has never been convicted of anything regarding violations of pollution standards.'

Serena lifted a brow, singling out the word 'convicted.' Tristar had never been convicted, that wasn't to say they had never been charged or had never committed any crimes. They had simply never been convicted, a fact that made her wonder what lengths they may have gone to to keep blemishes from their record. If Len Burke was an example of the kind of man they hired to make their acquisitions, she could well imagine the sharks they retained on their legal staff to help them work around inconveniences like EPA regulations.

Her gaze moved to Mason, the fledgling politician whose campaign would rely heavily on Tristar. She wondered if he realized just how neatly he was being maneuvered. Tristar was providing him with a platform on which to run. Directly or indirectly they would be providing him with funding. Had it occurred to him that eventually they would call in those markers?

'Isn't it true Tristar would dig a navigation canal that would contribute to the demise of the swamp?' she asked.

Burke snorted and shook his head. 'You'd put a few acres of worthless mud and snakes ahead of the lives of the people around here?'

'The swamp isn't worthless to everyone,' she said quietly, thinking of the look in Lucky's eyes as he'd shown her his special place that morning. 'It's an ecosystem that deserves respect.'

Shelby laughed without humor. 'My, you're the last person I would have expected to hear that from, Serena. Why, you've hated the swamp as long as I can remember. You moved all the way to Charleston to get away from it.'

Serena regarded her sister with a look that barely disguised anger and hurt. 'Be that as it may,' she said, 'we are getting ahead of ourselves, aren't we? The fact remains Gifford has strong feelings about heritage and tradition. He would prefer to see Chanson du Terre continue on as it always has.'

'How can it?' Shelby asked, tearing a biscuit into bite-size pieces. She looked askance at her twin. 'Are you going to come back from Charleston and farm it, Serena?'

'Of course not.'

'Then what do you suggest? Mason's future lies elsewhere. Who else is left to run it?'

'Shelby's right,' Mason said. 'Even if Gifford doesn't sell now, he'll only be delaying the inevitable. He's going to have to retire in the not too distant future. He'll be forced to sell in the end. Taking Tristar's offer now is the only practical thing to do. It's a very generous offer, certainly more than Chanson du Terre is worth as a going concern.'

'The place is falling down around Gifford's ears,' Shelby remarked. 'You can't help but have noticed. The house is in need of major restoration. Why, just look at the ceiling in this room for example.'

All eyes traveled upward and widened at the sight of the heavy brass chandelier hanging down from the center of a sagging, water-stained, peeling spot of plaster. It looked as if one good tug could bring the whole expanse crashing down on their heads.

'There are other alternatives to selling,' Serena said, bringing them back to the matter at hand. 'The land could be leased to another grower. The house must qualify for historical status; there's the possibility of grant money being available to restore it.'

'But to what end?' Mason questioned. 'When Gifford passes on, I trust he will leave the place to you and Shelby equally and Shelby has already stated she no longer wants it. Are you prepared to buy her out, Serena?'

'If you are, perhaps you'll just run along and get your checkbook, darlin',' Shelby suggested archly. 'I have a life to lead and I'd sooner get on with it than wait.'

Serena's mouth tightened as she looked at her sister. 'What happened to your dedication to the preservation of southern antiquities, sister?' she queried bitingly through a chilling smile. 'Did that committee meeting conflict with your facial appointments?'

Shelby slammed her fork down on the table and straightened in her chair, her mouth tightening into a furious knot. 'Don't you talk to me about dedication, Serena. You're the one who lives eight hundred miles away. You're the one—'

'Now, ladies,' Mason interrupted with the borrowed wisdom of Solomon shining in his eyes behind his glasses. 'Let's not regress to pointing fingers. The fact is neither of you will take over the running of the plantation. What we must concentrate on is how to deal with Mr. Burke's offer and how to deal with Gifford. Might you have any suggestions in that area, Lamar? Lamar?'

Canfield had dozed off over his mashed potatoes. Shelby rolled her eyes. Burke huffed in impatient disgust. Odille, making the rounds with a fresh gravy boat, gave the old attorney a bony elbow to the shoulder. He jerked awake, confusion swimming in his eyes as his gaze searched the table and settled on Serena.

'A lovely meal, Shelby,' he said with a smile. 'Thank you so much for asking me out.'

Serena groaned inwardly. If there had been any hope of finding a valuable ally in Gifford's attorney, it had just faded away.

'There's no place for sentiment in business,' Burke announced, helping himself to another mountain of sliced ham. 'The place will be sold in the end. Y'all might as well face the facts and take the money.'

'It's not our decision to make, Mr. Burke,' Serena said tightly.

He gave her a long look. 'Isn't it?'

'What are you saying?'

He lifted his shoulders and looked away from her toward Mason and Shelby. 'Just that Tristar's offer is firm. We want this piece of property. If you want to collect on that, I suggest you strengthen your powers of persuasion where your granddaddy is concerned – one way or another.'

The addendum had all the nasty connotations of a threat. Serena sat back in her chair, her gaze on Burke as he shoveled food into his mouth. Gifford had been right; a simple no was not going to deter the Tristar rep. She wondered as she caught her sister looking her way just what it was going to take to put an end to this business once and for all, and whether there would be anything left of her family when it was over.

12

Serena changed into her nightgown feeling as if she hadn't slept in a month. Dinner had been an exhausting ordeal, not to mention depressing. And with no progress for the trouble. Burke was still set on acquiring Chanson du Terre; Shelby and Mason were still bent on selling it to him. She was still caught in the middle.

She had been glad to escape to the quiet and comfort of her bedroom. The room hadn't been changed at all in the time she had lived away from Chanson du Terre. Like the rest of the house, it seemed to possess a stubborn agelessness that defied change. The walls were papered in a delicate vine and flower pattern over a background of rich ivory. The rug that covered the floor had been trod upon by generations of Sheridan feet. The cherry bed and its hand-tied net canopy had offered rest to the weary a century before. Serena found the idea comforting. The sense of constancy appealed to her, especially now, when she was feeling tired and uncertain about so many things. She could at least look around her room in the soft light of the bedside lamp and feel welcomed.

Belting her white silk robe around her, she went to stand in the open doorway leading onto the gallery, leaning against the frame as if she hadn't the strength left to support herself. The night beyond was dark and starless, the air heavy with the promise of rain and the scents of wisteria and honeysuckle. How many other Sheridan women had stood in this exact spot and looked out into the night, pondering their futures? How many would do so in years to come? None, if Len Burke got his way. And if Burke didn't get his way. . . ?

A soft knock on the door roused Serena from her tormented musings. She turned as Shelby stuck her head into the room.

'May I come in?'

A shrug was the only answer Serena could muster. She was exhausted. The prospect of yet another conversational wrestling match with her sister was not inviting.

Shelby came in and closed the door behind her, leaning back against it, an uncertain look in her dark eyes. She had shed her pumps and let her hair down, making her look young and sweet in her feminine dress. She still wore an array of expensive rings on her dainty hands and demonstrated her hesitancy by twisting her topaz around her finger.

'I'm only trying to be practical, Serena,' she said with a suddenness that made it seem as if she had launched into the middle of the conversation instead of the beginning. 'I should think you, of all people, would appreciate that. You've always been practical.'

'Practicality isn't the issue,' Serena said, coming away from the gallery door, sliding her hands into the deep pockets of her robe.

'Well, it should be. For heaven's sake, Serena, think about it!' Shelby insisted. She moved around the room with short, brisk strides, compulsively straightening things that didn't need straightening. 'The place will have to be sold eventually. Here we have a buyer ready to hand us money on a platter, and I can tell you as a real estate professional, they don't come along every day. There's nothing but good in this for everyone, and Gifford is standing in the way just to be stubborn!'

'He's worked this land all his life,' Serena pointed out calmly, playing the devil's advocate out of habit and necessity. 'He doesn't want to see it all wiped away.'

Shelby stopped her fussing and shot her sister a narrow sideways look, her mood flashing from businesslike to petulant to shrewd. 'He's manipulating you.'

Serena didn't argue the point; it was true. She was too caught up watching her sister's chameleon qualities, at once fascinated and horrified by the rapid changes. They pointed toward problems Serena found herself wanting to deny.

'He's just that way,' Shelby went on, absently rearranging things on the dresser to suit her own tastes. 'He's in his glory now, holding all of us hostage. He's a stubborn old man.'

'Would you give up your children for the sake of someone else's livelihood?' Serena asked.

Shelby turned toward her, offended and incredulous. 'Give up my children? Don't be ridiculous! Of course not, but it's hardly the same thing.'

'It is to Giff. This land is as much a part of him as we are. Why should he be expected to give it up?'

Shelby's face flushed and she stamped her foot on the rug. Her hands balled into fists at her side. 'Because it's what everyone else wants! Because it's going to happen anyway. For pity's sake, why doesn't he just give in?'

'Because he's Gifford.'

'Well, something has to be done, Serena,' she announced vehemently as she resumed pacing. 'He's just being unreasonable and it's hurting us all. I told you I thought he was going senile and I believe it. And I'm not the only one who thinks so.'

Serena thought back to Burke's threats of a competency hearing and frowned at her twin. She refrained from pointing out that a man who had the ability to manipulate so many people so neatly couldn't possibly be senile. Instead, she simply said, 'I will not see Gifford declared incompetent, Shelby. Don't even think about suggesting it.'

'It would serve him right,' Shelby said sourly, her lower lip jutting forward in a pout.

Serena was appalled by the suggestion and the attitude that accompanied it. She may not have been especially close to or fond of her sister, but still she didn't want to believe her own flesh and blood, her own twin capable of such callous selfishness. She stared at Shelby now, disgust and disbelief stark on her face. 'I can't believe your greed would push you to something so ugly.'

Shelby's eyes flashed wildly. Serena thought she could almost hear her sister's control crack. 'Greed? Greed!' Shelby shouted, stepping toward Serena. Her lovely ivory complexion turned a mottled red. Every muscle in her body seemed to go rigid. 'How dare you accuse me of greed! You're the greedy one! You and Gifford. Greedy and selfish! I want only what's best for everybody!'

Right, Serena thought. Businesswoman of the Year. Mason in the legislature. A healthy bank account and the unending gratitude of those who would profit from the deal. She didn't say any of those things, however. She stood silent, staring at her sister, a sick churning in her stomach.

Shelby paced back and forth along the length of the bed, huffing and puffing like a toy train. 'Isn't this just like you?' she said bitterly. 'You waltz in from Charleston and take Gifford's side just to please him and then you'll waltz back out and not give a damn that you've ruined everything for everyone else. You won't have to deal with it. You don't live here. You don't care. The rest of us have responsibilities here.'

'You don't seem to feel any responsibility toward Gifford or your family home or the environment,' Serena pointed out, knowing she would have been better off saying nothing. But she couldn't seem to find the cool restraint she used when confronted by an overwrought patient. She couldn't maintain objectivity with her own family, and the only way she could distance herself from them was in the physical sense. The minute she came back here she felt sucked into an emotional maelstrom, a thick familial quicksand that pulled her down from her safe perch above it all. It was a humbling experience and an exhausting one. She gave in to it now as her temper rose and her control slipped away.

'You know what the petrochemical industry has done down here already,' she argued. 'Fouling land and water—'

'Feeding people, providing jobs, keeping towns alive—'

'—elevating the cancer rate, destroying animal habitat—'

'Oh, for the love of Mike!' Shelby threw her hands up in exasperation. 'You sound like those lunatics up in Oregon, or wherever they are, harping on the loggers for scaring off a bunch of owls that don't have sense enough to go live someplace else. And all for a place you hate to begin with!'

Serena pulled herself back from the ragged edge of anger and sighed, crossing her arms defensively. 'Just because it's not a place I like to be doesn't mean I want it wiped off the face of the earth. There are people who still make their living out there, you know.'

Shelby sniffed indignantly. 'Poachers and white trash. If you ask me, Tristar would be doing us all a favor getting rid of them.'

Serena rolled her eyes. 'A very charitable attitude.'

'Practical. Practical,' Shelby reiterated with a decisive nod. She calmed visibly as she put on her businesslike persona again, folding her hands primly in front of her. 'It's the practical thing, Serena. And if you have no interest in staying here anyway, I don't see why you don't just side with us and get it over with. It's best for everyone. It's best for Gifford, if you come right down to it.

'He's seventy-eight years old and he's got a heart condition, for heaven's sake,' she said, warming to this new angle of showing concern for someone else. 'He shouldn't be out in the cane fields. He shouldn't have to worry himself sick over the weather and the insects and the price of diesel fuel and whether or not that old John Deere is going to make it another season. He should be taking it easy. He shouldn't have to think about anything but going fishing with Pepper and swapping stories with the men down at Gauthier's.

'He almost went bankrupt last year, you know,' she added, looking genuinely saddened. 'Many more things go wrong this year and he will. What good will all his stubborn pride do him then? It would kill him to go under. He can avoid it now, go out with dignity.'

Serena said nothing. Her sister's arguments were valid. They made perfect sense. They were neat and tidy and left no loose ends – except Gifford's heart's desire and the fate of Lucky's swamp. And how did one compare those things to the fate of a town? Was two hundred years of heritage more important than two hundred fifty jobs? Were a few jobs worth ruining a delicate wilderness that could never be replaced?

'I don't know,' she murmured half to herself.

She sat down on the foot of the bed and leaned against a slender post, twining her arm around it like a vine. She stared at her reflection in the mirror above the dresser, looking for answers that weren't forthcoming. She felt as if she had the weight of the world on her shoulders, and all she wanted to do was shrug it off and walk away, but she couldn't. She couldn't walk away from Chanson du Terre or her need to please Gifford or her complicated relationship with her sister.

'I don't know what to do,' she whispered, a feeling of bleak desolation yawning inside her like a cavern.

The image in the mirror was duplicated as Shelby sat down beside her.

They looked less like twins now, Serena thought, because she herself looked like hell. There were dark crescents beneath her eyes and she was pale and drawn. The emotional war was taking a toll on her. Shelby was bearing up better under the strain with the aid of a full complement of expensive cosmetics. She looked less troubled by the burden of it all, perhaps because she shouldered none of the load. Shelby had always possessed the convenient ability to shift blame elsewhere, so while she may have been frustrated with the current situation, she felt it was all someone else's fault. Serena had no doubt her sister slept like a baby. For all her talk of accepting responsibility, responsibility rolled off Shelby like water off a duck's back.

'My, you look all done in,' Shelby said softly, and her brows knitted in one of her rare shows of genuine concern.

She didn't look directly at Serena but assessed her appearance via the mirror, as if she were obsessed with their likenesses. It was a disturbing thing, and Serena forced herself to stand up and move to avoid it. She went to the French doors again and stood with her back against the frame.

'You didn't tell me you knew Lucky Doucet,' she said mildly, watching out of the corner of her eye for a reaction.

Shelby jerked around in surprise, a multitude of emotions sweeping over her face like clouds scudding across the night sky. 'What did he tell you?' she asked guardedly.

'Nothing much,' Serena conceded.

Apparently feeling safe, Shelby rose to her feet and moved in a leisurely manner, smoothing the bedspread, straightening the skirt of her dress. 'I went out with him a few times back when I was dating Mason to make Mason jealous,' she admitted without remorse. 'It was a long time ago. I never think about it. I mean, for heaven's sake, look at what became of him. I'm embarrassed to admit I ever knew him. Why did you want to know?'

'No reason.'

'Good Lord, Serena,' she said with genuine alarm. 'You're not involved with him, are you? He's dangerous. Why, you can't imagine the things people say about him!'

Serena expected she could imagine quite vividly what the average person would have to say about Lucky. They would look at him and see exactly what he wanted them to see, and 'dangerous' would only just begin to cover it. She had wondered if he had let Shelby see some other side of him. Obviously he hadn't.

It frightened her to think how happy that made her. This was dangerous territory – thinking she might be the one woman to reach beyond his barriers and touch his heart, taking joy in the knowledge that her sister had not been there before her. It was foolish. She had enough trouble without trying to take on a project like the reformation of Lucky Doucet. All he wanted from her was sex.

'He mentioned that he knew you,' she said. 'I was just curious, that's all.'

'Oh.' Shelby shrugged and headed for the door. 'Well, it was nothing,' she said, reducing the affair down to the level of importance it held for her. Lucky Doucet had served his purpose. She had gotten what she wanted. Nothing else mattered. 'Good night.'

'Good night.'

Serena watched her sister go. Nothing had been resolved. They had gone another circuit on the merry-go-round of their relationship once more, suffering through emotional ups and downs only to return to the place they had started.

She sighed as the door clicked shut and gasped in the next breath as someone grabbed her from behind. One brawny arm went around her waist and hauled her back into what seemed like a rock wall, and a hand clamped over her mouth, effectively snuffing out the scream that tore its way up the back of her throat.

'All dressed up for me, sugar?' Lucky said, his lips brushing her ear, his left hand moving restlessly over the silk that covered her belly. 'You shouldn't have.'

'Damn you,' Serena told him as he pulled his hand away from her mouth. She tried to twist around in his arms so she could hit him, but he held her in place with ridiculous ease. 'You scared the hell out of me.'

'Yeah, you oughta be scared of me,' he muttered, nuzzling the side of her throat.

He made that kind of comment again and again to convince her of the blackness of his character, but Serena was no longer willing to buy it. Now that she had caught glimpses of the real man, she was no longer willing to believe the myth. Her heart had, with a will of its own, set itself on that man beneath the dangerous façade. However futile it might have seemed, she wanted to latch on to the goodness she knew was inside him and draw it out.

That he still wanted to keep her away from who he really was made her angry – angry with him and angry with herself. Of all the men in the world, why did this one have to be the one to capture her heart? Two days earlier she hadn't even *liked* him. She wasn't sure she liked him now, but she couldn't escape the fact that she had fallen in love with him. It seemed impossible and foolishly romantic and very unlike the Serena Sheridan who lived a sane and orderly life in Charleston. But they weren't in Charleston and she wasn't the same person who had left there, she reminded herself with weary resignation.

'Stop it,' she said, her exhaustion with the whole situation showing in her voice.

'Stop what? This?' He rubbed his beard-roughened cheek against her skin again, breathing in the scent of her. 'Or this?' he asked, sliding his dark hand down over her belly to the juncture of her thighs where he stroked her boldly through her clothes.

Serena moaned at the sensations that burst and flowed inside her like floodwaters from a dam. In the span of one night Lucky had conditioned her body to respond to his without reserve. She wanted him instantly, wanted nothing more than to lie down and welcome him into her, to love him with every part of herself. But she forced herself to pull away from him, fighting to retain some small scrap of control, some tiny piece of sanity.

He let her go, chuckling wickedly, and sauntered over to her dresser, where he idly picked up and examined a perfume bottle as he watched her in the mirror from beneath his lashes.

Serena tightened the belt of her robe, staring hard at his reflection. 'Stop trying to scare me away from you,' she said.

'Was that what I was doing?' He made a face of surprise. 'Me, I thought I was on my way to gettin' you in bed.'

'You know what I mean.'

He shrugged and refused to comment, devoting more attention to her toiletries than to her argument. Frustration swelled inside her, but she refused to vent it, knowing that goading her was one of his favorite methods of keeping her at bay.

'What are you doing here? No poachers to thwart tonight?'

He gave her a black look by way of the mirror and picked up a tube of moisturizer. 'How was dinner?'

'Enlightening. Burke says Tristar has never been convicted of anything regarding pollution.'

'Oh, no,' he drawled. 'Just like they've never been convicted of bribing government officials or transporting illegal substances to un-licensed dumping sites. But if he said they've never done it, he's a liar.'

'He doesn't seem ready to give up on the idea of building here.'

'I'm sure he's not. They'd get a perfect site on the edge of nowhere, acres of dumping grounds in their backyard, and an eager young politician to boot.' He shook his head as he fingered the carved back of a rosewood hairbrush. '*Mais non,* he's not gonna give up.'

Serena moved to stand beside him, her gaze on his long artist's fingers as they touched her things. 'What else can he do?' she asked. 'Gifford says he won't sell and he means it. There's nothing Burke can do. Gifford can't be forced into selling.'

The instant she said it she remembered the look in the big Texan's eyes as he'd sat at their dinner table and told them Gifford would have to be persuaded. He struck her as a man who got what he wanted by whatever means were necessary, and her grandfather stood between him and his goal. How hard might he push? To what lengths might he be willing to go?

She pushed the disturbing questions from her mind and went to stand at the open door again, looking out into the night as if she might see an answer shining like a star in the darkness. 'He says the plant would employ two hundred fifty locals to start.'

'That's bullshit,' Lucky said. 'A hundred, mebbe. Seventy-five, probably. The rest would be company men. There aren't a lotta chemists and engineers standin' around on street corners here lookin' for jobs.'

'Still, that's more jobs than Gifford can provide. The boost to the local economy would be tremendous.'

'And the damage to the local environment would be devastating.'

Serena sighed and brought her hands up to rub the tension from her forehead. 'It's not as simple as I thought it would be.'

'It is simple,' Lucky argued adamantly. 'It's stupid simple. Black and white. Good guys and bad guys.'

Serena turned and faced him. 'Which are you. Lucky? I thought you didn't care about anyone or anything. You tell me you're a bad guy, then I find out you're out playing Lone Ranger in the night. You let me think you're some bad-ass poacher, then turn around and spout environmentalist propaganda at me. Who are you really?'

'Trust me, sugar,' he said. 'You don't wanna know.'

She met his scowl without flinching. 'I *do* want to know.'

'I told you before, Doc,' he said darkly, raising a finger in warning. 'Don' go lookin' inside my head. You won't like what you find.'

Serena stared at him, taking in the fierce set of his jaw, the intimidation in his stance . . . the brief flicker of uncertainty in his eyes – a wariness of her or of himself?

She could feel the dangerous desire to reach out to him shifting through her, a need to know that went beyond curiosity. A smart woman would have taken heed of his warning. A smart woman would have kept her distance. He had drawn the boundary line between them, and like a fool she stepped across it again, figuratively and literally, moving toward him, needing to know, needing to touch him.

'And what would I find in your heart?' she asked softly as she closed the distance between them.

'That I haven't got one,' he said, his face carefully blank.

Serena shook her head. 'I don't believe that. You go out of your way to help people. My God,' she said, gesturing to the bandanna still tied around his injured arm, 'you risk your life to help people.'

'Don' make me out to be some hero,' Lucky snapped, just barely resisting the urge to back away from her. 'I get paid back for what I do.'

'In French bread and cookies?'

'In privacy. People wander into my life and I get them out. That's all I do. That's all I care about,' he insisted, his inner tension crackling in his low, rough voice.

'Is that what you tell yourself, Lucky? You're a liar.'

'It's the truth.' He brought his hands up to take Serena by the shoulders, his fingers pressing on silk and tender flesh as if he might be able to physically force his opinion on her. His heart pounded with the necessity of it, the urgency of it. He leaned over her, his eyes as bright as a zealot's. 'I'm a devil, not a saint, and whatever heart I might have had once got ripped out by the roots a long time ago, sugar. Don' go lookin' for things that aren't there.'

Serena said nothing, but lifted a hand and splayed it across his chest, her fingers small and white against the black of his T-shirt. Her eyes locked on his as they both felt the frantic pounding behind his ribs, the evidence that shattered his lie more than any words could have.

Lucky gave a snarl of frustration and rage and battled within himself as fear swelled like a balloon inside him. He kicked it down, checked it ruthlessly, hardening himself against it with an effort that trembled through him like an earthquake. He gave Serena a shake.

'I don' give a rat's ass if you don' believe it,' he said in a voice like smoke. 'You wanna go diggin' through your psych books for explanations, do it on your own time. I didn't come here to get analyzed; I came here to get laid.'

His mouth swept down on hers, hard, seeking to punish, but he was met with no resistance, no fear. She was soft and sweet, yielding to him, melting against him, and that undid his anger as nothing else could have. He softened the kiss, making a sound of surrender in his throat as her lips parted beneath his in invitation. The kiss deepened and he felt himself going under, losing himself. His heart pounded and he clutched Serena to him, his mind swirling with the question of whether she was the stone that would sink him or the branch that would save him from drowning.

Neither, he told himself. She could be neither because this was desire and nothing more. She couldn't hurt him; she couldn't heal him. She could give him pleasure and he could help her forget her problems for a few hours. It was simple. Stupid simple. Black and white.

'I want you,' he whispered against her mouth.

He brushed his lips against her temple and turned her in his arms so she faced the mirror above the dresser. Serena stared at their reflections – Lucky, big and masculine behind her, his arms around her, his head bent down, his eyes on hers in the glass; and herself, dainty and feminine in his shadow, golden and white beside his darkness. She watched as his fingers untied the belt of her robe and stood motionless as he drew the garment back off her shoulders and let it fall to the floor. The gown she wore beneath it was silk and lace, a sheer white mist clinging to the curves of her body and hanging past her knees.

He stroked his hands down the front of her, cupping her breasts through the lace cups, kneading her stomach through the silk, sliding down over her hips, tracing every curve and line that expressed her femininity. He lowered his mouth to her shoulder, nibbling at her flesh, catching the narrow strap of the gown in his teeth and drawing it down. Serena watched as he feasted on her skin, kissing, nipping, licking, devouring every exposed inch. She bent her head to the side to give him access to her throat and moaned as he took it, his mouth moving fervently along the ivory column. He caught the other strap of her gown with his fingers and drew it down, then peeled the lace bodice away from her, letting it pool in a drift of white at her waist. He captured her breasts in his hands, lifting and squeezing them, plumping them together and flicking his thumbs across her nipples.

Serena's breath caught in her throat. She'd never been a party to anything so erotic. Her eyes, heavy-lidded and dark with passion, were locked on the image in the mirror. Lucky's big, tanned hands kneading her breasts, her nipples thrusting out swollen and red between his fingers. Arousal seared through her, hot and thick as she watched her own seduction and experienced every sensation at the same time.

He slid one hand down her rib cage and over her belly, pressing the white silk of her gown taut over her feminine mound. Serena leaned back against him, letting her thighs part as he slid his hand between them. He caressed her through the silk, moving the cool slick fabric against her most sensitive heated flesh. Then the gown was gone and through the haze of desire she watched his fingers stroke through the delta of tawny curls as the fever of need intensified inside her. With one arm banded across her ribs, he lifted her up against him and her head lolled back against his shoulder, rolling from side to side as he eased a finger deep into the warm, wet channel of her womanhood.

'Watch,' he whispered. 'Watch,' he said, his voice as smooth and smoky as whiskey, as seductive as a siren's song. 'This is what I want from you, *mon ange*.'

His eyes locked on hers in the mirror. He stroked her deeply, rhythmically, in time with her harsh breathing. Serena moaned and moved against his hand, her control gone, her instincts overwhelming her as Lucky took her closer to the edge.

She chanted his name, the words catching in her throat as she struggled for breath. Her breasts rose and fell in the image in the mirror. Her stomach quivered. Lucky's hand moved against her groin. His eyes watched her from beneath the rim of dark lashes, smoldering amber, hot and bright. Her gaze fastened on his mouth, blatantly sensual, carnal, his lips moist and parted slightly as he whispered to her.

'*Vien, chérie, vien, vien, vien . . .*'

Her climax hit her like a wave, breaking over her, knocking the breath from her. Her body stiffened in his arms and she would have cried out, but Lucky twisted her around and fastened his mouth over hers. He kissed her hungrily, savagely, bending her back over his arm, his free hand tangling in her hair as it spilled behind her.

In the next instant they were on the bed, Serena lying back on the cool sheets, Lucky with one knee on the mattress and one foot on the floor as he tore his T-shirt off and flung it aside. His jeans followed. He came to her magnificently naked, magnificently aroused, lowering himself over her and plunging himself into her in one smooth move that lifted her off the bed.

Serena arched up against him, taking everything he would give her and knowing in her heart it wouldn't be enough. She gave him her body, let him fill her again and again with the essence of what made him male. She welcomed the driving power of his thrusts, delighted in the feel of his muscled back beneath her hands, the hot musky scent of his body, the smoky taste of his kisses, but she longed for something more.

She looked up into his face and saw the torment there, the strain as he gave her his body and fought to withhold his soul. For an instant she could look into his eyes and feel the terrible struggle going on inside him, and it tore at her heart. There was no place here for reason or self-control. All she could give him was her love, no matter how foolish it seemed, no matter that she knew he wouldn't want to take it, no matter that she was certain her heart would get broken in the end.

As he moved powerfully over her and inside of her, she wrapped her arms around him and pressed her cheek against his chest, hanging on for dear life as longing tore through her shield of logic once and for all. She was in love with a man for the first time in her life, helplessly, hopelessly in love. He took her on a breathless climb to passion's very summit and soared with her over the edge, his big body straining against hers, his arms crushing her to him. And she let herself believe in that one brilliant moment that he could love her too.

13

She looked like an angel. Her hair spilled golden and silky across the pillow. Her lashes lay like tawny lace fans against her cheeks. Her mouth was soft and rosy, relaxed in sleep. Lucky looked down at her, something twisting painfully in his chest as he reached out to touch her but stopped himself, his fingers a scant inch above her face.

She was giving and caring, strong and brave, everything he'd ever given up on finding in a woman, and he couldn't allow himself to indulge in anything other than her body. That, of course, was heaven itself. What he felt when he was inside Serena was incredible. She took away the coldness, chased back the darkness, made him feel alive instead of caught in some bleak plane of existence. He could take her five times a day and never get enough of her. He'd never felt such an insatiable yearning for a woman, had never had his needs met with such sweet absolute surrender.

He wouldn't have believed it possible of the woman he'd first encountered in Gauthier's, but that cool, controlled woman wasn't who Serena really was. Too bad for him, he thought, his mouth twisting in a wry parody of a smile.

Serena wasn't cold and hard. She was a warm, golden temptation. Heaven was losing himself in her, hell was knowing he couldn't stay. She would want too much from him. She would want things he couldn't give. He couldn't let her get that close.

In the first place, he was terrified of what she would see – the things he'd done, the things he'd seen, the cold blackness that surrounded his soul and crept in on his mind. In the second place, he was terrified of what would happen. He had spent the past year putting himself back together, painstakingly reconstructing himself from the fragments Ramos's hell had left him in. Now those fragments balanced one against the other like a house of cards. One wrong move and it would all come crashing down.

He needed his peace, his solitude, his art. That was all. He had stripped his life down to those bare essentials because he couldn't tolerate anything more. He couldn't be around people because their presence irritated him, like air blowing across an exposed nerve. By necessity his focus had to remain inward, concentrating on holding himself together. He couldn't need a woman whose job was to poke around inside people's minds, ferreting out their secrets, taking them all apart to see what made them tick.

He slid from the bed without disturbing Serena, stepped into his jeans and zipped up, leaving the button undone. He dug a cigarette from the pocket of his T-shirt, hung it from his lip, and wandered across the room to the French doors that still stood open. Thunder rumbled in the distance, an appropriate accompaniment to everything that was going on inside him and around him; a portent of a coming storm within and without.

He had a bad feeling about this business with Chanson du Terre. He had from the beginning and it was only getting worse. Opposing forces were pushing against each other, building pressure. Something was going to have to give. Digging a match out of his pocket, he lit his cigarette and inhaled deeply, wondering which side would give in first.

Gifford Sheridan was an old man. Ferocious and hardheaded, to be sure, but an old man nevertheless. If he had a son to inherit or a granddaughter who wanted to stay, things might have looked better. As it was, the deck was stacked against him, against Chanson du Terre, against the swamp.

On the other side stood Tristar and Len Burke. Burke, who reminded Lucky too much of his old nemesis, Colonel Lambert, a man who had known no boundaries when it came to getting what he wanted. Where would Burke draw the line? And what of Shelby? Lucky knew all too well how far she was willing to go to get what she wanted.

Mason Talbot struck him as little more than a pawn to be used by Tristar and Shelby. He was too laid back to instigate anything. Too dimwitted in Gifford's opinion. But he would have his uses. He would make a perfect figurehead to rally the town around in favor of economic growth. And once Tristar was in place and Mason was ensconced in the legislature in Baton Rouge, he would make a very attractive spokesman for the chemical industry.

Lucky's gaze drifted back to the bed and Serena, who was frowning and mumbling in her sleep, her hand sweeping against the mattress where he had lain. The load had been dropped squarely on her slender shoulders, and while she seemed determined to uphold her grandfather's wishes, would she only be delaying the inevitable? She had said Gifford's ploy wouldn't hold her here. What would happen when she left?

'Lucky?' she whispered, rousing herself like a sleepy kitten. Blinking against the soft light, she sat up and combed back a handful of honey-gold hair from her eyes. Lucky watched and said nothing, savoring the sight of her as she drew the ivory cotton sheet up demurely over her breasts, a gesture that struck him as sweetly incongruous considering everything they'd done together in bed.

She tilted her head and blinked at him. 'What are you doing?'

'Havin' a cigarette,' he said. He took a deep drag and exhaled a plume of smoke in demonstration.

Serena frowned as she slid from the bed, wrapping the sheet around her like a Grecian gown. 'You smoke too much,' she chided him softly as she padded across the faded carpet. She cuddled against him, not waiting for an invitation, but sliding her arms around his lean waist and nuzzling her cheek against his bare chest. She tilted her head back to look up at him. 'You shouldn't smoke at all. It's bad for you.'

Lucky couldn't hold back a soft, incredulous laugh. He stared down into her earnest face, something like wonder rising inside him. He couldn't remember the last time he'd given a moment's thought to his health. Not because he doubted his own mortality, but because he didn't care. For a long, long time he'd felt as if he had nothing left to lose, including his own life. When he first returned from Central America, he spent night after night staring at a 9mm Beretta, his death awaiting him in a sleek black casing filled with hollow-point ammunition. The only thing that kept him from sticking the thing in his mouth and pulling the trigger was the knowledge of what it would have done to his parents, who were staunchly Catholic.

He had lived with death as a constant companion and now Serena stood looking up at him, warning him of the dangers of smoking.

'Why is that funny?' she asked, looking annoyed with him.

Lucky sobered. 'It's not.'

He turned without leaving her embrace and crushed his cigarette in a decorative china cup sitting on a stand. 'Happy?'

'Hardly.' Serena sniffed. 'That was my great-grandmother's teacup.'

'This old house is full of stuff like that, isn't it?' he asked, looping his arms loosely around her. 'Antiques, heirlooms, family treasures passed down and down.'

'Yes,' Serena answered, her own gaze wandering over a dozen things in this room alone that had seen generations of Sheridans come and go. 'It's like a microcosm of history. It ought to be renovated and opened to the public as a museum.'

'Instead, it could be razed and lost forever.'

She looked up at him, her brows pulling together over troubled dark eyes. 'Could we not talk about it for a while? I'm so tired.'

Lucky ran a hand over her hair, an unexpected wave of sympathy sweeping over him. He would have liked to have taken her away from all the problems, protected her, kept her all to himself for a little while, but that wasn't an option. He knew he should have steeled himself against the tenderness stirring inside him as he looked down at her, but he gave in to it for an instant, leaned down, and kissed her. She looked tired. She looked confused and battered. What could it hurt to offer her a little comfort?

Her lips were soft and warm beneath his. Eager, yearning. She clung to his kiss as if it might intoxicate her past thinking. She pressed herself against him as if she wished to be absorbed directly into his body. The desire to protect her rose up even stronger inside him and he tried to push it back. He couldn't be anyone's savior; he had all he could do just to hold himself together.

When he lifted his head he touched her cheek and murmured regretfully, 'I'm sorry, *chère*. I know you didn't ask for this fight.'

'It's mine by birthright, I suppose,' Serena said, drawing away from him. She wandered in the little pool of lamplight, absently touching objects on the table and dresser with one hand and clutching the sheet to her breasts with the other.

'It's ironic, you know,' she added, trying unsuccessfully to smile. 'I left here because I thought my life was somewhere else, because I didn't think I'd ever become my own person if I stayed. And here I am . . . ' She gestured to the room, to the house in general, looking around her with a vague sense of bewilderment. 'Here I am. They say you can't go home again. I can't seem to get away.'

'You'll be able to get away permanently if your sister has her way,' Lucky said, watching her with a hawkish gaze. 'Is that what you want – to be out from under the burden of your heritage forever?'

Serena looked around at the room, feeling the personality of the great house bearing down upon her. She was too tired to fight it. Resignation flowed through her and her shoulders sagged. She would be forever tied to this house in a way time and distance couldn't alter even if she wanted them to. This was her home. It would always be her home. Chanson du Terre was where her roots were and they went two hundred years deep.

'No,' she said softly.

She didn't want to see the old house destroyed. She didn't want to see strangers living here. She didn't want Tristar Chemical building a processing plant where the old slave quarters stood in silent testimony to past lives. She didn't want to see high wire fences surrounding what once had been cane fields. She wanted Chanson du Terre to be owned by a Sheridan; she just didn't want it to be her.

'Then you'd better be ready for a fight, sugar,' Lucky said. 'Len Burke means to have this land. He'll fight dirty to get it and your sister will be there right beside him.'

'It's not Shelby I'm worried about.'

He gave her a guarded look. 'Don't underestimate her, Serena. I don't think you realize what she might be capable of.'

Serena shrugged off his warning and the niggling doubts that had taken seed in her own mind over the past few days. Shelby was flighty and selfish, but she wasn't ruthless. 'She's my sister. I think I probably have a better idea of what she's capable of than you.'

'Did you think she was capable of abandoning you in the swamp?'

The jab found its target, hitting the nerve with stinging accuracy, but

Serena stubbornly shook it off. 'We've been over that ground before. She didn't intend anything bad to happen. Shelby doesn't think things all the way through. She doesn't consider all the consequences of her actions, just the immediate effect.'

Don't count on it, sugar, Lucky thought, but he kept the idea to himself. He supposed it was only natural for Serena to have a blind spot where her twin was concerned. What kind of person could look at their own flesh and blood and see evil? He only hoped that blind spot didn't keep her from seeing something truly dangerous before it was too late.

The explosion came just before dawn. It rattled the windows and shook the foundation of the old house. Serena was able to smell smoke before she was fully conscious. She shot up and out of bed, the instinct to flee danger pumping adrenaline through her bloodstream.

It took several seconds for her brain to catch up, sorting through the questions of where she was and what was the source of the danger. Her room was dark and in the aftermath of the blast the only sound was the rumbling of thunder. For a moment she thought that might have been all that had awakened her, but then the scent of smoke came again. It drifted in through the open French door, carried on a strong cold breeze that heralded the coming storm.

Grabbing her robe and throwing it on hastily, she rushed to the open door and looked out across the gallery and across the yard. A ball of orange glowed in the distance, and flames licked up the side of the machine shed. Shouts cut through the silence and men arrived at the scene, their shapes silhouetted against the brightness of the fire.

Serena whirled toward the bed, suddenly thinking of Lucky, but he was gone. His absence struck her like a physical blow, but there was no time to contemplate where he had disappeared to, or when or why.

She grabbed clothes out of the wardrobe without looking and jerked them on, not bothering with underwear. She stepped into her tattered espadrilles and ran out onto the gallery, down the steps, and across the garden, flying as fast as her legs would take her toward the building that was already engulfed in flames.

Workers were directing hoses at the conflagration by the time she got there, but to no avail. Fire was devouring the building. James Arnaud rushed back and forth between the workers, shouting to be heard above the roar, telling them to concentrate on wetting down the part of the enormous old wooden shed that wasn't already ablaze.

'What happened?' Serena yelled, grabbing his arm and his attention as he paced past her.

'Hell if I know,' he snapped, his thick dark brows set in a V over furious eyes. 'I heard the blast and came running. It was probably lightning. All I know is we've got most of our equipment in there and we're gonna lose it all if we don't get this fire put out!'

'Has anyone called the fire department?'

'They're on the way and they'd better get here fast. We might as well piss on this building for all the good we're doing.'

He shrugged her off then and went to help with the seemingly futile business of dousing the shed. Serena stood back helplessly, watching, squinting into the brilliance of the flames, the heat searing her cheeks even from a distance.

Above them the sky lit up with a network of white lines, and thunder boomed like cannon fire. Thick, rolling storm clouds were illuminated in the fluorescent glow of the lightning, black and swollen like enormous sponges.

'Come on, rain,' she shouted.

Mason came running from the house in pajamas and a robe, his thin brown hair standing up, his glasses askew. He wore a pair of polished oxfords but no socks.

'My God, this is terrible!' he said, tugging on the belt of his robe. He stared up at the blaze, the flames reflecting eerily in the lenses of his glasses. 'I've called the fire department. They're on their way.'

'I was just praying for rain,' Serena said. Fat drops splashed down on them from above and she turned her face up to the heavens.

Mason stared at the fire as it consumed the huge shed like an angry, voracious beast, devouring the walls, lapping at the heavy equipment within. 'All that machinery. I hope to heaven Gifford's insurance is up-to-date.'

The rain began to fall harder. In the distance came the sound of sirens.

Mason took Serena by the arm. 'We ought to get out of the way. There's nothing we can do here.'

She reluctantly backed away from the heat, feeling helpless as she thought of Gifford. She felt as if she were failing him somehow. It was absurd, she knew, but that didn't stop the old feelings of inadequacy from surfacing. Somehow she should have been able to prevent this. She should have been able to stop the destruction.

The rain came beating down now, cold and hard, soaking through the silk blouse she'd grabbed at random, matting her hair against her head, blurring her vision. Still the flames leapt into the night sky, roaring and crackling, mocking mother nature's efforts to put them out. There came a splintering sound and part of the roof caved in, sending a cloud of orange sparks billowing upward. Mason pulled harder on Serena's arm.

'Serena, come on!' he yelled urgently. 'There's nothing we can do. It's not safe here!'

He dragged her back a few more steps. Lightning lashed across the sky. Thunder exploded in a deafening blast. The wind picked up, shaking the trees and bending the tongues of flame that shot up from the burning building. The rain came harder in a fierce downpour, finally shrinking the fire, tamping it down. The first of the fire trucks roared up the driveway. Mason pulled Serena back another few steps.

'Let's go!'

They hadn't taken three steps toward the house when the second explosion came. In the periphery of her vision Serena saw the ball of flame burst through the ravaged wall of the building. From that point on what took only a split second in reality registered in her brain in slow motion – men running, fire rolling outward, lumber and shrapnel hurling in every direction.

She later remembered opening her mouth to scream, but not hearing anything. The invisible force of the explosion hit her in the back and flung her to the ground like a rag doll with Mason right beside her. She hit the ground with a bone-jarring bounce, gravel and crushed shell digging into her skin. Then everything went blessedly black.

'Total loss,' the claims adjuster said with the gravity of one imparting the death of a loved one. He stood in the doorway of the dining room, clipboard in hand, a small, apologetic man of forty-five with receding dark hair and eyes like a spaniel. There was soot on his hands and forearms and one big smudge of it across his high forehead.

He had arrived practically on the heels of the fire department, along with the neighbors. A fire was a major event in these parts, an occasion for people to gather and gawk and offer support to those who had suffered a loss. There was no two-week wait for the insurance man because chances were he would be standing there watching as the last of the rafters fell into the ashes.

'A total loss,' he repeated morosely. 'The building and everything in it. It's still smoldering in places.'

'Cool!' John Mason exclaimed, scrambling down from his seat. 'I'm gonna go see it!'

Shelby scowled at her son. 'You most certainly are not. You stay away from there, John Mason. Just look what happened to your father and your aunt Serena!'

Serena sent her nephew a meaningful look. She sat in her chair, still trembling, her ears ringing, pain biting into her body in various places. There were cuts and scrapes on her hands, knees, chin. Her cheeks and forehead wore a dark blush from the heat of the fire. She had yet to make it to the shower, and her hair hung like damp strings around her head. She still wore her ruined fuchsia silk blouse and red slacks.

All in all, she didn't make a pretty picture, and Mason had fared little better. She looked over at her brother-in-law as he sat staring down into his coffee cup with a vacant expression. His fine hair stood up in little shocks around his head. His robe was torn and dirty. There was a cut on his left cheekbone that stood out like a line of red ink against his ashen skin.

Serena imagined they both looked as if they had been mugged and left for dead, but they had to count themselves lucky. Two of the men who had been struggling to fight the blaze were now in the hospital, seriously injured by flying debris from the second explosion.

'Gifford had his insurance paid up, didn't he, Mr. York?' she asked, unsure whether she was whispering or shouting. She felt as if she were wearing cups over her ears.

York regarded her with his spaniel's eyes, looking like he was afraid she might call him a bad dog and send him away. 'Yes,' he said hesitantly. 'The premiums were paid up. There's no problem with that at all.'

'Are we to take it there is a problem elsewhere?'

'Er – well—' He shuffled his feet, then glanced down quickly to see if he tracked in mud. 'I'm afraid, yes, there is.'

'Oh, for pity's sake!' Shelby snapped as she poured herself a second cup of coffee. 'Spit it out.'

She sat in Gifford's place at the head of the table, prim and lovely in a green silk dressing gown, her hair twisted neatly in back, looking as if an explosion and fire were nothing to disturb her normal daily routine.

York swallowed hard. 'Well, I was just on the scene with the fire marshal, as y'all know, and there seems to be little doubt but that this was arson.'

'Arson?' Serena said in disbelief, a chill going through her. She shook her head, rejecting the possibility and all its ramifications. 'No. It was lightning.'

York looked woebegone. 'Ah – well – begging your pardon, Miss Sheridan, it wasn't. The fire was deliberately set. There really isn't any question of it. It was quite a sloppy job. You see,' he said, becoming more animated at the prospect of sharing some of his expertise, 'there was one big hot spot in the southwest corner of the shed and trailers leading out from it. That is to say, lines indicating a fuel path. There was alligatoring in the charred wood, giving the indication of rapid, intense heat, and signs of spalling in the concrete floor. It's very apparent that someone poured gasoline or a like substance all around and simply lit it up. And from what we could tell by the remains of the one tractor, a fuel path led directly to it. I'd have to say someone meant it to blow up.'

Serena sat back in her chair, pressing one hand to her lips and banding the other arm across her aching ribs. No one at the table said anything. She looked across at the chair Len Burke had occupied the night before, eating their food, drinking their wine, telling them that Gifford would have to be persuaded to sell – one way or another.

'You understand that until this matter is cleared up, my company won't be able to make a payment on your claim, I'm afraid. I'm sorry,' Mr. York said, sounding reluctant once again. Delivering bad news was evidently not his forte. He squeezed his clipboard. 'I really am sorry.'

'Mr. York,' Mason said, mustering a faint version of his affable politician's smile. 'Surely you don't believe one of the family is responsible for this horrible crime?'

'Oh, no, well – er – that isn't my place to judge. There will have to be a full investigation, you understand.'

'But Mr. York,' Serena said, trying to pull her mind away from thoughts of Burke, 'some of that equipment will have to be replaced immediately. How do you suggest we do that if your company isn't going to make good on the claim?'

York appeared to give earnest thought to the question, making a series of faces that caused the soot smudge on his forehead to wriggle like a shadow puppet. Finally he looked her in the eye and she thought he might burst into tears. 'I don't know,' he said. 'I'm sorry. Really I am.'

After several more rounds of questions, explanations, and apologies, the claims adjuster took his leave to have a second look at the rubble with John Mason hot on his heels.

'What a horrid little man,' Shelby said, selecting a muffin from the basket Odille brought in as if it were her most important task of the day. 'No wonder his wife is having an affair with the vice president of the bank.'

Serena shot her a look. 'Shelby, for heaven's sake, we have more pressing issues to discuss.'

'Serena's right, sweetheart,' Mason said gently.

'What's an affair?' little Lacey asked, staring owlishly up at her mother.

Shelby beamed a smile and stroked a hand over her daughter's blond curls. 'That's something cheap, trashy women do, darling. No need to worry your pretty head about it.'

'E-vil,' Odille intoned dramatically, drawing back from the table with the empty coffee urn clutched in her long, bony hands. Her turquoise eyes burned like blue flame, settling on each face in turn. 'Dat's what come dis house. E-vil. Lord have mercy on us all.'

On that ominous note she backed out of the room, her thin mouth stretched into a line of supreme disapproval.

'My God,' Shelby sniffed in affront, pulling together the lapels of her dressing gown. 'I don't know why Gifford keeps that woman on.'

'She's a witch,' Lacey said nonchalantly, reaching for a muffin. She dug one out of the basket and scampered out of the room, calling for her brother.

Serena rubbed her temples and sighed. 'Arson. Your Mr. Burke sending Gifford a little warning?'

There was a beat of stunned silence, then Mason came to life.

'Oh, Serena, you can't possibly believe Len Burke had anything to do with this!' he said with an incredulous laugh. 'Mr. Burke is a respectable businessman representing a respectable company. You can't honestly believe he's an arsonist!'

Serena looked at her sister and brother-in-law with grave eyes. 'Well, I certainly wouldn't want to believe the alternative.'

'That one of us might have done it?' Mason said, arching a brow above his glasses. 'Really, Serena, you've been spending too much time with your patients; you're becoming paranoid. Shelby and I were in bed. I don't mind saying I highly resent your entertaining such an insulting notion. Just because we're in favor of selling doesn't mean we'd burn the place to the ground.'

'My stars, Serena, is that what you really think of us?' Shelby said, her agitation building visibly as she stirred sugar into her coffee. Dots of color bloomed on her perfect cheekbones; her mouth tightened into a thin line. She glared at her sister, her demeanor of calm vanishing as instantly as mist. 'Accusing your own sister and brother-in-law! I don't know what's become of you up in Charleston. You're like a stranger to us!'

Serena pressed two fingers to her temples and sighed heavily. She was battered and exhausted. She felt as if all her tools for dealing with people had been stripped away from her. Certainly her energy for dealing with her twin's endless dramatic mood swings had been.

'Shelby, can we please dispense with the constant theatrics?' she said through her teeth. 'I didn't mean to accuse you. I was only saying that Mr. Burke would stand to benefit by this fire. It could have been set as a warning or with the express purpose of destroying the machinery. Either way, Gifford is out of money he can't afford to lose.'

'Well, I think it's preposterous,' Shelby pronounced indignantly. 'I find Mr. Burke perfectly charming.'

Serena couldn't find the strength to roll her eyes.

'The fire might not have had anything to do with the sale of the property,' Mason pointed out. 'Gifford has cultivated his share of enemies over the years. Why, not a month ago he had to let go of some of his hired men. It caused hard feelings, I can tell you. Then again, plenty of people stand to gain by Tristar coming here, Serena,' he said, contemplating his coffee. 'This is a small town; I imagine word is out by now. Gifford is preventing people from getting jobs. Someone might have decided to persuade him to change his mind.'

Serena pushed herself up from the table, her eyes on Mason, an unpleasant smile turning the corners of her mouth. 'My, what an interesting choice of words.'

'What are you going to do?' Shelby asked, looking up at her with suspicion.

'First, I'm going to take a long, hot shower. Then I'm going to go out into the swamp and get Gifford to come back here if I have to drag him by his hair.'

Lapsing into unconsciousness seemed like a more attractive choice, but Serena didn't see that she could afford the luxury of sleep. Forcing herself to plant one foot in front of the other, she pushed open the dining room door and left.

Shelby stared after her, waiting in breathless silence for the sound of a door down the hall closing.

'Well, that's just wonderful,' she said sulkily. 'She's going to bring Gifford back here. That's all we need. Damn her, why couldn't she just stay out of this?'

Mason reached for a muffin. 'Don't worry yourself about it, peach. This could turn out just fine. Gifford is bound to get disheartened sooner or later. If he comes back and sees the kind of damage that fire did, realizes what he's going to have to go through to replace the equipment and so on . . . he may just give up.'

'I certainly hope so, Mason. I certainly hope so.'

Serena let herself into her room, aching to fall across the bed and cry herself to sleep. Instead, she turned and nearly fell into Lucky. He grabbed her by the shoulders in a grip that could have bent iron and held her at arm's length, his gaze sweeping over her, wild and intense.

'*Mon Dieu*,' he muttered breathlessly. 'Look at you. Are you all right?'

'Oh, I'm fine except for the heart attack,' she said sarcastically. 'Is there something intrinsic in your makeup that compels you to frighten people? Did someone sneak up on you during your potty training or something?'

Lucky swore under his breath, letting go of her and turning to pace the bedroom floor. He ran a trembling hand over his hair and rubbed the back of his neck as he struggled to school his breathing to normalcy. 'I heard about the fire. Explosion. People being taken to the hospital.'

Serena bit back the flippant remark that sprang instantly to her tongue. She stood back and studied Lucky as he paced. He'd been afraid for her. It was clear in his eyes and the set of his mouth. It was clear in his struggle for control of his emotions. She made no comment but felt a flare of something like hope in her breast. The granite man who cared about no one had been frightened for her.

'I'm all right,' she said quietly. She let her knees give way and sank down on a little Victorian dressing stool, toeing off her ruined espadrilles and starting on the buttons of her blouse. She watched Lucky move back and forth along the bed, tension rolling off him like steam as he forcibly calmed himself. 'Where were you?'

'I had business to take care of.'

'You certainly have strange working hours.'

'I have a strange life,' he admitted dryly. 'You may have noticed.'

Serena arched a brow. 'What? Everyone I know lives in a swamp and picks their teeth with a commando knife.'

She dismissed his dark look and started to shrug off her blouse, but stopped herself as she realized two things simultaneously – she wasn't wearing anything underneath it and Lucky's eyes had suddenly settled, hot and glowing, on her chest. It wasn't that she felt modest around him. But a wild sensation fluttered in her middle. A deep, primal fear combined with excitement that took no notice of her need for control. Nor did it seem to care that the path it wanted to drag her down led to heartache. She managed to head it off at the pass and pushed herself to her feet, ignoring the protests of her aching legs.

'I have to take a shower,' she said, her fingers clutching her blouse together between her breasts.

Lucky stared at her. All the anxiety he had felt channeled itself into the one emotion he could understand and deal with – lust. When he'd heard about the explosion he'd nearly gone wild with thoughts of Serena lying burned and twisted among the rubble. Now she stood before him, looking bedraggled and a little bit afraid, but alive. Her dark eyes were wide and soft as she stared up at him.

He closed the distance between them with two long strides. His fingers pulled the blouse from her hand and peeled the two halves back as he pulled her gently into his embrace. With reverent care he bent and pressed his lips to each scratch that marred her face.

'I have to take a shower,' she mumbled again, her breath catching as Lucky's mouth settled on the pulse spot in her throat. 'I have to go to Gifford's.' She gasped and arched her back as his hand carefully claimed her breast, but tried valiantly to hold on to her train of thought. 'Will you take me?'

Lucky raised his head, his smoldering gaze capturing hers, an unconsciously tender smile turning one corner of his sensuous mouth. 'Oh, yeah, *chère*. I'll take you. Absolutely.'

14

'Arson!' Gifford exploded, his weathered face turning an alarming shade of red. 'By God, that tears it! That just tears it! I don't know what the hell this world is coming to. People got no respect for nothing anymore.'

He set aside the shotgun he'd been cleaning and rose from his lawn chair to pace in agitation. His hounds lay on the ground, one on either side of the chair, watching him move back and forth with their droopy eyes and somber expressions.

'That bastard Burke. I'll have his head on a pike before this is over. And that smarmy little Clifton York too,' he said, jabbing the air with a forefinger for emphasis. 'The nerve of that little weasel, refusing to pay the claim.'

Serena thought of the apologetic insurance adjuster and felt a pang of sympathy. 'Mr. York is only doing his job.'

'Practically accusing me of burning my own property,' Gifford ranted. 'By God, I'd eat dirt before I'd stoop to something so low. No Sheridan ever behaved in such a reprehensible manner – not counting the ones that got kicked out of the family, of course.'

'Of course,' Serena confirmed dryly. She stood before him with her arms crossed over the front of her wilting pink cotton blouse and her knees locked to keep her legs from buckling beneath her. The early morning storm had turned the cabin's meager yard to a soft ooze that squished up around the sides of her calfskin loafers. This trip was taking a heavy toll on her footwear on top of everything else. If she stayed much longer, she was going to have to go around in bedroom slippers.

'There was a time in this country when a man's honor meant something,' Gifford announced, as upset with having his reputation impugned as he was with having someone burn his machine shed to the ground. He planted his feet, jammed his hands at the waist of his jeans, and glared down at Serena as if it were all her fault standards had fallen to such an appalling level.

'I'm sure it's nothing personal,' she said. 'It's a clear-cut case of arson. Until they figure out who did it, the company can't pay.'

Gifford snorted. A shock of white hair tumbled across his forehead. His eyes were fierce. 'Until they figure out who did it. A blind halfwit could figure out who did it. Burke is responsible. Goddamn Texan. This state ought to have border regulations.'

'Burke has an alibi,' Lucky said unexpectedly. 'He was at Mouton's.'

Serena turned toward him, unable to hide her surprise. He was leaning indolently against the trunk of a big live oak, his eyes hooded and sleepy. He looked like a panther, all leashed strength and quiet intensity, waiting for some unsuspecting deer to wander past.

'How do you know that?'

He gave her a look that was flat and unreadable. His big shoulders rose and fell in a lazy shrug. 'Because I was there too, sugar.'

He'd left her bed to go to Mosquito Mouton's. Serena did her best to stem the rush of hurt. She had no hold on him, she reminded herself. Regardless of what her heart wanted, Lucky had clearly defined their relationship as just sex. Having agreed to those terms, she had no right to be angry with him or feel hurt that he hadn't chosen to hold her all night.

Business, he'd said. She wondered what kind of business one conducted at Mouton's in the wee hours of the morning. She wondered if it was the same kind of business he had been conducting the last time he'd been there – starting brawls, threatening people with knives.

'Of course he has an alibi,' Gifford said with disgust. 'A man like Burke does his own dirty work when he's coming up through the ranks, but he hires it out as soon as he can. It wouldn't be any mean feat to hire some local piece of trash to start a fire. People will do anything for a dollar these days.'

'Unfortunately, no one saw anything,' Serena said. 'Whoever did it managed to get away either before the first explosion or during the confusion afterward. I know I never thought of looking for a car or for anyone running away from the scene.'

'Maybe they never left the scene,' Lucky said quietly.

Serena sighed, blowing her breath up into the sweat-damp tendrils of hair that stuck to her forehead. She could feel Lucky's eyes on her, but she didn't look at him. They had already had this argument on the way to Giff's. She didn't for a minute believe Shelby had started the fire. It was simply impossible for her to picture Shelby slinging gas cans around and rigging machinery to blow up. But there may well have been a hired man capable of being bought off – by Burke, Serena insisted. Or the perpetrator may have been an outsider compelled by God knew what, a man who had simply blended in with the rest of the men while they had struggled to save the building.

'Well, there's no use speculating,' she said at last. 'The point is, this business is getting way out of hand. You have to come back home, Giff. I mean it this time.'

Gifford lifted one bushy white brow. 'Why? So you can cut and run?'

Serena refused to flinch. She stood toe to toe with the old man and said calmly, 'So you can face up to your responsibilities.'

'Why should I be any better at it than you are?' he asked sarcastically. 'Hell, I took my lessons from you, little girl. I didn't want to deal with it, so I left.'

'Stop it,' Serena snapped. She could feel the reins of her temper sliding through her exhausted grasp. Even in the best circumstances she had trouble dealing with Gifford in a controlled and rational manner. He knew exactly which buttons to push and he pushed them with a kind of malicious glee that infuriated her even further. She looked up at him now and held her anger in check with sheer willpower. 'You stop trying to lay all this guilt on me, Gifford. I've had it with your manipulation.'

'Oh? You *are* going back to Charleston, then?' he said with cutting mock-surprise. 'Leave your old grandfather to deal with arsonists and strong-arm tactics and treason among his own ranks.'

Serena ground her teeth and spoke through them. 'I'm not going anywhere.'

Gifford stared at her long and hard. 'Neither am I.'

The pressure built between them for another few seconds as their gazes locked and warred. Then abruptly Serena's temper erupted like a volcano. She kicked the lawn chair and let fly a very unladylike curse that sent the coon hounds scurrying for safety under the cabin.

'Damn you, Gifford,' she shouted, her hands knotting into useless fists in front of her. 'How can you be so stubborn!'

'It's a family trait.'

'Don't you dare be glib with me,' she warned, shaking a finger at him. 'This is serious.'

'I know exactly how serious it is,' Gifford said softly, abandoning his theatrics for cold, hard sobriety. 'I know exactly what's at stake here, Serena. I wonder if you do. You think I'm just being a contrary old fool. You think I'm enjoying all the havoc I'm wreaking on everyone's lives. I'm trying to save something that's been a part of this family for *two centuries.*'

'By sitting out here in the swamp?'

He shook his head, his impatience and weariness showing in his dark eyes and the set of his mouth. 'You don't get it, do you? I swear, for someone so intelligent you can be as thick as a red Georgia brick. I'm not talking about saving Chanson du Terre for the moment. I'm talking about it living on after me.'

Serena took in his words and their meaning, tears of anger and hurt and frustration rising in her eyes. She knew exactly what he meant. 'You can't make me want to come back here, Gifford. You can't force me to want to stay.'

'No,' he said softly. 'But I can make you see what the consequences will be if you don't. I can put it all in your hands. You can have the power of Caesar — does it live or does it die? Do two hundred years of heritage go on or do they get ground to dust? It will all be up to you, Serena. Sell it or save it.'

There it was. The cards were on the table. No more games. No more silent manipulation. He was laying it all at her feet and the thing she wanted most to do was turn and run. Serena stared up at him through a wavy sheen of tears and hated him at that moment almost as much as she loved him. She couldn't turn away. He meant too much to her. She couldn't stand the idea of disappointing him, of having him look at her and see a failure and a coward.

As a psychologist she could pick each of those thoughts apart, dissect them and diagnose them, and recommend therapy. But as a granddaughter, as a woman, she could only stand there and experience it. She felt as helpless and impotent as a child. She couldn't step back from it to examine it with the cool, objective eye of a neutral third party. She couldn't simply watch the storm from a safe distance. She was in the middle of it and there was no honorable way out.

'You think about that for a minute,' Gifford said, his face as stern and set as if it had been carved from granite. 'Then you come on inside the cabin. There's something that needs to be taken care of before you go back.'

He walked away, calling softly to his hounds. Serena stood facing the bayou, fighting the tears, trying to concentrate on the sound of footsteps and dog toenails on the worn boards of the gallery, the slam of the screen door, the sound of Marc Savoy singing on the radio, the call of an indigo bunting somewhere in the treetops nearby. Arms bound tight across her middle, she stared out at the muddy water and the profusion of spider lilies that grew along the opposite bank, and forced herself to hang on to the very last scrap of her pride and control.

Lucky watched her, everything inside him aching for her. Every feeling he had thought dead had been resurrected in the past few days and they ached and throbbed now, hypersensitive in their rebirth. He didn't welcome their return. It was easier, safer, not to feel at all. He resented their intrusion on his emotional isolation. He resented Serena for arousing them so effortlessly. But he couldn't look at her now and feel anger. Nor could he turn away. He couldn't look at her now and see how the calm, controlled woman from Charleston had been broken apart in a matter of days and not feel something – sympathy, empathy, compassion. . . .

He pushed himself away from the tree and went to stand behind her. He wrapped his arms around her, silently offering his strength, rocking her gently in time with the Cajun waltz that floated out through the cabin's screens.

Serena turned her face to his shoulder and squeezed her eyes shut against the tears, forcing two past her lashes to roll down her cheek and soak into Lucky's black T-shirt. The temptation was strong to just let go, to cry, to put the burden on his broad shoulders and ask him to take care of her problems the way he had taken care of Mrs. Guidry's poachers, the way he took care of the orphaned raccoons. But she didn't. Couldn't. He didn't want her problems. He had problems of his own. He didn't want involvement and he didn't want love. That knowledge made it all the more bittersweet to have his arms around her now, when she needed so badly to have someone to lean on.

Maybe he would change. Maybe he felt more for her than he wanted to admit. Maybe, when this business with Chanson du Terre was over, he would let her near enough to help him with the demons that haunted him.

And maybe pigs would fly.

She wasn't doing herself any favors falling into the trap of 'there but for the love of a good woman' thinking. She and Lucky had been thrown together by circumstances, had given in to physical needs, and when it was over they would go their separate ways – he into his swamp and she . . .

'I guess I'd better go in and see what new treat Gifford has in store for me,' she said, sniffing back the tears she wouldn't let fall. She turned in Lucky's arms and looked up at him, knowing with a terrible crystal-clear clarity that she had somehow, somewhere fallen in love with him. The thought hit her with a violent jolt every time it came. This big, brooding warrior with his panther's eyes and hooker's mouth, with his dark soul and heart of gold, had captured a part of her no other man ever had. Too bad he didn't want it.

They were greeted at the door of the cabin by the smell of warm beignets and strong coffee. While the battle of the Sheridans had been raging in the yard, apparently Pepper had been inside slaving over a hot stove. The old black man greeted Serena with a sad smile and a pat on the shoulder.

'You come on over here, Miz 'Rena. You looks like you could use some my coffee.'

Serena tried to smile. 'Could I have you inject it directly into my bloodstream, Pepper? I feel like I haven't slept in a month.'

'Po' Miz 'Rena,' Pepper muttered, shooting a damning glare at Gifford, who sat at the battered red Formica-topped table with a long envelope in front of him.

Serena pulled out a chrome-legged chair and sank down on a green vinyl seat that had cracked and torn and been repaired with duct tape. Gifford had taken the seat by the window that looked directly out onto the yard, and she wondered if he had seen Lucky holding her, but she dismissed the thought. Despite the way Gifford made her feel, she was no longer sixteen years old and under his guardianship. If she chose to have an affair with a man who looked and acted like a pirate, that was her own business.

She glanced around the cabin as Lucky took a seat and fished a cigarette out of his shirt pocket. Pepper kept up a running monologue in the background, drawling on pleasantly about the crawfish catch as he gathered up mismatched mugs and a big white enamel coffeepot. The coon hounds lay sprawled on the floor like rugs, looking up at Serena with mournful eyes. The furniture seemed haphazardly arranged around their gangly forms, worn and tattered armchairs with stuffing poking through in spots. The walls were unadorned except for mounted antlers and a gun rack grotesquely fashioned from a pair of deer forelegs.

Serena had always thought the cabin looked like her idea of a prison camp barracks with its tarpaper walls, pitted linoleum floor, and absence of niceties. It hadn't changed a lick in twenty-five years. It was the same floor, the same furniture, the same outdated appliances, the same arrangement of foodstuffs on the single shelf above the single cupboard, the same old round-edged black radio playing Cajun music and herbicide ads. Even the condiments on the table looked the same.

Gifford tapped his envelope against the tabletop, drawing Serena's eye away from the half-empty bottle of Tabasco sauce. It was a standard white business envelope with the return address printed in neat black script in the upper left-hand corner: LAMAR CANFIELD, ESQ. ATTORNEY AT LAW.

'This is yours.'

'What is it?' she asked suspiciously, loathe to reach out and touch the thing. She'd had enough unpleasant surprises to last her.

Gifford pushed it across the table. 'Look at it. Go on.'

She looked from her grandfather to Lucky, who was frowning darkly at the old man, and back to the envelope. Feeling as if she were about to take a step that couldn't be taken back, she picked it up and withdrew the folded papers. The document was ridiculously simple considering the power it wielded. It granted her power of attorney over Gifford's affairs, including the disposition of Chanson du Terre. It was stamped and signed on the appropriate lines in Gifford's bold hand and Lamar's, and it had been dated nearly three weeks previous. All it needed was Serena's signature to make it official.

Serena stared at it, feeling manipulated and used. It really was in her hands — a power she didn't want over a home that wouldn't let her go. Her first impulse was to throw the papers back in Gifford's face, but she didn't. Instead, she folded them neatly and put them back in the envelope. Without a word she stood and walked out.

'Why don't you put a little more pressure on her, Giff?' Lucky said sarcastically. 'Then we can all stand around and watch her crack.'

'She'll bear up,' Gifford said, lifting his chin. 'She's a Sheridan.'

'So's her sister.'

The old man sniffed and looked away, absently lifting a hand to rub the ear of a hound that had come to silently beg for attention.

Pepper clucked in disapproval as he slid down onto the chair Serena had vacated. 'Ain't no wonder she don' stay 'round here, you all the time pushin' her 'round dis way, dat way. Me, I'd go on to Charleston too.'

Gifford scowled at his friend. 'Then why don't you?'

''Cause if'n I left, there wouldn' be nobody 'round to listen to all your cussin' 'cept Odille, and she'd up'n kill you one fine day.'

'Smartass.'

Lucky ground his cigarette out in the blue tin ashtray on the table, crushing it with short, angry jabs, then skidded his chair back and stood up.

'I don' like your tactics, old man,' he said in a low, tight voice. He was reacting on instinct, he knew, not with any kind of rationale. Serena had been hurt and upset and that brought all those long-dormant protective feelings rushing to the fore. He didn't like it, but that didn't keep it from happening.

'I did what I had to do.'

'Without a thought to how Serena would feel about it.'

Gifford arched a brow, his dark eyes speculative. 'Since when do you give a fig about other people's feelings?'

Lucky said nothing. There was an answer lodged somewhere in his chest, but he refused to let it out or even look at it. He simply gave Gifford a long, disturbing look, then slipped out the door.

Serena was standing on the steps, looking out at the bayou, the infamous envelope tucked under one arm, her arms crossed over her chest. She looked pale and drawn, the dark smudges beneath her eyes a stark contrast to the youthful effect of the ponytail she wore. Lucky slid an arm around her and tilted her sideways against him.

'I don't want to go back just yet,' she said in a small voice.

'*Je te blâme pas*,' Lucky murmured, rubbing his hand up and down her arm. 'I don't blame you, sugar.'

'Can we go to your place?'

'*Oui*. If you like.'

'I need to get away for a while.'

She closed her eyes and pressed her head against him, and he felt that strange swelling, twisting feeling in his chest again.

'I'll take you away, *mon 'tite coeur*,' he said softly, and led her down the steps toward his pirogue.

Storm clouds were rushing in from the Gulf again as the pirogue slid in beside Lucky's dock. Fat and black, like dyed balls of cotton, they rolled north, thunder rumbling behind them. In a minute it would be raining, pouring, Serena thought as she looked up at the sky. And the minute after that it might be sunny and calm. The weather here seemed forever unsettled, unstable, adding to the impression of the swamp being a prehistoric place. Now, as the leaden clouds poured across the sky above, silence settled like a suffocating blanket all around. The trees went still. The birds went silent.

The rain started to fall as they crossed the yard, and by the time they had entered the house it was pounding down on the tin roof and splashing in through the window screens. Serena moved to close a window, but Lucky pulled her away.

'Let it rain,' he said, walking backward and drawing her with him toward the bed.

She looked up at him uncertainly. 'But the floor—'

'It's cypress; nothing can hurt it.'

They undressed each other to the accompaniment of the thunderstorm, slowly and quietly as the rain pounded down outside and the cool moist breeze blew in through the windows.

'I need you,' Serena whispered, head back, eyes closed against the weariness and turmoil that ached through her like a virus. She needed Lucky to sweep it all away, if only for a little while. She wanted to lose herself in the bliss of belonging to him, even if it was only temporary.

'I'm here,' he said, reaching behind her to release the clasp from her hair.

She sighed as he ran his fingers through her unbound tresses, spreading them across her bare shoulders. Rising on tiptoe, she returned the favor, pulling the leather lace from his queue and combing her hands through his curling black mane. He bound his arms around her, holding her high against his body, and kissed her slowly and deeply, then stood her away from him.

'*Viens ici, chérie,*' he whispered, sliding across the bed, holding his hand out to her.

Serena stared at him for a moment, mesmerized. He looked wild and dangerous, but she reached out and took his hand, welcoming its solid strength as she welcomed the strength of his arms when she settled herself on the bed and into his embrace.

They made love slowly as the rain fell. Lucky took complete command, letting Serena lie back to simply enjoy. He kissed her again and again, long, slow, deep kisses that left her breathless and languid. He lavished attention on her breasts, sucking gently at her nipples for what seemed like hours. Slowly he made his way down her body, kissing her everywhere with lingering, leisurely kisses, tasting her stomach, the point of her hip, the inside of her knee.

Lying between her legs, he slid his hands beneath her buttocks and lifted her slightly. He settled his mouth against her intimately, caressing her with his tongue, drinking in the taste of her. Serena arched her back and sighed at the exquisite pleasure. Desire swirled through her, building like the storm wind outside, sweeping her away to a place where there was nothing but herself and Lucky and this vibrant heat that burned inside her and exploded through her as he took her over the brink.

The shock waves were still pulsing when he slid up over her, caressing her body with his. She cried out when he entered her, not in pain, but in ecstasy as her muscles clenched and held him deep within her, caressing him, coaxing him toward his own completion.

Lucky ground his mouth against Serena's, catching her soft, wild sounds, giving her his tongue and the lingering sweet taste of her own body. The old bed creaked as he moved against her. Thunder rumbled overhead and rain hammered down on the tin roof, but those things receded into nothingness. Chanson du Terre, the past, the present, all faded away.

All Lucky could think of was Serena, her softness, her heat, the way she fit around him as tight as a silken glove, the way she welcomed him into her body and held on to him as if she would never let him go. All he could think of was giving her pleasure and letting that pleasure sweep him away.

He moved within her, slowly, gently, holding back his own release as he lured her toward another. Her hips moved against his. The tempo of her breathing quickened. He slipped a hand between them and rubbed his thumb against her most sensitive flesh, and she cried his name again as her ecstasy crested, taking Lucky with her. His body shuddered and stiffened as he poured his seed into her. He tightened his arms around her and thought he'd never felt quite so alive.

He turned onto his side as his muscles began to relax, and sank gratefully into the mattress. Physically, he was tired. Emotionally, he was exhausted from the constant war between feeling and trying not to feel. He gathered Serena close against him and wondered if she could sense him shaking inside.

Outside, the storm had passed. The thunder was rolling away to the north, leaving behind only the gentle sound of the rain. Inside, the storm of passion had passed and Serena lay in Lucky's arms, spent, too tired to face the feelings their lovemaking had kept at bay – all the emotions Gifford's actions had jerked loose, the pressure he had put on her, the conflicts over what needed to be done, the questions about family loyalty, the memory of the fire and all it meant. As he had promised, Lucky had taken her away from all that for a brief time, but now it all came rushing back.

The tears came as quickly as the spring shower had, and she let them fall without bothering to hide them or apologize for them. Lucky held her close, stroking her hair, brushing his lips against her temple. He whispered to her in French, soft words, comforting words, his low, purring voice almost as tangible a caress as his hand. It was just the respite she needed. Quiet compassion. Sheltering. Tender solace. The kind of consolation offered on an unspoken plane of understanding, offered with empathy, offered by a soulmate.

Serena felt her heart swell painfully at the thought. What they had was temporary, tenuous, a slice of their lives that seemed taken out of context. It was like a hothouse flower that had been forced to burst open overnight. Feelings had been magnified and time-accelerated. She wondered if what they had would die as quickly as it had come to life.

She knew the answer. It wrung a few extra tears from her heart and brought the words to her lips even though she knew she shouldn't say them. She shouldn't have become involved with him to begin with, but it was too late to change that and she couldn't change what was in her heart, no matter how pointless it was.

She sighed with a sense of fatalism and murmured against the base of his throat, 'I love you.'

The words ran into Lucky's heart like the blade of a knife. His hand stilled in the act of stroking her hair. Every muscle in his body tensed in rejection. 'Don't,' he said automatically.

Serena sat up, pulling the sheet over her breasts, and looked at him, her expression as carefully blank as his. 'Don't what? Don't love you or don't say it out loud?'

He shook his head as he climbed out of the bed and reached for his jeans. 'Don't,' he repeated as he pulled up the zipper. 'Don't say it. Don't think it.'

Serena watched him as he prowled the room, reading his unease in the set of his muscular shoulders and the tempo of his stride. He walked with his head down, eyes hooded, his hair partially obscuring his profile.

'Why not?' she asked, keeping her voice even.

He shot her a sideways glance. 'Because it isn't true. You can't love me. You don't know me. This' – he gestured toward the bed – 'this is just sex.'

'Not for me, it isn't.'

Lucky wheeled on her, his expression cruel, his eyes tormented. 'Well, it is for me,' he shot back, taking an aggressive step toward the bed. 'How's that, baby?' he asked sarcastically, raising his hands in question. 'Is that what you wanted to hear? You're a great lay, but that's all it is.'

The pain was instantaneous. Serena told herself she'd asked for it, but that hardly dulled the sting. Even seeing the tumult of contradictory emotions in Lucky's eyes wasn't much of a balm. This was his line of defense and he would cling to it to the bitter end. He didn't want to believe there could be something more between them even when he knew it already existed. He was afraid of it. He didn't want her seeing beyond his armor, didn't want her to touch him.

'It's just sex,' he repeated half under his breath as he retreated to pace along the foot of the bed.

'I don't believe you.'

'I don't care.'

'If you don't care, why does it upset you so much to hear me say I love you?'

He stopped in his tracks and turned his face to her with a look that would have chilled most men. 'Don't play shrink games with me, Serena.'

She didn't deny the charge, but shrugged and lifted her chin. If she'd been in possession of her common sense, she would have let the matter drop. But then, if she'd been in possession of her common sense, she never would have gotten into the pirogue with him at Gauthier's dock.

'I love you. That's how I feel. I needed to say it. I don't see why you're so upset,' she said defensively. 'I didn't ask you to say it back.'

Lucky snorted. '*Mais non*, but you expected me to.'

She stared at him, feeling an acute sense of sadness like a stone in her chest. 'No. I didn't.'

He swore in French and turned toward the window. 'I can't give you what you want, Serena,' he said, ignoring her answer. 'I don't have it in me.'

'Oh, I think you have it in you. You're just afraid to give it.'

'No,' he said, staring out at the rain. 'It's not there. It's gone. There's nothing there. I can't be the kind of man you need.'

'What do you know about the kind of man I need?'

'I know he isn't me.'

'What if you're wrong?'

He wheeled on her, letting all the frustration and pain and rage surface in one explosion of feeling. 'What do you know about me?' he roared. 'Nothing! You've pieced together some fantasy profile, made me out to be a hero when I'm nothing. I'm nothing but a man hanging on to his sanity by his fingertips. I'm nothing but a trained killer who might go off the edge in the blink of an eye. I don't have anything inside me but nightmares. Is that what you want? Is that the kind of man you need?'

Eyes wild, nostrils flaring, he stalked to the bed in a half crouch, meeting Serena at eye level. 'You wanna have a peek inside the man you think you love, Doc?' he whispered. 'You wanna know what makes me run?

'I spent a year in a private prison in Central America. My commanding officer arranged it because he was dirty and I was on to him. Our mission down there was one of those little soirées our government doesn't own up to. They told my family I was killed in a training accident. And for a year I sat in a filthy, rat-infested cell in total darkness. The only time they took me out was to torture me.

'Do you know what that does to a man's mind, Dr. Sheridan? Do you know what that leaves him with?' He straightened and slowly backed away. 'Nothing. Nothing. I don't have anything to give you. I live for myself, by myself, and that's the way I like it. I don't want your help and I don't want your love. The only thing I ever wanted from you was your body.'

328

He turned away from her and went back to the window, feeling bleak and empty.

Serena sat there for a long moment, absorbing his words, aching – not for herself, but for Lucky, for the sensitive young man who loved his family, the scholar, the artist who had had his life systematically destroyed. She hurt for the man he was now, tormented, frightened, alone. She wanted so badly to reach out to him, but she knew he would only push her away.

'If you wanted me to believe you were nothing but a heartless bastard, you should have left me at Gifford's that first night,' she said, a part of her wishing he had done just that.

'You got that right,' he answered derisively. 'I should have left you. But don't tell me I led you on, sugar. I told you from the first what this would be.'

'Yes, you did.' And from the first it had been a lie. They had come together in passion and anger and need, but it had never been as simple as 'just sex.' Never.

'Then keep your pretty words to yourself,' he muttered. 'I don't want to hear them. I have no need of your love.'

Serena wanted to cry. She'd never seen a man more in need of love. He pulled himself away from people, hid from the world. He had retreated to the solace of his swamp to heal his own wounds, but they weren't healing. They lay open and raw, and he retreated further still to some desolate place within himself. Her foolish heart ached to help him. The woman in her yearned to be the one to make a difference. But the psychologist knew it wouldn't happen and she knew why, small consolation though that was.

She didn't have the strength to fight the inevitable. All things considered, it seemed best to make the break there and then. Going on would be an exercise in futility, like beating her head against a brick wall. She had lost any kind of perspective that could have maintained a sexual relationship between them even if she had been able to stomach that kind of affair. And God knew she had other problems to take care of. She would chalk this up to being in the wrong place at the wrong time with the wrong man.

As she moved to gather her clothes, she studied Lucky, still standing framed by the curtainless window, and wondered bleakly how the wrong man could seem so right.

He turned and watched her, cast in a mix of silver light and black shadow that made a perfect portrait of him. 'Where do we go from here?'

Serena paused as she buttoned her blouse, considering options and answers, and decided to take his question at face value. 'Chanson du Terre.'

15

It was a long ride back. As Lucky stood silently behind her, Serena sat in the pirogue taking in the sights and sounds of the swamp. This would be her last trip through this wilderness that had haunted her for so many years. She had no intention of coming back for Gifford again. He had pushed things too far. Next time he would have to come to her. And as for any other reason she might venture out here, there wasn't any, she told herself, refusing the urge to turn around and look up at Lucky.

She focused instead on the swamp, looking past her instinctive fear at the primitive beauty, the delicacy, the place that Lucky loved. The rain had passed and the sun had returned with a vengeance, turning the place into a natural sauna. Moisture rose like steam from the surface of the water and dripped from the lacy festoons of Spanish moss. Wildflowers glistened, brilliant spots of color among the drab grays and browns. Serena wondered if Lucky had ever painted it this way.

They held their silence by tacit agreement until the landing at Chanson du Terre came into sight.

'What are you gonna do?' he asked quietly as he steered the boat in an arch for the dock.

'End it,' Serena said, still facing forward, her eyes on the big house. 'Send Burke packing, See that the matter of the fire and insurance claim are settled.'

'And then?'

She didn't answer him for a long moment. The pirogue snuggled in along the dock and settled. Finally she turned and looked up at him as she rose to her feet. 'Why should you care, Lucky? You got what you wanted.'

Lucky said nothing, but he stood wrestling with the emotions twisting inside him. He didn't care, he told himself. She could go back to Charleston, where she belonged. It didn't matter to him. He would have his swamp and his peace and no Sheridans to upset the placid surface of his life. He ignored the pain in his chest as Serena stepped from the boat and walked away without looking back. He didn't need her, couldn't need her, and that was the end of it.

With strong strokes of the push-pole he moved his pirogue away from the dock and turned south for Mouton's. It was going to be a good night for getting drunk and raising hell.

Serena crossed the yard slowly, her attention on the white Cadillac parked beside Shelby's BMW. Burke's, no doubt. As Giff had said, the man was as tenacious as a pit bull. And as charming. She wondered how he would take the news of her decision. Not well. He didn't strike her as a graceful loser.

Shelby was liable to take it badly too. She didn't like having her plans interfered with, particularly when personal glorification was at stake. She saw selling the plantation as the one and only means to achieve her goal of putting Mason in the legislature and putting herself on a public pedestal all in one fell swoop. She wouldn't be happy about having that means taken away from her. Added to that frustration would be the old feelings of competition between them. Gifford had played favorites, giving Serena the one tool that would have made all of Shelby's dreams come true.

Serena cursed Gifford for putting the land above all else. She cursed herself for coming back. But the die was cast now. The hand had been dealt and there was nothing to do but play it out.

They were gathered in the front parlor. Shelby was resplendent in a sleeveless red silk dress with a snug bodice and full skirt. Her hair was curled back neatly in a style that made her look like a movie star from the Carole Lombard era. Mason was in another one of his junior-senator outfits, charcoal slacks and an ivory shirt with the tie of some illustrious British regiment slightly askew at his throat. Burke wore the same western-cut suit he'd worn the previous night, but had opted to forgo the bolo tie. They turned as one toward Serena as she entered the room, their faces registering various expressions of surprise.

Shelby frowned. 'My word, Serena, is this how people dress for dinner in Charleston? You look a mess!'

Serena glanced down at her rumpled cotton blouse and black walking shorts that were creased and wrinkled. A quick peek in the gilt-framed mirror on the wall showed her hair escaping the bonds of its clip.

'Yes, I do look a mess. I'm sorry, but I just now got back from Gifford's,' she said, trying to mentally dismiss the afternoon spent with Lucky as easily as she omitted it from the conversation. 'You'll forgive me, Mr. Burke, for not being more presentable,' she said coolly. 'I'm tired and I'd rather not take the time to freshen up.'

'Gifford didn't return with you?' Mason asked, his brows lifting above the frame of his glasses.

'No.'

'What did he have to say about the fire?'

'Suffice it to say, he was upset.'

'But he didn't come back here to deal with it?' Burke said gruffly. He chewed on the end of his cigar and made a face like a bulldog. 'Damned strange, if you ask me.'

'I didn't ask you,' Serena said, too exhausted to adhere to the code of southern hospitality.

She watched his reaction with clinical interest. His jaw hardened. His eyes narrowed. She got the strong impression he didn't like taking guff from women.

Mason looked scandalized at her lack of manners. 'Serena! Mr. Burke is concerned with Gifford's mental state, as are we all.'

'I'm well aware of what Mr. Burke is concerned with. As to Gifford's mental state, I can assure you all he is as shrewd as ever.'

'He's behaving like a madman,' Shelby muttered, pouting. She lifted one bejeweled hand to play with the diamond pendant that hung from a gold chain around her neck. 'Stringing us all along, delaying the business proceedings. Mr. Burke is a busy man. He can't wait forever.'

'He doesn't have to wait at all,' Serena said, lifting the envelope she held so that everyone focused on it. 'Gifford has granted me power of attorney. I am to act on this matter as I see fit.'

Shelby gave a dramatic gasp, hand to her heart, but Serena pushed on, eager to get it over with and in no mood for her twin's theatrics. 'I don't see fit to sell this property to Tristar Chemical. Mr. Burke, I'm sorry your time here has been wasted.'

Burke turned scarlet. He pulled the cigar from his mouth and pointed it at Serena's face. 'Now, wait just a goddamn minute. You can't do that.'

'The courts would beg to differ. I didn't want the responsibility of this decision, but I have it and I've made up my mind.'

'I don't believe this,' Burke muttered. He wheeled on Mason. 'This deal was as good as done, Talbot. You talk some sense into her or you can kiss your trip to Baton Rouge good-bye.'

Mason looked nervous. He turned toward Serena, his affable smile contorting a little with uncertainty. 'Serena, let's not be hasty. I don't believe you've had time to take all the factors into consideration. There's a great deal at stake here.'

Serena gave him a level look. 'I know what's at stake, Mason. I think I see it more clearly than you do.'

'You!' Shelby snapped suddenly, drawing everyone's immediate attention. She glared at Serena, her knuckles turning white as she clutched a tumbler of scotch. She took a step forward. 'What do you know about anything? What do you know about having to live here? We're trying to do what's best for everybody.'

'You're trying to line your pockets and buy Mason a seat in the legislature,' Serena said succinctly. 'I have the power to stop you from sacrificing our heritage for your greed, and I'm using it. It's as simple as that, Shelby. I didn't want it to come to this, but I don't have any choice.'

Shelby advanced another step. Her perfect complexion was turning red in splotches that rose from the collar of her expensive dress to her hairline. 'You self-righteous little bitch,' she spat out. 'How dare you come waltzing back here, waving your morals like a banner, telling us what to do! We never asked for your interference.'

'No, you didn't,' Serena said, wondering if Lucky hadn't been right about them trying to get the deal through without her finding out about it until it was too late.

'Then why didn't you just stay out of it? Why didn't you just stay in your neat, clean little world in Charleston, ignoring us the way you always have?'

'I'm sorry,' Serena whispered, feeling her connection to her sister growing thinner and more brittle by the second. All she could think of was that it shouldn't have come to this.

'Sorry?' Shelby sneered, taking another step closer. 'Sorry!'

She flung her glass to the floor, heedless of the scotch that soaked into the rug in a dark stain. Stepping forward, she struck out with both hands, giving Serena a shove that sent her stumbling backward. Serena didn't try to defend herself physically or verbally. Words would do her no good; Shelby was well beyond seeing reason. Her rage was a tangible feeling in the air, like electricity building before an explosive storm. Serena watched in fascinated horror as the storm was unleashed.

'You don't see anything!' Shelby said, her voice rising in pitch and volume with each word as her control slipped further and further through her grasp. 'You don't care about this place. You never have. All you're doing is playing up to Gifford so he'll give you everything that ought to be mine!' She gulped a breath, half crying, her mouth twisting grotesquely as her fury built uncontrollably. 'You're trying to ruin everything for me just like you always have! God damn you! I wish you'd never been born!'

Serena stood motionless, not even trying to block the stinging slap her sister delivered. Shelby turned and fled the room, choking and sobbing. Serena didn't move. She stood in the electrified silence, struggling with her feelings, knowing at that moment that any slim hope she had held out for closeness with her twin had just been shattered.

Burke and Mason looked on, both men looking distinctly uncomfortable in the wake of female wrath. Mason recovered first, coming forward to gallantly offer his immaculate linen handkerchief. Serena took it, staring at it stupidly.

'There's blood,' he said, eyes downcast. 'The corner of your mouth.'

She dabbed it, but refused to look at the stain on the handkerchief. It was bad enough to know it was there. She focused instead on the envelope she still held and wondered if Gifford had any idea what he'd done.

'Serena,' Mason said softly. 'I realize you have a certain sentimental attachment to Chanson du Terre, but I've heard you say on more than one occasion that you wouldn't change your life because of it. We've discussed the practicality of selling, particularly now, when the plantation isn't doing well to begin with and the market is so bleak. And now there's the fire damage to consider—'

'Yes, what about that fire damage?' Burke interrupted. 'Can Gifford afford to cover the loss himself?'

Serena lifted her eyes and fixed them on the Texan. 'I think, Mr. Burke, the only aspect of the fire you need to concern yourself with is whether or not your name can be attached to it.'

He didn't appear the least bit shocked by her accusation, which was as good as an admission of guilt to Serena.

'I wasn't anywhere near here when the fire started,' he said, glancing idly at the end of his cigar. It had gone out. He frowned and went on calmly. 'I've got witnesses. It won't do you any good to try to prove otherwise.' His eyes hardened to stone as he stared down at her and repeated with emphasis, 'It won't do you any good at all.'

Serena arched a brow. 'Is that a threat, Mr. Burke?'

'It's a fact, sweetheart.'

She gave him her coolest look, not letting him see her questions about how far he might be compelled to go to get what he wanted. After a moment she stepped back from him and said, 'I believe I've had enough of your company to last me, Mr. Burke. It's been a very long and trying day. I'm going to call it an evening. Mason will show you out. And since your business here is finished, I won't expect to see you back again. Good night.' She nodded to her brother-in-law. 'Mason.'

She felt their eyes on her back even after she'd slipped out the door.

'What do you propose to do about this, Talbot?' Burke demanded in a low, rough voice, his glare bearing down on Mason like a spotlight. 'You blow this deal and you can just bend over and kiss your political ass good-bye.'

'Now, Len,' Mason said in his most soothing tones. He gamely resurrected his smile and turned toward the sideboard to pour his guest a drink. 'I'm sure I can get Serena to see reason. She just needs a little time, that's all. She's allowed Gifford to manipulate her. Once she realizes that and looks at the situation from a fresh perspective, I'm confident she'll see things our way.'

Burke gave him a long cold look. 'She'd better.'

Shelby paced the bedroom, her agitation showing in every step. The room was a shambles. At the peak of her rage she had tipped over every chair, torn the coverlet from the bed, pulled every article of clothing from the closet and dresser and flung them everywhere. Her path was now littered with designer-label suits and dresses that had been worn no more than twice. She ground the delicate fabrics beneath the heels of her pumps as she stalked the floor.

'Damn her. Damn her. I hate her!' she ranted, snatching a bottle of Chanel from the dresser and hurling it against the wall. It shattered, immediately engulfing the room in a sickening cloud of fragrance as the perfume soaked into the wallpaper in an oily stain.

Mason sat on the edge of the bed with his hands clasped lightly between his knees. He watched his wife's awesome display of temper with a properly concerned look knitting his brows and curling down the corners of his mouth. She whirled toward him, her eyes wild, her face contorted in a mask of rage.

'*Do something!*' she screamed, then lowered her voice to a hissing whisper. 'Do something, damn you! Don't just sit there looking pretty while Serena ruins everything I ever wanted!'

'Now, Shelby sweetheart, calm yourself—'

'Don't tell me to calm myself. If everyone calmed themselves as often as you said, we'd all be catatonic. This isn't the time to be calm! This is the time for action. We have to do something. Our future is riding on this.'

'I know that, peach,' Mason said, his gaze drifting wistfully over the expensive wardrobe Shelby had trampled into the floor.

'Of course, if you made more money in your law practice or if your parents hadn't lost their fortune in that silly oil bust, we wouldn't be in this mess.'

Mason hummed a noncommittal note.

'I wish we could just pretend Serena had never come here,' she muttered, resuming her pacing. She ran her fingers through her hair again and again, dislodging pins that fell silently into the drift of fabric she waded through. 'I wish she would just disappear. Gifford should have given that power of attorney to me. It's my future that's tied to this place, not Serena's. He should have given it to me, but no, he gave it to her and she doesn't have sense enough to see what's right.'

'Let's not fret over it now,' Mason said softly, standing and reaching for her hand. He drew her across a bright pink suit that still bore the price tag and pulled her into his arms. 'Let's sleep on it,' he said, brushing his lips against her temple. 'It'll all work out, peach. You'll see.'

'Yes,' Shelby said, suddenly utterly calm as she leaned against her husband. 'I will see.'

16

'Telepone call, Miz 'Rena,' Odille announced as she stepped into the dining room.

Shelby's head snapped up from a brooding contemplation of her crawfish bisque. 'Honestly, Odille, you know better than to interrupt dinner—'

'It's all right,' Serena said, pushing her chair back from the table with unseemly haste. 'I was finished anyway.'

She dropped her napkin over the plate she'd barely touched and turned to the housekeeper, who was giving Shelby a smug glare. 'I'll take it in the hall, Odille. Thank you.'

Walking out of the dining room and into the hall, Serena felt as if she'd just left a pressurized chamber. She'd never been so glad to escape a meal in her life. The day had been an especially trying one. She'd spent hours with the insurance investigator and the state fire marshal going over the particulars of the fire, walking through what was left of the machine shed. She'd spent another few hours on the telephone in Gifford's office soliciting aid in the form of equipment from neighboring planters. Then there had been the trip to the bank to really brighten the day. In addition to these pleasant chores she'd had to contend with Shelby's fire and ice moods and Mason's diplomatic lobbying for her to change her mind about selling the land.

Dinner had been the crowning glory. How anyone in that dining room had managed to choke down a single bite of food was beyond her. Serena was more than happy to have an excuse to get away. She could have kissed Odille's feet for interrupting.

She stopped at the hall table and picked up the receiver, expecting to hear the voice of one of the planters she had spoken with that day.

'This is Serena Sheridan. How may I help you?'

'You got it backward,' the man said in a hushed voice. 'I want to help you.'

A chill ran down Serena's spine. Her hand tightened on the receiver. 'Who is this?'

'A friend.'

The voice was dark and rough, not the voice of a friend, but the voice of a stranger. Serena steeled herself against the tingles of fear running through her and spoke in the most businesslike tone she could manage. 'Look, either you give me your name or I'm hanging up.'

'You're not interested in information that could tie Burke to your fire?'

Serena's heart picked up a beat. She swallowed hard. 'I'm listening.'

'Meet me at the back edge of that cane field that runs along the bayou in half an hour.'

'Isn't there some other way of doing this?' she asked. The idea of meeting an anonymous caller in the middle of nowhere held no appeal at all. 'Can't you tell me what you know now?'

'You can't see evidence over the phone, lady,' he answered impatiently. 'Do you want it or not? It's no skin off my nose if the insurance company never pays off.'

In the end Serena agreed to the meeting. She decided she would have James Arnaud follow her at a distance in case there was trouble. She didn't like the idea of meeting the man behind the voice, but she couldn't take the chance of dismissing evidence that would clear the way for the claim to be settled. The future of Chanson du Terre rode on getting that money. The plantation had become Serena's responsibility. She would do whatever she had to do.

She left the house without a word to anyone and walked to Arnaud's house only to be informed by a gum-chewing teenage daughter that the manager had gone to the hospital to visit the two men who had been injured in the explosion. Serena thanked the girl and wandered down the drive, wondering what to do. She could ask one of the other hired men to go with her, but she had no way of knowing which one of them might have been Burke's accomplice. She thought about skipping the meeting, but there was no guarantee her informant would try again.

The claim had to be settled. There was no question of that. Gifford wouldn't be able to cover even a fraction of the cost to replace the machine shed, let alone the machinery that had been burned inside it.

There was no choice for her to make. Taking a deep breath and squaring her shoulders, she set off for the rendezvous spot with determined strides.

No one was waiting for her when she arrived ten minutes later. Serena found herself standing at the end of the canebrake, shifting her weight nervously from one foot to the other. She didn't like being there. Even if it had been the middle of the day, she wouldn't have liked it. This particular field wasn't far from the plantation buildings, but the buildings were out of sight, giving one the impression of total wilderness. The money-green stalks of cane were already tall and grew thickly across the field to the south. To the north, Bayou Noir made a dog-leg cut into Sheridan property, partially isolating this field from the others. The mass willow trees along the bank of the bayou increased the sense of isolation.

Even at high noon this wasn't a place she would have chosen to be. It wasn't noon. The sun had begun its fireball descent. It would be night soon and she stood alone at the end of an equipment lane between a cane field and a black bayou, listening to the melodious call of a red-winged blackbird as the setting sun spilled orange light over everything.

She swung around, her breath catching hard in her throat at a rustling in the tall reeds along the bank. A blue heron rose, eerily silent, its long, spindly legs stretching out behind it as it sailed away. Serena forced herself to exhale slowly. It wasn't an alligator. It wasn't a snake.

It wasn't her informant.

Serena stroked her fingers along the canister of Mace inside her purse. Her ex-husband had given it to her as a gift when she'd begun her pro bono work at the mental health clinic. Romantic devil. The neighborhood where the clinic was located was a bad one, and she occasionally worked late. Paul had been concerned for her safety and Serena had to admit there had been times when she'd been concerned herself, but she had yet to use his gift. She touched it now only to reassure herself. She didn't really believe she would need protection.

She had already considered the possibility of a trap and dismissed it. Burke wouldn't be foolish enough to try something so close on the heels of the fire. It would point directly to him. Still, it didn't hurt to be prepared.

She heaved a long sigh and scanned the ground around her, looking for snakes. There were long black indigo snakes out here that hunted mice among the cane stalks. They weren't poisonous, but she had no desire to encounter one just the same. There were cottonmouths along the bayou that came out at night and copperheads that commanded the floor of the woods. The idea of them made her skin crawl and fear knot at the back of her throat. They wouldn't come looking for her, Serena reminded herself, doing her best to swallow the impending panic attack.

Where was her damned informant?

The sound of an outboard motor idling down drew her attention to the north. She tried to peer through the tangled ribbons of willow branches to make out the boat and its occupant, but it was impossible to see well. Already the light was fading along the bayou, and all she could make out was bits of color and shape.

She had for some reason assumed the man would be coming the same way she had, by foot down the lane. In the back of her mind she had decided he was an employee of Chanson du Terre. She had imagined he had chosen this spot for the meeting because it was near the plantation buildings and yet secluded enough so they wouldn't be seen. She had given no thought to the bayou or a boat, and she cursed her lack of foresight as a sudden chill swept over her from head to foot.

'Well, lookee here, Pou,' Gene Willis said, a leering smile twisting the hard line of his mouth as he parted the weeds and willow branches and

338

stepped into the clearing. Pou Perret scuttled along at his heels like a pet weasel, his droopy eyes darting furtively all around, his mustache twitching as if he were scenting the air for danger. 'If it ain't Lucky Doucet's lady. Fancy meetin' you here, Miz Sheridan.'

Serena eyed the pair warily, her hand closing around the Mace. She recognized them from Mouton's. She doubted she would ever get the scene out of her head: Lucky with a knife in his hand, this big red-haired man lunging for him, the little scruffy one swinging a broken bottle, a wild gleam in his eye. They might have been the kind of men one would hire to start a fire or commit any number of other criminal acts, but they didn't seem like the sort to come forward with information – unless it was for a price.

'How much do you want for the information?' she asked, trying to sound calm and businesslike despite the way she was beginning to tremble from the inside out.

'You hear that, Pou?' Willis went on smiling, sauntering closer. He moved with all the grace of a bear and looked nearly as strong. Serena's gaze focused on his hands. They were huge and ugly, raw-looking with fingers like sausages. 'The lady wants to pay us. I can't remember the last time a *lady* wanted to give me anything, can you?'

Pou apparently took it as a rhetorical remark. He said nothing, but Serena could feel his eyes on her, hot and feral like an animal's. He moved slowly toward her and to her right, his hands behind his back.

'Isn't that what you came here for?' she said, trying to buy time. She forced herself to stand her ground and gripped her can of Mace with a sweaty hand. 'Money?'

Willis grinned, an expression that had undoubtedly looked evil even when he'd been in the cradle. One sinisterly arched red brow climbed his forehead while the other hung low over a narrow eye. 'No, Miz Serena. We're already gettin' paid. And hell,' he added with a nasty laugh, 'this is a job I'd do for free.'

They were moving closer, slowly, menacingly. Serena took a half step back. Fear climbed high in her throat. 'I'll pay you double.' She wasn't sure how they were supposed to be earning their money, but she was fairly certain it would be worth paying them double *not* to do their jobs.

Pou shot a glance up at Willis, looking for a reaction. Willis pretended to consider her offer, humming and making an exaggerated face. After a minute he shook his head and smiled at her again.

'Naw, I don't think so,' he said, rubbing one of his ugly hands across his massive jaw. 'You see, the perks of this job are so much better than money. Ain't that right, Pou?'

Perret flinched a little at the sound of his name, tearing his gaze off Serena once again to look up at his partner. 'Jesus, Willis, let's just do it,' he whined, suddenly nervous again. 'Me, I don' wanna be hanging 'round here if that son of a bitch shows up. He'll kill us!'

'If you're looking for Lucky, he could be here any minute,' Serena said. It wasn't much of a threat, but she was beginning to feel a little desperate.

Willis just smiled and inched a little closer. 'Nice try, sweetheart, but I know exactly where Doucet is. He's at Mouton's with a whiskey bottle and a peroxide blonde who could suck the brass off a doorknob. I don't think he'll be joining us any time soon. Too bad for him. He's gonna miss one hell of a party.'

Serena felt a painful lurch in her middle at the thought of Lucky with another woman. Her concentration broke for just an instant, and in that instant Gene Willis reached out and grabbed her, his big ugly hand manacling her left wrist.

She reacted instantly, pulling the Mace from her purse and hitting the button as she swung it wildly toward Willis's face. He knocked her hand aside with a swift, hard blow that numbed her arm to the elbow and sent the can and her purse sailing, but he was a split second late. The spray caught him in the left eye and he let her go and reeled backward, howling like a wounded beast.

Serena turned and ran. Her heart was in her throat. Her blood roared in her ears. Her body felt as if it belonged to someone else, someone who didn't realize the kind of danger she was in. Her legs wouldn't move fast enough. Her lungs wouldn't draw enough breath for her to scream. She ran down the lane, stumbling because the loafers she wore weren't designed for flight.

Behind her she could hear Willis swearing and shouting at his partner, 'Get her, damn you!' Then came the pounding of feet.

She couldn't hope to outrun him. The lane stretched before her, looking longer and longer with not a building in sight. Her only options were to jump in the bayou and swim for it or try to lose herself in the cane. The cane led back to people. She thought of the indigo snakes and hesitated. There was no other choice. As Perret's footfalls rushed up on her, she veered suddenly to the left, diving for the cover of the sugarcane.

Perret tackled her from behind, his shoulder hitting her in the middle of the back, driving her forward and knocking her off her feet. She hit the ground with a thud that jarred every part of her. Her captor landed on top of her, the force of his weight blurring her vision and knocking the air from her lungs. Before she could even think of moving he had his knee planted between her shoulder blades, pinning her to the hot, moist earth.

He used a dirty bandanna for a gag, tying it roughly behind her head, incorporating strands of hair into the knot so that no matter how still Serena tried to be, it pulled. Tears of fear and pain flooded her eyes as Perret bound her hands tightly behind her back. They rose up in her throat and she choked and gagged, discovering very quickly that she wouldn't be allowed the luxury of crying. The bandanna with its foul, sour taste hindered not only speech but breathing and swallowing.

Perret rose and pulled her up with him, using the gag like a bridle on a horse. He curled his fingers into the back of it, pulling it unbearably tight, twisting her hair along with it, and jerked her to her feet and steered her back toward Willis.

The big man had regained his feet, but stood half doubled over, one hand pressed to his injured eye. The glare in his good eye was murderous, and Serena suddenly understood why some self-defense instructors preached cooperation rather than aggression. Whatever Willis had had in store for her was nothing compared to what was going through his mind now.

She tried to stop before she got too close to him, but Perret shoved her forward and she had no way of catching herself. Willis knocked her to her knees with a single backhanded blow across the face that brought more tears and the taste of blood.

'You bitch,' he growled, clutching at his eye. 'You're gonna pay for this. You're gonna pay till you wished you'd never been born a woman.'

Serena managed to turn and raise herself up as he swung his foot at her. The kick caught her shoulder instead of the side of her head. Pain exploded through her at the blow and then again as she went facefirst to the ground, unable to break the fall.

'Get her in the boat,' Willis ordered, and staggered away, still rubbing at his eye.

Perret once again took hold of her makeshift bridle and hauled her to her feet. They loaded her with a minimum of ceremony into a battered aluminum-hulled boat with a massive outboard motor hanging off the back. It was the kind of thing poachers might use, Serena suspected, with enough horsepower to outrun the game warden – or the odd Lone Ranger. The boat was loaded with traps and tarps, empty whiskey bottles and crushed beer cans. There were a number of small holes in the side above the water line that may well have been caused by bullets. It reeked of swamp water and fish. Perret forced her to sit on the bottom on a wadded-up piece of damp black canvas with her back against the side of the boat, the unadorned edge biting into her spine. Then Pou started the motor and piloted them away from the bank while Willis attempted to flush the Mace from his eye with beer.

The fear that rose inside Serena threatened to swallow her whole. She could feel it growing stronger, clawing at her, tearing at her mind as the boat carried her away from Sheridan land. She wanted to scream, but the screams caught in the back of her throat and choked her. She wanted to run, but there was nowhere to run to; there was nothing around her but black water and swamp.

God, they were taking her into the swamp! The terror she normally felt at the prospect of going out there doubled, then tripled. She better than anyone knew how easy it was for a person to become lost. By the time anyone realized she was missing, it would be virtually impossible to find her. Willis and Perret could do anything they wanted. There would be no witnesses. There would be no one to hear her screams. Suddenly her future looked worse than anything her nightmares had ever conjured.

She wondered wildly what their orders were. What exactly had Burke paid them to do? Scare her into selling? Get her out of the way while he made a deal for the land? Use her as a hostage with Chanson du Terre as her ransom price? It seemed unlikely. Too dangerous to Burke and to Tristar. That left only one possibility. Burke would get her out of the way – permanently.

That deduction brought another wave of fear. Tears gathered in her eyes, but she fought them back. Control. That was her only hope – to keep her head, to keep her cool, to look for the opportunity to escape.

With effort she forced the fear back, compressed it and shoved it into a mental compartment and shut the door. Fear would get her nothing. It was a waste of time and energy. It would do her no good to cry and shake. It would do no good to wish for a rescuer. Lucky wasn't going to swoop down from a tree and save her. He was at Mouton's drowning his sorrows, and she was on her own. She could save herself or she could be tortured and killed. It was as simple as that.

Still trembling, she forced herself to look around and take in landmarks. If she concentrated hard enough, she might be able to memorize the route they were taking and retrace it once she managed to get away. She thought it was the same way Lucky had gone to get her to Gifford's, but she wasn't sure. It was growing darker by the second, making it very difficult to see, and the bayou branched off too many times for her to be certain of the turns.

The swamp closed in around them, dark and silent beyond the puttering of the motor. Perret slowed the boat to a crawl as he negotiated the way among a stand of cypress. Willis sprawled in one of the boat's two bucket seats, facing Serena. He had stopped using the beer from his cooler to rinse his eye and had started drinking it instead.

Serena could feel his gaze on her, lingering on her breasts. She tried to shrug it off, but the feeling clung as tenaciously as the mosquitoes that were feasting on the exposed skin of her throat and face. She had worn a long-sleeved blouse and slacks, knowing better than to go out into the fields at dusk uncovered, but she had forgotten Lucky's warning about her perfume. She had dabbed some on after her shower, needing to feel feminine after a day of grubbing around in the ashes of the machine shed, and hadn't thought to wash it off before leaving the house.

Willis slid down from his perch to kneel on the tarp in front of her. Serena eyed him warily. His left eye was nearly swollen shut, giving him an even more monstrous appearance than before. Beer had spilled unheeded over his shirt, adding to the sour stench of his sweat. He raised a hand and brushed his rough-skinned knuckles along her jaw, smiling like a snake in the fading light.

'They don't call that Cajun bastard Lucky for nothing, do they?' he said. 'You're some fancy piece.'

Serena fought the urge to shrink away from his touch. An animal like Willis would feed on fear. She bit down on the gag and schooled her features into what she hoped was a blank mask.

'What would a lady like you see in that coonass trash anyway?' he asked, his eyes roaming over her as if the answer might be written somewhere on her body. His leering grin spread across his thin, hard lips and his good eye lit up. 'I'll bet he's hung like a stallion. Do proper ladies like you go for that? A man with the right kind of tool for the job? Who would'a guessed?'

He chuckled, apparently as amused by her lack of response as he would have been by a protest.

'You know,' he went on, still stroking her jaw, 'when I was up in Angola I had a picture of a pretty blonde on the wall of my cell. I used to dream about doing her every night. She looked a lot like you . . . only she was naked.'

He lowered his hand from her chin to the first button on her white silk blouse and popped it open with a flick of thumb and forefinger. Bile rose in Serena's throat, but she swallowed it as another pearl button gave way and another. She bit down harder on the gag and stared straight ahead as Willis opened her blouse and feasted his eyes on her breasts.

'Nice,' he whispered, leaning closer. He traced the lacy edge of her bra once, then again, this time dipping his finger inside the fabric to caress the slope of her breast. 'I can hardly wait to see the rest.'

Serena couldn't stop the involuntary shiver that rippled across her skin. The thought of this man putting his big ugly hands all over her body, touching her softest, most private flesh, was utterly repulsive.

Willis caught the reaction and gave a laugh that held more menace than humor. He engulfed one breast in his hand and gave it a squeeze that bordered on painful.

'You might as well get used to it, Lady Serena, 'cause ol' Pou and me are gonna have you every way there is before we're through with you.'

She nearly vomited at the mental images his warning conjured. Serena had counseled rape victims. She'd heard tales of abuse that had made her wonder what kind of God allowed such atrocities. Details came back to her now, vivid and horrible. She flicked a glance over the side of the boat at the inky water and wondered fleetingly if she wouldn't be better off drowning herself now.

It was then that they finally reached their destination. Perret guided the boat in alongside a ramshackle dock and cut the engine. Willis hefted himself and his beer cooler out of the boat and started up the incline toward the cabin, leaving Serena for his lackey. Pou's eyes fastened on the open front of her blouse and he reached out to touch her, but pulled back at the sound of Willis's voice.

'Wait till we get her inside,' he ordered. 'Goddamn mosquitoes are driving me nuts.'

The cabin looked abandoned. A tar-paper shack on stilts, it was the sort of place Serena had imagined Lucky living in before she'd seen his house. The yard was little more than mud and stringy grass. It was littered with junk – beer cans and bottles, tires, an old refrigerator with the door hanging open. There was a rusted car of indeterminate age sitting some distance away in a stand of weeds.

A car. That had to mean there was a road. But what good would a road do her if she was on foot? They would run her down just as they had before. Her only hope would be to lose herself in the woods.

What a hope – to lose herself in the dead of night, bound and gagged, in a wilderness that terrified her. Her old fear stirred strongly, but the new one was even worse. She had survived the swamp before; she would not survive what Willis and Perret had in store for her.

Willis had gone inside. Perret steered her across the yard, his fingers wound into the back of the gag again, pulling her hair. He was a small man, only about as tall as she was and thin, anemic-looking. His chest had a sunken look and his dirty jeans clung low on nonexistent hips. He wouldn't be nearly as strong as Willis, but he was quick. If she could manage to get free of him, she would have to do a better job of escaping than she had the first time.

Serena stepped up her pace toward the cabin so he was no longer shoving her along, but quickening his step.

'You in a hurry, *chère?*' he asked, laughing, displaying an alarming array of crooked rotten teeth. 'Me too.'

Sticking her right foot out to trip Perret, Serena pulled up abruptly and twisted her upper body sharply away to the left. One second Perret was chortling like a fiend, enjoying his dominance over her, the next second he was on the ground, tangled among a mess of old tires and rusty chicken wire.

Serena wasted no time looking back to see if he was coming after her. She dashed into the woods and ran blindly, dodging trees at the last second, stumbling over roots. She zigzagged, cut back, turned again, and ran on. Branches cut at her face and tore at her clothes. There was no light, only darkness and the blacker shapes of trees. She slammed her shoulder into one and had to stop and double over while pain rocked through her.

Crouching there against the trunk of a persimmon tree, she took quick stock of her various aches, all of them renewed by this latest blow. Her hands had started to go numb behind her back, but she was very aware of her right forearm where Willis had struck to dislodge the can of Mace. It felt as if it had been hit with an ax handle. Her left shoulder had taken

Willis's boot and now the tree trunk as well, and it throbbed relentlessly. Her muscles had started to cramp from the awkward position of her arms. There were a dozen other assorted pains, but at least she was alive and free. For the moment.

Her breath soughed in and out of her lungs, muffled by the gag. The cloth had loosened somewhat from Perret pulling on it, and Serena thought she might be able to work it free. She pressed her face against the trunk of the tree and rubbed her cheek against it, trying to work the bandanna down. The hard, scaly bark of the tree scraped her skin, but she persisted. Progress came gradually, but the gag finally fell free of her mouth. Still knotted into her hair in back, it hung like a noose around her neck. She leaned over and spat, trying in vain to get the taste of it out of her mouth.

Something slithered in the underbrush to her right, and Serena bolted, straining to see in the velvet darkness. She could hear the movement but couldn't tell what it was or precisely where it was. Memories crowded in her mind and tears rose up the back of her throat as she scanned the darkness all around, wondering wildly what awaited her. The swamp came alive at night, alive with hunters and the hunted.

'God, that's me,' she whispered, tears of despair stinging her eyes.

She didn't have the benefit of natural camouflage most animals of the swamp possessed. She had to stand out like a beacon in the night in her white blouse and khaki slacks.

Some distance behind her she could hear someone crashing through the growth. As she forced herself to press on, she wondered if Perret had come after her on his own or if Willis had joined him. She changed directions again and started running.

If only she could see. If only she had the use of her hands. If only she weren't so damned scared. If only Lucky were there.

Lucky. She wondered if she'd ever see him again. It seemed a stupid thing to think of, all things considered, but she wondered if he had any idea how much she loved him. She wondered if she'd had any idea herself before now. Running for her life put a lot of things into perspective, and she found herself making promises to God. *If I get out of this, I'll patch things up with Shelby, I'll forgive Gifford, I'll give more to charity, I'll try harder to reach Lucky.*

She would see him again if she kept running. She had to believe that. If she kept running, everything would turn out all right. She would be safe, Burke would get caught, she would see Lucky again. If she kept running. If she got away.

The night air was like fire in her lungs. She could no longer hear anything except her own breathing and the thunderous beating of her heart. Her head was pounding. The damp, musty scent of the forest filled her nostrils. The spongy ground seemed to dip and rise beneath her feet.

345

She felt completely disoriented, almost dizzy, hanging somewhere between hysteria and delirium.

She thought that if she could somehow get to Lucky's house she could use his CB radio to call for help or maybe she could find his gun. But she didn't make it to Lucky's house. An exposed root caught the toe of her loafer and pitched her headlong into the blackness. She landed on her face at the booted feet of Mean Gene Willis.

17

'Come on, sweet stuff, let's go somewhere we can have us a little private party.'

Lucky regarded the blonde draping herself over his left side with ill-concealed impatience. The woman had no self-control and less sense of danger. She had approached him the instant he'd settled himself behind the corner table at Mouton's, too stubborn or too stupid to notice that everyone else in the place was giving him a wide berth. As well-endowed as she was in other respects, she had obviously gotten severely short-changed in the brain department. The woman couldn't take a hint. He had snarled and snapped at her, but the efforts had bounced off her shield of stupidity, leaving her unmoved.

It was aggravating. He hadn't come looking for an easy lay; he'd come looking for trouble. He had come in to soak his temper in cheap booze and hope some big fool would strike a spark to it and pick a fight with him. He felt a need to hit something. It was what he'd done the night before, and it was what he planned to continue to do with his nights until he got it out of his system.

The blonde had other ideas.

She leaned against him, tilting her head back and squeezing her breasts together with her upper arms to best display her cleavage. The black tank top she wore seemed to have been intended for a flat-chested twelve-year-old. It rode up well above the waistband of her skin-tight jeans and made it abundantly clear to one and all that she found wearing a bra too restricting. She seemed to have difficulty keeping her eyes open, probably due to the thickness of her blue eye shadow and the weight of her false lashes. Her silvery-blond hair – brown at the roots – had been teased and tormented into a frightening confection and lacquered into place with enough spray to put a hole in the ozone the size of Lake Pontchartrain. The earrings dangling from her lobes looked like small chandeliers.

Lucky heaved a sigh of disgust. The woman had no class. She smelled like dime-store perfume and stale smoke, and she'd drunk most of his whiskey. She was pretty enough in a cheap, hard sort of way, and she had a body that had undoubtedly turned a head or two, but she roused nothing in him except irritation. She might have done better if she'd shown a little style, a little cool, if she'd presented herself as a . . . lady. Like Serena.

He swore a vicious oath in French and tossed back what was left of his drink. What did he need with a *lady?* What did he need with a woman who wanted to touch his rawest nerves and memories? She was nothing but trouble. She would never let him alone. She would never allow him the emotional distance he needed to maintain. He'd told her from the beginning what she would get from him, and still she'd dug for more. She wanted love and he wanted nothing to do with it. End of story.

So why was he brooding about her? a mocking inner voice asked. Why was he wondering how she had handled Burke and how she was bearing up with Shelby? Why did he want to know if she had exhausted her supply of strength, if she was in need of a shoulder to lean on?

He swore again and shrugged the blonde off, reaching for the bottle of whiskey on the table before him. The blonde – her name had gone in one ear and out the other – sat back with a coy look and helped herself to his cigarettes.

'You're a tough guy,' she observed, blowing smoke at the ceiling in a pose that was calculated to show off her profile. 'A loner.' Her shoulders swayed, and unencumbered breasts bounced in time to the frantic Zydeco tune blasting from the jukebox.

Lucky shot her a sardonic look. 'What are you? Einstein's daughter?'

She went on with her seduction routine as if he hadn't spoken. 'I like a tough guy. I don't mind a little adventure, if you read me.'

'Like a book.'

'So-oo-o . . .' She drew the word into three syllables, squirming a little on her chair and giving him a dazzling smile, raising her carefully plucked eyebrows in question.

Lucky's answer was forestalled by the arrival of Skeeter Mouton. Skeeter pulled up a chair on Lucky's right and settled his bulk on it, mopping the sweat off his forehead with a bar rag. A smile lit up in the center of his beard like a crescent moon, but it didn't reach his dark eyes.

'Hey, Lucky, where you at?'

Lucky ignored the greeting and poured himself another drink. 'You been waterin' the whiskey again, Skeeter.'

The bartender clutched his heart dramatically. His round face tightened in a wounded expression. 'Me? *Mais non!* Madame Mouton, she keeps the books, she waters the liquor. How can you accuse me of such a thing when me, I come all the way over here to give you information?'

'Information 'bout what?'

'Your two friends.'

It was on the tip of Lucky's tongue to tell Mouton he didn't care what Willis and Perret were up to. He was all through fighting other people's battles. From now on he was adhering to a strict code of isolationism. No more damsels in distress. No more plantations to save. He was living for himself; the rest of the world could go to hell. But Skeeter went on, oblivious of Lucky's inner thoughts.

'They had them a little meetin' s'afternoon.'

'Who with?' Not that he cared. He was just mildly curious, that was all. He directed his gaze across the crowded smoky room to where Len Burke sat deep in angry conversation with Perry Davis. 'With him?'

Mouton shook his head. '*Non*. The big oil man, he been right here the whole time. The other two, they got a call and went out, come back a while later smilin' like 'gators and throwin' money 'round. This was all just before you got here. You walk in, they slip out the side.'

'So?'

The round man shrugged and rolled his eyes, digging a folded bill out of a pocket on his apron. He waved it under Lucky's nose as if the smell of it might rouse him to show greater interest. 'So this is the bill they tipped their waitress with. 'Toinette, she was just showin' it to me 'cause she never had a tip so big. She 'bout fainted.' He gave a snort of disapproval. 'A twenty-dollar tip. Talk about!'

Lucky glanced at the bill in irritation. It was crisp and new, the kind of money decent people carried. In his experience, trash like Willis carried money that looked as dirty as the kind of deals that brought it to them. If Willis was leaving fresh twenties for cocktail waitresses, then it was a good bet there were lots more where this one had come from. He would have had to come into a tidy sum to inspire that kind of generosity. Gene Willis wasn't known for his philanthropy.

''Toinette, she says Willis had a roll of those as thick as a 'gator's tail. Me, I don' figure he got 'em sellin' Bibles and he ain't been on the bayou since the night you shot up his boat full o' holes, so he didn' get 'em from stealin' crawfish. Somebody payin' him this kinda money . . .' Mouton shrugged and mopped his forehead. 'Must be some kinda dirty job, *oui?*'

Lucky stared at the bill, rubbing the stiff paper absently between his fingers. This could have been the final payment for starting the fire, but if so, Willis and Perret would still be here, swilling Mouton's watered whiskey and playing *bourré* in the back room; the night was young. *Non*. This was payment for something else, something they were undoubtedly doing that very minute.

'You don' know what they were up to?'

Skeeter shook his head, frowning. 'No good, dat's for sure. Willis, he said somethin' 'bout meetin' a lady. I didn' pay him no mind. What lady would meet with the like of him?'

Shelby, Lucky answered mentally. Serena was right, her sister would probably not have started the fire herself. The job was too dirty and physical. Shelby would have considered it well beneath her. But she wouldn't have hesitated to pay someone else to do it. And now she was paying them for another job.

'They took outta here, headed up the bayou.' Skeeter tilted his head, his dark eyes twinkling as he chuckled. 'You sure put the air-conditioning in dat one, *cher*. Willis, he ain't never gonna get all them bullet holes patched up.'

The blonde, who had remained blessedly silent for all of five minutes, perked up suddenly at the mention of Willis's name. She leaned across the table toward Skeeter, making certain to twist herself around so Lucky could have another look at her amazing cleavage. 'You know Mean Gene? He's a rowdy son of a bitch, ain't he?'

She threw her head back and gave a laugh that bore an unfortunate resemblance to the braying of a mule.

Lucky turned on her slowly, his eyes glittering. The dangerous look had caused more than one man to back away from him. The blonde just gave him a wink and a grin.

'How do you know Willis, *chère?*' he asked, his voice silky.

'Well, shoot, I know him *every* way.' She gave her donkey laugh again and slapped Lucky on the arm. 'He's the one set me on to you, Ace. Said he reckoned you'd be needin' a woman 'cause yours was goin' someplace.' She flashed him her brightest smile and ran her hand up his thigh. 'Remind me to thank him later.'

Everything inside Lucky went cold and still. He murmured a prayer in French and stood up slowly, like a man in a daze, his hands clutching the edge of the table.

18

The powerboat roared through the swamp at a speed that wouldn't have been prudent even in daylight. The water was an obstacle course of snags and deadheads and cypress knees that were hidden now by the high water level. Lucky opened the throttle a little more and eased the wheel right, then left to narrowly avoid hitting a log. He focused straight ahead, trying to channel all his energy into navigating the boat. He knew this swamp better than anyone. All he had to do was focus, visualize the path and react mentally a split second before he needed to react physically.

He had run out of Mouton's like a man with the devil at his heels, stopping at his pirogue only long enough to grab his gear bag before commandeering the craft he was piloting now. He wore his infrared glasses, which allowed him to make out something of his surroundings, but not enough considering the speed he was traveling. The 9mm Beretta was strapped to his shoulder. He would have liked to have his rifle, but it wasn't something he kept in the pirogue and there was no time to go get it.

He had known the instant the pieces had come together back at Mouton's that time was of the essence. What he'd found at Chanson du Terre had confirmed his worst fears. Odille had seen Serena leave the house and walk down the lane toward Arnaud's. The Arnaud girl had watched her walk off toward the bayou. At the end of the service lane along the bayou Serena's purse had been lying abandoned, a can of Mace not far away.

Willis and Perret had her. Lucky thought he had a good idea of where they would take her. Willis had a place where he kept his fighting cocks. It was supposed to be a secret hideout, so they would undoubtedly feel perfectly safe taking Serena there. They wouldn't count on Lucky knowing the place. They wouldn't count on him turning down the attentions of the blonde either. He would have the element of surprise. He only hoped he wouldn't be too late.

The thought of Willis and Perret with their hands on Serena filled his head with a red haze, and he had to make a conscious effort to pull back from the image. Rage was ready to consume him. He could feel it roaring at the edges of his control, ready to sweep in and obliterate all else. He had to keep it leashed. He wouldn't do Serena any good if he came tearing in like a wild animal.

He called on old skills and instincts, reached deep within himself for a sense of dead calm. This was a mission. He would get the boat through the swamp. He would find Willis and Perret. He would kill them for touching his woman.

His woman.

He was in love with Serena Sheridan. He had been able to deny it before, but knowing Serena was in jeopardy put everything into perspective. What he felt for her went deeper than desire. It had from the first. That knowledge brought no comfort or joy to Lucky's heart. In fact, what it made him feel was bleak and desperate. He could offer her nothing. He was little more than a shell of a man, just managing to get himself from one day to the next. How could he take on the responsibility of love, of a wife? He didn't want it, couldn't handle it. Love changed nothing.

He cursed it as he swung the wheel of the boat to dodge a cypress knee at the last second. The only thing this love was doing was distracting him from his task. If he wasn't careful, it would get both himself and Serena killed.

The bayou took a slow bend to the east, and Lucky throttled down, instantly cutting the roar of the motor. He would go on foot from here. Guiding the boat in along the bank as close as he could, he shut it off and stuffed the key in the pocket of his fatigue pants. He tied the boat to an overhanging willow branch and jumped to shore.

As silent as a stalking cougar he moved through the woods, his mind playing back fragments of other missions. For the briefest instant he could smell the rain forest, hear the distant sounds of guerrilla gunfire. He felt his mind start to slip, but he pulled it back with an effort. If ever there had been a time for him to hang on to his sanity, it was now. He pulled the Beretta from its holster and cradled its familiar weight in his hand as he made his way through the dense growth.

It was a warm, still night. The air was heavy with the scent of honeysuckle and mud. The songs of frogs and insects combined into one high-pitched hum that floated across the whole swamp. Lucky strained to catch other sounds, thinking Willis might have stationed Perret somewhere as a lookout, but all he heard was the normal range of rustlings and squawkings that filled the nights. There were no shouts, no screams.

The last thought raised a knot in Lucky's throat. *Bon Dieu*, he couldn't bear the idea of Serena suffering at the hands of men like Perret and Willis. They were little more than animals – cruel, cunning, base. They would enjoy terrifying her simply because that was their nature, but they would take added pleasure in hurting her because they knew she was his.

They would make her pay for everything he'd done to thwart their poaching business.

For one excruciating second he had a clear picture in his mind of Serena tied down, her face twisted in pain, a scream tearing from her throat, tears streaming from her eyes. His vision blurred and he pressed the heels of his hands to his temples and forced back the image and the terrible rush of fear that accompanied it.

He would kill Shelby for this. The thought drifted like smoke around the dark edges of his mind. She had bought her own sister's death. Serena had been an inconvenience to her, just as his baby had been an inconvenience to her, nothing more than a stumbling block in the path of her goal. The idea brought a rush of hatred burning through him. He gritted his teeth and fought it under control. This was no time for emotion. He needed to pull himself into the eye of the storm, be calm, detached, focused.

He stopped and leaned back against the trunk of a tree for a moment, willing his body to relax. Taking a long deep breath, he cleared his mind of everything but cool white light.

Serena stumbled through the door of the cabin and fell across the dirty linoleum floor as Willis released her. The only light in the place came from behind the cracked yellow shade of an ancient black iron floor lamp in one corner. The room was filthy and smelled of mice and urine. A low green sofa squatted above the pitted linoleum floor with stuffing and springs sticking up through the cushions. A coffee table made from a heavily shellacked slab of wood sat in front of it. On the opposite side of the room stood a bed with a rusty iron headboard and footboard. There were no sheets, just a thin mattress covered with stained ticking.

Not the kind of place she had ever imagined staying in, let alone dying in, Serena thought as she struggled to her knees. Her gaze swept around the room automatically looking for an escape route. There was a back door, but it looked an awfully long way away as Willis stepped in front of her. He reached down and hauled her up off the floor by her sore arm and shoved her onto the bed.

'Make yourself comfortable, sweetheart,' he said, chuckling.

'It's kind of hard to be comfortable with my hands tied this way,' Serena said, blocking the pain as she pulled herself into a sitting position on the edge of the mattress. 'You might as well untie me. I know when I'm beaten. I obviously can't get away from you.'

'That's right.' Willis bent over the coffee table, then turned to face her with a whiskey bottle in one hand and his revolver in the other. A smile of smug triumph twisted his mouth. 'You can't get away. And with your hands tied, you can't get a hold of a gun either, and you can't scratch our eyes out while we have our little bit of fun. Nice try, Miz Sheridan, but no go. I like you just the way you are.'

He took a swig from the bottle, whiskey dribbling down his chin as he swaggered toward the bed. Serena watched him warily, trying to gauge his level of intoxication. He'd had several cans of beer on the way. He may have been drinking before that as well. If he drank enough, he might not be able to participate in the festivities, but there was still Perret to contend with.

He stood in the doorway with the shotgun in his hands, laughing nervously as he watched Willis advance on her. Serena was almost more afraid of him than she was of Willis. Willis was cruel and calculating, but Perret had a wild gleam in his eye when he looked at her that made her think he was teetering on the brink of a dangerous kind of frenzy.

Willis sat down beside her, his thigh pressing against hers, his hip brushing her hip. He braced himself upright with the whiskey bottle against the mattress and leaned over into Serena's face. The smell of his breath and the sour scent of his body was enough to make her want to draw back, but she held her ground. As long as she kept her mind working and the fear at bay, she had a chance. The second she buckled under the weight of terror, she would be lost; they would be on her like wolves on a lamb.

'See, if I untied you,' Willis said, his mouth a scant inch above hers, 'then you might just try to stop me from doing this.'

He brought the pistol up, and Serena's heart lodged in her throat as he drew the end of the barrel slowly along her jawline, down her throat, over her breastbone. He traced the lacy edge of her bra, the cold steel pressing into the flesh of her breast. A shudder passed through her from head to toe, and Willis smiled and chuckled.

'You like that, Lady Serena?' he asked, stroking the gun barrel across her nipple. 'You'll like this even better.'

Serena breathed a sigh of relief as he set the .38 aside on the bed, but gasped in the next instant as he grabbed her by the hair and pulled her backward onto the mattress. He leaned over her, looking like something from a horror movie with his twisted smile and one eye swollen shut. Chuckling low in his throat, he raised the whiskey bottle over her. Serena tensed and squeezed her eyes shut, waiting for the blow, but none came. Whiskey splashed onto her chest, soaking into the fabric of her bra and running in rivulets down her sides. The scent of it filled her nostrils.

Willis bent over her and took her nipple into his mouth, sucking hard at her through the wet silk. He jammed a knee between her thighs, forcing her legs to part and lowered himself onto her, grinding his erection against her.

Serena fought the tears that stung the backs of her eyes as the last of her hope was crushed beneath the weight of Gene Willis. She'd had her chance to escape, and she'd blown it. She wished they had simply killed her. She wished that the last thing she was to endure on this earth wasn't defilement and debasement. She didn't want to die with rape as her last memory.

Close your eyes and think of England. That was the line Victorian women had been schooled to remember in the face of sexual relations. *Close your eyes and think of Lucky*. The tears pressed harder for release as Willis sucked noisily at her breast and thrust himself against the apex of her thighs. Serena bit her lip until she tasted blood. Revulsion shuddered through her and rose in her throat to gag her. This was violence in one of its ugliest forms.

'Hey, who says you get her first?' Perret demanded, suddenly looming up behind Willis. His droopy eyes were narrowed and his mustache twitched as he worked his jaw angrily from side to side. The shotgun was still clutched loosely in his hands and his fingers twisted on the stock and barrel.

Willis raised his head from Serena's breast, but didn't deign to look at his partner. '*I* say I get her first,' he said, his tone low and dangerous.

Serena watched Perret with interest as his face flushed and his mouth moved back and forth as if he were working up the nerve to spit the words out. The feral gleam in his dark eyes intensified as his gaze fastened on her chest and the wet fabric that covered her breasts. 'You said before, I'd get her.'

'The hell I did,' Willis grunted. He ground his hips against Serena's and began to lower his head again, dismissing the man behind him.

'You did!' Perret insisted. 'You said I could have her first.'

'Looks to me like his promises don't mean very much,' Serena said. Her deflated hopes lifted a fraction. Her skill with minds and words was the only weapon she had. If she could turn the two men against each other, she might yet have a slim chance to live through this ordeal, and a slim chance was better than no chance at all.

Willis scowled at her. 'You shut up.'

'Why should I listen to you?' she countered. 'He's the one with the shotgun.'

'That's right,' Pou said militantly, his hand stroking up and down the barrel of the gun. 'Me, I got the shotgun, Willis. Get off her. I wanna do her first.'

'Go to hell.'

'I can shoot you, you lyin' bastard!' He swung the barrel of the shotgun around as if he had every intention of making good on his threat, but instead of pulling the trigger, he jabbed the nose of the gun in Willis's back.

Willis swore through his teeth. 'All right. Jesus, let me up.'

Perret stepped back and lowered the gun. Willis rose slowly, adjusting his jeans, glaring at the smaller man. In a quick move that belied his cumbersome size, he snatched the shotgun away by the barrel and swung the stock end at his partner like a baseball bat, narrowly missing Pou's head as he ducked back.

'You stupid coonass trash!' Willis shouted. 'You can't even get her from the goddamn boat to the house without screwing up! You can damn well wait your turn!'

'You said I got her first!' Perret shouted back.

Serena watched them argue. They yelled back and forth, issuing threats and insults, all the while inching away from the bed and toward the other side of the room. Nothing stood between her and the front door. She could make another run for it. She doubted she would get away, but there was a chance. Perhaps they would shoot her instead of chasing after her, too, and that seemed infinitely preferable to suffering the kind of violation they had planned.

She leaned forward, bracing herself to make a running start. Willis turned suddenly and set the shotgun beside the door. He sent an angry glance Serena's way.

'All right, all right,' he snapped, waving his hands in Perret's face to shut him up. 'We'll flip for first chance.'

He dug a quarter from his pocket and Perret snatched it away from him to make sure it wasn't two-headed. Willis grabbed it back and sent it into the air with a flick of his thumb.

Serena sprang from the bed and lunged for the door.

Perret wheeled toward her.

The quarter never landed.

The back door of the shack swung open. A shot exploded through the air and the coin vanished. Serena's heart leapt into her throat as she jerked around and saw Lucky standing there. He was danger personified in fatigue pants and a black T-shirt, mud smeared across his face and arms, a sleek black gun clutched in his hands.

Perret screamed as if he were seeing an apparition from hell. Whirling toward the door, he reached out for the shotgun propped against the wall. The gun in Lucky's hands bucked once and Pou screamed again as a bullet tore into his shoulder. He fell headfirst through the screen door and landed sprawled on the steps whimpering and crying.

Willis lunged for Serena, one brawny arm catching her around the neck. The momentum of his body carried her backward and to the floor, and they landed against the side of the bed, sending it skidding sideways. The .38 was in his hand and swinging in Lucky's direction before Serena could blink. Acting on adrenaline and instinct, she shoved backward with all her might, throwing Willis off balance. His shot went into the ceiling, sending down a rain of disintegrated Sheetrock.

Serena twisted out of his grasp and hurled herself toward the door, scrambling to get up from her knees. Her ears were ringing from the deafening sound of the shots and the pulse roaring in her veins. She didn't hear Willis behind her, but she felt his meaty hand close on her ankle and yank her leg out from under her. As she fell she turned her shoulders and saw Willis coming down toward her, the gun pointed at her head.

Everything went into slow motion then, time stretching out with its weird elasticity. The gun bore down on her, and behind it Willis's face, ugly and distorted with rage. His mouth opened as he shouted something at her she couldn't hear. Then Lucky flew in out of nowhere. He hit Willis like a freight train and they both went sprawling across the pitted linoleum, Willis's gun flying out of his hand and spinning across the floor like a top.

Lucky hauled Willis up off the floor by his shirtfront and slammed him back against the wall of the cabin. He had dropped his own gun and pulled his knife, pressing the deadly edge of the blade to the man's throat.

Willis's whole body trembled visibly. His face turned gray, and sweat popped out on his forehead and ran down his face like water on the waxy skin of a pumpkin. In a harsh whisper he invoked the names of various members of the holy family as he stared bug-eyed into the face of death.

'Oh, I wouldn' be callin' on them, *cher,*' Lucky said, chuckling softly. A frightening smile lit his panther's eyes and curled the corners of his lips. He caressed Willis's throat with the blade of the knife. 'Me, I got a feelin' you're not exactly on the A list up there.'

Willis swallowed convulsively, his Adam's apple scraping the razor edge of the knife. 'Jesus, Doucet,' he whispered frantically. 'I'm not armed. This is murder.'

Lucky's eyes were cold and bright. 'You think I care? There isn't gonna be enough of you left for anyone to prove it. You touched my woman, Willis. I'm gonna kill you. I just wish I could take my time doin' it.'

'Lucky.' Serena's voice floated to him from across the room. Tremulous and soft, it barely penetrated the edge of his consciousness, like a voice from another dimension. 'Lucky, don't do it.'

He glanced at her as she came into the periphery of his vision. There were scratches all over her face and neck. Her blouse was torn and dirty and hung open down the front. There was a bloody cut at the corner of her mouth and her lower lip was swollen. Her eyes, her beautiful, soft doe eyes were filled with terror and pain. The maelstrom of his fury surged through Lucky with renewed force.

'He did this to you,' he snarled through his teeth.

Serena said nothing, terrified that her answer would push him over the edge. She could see a part of him fighting to keep the wild rage at bay. The rage flashed in his eyes and rippled in his muscles; his whole body was rigid with it.

He turned back to Willis. 'I'll see you in hell, Willis,' he whispered, his voice silky-soft. 'But you're gonna get there a long way ahead of me.'

He let the knife bite into the man's skin. Several drops of blood beaded on the blade and ran down it to drip like teardrops onto Willis's shirt. Willis's mouth trembled as he let out a pitiful whimper.

Lucky stared at the blood as the scent of it filled his nostrils. Images whirled in his mind – Colonel Lambert, Amalinda Roca, Shelby. He saw each of their faces in the bright red drops, their eyes wild, mouths laughing. He saw fragmented pictures from his past – other enemies, other battles, other deaths. He felt the cold black ooze seeping in around the edges of his mind, threatening to wash in on him like a wave and sweep him away forever. His hand tightened on the hilt of the knife. Willis sucked in a breath.

Then Serena's voice came again, like a siren's call. 'Lucky, no. Leave him for the sheriff. He isn't worth it.' She stepped closer, looking up at him with her battered face, tears swimming in her eyes. 'Please, Lucky,' she whispered. 'I need you. I love you.'

'He hurt you,' he said, enunciating each word with painful deliberation. He kept his eyes on the knife. The storm raged inside him, pulling at him, tearing at him, and the blackness swirled at the edge of his mind like blood. 'He hurt you.'

'Not as much as this will.'

The knife bit a little deeper. Willis made a strangled sound in his throat. Blood trickled across the blade. Lucky stared at it, fascinated, horrified. The blackness swept in a little closer, dimming his vision. He was tired of fighting it. It would be so much easier for everyone if he just let it take him once and for all.

Serena's voice came to him again, so softly it was as if she had somehow spoken the words inside his head. 'I'm safe, Lucky. You saved me, now save yourself. Don't do this.'

A part of him wanted to let the knife go deeper. In his mind's eye he could see the blood flowing, swirling up to drown him, just like in his nightmare. It would wash over him and then he would be gone, no more battles to fight, no more betrayals to endure, no more love to forsake. His hand trembled on the hilt. He could feel his control bending, bowing under the weight.

'Hang on,' Serena whispered. 'Please hang on, Lucky.'

She stared at him, tears streaming down her face, afraid that if she blinked she would lose him. She could feel the tension vibrating around him. His fierce gaze was on Willis, but she didn't think Willis was what he was seeing. The expression in his eyes was something that came from looking inward and seeing the things one feared most. The most deadly struggle going on in the room was the one Lucky was waging with himself, and if he lost it, Serena had the terrible feeling he would be lost forever. A part of her would not have mourned for a second if Gene Willis had met his end, but revenge was nowhere near worth the price it was going to cost her.

'Hang on, Lucky,' she said again, drawing on some deep reservoir inside her for calm. 'You can beat it.'

'I'm tired,' he whispered, his eyes bleak and afraid as he looked through the face of Willis.

'I know,' Serena said, taking another half step toward him. 'I know you're tired, but you're stronger than you know. You're better than you know. You can beat it for good. Pull back from that edge. Please, Lucky, for me, for your family, for yourself. Pull back. You can do it. I know you can.'

Lucky stared at the blade of the knife, at the blood dribbling across it. He could feel himself teetering on the precipice, the ground crumbling beneath his boots. The abyss of madness beckoned, but on the other side Serena lured him back with strong, soft words, with the love he wanted so desperately to hang on to; the love he knew he could never keep. The pressures of the conflict built within him like steam until he was shaking from the force of it, as if he might explode at any second, and it kept building and building.

With a great roar of anguish he pulled the knife back and plunged it into the wall beside Willis's head. He pushed himself away from his captive and Willis crumpled to the dirty floor in a dead faint.

Lucky stepped back, swaying unsteadily on his feet as the darkness rushed to the outer boundaries of his mind and vanished in a blinding flash of light. He turned toward Serena, feeling strangely weak and disoriented, as if some vital electrical force had been suddenly drained from his body.

Serena tried to smile at him through the rain of tears streaming down her face. 'I've never been so glad to see anyone in my life,' she whispered.

Lucky drank in the sight of her, feeling her every cut and bruise as if it were his own. He wanted to heal her. He wanted to take her back in time and protect her from this nightmare and prevent her from witnessing what she had just witnessed. He wanted a lot of things at that moment – to be stronger, to be whole, to be the kind of man who could have had a future with a woman like Serena – but he contented himself with knowing she was alive and safe, and he pulled her into his arms to prove it to himself.

'*Merci Dieu*,' he whispered, burying his lips in her hair. His whole body was trembling from the internal battle he had just been through. His breath came in shallow gasps. Tears squeezed through the barrier of his lashes. He tightened his arms around Serena as if he were trying to absorb her into his being. '*Je t'aime. Je t'aime, ma douce amie*.'

I love you. Serena pressed her cheek to his chest and cried with a mixture of joy and relief and belated fear. Lucky loved her. She was safe. He was safe. They would have a chance at tomorrow together. But there was so much more left to face and so many feelings still to be dealt with, not the least of which were her feelings about what she had experienced tonight. They rushed to the fore now that she was in the shelter of Lucky's arms.

'I've never been so afraid,' she mumbled against his chest as the tears came harder.

'I know. I know, *mon chérie*. It's all right now. Everything's all right. You're safe.' He pressed fervent kisses to her temple, her cheek, her lips, trembling at the sweet taste of her. He couldn't get enough of just touching her, holding her, breathing in the faint scent of her perfume. With one shaking hand he began to carefully brush the leaves and twigs from her hair.

'Lucky?'

'*Oui.*'

'I really like having you hold me,' Serena said, twisting a little in his iron grasp, 'but do you think you could untie me first? I'd kind of like to hold you too.'

Lucky pulled back abruptly, swearing in French. He turned Serena around and dealt with the cord that bound her hands. She almost cried at the pain as feeling came rushing back into her fingers and her shoulders were allowed to sag forward, but decided she was too glad to be alive to cry about it.

They dealt with Willis and Perret quickly. Lucky dragged Pou back inside and grumbled while Serena did a cursory first aid job on the man's bullet wound. Then he bound both men hand and foot and tied them each to a bedpost.

'Let's get out of here,' he said when the task was accomplished and the two thugs sat on the floor glaring up at him. 'I'll bring the sheriff back later for these two.'

Serena nodded. Now that the danger had passed, she was feeling the effects of what she had been through. She ached all over and felt vaguely dizzy and rubber-legged. Lucky seemed to sense her fatigue and without a word swept her up in his arms. With long, purposeful strides he carried her away from the shack and into the woods.

He wound his way through the tangle of dark forest silently, surely. Serena put her arms around his neck and laid her head against his shoulder, marveling at the sense of safety she felt with him in this place she had feared for so long. But gradually the feeling of safety gave way to a subtle foreboding.

Lucky hadn't spoken a word since leaving the cabin. Serena thought she could actually feel him withdrawing from her. He might have, in a moment of intense emotion, told her he loved her, but she had the terrible feeling that love was something Lucky was more likely to shy away from than embrace. He had told her before that he didn't want her love, that he didn't have anything left inside him to give her. The discovery that he was capable of feeling would not be welcome to a man who had sentenced himself to emotional exile.

She sighed wearily at the thought that while the battle for her life was over and won, the battle for her heart was a long way from being over.

'Hey, it's a real boat,' she said in a weak attempt at levity as they emerged from the woods at the edge of the bayou and she saw the powerboat sitting in the black water. 'It's got a motor and everything.'

Lucky eased her over the side and set her on her feet, then frowned as he pulled himself into the boat and dug the keys out of his pocket. 'They have their uses,' he said shortly.

'Yes, they do. Be sure and thank the owner on my behalf for loaning it to you.'

'Can't.'

'Why not?'

''Cause I stole it.'

'You what?' Serena clamped her mouth shut and sank down into one of the passenger seats, feeling giddy at the idea that Lucky would commit a felony on her behalf. It had definitely been too long a day. She needed to go to bed and sleep for a year. Unfortunately, there was no time for that.

'How did you know they had me?' she asked, wrapping her arms around herself to ward off the chills that were beginning to rack her body now that she was away from Lucky's warmth.

Lucky didn't answer her until he'd found a blanket stowed in one of the boat's cubbyholes. He draped it around Serena's shoulders and tucked it carefully around her legs. 'The distraction they sicced on me had a big mouth and a little brain.'

'And could she really suck the brass off a doorknob?' Serena asked, unable to keep the sarcasm from her tone.

'I wasn't interested in finding out.' He tipped her chin up and tried to read her face in the dim light of the moon. 'Were you jealous?'

'Yes,' she answered honestly.

He didn't respond to that, but turned and prepared to start the boat.

'We'll need to tell the sheriff about Burke too,' Serena said, finding practical ground safer footing than probing the uncertain territory of their relationship. 'I think Burke is the one who paid Willis and Perret to – to—'

'No. He didn't. Skeeter Mouton says Burke was in the roadhouse when Willis and Pou left for their meeting this afternoon.' Lucky turned around and sat back against the console of the boat, crossing his arms over his massive chest. The look he leveled at Serena was serious. 'I think you'd better face facts, Serena. Shelby did this.'

Serena's heart gave a painful jolt. 'No.'

'You stood in her way, so she arranged to get rid of you.'

'No,' she said again, shaking her head. She didn't want to believe it. She didn't even want to consider the possibility. It was one thing to know she would never be close with her twin, it was something else to accept that her twin had tried to have her killed. She knew Shelby was emotionally unbalanced; there was no denying that after the scene over the power of attorney, but murder? Serena couldn't bring herself to believe that.

'How would Shelby ever have hired men like Willis and Perret?' she argued. 'She wouldn't go near a place like Mouton's.'

'She wouldn't have to. All she need do is call up your "family friend" Perry Davis.'

'Perry Davis?' Serena said, bewildered. 'But Perry is—'

'Crooked as a dog's hind leg,' Lucky finished. 'He finances his nasty little gambling addiction by taking payoffs from poachers. He wouldn't have any trouble finding the right men for a dirty job. No trouble a'tall.'

Serena leaned over and rubbed her temples. This was all happening too fast. It was overwhelming. In the span of just a few days her entire orderly world had been flipped upside down and inside out. Now Lucky was telling her a man she would have trusted was a criminal.

'What was to stop Burke from using Perry as a middleman?' she asked, lifting her head as the question sorted itself from the chaos in her mind. 'He wouldn't want to be linked directly with people like Willis and Perret. It doesn't mean anything that he didn't meet with them himself. He paid them to start the fire and he paid them to kidnap me.'

'I don't think so, sugar,' Lucky said. 'But we'll find out soon enough.'

They arrived at Lucky's house sometime later. Serena had no idea of the hour. The night had taken on an endless quality. She sat huddled in the passenger seat of the boat with the blanket wrapped tightly around her while Lucky quietly piloted the boat through the swamp. Neither spoke. When they reached his dock, Lucky tied the boat and carried Serena into the house.

Serena didn't even think of protesting. The aftershock of what had happened, the knowledge of what might have happened, the questions of who had caused it all to happen bombarded her nerves until it was all she could do to keep from falling completely apart. Having Lucky hold her was the best medicine she could have thought to prescribe.

He carried her into the bathroom and undressed her carefully. She kept her eyes on his artist's hands, long and strong and infinitely gentle, as they peeled away her torn, soiled blouse and the whiskey-soaked bra. She thought of the way Willis had touched her and shivered.

'Are you afraid of me, *chère?*' Lucky asked softly.

Serena shook her head. 'No. It's just that—' She broke off as another shudder of revulsion trembled through her and tears swam up to blur her vision. 'He . . . touched me. And I feel . . . so . . . dirty.'

Lucky bent his head and kissed the teardrops falling from her eyes. He whispered to her in his low, soothing voice. 'It's all right, *chérie*. I'll take it all away.'

He filled the small clawfooted tub with warm water scented with a fragrant oil taken from a mysterious brown bottle in the medicine cabinet. When the water was ready, he finished undressing Serena and carefully placed her in the tub.

The water felt like heaven, warm and soft and soothing. The fragrance of the oil drifted up in the steam, filling her head and taking away the remembered smells of sweat and liquor and fear. Serena closed her eyes and leaned back, relaxing for the first time in what seemed like weeks. Lucky leaned over her with one arm around her shoulders and carefully washed away all the dirt. He ran the cloth gently over her face, soothing her with his touch as he washed all the places that had been scratched and bruised. With infinite care he touched the cut at the corner of her mouth, ran the cloth down her throat, stroked it over her breasts. As he pressed soft kisses to her temple, he brought the warm, scented water up in his cupped palm to pour it down over her skin again and again in a cascade of cleansing, healing fluid.

Serena didn't speak for fear of breaking the spell. She allowed Lucky to touch her, to try to take away all evidence and memory of what had happened. She leaned into his strength, absorbed his gentleness, soaked up the love he was giving her, hoarding it away in her heart. Tomorrow loomed on her horizon like a storm gathering at the edge of the swamp, making these moments all the more precious to her. She savored each one and prayed what was left of the night would last forever.

When the water cooled, Lucky lifted her from the tub and dried her, then wrapped her in a towel and sat her down on the commode to carefully comb the tangles from her hair. He tended to the worst of her cuts with more of the mysterious oil from the cabinet, then carried her to his bed.

Serena snuggled into his embrace when he slid in naked beside her, letting her arms find their way around his waist. Her head nestled into his shoulder as if it had been made to fit there.

'Lucky?' she whispered.

'Hush, *chérie*,' he murmured. 'You need to sleep.'

'No. I need you.' She lifted her head and found his eyes in the soft light from the candle beside the bed. 'Make love to me, Lucky. I need to feel you. I need to have you love me. I need to have it feel good and right. Please.'

Lucky studied her face in the glow of the candle's flame. His heart nearly burst at the earnest plea in her soft, dark eyes. *Dieu*, he loved her so! He hadn't thought it possible for him to feel such emotion again, but now he ached with it in his muscles, in his bones, in his blood; he could taste it bittersweet upon his tongue. He loved her. And while there was precious little he could give her, he could give her this: his touch, his body, a memory of tenderness to take away the pain.

'Please, Lucky,' she whispered.

Turning onto his side, he lowered his head and kissed her slowly as he stroked his hand down her side. He made love to her with a patience he hadn't known he possessed, with a tenderness he had long denied. He caressed her and kissed her endlessly, until Serena took the initiative and guided him to the soft heat between her thighs. He slid into her, his breath catching at the exquisite sense of being one with her, and he loved her slowly and gently, until they were both replete.

He didn't withdraw from her afterward, but held her close, stroking her hair, brushing whisper-soft kisses to her temple.

'I love you,' she whispered as she finally gave in to sleep.

Lucky gazed down at her as the candle on the stand guttered and died and darkness swept in around them.

'*Je t'aime, mon coeur*,' he whispered into the silence.

19

'I must say, I'm a trifle baffled by this sudden change of heart,' Lamar Canfield drawled, his dark eyes wandering back and forth between the people who had summoned him to Chanson du Terre at such an unseemly hour of the morning. Young people had no sense of propriety. In the days when manners had still been in vogue, no one would have dreamed of calling on a person before nine o'clock.

He stared at the young woman seated behind Gifford Sheridan's massive cherry desk. She looked cool and composed in a forest-green suit with simple straight lines and a champagne silk blouse. There was a single strand of pearls at her throat. Her honey-blond hair was neatly contained at the back in a French twist. Her mouth lifted at the corners in a placid smile, but she twisted the large topaz ring she wore around and around on her finger, giving away her inner tension.

'It's really quite simple, Mr. Canfield,' she said with deliberate calm. 'As you know, Gifford has granted me power of attorney. I am to settle this matter as I see fit. Now, I have examined all the options and taken into consideration all factors, and the only logical, *practical* conclusion is to sell the property to Mr. Burke's company.'

Lamar shifted in his chair, the leather squeaking and sighing as he crossed his thin legs at the knee. He stared up at a water spot on the ceiling for a moment, then returned his gaze to his hostess, looking as if he were about to speak. He opened his mouth, shut it, frowned darkly for a second.

'Is there some problem, Mr. Canfield?' Len Burke demanded to know. He sat in the matching wing chair three feet from the aged attorney, obviously nursing a hangover. The whites of his eyes – what could be seen of them through his squint – had turned bloodred. The color of his complexion matched the green-brown wrapper of his unlit cigar.

Lamar regarded him with the same condescension he usually reserved for common ruffians. 'It seems to me, Mr. Burke, to be a rather abrupt change of loyalties. Why, just the other night Miss Sheridan seemed nothing short of appalled by the prospect of Chanson du Terre falling into your hands.'

Burke scowled at him. 'Yeah, well, she's changed her mind. Woman's prerogative.'

'I have changed my mind, Mr. Canfield,' she assured him.

'I see,' Lamar said gravely. He sat forward in his chair, straightening the lapels of his seersucker jacket. 'I must say, I am exceedingly disappointed by this, Shelby.'

'Serena,' she hastened to correct him.

'Yes, of course. Serena. I know what your grandfather had hoped to accomplish by giving this responsibility to you. He's going to be *very* unhappy,' Lamar declared dramatically, shaking his head in disapproval.

Shelby's eyes flashed and the line of her mouth tightened slightly. 'Well, it serves him right, if you ask me,' she snapped.

Mason stepped in diplomatically, his innocuous smile spreading like sunshine across his face as he strolled behind the desk. 'What Serena means to say, Lamar, is if Gifford is willing to give the power of the decision to someone else, then he must be prepared to face the consequences of that decision.'

'Amen.' Burke hauled a cowhide briefcase the size of a calf onto his lap and popped it open. 'Now, can we get on with the paperwork? I have everything drawn up here in the terms we agreed on. All I need is a couple of signatures and we can call it a done deal.'

He extracted a thick sheaf of papers, flipped to the final page, and handed the document across the desk to be signed.

'I'm surprised your sister hasn't come in to witness the transaction,' Lamar said with just the barest edge of sarcasm in his voice as he watched his hostess take up a pen. 'Her moment of triumph, so to speak.'

His remark won him a cutting glare, but no comment from the woman behind the desk.

'I'm afraid Shelby is indisposed this morning. She's resting,' Mason said. 'One of her migraines. Poor dear, she suffers terribly.'

'Well, I'm sure she deserves it,' Lamar said absently. He regarded the shocked expressions directed at him with bland innocence. 'The extra rest,' he clarified. 'I'm sure she deserves it.'

From the breast pocket of his suit he extracted a pair of wire-rimmed spectacles that looked as old as he did. He perched them on his nose and squinted down at the document that was thrust before him. The tension level in the room climbed faster than the temperature on a hot July day as one moment stretched into the next and Lamar showed no sign of picking up a pen. His gaze fixed on the signature; he hummed a bit.

'I'll need to see your signature on the power of attorney.' He glanced up and smiled benignly. 'A mere formality, of course.'

'Of course. I have it right here.' She slid the paper across the desk and sat back, forearms on the blotter, the fingers of her left hand twisting her topaz ring around and around.

Lamar examined both signatures with painstaking care, humming. 'Yes, they appear to match.'

'Of course they match,' Shelby snapped.

'Lamar is only looking out for his client's best interests,' Mason said placidly.

Canfield nodded. 'That's right, Serena.'

'Shel—' She clamped her teeth together abruptly and spoke through them. 'Shall we get on with it, Mr. Canfield? Mr. Burke is a busy man. I'm sure he'd like to be on his way.'

'That's right,' Burke growled. 'Sign it, I'll present the check and get the hell out of here. I've had enough of Lou'siana to last me.'

The venerable old southerner frowned at the Texan. 'I can assure you, sir, the feeling is mutual, but I would be entirely remiss in my duties if I did not read the entire document before signing.'

Burke's face flushed a shade that clashed horribly with his bloodshot eyes. Shelby made a little squeal of frustration. Mason cleared his throat carefully and made a steeple with his fingers.

'If you feel it's necessary, Lamar,' he said.

Lamar looked at them all with exaggerated bewilderment. 'Well, I'm not entirely certain. Perhaps I should consult with the real Serena.'

The faces of the three went simultaneously white as the door to the study swung open and Serena and Lucky stepped into the room. Shelby's eyes riveted on her sister and she gave a gasp of surprise.

'Serena! But you're supposed to be—'

'Dead?' Serena supplied, barely able to speak the word above a whisper. She couldn't bring herself to look at her twin, but fixed her gaze on Burke as if she might be able to compel him to confess just by looking at him. Her heart was pounding with desperate urgency. It had to be Burke. It had to be.

'No,' Shelby said. 'Gone. Out of the way.'

'Is that what Mr. Burke told you? That he'd hired someone to get me out of the way?'

'I don't know what you're talking about,' Burke said belligerently, uncomfortably shifting his bulk in the leather wing chair. 'I didn't hire anybody to do anything. Whatever went on was all their idea.' He motioned to Shelby and Mason with a thrust of his cigar.

'I'm sure I don't know anything about anybody getting killed!' Shelby said indignantly, the fingers of her left hand fussing with the pearls at her throat. Color rose to mottle her face with polka dots.

Serena swung toward her sister, a sick foreboding churning in the pit of her stomach. *Oh, God, please don't let it be . . .* Shelby's glance hit her squarely for one brief, naked second, then darted off.

'I – I don't know anything about that,' she insisted breathlessly.

'Don't you, Shelby?'

Serena could feel Lucky's presence behind her. She could feel his heat and his anger. He stepped past her and moved with restrained power toward the desk.

'You don't know anything about how Gene Willis and Pou Perret were gonna take your sister, your own flesh and blood, your *twin*, out into the swamp and rape her and kill her and dump her body where no one would ever find it?' he said, fury strumming through his words. He planted his hands on the desk and leaned across it aggressively. When he spoke again it was in a voice like smoke shot through with strands of steel. 'You don't know anything about that, Shelby? Perhaps I can refresh your memory for you.'

Shelby's complexion had gone ashen beneath her makeup. The blush that had been applied with delicate skill across her cheekbones stood out like slashes of red paint. Her eyes were wide with fear. She pressed herself back into her grandfather's chair in an attempt to escape the intensity of the man before her.

'I – I don't know what you're talking about,' she said, her voice trembling. 'You're crazy. Everyone says so.'

'*Mais* yeah, *chère*, I'm crazy,' Lucky whispered, leaning closer. 'There's no tellin' what I might do for revenge.'

Tears sprang into Shelby's eyes.

'Lucky, stop it,' Serena ordered. She was afraid of what Lucky's prodding would uncover. God help her, she was afraid he was right. She wanted with all her heart for him to be wrong. The idea that her own sister wanted her dead cut like a knife in the deepest part of her soul. She didn't want it to be true. She didn't want to have to face it, not after everything else she had been forced to face in the past week. She didn't think she would be able to stand it.

Lucky turned on her, his face tight with fury. 'Stop it?' he shouted. '*Mon Dieu!* She tried to have you murdered!'

'No!' Shelby screamed, slamming her fists down on the desk. 'They were supposed to get her out of the way, that's all! Tell them, Mason,' she said, swiveling her chair toward her husband. 'You said we'd get her out of the way. You never said anything about murder! Tell them!'

Time seemed to stand still for a second as all eyes turned to Mason Talbot. He stood beside his wife, looking resigned. He tucked his hands into the pockets of his rumpled chinos and rocked back on his heels as he looked down at Shelby.

'Now, peach,' he said in a weary tone. 'As usual, you haven't thought ahead. What did you think would happen once Serena returned? Why, she would have ruined everything, of course. We couldn't have her coming back.'

Shelby looked stunned. 'But she's my sister!'

'You hate her,' Mason pointed out.

Shelby frowned. 'Well, yes, but she's my sister. I wouldn't kill her!

Mason, how could you think such a thing?' She admonished him as if he were a naughty child.

'You wanted me in the legislature,' he said, his voice growing tighter. 'You wanted to live in Baton Rouge. We don't have the money for those things, Shelby, not with your spending habits and a new house and an old one that hasn't been sold. But you never think about anything as vulgar as money, do you? All you're interested in is getting what you want and damn the cost.

'What the hell was I supposed to do?' he shouted, the calm façade cracking finally under the strain. He stared down at her with a tortured expression. 'What was I supposed to do, Shelby? I had it all laid out in front of me, there for the taking, the opportunity to give us everything we wanted in one shot. And you were standing right behind me, pushing and pushing. What was I supposed to do?'

The full import of what they had done and what all the ramifications might have been hit Shelby in that moment. Serena could see comprehension dawn in her sister's eyes as if suddenly revealed to her in a vision. As Mason had said, Shelby hadn't thought ahead. As she had always done, she had planned only as far as the moment, not even considering the long-term consequences. She sat there now, looking like a little girl who had been given an unpleasant surprise – stunned, hurt, disillusioned.

Serena looked away as an expression of horror twisted Shelby's features, and she turned from her husband, buried her face in her hands, and began to sob. Tears rose in Serena's eyes.

'What about Gifford?' Lucky asked, his attention still focused on Mason.

Mason pushed his glasses up on his nose and tried to compose himself. He answered absently, as if he were explaining nothing more earth-shattering than plans for a picnic. 'He would have become despondent over Serena's disappearance and the loss of the plantation. Poor man. He probably would have committed suicide.'

Serena listened in stunned silence. She shook her head as a sense of vertigo seized hold of her for an instant. Another facet of her well-ordered life shattered. Mason. Staid, stoical, kind Mason Talbot, a man she had always liked and trusted, had paid to have her killed. He had allowed his greed and his love for Shelby to mutate into an ugly catalyst that had driven him to murder.

'And the fire?' Lucky prodded.

Mason ducked his head. His shoulders sagged. 'I believe I've said enough without having my attorney present,' he said softly.

'That's all right, Mason,' Sheriff Hollings said as he sauntered into the room with a pair of deputies at his heels. 'I've heard all I need to hear for now.'

Serena watched with a sense of disbelief as the officers each took charge of one perpetrator. Burke protested loudly as handcuffs were slapped on his wrists. Mason said nothing. Shelby fell sobbing across the desk and had to be helped to her feet by the sheriff.

'This is all your fault!' she shouted at Serena as they were being led from the room. Her face was awash in tears and mascara, her mask of beauty melting away to reveal her hate and inner torment. 'You never should have come back! None of this would have happened if you hadn't come back!'

There was nothing Serena could think of to say. She stared at her twin and felt a terrible aching hollowness inside. They should have been closer than sisters, but they were poles apart. The only thing left between them now was bitterness and pity and regret.

Lucky came up beside her and put his arm gently around her waist, silently inviting her to lean against his strength. They stood together and watched as the officers herded their prisoners toward the door with the sheriff drawling, 'Y'all have the right to remain silent. Anything you say can and will be used against you in a court of law. . . .'

Lamar rose slowly from the leather wing chair, scratching his chest. 'I believe I'll go and return this little microphone to Sheriff Hollings. Simply amazing the technology the police have at their disposal these days.' He gave Serena an apologetic look and patted her shoulder with a wrinkled hand. 'I truly am sorry, my dear, about all that's happened here today. What a terrible shock it must be to you.'

'Yes,' Serena murmured. 'Thank you for your help, Mr. Canfield.'

'Don't mention it. I was merely performing my civic duty. If you need any further assistance, don't hesitate to call.' He rolled his eyes heavenward and heaved a dramatic sigh. 'I may have every appearance of a dotty old codger, but I believe I still have a few tricks up my sleeve.'

Serena managed a pale smile as she watched the elderly lawyer stroll gracefully into the hall, Panama hat in hand. She listened as he exchanged a few lines of banter with Odille on his way out. Then the house fell into silence.

She could feel the power of Lucky's gaze on her as she went to the French doors. Trying to block the sound of departing squad cars from her mind, she looked through the panes of glass past the gallery, across the lawn. The bayou was a dark ribbon at the feet of the trees. The sky was a turbulent patchwork of rapidly changing cloud formations and patches of blue; it looked as unsettled as she felt.

She felt as if her life had been thrust into the winds of a hurricane. Everything had blown apart – her family, her image of herself, her sense of control over her own destiny – everything lay in fragments around her and she didn't know where to begin to pick up the pieces. She had come here for a few days of vacation. Instead, her life had been irreparably altered; *she* had been irreparably altered.

'What happens now?' Serena heard herself ask the question, but it felt as if it had come from someone else. She couldn't imagine why it would have come from her; she didn't think she really wanted to hear Lucky's answer.

'There'll be a hearing,' he said, deliberately choosing the mundane interpretation of the question. 'They'll be charged. Bail will be set – for Burke and Shelby at least.'

Serena glanced back at Lucky. He was sitting back against the desk, turning a smooth glass paperweight over in his hands, his gaze steady on her.

'I never would have suspected Mason,' she murmured. 'Never.'

'No one would have.' He put the paperweight down and came to stand behind her at the glass doors, his face grave. 'No one can guess the kind of things pressure can drive a man to do,' he said softly. 'I'm sorry about Shelby, Serena. I have my own grievance with her, but I know she's your sister and it must hurt.'

Tears stung Serena's eyes as she nodded. 'I always wished we would have been as close as twins are supposed to be. We never were. Now we never will be. What's happened will always be between us.'

Lucky slid his arms around her and leaned down to kiss her cheek. 'I told Hollings I'd take a deputy out to where we left Willis and Perret.'

Serena nodded, rubbing her hands over her upper arms as if to warm herself through the fabric of the soft faded chambray shirt she had borrowed from Lucky's wardrobe. It hung to her knees, and she had needed to fold the cuffs back five times to reveal her hands, but it had been a big improvement over her ruined silk blouse and the memories attached to it. She hadn't been able to look at that pile of clothing without shuddering. Lucky had taken the garments outside and burned them, then loaned her his shirt and a pair of old gray sweat pants.

'I suppose I should go and change,' she said. 'You'll be wanting your shirt back.'

'Keep it.'

The words seemed innocuous enough, but Serena felt what was coming as surely as if he had just held up a red flag. This was it. This was going to be the moment Lucky chose to end it. He would say good-bye and ride off into the swamp without looking back, and she would be left with a broken heart and an old blue workshirt.

'A souvenir?' she asked dryly, looking up at him over her shoulder. 'Something I can pack away in my hope chest and take out whenever I want to remember you fondly?'

Lucky stepped back, frowning. 'Serena, don't.'

'Don't what?' She arched one golden brow. 'Don't remember you fondly? Don't remember you at all? You want me to pretend I never fell in love with you? Is that what you're going to do, Lucky? Pretend you never told me you loved me?'

'I told you from the beginning what we could have.'

She held up both hands to ward off his words. Anger rushed into her head and pounded like mallets in her temples. 'Don't you try to feed me that line again. I'm ready to gag on it! I don't care what boundaries we set. I don't care that it's been only a matter of days. What we have goes way beyond sex, and you know it.'

'I know it can't work,' he insisted, glaring at her.

She returned his hard gaze, matching his stubbornness ounce for ounce. 'You won't let it work.'

Lucky spun away, his hands raised as if to strangle somebody as his temper surged. She was going to make this as difficult as possible for them both. She wouldn't just accept the facts and meekly walk away. No, no, she would tear them all apart and analyze them and try to find a cure.

'Dammit, Serena, you saw what happened out there last night,' he said tightly. He stared down at his boots because he was too ashamed to look her in the eye. 'Is that the kind of man you want for a husband? Next time I might just slip off that edge.'

'I saw what happened,' Serena said softly, aching for him. 'And I saw you get through it. You saved my life. And I watched you take care of me afterward, and I was there when you made love to me too. What happened with Willis doesn't make me love you less, Lucky. If anything, it makes me love you more.'

Lucky shook his head impatiently as he paced before her. 'That's not love. That's pity. I know what you see when you look at me, Serena – some poor, crazy bastard who needs someone to take care of him.'

'Damn you, Lucky Doucet,' Serena snarled. She came around in front of him and grabbed the waistband of his jeans to keep him from walking away. She glared up at him, her face scratched and bruised, fury in her eyes. 'I will thank you to stop interpreting my feelings for me. I don't pity you, you pity yourself. You're so damn proud and stubborn, you can't bear the idea that you're not perfect, that you have flaws and frailties like everyone else. You make me mad as hell, but I love you. You're strong and good and tender under all that macho bullshit. And you love me. Look me in the eye and tell me you don't.'

He knew he should have done it, but he couldn't. He couldn't look down into that beautiful battered face and tell her he didn't love her, when he loved her more than life. But he couldn't give her what she deserved either.

'I can't give you the kind of life you deserve.'

'I deserve to have the man I love.'

'I live in the swamp,' he said. 'I can't tolerate people. I'm lucky if I get through a day without comin' half unglued. What kind of future can I give you? What do I have to offer you, Serena?'

Her answer was simple and devastating. 'Your heart.'

Lucky closed his eyes like a man in pain.

'Don't try to tell me you don't have one. You're just afraid to give it,'

Serena said, tears rising again to tighten her throat and sting the backs of her eyes. 'I know what it is to be afraid, Lucky,' she whispered.

He shook his head, refusing to look at her, the muscles of his jaw working.

'Yes,' Serena insisted. She stared up at him earnestly, her heart in her eyes. 'I know how it feels. I know what it's like to feel it take hold and let it control you. I also know I could help you conquer it – not because I'm a psychologist, but because I'm the woman who loves you.'

'I've got to go,' he muttered, looking away, his face a taut, unreadable mask.

Serena felt futility pull down on her like a weight. He wasn't going to give in. He was going to withdraw into himself and close the door on her as he had countless times in the past few days, and none of the tools of her trade would be able to pry it open. Her love was the only key she had, and Lucky was making it clear not even that would unlock the chains that bound him to his past.

'Hiding isn't the answer, Lucky,' she said sadly. 'You're a good man, a strong man, a man with talents. You've got so much to offer if you'll only stop running from who you really are.'

'Let me go, Serena,' he said softly. 'You'll be better off.'

She stepped back from him, lifting her chin defiantly as she tried to sniff back her tears. 'You think you're doing this for me? Your nobility is sadly misplaced. I don't want it. I want a future with you. We could have so much more than you're willing to give us, Lucky. You let me know when you're ready to accept that. I'll be here waiting.'

Lucky's gaze sharpened on her. 'You're not goin' back to Charleston?'

'No.' Serena hadn't been certain of an answer until that very second, but it came out strong and sure, the only decision she could have made. 'I'll have to go back to settle my affairs, but that's all. Chanson du Terre is my home. I have responsibilities here, and roots. It's time I faced that and accepted myself for who I am inside instead of who I am in Charleston. I'm all through being a coward. You let me know when you are.'

She gave him one last long look, then started for the door.

A deputy stuck his head in the open doorway. 'Hey, Lucky, the boat's here. You ready to go?'

Serena stopped and stood there, waiting to hear his answer as if it were the answer to the question in her heart. The silence dragged on.

'Yeah,' he said at last, his voice soft and heavy. 'Let's get outta here.'

20

'Serena? Is that you?' Gifford bellowed from the depths of his study.

Serena paused outside the open door, suitcases in hand. 'Yes, Giff, it's me,' she called back wearily.

'Hey, Miz 'Rena,' Pepper called, grinning at her from his position in a leather wing chair. He lifted his coffee cup to her in salute. 'Mighty good to have you back.'

'Thanks, Pepper.' She wished she could have said it felt good to be back, but all she felt at the moment was exhausted. She thought she could have just lain down on the old Oriental rug between the two blue tick hounds and slept for a week or three. The hounds looked up at her with woeful expressions. One mustered the ambition to woof softly, then fell over on his side, exhausted from his effort.

Gifford abandoned the blueprints on his desk and strode across the room toward her. He looked as vibrant and healthy and cantankerous as ever. There was a flush of color on his high cheekbones. His eyes gleamed with a fierce intelligence. His white hair was in a state of disarray that told of numerous finger combings.

'Where the hell have you been?' he demanded to know. 'You were due back two hours ago. Odille waited supper as long as she could.'

'I'm sorry. My flight was delayed.'

'They don't have telephones up in Charleston?' Gifford said with characteristic sarcasm. He gave her an admonishing glare, took her suitcases away from her, and started down the hall with them.

Serena had all she could do to dredge up the energy to catch up with him. The man was nearly eighty and she thought he could probably work her right into the ground on his worst day. He was amazing.

He stopped at the door to her room and set her luggage down. 'You had an old man worried he might have scared you off for good,' he said gruffly as he straightened and looked her in the eye. The glare had softened grudgingly with lights of love and unspoken apology.

'No,' Serena said with a weary smile. 'You can't scare me, you old goat. I'm no coward.'

'Damn right you're not.' Gifford's shoulders straightened with pride. 'You're a Sheridan, by God.'

He looked at her for a long moment then, and sighed, all the bluster going out of him. He raised his weathered old hands and cupped her shoulders gently. 'I'm glad you're back, Serena. I know I pushed and bullied you into it, but you still could have said no in the end. I'm glad you didn't.'

Serena slid her arms around his lean, hard waist and hugged him. What had happened had changed their relationship and complicated it, but when all that was stripped away, the most important fact remained.

'I love you,' she whispered, pulling back.

Gifford reddened and looked at his feet, grumbling, uncomfortable with voicing such feelings to a person's face.

'You gonna go after that big Cajun?' he asked suddenly.

The question took Serena by surprise, hitting her too suddenly for her to give a controlled response. She shook her head and looked at the floor, afraid of what her grandfather might pick up from her unguarded expression.

'What's the matter? He's not good enough for you 'cause he doesn't wear silk suits and read *The Wall Street Journal?*'

That brought Serena's chin back up. She glared at Gifford, realizing belatedly that he was once again playing her like a finely tuned fiddle. 'That's not it and you know it,' she said evenly.

'He's had some rough times, but Lucky's a good man,' Gifford said gruffly.

'I know he is. Maybe someday he'll figure that out for himself. I can't push him into believing it.'

'Do you love him?'

'Yes.'

Gifford frowned, his bushy white brows pulling together in a V of disapproval above his dark eyes. 'You want him, but you're not going after him?'

'We're talking about a relationship, not a big-game hunt,' Serena said dryly. 'I can't go out in the swamp with a dart gun and bring him back to live in captivity. I can't drag him back here and force him to love me. Lucky has a lot of things from his past he needs to work out for himself. When he does – if he does – then maybe he'll see what we could have together.'

'Well, I hope so.' Gifford's frown softened, and he rubbed his chin. 'I sure as hell don't want to think I dumped you on his doorstep just to get your heart broken. I was counting on getting some great-grandchildren out the deal.'

'Gifford!' Serena gasped, her cheeks blooming delicate pink.

The old man showed no signs of remorse. He didn't even have the grace to look guilty.

'You look as peaked and thin as a runt pup,' he complained, his gaze raking her head to toe. 'I'll have Odille heat you a plate of food.'

Serena shook her head in amazement. 'Don't bother her,' she said absently. 'I ate on the plane.'

Gifford snorted his disapproval and moved off down the hall in the direction of the kitchen. 'Wouldn't feed that trash to my hounds.'

Serena watched him go. One of the reasons she had decided to move back home was that she had figured Gifford would need her after everything that had happened. What a joke that was. It was quite clear he could take care of himself. She was going to have to stay on her toes just to keep up with him.

She dragged her suitcases into her bedroom, where she kicked off her shoes, stripped off her travel-wrinkled suit, slipped on her robe, and set about the business of unpacking before she collapsed under the weight of her fatigue.

She went about the task methodically, mechanically. It seemed most of her movements these days were mechanical. She was operating on automatic, taking care of day-to-day matters with an obvious lack of enthusiasm. In her logical, educated mind she knew this lethargy would pass eventually. In the meantime, she simply had to suffer through it, going through each day only to get to the next. It wasn't fun, but it was better than nothing. In her more philosophical moments she reflected it would give her added empathy for her patients in the future – as soon as she had some patients.

She had gone back to Charleston to tie up all the loose ends there, to resettle her patients with new therapists, to sell her condo and say good-bye to friends. All had been accomplished with minimal flap. Tomorrow she would drive up to Lafayette and start looking for office space. She should have been looking forward to the task, but she couldn't come up with any emotion to dent the numbness inside.

Too much had happened in too short a time. Her emotions had gone on overload and shorted out. It was a defense mechanism. It hurt to feel, therefore her mind had shut down the capacity to feel. The only time her emotions turned back on was late at night, when she was too tired and too lonely to keep them at bay. Then they rushed back in a high-voltage surge of pain that left her feeling even more drained and beaten.

A month had passed since the crisis at Chanson du Terre had come to a head. There would still be the trials to get through – Mason, Willis and Perret, Perry Davis, who had in fact been Mason's middleman in hiring the two thugs. Len Burke had gotten off scot-free. There had been no hard evidence connecting him to any crime other than greed. Shelby had already pleaded guilty to a minimal charge of conspiracy and been given a suspended sentence. She and her children had gone to stay with Mason's parents in Lafayette. The Talbots had raised Mason's bail and were reportedly calling in long-due favors to get him the best defense attorneys money could buy. Rumors abounded about deals to avoid the scandal of a trial, but there had been no official word.

Serena found herself oddly incurious about it. She wasn't interested in punishment or restitution. The trust she had lost, the disillusionment she had suffered, couldn't be repaired or replaced. She wanted only to put it all behind her and get on with her life.

Gifford had reinstated himself in the house and was going on as if all that had happened was already little more than a dim memory. He was engrossed in planning the new machine shed as well as in ordinary plantation business. Pepper and James Arnaud had him thinking about crawfish as a new cash crop to rotate with the sugarcane.

As it always did, life gradually returned to normal, healing over the wound and leaving only hidden scars behind to remind those who had lived through the trouble.

Serena placed a final stack of lingerie in the dresser and closed the drawer. As she lifted her head her gaze caught on her reflection in the beveled mirror. It was amazing. She looked no different than she had before all this had begun. The cuts and scratches of her harrowing night in the swamp had long since healed, leaving her skin unmarred. It seemed as if there should have been some lasting sign of that whole momentous chapter in her life plain on her face for all the world to see, but the scars were on the inside, on her heart.

Lucky had gone away with the deputy that day and never returned. Serena had been angry, hurt, heartbroken. She had considered going out into the swamp to get him, but had decided against it in the end. It went against her grain to give up on him, but she knew she was right in not pushing him. It had to be Lucky's decision to come back to her. She couldn't force him to love her enough. She couldn't force him to want to have a future. He had to decide his life was empty without her. He had to see that hiding from the world wasn't the answer to his problems.

It had become painfully obvious he was not going to make those decisions.

Maybe she'd been wrong about him. Maybe he didn't love her after all. Maybe what they'd had together had been nothing more than desire magnified and intensified by the circumstances. Maybe she was the only one who had felt something that went beyond passion. Maybe she was the only one left feeling empty.

Even as she opened the dresser drawer and pulled out the faded blue workshirt, Serena chastised herself. This wasn't very healthy behavior. It was certainly no way to get over a broken heart. But her inner critic wasn't very stringent. Some deeper wisdom told her she needed time to heal. None of her practical therapy methods were going to change the fact that she still loved Lucky Doucet or that she missed him or that she hurt because of losing him. No amount of counseling could change the fact that she needed to feel close to him now at the end of a long day, when she was feeling tired and in need of a broad shoulder to lean on. So she didn't stop her hands from lifting the old blue workshirt from the drawer, nor did she try to stop herself from bringing it up to brush the soft chambray against her cheek and breathe in the scent of it.

Hardly an hour went by that she didn't think of Lucky, wondering what he was doing, if he was all right, if he was still chasing poachers. She couldn't help thinking about him, picturing him standing at the back of his pirogue, poling silently through the swamp, or sitting in his studio staring moodily at a canvas. She couldn't help thinking about him, wondering what he was doing, if he ever missed her.

He had done what he thought was the right thing, the noble thing, in leaving her. Ironic, considering how determined he had been to convince her he was no good. Sometimes it made her angry when she thought of it – how high-handed he'd been in deciding what was best for her – and sometimes it made her ache with sadness that he'd seen himself as so unworthy of her love. Sometimes she told herself he might have known best and she should just give up on him and get on with her life. But she could never manage to tell herself that at night when she lay in her bed, staring into the darkness.

Hugging the shirt to her chest, she closed her eyes and sighed as the pain penetrated the protective wall she'd built around her heart. The scents and sounds of the summer night drifted in through the open French doors. And with them came the memory of the night she and Lucky had made love in this room.

No other man had ever made her feel the way Lucky did. No other man had ever gotten past her barrier of cool control and brought out the true woman in her. It didn't make sense. He was the last man she would have imagined falling in love with, dark, dangerous, rough-edged. And she would never have believed herself capable of falling so hard and so quickly. It defied logic. She could find no pat, analytical answer, but it was true nevertheless. No man had ever made her feel so alive, so filled with passion and yearning to be a part of another soul. She knew with a deep, sad certainty no man ever would.

All dressed up for me, sugar?

The words came to her like smoke, like mist on the bayou. Serena stared into the mirror and imagined she saw him standing behind her, his hot amber gaze roaming over her body, his artist's hands coming up to cup her shoulders and pull her back against him. She closed her eyes as she clutched the shirt to her chest and for just a second imagined his arms around her.

'Serena?'

Her heart jolted in her chest as she swung toward the door.

'Shelby.' She couldn't hide the surprise in her voice or any of the other feelings that sprang up at her sister's sudden appearance in the doorway. They had had no direct contact since that fateful day in Gifford's study. Serena hadn't been able to find it in her to be the one to take the initiative, and Shelby had shown no desire to do so either. Serena had wondered how long they would go on in limbo. It appeared her question was about to be answered.

'May I come in?' Shelby asked, sounding as formal as a stranger.

'Yes. Of course,' Serena said, folding her arms in front of her, Lucky's shirt caught between them.

'I came by to pick up the last of our things,' Shelby explained as she stepped in and closed the door behind her.

Serena made no argument, even though she knew all of Shelby's and Mason's things had long since been packed and sent to the Talbot home in Lafayette. Shelby had taken the crucial first step. What difference did it make if she had felt the need for an excuse?

Serena watched her sister as she moved slowly around the room, Shelby's normal energy level subdued as she straightened a doily here, a lampshade there. As always, she was impeccably dressed in a delicately printed sundress with a full skirt. Every honey-gold hair was in place, smoothed into a chignon at the back of her head. Noticeably absent from her ensemble was the expensive jewelry she so loved. The only ring she wore was her engagement diamond.

Serena watched her with a strangely detached curiosity. The initial rush of confusing emotions had subsided, leaving her feeling blank and empty again, vaguely wary of her sister's motives.

'I suppose you're still angry with me,' Shelby said. Her tone of voice was almost annoyed, as if she didn't believe Serena had a right to be angry, but her movements and quick sideways glances said she was nervous about what the answer to her statement would be.

'No,' Serena said, turning to watch her in the mirror.

Shelby looked up and frowned at her. 'Serena the Good,' she said bitterly. 'I should have expected as much. Forgive all those who sin against you.'

'I didn't say I'd forgiven you. I said I wasn't angry. Anger isn't what I feel when I think about you.'

'What do you feel?'

Serena was silent for a long moment as she contemplated her answer. 'I don't know if it has a name. It's like grief, I guess, but different, worse in a way.'

Their eyes met in the mirror and Shelby suddenly looked genuinely sad.

'We were never very good at being sisters, were we?' she said softly.

Serena shook her head. 'No. I'm afraid we never were.'

Shelby moved several steps closer, until they stood side by side, close but not touching, alike but not the same. Her gaze riveted on their images in the looking glass. 'How can we look so much alike and be so different inside?' she whispered as if she were asking the question of herself.

Serena said nothing. There were no easy answers. As a psychologist, she could have cited any number of theories on the subject, but as a sister none of them meant anything. As a sister all she knew was that she and her twin were standing on opposite sides of a chasm that was too wide and deep to be bridged. There might have been a point in their past when they could have found some common ground and reached across, but that time was gone and they both knew it.

'I wish things hadn't gone so wrong,' Shelby said, her dark eyes filling.

That was as much of an apology as she was going to get, Serena thought sadly. There would be no remorse, no expression of regret for what had happened, for what could have happened. Shelby was incapable of taking blame. She was like a thief who was sorry the police had caught her red-handed, but not sorry she'd committed the crime. She was only sorry things had gone wrong.

'Me too,' Serena said softly, knowing they had very different ideas about what had gone awry. The blank slate of her emotions filled suddenly with a complex mix of feelings, like a tide rushing in, and, as she had said in answer to Shelby's earlier question, the strongest was something like grief. They may both have been physically alive, but whatever had been between them was dead and she wanted to mourn it like a lost soul.

'My word, Serena,' Shelby murmured, still staring at their reflections in the mirror, 'you look all done in.'

'I'll be all right.'

'Yes, I'm sure you will be.'

'Will you?'

'We'll manage,' Shelby said, lifting her chin a defiant notch.

She moved back a step. The distance between them widened. Her reflection in the mirror grew smaller. When she reached the door and turned the knob, Serena found her voice.

'Shelby?' Their eyes met again in the glass. 'Take care.'

A single tear rolled down her sister's cheek and a faint smile touched her mouth. 'You too.'

Serena watched her go, feeling as if she were losing a part of herself she'd never really known. Then, bone-weary and heartsick, she crawled onto the bed, curled up with Lucky's shirt, and did the one thing she did really well these days – she cried herself to sleep.

Gifford slipped into the room quietly. He set the plate he was carrying on the dresser and walked around the end of the bed to look down at his sleeping granddaughter. The tears were still damp on her cheeks, her breathing still shaky. She held an old blue workshirt wadded up in her hands, reminding him of when she'd been no more than a toddler, dragging a ragged yellow security blanket around the house with her everywhere she went.

He remembered the day they'd put her mother in the ground, how he had slipped in that night to check on the girls because Robert had been too lost in his grief to think of it. He had found Serena asleep on top of the covers, still wearing the little black velvet dress and white tights she'd worn to the funeral, one patent leather shoe on and one off. The tears had still been damp on her cheeks, and she had clutched in her hand that ragged old blanket.

He remembered it like it was yesterday even though tonight he felt every one of the years that had passed since then. The love he'd known for Serena that night hadn't lessened a whit. It didn't matter that Serena had grown into a woman or that life had complicated things between them. He still experienced her pain more sharply than if it had been his own. His grief over what Shelby had done was magnified by the grief he knew Serena was feeling. Her pain over Lucky's defection was more than enough to break his own heart.

He knew he had pushed her over the years and bullied and manipulated her, but he hadn't done anything without loving her, and he just about couldn't bear to see her suffering. He couldn't change what had happened between them, and he couldn't mend the rift between her and Shelby, but he could do his best to knock some sense into that big Cajun rogue. In fact, it was the least he could do, all things considered.

Careful not to wake Serena, he leaned across the bed and pulled the coverlet back over her. He looked at her again, turned slowly, and shuffled out of the room, taking the dinner plate with him and shutting the light off on his way out.

Lucky checked the rope attached to the nose of the half-submerged rowboat one last time, then slogged out of the bayou and onto the bank. The day was hotter than summer in Hades. The sun beat down on the bare skin of his back through a haze of humidity, burning him an even darker shade of brown. Sweat rolled off him. He pulled on a pair of worn leather work gloves and took up the end of the rope he had looped around the trunk of an oak tree, paying no attention to his discomfort. He focused his mind on his job.

He'd been hauling junk up out of the bayou for weeks now, working literally from sunup to sundown, cleaning up dozens of sites careless people had chosen for disposing of such things as old refrigerators, iron bedsteads, stoves, mattresses, bicycles, and tires. It was a job that needed doing and one that he could devote himself to and exhaust himself with in the hopes of gaining a few hours of sleep at the end of the day.

When the job called for it, he used a gas-powered winch, but he fell back on it only after he'd spent a good long while trying to pull the object out by himself – no matter what it happened to be. The exertion cleared his mind and made certain the overriding pain he felt was in his muscles.

He took up the rope now and tightened the slack gradually until he was leaning back hard against it, straining to inch the boat up out of the water. He heaved, his every muscle standing out, physical pain blocking all thought from his mind. Beads of sweat slipped past the bandanna he wore around his forehead, stinging his eyes. He leaned back, pulling until his blood was roaring in his ears. He didn't even hear the outboard motor till the bass boat was nearly to the bank.

From the corner of his eye he saw Gifford and groaned inwardly. Why couldn't the world just leave him alone? He adjusted his grip on the rope and heaved backward again, doubling his concentration on his task, dragging the boat up another six inches toward the bank. The sound of the outboard ceased abruptly, but Lucky worked on as if he were completely oblivious of Gifford Sheridan's presence.

'I had me a mule once could pull like that,' the old man drawled. 'He was a damn sight smarter than you, though, I reckon.'

Lucky sucked in a lungful of humid air, adjusted his grip, and hauled back on the rope again, the corded muscles in his neck and shoulders standing out as he pulled. The nose of the old rowboat lunged forward as the back end pulled free of the mud. Within a couple of minutes he had the dilapidated craft halfway ashore. He dropped the rope then and went to tip the water out of the boat. Gifford sat patiently watching him from under the brim of a battered old green John Deere cap.

'What are you doin' here?' Lucky growled, not looking up from his task. He pulled a small anchor from inside the boat and heaved it onto the bank. 'I thought you got everything you wanted, old man.'

'What would it matter to you if I did or didn't? Everybody knows you don't give a damn about anyone but yourself.'

Lucky said nothing as he drained the boat. He didn't need this. His life was miserable enough without having this cantankerous old man chewing his tail. He'd done what he had to do. That was the end of it.

'You broke her heart,' Gifford said succinctly.

Lucky flinched inwardly, the words like a whip across tender flesh. He focused on the junk in the boat as he stood there waist-deep in the bayou. 'I didn't ask her to fall in love with me.'

'No, but she did anyway, didn't she? God knows what she sees in you. I look at you now and all I see is a stubborn, selfish man too caught up in his penance to see he doesn't have anything left to pay for.' Gifford shrugged and sighed, his shrewd dark eyes on Lucky the whole time, never wavering. 'Hell, I don't know, maybe you like pain. Maybe you like thinking you could have had a decent life with a wonderful woman, but you passed it all up to suffer. Catholics do like their martyrs.'

He didn't so much as bat an eye at the murderous glare Lucky sent him. The old man sat leaning forward with his forearms on his thighs and his big hands dangling down between his knees, as calm as if he were sitting over a fishing pole waiting for a bite. Lucky turned abruptly and waded ashore, dragging the old rowboat with him. When the boat lay on its side like the carcass of a whale, he turned back toward Gifford.

'I did what was best.'

Gifford snorted. 'You did what was easiest.'

'The hell I did!' Lucky snapped, taking an aggressive step toward the bow of the bass boat. 'You think I wanted to walk away from her? No. But what kind of life could I give her? What kind of husband would I be?'

'Not much of one until you get yourself straightened out. I don't see any sign of that happening any time soon,' Gifford said sarcastically. 'I guess I can just go on home and tell Serena she's crying herself to sleep at night for no good reason.'

The blow was on target, even more so than Gifford could have hoped. Lucky had heard Serena's tears. He had found himself on the gallery of Chanson du Terre late one night, just to catch a glimpse of her, just to ease that one longing a little. He'd seen her curled up on her bed, crying into the shirt he'd left behind. He'd told himself then he'd done the right thing; he didn't deserve her tears. But the sound of them, the idea of them, had been enough to tear his heart in two.

'I can't give her what she needs,' he said, staring down at his boots.

'What do you think she needs, Lucky? Money? An executive husband? Serena can make her own money. If she wanted an executive, she could have had one long before now. All she needs is for you to love her. If you can't manage that, then, by God, you are one sorry soul indeed.'

'She knows I love her,' Lucky admitted grudgingly.

'Then come back.'

'I can't.'

Gifford swore, his patience wearing thin in big patches. 'Goddammit, boy, why not?'

Lucky gave him a long, level look. The corner of his mouth curled up in a faint sardonic smile. 'I got my reasons.'

The old man's jaw worked and his face flushed, but he held his temper in check. 'Well, Lucky,' he said at last on a long sigh, 'you have a nice life out here all by yourself.' He reached around for the starter rope, his fingers closing over the handle. 'Don't worry about Serena. She'll buck up. She's a Sheridan.'

The engine sputtered, then roared to life, and Gifford calmly rode away, leaving Lucky feeling as unsettled as the bayou in the churning wake of the outboard motor.

The feeling still hadn't subsided by sundown when he abandoned his job for the day and made his way home. It hadn't lessened any by midnight when he sat on the floor of his studio drinking and staring morosely at his paintings in the moonlight. He had managed to keep the worst of his feelings at bay these past few weeks, denying them, dodging them, burying them, but now they rose to the surface like oil on the bayou. They clung to him, refusing to be ignored even as he tried to study the painting on the easel before him.

He hadn't painted in weeks. He had expected to find the same peace in it as he had after returning from Central America, but when he'd taken up the brush and applied it to the canvas he'd felt nothing to compare with the peace he had found so briefly in Serena's arms. That kind of peace he never expected to find again.

That had been an unwelcome revelation. The solace he had once found in this place was lost to him. He had retreated from the love Serena had offered him and found not peace, but misery in the form of a terrible wrenching loneliness that felt as if a vital part of him had been torn out and taken away.

He couldn't go out into the swamp without thinking about the way she had given him her trust there in the place she had been so afraid of. His house was haunted by her memory. He hadn't slept a night in his bed because he couldn't lie there without remembering the feel of her body against his. Every time he turned he thought he caught the scent of her perfume in the air. He could feel her presence but he couldn't touch her, couldn't see her, couldn't take her in his arms and have her chase away the darkness in his soul.

'Damn you, Serena,' he muttered, pushing himself to his feet.

The emotions rose higher and hotter inside him, tormenting him. He paced back and forth before the easel with his head in his hands as he realized with a sense of panic there was no escape. He could work till he dropped and the feelings would still be there inside, waiting for a chance to torture him. He could drink himself unconscious and they would still come to him through the haze of oblivion.

Crying out in fury and frustration, he grabbed the unfinished painting from the easel and smashed the edge of it against the floor with all his strength, snapping the stretcher like a toothpick. He let the ruined mess drop from his hands and backed away from it blindly.

'Damn you, Serena!' he shouted to the heavens. He whirled toward his work table and swept an arm across it, knocking bottles and brushes to the floor. And he shouted in anguish above the crash, 'Damn you! Damn you!'

He stumbled back across the room, reeling at the inner pain, exhausted from fighting his feelings. Slowly he sank back down to the floor, on his knees on the dropcloth where they had first made love, feeling as bleak and desolate inside as he had ever in his life. He tilted his head back, turning his face up toward the skylights and the cold white light of the moon. Tears trickled from the outer corners of his eyes, across his temples, into his hair.

He hadn't asked to fall in love. All he had wanted was to be left alone. Now he was so alone, he couldn't stand it.

This was hell on earth, and Gifford had the gall to accuse him of taking the easy way out.

Serena had called him a coward. She'd said he pitied himself, that he was afraid to give their love a chance to work.

Of course he was afraid. He had known they would only end up hurt in the end, and he'd had enough pain to last him a lifetime.

But Serena was hurting now, despite his noble sacrifice, and he'd never lived through this kind of agony. It was far worse than anything Ramos and his buddies had dished out because it was relentless and unreachable and nothing relieved it. He ached with missing Serena. He ached with the need to touch her. He ached with guilt and the knowledge that she was right.

He was a coward. He'd been afraid to feel again. He had been afraid to let Serena get close to him for fear of what she would see, but she had seen every part of him, every side of him – good and bad – and she'd still loved him.

What kind of fool was he to let a woman like that get away? What kind of fool was he to go on suffering like this?

A noble fool who had pushed away the woman he loved for her own good. A frightened fool who had been too wary of love. A fool who had nothing to offer her but himself because his life had been stripped down to mere existence.

Where did he go from here?

Lucky stared long and hard at the painting on the floor before him. It lay in a crumpled, twisted heap, ruined, worthless. He could throw it out or he could try to salvage it, restretch the canvas, start over on the painting.

A sense of calm settled inside him as the answers came to him.

If Serena deserved a better man than he was, then he would have to become a better man. If his life offered her nothing, then he would have to change it, because he didn't want to live without her. He didn't want to be a martyr to his past. It had taken so much from him already – his youth, his hope, his family – he couldn't let it take Serena too.

The time had come to leave it behind and try to take that first step forward. He had a long way to go before he would feel whole and healed, but he would never get there if he didn't take that first step, and his life wouldn't be worth living if he stayed where he was.

Slowly he reached for the ruined canvas and pushed himself to his feet.

21

Serena stood on the sidewalk, looking up at the sign above the black lacquered door. RICHARD GALLERY was spelled out in flowing gold script on a black background. The building was three narrow stories of old brick sandwiched between similar buildings that had been lovingly restored more than once in their long histories. There was ornate grillwork over the windows, and flower boxes spilling scarlet geraniums and dark green ivy over their edges. Two doors down, a young man sat on a stoop playing a saxophone for tips. Just beyond him locals and tourists alike had begun to gather for dinner at a sidewalk café. A mule-drawn carriage clomped by on the street, its driver reciting the history of the area for his passengers. Just another hot summer night in New Orleans.

The French Quarter address of the building matched the one on the invitation she held in her hands, but still Serena hesitated. It had been four months since she'd last seen Lucky. He had made no attempt to get in touch with her until now, and this could hardly be construed as personal contact – an engraved invitation sent out by an art gallery. All it meant was that she was on his mailing list. How flattering.

A group of tourists brushed past her, laughing and chattering, parting to go around her like a stream around a boulder. Serena didn't move. She looked at the invitation in her hands, remembering how she felt when she first opened it. There was a mixture of joy and sadness – joy that Lucky had taken this step, that he was making an effort to put his life on track, sadness that she wasn't being included in that life.

She acknowledged the fact that she wasn't getting over him. She was getting on with her life without him, but she doubted she would ever be completely free of him. In fact, she knew she never would be. She was carrying his child.

She nibbled her lip and stared at the door of the gallery. All the way to New Orleans she had told herself she was going for Lucky's sake, to show her support. But the truth was this was an opportunity to see him on somewhat neutral ground, and she needed that. She told herself she would be calm and cool and tell him that while he was going to be a father, she expected nothing from him. She would be the picture of sophistication and poise, and then she would probably pass out.

'So, are we going to go inside or is this all you wanted to see?'

Serena jumped at the sound of the voice. She glanced around at the man who had insisted on accompanying her to New Orleans. Blond and handsome, David Farrell looked down at her with kind eyes and a gentle smile curving his wide mouth.

She had joined David and another psychologist in practice in Lafayette, and they had quickly become good friends. David was easy to talk to, understanding, intuitive. Serena had found herself confiding in him within days of meeting him, something that was very unlike her. There was something about him that seemed so trustworthy, so nonthreatening, everyone wanted to confide in him. It was a trait that made him very successful in his profession and popular with his friends. Serena had it on good authority he was considered prime husband material by every single woman in Lafayette.

He had insisted on driving with her to New Orleans to give her moral support. Now he stood beside her with his hands in his pants pockets, waiting patiently for a response. Serena gave him a look.

'Yes, we're going inside. I just wanted to be certain this is the place, that's all.'

David raised his eyebrows. 'Mmm.'

'Save it for your patients, Dr. Farrell,' she said dryly, and led the way inside.

The gallery was cool and light. Stark white walls were used as backdrops for the paintings, lights were strategically spotted toward the works, bleached wood floors were polished to a brilliant sheen. An impressive number of people milled around, admiring Lucky's work, talking, nibbling on dainty canapes and sipping white wine from tulip-shaped glasses. Cajun music floated out of cleverly hidden speakers, too soft to be appreciated.

Serena found herself missing the bayou country, and she smiled a little at the thought. This was the kind of life she had enjoyed in Charleston, but she found herself wishing she were sitting on the gallery at Chanson du Terre, listening to Pepper and Gifford argue with a blaring two-step playing in the background.

She couldn't imagine Lucky in these surroundings. He was too big, too wild, too elemental. She moved through the crowd half expecting to see him in fatigue pants and no shirt.

'He's very talented,' David said over her shoulder.

They had stopped beside a study of the bayou cast in the last bronze light of sunset. Serena looked at the painting, remembering the day she had first seen Lucky's work, remembering how it had drawn her in, remembering how they had made love at the foot of his easel.

'Yes,' she murmured. 'He's very talented. I'm glad he finally realized that.'

'It looks like a lot of people are realizing it tonight. I think your Mr. Doucet is going to be a reasonably wealthy man. Have you seen him yet?'

'No.'

'Well,' David said, snatching a glass of wine from the tray of a passing waiter, 'just say the word and I'll melt into the background.'

Serena went abruptly still. She felt Lucky's gaze hit her like a spotlight, and she turned slowly, her breath catching in her throat as her eyes met his halfway across the room. He stared at her as if she were the only woman on earth, completely ignoring the two gallery patrons who had been speaking to him. A vague dizziness swirled through Serena's head as he came toward her. He moved with the grace of a big cat, with a sense of leashed power that was out of place in this setting, but even the city folk knew enough to get out of his way.

Serena steeled herself against the wild mix of emotions seeing him set loose inside her. She gave him a wry look and said, 'Gee, they even got you to wear a shirt. This is a special occasion.'

He frowned at her, but smoothed a hand over the tie he had already pulled loose around the collar of his dress shirt. He looked devastatingly handsome in his pleated coffee-colored linen trousers, ivory shirt, and brown silk tie. His hair was still unruly, still long, but the boot lace that normally tied it back had been replaced by something a little more discreet. Serena felt a nervous flutter in her stomach. She wasn't sure she knew this Lucky. She found herself wishing he had indeed come in fatigue pants.

'I wasn't sure you'd come,' he said gruffly. His gaze raked over the man standing beside her. His jaw tightened.

'Of course I came. I got my invitation,' Serena said, sarcasm edging her voice. She held the envelope up to him as proof. 'I brought a friend with me. I hope you don't mind. This is David Farrell. David, Lucky Doucet.'

David stuck his hand out. 'It's a pleasure.'

Lucky said nothing. Tension rolled off him in waves.

Fighting a smile, David stepped back. 'Well, I believe I'll have a look around. You two probably have some catching up to do.'

Serena watched him move off into the crowd, then turned back toward Lucky. He was watching her, his gaze as disturbing as ever. Even after all this time Serena could feel her body responding to his nearness. Her heart had picked up a beat. She felt hot and too aware of her every nerve ending.

Forcing herself to ignore the sensations, she looked up at him with genuine warmth in her eyes. 'Congratulations on the show, Lucky. I know what it means. I'm very happy for you.'

Lucky said nothing for a long moment. He was too caught up in looking at Serena. He had lain awake nights aching to see her, but he hadn't allowed himself to go to her, not until he had something to offer her. Now he drank in the sight of her, absorbing everything about her – her honey-colored hair in its smooth twist, the delicate rose of her cheeks and mouth, the liquid brown of her eyes, the stubborn tilt of her chin. She was dressed in one of her neat business suits, a navy blue skirt and boxy double-breasted blazer, and Lucky caught himself picturing her in nothing but the old blue workshirt he'd left with her. He wondered bitterly if he would ever get the chance to see her wear it, wondered if she had worn it for her 'friend.'

'You look good,' he said, trying to decide what it was about her that seemed subtly different.

'So do you,' she whispered.

'How's Giff?'

'Fine.'

Bon Dieu, he thought, there was so much he wanted to say to her, but he stood like an oaf exchanging bland pleasantries as if she were little more than a stranger to him. Maybe when he had gotten his fill of looking at her – as if that could ever happen – the words would come. But then, he'd never been much for talk. What he wanted to do was kiss her. He wanted to take her in his arms and feel her against him, soft and warm. He wanted to pull the pins from her hair and run his hands through the silk. He wanted to lay her down and join his body with hers and feel that incredible sense of peace he'd known only with her.

But she had come with another man.

A finger poked Lucky's biceps and he turned his head to glare at the gallery owner, Henri Richard, a slender man in his forties who was just a little too cosmopolitan for Lucky's tastes. Lucky had needed to remind himself too many times over the last few weeks that the man was the owner of one of the best galleries in the city and that Danielle, Lucky's sister-in-law, had gone to a great deal of trouble to get the two of them together. Respect for Danielle was about the only thing that had kept him from telling Richard to go hang himself. That and the fact that this was his big chance to show Serena he was ready to turn his life around.

Richard ignored Lucky's glower and motioned to the exotic-looking woman standing beside him. 'You really must meet Annis, Lucky,' he drawled. 'She's the art critic for the *Times*.'

'They don' teach manners where you come from?' Lucky asked in a silky voice. 'I was speaking with Miz Sheridan, here.'

Richard's high cheekbones reddened. The art critic eyed Lucky with open interest.

Richard took a step closer to Lucky and spoke in a low, stiff whisper. 'Annis is a very important person in the art community.'

'Then I'm sure you won't mind kissing her ass,' Lucky muttered. 'Me, I've got better things to do.'

Serena cleared her throat delicately. 'Lucky, I can see you're busy. We can talk later.'

'We can talk now,' he said, swinging toward her, a dangerous look in his eyes. He took her by the arm and started for the back door. 'Let's get outta here. I can't breathe in this place.'

'But your show—'

'Can take care of itself.'

'Lucky!' Serena protested through her teeth, trying not to attract too much attention to them. 'These people came here to see you.'

Lucky kept moving, his brows low over his eyes, jaw set. 'If they came for the paintings, fine. If they came for the free booze, I don't care. If they came to gawk at me, they can take a flying leap; I'm not on display.'

The guests parted like the Red Sea as he made a beeline for the door with Serena hurrying to keep up with him. They cut through the small kitchen, past the curious stares of the catering people and out into the courtyard that was shared by several buildings on the block.

Cobbled paths radiated out from a central stone fountain that gurgled gently. The warm evening air was fragrant with the scents of the flowers blooming in riotous profusion all around. Strategically placed brass lanterns had just begun to glow as the natural light faded.

'You're fortunate it's considered amusing for artists to be rude and eccentric,' Serena commented dryly as Lucky led her toward a bench at the far corner of the garden.

'Yeah, I'll be a real hit, won't I?'

'A sensation. Do you think I might get the feeling back in this arm anytime soon?'

Lucky swore in French and let go of her abruptly as they reached the wrought iron bench that was sheltered by an arbor of bougainvillea. 'I get a little tense in a crowd,' he said by way of an apology.

Serena gave him a gentle smile. 'It looked to me like you were doing just fine.'

His big shoulders rose and fell in an uncomfortable shrug. 'I'm working at it.'

That dangerous need to reach out to him surfaced in Serena. She wanted to offer him her support. She wanted to offer him a hug and tell him how proud of him she was. But she made herself sit down on the bench instead. Lucky had managed just fine these past months without her. It was clear he was making a real effort to work through the problems his past had left him with. Serena told herself she could be glad for him, but she couldn't allow herself to share in his victory. If she was to survive, she would have to keep her distance from him emotionally as well as physically.

'You've been all right?' he demanded abruptly, his amber gaze boring down on her like a searchlight from above.

'Sure,' she answered slowly and without conviction. 'I've been fine.' If *fine* meant heartsick and lonely. She could have told him the truth, but she had promised herself she would hang on to her pride, at least.

The quiet of the garden closed in around them. The fountain babbled to itself. From beyond the building came the faint sounds of the city – a car honking, someone calling across a courtyard, jazz drifting out a window somewhere above them.

Lucky heard none of it. He stood there, uncomfortable in his new shoes, wondering if he'd missed his chance at a future with the only woman he'd ever really loved.

'I've missed you,' he said suddenly.

Serena stared at him in amazement. She thought her heart might have stopped. She knew she quit breathing.

'I've missed you like hell, Serena.'

'Then why didn't you come to me?' she asked, some of the pain she'd known these last months rising up to tighten her throat on her words.

'I couldn't. I had nothing to offer you. I couldn't come to you in pieces.'

'I loved you anyway.'

'Do you love me still?' Lucky asked. His gaze captured hers and held it prisoner as he waited for her answer.

'I've spent the last four months trying to get over it.'

'And have you?'

Serena said nothing. She stared up at him, hating him for doing this to her, for knocking down all the walls she had spent these last weeks building, for taking away her pretense of calm control. He leaned down over her, bracing one knee against the seat of the bench, his arms effectively corraling her in place.

'Have you gotten over me, Serena?' he asked, his voice soft and smoky.

Serena tried to turn her head away, but he caught her chin with one hand and tilted it up so she had no choice but to look at him.

'No,' she whispered, trembling inside. A lone tear teetered on the barrier of her lashes, then spilled over, washing away her last hope of keeping her pride intact. 'No.'

'Then what the hell are you doin' here with another man?'

The jealousy in his tone was unmistakable. Serena's eyes widened. 'David? He's just a friend. We work together.'

'You're not lovers?'

'No!' she snapped in annoyance. 'Not that it's any of your business.'

Lucky took a step back from her, jamming his hands at the waist of his trousers. His scowl darkened from black to bottomless. 'It damn well *is* my business, *chère*.'

'Oh, is that right?' Serena said sarcastically, one brow rising in mocking inquiry. 'And why is that?'

'Because I love you!' Lucky roared.

The night seemed to go perfectly still. Serena stared up at him, unable to speak, unable to move a muscle. Lucky stared back, his chest heaving.

'I love you,' he said again softly, without the anger.

Slowly Serena rose from the bench, never taking her eyes off Lucky. 'I'd given up hope on you,' she murmured. 'I waited and waited for you to come back.' She shook her head as tears flooded her eyes and blurred her vision. 'Say it again,' she whispered as she went into his arms. 'Please say it again.'

'I love you.' Each word was a kiss against her temple as Lucky held her close and gloried in the feel of her against him. *'Je t'aime, ma chérie. Je t'aime.'*

He crushed her to him, finding her mouth with his and kissing her deeply, roughly, with all the hunger pent up over the long months without her. His tongue rubbed against hers, drinking in the sweet taste of her, then he pulled back a fraction of an inch and kissed the tears from her cheeks and lashes.

'Don' cry, *chère*. Don' cry,' he said. 'It's all right now.'

Serena couldn't help herself. The rush of emotion was too strong, her control too fragile. She pressed her face into Lucky's broad shoulder and cried as the flood of feelings swept through her. She clung to Lucky, welcoming his strength, thanking God for the pleasure of having his arms around her again.

'Marry me, Serena,' he said, his voice tight and smoky with emotion. 'I need you so. I can turn my life around a hundred eighty degrees and it still won't be worth a damn without you in it. Marry me.'

Serena lifted her head from his shoulder and managed a tremulous smile as she looked up at him. He was a hard man, stubborn, proud; life with him would never be easy or dull, but life without him hardly seemed worth the effort. She loved him beyond all reason, but then, reason had nothing to do with love. Her heart had looked beneath the surface and seen a man worth reaching out to. Now he was reaching out to her.

'Marry me, Serena,' he said again.

'Yes,' she whispered.

'Have my children.'

'Yes.' Her smile widened as she took his hand and drew it around to the slight swell of her stomach.

She didn't have to say a word. Lucky read the message in her eyes. Warmth flowed through him as he pictured her holding their child, nursing a dark-haired baby at her pretty breast. Suddenly the life he had nearly thrown away seemed worth living. He pulled Serena close and held her for a long moment as the power of the love he felt swept through him like a cleansing wind, blowing away the last traces of darkness from his heart.

When he leaned back from her, Lucky brushed the last of Serena's tears away with his thumbs. His expression was a mask of concern. 'I don' know what kind of a husband I'll make for you, *chère*,' he admitted. 'I've been alone a long, long time. Longer than you know.'

'It's all right,' Serena said, lifting a hand to touch the smooth, hard plane of his cheek. 'You won't be alone anymore.'

'I'll have my lady with me.'

'Always.'

Author's Note

I hope you enjoyed the setting of *Lucky's Lady* as much as I enjoyed painting a picture of it for you with words. South Louisiana is a unique environment with a unique history and a unique and rich mix of cultural backgrounds. I have tried to portray some of this cultural diversity to the reader through the use of local dialects – in particular, through the use of a number of Cajun French words and phrases.

Cajun French differs from standard French much as Elizabethan English differs from the English we speak today. The language evolved separately from its mother tongue and has retained many antiquated words and phrases as well as incorporating new ones from other languages. There are many subdialects because this language was passed on for generations only orally. About sixty percent of the words in the Cajun vocabulary can be found in a standard French dictionary. The rest are unique to the patois.

Only recently have any attempts been made to preserve the language by writing it down, and those attempts have been embroiled in controversy. Arguments abound over how to go about saving the language, which dialect is the most correct, and whether or not the language should be saved at all. There are those who look upon it with disdain and call it simply 'bad French.' Personally, I look upon it as a unique part of a unique heritage, something that deserves to be preserved.

My sources for the Cajun words and phrases used in *Lucky's Lady* include *Conversational Cajun French* by Harry Jannise and Randall P. Whatley as well as translations of various Cajun folksongs performed by the group Beausoleil (translations by Sharon Arms Doucet, Barry Ancelet, and Ann Savoy). My thanks to these people for their work in keeping Cajun French alive.

Glossary of Words and Phrases
Used in This Book

allée	avenue, path
allons	let's go
américaine	american
baire	mosquito netting
bien, ma chère, casse pas mon coeur	now, my dear, don't break my heart
bon Dieu	good God
bonsoir	good night
bourré	a Cajun card game
c'est assez	that's enough
c'est bien	that's all right
c'est ein affaire à pus finir	it's a thing that has no end
c'est pas de ton affaire	that's none of your business
c'est toi que j'aime	it's you I love
Chanson du Terre	song of the earth
cher/chère/chère catin/chérie	dear/darling/etc.
coonass	a generally derogatory slang term for Cajun
Dieu	God
espèsces de tête dure	you hardheaded thing
foute ton quant d'ici	get away from here
grenier	attic
il n'a pas rien il va pas faire	there's nothing he won't do

j'aime te faire l'amour avec toi	I'd love to make love with you
je t'aime	I love you
je te blâme pas	I don't blame you
ma douce amie	my sweet love
mais non	but no
mais yeah	but yes
ma jolie fille	my pretty girl
maman	mama
ma petite	my little one
merci Dieu	thank God
mon ami	my friend
mon ange	my angel
mon coeur	my heart
mon 'tite coeur	my little heart
m'sieu	shortened form of *monsieur* mister
non	no
oui	yes
pas de bétises	no joking
pichouette	little girl
rien	nothing
sa c'est de la couyonade	that's foolishness
vien	come
viens ici	come here

CRY WOLF

Author's Note

Anyone familiar with my work knows I have a special affection for that part of Louisiana known as Acadiana. My interest has roots in family, even though it was the music that first drew my attention, and branches into history, linguistics, and a love for unique and fragile environments. In *Cry Wolf*, as in my previous books set in south Louisiana, I have done my best to bring to you the feel and flavor of bayou country. I have made a special effort to portray some of the cultural diversity of the area through the use of local dialects – in particular, through the use of a number of Cajun French words and phrases. A glossary of these words and phrases can be found at the back of the book.

Cajun French is a distinct language born in France and raised in Louisiana. About sixty percent of the words in the Cajun vocabulary can be found in a standard French dictionary. The rest are unique to the patois, words and phrases that evolved out of necessity to fit the environment and the people living in it.

My sources for the Cajun French used in *Cry Wolf* include *Conversational Cajun French* by Harry Jannise and Randall P. Whatley, and *A Dictionary of the Cajun Language* by the Reverend Monsignor Jules O. Daigle, M.A., S.T.L., a complete source and especially wonderful defense of a language that deserves to live on and flourish.

In a world where we are increasingly pressured to conform and homogenize, ethnic diversity is a precious gift. My sincere thanks to the people who strive to preserve and nourish such endangered species as the Cajun language. *Merci boucoup*.

Tami Hoag

All things are taken from us, and become
Portions and parcels of the dreadful Past.

Alfred, Lord Tennyson
The Lotus-Eaters

Prologue

The bâteau *slides through the still waters of the bayou. Still, black waters as dark as the night sky. As dark as the heart of a killer. In the water stand the cypress, rank upon rank, tall sentinels as motionless and silent as death. Behind them, on the banks, the weeping willows, boughs bowed as if by grief, and the live oak with their twisted trunks and gnarled branches, looking like enchanted things eternally frozen in a moment of agony. And from their contorted limbs hangs the moss, gray and dusty and tattered, like old feather boas left to rot in the attic of some long-forgotten, long-ruined mansion.*

All is gray and black in the night in the swamp. The absence of light, the reflection of light. A sliver of moon is wedged between high clouds, then disappears. Stillness descends all around as the boat passes. Eyes peer out from the reeds, from the trees, from just above the surface of the water. Night is the time of the hunter and the hunted. But all the creatures wait as the bâteau *slips past them, its motor purring, low and throaty, like a panther's growl. The air of expectation thickens like the mist that hovers between the trunks of the tupelo and sweet gum trees.*

One predator has struck this night, cunning and vicious, with no motivation but the thrill of holding another's life and savoring the power to snuff it out. The creatures of the swamp watch as the predator passes, as the scent of fresh blood mingles with the rank, metallic aroma of the bayou and the sweet perfume of wild honey-suckle, jasmine, and verbena.

The motor dies. The boat skirts a raft of water hyacinth, noses through the cattails and lily pads, and sidles up to the muddy bank, where ferns and creepers grow in a tangled skein. Somewhere in the distance a scream tears through the fabric of the night. Like an echo. Like a memory. The predator smiles, fondly, slyly, thinking not of the nutria that issued the sound, but of the woman lying dead on the floor of the bâteau.

Another kill. Another rush. Another dizzying high. Power, more seductive than sex, more addictive than cocaine. Blood, warm and silky, sweet as wine. The pulse of life rushing with fear, pounding, frantic . . . ebbing, dying . . .

The body is dragged to the bank, left near the end of a crushed clamshell path that glows powdery white as the moon flashes down once again like a searchlight — there and gone, there and gone. Its beam illuminates a dark head of hair, damp and disheveled with no trace of the style that had been so painstakingly sculpted and sprayed hours ago; a face, ghostly pale, cheeks rouged clownishly, lipstick smeared, mouth slack, eyes open and staring, unseeing, up at the heavens. Looking for mercy, looking for deliverance. Too late for either.

She will be found. In a day, maybe two. Fishermen will come to fill their creels with bream, bluegill, sac-a-lait. They will find her. But none will find her killer.

Too cunning, too clever, beyond the laws of man, outside the realm of suspicion this predator stalks. . . .

1

'I'll kill him.'

The hound sat in a pile of freshly dug earth, azalea bushes and rosebushes scattered all around like so many tumbleweeds, a streamer of wisteria draped around his shoulders like a priest's amice. Looking up at the people on the veranda with a quizzical expression, he tilted his head to one side, black ears perked like a pair of flags on the sides of his head. A narrow strip of white ran down between his eyes – one pale blue, one green – widening over his muzzle. His coat was a wild blend of blue and black, trimmed in white and mottled with leopard spots, as if Mother Nature hadn't been able to make up her mind as to just what this creature would be. As people spilled out the French doors of the elegant brick house known as Belle Rivière, he let out a mournful howl.

'I swear, I'll kill him,' Laurel Chandler snarled, her gaze fixed on the dog.

Rage and fury burned through her in a flash fire that threatened to sear through all slim threads of control. Two days she had been working on that garden. Two days. Needing desperately to do something and see an immediate, positive result, she had thrown herself into the task with the kind of awesome, single-minded determination that had taken her so far so fast as a prosecuting attorney. She had set herself to the towering task of reclaiming Aunt Caroline's courtyard garden in time to surprise her.

Well, Caroline Chandler had returned to Bayou Breaux from her buying trip, and she was surprised all right. She stood to Laurel's left, a tiny woman with the presence of a Titan. Her black hair was artfully coiffed in a soft cloud of loose curls, makeup applied deftly and sparingly, accenting her dark eyes and feminine mouth. She seemed barely forty, let alone fifty, her heart-shaped face smooth and creamy. She folded the fingers of her right hand gently over Laurel's clenched fist and said calmly, 'I'm sure it was looking lovely, darlin'.'

Laurel attempted to draw in a slow, calming breath, the way Dr. Pritchard had taught her in relaxation therapy, but it hissed in through her clenched teeth and served only to add to the pressure building in her head and chest.

'I'll kill him,' she said again, jerking away from her aunt's hold. Her anger trembled through her body like an earthquake.

'I hep you, Miz Laurel,' Mama Pearl said, patting her stubby fingers against her enormous belly.

The old woman sniffed and shifted her ponderous weight back and forth from one tiny foot to the other, the skirt of her red flowered dress swirling around legs as thick and sturdy as small tree trunks. She had been with the Chandler family since Caroline and Jeff Chandler were children. She lived with Caroline not as an employee but as a member of the family, running Belle Rivière like a general and settling comfortably if testily into old age.

'Dat hound make nothin' but trouble, him,' she declared. 'All the time rootin' in my trash like a pig, stealin' off the clothesline. Nothin' but trouble. Talk about!'

Laurel barely heard the woman's chatter. Her focus was completely on the Catahoula hound that had destroyed the first constructive thing she had accomplished since leaving Georgia and her career behind. She had come back to Louisiana, to Bayou Breaux, to heal, to start over. Now the first tangible symbol of her fresh start had been uprooted by a rampaging mutt. Someone was going to pay for this. Someone was going to pay dearly.

Letting out a loud primal scream, she grabbed her brand-new Garden Weasel and ran across the courtyard swinging it over her head like a mace. The hound bayed once in startled surprise, wheeled, and bounded for the back wall, toenails scratching on the brick, dirt and debris flying out behind him. He made a beeline for the iron gate that had rusted off its hinges during the time Belle Rivière had been without a gardener, and was through the opening and galloping for the woods at the bayou's edge before Laurel made it as far as the old stone fountain. By the time she reached the gate, the culprit was nothing more than a flash of blue and white diving into the cover of the underbrush, sending up a flock of frightened warblers to mark his passing.

Laurel dropped the Garden Weasel and stood with her hands braced against the gate that was wedged into the opening at a cockeyed angle. Her breath came in ragged gasps, and her heart was pounding as if she had run a mile, reminding her that she was still physically weak. A reminder she didn't appreciate. Weakness was not something she accepted well, in herself or anyone else.

She twisted her hands on the rusting iron spikes of the gate, the oxidizing metal flaking off against her palms as she forced the wheels of her mind to start turning. She needed a plan. She needed justice. Two months had passed since the end of her last quest for justice, a quest that had ended in defeat and in the ruination of her career and very nearly her life. Two months had passed since she had last used her mind to formulate a strategy, map out a campaign, stock up verbal ammunition for a cause, and the mental mechanisms seemed as rusty as the gate she was hanging on to with white-knuckled fists. But the old wheels caught and turned, and the momentary panic that she had forgotten what to do passed, a tremor that was there, then gone.

'Come along, Laurel. We'll go in to supper.' Caroline's voice sounded directly behind her, and Laurel flinched from nerves that were still strung too tight.

She turned toward her aunt, one of the few people in the world who actually made her feel tall at five foot five. 'I've got to find out who owns that dog.'

'After you've had something to eat.'

Caroline reached out to take hold of her niece's hand, heedless of the rust coating her palms, heedless of the fact that Laurel was thirty years old. To Caroline's way of thinking, there were times when a person needed to be led, regardless of age. She didn't care for the obsessive light glazing over Laurel's dark blue eyes. Obsession had landed the girl in a quagmire of trouble already. Caroline was determined to do all she could to pull her out.

'You need to eat something, darlin'. You're down to skin and bones as it is.'

Laurel didn't bother to glance down at herself for verification. She was aware that the blue cotton sundress she wore hung on her like a gunny sack. It wasn't important. She had a closet full of prim suits and expensive dresses back in Georgia, but the person who had worn them had ceased to exist, and so had the need to care about appearances. Not that she'd ever been overly concerned with her looks; that was her sister Savannah's department.

'I need to find out who owns that dog,' she said with more determination than she'd shown in weeks. 'Someone's got to make restitution for this mess.'

She stepped over the handle of the Garden Weasel and around her aunt, pulling her hand free of the older woman's grasp and heading back down the brick path toward the house. Caroline heaved a sigh and shook her head, torn between disgust and admiration. Laurel had inherited the Chandler determination, also known in moments such as this as the Chandler pigheadedness. If only Jeff had lived to see it. But then, Caroline admitted bitterly, if her brother had lived, they may well not have been in this mess. If Laurel's father hadn't been killed, then the terrible course of events that had followed his death would never have been set in motion, and Laurel and Savannah would in all likelihood have become very different from the women they were today.

'Laurel,' she said firmly, the heels of her beige pumps clicking purposefully against the worn brick of the path as she hurried to catch up. 'It's more important that you eat something.'

'Not to me.'

'Oh, for—' Caroline bit off the remark, struggling to rein in her temper. She had more than a little of the Chandler determination herself. She had to fight herself to keep from wielding it like a club.

Laurel stepped up on the veranda, scooping a towel off the white wrought-iron table to wipe her hands. Mama Pearl huffed and puffed beside the French doors, wringing her plump hands, her light eyes bright with worry.

'Miz Caroline right,' she said. 'You needs to eat, chile. Come in, sit down, you. We got gumbo for supper.'

'I'm not hungry. Thanks anyway, Mama Pearl.' She settled her glasses in place and combed her dark hair back with her fingers, then sent the old woman a winning smile as adrenaline rushed through her. The anticipated thrill of battle. 'I've got to go find the hound dog that owns that hound dog and get us some justice.'

'Dat Jack Boudreaux's dog, him,' Mama Pearl said, her fleshy face creasing into folds of disapproval. 'He's mebbe anyplace, but he's most likely down to Frenchie's Landing, and you don' need dat kinda trouble, I'm tellin' you, *chère*.'

Laurel ignored the warning and turned to kiss her aunt's cheek. 'Sorry to miss supper your first night back, Aunt Caroline, but I should be back in time for coffee.'

With that she skipped around Mama Pearl and through the French doors, leaving the older women standing on the veranda shaking their heads.

Mama Pearl tugged a handkerchief out of the valley of her bosom to blot the beads of perspiration dotting her forehead and triple chins. 'Me, I don' know what gonna come a' dat girl.'

Caroline stared after her niece, a grim look in her large dark eyes and a frown pulling at her mouth. She crossed her arms and hugged herself against an inner chill of foreboding. 'She's going to get justice, Pearl. No matter what the cost.'

2

Things were hopping at Frenchie's. Friday night at Frenchie's Landing was a tradition among a certain class of people around Bayou Breaux. Not the planter class, the gentlemen farmers and their ladies in pumps and pearls who dined on white damask tablecloths with silver as old as the country. Frenchie's catered to a more earthy crowd. The worst of Partout Parish riffraff – poachers and smugglers and people looking for big trouble – gravitated over to Bayou Noir and a place called Mouton's. Frenchie's caught everyone in between. Farmhands, factory workers, blue collars, rednecks all homed in on Frenchie's on Friday night for boiled crawfish and cold beer, loud music and dancing, and the occasional brawl.

The building stood fifty feet back from the levee and sat up off the ground on stilts that protected it from flooding. It faced the bayou, inviting patrons in from fishing and hunting expeditions with a red neon sign that promised cold beer, fresh food, and live music. Whole sections of the building's siding were hung on hinges and propped up with wooden poles, revealing a long row of screens and creating a gallery of sorts along the sides.

Even though the sun had yet to go down, the crushed shell parking lot was overflowing with cars and pickups. The bar was overflowing with noise. The sounds of laughter, shouting, glass on glass underscored a steady stream of loud Cajun music that tumbled out through the screens into the warm spring night. Joyous and wild, a tangle of fiddle, guitar, and accordion, it invited even the rhythmically challenged to move with the beat.

Laurel stood at the bottom of the steps, looking up at the front door. She had never set foot in the place, though she knew it was a regular haunt of Savannah's. Savannah, who made a career of flouting family convention. She may even have been sitting in Frenchie's at that moment. She had slipped out of Aunt Caroline's house around five, dressed like a woman who was looking for trouble and fairly glowing at the prospect of finding it. All she had told Laurel was that she had a date, and if all went well, no one would see her before noon Saturday.

Suddenly the hound skidded around the corner of the gallery and came to a halt, looking wide-eyed straight at Laurel. If she'd had any misgivings about coming to Frenchie's Landing – and she'd had a few – sight of the marauder dispelled them. She was on a mission.

A trio of men in their twenties, dressed and groomed for a night on the town, walked around her and started up the steps, laughing and talking, telling ribald jokes in Cajun French. Laurel didn't wait for the punch line. She rushed after them and snatched at the sleeve of the biggest one, a bull of a man with a close-cropped black beard and a head of hair as thick as a beaver pelt that grew down over his forehead in a deep V.

'Excuse me,' Laurel said. 'But could you tell me who that hound belongs to?'

He cast a glance at the dog on the gallery, as did his companions.

'Hey, dat's Jack's dog, ain't it, Taureau?'

'Jack Boudreaux.'

'*Mais* yeah, dat one's Jack's,' Taureau said. His look softened, and a grin tugged across his wide mouth as he gave Laurel a once-over. 'What, you lookin' for Jack, sugar?'

'Yes, I guess I am.' She was looking for justice. If she had to find this Jack Boudreaux to get it, then so be it.

'Dat Jack, he's like a damn magnet, him!' one of the others said.

Taureau snorted. '*Son pine!*'

They all shared a good male belly laugh over that.

Laurel gave them her best Cool Professional Woman look, hoping it wasn't completely ruined by her baggy dress and lack of makeup. 'I didn't come here to see his penis,' she said flatly. 'I need to discuss a business matter with him.'

The men exchanged the kind of sheepish looks boys learn in kindergarten and spend the next thirty years honing to perfection, their faces flushing under their tans. Taureau ducked his big head down between his shoulders.

'Am I likely to find him in there?' Laurel nodded toward the bar's front door as it screeched back on its hinges to let out an elderly couple and a wave of noise.

'Yeah, you'll find him here,' Taureau said. 'Center stage.'

'Thank you.'

The smoking reform movement had yet to make inroads in south Louisiana. The instant Laurel stepped into the bar, she had to blink to keep her eyes from stinging. A blue haze hung over the crowd. The scent of burning tobacco mingled with sweat and cheap perfume, barley and boiled crawfish. The lighting was dim, and the place was crowded. Waitresses wound their way through the mob with trays of beers and platters of food. Patrons sat shoulder to shoulder at round tables and overflowing booths, laughing, talking, stuffing themselves.

Laurel instantly felt alone, isolated, as if she were surrounded by an invisible force field. She had been brought up in a socially sterile environment, with proper teas and soirees and cotillions. The Leightons didn't lower themselves to having good common fun, and after her father had died and Vivian had remarried, Laurel and Savannah had become Leightons – never mind that Ross Leighton had never bothered to formally adopt them.

Caught off guard for an instant, she felt the old bitterness hit her by surprise and dig its teeth in deep. But it was shoved aside by newer unpleasant feelings as her strongest misgivings about coming here surfaced and threatened to swamp her – not the fear of no one's knowing her, but the fear of *everyone's* knowing her. The fear of everyone's recognizing her and knowing why she had come back to Bayou Breaux, knowing she had failed horribly and utterly . . . Her breath froze in her lungs as she waited for heads to start turning.

A waitress on her way back to the bar bumped into her, flashing a smile of apology and reaching a hand out to pat her arm. 'Sorry, miss.'

'I'm looking for Jack Boudreaux,' Laurel shouted, lifting her eyebrows in question.

The waitress, a curvy young thing with a mop of dark curls and an infectious grin, swung her empty serving tray toward the stage and the man who sat at the keyboard of an old upright piano that looked as though someone had gone after it with a length of chain.

'There he is, in the flesh, honey. The devil himself,' she said, her voice rising and falling in a distinctly Cajun rhythm. 'You wanna join the fan club or somethin'?'

'No, I want restitution,' Laurel said, but the waitress was already gone, answering a call of 'Hey, Annie' from Taureau and his cohorts, who had commandeered a table across the room.

Homing in on the man she had come to confront, Laurel moved toward the small stage. The band had slowed things down with a waltz that was being sung by a small, wiry man with a Vandyke and a Panama hat. A vicious scar slashed across his face, from his right eyebrow across his cheek, misshaping the end of his hooked nose and disappearing into the cover of his mustache. But if his face wasn't beautiful, his voice certainly was. He clutched his hands to his heart and wailed out the lyrics in Cajun French as dancers young and old moved gracefully around the small dance floor.

To his right Jack Boudreaux stood with one knee on the piano bench, head bent in concentration as he pumped a small Evangeline accordion between his hands.

From this vantage point Boudreaux looked tall and rangy, with strong shoulders and slim hips. The expression on his lean, tanned face was stern, almost brooding. His eyes were squeezed shut as if sight might somehow hinder his interpretation of the music. Straight black hair tumbled down over his forehead, looking damp and silky under the stage lights.

Laurel skirted the dancers and wedged herself up against the front of the stage. She thought she could feel the inner pain he drew on as he played. Silly. Easily half of Cajun music was about some man losing his girl. This particular waltz – 'Valse de Grand Mèche' – was an old one, a song about an unlucky woman lost in the marsh, her lover singing of how they will be together again after death. It wasn't Jack Boudreaux's personal life story, and it wouldn't have concerned her if it had been. She had come to see the man about his dog.

Jack let his fingers slow on the keys of the accordion as he played the final set of triplets and hit the last chord. Leonce belted out the final note with gusto, and the dancers' feet slowed to a shuffle. As the music faded away and the crowd clapped, he sank down on the piano bench, feeling drained. The song brought too many memories. That he was feeling anything at all told him one thing – he needed another drink.

He reached for the glass on the piano without looking and tossed back the last of a long, tall whiskey, sucking in a breath as the liquid fire hit his belly. It seared through him in a single wave of heat, leaving a pleasant numbness in its wake.

Slowly his lashes drifted open and his surroundings came once more into focus. His gaze hit on a huge pair of midnight blue eyes staring up at him from behind the lenses of man-size horn-rimmed glasses. The face of an angel hid behind those ridiculous glasses – heart-shaped, delicate, with a slim retroussé nose and a mouth that begged to be kissed. Jack felt his spirits pull out of their nosedive and wing upward as she spoke his name.

She wasn't the usual type of woman who pressed herself up against the stage and tried to snag his attention. For one thing, there was no show of cleavage. It was difficult to tell if she was capable of producing cleavage at all. The blue cotton sundress she wore hung on her like a sack. But imagination was one thing Jack Boudreaux had never been short on. Scruples, yes; morals, yes; imagination he had in abundance, and he used it now to make a quick mental picture of the woman standing below him. Petite, slim, sleek, like a little cat. He preferred his women to have a little more curve to them, but there was always something to be said for variety.

He leaned down toward her as he set the accordion on the floor and unfurled the grin that had knocked more than a few ladies off their feet. 'Hey, sugar, where you been all my life?'

Laurel felt as if he had turned a thousand watts of pure electricity on her.

He looked wicked. He looked wild. He looked as though he could see right through her clothes, and she had the wildest urge to cross her arms over her chest, just in case. Annoyed with herself, she snapped her jaw shut and cleared her throat.

'I've been off learning to avoid Lotharios who use trite come-on lines,' she said, her arms folding over her chest in spite of her resolve to keep them at her sides.

414

Jack's smile never wavered. He liked a girl with sass. 'What, are you a nun or somethin', angel?'

'No, I'm an attorney. I need to speak to you about your dog.'

Someone in the crowd raised a voice in protest against the absence of music. 'Hey, Jack, can you quit makin' love long enough to sing somethin'?'

Jack raised his head and laughed, leaning toward the microphone that was attached to the piano. 'This ain't love, Dede, it's a lawyer!' As the first wave of laughter died down, he said, 'Y'all know what lawyers use for birth control, doncha?' He waited a beat, then his voice dropped a husky notch as he delivered the punch line. 'Their personalities.'

Laurel felt a flush of anger rise up her neck and creep up her cheeks as the crowd hooted and laughed. 'I wouldn't make jokes if I were you, Mr. Boudreaux,' she said, trying to keep her voice at a pitch only he could hear. 'Your hound managed to do a considerable amount of damage to my aunt's garden today.'

Jack shot her a look of practiced innocence. 'What hound?'

'*Your* hound.'

He shrugged eloquently. 'I don't have a hound.'

'Mr. Boudreaux—'

'Call me Jack, angel,' he drawled as he leaned down toward her again, bracing his forearm on his thigh.

They were nearly at eye level, and Laurel felt herself leaning toward him, as if he were drawing her toward him by some personal magnetic force. His gaze slid down to her mouth and lingered there, shockingly frank in its appraisal.

'Mr. Boudreaux,' she said in exasperation. 'Is there somewhere we can discuss this more privately?'

He bobbed his eyebrows above dark, sparkling devil's eyes. 'Is my place private enough for you?'

'Mr. Boudreaux . . .'

'Here's another trite line for you, angel,' Jack whispered, bending a little closer, holding her gaze with his as he lifted a finger and pushed her glasses up on her nose. 'You're pretty when you're pissed off.'

His voice was low and smoky, Cajun-spiced and tainted with the aroma of whiskey.

Drawing in a slow, deep breath to steady herself, she tilted her chin up and tried again. 'Mr. Boudreaux—'

He shot her a look as he moved toward the microphone once again. 'Lighten up, angel. *Laissez les bon temps rouler.*'

The mike picked up his last sentence, and the crowd cheered. Jack gave a smoky laugh. 'Are we havin' fun yet?'

A chorus of hoots and hollers rose to the rafters. He fixed a long, hot look on the petite tigress glaring up at him from the edge of the stage and murmured, 'This one's for you, angel.'

His fingers stretched over the keys of the battered old piano, and he pounded out the opening notes of 'Great Balls of Fire.' The crowd went wild. Before the first line was out of his mouth, there were fifty people on the dance floor. They twirled and bounced around Laurel like a scene from *American Bandstand*, doing the jitterbug as if it had never gone out of style. But her attention was riveted on the singer. Not so much by choice as by compulsion. She was caught in the beam of that intense, dark gaze, held captive by it, mesmerized. He leaned over the keyboard, his hands moving across it, his mouth nearly kissing the microphone as his smoky voice sang out the lyrics with enthusiasm, but all the time his eyes were locked on her. The experience was strangely seductive, strangely intimate. Wholly unnerving.

She stared right back at him, refusing to be seduced or intimidated. Refusing to admit to either, at any rate. He grinned, as if amused by her spunk, and broke off the eye contact as he hit the bridge of the song and turned his full attention to the piano and the frantic pace of the music.

He pounded out the notes, his fingers flying up and down the keyboard expertly. All the intensity he had leveled at her in his gaze was channeled into his playing. The shock of black hair bounced over his forehead, shining almost blue under the lights. Sweat gleamed on his skin, streamed down the side of his face. His faded blue chambray shirt stuck to him in dark, damp patches. The sleeves were rolled back, revealing strong forearms dusted with black hair, muscles bunching and flexing as he slammed out the boogie-woogie piece with a skill and wild physical energy rivaling that of Jerry Lee Lewis himself.

Making music this way looked to be hard work physically and emotionally. As if he were in the throes of exorcism, the notes tore out of him, elemental, rough, sexy, almost frightening in intensity. He dragged his thumb up and down the keyboard, stroking out the final long, frenzied glissando, and fell forward, panting, exhausted as the crowd whistled and howled and screamed for more.

'Whoa—' Jack gulped a breath and forced a grin. '*Bon Dieu*. It's Miller time, folks. Y'all go sit down while I recuperate.'

As a jukebox kicked in, the rest of the band instantly dispersed, abandoning the stage in favor of a table that was holding up gamely under the weight of more than a dozen long-necked beer bottles and an assortment of glasses.

Leonce clapped Jack's shoulder as he passed. 'You're gettin' old, Jack,' he teased. '*Sa c'est honteu, mon ami.*'

Jack sucked another lungful of hot, smoky air and swatted at his friend. 'Fuck you, *'tit boule.*'

'No need.' Leonce grinned, hooking a thumb in the direction of the dance floor. 'You got one waitin' on you.'

Jack raised his head and shot a sideways look at the edge of the stage. She was still standing there, his little lawyer pest, looking expectant and unimpressed with him. Trouble – that's what she looked like. And not the kind he usually dove into headfirst, either. A lawyer. *Bon Dieu*, he thought he'd seen the last of that lot.

'You want a drink, sugar?' he asked as he hopped down off the stage.

'No,' Laurel said, automatically taking a half step back and chastising herself for it. This man was the kind who would sense a weakness and exploit it. She could feel it, could see it in the way his dark gaze seemed to catch everything despite the fact that he had been drinking. She drew deep of the stale, hot air and squared her shoulders. 'What I want is to speak with you privately about the damage done by your dog.'

His mouth curved. 'I don't have a dog.'

He turned and sauntered away from her, his walk naturally cocky. Laurel watched him, astounded by his lack of manners, infuriated by his dismissal of her.

He didn't glance back at her, but continued on his merry way, winding gracefully through the throng, stealing a bottle of beer off Annie's serving tray as he went. The waitress gave an indignant shout, saw it was Jack, and melted as he treated her to a wicked grin. Laurel shook her head in a combination of amazement and disbelief and wondered how many times he had gotten away with raiding the cookie jar as a boy. Probably more times than his poor mother could count. He stepped through a side door, and she followed him out.

Night had fallen completely, bringing on the mercury vapor lights that loomed over the parking lot and cloaking the bayou beyond in shades of black. The noise of the bar faded, competing out here with a chorus of frog song and the hum of traffic rolling past out on the street. The air was fresh with the scents of spring in bloom – jasmine and wisteria and honeysuckle and the ripe, vaguely rank aroma of the bayou. Somewhere down the way, where shabby little houses with thin lawns lined the bank, a woman called for Paulie to come in. A screen door slammed. A dog barked.

The hound leaped out at Laurel from between a pair of parked pickup trucks and howled at her, startling her to a skidding halt on the crushed shell of the parking lot. She slammed a hand to her heart and bit back a curse as the big dog bounded away, tail wagging.

'That dog is an absolute menace,' she complained.

'Don' look at me, sugar.'

He was leaning back against the fender of a disreputable-looking Jeep, elbows on the hood, bottle of Dixie dangling from the fingers of his left hand.

Laurel planted herself in front of him and crossed her arms, holding her silence as if it might force a confession out of him. He simply stared back, his eyes glittering in the eerie silvery light that fell down on him from above. It cast his features in stark relief – a high, wide forehead, sardonically arched brows, an aquiline nose that looked as if it might have been broken once or twice in his thirty-some years.

His mouth was set in sterner lines again above a strong, stubborn-looking chin that sported an inch-long diagonal scar. He looked tough and dangerous suddenly, and the transformation from the laughing, affable, wicked-grinned devil he'd been inside sent a shiver of apprehension down Laurel's back. He looked like a streetwise, predatory male, and she couldn't help second-guessing her judgment in following him out here. Then he smiled, teeth flashing bright in the gloom, dimples cutting into his cheeks, and the world tilted yet again beneath her feet.

'I have it on good authority that hound belongs to you, Mr. Boudreaux.' She dove into the argument, eager for the familiar ground of a good fight. She didn't like being caught off balance, and Jack Boudreaux seemed to be a master at throwing her.

He wagged a finger at her, tilting his head, a grin still teasing the corners of his mouth. 'Jack. Call me Jack.'

'Mr.—'

'Jack.' His gaze held hers fast. He looked lazy and apathetic leaning back against the Jeep, but a thread of insistence had woven its way into the hoarse, smoky texture of his voice.

He was distracting her, but more than that, he was trying to do something she didn't want – put the conversation on a more personal level.

He shifted his weight forward, suddenly invading her personal space, and she had to fight to keep from jumping back as her tension level rose into the red zone. She gulped down her instinctive fear and tilted her chin up to look him in the eye.

'I don't even know your name, *'tite ange,'* he murmured.

'Laurel Chandler,' she answered, breathless and hating it. Her nerves gave a warning tremor as control of the situation seemed to slip a little further out of her grasp.

'Laurel,' he said softly, trying out the sound of it, the feel of it on his tongue. 'Pretty name. Pretty lady.' He grinned as something like apprehension flashed in her wide eyes. 'Did you think I wouldn't notice?'

She swallowed hard, leaning all her weight back on her heels. 'I – I'm sure I don't know what you mean.'

'Liar,' he charged mildly.

With his free hand he reached up and slid her glasses off, dragging them down her nose an inch at a time. When they were free, he turned them over and nibbled on the earpiece absently as he studied her in the pale white light.

Her bone structure was lovely, delicate, feminine, her features equally so, her skin as flawless as fresh cream. But she wore no makeup, no jewelry, nothing to enhance or draw the eye. Her thick, dark hair had been shorn just above her shoulders and looked as though she gave no thought to it at all, tucking it behind her ears, sweeping it carelessly back from her face.

Laurel Chandler. The name stirred around through the soft haze of liquor in his brain, sparking recognition. Chandler. Lawyer. The light bulb clicked on. Local deb. Daughter of a good family. Had been a prosecuting attorney up in Georgia someplace until her career went ballistic. Rumors had abounded around Bayou Breaux. She'd blown a case. There'd been a scandal. Jack had listened with one ear, automatically eavesdropping the way every writer did, always on the alert for a snatch of dialogue or a juicy tidbit that could work itself into a plot.

'What are you wearing these for?' he asked, lifting the glasses.

'To see with,' Laurel snapped, snatching them out of his hand. She really needed them only to read, but he didn't have to know that.

'So you can see, or so the rest of us can't see you?'

She gave a half laugh of impatience, shifting position in a way that put another inch of space between them. 'This conversation is pointless,' she declared as her nerves stretched a little tighter.

He had struck far too close to the truth with his seemingly offhand remark. He appeared to be half drunk and completely self-absorbed, but Laurel had the sudden uncomfortable feeling that there might be more to Jack Boudreaux than met the eye. A cunning intelligence beneath the lazy facade. A sharp mind behind the satyr's grin.

'Oh, I agree. Absolutely,' he drawled, shuffling his feet, inching his way into her space again. His voice dropped a husky, seductive note as he leaned down close enough so his breath caressed her cheek. 'So let's go to my place and do something more . . . satisfying.'

'What about the band?' Laurel asked inanely, trembling slightly as the heat from his body drifted over her skin. She held her ground and caught a breath in her throat as he lifted a hand to tuck a strand of hair behind her ear.

He chuckled low in his throat. 'I'm not into sharing.'

'That's not what I meant.'

'They can play just fine without me.'

'I hope the same can be said for you,' Laurel said dryly. She crossed her arms again, drawing her composure around her like a queen's cloak. 'I'm not going anywhere with you, and the only satisfaction I intend to get is restitution for the damage your dog caused.'

He dropped back against the Jeep in a negligent pose once more and took a long pull on his beer, his eyes never leaving hers. He wiped his mouth with the back of his hand. 'I don't have a dog.'

As if on cue, the hound jumped up into the driver's seat of the open Jeep and looked at them both, ears perked with interest as he listened to them argue culpability for his crimes.

'A number of people have identified this as your hound,' Laurel said, swinging an arm in the direction of the culprit.

'That don' make him mine, sugar,' Jack countered.

'No less than four people have named you as the owner.'

He arched a brow. 'Do I have a license for this dog? Can you produce ownership papers?'

'Of course not—'

'Then all you have are unsubstantiated rumors, Miz Chandler. Hearsay. You and I both know that'll stand up in a court of law about as good as a dead man's dick.'

Laurel drew in a deep breath through her nostrils, trying in vain to stem the rising tide of frustration. She should have been able to cut this man off at the knees and send him crawling to Aunt Caroline's house to apologize. He was nothing but a liquored-up piano player at Frenchie's Landing, for Christ's sake, and she couldn't manage to best him. The anger she had been directing at Jack started turning back her way.

'What'd ol' Huey do, anyhow, that's got you so worked up, angel?'

'Huey?' She pounced on the opening with the ferocity of a starving cat on a mouse. 'You called him by name!' she charged, pointing an accusatory finger at Jack, taking an aggressive step forward. 'You named him!'

He scowled. 'It's short for Hey You.'

'But the fact remains—'

'Fact my ass,' Jack returned. 'I can call you by name too, *'tite chatte.* That don' make you mine.' Grinning again, he leaned ahead and caught her chin in his right hand, boldly stroking the pad of his thumb across the lush swell of her lower lip. 'Does it, Laurel?' he murmured suggestively, dipping his head down, his mouth homing in on hers.

Laurel jerked back from him, batting his hand away. Her hold on her control, slippery and tenuous at best these days, slipped a little further. She felt as if she were hanging on to it by the ragged, bitten-down remains of her fingernails and it was still pulling away. She had come here for justice, but she wasn't getting any. Jack Boudreaux was jerking her around effortlessly. Playing with her, mocking her, propositioning her. God, was she so ineffectual, such a failure—

'You didn't do your job, Ms. Chandler. . . . You blew it. . . . Charges will be dismissed. . . .'

'Come on, sugar, prove your case,' Jack challenged. He took another pull on his beer. *Dieu,* he was actually enjoying this little sparring match. He was rusty, out of practice. How long had it been since he had argued a case? Two years? Three? His time away from corporate law ran together in a blur of months. It seemed like a lifetime. He would have thought he had lost his taste for it, but the old skills were still there.

Sharks don't lose their instincts, he reminded himself, bitterness creeping in to taint his enjoyment of the fight.

'It – it's common knowledge that's your dog, Mr. Boudreaux,' Laurel stammered, fighting to talk around the knot hardening in her throat. She didn't hold eye contact with him, but tried to focus instead on the hound, which was tilting his head and staring at her quizzically with his mismatched eyes. 'Y-You should be man enough to t-take responsibility for it.'

'Ah, me,' Jack said, chuckling cynically. 'I don' take responsibility, angel. Ask anyone.'

Laurel barely heard him, her attention focusing almost completely inward, everything else becoming vague and peripheral. A shudder of tension rattled through her, stronger than its precursor. She tried to steel herself against it and failed.

Failed.

'You didn't do your job, Ms. Chandler. . . . Charges will be dismissed. . . .'

She hadn't proven her case. Couldn't make the charges stick on something so simple and stupid as a case of canine vandalism. Failed. Again. *Worthless, weak . . .* She spat the words at herself as a wave of helplessness surged through her.

Her lungs seemed suddenly incapable of taking in air. She tried to swallow a mouthful of oxygen and then another as her legs began to shake. Panic clawed its way up the back of her throat. She pressed a hand to her mouth and blinked furiously at the tears that pooled and swirled in her eyes, blurring her view of the hound.

Jack started to say something, but cut himself off, beer bottle halfway to his lips. He stared at Laurel as she transformed before his eyes. The bright-eyed tigress on a mission was gone as abruptly as if she had never existed, leaving instead a woman on the verge of tears, on the brink of some horrible inner precipice.

'Hey, sugar,' he said gently, straightening away from the Jeep. 'Hey, don' cry,' he murmured, shifting uncomfortably from foot to foot, casting anxious glances around the parking lot.

Rumor had it she'd been in some posh clinic in North Carolina. The word 'breakdown' had been bandied all over town. Jesus, he didn't need this, didn't want this. He'd already proven once in his life that he couldn't handle it, was the last person anyone should count on to handle it. *I don' take responsibility. . . .* That truth hung on him like chain mail. He leaned toward Frenchie's, wanting to bolt, but his feet stayed rooted to the spot, nailed down by guilt.

The side door slammed, and Leonce's voice came across the dark expanse of parking lot in staccato French. 'Hey, Jack, *viens ici! Dépêche-toi! Allons jouer la musique, pas les femmes!*'

Jack cast a longing glance at his friend up on the gallery, then back at Laurel Chandler. 'In a minute!' he called, his gaze lingering on the woman, turmoil twisting in his belly like a snake. He didn't credit himself with having much of a conscience, but what there was made him take a step toward Laurel. 'Look, sugar—'

Laurel twisted back and away from the hand he held out to her, mortified that this man she knew little and respected less was witnessing this – this weakness. God, she wanted to have at least some small scrap of pride to cling to, but that, too, was tearing out of her grasp.

'I never should have come here,' she mumbled, not entirely sure whether she meant Frenchie's specifically or Bayou Breaux in general. She stumbled back another step as Jack Boudreaux reached for her arm again, his face set in lines of concern and apprehension, then she whirled and ran out of the parking lot and into the night.

Jack stood flat-footed, watching in astonishment as she disappeared in the heavy shadows beneath a stand of moss-draped live oak at the bayou's edge. Panic, he thought. That was what he had seen in her eyes. Panic and despair and a strong aversion to having him see either. What a little bundle of contradictions she was, he thought as he dug a cigarette out of his shirt pocket and dangled it from his lip. Strength and fire and fragility.

'What'd you do, *mon ami*?' Leonce shuffled up, tugging off his Panama hat and wiping the sweat from his balding pate with his forearm. 'You scare her off with that big horse cock of yours?'

Jack scowled, his gaze still on the dark bank, his mind still puzzling over Laurel Chandler. 'Shut up, *tcheue poule.*'

'Don' let it get you down,' Leonce said, chuckling at his own little pun. He settled his hat back in place, and his fingers drifted down to rub absently at the scar that ravaged his cheek. 'Women are easy to come by.'

And hard to shake – that was their usual line. Not Laurel Chandler. She had cut and run. Even as his brain turned the puzzle over and around trying to shake loose an answer, Jack shrugged it off. His instincts told him Laurel Chandler would be nothing but trouble when all he really wanted from life was to pass a good time.

'Yeah,' he drawled, turning back toward Frenchie's with his buddy. 'Let's go inside. I need to find me a cold beer and hot date.'

3

'*Laurel, help us! Laurel, please! Please! Please . . . please . . .*'

She'd had the dream a hundred times. It played through her mind like a videotape over and over, wearing on her, tearing at her conscience, ripping at her heart. Always the voices were the worst part of it. The voices of the children, frantic, begging, pleading. The qualities in those voices touched nerves, set off automatic physiological reactions. Her pulse jumped, her breath came in short, shallow, unsatisfying gasps. Adrenaline and frustration pumped through her in equal amounts.

Dr. Pritchard had attempted to teach her to recognize those signals and defuse them. Theoretically, she should have been able to stop the dream and all the horrible feelings it unleashed, but she never could. She just lay there feeling enraged and panic-stricken and helpless, watching the drama unfold in her subconscious to play out to its inevitable end, unable to awaken, unable to stop it, unable to change the course of events that caused it. Weak, impotent, inadequate, incapable.

'*The charges are being dropped, Ms. Chandler, for lack of sufficient evidence.*'

Here she always tried to swallow and couldn't. A Freudian thing, she supposed. She couldn't choke down the attorney general's decision any more than she could have chewed up and swallowed the *Congressional Record*. Or perhaps it was the burden of guilt that tightened around her throat, threatening to choke her. She had failed to prove her case. She had failed, and the children would pay the consequences.

'*Help us, Laurel! Please! Please . . . please . . .*'

She thrashed against the bed, against the imagined bonds of her own incompetence. She could see the three key children behind the attorney general, their faces pale ovals dominated by dark eyes filled with torment and dying hope. They had depended on her, trusted her. She had promised help, guaranteed justice.

'*. . . lack of sufficient evidence, Ms. Chandler . . .*'

Quentin Parker loomed larger in her mind's eye, turning dark and menacing, metamorphosing into a hideous monster as the children's faces drifted further and further away. Paler and paler they grew as they floated back, their eyes growing wider and wider with fear.

'*Help us, Laurel! Please . . . please . . . please . . .*'

'. . . *will be returned to their parents* . . .'

'No,' she whimpered, tossing, turning, kicking at the bedclothes.

'*Help us, Laurel!*'

'. . . *returned to the custody of* . . .'

'No!' She thumped her fists against the mattress over and over, pounding in time with her denial. 'No! No!'

'. . . *a formal apology will be issued* . . .'

'NO!!'

Laurel pitched herself upright as the door slammed shut on her subconscious. The air heaved in and out of her lungs in tremendous hot, ragged gasps. Her nightgown was plastered to her skin with cold sweat. She opened her eyes wide and forced herself to take in her surroundings, busying her brain by cataloging every item she saw – the foot of the half-tester bed, the enormous French Colonial armoire looming darkly against the wall, the marble-topped walnut commode with porcelain pitcher and bowl displaying an arrangement of spring blooms. Normal things, familiar things illuminated by the pale, now-you-see-it-now-you-don't moon shining in through the French doors. She wasn't in Georgia any longer. This wasn't Scott County. This was Belle Rivière, Aunt Caroline's house in Bayou Breaux. The place she had run to.

Coward.

She ground her teeth against the word and rubbed her hands hard over her face, then plowed her fingers back through her disheveled mess of sweat-damp hair.

'Laurel?'

The bedroom door opened, and Savannah stuck her head in. Just like old times, Laurel thought, when they were girls and Savannah had assumed the role of mother Vivian Chandler had been loath to play unless she had an audience. They were thirty and thirty-two now, she and Savannah, but they had fallen back into that pattern as easily as slipping on comfortable old shoes.

It seemed odd, considering it was Laurel who had grown up to take charge of her life, she who had struck out and made a career and a name for herself. Savannah had stayed behind, never quite breaking away from the past or the place, never able to rise above the events that had shaped them.

'Hey, Baby,' Savannah murmured as she crossed the room. The moon ducked behind a cloud, casting her in shadow, giving Laurel only impressions of a rumpled cloud of long dark hair, a pale silk robe carelessly belted, long shapely legs and bare feet. 'You okay?'

Laurel wrapped her arms around her knees, sniffed, and forced a smile as her sister settled on the edge of the bed. 'I'm fine.'

Savannah flipped on the bedside lamp, and they both blinked against the light. 'Liar,' she grumbled, frowning as she looked her over. 'I heard you tossing and turning. Another nightmare?'

'I didn't think you were coming home tonight,' Laurel said, railroading the conversation onto other tracks. She tossed and turned every night, had nightmares every night. That had become the norm for her, nothing worth talking about.

Savannah's lush mouth settled into a pout. 'Never mind about that,' she said flatly. 'Things got over quicker than I thought.'

'Where were you?' Somewhere with smoke and liquor. Laurel could smell the combination over and above a generous application of Obsession. Smoke and liquor and something wilder, earthier, like sex or the swamp.

'It doesn't matter.' Savannah shook off the topic with a toss of her head. 'Lord Almighty, look at you. You've sweat that gown clean through. I'll get you another.'

Laurel stayed where she was as her sister went to the cherry highboy and began pulling open drawers in search of lingerie. She probably should have insisted on taking care of herself, but the truth of the matter was she didn't feel up to it. She was exhausted from lack of sleep and from her encounter with Jack Boudreaux. Besides, wasn't this part of what she had come home for? To be comforted and cared for by familiar faces?

Much as she hated to admit it, she was still feeling physically weak, as well as emotionally battered. Coming unhinged was hard on a person, she reflected with a grimace. But as Dr. Pritchard had been so fond of pointing out, her physical decline had begun long before her breakdown. All during what the press had labeled simply 'The Scott County Case' she had been too focused, too obsessed to think of trivial things like food, sleep, exercise. Her mind had been consumed with charges of sexual abuse, the pursuit of evidence, the protection of children, the upholding of justice.

Savannah's disgruntled voice pulled her back from the edge of the memory. 'Crimeny, Baby, don't you own a nightgown that doesn't look like something Mama Pearl made for the poor out of flour sacks?'

She came back to the bed holding an oversize white cotton T-shirt at arm's length, as if she were afraid its plainness might rub off on her. Savannah's taste in sleep-wear ran to Frederick's of Hollywood. Beneath the gaping front of her short, champagne silk robe, Laurel caught a glimpse of full breasts straining the confines of a scrap of coffee-colored lace. With a body that was all lush curves, a body that fairly shouted its sexuality, Savannah was made for silk and lace. Laurel's femininity was subtle, understated – a fact she had no desire to change.

'Nobody sees it but me,' she said. She stripped her damp gown off over her head and slipped the new one on, enjoying the feel of the cool, dry fabric as it settled against her sticky skin.

An indignant sniff was Savannah's reply. She settled herself on the edge of the bed once again, legs crossed, her expression fierce. 'If I ever cross paths with Wesley Brooks, I swear I'll kill him. Imagine him leaving you—'

'Don't.' Laurel softened the order with a tentative smile and reached out to touch the hand Savannah had knotted into a tight fist on the white coverlet. 'I don't want to imagine it; I lived it. Besides, it wasn't Wes's fault our marriage didn't work out.'

'Wasn't his—!'

Laurel cut off what was sure to be another tirade defaming her ex-husband. Wesley claimed he hadn't left her, but that she had driven him away, that she had crushed their young marriage with the weight of her obsession for The Case. That was probably true. Laurel didn't try to deny it. Savannah automatically took her side, ever ready to battle for her baby sister, but Laurel knew she wasn't deserving of support in this argument. She didn't have a case against Wes, despite Savannah's vehemence. All she had was a solid chunk of remorse and guilt, but that can of worms didn't need to be opened tonight.

'Hush,' she said, squeezing Savannah's fingers. 'I appreciate the support, Sister. Really, I do. But don't let's fight about it tonight. It's late.'

Savannah's expression softened, and she opened her hand and twined her fingers with Laurel's. 'You need to get some sleep.' She reached up with her other hand and with a forefinger traced one of the dark crescents stress and extreme fatigue had painted beneath Laurel's eyes.

'What about you?' Laurel asked. 'Don't you need sleep, too?'

'Me?' She made an attempt at a wry smile, but it came nowhere near her eyes, where old ghosts haunted the cool blue depths. 'I'm a creature of the night. Didn't you know that?'

Laurel said nothing as old pain surfaced like oil inside her to mingle with the new.

With a sigh Savannah rose, tugged down the hem of her robe with one hand and with the other pushed a lock of wild long hair behind her ear.

'I mean it, you know,' she murmured. 'If Wesley Brooks showed up here now, I'd cut his fucking balls off and stuff 'em in his ears.' She cocked her fingers like pistols and pointed them at Laurel. 'And *then* I'd get mean.'

Laurel managed a weak chuckle. God, how Vivian would blanche to hear language like that from one of her daughters. Daughters she had raised to be debutantes. Sparkling, soft-spoken belles who never cursed and nearly swooned in the face of vulgarity. Vivian had expected sorority princesses, but God knew Savannah would eat dirt and die before she pledged to Chi-O, and she doubtless lay awake nights dreaming up ways to shock the Junior League. Laurel had been too busy to pledge, consumed by her need to get her law degree and throw herself into the task of seeing justice done.

'Would you prosecute me?' Savannah asked as she reached for the lamp switch.

'Be kind of hard to do, seeing how I don't have a job anymore.'

'I'm sorry, Baby.' Savannah clicked off the lamp, plunging the room into moonlight and shadows once again. 'I wasn't thinking. You shouldn't be thinking about it, either. You're home now. Get some sleep.'

Laurel sighed and pushed her overgrown bangs back off her forehead, watching as Savannah made her way to the door with her lazy, naturally seductive gait, her robe shimmering like quicksilver. ''Night, Sister.'

'Sweet dreams.'

She would have settled for no dreams, Laurel thought as she listened to the door latch and her sister's footsteps retreat down the hall. But no dreams meant no sleep. She checked the glowing dial of the old alarm clock on the stand. Three-thirty. She wouldn't sleep again tonight no matter how badly her body needed to. Her mind wouldn't allow the possibility of another rerun of the dream. The knowledge brought a sheen of tears to her eyes. She was so tired – physically tired, emotionally exhausted, tired of feeling out of control.

With that thought came the memory of Jack Boudreaux, and a wave of shame washed over her, leaving goose bumps in its wake. She'd made an ass of herself. If she was lucky, he was too drunk to remember by now, and the next time she saw him she could pretend it never happened.

There wouldn't be a next time if she could help it. She knew instinctively she would never be able to handle a man like Jack Boudreaux. His raw sexuality would overwhelm her. She would never be in control – of him or the relationship or herself.

Not that she was interested in him.

Tossing the coverlet and sheet aside, she swung her legs over the edge of the bed, went to the French doors, and pulled them open. The night was comfortably warm, fragrant with the scents of spring, hinting at the humidity that would descend like a wet woolen blanket in another few weeks. The magnolia tree near the corner of the house still had a few blossoms, creamy waxy white and as big as dinner plates set among the broad, leathery, dark green leaves.

She had climbed that tree as a child, determined to find out what the experience was all about. Tree climbing was forbidden at Beauvoir, the Chandler family plantation that lay just a few miles down the road from Belle Rivière. Tree climbing was not something 'nice girls' did – or so said Vivian. Laurel shook her head at that as she wandered out onto the balcony. *Nice girls. Good families.*

'*Things like that don't happen in good families. . . .*'

'*Help us, Laurel! Help us. . . .*'

The past and the present twined in her mind like vines, twisting, clinging vines attaching their sharp tendrils to her brain. She brought her hands up to clamp over her ears, as if that might shut out the voices that existed only in her head. She bit her lip until she tasted blood, fighting furiously to hold back the tears that gathered in her eyes and congealed into a solid lump in her throat.

'Dammit, dammit, dammit . . .'

She chanted the word like a mantra as she paced the balcony outside her room. Back and forth, back and forth, her small bare feet slapping softly on the old wood. Weakness surged through her like a tide, and she fought the urge to sink down against the wall and sob. The tears choked her. The weakness sapped the stability from her knees and made her curl in on herself like a stooped old woman or a child with a bellyache. The memories bombarded her in a ferocious, relentless cannonade – the children in Scott County, Savannah and their past. *'Nice girls.' 'Good families.' 'Be a good girl, Laurel.' 'Don't say anything, Laurel.' 'Make us all proud, Laurel.' 'Help us, Laurel. . . .'*

No longer able to fight it, she turned and pressed herself against the side of the old house, pressed her face against it, not even caring that the edges of the weathered old bricks bit into her cheek. She clung there like a jumper who had suddenly remembered her terror of heights.

'Oh, God,' she whimpered as the despair cracked through her armor and the tears squeezed past the tightly closed barriers of her eyelids. 'Oh, God, please, please . . .'

'Help us, Laurel! Please, please, please . . .'

Her fingertips, then her knuckles scraped the brick as her fingers folded into fists. She sobbed silently for a moment, releasing a small measure of the inner tension, then swallowed it back, gagging on the need to cry even as she ruthlessly denied herself the privilege. She pushed herself away from the building and turned toward the balcony, swiping the tears from her face with the heels of her hands.

Dammit, she wouldn't do this. She was stronger than this. She had come here to take control of her life again, not to fall apart twice in one night.

Using anger to burn away the other emotions, she turned and slammed her fist against one of the many smooth white columns that supported the roof of the balcony, welcoming the stinging pain that sang up her arm.

'Weak – stupid – coward—'

She spat out the insults, her fury turning inward. She kicked herself mentally for her failures as she kicked the column with her bare foot. The pain burst through her like a jolt of electricity, shorting out everything else, breaking the thread of tension that had been thickening and tightening inside her.

Gulping air, she bent over the balustrade, her fingers wrapping tightly around the black wrought-iron rail. In the wake of the pain flowed calm. Her muscles trembled, relaxing as the calm shimmered through her. Her heartbeat slowed to a steady bass-drum thump, thump, thump.

'Sweet heaven, I have to *do* something,' she muttered. 'I can't go on like this.'

That truth had precipitated her leaving the Ashland Heights Clinic. Her stay there had been peaceful, but not productive. Dr. Pritchard had been more interested in digging up the past than in helping her fix her miserable present. She didn't see the point. What was done was done. She couldn't go back and fix it no matter how badly she wanted to. What she needed to do was push it behind her, rise above it. Move forward. Do something. Do what?

Her job was gone. The fallout from The Case had fallen directly on her. She had been stripped of power, profession, credibility. She had no idea what would become of her, what she would ultimately do or be. Her job had been her identity. Without it she was lost.

'I've got to do something,' she said again, looking around, as if an answer might appear to her somewhere down the dark corridor of the balcony or in the trees or the garden below.

Belle Rivière had been built in the 1830s by a local merchant to placate his homesick young wife who had grown up in the Vieux Carré in New Orleans. The house was designed to emulate the elegant splendor of the French Quarter, right down to the beautiful courtyard garden with its fountain, and brick walls trimmed with lacy black wrought-iron filigree. The garden Laurel had spent two days trying to put to rights only to have Jack Boudreaux's dog – *allegedly* his dog – uproot her efforts. Damn hound.

Damn man.

The garden had been maintained sporadically over the years. Laurel remembered it as a place of marvelous beauty during her childhood when old Antoine Thibodeaux had tended it for Aunt Caroline. As lush and green as Eden, spray billowing from the fountain, elegant statues of Greek women carrying urns of exotic plants. Antoine had long since gone to his eternal rest, and Caroline's latest gardener had long since gone to New Orleans to be a female impersonator on Bourbon Street. Caroline, absorbed in her latest business venture, an antiques shop, hadn't bothered to hire anyone new.

Laurel had seen it as the perfect project for her, physically, psychologically, metaphorically. Clear away the old debris, prune off the dead branches, rejuvenate the soil, plant new with a hopeful eye to the future. Resurrection, rebirth, a fresh start.

She stared down at the mess Huey the Hound had left and heaved a sigh. Young plants torn up by the roots. She knew the feeling . . . .

'Where are you taking Daddy's things, Mama?'

'To the Goodwill in Lafayette,' Vivian Chandler said, not sparing a glance at her ten-year-old daughter.

She stood beside the bed that had been her husband's, smartly dressed

429

in a spring green shift with a strand of pearls at her throat. She looked cool and sophisticated, as always, like a model from out of a fashion magazine, her ash blond hair combed just so, pale pink lipstick on. She propped her perfectly manicured hands on her hips and tapped the toe of one white pump against the rug impatiently as she supervised the proceedings. Tansy Jonas, the latest in a string of flighty young maids, hauled load after load of suits and shirts and slacks out of the closet to be sorted into piles.

'Of course, we'll have to take some of it to the church,' Vivian said absently as she considered the armload of dress shirts weighing down poor Tansy. Tansy wasn't more than fifteen, Laurel reckoned, and thin as a willow sapling. The girl seemed to weave beneath the burden of silk and fine cotton cloth, her black eyes going wider and wider in her round dark face.

'It's expected,' Vivian went on, inspecting the state of collars and cuffs, oblivious to Tansy's discomfort. 'The Chandlers having always been the leading family hereabouts, it's our duty to contribute to the less fortunate in the community. Why, just the other day, Ridilia Montrose was asking me if I hadn't donated Jefferson's things,' she said, frowning prettily. 'As if she thought I wasn't going to. She's got a lot of nerve, and I would have told her so if I weren't a lady. Imagine her looking down on me when everybody in town knows they nearly went bankrupt! And what a shame that would have been, because that daughter of hers has teeth like a mule, and it's going to cost a fortune to fix them.'

She selected a pair of striped shirts, impervious to the pleading look on the maid's face, and tossed them into one of several piles on the bed. 'I told her I just hadn't been up to sorting through Jefferson's things. Why, the mere thought of it had me on the verge of one of my spells. I can see, though, that I can't put it off a second longer, or there'll be tongues wagging all over town. I swear, that Ridilia isn't any better than she has to be.'

Continuing in the same breath, she said, 'Tansy, put the rest of those on the chair.'

'Yas'm,' Tansy murmured with relief, staggering away under the weight of the load.

'I'll sort through your father's things,' Vivian said to Laurel. 'Never mind that it could send me into a tail-spin. I'll donate to the church, but I'll die before I see no-account trash walking around Bayou Breaux in Jefferson's silk suits. They're going to Lafayette, and Ridilia Montrose can go to blazes.'

Laurel scooted off the seat of the blue velvet armchair before the maid could bury her alive. She didn't like this at all. Seeing all of Daddy's things pulled out of his neat closet and strewn around his room caused a hollow, churning feeling in her tummy. She had played in his closet more times than she could count, sneaking in there with her Barbie dolls, pretending his big shoes were cars or boats or space ships. It had been her secret place for when she wanted to be all alone. It smelled of leather and cedar and Daddy. She had sat cross-legged on the floor and felt the legs of his neatly hung pants brush across the top of her head, and pretended they were vines and that she was inside a secret cave in the jungle and that his belts were snakes. Now it was all being torn apart to be given to strangers in another town.

Chewing on a thumbnail, she sidled along the big mahogany bureau, her eyes on her mother. Vivian didn't look bothered at all by what she was doing, unless being cross counted. Laurel didn't think it did. It only meant that her mother would rather have been doing something else, not that this job made her sad. She said it might give her a spell, though, and that was a million times worse than just plain sad. It scared Laurel something terrible when her mother went into one of her blue spells – crying all the time, hardly ever getting out of her nightclothes, shutting herself up in her rooms – the way she had done when Daddy died.

Laurel secretly feared she was going to have the same kind of spells. She had felt that bad when Daddy died. She hadn't wanted to see anybody. And she had cried and cried. She had cried so hard, she thought she might just turn herself inside out the way Daddy had always teased her she would. She and Savannah had cried together. She had slipped into her sister's room through the door in the closet because Mama had told her more than once that she was a big girl now and had to sleep alone. She and Savannah had hid under the covers and cried in their pillows until they almost choked.

Ties came out of the closet next, a whole long rack of them that had hung on the clothes pole. The ties drooped down off the rack, nearly to Tansy's feet. The maid struggled to hold it up high, skinny arms over her head so as to give her employer a good look at the strips of silk. Laurel spotted the blue one with the big bug-eyed bass painted on it and almost giggled as she remembered her father wearing it. His lucky poker playing tie, he had always said with a wink and a grin. Vivian snatched it off the rack and threw it on the Lafayette pile.

'But Mama,' Laurel said, her heart sinking abruptly, 'that was Daddy's favorite!'

'I've always hated the sight of that tie,' Vivian grumbled, talking more to herself than to Laurel. 'I thought I'd die of embarrassment every time Jefferson put it on. To think of a man in his position going around in a necktie the likes of that!'

Laurel stepped alongside the bed and reached a hand out to brush her fingertips over the painted bass. 'But Mama—'

'Laurel, leave that be,' she snapped. 'Don't you have schoolwork?'

'No, Mama,' she murmured, inching back from the bed, staring longingly after the bass tie as her mother tossed three more on top of it.

'Can't you see I'm busy here?'

431

'Yes, Mama.'

She backed into the corner by the dresser again and pretended to be invisible for a while. She didn't want to be sent to her room. She wanted to be in here with Daddy's things – only she didn't want Mama and dumb old moony-eyed Tansy here rooting through everything.

She wiggled one foot over on its side and back, over and back, over and back, the way Mama always scolded her for on account of it would scuff up her shoes. Laurel didn't care. Mama was too busy throwing out Daddy's things to notice. Laurel wouldn't have cared anyway, because tears were filling up her eyes and she needed something to concentrate on so she wouldn't start to cry and get scolded for that. So she twisted her foot over and back, over and back, and chewed on her thumbnail even though there wasn't much left to chew on.

The fingers of her left hand moved along the top of the bureau, brushing against the edge of Daddy's jewelry case. Because it made her tummy hurt to watch Mama and Tansy, she turned and looked at the heavy wooden box with its fancy inlaid top and shiny brass latch. She stroked her small hand over its smooth surface and thought of Daddy, so big, so strong, always with a smile for her and a stick of Juicy Fruit gum in his pocket.

One big, fat tear teetered over the edge of her eyelashes and rolled down her cheek to splash on the polished bureau. Another followed. She couldn't think of Daddy's being gone forever. She missed him so much already. He was strength and safety and love. He didn't care if she scuffed up her shoes, and he always hugged her when she cried. Laurel couldn't bear the idea of losing him. She didn't want him gone to heaven with the angels the way Reverend Monroe had told her. Maybe that was selfish, and she felt bad about that, but not bad enough to give up her daddy.

Her small fingers fumbled with the latch, and she lifted the lid on the jewelry box. The box was lined with red velvet and filled with man things. Daddy's money clip, the two big chunky rings he never wore, his tie tacks and cuff links and some Indian-head pennies.

Laurel reached in and lifted out the red crawfish tie pin she had given him for Father's Day when she was seven. It wasn't worth much. Savannah had helped her buy it for three dollars at the crawfish festival in Breaux Bridge. But Daddy had smiled when he opened the box, and told her it would be one of his favorites. He had worn it to the father-daughter dinner at school that year, and Laurel had been so happy and proud, she could have burst.

'Laurel,' Vivian snapped, 'what are you into now? Oh, that jewelry box. I'd nearly forgotten.'

She shooed Laurel aside and made a hasty pass through the box, setting aside a pair of diamond cuff links, a signet ring, a diamond tie pin. Then she ordered Tansy to bring a shoe box and dumped the rest of the contents into it. Laurel watched in horror, tears streaming down her cheeks, the crawfish pin sticking her hand as she tightened her fist around it.

Vivian shot her a suspicious look. 'What have you got there?'

Laurel sniffed and tightened her fingers. 'Nothin'.'

'Don't you lie to me, missy,' Vivian said sharply. 'Good little girls don't tell lies. Open your hand.'

Be a good girl, Laurel thought, always be a good girl, or Mama gets cross. She bit her lip to keep from crying as she held out her hand and opened her fist.

Vivian rolled her eyes as she picked up the tie pin, pinching it between thumb and forefinger and holding it up as if it were a live bug. 'Oh, for pity's sake! What do you want with this piece of trash?'

Laurel flinched as if the word had struck her. Daddy hadn't called it trash, even if it was. 'But Mama—'

Her mother turned away from her, dropping the pin in the shoe box Tansy held.

'B-but Mama,' Laurel said, her breath hitching in her throat around a huge lump. 'C-couldn't I keep it j-just 'cause it was D-Daddy's?'

Vivian wheeled on her, her face pinched, eyes narrowed like a snake's. 'Your father is dead and buried,' she said harshly. 'There's no use being sentimental about his things. Do you hear me?'

Laurel backed away from her, feeling sick and hurt and dizzy. Tears spilled down her cheeks, and a hollow ache throbbed inside her heart.

'You're just being a nuisance in here,' Vivian went on, working herself into a fine lather. 'Here I am, doing my best to finish an awful job, a migraine bearing down on me, and pressures like no one knows. We have guests coming for dinner, and you're underfoot . . .'

The rest of what she had to say sounded like nothing to Laurel but blah blah blah. Her ears were pounding, and her head felt as though it might explode if she couldn't start crying hard real soon. Then Savannah was behind her, putting her hands on Laurel's shoulders.

'Come on, Baby,' she whispered, drawing her out the bedroom door. 'We'll go in my room and look at pictures.'

They went to Savannah's room and sat on the rug next to the bed, looking at a photo album full of pictures of Daddy Savannah had stolen from the parlor the day of Daddy's funeral. She kept it under her mattress and had told Tansy if she ever tried to take it out or tell Vivian about it, she would have a voodoo woman put a curse on her that would give her warts all over her face and hands. Tansy left it be and had taken to wearing a dime on a string around her neck to protect her from *gris-gris*.

They sat on the rug and looked at their father in the only way they would ever be able to see him again, and felt alone in all the world, like two little flowers pulled up by the roots.

That night Ross Leighton came to dinner.

Savannah sat with her back to her dressing table, one foot pulled up on the seat of the chair, one arm wrapped around her leg, the other hand toying with the pendant she never took off. Lost in thought, she ran the gold heart back and forth on its fine chain. Through the French doors that led onto the balcony she could just see Laurel leaning against a column down the way. Poor Baby. The Case had taken everything out of her – her pride, her fight, her self-confidence, her independence. Everything that had taken her away from here had been taken away from her, and now she was back. Poor lost lamb, weak and sorely in need of comfort and love. Just like old times. Just like after Daddy died and Vivian had offered as much solace as a jagged piece of granite.

Funny how time had run in a circle. All during their growing-up years Savannah had mothered and nurtured and protected, and Laurel had grown stronger and brighter and burned with ambition, reaching higher and going further, eventually leaving Savannah in the dust. But now she was back, in need of mothering and nurturing again.

She turned and looked at herself in the beveled mirror above her dressing table, taking in the tousled hair, the bee-stung lips she pumped with collagen at regular intervals. Her robe had slipped off one shoulder, baring creamy skin and the thin strap of her chemise. Her breasts were barely contained by the lacy cups, their natural shape augmented by silicone implants she'd had put in years ago in New Orleans. She traced a fingertip across her lower lip, then along the scalloped edge of lace, her nipple twitching at the slight contact, a response that triggered a quick, automatic fluttering between her legs.

Laurel had gone off to Georgia to gain fame and fight for justice. To do the family proud. And Savannah had stayed behind, carving out her reputation as a slut.

Shedding her robe, she crossed the room and lay down on the bed with the elegantly carved, curved headboard. Leaning back against a mountain of satin pillows, she lit a cigarette and blew a lazy stream of smoke up toward the ceiling. Life had come full circle. Laurel was home, and Savannah was being given the chance to be important again, to do something worthwhile. Her baby sister needed her. Life could be turning around for her at last. Now all she needed was for Astor Cooper to die.

4

Jack jerked awake, bolting against the cluttered mahogany desk, throwing his head back away from the black Underwood manual typewriter that had served as pillow for the last – what? hour? two? three? He looked around, blinking against the buttery light that filtered down through the canopy of live oak and through the sheer lace curtains at the window. He rubbed his hands over his lean face and cleared his throat, grimacing at the taste of stale beer coating his mouth. With his fingers he combed back his straight black hair, which was too thick and too long for south Louisiana this time of year.

The old ormolu clock on the bedroom mantel ticked loudly and relentlessly, drawing a narrow glare. Eleven-thirty. The respectable folk of Bayou Breaux had been up and industrious for hours. Jack had no memory of coming home. It might have been midnight. It might have been dawn when he had stumbled across the threshold of the old house the locals called L'Amour. He cast a speculative look at the heavy four-poster bed with its drape of *baire* carelessly stuffed behind the carved headboard. There might have been a woman dozing among the rumpled sheets. He had a vague memory of a woman . . . big blue eyes and an angel's face . . . fire and fragility . . .

There wasn't a woman in his bed, which was just as well. He was in no mood for morning-after rhetoric. His head felt as though someone had smashed it with a mallet.

The last thing he remembered was Leonce's leading him away from Frenchie's. He might have gone anywhere, done anything after that. Pain jabbed his temples like twin ice picks as he tried to remember. Funny, he thought, his mouth twisting at the irony, he drank to forget. Why couldn't he just leave it at that?

'Because you're perverse, Jack,' he mumbled, his voice a smoky rumble, made more hoarse than usual by a night of loud singing in a room where ninety percent of the people were chain smokers.

He pushed himself up out of the creaking old desk chair, his body doing some creaking and groaning of its own after God knew how many hours in a sitting position. He stretched with all the grace of a big lean cat,

435

scratched his flat bare belly, noted that the top button on his faded jeans was undone but left it that way.

The page in the typewriter caught his eye, and he pulled it out and studied it, frowning darkly at the words that must have seemed like gems at the time he had pounded them out.

She tries to scream as she runs, but her lungs are on fire and working like a bellows. Only pathetic yipping sounds issue from her throat, and they are a waste of precious energy. Tears blur her vision, and she tries to blink them back, to swipe them back with her hand, to swallow the knot of them clogging her throat as she runs on through the dense growth.

Moonlight barely filters down through the canopy of trees. The light is surreal, nightmarish. Branches lash at her, cutting her face, her arms. Her toes stub and catch on the roots of the oak and hackberry trees that grow along the soft, damp earth, and she stumbles headlong, twisting her head around to see how near death is behind her.

Too near. Too calm. Too deliberate. Her heart pounds hard enough to burst.

She scrambles backward, trying to get her legs under her. Her hands clutch at roots and dead leaves. Her fingers close on the thick, muscular body of a snake, and she screams as she tries to escape the triangular head and flashing fangs that strike at her. The stench of the swamp fills her head as the copper taste of fear coats her mouth. And death looms nearer. Relentless. Ruthless. Evil. Smiling . . .

Crap. Nothing but crap. With a sound of disgust Jack crumpled the page and hurled it in the general direction of the wastebasket – an old Chinese urn that may well have been worth a small fortune. He didn't know, didn't care. He had stumbled across it in the attic, buried under a decade's worth of discarded, moth-eaten clothing. Apparently it had been there some time, as it was a third full of the dead, decaying, and skeletal remains of mice that had fallen into it over the years and been unable to get out.

Jack owned antiques because the old decrepit house had come with them, not because he was culturally sophisticated or a conspicuous consumer or particularly appreciative of fine things. Material things had become irrelevant to him since Evie's death. His perspective of the world had shifted radically downhill. Another irony. For most of his thirty-five years he had fought tooth and nail to achieve a status where he could own 'things.' Now he was there and no longer gave a damn.

'*Dieu*,' he whispered, shaking his head and wincing at the pain, 'old Blackie must be sittin' in Hell laughin' at that.'

Bon à rien, tu, 'tit souris. Good for nothin', pas de bétises!

The voice came to him out of the past, out of his childhood. A voice from beyond the grave. He flinched at the memory of that voice. A conditioned response, even after all this time. Often enough a slurred line from Blackie Boudreaux had been followed up with a backhand across the mouth.

Jack pulled open the French doors and leaned against the frame, the smooth white paint cool against the bare skin of his shoulder. His eyes drifted shut as he breathed in the sweet green scent of boxwood, the fragrant perfume of magnolia and wisteria and a dozen other blooming plants. And beneath that heady incense lay the dark, insidious aroma of the bayou – a mixture of fertility and decay and fish. The scents, the caress of the hot breeze against his face, the chorus of bird song instantly transported him back in time.

He saw himself at nine, small and skinny, barefoot and dirty-faced, running like a thief from the tarpaper shack that was home. Running from his father, running to escape into the swamp, his bare feet slapping on the worn dirt path.

In the swamp he could be anyone, do anything. There were no boundaries, no standards to fall short of. He could conquer an island, become king of the alligators, be a notorious criminal on the run. On the run for killing his father, which he would have done if he had been bigger and stronger . . .

'Shit,' he muttered, stepping back into the bedroom.

He left the doors open and shuffled toward the bathroom some previous forward-thinking owner of L'Amour had converted from a dressing room back in the twenties. It still 'boasted' the original white porcelain fixtures and tile. Not much of a boast, considering all were dingy with age, cracked, and chipped. Fortunately, Jack's only prerequisite was that they work.

With the flick of a switch the boom box sitting on the back of the old toilet came to life, belting out the bluesy, bouncy Zydeco sound of Zachary Richard – 'Ma Petite Fille Est Gone.' Despite the fact that it jarred his aching head, Jack automatically moved with the beat as he filled the sink with cold water. The music defied stillness with its relentless bass rhythm and hot accordion and guitar licks.

Gulping a big breath, he bent over at the waist and stuck his head in the basin, coming up a minute later cursing in French and shaking himself like a wet dog. He gave himself a long, critical look in the mirror, debating the merits of shaving as water dripped off the end of his aquiline nose. He looked tough and mean in his current state, a look he didn't let many people see. The gang down at Frenchie's knew Jack the Party Animal. Jack with the ready grin. Jack the lady's man. They didn't know this Jack except through his books, and it amazed them that the Jack Boudreaux who was touted by the publishing world as the 'New Master of the Macabre' was *their* Jack.

He sniffed and tipped his head to one side, a wry half smile curving his mouth. '*Pas du tout, mon ami,*' he murmured. '*Pas du tout.*'

As he reached for his toothbrush, the music on the radio was cut short in midchorus.

'This just in,' the deejay said, his usually jovial tone stretched taut and flat by the gravity of the news. 'KJUN news has just learned of another

437

apparent victim of the Bayou Strangler. This morning, at approximately seven o'clock, two fishermen in the Bayou Chene area in St. Martin Parish discovered the body of an unidentified young woman. Though authorities have yet to release a statement, reliable sources on the scene have confirmed the similarities between this death and three others that have occurred in south Louisiana in the past eighteen months. The body of the last victim, Sheryl Lynn Carmouche, of Loreauville, was discovered—'

Jack reached over and hit the tape button. Instantly the frantic fiddle music of Michael Doucet whined through the speakers, snapping the tension, drowning out the grim news. He'd had enough grimness to last him. He had a stock stored up, ready to be called upon and brought down on his head like a ton of bricks any time he wanted. He didn't care to bring in more from outside sources.

Don't get involved. That was his motto. That and the traditional Cajun war cry – *laissez le bon temps rouler*. He didn't want to hear about dead girls from Loreauville. He couldn't give Sheryl Lynn Carmouche her life back. He could only live his own, and he intended to do just that, starting with a big shrimp po'boy and a bottle of something cold down at the Landing.

Sweat trickled between Laurel's breasts as she knelt in the freshly turned earth. It beaded on her forehead, and one drop rolled down toward her nose. She reached up with a dirty gloved hand and wiped it away, leaving a smear of mud.

No one would have spotted her for a once-aggressive attorney – a fact that suited her just fine. She wanted to lose herself in mindless manual labor, thinking of nothing but simple physical tasks like turning soil and planting flowers. She suspected she would appear to have bathed in dirt by the time she finished her work in the courtyard. There were worse things to become immersed in.

She poked at the root of a new azalea bush with a small hand spade, mixing in the special compost Bud Landry at the nursery had sent home with her – his own secret blend of God-knew-what that would grow anything, 'guar-un-teed.'

She spent most of the morning sweeping up yesterday's carnage and supervising the hanging of a new gate at the back of the courtyard. Not pausing for more than a sip of the iced tea Mama Pearl brought out for her, she swept and raked and piled. She then hauled the mess, one load at a time, to the edge of the small open field that lay to the east of Aunt Caroline's property, where she piled all the debris of her first two days' work, and would burn it all before it could become a haven to snakes and rodents.

She made a mental note to call city hall and check to see if she would need a permit. No one in Bayou Breaux had ever been much on that kind of formality, but times changed. She hadn't lived here in a lot of years. For all she knew the place could have been taken over by yuppies on the run from suburban life. Or the Junior League might have decided environmentalism was in vogue – so long as it didn't interfere with their husbands' businesses. Laurel could well imagine her mother leading the crusade against common folk burning brush while Ross Leighton polluted the bayou with chemicals intended to keep his cane crop money-green and safe from insects.

Thoughts of Vivian erased what was left of Laurel's smile. She had been in Bayou Breaux four days now without making a call to Beauvoir. That wouldn't be tolerated much longer. She had no desire to visit her childhood home or the people who resided there, but there was such a thing as family duty, and Vivian was bound to bring it down on Laurel's head like a club if she didn't make the expected pilgrimage soon.

The idea hardly overjoyed her. The fact that she would have to deal with Vivian and Ross, if only to sit at the same table with them for dinner, had been enough to make her reconsider the wisdom of coming back. But the instinctive need for a place that was familiar had overridden her aversion to seeing her mother and stepfather.

The thought of going off someplace on her own, someplace where her anonymity would be absolute, had been too daunting. Go someplace where the only company she would have would be herself? That was company she didn't want to keep just now. She had longed for the reassurance of Caroline Chandler's formidable personality and unconditional love. She had felt a need to see Savannah. She had missed Mama Pearl's fussing and truculence. The occasional encounter with Vivian and Ross seemed small enough penance to pay for the privilege of coming home.

With considerable force of will she shut the door on the topic and focused on other things. Her hands packed the soil around the roots of the azalea bush. The scents of ripe compost and green growth filled her nostrils. Across the courtyard bees were buzzing lazily over a wild tangle of rambling roses and wisteria that clung to the brick wall. A Mozart quintet drifted from the boom box she had left on the gallery of the house.

The heat grew a little thicker. She sweated a little harder. Overhead wispy clouds writhed and curled their way across the blue-sky, scudding northward on a balmy Gulf breeze. The quintet ended, and the news began, signaling the start of the lunch hour.

'Topping the news this hour: the discovery of another apparent victim—'

Laurel jerked her head around as the announcement was cut short. Savannah stood on the gallery, hands on her hips, a pair of square black Ray-Bans shading her eyes. She had pulled her wild hair up into a messy topknot that trailed tendrils along her neck and jawline, and had dressed with her usual flair in a periwinkle spandex miniskirt that hugged the curves of her hips and backside, and a loose white silk tank that managed to show more than it covered. A diamond the size of a pea hung just above the deep shadow of her cleavage, just below the necklace Daddy had given her years ago, and gold bangles rattled at her wrists as she shifted her weight impatiently from one spike heel to the other.

'Baby, what in the world do you think you're doing?'

Laurel pushed her bangs out of her eyes and flashed a smile. 'Gardening! What's it look like?'

She abandoned her tools and straightened up, dusting the loose dirt off the knees of her baggy jeans before heading for the gallery. Mama Pearl would cluck at her like a fat old hen if she tracked it into the house.

'You've spent the entire last two days gardening,' Savannah said, frowning. 'You're going to wear yourself out. Didn't your doctor tell you to relax?'

'Gardening is relaxing, psychologically. I've needed to do something physical,' she said, toeing off her canvas sneakers and stepping up beside her sister. In her heels Savannah towered over her. Laurel had always felt small and mousy in Savannah's presence. Today she felt like a grubby urchin, and the feeling pleased her enormously.

Savannah sniffed and made a comical face of utter disgust. 'Mercy, you smell like a hog pen at high noon! If you needed to do something physical, we could have gone shopping. Your wardrobe is begging for a trip to New Orleans.'

'I have plenty of clothes.'

'Then why don't you wear them?' Savannah asked archly.

Laurel glanced down at the shapeless cotton T-shirt and baggy jeans that camouflaged all details of her body. Most of what she had brought with her was designed for comfort rather than style.

'It wouldn't be very practical for me to do gardening in stiletto heels,' she said dryly, eyeing her sister's outfit. 'And if I had to bend over in that skirt, I'd probably get arrested for mooning the neighbors.'

Savannah looked out across the courtyard to L'Amour, the once-elegant brick house that stood some distance behind Belle Rivière on the bank of the bayou. The corners of her lush mouth flicked upward in wry amusement. 'Baby, you couldn't scandalize that neighbor if you tried.'

'Who's living there? I didn't think anyone would ever buy it, considering the history of the place and the state it was in the last time I saw it.'

L'Amour had been built in the mid-nineteenth century for a notorious paramour by her wealthy, married lover. By all accounts – and there were many versions of the tale – she died by his hand when he discovered she was also involved with a no-account Cajun trapper. Laurel had grown up hearing stories about the place's being haunted. No one had lived there in years.

'Jack Boudreaux,' Savannah answered, her smile turning sexy at the thought of him. 'Writer, rake, rascal, rogue. And when he gets to be old enough, I imagine he'll be a reprobate too. Come along, urchin,' she said, turning for the house. 'Go hose yourself down. I'm taking you out to lunch.'

Jack Boudreaux. Laurel stood on the veranda, staring at L'Amour.

'Baby, you coming?'

Laurel snapped her head around, a blush creeping up her cheeks like a guilty schoolgirl's. Concern tugged at Savannah's brows, and she pushed her sunglasses on top of her head.

'I think you've been out in the sun too long. You should have worn a hat.'

'I'm fine.' Laurel shook her head and dodged her sister's gaze. 'I'll just take a nice cool shower before we go.'

Cold shower indeed, she thought, shaken by her response to the mere mention of a man's name. Lord, it wasn't as though she had enjoyed their encounter. It had unnerved her, and in the end she'd made a fool of herself. Mortification should have been her reaction to the words 'Jack Boudreaux.'

She showered quickly and dressed in a pair of baggy blue checked shorts and a sleeveless blue cotton blouse. Barely ten minutes had passed by the time she trotted down the stairs and turned into the parlor, a room with soft pink walls and the kind of elegant details that put Belle Rivière on a par with the finest old homes in the South.

'. . . poor girl over in St. Martin Parish,' Caroline was saying in a low voice.

She sat in her 'throne,' a beautifully carved Louis XVI man's armchair upholstered in rose damask. Home from her regular Saturday morning at the antiques shop, she had settled in place, kicking off her black-and-white spectator pumps on the burgundy Brussels carpet and propping her tiny feet on a gout stool some woman in the eighteenth century had doubtless gone blind needle-pointing the cover for by lamplight. A tall, sweating glass of iced tea sat on a sterling coaster on a delicate, oval Sheraton table to her left.

'I turned the radio off before she could hear,' Savannah said, her voice also pitched to the level of conspiracy. She sat sideways on the camelback sofa, leaning toward her aunt, her long bare legs crossed.

'Before I could hear what?' Laurel asked carefully.

The two women jerked around, their eyes wide with guilty surprise. Savannah's expression changed to irritation in the blink of an eye.

'It should have taken you at least another twenty minutes to get ready,' she said crossly. 'It would have, if you'd bothered to put on makeup and do something with your hair.'

'It's too hot to bother with makeup,' Laurel said shortly, her temper rising. 'And I don't give a damn about my hair,' she said, though she

441

automatically reached up a hand to tuck a few damp strands behind her ear. 'What is it you didn't want me to hear?'

Aunt and sister exchanged a look that sent her ire up another ten points.

'Just something in the news, darlin',' Caroline said, shifting in her chair. She arranged the full skirt of her black-and-white dotted dress slowly, casually, as if there were nothing more pressing on her mind. 'We didn't see the need to upset you with it, that's all.'

Laurel crossed her arms and planted herself in front of the white marble fireplace. 'I'm not so fragile that I need to be shielded from news reports,' she said, tension quivering in her voice. 'I don't need to be cosseted from the world. I'm not in such a precarious mental state that I'm liable to fly apart at the least little thing.'

Even as she spoke the words, her mouth went dry at the taste of the lie. She *had* come here to be cosseted. Only just last night she had gone to pieces arguing with a no-account drunk about a no-account hound. *Weak.* She shivered, tensing her muscles against the word, the thought.

'Of course we don't think that, Laurel,' Caroline said, rising with the grace and bearing of a queen. Her dark eyes were steady, her expression practical, straight-forward with not a hint of pity. 'You came here to rest and relax. We simply thought those objectives would be more easily attained if you weren't dragged into the torrent of speculation about these murders.'

'Murders?'

'Four now in the last eighteen months. Young women of . . . questionable reputation . . . found strangled out in the swamp in four different parishes – not Partout, thank God.' She gave the information flatly and with as little detail as possible. Now that the cat was out of the bag, she saw no point in dancing around the issue with dainty euphemisms. Certainly her niece had dealt with cases as bad or worse in her tenure as a prosecuting attorney. But neither did she see the need to paint a lurid picture of torture and mutilation, as the newspapers had done. She only hoped the case wouldn't snag Laurel's attention. Coming away from the situation in Scott County, she didn't need to become immersed in another potboiler case of sex and violence.

'All in Acadiana?' Laurel asked, narrowing the possibilities to the parishes that made up Louisiana's French Triangle.

'Yes.'

'Are there any suspects?' The question was as second-nature to her as inquiring after someone's health.

'No.'

'Do they—'

'This doesn't concern you, Baby,' Savannah said sharply. She rose from the sofa and came forward, her pique doing nothing to minimize the sway of her hips. 'You're not a cop, and you're not a prosecutor, and

442

these girls aren't even dying in this jurisdiction, so you can just tune it out. You hear?'

It was on the tip of Laurel's tongue to tell Savannah she wasn't her mother, but she bit the words back. What a ludicrous statement that would have been. Savannah was in many ways more of a mother to her than Vivian had ever been. Besides, Savannah was only trying to protect her.

Hands on her hips, she tamped down her temper, sighing slowly to release some of the steam, feeling drained from what little fury she had shown. 'I don't have any intention of trying to solve a string of murders,' she assured them. 'Y'all know I have my hands full just managing myself these days.'

'Nonsense.' Caroline sniffed, tossing her head. 'You're doing just fine. We want you to concentrate on getting your strength back, that's all. You're a Chandler,' she said, seating herself once more on her throne, arranging her skirt just so. 'You'll be fine if your stubbornness doesn't get the better of you.'

Laurel smiled. This was what she had come to Belle Rivière for – Caroline's unflagging fortitude and ferocious determination. There were those around Bayou Breaux who compared Laurel's aunt to a pit bull – a comparison that pleased Caroline no end. Caroline Chandler was either loved or hated by everyone she knew, and she was enormously proud to inspire such strong reactions, whatever they were.

'We're going to lunch, Aunt Caroline,' Savannah said, slinging the strap of her oversize pocketbook up on her shoulder. The Ray-Bans slid back into place, perched on the bridge of her nose. 'Come along? Mama Pearl's gone to a church meeting.'

'Thank you, no, darlin'.' Caroline sipped her tea and smiled enigmatically. 'I have a luncheon appointment with a friend in Lafayette this afternoon.'

Savannah tipped her glasses down and arched a brow at Laurel, who just shrugged. Caroline's friends in other towns never had names – or genders, for that matter. Because she'd never been married, or even seriously involved with any of the local men, Caroline's sexual preferences had long been a source of speculation among the gossips of Bayou Breaux. And she had always staunchly, stubbornly refused to answer the question one way or the other, saying it was no one's damn business whether she *was* or *wasn't*.

'What do you think?' Savannah asked as they slid into the deep bucket seats of her red Corvette convertible.

'I don't,' Laurel said, automatically buckling her seat belt. Savannah drove the way she lived her life.

Savannah chuckled wickedly as she put the key in the ignition and fired the sports car's engine. 'Oh, come on, Baby. You're telling me

443

you've never tried to picture Aunt Caroline going at it with one of her mysterious friends?'

'Of course not!'

'You're such a prude.' She backed out of the driveway and onto the quiet, tree-lined street that led directly downtown. Belle Rivière was the last house before the road stretched out into farmland and wetlands. But even up the street, where houses stood side by side, the only activity seemed to be the swaying of the Spanish moss that hung from the trees like tattered banners.

'Not wanting to picture my relatives engaging in sex doesn't make me a prude,' Laurel grumbled.

'No,' Savannah said. 'But it sure as hell makes you the odd one in the family, doesn't it?'

She let out the clutch and sent the Corvette flying down the street, engine screaming. Laurel fixed her eyes on the road and fought the urge to bring her hand up to her mouth so she could gnaw at her thumbnail.

Sex was the last thing she wanted to talk about. She would have preferred there were no such thing. It seemed to her the world would have been a much better place without it. It certainly would have been a better world for the children she'd fought for in Scott County, and for countless others. She tried to imagine what Savannah might have achieved with her life had she not become such a sexual creature.

Those thoughts brought a host of others bubbling to the surface and set her stomach churning. She tried to turn her attention to the familiar scenes they were passing at the speed of sound – a block of small, ranch-style houses, each with a shrine to the Virgin Mary in the front yard. Shrine after shrine made from old clawfoot bath-tubs that had been cut in half and planted in the ground. Flowers blooming riotously around the feet of white totems of the Holy Mother. A block of brick town houses that had been restored in recent years. Downtown, with its mix of old and tacky 'modernized' storefronts.

She didn't turn to look at the courthouse as they passed it, concentrating instead on the congregation of gnarled, weathered old men who seemed to have been sitting in front of the hardware store for the past three decades, gossiping and watching diligently for strangers.

The scenes were familiar, but not comforting, not the way she wanted them to be. She felt somehow apart from all she was seeing, as if she were looking at it through a window, unable to touch, to feel the warmth of the people or the solace of long acquaintance with the place. Tears pressed at the backs of her eyes, and she shook her head a little, reflecting bitterly on the defense of her mental state she had made to Caroline and Savannah in the parlor. What a crock of shit. She was as fragile as old glass, as weak as a kitten.

'I'm really not very hungry,' she murmured, digging her fingers into the beige leather upholstery of the car seat to keep her hands from shaking as the tension built inside her, the forces of strength and weakness shifting within, pushing against one another.

Not bothering with the blinker, Savannah wheeled into the parking lot beside Madame Collette's, one of half a dozen restaurants in town. She took up two parking spots, sliding the 'Vette in at an angle between a Mercedes sedan and a rusted-out Pinto. She cut the engine and palmed the keys, sending Laurel a look that combined apology and sympathy in equal amounts.

'I'm sorry I brought it up. The last thing I want is to upset you, Baby. I should have known better.' She reached over and brushed at a lock of Laurel's hair that had dried at a funny angle, pushing it back behind her ear in a gesture that was unmistakably motherly. 'Come on, sweetie, we'll go have us a piece of Madame Collette's rhubarb pie. Just like old times.'

Laurel tried to smile and looked up at the weathered gray building that stood on the corner of Jackson and Dumas. Madame Collette's faced the street and backed onto the bayou with a screened-in dining area that overlooked the water. The restaurant didn't look like much with its rusted tin roof and old blue screen door hanging on the front, but it had been in continuous operation long enough that only the true old-timers in Bayou Breaux remembered the original Collette Guilbeau – a tiny woman who had reportedly chewed tobacco, carried a six-gun, and dressed out alligators with a knife given to her by Teddy Roosevelt, who had once stopped for a bite while on a hunting expedition in the Atchafalaya.

Rhubarb pie at Madame Collette's. A tradition. Memories as bittersweet as the pie. Laurel thought she would have preferred sitting on the veranda at Belle Rivière in the seclusion of the courtyard, but she took a deep breath and unbuckled her seat belt.

Savannah led the way inside, promenading down the aisle along the row of red vinyl booths, hips swaying lazily and drawing the eyes of every male in the place. Laurel tagged after her, hands in the pockets of her baggy shorts, head down, oversize glasses slipping down her nose, seeking no attention, garnering curious looks just the same.

The scents of hot spices and frying fish permeated the air. Overhead fans hung down from the embossed tin ceiling, as they had for nearly eighty years. The same red-on-chrome stools Laurel remembered from her childhood squatted in front of the same long counter with its enormous old dinosaur of a cash register and glass case for displaying pies. The same old patrons sat at the same tables on the same bentwood chairs.

Ruby Jeffcoat was stationed behind the counter, as she always had been, checking the lunch hour receipts, wearing what looked to be the same black-and-white uniform she had always worn. She was still skinny and ornery-looking, hair net neatly smoothing her marcel hairdo, lips painted a shade of red that rivaled the checks in the tablecloths.

Marvella Whatley, looking a little plumper and older than Laurel remembered, was setting tables. There was a fine sprinkling of gray throughout the black frizz of her close-cropped hair. A bright grin lit her dark face as she glanced up from her task.

'Hey, Marvella,' Savannah called, wiggling her fingers at the waitress.

'Hey, Savannah. Hey, Miz Laurel. Where y'at?'

'We've come for rhubarb pie,' Savannah announced, smiling like a cat at the prospect of fresh cream. 'Rhubarb pie and Co-Cola.'

At the counter Ruby eyed Savannah's short skirt and long bare legs, and sniffed indignantly, frowning so hard, her mouth bent into the shape of a horseshoe. Marvella just nodded. Nothing much ever bothered Marvella. 'Dat's comin' right up, then, ladies. Right out the oven, dat pie. You gonna want some mo' for sho'. M'am Collette, she outdo herself, dat pie.'

The table Savannah finally settled at was in the back, in the screened room, where abandoned plates and glasses indicated they had missed the lunch rush. Out on the bayou, an aluminum bass boat was motoring past with a pair of fishermen coming in from a morning in the swamp. In the reeds along the far bank a heron stood, watching them pass, still as a statue against a backdrop of orange Virginia creeper and coffee weed.

Laurel drew a deep breath that was redolent with the aromas of Madame Collette's cooking and the subtler wild scent of the bottle brown water beyond the screened room, and allowed herself to relax. The day was picture perfect – hot and sunny, the sky now a vibrant bowl of pure blue above the dense growth of trees on the far bank. Oak and willow and hackberry. Palmettos, fronds fanning like long-fingered hands. She had nowhere to go, nothing to do but pass the day looking at the bayou. There were people who would have paid dearly for that privilege.

'We-ell,' Savannah purred as she surveyed the room through the lenses of her Ray-Bans, 'if it isn't Bayou Breaux's favorite son, himself.'

Laurel glanced across the room. At the far corner table sat the only other customer – a big, rugged-looking man, his blond hair disheveled in a manner that suggested finger-combing. He might have been fifty. He might have been older. It was difficult to tell. He had the look of an athlete about him – broad shoulders, large hands, a handsome vitality that defied age. He sat hunched over a spiral notebook, glaring down through a pair of old-fashioned round, gold-rimmed spectacles. His expression was fierce in concentration as he scribbled. A tall pitcher of iced tea sat to his left within easy reach, as if he planned on sitting there all day, filling and refilling his glass as he worked. Laurel didn't recognize him, and she turned back to Savannah with a look that said so.

'Conroy Cooper,' Savannah said coolly.

The name she recognized instantly. Conroy Cooper, son of a prominent local family, Pulitzer Prize-winning author. He had grown up in Bayou Breaux, then moved to New York to write critically acclaimed stories about life in the South. Laurel had never seen him in person, nor had she ever read his books. She figured she knew all she needed to about growing up in the South. She had listened to him tell stories on public radio once or twice and remembered not the tales he had told, but his voice. Low and rich and smooth, the voice of old Southern culture. Slow and comforting, it had the power to lull and woo and reassure all at once.

'He moved back here a few months ago,' Savannah explained in a hushed tone of conspiracy.

Her gaze was still directed at Cooper, her expression masked by her sunglasses. She trailed a fingertip up and down the side of the sweating glass of Coke Marvella had brought, a movement that reminded Laurel of a cat twitching its tail in pique.

'His wife has Alzheimer's. He brought her back here from New York and put her in St. Joseph's Rest Home. I hear she doesn't know her head from a hole in the ground.'

'Poor woman,' Laurel murmured.

Savannah made a noise that sounded more like indigestion than agreement.

The pie arrived, steaming hot with vanilla ice cream melting down over the sides to puddle on the plate. Laurel ate hers with relish. Savannah picked and fiddled until the ice cream had completely returned to its liquid state and the pie was a mess of pinkish lumps and crust that resembled wet cardboard.

'Is something wrong?'

She started at the sound of Laurel's voice, dragging her gaze away from Cooper, who had yet to acknowledge her presence. 'What?'

'You're not eating your pie. Is something wrong?'

She flashed a brittle smile and fluttered her hands. 'Not a bit. My appetite just isn't what I thought it was, that's all.'

'Oh, well . . .' Laurel shot a considering glance at Cooper, huddled over his writing. 'I was thinking I would just run up the street to the hardware store. Aunt Caroline needs a new garden hose. You wanna come?'

'No, no, no,' she said hastily. 'You go on. I'll meet you at the car. I'm going to have Madame Collette box up one of these pies and take it home for supper.'

Savannah forked up a soggy bite of pie and watched as Laurel ducked through the doorway, leaving her alone with the man who had effortlessly snared her heart and seemed determined to break it.

Anger shimmered through her in a wave of heat, pushing her toward recklessness. She wanted him to look at her. She wanted to see the same kind of hunger in him that she felt every time she saw him, every time she thought of him. She wanted to see the same raw longing burning in his eyes. But he just sat there, writing, oblivious of her, as if she weren't any more important than a table or a chair.

447

She rose slowly, smoothing her short skirt, her every movement sensuous, sinuous. For all the good it did her. Cooper went on scribbling, head bent, brows drawn, square jaw set.

Slowly she sauntered across the room, stiletto heels clicking on the linoleum floor. She tossed her sunglasses down beside his notebook, and slowly raised the hem of her skirt, inch by inch, revealing smooth, creamy thighs and a thicket of neatly trimmed dark curls at the juncture of those thighs.

Cooper bolted in his chair, dropping his pen and nearly overturning the pitcher of tea at his elbow. 'Jesus H. Christ, Savannah!' The words tore from his throat in a rough whisper. He glanced automatically toward the door for witnesses.

'Don't worry, honey,' Savannah purred, sliding the fabric back and forth across her groin. 'There's nobody here but us adulterers.'

He reached across the table with the intent of pulling the skirt down to cover her, but she inched away from him and slowly moved around the end of the table, her back to the door.

'Like what you see, Mr. Cooper?' she murmured in a voice like honey, wicked mischief flashing in her pale blue eyes. 'It's not on the menu, but I'd give you a taste if you asked me real nice.'

Blowing out a sigh, Cooper sat back and watched as she lowered one knee onto the chair beside his. The initial shock had subsided, and his usual air of calm settled over him as comfortably as the old tattersall shirt he wore. It was Savannah's nature to shock. Overreacting only pushed her to be more outrageous, like a naughty child seeking attention. So he settled himself and looked his fill, knowing he would see anyone intruding on the moment quickly enough to act before they could be caught.

'Maybe later,' he drawled. 'Tonight, perhaps.'

She pouted, staring at him from under her lashes. 'I don't want to wait that long.'

'But you will. That'll only make it better.'

He reached out again, slowly, casually, and drew his fingertips up a few smooth inches of leg, meaning to tug the skirt down out of her grasp, but she caught his hand and guided it between her thighs.

'Touch me, Coop,' she whispered, leaning against him, pressing her cheek down on top of his head. She wound her right arm around the back of his neck, anchoring his face against her breasts as her hips began to move automatically, rhythmically against his hand. 'Please, Coop . . .'

She was hot and silky, her body instantly ready for sex. She moved against him wantonly. Cooper had no doubt that she would have straddled him on the spot if he would have allowed it, without a care as to who might walk in on them. The idea held a strong fantasy appeal, he thought, grimacing, as desire pooled and throbbed. But he wouldn't follow through.

448

He thought that might be the only thing that set him apart from the sundry other men Savannah had cast her spell over – that he somehow managed to maintain the voice of reason in the face of her overwhelming sexuality, instead of losing himself in it.

'Please, Coop,' Savannah breathed. She traced the tip of her tongue along the rim of his ear, panting slightly as need gathered in a knot in the pit of her belly.

The need swirled around her like a desert wind, heating her skin. She wanted to tear her blouse open and feel his mouth, wet and avid, on her breasts. She wanted to impale herself on his shaft and go wild with the pleasure of it. She wanted . . . wanted . . . wanted . . .

Then he pulled his hand away and stood, disentangling himself from her, and the want congealed into a hard ache of frustration.

'You're such a bastard,' she spat, jerking her skirt down, straightening her top. A strand of hair fell across her face and stuck to her sweat-damp cheek. She tucked it behind her ear.

Cooper pulled his glasses off and began cleaning the steam from them, methodically rubbing the lenses with a clean white handkerchief. He looked at her from under his brows, his gaze as blue as sapphire, as steady as a rock. 'I'm a bastard because I won't have sex with you in a public place?'

Savannah sniffed back the threat of tears, furious that he had the power to make her feel shame. 'You wouldn't even look at me across the goddamn room! You wouldn't even give me a civil "Good afternoon, Miz Chandler."'

'I was concentrating,' he said calmly.

He settled his spectacles back in place, folded the handkerchief, and returned it to the hip pocket of his khaki pants. That task accomplished, he gave her a tender look, the corners of his mouth tilting up in a way that was, despite his fifty-eight years, boyish and unbelievably charming. 'I'm a sorry excuse for a man if my work can so involve me that I miss one of your entrances, Savannah.'

He reached out a hand and touched her cheek with infinite gentleness. 'Forgive me?'

Damn him, she would. That low, cultured drawl wrapped around her like silk. She could have curled up beside him and listened to him talk for a hundred years, glad just to be near him. She sniffed again and looked at him sideways.

'What are you working on? A short story?'

Coop picked up the notebook as she reached for it and closed it, forcing a grin. 'Now, darlin', you know how I am about letting anyone read my work. Hell, I don't even let my agent read it until it's done.'

'Is it about me?' The storm clouds gathered and rumbled inside her again. 'Or is it about Lady Astor?' she asked petulantly, giving her head a toss as she moved restlessly away from the table.

449

She paced along the screened wall, oblivious to the shabby pontoon tour boat that was ferrying a load of unsuspecting tourists up the bayou and into the sauna that was the swamp at midafternoon.

'Lady Astor Cooper,' she sneered, planting her hands on her hips. 'Patron saint of martyred husbands.'

'Better I martyr myself to my marriage than to my cock.'

'Are you implying that's what I do?' she demanded. 'Martyr myself to sex?'

Cooper hissed a breath in through his teeth and made no comment. They were treading on dangerous ground. He had his own theories about Savannah's sexual motives, but it would do no good to share them with her. He could too easily envision her in a rage of hurt and hysteria, wildly lashing out. And he had no desire to hurt her. For all her faults, he had fallen in love with her. Hopeless love in the truest sense.

'Well, I've got news for you, Mr. Cooper,' she said, leaning up into his face, her lovely mouth twisted with bitterness. 'I get fucked because I like getting fucked, and if you don't want to do it, then I'll go find someone who will.'

He caught her arms and held her there for a moment as she breathed fury into his face, steaming his glasses all over again. A deep, profound sadness swelled inside him and he frowned. 'You make yourself miserable, Savannah,' he murmured.

She shivered inside, trying to shake off the chill of the truth. Coop saw it, damn him. He caught her eyes with that worldly-wise, world-weary, worn blue gaze, and saw he'd struck a nerve. She jerked away from him and grabbed her sunglasses off the table.

'Save your insights for your work, Coop,' she said waspishly. 'It's the only place you really let yourself live.' She jammed the Ray-Bans in place and flashed him a mocking smile. 'Have a nice day, Mr. Cooper.'

She whirled out of Madame Collette's in a huff and a cloud of Obsession, not bothering to pay the bill. Ruby Jeffcoat knew who she was, the dried-up old bitch. She'd just add it to the tab and tell every third person she saw what a slut Savannah Chandler was, prancing around town in a skirt cut up to her crotch and no bra on.

Laurel pushed herself away from the side of the Corvette as Savannah stormed across the parking lot, all pique and no pie in sight. She looked furious, and Laurel had a strong hunch it wasn't anything to do with the restaurant, but one of its patrons. Conroy Cooper. Old enough to be their father Conroy Cooper. Married Conroy Cooper.

Oh, Savannah . . .

'Let's get the hell out of here,' Savannah snarled. Tossing her purse behind the seat, she jerked open the driver's door and slid in behind the wheel.

Laurel barely had time to get in the car before the 'Vette was revved and rolling. They hit Dumas, and Savannah put her foot to the floor, sending the sports car squealing away from Madame Collette's, leaving a trail of rubber.

'Where are we going?' Laurel asked as casually as she could, considering she had to shout to be heard above the roar of the wind and the engine.

'Frenchies,' Savannah yelled, pulling the pins from her hair and letting them fly. 'I need a drink.'

Laurel buckled her seat belt and held on, not bothering to comment on the fact that it didn't look as though they'd be having rhubarb pie for supper, and trying her damnedest not to think about Jack Boudreaux.

5

'Jesus saves!'

'Jesus lives!'

'Jesus Christ,' Savannah snarled as she stopped in her tracks, propped a hand on one hip, and took a look at the scene outside Frenchie's.

Patrons crowded the gallery, staring down, bemused at a dozen protestors who were toting signs bearing such intelligent slogans as 'Close Frenchie's. End Sin.' The picketers were gathered in a knot at the bottom of the steps, putting on a show for the camera of a Lafayette television station, chanting their slogans in a vain attempt to drown out the swamp pop music that spilled through the screens.

In the center of the righteous stood the ringleader of their band, Reverend Jimmy Lee Baldwin, resplendent in a white summer suit, fresh out of the JC Penney catalog. Two thousand dollars' worth of too-white caps shone as he spoke to a reporter who looked as though he used enough hair spray to put his own personal hole in the ozone.

Jimmy Lee was good-looking, standing an inch or two past six feet tall, and had once been lean and athletic, though in the years since high school basketball, firm muscle had softened. He wore his tawny hair slicked straight back from his face, drawing attention to his eyes, which were the color of good scotch, and to the dazzling dental wonders that lined his smile like big white Chiclets.

Though he was barely thirty-eight, lines of dissipation were etched deeply beside those tawny eyes and around a mouth that had a certain weakness about it. Between the teeth and the tan that looked as though he'd gotten it down at the Suds 'n' Sun Laundromat/Tanning Parlor, Jimmy Lee looked just a little too tacky to be truly handsome. Not that anyone could ever have convinced him of that.

'Who is it?' Laurel asked, shoving her glasses up on her nose. The sight of the white news van automatically made her nervous. The irrational fear that they had come here to track her down flashed through her mind, but she resolutely crushed it out with the gavel of practicality. She wasn't news any longer.

'The Reverend Jimmy Lee Baldwin. Saver of lost souls, purveyor of heavenly blessings, leader of the Church of the True Path.'

'I've never heard of it.'

'No. I reckon Georgia had its own religious screwballs. The Revver showed up here about six months back and started to gather himself a flock. He's got his own show now on local cable up in Lafayette. Fixin' to be a big star in the televangelist ranks, he is.'

Savannah dug a cigarette out of her pocketbook and lit it, taking a long, considering drag as she stared at Jimmy Lee through her sunglasses. He was on a roll, gesturing like a wild man as he began ranting about the dens of iniquity.

'Come on, Baby,' she said on a breath of smoke. 'I need to get me that drink.'

Laurel started for the side door, having no desire to call attention to herself by crashing a picket line. But Savannah made a beeline for the action, miniskirt twitching across her thighs, hips swaying alluringly. She gave her head a toss, fluffing her long, wild mane with her free hand as she went. She looked like a walking ad for wanton sex and decadent living. Laurel bit back a groan and followed her. Trouble had always been a magnet to Savannah, and she was headed toward this mess with a sly smile teasing the corners of her mouth.

Her approach did not go unnoticed. Almost immediately a chorus of wild cheers and wolf whistles rose from the men on the gallery. Of the group involved in the protest, the reporter saw her first, his head snapping around in a classic double take as he held the microphone in front of Reverend Baldwin. He elbowed the cameraman, who swung his lens in her direction. Reverend Baldwin broke off in midtirade, clearly annoyed to have his moment in the spotlight cut short. He recovered quickly, though, and moved to turn the situation to his advantage.

'Sister, sister, be redeemed!' he called dramatically. 'Let Christ Jesus quench your thirst.'

Savannah stopped a scant six inches from the minister, cocked a hip, and blew a stream of smoke in his face. 'Honey, if He shows up in the next five minutes with a Jax long-neck, I'll be glad to let Him quench my thirst. In the meantime Frenchie can serve that need just fine.'

She blew a kiss to the camera while the crowd on the gallery howled laughing, and sauntered on, the picketers-turned-gawkers parting like the Red Sea to let her pass on up the steps. Laurel tried to hurry after her before the faithful closed ranks on their leader again, but Baldwin caught her by the arm.

'Turn to God, young woman. Find the True Path! Let the Lord quench the thirst in your soul with conviction and righteousness!'

Laurel looked up at him, her brows pulling together in annoyance. She had no patience for the likes of Jimmy Lee Baldwin. Televangelists ranked a notch lower than disreputable used-car salesmen in her book, bilking the poor and the elderly out of what limited funds they had, selling them the kind of salvation God offered free of charge in the Bible.

She hadn't come here looking for a fight. In fact, she would have given anything to have passed unnoticed through the throng. But she wasn't about to be used as a pawn. She pulled in a deep breath and felt the fire that had been turned low leap inside her.

'I have convictions of my own, Mr. Baldwin,' she said, smiling inwardly as he jerked his head around and looked at her as if she were a mute suddenly healed. He hadn't expected her to stand up to him. 'All of them more important than the sale of perfectly legal alcoholic beverages in a licensed establishment.'

Jimmy Lee recovered admirably from his shock. 'You condone the sin of drink, lost sister? May the Lord have mercy—'

'If I'm not mistaken, it was Christ who changed the water into wine at the wedding at Cana. John, chapter two, verses one to eleven. Liquor itself isn't bad, Reverend, just the foolish acts committed by those who overindulge. And alcoholism is an illness, not a sin. Perhaps God should have mercy on *your* soul for suggesting otherwise.'

He bared his snowy-white teeth at her in what would pass for a smile on videotape, she supposed, and his fingers tightened on her upper arm, telegraphing his anger. 'I come only as God's soldier in the war to save men's souls. Our battlegrounds are the dens of iniquity where men's weaknesses are exploited for monetary gain.'

'If you're only interested in saving *men's* souls, then perhaps you could take your hand off me,' she said dryly, pulling free of his grasp. 'As to exploiting people's weaknesses for monetary gain, my interests run more in the direction of the disposition of monies solicited by television preachers. I wonder what the Lord would have to say about that.'

As the audience on the gallery cheered, Baldwin flushed red. His mouth tightened, and the whiskey-brown eyes, which had moments ago glowed with the bright lights of glory, hardened like amber. He took a step back from her, admitting defeat as far as Laurel was concerned. She gave him one last hard look and started to turn for the steps, but the reporter outflanked her, and she flinched away from the light of the hand-held strobe an assistant shot up behind the cameraman.

'Miss, Doug Matthews, KFET-TV, can we please get your name?'

Memories of other times and other cameras flashed through Laurel's mind. Reporters pressing in on her, yapping and jumping at her like a pack of hounds. Questions, accusations, snide remarks, hurled at her from all sides like darts.

'No,' she murmured, fighting the tightness that suddenly squeezed her chest. 'No, please just leave me alone.'

Savannah stepped down off the gallery and pushed the cameraman's lens down. 'Leave my sister alone, sweetheart,' she said, her gaze leveled on the reporter, 'else I'll take that cute little microphone and shove it up your tight little ass.'

Hoots and shouts issued from Frenchie's patrons. Gasps rippled through the crowd of believers as the Chandler sisters went up the steps and into the bar.

Jimmy Lee stepped away from them, dragging Doug Matthews with him. 'You'll take that shit out, or I'll beat her to that goddamn microphone,' he growled, looming over Matthews, who was jockey-short and coward-yellow.

Doug Matthews sent him a contentious look, making a token show of journalistic integrity as he smoothed a hand carefully over his blond hair. 'It's news, Jimmy Lee.'

'So is your penchant for pretty young men.' His eyes darted to his throng of disgruntled followers who were milling around the parking lot looking as though their parade had been hailed on. 'Fuck news. This is supposed to be the launch of my big campaign against sin. I'm not gettin' shown up by some little skirt in horn-rimmed glasses. You take that tape and cut and paste until I look like Christ himself forgiving Mary Magdalene.' He cuffed Matthews on the chest, scowling ferociously. 'You got that, Dougie?'

Matthews pouted and rubbed at the sore spot, carefully straightening his turquoise tie. 'Yeah, yeah. I got it. I wonder who she was, anyway. She sure as hell cleaned your clock.'

Jimmy Lee rubbed his knuckles against his chin, his gaze on the screen door the two women had gone through. 'Sister,' he murmured, the oily wheels of his mind whirring like windmills. 'Savannah Chandler's sister.' Awareness dawned, and he brightened considerably as the seeds of a plan took root. 'Laurel Chandler.'

'Poor Jimmy Lee,' Savannah said without sympathy as they stepped into the cool, dark interior of Frenchie's. 'He's only trying to rid the town of impurities, immoralities, and prurient behavior. He's a firsthand expert on prurient behavior.' Sliding her sunglasses down her nose, she looked at Laurel and smiled wickedly. 'And I ought to know, 'cause I've gone to bed with him.'

'Savannah!'

'Oh, Baby, don't look so scandalized.' She chuckled as she glanced around the room for a choice place to roost. 'Preachers get the itch too. And let me tell you, Jimmy Lee likes his scratched in some of the most inventive ways. . . .'

She sauntered toward a table, feeling a little bit mean and a little bit vindicated. Coop had rattled her, something she didn't like at all. Making a fool out of Jimmy Lee went a long way toward making up for the scene at Madame Collette's. And truth to tell, shocking Laurel made up the rest. Laurel, such a good girl. Laurel the upstanding citizen. Laurel the golden child. It did her good to get thrown for a loop every once in a while. Let her see how the other half lived. Let her think *There but for the grace of God and Savannah*. . . .

455

The crowd in the bar greeted her like the conquering heroine, calling to her, raising their glasses. A sense of warmth and importance flowed through her. This was her turf. These were her people, much to the dismay of Vivian and Ross. Here she was appreciated. She smiled and waved, the kind of all-encompassing, regal gesture of a beauty queen.

'Hey, Savannah!' Ronnie Peltier called from over by the pool table, where he stood leaning on the butt of his cue. 'Dat's some tongue you got on you, girl.'

'So I've been told, honey,' she drawled.

He grinned and shifted his weight. 'Oh, yeah? Well, why you don' come on over here, *jolie fille*, and show me?'

Savannah tossed her head and laughed, assessing his charms all the while. Ronnie was big where it counted and cute as could be. Conroy Cooper could go to hell. She had just found herself a fun-loving Cajun boy to play with.

Leonce Comeau swiveled around on his barstool and slid his hand down her back as she passed. 'Hey, Savannah, when you gonna marry me? Me, I can't live without you!'

She slid him a sly look over her shoulder, mentally shuddering at the grotesque scar that bisected his face, the long, shiny-smooth pink line that began and ended in strange knots of flesh. 'If you can't live without me, Leonce, then how come you ain't dead yet?'

'*I yi yiee!*' He clutched his hands to his heart as if she'd shot him, a big grin splitting across his bearded face. 'You heartless bitch!'

Laurel watched the proceedings with a sinking heart and a churning stomach. It tore her up to see this side of her sister – the seductress, the slut. Savannah had so much more to offer the world than her sexual prowess. Or she once had. Once she had been full of promise, full of hope, bright-eyed at the possibilities life had to offer. Once upon a time . . .

'You want a toothpick, *'tite chatte*?'

The voice was unmistakable. Whiskey and smoke and a vision of black satin sheets. His breath was warm against her cheek, and she jerked around, cursing herself for bolting.

'Why would I want a toothpick?' she demanded indignantly.

Jack grinned at the flash of temper in her dark blue eyes. It was a hell of an improvement over the sadness and guilt he'd glimpsed there a moment before. For a moment she had looked like a lost child, and the impact of that impression had slammed into him like a truck. Not that he really cared about her, he assured himself. Miss Laurel Chandler was hardly his type. Too serious by half. Too driven. He liked a girl who liked her fun. A few good laughs, a nice healthy round of mattress thumping, no strings attached. Laurel Chandler was a whole different breed of cat – as evidenced by the mincemeat she'd made of Jimmy Lee Baldwin.

'Why, to pick all those pieces of Jimmy Lee out your teeth, sugar,' he

456

said. 'You sure chewed him up and spit him out. Remind me not to get on your bad side.'

She scowled. 'You're already on my bad side, Mr. Boudreaux.'

'Then why I don't just buy you a drink, angel, and we can make up?' he suggested, smiling, leaning down just a little closer than he should have. Her frown tightened, but she held her ground.

'I'd rather be left alone, thank you very much,' Laurel said primly, avoiding those dark eyes that had managed to see past her carefully erected defenses once already. She fixed her gaze on one deep dimple and did her best to ignore its blatant sex appeal.

'Oh, well, then you came to the wrong place, sugar.'

He draped an arm casually around her shoulders and steered her toward the bar, completely ignoring her wishes. She held herself stiffly, resisting his herding. She looked up at him sideways. He wore a battered black baseball cap that had '100% Coonass' machine embroidered on the front in glossy blue thread. A blood red ruby studded the lobe of his left ear. The wild Hawaiian print shirt he wore hung completely open, revealing a broad wedge of tan chest, well-defined muscle lightly dusted with black hair, a belly that looked as hard and ridged as a washboard. A line of silky-looking hair curled around his belly button like a question mark and disappeared into the low-riding waist of his faded jeans, as if beckoning curious female eyes to wonder about the territory that lay beyond.

She jerked her gaze away, pushing her glasses up on her nose in an attempt to hide the blush that bloomed instantly on her cheeks.

He wasn't her type at all, she reminded herself. He wasn't the kind of man she usually allowed to touch her. He wasn't the kind of man she would ordinarily have known at all. And he wasn't charming her. She was only letting him shepherd her toward the bar because she didn't want to watch Savannah seducing the pool players.

'Talk about chewing ass,' he said, an unholy light in his eyes. 'What's black and brown and looks good on a lawyer?' Laurel shot him a scowl, which he fielded with an incorrigible grin. 'A doberman.'

The laugh that rolled out of him may as well have been a pair of hands that skimmed boldly over her. Laurel ground her teeth at her unwanted reaction, berating her body for its inability to judge character.

'Hey, Ovide!' Jack called. 'How 'bout a drink here for our little tigress?'

Laurel blushed again at the name and climbed up on a barstool, figuring she would at least be rid of Jack Boudreaux's touch now. She was wrong. He merely stood beside her, arm hooked around her loosely but possessively. Worse than standing beside him, she was now at eye level with him, and he didn't hesitate to lean close and murmur in her ear.

'That's Ovide,' he said, his voice as low and intimate as if he were whispering words of seduction. He fished a cigarette out of his shirt pocket and dangled it from his lip. ' "Frenchie" Delahoussaye. The man you were stickin' up for out there.'

The man behind the bar was in his late sixties, short and stout with sloping shoulders and no neck. He was bald as a cue ball on top, with shaggy steel gray hair ringing the sides of his head and sprouting in fantastic tufts from his ears. A cloud of curly gray hair spilled out of the V of his plaid shirt, and a thick mustache draped across his upper lip and trailed down past the corners of his mouth. His eyebrows were so bushy, they could have been pads of steel wool glued to his forehead. He looked like a nutria that had taken human form by enchantment. He moved purposefully if slowly, filling tall mugs with beer from a tap.

In contrast, the woman behind the bar with him moved at the speed of light, dashing to fill glasses, grab a pack of cigarettes, call an order for a po'boy back through the window to the kitchen. She was younger than Ovide, though not by a lot, and her face showed every day of her years, with lines etched beside her eyes and thin mouth that was painted poppy orange to match her tower of hair. Her skin had the leathery look of a lifelong smoker. It was stretched taut and shiny against the bones of her skull, giving added emphasis to the large dark eyes that bulged out of her head as if she were perpetually startled. Despite her obvious age, she was still petite, with a hard, sinewy body beneath tight designer jeans from the seventies and an electric blue satin western shirt.

She snatched the two mugs from Ovide and plunked one down on the bar in front of Laurel, scolding Frenchie nonstop.

'What'sa matter wit' you, Ovide? Jack, he don' wan' no damn glass, him!'

She snatched a long-neck bottle of Pearl from the cooler and popped the top off while she grabbed a rag with the other hand and wiped a trail of water off the bar, her mouth going a mile a minute.

'Ovide, he don' know which way is up, *cher*, what wit' all this preacher and ever'ting all the time carryin' on outside our door.' She sucked in a breath and cast a glance heavenward that looked more like annoyance than supplication. '*Bon Dieu,* what dis world comin' to wit' the like of dat Jimmy Lee callin' himself a man of the cloth? *Mais, sa c'est fou!* It pains me to see.'

She cocked a thickly penciled brow at Jack and chastised him for being remiss in his manners, as if he could have gotten a word in edgewise. 'So, *cher,* you gonna introduce me to *une belle femme* or what?'

Jack threw back his head and laughed, his arm automatically tightening around Laurel. She stopped breathing as her breast came into contact with his side.

'T-Grace,' he announced, 'meet Miss Laurel Chandler. Laurel, T-Grace Delahoussaye, Frenchie's right hand, left hand, and mouthpiece.'

T-Grace slapped at him with her wet towel, even as her attention held fast on Laurel. 'You say some pretty smart things to dat horse's ass Jimmy Lee, *chère*.'

'Miz Chandler is a lawyer, T-Grace,' Jack offered, a comment that made T-Grace lean back and eye Laurel as dubiously as if he had announced she was from outer space.

Laurel shifted uncomfortably on her stool and tried in vain to discreetly tug some of the wrinkles out of her blouse. 'I'm not practicing at the moment. I'm just in town to visit relatives.'

T-Grace eyed Laurel critically, then said, 'Ovide, he's jus' beside himself over dis "End Sin" thing with dat preacher and all,' as she accepted a tray of empty glasses from a waitress and whirled to set them next to the bar sink.

Laurel glanced at the impassive Ovide, who stood beside his wife, silently pouring drinks and lining them up on the bar for distribution. Either T-Grace was psychic or the man's moods were too subtle for normal human eyes to detect.

'You say some pretty hard things to make a man think, *oui*?' She gave a snort and swiped a fly off the bar with her rag. 'If dat Jimmy Lee can think. He's all the time so busy talkin', him, can't be nothin' much left in his head to think about. So you gonna be *our* lawyer, *chère*, or what?' she asked baldly, crossing her arms beneath her bosom impatiently while she waited for an answer.

Laurel gaped, stunned by the question, left speechless by T-Grace herself. The proposition was ludicrous. She wasn't a lawyer here in Bayou Breaux; she was just Laurel Chandler. The idea that she could be both was the furthest thing from her mind right now. She had come here to rest, to heal, not to take up the fight.

'Oh, no,' she said, shaking her head, nervously stroking a finger through the condensation on her beer mug. 'I'm sorry, Mrs. Delahoussaye. I'm only in town for vacation. All you really need to do is file a complaint for trespassing. If you feel you need help, I'm sure there are any number of local attorneys who would be glad to represent you.'

T-Grace sniffed and shot a look at Jack. 'Some less than there oughta be.'

He scowled at her, picking the unlit cigarette from between his lips to gesture with it. 'I told you, T-Grace, I couldn't if I wanted to. Besides, you don' need no lawyer. Jimmy Lee's just a pest. Ignore him, and he'll go away.'

The older woman stared hard at him, all pretense of teasing gone from her bulging dark eyes, leaving her looking old and tough as boot leather. 'Trouble don' jus go away, *cher*. You know dat good as me, *c'est vrai*.'

Laurel watched the exchange with interest. Jack's bad-boy grin had vanished into that hard, intense look she had glimpsed the night before. A look that clearly told T-Grace to back off, a look that most grown men would have heeded. T-Grace pretended to shrug it off and turned away from him. She glanced sideways at Laurel as she pulled a pair of bottles from the cooler and popped the tops off.

'Why for you wearin' dem big glasses, *chère*? You in disguise or what?'

She moved off to do a dozen tasks at once before Laurel could formulate any kind of answer. Laurel pushed the glasses up on her nose and frowned.

'It's not much of a disguise, angel,' Jack said.

'Not compared to yours,' Laurel returned. The best defense was a good offense. She didn't like being so easily read, and she had no intention of talking to Jack Boudreaux about her motives for doing anything. She certainly wasn't about to let him escape being questioned himself.

'Mine?' he scoffed. He shook his head, took a long drink of his beer, and wiped his mouth with the back of his hand. 'No disguises here. What you see is what you get, sugar.'

The wickedness returned, sparkling in his eyes, curling the corners of his mouth, digging those breath-stealing dimples into his cheeks. He leaned close, sliding his hand around to the small of her back. His fingers teased her through the thin cotton of her blouse, rubbing lazy circles.

'You like that promise, no?' he breathed, leaning closer still, his lips just brushing the shell of her ear. Laurel shivered, then gasped as his hand slipped beneath the hem of the loose-fitting blouse.

'No,' she said emphatically, batting his hand away. She gave him a look that had made better men back off and ground her teeth when he only smiled at her. 'Don't try to change the subject.'

'I'm not. The subject is us. I'm just tryin' to get past the talkin' stage, angel.'

'When hell freezes over.'

'Well, that devil, he's gonna feel a chill one of these days real soon.'

She arched a brow at him, thwarting the temptation to be either flattered or amused. 'Is that a fact?'

'Oh, absolutely,' he drawled, dark eyes shining.

His intent was clear. For reasons Laurel couldn't begin to fathom, he'd set his sights on her. Probably because she was the only female in his territory he had yet to notch his bedpost for. His arrogance was astonishing. But more astonishing was the vague sensation of arousal his words, his touch, his nearness conjured inside her.

It was a simple matter of physical needs, she rationalized, needs too long ignored and a handsome man all too willing to rectify the situation.

'You think too much, angel,' Jack said, replacing his cigarette. She was as transparent as glass, working out in her mind a logical excuse for the physical attraction that arced between them like electric sparks. He bumped her glass closer. 'Have a drink. Have a good time. Lighten up.'

His philosophy in a nutshell, Laurel thought. She was about to give him her opinion on the subject when Savannah appeared to her right, draped all over the Cro-Magnon pool player like a vine.

'Baby,' she drawled, her gaze fastened hungrily on Mr. Cuestick as she rubbed the flat of her hand over his chest. 'Me and Ronnie got plans for the evening.'

She sounded drunk, though they hadn't been in the bar long enough for that to have been the case. Drunk on arousal. Drunk on the need for sex. Laurel sighed and glanced down, finding no relief as Savannah's bare knee came into view – sliding up and down Ronnie's muscular thigh.

'What about supper?' she asked shortly.

'Oh . . . we'll eat later.' The pair of would-be lovers shared a laugh over that, ending the joke with a kiss, open mouths meeting briefly, tongues teasing. Ronnie's hand slid down from the small of Savannah's back to grope her ass, and she groaned deep in her throat.

'Fine,' Laurel murmured, turning to stare at her untouched beer. 'Just how am I supposed to get home?'

'Here. You can take the 'Vette.' The keys landed on the bar with a rattle. 'I'll get my own ride.'

Another round of salacious laughter. Laurel shook her head.

Savannah caught the action from the corner of her eye. Putting her enjoyment of Ronnie on hold for an instant, she turned her head, taking in the total package of sisterly disapproval.

'Don't knock it till you've tried it,' she said peevishly, forgetting about love, forgetting about Laurel's current state of frailty and her own vow to help her baby sister through it all. Right now *her* needs were all that mattered, and what she needed most was to get naked with Ronnie Peltier and forget all about her good girl sister and Conroy Cooper and wanting to be something she wasn't. 'Loosen up, Laurel. Have a little fun of your own for a change.

'Come on, Ronnie, sweetie,' she said, disentangling herself from him and taking him by the hand to lead him away like a prized stallion. 'Let's go.'

Laurel didn't turn to watch her leave. She sat staring at her drink, staring at Savannah's key ring with the little rubber alligator hanging from it by his tail. The gator looked up at her, jaws open, with a tiny boot lying on its red tongue. It was supposed to be a joke, but she didn't feel like laughing. There wasn't anything funny about people being swallowed up – by alligators or by their own demons.

The noise level in the bar suddenly seemed to increase in volume, the clank of glasses, the noise of the jukebox, the sounds of voices all becoming too loud for her ears. She grabbed the keys and pushed herself away from the bar.

Outside, the protesters had gone, and the news van with them. There was no sign of Savannah and Ronnie Beefcake. Out on the bayou someone was fishing among the spider lilies and water lettuce along the far bank. The sky that had been a fine clear blue earlier was now striped with clouds tumbling up from the Gulf. The wind had come up as well and shook the heart-shaped leaves of a redbud tree that grew at the edge of the parking lot, flipping them inside out.

Laurel stood for a long moment beside the door of the Corvette, just staring across the bayou, wondering if she'd made a mistake in coming back here. Time away had somehow softened memories of Savannah's penchant for self-destruction. The lure of familiar faces had outweighed the potential for resurrecting old pains, old guilt.

'*It's not your fault, Baby.*'

'*But he doesn't hurt me.*'

'*You're lucky and I'm not, that's all. Besides, I'd never let him hurt you. I'd kill him first.*'

'*Killing's wrong.*'

'*Lots of things are wrong. That doesn't stop people from doing them.*'

She raked a hand through her hair and rubbed at the tension in the back of her neck. She should have stayed home, stayed in the quiet seclusion of the courtyard at Belle Rivière. Maybe she could have talked Savannah into it, and they would still be there now as afternoon edged toward evening, sipping iced tea and lounging on the chaises, talking of nothing important. Or she could have taken her sister up on the idea of shopping. Anything would have been better than this outcome.

The *if onlys* piled up one atop the other, adding to the pile she'd started as a child, like live coral settling on dead to form a reef. The layers below were thick with remorse, hard with guilt. *If only she had stopped Daddy from going out in the field that day . . . If only she could make Mama see the truth . . . If only she could make the attorney general believe . . .*

If only she weren't so powerless, so weak . . .

She hung her head and closed her eyes for a moment. When she opened them again, she was staring at the foot pedals of the Corvette – all three of them – and yet another wave of impotence crashed through her. She had never learned to drive a standard transmission.

'Come on, angel,' Jack said as he materialized beside her. She shied away from him, but not before he slipped the keys from her limp fingers. He tossed them up in the air, catching them with one hand, and grinned like a pirate. 'Let's go for a spin.'

6

He hopped over the door and settled easily into the driver's seat, his graceful hands smoothing over the leather-wrapped steering wheel. Huey bounded over the passenger door and sat in the bucket seat, head up, mismatched eyes bright, ears perked, alert, and eager for adventure.

Laurel rushed around the hood of the car. 'Get that mangy hound out of my sister's car!' she demanded, yanking the door open. She tried to shoo the dog, but he only thought it was a game and yipped at her and wagged his tail in Jack's face as he play-bowed and batted a big paw at the hand she was waving.

'Get out, you flea-bitten, garden-digging, contrary mutt!' She leaned into the car and tried to haul him out bodily, straining and swearing as the dog wriggled and twisted and got his head up in her face and started to lick her.

'Uck!' Laurel jumped back, wiping slime off her face, shooting a glare at Jack. 'You could be a little more helpful.'

He shrugged and grinned. 'He's not my dog.'

A growl rumbled between Laurel's teeth. Huey gave her an incredulous look, whined a little, and jumped out of the 'Vette. Jack laughed, amused by her pique and glad to see something in her expression other than the bleakness that had been there a moment ago as she'd stood looking out at the bayou.

He had followed her out of the bar, intrigued by her reaction to Savannah's sudden 'date.' After the way she'd torn into Jimmy Lee Baldwin, he fully expected to see her chasing her sister down to give her what-for. He hadn't expected to see her standing by the car looking lost and in pain.

Not that that was the reason he had stepped forward and taken the keys from her hand. He wanted to put the Corvette through its paces, that was all. He had given up his Porsche when Evie died. It was too much a symbol of the attitude that had led to her death. He didn't miss the car, but he sometimes missed the raw power, the feel of a sleek machine jumping beneath him, hugging the curves, roaring down the highway. His Jeep got him where he was going, but there was nothing quite like a hot sports car for unleashing something wild in a man.

That was the reason he had snatched the keys from Laurel's hand. It wasn't because he wanted to offer her any kind of comfort. Hell, he wasn't even sure what her problem was. And he didn't want to know. He didn't get involved. If she had a beef with Savannah's taste in men – which encompassed almost the whole of the gender – then she would just have to take it up with Savannah. All he wanted from her was a little fun and the chance to study an intriguing character.

She stood looking at him with stern expectation, her small hand extended. 'The keys, Mr. Boudreaux.'

He had already put the key in the ignition and looked down now, flicking the little alligator into motion. 'But you can't drive this car, can you, sugar?'

'What makes you say that?'

''Cause you would'a left already. Hop in. I'll drive you home.'

'I have no intention of going anywhere with you. Give me the keys. I'll walk home.'

'Then I'll walk with you,' Jack said stubbornly. He pulled the keys back out and stuffed them into the pocket of his jeans as he climbed out. 'Pretty ladies shouldn't go walking 'round these parts alone just now,' he said, giving her a look of concern he would never admit to. 'But I'll warn you, sugar, Savannah's gonna be none too pleased to hear you left her pet 'Vette in the parking lot at Frenchie's. There ain't liable to be nothin' left come morning.'

Laurel heaved a sigh and weighed her options. She could ride home with Jack Boudreaux, or she could walk home with Jack Boudreaux. There was no reliable taxi service in Bayou Breaux; a town where people were seldom in a hurry to get anywhere didn't warrant it. She didn't know anyone else at Frenchie's to ask for a ride home, and Aunt Caroline wasn't likely to be back from Lafayette to come and get her.

'Women shouldn't accept rides from men they barely know, either,' she said, easing herself down in the bucket seat, her gaze fixed on Jack.

'What?' he asked, splaying a hand across his bare chest, the picture of hurt innocence. 'You think *I'm* the Bayou Strangler? Oh, man . . .'

'You could be the man.'

'What makes you think it's a man? Could be a woman.'

'Could be, but not likely. Serial killers tend to be white males in their thirties.'

He grinned wickedly, eyes dancing. 'Well, I fit that bill, I guess, but I don' have to kill ladies to get what I want, angel.'

He leaned into her space, one hand sliding across the back of her seat, the other edging along the dash, corralling her.

That strange sense of desire and anticipation crept along her nerves. If she leaned forward, he would kiss her. She could see the promise in his eyes and felt something wild and reckless and completely foreign to her raise up in answer, pushing her to close the distance, to take the chance.

His eyes dared her, his mouth lured – masculine, sexy, lips slightly parted in invitation. What fear she felt was of herself, of this attraction she didn't want.

'It's power, not passion,' she whispered, barely able to find her voice at all.

Jack blinked. The spell was broken. 'What?'

'They kill for power. Exerting power over other human beings gives them a sense of omnipotence . . . among other things.'

He sat back and fired the 'Vette's engine, his brows drawn pensively as he contemplated what she'd said. 'So, why are you going with me?'

'Because there are a dozen witnesses standing on the gallery who saw me get in the car with you. You'd be the last person seen with me alive, which would automatically make you a suspect. Patrons in the bar will testify that I spurned your advances. That's motive. If you were the killer, you'd be pretty stupid to take me away from here and kill me, and if this killer was stupid, someone would have caught him by now.'

He scowled as he put the car in gear. 'And here I thought you'd say it was my charm and good looks.'

'Charming men don't impress me,' she said flatly, buckling her seat belt.

Then what does? Jack wondered as he guided the car slowly out of the parking lot. A sharp mind, a man of principles? He had one, but wasn't the other. Not that it mattered. He wasn't interested in Laurel Chandler. She would be too much trouble. And she was too uptight to go for a man who spent most of his waking hours at Frenchie's – unlike her sister, who went for any man who could get it up. Night and day, those two. He couldn't help wondering why.

The Chandler sisters had been raised to be belles. Too good for the like of him, ol' Blackie would have said. Too good for a no-good coonass piece of trash. He glanced across at Laurel, who sat with her hands folded and her glasses perched on her slim little nose and thought the old man would have been right. She was prim and proper, Miss Law and Order, full of morals and high ideals and upstanding qualities . . . and fire . . . and pain . . . and secrets in her eyes . . . .

'Was I to gather from that conversation with T-Grace that you used to be an attorney?' she asked as they turned onto Dumas and headed back toward downtown.

He smiled, though it held no real amusement, only cynicism. 'Sugar, "attorney" is too polite a word for what I used to be. I was a corporate shark for Tristar Chemical.'

Laurel tried to reconcile the traditional three-piece-suit corporate image with the man who sat across from her, a baseball cap jammed down backward on his head, his Hawaiian shirt hanging open to reveal the hard, tanned body of a light heavyweight boxer. 'What happened?'

What happened? A simple question as loaded as a shotgun that had been primed and pumped. What happened? He had succeeded. He had set out to prove to his old man that he could do something, be something, make big money. It hadn't mattered that Blackie was long dead and gone to hell. The old man's ghost had driven him. He had succeeded, and in the end he had lost everything.

'I turned on 'em,' he said, skipping the heart of the story. The pain he endured still on Evie's behalf was his own private hell. He didn't share it with anyone. '*Rogue Lawyer*. I think they're gonna make it into a TV movie one of these days.'

'What do you mean, you turned on them?'

'I mean, I unraveled the knots I'd tied for them in the paper trail that divorced them from the highly illegal activities of shipping and dumping hazardous waste,' he explained, not entirely sure why he was telling her. Most of the time when people asked, he just blew it off, made a joke and changed the subject. 'The Feds took a dim view of the company. The company gave me the ax, and the Bar Association kicked my ass out.'

'You were disbarred for revealing illegal, potentially dangerous activities to the federal government?' Laurel said, incredulous. 'But that's—'

'The way it is, sweetheart,' he growled, slowing the 'Vette as the one and only stop light in Bayou Breaux turned red. He rested his hand on the stick shift and gave Laurel a hard look. 'Don' make me out to be a hero, sugar. I'm nobody's saint. I lost it,' he said bitterly. 'I crashed and burned. I went down in a ball of flame, and I took the company with me. I had my reasons, and none of them had anything to do with such noble causes as the protection of the environment.'

'But—'

' "But," you're thinking now, "mebbe this Jack, he isn't such a bad guy after all," yes?' His look turned sly, speculative. He chuckled as she frowned. She didn't want to think he could read her so easily. If they'd been playing poker, he would have cleaned her pockets for her.

'We'll, you're wrong, angel,' he murmured darkly, his mouth twisting with bitter amusement as her blue eyes widened. 'I'm as bad as they come.' Then he flashed his famous grin, dimples biting into his cheeks. 'But I'm a helluva good time.'

The light had not yet turned green, but he floored the accelerator, sending the Corvette lunging forward like a thoroughbred bolting from the starting gate. A pickup coming down Jackson had to skid sideways to avoid hitting them. Its driver stuck his head out the window and shouted obscenities after them. Laurel grabbed the armrest and gaped at Jack. He laughed as he shifted the car, feeling wicked, feeling reckless. Miz Laurel Chandler needed some shaking up, and he was just the guy to do it.

They barreled down Dumas, the business district a blur. Laurel cut a glance toward the courthouse, fully expecting to see beacons flash on one of the parish cruisers in the parking lot, but they shot past without incident and headed toward the edge of town. Past the brick town houses, past the shrines to Mary, past the cutoff to L'Amour, past Belle Rivière, and into the country, where planters warred with the Atchafalaya for control of the land.

Apprehension clutched Laurel's stomach. She had taken a calculated risk getting in the car with Jack Boudreaux, but she thought her logic had been sound. Now other possibilities flashed in her mind. Maybe the killer hadn't been smart, just lucky. Maybe Jack was just plain crazy. Nothing he'd said or done so far in their short acquaintance could have convinced her otherwise.

God, wouldn't that be just the way? She would have survived every rotten thing that had happened in her life to date, fought her way through a breakdown, only to be done in by a disbarred lunatic.

She pushed the fear aside and let anger take hold.

'What the hell are you doing?' she yelled, twisting toward him on her seat. The needle on the speedometer had gone out of her range of vision.

'Taking you for a ride, angel!'

He pushed a cassette into the tape player, then settled back in his seat, right hand resting lightly on the steering wheel, left arm propped on the door frame. Harry Connick, Jr., blared out of the speakers – 'Just Kiss Me.' The road stretched out before them like a ribbon, flat and snaking around canebrakes and copses of trees, skipping over fingers of Bayou Breaux. Driveways to plantations blinked past, and the countryside grew wilder with every second.

Laurel looked behind her, toward rapidly retreating civilization, and kicked herself mentally for taking such a ridiculous chance.

'I don't want to go for a ride! I want to go home!' she shouted, smacking Jack hard on the shoulder with a fist. 'Turn this car around right now!'

'Can't!' he called back to her.

'The hell you can't!'

Jack started to shoot her another grin, but swallowed it as she reached into her purse and pulled out a gun.

'Jesus!'

'Stop the damn car!'

She looked mad enough to shoot him. Her dark brows were drawn together in a furious scowl, her mouth pressed into a thin white line. Her glasses were slipping down her nose, and the wind was tearing at her hair and making her blink, but none of that negated the fact that she had a stainless steel Lady Smith clutched between her dainty little hands.

He jerked his attention back to the road. They were coming up too fast on a sharp lefthand curve. He let off the gas and touched the brake, shifting down into fourth. The engine roared in protest, but the 'Vette came under control, rocking only slightly as it bent around the curve.

They might have made it if it hadn't been for the alligator taking up half the road.

'Shit!'

'Aaaahhh!'

He swerved to miss the gator, but they missed the end of the curve, as well, right-side wheels hitting the shoulder and yanking the 'Vette off the road. Jack fought with the steering wheel to keep the car upright, swearing a blue streak through clenched teeth. Their momentum sent them crashing through the dense undergrowth, the 'Vette bucking and rocking like a spooked horse, brush and grass and cattails whipping at the windshield. They finally came to rest at the base of a sweetgum tree, just inches from smashing into the trunk. Just beyond the tree the land became water.

'Oh, my God. Oh, my God,' Laurel muttered over and over. She was shaking like a palsy victim. The gun lay at her feet, and she stared at it, grateful she hadn't taken the safety off.

Jack leaned over and caught her chin in his hand, turning her face toward him. 'Are you okay? Are you all right?' he demanded, his voice harsh and low. He was breathing as hard as if he'd carried the car out here on his back.

Laurel looked at him, stunned, shaken. 'You're bleeding.'

'What?'

'You're bleeding.'

Lifting a hand, she brushed at a line of red above his left eye, smearing it with her thumb. He caught her by the wrist and drew back to see the blood on her hand, then looked in the cockeyed rearview mirror to check out the wound himself.

'Must'a hit the windshield.'

'You should have worn your seat belt,' Laurel mumbled, still too shaken to be coherent. 'You might have been killed.'

'No one would'a missed me, sugar,' he said darkly as he fought to get his door open. Swearing in French, he gave up and climbed over it to survey the damage to the car.

An ominous hiss sounded beneath the long, sleek hood; steam billowed out from under it. The paint job was shot, scratched all to hell by the bushes and saplings they had crashed through. The wheels would be out of alignment, and it would be a pure damn miracle if the undercarriage wasn't twisted.

'Oh, man, Savannah's gonna have my ass.'

'Not if I have it first,' Laurel said, stepping across the console to crawl over Jack's door. Hers was operational, but too near the trunk of a willow to get open. With both feet planted on the squishy, oozy ground, she faced Jack, her hands jammed on her hips and fury lighting a fire in her eyes. 'Of all the stupid, irresponsible—'

'Me?' He slapped his hands against his chest, incredulous. 'You were the one pointing the gun!'

'—moronic, sophomoric, juvenile things to do. I can't believe anyone would—' She broke off as he started laughing. 'What?'

He only laughed harder, wiping at his eyes, holding his stomach.

Laurel frowned. 'I don't see the least little thing funny about this.'

'Oh – yeah – you got a lawyer's sense of humor all right.' Jack straightened and tried to compose himself. 'The whole thing's ridiculous. Doncha see it? You, you prim little angel, pull a gun on me. We almost hit an alligator—' He broke off and started laughing again.

Laurel watched him, feeling her temper let go by degrees. They were safe. Savannah's car was worse for wear, but no one had been hurt. As anger and fear subsided, she began to see the lunacy of the situation. How would they ever explain it? She put a hand to her mouth and giggled.

Jack caught the motion and the stifled sound. He looked at her, at the sparkle in her eyes and the shaking of her shoulders as laughter tried to escape, and he felt as though he'd been hit in the head all over again. On impulse he reached out and pulled her hand down, grinning like an idiot at the bright smile that lit up her face. *Dieu*, she was pretty . . .

'I don't know what I'm laughing about,' she said, embarrassed.

'I don't care.' He shook his head, stepping closer. 'But you oughta do it more often, angel.'

Her glasses were askew, and he took them off as he moved closer still. Laurel stopped laughing . . . stopped breathing. Her gaze was locked on his face. Her body was very aware of his nearness, responding to it in ways that were instinctive and fundamentally feminine – warming, melting. She was backed up against the side of the car, caught between an immovable object and an irresistible force. He lifted a hand to stroke her hair, lowering his mouth toward hers inch by inch.

She should have moved. She should have stopped him. She didn't know much about this man, and what she did know was hardly good. He was – what had Savannah called him? – a writer, a rake, a rogue. He was a man with a reputation for seduction and a past that was probably shady, to say the very least. He had no business touching her, and she had no business wanting him to. She should have stopped him. But she didn't.

She shivered at the first touch of his lips, blinking as if the contact had given her a shock. He held her gaze, his eyes dark and intense, mesmerizing. Then he settled his mouth over hers, and thought ceased. Her eyes drifted shut. Her hands wound into the fabric of his shirt. Jack pulled her close, slanting his mouth across hers, taking possession of it. At the first intrusion of his tongue, she gasped a little, and he took full advantage, thrusting slowly, deeply, into the honeyed warmth of her mouth.

She tasted sweet, and she felt like heaven against him. Jack groaned deep in his chest and pressed closer. The scent of her filled his head. Not expensive perfume, but soap and baby powder. He spread his legs and inched closer, fire shooting through him as his thighs brushed the outside of hers and his groin nudged her belly.

The need was instantaneous and stronger than anything he'd known in a long time. Strong enough to make him think, something he generally avoided doing when he was enjoying a lady's charms. It was crazy to want like this.

Crazy . . . She'd had a breakdown. She was vulnerable, fragile. Like Evie had been.

Desire died like a flame that had been suddenly doused. Jesus, what kind of jerk was he? He didn't bother to answer that question. It was a matter of record. He was the kind of man who took what he wanted and never gave a thought to anyone else. Selfish, self-absorbed. He had no business touching her.

Laurel opened her eyes as Jack stepped away. She felt dizzy, weak, as shaken as she had been when the car had finally rolled to a halt. Like a woman in a daze, she lifted a hand and touched her fingers to her lips, lips that felt hot and swollen and thoroughly kissed. Her skin seemed to be melting – warm, wet – then she blinked and realized with no small amount of surprise that it had started to rain.

The sky that had shone in various shades of blue all day like a lovely sapphire had gone suddenly leaden. Weather in the Atchafalaya was always capricious. A perfect afternoon could yield to a hurricane by evening, or a tornado, or a shower. Showers could become torrential downpours in the blink of an eye.

'We should get the top up on the car,' she said blankly, her body not receiving any of her brain's commands to move.

Jack didn't move, either. He stood there in the rain looking tough and sexy. His cap was gone. His tousled black hair glittered with moisture. It ran down off his nose, dripped from his scarred chin. The bleeding on his forehead had stopped, leaving an angry red line. His eyes were dark and unreadable, and Laurel shifted nervously against the side of the car.

'I . . . I don't ordinarily just let men kiss me,' she felt compelled to explain. She didn't even kiss on the first date. It had taken Wesley months to coax her into bed, months before she had trusted him enough.

He grinned suddenly, once again transforming himself. 'Hey, I'm no ordinary guy,' he said, shrugging, arms wide, palms up.

They worked together to get the top up and secured on the 'Vette.

'We'll have to walk for help,' Jack said, raising his voice as the rain began to fall harder. 'This car, she's not gonna go nowhere, and the rain could keep up all night.'

Laurel said nothing, but followed him along the path they had mowed back out to the road, glad there was no sign of the alligator. She took a good look at her surroundings, getting her bearings from familiar landmarks. If you followed the dirt path into the woods to the north, you eventually came to the place where Clarence Gauthier kept his fighting dogs. A sign made from a jagged piece of cypress siding was posted on the stump of a swamp oak that had been struck by lightning and killed twenty years ago: 'Keep Out – Trespasser Will Be Ate.'

'Come on, sweetheart,' Jack said, nodding toward town.

'No.' Laurel shook her head and swiped at the rain drizzling down across her face. 'This way.' She turned and headed east.

'Sugar, there's nothin' that way but snakes and gators,' he protested.

A ghost of a smile turned the corners of her mouth. Snakes and alligators. And Beauvoir, her home.

Beauvoir made Tara look like low-rent housing. It stood at the end of the traditional *allée* of ancient, moss-draped live oak, a jewel of the old South, immaculately preserved and painted pristine white. A graceful horseshoe-shaped double stairway led from the ground level to the upper gallery of the house. Six twenty-four-foot-tall Doric columns stood straight and white along each of the four sides of the building, supporting the overhang of the Caribbean-style roof. Entrance doors, centered on both the upper and the lower levels of the house, boasted fanlights and sidelights and were flanked by two sets of French doors, which were themselves set off by louvered shutters painted a rich, money green. Three dormers with Palladian windows called attention to the broad-hipped slate roof. A glassed-in cupola crowned the architectural work of art.

Beauvoir was a sight to take the breath away from preservationists. Laurel thought it might have inspired something like awe or love in her, as well, if her father had lived. But the plantation had gone into her mother's control at his death, and Vivian had seen fit to bring Ross Leighton to it. Laurel doubted she would ever feel anything but regret and loss when standing before the facade of Beauvoir – regret for her father's untimely death, for the childhood she had endured instead of enjoyed, loss for the generations of tradition that would die with Vivian. Neither Laurel nor Savannah would ever live here again. The memories were too unhappy.

It was a pity. There were few houses of its ilk left. Fire and flood had claimed many over the years. Neglect had taken its share. The cost of keeping up a house of that size was an enormous financial burden in an area that had suffered too many lean years in the decades since the fall of the Confederacy. In modern times greed had claimed most of the rest. Many a fine old home had survived all else only to fall to the wrecking ball, making way for oil derricks and chemical factories.

Laurel walked up the drive, lost in thought, almost forgetting the man who walked beside her. She jumped a little when he spoke.

'If this is your home, how come you're not stayin' here?'

'That's none of your business, Mr. Boudreaux.'

Mr. Boudreaux again. The bright-eyed angel who had taken him halfway to heaven with a kiss was in full retreat. 'Just like it's none of my business why you're carryin' a gun around in your pocketbook?'

Laurel let silence be her answer. She had no intention of telling him the gun had been a necessary fashion accessory back in Georgia, when death threats had come in the mail as often as sweepstakes offers. Wesley had been appalled at the thought of her carrying a handgun. Jack Boudreaux had laughed. She herself saw the gun as a sign of weakness, but she carried it still, unable to part with the security it represented.

'You don' live here. Savannah don' live here. Who's left?'

She walked on for a moment. 'Vivian. Our mother. And her husband, Ross Leighton.'

Vivian. Jack arched a brow at the flat tone of voice. Not *our mother, Vivian,* but *Vivian.* A name spoken like that of an acquaintance – and one she was not overly fond of at that. There was a story there. Jack had never in his life called his mother anything but Maman right up to the day she died. A matter of respect and love. He heard neither in Laurel's voice, saw neither in her face. Her expression was tightly closed, giving away nothing, and her eyes weren't quite visible to him behind the rain-streaked lenses of her glasses.

She had grown quieter and quieter on the hike, not even rising to the bait of one of his lawyer jokes, but pulling in on herself and drawing a curtain of silence around her. Coming home wasn't eliciting the traditional joyous response. Her step didn't lighten, the closer they got. She marched along like a prisoner being escorted to the penitentiary.

And you would do the same, Jack, if you were walking down the path to that tarpaper shack on Bayou Noir.

It wasn't the dwelling that mattered. It was the memories.

That revelation made him glance once again at the woman who walked beside him. A grand house didn't guarantee happiness. She might have had as bleak a childhood as his own. The possibility stirred the threads that might have formed a bond between them if he hadn't known enough to snap them off. He didn't want bonds.

A white Mercedes sedan was parked in front of the house, looking like an ad layout for the car company, waiting for some elegant couple to emerge from the grand house so they could be whisked away in Bavarian-made opulence to some nearby exclusive restaurant for dinner. It was Saturday night, Laurel reminded herself. Dinner and dancing at the country club. Socializing with peers. As queen bee of Partout Parish society, Vivian had the night to lord it over the less wealthy. She wasn't going to care for an interruption to her plans.

Laurel tried to tamp down the automatic rise of anxiety as she pressed the lighted button beside the door. She could feel Jack's eyes on her, knew he was wondering why she would feel compelled to ring the bell at the house she had grown up in, but she offered nothing in the way of explanation. It was too complicated. She had ceased to feel welcome in this house the night her father died. Beauvoir was not a home; it was a house. The people in it were people she would sooner have considered strangers than family. And those were feelings that brought on an even more complicated mix of emotions – resentment and guilt warring within her for supremacy over her soul.

The servant who answered the door was no one Laurel had ever seen before. Vivian and Ross were not the kind of people who inspired great loyalty in their employees. Vivian fired maids and cooks with regularity, and those she didn't fire were usually driven away by her personality. This maid, a whey-faced zombie in a sober gray uniform, looked at her blankly when she announced herself and left the cool white entry hall without a word, presumably to go find her mistress.

'Fun girl,' Jack muttered, making a face.

Laurel said nothing. She stood where she had stopped just inside the door, dripping rainwater on the black-and-white marble floor. While Jack inspected the portrait of Colonel Beau Chandler that hung in a huge gilt frame over a polished Chippendale hall table, she caught a glimpse of herself in the beveled mirror that hung on the opposite wall above another priceless antique table. There was also a mirror at floor level, where antebellum belles had checked their hems and made certain their ankles weren't showing. Laurel wasn't concerned about her ankles. She winced inwardly as she took in her drenched hair and soggy blouse. A fist of anxiety tightened in her stomach. The same one she had felt as a child coming in from play with a grass stain on her dress.

'. . . *what's the matter with you, Laurel? Shame on you! Nice girls don't get stains on their clothing. You're a Chandler, not some common little piece of trash. It's your duty to conduct yourself accordingly. Now go to your room and get changed, and don't come down until I call for you. Mr. Leighton is coming to dinner . . . .*'

'Hey, sugar, you okay?'

She jerked her head around and looked up at Jack, who was eyeing her warily.

'You look like you saw a ghost,' he said. 'You're whiter than that big boat of a car sittin' outside.'

Laurel didn't answer him. The sound of a sharp, angry voice caught her ear, and she looked toward the door that led to the parlor, her blood pressure jumping higher with every word.

'. . . told you never to disturb me when I'm getting ready for a dinner engagement.'

'Yes, ma'am, but—'

'Don't you talk back to me, Olive.'

Silence reigned for several moments, expectation swelling in the air. Laurel pulled her glasses off and slicked a hand back through her hair, hating herself for giving in to the impulse.

'. . . be a good girl, Laurel. Always look your best, Laurel . . . .'

Vivian stepped out of the parlor. She was fifty-three now, but still looked like Lauren Hutton — cool, elegant, alabaster skin, and eyes the color of aquamarines. What outward beauty God had given her, plastic surgery was preserving well. Only a hint of lines beside her eyes, none near the sharply cut mouth that was painted a rich, enticing red. Her body looked as slender and hard as a marble wand, and was draped to perfection in emerald green silk. The simple sheath masterfully accented the sleek lines of her body.

The heels of her pumps snapped against the tile floor as she came toward them, her attention on the clasp of the diamond bracelet she was fastening. Then her head came up, and she touched a hand to her neatly coiffed ash blond hair, a gesture Laurel remembered from infancy.

Vivian's eyes went wide with shock. 'Laurel, what in God's name have you been doing?' she demanded, her gaze sliding down Laurel from the top of her wet head to the tips of her ruined canvas sneakers.

'We had a little accident.'

'Well, for heaven's sake!'

Vivian's gaze flicked to Jack and held hard and fast on him, disapproval beaming from her like sonic waves. Jack met her look with insolence and a slow, sardonic smile. His shirt still hung open. He stood with his hands jammed at the waist of his jeans and one leg cocked. Finally he gave a mocking half bow.

'Jack Boudreaux, at your service.'

Vivian stared at him for a second longer, obviously debating the wisdom of snubbing him. Jack would have laughed if it hadn't been for Laurel. He knew exactly what was going through Vivian Chandler Leighton's mind. He didn't quite fit into any of the neat little pigeon holes she usually assigned people to. He was notorious, disreputable; he wrote gruesome pulp fiction for a living; and he had a past as shady as the backwaters of the Atchafalaya. Women like Vivian would ordinarily have written him off as trash, but he was stinking rich. The Junior League didn't have an official category for riffraff with money.

'Mr. Boudreaux,' she said at last, nodding to him but not offering her hand. The smile was the one she had been trained to give Yankees and liberal democrats. 'I've heard so much about you.'

He grinned his wicked grin. 'None of it good, I'm sure.'

Ross Leighton chose that moment to make his appearance. He stepped out of his study down the hall, a glass of scotch in his hand, looking dapper and distinguished in a tan linen suit. He was of medium height and sturdy frame, with a ruddy face and a full head of steel gray hair he wore swept back in a style that suggested vanity.

'We have company, Vivian?' he asked, ambling down the hall, lord of the manor, usurper to the throne of Jefferson Chandler. He wore a big smile that tended to fool too many people. It didn't fool Laurel. It never had. It widened as he recognized her, and he came toward her, chuckling. 'Laurel! My God, look at you! You look like a drowned mouse.'

He bent to kiss her cheek, and she stepped away from him, sliding her glasses back on and tilting her chin up to a truculent angle.

Jack watched the exchange with interest. There had been no words of greeting or concern from any of them, and if looks could have killed, Ross Leighton would have been dead on the floor. Charming family.

'We had us a li'l car trouble,' Jack said, drawing Leighton's attention away from Laurel. 'You got a tractor I could borrow? If we don' get that car out'a where it is quick, the swamp she's gonna swallow it right up tonight.'

'It's a poor night to be out on a tractor,' Ross said, chuckling, bubbling over with condescending bonhomie.

Jack slicked a hand over his damp hair, then clamped it on Ross Leighton's shoulder, flashing a grin as phony as the older man's laugh. 'Ah, well, me, I don' mind gettin' a li'l wet,' he said, thickening his accent to the consistency of gumbo. 'It's not like I'm wearin' no five-hun'erd-dollar suit, no?'

Ross cast a pained look at the hand print on the shoulder of his jacket as he led the way back down the hall to his study so he could call the plantation manager and order him to go out in the rain with Jack.

Laurel watched them go, wishing she could have been anywhere but here. She wasn't ready to deal with Vivian yet. She would have liked another day, maybe two, just to settle herself and gather her strength. She would at least have liked to look presentable instead of like a drowned mouse. Damn Ross Leighton – with that one offhand remark he had managed to make her feel like a ten-year-old all over again.

'Laurel, what on earth are you doing out with that man?' Vivian asked, her voice hushed and shocked. She pressed a bejeweled hand to her throat as if to make certain Jack hadn't somehow managed to steal the diamond-and-emerald pendant from around her neck.

Laurel sighed and shook her head. 'It's nice to see you, too, Mama,' she said with the faintest hint of sarcasm. 'Don't worry about our well-being. Jack hit his head, but other than that we're fine.'

'I can see that you're fine,' Vivian snapped.

She turned and went back into the parlor, expecting Laurel to follow, which she did, reluctantly. Vivian lowered herself gracefully onto one of a pair of elegant wing chairs done in cream moiré silk. Laurel ignored the implied dictate to occupy the other. That was a trap. She was wet and presumably dirty. She knew better than to touch the furniture while she was in such an appalling state of dishabille. She stationed herself on the other side of the gold Queen Anne settee, instead, and waited for the show to begin.

'You've been in town for days without so much as calling your mother!' Vivian declared. 'How do you think that makes me feel?' She sniffed delicately and shook her head, pretending to blink away tears of hurt. 'Why, just this morning, Deanna Corbin Hunt was asking me how you were doing, and what could I say to her? You remember Deanna, don't you? My dear good friend from school? The one who would have written you a letter of recommendation to Chi-O if you hadn't broken my heart and decided not to pledge?'

'Yes, Mama,' Laurel said dutifully and with resignation. 'I remember Mrs. Hunt.'

'I can only imagine what they all think,' Vivian went on, eyes downcast, one hand fussing with a loose thread on the arm of the chair. 'My daughter home for the first time in how long, and she isn't staying in my home, hasn't even bothered to call me.'

Laurel refrained from pointing out that telephones worked two ways. Vivian was determined to play the tragically ignored mother. She had never been one to see ironies, at any rate. 'I'm sorry, Mama.'

'You should be,' Vivian murmured, casting big blue eyes full of hurt up at her daughter. 'I've been feeling just ragged with worry, not knowing what to think. I swear, it'd like to have given me one of my spells.'

Guilt nipped at Laurel's conscience at the same time the cynic in her called her a sucker. She'd spent her entire childhood tiptoeing around the danger of causing one of her mother's 'spells' of depression, and her feelings had engaged in a constant tug-of-war between pity and resentment. On the one hand, she felt Vivian couldn't help being the way she was; on the other, she felt her mother used her supposed fragility to control and manipulate. Even now, Laurel couldn't reconcile the polarized feelings inside her.

'How do you think it looks to my friends to have my daughter staying in town with her lesbian aunt, instead of with me?'

'You don't know that Aunt Caroline is a lesbian,' Laurel snapped. 'And what difference would it make if she were?' she asked, pacing away from the settee, away from her mother, and toward the mahogany sideboard, where half a dozen decanters stood on a silver tray. She wished fleetingly that her stomach could have handled a drink, because her nerves sure as hell could have used one about now. But she turned away from it and went to the French doors to look out at the rain and the gathering gloom of night.

'It's nobody's business who Aunt Caroline sees,' she said. 'Besides, I don't hear you complaining about the fact that your other daughter *lives* with Caroline.'

Vivian's perfectly painted mouth pressed into a tight line. 'I quit concerning myself with Savannah's actions long ago.'

'Yes, you certainly did,' Laurel mumbled bitterly.

'What was that?'

She bit her lip and checked her temper. No purpose would be served by pursuing this line of conversation now. Vivian was the queen of denial. She would never accept blame for her daughters' not turning out the way she had planned.

She pulled in a calming breath and turned away from the window, her arms folded tightly against herself, despite the fact that her clothes were soaking wet. 'I said, what's so wrong with Jack Boudreaux?'

Vivian gave her a truly scandalized look. 'What *isn't* wrong with him? For heaven's sake, Laurel! The man barely speaks the same language we do. I have it on good authority that he comes from trash, and that's no great surprise to me now that I've met him.'

'If he were wearing a linen suit, would he be respectable then?'

'If he were wearing any less of a shirt, I would ask him to leave the house,' she stated unequivocally. 'I don't care how famous he may be. He writes trash, and he is trash. Blood will tell, after all.'

'Will it?'

'My, you're snippy tonight,' Vivian observed primly. 'That's hardly the way I raised you.'

She rose and went to the sideboard to prepare herself a drink. For medicinal purposes, of course. Very deliberately she selected ice cubes from the sterling ice bucket with a sterling ice tongs and dropped them into a chunky crystal glass. 'I'm simply trying to guide you, the way any good mother would. You don't always seem to know what's best, but I would have thought you had better sense than to get involved with a man like Jack Boudreaux. God knows, your sister wouldn't hesitate, but you . . . Coming away from your little trouble and all, especially . . .'

'Little trouble.' Laurel watched her mother splash gin over the ice and dilute it with tonic water. The aroma of the liquor, cool and piney, drifted to her nostrils. Cool and smooth and dry, like gin, that was Vivian. Never mar the surface of things with anything so ugly as the truth.

'I had a breakdown, Mama,' she said baldly. 'My husband left me, my career blew up in my face, and I had a nervous breakdown. That's more than a "little trouble."'

True to form, Vivian sifted out the things she didn't want to discuss and discarded them. She settled on her chair once again, crossed her legs, took a sip of her drink. 'You married down, Laurel. Wesley Brooks was spineless, besides. You can't expect a man like that to weather much of a storm.'

'Wesley was kind and sweet,' Laurel said in her ex-husband's defense, not impressing her mother in the least.

'A woman should marry strength, not softness,' Vivian preached. 'If you had chosen a man of your own station, he would have insisted you give up law and raise his children, and none of this other unpleasantness would have happened.'

Laurel shook her head, stunned at the rationalization. If she had married her social equal, a well-bred chauvinist ass, then she could have avoided dealing with The Scott County Case. She could have given up the pursuit of justice and concentrated on more important things, like picking out a silver pattern and planning garden parties.

'We're having guests for dinner tomorrow.' Checking the slim gold watch she wore, Vivian set her drink aside and rose, delicately smoothing the wrinkles from her dress. 'The guest list will provide more suitable company than what you've been keeping lately.'

'I'm really not feeling up to it, Mama.'

'But, Laurel, I've already told people you would be here!' she exclaimed, sounding for all the world like a spoiled, petulant teenager. 'I was going to call you today and tell you all about it! You wouldn't deny me the chance to save face with my friends, would you?'

'Yes' hovered on her tongue, but Laurel swallowed it back. *Be a good girl, Laurel. Do the proper thing, Laurel. Don't upset Mama, Laurel.* She stared down at her squishy sneakers and sighed in defeat. 'Of course not, Mama. I'll come.'

Vivian ignored the dolorous tone, satisfied with the answer. A smile blossomed like a rose on her lips. 'Wonderful!' she exclaimed, suddenly fluttering with bright energy. She moved from table to mirror and back, smoothing her skirt, checking her earrings, gathering up her evening bag. 'We'll sit down at one – after Sunday services, as always. And do wear something nice, Laurel,' she added, casting a sidelong look at her wilted, rumpled daughter. 'Now, Ross and I are already late for our dinner reservations, so we've got to rush.'

'Yes, Mama,' Laurel murmured, gritting her teeth as her mother bussed her cheek. 'Have a nice evening.'

Vivian swept out of the room, regal, imperious, victorious. Laurel watched her go, feeling impotent and beaten. If she hadn't been such a coward, she would have told her mother years ago to go to hell, as Savannah had. But she hadn't. And she wouldn't. Poor, pathetic little Laurel, still waiting for her mother to love her.

She snatched a glass off the sideboard, intending to hurl it across the room at the fireplace, but she couldn't manage to let herself go even that much.

Don't break anything, Laurel. Mama won't love you. Don't say the wrong thing, Laurel. Mama won't love you. Do as you're told, Laurel, or Mama won't love you.

The front door closed, and she listened to the engine of the Mercedes fire and the car's tires crunch over the crushed shell of the drive. Then she set the glass down, put her hands over her face, and cried.

7

Jack stood in the doorway to the parlor, in the shadows of the now-darkened entry hall. The sound of Laurel's tears tore at him, raked across his heart, and drew not blood, but compassion. He knew nothing of this house, these people, but he knew what it was to be part of a dysfunctional family. He could remember only too well the bitter words, the angry fights, the air of tension that had made him and his sister tiptoe around the house, afraid that any sound they might make would spark an explosion from their father and bring the wrath of Blackie Boudreaux down on one or all of them.

He knew, and that was all the more reason he should have just left. Beauvoir was a nest of snakes. Only a fool would poke at it. He was no fool. He was many things, few of them admirable, but he was no fool.

Still, he didn't move. He stood there and watched as Laurel scrubbed the tears from her face and fought off the next wave of them. She fought to school her breathing into a regular rhythm, blinked furiously at the moisture gathering in her eyes, busied herself cleaning her glasses off with the tail of her shirt. *Dieu*, she was a tough little thing. She thought she was alone. There was no reason she shouldn't have just flung herself down on the fancy gold settee and bawled her eyes out if she wanted to. But she struggled to rein her emotions in, fought for control.

Before sympathy could take root too deeply, Jack pushed himself into motion.

'You ready to go, sugar?'

Laurel jumped at the sound of his voice. Fumbling, she put her glasses back on and smoothed a hand over her hair, which had begun to dry. 'I ... I thought you went to pull the car out.'

Jack grinned. 'I lied.'

Too aware of being alone with him, she stared at him for several moments while the grandfather clock across the room ticktocked, ticktocked. 'Why?'

He was prowling around the room, carelessly picking up knickknacks that had been in the family for generations, absently looking them over, setting them aside. He glanced up at her as he picked up a lead crystal paperweight and hefted it in his hand like a baseball.

"Cause I didn' like your *beau-père*. And I can't say I was all too fond of your *maman*, either.'

'They'll be crushed.'

'Naw . . .' He grinned that wicked grin again, tossed the paperweight up, and caught it with one hand. Laurel's heart jumped with it. 'They'll be pissed. Late for dinner.'

They *would* be pissed. Vivian especially so. Laurel fought the urge to smile, her mouth quirking like the Mona Lisa's. 'Well, you're easily amused.'

'So should we all be, angel. Life's too short.'

He was right beside her now, facing the opposite direction. His arm nearly brushed her shoulder as he reached out to touch something on the sideboard. She told herself to move, but before she could he turned and was behind her, his arms slipping around her, head bending down so he could whisper in her ear.

'So why don' we go find your old bedroom and spend some time amusin' each other, *catin*? Me, I'd like to get out'a these wet clothes and into somethin' . . . *warm* . . .'

A shiver feathered over her skin as his breath trailed down the side of her neck and right on down the front of her blouse, stirring those strange embers of desire inside her. She tried to step away from him, but he held her easily, pressing his hands flat against her stomach. He nibbled his way down the side of her neck, nuzzling aside the collar of her blouse to sample the curve of her shoulder, and her pulse jumped.

Jack gave a low, throaty chuckle. She sure as hell wasn't thinking about Lady Vivian now. 'Come on, sugar,' he murmured. 'There's gotta be a whole lotta empty beds in this big ol' barn.'

'And they're going to stay that way,' Laurel said. This time when she tried to escape his hold, he let her go. She shied away and turned to face him. 'How do you propose we get back to town?' she asked, trying to trample down all her tingling nerve endings with pragmatism.

Jack stuck his hands in his pockets and cocked a hip. 'I called Alphonse Meyette. Him and Nipper's gonna come tow the 'Vette back to the station. I told him to stop down to the Landing and have Nipper drive my Jeep out. I'll give you a ride home, darlin'.'

Laurel scowled at the devilish grin. 'Where have I heard that before?'

He leaned toward her, daring her to hold her ground, dark eyes snapping with mischief. 'I'd rather give you a ride upstairs,' he said, his voice dropping to a smoky rumble.

She couldn't help laughing at his audacity. Crossing her arms, she shook her head. 'I know all about your reputation with women, Mr. Boudreaux.'

He moved closer still, no more than inches from touching her, and she realized too late that he had her neatly trapped against the back of the settee. He planted a hand on either side of her and tilted his head as he

480

lowered it, his gaze holding hers like a magnet. 'Then how come we're not in bed yet?'

'God, the size of your ego is astonishing,' she said dryly.

The dark eyes sparkled, the smile widened, the dimples cut into his cheeks. He bobbed his eyebrows. 'You oughta see the rest of me.'

The humor did her in. If his statement had indeed been ego, she might have slapped him, she certainly would have singed his ears with a scathing commentary regarding her opinion of Neanderthals who thought a man's worth and a woman's willingness all came down to a few inches of penis. But it was humor in those dark eyes, inviting her to share the joke, not be the butt of it. She tried to give him a stern look and failed, giving over helplessly to giggles instead.

'If I didn't have such healthy self-esteem,' Jack said as he leaned a hip against the settee and crossed his arms, 'I might be offended.'

Laurel sniffed and pushed her glasses up on her nose, feeling better, feeling stronger. Vivian had knocked her badly off balance. Coming to Beauvoir had shaken loose too many feelings she wasn't ready to deal with. But Jack had distracted her from the dark emotional whirlpool that had threatened to suck her in, letting her get her legs back under her. She shot him a sideways glance, wondering if he had any idea she hadn't laughed in this house in twenty years.

The Corvette was extricated from the edge of the swamp with minimal fuss and towed away to Meyette's garage. Laurel watched the proceedings from the passenger's seat of Jack's Jeep with Huey the Hound sitting in Jack's spot behind the wheel. The rain had stopped, leaving everything dripping and glistening. The clouds had cleared a path for a melted bronze sunset that cast the swamp in silhouette. The air was fresh and cool, but the dark underlayment of the bayou lingered as always. Laurel shivered in her damp clothes as her attention drifted from the tow truck to the dense wilderness that lay around them. Without thinking, she raised a hand to nibble at her thumbnail.

She had grown up here on the edge of the Atchafalaya, but she had never felt a party to its secrets. The swamp was a world unto itself, ancient, mysterious, primal. She had always thought of it as an entity, not just an ecosystem. Something with a mind and eyes and a dark, shadowed soul. That impression closed in on her as Alphonse Meyette's tow truck rumbled off toward Bayou Breaux and quiet descended. The expectant, hushed silence of the swamp.

Thoughts of murder came, seeping into her like cold, and she shivered again and rubbed her hands over her arms as an image flashed through her head. A young woman lying out here, alone, dead, the swamp watching, knowing, keeping its secrets . . .

'Hey, ugly, outta my seat.'

Jack's voice snapped the terrible vision, and she jumped. Huey grumbled a protest and clambered between the seats to the back, where he curled up in a ball with his back to them.

'Not your dog.' Laurel rolled her eyes.

Jack grinned as he climbed behind the wheel, teeth flashing bright in the gloom. 'I can't help it if he finds my personality irresistible.' He tossed a dirty denim jacket across her lap. 'Put that on. I charmed Nipper out of it on your behalf.'

Laurel wasn't sure whether she should thank him or not. The jacket reeked of male sweat, cigarette smoke, and gasoline, but the Jeep was open, and the ride back was likely to be a chilly one, considering her damp state. She wrinkled her nose and shrugged into the coat. The sleeves hung past her fingertips.

'You okay?'

She glanced up from rolling the cuffs back.

'You looked a little peaked there a minute ago.'

'I was just thinking . . . about that girl they found . . .' And what it would be like to die out here with no one to see, no one to hear but the swamp. She kept that part of her thoughts to herself. She had too vivid an imagination, put herself too easily in the place of others. Not a good trait for someone who had to deal with the victims of violent crimes. It was that inability to draw the line between sympathy and empathy that made her vulnerable.

'Bad business, that,' Jack said softly, his hand on the key, his eyes scanning the darkening swamp.

A barred owl called four round notes, then lifted off from the branches of a nearby cypress tree, its wide wings beating the air, barely making a sound. Laurel pulled the smelly jacket tighter around her.

'Did you know any of them?'

He shot her a hard glance. 'Are you questioning me, counselor? Should I have a lawyer present?'

Laurel pushed past the question of whether his tone held sarcasm or defensiveness, not sure she wanted to know the answer. 'I'm asking an innocent question. Self-professed lady's man that you are, it wouldn't seem too unreasonable that you would have known one of the victims.'

'I didn't. None of them were from here.'

Four bodies. Four parishes in Acadiana, but not Partout. No victims from Partout Parish, no victims found here. Laurel couldn't help wondering if that was by chance or by design. If Partout Parish might be next on the killer's list. She looked at the wilderness around them and thought again about the terrible loneliness of dying out here.

The swamp was an unforgiving place. Beautiful, brutal bitch. Steamy and seductive and secretive. Death here was commonplace, a part of the cycle. Trees died, fell, decayed, became a part of the fertile ground so more trees could grow from it. Mayflies were eaten by frogs, frogs by snakes, snakes by alligators. No death would find sympathy here. It was a place of predators.

She glanced at Jack. Jack, who had teased her out of her mood at Beauvoir. Jack, with his devil's grin. He wasn't grinning now. That mask had fallen away to reveal the intensity that she suspected was the core of him. Hard. Hot. Shadowed.

'The only place I kill people is on paper, sugar,' he said. He pulled a cigarette from his shirt pocket, dangled it from his lip.

The word 'liar' rang in his head as he swung the Jeep around in a U-turn and headed for town.

Savannah stood outside the French doors of Coop's study, hiding among the overgrown lilac bushes beside the comfortable old house, watching as he worked. He sat at his desk, hunched over his notebook, a cigar smoldering in the ashtray, a snifter of brandy sitting beside it. The desk lamp was the only light on in the house, creating an oasis of soft, buttery light around him. Through the glass he seemed like a dream, a warm, golden dream she would never be able to grasp and hold on to. Always held at bay by an invisible barrier. Her past. His devotion to his wife.

Damn Astor Cooper. Why couldn't she just die and be done with it? What a cruel bitch she was, hanging on to him with her invisible threads when she was nothing more than a shell. She may have been a lovely woman in her time. Savannah imagined her as being sweet and demure and gracious. Everything *she* wasn't. Respectable, the perfect wife, the perfect hostess. But Coop's wife was nothing now, and she could give him nothing but heartache. Her mind was gone. Only her body lived on, functioning automatically, tended by nurses.

I could give him something. I could give him everything, Savannah thought, absently smoothing her hands down her wrinkled silk tank.

Like she had given Ronnie Peltier everything?

She tightened her jaw at the bitter inner voice, tightened her hold on the lilac branch. She'd had sex with Ronnie because she had wanted to, needed to. There was nothing to feel guilty about. Not the way she had offered herself, not the way she had given herself, not the greedy, insatiable way she had taken him.

'*It's what you were made for, Savannah. . . . You always want it, Savannah. . . .*'

That was the truth. The truth that had been burned into her brain night after night. She was a born seductress, built for sin. There was no use fighting her true nature.

She hadn't fought it tonight. The scents of sex and Ronnie's Aqua Velva after-shave lingered on her in testimony to the fact. They hadn't even made it to his trailer house before succumbing to their passions. Savannah had made him pull his truck in around back of the old lumber yard and climbed on him right there on the bench seat of his Ford

Ranger. Ronnie made no protest, asked for no explanations. That was what she liked about young men – they were uncomplicated. There were no moral millstones weighing down Ronnie Peltier. He was perfectly willing to drop his Levi's and just go at it for the sheer fun of it.

Arousal and shame grappled for control within her, twisting, struggling against each other, and tears rose in her eyes, blurring her vision of Coop as he sat writing.

'Damn you, Conroy Cooper,' she mumbled, hating the feelings writhing inside her, and directing that hate at Coop. It was his fault. If she hadn't fallen in love with him, if he weren't so damn noble . . . He was the one who made her feel like a whore.

No. She *was* a whore. She had been born a whore and trained to perfection. Cooper made her ashamed of it.

Crying silently, she pushed herself away from the lilac bush and sidled along the house like a thief. She pressed herself against the clapboard siding and crept along to the edge of the French doors, where she pressed her face against the glass.

Cooper straightened his back slowly, wincing as he set his pen aside. His brain felt numb and empty, like a sponge that had been wrung out by merciless hands. The analogy struck him as one last drop of inspiration, and he started to reach for his pen again to scribble it down when a movement at the French doors caught his peripheral vision.

'Savannah?' He mumbled her name to himself, straining his eyes against the darkness that cloaked her features. Of course it was. She would come to him now in contrition, as she always did after one of her little blowups. And he would take her back and comfort her. They had gone through this cycle before. Savannah was a creature of habit. He frowned at the thought that her habits included self-inflicted torment and degradation.

She fell into his arms the second he opened the doors, sobbing like a child. Cooper folded his arms around her and rocked her and murmured to her, his lips brushing softly against her wild mane.

'I'm sorry!' she cried, grabbing handfuls of his shirt in her fists. 'I'm so, so sorry!'

'Hush,' he whispered, his voice low and smooth and soothing. 'Don't cry so, darlin', you're breaking my heart.'

'You break my heart,' Savannah said, aching so, she felt completely raw inside. 'All the time.'

'No,' he murmured. 'I love you.'

'Love me.' She drew a shuddering breath and whispered the words again and again as scalding tears squeezed through the barrier of her tightly closed eyelids. 'Love me. Love me.'

Wasn't that all she had ever wanted? To be loved. To be cherished. And yet she gave herself away time and again to men who would never love her. Confusion boiled and swelled inside her, and she cried it out

484

against Cooper's solid chest, wrapping herself in his warmth, anchoring herself against his strength. She felt so lost. She wanted to be strong, but she wasn't. She wanted to be good, but she couldn't. The only thing she was good at was sex, and that wasn't enough to make Coop forsake his vows.

'Hush, hush,' he whispered, rocking her.

She smelled of sex and cheap cologne. She'd been with another man. He was neither surprised nor dismayed for his own sake. He didn't expect fidelity from Savannah. She was, by her own definition, a harlot. It saddened him, though, in a deeply fundamental way. Savannah was in many ways the embodiment of the South, he thought. Beautiful, wanton, stubborn, victimized . . .

'. . . Cooper?'

Savannah leaned back and looked up into his face, her fists still wound into the fabric of his shirt. He blinked at her, his thick blond lashes sweeping down behind his spectacles, clearing the glaze from his too-blue eyes.

'Damn you,' she snarled, pushing herself away. 'You're not even listening to me! You're off with *her* in your mind, aren't you? Off with Lady Astor. Pure, chaste Lady Astor.'

'I wasn't,' he said calmly. He went to the desk, dismissing her, and went about the business of putting his notebook and pen away, tamping out the last of a good cigar that had gone to waste.

'You'd rather she were here,' Savannah said bitterly. 'She wasn't off fucking Ronnie Peltier eight ways from Sunday tonight. No, she's sitting over at St. Joseph's, pretty as an orchid, dumb as a post—'

'Stop it!' Cooper's voice tore like thunder through the air. He wheeled and grabbed her by the arms and gave her a rough shake. He caught himself before he could shake her again and reined his temper in with an effort that made him tremble.

'Damn you, Savannah, why do you do this?' he demanded, his voice harsh, his fingers biting into the flesh of her arms. 'You beg for my love, then you make me want to hate you. Why can't you just take what I can give you and be happy with that?'

'Happy?' she whispered bleakly, looking up at him, her heart in her eyes. 'I don't know what that is.'

Cooper closed his eyes against a hot wave of emotion and pulled her against him, holding her tight.

'Don't hate me, Coop,' she said softly, sliding her arms around his waist. 'I do enough of that for both of us.'

'Shhh . . . Hush . . .' He brushed her hair back from her cheek and pressed a kiss to her temple, then to her mouth. 'I love you,' he said, the words barely more than a breath as his lips brushed against hers. 'I love you.'

'Show me.'

The hall clock ticked away the seconds of the night. Savannah listened to it in the stillness as she lay curled against Cooper's side. He was asleep, breathing deeply, one arm still holding her close. He looked older sleeping. With his vitality turned off, his athletic energy refueling, there was nothing left but the face that had weathered fifty-eight years of life.

For just a moment she imagined he was her father lying there, alive, holding her next to him. Jeff Chandler would have been fifty-eight if he had lived. And for a moment she allowed herself to wonder what her life would have been like. How different she might have been. She might have been the famous one of the Chandler sisters. She might have been an actress or a fashion designer. And Laurel . . . Laurel might not have needed to fight so hard for justice.

Poor Baby. Guilt nipped her as she thought of the way she'd left Laurel at Frenchie's. She really should have been home now, seeing to it that Laurel was getting some rest. Seeing to her sister's recuperation was her job now. But she had needed this time with Coop. Time without fighting, without words, with nothing but love between them.

There was never anything less than gentleness in his lovemaking. He was always so careful with her. No hurry. No frantic grappling. No rough urgency. Tenderness. Reverence. As if every time was her first time.

No, she thought, her mouth twisting into a parody of a smile. Her first time had been nothing like that.

'You want me, Savannah. I've seen the way you look at me.'

'I don't know what you mean—'

'Liar. You're a little tease, that's what you are.'

'I'm not—'

'Well, I'm going to give you what you're asking for, little girl.'

'No! I don't want you to touch me. I don't like that.'

'Yes, you do. Don't lie to me. Don't lie to yourself. This is what you were made for, Savannah. . . .'

And she had closed her eyes against the first burning pain and damned Ross Leighton to eternal hell.

Lady-killer . . . Killer . . . 'The only place I kill people is on paper.' . . . Liar . . . You're a liar, Jack. . . .

He paced the halls of L'Amour, oblivious of the wallpaper that was peeling off the walls, oblivious of the dust, the dank odor of mildew and neglect, oblivious of everything but his own inner torment. It snarled and snaked inside him like a caged beast, and there was nothing he could do about it but stalk the dark halls of the house. He couldn't set the beast loose because it terrified him to think what he might do – go mad, kill himself.

Kill himself. The idea had crossed his mind more than once. But he dismissed it. He didn't deserve the freedom death would offer. It was his punishment to live, knowing he was worthless, knowing he had killed the one person who had seen good in him.

Evie. Her face floated before his mind's eye, soft, pretty, her dark eyes wide and trusting. Trust – that cut at him like a razor. She had trusted him. She was as fragile as fine blown glass, and she had trusted him not to break her. In the end he had destroyed her, shattered her. Killed her.

A wild, indistinguishable cry tore up from the depths of him, and he turned and slammed his fist against the wall, the sounds of agony and impact echoing through the empty house. Empty, like his heart, like his soul, like the bottle of Wild Turkey dangling from the fingers of his left hand. The beast lunged at its barriers, and he whirled and flung the bottle and listened to it smash against a door down the hall.

'Worthless, useless, rotten . . .'

The image of Blackie Boudreaux rose up from one of the dark corners of his mind to taunt, and he stumbled from the hall, through a dark room, and out onto the upper gallery to escape it.

'Bon à rien, tu, bon à rien . . .'

The memory came after him like a demon, painfully sharp and so bright, he squeezed his eyes closed against it. He pressed his back against the brick wall, braced himself, held himself rigid until every muscle quivered with the effort, but nothing stopped the memory from coming.

His mother stood doubled over by the kitchen sink, blood running from her nose and lip. Tears swam in her eyes and streamed down her cheeks, but she didn't cry aloud. She knew better. Blackie didn't want to hear caterwauling; it made him meaner. Le bon Dieu knew he was mean enough in the best of times.

Jack clutched at her skirt, frightened, angry, ten years old. Too small to do anything. Worthless, useless, good for nothing. Good for hating. He figured he was an expert at that. He hated his father with every cell of his body, and that hate launched him away from his mother's trembling legs and into Blackie's path as he advanced, arm drawn back for another blow.

A high-pitched scream pierced the air as Marie came running in. Jack didn't glance at his little sister, but yelled for her to get out as he flung himself at their father. He wished he were bigger, stronger, big enough to hit Blackie as hard as Blackie hit Maman, but he wasn't. He was just a puny runt kid, just like Papa always told him.

That didn't mean he wouldn't try.

He balled his fists, meaning to pound his old man as best he could, but Blackie had other ideas. He swung the arm he had pulled back to strike his wife with, instead backhanding Jack across the face, knocking him aside like a doll.

Jack hit the floor, his head spinning and throbbing, tears clouding his vision, hate burning through him like acid.

Then suddenly he wasn't ten anymore. He was a teenager, and he got to his feet and grabbed the iron skillet off the stove and swung it with both hands as hard as he could. . . .

He jerked as his mind slammed the door on the memory.

'The only place I kill people is on paper, sugar. . . .'

From where he stood in the deep shadows of the gallery he could see Belle Rivière. He could see across the darkened courtyard to the back door, where the outside light was still burning. All the windows were dark. Sane people were in bed at this hour. Laurel was in bed.

'And I sit in the still of the night and howl at the moon,' he mumbled, sliding down to sit on the weathered floor of the gallery. Huey materialized from the shadows and sat down beside him, a grave look on his face, pendulous lips hanging down.

'You don' know enough to stay away from the like of me, do you, stupid hound?'

Laurel knew enough. She was wary of him.

'And well you should be, *mon ange*,' he murmured, staring across at the black windows of Belle Rivière.

She had let him kiss her, had let him get close, but in the end she had shied away. Just as well for her sake. He was a user and a cad. *Lady-killer . . . killer.*

The word simmered in his brain as he pushed himself to his feet and went inside to work.

8

Savannah took the demise of her Corvette with remarkable good grace. It was news of who had been driving she took exception to.

'Jack?' She arched a brow, stiffening slowly but visibly, her back straightening. She sat on Laurel's bed, wearing her champagne silk robe open over a black lace teddy, looking like an ad for Victoria's Secret with her hair mussed and her lips kiss-swollen. 'What the hell were you doing out on the bayou road with Jack Boudreaux?'

'A question I asked myself as we hurtled along like some kind of rocket test car on the salt flats,' Laurel grumbled as she studied herself with a critical eye in the cheval glass.

The skirt she wore was soft and flowing with a pattern of mauve cabbage roses and deep green leaves on an ivory background. The waist was riding at the top of her hips, and the hem hung nearly to her ankles. Weight loss was hell on the wardrobe. It would have to do. She hadn't brought many good outfits with her. At any rate, the petal pink cotton summer sweater was baggy enough to hide the sagging waist. She heaved a sigh of resignation and looked at her sister via the glass.

'I can't drive a stick. He offered – no, he *commandeered*,' she corrected, irritated all over again with his highhandedness. If he hadn't been so pushy, she never would have ended up kissing him, never would have ended up staring at the ceiling half the night.

Savannah frowned, hit unaware by a jolt of jealousy. Frenchie's was her territory, her little kingdom of men. Jack Boudreaux was a member of her court. She didn't like the idea of his sniffing around her baby sister, especially when he had yet to come sniffing around *her*. And she didn't like the idea of sharing Laurel, either. Laurel had come home to her big sister for love and comfort, not to Jack Boudreaux.

'He's trouble,' she said, rising to come and stand behind Laurel. 'Stay away from him.'

Laurel shot a curious look over her shoulder as Savannah fussed with the lace collar of her sweater. 'Yesterday you seemed charmed enough by him.'

'It's one thing for me to be charmed by him. I don't want him charming you, Baby. The man's a cad.'

Savannah the great protector. Always watching out for her while no one watched out for Savannah. A cad was good enough for Savannah, or a pool shark ten years her junior, or a married Pulitzer Prize-winner old enough to be her father. Laurel chewed back the urge to say something she knew she would regret. She loved her sister, wanted something better for her than the life Savannah had chosen for herself, but now was not the time to say so. She had enough on her mind thinking of the dinner she had no appetite for.

'You said he was a writer. What does he write?'

'Oooh,' Savannah cooed, a wicked smile curling the corners of her mouth and sparkling in her eyes. 'Deliciously gruesome horror novels. The kind of stuff that makes you wonder how the man sleeps nights. Don't you ever go to the bookstores, Baby? Jack's practically always on the best-seller lists.'

Laurel couldn't remember the last time she'd read anything that wasn't written in legalese. The Case had consumed all her time, pushing all else out of her life – her hobbies, her friends, her husband, her perspective . . . at any rate, she wasn't given to reading the kinds of books that kept people up wide-eyed with fear of everything that went bump in the night. She didn't need to pay money to be horrified and get depressed. She dealt with enough real-life horrors. Depression was something she could get for free.

She tried to reconcile her image of Jack, the piano-playing, car-stealing, kiss-stealing rogue, with her mental image of what a horror novelist would be like, and couldn't. But there was another Jack, the man she had caught glimpses of at odd moments. A harder, darker man with an inner intensity that unnerved her. Just the memory of that man brought out a strange skittishness in her, and so she dismissed all thoughts of him and concentrated instead on the matter at hand.

She looked at herself in the mirror again, deciding she looked like a little girl playing dress-up in her mother's clothes. Not that Vivian had ever allowed them to do such a thing. Savannah rummaged through a drawer in the walnut commode and came back with two safety pins. She made a pair of pleats in the front waist of the skirt and secured them, hiding the pins with the hem of the sweater.

'Instant fit. Old fashion-model's trick,' she said absently, studying Laurel with sharp scrutiny.

'Why didn't you stick with it?' Laurel asked.

'You'll wear my new gold earrings,' she muttered, then snapped her head up. 'What? Modeling?'

'You had a good thing going with that agency in New Orleans.'

Savannah sniffed, lifting one shoulder in a casual shrug while she picked up a makeup brush and a pat of blusher and expertly dusted soft mauve along Laurel's cheekbones. 'Andre loved me for my blow jobs, not my portfolio. I wasn't good enough – at modeling, that is. I happen to give the world's greatest blow job.'

Laurel didn't comment, but Savannah caught the tightening of her jaw, the thinning of her mouth. Disapproval. It stung, and she resented it. 'Do what you do best, Baby,' she said, a fine razor edge to her voice. 'Your thing is justice. My talents lie elsewhere.

'Now, let's take a look at you,' she said briskly, setting the makeup aside. 'I can't imagine why you're going to this. I would have told Vivian to go to hell.'

'You have,' Laurel said flatly. 'On numerous occasions.'

'So it's your turn. She jerks you around like a dog on a leash—'

'Sister, please.' She closed her eyes briefly. Lord, if she wasn't up to this fight, what in hell would she do at Beauvoir? A tremor of nerves rattled through her. Dinner with Vivian and company was like dancing through a mine field. God, she thought derisively, how had she ever survived in the courtroom when she was such a coward?

'I could have said no,' she said wearily, 'but I don't need the trouble. One meal, and I'm off the hook. I might as well get it over with.'

Savannah made a noncommittal sound. 'Well, please borrow my new gold earrings, and for chrissakes, don't wear those awful Buddy Holly glasses. They make you look like that little chicken in the Foghorn Leghorn cartoons.'

Laurel arched a brow. 'You don't want me to go, but you want me to look good?'

Her pale eyes turned hard and cold, and a bitter smile cut across her lush mouth. 'I want Vivian to look at you and feel like the dried up old hag she is.'

Laurel frowned as Savannah went to fetch the earrings from her room. They had always been adversaries – Savannah and their mother. Vivian was too selfish, too self-absorbed to have a daughter as beautiful, as attractive to men as Savannah was. Their rivalry was yet another unhealthy facet in an unhealthy relationship. That rivalry was one reason Laurel had always downplayed her own looks. Always the little diplomat, she hadn't wanted to rock an already listing boat by attracting attention to herself. Her other reason wasn't so noble, she admitted, scowling at herself in the mirror.

If I'm not as pretty as Savannah, then Ross will leave me alone. He picked Savannah, not me. Lucky me.

There wasn't a word for the kind of guilt those memories brought, Laurel thought as Savannah returned. Her robe had slipped off one shoulder as she fiddled with the earrings, revealing a hickey the size of a silver dollar marring her porcelain skin. Laurel's stomach knotted, and she wondered how she was ever going to choke down pot roast.

Sunday dinner at Beauvoir was a tradition as old as the South. The

491

Chandlers had always attended Sunday services – as much out of a sense of duty and obligation to the community as out of reverence for the commandments – then a chosen few would be invited to dine at Beauvoir and pass the day away in genteel pursuits. There were no Chandlers left at Beauvoir, but the tradition endured, a part of Vivian's twisted sense of social responsibility.

If only she had possessed a fraction of that sense of responsibility for her own family, Laurel thought as she stood on the veranda and rang the bell. It had begun to rain again, and she listened to it as she waited, hoping in vain that the soft sound would soothe her ragged nerves. She thumbed a Maalox tablet free of the roll in her skirt pocket and popped it in her mouth.

The downtrodden Olive answered the door, as gray and gloomy as the afternoon, looking at Laurel with dull eyes, as though she had never seen her before. Laurel tried to give her a sympathetic smile as she stepped past the woman and headed toward the main parlor, visions of old zombie movies flickering in the back of her mind.

This would be the perfect setting for a horror movie or a horror novel. The old plantation on the edge of the swamp, a place of secrets, old hatreds, twisted minds. A place where tradition was warped into something grotesque, and family love curdled like spoiled cream. She tried to imagine Jack writing it, but could picture him only in a Hawaiian shirt with his baseball cap on backward and that cat-that-got-the-canary grin on his face. The image brought a ghost of a smile to her lips as she pictured him here, in the main parlor of Beauvoir, observing the assembled guests.

That he wouldn't exactly fit in was the understatement of the year. Ross stood near the sideboard looking freshly pressed and perfectly groomed in a silver-gray suit. He was the model of the well-bred, distinguished Southern gentleman, right down to his neatly manicured fingernails. The easy, patronizing smile. The aura of authority.

Laurel dragged her gaze away from him, sure the hate she felt for him was strong enough, magnetic enough to draw the attention of everyone in the room. She focused instead, briefly, on the other guests, quickly sizing them up in a way that was automatic to her. As a prosecuting attorney she'd had to draw swift and accurate impressions of victims, perpetrators, prospective witnesses, defense attorneys. She did so now for many of the same reasons – to give herself an edge, to formulate a strategy.

The man Ross was speaking with wore a clergyman's collar. He was small and thin and balding, and nodded so often in agreement with Ross's pontificating that he looked as if he had some kind of nervous condition. She labeled him as weak and obsequious and moved on.

A middle-aged couple stood behind the settee where Jack had corralled her the night before. A pair of plump, pleasant faces – the man's slightly sunburned, the woman's pale and perfectly made up. The woman wore a pale pink suit with a flared jacket that looked too crisp not to be brand-new, and her black hair had that wash-and-set roundness achieved by an hour of teasing and back-combing in a chair at Yvette's House of Style. Her gaze strayed continually, covetously to the obvious signs of wealth in the room. They would be neighbors, Laurel guessed. Planters, but not on a par with the massive Chandler-Leighton holdings. People who would be suitably humbled and impressed with an invitation to Beauvoir.

She moved on to Vivian, enthroned in her wing chair, looking cool and sophisticated in a royal blue linen dress. The other wing chair was occupied by a tall, dark-haired man who sat slightly turned, so that Laurel couldn't see his face. Before she could shift positions to get a quick look at him, Vivian caught sight of her and rose from her chair, the corners of her mouth curling upward in her version of a motherly smile.

'Laurel, darlin'.'

She came forward, hands extended. Dutifully, Laurel took hold of her mother's fingers and suffered through the ritual peck on the cheek as they became the focal point in the room.

'Mama.'

'We missed you at services this morning.'

'I'm sorry. I wasn't feeling up to it.'

'Yes, well . . .' Vivian kept the thin smile in place. Only Laurel caught the censure in her gaze. 'We know you need your rest, dear. Come meet everyone. Ross, look, Laurel is here.'

Ross came forward, his smile like a banner across his face. 'Laurel, darlin', aren't you looking pretty today!'

He put a hand on her shoulder, and she moved deftly away, not willing to suffer his touch for anyone's sake. 'Ross,' she murmured, tipping her head to avoid making eye contact with him.

The clergyman was introduced as Reverend Stipple. His handshake was as soft as a grandmother's. The couple, Don and Glory Trahern, had recently taken over the plantation of Glory's uncle, Wilson Kincaid, whom Laurel remembered vaguely as a friend of her father's. Don Trahern seemed a nice mild-mannered sort. Glory was obviously courting Vivian's favor, smiling too hard and gushing too many pleasantries. Laurel murmured the requisite greeting, then found her gaze straying to the last of the group to be introduced.

The little circle of guests opened to make way for him, everyone looking up at him as if he were the crown prince of some foreign place come to grace poor little Bayou Breaux with his presence.

'. . . and our guest of honor today,' Vivian said. 'Stephen Danjermond, our district attorney. Stephen, my daughter Laurel.'

A setup. Laurel felt as though she'd been blindsided. She had expected Vivian's usual assemblage of minor local royalty. She hadn't expected her mother to play this game. She and Danjermond were the only people in the room younger than forty-five. The only two people conspicuously unattached. She felt like a fool, and she felt like leaving. But she gritted her teeth and held her hand out, tilting what she hoped was a blandly pleasant look up at the district attorney.

'It's a pleasure to meet you, Mr. Danjermond.'

'The pleasure is mine,' he said smoothly.

His gaze caught hers like a tractor beam and held it, steady, unblinking, calm. Flat calm, like the sea on a windless day. His eyes were a clear, odd shade of green. The color of peridot, fringed by thick, short lashes and set deep beneath a strong, straight brow. He was strikingly handsome, his face a long rectangle with a strong jaw and a slim, straight nose. His mouth was wide and mobile, curving up on the ends in a sensual, almost feline way.

He would be a formidable opponent in the courtroom. Laurel knew it instinctively, could feel the power of his personality in his gaze even while she could read nothing of his thoughts. She started to draw her hand back, but he held on to her – lightly but firmly, closing both his long, elegant hands over her much smaller one.

'I've heard so much about you,' he said. 'I've been looking forward to meeting you, Laurel.'

There was something almost intimate in his tone. His voice was a warm, well-schooled, well-modulated baritone that vibrated with the ring of old Southern money.

'Stephen is from New Orleans,' Vivian said brightly, raising her voice a fraction as thunder rumbled overhead. 'I met his mother years ago – though no one will get me to confess how many years,' she added coyly, lashes fluttering. 'Back when I spent summers with my cousin, Tallant Jordan Hill. You remember Cousin Talli, don't you, Laurel? Her father was in oil, and his brother was the one who made such a fortune in the silver market and then lost it all on the New York Stock Exchange? It was such a scandal!

'Laurel was a junior bridesmaid in Cousin Talli's second wedding,' she explained. Glory Trahern hung on every word. Everyone else's eyes had begun to glaze over. 'Her first husband was crushed to death, you know, Lord, it was a horrible thing! But Talli bounced back and remarried well.

'A remarkable woman, Talli. She introduced me to Stephen's mother at a soiree. A lovely woman, just a precious, lovely woman! As it turns out, we had both attended Sacred Heart, but she was several years older than I, and we ran in different circles.

'The Danjermonds have been in shipping for years,' she said in conclusion, mention of business making the men tune in once again.

'Shipping and politics,' Danjermond said. To his credit, he had managed to smile all the way through Vivian's monologue. 'My elder brother, Simon, went into the shipping business. That left politics for me.'

The rest of the cast cooed and bobbed their heads approvingly. Laurel bristled. He still held her hand, and she couldn't pull it loose without creating a scene. She brought her chin up a notch and looked him hard in the eye.

'I've always been of the belief that a prosecuting attorney's first loyalty is the pursuit of justice, not public office.'

Glory Trahern sucked in a little gasp and put a hand to the bow at her throat as if it were choking her. The rest of the party stood staring at Laurel with owl eyes, except Vivian, whose stare more resembled a she-wolf's. Only Danjermond himself seemed unoffended. His smile curled a little deeper at the corners of his mouth.

'I'd heard you were quite the champion for Lady Justice.'

'That was my job,' she said flatly, refusing to be charmed. 'And yours.'

He tipped his head, conceding the point. 'So it is, and my record speaks for itself. The good people of Partout Parish can attest to that.'

'We certainly can, Stephen,' Vivian chirped.

Beaming a smile at him, she stepped to his side and slipped her arm through his, as if she had decided Laurel wasn't worthy of him so she was taking him back. Laurel pulled her hand free and crossed her arms, thinking she might have been amused if she hadn't been so damn angry with her mother to begin with.

'Your record is impeccable,' Vivian went on, glowing proudly at him, as if she were somehow responsible for this paragon of manhood. 'I declare, I don't know how we'd get along without you. While all around us crime is running rampant throughout Acadiana, Partout Parish has become a virtual haven for the law-abiding.'

'I swear,' Glory Trahern gushed, leaning over to touch Danjermond's arm as if he were a lucky charm. 'I hardly dare to set foot across the parish line, what with all these murders going on around us.'

Danjermond's green eyes glowed with amusement as he met Laurel's skeptical stare. 'You see, Laurel, the advantage of having a politically ambitious district attorney? I have to do my job well, or no one will vote for me when I run for office.'

The comment drew chuckles all around. Vivian patted his sleeve, pleased with his benevolent good humor. Laurel managed a smile. Stephen Danjermond was hardly the first politician to train for the job in the district attorney's office. She was hardly up to arguing philosophy with him at any rate. She had come here to put in her required appearance, that was all. By the looks Vivian was sliding her, she figured she would do well to stick to that plan.

Be a good girl, Laurel. Don't rock the boat, Laurel. Always say the right thing, Laurel.

Olive slunk into the room, looking almost apologetic, and announced in a meek monotone that dinner was ready, flinching like a whipped dog as lightning flashed outside the tall French doors.

'Well, I certainly have an appetite!' Ross announced with a blazing smile. He slapped Reverend Stipple on the shoulder. 'How about you, Reverend?'

The minister bobbed his head like a window ornament in the back of a hopped-up Chevy. 'I surely do.'

Everyone moved on toward the dining room, Vivian leading Danjermond ahead, then returning without him to herd the rest of her guests out of the parlor. She snagged Laurel by the arm and held her back as the others continued down the hall, chatting amicably.

Laurel closed her eyes briefly and bit down on a sigh.

'Laurel Leanne! How dare you be rude to a guest in this house!' Vivian snapped, her voice a harsh whisper, her bony fingers biting into Laurel's arm. 'Stephen Danjermond is an extremely important man. There's no telling how far he will go in politics.'

'That doesn't mean I have to agree with him, Mama,' Laurel pointed out, knowing it wouldn't do her any good. Her mother's code demanded that ladies be agreeable regardless. It wouldn't have mattered if Stephen Danjermond's politics had rivaled Adolf Hitler's for extremism.

Vivian pinched her lips together and narrowed her eyes. 'Be civil to him, Laurel. I raised you to be a lady and won't tolerate less in this house. Stephen is educated, powerful, from a very good family.'

Translation: Stephen Danjermond was a prize catch. No doubt every debutante in the parish had her sights set on him. Laurel wanted to tell her mother that she wasn't fishing, but she kept the comment to herself. Somehow it had never occurred to Vivian that she might need time to heal in the wake of all that had happened to her.

'I'm sorry, Mama,' she murmured, not wanting to prolong the argument.

'Oh, well,' Vivian said with a sigh, her temper cooling as abruptly as it had flared up. 'You've always had your headstrong moments. You're just like your father that way.'

She reached up to brush lightly at Laurel's bangs, her expression softening into one of her rare, truly motherly looks. 'You do look pretty today, darlin'. This shade of pink becomes you.'

Laurel said thank you, hating herself for letting the compliment mean anything to her. She never seemed able to escape that childish need for her mother's approval.

A weakness. One of many.

She glanced at her watch as Vivian took her by the arm and led her out of the room, wondering how soon she could leave. This emotional tug-of-war wasn't what she needed to get herself back on track.

It's just a dinner, just a couple of hours. Get through it and go home.

The dining room was as elegant as the parlor, as filled with heirlooms and oil portraits of Chandlers dead and gone. The Hepplewhite table and shield-back chairs shone from two centuries of hand-polishing. Footfalls sounded against the cypress floor and bounded up to the twelve-foot ceiling. Glory Trahern stared up as if she were trying to see them rather than calculating the worth of the blown glass chandelier. Her husband snatched her arm and herded her toward a chair.

Not surprisingly, Laurel found herself seated directly across from Stephen Danjermond, who had the place of honor – at the right hand of Vivian, who sat at one end of the table, opposite Ross. Laurel slid into her chair and focused on her Wedgwood plate, uncomfortably aware of the handsome, elegant, articulate man across from her, wishing she had worn her glasses. She didn't want to attract his attention any more than she had wanted to attract the attention of her stepfather two decades ago. There was no room in her life for a man right now.

The image of Jack's mocking smile appeared before her mind's eye, and she frowned and speared a stalk of baby asparagus.

The topic of law and order had survived the trip down the hall, and the participants discussed the dynamic duo of Partout Parish – Sheriff Duwayne Kenner and District Attorney Danjermond – pleased and proud of the fact that crime here was being kept to a minimum.

'People can say what they will about Kenner's personality,' Ross said with his usual air of supreme authority, 'but the man does his job. I dare say if those killings had taken place in our parish, Kenner would have had the man responsible by now.'

'Perhaps,' Danjermond murmured as Olive collected his salad plate and slunk away. 'He would certainly do his utmost. He's a very capable man, and tenacious as they come. However, we have to remember that killers of this sort are notoriously clever. Brilliant even.'

'Sick,' Glory Trahern said, fussing with her bow as she shivered. 'Crazy and sick, that's what he is.'

He tipped his head, conceding the possibility. 'Or cold. Emotionless. Soulless.' He turned his intense, mesmerizing gaze on Laurel. 'What do you think, Laurel? Is our Bayou Strangler crazy or evil?'

Laurel twisted her napkin in her lap, wishing herself away from this conversation, afraid that it would gradually turn her way and the Traherns and Reverend Stipple and Stephen Danjermond would want to hear all about her life as 'the prosecutor who cried wolf.' 'I . . . I couldn't say,' she murmured. 'I don't have enough knowledge about the cases to form an educated guess.'

'There is a difference, though, don't you agree?' he prodded, the insistence in his voice subtle, smooth, strong. 'While society deems all murderers insane to one degree or another, the courts have a different criterion. In the eyes of the law, there is a distinct difference.

'You believe in evil, don't you, Laurel?'

Laurel met his steady gaze, uneasiness drifting through her. She didn't want to be drawn into this conversation, but Danjermond held her attention, and the other diners waited expectantly. She could feel their eyes, sense the pressure of their held breath. Thunder rolled through the leaden skies outside. The rain came a little harder.

'Yes,' she said softly. 'Yes, I do.'

'And good must triumph over evil. That is the foundation of our judicial system.'

Yes, but it didn't always. She knew that better than most, and so she held her tongue and glanced away, and Danjermond's cool green eyes held fast on her, speculating.

'Speaking of good and evil,' Laurel said, catching the eye of Reverend Stipple, 'what do you make of Jimmy Lee Baldwin, Reverend?'

'As much as I hate to speak ill of anyone, my own opinion of him is less than complimentary,' the minister said as he served himself a portion of beef. 'He's a bit too fancy for my tastes. However, his television ministry does reach out to the homebound and calls back those who may have left the fold of Christ on the wayward paths of life.'

One opinion was canceled out by the other, but Laurel bit her tongue on the urge to point that out. *Just do your time and get the hell out of here.*

'And he *is* campaigning against sin in the community,' Reverend Stipple went on, looking as though he might just convince himself to like Baldwin after all.

Laurel thought of Savannah's comment about Jimmy Lee Baldwin's twisted sexual preferences and held her tongue as the potatoes came her way.

'I hear he's going to try to close down Frenchie's Landing,' Glory Trahern said, her eyes lighting up at the chance to pass on gossip.

'Yes,' Laurel said, 'and the owners are very upset about it.' At least T-Grace Delahoussaye was upset. She had to take T-Grace's word for it that Ovide was upset.

'You've been there?'

Laurel winced inwardly at Vivian's tone, but pushed the fear of her mother's reaction aside. She was a grown woman, able to go where she chose. 'I had to see a man about a dog,' she said, cutting the one thin slice of roast she had taken. 'While Frenchie's doesn't compare with the country club, it hardly seemed the den of sin Mr. Baldwin is trying to make it out to be.'

'It's nowhere for respectable people to go,' Vivian commented, her face tight with disapproval.

'I see your point, though, Laurel, darlin',' Ross announced. 'Skeeter Mouton's is by far the most notorious place in the parish. If Baldwin were serious about this war against sin, Mouton's would be the likely target. I suspect, however, that Mr. Baldwin knows too well the kind of trouble he'd be asking for poking at that hornets' nest. He'd get himself killed.'

'Instead, he's harassing a legitimate business.'

'Are you taking up the Delahoussayes' cause, Laurel?' Danjermond asked mildly.

Laurel met his steady gaze once again. 'I'm not practicing at the moment, but someone should take up their cause.'

He shrugged slightly. 'I can't act on their behalf unless they make a formal complaint. You might pass that information along. It isn't against the law to preach; trespassing is another matter.'

'Yes, I already have made that suggestion to them.'

He smiled slowly, as if to tell her he knew her far better than she knew herself. 'So you *are* taking up their cause, aren't you, Laurel?'

The truth of his statement stopped her short for a second, but she shook it off. 'I merely made a suggestion.'

'Stephen has more important causes to take up. Don't you, Stephen, dear?' Vivian said, reaching out to pat his hand approvingly. 'Why don't you tell us about the state attorney general's appointing you head of the Acadiana drug task force?'

The meal progressed at a snail's pace. Laurel picked at her food and glanced at her watch every thirty seconds. Finally, they left the table and went back to the parlor for coffee. While Vivian bossed Olive around and the Traherns settled on the gold settee, Laurel roamed to the French doors and stood with her cup in her hand, staring out wistfully at the rain-washed garden. The thundershower had passed. When she escaped, she would go back to Belle Rivière and take a book out to the courtyard and sit in a corner reading and absorbing the quiet, the scent of rain, roses, and wisteria.

'Is the company really all that unpleasant?'

She started and glanced up, surprised to find Danjermond standing so close beside her. He had abandoned his coffee and stood with his hands tucked into the pockets of his fashionable pleated trousers.

'No, not at all,' Laurel said quickly.

Danjermond smiled like a cat. 'You're not a terribly good liar, Laurel. Tell the truth now. You'd rather be elsewhere.'

'I admit I didn't come back to Bayou Breaux to socialize.'

'Then it's my good fortune you made an exception in this case. Unless I'm the reason you're staring so longingly out that window, wishing yourself away.'

'Of course not.'

'Good, because I was about to suggest we get together in a more intimate setting one evening soon. A candlelit dinner, perhaps.'

'I hardly know you, Mr. Danjermond.'

'That's the whole point of intimate dinners, isn't it? To get to know each other. I'd like to find out more about your views, your plans, yourself.'

'I have no plans for the moment. And I don't care to discuss my views. I'm not trying to be rude,' she said, lifting her free hand in a gesture of peace. 'The fact of the matter is I was recently divorced and have been through a great deal in the past year. I'm simply not up to a date at this point.'

'Or a job offer?' he queried, lifting a brow, seeming not the least affected by her rejection of him personally.

Laurel tucked her chin back and eyed him with more than a hint of suspicion. 'Why would you offer me a job? We've only just met.'

'Because I can always use another good prosecutor in my office. The Scott County case notwithstanding, you have an excellent record. Your work on the Valdez migrant worker case was outstanding, and you went far above and beyond the call of duty investigating the rape of that blind woman back when you were little more than a clerk for the DA's office in Fulton County.'

She had been barely out of law school. It was ancient history. The fact that he had for some reason dug that deeply into her past brought a return of the uneasiness she had felt earlier. She crossed her arms in front of her, careful not to dump coffee down the front of her sweater. 'You seem to have an inordinate knowledge of my career, Mr. Danjermond.'

'I'm a very thorough man, Laurel.' He smiled again, that even, handsome smile. 'You might say attention to detail has gotten me where I am today.'

To the DA's office in backwater Louisiana? It seemed an odd thing to say, considering Stephen Danjermond had Bigger Things written all over him. With his pedigree and family connections, Laurel would have expected him to be firmly entrenched in Baton Rouge or New Orleans.

'There is a method to my madness, I assure you,' he said, reading her silence with amazing accuracy. 'Ambitious prosecutors are a dime a dozen in New Orleans. Acadiana offers me the chance to shine on my own. And there are unique problems here, problems I feel I can help control – drug smuggling, gun running. There is a certain element in the bayou country that remains largely uncivilized. Bringing that faction to heel and making them realize the days of Jean Lafitte are long past is a worthy goal.'

'And one that will attract the attention of the powers that be.'

His broad shoulders rose and fell. '*C'est la vie. C'est la guerre.* To the victor go the spoils.'

'I know how the game is played, Mr. Danjermond,' Laurel said in a cool tone. 'I'm not naive.'

'No, you're an idealist. A much more difficult lot in life. Better to be a cynic.'

'Is that what you are? A cynic?'

'I'm a pragmatist.' He held her gaze and let the silence build between them until Laurel had to fight herself to keep from stepping back. 'Will you consider my offer?'

She shook her head. 'I'm sorry. I'm flattered, but I can't think about work yet.'

'But it's not just work to you, is it, Laurel? The pursuit of justice is a calling for you, an obsession,' he said. 'Isn't it, Laurel?'

The question was too personal. She was feeling too sensitive. He stood a little too close, watched her too intently. He looked relaxed, and yet she had the impression of leashed power beneath his calm facade. He was too . . . everything. Too tall, too handsome, too charming. Too still.

She glanced at the platinum Rolex strapped to his wrist, and relief flooded through her. 'I'm afraid I have to be leaving now, Mr. Danjermond. I promised my aunt I'd help her with some things this afternoon. It was a pleasure meeting you.'

'Until we meet again, Laurel.'

When donkeys fly, she thought. She hadn't come home for challenges or entanglements or trouble. She backed away another step, some primal instinct keeping her from turning her back too quickly on Stephen Danjermond. He watched her, calm amusement lighting his green eyes, and she turned then, simply to escape looking at his too-handsome face, turned just as Savannah walked in the door.

9

Tension, like electricity, filled the room instantly, tightening skin, raising short hairs, freezing breath. The initial shock held everyone motionless, speechless, then Olive rushed into the room, chalk-faced, eyes brimming with tears.

'I didn't let her in, Mrs. Leighton!' she wailed. 'I didn't! She shoved me!'

Vivian grabbed the maid by the arm and hustled her out into the hall. Savannah watched them go, a smirk tugging at the corners of her lush mouth. The initial responses to her appearance made it worth the trouble she had taken to get out here. She could have turned right around and left, only she wasn't satisfied. She wanted to tear through this little civilized, socially correct affair like a tornado and carry her baby sister off with her when she went. Damned if she was going to let Vivian dig her claws into Laurel or let Ross get within two feet of her.

She looked past the shocked faces of Glory and Don Trahern and Reverend Stipple, to her dear old stepdaddy. Ross's expression was guarded, like that of a poker player bluffing on a busted hand. He still wanted her. She was sure of that, and she smiled at him to let him know she knew. To remind herself he had chosen her over his wife, over her mother. To reinforce the truth in her own mind – that she was a born whore and would never be anything else. And she reveled in the moment, in making him wonder, making him squirm.

Feeling smug, she strolled into the room, her gait loose, hips swinging. She had dressed for the occasion in a scandalously short, sleeveless dress that was white with large red amaryllis blossoms splashed across it, and fit her like skin on a sausage. Aside from her red stiletto heels, it was the only article of clothing she wore. She had looped a long strand of pearls carelessly around her neck to accompany her ever-present pendant, and brushed her hair upside down so that it was now like a cloud around her shoulders, wild and sexy. Her Ray-Bans completed the outfit, hiding her eyes, giving her an air of mystery.

'Savannah,' Laurel said, finding her tongue at last. She studied her sister and chose her words carefully. 'We didn't expect to see you.'

'I had a change in plans,' Savannah said evenly. 'I need to borrow your car, Baby. Seeing how mine is temporarily out of commission.'

'Of course.' Laurel took a step toward the door. 'You can give me a ride back to Belle Rivière. I was just leaving.'

'So soon?' Savannah cooed, disappointment plumping out her lower lip as she slid her sunglasses down her nose and stroked a gaze down Stephen Danjermond. 'I haven't even been properly introduced.'

Laurel bit her tongue and held her temper, saying a quick prayer that her sister wouldn't do anything more outrageous than she already had. She slipped an arm through Savannah's, intent on controlling her in some way.

'Stephen Danjermond, my sister, Savannah. Savannah—'

'District Attorney Danjermond,' Savannah murmured, preening like a cat, offering her free hand to the man Vivian had obviously marked for Laurel. 'Such a pleasure, Mr. Danjermond. Savannah Chandler Leighton at your . . .' Her gaze slid down the long, lean, elegant length of him, lingering suggestively. '. . . service.'

'Miss Leighton?' One dark brow rose a fraction. 'You go by your stepfather's name?'

'Oh, yes,' Savannah purred, stroking the palm of his hand with her fingertip. She shot a look at Ross across the room. 'I owe my stepdaddy *so* much after all.' She lifted one shoulder in a casual shrug. 'Ross made me what I am today, you know.'

'Savannah.' Vivian's voice cut across the parlor like a scimitar. She stood rigid and queenly beside her chair, hands clasped tightly in front of her. 'What a surprise to see you here.'

'Yes, I expect it is,' Savannah drawled sweetly, cocking a hip and planting her hand on it in a belligerent stance that perfectly mirrored her attitude. 'Seeing how you told me once to get the hell out of this house and never come back.'

Laurel flinched inwardly as her stomach knotted with tension. She moved toward her sister, reaching out to put a hand on Savannah's arm. 'Savannah, please, let's just go.'

'Yes,' Vivian snapped, her alabaster complexion mottling red with anger. 'Please do go. If you can't keep a civil tongue in your head and behave as a lady, you are *not* welcome here.'

Savannah shrugged off Laurel's hand and sauntered toward the door, stopping within a yard of their mother. All the old bitterness seethed up inside her like acid, boiling and churning, eating away at her. Her face twisted into a sour mask. 'I've never been a lady in this house, and I used to be *welcome* day and night.'

'*Sister, please,*' Laurel whispered, taking hold of Savannah's wrist. Her gaze darted between the raw fury and sheen of tears in Vivian's eyes to Ross, who stood across the room, suddenly fascinated by the pattern in the Aubusson rug. '*Please*, let's go.'

The tremor in Laurel's voice was the only thing that kept Savannah from lighting into her mother and shouting to the very proper guests that she was what she was because Ross Leighton had mounted her four times a week from the day she turned thirteen. And her very proper, perfect belle mother had never even suspected – because Vivian saw only what she wanted to see.

Vivian and Ross deserved whatever humiliation she brought them. But now was not the time. Poor Baby, always the peacemaker; she didn't need the tension. Savannah had, after all, come here to rescue her. Besides, she preferred to torture her mother and stepfather in little, never-ending ways.

'Come on, Baby,' she murmured, sliding an arm around Laurel.

They walked out of the parlor in no particular hurry, down the hall past Olive, who stood red-eyed, her flat face pale and wet, her stringy red hair clinging to her cheeks. The maid glared at Savannah. Savannah just laughed.

Laurel wanted to run and fling the door open and sprint for her car, but she was stuck beside Savannah, moving with nightmarish delibera-tion, their shoes clicking against the marble floor. She didn't dare try to rush. When Savannah was in one of her moods, there was no telling what she might do, what might set her off. Outside, the sun was breaking through. The low clouds that had brought the shower were already tearing apart into thin, gauzy strips and floating away. Humidity hung in the air like steam, thick and hard to breathe, intensifying the rich green scents of boxwood and bougainvillea. Savannah paused on the veranda as if she had all day and surveyed what might have been her kingdom if their father had lived.

Laurel saw it too. The broad sweeping emerald lawn, the lush semitropical growth of the cypress swamp beyond, the broad money green leaves of the sugarcane that stretched off in the other direction beyond the pecan grove. Home to generations of Chandlers. Generations that would end with them.

'Why did you have to do that?' she asked.

Savannah slid her sunglasses off and arched a brow. 'Why? Because they deserved it. I came here to save you.'

'Save me?' Laurel shook her head. 'I was doing just fine. It was only a dinner. I was about to leave.'

'Well, isn't that gratitude?' Savannah said sarcastically, cocking her hip. 'I did what you've never had the nerve to do – I stood up to them—'

'I don't see the point in making a big public scene—'

'You wouldn't, would you?'

The remark cut Laurel to the bone. She sucked in a breath and looked away, guilt and anger twining inside her like vines. It wasn't fair of Savannah to blame her for not having been abused by Ross, but it was unpardonable that Laurel felt lucky for the same reason. The cycle of feelings never ended.

'Let's just go home and start the afternoon over, okay?' Start over. That was what she had come to Bayou Breaux to do. Why had she thought she would be able to start over in a place where the past never went away? She wanted to think they could all rise above it and move on, but with every moment she spent here, she felt it pulling at her more and more, like quicksand, like the thick mud of the swamp, sucking her down, draining her strength.

Savannah climbed in on the driver's side of Laurel's black Acura, her dress riding up her bare thighs. Laurel went around the hood and slid into the passenger's seat, her eyes on the veranda of Beauvoir. Olive stood at the main door, glaring at them. There was no sign of Vivian, who was doubtless in the parlor, trying to smooth things over as best she could with her guests.

Poor Mama, always so afraid of what people would think.

'How did you get out here?' she asked absently.

Savannah started the car and swung it around the circular drive, flinging a wave of crushed shell across the yard. She eased off the accelerator as they headed down beneath the canopy of the live oak.

'Ronnie Peltier gave me a ride.' She laughed at that and draped her left arm casually along the open window. 'I gave him three rides last night. I figured he owed me.'

Laurel blew out a sigh and speared a hand back through her hair. 'I wish you wouldn't do that.'

'What? Have sex with Ronnie Peltier?'

'Tell me about it. I don't want to hear it, Sister.'

'Christ, Baby,' Savannah snapped. 'You're such a prude. Maybe if you *had* sex once in a while, you wouldn't be so uptight about it.' She barely slowed for the turn onto the bayou road, wheeling out in front of a four-by-four truck and squealing away from it as a horn blasted indignantly. 'Maybe you ought to take that long, tall district attorney for a ride. He had a look about him.' She smiled slowly, savoring the idea of going a round or two with Stephen Danjermond herself. 'I'll bet he's got a ten-inch cock and screws with his eyes open.'

'I'm sure I don't care,' Laurel grumbled.

'Yeah? Well, I'll bet Vivian cares. A fine, upstanding, well-bred man like Mr. Danjermond. She'd hand you over to him on a platter if she could. Think about it. She could marry you off to a man with money, power, prestige, a big future in politics, and snuff out the last embers of your big scandal all at once. How perfectly neat and tidy and cold – just the way Vivian likes things.'

There was nothing for Laurel to say. She had seen Vivian's game for what it was, too, and it didn't bear comment as far as she was concerned. She had no intention of letting her mother manipulate her – except that she already had. The thought struck her like a hammer to the chest. She had gone to Beauvoir to placate Vivian. Nothing that had happened during the course of that visit could be undone. Because of Vivian, Danjermond was interested in her personally and professionally. Because of Vivian, Savannah had caused a scene, and now there was this tension between them, calling to mind the wedge that would forever both bind them together and hold them apart – Ross's abuse.

'I never should have come back,' she whispered.

'Baby, don't say that!' Savannah exclaimed, stricken by the thought. She shoved her Ray-Bans on top of her head and stared at her sister, taking her eyes off the road for a full ten seconds. 'Don't say that. You needed to come home. I'm going to take care of you, I promise.' She changed hands on the steering wheel and reached across to brush her fingers over Laurel's hair. 'That's all I was doing at Beauvoir – taking care of you, protecting you from Vivian. We'll start all over, starting now. It'll just be you and me and Aunt Caroline and Mama Pearl. We won't do anything but have fun. It'll be just like old times.'

Laurel caught her sister's hand and kissed it and hung on tight while Savannah's attention cut back to the road. *Just like old times. Old times here are not forgotten. . . . But they should be . . .*

'I-I d-didn't mean for Mama to c-catch me! I-I thought she was g-gone to her m-meeting!' Laurel clutched at her sister, crying, miserable, desperate, her cheek still stinging and burning from the slap of Vivian's hand.

She'd done wrong. Mama was furious with her. Heaven only knew but that she might end up having a spell. And it would be all my fault, Laurel thought. She knew she wasn't supposed to have the pictures of Daddy out in the parlor, 'cause if Mr. Leighton saw them, he wouldn't like it. She winced again as the memory swooped down on her like a hawk . . . . .

Vivian stepped into the room with a smile on her face, a smile that vanished as she saw what Laurel was playing with. The photo album, the crawfish tie pin, the bass tie Savannah had stolen out of the boxes for the Lafayette Goodwill. All their little bits of Daddy. They kept them up in Savannah's room, but just once Laurel had wanted to take them down to the parlor and sit by the window where Daddy had held her on his lap on rainy days and told her funny stories that he made up off the top of his head.

'Laurel, what are you doing?' Vivian asked, drifting across the room. She'd been to her hospital auxiliary meeting. She always wore her double pearls to the hospital auxiliary. They clicked together like teeth chattering as she came toward Laurel, her face turning red beneath her perfect makeup as her gaze settled on the collection of mementos. 'Where did you get these things?'

'Um . . . um . . .' Laurel's fingers curled around the edge of the photo album, and she pulled it protectively against her, but it was too late. Vivian jerked the book away from her and gasped.

'Where did you get this? What is it doing out here? Shame on you for dragging this out!' She slammed the album closed and tossed it onto the seat of the old red leather wing chair that had been Daddy's favorite.

She pressed her hands to her cheeks and paced in a short line back and forth, back and forth, as nervous as a racehorse, her eyes flashing with something like panic. 'Shame on you for bringing that out! Mr. Leighton is new to this house, and you're dragging out all this! What would he think if he saw this?'

Laurel didn't really care what Mr. Leighton thought. She didn't like him. Didn't like his staying in Daddy's room. Didn't like the way he patted her head. Didn't like the way he looked at Savannah. She didn't want him at Beauvoir.

'I don't like him!' she blurted, popping up from her seat on the floor, anger making her feel like she could grow to be ten feet tall and mean as an alligator. 'I don't like him and don't care what he thinks!'

The slap came hard and fast and turned her head. Tears rushed up from deep inside and poured down her face, her cheek stinging and half numb. Vivian grabbed her by the shoulders and gave her a shake.

'Don't you *ever* say that!' she said fiercely, her eyes bright with temper and tears. 'Your father is dead. Mr. Leighton is head of this house now, and you will be a good girl and mind him and show respect. Do you understand me, Laurel Leanne?'

Laurel stared at her, wishing she didn't have to say yes. Wishing she could dare say no and still have Mama love her. But she couldn't, and she knew it. Mama already didn't love Savannah most of the time.

'Do you understand me?' she repeated, her voice trembling, on the verge of the kind of hysteria that always came before one of her spells.

'Y-yes, Mama,' Laurel stammered, anger and sorrow tumbling together inside her like a pair of fighting cats. 'I-I'm sorry, Mama.'

That quickly, Vivian's temper cooled visibly. Her hold on Laurel's arms eased. She bent down awkwardly, so as not to wrinkle her new hot pink dress, and stroked Laurel's hair back from her forehead again and again, wiping tears into it. A trembling smile wobbled across her perfectly painted mouth. 'That's my girl. I know you'll be a good girl. You know what's important, don't you, Laurel? You're always such a good girl,' she whispered, sniffling. 'Mama's little pet. You run along now and play elsewhere.'

And Laurel had run. She had run out to find Savannah in the rickety old boathouse down on the bank of the bayou. They sat in the old wooden *bâteau* Daddy had let them use, and Savannah hugged her and wiped her tears. Laurel desperately wanted her to say everything would be all right, but Savannah had stopped saying that after Vivian and Ross had come back from their honeymoon.

So many things had changed so fast. Daddy gone. Ross Leighton taking his place. Some nights it just scared her so to think of it that she couldn't sleep, and she tried to sneak into Savannah's room as she always had, but Savannah kept the secret door locked now and wouldn't tell her why.

'I wish we could take the boat and float all the way to New Orleans,' she mumbled against her sister's shoulder. 'I wish we could run away.'

'We can't,' Savannah murmured, stroking her hair.

'We could go and live with Aunt Caroline.'

'No,' she whispered, staring out at the water. 'Don't you see, Baby? There's no getting away.'

The way she said it made Laurel scared all over again, and she shivered and looked up at her sister, feeling all hollow and achy inside at the sadness in Savannah's eyes. Then Savannah smiled suddenly and tickled her.

'But we can go out on the bayou and pretend we're shipwrecked on a jungle island,' she said, twisting around to untie the *bateau* from its mooring.

And they let the boat drift out of the old cypress shed that looked like a junk heap and smelled like fish, and headed up the bayou to a place where they could pretend the world was perfect and Ross Leighton didn't exist.

'Dat Armentine Prejean, she kin cook, her,' Mama Pearl declared, shaking her wooly head as she snapped beans into a plastic bucket wedged between her tiny feet. 'She don' cook nothin' good for Vivian, but she kin cook, I tell you. If she wasn' cookin' for Vivian, you would'a ate her dinner, *chère.*'

Laurel glanced up from the shrimp salad she was picking at. She had changed out of her skirt into a pair of faded denim shorts and a loose purple cotton blouse, and was feeling comfortably inconspicuous again with her glasses perched on her nose. Everyone had trailed out onto the back gallery of Belle Rivière and settled in, cocooned in the quiet of the courtyard and the warmth of the afternoon. 'The meal was fine, Mama Pearl. I just didn't have much of an appetite, that's all.'

Pearl snorted, her fleshy face folding into creases of supreme disapproval. 'Nothin' but bones, you. You gonna dry up an' blow away if you don' get some fat on you.'

Savannah stretched back on the cushioned lounge and set her book aside. 'Aw, you know what they say, Mama Pearl, a girl can't be too rich or too thin.'

Pearl snorted again. '*Sa c'est de la couyonade.*'

Caroline twirled the ice in her glass of tea, her dark eyes carefully fixed on Laurel. 'We saw you on the news last night, darlin'. Standing toe to toe with that televangelist.'

Pearl cackled and slapped her knees. 'You give him good, talk about! Even knowed your Bible verse! *Ma bon fille!* I tell ever'body at church dis mornin', dat's *my* girl!'

Laurel made a face that was a cross between a smile and a frown and said nothing. What little appetite she had managed to work up for the shrimp salad fled, and she laid her fork across the plate.

'The Delahoussayes are good people,' Caroline said evenly. She let that hang in the air while she recrossed her legs and arranged the hem of her slim pale yellow skirt. 'Would it be difficult to stop Baldwin from harassing them?'

Laurel shrugged. 'Maybe not. They could talk to Judge Monahan. But that doesn't stop Baldwin from waging his war against sin in other ways.'

'A little action is better than a whole lot of talk,' Caroline said. She took a sip of her tea and set it back down, tracing a fingertip down the side of the sweating glass.

'Lord knows, *action* is right up the Revver's alley,' Savannah said dryly, winning herself a frown from Laurel. 'If Jimmy Lee is a man of God, then the Marquis de Sade is right up there in heaven, tying the lady angels to the pearly gates and licking his lips.'

Mama Pearl flung a bean down and scolded Savannah in a rapid stream of Cajun French that rolled off Savannah like water off a duck. Inside the house the telephone rang. Savannah unfolded herself from the chaise in no particular hurry and went to answer it. Pearl collected her bucket and waddled in after her, muttering under her breath.

Laurel quelled the urge to go after them. She could feel Caroline's gaze weighing on her.

'You still belong to the Louisiana Bar Association, don't you?' her aunt asked innocently.

'Yes, but I'm not ready to take anything on,' Laurel argued, her fingers curling into fists on the glass table-top. 'I don't need the trouble.'

Caroline rose, brushing an imaginary crumb from her loose-fitting chocolate silk tunic. She moved a step toward the house, glancing at Laurel as if in afterthought. 'Neither do the Delahoussayes.'

Laurel ground her teeth as her aunt sauntered through the French doors that led directly into her study. 'I came here to rest,' she muttered, crossing her arms and sitting back in her chair. 'I came here for peace and quiet.'

No one answered her. Mama Pearl had gone off to the realm that was her kitchen. Even as Laurel thought of seeking out Savannah so she could vent her spleen, she heard the Acura start and squeal away from the front of the house. Aunt Caroline had given her words of wisdom and retreated.

Suddenly restless, Laurel stood and paced along the gallery for a moment. The afternoon breeze caught at the hem of her blouse, stirred the trailing fronds of a hanging fern, fluttered the pages of Savannah's abandoned book. Sorely in need of a distraction, Laurel bent and snatched up the paperback.

Evil Illusions by Jack Boudreaux.

The cover depicted the swamp at night, misty and dark, the water shining like black glass under a pale moon. Among the dense growth along the bank, a pair of eyes peered out, glowing red. The artwork was enough to make Laurel shiver. She turned the book over and read the back copy as she stepped down off the gallery and wandered along a brick path toward the back of the courtyard.

Master of suspense, New York Times best-selling author Jack Boudreaux creates another spine-tingling read guaranteed to keep the bravest cynic awake nights.

Something is stalking the town of Perdue, Louisiana, preying on children and spreading a terror that threatens to tear the town apart. By day Perdue maintains the facade of a picture-perfect small town, but appearances are illusion, and evil lurks in the woods beyond, waiting for the sun to set.

Beautiful young widow Claire Fontaine has come to Perdue with her daughter to claim an inheritance the locals say is cursed. Haunted by a violent past, she hopes to make a fresh start. But even as she begins a new career as a nurse practitioner in the local clinic, a shadow is falling across her path to happiness. A shadow of menace . . . and death.

As terror tightens its grip on the town, Claire must decide whom she can trust. Is the dashing Dr. Verret a worthy candidate . . . or a killer? Is resident magician Jalen Pierce a harmless huckster, or is his innocent guise . . . an Evil Illusion . . . ?

Intrigued, Laurel settled back on a stone bench in a corner of the courtyard and opened the book at random.

Night clutches the swamp in a grip as cold and black as death. Fingers of mist slither among the trunks of the cypress like ghostly snakes. From somewhere in the distance comes a roar that calls to mind prehistoric times, primeval swamps, ancient monsters.

Fear runs in rivulets down Paula's back. As she sits in the bâteau, *waiting, watching, a sense of evil presses in on her. It is thick and heavy in the air. As thick as the mist. As suffocating as a blanket. She claws at the collar of her blouse and tries to swallow, swings around at a rustle in the underbrush behind her.*

A nutria screams as it meets its death. A cottonmouth breaks the surface of the bayou, its long, lithe body wrapped around the thrashing body of a bullfrog. Overhead a winged black shape swoops down from the branches of a tree. Another night predator. An owl . . . a bat . . . something hideous . . . something terrifying

. . . And a scream rips from Paula's throat. Hot, wild, raw. A scream like the nutria's. The scream of prey. Heard by no one. Swallowed up by the night.

'I'm flattered.'

Laurel jumped, her heart leapfrogging into her throat. Jack stood not two feet away, leaning indolently against one of Aunt Caroline's Grecian lady statues, his hands in the pockets of his worn jeans, one leg cocked. He looked tough and sexy in a faded black T-shirt depicting a dancing alligator and the slogan 'Gator Bait Bar. *Restaurant et Salle de Danse.*' The cut above his left eye only added to his aura of dangerous mystery, and somehow complemented the tiny ruby that winked blood red on his earlobe.

Laurel gathered her indignation and hopped to her feet, slapping the book shut. 'You scared the life out of me!'

Jack grinned at her outrage. 'My editor will be glad to hear it. She pays me bags full of money to scare people.'

'That's not what I meant, and you know it. What do you think you're doing, sneaking up on me?'

He pressed his hands to his heart and looked too innocent to be believed. 'Me, I was just walking along, thinking to myself I oughta do the neighborly thing and stop by for a visit.'

She crossed her arms and tapped her toe, eyeing him with open suspicion. Jack stepped closer, lifted the book from her fingers, and tossed it onto the bench.

'You know what your problem is, sugar?' he murmured, sliding his arms around her. She jumped, eyes wide at his nerve, and tried to bolt back, but he locked his hands behind her at the small of her back and held her easily. His wicked smile cut across his face. 'You're too tense. You gotta loosen up, angel.'

'Let go of me,' Laurel demanded, holding herself as rigid as a post as her nerve endings snapped like whips in response to his nearness.

'Why? I like holding you.'

'I don't want to be held. I don't like to be held.'

He studied her expression for a long while, reading something like fear. Fear of him? Or was it something deeper, more fundamental? Fear of intimacy, maybe. Fear that she might actually enjoy it.

'Liar,' he said softly, but set her free just the same. She should have been afraid of him. He was a user and a bastard. If he'd had a shred of decency, he would have left her alone. But she intrigued him, little bundle of contradictions that she was. And he wanted her. He couldn't escape that fact, and he didn't want to deny it.

He pulled his cigarette out from behind his ear and dangled it from his lip as he bent to retrieve the book. *Evil Illusions*, his latest best-seller, for all it meant to him. He wrote to kill time, to give himself some outlet, some way to vent what was inside him. He had never set out to become a success, an attitude that drove his editor insane. She wanted him to go on tour, to play the celebrity. He refused. She wanted him to court booksellers and distributors. He stayed home. His attitude exasperated her, but Jack just laughed it off and told Tina Steinberg she had enough energy, enthusiasm, and ambition for both of them.

'Are you ever going to smoke that cigarette?' Laurel snapped.

Jack glanced at her from under his brows and grinned, cigarette bobbing. 'Nope. I quit two years ago.'

'Then why do you keep sticking that cigarette in your mouth?' she asked peevishly.

His gaze held hers and all but caressed it, devilish lights dancing. 'I've got an . . . oral fixation. You wanna help me out with that, sugar?'

Laurel scowled at him and at the wave of liquid heat that washed through her as her gaze strayed to the sexy curve of his lower lip and she remembered the feel and taste of his mouth on hers.

'Why horror?' she asked suddenly, reaching out to tap a finger against the book cover.

A wry smile pulled at one corner of Jack's mouth. *Because it's my life. Because it's what lives inside me. Dieu*, she'd run like a rabbit if he told the truth. Lucky he'd never had any particular aversion to lying.

'Because it sells,' he said, tossing the paperback down on the bench.

Better she think of him as a mercenary than a lunatic. A mercenary probably still stood a chance of getting her into bed. And a mercenary he was, after all. Hadn't he spent half the afternoon rummaging through old newspapers, studying Miss Laurel Chandler's life as a prosecuting attorney? Not because he wanted to know more about her as a person, he told himself, but because he found her intriguing as a character. He had even jotted down a few notes about her for future reference, thinking she would make a fascinating heroine with her mix of fragility and strength.

'Come on, *'tite chatte*,' he said, nodding toward the back gate. He caught her small hand in his and started walking.

Laurel dug her heels in and scowled at him. 'Come on where?'

'Crawfishin'.'

She tried in vain to tug her hand away even as her feet took a step in his direction. 'I'm not going crawfishing with you. I'm not going anywhere with you!'

'Sure you are, sugar.' He grinned like the devil and drew her another step toward the gate. 'You can't stay holed up in this garden forever. You gotta get out and live with the common folk.'

She gave a sniff. 'I don't see much of anything common about you.'

'*Merci!*'

'It wasn't a compliment.'

'Come on, angel,' he cajoled, changing tacks without warning. He sprang toward her, landing as graceful as a cat, and swung her into a slow dance to music only he could hear. 'Me, I'm jus' a poor Cajun boy all alone in this world,' he murmured, his voice warm and rough like velvet, his accent thickening like a fine brown roux. He captured her gaze with his and held it, his head bent so that they were nearly nose to nose. 'Woncha come crawfishin' with me, *mon coeur*?'

Temptation curled around her and drew her toward him. It seemed insane, this attraction between them. She didn't want a man in her life right now. She had all she could do to manage herself. And Jack would not be managed. He had a wildness about him, an unpredictability. He could tell her he had suddenly decided to fly off to Brazil for the day, and she wouldn't have been a bit surprised. No, he was no man for her.

But his offer was tempting. She could almost feel the mud between her toes, smell the bayou, feel the excitement of lifting a net full of clicking, hissing little red crawfish out of the water. It had been years since she'd gone. Her father had taken her and Savannah – against Vivian's strident objections. And she and Savannah had snuck away on their own a time or two after he had died, but those times were so distant in the past, they no longer seemed real. Now Jack was offering. Good-time Jack with his devil's grin and his air of *joie de vie*.

She looked up at him, and her mouth moved before she could even give it permission. 'All right. Let's go.'

10

They rode in Jack's Jeep down the bayou road, turning off on a narrow, overgrown path a short distance before the site of their accident. Lined with trees, rough and rutted, it had Jack slowing the Jeep to a crawl, and Huey jumped out of the back, eager to begin his exploration of this new territory. Laurel hung on to the door as the Jeep bounced along, her attention on the scenery. She knew the area. Pony Bayou. So named for a prized pony owned by a local Anglo planter back in the late seventeen hundreds. The pony was 'borrowed' by a Cajun man who planned to use the stallion for breeding purposes. A feud ensued, with considerable bloodshed, and all for nought as the pony got himself mired in the mud of the bayou and was devoured by alligators.

Despite its gruesome history, Pony Bayou was a pretty spot. The stream itself was narrow and shallow with low, muddy banks and a thick growth of water weeds and flowers. A perfect haven for crawfish, as was evidenced by the presence of two beat-up cars parked along the shoulder of the road. Two families were trying their luck in the shallows, their submerged nets marked by floating strips of colored plastic. Half a dozen children chased each other along the bank, shrieking and laughing. Their mothers were perched on the long trunk of an ancient brown Cadillac, swapping gossip. Their fathers leaned back against the side of the car, drinking beer and smoking nonchalantly. Everyone waved as Laurel and Jack rumbled past in search of a spot of their own. Laurel smiled and waved back, glad she had come, feeling lighter of heart away from the aura of her family.

They parked the Jeep and gathered their equipment as if this were an old routine. Laurel pulled on a pair of rubber knee-boots to wade in, grabbed several cotton mesh dip nets, and clomped after Jack, who had nets tucked under his arm and carried a cooler full of bait. Huey bounded ahead, nose scenting the air for adventure. Jack scolded him as the hound splashed into the bayou, and Huey wheeled and slunk away with his tail tucked between his legs, casting doleful looks over his shoulder at Jack.

Jack scowled at the dog, not appreciating the fact that he felt like an ogre for spoiling Huey's fun. Laurel was giving him a look as well.

'There won' be a crawfish between here and New Iberia with him around,' he muttered.

'Depends on how good a fisherman you are, doesn't it?' She lifted a brow in challenge.

'When you grow up fishin' to keep your belly full, you get pretty damn good at it.'

Laurel said nothing as she watched him bait the nets with gizzard shad and chicken necks. He had grown up poor. Lots of people had – and did – in South Louisiana. But the hint of defensiveness and bitterness in his tone somehow managed to touch her more than she would have expected it to.

There was such a thing as being poor and happy. After her father had died, Laurel had often offered God every toy she possessed, every party dress, for the chance to have parents who cared more about her and Savannah than they did about wealth. She had known a number of families whose parents worked on Beauvoir, who had little and still smiled and hugged their children. The Cajuns were famously *un*material-istic and strongly family-oriented. But she had a feeling this had not been the case with Jack's family.

Curiosity itched inside her, but she didn't ask. Personal questions didn't seem wise.

They each took a net out into the water, spacing them a good distance apart. Jack worked quickly and methodically, the ritual as second-nature to him as tying his shoes. Laurel kept stumbling over tangles of alligator weed that was entwined with delicate yellow bladderwort and water primrose. The spot she had chosen to drop her net was choked with lavender water hyacinth that fought her for control of the net.

'Uh-huh,' Jack muttered dryly, suddenly beside her, reaching around her, enveloping her in his warm male scent. 'I can see you grew up eating store-bought crawfish.'

Laurel shot him an offended look. 'I did not. I'll have you know, I've done this lots of times. Just not in the last fifteen years, that's all.'

Jack set the net and helped her wade back to shore, balancing her when the roots and reeds caught at her boots. When they were back on solid ground, he gave her a dubious look.

'I saw where you grew up, sugar. I can't picture any daughter of that house wading for mudbugs.'

'That just shows what a reverse snob you are,' Laurel said as she stepped out of the hot boots and let her bare feet sink into the soft ground of the bank. 'Daddy used to take Savannah and me.'

She leaned back against the side of the Jeep and stared across the bayou, thinking of happier times. On the far bank lush ferns and purple wild iris grew in the shade of hardwood trees dripping moss and willows waving their pendulous ribbons of green. In brighter spots black-eyed Susans and white-topped daisy fleabane dotted the bank like dollops of sunshine.

Somewhere along the stream a pileated woodpecker began drumming against a tree trunk in search of an insect snack and the racket startled a pair of prothonotary warblers from their roost in a nearby hackberry sapling. The little birds fluttered past, flashes of slate blue and bright yellow.

'What happened to him?' Jack asked softly.

Emotion solidified in Laurel's throat like a chunk of amber. 'He died,' she whispered, the beautiful growth along the far bank blurring as unexpected tears glazed across her eyes. 'He was killed . . . an accident . . . in the cane fields . . .'

One swift, terrible moment, and all their lives had been changed irrevocably.

Jack watched the sadness cloud her face like a veil. Automatically, he reached for her, curled his arm around her shoulder, pulled her gently against his side. 'Hey, sugar,' he murmured, his lips brushing her temple. 'Don' cry. I didn' mean to make you cry. I brought you out here to make you happy.'

Laurel stifled the urge to lean against him, straightening away instead, scrubbing at the embarrassment that reddened her cheeks. 'I'm okay.' She sniffed and shook her head, smiling against the desire to cry. 'That just kind of snuck up on me. I'm okay.' She nodded succinctly, as if she had managed to convince herself at least, if not Jack.

He watched her out of the corner of his eye. Tough little cookie, bucking up when she wanted to crumble. She was a fighter, all right. He had learned that not only by experience, but through his reading. According to the papers he had culled out of his collection of a year's worth, she had been as tenacious as a pit bull going after the alleged perpetrators in the Scott County case. She had driven her staff mercilessly, but worked none harder than she worked herself in the relentless – and, as it had turned out, futile – pursuit of justice. He couldn't help wondering where that hunger for truth and fairness had come from. Reporters had described it as an obsession. Obsessions grew out of seeds sown deep inside. He knew all about obsessions.

'How old were you?' he asked.

Laurel pulled up a black-eyed Susan and began plucking off the petals methodically. 'Ten.'

He wanted to offer some words of sympathy, tell her he knew how tough it was. But the fact of the matter was, he had hated his father and hadn't mourned his passing for even a fraction of a second.

'What about you?' Laurel asked, giving in to her curiosity on the grounds of good manners. He had asked her first. It would have been rude not to ask in return. 'Do your parents live around here?'

'They're dead,' Jack said flatly. 'Did he want you to be a lawyer, your daddy?'

Laurel looked down at the mutilated flower in her hand, thinking of it

516

as a representation of her life. The petals were like the years her father had been alive, all of them stripped away, leaving her with nothing but ugliness. 'He wanted me to be happy.'

'And the law made you happy?'

She shook her head a little, almost imperceptibly. 'I went into law to see justice done. Why did you go into it?'

To show my old man. 'To get rich.'

'And did you?'

'Oh, yeah, absolutely. Me, I had it all.' *And then I killed it, crushed it, threw it all away.*

Jack shifted his weight restlessly from one squishy wet sneaker to the other. She was turning the tables on him, neatly, easily, subtly. He shot her a glance askance. 'You're good, counselor.'

Laurel blinked at him in innocence. 'I don't know what you mean.'

'I mean, *I'm* the one asking the questions, so how come I'm all of a sudden giving answers?'

Her mouth turned down in a frown. 'I thought this was a conversation, not an interrogation. Why can't I ask questions?'

'Because you won' like my answers, sugar,' he said darkly.

'How will I know until I hear them?'

'Trust me.'

Laurel took advantage of the silence to study him for a moment as he stared out at the brown water, that intense, brooding look on his face. The feeling that he was two very different men struck her once again. One minute he was the wild-eyed devil who wanted nothing more than to get into trouble and have a good time; the next he was this closed, dark man who kept the door shut on the part of himself he didn't want anyone to see. She found herself wanting to know what was on the other side of that door. A dangerous curiosity, she thought, pulling herself back from asking more questions.

Down the bank Huey suddenly bounded out of a stand of cattails and coffee weed, baying excitedly. The children who had been chasing around their parents' cars farther downstream came running, squealing with excitement to see what the hound had discovered, shrieking delightedly when they found the dog's quarry was a painted turtle with a spotted salamander riding on its back.

The turtle lumbered along, ignoring the sniffing hound, its lethargic gait seeming out of sync with its gaudy coloring. Its ebony-green shell shone like a bowling ball and was crisscrossed with a network of reddish-yellow lines. A broad red stripe stroked down the center of it from head to tail. The salamander flicked its long tongue out at the dog, sending Huey into another gale of howls that in turn set the children off again.

Poor Huey couldn't seem to figure out why the turtle didn't spring away from him so he could give chase. He batted a paw at it and yipped in surprise as the salamander shot off its hard-shelled taxi and skittered into the tall weeds. The hound wheeled and ran, bowling over a toddler in his haste to escape.

Being the closest adult, Laurel automatically went to the little girl's aid. She hefted up twenty pounds of squalling baby fat and perched the child on her hip as if it were the most natural thing in the world.

'Don't cry, sweetie, you're okay,' she cooed, stroking a mop of black curls that were as soft as a cloud.

The little girl let out a last long wail, just to let the world know she had been sorely mistreated, then subsided into hiccups, her attention suddenly riveted on her rescuer. Laurel smiled at the swift change of mood, at the innocence in the chubby face and the wonder in the round, liquid dark eyes. A muddy little hand reached up and touched her face experimentally.

'Jeanne-Marie, are you okay, *bébé*?' The child's mother rushed up, her brows knit with worry, arms reaching out.

'I think she was just startled,' Laurel said, handing the baby over.

After a quick inspection satisfied her parental concern, the young woman turned back to Laurel with a sheepish look. 'Oh, look! Jeanne-Marie, she got you all dirty! I'm so sorry!'

'It's nothing. Don't worry about it,' Laurel said absently, reaching out to tickle Jeanne-Marie's plump chin. 'What a pretty little girl.'

The mother smiled, pride and shyness warring for control of her expression. She was herself very pretty in a curvy, Cajun way. 'Thank you,' she murmured. 'Thank you for picking her up.'

'Well, I'm sure the dog's owner would apologize to you,' Laurel said dryly, shooting Jack a glance over her shoulder. 'If he would ever admit the dog is his.'

The woman was understandably baffled, but nodded and smiled and backed away toward the rest of her group, telling Jeanne-Marie to wave as they went.

Laurel waved back, then turned toward Jack, a smart remark on the tip of her tongue. But he had a strange, stricken look on his face, as if he had seen something he hadn't been at all prepared for.

'What's the matter with you?' she said instead. 'Do you have a phobia of children or something?'

Jack shook himself free of the emotion that had gripped him as he had watched Laurel with little Jeanne-Marie. *Dieu*, he felt as though he'd taken an unexpected boot to the solar plexus. She had looked so natural, so loving. The thought had crossed his mind instantly, automatically, that she would make a wonderful mother – as Evie would have if she had ever gotten the chance. If their child had ever been born. Thoughts he didn't usually allow himself during daylight hours. Those were for the night, when he could dwell on them and beat himself with them and cut his soul to ribbons with their razor-sharp edges.

'A – no,' he stammered, blinking hard, scrambling for a mental toehold. He shrugged and flashed her a smile that was pale in comparison to his usual. 'Me, I just don' know much about babies, that's all.'

Laurel gave him a look. 'I'll bet you know all about making them, though, don't you?'

'Ah, *c'est vrai*. I'm a regular expert on that subject.' His grin took hold, cutting his dimples deep into his cheeks. He looped his arms around her, catching her by surprise, and shuffled closer and closer, until they were belly to belly. 'You want for me to give you a demonstration, sugar?' he drawled, his voice stroking over her like long, sensitive fingers.

Laurel swallowed hard as raw, sexual heat swept through her.

'You certainly have a high opinion of your own abilities,' she said, grabbing frantically for sass to ward off the other, more dangerous feelings.

He lowered his head a fraction, his dark eyes shining as he homed in on her mouth. 'It ain't bragging if you can back it up.'

Laurel's pulse jumped. 'I'll back *you* up,' she threatened with a look of mock consternation. She planted both hands against his chest and shoved.

He didn't budge. Just grinned at her, laughing. Fuming, she pushed again. He abruptly unlocked his hands at the small of her back and she let out a little whoop of surprise as she stumbled backward. Momentum carried her faster than her feet could catch up, and she landed on her fanny in a patch of orange-blossomed trumpet creeper. Peals of high-pitched laughter assured her that the children had witnessed her fall from dignity. Before she could even contemplate resurrecting herself, Huey bounded out of a tangle of buttonbush and pounced on her, knocking her flat and licking her face enthusiastically.

'Ugh!' Laurel snapped her head from side to side, in a futile attempt to dodge the slurping dog tongue, swatting blindly at the hound with her hands.

'*Arrête sa! C'est assez! Va-t'en!*' Jack was laughing as he shooed Huey out of the way. The hound jumped and danced and wiggled around their legs as Jack stretched out a hand to Laurel and helped her up. 'You can't get the better of me, *catin*.'

Laurel shot him a disgruntled look. 'There is no "better" of you,' she complained, struggling to keep from bursting into giggles. She never allowed herself to be amused by rascals. She was a level-headed, practical sort of person, after all. But there was just something about this side of Jack Boudreaux, something tempting, something conspiratorial. The gleam in his dark eyes pulled at her like a magnet.

'You only say that 'cause we haven't made love yet,' he growled, that clever, sexy mouth curling up at the corners.

'You say that like there's a chance in hell it might actually happen.'

The smile deepening, the magnetism pulling harder, he leaned a little closer. 'Oh, it'll happen, angel,' he murmured. 'Absolutely. Guar-un-teed.'

Laurel gave up her hold on her sense of humor and chuckled, shaking her head. 'Lord, you're impossible!'

'Oh, no, sugar,' he teased, slipping his arms around her once again. 'Not impossible. Hard, mebbe,' he said, waggling his brows.

The innuendo was unmistakable and outrageous. Their laughter drifted away on the sultry air, and awareness thickened the humidity around them. Laurel felt her heart thump a little harder as she watched the rogue's mask fall away from Jack's face. He looked intense, but it was a softer look than she had seen there before, and when he smiled, it was a softer smile, a smile that made her breath catch in her throat.

'I like to see you laugh, *'tite ange*,' he said, lifting a hand to straighten her glasses. He brushed gently at the smudge of mud Jeanne-Marie had left on her cheek. His fingertips grazed the corner of her mouth and stilled. Slowly, deliberately, he hooked his thumb beneath her chin and tilted her face up as he lowered his mouth to hers.

Not smart, Laurel told herself, even as she felt her lips soften beneath his. She wasn't strong enough for a relationship, wasn't looking for a relationship. She couldn't have found a more unlikely candidate in any event. Jack Boudreaux was wild and irreverent and unpredictable and mocked the profession and system she held such respect for. But none of those arguments dispelled the fire that sparked to life as he tightened his hold on her and eased his tongue into her mouth.

Jack groaned deep in his throat as she melted against him. His little tigress who hissed and scratched at him more often than not. She didn't want him getting close, but once the barrier had been crossed, she responded to him with a sweetness that took his breath away. He wanted her. He meant to have her. To hell with consequences. To hell with what she would think of him after. She wouldn't think anything that wasn't the truth – that he was a bastard, that he was a user. All true. None of it changed a damn thing.

He tangled one hand in her short, silky hair and started the other on a quest for buttons. But his hand stilled as a high-pitched, staccato burst of sound cut through the haze in his mind. Laughter. Children's laughter. Jack raised his head reluctantly, just in time to see round eyes and a button nose disappear behind the trunk of a willow tree.

Laurel blinked up at him. Stunned. Dazed. Disoriented. Her glasses steamed. 'What?' she mumbled, breathless, her lips stinging and burning, her mouth feeling hot and wet and ultrasensitive – sensations that were echoed in a more intimate area of her body.

'Much as I like an audience for some things,' Jack said dryly, 'this ain't one of those things.'

Another burst of giggles sounded behind the tree, and Laurel felt her cheeks heat. She shot him a look of disgust and gave him an ineffectual shove. 'Go soak your head in the bayou, Boudreaux.'

He grinned like a pirate. 'It ain't my head that's the problem, *ma douce amie.*'

She rolled her eyes and sidled around him, lest he try anything funny, heading back to the Jeep and her boots. 'Come on, Casanova. Let's see if you can catch anything besides hell from me.'

They went back into the water, and Jack lifted the first of the nets, revealing a good catch of fifteen to twenty crawfish. The little creatures scrambled over one another, hissing and snapping their claws. They looked like diminutive lobsters, bronze red with black bead eyes and long feelers. Laurel held an onion sack open while Jack poured their catch in. They moved down their row of nets, having similar luck with each. When they were through, they had three bags full.

By then the sun had turned orange and begun sliding down in the sky. Dusk was coming. With it would come the mosquitoes. Ever present in the bayou country, they lifted off the water in squadrons at sunset to fly off on their mission for blood.

Laurel arranged things neatly and efficiently on her side in the back of the Jeep. Jack tossed junk helter-skelter. The bags of crawfish were stowed with the rest of the gear, an arrangement Huey was extremely skeptical of. The hound jumped into his usual spot and sat with his ears perked, head on one side, humming a worried note as he poked at the wriggling onion sacks with his paw.

On their way back out to the main road Jack stopped by the old Cadillac and gave one bulging bag to the families, who probably relied on their catch for a few free meals. The gift was offered without ceremony and accepted graciously. Then the Jeep moved on, with several children chasing after it, flinging wildflowers at Huey, who had garnered a daisy chain necklace in the deal.

The whole process was as natural as a handshake. Reciprocity, a tradition that dated back to the Acadian's arrival in Louisiana, a time when life had been unrelentingly harsh, the land unforgiving. People shared with friends, neighbors, relatives, in good times and bad. Laurel took in the proceedings, thinking that since her father's death, no one at Beauvoir had ever offered anyone anything that didn't have strings attached.

'That was nice,' she said, sitting sideways on the seat so she could study his response.

He shrugged off the compliment, slowed the Jeep for the turn onto the main road, pulled his cigarette out from behind his ear, and dangled it from his lip. 'We caught more than we need. They got a lotta mouths to feed. Besides,' he said, cutting her a wry look, 'I don' want 'em gettin' any ideas about suing me for Huey traumatizing their *bébé.*'

'How could they sue if he's not your dog?' Laurel asked sweetly.

'Tell it to the judge, angel.'

'I may just do that,' she said, crossing her arms and fighting a smile. 'There's still the little matter of my aunt's flower garden. . . .'

'Only through God may you be set free, brothers and sisters!' Jimmy Lee let the line echo a bit, loving the sound of his own voice over loudspeakers. Never mind that they were cheap, tinny-sounding loudspeakers. Once the money started rolling in for his campaign against sin, he would go out and buy himself new ones. And a new white suit or two. And a fancy French Quarter whore for a weekend. . . . Yes, indeed, life was sure as hell going to be sweet once the money came rolling in.

He had no doubt he would be rich and famous. Despite the betrayal of that little faggot Matthews, who had run the 'news' version of Saturday's debacle instead of the version Jimmy Lee had envisioned on the ten o'clock report. Jimmy Lee was too good-looking not to make it, too charismatic, too good at pretending sincerity. He had it all over the other televangelists. Jim Bakker was a fool and had gotten his ass thrown in prison to prove it. Swaggart was careless, picking up prostitutes on the street. They had both fallen by the wayside, opening the road to fame and fortune for Jimmy Lee Baldwin. In another five years he'd have himself a church that would make the Crystal Cathedral look like an outhouse.

The followers of the True Path cheered him, looking up at him as though he were Christ himself. Some wore looks of near-rapture. Some had tears in their eyes. All of them were saps. In another era he would have made a fortune selling snake oil or the empty promise of rain to drought-plagued farmers. He was a born con man. But in this the age of self-awareness and the search for inner peace, religion was the ticket. As L. Ron Hubbard had once said, if a man wanted to get rich, the best way was to form his own religion. Jimmy Lee looked out on the pathetic, avid faces of his followers and smiled.

'That's right, my friends in Christ,' he said, walking to the other end of the rented flatbed truck that was serving as his stage for the afternoon. 'Only through faith. Not through liquor or drugs or sins of the flesh!'

He loved the way he could build a sentence to a thundering crescendo. So did his faithful. There were women in the crowd who looked positively orgasmic over the magic of his voice.

'That's why, my beloved brothers and sisters,' he said softly.

He raised his crumpled handkerchief to his face and blotted away the sweat that was running down his forehead. The day had turned into a damn steambath. His white shirt was soaked through. His cheap linen-look jacket hung on him like damp wallpaper. He wanted desperately to take a cool shower and lie naked on his bed with a lovely young thing reviving his energies with her sweet hot mouth. But for the moment he was stuck on the back of this flatbed truck with the sun beating down on him, boiling the sweat on his skin. The first thing he was going to do when he was rich and famous was move his ministry the hell away from Louisiana.

'That's why we have to do this battle. That's why we have to vanquish our wicked foe who would lead us all into temptation and deliver us into the hands of evil. That's why we must smite down the dens of iniquity!'

He swung his arm in the direction of Frenchie's, which was across the parking lot behind him, and his small gathering of devout cheered like the mob at Dr. Frankenstein's door. Such eager little sheep. Jimmy Lee grinned inwardly.

Laurel climbed out of the Jeep, took several swift, angry steps toward the gathered crowd, then stopped in her tracks, the soles of her sneakers crunching on the fine white shell. Her every muscle tensed as her conscience warred with the part of herself that was preaching self-protection. This wasn't her fight. She wasn't up to handling a fight. But it made her so damn mad. . . .

'You fixin' to whup him onstage this time, *'tite chatte*?' Jack asked, curling a hand around her fist and lifting it experimentally.

She shot him a look of pure pique and jerked away. 'I'm going to have the Delahoussayes call the sheriff. If no one else is going to help them, that's the least I can do.'

Jack shrugged. 'Go ahead, darlin'. For all the good it'll do.'

'It most certainly will do good.'

He rolled his eyes and trailed after her as she marched onward. 'You haven't met Sheriff Kenner, have you, sugar?'

Laurel considered the question rhetorical. She couldn't see that it would make any difference. Baldwin and his congregation were trespassing. Trespassing was against the law. The sheriff's job was to uphold the law. It was as simple as that.

They had to pass Baldwin's makeshift stage on the way to the bar. Laurel held her head high and fixed the self-styled preacher with a baleful glare.

Jimmy Lee had caught sight of her the second she had wheeled into the lot with Jack Boudreaux. Laurel Chandler. God was smiling down on him today, indeed.

He waited until she was almost even with the truck before calling out to her. 'Miss Chandler! Miss Laurel Chandler, please don't pass us by!'

She shouldn't have slowed down. She should have kept right on marching for the bar. She didn't want to go any deeper into this than she was already. But her feet hesitated automatically at the sound of her name, and something pulled her toward Jimmy Lee Baldwin. Not his charisma, as he would probably have preferred to believe. Not his air of authority. But something that had been with her since childhood. The need to stand up to a bully. The need to try to make people see a charlatan for what he was. The need to fight for justice.

She turned and marched right up to the front of his stage and glared up at him.

'Join us, sister,' Jimmy Lee said, holding his hand out toward her. 'I don't know what hold this vile place has over you, but I know, *I know* you are a good person at heart.'

'Which is more than I can say for someone bent on harassing law-abiding citizens,' Laurel snapped.

'The law.' Jimmy Lee bobbed his head, a grave expression pulling down his handsome features. 'The law protects the innocent. And the guilty would hide like wolves in sheep's clothing, hide behind the law. Isn't that true, Miss Chandler?'

Laurel went still. His eyes met hers, and a chill of foreboding swept over her skin despite the heat of the day. He knew. He knew, and the bastard was going to use it to his own end. Without looking, she could feel the curious eyes of his fifty or so followers falling on her. He knew. They would know. That she had failed. That justice had slipped from her grasp like a bar of wet soap.

'My friends . . .' Baldwin's voice came to her as if from a great distance down a long tin tunnel. 'Miss Chandler has herself been a soldier in the fight against the most heinous of crimes, crimes against innocent children. Crimes perpetrated by depraved souls who would masquerade among us, showing us righteous faces by day and by night subjecting our children to unspeakable acts of sex! Miss Chandler knows of our fight, don't you, Miss Chandler?'

Laurel barely heard him. She could feel the weight of their gazes press in on her, the weight of their judgment. She had failed. '. . . *unspeakable acts of sex.* . . .' She shivered as she felt herself drawing inward, pulling in to protect herself. ' . . . *unspeakable acts of sex.* . . .' '*Help us, Laurel! Help us . . .*'

Jack watched her go pale, and he damned Jimmy Lee to eternal hell. His own personal philosophy of life was live and let live. If Jimmy Lee wanted to make a buck off God, that was his business. If people were stupid enough to follow him, that wasn't Jack's problem. He would have gone right on ignoring Baldwin and his band of lunatics. He wasn't out to fight anyone's fight. But the bastard had gone too far. He had somehow, some way managed to hurt Laurel.

Before he could even fathom what lay beneath his response, Jack hopped onto the hood of Baldwin's borrowed truck and proceeded to climb over the cab. He jumped down onto the flatbed, landing right smack behind Jimmy Lee, who bolted like a startled horse, but didn't move quickly enough to get away.

Jack caught hold of Baldwin's arm and deftly twisted it behind the preacher's back in a hold he had learned the hard way – from his old man. He grinned at the man like a long lost brother and spoke through his teeth at a pitch only Jimmy Lee could hear. 'You got two choices here, Jimmy Lee. Either you can suddenly succumb to the heat of the day, or I'll break all the fine, small bones in your wrist.'

Baldwin stared into those cold dark eyes, and a chill ran down him from head to toe. He'd heard rumors about Jack Boudreaux . . . that he was wild, unpredictable, affable one minute and mean as sin the next.

Boudreaux was, by all accounts of the people who read his books, seriously unbalanced. The hold tightened on his wrist, and Jimmy Lee thought he could feel those small bones straining under the pressure.

'That's right, Jimmy Lee' – the smile chilled another degree – 'I'd sooner break your arm.'

Restless murmurs began rumbling through the crowd like distant thunder. The preacher ground his teeth. He was losing his momentum, losing his hold on them. Damn Jack Boudreaux. Jimmy Lee had had them on the brink of a frenzy, champing at the bit to launch him on the road to televangelist greatness. He cast a glance at his followers and back at the man beside him.

'Sin,' he said, and the pressure tightened. 'I-I can feel the heat of it!' He rolled his eyes and swayed dramatically on his feet. 'Oh, Lord have mercy! The heat of it! The fires from hell!'

Jack let him go and watched with a mixture of cynicism and satisfaction as Baldwin staggered away across the flatbed. Obviously a disciple of the William Shatner/Captain Kirk school of acting, Baldwin stumbled and swayed, contorting his face, wrenching his back, calling out in staccato bursts as his audience gasped in alarm. Several women screamed as he finally collapsed onto the bed of the truck and writhed for another thirty seconds.

People rushed for the stage. Jack strolled across to the prostrate form of the preacher and calmly snatched up the microphone.

'Hey ever-body! Come on inside and douse those fires of hell!' he called, grinning like the devil. 'Drinks are on me! *Laissez le bon temps rouler!* And tell 'em Jack sent you!'

The contingent of Frenchie's patrons who had been standing at the back of the crowd or lounging on the gallery sent up a wild chorus of hoots and cheers and made a mad dash for the bar. Jack hopped down off the truck. Laurel didn't even look up at him, but turned and started back for the Jeep.

'Hey, sugar, where you goin'?'

'Home. Please,' Laurel said, emotion tightening around her throat like a vise. There was a pressure in her chest, in her head. She wanted – needed – to escape.

Jack caught her by the arm and shuffle-stepped alongside her. 'Hey, hey, you can't run off, spitfire. T-Grace is gonna have the place of honor all set for you.'

'What for?' She stopped and wheeled on him, her body vibrating with tension, her face set in lines of anger and something like shame tinting the blue of her eyes. 'I failed. I lost.'

Jack's brows pulled together in confusion. 'What the hell are you talkin' about? Failed? Failed what?'

She'd choked. She'd lost it. If it hadn't been for his coming to the rescue, there was no telling what humiliation she might have suffered. She felt as if

Baldwin had reached right into her and pulled out that part of her past to hold it up to his followers like a science experiment gone wrong.

'You stood up to him, Laurel,' Jack said softly. 'That was more than anyone else was willing to do. So you didn't deliver the knockout punch. So what? Lighten up, sugar. You're not in charge of the whole damn world.'

His last line struck a chord, brought back a memory from her stay at the Ashland Heights Clinic, brought back Dr. Pritchard's voice. How egotistical of her to think that she was the center of all, the savior of all, that the outcome of the future of the world rested squarely on her shoulders.

She was overreacting.

She had come here to heal, hadn't she? To take control of her life again. If she ran now, from this, she would be giving in to the past when she had vowed to rise above it.

She looked up at Jack, at the concern in his eyes, and wondered if he even knew it was there.

'Thank you,' she murmured. She wanted to reach up and touch his cheek, but it seemed a dangerously intimate thing to do, and so curled her fingers into a loose fist instead.

Jack eyed her suspiciously. 'For what?'

'For rescuing me.'

'Oh, no.' He shook his head and backed away from her a step, raising his hands as if to ward off her gratitude. 'Don' make me out to be a hero, sugar. I had a chance to make a fool outa Jimmy Lee, that's all. Me, I'm nobody's hero.'

But he had saved her – several times – from her own thoughts, her own fears, from the dark mire of depression that pulled at her. Laurel studied him for a moment, wondering why he preferred the image of bad boy to champion.

'Come on, 'tite ange,' he said, jerking his head toward the bar. 'I'll buy you a drink. Besides, I've got a lawyer joke I just remembered I wanted to tell you.'

'What makes you think I want to hear it?'

Jack slid an arm around her shoulders and steered her toward Frenchie's. 'No, no. I know you don't wanna hear it. That's half the fun of tellin' it.'

Laurel laughed, the tension going out of her by slow degrees.

'What's the difference between a porcupine and two lawyers in a Porsche?' he asked as they skirted around Baldwin's truck. 'With a porcupine, the pricks are on the outside.'

They crossed the parking lot, Jack laughing, Laurel shaking her head, neither one aware that they were being very carefully watched.

11

Savannah sat in a far corner of the bar, an aura of silence enveloping her like a force field, while all around her the air was filled with raucous sound. Filé was blasting out of the jukebox – 'Two Left Feet.' Billiard balls smacked together, people shouted to be heard above the general din. Savannah blocked it all out. Anger simmered inside her, hot and bitter and acidic.

The call from St. Joseph's had broken in on her time with Cooper like an unwelcome news bulletin. Mrs. Cooper was suddenly having a bad spell, and couldn't Mr. Cooper please come? He had been there all morning and half the afternoon as it was. Selfish, greedy bitch. It wasn't enough that she had to hold on to him mentally, she had to drag him away physically, as well.

'I hate her,' Savannah snarled, the feeling too strong to keep bottled up inside.

No one noticed she'd spoken at all. No one was paying any attention to her.

She took a gulp of her vodka tonic and did a slow reconnaissance of the room through the dark lenses of her sunglasses. The place was crowded for a Sunday evening. Thanks to Laurel. Laurel. Everybody's little heroine. Everybody's little savior.

The anger burned a little hotter, flared up as she tossed another splash of alcohol on the flames. The irony was just too bitter. Laurel was what she was because of Savannah. She was the chaste and pure one because Savannah had been her savior, her protector.

She stared hard toward the bar, where her Baby was being toasted and cheered by T-Grace and the regulars. And Jack Boudreaux stood by her side, the least likely white knight she'd ever seen. Baby was supposed to be home, brooding, hiding, weak, and in need of her big sister for comfort and support. Damn her. She was getting stronger by the day, by the minute, snatching away Savannah's chance to be the stronger one, to play the role of protector again, to rise above her station of town tramp and be somebody important.

She picked a matchbook up off the table and mutilated it while she watched the way Jack hovered over Laurel, touching her shoulder, the small of her back, leaning close to whisper something in her ear then throwing his head back and laughing as she slugged him on the shoulder.

He had never whispered anything in Savannah's ear, damn his miserable Cajun hide. She would have given him the ride of his life, but he'd never shown any interest in her beyond the casual flirting he did with every female on the planet. He was sure as hell showing an interest in Baby, and Savannah didn't like it one damn bit.

'Damn you, Baby,' she muttered, polishing off the last of her drink.

'You talkin' to me, *ma belle*?' Leonce bent over her from behind, sliding one bony hand down over her shoulder to fondle her breast.

'Damn right, you jerk,' she complained. 'You're not paying any attention to me at all.'

His scar repulsed her. It constantly drew her eyes to the grotesque lumps at either end of it and the misshapen end of his nose in between. She'd heard a story once that a woman had given him the mark with the business end of a broken bottle, but Leonce seemed to bear no ill will toward the gender. He came on to anything in panties.

'I'll pay anything you want if you get naked with me, *chère*.'

Whore. You're nothing but a whore, Savannah . . .

Her anger spiked, breaking through her facade of boredom. She wasn't for sale. She did what she wanted when she wanted with whomever she wanted because she *wanted* to. Which made her a slut, not a whore. The bitter distinction burned in her stomach like an ulcer, and confusing, conflicting emotions twisted and writhed in her chest, the pressure building like steam in a radiator.

Needing to take it out on somebody, she grabbed a chunk of Leonce's beard and gave it a vicious twist, wringing a howl out of him. He staggered back the instant she let go and crashed into a pool player getting ready to take a shot, earning himself a jab with a cue stick and an earful of four-letter words.

Leonce ignored the other man, his glare fixed on Savannah as he rubbed his cheek. 'What the hell you do dat for?'

Savannah stood up, kicking her chair back. 'Go fuck yourself, Scarface. Save your money to buy yourself a brain, you asshole.'

She snatched up her glass and threw it at him, bouncing it off his shoulder as he ducked away.

'Crazy bitch!' he yelled as sneers and chuckles rumbled behind him. 'You goddamn crazy bitch!'

Savannah ignored him, snatched up her pocketbook, and went on the prowl. She didn't need to settle for Leonce Comeau; there were plenty of younger, good-looking bucks who would appreciate her company and her expertise. Her gaze caught on Taureau Hebert across the room, regaling his buddies with the tale of his latest run-in with the game warden.

She'd had her eye on him for a while now. He hadn't been nicknamed

Bull for nothing. He was all of twenty-three and built for service from his mile-wide shoulders on down. It seemed like the perfect time to put him to the test.

But as she set off, hips swaying, tossing her wild mane back over her shoulder, concentrating all her considerable energy into the total package of allure, Annie Delahoussaye-Gerrard bounced into the picture, and the men at Taureau's table snapped their heads around to ogle her cleavage as she served their drinks and flirted with them.

Savannah fought off the wild urge to scream. This was *her* territory. Who the hell did this cheap little waitress think she was, anyway?

Young and pretty, that's who she was. And she had a sunny smile and a sweet laugh. Like her mother, T-Grace, Annie favored her clothes a size too small, pouring her ample curves into tight jeans and tank tops that left nothing to the imagination. A tangle of fake gold chains hung around her throat, and she wore a cheap ring on nearly every finger. No style at all, Savannah thought bitterly as she fingered the long strand of real pearls she wore and briefly contemplated wrapping them around Annie Gerrard's pretty young throat.

The little bitch had no business sniffing around the men here. She had a man of her own, a husband. Savannah very conveniently forgot the fact that Tony Gerrard – Annie's husband – had only just been released from a stay in the parish jail for knocking her around, and rumors of a divorce were in the air.

She strolled around behind the table, slipping in between Taureau and the waitress, sliding an arm around Taureau's thick, sunburned neck as if they were longtime lovers. She ignored his startled expression and fixed a hard-eyed look on Annie. 'Why don't you run along and get me a fresh vodka tonic, sweetheart? That *is* your job here, isn't it?'

Annie narrowed her dark eyes and propped her empty tray on her well-rounded hip. '*Mais yeah*, that's my job,' Annie sassed, looking her adversary up and down with undisguised contempt. 'What's yours, *grand-mère*? Molesting young men?'

Savannah didn't hear the obscenities that spewed from her own mouth. With a blood red haze clouding her vision, she launched herself at the waitress, grabbing a handful of overpermed dark hair. She swung her other arm in a wild, roundhouse punch that connected solidly with Annie's ear.

Taureau and his buddies shot up out of their chairs, eyes round with astonishment. Someone yelled 'Cat fight!' above the blare of the jukebox. There was another call of '*Grand rond!*' and instantly a circle of spectators formed around the two women as they crashed into a table, sending bottles and glasses flying. Beer spilled in a foaming river across the wood floor, making the footing treacherous and giving an advantage to Annie, who was in sneakers.

Savannah didn't notice herself slipping. Her perceptions had become strangely distorted, her vision zooming close up on her adversary, hearing nothing but a loud, chaotic babble of sounds – screeches and screams and crashing. She felt nothing – not the other woman's hand yanking on her hair or fingernails biting into her flesh or toe connecting with her shin – nothing but the white-hot rage that roared within. She swung and clawed and shouted, holding on tight to whatever part of Annie Gerrard she could grab, and they spun, stumbling around the circle of spectators like wind-up dolls run amok.

T-Grace let out a sound that was something between fury and a war cry as she barreled out from behind the bar, elbows flying into the ribs of anyone who didn't get immediately out of her way. She plunged through the crowd, shouting at the top of her lungs, her eyes bulging wildly as she rushed to save not her daughter but her glassware and furniture. Annie could take care of herself.

Laurel jerked around on her barstool to see what the commotion was all about, and her heart clutched in her chest as a red-on-white dress caught her eye. 'Oh, my God, Savannah!'

Without a thought to her own safety, she launched herself off the stool and dove into the crowd. Jack swore under his breath as he grabbed her from behind and swung her out of his way. He made it to the melee about the same instant as T-Grace, and they danced around the combatants, angling to get a hold on one or the other of them to pull them apart.

An old hand at brawls, T-Grace was less than diplomatic. She didn't hesitate to land a few blows of her own or grab a handful of Savannah's hair as she struggled to get her youngest child extricated from the fight that was smashing up the bar and putting a hold on drink orders.

Jack jumped in behind Savannah and wedged an arm between the two women, getting bitten for his efforts. An elbow caught him above the left eye as they lurched around the circle like rugby players in a scrum, reopening the cut he'd gotten crashing Savannah's 'Vette. He gritted his teeth and cursed a blue streak through them, wondering what the hell had compelled him to get involved in this mess in the first place. He wasn't a fighter; he was an observer. If two women wanted to tear each other's hair out, he usually just stood back and took mental notes. He winced and swore in French as a spike heel dug into his instep. He wouldn't have to take mental notes this time; his body was going to be a pictorial essay on the intricacies of a barroom cat fight. An elbow dug into his ribs, and he grunted and angled for a better hold while his feet slipped precariously in the spilled beer.

Laurel hovered on the edge of the action, her stomach twisting, her breath like two hard fists in her lungs, disjointed thoughts shooting through her mind like shrapnel. She hadn't even been aware of Savannah's presence in the bar. Seeing her like this, locked in combat with another woman, was too surreal to be believed. She brought a hand up to her mouth and bit down hard on her thumbnail.

Suddenly an explosion rent the air, followed by a chorus of screams, and everyone went absolutely still for a split second. Laurel was sure her heart stopped, sure one of the women had fired and someone had been killed. But the fighters broke apart, Savannah with Jack dragging her backward, T-Grace with her daughter in a choke hold. Heads turned toward the bar.

Ovide held a smoking .38 in one meaty fist. The gun was pointed toward the ceiling, and a telltale plume of plaster dust was floating down. The bartender's face was as impassive as ever. He looked like a ridiculous cartoon character standing there, his walrus mustache drooping down, tufts of white hair sprouting out of his ears. He didn't say a word as his patrons stared at him, but set the gun down behind the counter, calmly picked up a glass, and went on drying it with the rag he had never bothered to put down.

T-Grace gave her daughter a rough shake. 'Fightin' with the customers. Talk about!'

Annie wiped a drizzle of blood from her nose with the back of her hand, her gaze, still hot and angry, locked on Savannah Chandler. '*She* started it, Maman—'

T-Grace cut her daughter off with a wild-eyed look. 'I don' wanna hear no more. Get on with you! Go fix yourself up.' She gave her daughter a shove in the direction of the ladies' room and clapped her hands over her head as she turned back toward the rest of the crowd. '*Allons danser!*' she ordered as Roddie Romero and the Rockin' Cajuns wailed out of the jukebox.

The bar patrons drifted back to their prefight activities, several couples taking T-Grace's command to heart and swinging out onto the dance floor to work off the excitement by working themselves into a sweat.

Adrenaline was still scalding the pathways of Savannah's blood vessels. She felt wild and irrational and didn't give a damn who saw it or what anybody thought. She shot Jack a pointed look over her shoulder. 'If you wanted to put your hands on me, Jack, all you had to do was say so.'

He let go of her abruptly. His face was set in stern lines. He pulled a handkerchief out of his hip pocket and offered it to her. 'Your lip is bleeding.'

Savannah just stared at him, recklessness rolling through her in big waves. Very slowly, very deliberately, she ran her tongue along her bottom lip, licking the blood away.

'You want to do that for me, Jack?' she murmured seductively, swaying toward him. 'I'll bet you go for that sort of thing, don't you? Writing all those bloody, gruesome books gives you a taste for it, doesn't it, Jack?'

Jack said nothing. He had thought more than once of succumbing to

Savannah Chandler's charms, but always something made him steer clear at the last second. Some instinctive wariness made him keep his distance. He hadn't understood until that second it was fear. Not of the woman, but of what they might become together. She would pull him over the edge with her, then only *le bon Dieu* knew what would happen as they tumbled together into madness. A cold chill trickled down his back at the thought.

'We're two of a kind, you and me, Jack,' she whispered, holding his gaze.

Laurel arrived at her sister's side, pale as chalk, frightened and furious, trembling as she reached out to touch Savannah's arm. 'My God, are you all right? You're bleeding! Jesus, Savannah, what were you thinking?'

Savannah shrugged off the touch and glared at her. 'I wasn't,' she snapped. 'That's your department, Baby. You think, I act. Maybe if someone could put us together, we'd be a whole person.'

She spun away and bent to snatch up her red calfskin pocketbook from the floor, not in the least bit concerned that the hem of her dress rode all the way up to her bare ass as she did so. Laurel's breath caught in her throat, and she took a step toward her sister meaning to pull the skirt down to her knees if she could.

'Savannah, for God's sake!'

Savannah gave a derisive sniff as she dug a cigarette and slim gold lighter out of her bag. 'God's got nothing to do with it, Baby,' she said as she lit up. She took a deep, calming drag and blew the smoke toward the ceiling, never taking her eyes off Laurel. 'He's a sadist, anyway. Haven't you realized that by now?' She smiled bitterly, a smile made gruesome by the bright red blood staining her lush lower lip. 'The joke's on us.'

Satisfied with having the last word, she turned on her red stiletto heel and strolled out the front door as calmly as if nothing had happened at all.

'She gonna come to grief, dat one,' T-Grace said, her voice vibrating with anger. She stood beside Laurel with her hands jammed on her hips, electric blue cowboy boots planted apart. Her tower of red hair was listing perilously to the left. Her leathery face was suffused with color, and her dark eyes bugged way out, making her look as if some invisible hand had her by the throat.

Laurel didn't bother to argue the point. Her heart sank at the thought that it was quite probably true. Savannah seemed bent on destroying herself one way or another, and Laurel had no idea what to do to prevent it. She wanted to believe she could stop it. She wanted to believe they could control their own destinies, but she didn't seem to have control of anything. She felt as if she were trying to stop a crazily spinning carousel by simply reaching out and grabbing it. Every time she caught hold, it flung her to the ground.

'I'm sorry, Mrs Delahoussaye,' she murmured. 'Please be sure to send the bill for damages to my aunt's house.'

T-Grace wrapped an arm around her and patted her shoulder, instantly the surrogate mother. 'Don' you be sorry, *chère*. You don' got nothin' be sorry 'bout, helpin' us out like what you did with dat damn Jimmy Lee. You come an' eat some crawfish, you. You so little, I could pick up over my head.'

'T-Grace,' Jack said, resurrecting his smile with an effort, 'who you tryin' to fool? You could pick *me* up over your head and dance the two-step.'

She shook a bony finger at him, fighting the smile that pulled at her thin ruby lips. 'Don' you tempt me, *cher*. You so full of sass, I jus' might show you who's boss, me. You come on sit down 'fore dat bump on your head make you more crazy than you already is.'

As they wound their way through the throng, T-Grace snatched hold of Leonce and ordered him to mind the bar. Leonce swept off his Panama hat and made a courtly bow, the tails of his Hawaiian shirt drooping low. He came up with a big grin that split his Vandyke and gave Jack a punch on the shoulder.

'Jumpin' into cat fights, talk about! What you gonna do next, Jack? Mud wrasslin' with women and alligators?'

Jack scowled at his friend, reached out with a quick hand, and flipped Leonce's hat off Leonce and onto his own head, leaving Leonce blushing back across his balding pate. 'You're just jealous 'cause you were only the warm-up act.'

Comeau's face darkened at the reminder, his scar glowing an angry red like a barometer of his temper. He tried to snatch the hat back, grabbing air as Jack ducked away. 'Fuck you, Boudreaux.'

'In your dreams,' Jack taunted, laughing. 'Go water the liquor, *tcheue poule*.'

T-Grace whirled around and boxed his ear, knocking the hat askew. 'We don' water nothin' here, smart mouth.'

She hardly broke her stride, continuing toward a little-used side door, barking orders at a waitress along the way and signaling to her husband to join them. Jack rubbed his ear and shot her a disgruntled look from under the brim of the straw hat – a look that was tempered by a twinkle in his eye.

They went outside and across a stretch of parking lot to the bank of the bayou, where a picnic table and assorted lawn chairs sat, divided from the yard of a tidy little forest green house by the requisite flower shrine to Mary. The area was partially illuminated by cheap plastic Chinese lanterns alternated with yellow bug lights strung up between two poles. The sun had sunk, but night had yet to creep across the sky. The bayou was striped with bars of soft gold light and translucent shadow.

Ovide planted his bulk in a lawn chair and said nothing while T-Grace supervised the layout of food on the picnic table. Laurel hung back, uncertain, wary of why she was being treated as a guest. She glanced at her watch and started to back away.

'I appreciate the offer, Mrs. Delahoussaye, but I think I should probably go. I ought to find Savannah—'

'Leave her be,' T-Grace ordered. 'Trouble, dat's all what she'll get you, *chère*, sister or no.' Satisfied with the spread, she turned toward Laurel with her hands on her hips and a sympathetic look in her eyes. '*Mais yeah*, you gotta love her, but she'll do what she will, dat one. Sit.'

Jack put his hands on Laurel's shoulders and steered to the picnic table. 'Sit down, sugar. We worked hard catchin' these mudbugs.'

She obeyed, not because she was hungry or eager to please, but because she didn't want to think what she would do if she could find Savannah. She wanted to talk, but the talk would invariably turn into an argument. When Savannah was in one of her moods, there was no reasoning with her. A headache took hold, and she closed her eyes briefly against the pain.

'Eat,' T-Grace said, sliding a plate in front of her. It held a pile of boiled crawfish, boiled red potatoes, and *maquechou* – corn with chunks of tomato and peppers. The rich, spicy scents wafted up to tease Laurel's nostrils, and her stomach growled in spite of the poor appetite she'd had two seconds ago.

Jack tossed the Panama hat on the end of the table, straddled the bench, and sat down beside her, too close, his thigh brushing hers, his groin pressing against her hip. The air seeped out of her lungs in a tight hiss.

'She's a debutante, T-Grace,' he said. 'Probably don' know how to eat a crawfish without nine kinds of silver forks.'

'I do so,' Laurel retorted, shooting him a look over her shoulder.

Defiantly, she snapped off a crawfish tail, dug her thumbs into the seam, and split it open to reveal the rich white meat, which she pulled out and ate with her fingers. The flavor was wonderful, making her mouth water, evoking memories. In her mind's eye she could see her father wolfing down crawfish at the festival in Breaux Bridge, his eyes closed with reverent appreciation and a big smile on his face.

'You gonna be a real Cajun and suck the fat out'a the head?'

She jerked free of the bittersweet memory and scowled at Jack, who was slipping his arms around her to steal food off her plate. 'Go suck the fat out of your own head, Boudreaux. That ought to occupy you for a while.'

Ovide's mustache twitched. T-Grace slapped the arm of her lawn chair and cackled. 'I like this girl of yours, Jack. She got enough sass to handle you.'

Laurel tried unsuccessfully to scoot away from him. 'I'm afraid you've got the wrong idea, Mrs. Delahoussaye. Jack and I aren't involved. We're just . . .' She trailed off, at a loss for an appropriate word. Friends seemed too intimate, acquaintances too distant.

'You could say lovers, and we'll make good on it later,' he murmured in a dark, seductive voice, nuzzling her ear as he reached for another crawfish.

T-Grace went on, unconcerned with Laurel's definition of the relationship. 'A girl's gotta have some sass. Like our Annick – Annie, you know? She gets herself in a scrap or two, but she takes care of herself, *oui*? She's a good girl, our Annie, she jus' can't pick a good man is all. Not like her *maman*.'

She reached over to pat Ovide's sloping shoulder lovingly, her hard face aglow with affection. Ovide gave a snort that might have been approval or sinus trouble and tossed a crawfish shell into the bayou. A crack sounded from the dark water as a fish snapped up the shell.

'We raise seven babies in this house,' T-Grace announced proudly. 'Ovide and me, we work every day to make a good home, to make a good business. Now we got this damn Jimmy Lee making trouble for us, sayin' Frenchie's is the place where sin come from. Me, I'd like to send him to the place where sin come from. Ovide, he's gonna get the ulcer from worryin' 'bout what dat Jimmy Lee gonna do next.'

She patted her husband's shoulder again, brushed at the wild gray hair that fringed his head and poured out of his ear. She shot a shrewd, sideways look at Laurel. 'So, you gonna help us wit' dat or what, *chère*?'

The other shoe fell. Laurel felt trapped with Jack on one side and T-Grace staring her down on the other. She shifted uncomfortably on the bench, wanting nothing more than to escape. She shook her head as she abandoned her supper and extricated herself from the bench. 'I believe we've already had this conversation, Mrs. Delahoussaye. I'm not practicing law—'

'You don' gotta practice,' T-Grace said dryly. 'Jus' do it.'

Laurel heaved a sigh of frustration. 'Really, all you have to do is call the sheriff the next time Reverend Baldwin comes on your property—'

'Ha! Like dat pigheaded jackass would bother with the like of us!'

'He's the sheriff—'

'You don' understand, sugar,' Jack drawled. He swung his right leg over the bench and stretched his feet out in front of him, leaning his elbows back against the table. 'Duwayne Kenner only comes runnin' if your name is Leighton or Stephen Danjermond. He's got too many important meetings to bother with the common folk. He isn't gonna get mixed up with Jimmy Lee and his Church of the Lunatic Fringe unless a judge tells him to.'

'That's absurd!' Laurel exclaimed, rounding on Jack. 'That's—'

He raised his brows. 'The way it is, sweetheart.'

'He's sworn to uphold justice,' she argued.

'Not everybody has the same conviction about that you do.'

She said nothing, just stood there for a long moment. He had no such conviction. Jack made his own rules and probably broke them with impunity. He joked about the system, derided the people who tried to make it work. But he knew she didn't.

He watched her, his eyes a dark, bottomless brown, his expression intense. He was trying to read her. She felt as if those eyes were reaching right into her soul. Abruptly, she turned back toward T-Grace.

'There are several attorneys here in town—'

'Who don' give a rat's behind,' T-Grace said. She abandoned her plate on the ground, forfeiting her dinner to Huey, who crawled out from under the picnic table and laid claim to the crawfish. T-Grace ignored the dog, her hard gaze homing in on Jack. She walked up to him with her hands on her hips, her chin tipped in challenge. 'Jack here, he could help us, but here he sits on his cute little—'

'Jesus Christ, T-Grace!' Jack exploded. He got up from the bench so quickly, it tipped over backward with a crash that sent the hound scurrying for safe cover. 'I'm disbarred! What the hell am I supposed to do?'

'Oh, nothin', Jack,' she said softly, mockingly, not giving up an inch of ground. 'We all know you jus' wanna have a good time.' Daring more than any man would have, she reached up and patted his lean cheek. 'You go on and have a good time, Jack. Don' bother with us. We'll make out.'

Jack wheeled around in a circle, looking for some way to vent the anger roaring inside him. He wanted to yell at the top of his lungs, bellow like a wounded animal. He snatched a beer bottle off the table and hurled it, narrowly missing the bathtub shrine to the mother of God, and still the fury built inside him.

'Shit!'

T-Grace watched him with wise old eyes. 'That's all right, Jack. We all know you don' get involved. You don' take responsibility for nothin'.'

He glared at her, wanting to grab her and shake her until her bug eyes popped right out of her head. Damn her, damn her for making him feel . . . what? Like a cad, like a heel? Like a good for nothing, no-account piece of trash?

Bon à rien, T-Jack . . . bon à rien.

That's what he was. No good. He'd had that truth drilled into him since he was old enough to comprehend language. He had proven it true time and again. He had no business howling at the truth.

His gaze caught on Laurel, who stood quietly, her arms folded against her, her big eyes round behind her glasses. The champion for justice. Willing to sacrifice her reputation, her private life, her career, all for the cause. *Dieu, what she must think of me . . . and all of it true.*

That was the irony – and he had a finely honed appreciation for irony – that he was everything T-Grace accused him of and less, that he was exactly what he aspired to be, and now the image he had settled into was turning on him – or he was turning against it.

'I don' need this,' he snarled. 'I'm outta here.'

Laurel watched him stalk away, a little shaken by his outburst. A part of her wanted to go after him, to offer comfort, to ask why. *Not smart, Laurel.* She had enough trouble of her own without taking on the burden of Jack Boudreaux's darker side . . . or the plight of Frenchie's Landing. . . .

But as she turned back toward T-Grace, she couldn't bring herself to say no. It was no big deal, she told herself. Just a visit to the courthouse, a phone call or two. She wasn't taking on the world. Just a pair of honest, hardworking people who needed a little justice. Surely she was strong enough for that.

'All right,' she said on a sigh. 'I'll see what I can do.'

For once, T-Grace was speechless, managing only a smile and a nod. Ovide hefted himself out of his chair and dusted remnants of crawfish shells off his belly. Laying a broad hand on Laurel's shoulder, he looked her in the eye and growled, *'Merci, chère.'*

12

Jimmy Lee sat on the window sill, feeling sorry for himself, wearing nothing but his dirty white trousers and a frown. Sweat trickled in little streams down his chest to pool on his belly. He sipped at a glass of brandy, brooding, reliving his humiliation in his mind, tormenting himself with it. He had had that crowd in the palm of his hand, he thought, curling his fingers into a fist. Then that damn Chandler bitch had ruined everything. Of course, he had managed to salvage the situation with his quick thinking, but the moment of glory had been spoiled, just the same.

Women were the bane of his existence. Sluts and whores, all of them. Some came in more respectable packages than others, but they were all alike underneath the wrapping. Wicked as Eve, every last one of them.

He laughed a little at the biblical reference and tossed back a gulp of brandy. Shit, he was even starting to *think* like a preacher.

The night was still and hot as hell, the air electric with something like expectation. A dark restlessness shifted inside him and he lifted his glass and tried to douse the feeling with the last of his drink. The quiet pressed in on him, irritating raw nerve endings like fingernails on a chalkboard. He longed for the noise of New Orleans, the sounds and smells of Bourbon Street, the dirt and dark alleys of the Quarter, the places the tourists never saw.

A man could get anything he wanted in New Orleans, any way he wanted it.

But he was out here, stuck on the edge of the godforsaken swamp. He had an apartment up in Lafayette, but he had chosen Bayou Breaux as the spot to launch his campaign, and so had rented this one-room bungalow at the edge of nowhere in order to have some privacy.

Bayou Breaux had seemed the perfect choice for his 'War on Satan' – the heart of Acadiana, where good Christian people were as thick as ants on a watermelon rind, where times were a little lean these days because of the perilous state of the oil industry and the agricultural economy, where crime was pressing in and people needed something to grab onto and believe in. There were too many Catholics to suit him, but there were also busloads of fundamentalists fervent enough and gullible enough to believe anything. They were the core of his ministry. They would bankroll him into stardom and carry him there on their shoulders.

If Laurel Chandler didn't get in the way.

The screen door swung open with a creak and Savannah Chandler walked in, a seductive vision in her short flowered dress and red high heels. Her gaze scanned the shabby little room, taking in the dingy yellow walls, the cheap, mismatched furniture, the bottle of E & J on the battered coffee table, assessing the surroundings the same way she might judge a new boutique.

Finally she turned toward him, not saying a word, acting as if she had more right to be there than he did. She had eyes like a she-wolf – pale, translucent blue – and something in them sent a shiver of awareness down his spine. A white-hot flame that burned. A hunger that called to his own. A recognition of a common need.

'All dressed up and nowhere to go, Jimmy Lee?' she drawled.

'I could say the same to you.'

She shot him a sly look from the corner of her eye. 'No, you couldn't. I came here.'

'What for?'

'For a while.'

He said nothing as she skirted around the old iron bed, trailing a forefinger along the foot rail. She stared at him from under her lashes. He could feel the heat of her gaze on his face, on his bare chest, and he couldn't quite resist the urge to suck in his stomach. She came toward him, head down, her long wild hair tumbling over one shoulder, twining with the long strand of pearls she wore. Her hips rolled sensuously from side to side. The only sounds in the room were the click of spike heels against linoleum, the creak of the old ceiling fan as it turned, and the soft, seductive swish of fabric as it rubbed against skin.

Jimmy Lee held himself still as lust rose up inside him like a demon. She stopped a scant inch away. Her perfume mingled with the faint scent of brandy and the damp, earthy aroma of the swamp that drifted in through the window, and beneath it all lay the unmistakable musk of arousal – hers, his. . . .

'Your sister made a fool of me today,' he said, his voice low and whiskey-hoarse.

One corner of her mouth curled into a subtle sneer. 'You oughta be used to that, Jimmy Lee.'

He moved so quickly, she couldn't help gasping as his hand closed, tight and punishing, on her upper arm. 'I'm gonna be a star,' he said softly.

She didn't ignore the pain of his fingers biting into her flesh. Instead she drank it in, fed on it, smiled a little deeper. 'You're nothing but a two-bit hustler.'

'And you're nothing but a cheap piece of snatch,' he said. 'A whore without a price tag.'

She slapped him so hard that the blow sang up her arm and her palm burned like live ash. In one explosive move, Jimmy Lee was on his feet, his hand thundering down to return the slap. It snapped her head back and the split that had knitted together along her bottom lip cracked open, instantly filling her mouth with the sharp, thick taste of her own blood.

As if a door had been suddenly thrown open inside her, all the restlessness, the recklessness, the wildness rushed out on a wave of hate. Hate for him, hate for herself, an all-encompassing, drenching, drowning hate that washed away control, compunction, restraint. And all of it – the need, the hate, everything – glowed in her eyes as she turned her head and looked up at Jimmy Lee Baldwin.

He stared down at her for a long while, feeling again that strange kinship between them. Something dark, something evil. And it stirred arousal like nothing else he'd ever known. Desire rose up like a beast inside him, wild, rabid, unchained. A sound of animal need rose up the back of his throat as he pulled Savannah roughly against him and crushed her mouth with his.

She fought his embrace – not to escape, just to fight – but all her hands could grasp was the fever-hot, sweat-slick skin of his chest and upper arms, and she groped and clawed and pinched as the ripe male scent of him filled her head and his tongue filled her mouth.

Behind her back, his fingers worked frantically at the zipper of her dress. He pulled the tab down a few inches, then curled his fingers into the opening and tore it the rest of the way. He worked it past her shoulders and lower as he dragged his mouth from her lips to her throat. He grasped the neckline of the dress in both hands and jerked it down, hunger snarling inside him like a wild dog as her breasts sprang free, full and firm. He bent over and caught one turgid peak in his hot, avid mouth, sucking hard, wringing a frantic sound from her . . . and another and another. Winding his hand into her pearl necklace, he rubbed the cool, satiny beads across her other aching point.

Unsure of whether she wanted to hold him to her or push him away, Savannah shoved at his shoulders, tangled her hands in his slicked-back hair and pulled. This was a battle for her mind, for her soul, and desperation gripped her throat at the idea that she stood no chance of winning. *This is what you were born for, Savannah. Don't try to deny it. . . .*

For an instant she was back in her room at Beauvoir, and the man sucking greedily at her breast was her stepfather. She cried out, not at the assault of her body, but at the conflicting feelings that assaulted her. Her body responded to his touch, tingled and burned and ached. In the beginning she hadn't liked it, but over time she had come to see that Ross was right – this was what she was made for, this was what she was good at. But the pleasure that ribboned through her body brought with it a

540

wrenching shame. She was a whore. That was all she would ever be. That was all any man would love her for – sex.

She sobbed a little, feeling trapped, but she cast aside the sensation and let Ross's words balm her ravaged heart. '*You're so beautiful, Savannah. You're so much more woman than your mother. I want you all the time. Sometimes I think I'll go mad with need of you. . . .*'

Need of her. He needed her. He wanted her. The words gave her a sense of power, and she grasped it and hung on.

'You're wicked, Savannah,' Baldwin muttered, trailing his mouth down the slope of her breast, over the quivering muscles of her stomach. 'You're a witch the way you make a man want you.'

A wild, bitter laugh tore from her. She braced her hands against the window frame as Jimmy Lee went down on her. He caught the hem of her dress and shoved it up past her hips, so that it bunched around her waist. The strand of pearls hanging down between her breasts, she teetered on her red high heels, feet braced apart, head swimming dizzily, drunk on a mix of need and hate and self-pity and self-loathing and rapacious, insatiable arousal.

Jimmy Lee devoured her, as greedy and ravenous as a glutton at a feast. His tongue teased and flicked and probed, bringing her to the edge of orgasm but never beyond, never granting her satisfaction, only pushing the pain of unfulfilled arousal to its outer limits.

'I hate you, Jimmy Lee!' Her voice was little more than a rasp, as tormented as the rest of her body, as seized by desire and frustration. 'You're a son of a bitch.'

He tumbled her back across the creaking, sagging mattress of the old bed, falling across her, pinning her arms above her head with one hand. She struggled beneath him as he reached down with his free hand and stripped his belt from his trousers.

'You're nothing but a pervert, Jimmy Lee,' she taunted, her heart racing as he bound her hands to a rail on the iron headboard.

'It takes one to know one,' he growled.

She laughed, a throaty, seductive laugh, her cool, she-wolf eyes glowing with hunger and anticipation as he sat back, straddling her thighs, and unfastened his trousers. He didn't bother to take them off, but he did bother to protect himself, pulling a condom out of his pocket and slipping it on with practiced efficiency.

'Can't be too careful these days,' he said. He braced himself above her on his elbows and stared down at her, his breath coming in hard pants. 'My adoring public wouldn't take it too kindly if I caught something nasty from some alley cat who spreads her legs for every man in town.'

Savannah glared at him. 'I'll be sure to tell them you said that.'

'Who'd believe you?' he asked, contempt for her festering inside him like a boil. 'I'm their savior. You're just a bitch in heat.'

'*Don't bother telling anyone, Savannah. No one will ever believe you. . . .*

They'll see you for what you are — little slut, little prick teaser. . . . You're a bad girl, Savannah, and everyone knows it. . . . There's no use telling. We both know you seduced me. . . .'

She closed her eyes as the voice played in her head. She raised her hips as Jimmy Lee thrust into her . . . and hated herself.

The midnight moon cast a silvery sheen down on the trees, and the mist crept, soft and white, across the surface of the black water.

A lot of women were afraid of the swamp. A lot of *men* were afraid of the swamp. It didn't frighten Savannah. She felt something other than fear out here. Something ancient. Something that called to her and stirred her blood.

This place had always been her escape. This was where she and Baby had run to get away from home and the unhappiness there. Out here she felt free. She felt like a part of the swamp, like an animal — a deer or a bobcat or a copperhead snake. She wanted to take her clothes off and be naked here, be a part of it, a creature of the Atchafalaya.

Giving in to that primal desire, she slipped off the dress the Revver had ruined for her, tossed it on the hood of the car, and slicked her hands down over the curves of her naked body.

For a moment she closed her eyes and imagined what it would be like to lie down here on the mat of dead leaves and welcome her lover into her body beneath the light of the bayou moon. They would mate as all animals mated, without guilt, without inhibition, glorying in the pure excitement of it. She would scream out in ecstasy, her cries mingling with the eerie cacophony that carried across the swamp at night.

The mental image wrung a low moan from her, made her ache with need, a need Jimmy Lee hadn't been able to assuage no matter how many ways he used her — and he had used her in every way a man could use a woman. This was a need no man could quench, a need that was rooted deep in the core of her.

She threw her head back, lifting her face to the moon, tumbling her wild hair down her back. The restlessness stirred harder, hotter. The wildness pulled at her, drew on something deep within. She needed . . . needed . . . needed . . .

Need drives the predator. Not the need for food, but for sustenance of another kind. A need for blood, a taste for death. A need to punish, a desire to inflict pain. To watch pain grow like a cancer, from a simple response into something all-consuming. A need to control. To play God.

To play. A game. The thought brings a smile. The smile brings a chill to the prey. For every game there is a loser. The one bound and held captive knows the outcome before the game begins. For the victim there is no game, only anticipation, pain, terror, and, she prays, death. Please, death. Soon . . .

No one hears her screams. No one comes to her aid. There are no saviors in the swamp. Cruelty here is a way of life. Death as commonplace as snakes. Danger hidden in beauty. No salvation. No justice. Life. Death. The hunter and the hunted.

The knife gleams silver in the moonlight. The blade cuts delicately, with skill, slicing like a bow across the strings of a violin. The song it plays high-pitched and eerie. Human. A prelude to death.

And in the end, the instrument will fall silent, the prey will succumb. She will die as the predator believes she deserves to die – naked and defiled. Another dead whore left to rot in the swamp. A fitting end, a fitting place. And the predator will glide away in the bâteau, *silent, safe, the secret shared with only the trees and the creatures of the night . . .*

Laurel sat up suddenly, shaking, cold, her skin slick with sweat, her heart pounding. The nightmare faded as she grounded herself in reality, but the sounds of the children's cries still echoed in her mind, driving her from bed. She crossed to the highboy and pulled out another oversize T-shirt, trying to crowd the last of the dream from her brain. She was trembling violently, her stomach knotting with residual anxiety, and she cursed a blue streak under her breath, battling the weakness.

Her hand brushed across the bottle of tranquilizers tucked in among her underwear, left over from her stay at Ashland Heights. Dr. Pritchard had told her to take them when she needed help sleeping, but she wouldn't. No matter how badly she wanted to, she wouldn't take any. They were a crutch, another weakness, and she was so damn tired of being weak.

She changed quickly and went out onto the balcony, hoping to rejuvenate herself with fresh night air, but the air was heavy and warm, without a breath of a breeze. Folding her arms against herself to keep from shaking, she padded down to the French doors of Savannah's room and peeked in. The bed was unmade, the rich gold-and-ruby spread a tangled drift across the mattress, lace-edged satin pillows mounded along the ornate French headboard and tossed carelessly onto the floor. The rest of the room had Savannah's stamp of housekeeping draped everywhere in the form of discarded lingerie and articles of clothing that had been dragged out of the closet and abandoned in favor of something brighter, skimpier, sexier, trashier.

Fear cracked through the other emotions that were thick in Laurel's throat as a medley of lines played through her head. '*Murders?*' . . . '*Four now in the last eighteen months . . . Young women of questionable reputation*' . . . '*She gonna come to grief, dat one.*' . . .

She chewed hard on her thumbnail as she wrestled with the urge to call the police. She was being silly, jumping to conclusions. There was nothing unusual in Savannah's staying out past two – or all night, for that matter. She could have been anywhere, with anyone.

With a killer?

'Stop it,' she ordered, her voice a harsh whisper as she reined in the irrational urge to panic. Dammit, she wasn't an irrational person. She was logical and sensible and practical. Wasn't that what had saved her when she was growing up in the poisonous atmosphere of Beauvoir?

That and Savannah.

Her gaze fell again on the bed, and she jerked herself away and headed for the stairs that led down to the courtyard, her stride brisk and purposeful.

She was feeling unsettled, skittish. The evening at Frenchie's had rattled her, from her encounter with Baldwin to Savannah's fight to Jack's tirade to the role she had agreed to play for the Delahoussayes. Truth to tell, that probably had her the most on edge. Tomorrow she would have to go down to the courthouse and see about solving the problem of Jimmy Lee Baldwin. She would have to go to work as if she had never stopped, as if she hadn't left her last job in disgrace. She would go into the halls of justice and face the secretaries, the clerk of court, the judge, other attorneys, Stephen Danjermond.

She had been mulling over that prospect as she walked home from Frenchie's. With Jack nowhere to be found, and the last rays of day still seeping through the gloom of evening, she had set off for Belle Rivière on foot, hoping to walk off some of the anxiety and self-doubt. But after only two blocks, a bottle green Jaguar pulled alongside the curb, its passenger window sliding down with a hiss.

'Might I offer you a ride, Laurel?' Stephen Danjermond leaned across the soft gray leather seats of the car and stared up at her, his green eyes glowing like jewels in the waning light. He smiled, that handsome, perfectly symmetrical smile, tinting it with apology. 'As much as I enjoy bragging about our diminished crime rate in Partout Parish, I hate to see a lady take chances.'

'I could be taking a chance with you, for all I know,' Laurel said evenly, keeping her fists tucked in the deep pockets of her baggy shorts.

Danjermond regarded her with a touch of disappointment, a touch of amusement. 'I think you know me better than that, Laurel.'

She looked at him blankly, trying to cover her confusion. They had only just met, but somehow she knew if she pointed that out to him, he would only be more amused. She felt as if he were a step ahead of her in time, that she was coming into a play already in progress and missing her cue. If he could rattle her this much with a simple conversation, he had to be hell on wheels in a cross-examination. A man destined for great things, Stephen Danjermond.

She pulled open the door of the Jag and sank down into the butter-soft seat. 'I don't know you at all, Mr. Danjermond,' she murmured, her tone as cryptic as his expression.

'I intend to remedy that situation.'

He let the car ease along the deserted street, silent for a moment, the

Jag as quiet as a soundproof booth. He had shed his tailored suit for a knit shirt the color of jade and a pair of tan chinos, but he still looked immaculate, perfectly pressed.

'Dinner with your parents was an interesting occasion,' he said.

'They're not my parents,' Laurel blurted automatically, a hot flush stinging her cheeks as he looked at her with one dark brow raised in question. 'What I mean to say is, Ross Leighton isn't my father. My father passed away when I was small.'

'Yes, I know. Killed, wasn't he?'

'An accident in the cane fields.'

'You were close to him.' He stated it as a fact, not a question. Laurel said nothing, wondering how he knew, wondering what Vivian might have told him. Wondering if he was privy to Vivian's plans for the two of them.

He shot her another steady look. 'Your aversion to Ross,' he explained. 'I suspect you never accepted his taking your father's place. A child loses a beloved parent, resentment toward the usurper is natural. Though I should think you would have gotten over it by now. Perhaps there's something more to it?'

The answer was none of his business, but Laurel refrained from saying so. Her skills were rusty, but the instincts were still there. Danjermond's were honed to perfection. He didn't have conversations, he had verbal chess matches. He was never off duty. Every exchange was an opportunity to exercise his mind, sharpen his battle skills. She knew; she had been there. She had been that sharp, that focused. She knew an answer to this question would put her in check.

'I'm sorry about the scene my sister caused,' she said casually. 'Savannah does love to be dramatic.'

'Why are you sorry?' He stopped the Jag for the red light at Jackson and pinned her with a look. 'You aren't the one who caused the commotion. You have no control over your sister's actions, do you, Laurel?'

No. But she wanted to have. She wanted control. She wanted the components of her world to fit neatly into place. No messes, no unpleasant surprises.

Danjermond's gaze held fast on her. 'Are you your sister's keeper?'

She shook off the thoughts and kicked herself mentally for not seeing the potential hazards of this subject she had diverted them onto. 'Of course not. Savannah does as she pleases. I know she won't apologize for disrupting Vivian's gathering, so I will. I was merely taking up the gauntlet for etiquette.'

'Ah,' he smiled, looking out over the hood of the car, 'the gauntlet. You might have been a knight of the Round Table in a past life, Laurel. Galahad the Good, adhering to your strict code of honor.'

He seemed amused, and it irritated her. Did he think he was too urbane, too sophisticated for the quaint, provincial ways of Bayou Breaux – he the privileged son of old New Orleans money?

'Hospitality is the Southern way. I'm sure you were raised to have better manners than to, say, interrogate a guest,' she said sweetly, shifting to the offensive.

He looked surprised and pleased at her parry. 'Was I interrogating you? I thought we were getting acquainted.'

'Getting acquainted is generally a reciprocal process. You haven't told me anything about yourself.'

'I'm sorry.' He sent her a dazzling smile that had doubtless knocked more than one simple belle off her feet. Laurel reminded herself she was no simple belle, had never been. 'I'm afraid I find you such an interesting and enchanting creature, I lost my head.'

The sincerity in his voice was too smooth, too polished to be real. Laurel had the unnerving feeling that nothing on this earth could rattle Stephen Danjermond. There was that sense of calm around him, in his eyes, in the core of him. She wondered if anything could ever penetrate it.

'False flattery will get you nowhere, Mr. Danjermond,' she said, glancing away from him to her reflection in the mirror on the visor. 'I hardly look enchanting tonight.'

'Fishing for a compliment, Laurel?'

'Stating a fact. I have no use for compliments.'

He turned in at the drive to the carriage house that served as Belle Rivière's garage and let the Jag idle in park. 'Practicality and idealism,' he said, turning toward her, sliding his arm casually along the back of the seat. 'An intriguing mix. Fascinating.'

Laurel's fingers curled over the door handle as he studied her with those steady, peridot eyes. 'I'm so glad I could amuse you,' she said, her tone as dry as a good martini.

Danjermond shook his head. 'Not amuse, Laurel. Challenge. You're a challenge.'

'You make me feel like a Rubik's Cube.'

He laughed at that, but his enjoyment of her spunk was cut short as his pager went off. 'Ah, well, duty calls,' he said with a sigh of regret, punching a button on the small black box that lay on the seat between them. 'Might I beg the use of a telephone?'

He made his call in the privacy of Caroline's study and left immediately after, leaving Laurel feeling a mix of relief and residual tension. She had dreaded the prospect of introducing him to Aunt Caroline and Mama Pearl and having to sit through coffee and conversation. She had escaped that fate, but the tension lingered.

It lingered, still, as she wandered the cobbled paths of the garden in her bare feet. What a nightmare that Vivian saw them as a match.

Even if she had been in top form, Laurel wouldn't have wanted anything to do with him personally. He made her uneasy with those cool green eyes and that smooth drawl that never altered pitch or tempo. He was too composed when she felt as if she were scrambling on the side of a steep hill, scratching for a handhold. He was too intensely male, she supposed.

An image of Jack came to her, unbidden, dark, brooding, intense. Intensely male in a more basic, primal way than Stephen Danjermond . . . and desire stirred when she thought of him.

It made no sense. She had never been attracted to bad boys, no matter how seductive the gleam in their eyes, no matter how wicked their grins. She was a person who lived by the rules, stuck to them no matter what. There hadn't been a rule made Jack Boudreaux wouldn't go over, under, or around. She had always been one of the world's doers, tackling problems head-on. Jack's credo was to avoid as much responsibility as he could, to lay back and have a good time. *Laissez le bon temps rouler.*

It made no sense that she should feel anything toward him except contempt, but she did. The attraction was there, pulling at her every time he looked at her. Strong, magnetic, beyond her control. And that made her uneasy all over again. He was trouble on the hoof. A man with secrets in his eyes and a dark side he took great pains to camouflage. A man whose baser instincts ran just beneath the surface. Dangerous. She'd thought so more than once.

'Dreamin' about me, sugar?'

Laurel started, clutching at her heart as she whirled around. Jack stood just inside the back gate, leaning indolently against the brick gatepost. Shadows fell across his face, but she could feel him watching her reaction, and willed herself to relax and stand calm.

'You don't give a fig how much it sells,' she said, dryly. 'You write horror because you love to scare people. I'll bet you were the kind of little boy who hid in the closet and jumped out at his mother every time she walked past.'

'Oh, I hid often enough.' His voice came so softly, Laurel thought she was imagining it. Low and smoky and laced with old bitterness. 'My old man locked me in a closet for a couple of days once. I never tried to scare anybody, though. *Mais non.* My sister, Maman, and me – we were pretty much scared all the time as it was.'

His words, so casually delivered, hit Laurel with the force of a hammer. In just those few sentences he had painted a vivid and terrible picture of his childhood. With just those few words he had stirred within her compassion for a small, frightened boy.

He stepped out of the shadows, into the silvery light, his hands in his pockets, his shoulders sagging. He looked beat, drained. She had no idea what he had been doing in the time since he had stormed away from Frenchie's, but it had sapped his energy and etched lines of fatigue across his face.

'Oh, Jack . . .'

'Don't,' he said sharply, shaking off her sympathy. 'I'm not a little boy anymore.'

'I'm sorry,' she whispered.

'Why? You were Blackie Boudreaux in another life?' He shook his head again, took a step closer. '*Non, 'tite ange.* You weren't there.'

No. She had been busy surviving her own nightmare, but she wouldn't say that, wouldn't share it . . . had never shared it with anyone.

'What are you doing here?' she asked. 'What are you doing out at this hour?'

'Prowling.' He smiled slowly, his gaze roaming deliberately down from the top of her head to her tiny bare toes. 'On the lookout for ladies in their nightclothes.'

Laurel had forgotten her state of undress. Now that Jack had so graciously pointed it out to her, she was acutely conscious of the fact that beneath a thin T-shirt that fell shorter than a miniskirt, she wore nothing but a pair of lavender panties. His grin deepened and he bobbed his eyebrows, an expression that clearly said 'Gotcha.'

She crossed her arms and scowled at him. 'People can get shot creeping around backyards in the dead of night.'

Jack let his gaze melt down over her again, lingering on the plump curves of her breasts. 'Mmmm . . . you don' look armed, sugar, but you could be dangerous – to my sanity,' he growled.

Laurel tried to scoot away from him and found he had backed her around into a position that trapped her between an armless statue of a Greek goddess and the bench where he had caught her reading his book.

'I wasn't aware your sanity was in question,' she said sarcastically. 'The general consensus seems to be that you're crazy.'

He chuckled and inched a little closer to her. 'You got a lotta sass, *'tite chatte.* Come here and give me a taste.'

He didn't give her a chance to say no, but closed the distance between them and stole a kiss, slipping his arms quickly around her. Laurel reacted with an unfamiliar mix of desire and pique. Temper overruled temptation, and she started to bring her knee up to teach him the wisdom of asking for permission. Jack reacted instantly, twisting out of harm's way, throwing Laurel off balance. Before she could realize what he was doing, she was sprawled on top of him on the stone bench, her chin on his chest, eyes round with astonishment.

He sat with his back propped against the wall, one foot planted on the bench, one on the ground. He grinned at her. 'All right, sugar, have your way with me.'

'I'll thank you to let me up,' Laurel said primly, shoving against his chest.

'No,' Jack murmured, holding her, pulling her back down when she would have shot to her feet and stormed away. He wanted to hold her, needed to feel her softness against him. He pulled her close and nuzzled her ear while he rubbed a hand gently over her back. 'Stay,' he whispered. 'Don't go, angel. It's late, and I don' wanna be alone with myself.'

His strength wouldn't have kept her there, but the need in his voice was another matter altogether. It was subtle, couched in threads of humor, but there nevertheless. Laurel stilled against him, her eyes finding his in the moonlight, searching, wondering, a little wary.

'I never know who you are, Jack,' she said softly.

She wouldn't want to know who he really was, he thought. If she knew everything about him, she wouldn't stay. If she knew anything about him, she would steer clear, and he would never have the chance to hold her, to take some solace in the feel of her against him – never have the chance to lose himself, however briefly, in the sweet bliss of kissing her.

He couldn't run that risk tonight. He had spent too much time tearing up what was left of his conscience and flogging what was left of his soul. He felt too beaten, too battered, and she was too pretty and too good.

Too good for the like of you, Jack . . .

She stared at him, her eyes as dark as midnight, as uncertain as a child's. In spite of all she'd been through, an aura of innocence still clung about her like a fading perfume. Like Evie. God, what pain that thought brought with it! If he touched her, he would sully her innocence, destroy it as he had destroyed Evie. But he wasn't strong enough to be noble, wasn't good enough to do the right thing. He was a bastard and a user and worse, a man caught between what he was and what he wanted. And he was so damn tired of being alone . . . .

'You don' trust me,' he whispered, tenderly brushing her hair from her eyes. He grazed his fingertips along the delicate line of her cheekbone. 'You shouldn't. I'm bad for you.'

The warning was diluted to nothing by the sadness in his face. His mouth twisted into a half smile that was cynical and weary. His dark eyes looked a hundred years old. Bad Jack Boudreaux. The devil in blue jeans. Self-professed cad. Warning her away. He didn't see the paradox, but Laurel did. He was nobody's hero, but he would save her from himself.

She had spent too much of her life with people who claimed to be good and weren't. Jack claimed to be bad, but if he were truly bad, she would have known, would have sensed, wouldn't have wanted him to kiss her, to touch her, to hold her while the night lay warm and fragrant around them.

He's dangerous . . . .

Yes, she had thought that. And if Jack himself wasn't dangerous, then what she felt when he was this near surely was. She couldn't fall for him, not for his body or his tarnished soul or his allure of the forbidden. There was no room in her life for a rogue. She couldn't have her heart broken again; she was still trying to glue the pieces back together from the last time she had come apart.

She could feel it beating, thumping against Jack's chest through the thin fabric of her white T-shirt and his black one. She held her breath and counted the beats, her eyes on his, wondering why she didn't take her own advice and walk away.

'Well, hell,' he muttered, pulling her closer, 'you don' wanna believe me, I might as well prove it.'

The kiss was carnal from the first. Burning hot. Frankly sexual. He traced his tongue slowly around the inner edge of her lips, then slipped deeper, probing, exploring. Laurel tried to catch her breath and caught his instead, hot and flavored with the taste of whiskey.

He ran his hands over her back, chasing shivers, setting off new ones, sliding lower. Desire swelled inside her, pushing aside sanity, blazing a trail for more instinctive responses. She arched against him, losing herself in the kiss, in the moment. She tangled her hands in his hair. His hands slid over her buttocks, kneading, stroking. He caught the hem of her T-shirt and dragged it up, his knuckles skimming over the taut muscles of her back, skating along the sides of her rib cage.

Laurel felt as if she were tumbling through space, dizzy, hanging on tight to her only anchor. Then suddenly she was on her back with no roof but a sky full of diamond lights and branches strung with lacy moss, and Jack was at her breast, his tongue rasping against her nipple, his lips tugging gently. The sensation was incredible, setting off a flutter of something wild inside her, tearing away her self-control—

Control. Panic rose inside her. She never lost control. *Couldn't* lose control. She was no creature of passion like Savannah.

'No.' The word came out as a puff of nothing. She swallowed hard and tried again, pushing at Jack's broad shoulders as guilt and fear and a dozen other emotions twisted in her chest and tightened like vines around her lungs and throat. 'Jack, no.'

His hand stilled as his fingertips were sneaking under the waistband of her panties. He raised his dark, glittering eyes to meet hers, his mouth poised just above the taut, swollen bud of her nipple. Laurel tightened her every muscle against the desire to just let go. She brought a chilling dose of shame down on her own head to cool the fire.

What the hell was the matter with her, succumbing to the charms of a rake like Jack Boudreaux? On a stone bench in her aunt's courtyard, no less. She barely knew him, didn't trust him, wasn't even sure she liked him.

Jack watched her, watched the flash of panic, the wash of guilt. 'You want me, angel. I want you.' He shifted his weight, pressing his erection against her hip as proof of his statement.

'I . . . I don't.' Laurel bit down hard on the urge to panic. She kept her eyes locked on his, as if that contact somehow gave her a measure of control. Foolish. He outweighed her by eighty pounds. He could take what he wanted, as men had been doing since the dawn of time.

'*Tu menti, mon ange*,' he murmured, shaking his head. 'You lie to yourself, not me.'

His eyes held fast on hers as he touched the warm, dewy cleft of her womanhood.

'I think you proved your point,' she said bitterly. 'You're a bastard, and I want you anyway. You've made that fact very clear.'

That age-old weariness crept into his expression again, seeped outward from some deep, dark well inside him. '*Oui*,' he said. He slid his hand back up over her belly and pulled her T-shirt down, covering her. He smoothed the fabric gently, regretfully, his mouth twisting. 'And now I have the whole long night to wonder why I made it at all.'

13

Laurel checked her reflection in the hall mirror, frowning. She hadn't brought a suit home with her. The best she could do was a loose-fitting navy linen blazer over a white silk tank and a pair of taupe trousers. The outfit was more formal than she had ever planned to look during her stay here, less formal than she would ever have allowed herself on the job. No win.

It seemed she was stuck in a groove of no-win situations. She didn't want to tackle anything more mentally and emotionally taxing than gardening, but had given her pledge to T-Grace and Ovide. She had no intention of getting involved with a man, but had tossed and turned until dawn thinking about Jack, dreaming about Jack. Jack, with his devil's grin. Jack, with his brooding intensity. Jack, with weary dark eyes that had seen too much.

What if she hadn't said no?

'You look very lawyerlike.'

Laurel glanced around to find Caroline on her way out for the day. 'I don't want to do this,' she admitted glumly.

Caroline put her arm around Laurel's waist to give her a reassuring squeeze. 'You don't feel ready?'

'No.'

She reached up to tuck an errant strand of ash brown hair behind Laurel's ear, her heart aching a little. Beneath the discreet makeup, behind the lenses of her oversize spectacles, Laurel had the look of a child braced for the first day of school – trying to be brave, wanting to stay safe at home.

'I think maybe you're more ready than you know, darlin',' Caroline said gently. 'More time isn't going to change what happened. You'll never be able to get justice for those children. I think the best thing you can do is go and get justice for somebody else, then.'

Laurel heaved a sigh and nibbled her lower lip, chewing off the soft coral lipstick she had just applied. She couldn't think of a thing to say. The feelings were too jumbled. She wanted to stand there forever with Caroline's arm around her, with her aunt's love supporting her. This was what she had come home for, not to jump into trouble with a religious charlatan, not to fend off Vivian's machinations, not to be tempted by Jack Boudreaux. For love, for someone who would judge her far less harshly than she judged herself. For the first time in a long while she felt an acute stab of longing for her father, who had solved all her childish problems with a hug and a kiss and a stick of Juicy Fruit gum. But all she had left of him were a few old snapshots, his crawfish tie pin, and his sister – Caroline.

She drew in a slow, deep breath, tamping down the emotions, drawing up some strength, focusing on the few items scattered on the Chippendale hall table, and cataloging them to give her mind something to do besides wallow in sad memories – an ivory French-style telephone, a blue willow vase holding a spray of fresh-cut flowers, a pewter dish holding an assortment of car keys and a lone earring.

'I'll be all right,' she said, her gaze fastening on the earring. It was heart-shaped, large, tarnished silver studded with rhinestones and bits of colored glass. She fished it out of the dish as an excuse to change the topic. 'Is this yours?'

Caroline frowned at the gaudy bauble. 'Lord, no. It must be Savannah's.' She took a step back and gave her niece one last, long look in the eye, not in the least bit fooled by the diversion. 'You come down to the store and see me later if you need to talk, you hear?'

Laurel nodded. Caroline reached up and stroked her niece's cheek gently, her thumb just grazing one of the dark shadows of fatigue that arched beneath her eyes. 'I know how strong you really are, sweetheart,' she said softly, 'and I know you'll be all right. You're a Chandler, after all, and we're made of stern stuff. But don't expect to climb back all in one day, and don't forget that I'm here if you need me.'

'Thanks, Aunt Caroline,' Laurel murmured.

Caroline straightened her dainty shoulders, a gleam in her dark eyes and a wry smile curling her mouth. 'Thanks, nothing. You go kick the figurative shit out of that television preacher.'

A chuckle bubbled up inside Laurel, and she smiled. 'I'll do my best.'

As Caroline went out, Savannah came down the stairs, wearing a plum silk kimono trimmed with a band of ivory satin and wide ivory satin cuffs that fell past her wrists. Laurel watched her descent by way of the mirror as she repaired her lipstick, trying to assess her sister's mood. It had been near dawn before Savannah had come in, and she was obviously trying to fight off the aftereffects of her late night. She wore a blue gel eye mask to combat puffiness and took the stairs one careful step at a time. Her lips were swollen and red, and her hair was as wild as a witch's mane around her shoulders.

Their eyes met in the mirror, and Laurel bit down on the questions that sprang instantly to mind and the recriminations that came hard on their heels.

'Is this your earring?' She held up the heart-shaped bob as she turned away from the mirror.

Savannah said nothing as she padded barefoot down the hall. She stared blankly at the earring for a moment, flicked at it with a finger to set it swinging. 'It was in your car,' she said flatly. 'Where are you going?'

'Down to the courthouse to see about stopping Baldwin from harassing the Delahoussayes.'

'Christ, Baby, you barely know them.'

'I know all I need to know.'

'You're not supposed to be upsetting yourself with other people's problems.' *You're supposed to be letting me take care of you.*

Laurel opened her pocketbook and dropped in her lipstick and car keys. 'So,' she said with a shrug, 'I'll solve this one and go back to lying low. How's that sound?'

'Like a load of bullshit,' Savannah snapped. 'Let the Delahoussayes take care of themselves. They can damn well fight their own fights.' Her mouth bent into something like a smile. 'You saw that for yourself yesterday. That bitch Annie damn near gave me a bald spot.'

She lifted a hand to rub at her scalp, the sleeve of her kimono falling to her elbow. Laurel's eyes went round at the sight of her wrist. The delicate, porcelain skin was bruised and raw in spots.

'My God, Sister! What happened to you?' she demanded, snatching at Savannah's arm so she could get a better look.

Savannah bared her teeth, an expression made eerier by the blue mask she wore across her eyes like something left over from Mardi Gras. 'You don't want to know.'

'Yes, I do! What the hell—'

'No,' she said coolly. 'I distinctly remember you telling me you didn't want to hear about my sex life. You didn't want to hear that Ronnie Peltier has a cock like a jackhammer or that the Revver likes to play whip-me, whip-me games or that I like to do it with—'

'Stop it!' Laurel yelled. Flinging her sister's arm away, she stepped back, as if Savannah's admission was so repulsive, she couldn't stand the idea of touching her or breathing the same air. 'Dammit, Savannah, why do you have to do that? Why do you have to degrade yourself that way?'

'Because I'm a *slut*.' Savannah threw the word like a dagger, her temper tearing through what little self-control she had left. She stalked toward Laurel, eyes narrowed behind her mask, lips pulled back. 'I'm not a shining little bright-eyed heroine. I'm what Ross Leighton turned me into.'

'You're what you want to be,' Laurel fired back. 'Ross hasn't laid a hand on you in fifteen years—'

'How do you know?' Savannah sneered, backing her into the hall table. 'Maybe I still fuck him twice a week for old time's sake.'

'Shut up!'

'What's the matter, Baby? Don't you want to hear about how I spread my legs for our dear old stepdaddy so you wouldn't have to?'

The words stung like nettles in Laurel's heart. 'I didn't have any control over what Ross did to you,' she said, her voice choked with emotion. 'You can't blame me, and you can't blame yourself. It's stupid to spend the rest of your life punishing yourself for something that was beyond your control.'

Savannah stepped back, her expression beneath her mask a combination of cynicism and incredulity. 'My God, aren't you the little hypocrite?' she said softly. 'What the hell have you been doing with your whole damn life?'

Laurel stared at her, stunned, weak. Her knees felt like water, and her stomach tightened like a fist.

Mama Pearl rumbled into the hall, wringing her plump hands in a red checked dish towel, a scowl folding her forehead into burls of flesh. 'What the world goin' on out here?' she demanded. 'All I hear is yellin' an' cursin' like to burn the Almighty's ears! What goin' on?'

Savannah pulled her temper in and wrapped it tight around her as she adjusted the sash on her kimono. 'Nothing, Mama Pearl,' she said calmly. She picked a piece of dead leaf out of her hair and crumbled it between her fingers. 'I just came down to get a pot of tea.'

Mama Pearl looked to Laurel for corroboration. Laurel straightened her glasses and picked up her purse, her hand trembling visibly. 'I have to go,' she mumbled, refusing to meet anyone's eyes, focusing on maintaining some semblance of control.

She walked out of the house and into the sauna heat of midmorning on wobbly legs, thinking that after what she had just been through, a trip to the courthouse was going to be a piece of cake.

The air-conditioning in the sheriff's office was fighting a losing battle against the afternoon sun that came glaring in through the window. Sheriff Duwayne Kenner stood behind his desk with his hands on his slim hips, overseeing the futile attempts of two maintenance men who were trying to install a new venetian blind.

'Get the goddamn bracket straight,' he growled. 'And the left one's half an inch higher than the right. What the hell you boys thinkin' – that y'all can tip the whole goddamn courthouse so the shade'll hang straight?'

The maintenance man on the right shot a glance over his meaty shoulder, blinking at the sweat that dribbled down his shining dark forehead and into his eyes. His blue shirt was soaked down the back and sides, the tails crawling up out of the low-riding waistband of his pants, giving glimpses of a generous tube of fat around his middle. He gulped a breath and mumbled the expected, 'No, sir.'

The other man – younger, thinner, harder, darker – set his jaw at the word 'boy' and dropped his end of the blind so that the blazing sun struck Kenner full in the face.

'Jesus Christ!' The sheriff took a quick step back, snapping his head to the side and squeezing his eyes shut. The badge pinned to the chest of his sweat-stained khaki uniform shirt glinted like gold.

The younger man's mouth flicked up on the corners. 'I's sorry, Sheriff Kenner,' he said in an exaggerated drawl.

'Your sorry black ass,' Kenner grumbled under his breath. He jerked around, muttering about the squandering of tax dollars on equal opportunity programs, and faced the young woman who had come into his office a full five minutes ago to speak with him.

Laurel Chandler. Ross Leighton's stepdaughter. While Kenner curried favor with Leighton, he was in no particular hurry to listen to the girl. Everyone in town had heard about her – making wild accusations up in Georgia, blowing the case, losing her marbles over it. She was trouble. He could smell trouble a mile off – even when it was wearing perfume.

Laurel sat in the visitor's chair, sweat trickling down her sides and between her shoulder blades. Her linen jacket was wilted, her temper frayed down to the nub. While her morning's efforts had gone smoothly, she had a feeling Kenner was going to be a whole different story. He had the unmistakable aura of a redneck about him. He looked fifty, tough and sinewy, with the lean build of a cowboy. His steel gray hair was thinning fast on top, but she doubted anyone ribbed him about it. If Kenner had a sense of humor, the Klan backed the NAACP.

He regarded her with hard, dark eyes, his impatience charging the air around him, his mouth set in a grim line that would have done Clint Eastwood proud. 'What can I do for you, Miz Chandler?' he asked in a flat tone that indicated both his level of interest and his lack of willingness to do anything at all for her.

Laurel took a deep breath of stifling, sweat-tinged air and shifted on her seat. 'I wanted to make you aware of the situation between the Delahoussayes of Frenchie's Landing and Reverend Jimmy Lee Baldwin. He's been harassing them and disrupting their business. I've spoken with Judge Monahan on their behalf.'

Kenner perched a skinny buttock on one corner of his desk, picked up a pack of unfiltered Camels, and shook one out just long enough to hook his lip over. 'Seems a mite drastic,' he said, cigarette bobbing as he tore a match from a book and struck it.

'Baldwin is not only making a nuisance of himself, he's defaming the Delahoussayes and inhibiting their right to free trade.'

He took a deep pull on the cigarette, pretending to consider the facts as she had presented them. 'He hasn't hurt anybody, has he?'

'Is that your criterion for action?' Laurel asked coolly. 'You wait until someone has resorted to physical violence?'

Eyes narrowing to slits, Kenner blew twin streams of smoke out his slim nose and pointed a finger at her, shaking ash down on the cheap linoleum floor. 'I do a damn good job in this parish, Missy. Everywhere around us they got dead girls stacked up like cordwood and drug dealers crawling around thick as copperheads in canebreaks. You don't see that here, and I'll tell you why – 'cause I know damn well whose ass to kick.'

'I'm sure you do.'

'You're goddamn right I do.' He took a quick drag on his smoke and shot a glare over his shoulder at the maintenance men, who were making an unholy racket with the blind. 'And I'll tell you this – I got better things to do with my time than chase around after that television preacher, tellin' him where he can piss and where he can't.'

Laurel rose gracefully, smoothing the wrinkles from her trousers, schooling her temper. Kenner was hardly the first jerk she'd ever come up against. 'I don't care where he pisses, Sheriff,' she said smoothly. 'I don't care where he does anything, as long as he doesn't do it at Frenchie's Landing. Judge Monahan has granted a temporary injunction until the formalities can be taken care of. Diligent as you are, I expect you'll do everything in your power to see that Reverend Baldwin respects it.'

Kenner gave her a flat look, the muscles in his lean jaw working. His cigarette smoldered between his fingers, ribbons of blue smoke curling up into the stagnant air. 'I know who you are, Miz Chandler,' he said softly. 'I don't need some female with an overactive imagination running around my parish crying wolf every time she turns around and dud'n like the look of somebody.'

The jibe hit and stuck. Laurel tensed against it, steeled herself and her pride, and dug down for some of the grit she had been known for back in Scott County. Lifting her chin, she met Kenner's stare, unflinching. 'I don't make empty accusations, Sheriff. If I cry wolf, there'll be one coming to chew your skinny ass.'

He gave a snort of derision and stubbed out his cigarette, shooting another glare at the maintenance men, who had stopped working altogether to watch the confrontation.

'Get your lazy asses in gear and get that goddamn blind up before I get a heat stroke!'

Laurel turned and walked out, gritting her teeth as her stomach knotted and her nerves gave a belated tremor. The hall was cooler and darker. The courthouse had been built before the Civil War, and for a town the size of Bayou Breaux, it was an impressive structure, three stories of brick with Doric columns and a broad set of steps out front. Inside, the hallways were wide with soaring ceilings where old fans turned lazily to stir the humid air. The dark green plaster walls were decorated with a framed gallery of prominent citizens from the past.

For a moment Laurel leaned back against the cool, nubby plaster and rested her eyes, willing herself to relax. It didn't matter what Kenner thought of her. His opinion was no great surprise. She imagined a great many people held it. *The Prosecutor Who Cried Wolf.* The headline still made her angry, still made her want to lash out, to rail at those who had doubted her.

I wasn't wrong. They were guilty.

She wasn't wrong, she was a failure. That was the worst of it. Knowing that those children had been committed to terrible fates because she hadn't been able to prove it.

'*No one will believe you, Laurel. . . . Don't tell Mama.*'

For an instant she was twelve again, standing in the door to the parlor, watching Vivian fuss with an arrangement of calla lilies and delphinium. The secret was there inside her, a big gooey ball of words that clogged her throat. Savannah's warning rang in her ears – '*No one will believe you, Laurel. Don't tell Mama. She'll only get cross with you . . . .*' Helplessness and fear gripped her like icy hands, grappling with her sense of justice. She wanted to tell, thought she ought to, but she just stood there, watching Vivian frown and fuss, her temper slipping visibly as the flowers failed to please her. . . .

Sucking in air like a diver just breaking the surface, Laurel shoved herself away from the wall and turned into a shallow alcove, where a water fountain gurgled. She bent over and swallowed a mouthful of cool, over-chlorinated water, dampened her fingers, and patted her cheeks. Dismissing the memories, she dug through her pocketbook for a roll of Maalox tablets.

She would have to go to Frenchie's and explain things to T-Grace and Ovide. Maybe she would stop by the antiques shop and tell Aunt Caroline everything had gone well enough.

'Back in harness, so to speak, Laurel?'

She jumped at the sound of Stephen Danjermond's voice. She hadn't heard his approach, had been too focused on herself, she supposed. Closing her purse, she casually took a step back. 'Just doing a favor for some friends.'

'The Delahoussayes?' he asked, his smile telling her he already knew the answer. He stood half in shadow, his face half light and half dark, like a figure in a dream. Laurel found the effect unsettling. 'News travels fast in a town this size,' he said, sliding his hands in the pockets of his tailored charcoal trousers. 'I had a chat with Judge Monahan over lunch. He was very taken with you.'

'He was taken with the idea of making Reverend Baldwin's life unpleasant,' Laurel said. 'Some years ago his mother gave a sizable fortune to a man of Baldwin's ilk, and it was later discovered he spent the contributions of his flock on such things as air-conditioned dog houses and spiritual retreats to nude beaches on the French Riviera.'

'You sell yourself short, Laurel. I was discussing with him the possibility of your coming to work for me. The idea pleased him.'

She frowned a little. 'I wish you wouldn't have said anything. I told you, Mr. Danjermond, I'm not thinking about going back to work at this point.'

'But you're thinking about seeing justice done, aren't you, Laurel? A job title has little to do with it. You are who you are.'

The way he said it had a ring of inevitability, as if mankind's little play of the busy, bustling world was all superfluous to the core of life. The trappings could all be stripped away and everyone reduced to their very essence. She was the champion for justice.

'It's what matters most to you, isn't it?'

Laurel kept her answer to herself, feeling it would somehow give him an advantage in their chess game. She resettled her purse strap on her shoulder and shifted her weight toward the door. 'I ought to be on my way. I have to go tell T-Grace and Ovide what's going on and make sure Baldwin gets the message. I don't have a lot of faith that Kenner will do the job.'

Amusement lit the district attorney's eyes and widened his smile. He turned and started toward the door with her, checking his long, fluid strides to stay beside her. 'I assume it wasn't love at first sight between you and Duwayne.'

'He's a racist, a sexist, and a jerk,' Laurel said flatly.

'And he's very good at his job.'

'Because he knows whose ass to kick. Yes, he told me.'

They stepped out onto the broad portico. A capricious breeze slithered between the columns, riffling Danjermond's raven hair and playing with the end of his burgundy tie. He cut a handsome figure, Laurel admitted, athletic and elegant, perfectly at home in his tailored suit standing at the portal to the halls of justice. He would go far on looks alone, farther with a mind as sharp and clever as his. She really couldn't blame her mother for seeing him as a potential son-in-law. Vivian had been raised to believe in matches made for family allegiance and social prominence. Stephen Danjermond had to fit her requirements to a T.

'There's a trick to dealing with Kenner, you know,' he pointed out.

Laurel frowned. 'Yes, well, I don't think I'm going to grow a penis any time soon.'

Danjermond laughed, delighted with her plain talk. People never expected her to speak her mind, assuming that because she was petite and pretty, she was automatically shy and retiring. She had used that erroneous assumption to her advantage more than once.

'Heaven forbid!' He lifted a hand and cupped her chin, his thumb stroking along her jaw, sending a jolt of awareness through her. Sexuality, sensuality, hummed in the air around him as if he had suddenly turned up the power on his magnetism. 'You're delicate, lovely, exquisite just as you are, Laurel. Bright, forthright, brimming with integrity.'

559

'Kenner thinks I'm a troublemaker.' She backed away from him and turned to look out at the street.

'I'll speak with him.'

'No. I fight my own battles, thank you.'

'Yes, you do, Laurel. That's a matter of record.' His gaze turned speculative. The breeze died. 'The battle you fought in Scott County – should you have won?'

Laurel had to brace herself against the barrage of feelings his blunt question brought on. Yes, she should have won – for the children, for the name of right. But she hadn't been strong enough, and in the end evil had won out.

'They were guilty,' she said, and without another glance at Stephen Danjermond, she headed down the steps.

14

Laurel wheeled her Acura into Meyette's Garage, dreading the thought of getting out of the car's air-conditioned comfort. She had shed her jacket, but the day had simply turned too hot to move. It was a day to be spent in a cool room with quiet music and a good book. That image would remain in her imagination, however, shimmering like a mirage for another hour or so.

Savannah had brought the car home with a near-empty tank and a coat of mud splatters from God knew where. Laurel had decided she would fill up on her way to Frenchie's Landing and wash the car herself after the heat of afternoon had subsided. The prospect of doing something physical, simple, and gratifying held enormous appeal. Just herself and her car in the shade of the driveway, a bucket and a sponge, Mozart playing softly in the background . . .

She pulled up along pumps of a type most stations had traded in for newer models ten years ago and got out, sending a smile to the mechanic who stuck his head out from under the hood of a putty-color Ford.

'Hey, Miz Chandler.'

'Hey, Nipper.'

'I'll be right with you.'

'That's fine.'

He beamed a smile at her, strong white teeth flashing in a lean face that was covered with grime and running with sweat. He was twenty-five, with a flat-topped hedge of brilliant red hair. Laurel thought he was probably something of a local heartthrob when he was clean, but she had only ever seen him tinkering under the hood of a car, looking like Pigpen grown up.

Meyette's was the kind of station that didn't exist anywhere but small, out-the-way towns. City folk would have shied away from the shabby buildings, the dark, dirty, cavernous garage. They might have found the old chest-type Coca-Cola cooler that squatted on the gallery by the front door quaint and might have tried to wheedle the antique away from the old rube who ran the place, but they would have let their bladders burst before asking for the restroom key and would have starved before trying a stick of the homemade *boudin* sausage Mrs. Meyette sold over the counter in the office.

The thought offered a margin of security. While Cajun country had become a trendy tourist draw, there were still parts of home that would never be violated.

Laurel's gaze hit on Jimmy Lee Baldwin, who stood on the gallery of the garage, a bottle of Orange Crush in hand, and the word 'violated' reverberated in her head. Her enjoyment of her surroundings dimmed. She couldn't look at him without thinking of the things Savannah had said about him. The man was slime. His mere existence was a violation against decent people. Preaching salvation and performing lewd sex acts on the side was a kind of hypocrisy that touched off an almost uncontrollable fury in her.

Straightening away from the side of the building as she marched toward him, he smoothed a hand over his slicked-back tawny hair, at the same time pasting on his too-white smile, making the two actions seem like cause and effect. He had sweated through his white dress shirt and rolled up the sleeves in a futile attempt to battle the heat. His skinny black necktie hung limply around his neck, pulled loose at the collar, and the button beneath it was undone. The crease in his black trousers had melted out, the total effect leaving him looking like a rumpled and disreputable traveling salesman.

'Miz Chandler, what a pleasant surprise,' he said. He discreetly wiped the condensation from the soda bottle off on the side of his pants leg and offered his hand to her. He had given the subject of Laurel Chandler considerable thought as he had lain in bed this morning, the fan blowing across his naked body as he recuperated from his night's play. He wanted her if not as an ally, then at least out of the Delahoussaye camp. He was ready to pluck the rose of his future, but every time he reached for it, he was pricked by this lovely little thorn.

Laurel scowled at him as if he were holding out a dead rat for her inspection. 'I don't see much of anything pleasant about it, Mr. Baldwin.'

Jimmy Lee tightened his jaw against the urge to call her a snotty little bitch. He pulled his hand back and planted it at his waist. 'There's no need to be hostile. We're not enemies, Miz Chandler. In fact, we could be allies. We fight on the same side, you and I. Against evil, against sin.'

Laurel almost laughed. 'Save the sermons for the poor fools who believe in you. We're not on the same side, Baldwin. I have my doubts that we belong to the same species. From what I've heard about you and seen of you, I'd have to say you're more closely related to things that crawl out from under dead tree stumps. Don't waste your time trying to charm me. I've dealt with too many snakes not to know one when I see one.'

Fury burned hot in Jimmy Lee's belly. If there was one thing in this world he couldn't tolerate, it was a mouthy broad. He would have given just about anything for a chance to cuff her one, but he wouldn't have given up his shot at stardom, and Nipper Calhoun was too handy a witness.

He lifted his shoulders in a stiff shrug and stared down at her, his tawny eyes as cold and flat as gold coins. 'That's not what I've heard about you,' he said tightly. 'The way I hear it, you point fingers at random.'

The blow to her pride landed, but Laurel didn't bat an eyelash. She wouldn't give him the satisfaction. 'It doesn't matter what you've heard about me. All you need to hear is what Judge Monahan has to say. As of today you are hereby ordered to cease and desist your harassment of the Delahoussayes and are forbidden from setting foot on their property. I'm pleased to give you the news in person,' she said, flashing him a nasty smile. 'The paperwork will be delivered. You have yourself a real nice day, Mr. Baldwin.'

She turned and pranced away toward Meyette's office, prim little nose in the air. Jimmy Lee watched her go and felt all his carefully stacked plans for his big campaign tumble around him like a house of cards. Before he could stop himself, he had lunged after her and clamped a hand down on her shoulder, meaning to spin her around and tell her a thing or two about playing hard ball.

Jack stepped out of the shadows of the garage and hooked the toe of his boot in front of the preacher's ankle. As Laurel twisted away from the man's touch, Jack pulled back, and the Revver went sprawling, facedown in the dirt. Baldwin's breath left him in a painful grunt.

'Oh, hey, I'm sorry, Jimmy Lee,' Jack said without a drop of sincerity. 'I guess I wasn' lookin' where I was goin'.'

Baldwin shoved himself up onto his hands and knees, coughing and spitting dirt in between curses. He shot a vicious look at Jack over his shoulder, his face burgundy beneath the layer of gritty dirt.

'*Bon Dieu!*' Jack exclaimed with exaggerated shock. 'There's some words comin' out your mouth I never seen in the Bible!'

'I doubt you ever cracked the spine of a Bible, Boudreaux,' Jimmy Lee snarled. He hauled himself to his feet, trying in vain to dust his clothes off. His eyes locked on Jack in a stare as hard and cold as a billiard ball.

'Well,' Jack drawled, 'mebbe I never have read it, but I looked at the pictures.' He put on a quizzical look and scratched his head. 'Do you think Jesus got his tan at Suds 'n' Sun too?'

Jimmy Lee glared at him for a second, his jaw working to chew back his rage.

'What do you think, Miz Chandler?' Jack arched a brow at Laurel.

Laurel stared at him for several seconds, caught completely off guard by his appearance, to say nothing of his question. She hadn't expected to see him here, hadn't finished preparing herself for speaking to him after what had happened in the courtyard. She had strategies filed away in her brain for every kind of courtroom situation, but she had no strategies for near-miss sexual encounters. She had no string of lovers in her past to draw experience from. Her ex-husband was the only man she had ever been seriously involved with, and while Wesley was a good man, an intelligent man, a kind man, he wasn't the kind of man Jack was.

He was shirtless and tan. He held a cherry Popsicle in his left hand, his elegant musician's fingers deftly holding the stick so the thing wouldn't drip on him. He brought it to his mouth and nipped off a corner.

'This is quite a day for me,' he said, his dark eyes glittering with mischief. 'I get to see a lawyer speechless and a television preacher wearing his dirt on the *outside* for once.'

'I don't have to take this from you, Boudreaux,' Jimmy Lee said, his voice low and thrumming with anger. He raised an accusatory finger and shook it in Jack's face. 'Mr. Big-Shot Best-Selling Author. You're nothing but a no-account, alcoholic piece of trash. All the money in the world can't change that.'

'Naw,' Jack said, his pose deceptively casual, one leg cocked, his right hand propped at his waist. He heaved an exaggerated sigh and hung his head. 'A man is what he is.'

In the blink of an eye, he had Baldwin by the shirt front and slammed up against the side of the building. That quickly the mask of humor was gone, and in its place was a fury that burned like hot coals in the depths of his eyes.

'A man is what he is, Jimmy Lee.' He ground the words out between his teeth, his face inches from Baldwin's. 'You, you're a piece-of-shit con man. Me, I'm the guy who's gonna kick your balls up to your throat and knock your teeth down to meet 'em if you *ever* lay a hand on Miz Chandler again.' He let the fire shimmer in his eyes for a moment longer, then flashed an unholy smile. 'Have I made myself perfectly clear, Jimmy Lee?'

Slowly he loosened his hold on Baldwin's shirt front. Smiling affably, he made a token attempt to smooth out the fabric and brush off some of the dirt, then stepped back and dropped his hands to the waist of his jeans.

'Mebbe you just better go on home and change, Jimmy Lee. You don' want people lookin' at you and thinkin' you had a run-in with the devil and lost.'

He walked away a few paces and poked his toe at the Popsicle he had dropped, frowning. Dismissing Baldwin entirely, he dug some change out of his pocket and headed for the little white freezer that hummed laboriously beside the Coca-Cola cooler. He could feel Baldwin's eyes boring into his back, but didn't give a damn. There was nothing any two-bit cable TV preacher could do to him. He didn't run a business, and he already had a bad reputation. He shot an inquiring look at Laurel.

'You want a Popsicle, *'tite chatte*?'

'You're messing with the wrong man, Boudreaux,' Baldwin said, his voice trembling with rage and humiliation. 'You don't want to tangle with me.'

Jack flicked a glance at him, looking supremely bored with the whole scene. 'That's right, preacher. I don' want to tangle with you. I got better things to do with my time than scrape you off the bottom of my shoe, so mebbe you oughta just stay the hell outta my sight.'

Jimmy Lee shook his head, a strange look of amazement dawning on his face. 'You don't know who you're dealing with,' he muttered, then turned on the heel of his wingtip and stalked off toward his car.

Laurel watched him walk away, then turned toward Jack, stepping up onto the gallery. He stared down into the freezer as cold billowed up out of it in a cloud.

'For someone who claims not to be anybody's hero, you seem to spend an awful lot of time coming to my rescue,' she said.

'*Mais non*,' Jack mumbled, reaching in for a Fudgsicle. 'Me, I was just having a little fun with Jimmy Lee while my carburetor gets looked at.'

He didn't want her reading anything into his actions, he told himself. But the truth was that he didn't want to look at those actions too closely himself. He didn't want to dig too deep for the reason behind the rush of anger he'd felt when Baldwin had put his hand on her. He didn't own her, would never have any claim on her, and therefore had no business feeling jealous or overprotective.

Conditioned response. That was what it was. How many times had he rushed at Blackie when the old man reached out and put a hand on Maman or Marie? Countless times. They had called him their hero, too. But he hadn't been anything but a kid full of rage and hate. Small and weak and worthless, and Blackie had shaken him off more times than not. He wasn't small or weak anymore. The feeling of slamming Baldwin up against the building had sent a rush of adrenaline and power through him that was still buzzing in his veins.

He glanced at Laurel as he unwrapped his treat, trying to defuse her concentration with a teasing smile. 'Besides, I didn't want you to pull your gun out and shoot him. Day's too hot to have a corpse laying around out in the sun.' She made a disgusted face, and he chuckled to himself. 'Popsicle or Fudgsicle, angel? What do you think?'

Laurel narrowed her eyes as he blatantly dismissed her line of questioning. 'I think you ought to make up your mind, Jack,' she said. 'Are you a good guy or a bad guy?'

'That all depends on what you want me for, darlin',' he murmured, his voice rough and smooth at once, beckoning a woman to reach out and touch him.

Laurel's heart beat a little harder; nerve endings he had awakened and tantalized the night before stirred restlessly. She frowned at him. 'I don't want you for anything.'

Jack leaned across the open freezer, 'It's a good thing you're not under oath, counselor,' he whispered.

'Close the freezer, Boudreaux,' she said sarcastically, 'before your hot air melts all the Popsicles.'

She went into the station and paid for her gas, spending a few moments chatting with Mrs. Meyette, who asked after Aunt Caroline and Mama Pearl, told her she was too thin, and made her take half a dozen sticks of *boudin* with her. When she came out, Jack was nowhere in sight.

She staunchly refused to acknowledge the disappointment that slid down through her. She had better things to do with her time than spar with him, and she had to assume he had better things to do, as well. He was supposed to be some hot-shot best-selling author, but he never seemed to work. It seemed to her he was always at Frenchie's or giving her a hard time. And it took no imagination at all to picture him spending the rest of his time sprawled in a hammock asleep with that awful hound sacked out right beneath him.

Trying like a demon *not* to picture him at all, she drove home and changed out of her slacks into a cool gauzy blue skirt and a loose-fitting pale blue cotton tank. The house was silent, the shades drawn. Mama Pearl had left a note on the hall table: *Gone to card club. Red beans and rice in the pot. Eat, you!* Monday. Wash day. Red beans and rice for supper. Laurel smiled at the comfort of tradition.

There was no sign of Savannah. Laurel wasn't sure whether to be disappointed or relieved. She didn't like the memories from their morning's argument lingering in her mind like acrid smoke, but she didn't know how they would clear the air, either. They had both said things that would have been better left unsaid. They couldn't go back and change their childhoods. Laurel wanted to leave it all in the past, to start fresh, but Savannah dragged her past around with her like an enormous overloaded suitcase.

And so do you, Baby. She could almost hear her sister's voice, angry, accusatory.

'What the hell have you been doing with your whole damn life?'

Looking for justice.

There was a difference, she insisted. She was an attorney; that was her job. She wasn't trying to change the past. She wasn't trying to atone for anything.

The word 'liar' drifted through her mind, and she slammed down on it before it had the chance to do more than rattle her nerves. She had to go out and take care of some business. No doubt by the time she got home, Savannah would be here, begging forgiveness for the nasty things she'd said, promising she hadn't meant any of them. That was the way their fights usually ran. That was the way Savannah's temper ran – hot and cold, from emotional conflagration to contrition in a flash. She was probably off somewhere right now thinking about coming home to red beans and rice and a side order of apologies.

Savannah stared out at the heat. It seemed so thick, so oppressive, she thought she could see it hanging in the air above the bayou, pressing down on everything. It permeated the cabin, seeping in through the screens, soaking into everything, bringing with it the wild, feral scent of the swamp.

She brushed at the stray tendrils of hair that had escaped her topknot and shifted restlessly from one bare foot to the other. Sweat coated her skin like a fine mist, despite the fact that she wore nothing but a pair of ragged cut off jeans and a black bandeau bikini top with a sheer white blouse hanging open over it.

The quiet was getting to her. She had promised Coop she wouldn't disturb him, but the day had come to a complete standstill. Even the birds had fallen silent beneath the blanket of heat. The sense of expectation that was so much a part of the swamp had thickened until everything waited, breath held, for something unknown, unseen.

The two-room cabin squatted on stilts above the murky green water. From Savannah's vantage point, no solid land was visible, only bald cypress, their thick hard trunks thrusting up from the water, scruffy, stubby branches sticking out like deformities, knobby knees jutting out at the bases. They looked like tortured creatures that had been cast under an enchantment and petrified so that they resembled death. Floating on the surface around their trunks were sheets of delicate green duckweed and rafts of water hyacinth, shimmering violet and looking deceptively fragile beneath the brutal sun. Lily pads lay scattered like an array of deep green Frisbees tossed randomly across the bayou.

She could see a partially submerged log lying at the edge of a thicket of cattails and knew it could well be an alligator. Not far to the south, the jagged stump of a dead cypress had become home to a nest of herons, and the pair posed there, motionless, looking like a woodcarver's exquisite craftings, their long necks arched and tucked, black beaks as straight and slender as fencing foils.

The birds' stillness irritated Savannah. She wanted them to squawk and fly away, huge wings beating the air. She wanted the gator to lunge for one of the fish that dimpled the surface of the water as they rose unseen to catch insects. She wanted the air to stir, wanted to see the reeds sway. Most of all she wanted Coop to move.

He sat at a rough plank table that was pushed up against one screened wall, staring out, making notes from time to time, nearly as motionless as the surroundings. He had bought the cabin as a fish camp, but he never fished when he met her here. He mostly stared. 'Absorbing the profound intensity of life in the swamp,' he'd explained once. He would sit there for hours, seemingly doing nothing, then he would come to her and they would make love on the old moss-stuffed mattress.

This was their secret hideaway; an idea that usually appealed to Savannah. She liked going out on the bayou in her old flat-bottomed aluminum boat, not saying anything to anybody, winding her way into the dense, lush wilderness to meet her lover. But today something about the arrangement grated on her. She blamed it on the fight she'd had with Laurel.

'Why do you have to do that? Why do you have to degrade yourself that way?'

She jerked around and burned a hole in Cooper's broad back with her glare. 'Haven't you stared out that screen long enough?'

Coop sat back, wincing a little at the stiffness that had settled in his joints. He scratched a hand back through his blond hair like a man just waking from a long, deep sleep, and looked at Savannah over his shoulder. He was struck as always by her raw sexuality and by the soft, stunning natural beauty she had seen fit to make slightly grotesque with collagen and silicone. She was so alluring, so flawed, she never failed to captivate him utterly.

He longed to turn and jot those thoughts down in his notebook, but he refrained. Savannah's mood seemed as volatile as the weather – a tense stillness that hid a building storm. Instead, he put down his pen, rose and stretched.

'I don't mean to ignore you, love,' he mumbled in his low, smooth voice. 'But I have to get my notes made. I'm doing an APR broadcast from N'Awlins next weekend.'

Savannah's eyes lit up like a child's. 'You'll take me with you?'

It was more a statement than a question. Coop doubted she even heard him when he said, 'We'll see.' She was already racing ahead, making plans for them to meet in one of the cottages of the Maison de Ville, chattering about dinner in her favorite restaurants, the shopping she would do, the clubs they might visit.

Of course, he wouldn't take her. While he loved her, he knew that love must be contained within very definite boundaries. If he allowed it to escape the small pen of Bayou Breaux, it would run wild and in its delirium destroy itself and them. Like a fine wine, it was something to be sipped and savored. Savannah would drink it all in greedy, sloppy gulps, spilling it down her, splashing it all over, laughing madly.

He stroked a hand over the back of her head down to her neck and smiled with pleasure as she arched into his touch like a cat.

'Let's get you out of these clothes,' he murmured, stepping away from her, reaching for one cuff of the gossamer blouse she wore.

'No.' Savannah pulled her hand back, smiling shyly to cover her shame. Laurel's words were too fresh in her mind. Coop would think the same when he saw the marks on her wrists – that she degraded herself. She didn't want to hear that from him, not today. Today she wanted to pretend they had a normal life. She sent him a coy look. 'I want to wear it for you.'

He said nothing, but stood and watched as she shed the bikini top and the cutoffs, leaving only the sheer white blouse to cover her. The picture she presented was more tantalizing than if she had been completely naked. She knew because she had stood in front of the mirror in her room and studied the look. Provocative. Dressed but not decent. The sheer fabric was a misty barrier that invited a man to reach past it to the treasures of her lush feminine body.

Time lost its meaning for her. They could have been in bed a week. She wanted it to last forever. With his slow, gentle lovemaking, Cooper made her think it *could* last forever, that they had all the time in the world instead of just a few stolen hours.

And time meant nothing as they lay together afterward, skin sticky with their mingled sweat, the air redolent with the exotic musk of sex and perfume, the dusty scent of the moss-stuffed mattress. They lay touching, despite the heat, limbs tangled, hearts thudding slowly, their breathing shallow, as if to keep from disturbing the peace that had settled around them.

This was happiness, Savannah thought, being here with Coop. She loved him so much it frightened her. Too good to be true. Too good to be hers. Sex with him was so different from what she sought out with others. With others she felt wild, wicked. With Coop there was nothing depraved, debauched, dissipated, dissolute. She felt all the things she had spent her life yearning for but never finding. She shivered a little at the thought. Too good to be true.

'Will you marry me, Coop?' The words seemed to spill directly out of her overflowing heart, and instantly a part of her wished them back, because she knew deep down what his answer would be.

The air hummed with silence for a few moments, then with the electric whine of cicadas, then with the tension of an answer unspoken. Tears stung Savannah's eyes and seared her heart like acid, and all the gold wore off the afterglow, leaving her feeling like what everyone said she was – a slut, a whore, not deserving of anything like the love of a good man.

'*Why do you have to degrade yourself that way?*'
Because that's what whores do, Baby.

Coop sighed and sat up with his back against the headboard as Savannah got out of bed. 'I can't give you that commitment, Savannah,' he said sadly. 'You know that. I have a wife.'

She stepped into her shorts and jerked them up, her fingers fumbling with the fastenings as she shot him a burning look from under her lashes. 'You have a vegetable.'

'I can't abandon her, Savannah. Don't ask me to.'

Frustration swelled and burst inside her like a festered wound, its hot, caustic poison shooting through her, penetrating every muscle, every fiber. Unable to stand it, she clamped her hands on her head and doubled over, a wild animal scream tearing from her throat.

'She doesn't even know who you are!' she sobbed.

He just sat there, looking handsome and sad, his blue eyes locked on her as if he were gazing at her for the very last time, memorizing her every feature.

'But I know who I am,' he whispered, that low, smooth voice capturing futility and fatalism and a sense of inevitability she recognized but didn't want to hear.

He would never leave Astor as long as she was alive. And Savannah knew he would never marry her because wife was not the role he had cast her in in his real-life drama of the South. Unless she could purge herself somehow, cut out and dispose of what she had been all these years, and that seemed as impossible a task as cutting out a piece of the ocean.

She stared at him through tear-washed eyes for several silent moments, thinking she could feel her heart shatter like a glass ornament. Then she turned and left the cabin without a word, hating him, hating herself for what she was . . . and for what she would never be.

15

Frenchie's was a madhouse. Annie had failed to show up for work, and one of the other waitresses was out sick, leaving T-Grace to wait tables herself. She stormed around the bar at a lightning pace, slinging plates of red beans and rice, serving beer, taking orders and barking out her own as she went. The heat and humidity had combined with her short temper to leave her looking frazzled and dangerous. Her red hair was a cloud of frizz around her head. Her eyes looked ready to pop out of her heat-polished face. She stopped in a clearing between tables and brushed her bangs off her forehead with the back of a hand, blowing a cooling breath upward as Laurel approached her.

'You get dat Jimmy Lee thrown in jail or what, *chère?*' she asked without preamble.

'He's been officially warned off,' Laurel said, raising her voice to be heard above the racket of pool games, loud talk, and jukebox Zydeco.

T-Grace gave a derisive snort and propped a hand on her skinny hip. 'Ovide, he warn dat bastard's ass off with some buckshot next time he come 'round.'

'I wouldn't advise that,' Laurel said patiently, silently thankful the Delahoussayes hadn't already resorted to such measures. The Cajuns had their own code of folk justice, a tradition that predated organized law enforcement in these parts. 'If he bothers you again, call the sheriff and press charges.'

'If he bothers us again,' T-Grace said, a sly smile pulling at one corner of her thin mouth, 'we're gonna need to hire more help. All dat rantin' and ravin' what he done on television was like free advertisin' for Frenchie's. My Ovide, he's in a panic tryin' to serve ever'body.'

Laurel turned to see Ovide, stoic as ever, planted behind the bar, filling mugs and popping the tops off long-neck bottles, sweat beading on his bald spot like dew on a pumpkin. Leonce was playing backup bartender, his Panama hat tipped back on his head. As he slid a bottle across the bar to a customer, a grin slashed white across his close-cropped beard in counterpoint to the scar that ran red across his cheek.

'So what's the difference between a dead lawyer and a dead skunk in the middle of the road?' the customer asked. 'There's skid marks in front of the skunk.'

Leonce howled at the old joke and moved to dig another beer out of the cooler. Jack swiveled around on his bar stool, grinning like the Cheshire cat as his gaze landed smack on Laurel. He had made a token concession to the 'No Shirt, No Shoes, Get the Hell Out' sign that hung on the wall behind the bar, but the red team shirt from the Cypress Lanes Bowling Alley hung open down the front, framing a wedge of muscular chest and flat belly.

T-Grace reached out and patted Laurel's cheek, her eyes glowing as they darted between *une belle femme* and Jack. '*Merci, ma petite.* You done a fine job, you. Now come sit you pretty self down and have some supper before the wind comes up and blows you away, you so little!'

She took hold of Laurel's arm with a grip that could have cracked walnuts and ushered her to the bar, where she ordered Taureau Hebert to go in search of some other place to sit his lazy behind, thereby vacating the seat next to Jack.

'Hey, Ovide!' Jack called, his devilish gaze on Laurel. 'How 'bout a champagne cocktail for our heroine here?'

Laurel gave him a look and busied her hands arranging her skirt. Ovide slid a foaming mug of beer in front of her. Jack leaned over conspiratorially and murmured, 'What he lacks in sophistication, he makes up for in sensitivity.'

A chuckle bubbled up, and Laurel shook her head. She couldn't seem to stay mad at him, no matter what he did or said or made her feel.

'Don't you ever work, Boudreaux?' she asked, frowning at him.

His grin stretched, dimples biting deep in his lean cheeks. 'Oh, yeah. Absolutely. All the time.' He leaned closer, bracing one hand on the back of her stool, resting the other on her knee. His voice dropped a husky notch, and his breath tickled the side of her neck. 'I'm workin' on you now, *'tite chatte.*'

Laurel arched a brow. 'Is that right? Well,' she drawled, poking him hard in the ribs with her thumb, 'you've been laid off, hot shot.'

Jack rubbed his side and pouted. 'You're mean.' His scowl, however, was ruined by the gleam in his eyes as he added, 'I like that in a woman.'

'You mind your manners, Jack,' T-Grace said with a wry smile as she set a steaming plate of food down in front of Laurel. 'This one, she's gonna show you what's what, just like what she did wit' dat damn preacher.'

Jack grinned and winked at Laurel, and she felt a wave of warmth sweep through her that had nothing to do with the heat of the day. It had to do with laughter, with friends, with a sense of belonging. The realization flashed like a light bulb going on above her head. She couldn't remember the last time she had felt welcome anywhere besides Aunt Caroline's house.

In Scott County she had always been an outsider, and then a pariah as she had leveled accusations at people no one wanted to believe capable of evil. She had told herself it didn't matter, that the only thing that mattered was justice, but it *had* mattered. She would have given anything back then to have someone in the community believe in her, support her, smile at her, joke with her.

She thought back to the first night she had come in here and remembered the sense of isolation that had enveloped her and the loneliness that had accompanied it. In just a matter of days the people here had accepted her, and acceptance was something she had ached for. She had called that need a weakness, but maybe it wasn't so much weak as it was human.

Dr. Pritchard's voice came back to her, soft and steady. *'You're not perfect, Laurel, you're human.'*

'So, you managed to save the day again, did you, Baby?'

Savannah's voice cut sharply into her thoughts. Laurel turned toward her sister, a fist of anxiety tightening in her belly. Savannah stood with a tall drink in one hand, the other propped on her hip. Her breasts were threatening to spill over the edge of her black bikini top, the sheer blouse she wore over it offering no backup modesty. Her hair was a mess, falling out of its topknot in curling dark ribbons.

'It was nothing so dramatic as that,' Laurel said, automatically downplaying her accomplishment, as she had done all her life.

'Come on, Baby,' Savannah said with a tight, unpleasant smile, her pale blue eyes shining too bright.

'Don't be modest. We're a helluva team, you and me. You knock 'em on their butts, and I screw their brains out.'

Laurel clenched her jaw and squeezed her eyes shut for an instant, trying to gather strength and patience. Jack caught the action and turned to Savannah with a frown.

'Hey, sugar, why you don' give it a rest for one night, huh?'

'Ooooh!' Savannah drew back with an exaggerated expression of mock fear, pressing her free hand to her throat. 'What's this? Jack Boudreaux rising to an occasion that doesn't have its legs spread for him?'

'Bon Dieu,' he muttered, shaking his head.

'What?' Savannah demanded, two vodka tonics beyond reason, too upset with the turns her life was taking to give a damn. 'I'm too crude for you, Jack? That's hard to imagine, considering the way you butcher people in your books. I can't imagine anything offending you.'

She wedged herself between his stool and Laurel's, deliberately brushing his arm with her breast, sending him her most sultry expression. 'We ought to go a couple rounds, Jack,' she purred, raking a hot gaze from his crotch to his belly to his bare chest, finally landing on his face. 'Just to find out.'

He met her look evenly, his dark eyes intense, his mouth set in a grim line.

Laurel slipped down off her stool, doing her best to control the fine trembling in her limbs. 'Sister, come on,' she said, trying to take the glass from Savannah's fingers. 'Let's go home.'

Savannah turned on her, angry that Laurel was always the one with the cooler head, always in control, always respectable and bright and perfect.

'What's the matter, Baby? Am I being an embarrassment?' she asked, as angry with herself as she was with Laurel. 'You'll never say so in here, will you? Don't make a public scene. Don't call attention to yourself. Never air the dirty laundry in plain sight. Christ,' she sneered, 'you're just as bad as Vivian.'

She jerked her hand free of Laurel's grasp, sloshing vodka and tonic over the rim of her glass, her expression something that bordered so closely on hate that it took Laurel's breath away.

'You go on and be little Miss Prim and Proper,' she sneered, her voice laced with venom. 'Always do the right thing, Laurel. Me, I've got better ways to spend my time.'

She whirled around, almost losing her balance, the vodka numbing her equilibrium, as well as her inhibitions. Willing the floor to stop pitching, she walked away, her sights set on the pool players, her hips swinging, a hard laugh ringing out of her as she caught sight of Ronnie Peltier.

Laurel pressed a hand to her mouth and tensed against the emotions that were buffeting her like hurricane winds. She couldn't seem to get ahead. Every time she thought she was getting her feet under her, she got knocked back a step. She pulled in on herself, not hearing the noise of the bar, not seeing the look of concern Jack was giving her. All she heard was her pulse roaring in her ears. All she saw was the mistake she had made in coming home.

Without a word she turned and walked out of the bar. She didn't allow herself to think of anything at all as she crossed the parking lot. She just put one foot in front of the other until she had reached the levee, then she stood on the bank and stared out at the bayou, working furiously to tamp down the feelings Savannah had torn loose. It didn't do any good to get upset. Savannah was who she was. Her problems were rooted in a past she refused to let go of, was perhaps incapable of letting go of. She had her moments when she would say anything, do anything, and damn the consequences. It was pointless to let any of that get to her.

But it hurts, a small voice inside her said. The voice of a little girl who had only her big sister to rely on for love and comfort. The big sister who looked out for her, who protected her, who sacrificed for her.

But who looked out for Savannah?

Laurel bit her lip against the pain, squeezed her eyes shut against it. She pressed her hands over her face and stood there trembling, afraid if she even breathed, the dam would burst and she would dissolve into a quivering mass of weakness and guilt and pain.

Jack stood behind her on the levee, his feet rooted to the spot as he watched her struggle. He should have left her alone. There was no way in hell he wanted to get caught in the middle of what had gone on in the bar. But he couldn't seem to make himself turn around. He damned Savannah for being such a bitch, damned Laurel for being so brave, damned himself for caring. No good could come of it for any of them. But even as he was convincing himself of that fact, his feet were moving forward.

'She's drunk,' he said.

Laurel hugged herself, her eyes fixed on the far bank of the bayou. 'I know. She's got problems that go back a long way. I've been gone a long time. I didn't realize she was this . . . troubled,' she murmured, searching desperately for a word that seemed safe, a word that skirted way around the one that came strongest to mind. 'If I'd known, I don't think I would have come back now.'

She braced herself against the wave of guilt that admission brought. *Selfish, weak, coward.* She should have been willing to help Savannah, regardless of her own fragile state. She owed her sister that much and more. Much, much more.

Jack stepped closer. His hands settled on her shoulders, so slim, so delicate, so strong, and still he told himself he should just go on back into Frenchie's and order himself another beer. 'I can't see you running from trouble, *'tite chatte.'*

Laurel stood still for his touch, while she told herself not to. His hands were big and warm, his long, musician's fingers gentle and soothing. Comforts she didn't deserve. Despair rose on a tide inside her. 'Why do you think I came home in the first place?' she asked, her voice choked with the shame of it.

Because she needed a place to hide, a place to heal, Jack thought, but he said nothing of the sort. It didn't seem wise to let her know he'd been reading up on her, thinking about her. She didn't need a mercenary right now. She needed a shoulder. Cursing himself for a fool, he turned her around and offered his.

'Come here,' he growled as he pulled her glasses off and folded his arms around her.

Laurel squeezed her eyes shut against the tears, refusing to let them fall. She told herself not to succumb to the temptation of leaning on him, but her arms slipped around Jack's lean waist just the same. It felt too good to be held, to let someone else be strong for a minute or two. Ironic that that someone was Jack, the self-professed antihero. She might have pointed that out to him if she hadn't felt so damn weak.

Trembling with the effort of holding it all at bay, she pressed her cheek to his chest, to the soft washed cotton of his bowling shirt. She concentrated on the sound of his heartbeat, the feel of the taut muscles in the small of his back, the scent of Ivory soap underlying the subtle tang of male sweat.

'You've had a hard day, huh, *mon coeur*?' Jack murmured, his lips brushing her temple, her faint perfume filling his head. She was so delicate in his arms, he couldn't believe she was strong enough to take on the burdens she had. It killed him to think of her trying. 'You oughta be more like me,' he muttered. 'Don't give a damn about anyone but yourself. Let people do what they will. Take what you want and leave the rest.'

'Oh, yeah?' Laurel scoffed, leaning back to look up at him. 'If you're so tough, what are you doing standing here holding me?'

He grinned and swooped down to nip at the side of her neck, surprising a little squeal out of her. 'I like the way you smell,' he whispered, nuzzling her cheek, skimming his hands up and down her back.

Laurel squirmed and wriggled, laughing, finally breaking free of his hold. Snatching her glasses out of his hand, she danced a couple of steps back from him, her gaze suddenly catching on his. While her heart beat a little harder, her laughter faded away, and something warm and seductive and invisible pulled at her, like the allure of the moon on the tides.

'I told you, sugar,' he said, lifting his shoulders in a lazy shrug. 'Me, I just like to have a good time. And you strike me as a lady in serious need of a good time.' He shuffled a step closer, held a hand out to her. 'Come on, angel. Let's you and me go and have us some fun.'

She eyed him warily. 'Fun? What's that?'

She couldn't remember the last time she'd done anything just for fun. Her work had consumed her life for so long, then had come the struggle just to keep herself from falling into a million tiny broken bits. And since she had come home, her focus had been on doing constructive things. She had enjoyed her time in the garden, but the goal had been to accomplish something tangible, a success she could see.

Jack ducked around behind her and got her by the shoulders, steering her down the levee toward the dock. 'You need a lesson from the master, sweetheart. I'll teach you all about havin' fun.'

Reluctantly letting him herd her along, Laurel shot him a skeptical look over her shoulder. 'Would this "fun" you're alluding to be of a sexual nature?'

His dimples flashed. 'I sincerely hope so.'

'I'm out of here.' She changed directions deftly, ducking under his arm and marching back up the levee toward the parking lot.

'Aw, come on, '*tite ange*,' Jack begged, jogging around to cut her off. He gave her his most sincere look, pressing his hands to his heart. 'I'll behave myself. Promise.'

Laurel gave a sniff of disbelief. 'Are you going to try to sell me swampland, too?'

'No, but I'll show you some. I thought we could take a nice relaxing sunset boat ride.'

'Go into the swamp at sunset? Are you crazy? The mosquitoes will cart us off and carve us up for dinner!'

'Not in the boat I have in mind.'

She gave him a long, considering look, amazed that she could even be considering his offer. She didn't trust him an inch. But the idea of a leisurely cruise on the bayou, of escaping to the wilderness that had been her refuge as a child, held a strong appeal. And Jack himself was temptation personified.

'Come on, sugar,' he cajoled, his head tipped boyishly, an irresistible smile canting his lips. He held his hand out to her. 'We'll pass a good time.'

Three minutes later they were climbing aboard a boat that was essentially a small screened porch on pontoons. The roof was waterproof canvas in a jaunty red-and-white stripe. A pair of redwood planters filled with geraniums and vinca vines sat as decoration flanking the door to the screened area.

'This is *your* boat?' Laurel asked, not bothering to hide her skepticism.

Jack reached under the velvety leaves of a geranium, plucked out the starter key, and blew the dirt off it. 'No.'

'No?' she followed him into the cabin. 'What do you mean, no? You're *stealing* this boat?'

He frowned at her as he started the engine and gunned the throttle. 'I'm not *stealing* it. I'm *borrowing* it.' Laurel rolled her eyes. 'Lawyers,' he grumbled, scowling as he concentrated on piloting the pontoon away from the dock. 'Relax, will you, angel? The boat belongs to Leonce.'

With the issue of ownership out of the way, Laurel sank down on one of the deep cushioned benches that faced each other in front of the console. She tried to concentrate on the passing scenery – the businesses that backed onto the bayou and the ramshackle boat houses that were tucked along the bank behind them; the houses that lined the bank farther down, many with people in the yard gardening or talking with neighbors or watching children play. Normal scenes of people with normal lives. People who had ordinary backgrounds and boring jobs.

The thought struck a pang of envy inside her that hummed and vibrated like a tuning fork. If she had had a boring job, an ordinary background, maybe she and Wesley would still be together. Maybe they would have a child by now.

Sighing, she toed her shoes off, pulled her feet up on the bench, and tucked them under her, settling in, unconsciously letting go of the tension and easing into melancholy. Slowly, the fierce grip she held on her mind eased, and her thoughts drifted. They passed L'Amour, the brick house looking vacant and lonely standing amid the moss-draped live oak and magnolia trees. Huey watched them pass from the bank, a woebegone

577

expression on his face. Then civilization grew scarce – the occasional plantation house visible in the distance, the odd tarpaper shack teetering above the black water on age-grayed pilings.

The scenery grew lusher, wilder. Trees crowded what land there was, shoulder to shoulder, their crowns entangling into a dense canopy of green that blotted out the evening sun, leaving the ground below them veiled in darkness. Sweet gum and persimmon and water locust, ironwood and redbud and a dozen other species with buttonbush and thorny dewberry and greenbriar skirting their bases. The banks were thick with patches of yellow spiked cane and coffee weed, fan-fronded palmetto trees and verdant ferns. Vines and flame-flowered trumpet creeper braided together along the edge like embroidery, and the shallows grew thick with spider lilies and water lettuce.

The bayou branched off again and again, each arm reaching into another pocket of wilderness. Some of the channels were as wide as rivers, others narrow trickles of streams, all of them part of a vast labyrinth of no-man's-land. The Atchafalaya was a place where it seemed the world was still forming, ever-changing, metamorphosing, and yet always primitive. Laurel could never come out here without feeling transported back in time. That had always been the appeal for her, to escape to a time when none of her problems existed. The swamp worked its magic on her again, pulling her into another dimension, leaving all her troubles in the distance as the pontoon chugged along.

They passed through a shadowy corridor of trees where no land was visible at all, giving testimony to the constant battle here between water and earth. A cat squirrel vaulted from one gray trunk to the next, skittering around behind it to peek its head around and stare at the passing boat. Birds darted everywhere, warblers and wildly painted buntings and orioles; flashes of color in the gloom, flitting among the lacework of branches.

Finally, they emerged from the natural bower into an area where the bayou grew wide, looking more like a lake than a stream. Jack maneuvered the pontoon into a spot near the south bank, positioning them so they had a panoramic view of the swamp as the sun slid down in the west. He cut the grumbling motor and stepped out of the cabin to cast the anchor over the side. When he returned, he sank down beside Laurel, stretching his legs out in front of him, laying his arms along the back of the bench.

'It's beautiful, no?' he said softly.

'Mmmm . . .'

The sky was an artist's palette of color. The eastern horizon was a deep, luxurious purple that gave way to azure that faded into a smoky white that grew deeper and deeper orange to the west, where the sun was a huge ball of flame. Before them lay the swamp, desolate, beautiful, full of secrets. Laurel soaked it all in, absorbed the quiet of it, let the peace of it seep into her. The pontoon swayed gently on the current and the tension leeched out of her, leaving her limbs feeling heavy and relaxed.

In the absence of motor noise, the bayou chorus began. Crickets trilled in the reeds, an unseen string section. Then came the bass *chug-a-rum* of the bullfrog, then the rattling banjo twang of the green frog. From a distance came the occasional accompaniment of bird calls, and nearer the boat the low hum of mosquito squadrons lifting off the surface of the dark water to fly their sunset sorties.

'Savannah and I used to come out here when we were kids,' Laurel said softly. 'Never too far from home. Just far enough so we thought we were in another world.'

To escape. Jack heard the words. They hung in the air, there for anyone who knew the secret desires of unhappy children. 'Me too,' he said. 'I grew up over on Bayou Noir. I spent more time in the swamp than I did in the house.'

To escape, Laurel thought. They had that in common.

'I had a secret hideout,' he admitted, staring out past the swamp to another time. 'Built it out of peach crates and planks I robbed from a neighbor's pasture fence. I used to go out there and read my stolen comic books and make up stories of my own.'

'Did you write them down?'

'Sometimes.'

All the time. He had scribbled them down in notebooks and read them aloud to himself with a kind of shy pride he had never experienced in anything else. He'd never had anything to be proud of. His daddy was a piss-mean, drunken, good-for-nothing son of a bitch who had told him time and again he would never be anything but a good-for-nothing son of a son of a bitch. But his stories were good. That realization had been a surprise as wonderful as the Christmas his *maman* had given him a real cap gun – which he also kept at his hideout. More wonderful, really, because the stories came from him and proved he was worth something.

Then had come the day Blackie had followed him out to his secret hideaway. Drunk, as usual. Mean, as always. And the hideout was smashed, and the comic books and his stories and the dreams that were attached to them plunged into the bayou.

As worthless and useless as you are, T-Jack . . .

Laurel watched his face, saw the way his jaw hardened against some unpleasant memory, saw the anger in his dark eyes and the vulnerability that lay beneath it, and her heart ached for him. The few words he had spoken about his childhood had sketched a bleak picture. She could only guess that what was passing before his mind's eye now was a chapter from that time.

'Daddy had an old *bâteau* with a little trolling motor on it,' she murmured to break his tension. 'He taught Savannah how to work it. It was our secret, because Vivian would never have approved of her daughters doing such a thing. After he died, we used to sneak away and go out in it all the time. It made us feel closer to him somehow.'

And far away from Beauvoir.

Jack turned toward her, shifting his weight on the bench, searching her face with his gaze. She looked a little embarrassed, as if she had never told anyone this particular secret before. The idea pleased him in a way he shouldn't have allowed, but he didn't try to stop it.

'When I was a kid, I used to think my family would be great if only we had money,' he said. 'I thought every problem we had was because we were poor. That wasn't true at all, was it?'

'No,' she whispered, bleakly.

She stared down at her hands, fingering a thumbnail that had been bitten to the quick. She looked small and tired and vulnerable, not strong enough to fight off all the feelings coming home had churned up. She had gone off to create a life for herself, never suspecting that life would chase her right back to the problems she had been escaping from.

'*Dieu*,' Jack muttered, letting his arm slip off the bench and around Laurel's shoulders: 'I'm not doin' my job very well, am I?' he asked in a teasing voice while he massaged her shoulder. He leaned down close and nuzzled her ear. 'I brought you out here to have fun, to make you happy.'

Warmth bloomed inside Laurel. She told herself she didn't want it, but the voice wasn't stern enough to make her move away from him. She shot him a wry look. 'I think you brought me out here with ideas of raiding my panties.'

He grinned an unholy grin, his eyes shining like polished onyx in the fading light. '*Mais oui, mon coeur*,' he murmured, his smoky voice purring deep in his throat as he slipped his other arm around her. 'That's how I plan to make you happy.'

Had any other man made such a statement to her, she would have cut him off at the knees with her rapier tongue and sent him crawling home. Jack's arrogance, tempered with his sense of humor, only made her want to go along on whatever wild adventure he suggested. That wasn't the smart thing or the safe thing, but it was the most tempting thing. As his lips found her throat and he began to kiss her with teasing little taste-testing kisses, the temptation grew stronger.

'I thought—' She broke off at the breathless sound of her voice, cleared her throat, and tried again. 'I thought you were going to be on your best behavior.'

He chuckled wickedly against her neck, sliding a hand up and down her upper arm, his thumb brushing seductively against the side of her breast. 'Sugar, this *is* my best behavior.'

A shudder of pure longing went through her. She had ignored her physical needs for so long, she had forgotten what it was to want a man.

No, her mind insisted, the correction cutting through the haze of desire, she had *never* known what it was to want a man. Not the way she wanted Jack. She had grown up subduing herself sexually, avoiding something she had seen only the ugly side of. Her marriage to Wesley had been a marriage of friends, passionless on her part because she didn't think herself capable of passion.

She'd been wrong. As Jack trailed kisses down the column of her throat to the sensitive curve of her shoulder, passion came to life inside her like a fire that had been smoldering beneath cold ash. It startled her, frightened her. She didn't want to want him. She had never wanted to think of herself as being vulnerable to the lure of sex.

'You told me not to trust you,' she said, trying to stiffen muscles that had begun to melt with the warmth of desire. 'You said yourself, you're bad for me.'

'Well, you can't listen to me, darlin',' he murmured, kissing his way back up her neck to her ear. He traced the tip of his tongue around the rim of the delicate shell, drew the lobe between his lips and sucked gently. 'I'm a writer; I tell lies for a livin'.'

'Then I should know better than to get within an arm's length of you.'

'Why? We don't need to talk at all for making love. Bodies don't tell lies, sweetheart.' To prove his point he caught her hand and drew it to the front of his jeans, pressing her palm against his erection, holding her there while he feathered kisses along her jaw to the corner of her mouth and probed delicately with the tip of his tongue. 'I want you, angel,' he whispered seductively. 'That's no lie.'

She snatched a breath and forced herself to stand instead of succumb. Her legs wobbled beneath her, and she was glad her flowing, gauzy skirt hid her quaking knees. She folded her arms across her middle, holding herself together, keeping her hands from reaching out to him.

'I don't have casual sex with men who are admittedly liars and bastards,' she said, struggling for and not quite managing the calm, cutting voice that had won her more than one court case.

Jack looked up at her from the bench, eyes wide with false innocence. He splayed his hands against his chest and rose with careless grace, stalking her across the narrow confines of the pontoon.

'Did I say I was a liar?' he asked with disbelief. 'Oh, no, *chère*,' he purred, backing her into the console. 'I meant to say I was a *lover*. Come here and let me show you.'

Laurel shook her head, sidestepping him as he reached for her, amazed at his ability to change personas – teasing, then sober, then seductive, then teasing again. It was almost more unnerving than his ability to make her want him. 'Last night you warned me away from you. Today you act as if it never happened. Who are you this time, Jack?'

His expression grew serious, intense, as he stared down at her, and a tremor went through her. This Jack looked like a dominant male, a predator, capable of anything. 'I'm the man whose gonna make love to you until you forget every stupid thing I ever said,' he muttered.

If he had tried to snatch her against him, she would have bolted. If he had stepped too close, she would have kneed him. If he had tried to force her, she would have done her best to get her hands on the gun in her purse and shoot him. But he did none of those things. Instead, he lifted his hand and cupped her cheek, the fire in his eyes softening to tenderness.

'Let yourself live a little bit, angel,' he whispered. 'Live. Not for work, not for somebody else's cause. For the moment. For yourself. Reach out and take something you want for once.'

Then he lowered his head and kissed her, softly, gently, experimentally. His lips, firm and smooth and oh-so-clever, moved against hers, rubbed over hers, seduced hers into softening and responding. He inched a step closer, raising his other hand and sliding his fingers back into her silky hair.

'Kiss me back, *mon coeur*,' he commanded on a phantom breath. 'There's no reason you shouldn't.'

Just that she didn't trust him or respect him or want the complication of an affair in her life, she thought dimly. But she gave voice to none of those reasons, thinking that they didn't really have much to do with the here and now. *Let yourself live a little bit, angel.* . . .

She'd been so careful for so long, she couldn't believe she was being seduced by a rogue like Jack. But then that was his allure, wasn't it? He was bad for her. He was wicked. And she had always followed the rules, made the correct choices, done the right thing.

Reach out and take something you want for once.

Jack's mouth moved insistently over hers, coaxing, luring, tempting, offering pleasure, promising bliss, guaranteeing an hour or two of blessed oblivion of the problems in her life. And God knew she wanted him.

Hesitantly, she obeyed his command, rising on tip-toe, relaxing her lips beneath his. Her fingers curled into fists, gathering the fabric of his shirt in bunches. Then he slid his arms around her, anchoring her against him, holding her safe and secure as she opened to him.

Jack groaned at her surrender and deepened the kiss. With a slow, sensuous stroke, he eased his tongue into her mouth, probing deeply, suggestively. She answered him with a tentative foray of her own, her tongue tracing his lower lip, dipping inside his mouth.

He wanted her, had wanted her from the first, this angel with her alluring combination of fire and fragility. He wanted her in a way he hadn't wanted a woman in a long time – possessively, obsessively. He wanted her to be his in a way she had never been any other man's. He would have seen it as dangerous thinking if he had been able to think at all.

Without breaking the kiss, he took her glasses off and set them aside on the steering console, then guided her hands down to his waist and abandoned them there as he shrugged his shirt off and tossed it aside. He gasped a little at the feel of her hands, so cool and soft, gliding back up his chest.

Laurel explored the smooth, hard planes and ridges of his body, marveling at the strength there, marveling at her own response to his fever-hot skin. She couldn't get enough of touching him, wanted to press into him and feel that strength and heat against the length of her and absorb it through her skin. When he lifted the hem of her top, the sound she made in her throat wasn't protest, but the eager anticipation of pleasure. Naked from the waist up, she moved into him, what was left of her breath vaporizing in her lungs as her breasts flattened against him.

Jack growled low in his throat as he kissed her. Like a sculptor admiring a work of art, he traced his hands down her back, caressing, exploring, interpreting every graceful curve, every plane and hollow. Lifting her into him, he pressed her hips to his, pressed her into his arousal, letting her know how badly, how urgently, he wanted her. He felt her tongue dip into the hollow at the base of his throat, and the flames of desire licked at his sanity.

Need making his fingers clumsy, he fumbled with the button and zipper at the back of her skirt and pushed the garment out of his way. At last she was naked in his arms. He stood back for a moment and drank in the sight of her with greedy eyes.

She was slender and sleek, but there was no mistaking her feminine curves – or her uncertainty about showing them to him. A delicate blush rose up her neck into her cheeks as he studied her, as if she were afraid he would somehow find her lacking.

'*Viens ici, chèrie*,' he whispered, holding out his hand to her. 'Come here before your beauty undoes me.'

He pulled her tight against him, kissing her greedily, hungrily, letting her know his words were more than just the clever prattle of an experienced Lothario. They were truth.

Slowly he lowered her to the red flowered cushions of the bench that was directly behind her, following her down, sprawling over her. She arched her back off the cushion as he found her breast with his mouth, capturing her nipple between his lips and sucking hard on the turgid tip, then sucking gently, massaging her with his tongue.

Laurel tangled her hands in his dark hair and moved restlessly beneath him, soft, wild sounds of yearning keening in her throat. She wrapped her legs around him, lifting her hips against his belly, seeking contact, seeking to assuage the urgent ache that burned at the core of her desire.

He stroked the swollen petals of her woman's flesh tenderly, seductively, opening her to his touch like a precious, fragile flower. She gasped with pleasure as he eased two fingers into the hot, tight silken pocket between her thighs. Then he found the sensitive bud of her desire with his thumb, tapping against it with the slightest of touches, then rubbing gently until she was breathless.

'You like this, sugar?' he whispered, stroking deep, then easing slowly out of her, opening her, stretching her.

'Yes – no—' she gasped, lifting her hips.

'Enjoy it, darlin'. Let yourself go,' he coaxed. 'Let me make you happy,' he murmured. He kissed her quivering stomach, mouth open, hot, wet, tongue dipping into her navel. 'Are you ready for me, angel?'

'Yes. Jack, please . . .'

She gulped a breath and strained against the fist of desire that tightened and tightened within her. She'd never wanted like this. When Jack sat up, reaching for the button on his jeans, Laurel reached out to help him. Sitting up, she pressed fervent kisses to his chest as she closed her fingers around his thick, pulsing shaft.

Jack's control broke at the feel of her small hand stroking him. He tumbled her back on the cushion, pushed her hand aside and guided himself, squeezing his eyes shut as he eased into her.

'*Mon Dieu*, you're tight!'

Laurel moaned. 'I'm a little tense,' she said breathlessly. 'It's been a long time for me.'

Her admission caught Jack by the heart and squeezed. 'No,' he said, bending down to kiss her. 'It's the first time. Our first time. Just relax and enjoy, darlin'.'

Laurel closed her eyes and wrapped her arms around him as he began to move against her and within her. He kissed her deeply, then playfully. He nipped the side of her neck, murmured hot, sexy words to her as they moved together. The pleasure built and intensified, swelling inside her until she could barely breathe for the pressure of it.

Jack's kisses grew more urgent, more carnal, his thrusts deeper, driving, straining, filling her to bursting. The time for play faded, paled in the face of something hot and intense that enveloped them and threatened to consume them. Something like fear gripped Laurel by the throat, and she tightened her hold on him, not sure where this was taking her or what would happen after.

'Don't fight it, sweetheart,' he whispered urgently. He rubbed his cheek against hers, swept her hair back from her face, kissed her temple. 'Don't fight it. Let it happen. Take us to heaven, angel.'

Not giving her a choice, he slipped a hand between them and touched the tender nerve center of her desire, taking her over the edge. Taking them both over the edge.

'*Mon Dieu*, angel.'

Even in the dim light of dusk he could see the color rise into her cheeks as she turned her face away from him. 'Oh, no, sweetheart,' he said softly, skimming his fingertips along her jaw. 'Don' be shy with me now. Don' be embarrassed. That was beautiful. That was perfect.'

'I'm not very good at this,' she mumbled, still not looking at him, despite the gentle pressure he applied to her chin.

'At what? Sex?'

That, too, Laurel thought, chagrined. 'Talking afterward.'

'Your ex-husband, he was a mute, or what?'

She laughed at that because she was still feeling embarrassed and because laughter was what Jack had been aiming for with his teasing. He tickled the side of her neck, and she cringed, turning toward him at last. 'No. He just never had much to say afterward.'

Jack looked down into her face, reading vulnerability there in her wide dark eyes, and it tugged at his heart. So fiery, so sure of herself in other ways, she was uncertain about this most natural and basic aspect of her femininity. How different she was from Savannah, whose expertise in the bedroom was the stuff of legends. He wanted to know what forces had shaped their lives to make them so different from one another, but this wasn't the time to ask. This was the time to reassure.

'What was he – paralyzed from the neck down?' he queried dryly.

No, Laurel thought, he was sweet and kind and honest, and he'd tried his best to make their marriage work, but she had failed him in so many ways. What she had felt with Wes was friendship and a sense of emotional security, not all-consuming passion. She had used him to anchor her life and had given him little in return, had in fact turned on him when The Case had been at its most stressful, all but pushing him out of her life.

'Hey, sugar . . .' Jack murmured. 'Don' look sad, angel. I didn' mean to drag up bad memories.'

If it weren't for bad memories, I'd have no memories at all. She looked away from him and tensed herself against the ridiculous urge to cry at his concern.

'We've all of us got bad memories,' he said. 'But they don' belong here, between us. We came out here to have fun, remember?' His fingers found another ticklish spot along her ribs and tortured a little smile out of her. 'We were doin' pretty damn good there for a while, no?'

'Yes,' she whispered, the corners of her mouth turning up in pleasure, in embarrassment.

'That's it,' he praised her in a warm, seductive voice. Settling himself on top of her, he lowered his head until they were nose to nose, lips to lips. 'Smile for me.' He smiled as she did. 'Kiss me,' he whispered, groaning with pleasure as she complied.

Her breath caught as he shifted his hips and eased into her again. Need took precedence over old memories. *Reach out and take something you want for once.* She wanted this. She wanted Jack – for now, for the pleasure he could give her and the bliss that transported her mind away from the problems that plagued her. Heaven, he called it. She arched her hips against his, closed her eyes, and held on to him for the return trip.

Midnight was nearing when they finally dressed. The process was complicated with much touching and teasing and long pauses for kisses and hot, whispered words. Laurel felt like a teenager – not the quiet, serious teenager she had been, but an ordinary, hormone-crazed teenager out for a night of forbidden fooling around with the class bad boy. Jack played his role to the hilt, trying to take off every article of clothing she put on, trying to talk her into spending the night on the bayou with him.

'Come on, sweetheart, stay with me,' he coaxed, murmuring the words against her throat as he dragged the hem of her blouse upward, stroking his fingers up her sides toward her breasts. 'We're just gettin' started . . . .'

Laurel's sense of responsibility was too ingrained, and she wriggled out of his grasp and reached for her glasses on the steering console, settling them on her nose and settling the issue.

'If I don't get back soon, Aunt Caroline and Mama Pearl will worry,' she said, brushing futilely at the wrinkles in her clothes. 'You don't want them sending the sheriff out looking for us, do you?'

Jack jammed his hands at his waist, the picture of a disgruntled male who was too sexy for his own good. He wore nothing but his jeans, and they weren't quite zipped. 'Kenner couldn't find his own ass in the dark, let alone us.'

'He could get lucky.'

'But I'm not gonna,' he grumbled.

'You already have.'

Instantly he grinned his wicked grin and backed her against the console. '*Mais yeah*, angel.' He chuckled, dipping his head to nibble her neck again. 'And I like my odds for another go.'

Laurel ducked away before he could get his arms around her. 'Go weigh anchor, sailor, before I pull my gun on you.'

Purring low in his throat, he sprang toward her and stole a kiss, dancing deftly away when she would have slugged him. 'I love it when you boss me around.'

She snatched up a pillow from the bench and hurled it at his head. Jack darted outside and used the door for a shield, chuckling the whole time.

Giving up on the idea of seducing her again, he went about the business of pulling up the anchor, cursing under his breath as it caught on something tangled in the reeds. He hauled back on the nylon rope, damning people who used the swamp for a garbage dump. The anchor finally pulled free, and he hauled it aboard. Minutes later the motor was puttering and the pontoon eased away from the bank and headed west . . .

. . . and the body of a naked woman, brutally tortured, cruelly slain, buoyed by the dense growth beneath her, floated out of the reeds and bobbed in the wake of the boat, her sightless eyes staring after them, her arm outstretched toward them in a plea for help that was much too silent and far too late.

16

The sun shone, butter yellow, a soft, indistinct ball on the far side of the morning haze. Laurel sat at the table on the gallery, staring out across the courtyard, through the back gate, and toward the bayou, where the mist hung in gauzy strips above the water and wound like ribbons of smoke through the trees. She stared toward the bayou . . . and L'Amour.

The old brick house stood stately and alone, half hidden by trees and shrubbery that had been allowed to encroach during generations of neglect. From the branches of one gnarled live oak hung two dozen or more neckties, their tails fluttering in the slight breeze – a testimony to Jack's abdication from the world of corporate law, she supposed. She certainly couldn't imagine him putting on a tie, much less a suit, in his current phase – the rebel, the rogue. But she thought of him younger, intense, hungry to prove himself, and the image came quite easily. Jack, elegant in double-breasted gray silk. Handsome, yet rough around the edges. Educated, but with some aura of that boy who had grown up wild on the edge of the swamp. Like a panther that had been domesticated, always with a shadow of his former self nearby, the air of danger lingering around him.

She wondered what had driven him from that world he had worked so hard to conquer. She wondered if it was wise to care.

She shifted on her cushioned chair, curling her feet beneath her, and lifted her tea cup with both hands to take a sip of Earl Grey. The rest of the household would be stirring soon. Caroline would be subjecting her body to the contortions of her daily yoga regimen. Mama Pearl would be shuffling around her kitchen in a cotton shift and terrycloth slippers, starting the coffee, setting out a bowl of chilled fruit, grumbling to herself about the state of the world while the morning news came over the radio. But for now, the gallery and the morning belonged to Laurel, and she relished the peace. Unable to sleep past four o'clock, she had showered and dressed.

She had expected to feel a certain amount of turmoil concerning her night of lovemaking with Jack. After all, she had never been one to indulge in reckless passion – had, in fact, disdained and avoided it. But sitting in the dewy-soft quiet of the courtyard, she could find no regrets, no recriminations. He had offered something she wanted, needed – not just sex, but a release from other tensions – and she had accepted. And it had been wonderful . . .

'People who get up this early shouldn't look so happy.'

Savannah stood in the open French doors to the hall, looking sleep-rumpled and groggy in her champagne silk robe. Her hair tumbled around her shoulders in wild disarray, and mascara smudges ringed her eyes. She looked tough, dissipated by dissolute living, like a hooker the morning after. The glow of excitement had diffused, the allure had vanished with the moon.

She pushed herself away from the door and stepped out onto the gallery, barefoot, one hand tucked into the deep pocket of her robe, the other toying with the heart on her necklace.

Laurel tried to think of an innocuous comeback line, but she couldn't get past the hurt that still lingered from the night before. 'Would you like some tea?' she asked quietly.

Savannah shook her head, her lips tightening against a bittersweet smile. That was Baby, falling back on good manners to hide her feelings. If all else failed her, she would at least be a gracious hostess. Such a little belle. Vivian would have been proud of her.

'I want to apologize for yesterday. I said a lot of things I shouldn't have.' The words came out in a rush of embarrassment and contrition. She busied her fingers twisting the sash of her robe. 'And I never should have been such a bitch to you last night, but I was just feeling so hurt and so damn angry—'

Laurel set her cup down and rose, concern knitting her brows. 'I didn't mean to hurt you, Sister—'

'No, not you, Baby. Cooper.' She stared down at the table through a bright sheen of tears, feeling as fragile as Laurel's china teacup. 'I don't know what I'm going to do,' she said, trying to smile, shaking her head at the futility of it all. 'I love that man something awful.'

She turned and walked away a few steps, breathing deep of the sweet, dew-damp scents of the garden – flowers and sweet olive and boxwood – green, vibrant scents of life. As if she could scrub away the feeling of despair that clung to her, she rubbed her hands over her face. But a dozen other feelings gurgled up inside her like tainted water from an underground spring – guilt and anger, remorse and jealousy. She didn't want any of it.

Trying to tamp it all down, she turned back toward Laurel, who stood watching her with wide eyes and a serious face. For just an instant she was that same little waif who had looked to Savannah for love and support when they had no one else to turn to, and Savannah felt a welcome rush of strength.

'It doesn't matter,' she said, finding a smile for her baby sister. 'It doesn't have anything to do with us. I won't let anything come between us.'

Laurel went into her sister's arms, vowing to say nothing about Conroy Cooper or any other man Savannah involved herself with. She couldn't change Savannah, couldn't change the way Savannah thought about her past, and those were not the reasons she had come home in the first place. This was what she had come for, she thought as she hugged her sister – unconditional love and support. That had to work both ways. And so she said nothing about the scent of stale perfume and stale sex that clung to Savannah.

'I won't let anything come between us,' Savannah said again, vehemently, her embrace tightening around Laurel's slender frame.

'You might let some air come between us,' Laurel teased. 'You're squeezing the life out of me.'

A nervous laugh rattled out of her, and she loosened her hold, stepping back, settling her hands on Laurel's shoulders. 'Maybe I will have a cup of that tea, after all. We can sit out here and chat. You've made the garden so pretty again. We'll make some plans.'

She rushed back into the house, hurrying as if she were afraid the moment would pass and the wall of tension would rise up between them again. Laurel settled into her chair, reaching for the matchbook she had found on the seat of her car the night before. Savannah's, she supposed. She turned it around and around in her fingers, absently, just something to busy her hands. Not five minutes passed before Savannah returned with a tray bearing the teapot, a cup for herself, and a plate heaped with powdery *beignets*.

'These are left over from yesterday,' she chattered, arranging everything to her satisfaction on the table. 'I just popped them into the microwave to warm them up and sprinkled fresh sugar on them. Have one,' she ordered, suddenly full of life and hope. 'Have half a dozen. If anyone ever needed to load up on Mama Pearl's cooking, it's you, Baby. You don't have an ounce to spare.'

Laurel tossed the matchbook down on the tabletop between them and reached for a *beignet*. 'You left that in the car.'

Savannah picked it up and sat back, studying it idly as she nibbled on the corner of her breakfast. She said nothing for a long moment, staring at the blood red square blankly, then dropped it. 'I use a lighter.'

A vague sense of unease shifted through Laurel. She set her *beignet* aside on her napkin, her gaze moving from her sister's expressionless face to the matchbook. An elaborate Mardi Gras mask was stamped in black above the words 'Le Mascarade' and a French Quarter address in New Orleans. 'If it's not yours, then how did it get in my car?'

A careless shrug was her only answer. Savannah pushed her chair back from the table and rose. 'I forgot the sugar for my tea.'

As she padded back into the house, Laurel fingered the matchbook, a strange chill pebbling the flesh of her arms with goose bumps.

'*Bonjour, mon ange.* For you.'

Laurel gasped as a perfect red rose appeared before her. She hadn't heard Jack's approach, hadn't even caught a glimpse of him from the corner of her eye. His ability to appear and disappear seemingly from and into thin air rattled her, and she narrowed her eyes to compensate with annoyance.

'You damn near gave me a heart attack.'

Jack frowned, leaning over her, breathing in the clean scent of her hair. 'Is that any way to thank a man for bringing you flowers?'

She gave a little sniff of disdain but accepted the rose. 'You probably stole it from one of Aunt Caroline's bushes.'

'It's no less a gift,' he said, leaning closer, his gaze fastening on her lips.

Anticipation fluttered in her throat. 'How can it be a gift if it's something I already possessed?'

He lowered his head another fraction of an inch, closing the space between them to little more than a deep breath. His lashes drifted down, thick and black. 'Isn't that just like a lawyer?' he whispered. 'If I offered you the moon, you'd probably want to see my deed to it.'

Any retort she might have made was lost. Any thought she might have had in her head vanished as Jack settled his mouth against hers. He kissed her deeply, intimately, leisurely, reminding her graphically and frankly of the intimacy they had shared the night before.

When he lifted his mouth from hers at last, he made a low, purring sound of satisfaction in his throat, then chuckled wickedly. 'Why you blushin', *ma jolie fille*?' he asked, his voice dark and smoky. 'You gave me a helluva lot more than a kiss last night.'

'But you probably didn't have an audience, did you, Jack?' Savannah asked sharply. She stepped out from behind a pillar and set a silver sugar bowl on the table, never taking her eyes off him. She picked up the red matchbook and tapped it against her cheek. 'Or have you led my baby sister that far astray?'

He straightened, his eyes cold, his face set in a stony mask. 'That's none of your damn business, Savannah.'

'Yes, it is,' she argued. 'I won't have you fucking my baby sister, Jack.'

'Why is that? Because I didn't do you first?'

She threw the matchbook down, color rising high into her cheeks. 'You son of a bitch.'

'Stop it!' Laurel snapped, shoving her chair back and rising to her feet. She turned toward her sister, a part of her shocked by the pure hatred she saw burning like pale blue flame in Savannah's eyes as she stared at Jack, a part of her too annoyed to pay attention to it. 'Sister, I appreciate your concern, but I'm a big girl. I can take care of myself.'

Savannah blinked at her, looking stunned. 'No, you can't. You need me.'

'I need your support,' Laurel qualified. 'I don't need you screening my dates.'

Savannah picked out four words from the rest and drove them through her own heart like a stake. '*I don't need you.*' Baby didn't need her, didn't want her, preferred the company of Jack Boudreaux. Panic clawed through her, and fury poured out of the wounds as hot and red as blood. Her one chance to do something important was being snatched away from her. Everything she wanted was always beyond her reach. Coop. Laurel. Baby was turning away from her for a man. And she was left with nothing, just another slut like every other slut in south Louisiana.

'After all I've done for you,' she muttered, her lush mouth twisting at the bitterness, at the irony. 'After all I've done for you, you don't need me.'

Laurel's jaw dropped. 'That's not what I said!'

'Well, fine,' Savannah went on. 'You go on and have a high old time with him and just forget about me. I don't need you, either. You're nothing but an ungrateful little hypocrite, and I can't think why I ever would have saved you from anything.'

Tears shone like diamonds in her eyes. She caught at her artificially plump lower lip with her teeth, raking color into it. 'I never will again,' she vowed, her voice choked and petulant. 'You can count on that. I *never* will again.'

'Savannah!' Laurel started after her as she whirled and ran into the house, but Jack caught her by the shoulder.

'Let her go, angel. She's in no mood to listen. Let her cool off.'

Seconds later the Acura roared to life at the side of the house, and then came the angry screech of tires on asphalt.

Laurel turned and slammed her fist into Jack's shoulder, not to punish him, but because she needed to hit something, anything. 'I don't understand what's going on with her!'

'She's jealous.'

'No,' she murmured, leaning into him as the anger seeped out of her muscles, leaving her trembling. 'It's not as simple as that.'

'Yeah, well . . .' He heaved a sigh and slipped his arms around her, resting his chin atop her head. '*C'est vrai*, life's a bitch. Nothin's ever simple. . . .'

Certainly not in Laurel's life. She seemed interminably tangled in a web of obligations. He wanted to cut her loose, if only for a little while, give her a break . . . have her all to himself so he might pretend she could be his.

'Except fishin',' he said, going with the impulse that had brought him here at this ungodly hour in the first place. 'You ready to come fishin' with me, *ma petite?*'

'I never said I'd go fishing with you,' Laurel said, frowning.

'Sure you did. Last night.' He tucked a knuckle under her chin and tipped her face up. 'You whispered it in my ear while we were makin' love. You said I could take you anywhere. I'm taking you fishin'.'

They went out in a *pirogue* Laurel had more than a few reservations about. Slender and shallow as a pea pod, it was made of weathered cypress planking and bobbed like a cork on the inky, oily surface of the bayou. Laurel stood on the dock for a long moment, looking dubious, as Jack loaded fishing gear into the bow.

'Are you sure this thing is safe?'

'Oh, absolutely,' he drawled, adding a cooler to the cargo in the nose of the boat. The *pirogue* dipped and swayed on the water as if protesting even that slight load. Unconcerned, Jack climbed in, braced his feet, and reached a hand up to help her aboard. 'An old friend of mine made this *pirogue* for me. As he would say. "This boat, she rides the dew." '

Laurel swallowed hard as she stepped down into the craft and felt it bob beneath her. She grabbed hold of Jack's biceps for an instant to steady herself and to pull him with her if she went overboard. 'Was he sober at the time?'

'Hard to say,' Jack mused, easing her down on the boat's plank seat. He jammed a red USL Ragin' Cajuns baseball cap down on her head and stepped deftly over the seat to take up the push-pole at the stern. 'Ol' Lucky Doucet, he used to be some kind of wild.'

He pushed off, and they moved away from the dock, the *pirogue* seeming to skate across the water, as graceful as a blade on ice. Laurel took a deep breath and willed herself to relax.

'Used to be?' Tipping the oversize cap back on her head, she twisted around to look at him. 'Is he dead?'

'Naw, he's married. Got himself a beautiful wife, a little daughter, another baby on the way.'

'Busy man,' Laurel said dryly.

Happy man, Jack thought, sinking the fork of the push-pole into the muddy bottom and sending the *pirogue* gliding forward. A hard, hollow ball of longing lodged in his chest, taking up valuable air space, and he scowled and did his best to smash it with a mental mallet of self-punishment. He'd had his chance, and he'd blown it in the worst possible way. He didn't deserve another.

Pushing the dark thoughts from his mind, he turned his attention on Laurel and all the little puzzle pieces he had yet to find to complete his picture of her. She sat on the hard plank seat of the *pirogue* with the posture of a debutante, her gaze scanning the far bank of the bayou, where an alligator was sunning itself. Even in her baggy clothes and the too-big cap she looked feminine and graceful. He shook his head at that, a wry smile tugging at one corner of his mouth.

She wasn't his type. Not at all. These days he usually went for curvy, carefree girls with big breasts and uncomplicated brains, women who wanted nothing more from him than a good tussle between the sheets. He didn't know what Laurel Chandler would want. She claimed she wanted nothing from him, and yet he felt something about her drawing on him like a magnet. Instinct told him his curiosity could be dangerous, but the warning wasn't strong enough to overpower the attraction. Besides, he told himself smugly, he couldn't get in any deeper than he wanted to.

He piloted the *pirogue* to a favorite fishing hole, a place where willows shaded the banks, and bass, bream, and crappie cruised among the cypress stands and wallowed in the sluggish water edging the thickets of reeds and cattails. Laurel passed on the offer of a pole and instead pulled *Evil Illusions* out of the canvas tote bag she had brought with her. The morning passed to the trill of cicadas, the whine of a fishing reel, the splash of fish fighting against a future in a frying pan. Conversation became as sporadic and desultory as the breeze.

Laurel found the quiet soothing in the wake of Savannah's blow-up. With an effort she pushed the questions about her sister's behavior to the back of her mind and tried to lose herself in the pages of Jack's book. Not a difficult thing to do. Despite his show as a simple Cajun boy, he was an excellent writer, talented, clever. He had the ability to pull the reader into the story as if through a portal into another dimension. The visual images were sharp, dark; the emotions so thick and electric, they left her skin tingling. The fear that built from paragraph to paragraph was almost unbearably intense. The sense of evil that overshadowed it all was at once subtle, insidious, and overwhelming.

Strong impressions from a man who claimed he didn't care much about anything that went on in the world around him except having a good time. No, she thought, watching as he cast gracefully toward the edge of a tangle of water hyacinth, these impressions, these dark fantasies didn't come from Jack the Party Animal. They came from the other Jack. The man with the burning gaze and the aura of danger. The man who stood silent and watchful behind the facade of the rogue.

'Where does it come from?' she asked as they spread a blanket on shore, preparing to have lunch.

'What?'

'What you write.'

Everything about him went utterly still for a split second, as if her question had literally stopped him cold. But he recovered so quickly, Laurel almost convinced herself she had imagined the response.

'It's just made up,' he said, smoothing a corner of the blue plaid blanket. 'That's why they call it fiction, sugar.'

'I don't believe you just sit down, put your hands on a keyboard, and come up with that stuff.'

'Why not?'

'Because it's too good.'

He gave a dismissive shake of his head. 'It's a talent, a trick, that's all.' Some trick, he thought bitterly. Just sit down at the typewriter and open a vein. Bleed out all the poison that simmered inside him.

Laurel knelt on the blanket, studying him with her head tilted on one side. 'Some writers say it's like method acting. That they mentally live through every action and emotion.'

'And others will tell you it's like doing paint-by-numbers.'

'What do *you* say?'

'I say, I'm too damn hungry to play twenty questions,' he growled, stalking her across the blanket on his knees. A wicked smile played at the corners of his mouth and carved his dimples into his lean cheeks.

Nerve endings on red alert, Laurel held her ground as he approached. It seemed amazing to her, the way her body came alive and aware of him. Her heart picked up a beat, her breasts grew heavy and tingled with electricity.

'What's for lunch?' she asked breathlessly as he stopped before her, a scant inch of charged air separating them.

'You.'

He knocked the baseball cap from her head with a flick of his wrist. Then she was in his arms, immersed in his embrace, lost in his kiss. It occurred to her vaguely that he was trying to distract her from her line of questioning, but she couldn't bring herself to object to his method. His touch unleashed a host of needs that had lain dormant inside her until last night. Now they leaped and twisted, wild with the prospect of freedom.

Afterward they dozed exhausted, replete. Jack settled on his side with one leg thrown across Laurel's. She turned toward him and curled one small hand against his chest, too hot to cuddle, but needing to maintain contact with him. And they lay there in the quiet, in the heat, listening to the cicadas and the songbirds and the pounding of their own hearts.

A belated tremor of fear rumbled through Laurel. Fear of the control she had lost so completely. Fear of the incredible pleasure Jack had given her. An old fear that had its roots in a time of her life when she had seen sex as only a negative experience. She knew better now, but old fears never quite died – they just hid in dark corners of the mind and waited for the chance to slip out. Deliberately, she dismissed it and blinked her eyes open to look at Jack.

He lifted a hand and touched her cheek, idly brushing back a strand of hair. 'Where'd you go, *'tite chatte*?' he whispered, his brows drawing together.

'Nowhere important,' she said, dodging his gaze.

'Back to Georgia?'

'No.'

'But you do go back there, in your mind, *oui*?'

She thought about that for a moment, debating the wisdom of revealing anything about that time in her life. A part of her wanted to guard the secrets, hide the past, protect herself. But it seemed ironic to try to hide anything from a man who had shared the most private parts of her body, who had taken her to dizzying heights of pleasure and held her safe in his arms as they floated together to earth. She had opened her body to him, now she opened another part of her, tentatively, hesitantly, feeling more vulnerable than a virgin.

'It comes to me sometimes,' she said at last. She sat up and began dressing, not wanting to feel any more naked than was necessary.

Jack hitched his jeans up and zipped them, leaving the button undone. 'Can you talk about it?'

She shrugged, as if it were unimportant or easy, when it was far from being either. 'I guess you read about it in the papers.'

'I read some of what the papers had to say, but I've been around the block a time or two, sugar. I know there's a helluva lot more to any story than sound bites and photo ops.'

Dressed, Laurel sat on the blanket with her arms wrapped around her knees and stared at the bayou. A squadron of wood ducks banked around in tight formation and came down with wings cupped and feet outstretched. They hit the water in unison and skied several feet, finally settling down to paddle away, chuckling among themselves.

'It started with three children and a story about a "club" that met once a week,' she began, bracing herself inwardly against what was to come. Even now, months after the case had been taken away from her, the details had the power to sicken her, the images came back as bright and ugly as ever. Her hands tightened against her shins until her knuckles turned white.

'The allegations were incredible. Child pornography. Sexual abuse. The children had been sworn to secrecy. Small animals had been slaughtered in front of them, killed and torn apart, as a demonstration of what might happen if they talked. But they became more frightened of what might happen if they *didn't* talk.

'They came to me because I had been to their school during career week. I had talked about justice, about doing the right thing and fighting for the truth.' Her mouth twisted at the irony. 'The poor little things believed me. I believed myself.'

She could still see them, all those little faces staring up at her from the floor of the gymnasium, their eyes round as they absorbed her sermon on the pride and nobility of working to see justice served. She could still feel that sense of pride and self-righteousness and naivete. She had still believed then that right would always win out if one worked hard enough, believed strongly enough, fought with a pure heart.

'Nobody wanted me to touch their story. The adults they were accusing were above reproach. A teacher, a dentist, a member of the Methodist church council. Fine, upstanding citizens – who just happened to be pedophiles,' she said bitterly.

'What made you believe them?'

How could she explain? How could she describe the sense of empathy? She knew what it was to hold a terrible secret inside, because she had held one of her own. She knew what courage it took to let the secret out, because she had never been able to muster it.

The guilt twisted like a knife inside her, and she squeezed her eyes shut against the pain. She had never found the strength to brave her mother's unpredictable temperament or risk her mother's love.

'Don't tell Mama, Laurel. She won't believe you. She'll hate you for telling. She'll have one of her spells, and it will be all your fault.'

If she hadn't been such a coward, if she had done the right thing, the brave thing . . .

A picture of Savannah swam before her eyes, rumpled, seductive, playing the harlot with a tragic sense of reckless desperation underlying her sexuality.

She pushed to her feet and walked down to the edge of the water, wanting to escape not only Jack and his questions, but her past, herself. He followed her. She could sense him behind her, feel his dark gaze on her back.

'Why did you believe them, Laurel?'

'Because they needed me. They needed justice. It was my job.'

The denial of her own feelings built a sense of pressure in her chest that grew and grew, like an inflating balloon. It crowded against her lungs, squeezed her heart, closed off her throat, pushed hard on the backs of her eyes. She had crushed it out before, time and again. She had railed at Dr. Pritchard for trying to make her let it out.

'I wasn't atoning for anything. I had a job to do, and I did it. My childhood had nothing to do with it.'

He just gave her that long, patient look that held both pity and disappointment. And she wanted to pick up one of the fat psychology books from his desk and hit him in the face with it.

'I didn't come here to talk about ancient history. I want help for what's happening now.'

'Don't you see, Laurel? The past is what this is all about. You wouldn't be where you are today if not for where you started and what went on there.'

'I'm not trying to atone for anything!'

She tried to suck in a breath, but her lungs couldn't expand to accommodate the humid air. The pressure was so great, she wondered wildly if she would simply explode.

Control. She needed control.

Ruthlessly, she tried to push aside the other thoughts and concentrate on simply relating the facts in a way that would satisfy Jack and keep her emotional involvement to a minimum.

'We worked day and night to build a case. There was evidence, but none of it could be tied directly to the accused. And the whole time, they were soliciting sympathy in the community, claiming to be the victims of a witch hunt, claiming that I was trying to climb on their backs to the state attorney general's office.' Her hands balled into tight fists at her sides as she tried to leash the fury building inside her. Her whole body trembled with the power of it. 'God, they were so slick, so clever, so smug!'

So evil.

You believe in evil, don't you, Laurel?

She clenched her teeth against the need to scream.

. . . and good must triumph over evil . . .

'All we really had was the testimony of the children.'

She snatched half a breath, feeling as if her lungs would burst.

'Children aren't considered reliable witnesses.'

Don't bother telling, Laurel. No one will believe you.

'Parker – the state AG—' She was gasping now, as if she had run too far too fast. A fine sheen of sweat coated her skin, sticky and cold. 'He took the case away from me – It – was politically explosive – He said I – I – couldn't handle it—'

Jack stepped closer, his heart pounding with hers, *for* her. He could feel the tension, brittle in the air around her, snapping with electricity. He reached out to lay a hand on her shoulder, and she jolted as if he had given her a shock.

'You did the best you could,' he said softly.

'I lost,' she whispered, the words lashing out of her like the crack of a whip, the anguish almost palpable. Shaking violently, she raised her fists and pressed them hard against her temples. 'They were guilty.'

'You did your best.'

'It wasn't good enough!' she screamed.

The ducks departed in a flurry of wings and splashing water. Egrets and herons that had been wading in the shallows for fish took flight and wheeled over the bayou, squawking angrily at the disturbance. Laurel twisted away from Jack's touch and ran along the bank, stumbling, sobbing, frantic to escape but with nowhere to run. She fell to her knees in the sandy dirt and curled over into a tight ball of misery, dry, wrenching sobs tearing at her throat.

For a moment Jack stood there, stunned by the depth of her pain, frightened by it. Instinct warned him off, like an animal scenting fire. He didn't want to get too close to it, didn't want to risk touching it, but an instant after that thought had passed through his head, he was kneeling beside her, stroking a hand over the back of her head.

'Darlin', don't cry so,' he murmured, his voice a hoarse rasp. 'You did your job. You did what you could. Some cases you win, some you don't. That's just the way the game goes. We both know that.'

'It isn't a game!' Laurel snapped, batting his hand away. She glared at him through her tears. 'Dammit, Jack, this isn't Beat the System, it's justice. Don't you see that? Justice. I can't just shrug and walk away when the bet doesn't pan out. Those children were counting on me to save them, and I failed!'

It was a burden with the weight of the world, and she crumpled beneath the pressure of it.

Gently, Jack drew her into his arms and rocked her. He kissed the top of her head and stroked her hair and shushed her softly, and time passed by them, unnoticed, unmarked.

Justice, he thought cynically. What justice was there in a world where children were used and abused by the people who were supposed to protect and nurture them? What justice was there when a woman as noble, as brave, as truehearted as the one in his arms suffered so for the sins of others? What justice allowed a man the like of himself to be the only one here to offer her comfort?

There was no justice in his experience. He had never seen any evidence of it growing up. As an attorney, he had been trained to play the court system like an elaborate chess game, maneuvering, manipulating, using strategy and cunning to win for his client. There had been no justice, only victory at any cost.

If there was such a creature as justice, he thought, then it had an exceedingly sadistic sense of humor.

17

They saw the commotion all the way from the dock at Frenchie's Landing. Cars were parked up and down the road. A crowd of considerable size had gathered. From that distance only the indistinct crackle of a voice could be heard through a bad speaker system; not individual words, just the rise and fall of pitch and tempo, but there was no mistaking the fact that something exciting was going on at the former Texaco station that had only yesterday stood empty across the road from Frenchie's.

Laurel glanced at Jack – something she had been avoiding doing all afternoon, since the humiliation of breaking down in front of him. His shoulders rose and fell in a lazy shrug. He was the picture of indifference with his khaki shirt hanging open, baseball cap tipped back on his head, stringer of glossy fish hanging from his fist.

He had no interest in what was going on across the road. His focus was on Laurel and the curious shyness that had come over her. He had never known a woman who didn't shed tears with gusto and impunity. Yet Laurel had shrunk from her emotional outburst – and from him – clearly embarrassed that she had shown such vulnerability in front of him.

He wondered if she ever cut herself an inch of slack. She demanded perfection of herself, a goal that was simply unattainable for any mortal human being. A trait he should have steered well clear of. *Le bon Dieu* knew he was the farthest thing from perfect. But he caught himself admiring her for it. She seemed so small and fragile, but she had a deep well of strength, and she went to it again and again, and accepted no excuses.

That's more than you can say for yourself, mon ami.

They crunched across the crushed shell of the parking lot another few yards, aiming for the bar, but Laurel's gaze held fast on the goings-on across the road. Spectators milled around, craning their necks for a better look at something. An auction, perhaps, she thought, though she couldn't recall seeing anything at the old gas station worth buying. The place had been stripped bare and abandoned back in the seventies, during the oil embargo. Then one word crackled across the distance, and stopped her dead.

'. . . damnation!'

She sucked in an indignant breath and let it out in a furious gust. 'That son of a bitch!'

Before Jack could say a word, she wheeled and made a beeline toward the station, her shoulders braced squarely, her stride quick and purposeful. He should have just let her go. He stood there for a second, intending to do just that. He wanted to drop off the fish for T-Grace and have himself a tall, cold beer. He didn't want to stick his nose into some damned hornet's nest. But as he watched Laurel stomp away, he couldn't put from his mind the image of her in his arms, weeping against his chest because she hadn't been able to give Lady Justice the miracle of sight.

Swearing under his breath, he tightened his grip on the stringer of dripping fish and jogged to catch up with her.

'He's not on the Delahoussayes' property,' he pointed out.

Laurel scowled. 'He'd damn well better have a lease on that place and a permit to hold a public demonstration,' she snarled, secretly hoping he had neither so she could get Kenner on him.

'You've done your part, angel,' Jack argued. 'You got him out of Ovide's hair – such as it is. Why you don' just leave him be and we can go have us a drink?'

'Why?' she asked sharply. 'Because I'm here. I'm an officer of the court and have an obligation to the Delahoussayes.' She shot him a glare. 'Go have your drink. I didn't say you had to come with me.'

'*Espèces de tête dure*,' he grumbled, rolling his eyes.

'Yes, I am,' she said, never slowing her stride. 'Hardheadedness is one of my better qualities.'

Baldwin and his followers hadn't wasted any time. The tall 'For Sale or Lease' sign that had stood propped in the front window of the station had been replaced with one that read 'End Sin. Find the True Path.' The door to the garage was open, and a stage had been hastily built across its mouth, giving Jimmy Lee a dark, dramatic background for his ranting and pacing routine.

His followers had gathered on the cracked concrete outside, crowding together despite the heat. Many of the women pressed toward the stage for a closer look at him, their faces glowing with sunburn and adulation. And Jimmy Lee stood above them all, drenched in sweat and glory, his hair slicked back and his caps gleaming white in the late afternoon sun. He stalked across the stage, his white shirt soaked through, his tie jerked loose, pleading with his followers to march valiantly on beneath the weight of their respective crosses, urging them to lighten his load by donating to keep the ministry going.

'I will fight on, brothers and sisters! No matter how Satan may try to smite me down, no matter the obstacles in my path, no matter if I have nothing with which to fight my battle except my faith!' He let his declaration ring in the air for a few seconds, then sighed dramatically and stood with shoulders drooping. 'But I don't want to fight this battle alone. I need your help, the help of the faithful, of the brave, of the devout. Sad as I am to admit it, we live in a world ruled by the almighty dollar. The ministry of the True Path cannot continue to bring the good news to untold thousands of believers each week without money. And without the ministry, I am powerless. Alone, I am only a man. With you behind me, I am an army!'

While the faithful and the devout applauded Baldwin's acting skills, Laurel skirted around the edge of the mob. She watched them with a mix of anger and pity – anger because they were gullible enough to listen to a charlatan like Baldwin, and pity for the very same reason. They needed something to believe in. She didn't begrudge them that. But that they had chosen to believe in a perverted con man made her want to knock their heads together.

She didn't see the cameras until it was too late. Her gaze caught first on the van parked alongside the garage. It bore the call letters of the Lafayette cable television station that was home to Baldwin's weekly show. Then her eye caught one of the video cameras that was capturing the spectacle for the home audience. By then she was nearly at the front of the throng, and Baldwin had already spotted her.

His gaze, luminous gold and glowing with the light of fanaticism, flashed on her like a spotlight, and he broke off in midsentence. The anticipation level of the crowd rose with each passing second of his silence. The cheap sound system underscored it all with a low, buzzing hum.

Laurel froze, her heart picking up a beat as both the cameraman and Jimmy Lee moved toward her. She could feel the cyclops eye of the camera zooming in on her, could feel the heat of Baldwin's gaze, could feel the additional weight of a hundred pair of eyes as one by one the crowd turned toward her. She braced herself and drew in a slow, deep breath.

'Miz Laurel Chandler,' he said softly. 'A woman of intelligence and deep convictions. A good woman drawn in by deception to battle on the side of Satan.'

Gasps and murmurs ran through the crowd. The woman standing closest to Laurel stepped back with a protective hand to her bosom.

'I don't think Judge Monahan will be too pleased with the comparison,' Laurel said archly, crossing her arms. 'But you're probably amused, being an expert at drawing in good people by means of deception, yourself.'

Those close enough to hear her began to grumble and boo. Baldwin cut them off with a motion of his hand. 'Condemn not, believers!' he shouted. 'Christ himself, in his infinite wisdom, preached forgiveness for those who would hurt you. He has counseled me in matters of forgiveness—'

'Has He counseled you in matters of the law?' Laurel queried. 'Do you have any right to be on this property, holding this assembly?'

Something ugly flashed in Baldwin's eyes. He didn't like her interrupting his divinely inspired lines. *Tough shit, Jimmy Lee.*

'We have every right, lost sister,' he said tightly. 'We have legal rights, granted by man. We have moral rights, granted by God Himself, to gather in this humble setting and—'

'Appropriate setting,' Jack drawled. He stepped around Laurel to lean indolently against the edge of Jimmy Lee's stage, the stringer of fish still swinging from his fist. 'You always did give me gas, Jimmy Lee.'

He was near enough that the mike picked up the last of his words, and people at the back of the crowd, who had come only out of curiosity, burst out laughing.

Jimmy Lee's face flushed a dark blood red beneath his artificial tan. His mouth quivered a little as he fought to keep from sneering at the man who was leaning lazily against his platform. Damn Jack Boudreaux. Damn Laurel Chandler. She was the troublemaker, the little bitch. Boudreaux only came along sniffing after her. But as much as he wanted to drag out all the dirt on Laurel Chandler, Jimmy Lee kept himself in check. His followers wouldn't tolerate an attack on a woman of her standing. Boudreaux, on the other hand, was a whole different breed of cat.

He smiled inwardly, a feral, vicious smile. 'Do I indeed, Mr. Boudreaux?' he asked. 'Shall I tell you what your books do for me? They sicken and disgust me, as they do any good Christian. The content is vile, brutal, a celebration of evil and an instruction manual in the ways of Satan. Or are you here to tell us you've given up that path of wickedness?'

A slow grin spread across Jack's face. He plopped his fish down on Jimmy Lee's wing tips, sending him scooting backward, and hopped onto the stage to sit with his legs swinging over the edge. 'Well, hell, Jimmy Lee, that's sort of like askin' you if you've quit stealin' people's money. The way the question is phrased, denial is an admission of guilt. Having been an attorney in a previous incarnation, I know better than to answer.' He tipped his head and treated Baldwin to a merciless, wicked grin so hard and sharp, it could have cut glass. 'Me, I'm just amazed to hear you know how to read.'

Another volley of laughter sounded at the back of the crowd and rippled forward. Jimmy Lee clenched his jaw against a stream of profanity. His fist tightened around his microphone while he indulged himself in the fantasy that it was Boudreaux's windpipe he was crushing.

'Evil is no laughing matter,' he said sternly. He turned his gaze back out across the small sea of faces that had gathered to hear him and pointed hard at Jack. 'Do we want our children growing up on the kind of twisted and depraved tales this man tells? Tales of murder and mutilation and horrors that should surely be beyond the imaginings of decent people!'

'Hey, Jack!' Leonce called out from near the dusty old gas pumps. 'What's the name o' dat book?'

'*Evil Illusions!*' Jack called, laughing. 'On sale everywhere for five ninety-nine!'

'And he laughs and makes money off this filth!' Jimmy Lee shouted to the devout above the laughter of the others. 'What other sins might a sick mind like that commit? We hear every day about crimes against women and children in this country. Our own Acadiana is being terrorized by an animal who stalks and murders our women. And where do creatures like that get their ideas for their crimes?'

The grin vanished from Jack's face. He met Baldwin's gaze evenly, never breaking the stare as he rose to his feet and closed the distance between them, booting the fish aside. Hostility rolled off him in hot waves.

'You better watch your mouth, preacher,' he growled, gently pushing Baldwin's microphone aside. 'You never know what kind of revenge a sick mind like mine might come up with.'

Jimmy Lee savored the small victory of striking a nerve, meeting Jack's hard stare with a smugness that came from having the safety of a crowd around him. 'I'm not afraid of you, Boudreaux.'

'No?' Jack arched a brow. 'Are you afraid of the words "slander suit"? You'd better be, Jimmy Lee, because I could have my lawyers tie you up in court for the rest of your unnatural life. I wouldn't leave you a pot to piss in, and this preacher act of yours will have been for nothing.'

Baldwin narrowed his eyes. A muscle twitched in his jaw. 'It's a free country, Boudreaux. If I think reading trash pushes unstable minds to commit unspeakable acts, I can say so.'

'Uh-huh. And if you utter my name in connection with those unspeakable acts, I'll have the right to beat the ever-lovin' shit out of you – figuratively speaking.' He smiled like a crocodile and lifted Jimmy Lee's hand so that the mike picked up his next words. 'Mebbe you oughta try to cast the demons outta me, Jimmy Lee. Run 'em into some pigs or somethin'. Give the folks their money's worth.' Baldwin glared at him. 'No? Well, that's okay, Jimmy Lee.'

He bent and snatched up the stringer of fish and swung them hard at Jimmy Lee. Baldwin barely had time to react, catching the slimy mass against his belly with a grunt and a grimace.

'There you go,' Jack said. 'Now you get yourself a couple'a loaves of bread, and mebbe you can do *that* miracle.'

Howls of laughter went up from the back of the crowd. Laurel pressed a hand over her mouth and tried to contain herself. Jack hopped down off the stage and sauntered toward her, slipping a cigarette out of his shirt pocket and dangling it from his lip.

'You are *so* bad!' she whispered as he turned her by one arm and escorted her away from the crowd.

His dark eyes sparked with mischief as he slanted a look at her. 'That's what makes me *so* good, sugar,' he drawled. 'Now let's go get that drink you owe me.'

They hadn't taken three strides toward the road when a terrible scream split the air – piercing, blood-curdling, a sound that cut straight to the bone. Laurel pulled herself up, chilled and shaken, her hand grasping Jack's forearm, her heart thundering in her breast. She could hear the crowd behind her murmuring, gasping, shuffling their feet on the concrete as they turned. Then the scream came again and again. It emanated from Frenchie's, a terrible, keening wail, that carried in it a note instinctively understood by all, and everyone stood, breath held, waiting.

Laurel's grip tightened on Jack's arm as she spotted the Partout Parish cruiser parked out front. Sheriff Kenner walked out of the bar and down the steps, his mirrored aviator sunglasses glinting in the sun. The side door on the building slammed, and a thin young man in surfer shorts and a neon green shirt jumped the rail and came barreling across the parking lot, running as if the devil were at his heels, his face chalk white, shirttails flying.

The front door swung open again, and T-Grace literally hurled herself out onto the gallery, screaming, 'My *bébé*! My *bébé*!' She fell to her knees, smashing her fists against the floor over and over, wild, terrible sobs tearing up from her very soul. Then Ovide stumbled out onto the gallery, feeling his way like a blind man. Finding his wife with his hands, he sank down behind her, tilted his face heavenward and cried out, '*Bon Dieu avoir pitié!*'

'Oh, God, Jack,' Laurel whispered, tears crowding her throat and pressing at her eyes. The feeling that swelled inside her as she turned toward him was unmistakably grief, and a small, disconnected part of her brain marveled at the body's ability to react so strongly to something as yet unannounced.

Seconds later the young man who had dashed out of the bar arrived with the news: Annie Delahoussaye-Gerrard, who had not been seen since Sunday night, had been found. Her nude, brutalized body had been discovered by a pair of hikers along the bank of the bayou.

The murder rocked the town of Bayou Breaux to its core. As the terror of the Bayou Strangler had gripped other parts of Acadiana, residents here had felt immune. Partout Parish had seemed a safe haven, a magical place where bad things didn't happen. In the time it took Annie Delahoussaye-Gerrard to gasp her last breath, the illusion of safety had vanished. The world tilted on its axis, and the residents of Bayou Breaux cast about frantically for something to hang on to.

That evening the streets were abandoned. Businesses closed early. People went home to be with their families. Doors that had never been locked before were bolted shut against the threat of evil that lurked along the dark, misty banks of the bayou.

T-Grace, inconsolable in her grief, had to be carried to her bed and sedated. As if the news had been carried to them on telepathic waves, the rest of the Delahoussaye children began arriving. The family banded together to mourn, to offer each other strength, to fill the tiny house where they had all been raised and try to banish the emptiness left by that one missing face.

The bar was not open, but a core of regulars gathered inside in much the same way as the Delahoussaye clan in their home. They were family of sorts – Leonce and Taureau, Dede Wilson and half a dozen others. Annie had been one of them, and now she had been torn from the fabric of all their lives, leaving a ragged, ugly hole.

Leonce took charge of the bar, dispensing drinks without a trace of his usual carefree grin. His Panama hat hung on the rack by the front door, removed out of respect, and he had traded his trademark aloha shirt for a somber black T-shirt. The rest of the group sat at or near the bar, everyone avoiding the dance floor and stage, except Jack. He sat on the piano bench, drinking Wild Turkey and playing soft sad songs on his small Evangeline accordion.

Laurel watched him from her perch on the corner barstool. He sat with his head bent, his graceful hands working the instrument, squeezing out notes so poignant, it seemed to be weeping. He hadn't said ten words since the announcement – to her or to anyone. Despite the fact that he remained physically present, she couldn't get away from the feeling that he had gone into retreat. He had pulled in on himself and closed all doors and shutters, the same as the residents of Bayou Breaux had locked up their homes. His face was a stark, blank mask, offering nothing, giving nothing away. There was no sign of the man who had teased her or the man who had held her while she cried. She nibbled on a thumbnail and wondered where he'd gone . . . and wished he hadn't gone there without her.

She felt like an outsider again. The others all had their memories of Annie to bind them together, common tales and common experiences. She hadn't known Annie. Until recently, her life had never crossed paths with any of the people who thought of a place like Frenchie's as a second home.

An old feeling came back to her from childhood, a memory of herself and Savannah dressed in their matching Sunday best, standing on the sidewalk out front of the church, watching with longing while other children ran and played in the park adjacent to the church grounds.

'Can't we play, too, Mama?'

'No, darling, you don't want to get your pretty dress all dirty, do you?'

Vivian, in a red-on-white dot dress that matched her daughters', an elegant wide-brimmed white hat perched just so on her head, bent and smoothed a sausage curl behind Laurel's ear. 'Besides, sweetheart, those aren't the kind of children you should play with.'

'Why not?'

'Don't be silly, Laurel.' She smiled that brittle smile that always made Laurel's tummy knot. 'They're common. You're a Chandler.'

A stupid memory, she thought, trying to crush the residual vulnerability. This was a time of tragedy for the Delahoussayes; she had no business feeling sorry for herself. Besides, no one in their right mind would *want* to be included among the mourners.

'Here you go.'

Laurel looked up and blinked at the tumbler of milk Leonce had set on the bar before her.

'My grandpapa, he had an ulcer,' he said softly. He put his elbows on the bar and leaned toward her, a knowing look raising one dark eyebrow and the knot of scar tissue that interrupted it. 'He used to rub his belly same as what you're doin'. When he ran out of the cabbage juice the local *traiteur* used to give him, he drank milk.'

Laurel shot a guilty glance at the hand she had absently pressed to her middle. 'I'm fine,' she said, wrapping both hands around the cold glass. 'But thank you, anyway, Leonce.'

He took a deep drag on his cigarette and sighed out a cloud of pale smoke, staring across the room at nothing. 'I can't believe she's gone, snatched away from us just like dat,' he said, snapping his fingers.

'Were you close?'

He smiled sadly. 'Ever'body loved Annie.'

Laurel sipped her milk and looked at Jack out of the corner of her eye, wondering if he had loved Annie. 'She was married, wasn't she?'

'Oh, yeah, but Tony, he didn' treat her good, so all bets were off, if you get my drift.'

He took another pull on his smoke and crushed the butt out in a Jax Beer ashtray. Lost in memories for a moment, he lifted a hand to rub absently at the scar on his cheek. 'Annie, she liked to pass a good time,' he murmured. 'She wasn' a bad girl. She just liked to pass a good time, is all.'

Meaning she cheated on her abusive husband. Automatically, Laurel's mind sorted and filed the facts, formulated theories. Old habit. Comforting in its way. There was solace, consolation to be found in making sense of tragedy. Murders could be solved. Justice could be served.

But nothing would ever bring Annie back.

The side door near the kitchen opened, and Ovide stumbled in like a zombie. He looked twenty years older and frail, despite his bulk. The hair that fringed his head stood out in an aura of silver. The ruddy color had leeched out of his face, leaving his skin a ghostly shade of gray.

Talk stopped, and everyone looked to him expectantly. Everyone except Jack, who hunched over his accordion, playing 'Valse de Grand Meche.' Ovide just stood there looking lost and confused, as if he had no idea where he was or what he was doing there. Leonce went to him and took hold of his arm, speaking to him softly in French. He didn't appear to listen, but looked around the bar at the people who had gathered to talk, at Jack, who had set himself apart. Finally, his gaze settled on Laurel.

'*Viens ici, chérie*,' he murmured, holding a hand out toward her. 'T-Grace, she wants to see you.'

Laurel just barely kept from looking over her shoulder to see if there was a more likely person standing behind her. 'Me?' she murmured, touching her chest.

'*Oui*, come. Please.'

With a heavy, black feeling of foreboding pressing down on her, and with the ironic thought that she was going to be included after all, she slid down off her stool.

They entered the Delahoussaye home through the kitchen, which proved to be the largest room of the house. Inappropriately cheerful and bright, the rich aroma of coffee and the spicy bite of *etouffée* lingered in the air. The walls sported yellow-and-white checked paper and a boggling array of knickknacks that ranged from plastic praying hands to thimbles from Las Vegas to salt-and-pepper sets in the guise of squirrels and chickens – all of it striking Laurel as being painfully sweet and too revealing about the woman who had raised her children in this house.

Delahoussaye children and grandchildren filled the benches at the long harvest table in the center of the room. Sleepy-eyed children sat on the laps of parents or elder siblings. The glare of the fluorescent light washed the color from all their faces, emphasizing eyes that had been cried raw and red. Laurel envied them their family, but not the grief that hung like a pall around them.

'I'm so sorry,' she whispered, apologizing for both their loss and her intrusion on this private time.

Her words triggered a flood of tears from a woman who might have been Annie's twin – apple cheeks and corkscrew curls, a tank top two sizes too small. A brawny husband folded his arms around her and the dark-haired baby who sat on her lap and rocked them both. At the other end of the table, a younger version of T-Grace stood abruptly and looked straight at Laurel.

'Thank you for coming,' she said automatically. 'I'll make us a fresh pot of coffee.'

She set about the task with the frenetic energy of someone trying to keep a step ahead of inner demons. Laurel recognized the signs from experience, and she felt empathy drawing on her, pulling at her limited reserve of strength.

She followed Ovide through the cramped living room, where two boys of about ten sat on the floor watching an age-old rerun of *Star Trek* on a television that had the sound turned so low, the actors seemed to be whispering. A toddler had been settled to sleep on the green plaid sofa with a nubby orange afghan covering all but her face and the fist pressed against her mouth as she sucked her thumb.

T-Grace lay in bed in a room that would have been considered a closet at Beauvoir. Meager light from a red glass Spanish-look lamp on the nightstand glowed off the imitation walnut paneling that displayed gold plastic candle sconces and gaudy metal butterflies. The smell of mothballs and cheap perfume permeated the air. Clothes were folded and stacked in precariously tipping piles on every available surface, giving the cramped little room the feel of a storage cupboard at the Salvation Army store.

When Laurel stepped through the door, her breath caught hard in her throat. Her first thought was that T-Grace had died of shock and heartbreak, and she could only wonder why Ovide had dragged her over here to view the body. The woman lay propped against half a dozen pillows, her bulging eyes staring into nothingness, her thin mouth hanging slack, as if she had been stricken down midsentence. Her orange hair stood up in thin, ratty tufts around her head. Then she stirred, lifting a hand from the green chenille bedspread, and Laurel forced herself to move farther into the room.

'I'm so sorry, T-Grace,' she said softly as she took the woman's hand and settled a hip on the edge of the bed.

T-Grace rolled her head from side to side on the pillow, too sedated to do much more. 'My poor, poor *bébé*. She's gone from us. Gone from dis world,' she mumbled. 'I can't bear it.'

'You should try to rest,' Laurel whispered, unable to find adequate words that could soothe a mother's suffering.

'There is no pain like to lose a child,' T-Grace said, her eyes filling. She made no move to brush the tears away. They spilled down her sunken cheeks and trickled back along her jaw. What little energy she had left she concentrated into speech. 'I would give myself a hundred times in her place.'

Laurel bit her lip and held tight to the hand that seemed so frail in hers.

'Someone gotta pay for dis.'

'They'll catch the man,' Laurel said thickly, to placate T-Grace and to reassure herself. Someone would pay. Justice would triumph in the end. It had to.

But not soon enough for Annie.

T-Grace looked her square in the face, a glimmer of her old fire flickering in her eyes. 'You gonna help us wit' dat, *chère*, or what?'

Panic booted Laurel in the stomach. 'What can I do, T-Grace? I'm not a deputy. You don't need a lawyer.' *You don't need me. Please, please, don't ask me to get involved in this.*

'My Ovide and me, we don' trust dat jackass Kenner,' T-Grace said. 'You go, you make sure he's doin' right by our poor *bébé* Annick.'

Laurel shook her head. 'Oh, T-Grace—'

T-Grace gathered the last of her strength and lunged ahead, grasping at Laurel with hands as cold and bony as death. 'Please, Laurel, help us!' she exclaimed, desperation ragged in her voice. 'Please, *chère, s'il vous plaît!*'

The words rang in Laurel's head, clashing with the pleas she heard every night in her sleep. She pushed herself to her feet as T-Grace fell back on the pillows, and backed away from the bed, fighting to keep herself from running out. Tears crowded her eyes and throat, and she tried to fight them back with reason. This wasn't the same as Scott County. She wouldn't be taking on the investigation or trying to shoulder the burden of proof. All they were asking was that she keep an eye on things for them.

Still, her first, her strongest instinct was to say no, to protect herself. *Selfish. Coward. Weak.*

'*Please, help us, Laurel. . . .*'

'*You'll never be able to get justice for those children . . . go and get justice for somebody else. . . .*'

She looked at T-Grace, lying on the bed like a corpse, her incredible energy sapped from her by grief. Then she turned to Ovide, who stood in the doorway, looking old and lost and helpless. She had the power to help them in some small way – if she could get past her own weakness.

'I'll do what I can.'

Jack had forsaken the accordion for the piano by the time Laurel came back to the bar. His fingers moved slowly, restlessly, caressing the keys. His head was tipped back, his eyes closed. The old upright piano that was more accustomed to belting out boogie-woogie whispered the opening movement of Beethoven's Moonlight Sonata, dark, brooding, quiet, sad.

The last of the people who had gathered to talk were on their way out the front door as Laurel walked in the side. Only Jack remained, and Leonce, who was turning out lights and putting the chairs up, sweeping as he went.

He glanced up at her, leaning against his broom, his scarred face in the shadows, a Dixie sign glowing red neon behind him. 'Hey, *chère*, you want a ride home?' he asked softly. 'Me, I don' think ol' Jack oughta get behind a wheel, you know?'

'That's okay, Leonce,' she murmured. 'We didn't drive. A long walk will do us both good.'

He dropped his gaze to the broom bristles and started sweeping again before she could read anything in his expression. 'Suit yourself.'

Laurel tucked her hands in the pockets of her shorts and wandered to the stage. Jack made no move to acknowledge her presence, even when she sat down beside him on the piano bench. He went on playing like a man in a trance, his long fingers stroking the yellowed keys with the care of a lover. The song rose and fell, melodies twining around one another, wrapping around Laurel and drawing her into another world, a world of stark poignancy and bittersweet emotion. Every note swelled with longing. A crushing pain filled the silences in between.

This was what hid behind the other Jack, the man with the haunted eyes and the aura of danger – loneliness, anguish, artistry. The realization struck a chord deep within her, and she closed her eyes against the pain. How many other layers were there? How many Jacks? Which one was at the core of the man? Which one held his heart?

She closed her mind to the questions and laid her head against his shoulder, too overwhelmed by feelings to think. She had held herself in tight check all evening, not allowing herself to react to Annie's murder or any of the emotions that had tried to surface since. But now, with no witnesses except a man who had already seen her cry, she stopped fighting. The feelings rushed up through her chest to her throat and clogged there in a hard lump. The tears came, not in a torrent, but in a painful, stingy trickle, spiking her lashes and dampening her cheeks.

Jack's hands slowed on the keyboard as the piece softened to its close. His fingers crept down to touch the final note, a low minor chord that vibrated and hung in the air like the echo of a voice from the dark past.

'Did you care about her?' Laurel asked, the question slipping out without her permission. Her breath held fast in anticipation of his answer.

'You mean, did I sleep with her?' Jack corrected her. He stared at the black upper panel of the piano, willing himself to see nothing, not the wood, not the ghost of Annie's sunny smile, nothing. 'Yeah, sure,' he said, his voice flat, emotionless. 'A couple times.'

His answer stung, though she told herself it shouldn't have. He was a rake, a womanizer. He'd probably slept with half the women in the parish. It shouldn't have meant anything to her. She pushed the reaction aside and tried to decipher what he might be feeling in the aftermath of the death of a woman he had known – intimately – whose parents were friends of his.

'I'm sorry,' she whispered.

'Be sorry for Annie, not for me. I'm alive.' For all the good he did anybody. His mouth twisted at the irony, and he reached for his whiskey to numb the ache. The liquor went down, as smooth as silk, to pool in his belly and send a familiar warmth radiating outward.

'I'm sorry for T-Grace and Ovide,' Laurel said, recalling too vividly the scene that had been played out on the gallery, remembering too clearly the desperation in T-Grace as she begged for help. 'They asked me to be their liaison with the sheriff.'

'And you agreed.'

'Yes.'

'Naturally.'

Even though he settled his fingers on the piano keys once again and started to play something slow and bluesy, she caught the caustic note in his voice. Slowly she straightened away from him, her gaze hard and direct. 'What's that supposed to mean?'

Jack didn't bother looking at her. He could feel the defensiveness going up like a wall around her, just as he had intended. 'It means you're a good little girl, doin' the right thing.'

'They're friends,' she said shortly. 'They asked me for a favor. It seemed a small enough thing to give them in light of the fact that their daughter has just been murdered. They don't understand police procedure. They don't trust the system to work for them.'

'Imagine that,' he drawled sardonically.

Laurel bristled. 'You know, I'm sick of your smartass remarks, Jack. It may not be perfect, but it's the only system we've got. It's up to people like you and me to make it work.'

He went on playing, wishing it would release some of the tension that was coiling inside him like a copperhead about to strike. He was feeling mean. He was feeling too sensitive, as if all his nerve endings had been exposed and rubbed raw. His strongest instinct was not to let anyone near. He wanted to draw himself into that small, dark room inside himself, as he had when he'd been a boy waiting for the thundering hand of Blackie Boudreaux to come down on him. He wanted to go to that place where no one could touch him, no one could hurt him, where he couldn't feel and didn't care.

But Laurel Chandler sat beside him, prim and properly affronted by his lack of faith in her precious system of jurisprudence. Damn her.

'It didn't work very well for you, did it, *'tite chatte*?'

The slyness in his tone cut Laurel to the quick, and pain flowed through her at the thought that she had shared that experience with him – had trusted him with that fragile, damaged part of her heart – only to have him use it against her.

'Fine,' she said. She hit the keyboard with her fists, pounding out a discordant tangle of notes as she rose from the bench. 'The system sucks. So we should just throw our hands up and let crime run rampant?' She paced behind him, trying to channel the hurt into anger. An argument was something she could grasp and wield with skill. More productive than grief or fear. 'That would be great, Jack. Then we could all do what you do – sit around and do nothing while our society comes apart at the seams.'

He arched a brow as he swung around on the bench to face her. Stretching out with deceptive laziness, he leaned his elbows back against the piano and crossed his ankles in front of him. 'What?' he demanded belligerently. 'You think I should do somethin'? What would you have me do? Wave a wand and bring Annie back to life? I can't. Shall I look into a crystal ball and see who killed her? I can't do that, either. See, sugar? It's like my old man always told me – I'm just fuckin' good for nothin'.'

'How convenient for you,' Laurel snapped, ignoring the softer part of her heart that ached for Jack the abused child. She was too angry with him to feel sympathy. He reminded her too much of Savannah, wallowing in the polluted waters of her past instead of picking herself up and doing something positive with her life. 'You don't have to take responsibility for anything. You don't have to aspire to anything. If the going gets tough, you can always turn around and blame your past. You don't have time to care about anyone else because you're so damn busy feeling sorry for yourself!'

He was on his feet and towering over her so quickly, she barely had time to suck in a breath of surprise. Common sense demanded she back away from him, the way she might back away from a panther encountered in the wild. But a deeper instinct made her hold her ground, and a tense, itchy silence descended between them.

He stared at her long and hard, his chest heaving with temper, his jaw set so rigid that the scar on his chin glinted like silver in the faint light. But the fire that had flared in his dark eyes died slowly, leaving that age-old abject weariness. The corners of his mouth cut upward in a bitter imitation of a smile.

'You don' want me to care about you, sugar,' he murmured. 'Everybody I ever cared about is dead.' He raised a hand to caress her cheek, and she started at his touch. 'See? I told you I'd be bad for you. You should have listened.'

She batted his hand away and took a step back. He was trying to frighten her. The same man who had only hours ago wooed her with his wicked smile – No. Not the same man.

Angry with his chameleon act, angry that he would try to scare her, angry with herself for giving a damn what he did, she gave him one last look of defiance. 'Play your games with someone else, Jack. I'm going home.'

He watched her hop down off the stage and head for the front door, telling himself to let her go, telling himself he was better off not caring that she would walk out into the night alone. But he couldn't quite pull the door shut on that little room. He couldn't quite get the images out of his mind – Annie . . . Evie . . . Lost forever. The need to protect Laurel pulled against the need to protect himself, stretching his nerves as taut as violin strings, and he trembled with the tension of it, waiting for the thread to simply snap.

Laurel kept on walking, her head up, her slim shoulders squared, her tiny feet barely making a sound as her sneakers struck the floor. So small, so fragile, so fiercely determined to take on every rotten thing the world tossed her way.

Swearing under his breath, Jack jumped off the stage. He caught up with her in half a dozen strides and grabbed hold of her arm, halting her progress toward the door.

'I'll walk you.'

'Why?' she demanded, glaring up at him. 'What are you going to do, Jack? Protect me? You just finished telling me how dangerous you are. Why would I go with you, anyway? You're drunk.'

His hand tightened on her arm. His temper boiled hotter, harder as the warring factions within him fought between the urge to throttle her or crush her against him.

'I'm not that drunk,' he growled. 'I said, I'll walk you home.'

'And I asked you why,' Laurel said, too angry to be cautious. A small, rational corner of her brain told her she was taunting a tiger, but she didn't listen. Something inside her was pushing her to recklessness. She didn't understand it, wasn't sure she *wanted* to understand it, but she couldn't seem to stop it. 'Why?'

His nostrils flared. His brows pulled ominously low over his eyes. He looked like the devil glaring down at her, the hard planes and angles of his lean face cast in sharp relief. 'Don't be stupid. Women are gettin' killed. Do you wanna be one of them?'

'What's it to you one way or the other, Jack?' she returned. 'You don't care about anyone but yourself. After they find my body, you can drink a quart of Wild Turkey in my honor and tell people you slept with me a couple of times.'

The leash on his control stretched to the breaking point. Rage rumbled through him like thunder, shaking him, swelling in his chest, roaring in his ears. He gripped her shoulders with both hands, trembling with the need to shake her like a rag doll and hurl her aside, out of his life.

'Damn you,' he snarled, not even sure whether he was cursing Laurel or himself. 'If you wanted an idealist, you shoulda gone shoppin' in a better neighborhood, sugar. I'm a bastard and a user and a cynic—'

'Why do you want to walk me home, Jack?' she demanded, matching him glare for glare.

'Because I've got enough corpses on my conscience to last me!'

A thick, heavy silence hung in the air around them as their gazes held. Jack's expression was fierce, wild. His fingers bit into the tender flesh of Laurel's upper arms. She had the feeling that he could have snapped her in half like a twig. She had never been quite so aware of the differences in their sizes, had never felt quite so physically fragile.

I've got enough corpses on my conscience to last me . . . The words sank into her brain one by one to be scrutinized, and a chill ran through her.

She stared at him for a long moment, watching him struggle to rein back the beast that was his temper. As his breathing slowed, she forced herself to relax by degrees, and breathed easier herself as his grip loosened.

'Would you care to elaborate on that statement?' she asked softly.

Very deliberately he lifted his hands from her shoulders and turned away from her. 'No, I wouldn't,' he said, and he headed for the door.

They walked the dark, deserted streets to Belle Rivière in silence, not speaking, not touching. Jack had closed himself off entirely. Laurel watched him surreptitiously, wondering, the wheels of her lawyer's mind whirling as she scrambled for a logical explanation, her heart swearing there had to be one.

He walked her to the courtyard and held the gate open for her. She stepped into the garden, trying desperately to think of something to say that would somehow ease the tension between them, but when she turned to say it, he was gone. Without a word he had slipped into the black shadows of the trees that stood between Belle Rivière and L'Amour.

Time slipped by unnoticed as she stood with her hands wrapped around the iron bars of the gate, staring toward the brick house that stood on the bank of the bayou. No lights came on in the windows.

Everyone I ever cared about is dead.

I've got enough corpses on my conscience to last me . . .

Who had he lost? Who had he cared about? Why were their deaths on his conscience?

The only thing she knew for certain was that it wasn't wise of her to want that knowledge. She had all she could handle just getting herself from one day to the next. She didn't need the kind of trouble that was brewing between herself and Savannah. She didn't want to get involved with the Delahoussayes or a murder investigation. She wasn't strong enough to endure a relationship with a man like Jack. He had too many facets, too many secrets, too many shadows in his past, too much darkness in his soul.

And still she felt attraction to him pulling on her like a magnetic force.

'Oh, God,' she whispered, closing her eyes and pressing her forehead against the cool iron bars of the gate. 'I never should have come back here.'

A scrap of cloud scudded across the sliver of moon. A sultry breeze whispered through the branches of the trees. A chill raced over Laurel's flesh, and she looked up abruptly, sensing . . . something. She strained her eyes, staring into the darkness, seeing nothing, but sensing . . . a presence. The sensation lingered like a dark, intent gaze, and the hair rose on the back of her neck.

'Jack?' she called, a faint quiver of doubt vibrating in her voice.

Silence.

'Jack? Huey?'

Nothing but the heavy feeling of eyes.

Somewhere in the woods beyond L'Amour a screech owl called, its voice like a woman's scream. Laurel swallowed hard as her heart climbed into her throat. Slowly, she backed toward the house, sliding her feet on the uneven brick pathway to keep from tripping. As she scanned the shadows of the courtyard for unfamiliar shapes, she chided herself for spooking so easily, trying not to think about the fact that Annie's body had been discovered not so very far from here.

It seemed to take forever to reach the gallery, but when she did, she felt like a child reaching the safe place in a game of tag. Relief swirled through her in a dizzying wave as she slipped into the house and locked the French doors behind her.

The predator is cloaked in shadows. A creature of the night. A creature of darkness. Watching. Waiting. Contemptuous. Smug.

The adversary has been chosen. Good, golden, champion of justice. But goodness and justice have nothing to do with this game. In this game, only the strong and the clever survive.

18

Tony Gerrard sat hunched over the small table in the interrogation room like a sullen sixteen-year-old hood in detention. His curly black hair was renegade length, his wide jaw shadowed blue by his beard. The sleeves of his faded denim work shirt had been cut off to reveal bulging biceps adorned with the artistic handiwork of Big Mamou of Mamou's Tattoos fame. His right arm proudly proclaimed him to be 100% Coonass. An alligator lounged on his left, seeming to come to life as he reached for an ashtray to tap off his cigarette. The gator stretched and twisted, all but bellowing before shrinking back into complacency.

In truth Tony hadn't changed a bit in the ten years since he'd dropped out of high school. Physically, he had matured early, reaching his full height of five feet eight and bulking out with muscle the instant his hormones had sprung to life. Psychologically, he hadn't matured at all. His temper was still the volatile and unpredictable creature of an adolescent. He used his penis like a homing device, and his idea of a good time invariably included sports, crude humor, and mass quantities of beer.

He'd been in trouble off and on since junior high, but his trouble had never amounted to much, to his way of thinking – a few smashed cars, the occasional fist fight. Twice he had been hauled in for pushing Annie around, but he had never hurt her badly. The court never wanted to hear it, but she'd always given as good as she got, the little hellcat.

He smiled a little at the memory of her hurling beer cans at him, swearing at him a mile a minute. But the smile twisted into a knot of pain as he reminded himself that Annie wouldn't be around to throw anything at his head anymore.

He stared down at the plain gold wedding band on his left hand, unable to look away from it, unable to stop from twisting it around and around on his finger.

'You can take that off and hock it, Tony,' Sheriff Kenner drawled, planting a boot on the seat of the only other chair at the table. He rested his forearms on his lean thigh and looked at Tony sideways, feeling exhausted and mean. He'd gotten two hours' sleep since the discovery of the body. 'You're not married anymore.'

Tony just sniffed and looked away.

'Divorce would have been cheaper,' Kenner said, watching his man with narrowed eyes. 'You don't have jack shit to sue for. Might have lost your truck, is all. You're gonna pay now, boy. They'll throw your pretty ass in Angola Pen, and you'll pay for the rest of your miserable life.'

Tony blinked at the itchy pressure in his eyes, never glancing Kenner's way, and mumbled, 'I didn't kill her.'

'Sure you did. You just spent six weeks in our little parish hotel 'cause of the missus. You had six weeks to get up a good head of steam. You got out, went to pay her back, got a little carried away . . .'

'I didn't kill her.'

'Tell me, Tony, what's it like to wrap a scarf around a woman's throat and choke the life out of her? Did you watch her face? Did you watch her turn color, watch her eyes bug out as she realized the man she married was gonna kill her?'

'Shut up.'

'Did you like the sounds she made, Tony?'

'Shut up.'

'Or did you like it better when she was begging you to stop using that knife on her?'

'Shut up!' Tony exploded to his feet, sending his chair skittering backward on the linoleum. His face contorted with rage, and spittle flew as he shouted, 'Shut the fuck up!'

Kenner pounced like a wolf, grabbing him by the back of his thick neck and digging his fingertips in. As Tony gasped at the pain shooting down his spine, Kenner leaned in close, invading the man's personal space in every way he could. 'No, you shut up, dickhead!' he bellowed in Gerrard's ear. 'Shut up and sit down.' He let go of Tony's neck and shoved the old wooden straight chair back under him just in time to catch him.

Tony hit the seat of the chair so hard, it felt like a baseball bat hitting his balls. Another swarm of red and blue dots swirled before his eyes. He swallowed hard and propped his elbows on the scarred table, hanging his head and rubbing weakly at the back of his neck. What was left of his cigarette smoldered in the ashtray, the smoke nauseating him.

Kenner walked away to an old army green metal desk that squatted along one wall of the barren room and picked up a manila file folder. He took his time about it, believing firmly in fucking with a perp's mind. Tony Gerrard wanted out of this room. Let him think that wasn't going to happen any time soon. Let him think that the reason the cops figured they had all the time in the world to question him was because they were damn certain he did the deed.

'You're a sad sack of shit, Tony,' he muttered, thumbing through the file. 'Getting off on this kind of sick torture stuff.'

'I didn't do it,' Tony whispered, pinching the bridge of his nose. He wanted to cry, and he hated Kenner for that. He wanted out of this crackerbox of a room. He wanted to stop thinking about Annie and words like 'torture' and 'murder.'

'Hell, everybody knows you knocked her around.'

'But I never would'a done—' He broke off and swallowed hard as the gossip came back to him in an ugly rush. Everyone in town was talking about what those hikers had found. 'I never would'a done that. Never.'

'You mean, this?' Kenner pulled the crime scene Polaroids out of the file and tossed them on the table.

For one long, terrible second Tony stared at the body of his wife, his brain cataloging the gruesome atrocities – the scarf knotted around her throat, the cuts the knife had made in her breasts and belly and thighs. In that one second the images were forever branded into his memory. The skin, unnaturally pale, mottled with bruises, sliced open in places, torn and ragged in others. And her eyes. Those beautiful big brown eyes, frozen in a stare of pure horror.

'She probably looks worse than when you dumped her body,' Kenner said coldly. 'She was in the bayou a couple days. Lucky there was anything left, what with the fish and the gators and—'

Tony swept the pictures off the table with a cry of anguish, then turned and vomited on the floor, his guts wrenching at the images flashing through his head.

'Annie! Oh, God, Annie!' he cried, the sobs tearing up from his heart. He rose in a half crouch, doubled over by the terrible pain of loss, and stumbled away from the table to sink down on his knees in the corner.

Kenner frowned and sighed. He picked up the snapshots, careful not to look at them, and slipped them back in the folder. The hot, acidic scent of Tony's stomach contents burned his nostrils, but that wasn't what left the bad taste in his mouth.

He had wanted Gerrard to be guilty, had honestly believed he could have committed the crime. A confession would have justified what he had just put Tony Gerrard through. It was a hell of a lot more gratifying to torment a guilty man than a grieving husband.

'You're free to go,' he said in a low voice, then let himself out of the room.

The next door down the hall opened, and Danjermond walked out looking cool and composed, unaffected by what he had seen through the two-way glass.

'My God, you're a ruthless bastard,' he drawled mildly.

Kenner watched him straighten a shirt cuff and align his onyx cuff link with the top stitching. 'No,' he said. 'Whoever killed Annie Delahoussaye-Gerrard is a ruthless bastard. I just mean to catch him.'

Danjermond glanced at him from under his brows. 'You don't think Gerrard is guilty?'

He shook his head as he dug a cigarette out of his shirt pocket and hung it from his lip. 'You saw him.'

'He could be acting. Or perhaps what we witnessed was abject remorse.'

'If he's acting, then he deserves the goddamn Academy Award.' He struck a match and cupped his hands around his cigarette as if he were standing outside in a stiff wind. To banish the sour taste and smell that lingered in his senses, he drew the smoke deep into his lungs and exhaled through his nostrils. 'I got a call in to the sheriff in St. Martin Parish, where they found that last dead girl. A hundred says the same piece of shit did this one.'

He tossed his match down on the floor and ground it to shreds with the toe of his boot. 'I'll catch the son of a bitch,' he swore. 'Nobody does this in my parish and gets away with it.'

The very corners of Danjermond's mouth curled in a sardonic, unamused smile. 'I appreciate your attitude. Killers running around loose don't do my career any good, either.'

Kenner shot him a hard look, his eyes mere slits in his lean, leathery face. 'Fuck your career, Danjermond. I got a wife and two daughters. This maniac comes sniffing around my turf, I'll tear his goddamn throat out.'

He turned and headed for his office. Danjermond fell in step beside him, his stride fluid and graceful beside the sheriff's cowboy swagger. 'Our constituents can be grateful you have the sensibilities of a pit bull, Sheriff.'

'Yeah, and I'm mean enough to take that as a compliment.' He glanced through the window into his office and pulled up short of the door, a headache instantly piercing his temples as he caught a glimpse of Laurel Chandler's profile through the venetian blind. 'Shit. This is all I need. She's probably here to tell me Jimmy Lee Baldwin did it.'

Danjermond gazed between the slats of the blinds, taking in the feminine lines of Laurel Chandler's face and the determined set of her chin. She sat in the chair beside Kenner's desk with her legs crossed, and bent as he watched to scratch a spot on her stockinged calf. 'She does have a reputation for being . . . dogged.'

Kenner snorted and stubbed his cigarette out in the dirt of a potted orange tree that sat beside his secretary's desk. 'She has a reputation for causing trouble, and I don't want any more than I've already got.'

Laurel emerged from her interview with Kenner feeling like she'd just gone three rounds with Dirty Harry. How the man had ever won an election was beyond her. He certainly hadn't gone the route of charming the voters. More likely they had been afraid not to vote for him. A territorial sort, he'd torn into her first for invading his office. Then had come the 'I have better things to do' speech. He calmed down only marginally when she explained herself, explained that the Delahoussayes didn't understand procedure and only wanted someone to act as go-between on their behalf.

Grudgingly he gave her the barest of details concerning the investigation. Because of the priority nature of the case, the autopsy was already being performed. He couldn't say when the body would be released. He wouldn't say if they had any solid physical evidence. No arrests had been made.

'You brought Tony Gerrard in for questioning.'

He narrowed his eyes at her. She couldn't even see the pupils. A muscle ticked in his cheek.

'It's common knowledge, Sheriff. This is a small town.'

He lit a cigarette and slowly went through with the ritual of shaking out the match and taking his first deep drag. 'We brought him in. Had a little chat.'

'I suppose you're aware that his wife had had relationships with a number of other men.'

'You gonna tell me they all did it? It was a goddamn conspiracy, right? You're big on that kind of bullshit.'

'I'm not telling you anything.'

She wanted to tell him to do the anatomically impossible, she thought as she marched down the hall. He had her pegged as a head case, and everything she said he twisted into the ineffectual babblings of a hysterical woman. He wouldn't have believed her if she had told him the earth was round. Of course, Neanderthal that he was, he probably had doubts about that anyway. A nasty insinuation concerning the species residing in Kenner's family tree ran through her head, and she smiled a little at the mental image of orangutans with slitted eyes and cigarettes dangling from their nonexistent lips.

'I've seen people convicted on the basis of a smile like that one.'

Danjermond stepped out of the water fountain alcove, seeming to materialize out of nothing. Laurel's heart jolted, but she managed to keep from shying sideways. She looked up at the district attorney, finding the quiet amusement in his clear green eyes both irritating and inappropriate – just as her smile must have looked.

'I should probably be fined at the very least,' she said with a rueful look. 'Psychic defamation of character.'

He tipped his head. 'Not on the books in the state of Louisiana.'

'Then I'm off the hook as long as Kenner can't read minds.'

'I believe his talents lie in other areas.'

Laurel sniffed and crossed her arms, allowing a little of her anger to sizzle up. 'Yes, I'm sure he's a whiz with a rubber truncheon and thumbscrews, but that's not my idea of a good time.'

'No?' Danjermond chuckled, then the sound faded away and a heavy silence fell between them like a blanket of humidity. His gaze turned speculative and held fast on her face, searching, probing. 'What is, Laurel?' he asked softly.

Something about his question froze her tongue to the roof of her mouth. She had the feeling, as she looked up into that calm, stunningly handsome face that he was running possible scenarios through his head. Hot, dark, erotic. The air around them seemed suddenly charged with his powerful sexuality. She felt it envelop her, felt it penetrate the skirt and blouse she wore and stroke over the silk beneath. A delicate shiver of arousal rippled through her, followed closely by something like revulsion. She wasn't sure she understood either.

'We might discuss it over lunch,' he said quietly, his gaze lingering on her mouth, as if he were imagining watching her lips close over a red, ripe strawberry. He stroked the fingertips of one hand along the stylish silk necktie he wore, smoothing it with a lover's caress. His voice softened to the texture of velvet. 'Or after.'

'That seems a highly improper suggestion, Mr. Danjermond,' Laurel said coolly, wishing fervently that someone else would happen out into the hall and break the sexual tension or at least witness it. But then she had the eerie feeling that no one else would see it or sense it. The signals he was sending out were for her alone.

Sliding his hands into the pockets of his coffee brown trousers, he smiled that all-knowing feline smile that made her feel as if he were a superior life-form who had taken the guise of a mere mortal for amusement. 'I don't believe I've broken any rules by asking you to lunch.'

Once again he had neatly maneuvered her into a corner. The realization annoyed her. If she wanted to make an argument against his statement, she would have to be the one to bring up the topic of sexual tension and implied propositions.

Or maybe she was just imagining the whole thing. Perhaps she had taken such an aversion to Vivian's notions of him as a son-in-law, she was reading into everything he said. Whatever the case, she didn't want to deal with him; she didn't have the energy.

'Thank you for the invitation,' she said smoothly. 'But I'm afraid I already have plans.'

One straight brow lifted. His gaze seemed to intensify, his pale green eyes glowing like precious stones held up to the sun. 'Another man?'

'My aunt. Not that it's any of your business.'

He treated her to a full-fledged smile that was perfectly even, perfectly symmetrical, bright, white, handsome as she imagined all the Danjermonds had been since the days of the Renaissance. 'I like to know if I have competition.'

'I told you before,' Laurel said, edging toward impatience. 'I'm not looking to get involved with anyone at the moment.'

The word 'liar' rang in her head, and she had the distinct feeling

Stephen Danjermond heard it, too. But he would have to call her on it. She wasn't bringing up the subject of Jack Boudreaux. Today she honestly wished she'd never heard the name.

'Sometimes we get things we are not necessarily expecting, though, don't we, Laurel?' he said.

He didn't like her rebuff. She could hear the faintest edge in his smooth, cultured voice, and behind the affable smile his eyes had a coldness about them that hinted at temper. Too bad. She had no intention of becoming entangled with him – emotionally or otherwise.

'Annie Delahoussaye certainly got something she wasn't expecting,' she said, neatly shifting gears to business. God, how appalling that murder seemed safer territory than personal relationships.

'You're here on her behalf, Laurel? For someone who claims not to be interested in going back to work you certainly are spending a great deal of time in the court-house.'

'Her parents asked me to act as their liaison with the sheriff's department,' she said. 'They're devastated, naturally, and Kenner is less than forthcoming, to say nothing of the fact that sympathy is a completely foreign concept to him.'

Danjermond nodded thoughtfully. 'He's a hard man. He would tell you there's no place for sympathy in his work.'

'Yes, well, he'd be wrong.'

'Would he?' he asked, looking doubtful. 'Sympathy can sometimes be equated with weakness, vulnerability. It can draw a person into situations where perspective becomes warped and emotion takes over where logic should rule. We're taught in law school not to allow ourselves to become emotionally involved, aren't we, Laurel? As you well know, the results can be disastrous.'

He couldn't have cut her more cleanly if he had used a scalpel. And he'd done it so subtly, seemingly without effort. And once again, Laurel could say nothing without incriminating herself. She had the distinct feeling he was punishing her for turning down his invitation, but she could hardly accuse him. The best thing she could do was concede to an opponent she was no match for and get the hell out.

She took a very rude, very deliberate look at her watch and said flatly, 'Oh, my, look at the time. I have to be going.'

Danjermond gave her a mocking little half bow. 'Until we meet again, Laurel.'

She left the courthouse feeling battered. Kenner had been bad enough, but she couldn't encounter Stephen Danjermond without feeling she had walked into a tiger's cage. He was beautiful, charismatic, but there was a strength, an ego, a temper there beneath the handsome stripes. This time he had reached out and swiped at her with his elegant paw, and she felt as if his claws had sliced into her as sure and sharp as razor blades. She thanked God she would never have to face him in a courtroom.

The Acura was parked beneath the heavy shade of a live oak at the edge of the courthouse lot. Laurel slid behind the wheel, and the tension that had gripped her in its fist all morning finally let go, leaving her feeling like a puddle of melted Jell-O. She stared across the street for a moment, watching the weathered old men who sat on their bench in front of the hardware store.

They gathered there every morning in their summer hats and short-sleeved shirts, suspenders holding up baggy dark pants. Laurel knew the faces had changed over the years, but she could remember old men sitting there when she had been a small child. They took their places on the bench to watch the day go by, to swap stories and gossip. Today they looked grim, unsmiling, wary of every car that drove past, watchful of strangers. A woman emerged from the store, holding the hand of a daughter who had probably considered herself too old for it just yesterday.

Annie Delahoussaye was on a lot of minds today.

Was she on Jack's mind?

'Shit,' Laurel whispered, her lashes drifting down as weariness weighed like lead on her every muscle — most especially her heart. His image drifted into her mind without her permission, that haunted, brooding look in his eyes, his face hard. She'd seen that look all night, heard his harsh, smoky voice. *I've got enough corpses on my conscience. . . .*

He might have been referring to his work, but he had played the cynical mercenary hack every time she brought the subject up. He wrote horror for the money. He would claim he had no trouble distinguishing fact from fiction. Her thoughts turned back to what little mention he'd made of his life as corporate attorney for Tristar Chemical. Hardly a violent occupation. Still, every time she started to dismiss it, something pulled her back. He had crashed and burned, he'd said, and taken the company down with him. Why?

Intuition told her she would find some of the answers she was looking for in Houston, where Tristar had its headquarters. She had acquaintances there, could make a phone call. . . . Practicality told her not to look. She was far better off leaving Jack and his moods alone. He obviously had problems he needed to work out — or wallow in, as seemed to be his choice. They would be disastrous together, both of them wounded, looking to each other for strength that simply wasn't there. He didn't want her anyway. Not in any permanent sense. They had had some fun together, 'passed a good time' as the Cajuns said. That was all Jack wanted.

She ignored the way that knowledge stung, and reached for the ignition, firing the car's engine and air-conditioning to life. How many times had she said she wasn't looking for a relationship? She was in no emotional condition to enter into one. That she had taken him as a lover was a whole other matter, a matter of letting herself live, of taking

623

something for her own pleasure. She told herself she wanted nothing more than that from him, and did her damnedest to forget the way his arms had felt around her while she cried.

Lunch consisted of stuffed tomatoes and garden-fresh salad that no one seemed to have an appetite for. They sat at the glass-topped table on the back gallery, looking out at the courtyard where old growth was flourishing, now that it was free of choking weeds, and new flowers were growing fuller and more vibrant by the day.

Whether deliberately or subconsciously, Laurel thought Caroline had chosen to eat out here so they would be surrounded by positive affirmations of life and beauty when talk around town all morning had been of death and ugliness. They could sit and feel the breeze sweep under the shade trees and along the gallery, bringing with it the heavy perfume of sweet olive and gardenia. They could listen to the songs of the warblers and buntings and look out on the abundance of life in the garden and try to counterbalance thoughts of death.

'Me, I dunno what dis world comin' to,' Mama Pearl grumbled, wagging her head. She dug a good-size chunk of chicken out of her tomato with a ferocious stab of her fork, but she didn't bring it to her mouth. Setting the fork aside, she heaved a sigh and rubbed a plump hand across her lips, as if to push back the words that might have spilled out. As tears rose, her eyes darted to the courtyard and she stared hard at the old stone fountain with its grubby-faced cherubs cavorting around the base.

Caroline toyed with her salad, turning a ring of black olive over and over with the tines of her fork. Her usual air of command seemed dimmed, subdued by the weight of events, but she was still the head of Belle Rivière, their leader, their rock, and she rose to the occasion as best she could. Drawing in a deep breath to fortify herself, she squared her dainty shoulders beneath the soft white chiffon blouse she wore.

'The world has been a violent place since the days of Cain,' she said quietly. 'It's no worse today. It only seems so because the violence has hit so close to home.'

Mama Pearl gave her a sharp look of disapproval and hefted her bulk up from the table, scraping her chair back. 'You tell dat to T-Grace Delahoussaye. I gots to check my cake.'

Grumbling under her breath, she waddled into the house, her red print cotton shift swishing around her with every step. Caroline watched her go, feeling helpless to do anything to alleviate the grief and worry and anger that had tempers running short and fears running close to the surface of everyone she knew. She turned her gaze to Laurel, who was picking at her chicken salad.

'How are you doing, darlin'?'

'Fine.' The answer was automatic. Caroline ignored it and waited patiently for something closer to the truth.

Resigning herself to the inevitable. Laurel set her fork aside and rested her forearms on the cool glass of the tabletop. 'I feel stronger than I did,' she said, a little amazed by the admission. 'But with all the things that have happened . . . everything I feel myself getting dragged into . . . A part of me would like very much to run away to a resort someplace where I wouldn't know a soul.'

In a gesture of love and an offer of support, Caroline reached across the table and twined her fingers with her niece's. 'But you won't.'

To leave now, with her word given to the Delahoussayes, with tension between her and Savannah, would be the coward's way out. She couldn't walk away and live with herself. 'No, I won't.'

Caroline squeezed her hand, her heart brimming with love, with sympathy. 'Your father would have been so very proud of you,' she said, her voice suddenly husky with emotion. 'I'm proud of you.'

Laurel couldn't think of a single thing she had done to be proud of, but she didn't say so. She didn't say anything for a minute for fear she would burst into tears. For a long moment she stared off at a particularly beautiful cluster of purple clematis that was twining around one of the gallery pillars, and just hung on to her aunt's hand, savoring the contact and the strength that passed to her from someone who loved her unconditionally.

She suspected a great many people in Bayou Breaux were paying special attention to family today, having been struck aware that loved ones could be snatched away in a heartbeat with feelings left unspoken and dreams never realized. Today, life would seem more precious, more urgent, something to be clung to and relished.

Bringing her emotions back in line, she gently extricated her fingers from Caroline's and reached for the stack of mail she had picked up at the post office on her way to the courthouse. 'You've got some interesting-looking letters today,' she said, sorting through the stack. She plucked out several fine-quality envelopes, each with a different postmark – Biloxi, New Orleans, Natchez – all of them addressed in flowing, feminine script, one smelling faintly of jasmine.

Caroline accepted them, a soft smile turning her lips as she perched her reading glasses on her slim, upturned nose and scanned the addresses. 'How lovely to hear from friends on such a terrible day.'

'Old friends from school?' Laurel asked carefully, watching closely as her aunt used a table knife to open the pink one. 'Or business?'

'Mmm . . . just friends.'

Laurel chided herself for her curiosity. Caroline's privacy was her own. Of course, Savannah might have just asked her outright.

'I can't believe Savannah is sleeping in so late,' she murmured, wondering if today might not be the perfect time to start mending the tears in their relationship. Arguments seemed petty and pointless in the face of death, and life seemed so finite. They could take the rest of the day and drive down to Cypremort Point for bluepoint crabs and a view of the gulf at sunset. They would sit together with the salty breeze on their faces and in their hair, and talk and watch the saw grass sway in the shallows while gulls wheeled overhead. 'Do you think I dare wake her up on the pretense of delivering her Visa bill?'

'Hmm? Oh, a—' Caroline glanced up from her letter. 'Savannah isn't here, darlin'.'

'Where did she go?' Laurel asked, annoyed that the perfect day that had painted itself in her mind was going to be put off. 'More to the point, *how* did she go? I had the car all morning.'

'I'm not sure. Perhaps she had a friend pick her up. I couldn't say; I was at the store. Did you have plans?'

'No. It's just that we've been talking about spending some time together. She wanted to do something yesterday, and then Jack showed up.'

'She left here in a state yesterday, I do know that,' Caroline said, folding back a sheet of pink stationery. 'I take it she doesn't approve of your seeing Mr. Boudreaux.'

'I don't think Jack is her problem.' Concern tugged at the corners of Laurel's mouth and furrowed her brow. She wrestled for a moment with the thoughts that had been troubling her since Savannah's blowup, finally deciding they were best shared. 'I'm worried about her. She seems so . . . volatile. Up one minute and down the next. She got into a fight with Annie Gerrard Sunday. A *fist fight*! Aunt Caroline, I'm frightened for her.'

And for myself, she thought, in a small way. The child in Laurel had always depended on Savannah. That child felt lost at the prospect of Savannah's not being dependable any more.

Caroline set her letters aside and slipped her reading glasses off, her expression somber. 'She was seeing a psychiatrist in Lafayette for a while. I think she might have gotten help there, but she wouldn't stay with it.'

Naturally. Just as she never stayed with a job or anything else that might have given her help or a sense of purpose that didn't involve sex. Laurel's hands fisted on the tabletop, and she wished for something she could hit to let off some of the impotent anger that was building inside her. 'She's determined to let the past rule her life, dictate who she is, what she is. We had an awful fight about it the other day. I lost my temper, but it makes me angry to see her throw her life away for something that ended fifteen years ago.'

For a moment Caroline said nothing. She sat quietly toying with one of the heavy gold hoops that hung from her ears and let Laurel's statement hang in the air, let it sink in not for her own benefit, but for her niece's.

'Tell me,' she said at last. 'Do you not still see those children from Scott County in your sleep?'

The abrupt change of subject jolted Laurel for a second. The question brought the faces up in her memory, and she had to force them back into the little compartment she tried to stow them in during the day. 'Yes,' she murmured.

'But that's over and done with,' Caroline said. 'Why can't you let them go?'

'Because *I* failed them,' Laurel said, tensing against the guilt. 'It was *my* fault. I deserve to be haunted by that—'

'No,' Caroline cut her off sharply, her dark eyes bright with the strength of her feelings. 'No,' she said again, softening her tone. 'You did all you could. The outcome was not in your hands. You had no control over the attorney general or the lack of evidence or what other members of the community did, and yet you blame yourself and let that part of your past torment you.'

Laurel didn't try to argue her culpability; she knew what the truth was. The point her aunt was making had little to do with her, anyway.

'Are you saying Savannah blames herself for the abuse?' she asked, incredulous at the thought. 'But what happened was Ross's fault! He forced himself on her. She couldn't possibly believe that was her fault.'

Caroline stroked a fingertip thoughtfully along her cheekbone and raised a delicately arched brow. 'You think not? Savannah is a beautiful, sensual, sexual creature. She always has been. Even as a child she had a certain power over men, and she knew it. You think she hasn't blamed herself for being attractive to Ross or that Ross hasn't taken every opportunity to blame her himself? He is and always has been a weak man, taking credit that isn't his due and shedding blame like water off a duck's back.'

A fresh spring of hate for Ross Leighton welled up inside Laurel, and she recognized that a large part of her anger was for the fact that Ross had never been made to pay for his crime. Justice had never been served. Some of the blame for that was hers, she knew, and the guilt for that was terrible.

If only she had found the courage to tell their mother or go to Aunt Caroline. But she hadn't. Vivian was still in ignorance of her husband's atrocities. Caroline had found out the truth years after the fact. There had been no justice for Savannah . . . so Laurel had spent her life seeking justice for others.

I'm not trying to atone for anything!

God, what a lie. What a hypocrite she was.

Caroline rose gracefully from her chair, tucking her letters into a patch pocket on the full yellow skirt that hugged her tiny waist and swirled around her calves. She came around the table and slipped her arms around Laurel's shoulders, hugging her tight from behind. 'The past is always with us, Laurel,' she said gently. 'It's a part of us we can't ignore or abandon. And it's not always easy to keep it behind us, where it belongs. You'd do well to remember that for yourself, as well as for your sister.'

She pressed a kiss to her temple and went inside, leaving Laurel alone on the gallery to listen to the bird-song and to think.

When her thoughts had chased each other around her brain sufficiently to give her a headache, Laurel turned her attention back to the mail, thumbing through the bills and pleas from missions. At the back of the stack was a plain white envelope with no address, return or otherwise.

Puzzled, she opened the flap and extracted not a letter, but a cheap gold necklace with a small golden butterfly dangling from it. She lifted the chain and watched the butterfly turn and sway, and a strange shiver passed over her, like a chill wind that had slipped out of another dimension to crawl over her skin.

The wheels of her mind turned automatically, searching for the most logical explanation for the necklace. It was Savannah's – though Savannah's tastes were much more expensive. She had forgotten it on the seat of the car – but why was it sealed in an envelope?

No answer satisfied all the questions, and none explained the knot of nerves tingling at the base of her neck.

In his office in the Partout Parish courthouse, Duwayne Kenner leaned over his desk, hammers pounding inside his temples, acid churning in his gut. He leaned over the fax copies of crime reports from four other parishes. His eyes scanned the photographs the sheriff from St. Martin had brought along with him of Jennifer Verret, who had been found dead Saturday morning, strangled with a silk scarf and mutilated. On the other side of the desk, Danjermond stood looking pensive, twisting his signet ring around on his finger.

'There's no doubt in my mind,' Kenner growled, his voice turned to gravel by two packs of Camels. 'We're dealing with the same killer.'

'Everything matches?'

'So far. We'll have more details when the lab reports on Annie Gerrard come in, but it's all there – the silk scarf, the same pattern of knife wounds. Most importantly, details that were kept away from the press match, eliminating the possibility of a copycat.'

'Such as?'

'Such as the markings on the wrists and ankles, and the fact that each woman had items of jewelry taken off her body. Sick bastard likely keeps them as souvenirs,' he mumbled, his eyes narrowing to slits as he took in the savagery one human being could commit against another. 'Well, by God, I'll find out when I catch him. I swear I will.'

19

One of Vivian's more annoying traits was her sporadic attempts at spontaneity. Laurel recalled the times during her childhood when her mother would snap out of her day-in-day-out routine of clubs and civic responsibilities and life as mistress of Beauvoir, and scramble frantically to do something spontaneous, something she thought terribly clever or fun, which the events seldom proved to be. There was always an air of desperation about them and a set of expectations that were never achieved. Not at all like the spur-of-the-moment notions of Laurel's father, which had always been unfailingly wonderful in one way or another, never planned, never entered into with a set of criteria or goals.

'Seize the moment and take what it gives you,' Daddy had always said with a simple joy for life glowing in his handsome face.

Vivian had always seized her moments with grasping, greedy hands and tried to wring out of them the things she wanted. Laurel had always felt sorry for her mother because of it. It wasn't in Vivian's makeup to be spontaneous. That she felt compelled to try, and tried too hard, had always left Laurel feeling sad, particularly when one of Vivian's failed attempts led her into yet another spell of depression.

Perhaps that was why, when Vivian had called to invite her to have dinner out with her – dinner and 'girl talk,' God forbid – Laurel hadn't managed to find an excuse during that slim five-second window of opportunity when lies can go undetected over the phone lines. Or perhaps her reasons had more to do with the day and the thoughts she had had of family and the fickleness of life.

Savannah would have no doubt had a scathing commentary on the subject. But as Savannah had yet to return from wherever she had spent the day, Laurel didn't have to listen to it. She accepted the invitation with an air of resignation and did her best to turn off the internal mechanism of self-examination.

They sat in one of the small, elegant dining rooms of the Wisteria Golf and Country Club, chatting over equally elegant meals of stuffed quail and fresh sea bass. The club was housed in a Greek revival mansion on what had once been the largest indigo plantation in the parish. The house and grounds had been meticulously restored and maintained, right down to the slave cabins that sat some two hundred yards behind the mansion and now served as storage sheds for garden equipment and between-round hangouts for the caddies – who were quite often black youths. No one at Wisteria worried about offending them with the comparison between caddies and slaves, and there were no other people of color to be offended other than hired help, because Wisteria was, always had been, and always would be an all-white establishment.

Laurel poked at her sea bass and thought longingly of bluepoint crabs and the colors of the Gulf sky at sunset, the sound of the sea and gulls, the tang of salt air. Instead, she had a grouper glaring up at her from a Limoges plate, green velvet portieres at tall French doors, a Vivaldi concerto piping discreetly over cleverly hidden speakers, and the artificial cleanliness of central air-conditioning. Her mother sat across from her, completely in her element, ash blond hair sleekly coiffed, a vibrant blue linen blazer bringing out the color of her eyes. Beneath the jacket she wore a chic white sheath splashed with the same shade of blue. Sapphire teardrops dripped from her earlobes.

'The world has gone stark raving mad,' Vivian declared, spearing a fresh green bean. She chewed delicately, as a lady should, breaking her train of thought absolutely to savor the taste of her food. After washing it down with a sip of chardonnay, she picked up the thread of the conversation and went on. 'Women being murdered in our backyards, practically. Lunatics running loose through town in the dead of night.

'Tell me why on earth anyone would want to vandalize St. Joseph's Rest Home, scaring those poor elderly people witless.'

Laurel went on point like a bird dog, straightening in her chair, her fork hovering over her mutilated fish. 'St. Joseph's?'

'Yes.' Vivian went on with appropriate disgust as she took a knife after her quail and dismembered it. 'Spray-painted obscenities outside one of the rooms, left a terrible mess on the lawn that I simply won't even speak of in public or anywhere else, banged on the windows, shouting and carrying on. It was an absolute disgrace, the things that were done.'

'Did they catch this person?' Laurel asked carefully.

'No. She ran screaming into the night.'

Foreboding quivered down Laurel's spine. 'She?'

'Oh, yes. A woman. Can you imagine that? I mean, one might expect a certain kind of hooliganism from a young man, but a woman?' Vivian shuddered at the thought of the natural order of things being so badly twisted. 'I volunteer at the library, as you know. This was my day to take books to the rest home. Ridilia Montrose assists the activities coordinator there on Wednesdays. You remember Ridilia, don't you, Laurel dear? Her daughter Faith Anne was the one who had such extensive orthodontia and then wound up being elected homecoming queen at Old Miss? Married a financier from Birmingham? Ridilia says it was most definitely a female, according to the night staff.'

630

She pressed her lips into a thin line of disapproval and shook her head, setting her sapphires swinging. 'Terrible goings-on. I swear, some people just breed indiscriminately and let their children grow up running like wild dogs. Blood will tell, you know,' she said, as she always said. And, as always, it made Laurel grit her teeth on a contradiction she had been trained not to voice. 'Anyway, the person I feel most sorry for is that poor Astor Cooper. All this went on right outside her window. Can you imagine?'

What little Laurel had eaten of her meal turned into a lump of grease in her stomach. 'Astor Cooper?' she managed weakly as her mind pieced together facts without her consent.

'Yes. Her husband is Conroy Cooper, the Pulitzer Prize-winning author? Such a charming man. So generous to the local charities. It's just a tragedy that his wife has to be so afflicted. Alzheimer's, you know. And I'm told her people up in Memphis are just lovely. It's such a shame. Ridilia said Mr. Cooper was absolutely beside himself over the vandalism. He's so very loyal to his wife, you know. . . .'

Laurel placed her hands in her lap, fighting the urge to grip the table to steady herself. While her mother sat across from her, going on about Conroy Cooper's sterling character, that same voice drifted out of the back of her mind, admonishing her for her manners. *Young ladies do not lay their hands on the table, Laurel. . . .* Then Savannah's face came to mind, her expression sly. *His wife has Alzheimer's. He put her in St. Joseph's. . . . I hear she doesn't know her head from a hole in the ground.*

Sick dread ran down her throat like icy fingers. It couldn't be, she told herself. It simply couldn't be. Savannah had her problems, but she wouldn't resort to – As if to mock her defense, her memory hurled up a picture of her sister locked in combat with Annie Delahoussaye, screaming like a banshee and whirling like a dervish around Frenchie's.

'Laurel? Laurel?' Her mother's sharp tone prodded her back to reality. Vivian was frowning at her. 'André would like to know if you've finished with your fish.'

'I'm sorry.' Laurel scrambled to compose herself, ducking her head and smoothing her napkin on her lap. She glanced up at the patient André, who watched her with soulful brown eyes set in a bloodhound's face. 'Yes, thank you. It was excellent. My apologies to the chef that I was unable to finish it.'

As the dinner plates were whisked away and the tablecloth dusted for crumbs, Vivian studied her daughter and sipped her wine. 'I hear you've been to the courthouse twice this week. They're seeing more of you than I am.'

An untrained ear may not have picked up the note of censure. Laurel received it loud and clear. 'I'm sorry, Mama. I got caught up helping the Delahoussayes.'

'Hardly the sort of people—'

Laurel brought a hand up to stop her like a crossing guard. 'Can we please skip this conversation? We're not going to agree. We'll both end up angry. Could we just not have it?'

Vivian straightened into her queen's posture on her chair, her chin lifting, her eyes taking on the same cold gleam as the sapphires she wore. 'Certainly,' she said stiffly. 'Never mind that I have only your best interests at heart.'

That Vivian had never had any interests at heart but her own was a truth Laurel chose to keep to herself. If she provoked her mother into an argument in public, she would never be forgiven. A part of her thought she shouldn't care, but the plain truth was Vivian was the only mother she had, and after a lifetime of walking on eggshells to gain approval, to garner what Vivian would consider love, she was probably not going to change. Just as Vivian would never change.

The pendulum of Vivian's moods swung yet again as she turned toward the entrance to the dining room. Like the sun coming out from behind a thunderhead, a smile brightened her face. Laurel turned to get a look at whoever had managed to perform such a miracle and caught another unpleasant surprise square on the chin.

'Stephen!' Vivian said, offering her beringed hands to Danjermond as he strode to their table. He took them both and bent over one to bestow a courtly kiss. Vivian beamed. All but purring, she turned toward Laurel. 'Look, Laurel dear, Stephen is here! Isn't this a lovely surprise?'

In a pig's eye. Laurel forced a smile that looked as if she had a lip full of novocaine. 'Mr. Danjermond.'

'Stephen, you're just in time for dessert. Do say you'll join us.'

He treated her to a dazzling square smile. 'How could I decline an offer to spend time with two of the most beautiful belles in the parish?'

Vivian blushed on cue and batted her lashes, impeccably schooled in the feminine art of flirtation. 'Well, this belle needs to powder her nose. Do keep Laurel company, won't you?'

'Of course.'

As she walked away from the table, Danjermond slid into the empty chair to Laurel's right. He was, as she was, dressed in the same clothes he had worn to the courthouse that morning – the coffee brown suit, the ivory shirt and stylish tie – but he had somehow managed to come through the day without a wrinkle, while Laurel felt wilted and rumpled. Something about his elegance made her want to comb her hair and take her glasses off, but she refrained from doing either.

'You're angry with me, Laurel,' he said, simply.

Laurel crossed her legs and smoothed her skirt, taking her time in replying. Outside, a squall line had tumbled up from the Gulf and was threatening rain. Wind pulled at the fingers of the palmetto trees that lined the putting green. She stared out at them through the French doors, debating the wisdom of what she wanted to say.

'I don't like the games you play, Mr. Danjermond,' she said at last, meeting his cool green gaze evenly.

He arched a brow. 'You think my being here is part of a conspiracy, Laurel? As it happens, I dine here often. You do concede that I have to eat, don't you? I am, after all, merely human.'

The light in the peridot eyes danced as if at some secret amusement. Whether it was her he was laughing at or the line about his being a mere mortal, she couldn't tell. Either way, she had no intention of joining in the joke.

'Anything new on the murder?' she asked, toying with the stem of her water glass.

He plucked a slice of French bread from the basket on the table, tore off a chunk, and settled back in his chair with the lazy arrogance of a prince. Chewing thoughtfully, he studied her. 'Kenner released Tony Gerrard. He feels the murder is the work of the Bayou Strangler.'

'And what do you think? You don't think Tony Gerrard might have pulled a copycat?'

'No, because if he had, he would have screwed up. Our killer is very clever. Tony, regrettably,' he picked a white fleck of bread off his tie and flicked it away, 'is not.'

'You sound almost as if you admire him – the killer.'

He regarded her with a look of mild reproach. 'Certainly not. He intrigues me, I admit. Serial killers have fascinated students of criminal science for years.' He tore another chunk off the fresh, warm bread, closed his eyes, and savored the rich, yeasty aroma of it before slipping it into his mouth. As he swallowed, his lashes raised like lacy black veils. 'I'm as horrified by these crimes as anyone, but at the same time, I have a certain' – he searched for the word, picking it cleanly and carefully – '*clinical* appreciation for a keen mind.'

As he said it, Laurel had the distinct impression that he was probing hers. She could feel the power of his personality arching between them, reaching into her head to explore and examine.

'What do you think of sharks, Laurel?'

The change of direction was so abrupt, she thought it was a wonder she didn't get a whiplash. 'What should I think of them?' she said, annoyed and puzzled. 'Why should I think of them at all?'

'You would think of them if you found yourself overboard in the ocean,' Danjermond pointed out. He leaned forward in his chair, warming to his subject, his expression serious. 'In all of nature, they are the perfect predator. They fear nothing. They kill with frightening efficiency.

'Serial killers are the sharks of our society. Without souls, without fear of recrimination. Predators. Clever, ruthless.' He tore off another chunk of bread and chewed thoughtfully. 'A fascinating comparison, don't you think, Laurel?'

'Frankly, I think it's stupid and dangerously romantic,' she said bluntly as her temper began to snap inside her like a live wire. Ignoring the dictates of her upbringing, she planted her fists on the table and glared at the district attorney. 'Sharks kill to survive. This man is killing for the pure, sick enjoyment of seeing women suffer. He needs to be stopped, and he needs to be punished.'

Danjermond scrutinized her pose, her expression, the passion in her voice, and nodded slightly, like a critic approving of an actor's skills. 'You were born for the prosecutor's office, Laurel,' he declared, then his gaze intensified, sharpened, as if he had sensed something in her. Slowly, gracefully, he leaned forward across the table until he was just a little too close. 'Or were you *made* for it?' he murmured.

Laurel met his gaze without flinching, though she was trembling inside. The air between them vibrated with Danjermond's potent sexuality. He was close enough that she could pick up the hint of a dark, exotic cologne. Somewhere outside the cube of tension that boxed them in, thunder rumbled and fat raindrops spat down out of the clouds. The wind hurled handfuls under the veranda, pelting the panes in the French doors.

'You do fascinate me, Laurel,' he whispered. 'You have an astonishing sense of chivalry for a woman.'

Vivian chose that moment to return to the table, and Laurel thought that if she was never grateful to her mother for anything else, she was grateful for this interruption. Stephen Danjermond made the short hairs stand up on the back of her neck. The less she had to be alone with him, the better.

He sat with them for coffee. Vivian ordered bread pudding and enjoyed it with a side order of political talk and chatter about the upcoming League of Women Voters dinner. Laurel sat studying the stubs of her finger-nails, wishing she were anywhere else. Her thoughts turned unbidden to Jack, and she wondered, as she stared out at the rain, where he was tonight, what he was feeling.

Judge Monahan and his wife were shown into the dining room, capturing Danjermond's attention, and the district attorney abandoned them for more influential company. While Vivian took care of the bill, Laurel took her first deep breath in thirty minutes.

They walked out onto the veranda together and stood watching as the valets dashed out into the rain to retrieve their cars.

'This was lovely, darling,' Vivian said, smiling benevolently. 'I'm glad we could have this evening together after that unpleasantness with your sister Sunday. I swear, I don't know at times how she could even be mine, the way she behaves.'

'Mama, don't,' Laurel snapped, then softened the order with a request. 'Please.'

Instead of pique, Vivian chose to move on as if Savannah had never been mentioned at all. 'I'm so glad Stephen was able to join us for a little while. He's very highly thought of in these parts and in Baton Rogue, as well. With his family connections and his talent, there's no telling how far he might go.' Her white Mercedes arrived under the portico, but she made no move toward it, turning instead to give her daughter a shrewd look. 'As I walked across the dining room tonight, I couldn't help thinking what a handsome couple the two of you would make.'

'I appreciate the thought, Mama,' Laurel lied, 'but I'm not interested in Stephen Danjermond.'

Disapproval flickered in Vivian's light eyes. She reached up impatiently and brushed at a wayward strand of Laurel's hair, succeeding in making her feel ten years old. 'Don't tell me you're interested in Jack Boudreaux,' she said tightly.

Laurel stepped back from her mother's hand. 'Would it matter if I were? I'm a grown woman, Mama. I can chose my own men.'

'Yes, but you do such a poor job of it,' Vivian said cuttingly. 'I asked Stephen about Jack Boudreaux—'

'Mama!'

'He told me the man was disbarred from practicing law because he was at the heart of the Sweetwater chemical waste scandal in Houston.' Laurel's eyes widened automatically at the name 'Sweetwater.' Gratified, Vivian went on with relish. 'Not only that, but it isn't any wonder he writes those gruesome books. Everyone in Houston says he killed his wife.'

If her mother said anything after that, Laurel didn't hear it. She didn't hear the murmured words of parting, didn't feel the compulsory kiss on her cheek, noticed only in the most abstract of ways that Vivian was being ushered into her car and the gleaming white Mercedes was sliding out into the darkening night.

She stood on the veranda in a puddle of amber light from the carriage lanterns that flanked the elegant carved doors to the Wisteria. Beyond the pillars that supported the roof, rain pounded down out of the swollen clouds and splattered against the glossy black pavement of the drive. And it was Jack's voice she heard. *'I've got enough corpses on my conscience. . . .'*

He wanted to kill somebody.

Jimmy Lee stalked the confines of his steamy, shabby bungalow in his underwear, frustration bubbling inside him, gurgling in a low growl at the back of his throat as he recounted all the shit mucking up his road to fame and fortune.

The cheap secondhand television he had picked up at Earlene's Used-a-Bit sat on an old crate in the corner. Instead of his own regularly scheduled hour of glory, the screen was filled with the flickering image of Billy Graham on a crusade to save the heathen communist souls of

Croatia. A rerun hastily dug up to take the place of the fiasco that had been taped the day before at the old Texaco station.

The horizontal hold was slipping like fingers on a greased pig, the picture jumping up, catching, jumping up, catching. Passing the set on his circuit around the room, Jimmy Lee gave it a smack along the side that served only to send the volume blaring.

Swearing, he fumbled with the knob, managing to break it off in his hand. The control on his temper snapped just as readily, and he grabbed a lamp off an imitation wood end table and hurled it at the wall, the horrific crash drowning out Billy Graham right in the middle of his rage against the excesses of modern life.

Fuck Billy Graham. Jimmy Lee turned from the set, ignoring it even though it was rattling with the wrath of the master televangelist. The guy had one foot in the grave. He was old hat, passé, not in touch with what needy fanatics of the nineties wanted. In another few years, Jimmy Lee would be the one crusading around the world, begging the faithful of all races to stand up and be counted – and, most importantly, to stand up and have their money counted.

He'd be there, at the top, at the pinnacle, worshiped. And he wouldn't wear anything but tailor-made white silk suits. Hell, he'd even have tailor-made white silk underwear. He did love the feel of cool white silk. He'd have sheets of silk and curtains and white silk socks and white silk ties. Silk, the feel of money and sex. White, the color of purity and angels. The dichotomy appealed to him.

He'd get there, he promised himself, no matter what he had to do, no matter who got in his way.

Immediately several faces came to mind. Annie Delahoussaye-Gerrard, whose corpse had upstaged him in the local news. Savannah Chandler, whose taste for adventure dragged his thoughts away from his mission. Her sister, Laurel Goody Two Shoes, who plagued him like a curse. Bitches. His life was infested with bitches. Good for nothing but slaking a man's baser needs. On the television, a fat white broad who looked like Jonathan Winters in drag was belting out a chorus of 'How Great Thou Art.' Inside Jimmy Lee, the restless hunger burned. The night beckoned like a harlot, hot, stormy, tempestuous, and he cursed women in his best televangelist voice for leading him into temptation.

Jack prowled the grounds of L'Amour, too restless to be hemmed in by walls. He hadn't slept in . . . what? Two days? He'd lost track of time, lost track of everything but thoughts of death and worthiness . . . and Laurel. He couldn't get her out of his mind. Such indomitable honor, so much courage. He couldn't help caring about her. She was too pure, too brave, too good.

Too good for the like of you, T-Jack . . .

Dieu, what irony, as twisted as a lover's knot, that the most caring thing he could do for her would be to not care about her at all. Everything he touched died. Everything he wanted withered just within his grasp. He had no right to take her as part of his penance for other sins.

He walked down to the bank of the bayou and stood in the deep moon shadows of the live oak, staring out at the glassy water, the *pirogue* that bobbed at the end of the dock. The night sang around him, a chorus of frog song and insects in between thundershowers. A breeze teased the ends of the moss that hung down from the branches, and they swayed heavily, like ropes on the gallows.

He could see Evie's face hanging there in front of him, pale and pretty even in death, her beautiful dark eyes full of accusation and anger and disappointment. Evie, so trusting, so loving. He had loved her so carelessly, had taken so casually the precious gift she had made of her heart. Shallow, selfish bastard that he was, he had taken all she offered as if it were his due, part of the spoils of his success.

The guilt that weighed on him was heavier than anything in this world. It pressed down on him from above, in on him from all sides. He jerked around in a circle, looking for an escape route and finding none. He tried to back away, but came up against the rough trunk of the live oak, the bark biting into his back through the thin fabric of his T-shirt as the guilt pressed in on him.

Tipping his head back, he closed his eyes tight against the pain, and scalding tears trickled in a stream across his temples and into his hair. There were no adjectives in his writer's mind to describe the anguish, no words for the way it raked through his heart.

'*Bon Dieu, Evangeline, sa me fait de le pain. Sa me fait de le pain.*'

He whispered the words over and over, a hoarse, broken chant for forgiveness, a mantra for relief from the terrible weight of his remorse. But he was granted no pardon. He knew he deserved none, because no matter how sorry he was, Evie would always be dead. And all the dreams she had dreamed would be dead. And all the babies she had planned to love would never be at all.

Because of him.

'*Sa me fait de le pain,*' he mumbled, his face contorting against the pain. He turned into the trunk of the tree and pressed his cheek against the corrugated surface, clinging to the tree as regret wrung tears from him with merciless hands.

Sweet, sweet Evie, his wife.

Sweet, sweet Annie, like family.

Sweet, sweet Laurel . . .

Bad Jack Boudreaux. Never good enough. Not worthy of love, never meant for a family. Never anything a decent woman should want. A bastard, a cad, a killer.

What a cruel lie to think he could have anything. Better not to care at all than watch something so precious, something so deeply desired, slip through his grasp like smoke, like a magician's trick – there and gone in a heartbeat.

As fragile as life – there and gone in a heartbeat.

Whining softly with concern, Huey padded up to him and nosed the hand that hung limp at his side, sniffing for trouble or a treat. The dog's rough pink tongue slid along his palm hesitantly, offering comfort and sympathy, and Jack pulled away.

'Get outta here,' he growled, swinging an arm at the dog.

The hound scuttled back clumsily, ears cocked, his head tilted in a quizzical expression. He woofed softly, falling into a play-bow and wagging his slender wand of a tail.

'Get outta here!' Jack roared.

All the anger and hurt that had gathered into a hard ball inside him burst like a nova and sent a hot, white rage through him. It tore out of him in a wild cry, and he lashed out at the dog, the toe of his boot just grazing Huey's rib cage. The dog let out a yelp of betrayal and fright, and ran ten feet away to stand cowering, looking at Jack with his mismatched eyes as hurt and innocent as a child's.

'Get the hell away from me!' Jack snapped. 'I don' have a dog! I don' have a dog,' he repeated, the adrenaline spent, his voice a ragged whisper. 'I don' have nothin'.'

And he turned and walked away from the hound, from L'Amour, and disappeared into the shadows of the night.

20

Thunder rolls like distant cannon fire. Clouds scud across the night sky like tattered wisps of smoke. The battlefield runs red.

The captive taunts and screams in the night in the swamp. Agony like a wild euphoria fills the air with electricity and the sweet, cloying scent of blood. Desperation and hate. Need and desire. Emotions twist and tear apart, overwhelming both captive and captor. The walls of the shack tremble with the terrible power of dark needs unleashed in the predator and in the prey lashed to the bed.

More than the hunter had bargained for. Madness strips away control, pulls even the soulless over its edge and into the maelstrom.

Outside, the wind rips through the trees, lays flat the slender stalks that grow in the shallows. The creatures of the night bolt and shy, heads turning, eyes wide, nostrils scenting the air as they turn toward the eye of a vortex of violence. The moon punches a hole in the blackness, but the thunder rolls nearer, and lightning fractures the sky like cracks in glass.

The storm comes. Without. Within. Savage and wild. Screaming. Slashing. Rain pelts the bayou and tears at tender growth. Blood spatters walls, prey, and predator. The silk tightens. The end rushes up from the black depths of hell. The moment explodes with power unimagined. With triumph, with defeat, with release from torment – torment from within and without.

The wind dies. The storm wanes. The need ebbs. Control settles in place like dust. Calm returns, and logic with it.

Another dead whore for the unsuspecting to find. Another crime committed to go unsolved. The predator smiles in the blood-drenched night. An adversary might suspect, but none will believe her.

Laurel didn't awaken, she was torn from sleep. In the middle of a dark, disturbing dream, cold, frantic hands reached into her psyche and pulled her out of one realm of existence and into another. She emerged gasping for air, like a swimmer breaking the surface after a long dive in frigid waters. The air around her was warm and moist, a pocket of heat and humidity that had sucked in through the French doors to escape the storm. The room was dark and still, a stillness that held something other than simple quiet. Loss. She felt alone in a way she had never felt before in her life, and her thoughts turned automatically toward Savannah. She had never been alone; she had always had Savannah.

Heart bumping hard against her breastbone, she fought to untangle her legs from the sheet and raced out onto the balcony in nothing but the camisole and slip she had fallen asleep wearing. Down the corridor she ran to the set of doors that opened into her sister's room. She fumbled with the latch and threw them back, stumbling as she pitched herself into the bedroom.

The stillness lingered here, too, hanging like a shroud. An unseen hand closed around Laurel's throat as she looked around the room. The bed was unmade, empty, the covers left in a drift, pillows strewn everywhere. It looked the same as the last time she had seen it. She tried to swallow the fear that crowded her tonsils and turned slowly, taking in the jumble of jars and pots and bottles on the dressing table, the discarded clothes draped over chairs and abandoned on the floor. There was no way of telling when last Savannah had occupied the room.

A chill raced over her and seeped bone-deep into her. Tears pooled in her eyes. She twisted her hands together, pacing beside the bed. 'Don't be stupid, Laurel,' she muttered, her voice cutting and harsh. 'Savannah has slept elsewhere more times than you can count. Just because she isn't here tonight – that doesn't mean anything. She's with a lover, that's all.'

To distract herself, she tried to think of which one it might be. Ronnie Peltier with his jackhammer penis. Taureau Hebert – the man Savannah had fought over with Annie. Jimmy Lee Baldwin – who preached morals and played bondage games. Conroy Cooper – whose invalid wife had been terrorized only the night before.

The tag lines that accompanied each name swarmed in Laurel's mind like gnats. She was trained to add up facts as an accountant does a row of figures. She was trained to put puzzle pieces together in her sleep. Tonight she wanted to do neither. The subtotal of the column, the picture that began to take shape – both gave an answer she didn't want to know.

Standing beside the bed, she leaned over and gathered up Savannah's champagne silk robe, bringing the elegant fabric to her cheek. Cool, soft as a whisper, smelling of Obsession. She didn't want to think that Savannah was ill. She didn't want to face the truth that the sister who had mothered her and shielded her had declined to this point without her doing anything but judging. How many times had she wished Savannah would block out the past, rise above it, get beyond what Ross Leighton had done to her? While Laurel herself had lived to atone for that same past, ignoring her martyrdom, calling it a career.

Tears spilled across the silk, and she wished with all her heart her sister would walk through the door so she could go into Savannah's arms and beg her forgiveness. But no one came through the door. Only the empty room heard her cry.

Drained, she tossed the robe back on the rumpled bed and wandered back out onto the balcony. The latest fit of rain had passed, leaving everything dripping. Moonlight caught on droplets, turning them to diamonds. The wind rustled restlessly in the trees. Laurel curled an arm around the pillar outside her own room and leaned against it, her gaze traveling the distance to L'Amour.

Some people said it was haunted. She wondered if the ghosts that haunted Jack had anything to do with the history of the house, or if they were his own, brought here with him from Texas.

He'd been at the heart of the Sweetwater incident, Vivian had said. Sweetwater was a Houston subdivision built by developers that touted the good life, a place to raise families. A little piece of heaven that backed onto a little piece of hell. Illegally buried in the field beyond, drums of chemical waste poisoned the ground. Laurel hadn't followed the case except in snatches caught on the nightly news. She had been wrapped up in legal battles of her own. She remembered the barrels had been almost impossible to trace. The trail had led from dummy company to dummy company.

Jack had unraveled the snare for the feds. He was the best man for the job, she supposed, because, if Vivian's information was correct, he had been the one to lay the paper trail away from Tristar. If she hadn't known him, she would have called him a dozen names. Ruthless, godless, greedy bastard would have been one of the nicer ones. But she did know him. She knew he had clawed his way up through the ranks because he thought he needed to prove himself. What must it have done to him to reach the peak only to find out he was on the wrong mountain? He said he had crashed and burned and taken the company down with him.

And his wife?

The word lay bitter on Laurel's tongue. She might have said she didn't want him, didn't want any kind of a lasting relationship, but the bald truth was she didn't want to think of his loving someone else.

But had he loved her, or had he killed her?

A light winked on in one of the second-story windows of L'Amour, faint, as if it came from a room within the depths of the house. Faint, yet it pulled at her like a beacon. She needed to know who he really was. Which Jack stood behind the final facade? The shark, the rogue, the man who claimed he didn't care about anyone but himself, or the man who had held her and offered her comfort, who had come to her rescue, who had distracted her from problems and fears?

She couldn't see him as a killer. Killers didn't warn potential victims away or walk them home to keep them safe. No, 'homicidal' wasn't a word she could apply to Jack. Troubled. Angry. Wounded.

Wounded. The word struck a chord inside her. The light in the old house beckoned.

Jack climbed the stairs to the second floor, bone tired, his body aching, begging for sleep. But he knew his mind would never grant the wish. Not tonight. Ignoring the rustlings of mice in a pile of fallen wallpaper down the hall, he shuffled into his bedroom and flicked on the lamp that perched on his desk a level above the old black Underwood typewriter. A white page glared up at him, reminding him not of deadlines or plot twists, but of Jimmy Lee Baldwin. Jimmy Lee standing above his devoted followers, asking them where demented minds get the inspiration to kill.

Their eyes meet in the dim light of the woods. Predator and prey. Recognition sparks. Realization dawns. Awareness arcs between them. Strange needs commingle. Dark desires intertwine. It is understood that the game will end in death. She opens her arms to welcome it, to end the torment that has haunted her life.

A slim silver blade gleams in the dark. . . .

What followed was death, presented in a way that was disturbingly seductive, poetically artistic, gruesome and graphic, and frightening as hell.

That was his job – to frighten people, to keep them awake nights and tighten their nerves until every sound heard in a lonely house held the potential for unspeakable terror. People called it entertainment, not inspiration. He wouldn't think otherwise. To believe it inspired meant to take responsibility, and everybody knew Jack Boudreaux didn't take responsibility for anyone or anything.

'They say she never met him here.'

Jack's head came up, and he looked toward the door, not entirely certain what he was seeing was real. Laurel stood just outside the chipped white door frame, against a background of black. A pale portrait of a woman in a flowing skirt painted with old cabbage roses, a blue cotton blouse with the tails hanging down. She was a vision, an angel, something he should never have touched. Better to have longed from a distance and had her only in his imagination. No one could take that away.

'Madame Deveraux,' she said and took a step nearer. 'Her wealthy, married lover, August Chapin, built this place for her. Everyone in the parish knew. He flaunted his obsession for her, much to the shame of his poor wife.'

Jack found his voice with an effort. 'She never met him here?'

'Mr. Chapin, yes. The man she truly loved, no.' She walked into the room slowly, lingering by the tall French doors, out of the glow of the desk light. 'She loved a man named Antoine Gallant. A no-account Cajun trapper. He refused to set foot in the house Chapin built to house her as a whore. They met in secret in a cabin in the swamp.

'Of course, they were found out. His pride smarting sorely, Chapin challenged Gallant to a duel, which he meant to win by tampering with the pistols. Madame Deveraux learned of the plot just minutes before the duel was to take place. She rushed to warn her love, but the men had already stepped off the distance and had turned to take aim. In order to save Antoine, she hurled herself in front of him and took Chapin's shot herself. She died in Antoine's arms.'

She wandered to the old rolltop desk and stood behind it with her hands resting on the high back. Her expression was somber, searching as she slowly scanned the room with her eyes. 'I grew up hearing her spirit still haunted this house.'

Jack shrugged, avoiding the penetrating stare she turned on him. 'I haven't seen her.'

'Well,' she murmured, 'you have ghosts of your own.'

Oui. More than you know, angel.

'Someone mentioned Sweetwater today,' Laurel said, treading carefully. 'You were Tristar's man, weren't you?'

He smiled bitterly and took a bow, backing away from the desk. '*C'est vrai*, you got it in one, sugar. Jack Boudreaux, star shyster. Wanna bury some poison and get away with it? I'm your man. I can tie the trail in a Gordian knot that loops around and around, and twists and doubles back and dead-ends. Holding companies, dummy corporations, the works.' He jammed his hands at the waist of his jeans and stared up at the intricate plasterwork medallion on the ceiling, marveling not at it but at his own past life. 'I was so clever, so bright. Working my way up and up, never caring who I stepped on as I climbed that ladder. The end always justified the means, you know.'

'In the end, you brought them down.'

One dark brow curving, he pinned her with a look. 'And you think that makes me a hero? If I set houses on fire, then put the fires out after the people inside had all burned, would I be a hero?'

'That would depend on your motives and intent.'

'My motives were selfish,' he said harshly, pacing back and forth along the worn ruby rug. 'I wanted to be punished. I wanted everyone associated with me to be punished. For what *I* did.'

'To the people in Sweetwater?' she asked cautiously, studying him from beneath the shield of her lashes.

He halted, watching her intently out of the corner of his eye, old instincts scenting a trap. 'Where are you trying to lead me, counselor?' he asked, his voice a low, dangerous purr. Slowly, he moved toward her, his gait deceptively lazy, his gaze as hard as granite behind a devil's smile, one hand raised to wag a finger in warning. 'What kind of game are you playin', *'tite chatte*?'

Laurel curled her fingers into the fabric of her skirt and faced him squarely, her face carefully blank. 'I don't play games.'

Jack barked a laugh. 'You're a lawyer. You're trained to play games. Don't try to fool me, sugar. You're swimmin' with a big shark now. I know every trick there is.'

He stopped within inches of her, leaning down, meeting her at her level, his nose almost touching hers. In the soft lamplight his eyes sparkled like onyx, hard and fathomless.

'Why don' you just ask me?' he whispered, his whiskey-hoarse voice cutting across her nerve endings like a rasp. 'Did you kill her, Jack? Did you kill your wife?'

She swallowed hard and called his bluff, betting her heart on his answer. 'Did you?'

'Yes.'

He watched her blink quickly, as if she were afraid to take her eyes off him for even a fraction of a second. But she held her ground, brave and foolhardy to the last. And his heart squeezed painfully at the thought. She was waiting for a qualification, something that would dilute the truth into a more palatable mix.

'I told you I was bad, angel,' he said, stepping back from her. 'You know what they say, blood will tell. Ol' Blackie, he always told me I'd be no good. I shoulda listened. I coulda saved a whole lotta people a whole lotta grief.'

He drifted away from her in body and mind, losing himself in a past that was as murky as the bayou. Wandering across the room, past the heavy four-poster with its sensuous drape of white netting and its tangle of bed-clothes, he found his way to another set of French doors and stood looking out into the dark. The wind had come up again and chattered in the branches of the trees, a natural teletype of the next storm boiling up from the Gulf. Lightning flashed in the distance, casting his hard, hawkish profile in silver.

Laurel moved toward him, skirting the foot of the bed. She should have left him. Regardless of the details she was waiting to hear, he was trouble. She may even have had cause to be frightened of him – Jack, with his dual personality and his dark secrets, a temper as volatile as the weather in the Atchafalaya. But she took another step and another, her heart drumming behind her breastbone. And the question slipped past her defenses and out of her mouth.

'What was her name?'

'Evangeline,' he whispered. Thunder rattled the glass in the windows, and rain began to fall, the scent of it cool and green and sweet. 'Evie. As pretty as a lily, as fragile as spun glass,' he said softly. 'She was another of my trophies. Like the house, like the Porsche, like crocodile shoes and suits from Italy. It never penetrated the fog that she loved me.' He ducked his head, as if he still couldn't believe it.

'She was the perfect corporate wife for a while. Dinner parties and cocktail hours. Iron my shirts and brew my coffee.'

Amazed by the sting of his words, Laurel wrapped an arm around an elegantly carved bedpost and anchored herself to it. This woman had shared his life, his bed, had known all his habits and quirks. But she was gone now, forever. 'What happened?'

'She wanted a life with me. I loved my work. I loved the game, the challenge, the rush. I was in the office by seven-thirty. Didn't go home most nights until eleven, or one, or two. The job was everything.'

'Evie started telling me she wasn't happy, that she couldn't live that way. I thought she was temperamental, cloying, selfish, punishing me for working hard so I could give her fine things.'

Regret burned like acid in his throat, behind his eyes. He clenched his jaw against it, whipped himself mentally to get past it. 'The first Sweetwater story had broken, and I was working like mad to cover the company's ass in triplicate. I barely took time to shave or eat.'

Tension rattled through him like the thunder shaking the window-panes as the scenes played out in his memory. His emotions rushed ahead frantically, knowing the ending, torn between the need to protect himself and the need to punish. He drew in a sharp breath through his nostrils and curled a fist into the fragile old lace of the curtain.

'One night I came home in a bitch of a mood. Two o'clock. Hadn't had a meal all day. There wasn't anything in the kitchen. I went looking for Evie, spoiling for a fight. Found her in the bathroom. In the tub. She'd slit her wrists.'

'Oh, God, Jack.' Laurel's arm tightened around the pillar. She brought a hand to her mouth to hold back the cry that tore through her, but the tears still flooded and fell. Through them she watched Jack struggle with the burden of his guilt. His broad shoulders were braced against it, trembling visibly. In the lightning glow she could see his face, his mouth twisting as he fought, chin quivering.

'The note she left was full of apologies,' he said, his voice thickening, cracking. He cleared his throat and managed a bitter smile. ' "I'm sorry I couldn't make you need me, Jack. I'm sorry I couldn't make you love me, Jack." Sorry for the inconvenience. I think she did it in the bathtub so she wouldn't leave a mess.'

This time when the urge came, Laurel let go of the post and let herself go to him. 'She made her own choice, Jack,' she murmured. 'It wasn't your fault.'

When she started to lay her hand against the taut muscles of his back, he twisted away and swung around to face her. His eyes were burning with anger and shame, swimming with tears he refused to let fall.

'The hell it wasn't!' he roared. 'She was *my* responsibility! *I* was supposed to take care of her. *I* was supposed to look out for her. *I* was supposed to be there when she needed me. *Bon Dieu*, I might as well have taken the blade to her myself!'

He whirled and cleared a marble-topped table with a violent sweep of his arm, sending antique porcelain figurines crashing to their doom on the cypress floor. Laurel flinched at the sound of shattering china, but didn't back away.

'You couldn't have known—'

'That's right, I couldn't have,' he snapped. 'I was never there. I was too busy manipulating the illegal disposal of toxic waste.' He threw back his head and laughed in sardonic amazement. 'Jesus, I'm a helluva guy, aren't I? Huh? A helluva match for you, Lady Justice.'

She pressed her lips together and said nothing. She couldn't condone what he'd done at Tristar – it was both illegal and immoral – but neither could she find it in her to condemn him. She knew what it was to get caught up in the job, to be driven to it by demons from the past. And she knew what guilt could do to a person, the changes it could wreak, the pain of it eating inside.

'You didn't kill her, Jack. She had other choices.'

'Yeah?' he asked, his voice thin and trembling, his face a mask of torment. 'And what about the baby she was carrying? Did he have a choice?'

The pain was as sharp as ever. As sharp as the razor blade that had ended his dream of a wife and a family. It sliced at his heart, severed what was left of his strength. He turned back to the French doors and leaned into the one that stood closed, pressing his face against the cool glass, crying silently while rain washed across the other side, soft and cleansing, never touching him. He could still see the pathologist's face, could still hear the disbelief in his voice. '*You mean she hadn't told you? She was nearly three months along . . .* '

His child. His chance to atone for all his father's sins. There and gone before he even had the joy of knowing. Gone because of him, just as Evie was gone because of him.

Not for the first time he thought he was the one who should have sliced open a vein and drained his life away.

Laurel slipped her arms around his waist and pressed her cheek against his back, her tears dampening the soft cotton of his T-shirt. She could see it all so clearly. Jack, so eager to prove himself, scrambling up that sheer granite face of the odds that were stacked against his making anything of himself. Then all of it crumbling beneath him, sucking him down and crushing him with the weight of the debris. He must have thought he'd had everything he ever wanted right in the palm of his hand, and then it was swept away, and every line of degradation his father had ever hammered into him must have come rushing back.

He shoved her away so suddenly, so unexpectedly, Laurel nearly fell. She stumbled back against the table, her shoes crunching over a fortune in shattered porcelain. Jack wheeled on her, his face dark with rage.

'Get out! Get outta here! Get outta my life!' he shouted in her face. 'Get out before I kill you too!'

Laurel just stared at him, at the wild gleam of pain in his eyes, the muscles and tendons that stood out in his neck, the heavy rise and fall of his chest as he breathed. She should have run like hell. Inside he was as fractured as any of the statuettes grinding to dust beneath her feet. She wasn't in much better shape herself. She certainly wasn't strong enough to take on his healing too.

She should have run like hell. She didn't.

She fell in love.

He was trying to push her away, not because he didn't care, but because he cared too much; not because he didn't feel, but because his heart was so badly battered. Losing her heart to him wasn't the smart thing or the timely thing. It wasn't the choice she would have made with her logical, practical attorney's mind, but logic had nothing to do with it.

She met his pain and fury with her chin up and her eyes clear. 'Why should I go?'

Jack stared at her, dumbfounded. He thought he could actually feel the gears in his mind slipping. 'Why?' he repeated, incredulous. He swept his hands back over his hair, turned around in a circle, stared at her some more. 'How can you ask that? After all I've just told you, how can you stand there and ask that?'

'You didn't kill your wife, Jack,' she said gently. 'You didn't kill your child. You're not going to kill me, either. Why should I leave?'

'I can't have you,' he whispered, more to himself than to Laurel.

She stepped up to him, calm and fearless, and whispered, 'Yes, you can.'

He wanted to tell her she didn't understand. He couldn't have her, couldn't care, because he didn't deserve her and because everything he ever wanted was ripped away from him in the end anyway. He didn't need the pain, didn't think he could stand it. But he said none of those things. The words simply wouldn't come.

All he could think as he stared down into that earnest, angelic face was that he wanted to hold her. Just for a little while. Just for what was left of the night. He wanted to hold her, and kiss her, and find some comfort in her body.

Use her.

He'd be a bastard to the very end, he thought. No use fighting his true nature. It wasn't as if he hadn't warned her.

It wasn't as if he didn't need her . . . .

Longing welled inside him, and he reached out to touch her, to ease the ache, to fill the hole in his heart if only temporarily. She sank against him, so small, so fragile. His . . . for the moment . . . for the night . . . for a memory he could hold forever.

Outside, the storm shook the night with sound and fury, but in this room all was stillness except the beating of hearts, the caress of flesh against flesh. Mist blew in through the open door and settled like silver dew, shimmering on the cypress floor when the lightning flashed, but all that touched them was a warmth that glowed from needs within.

Every sense was heightened. Every sense was filled. The fragrance of her skin. The hardness of his muscle. The taste of tears, of gentleness, of desire. The sound of breath catching. The growl of passion. The contrast of light skin on dark. The delicate lacework of her lashes as they swept against her cheek. The planes and angles of his beard-shadowed jaw. Laurel immersed herself in it all. Jack soaked it up greedily.

He touched her like a blind man trying to see with his fingertips, tracing the lines and gentle curves. Fingers fanned wide, he skimmed her jaw, her throat, the slope of her shoulders. He cradled her breasts then let his touch flow downward, over her ribs to her tiny waist, along the subtle flare of her hips.

As he mouthed phantom kisses across her eyelids, along her jawline, his fingers explored her most tender flesh. Laurel whispered his name, and need shuddered through them both.

He wouldn't be an easy man to love. He had branded himself unworthy, thought of himself only in terms of his flaws. He would push her away in the name of caring, break her heart and call it fate. But she went to him. She went to him and offered him everything she was, everything her heart could hold. Without words. Without strings.

He took her in his arms, and they fell across the bed. Springs creaked, linens rustled. The storm rolled on toward Lafayette, thunder sounding like the faint echo of hoofbeats, rain hissing like the sound of steam.

One arm hooked behind her gracefully arching back, Jack bent himself over her and took her breast in his mouth. Her nipple budded beneath the coaxing of his tongue, beneath the wet silk of her camisole, and he drew on it hotly, greedily.

His fingers caught in the hem of the garment and pulled it up. She lay back and stretched her arms above her head. He pushed the camisole to her wrists and held it there, held her there, pinned to the mattress. His eyes locked on hers as he kneed her legs apart and settled his hips against hers.

Laurel's breath fluttered in her throat, not with fear but with anticipation. He would never hurt her physically. He would break her heart – of that she had little doubt – but she trusted him implicitly with her body. She offered herself totally, opened herself, wound her legs around his hips.

And he filled her. Slowly. Inch by inch. His eyes on hers. Giving her the essence of his maleness, being welcomed and embraced by the warm, tight glove of her woman's body. Pressing deeper, deeper, until she gasped his name. When the joining was complete, he cast the silk aside and gathered her to him in a crushing embrace.

It went on forever. It could never have lasted long enough. They moved together, body to body, need to need, heart to heart. Scaling peaks of pleasure, soaring from height to dizzying height.

Jack lost himself in the heat, in the bliss, in the comfort she offered him without words. He gave himself over to desire, thought nothing of right or wrong, only of Laurel. So sweet, so strong. He wanted to give her everything, be everything for her. He wanted to press her to his heart and never let her go. She filled up the hole inside him, flooded all the pain away, made him believe for a moment he could start over . . . with her . . . have a family . . . have peace . . . find forgiveness.

Foolish thoughts. Foolish heart. But for this night he would cling to them as he clung to the woman in his arms, and soothe his aching soul with visions of love.

21

Laurel slipped from the bed at dawn and dressed silently in the soft light that filtered through the French doors and lace curtains. For a long while she stood by the balcony door and just studied him, as an artist might study a subject before putting brush to canvas, taking in everything about the man, the mood. The light seemed the color and consistency of fine sand, golden and grainy, and it didn't quite penetrate the shadows of the graceful four-poster. Jack lay sprawled on his belly taking up most of the bed, his face buried in the crook of his arm. His bronzed back was a sculpture of lean, rippling muscle. The sheet, a drift of white, covered only a section of thigh and hips. One leg was bent at the knee, thigh and calf strong, masculine, dusted with rough, dark hair.

Laurel memorized the way he looked in that moment, this first morning after she'd fallen in love with him. It didn't seem any wiser today than it had in the night. She had no idea where these feelings would lead, but she wouldn't deny to herself that she felt them. She'd lied to herself enough in her lifetime. She had, however, refrained from telling Jack, knowing without being told that he wouldn't want to hear it.

Her heart squeezed painfully at the thought, but she pushed the pain away. She would let things take their natural course. The feelings were too new, too sensitive to be trod upon by something as heavy as practicality or an awkward morning-after scene.

She touched two fingers to her kiss-swollen lips and wondered how she had gotten in so deep so fast with a man like Jack Boudreaux. They were opposites in many ways, too alike in others. An unlikely match drawn together by pain, bound by something neither of them would speak of – love.

It had to have been love in his touch during the long, sultry night. The tenderness, the poignancy, the sweetness, the desperation – in her logical, analytical mind, those components added up to more than mere lust, she was sure. Just as she was sure Jack would never acknowledge it and she would never speak the word. Not now. Not when he was so certain he didn't deserve anything good. She wouldn't try to bind him to her with words and guilt. He had enough guilt of his own.

Unbidden, thoughts came of the wife and child he had lost, and she ached for him so, she nearly cried out. She knew about loss, and she knew about blame. She thought of the unloved, battered boy he had been, and the frightened, emotionally neglected little girl in her wanted to reach out and gather him close. And she knew if Jack had suspected any of what she was thinking, he would have done his damnedest to chase her away. He hoarded his pain like a miser, stored it deep inside, and shared it with no one. It stayed stronger that way, more potent, more punishing. She knew.

God, why him? Why did she have to go and fall in love with a man like Jack at a time like this, when all she really wanted to do was get her feet back under her and get her life back on track – any track?

No answer came to her as dawn broke over the bayou in ribbons of soft color. No answer but her heartbeat.

In the frame of the open French door a small dark spider was carefully spinning a web of hair-fine silk that glistened in the new light with crystal beads of morning dew. Laurel watched for a moment, thinking of her own attempt to build a new life. She had come home to heal, to start over, and she felt as if she were as fragile, as vulnerable as that newly spun web. She looked for toe-holds and tried to weave back together all that had been torn asunder inside her, but the slightest outside force would tear it all apart again, and once again she would be left with nothing.

Her gaze shifted to Jack, who was still asleep – or pretending to be – and she felt that tenuous foundation tremble beneath her. With a heavy, tender heart, she tiptoed out of the room and left the house.

As he heard the hollow echo of the front door closing, Jack turned over slowly and stared up at the morning shadows on the ceiling. He wanted to love her. His heart ached for it so, it nearly took his breath. It surprised him after all this time, after all the hard lessons, that he could still be vulnerable. He should have been able to steel himself against it. He should have known enough to turn her away last night. But he had wanted so badly just to hold her, just to take some comfort in her sweetness.

He had wanted her from the first. Desire he understood. It was simple, basic, elemental. But this . . . this was something he could never be trusted with again. And because he knew that, he had somehow believed he would never be tempted. Now he felt like a fool, betrayed by his own heart, and he kicked himself mercilessly for it. *Stupid, selfish bastard* . . . He couldn't allow himself to fall in love with Laurel Chandler. She deserved far better than him.

And maybe, a lost, lonely part of him thought as the pain of those self-inflicted blows burst through him, maybe after all the penance he had done, he deserved to be left in peace.

Laurel went up to her room via the courtyard and balcony, not wanting to alert anyone else in the house that she was only just returning. Preoccupied with turbulent thoughts of Jack and the night they had spent together, she took a long, warm shower, then dressed for the day in a pair of black walking shorts and a loose white polo shirt. She assessed her looks in the mirror above the walnut commode, seeing a woman with troubled eyes and damp, dark hair combed loosely back.

There should have been some external sign of the changes made inside her during the last few days – the strength she had regained fighting for her new friends, the humility that remained after her pompous ideas concerning Savannah's life had been shattered, the uncertainty in her heart about her own future.

With a sigh she dropped her gaze to the small china tray on the commode where she had left the little pile of oddities she'd come across recently. The gaudy earring no one would lay claim to, the matchbook from Le Mascarade she had found in her car, the necklace that had come in the plain white envelope. At a glance they seemed unrelated, harmless, but something about the way they had simply appeared made her uneasy. Looks could be deceiving. An earring with no mate. A match-book with a name that conjured images of people in disguise. A necklace. There was no thread to tie the items to one another other than the mystery of their origin.

She lifted the necklace, draping the flimsy chain over her index finger. The little butterfly wobbled and danced in a bar of light that slanted through the door. It was probably Savannah's, she told herself again. She'd left it somewhere with a lover. She was notoriously careless with her things. The man had sent it . . . in an envelope with no address. No. It had to have been left in the car. Unless the Bayou Breaux post office was employing psychics, blank envelopes didn't get delivered.

The obvious solution was to simply ask Savannah herself. Forgetting the hour, Laurel marched down the balcony to her sister's room and let herself in.

The bed was empty. The sheets were tangled. The same abandoned clothes littered the chairs and floor. The same sense of stillness as had been there the night before hung, damp and musty in the air.

The memory of that stillness hit Laurel like a wall. It had seemed so surreal, she had almost convinced herself it had been a dream, but here it was again with panic hard on its heels. Savannah hadn't slept in this bed. When was the last time anyone in the house had seen her? She had returned the Acura sometime Tuesday night or Wednesday morning – How did anyone know that? The car had been in the drive Wednesday morning, but no one had actually seen Savannah that day.

'Murders?' '. . . four now in the past eighteen months . . . women of questionable reputation . . . found strangled out in the swamp . . .'

'Oh, God,' Laurel whispered as tears swam in her eyes and crowded her throat till it ached.

She clutched the little necklace in her fist and bit down hard on a knuckle as wild, terrible, conflicting images roared around in her head like debris caught up in a tornado wind. Savannah lying dead someplace. Savannah locked in combat with Annie Gerrard, her eyes glazed with blood lust. T-Grace screaming on the gallery at Frenchie's. Vivian relating the tale of the vandal at St. Joseph's rest home. '*Blood will tell.*' Blood. Blood from wounds. Blood red – the color of the matchbook from Le Mascarade. Savannah's face blank as she tossed it on the table. '*I use a lighter. . . .*' Savannah, finally pushed over that mental edge after all these years because of that son of a bitch Ross Leighton. Savannah, used by men, by Conroy Cooper, by Jimmy Lee Baldwin, who liked his women bound . . . .

All of it whirled around and around in Laurel's mind like fractured bits of glass in a kaleidoscope, every picture uglier than the one before it, every possibility too terrible to be true. And over it all came the harsh voice of logic, scolding her for her foolishness, for her lack of faith, for her lack of evidence. All she really knew was that her sister wasn't home, and no one in the family had seen her since Tuesday. The only logical thing was to go looking for her.

She seized on the notion with a rush of relief and resolve. Don't fall apart, *do something*. Get results. Solve the mystery.

Focused, all the tension drawn into a tight ball of energy that lodged in her chest, she left the room and went to her own to get shoes and her purse. She would leave the back way, she thought as she trotted down the steps to the courtyard. No use alarming Aunt Caroline or Mama Pearl. She would find Savannah, and everything would be all right.

Mama Pearl was up already, shuffling out onto the gallery with a cup of coffee and the latest *Redbook*. She caught sight of Laurel the instant her sneaker touched ground at the foot of the stairs.

'Chile, what you doin' up dis hour?' she demanded, her brow furrowing under the weight of her worry.

Laurel pasted on a smile and stepped toward the back gate. 'Lots to do, Mama Pearl.'

The old woman snorted her disgust for modern femininity and tossed her magazine down on the table. 'You come eat breakfast, you. You so little, the crows gonna carry you 'way.'

'Maybe later!' Laurel called, waving, picking up the pace as she turned for the back gate.

She thought she could still hear Mama Pearl grumbling when she was halfway to L'Amour. It might have been her stomach, but she doubted it; it had gotten too used to being empty. Out of habit, she dug an antacid tablet out of her pocketbook and chewed it like candy.

She had left Jack to avoid the awkwardness of morning-after talk. What had passed between them during the night had gone far beyond words and into a realm of unfamiliar territory. But this was safe ground. She wanted to ask his opinion, tap his knowledge. It was like business, really. And friendship. She wanted his support, she admitted as Huey bounded between a pair of crepe myrtle trees and bore down on her with his tongue lolling out the side of his mouth and a gleam in his mismatched eyes.

The hound crashed into her, knocking her into the front door with a thud. As she called him a dozen names that defamed his character and his lineage, he pounced at her feet, yipping playfully, snapping at her shoelaces. He whirled around and leaped off the front step, running in crazy circles with his tail tucked, clearly overjoyed to see her. Laurel scowled at him as he dropped to the ground at the foot of the step and rolled over on his back, inviting her to scratch his blue-speckled belly.

'Goofy dog,' she muttered, giving in and bending over to pat him. 'Don't you know when you're being snubbed?'

'Love is blind,' Jack said sardonically, swinging the door open behind her.

He was in the same rumpled jeans. No shirt. He hadn't shaved. A mug of coffee steamed in his hand. As Laurel stood, she could see that the brew was as black as night. She breathed in its rich aroma and tried to will her heartbeat to steady. He didn't look pleased to see her. The man who had held her and loved her through the night was gone, replaced by the Jack she would rather not have known, the brooding, angry man.

'If you've got some milk to cut that motor oil you're drinking, I could use a cup myself.'

He studied her for a minute, as if trying to decipher her motives, then shrugged and walked into the house, leaving her to follow as she would. Laurel trailed after him down a long hall, catching glimpses of rooms that had stood unused for decades. Water-stained wallpaper. Moth-eaten draperies. Furnishings covered with dustcloths, and dustcloths thick with their namesake.

It was as if no one lived here, and the thought gave her an odd feeling of unease. Certainly Jack, *The New York Times* best-selling author, could afford to have the place renovated. But she didn't ask why he hadn't, because she had a feeling she knew. Penance. Punishment. L'Amour was his own personal purgatory. The idea tugged at her heart, but she didn't go to him as she longed to. His indifference to her presence set the ground rules for the morning – no clinging, no pledges.

He led her into a kitchen that, unlike the rest of the house, was immaculate. The red of the walls had faded to the color of tomato soup, but they were clean and free of cobwebs. The refrigerator was new. Cupboards and gray tile countertops had been cleaned and polished. The only sign of food was a rope of entwined garlic bulbs and one of red peppers that hung on either side of the window above the sink, but it was a place where food could be prepared without threat of ptomaine.

He pulled a mug down from the cupboard and filled it for her from the old enamel pot on the stove. Laurel helped herself to the milk – a perfect excuse to snoop. Eleven bottles of Jax, a quart of milk, a jar of bread-and-butter pickles, and three casseroles, each bearing a different name penned on a strip of masking tape like offerings for a church pot luck supper. Lady friends taking care of him, no doubt. The thought brought a mix of jealousy and amusement.

She leaned back against the counter, stirring her coffee. 'Have you seen Savannah since the other morning when she left in such a huff?'

'No. Why?'

'I haven't, either. Nor has Aunt Caroline or Mama Pearl.' She fiddled with her spoon as the nerves in her stomach quivered. She fixed her gaze on Jack's belly button and the dark hair that curled around it. 'I'm a little concerned.'

He shrugged. 'She's with a lover.'

'Maybe. Probably. It's just that . . .' She trailed off as the suspicions and theories tried to surface. She wished she could share it all with him, but he wasn't in a sharing mood, and faced with the stony expression he was wearing, she couldn't bring herself to tell him any of it. She felt alone; the one thing she had come to him to avoid. '. . . with all that's been going on, I'd feel better knowing for certain.'

'So what do you want from me, sugar?' he asked bluntly. 'You know for a fact she's not in my bed.'

'Why are you doing this?' she demanded, setting her cup aside on the counter. She halved the distance between them, hands jammed on her hips.

'What?'

'Being such a bastard.'

Jack arched a brow and grinned sharply. 'It's what I do best, angel.'

'Oh, stop it!' she snapped. 'It's too early in the morning for this kind of bullshit.' She dared another step toward him, peering up at him in narrow-eyed speculation. 'What did you think, Jack? That I was coming over here to ask you to marry me?' she said sarcastically. 'Well, I'm not. You can relax. Your martyrdom is safe. All I want is a little help. A straight answer or two would be nice.'

He scowled at her as the martyrdom barb hit and stuck dead center. Giving in to the need to escape her scrutiny, he abandoned his coffee and sauntered across the room to pull a beer from the fridge.

'What do you want me to say?' he asked, twisting off the top with a quick motion of his wrist. 'That I know who was screwing your sister last night? I don't. If I were to hazard a guess as to the possible candidates, I could just as well hand you a phone book.'

'Oh, fine,' Laurel bit back. She stalked him across the room like a tiger. Fury bubbled up inside her, and she wished to God she were big enough and strong enough to pound the snot out of Jack Boudreaux. He deserved it, and it would have gone a long way to appease her own wounded pride. 'You're a big help, Jack.'

'I told you, sugar, I don' get involved.'

'What a crock,' she challenged, toe to toe with him now, leaning up toward him with her chin out and fire in her eyes. She might have been uncertain treading the uneven ground of their suddenly formed relationship, but she knew what to do in an argument. 'You're dabbling around the edges everywhere, Jack – with Frenchie's, with the Delahoussayes, with Baldwin, with me. You're just too big a coward to do more than get your feet wet.'

'Coward?' He gaped at her, at the sound of the word. He described himself in many ways, few of them flattering, but 'coward' was not on the list.

Laurel pressed on, shooting blind, fighting on instinct. Her skills were rusty, and she had never been good at keeping her heart out of a fight, anyway. It tumbled into the fray now, tender and brimming with new emotion. The words were out of her mouth before she could even try to rope them back. 'Every time it starts looking like you might have a chance at something good, you turn tail and run behind that I-don't-give-a-damn facade.'

'A chance at something good?' Jack said, his gaze sharp on hers, his heart clenching in his chest. 'Like what? Like us?'

She bit her tongue on the answer, but it flashed in her eyes just the same. Jack swore under his breath and turned away from her. Struggling for casual indifference, he shook a cigarette out from a pack lying on the counter and dangled it from his lip. '*Mon Dieu*, a couple'a good rolls in the sack and suddenly—'

'Don't!' Laurel snapped. She held a finger up in warning and pressed her lips together hard to keep them from trembling. 'Don't you dare.' She gulped down a knot of tears and struggled to snatch a breath that didn't rattle and catch in her throat. 'I didn't come here to have this fight,' she said tightly. 'I came here because I thought you might be able to help me, because I thought we were friends.'

Jack blew out a huff of air and shook his head. 'I can't help anybody.'

Laurel tugged her composure tight around herself. Damned if she'd let him make her cry. 'Yeah? Well, forgive me for asking you to breach the asshole code of conduct,' she sneered. 'I'll just go ask Jimmy Lee Baldwin flat out if he had my sister tied to his bed the past two nights. I'll just go knock on every goddamn door in the parish until I find her!' She held up a hand as if to ward off an offer that was not forthcoming. 'Thanks anyway, Jack,' she said bitterly, 'but I don't need you after all.'

He watched her storm out of the kitchen and down the hall, a frown tugging at his mouth, a lead weight sinking in his chest. 'That's what I've been tellin' you all along, angel,' he muttered, then he turned and went in search of matches.

Coop stared into his underwear drawer, frowning at the array of serviceable cotton Jockey shorts and boxers and the little silk things Savannah had bought him. He lifted out a white silk G-string, dangling it from his finger, shaking his head. He'd felt stupid as hell wearing it, too big and too old and too set in his ways. But as he dropped it in the wastebasket beside the dresser, he felt a little twinge of regret, just the same.

She wouldn't be back this time. The fight to end all fights had been fought. It was over, once and for all.

Too bad, he thought as he stared out the window. He had loved her. If only she had been able to take that love for what it was worth and find happiness. Of course, that restless, insatiable quality had been one of the things to draw him to her in the first place. So needy, so desperate to assuage that need, so utterly, pitiably incapable of filling that gaping hole within her heart.

He sighed as his mind idly drew character sketches of Savannah, and his gaze fell through the window, taking in the details of the setting. The bayou was a strip of bottle green beyond the yard, and beyond the banks lay the tangled wilderness of the Atchafalaya. Wild and sultry, like Savannah, unpredictable and deceivingly delicate, fragility in the guise of unforgiving toughness.

He thought he ought to write the image down, but he couldn't work up the ambition to go and get his notebook. Instead, he let the lines fade away and tended to his packing. Five pair of shorts, five pair of socks, the tie bar Astor had given him the Christmas before she forgot his name.

Astor. God, how different she had been from Savannah. She had always worn her fragility like a beautiful orchid corsage, as if it were the badge of a true lady, a sign of breeding. Her toughness had been inside, a stoic strength that had borne her through the stages of her decline with dignity. She would have disapproved of Savannah – silently, politely, with a tip of her head and a cluck of her tongue. But he imagined Astor would have forgiven Savannah her sins. He wasn't so sure the same could be said for his case. He had made his wife a pledge, after all.

The doorbell intruded on his musings, and Coop abandoned the closet and his shirt selections to answer it, never expecting to find Laurel Chandler standing on the stoop.

'Mr. Cooper, I'm Laurel Chandler,' she said, all business, no seductive smile, no gleam of carnal fire in the eyes behind the oversize, mannish spectacles.

'Yes, of course,' he said. Remembering his manners, he stepped back from the door. 'Would you care to come in?'

'I'll be blunt, Mr. Cooper,' Laurel said, making no move to enter the house. 'I'm looking for my sister.'

Coop sighed heavily, wearily, feeling his age and the weight of his infidelity bearing down on his broad shoulders. 'Yes. Do come in, Miz Chandler, please. I'm afraid I'm in a bit of a hurry, but we can talk as I pack.'

Determined to dislike him, Laurel stepped past him and into the entry hall of a lovely old home that held family heirlooms and an ageless sense of loneliness with equal grace. Everything was in its place and polished to a shine, with no one here to see it. A grandfather clock ticked the seconds away at the foot of the stairs, marking time to the end of a family. Cooper and his wife had no children. When they were gone, so would be the memories they had made in this house over the generations.

She cast a hard glance at Conroy Cooper. Behind the lenses of his gold-rimmed glasses, he met her gaze with the bluest, warmest, saddest eyes she had ever seen, and he smiled, wistfully, regretfully. It wasn't difficult to see what had attracted her sister. He was a big, strong, athletic man, even at an age that had to be near sixty. His face had probably taken young ladies' breath in his heyday. A strong jaw and a boyish grin. Now it was a map etched with lines of stress and living. No less handsome; more interesting. He stood there in rumpled chinos with one leg cocked, his head tipped on one side. A gray T-shirt with a faded Tulane logo spanned his shoulders and hung free of his pants.

'I am certain you are well aware of my relationship with your sister,' he drawled, that smooth, wonderful voice rolling out of him, rolling over Laurel like sun-warmed caramel. She steeled herself against its effects. 'And you think less of me for it.'

'You're an adulterer, Mr. Cooper. What am I supposed to think of you?'

'That perhaps I loved Savannah as best I could while trying to keep a promise to a woman who no longer remembers me or anything of the life we once had together.'

Laurel pressed her lips together and looked down at her shoes, dodging the steady blue gaze.

'Savannah once told me you thought in absolutes,' he said. 'Right or wrong. Guilty or not guilty. Life isn't quite so black and white as you would like for it to be, Laurel. Nothing is as absolute in reality as it is in our minds in our youth.'

'Loved,' Laurel repeated, seizing on the thought to fend off any pangs of contrition his words may have inspired. She raised her head and looked at him sharply again. 'You said *loved*. Past tense.'

'Yes. It's over.' He ran a hand back through his blond hair, glancing at the clock as it ticked away another few seconds. 'I don't mean to be rude, but I have to be in N'Awlins this afternoon. If you'll excuse my back, I'll lead the way.'

As she followed him into his bedroom, a feeling of something like déjà vu stole over her. The furnishings were big and masculine. The smell of leather and shoe polish underscored the faint woodsy tang of aftershave. Like Daddy's room back home before Vivian had dismantled it and given it over to Ross.

A duffel bag sat open on the white counterpane on the bed, giving her a peek of white cotton and polished wingtips. Cooper went to the closet and selected three shirts, which he hung neatly in a black garment bag on the closet door.

'She wanted to go with me on this trip,' he said. 'Of course, I had to tell her no. She knew very well the boundaries of our relationship. If you think she took the news well, I should point out to you that I used to have a collection of fine antique shaving mugs left to me by my grandfather. I kept them in that cabinet next to the bathroom door.'

The curio cabinet stood, an empty frame with no glass in its sides and no antique shaving mugs within. All signs of the destruction had been vacuumed away, but Laurel could very easily picture her sister hurling mugs at Cooper's head. She had that kind of rage in her, that kind of violence.

Fingers of tension curled around her stomach and squeezed.

'When did this argument take place?' she asked, turning to face Cooper once again.

He hung a pearl gray suit in the garment bag and smoothed the sleeves. 'Tuesday. Why?'

'Because I haven't seen her since Tuesday morning.'

He pulled another suit from the closet and added it to the bag, frowning as his mind rushed to plot out scenarios. 'Then she's probably gone on to N'Awlins. I wouldn't put it past her to think she could disrupt my stay.'

'She didn't have a car.'

'She may have caught a ride with a friend.' His mouth compressed into a tight line as he zipped the bag shut. 'Or another man. You might check with the Maison de Ville. She likes to stay in the cottages there.'

'Yes,' Laurel murmured. 'I know.'

They had stayed there the spring before their father died. A family outing, one of the few she remembered happily. She could still hear Vivian going on about how movie stars sometimes stayed there. She could still see the thick-walled cottages and the courtyard, could still hear the noise and smell the ripe smells of New Orleans as she had perceived them then, through the senses of a child.

Cooper pulled the garment bag down from the closet door, folded and latched it securely. Laurel watched his hands. They were thick and strong with square-cut nails. The hands of a farmer or a carpenter, not a writer. A gold band, burnished with age, circled the third finger of his left hand.

'How is your wife?'

His head came up sharply, eyes shining with interest and surprise as he studied her. He swung the bag onto the bed beside the duffel.

Laurel picked at her ravaged thumbnail absently, uncomfortable with the topic and his scrutiny. 'I heard about the incident at St. Joseph's. I'm sorry.'

Coop nodded slowly, finding it interesting that Laurel would apologize for the actions of her sister. They were two sides of the same coin – one light, one dark; one driven by angst to acts of justice, one to strange fits of passion. Laurel subdued everything feminine about herself; Savannah flaunted and magnified. Laurel held everything within; Savannah knew no boundaries and no control.

'She's doing well enough,' he said. 'One of the few saving graces of her illness is that she forgets unpleasantness almost as quickly as it happens. It's the rest of us who have to go on with bad memories lingering like the smell of smoke.'

The past was gone, but its taint was stubborn and pervasive. An apt analogy, Laurel thought as she left the house.

She slid behind the wheel of her car and just sat there for a moment, her mind trying to go in eight directions at once. Cooper thought Savannah had gone to New Orleans. It didn't feel right. Savannah had always treated a trip to New Orleans as an event, something to fuss over and pack and repack for. She would have told Aunt Caroline, promised to bring back something outrageous for Mama Pearl just to hear the old woman huff and puff. She wouldn't have slipped away like a thief in the night, regardless of who she had gone with.

She would call the Maison de Ville, just to be sure, but there were other possibilities, and one of them was Jimmy Lee Baldwin.

Jimmy Lee stretched out across his rumpled bed and groaned. He felt near death with exhaustion. He smelled of rank, ripe sweat with an undertone of liquor and an overtone of sex. Without question, he needed a long shower before his lunch meeting with his deacons. Deacons. Christ, the saps would go nuts over that title.

'You're fucking brilliant, Jimmy Lee,' he snickered, staring up at the creaking old ceiling fan as it strained to stir the stale air. 'You're a Grade A-mazing, God damntastic genius.'

It was the sign of a man who would go far. When things turned sour, he found a way to sweeten the deal. The taping at the Texaco station hadn't turned out the way he had planned, but ultimately it was going to be to his advantage. He would make sure of it.

The brainstorm had come in the middle of a wild, hard fuck. In a way, he had a whore to thank, ironic as that seemed. The answer to his troubles was what she had begged from him – mercy, sympathy. He would play on the sympathies of his followers. He didn't believe in giving sympathy himself. Go for the throat. Look out for Number One. Those were his mottoes. But the American people had traditionally loved an underdog. He would get a few key puppets whipped into a frenzy for his flagging cause, they would rally the troops, and he'd be back on track in nothing flat.

He smiled a wicked smile as he pictured it. The looks on their gullible, stupid faces as he poured his heart out to them about the plight of his ministry and his campaign to end sin. His cause was being sabotaged by

Satan in the guise of Jack Boudreaux. He was being thwarted and made to look a fool at every turn, and he just didn't know if he had the heart to go on alone. Perhaps if one or two good men would be willing to shoulder some of his burden by filling the role of deacon . . . Their eyes would go wide, and their faces would shine with imagined grace.

The timing was perfect. Discovery of a mutilated female in their own backyards tended to turn people's thoughts to God and to vengeance. They would want a leader and a scapegoat, and Jimmy Lee intended to give them both.

He sat up just enough to snag the paperback off his nightstand and fell back across the lumpy mattress, thumbing through the pages.

Blood ran in rivulets, pearling and tumbling in the knife's wake. She tried to scream, but the sound vibrated only in her mind. Her throat was raw. Silk filled her mouth, like a stopper in a bottle, and the tie of the gag pulled her lips back in a macabre smile. . . .

'Twisted stuff, Jack my man.' He chuckled as he folded down the corner on the page.

This was all playing right into his hands. He fantasized about all the possibilities as he stripped and showered in the grungy, mildew-coated shower stall. Jack Boudreaux would get pinned for the murders. Jimmy Lee would be a hero. Free publicity. Fan mail. The faithful would come out of the woodwork and follow him anywhere, do anything for him. What a perfectly wonderful dream.

He was a happy and satisfied man as he dressed. He even hummed a few bars of an old gospel tune as he polished off the knot in his tie and stood back to critique his look in the mirror above the bathroom sink.

His tawny hair was slicked back, his cheeks perfectly tan and clean-shaven. He flashed a smile, euphoric as always with the dental wonders he had invested in. He looked, quite simply, perfect. The shirt and tie were neat, but the knot was just slightly loose and askew. The suit was sufficiently limp with just enough wrinkles to make him look a little downtrodden. He took a deep breath and let it out slowly, letting his shoulders sag and the muscles of his face droop into a worried frown. For a crowning touch, he mussed his hair a little in front, flicking a few strands loose to tumble across his forehead.

The deacons wouldn't know what hit them.

Someone banged on the screen door, and Jimmy Lee let whoever it was wait a few seconds, setting the mood. It was probably one of his chosen come to check on him. He had sounded despondent when he'd called them this morning. He shambled out of the bathroom, head hanging low, hands dangling by his sides.

Laurel Chandler stared in at him through the screen. She didn't look the least bit sympathetic. She looked like trouble.

'Miz Chandler,' he said, pushing the door open. 'What a surprise to see you here.'

'Yes, I suppose you'd be less surprised to see my sister,' Laurel said. She stepped across the threshold, staying as far away from Baldwin as she could, never turning her back to him for a second. From the corners of her eyes, she did a quick reconnaissance of the shabby bungalow, her gaze lingering a second on the old bed with its scrollwork iron headboard and footboard.

Jimmy Lee let the door bang shut. His face carefully blank, his gaze steady on the woman who looked up at him with undisguised contempt, he pushed back the sides of his suit coat and planted his hands at his waist. 'Just what is that supposed to mean?'

'Exactly what you think it means.'

'You're suggesting I have a relationship with your sister?'

'No. I'm saying you have sex and play bondage games with my sister.'

His reaction was something that artlessly combined incredulous laughter and choking astonishment. Jaw hanging slack, head wagging, he staggered back a step, as if her words had struck him physically and dazed him. 'Miz Chandler, that's simply outrageous! I am a man of God—'

'I know exactly what you are, Mr. Baldwin.'

'I think not.'

'Are you calling my sister a liar?' she challenged, planting her hands on her slim hips.

Jimmy Lee bit his tongue and assessed the situation. Back in his youth, when he'd hustled small-time for pocket money, he had prided himself on being able to read a mark in nothing flat. What he saw behind the glasses, in the depths of Laurel Chandler's deep blue eyes, behind the temper and the intelligence, was a hint of vulnerability. Maybe she didn't approve of Savannah's freewheeling sex life. Maybe she was every bit as prim as she appeared to be. Maybe she didn't quite trust Savannah's sanity.

He sighed dramatically and slipped his hands into his trouser pockets, forcing his shoulders down. Letting her hang for a minute, he turned away from her – not so far that she couldn't see him furrow his brow and frown, as if in contemplation.

' "Liar" is a harsh word. I think your sister is a very troubled woman. I don't deny she's come to me. I've tried to counsel her.'

'I'll bet you have.'

Her whole body vibrating with temper, Laurel took a slow turn around the room. When she came to the foot of the unmade bed, she stopped and curled her fingers over the curving bow of the foot rail. It was bumpy with layers of old paint, rough in spots where the rust was coming through. She gave it a yank, testing for sturdiness, and shot a look at Baldwin over her shoulder.

'Psychiatrists still favor using a couch for their sessions. I guess you decided to take it a few steps further.'

She gave the bed another shake, but turned her back to it the instant her imagination began to picture Savannah there with her wrists bound.

Annie Gerrard had been bound by her wrists too.

She settled her right hand on her pocketbook and pressed the pocketbook against her hip, imagining that she could feel the outline of her Lady Smith through the glove-soft leather.

'Do you know what I think of men who have to tie women up in order to feel superior to them?' she asked, giving Baldwin the same look that had cracked more than one defendant's story. 'I think they're spineless, twisted, despicable scum.'

A muscle ticked in Jimmy Lee's cheek. In his pockets he balled his hands into fists. His temper strained with the need to use them. 'I told you, I've never had anything to do with your sister sexually. Only the Lord can decipher what might go on in a mind like Savannah's. I don't doubt but that she's capable of saying – of doing – anything at all. But I'm telling you, as God is my witness, I have never laid a hand on her.'

'God is a very convenient witness,' Laurel said dryly. 'Difficult to cross-examine.'

Baldwin's tawny brows scaled his forehead. He all but raised a finger and declared her a blasphemer. 'You would doubt the Lord?' he gasped, incredulous.

The act was lost on Laurel. 'I would doubt you,' she said. 'I came here to ask if you've seen Savannah in the last couple of days, but I can see I'm wasting my time waiting for a straight answer. Perhaps Sheriff Kenner will have better luck.'

She hadn't taken three steps past him when his hand snaked out and caught her by the shoulder. Laurel twisted around, chopping at his arm as she had been taught in self-defense class, breaking his hold. He glared at her, but made no move to touch her again.

'I haven't seen your sister,' he said, struggling to maintain a facade of calm. 'That's God's honest truth. No need to drag the sheriff out here.'

Laurel took another step back toward the door and inched her hand into her purse. Her heart was thumping. Her palms were sweating. She hoped to hell she would be able to hang on to the gun if the need arose.

'Why don't you want him out here? Skeletons in your closet, Reverend?'

'Scandal is deadly in my position,' he said, following her retreat toward the door. 'Even though I've done nothing wrong, people tend to believe where there's smoke, there's fire.'

'They're usually right.'

'Not in this case.'

'Save your breath, Baldwin,' she sneered. 'You couldn't win me over if you turned water into wine right before my very eyes. You're a charlatan and a fraud, and if I didn't have better things to do with my time, I'd make certain the whole damn world found out about it.'

She could ruin him. The thought hit Jimmy Lee like a brick in the belly. His stomach twisted into a knot. His shot at wealth and glory could be dead in the water. No one would believe her sister, but people would at least pause to listen to Laurel Chandler. They might dismiss what she said after, since she had a reputation for crying wolf, but the damage would be done.

The press would focus on him. Despite the pains he had always taken to disguise himself, some whore would recognize him on the news and sell a juicy story to the *Enquirer*. Christ, he wished he'd never set eyes on a Chandler woman in his life. Bitches and whores, both of them. He wanted to choke the life out of this one, the pompous little do-gooder.

As the picture flashed like a strobe in his brain, his hold on his temper broke with a snap. He opened his jaws in a snarl that was made only more eerie by the white of his too-perfect caps. A red haze filmed across his eyes, and he lunged toward her, growling, 'You little bitch.'

Heart catapulting into her throat, Laurel stumbled backward to give herself room. Staying just out of Baldwin's reach, she jerked the Lady Smith from her purse and held it chest-high, with both hands wrapped around the grip.

Jimmy Lee's eyes bugged out at the sight of the gun. 'Jesus Fucking Christ!'

'Amen, Revver,' Jack drawled.

Adrenaline was searing his veins. He wanted nothing more than to throw the door open, tackle Baldwin, and pound the life out of him for whatever he had done to spook Laurel, but he held the machismo in firm check. Laurel and her purse pistol had the situation under control. Sort of. Her hands were trembling badly.

With deliberately, deceptively lazy movements, Jack drew open the screen door and propped himself up against the jamb.

'And if you think she can't use it, you better think again, Jimmy Lee,' he said. 'She'll shoot your balls off and feed 'em to stray dogs.'

Jimmy Lee glared at him with a look of pure, unadulterated hate. 'I didn't ask you in, Boudreaux.'

Jack arched a brow in amusement. 'Oh, yeah? Well, you gonna do somethin' 'bout that, Jimmy Lee? Ms. Smith & Wesson might have somethin' to say 'bout that.'

'Isn't that just like you – hiding behind a woman,' Baldwin sneered. He raised an impotent finger in warning. 'You take my word for it, Boudreaux. You won't be able to hide much longer.'

He had a card up the sleeve of that cheap suit. Jack could tell by the gleam in his eyes. He couldn't imagine what it was, but he couldn't imagine that he'd give a damn, either. He blinked wide in mock fear and splayed a hand across his heart.

'Did you hear that, Miz Chandler? Why I do believe the good reverend just threatened me.' With the same casual grace, Jack reached out and gently pushed her hands and the gun down so the barrel pointed at the floor. 'Sugar, mebbe you could wait outside for me. I think Reverend Baldwin and I need to clear up this little misunderstanding.'

Laurel looked up at him, more curious as to why he had shown up than what he was going to do to Jimmy Lee Baldwin. She probably should have stood her ground or made him leave with her. After all, assault was against the law, and she was sworn to uphold the law. But she glanced over at Baldwin and felt a surge of something primal and angry, and for once turned her back on rules and regulations. She didn't like the things Baldwin had intimated about Savannah – even if she knew deep down they may well have been true.

She slipped the Lady Smith back into her pocketbook and without a word turned and left the bungalow.

Jack settled his hands at the waist of his jeans and waited for the echo of the screen door slamming to fade away before he turned fully toward Jimmy Lee. Jimmy Lee, who believed the best defense was a good offense, snatched up the mostly empty bottle of E&J brandy off the three-legged coffee table and brandished it like a big glass club.

'Get the hell out of my house, Boudreaux.'

'Not before we have us a little chat.' Jack circled Baldwin slowly, moving in on him by imperceptible degrees. He didn't appear threatening. He scuffed his boots along on the gritty linoleum, his head down, as if he had nothing better to do than count the cigarette burns in the floor. 'Now, Jimmy Lee, I don' know what you did to make Miz Chandler pull her little peashooter on you, but it had to be somethin' bad – her being such a law-abiding sort and all.'

'I didn't do shit to her,' Jimmy Lee snapped, turning, turning, to keep Boudreaux in front of him. His fingers flexed on the neck of the brandy bottle. 'She's unbalanced. She was in an asylum, you know. She's nuts, just like her sister.'

Jack shook his head in grave disappointment, still shuffling along, still turning, still moving in a little at a time. 'You're impugning the character of a fine, upstanding woman, Jimmy Lee. Even I have to take exception to that.'

Jimmy Lee made another quarter turn, wondering dimly at the way the floor seemed to dip beneath his feet. 'I don't give a rat's ass what you take exception to, you coonass piece of shit.'

Jack suddenly moved toward him, and Jimmy Lee swung the heavy, unwieldy brandy bottle. He did so with gusto, imagining the mess it would make of the Cajun's head, but he missed badly, throwing himself off balance in the process.

Jack ducked the blow easily. Quick and graceful as a cat, he stepped around Baldwin, caught hold of the preacher's free arm, twisted it up high behind him, and ran him face-first into the rough plaster wall. The bottle shattered and fell to the floor in tinkling shards, the last of the brandy soaking into Baldwin's wingtips.

'I told you once to leave Laurel Chandler alone,' Jack growled, his mouth a scant inch from Baldwin's ear. 'You shouldn't make me tell you twice, Jimmy Lee. Me, I don' have that kind of patience.'

Jimmy Lee tried to suck in a watery breath. His face was mashed against the nubby plaster, and he was sure he'd chipped at least three of his precious caps. While the blood pounded in his head and spittle bubbled between his ruined teeth and down his quivering chin, he damned Jack Boudreaux to hell and plotted a hundred ways to torment him once they were both there.

'I mean it, Jimmy Lee,' Jack snarled, jerking his arm up a little higher and wringing a whimper out of him. 'If you give her another moment's trouble, I'll rip your dick off and use it for crawfish bait.'

He gave one last little push, then stepped back and dusted his palms off on his thighs as Baldwin stood, still facing the wall, doubled over, clutching his arm.

'Hope I don' see you 'round, Jimmy Lee.'

Jimmy Lee spat on the floor, a big gob of blood and saliva flecked with fragments of porcelain. 'God damn you to hell, Boudreaux!' he yelled around the thumb that was feeling gingerly for the sorry condition of his caps.

Jack waved him off and walked out and away from the bungalow.

'I don't want to know one thing about it,' Laurel said as she came toward him from the base of a huge old magnolia tree. 'If I don't know anything, I can't be called to testify.'

'He'll live,' Jack said sardonically. They walked toward the vehicles they had left on the scrubby lawn beside Baldwin's beat-up Ford. Huey sat behind the wheel of Jack's Jeep, ears up like a pair of black triangles, mismatched eyes bright. Jack shot Laurel a sideways glance. 'You okay?'

Laurel gave him a look. 'What are you doing here, Jack? Two hours ago you weren't even willing to give me a straight answer, let alone ride to my rescue.'

He scowled blackly, caught in a trap of his own making. He should have stayed the hell out of it, but as he sat at his desk, smoking the first pack of Marlboros he had allowed himself in two years, trying to conjure up a violent muse, he hadn't been able to get the image out of his head – Laurel charging at Baldwin with the courage of a lion and the stature of a kitten. Baldwin was a con man, but that didn't mean he wasn't capable of worse, and try as he might to convince himself otherwise, Jack couldn't just stand back and let her take a chance like that alone.

'I followed you,' he admitted grudgingly. 'I don' want to get involved, but I don' want to see you get hurt, either. I've got enough on my conscience.'

Too late for that, Laurel thought, biting her lip. He had hurt her in little ways already. He would break her heart if she gave him the chance, and damn her for a fool, some part of her wanted to give him that chance. Knowing everything she knew about him. Even after everything they had said in his kitchen. She couldn't think of his tenderness in the night, of the vulnerability that lay inside that tough, alley-cat facade, and not want to give him that chance.

'Why, Mr. Boudreaux,' she said sardonically, gazing up at him with phony, wide-eyed amazement, 'you'd better watch yourself. One might deduce from a statement such as that one that you actually feel concern for my well-being. That could be hazardous to your image as a bastard.'

'Quit bein' such a smartass,' he growled, his expression thunderous. 'I didn't like the idea of you comin' out here alone. Ol' Jimmy Lee, he might not be as harmless as he seems, you know.'

'He might not be harmless at all,' Laurel muttered, turning her gaze back toward the shabby little bungalow.

Reverend Baldwin was into kinky sex and bondage, and he had an ugly temper. He also had a near-perfect cover. Who would ever suspect a preacher of murder?

'Murder.' The word made her shudder inside. She had come here looking for her sister, and now she was thinking of murder. She wouldn't begin to allow the two subjects near one another in her mind. In any regard.

'Well, whatever your reasons, thank you for coming.'

They seemed beyond the formality of thanks, and it hung awkwardly between them. Laurel pushed her glasses up on her nose and shuffled toward her car. Jack shrugged it off and curled his fingers around the door handle of the Jeep.

'Where you goin' lookin' for trouble next, angel?' he asked, calling himself a fool for caring.

'To the sheriff,' she said, already steeling herself for the experience. 'I think he and I need to have a little chat. Want to come?'

It was a silly offer. She had no business feeling disappointed when he turned her down, but she didn't want to break the fragile thread of communication between them. *Foolish*. Even as she chastised herself, her fingers snuck into her purse and came out with the red match-book. She offered it to him, simply to feel his fingertips brush against hers.

'Would you happen to know anything about this place?'

Jack's expression froze as he stared down at the elaborate black mask and the neat script title. 'Where'd you get this?'

Laurel shrugged, her mouth going dry as his tension was telegraphed to her. 'I found it. I think Savannah left it in my car, but she wouldn't admit it was hers. Why? What kind of place is it?'

'It's the kind of place you don' wanna go, sugar,' he said grimly, handing it back to her. 'Unless you like leather and you're into S&M.'

667

22

Kenner lit his fifth cigarette of the day and sucked in a lungful of tar and nicotine. His eyeballs felt as if they'd been gone over with sandpaper, his vocal cords as if they'd grown bark. He had ice picks stabbing his brain and a stomach full of battery acid disguised as coffee. In comparison, a rabid dog had a pleasant attitude. He was getting nowhere with the Gerrard murder, and it pissed him off like nothing else – except maybe Laurel Chandler.

He stared at her through the haze of smoke that hovered over his cluttered desk, his eyes narrowed to slits, his mouth twisting at the need to snarl.

'So you think Baldwin killed your sister and all them other dead girls?'

Laurel bit back a curse. Her fingers tightened on the arms of the visitor's chair. 'That isn't what I said.'

'Hell, no,' Kenner barked, shoving to his feet. 'But that's what you meant.'

'It is not—'

'Jesus, I've been just waiting to hear this—'

'Then why don't you listen?'

'—haven't I, Steve?'

Danjermond, lounging against a row of putty-color file cabinets, tightened his jaw at the shortening of his name. Kenner didn't notice. He'd been looking for an excuse to blow off some steam. First someone had the balls to kill a woman in his jurisdiction. Then he'd had to let Tony Gerrard walk. Then every hoped-for lead had piddled into nothing. Now this. He let his temper have free rein, not giving a damn that Laurel Chandler was connected. Ross Leighton himself said the girl was a troublemaker, said she always had been.

'I've just been waiting for you to come charging in here, pointing fingers and naming names.'

'I'm only trying to give you information. It's my civic duty—'

'Fuck that, lady.' He cut her off, leaning over the desk to tap his cigarette off in the ashtray. 'You're trying to make trouble, same as you did up in Georgia. Point your finger, shoot your mouth off, get your name in the paper. You get off on that or something?'

Laurel ground her teeth and cut a look Danjermond's way, wondering why the hell he didn't do something. 'I never said Baldwin killed anyone. I just thought you might like to know—'

'That he's some kind of pervert. A preacher.' Kenner snorted his derision and shook his head as he pulled hard on his smoke. 'What was it up in Georgia? A dentist? A banker? Is there anyone you *don't* suspect of being a pervert?'

'Well, I doubt you are,' Laurel snapped, coming up out of her chair. She planted her hands on Kenner's littered desktop and met him glare for glare. 'Why should you resort to perversity when you obviously have a license to fuck over anyone you want!'

While Kenner snarled and foamed at the mouth, her gaze cut again to Danjermond, who had the gall to be amused with her. She could see it in the translucent green depths of his eyes, in the way the corners of his mouth flicked upward ever so slightly. He roused himself from his stance against the file cabinets and came forward, turning his attention on Kenner.

'Now, Duwayne,' he said calmly. 'Miz Chandler came in here with the best of intentions. If she believes she has information pertinent to the case, you ought to listen.'

'Pertinent to the case!' Kenner made a contemptuous sound in his throat and smashed out his cigarette in the overflowing plastic ashtray. 'Savannah Chandler says the preacher gets off on tying women up. Savannah Chandler. Jesus, everyone in town knows she's got screws as loose as her morals!'

Fury misting her vision red. Laurel all but dove for his throat. 'You son of a bitch!'

Kenner shrugged. 'Hey, I'm not saying anything that idn't common knowledge.'

'But you're not saying it very tactfully,' Danjermond pointed out, frowning.

'Shit, I don't have time to be David Fucking Niven. I've got a murder to solve.' He snagged another Camel from the pack and lit it with a match, his gaze hard on Laurel. 'Leave the investigating to me, *Ms.* Chandler.'

'Fine,' Laurel said through her teeth. 'But it would probably be helpful if you would take your head out of your ass so you could see to do it.'

Kenner's color deepened to burgundy. He snatched his cigarette from his lip and shook it at her, raining ash down on his desktop and the drift of papers strewn across it. 'You want a little advice on where you might find your sister? I wouldn't look any farther than a few dozen bedrooms.'

'And that's what you would have said about Annie Gerrard, too, isn't it?' Laurel felt a little surge of triumph as the hit scored. A muscle flexed in Kenner's jaw, and he glanced away. 'Yeah, Annie liked to sleep around a little. Look where they found her.'

Kenner turned his back on her and stared out through the slats in the crooked Venetian blind. Danjermond came around the end of the desk and caught her gently by the arm. 'Perhaps it would be better if you and I discussed this in my office, Laurel.'

Gracefully, he turned her toward the door and ushered her into the outer office, where Kenner's secretary, Louella Pierce, sat with nail file in hand, absorbing every detail of the melee so she would be able to relate it blow by blow to everyone in the break room. A couple of uniformed officers looked up from the paperwork on their desks with smirks on their faces.

Adrenaline still pumping, Laurel glared at them. 'What the hell are you looking at?'

Eyebrows shot up as heads ducked down. Danjermond continued into the hall without pause, herding her along. His grip on her arm seemed deceptively light, but when she tried to discreetly pull away, she couldn't.

'I'll thank you to let me go, Mr. Danjermond,' Laurel said softly, angrily, her eyes flashing fiercely as she looked up at him. 'I didn't appreciate your little Good Cop-Bad Cop routine back there. I'm not some wide-eyed civilian walking in here with a head full of gossip.'

'No,' he said calmly, never altering his stride or his expression, but there was something hard in his gaze as he glanced down at her. 'You're a former prosecutor with a reputation for making allegations you can't back up. How did you expect him to react?'

There was considerable activity in the hall. Court was in session, but in addition to the usual cadre of attorneys and clerks and stenographers, there were reporters hovering like vultures, waiting for some meat on the latest of the Bayou Strangler's cases. Laurel sensed their presence. Her stomach tightened, and the hair on the back of her neck rose as she felt eyes turn her way – eyes that brightened with feral anticipation at the sight of her walking arm in arm with the parish's golden boy district attorney. Just as in old times, they homed in, scrambling to switch on tape recorders, fumbling for pencils and notebooks. They came forward in a rush, sound bursting out of them like a television that had suddenly been turned on high volume.

'Mr. Danjermond!'

'Ms. Chandler!'

'—is there any connection—?'

'—are you aiding in the investigation—?'

'—have there been any new leads—?'

Danjermond walked on, calm as Moses strolling through the Red Sea. 'No comment. We have no comment to make at this time. Ms. Chandler has no comment.'

Hating herself for it, Laurel leaned into him and let him take the brunt of the media storm. He guided her into his outer office, and while he dealt the press a final, frustrating 'No comment' at the door, she made a beeline past the curious gaze of his secretary and went into the quiet of his inner sanctum.

The details of the office penetrated only peripherally – hunter green walls, heavy brass lamps, dark leather chairs, the smell of furniture polish and cherry tobacco, a place for everything and everything in its place. The shades were drawn, giving the room the feeling of twilight. The mood of the room may have soothed her, but she was too caught up in the churning memories and emotions and self-recriminations. The way she had lost her temper with Kenner was too reminiscent of scenes from Scott County – fights with the sheriff, tirades unleashed on her assistants and colleagues.

She gulped a breath and stopped her pacing, bringing up both hands to press them against her temples. As in a dream, she could see herself tearing her office apart, wild, ranting, throwing things, smashing things, screaming until her assistant, Michael Hellerman, had called in Bubba Vandross from security to come and subdue her.

After months of riding that mental edge, she had gone over. She wasn't on the brink now, but she was damn close. The frustration of trying to deal with Kenner pushed a button. She had no control over him, and control was the one thing she had needed most since her father had died.

And then the press. God, would she never escape the loop of recurrences? If she had gone to Bermuda instead of Bayou Breaux, would she now be standing in the magistrate's office, embroiled in some island intrigue?

She let out a shuddering breath and tried to let go some of the tension in her shoulders. She needed to regroup, to think things through. She needed to find Savannah and dispel the dark shadows lurking in the back of her mind.

She ran a hand over the soft leather of her pocket-book, thinking of the odd trinkets she had dropped into it – the earring, the necklace, the matchbook. She had shown none of them to Kenner, knowing he would only have taken them as further proof of her mental instability. They might have come from anywhere. They might all have been Savannah's.

The matchbook lingered in her mind. Jack turning it over with his nimble musician's fingers. His expression going carefully blank at the sight of the name. A leather bar in the Quarter. Secretive, seclusive, exclusive. A place where masks were commonplace and anything might be had for a price or a thrill. He had been there doing research for a book.

He had pinned her arms above her head, held her down as he joined their bodies. . . .

Jimmy Lee Baldwin was into bondage, Savannah said.

Savannah had allowed herself to be tied up. . . .

Nausea swirled around Laurel's stomach, and she leaned against an antique credenza and closed her eyes.

'Would you care for a brandy?'

She jerked her head up as Danjermond closed the door softly behind him.

'For medicinal purposes, of course,' he added with a ghost of a smile.

'No,' she said, stiffening her knees, squaring her shoulders. 'No, thank you.'

He slid his hands into the pockets of his trousers and wandered along a wall of leather-bound tomes. 'Forgive me for being less than supportive in Kenner's office. I've learned the best way to handle him is not to handle him at all.' He shot her a sideways look, taking her measure. 'And I admit I wanted to see you in action. You're quite ferocious, Laurel. One would never suspect that looking at you – so delicate, so feminine. I like a paradox. You must have taken many an opponent by surprise.'

'I'm good at what I do. If the opposition is taken by surprise by that, then they're simply stupid.'

'Yes, but the plain fact is that people draw certain conclusions based on a person's looks and social background. I've been on the receiving end of such impressions myself, being from a prominent family.'

Laurel arched a brow. 'Are you trying to tell me you may be a son of the Garden District Danjermonds, the shipping Danjermonds, but at heart you're just a good ol' boy? I have a hard time believing that.'

'I'm saying one can't judge a book by its cover – pretty or otherwise. One never really knows what might hide behind ugliness or lurk in the heart of beauty.'

She thought again of Savannah, her beautiful sister, spinning around Frenchie's with Annie Gerrard in a headlock, smearing excrement on the wall of St. Joseph's rest home outside Astor Cooper's window, screaming obscenities in the moonlight. Sighing, she closed her eyes and rubbed at her forehead as if she could scrub her brain clean of doubt.

'I'll do what I can to influence Kenner,' Danjermond said softly.

He was behind her now, close enough that she could sense his nearness. He settled his elegant hands on her shoulders and began to rub methodically at the tension. Laurel wanted to bolt, but she held her ground, unsure of whether his gesture was compassion or dominance, unsure of whether her response was courage or acquiescence.

'I can't make any promises, though,' he said evenly. 'I'm afraid he has a valid point concerning the information on Baldwin. Your sister has something of a credibility problem. Particularly as she's gone missing. You know all about credibility problems, don't you, Laurel?'

She jerked away from his touch and turned to face him, her anger blazing back full force. 'I can do without the reminder, thank you, and all the other little snide remarks you so enjoy slipping into our conversations like knives. Just whose side are you on, anyway?'

'Justice takes the side of right. Nature, however, chooses strength,' he pointed out. 'Right and strength don't always coincide.'

He let that cryptic assertion hang in the air as he opened a beautiful cherrywood humidor on his desk top and selected a slim, expensive cigar. 'The courtroom often more resembles a jungle than civilization,' he said as he went about the ritual of clipping the end of the cigar. 'Strength is essential. I need to know how strong you are if we're going to work together.'

'We're not,' Laurel said flatly, moving toward the door.

He slid into his high-backed chair, rolling his cigar between his fingers. 'We'll see.'

'I have other things to see to,' she snapped, infuriated by his smug confidence that she wouldn't be able to resist the lure of his offer or the lure of him personally. 'Finding my sister for one, since the sheriff's department is obviously going to be of little help.'

A lighter flared in his hands, and he drew on the cigar, filling the air with a rich aroma. 'I wouldn't worry overmuch, Laurel,' he said, his handsome head wreathed in fragrant, cherry-tinted smoke. 'She may well have gone to N'Awlins, as her lover suggested. Or perhaps she's enjoying the charms of another man. She'll turn up.'

But what condition would she be in when she did? The question lodged like a knot in Laurel's chest. If Savannah had gone off some inner precipice, what would be left to find? The possibilities sickened her. One thing was certain – Savannah wouldn't be the sister Laurel had always leaned on. The child within her wept at the thought.

Prejean's Funeral Home was typical in Acadiana. Built in the sixties, it was a low brick building with a profusion of flower beds outside and a strange mix of sterility, tranquillity, and grief within. The floors were carpeted in flat, industrial-grade, dirt brown nylon, made to last and to deaden the sounds of dress shoes pounding across it. The ceilings were low-hung acoustical panels that had absorbed countless cries and murmured condolences.

Prejean's had two parlors for times that were regrettably busy, and a large kitchen that, if people had known how closely it resembled the embalming room, may well have gone unused. But, as with every social situation in South Louisiana, food was served for comfort and for affirmation of life. Women friends of T-Grace's, neighbors, fellow parishioners from Our Lady of the Seven Sorrows Catholic church would be in the kitchen brewing strong coffee and making sandwiches. Laurel knew Mama Pearl had brought a coconut cake.

Those who had come to pay respects to the Delahoussayes gathered in the Serenity room. The casket was positioned at the front of the room beneath a polished oak cross. Closed, the lid was piled high with white mums and gardenias, as if to discourage anyone from trying to lift it. Candles flickered at either end in tall brass candelabras.

People stood in knots of three and four at the back of the room, distancing themselves from death as much as they could while still supporting the family with their presence. Up front, more serious mourners sat in rows of chrome-and-plastic chairs that interlocked like Lego toys. Enola Meyette led the chanting of the rosary, a low murmur of French that underscored whispered conversations and muffled sobs.

T-Grace sat front and center in an ill-fitting black dress, her face swollen, her red hair standing out from her head as if she had been given an electric shock, her eyes huge and bloodshot. She was supported on one side by a burly son. To her right, Ovide sat in a catatonic state, his mouth slack, shoulders drooping beneath the weight of his grief.

Laurel's heart ached for them as she made her way through the throng to pay her respects. She knelt before T-Grace and took hold of a bony hand that had to be as least as cold as that of the daughter lying dead in the casket.

'I'm so sorry, T-Grace, Ovide,' she whispered, tears rising automatically. She had been schooled from childhood to keep her emotions politely concealed. Even at her father's funeral, Vivian had admonished her and Savannah to cry softly into their handkerchiefs so as not to make spectacles of themselves. But the day had been too long, and she was too tired and keyed-up for anything but a modicum of restraint.

T-Grace looked down on her, valiantly trying to smile, her thin mouth twisting and trembling with the effort. '*Merci*, Laurel. You're all the time so good to us.'

Laurel squeezed the hand in hers and pressed back the emotions crowding her throat. 'I wish I could do more,' she whispered, feeling impotent.

She turned to Ovide, trying to think of something to say to him, but his eyes were on his daughter's casket, glazed with a kind of numb shock, as if he had only just realized how permanent Annie's absence would be.

As Mrs. Meyette began another decade of the rosary, Laurel rose and moved off toward the back of the room, restless and uncomfortable as she always had been with the rituals of death. She scanned the crowd, looking for Jack, but not finding him. She didn't know if she was more disappointed for T-Grace and Ovide or for herself. Stupid. How many times had he told her she couldn't count on him? .

How many times had he made a lie of his own words?

He was a con man in his own right, playing a shell game with his personality. Distract the mark with the appearance of a rogue, while under one shell hid a heart filled with compassion and under another one compressed with grief and guilt. The shells swept and danced beneath his clever hands. Now you see it, now you don't. Which one held the real Jack? Would he ever let her close enough to find out?

She felt a little guilty, thinking about him during a wake, but in that moment she would have given just about anything to feel his arms slip around her, to hear his smoky voice murmur something irreverent in her ear. She was tired and worried, and she wanted very badly to share those fears with someone.

A call to Maison de Ville in New Orleans had assured her Savannah wasn't staying there. A call to Le Mascarade had gotten her nothing but a derisive laugh. Patrons names were confidential. She had tracked down Ronnie Peltier, who was hefting sacks at Collins Feed and Seed. He hadn't seen Savannah since Tuesday night. She had come to his trailer in a temper and left an hour or two later. He claimed he hadn't seen her since.

Laurel spotted him standing with a group of cronies across the room – Taureau Hebert and several other regulars from the bar. They looked young and uncomfortable in neckties. Their eyes avoided the casket at the front of the room.

'It's fascinating, isn't it?'

She jumped as Danjermond's voice sounded low and soft in her ear. He stood beside her, looking as perfectly pressed as he had that morning, his suit immaculate, tie neat. Laurel felt wilted and rumpled beside him even though she had showered and changed into a skirt and fresh blouse before coming. That effect alone was enough reason to avoid him, as far as she was concerned.

'All the different defense mechanisms people develop to deal with death,' he said, frowning slightly as his gaze moved over the gathering of the faithful and the bereaved. 'A dose of religion, gossip, and jokes served up with coffee and a slice of pie afterward.'

'People take comfort in ritual,' Laurel said, trying to sidle away from him, but he had her neatly trapped between himself and a potted palm.

'Yes, that's true,' he murmured, his sharp green gaze taking in the tableau of grief at the front of the room. T-Grace had begun to sob again, and her children gathered around her. Mrs. Meyette raised her voice, but never broke cadence in the recitation of the Hail Marys.

'Are you here in an official capacity or just out of morbid curiosity?'

He arched a brow at her sarcasm. 'Would you rather Kenner had come to represent Partout Parish?'

'Not even he would be that callous.'

T-Grace let out a series of soul-raking, ear-piercing wails, and one of her sons and Leonce Comeau half dragged her from the room. They were followed by old Doc Broussard, toting his black bag, and Father Antaya, each of them ready to dispense his own brand of medicine.

'Any sign of your sister, yet?' Danjermond asked.

'No, but if you'll excuse me, I see someone who may be able to help me.'

Calling on skills honed at countless cocktail parties, Laurel slipped away from him before he could voice a protest and worked her way through the crowd to the front of the room. The final amen was uttered, and those who had been praying rose stiffly, beads clacking as they stored their rosaries in purses, pouches, pockets.

Leonce came back into the room, his marred face grim, his bald spot shining with sweat. He pulled a red handkerchief out of his hip pocket and dabbed at the moisture. He had thrown a black jacket on over his black T-shirt and jeans, and shoved the sleeves to his elbows, making him look more like an artist or a rock star than a mourner.

'Hey, *chère*, where y'at?' he said, managing a weary smile as he settled a hand on Laurel's arm. 'Jack here?'

'No.'

His gaze cut away so she couldn't see the hope that sparked in his eyes. He looked to the coffin, gleaming polished oak beneath its drape of waxy gardenias and frayed mums. 'I shoulda guessed not. Jack, he don' do funerals. Been to one too many, I guess.'

Laurel made a noncommittal sound. 'How's T-Grace?'

'She's laying down in old man Prejean's office.' He shook his head, still amazed. 'Dat's some kinda scream she got, no?'

'I imagine losing a child tears loose a lot of things inside.'

'Yeah, I guess.' His dark gaze settled on the casket again because he was a little superstitious about turning his back on it. 'Poor Annie,' he murmured. 'Teased one dick too many. All she wanted was to pass a good time. Look what it got her.'

The implication made Laurel frown: No one asked to be tortured and killed. No woman deserved the kind of end Annie had met, regardless of what kind of life she had led. That thought bled into thoughts of Savannah, and Laurel's heart thumped at the base of her throat.

'Leonce, have you seen Savannah lately?'

He jerked around toward her, his brows slashing down over his eyes in a way that made his scar seem longer and more prominent. 'Hey, yeah, I gotta talk to you 'bout dat one,' he said ominously.

Taking her by the arm again, he led her out the door and into the shadows of the hall that led to the room where Prejean practiced his craft of readying people for the great beyond. The skin prickled at the base of Laurel's neck, and she cast a nervous glance back toward the Serenity room.

Leonce let go of her and stepped back, one hand propped at his waist, the other unconsciously touching his cheek, fingertips rubbing at the scar as if it might be erased. 'Tuesday night I'm comin' back from Loreauville – me, I sing with a band down there sometimes, you know? – and I'm drivin' down Tchoupitoulas 'bout a block from St. Joe's home. Here comes Savannah runnin' 'cross the grass, 'cross the street right in front of me. I damn near hit her. I lean out the window and I yell, "Hey, what's a matter wit' you, *chère*? You gone crazy or somethin'?"'

Laurel felt as if an anvil had dropped on her from a great height. This wasn't the story she had wanted to hear. She wanted him to tell her he'd

676

seen her sister driving off to Lafayette to visit friends or leaving with a lover for a tryst in New Orleans. She didn't want confirmation of a suspicion that made her weak with dread.

Leonce was watching her, waiting for some kind of response. She somehow managed to open her mouth and make words come out. 'Did she answer you?'

'Oh, yeah,' he snorted. 'She comes around the side window and tells me why don't I go fuck myself. How you like dat?'

'I don't,' Laurel murmured. She blew out a breath and combed her fingers back through her hair, walking in a slow circle around Leonce, her mind working automatically to assimilate the story into the other facts and pieces she'd stored away. Tears rose in her eyes as the nerves in her stomach twisted tight around a hot lump of fear.

'Hey,' Leonce drawled, spreading his hands wide. 'I didn' mean to upset you, *chère*. I just thought you oughta know.' He reached out to her, offering comfort and concern. Curling his fingers over her shoulder, he let his thumb brush against the pulse point in her throat. 'You wanna go get a drink or somethin' and talk about it? Me, I'm a pretty good listener.'

While the idea of escape appealed to her enormously, the idea of escaping with Leonce did not. There was just enough male interest in his big dark eyes to override the sympathy he was offering. And truth to tell, as ashamed as it made her feel, she didn't like looking at him. The scar continually drew her eye – the smooth, shiny quality of it, the grotesque burls of scar tissue that left brow and nose and lip slightly misshapen.

'We can go someplace dark,' he said, the musical quality of his voice flattened and hard. His fingers tightened briefly on her shoulder, then he jerked them away.

Laurel felt an immediate kick of guilt. 'No, Leonce, I didn't mean—'

'Is everything all right, Laurel?'

Danjermond stood at the end of the hall, half in light, half in shadow, his steady gaze shifting slowly from her to Leonce and back. Leonce swore under his breath in French and pushed past her, heading for a side exit.

Laurel heaved a sigh and pushed her glasses up on her nose. 'Yes, everything is just peachy.'

'I was just leaving,' he said, producing the keys to his Jag and dangling them from his hand. 'Would you care to join me for a nightcap or a cup of coffee?'

She shook her head, amazed at his inability to grasp the concept of the word 'no.' 'Your persistence is astounding, Mr. Danjermond.'

He smiled that feline smile. She could almost imagine him purring low in his throat. 'As I've said, nature rewards strength and tenacity.'

'Not tonight she doesn't.' Laurel slipped her hand into her pocketbook and brushed the chain of the butterfly necklace away from her tangle of keys. 'I'm going home.'

Danjermond inclined his handsome head, conceding. 'Some other time.'

When hell freezes over, Laurel thought as she walked out. The sky was purple and orange in the west. The light above the parking lot was winking on with a series of clicks and buzzes. She unlocked the door of the Acura and slid behind the wheel, thinking she would rather have gum surgery than go out with Stephen Danjermond. A date with him would have to be like consenting to have her brain poked with needles. She wondered if he had ever had a conversation that didn't run on three levels simultaneously. Perhaps as a child – if he had ever been a child. The Garden District Danjermonds probably frowned on childhood the same way her own mother had.

Odd, she thought, that they would have that in common and turn out so very different from one another. But then she'd already seen firsthand that shared experiences didn't guarantee shared responses. She and Savannah could scarcely have been less alike. Thousands of teenage girls were molested by stepfathers or other men in their lives; not all of them responded the way Savannah had. Statistics showed that abused boys grew into abusive men, but she couldn't picture Jack beating a child – he had wept over the one he had lost without knowing.

Jack. She wondered where he was, if he was privately mourning the loss of a friend or if he was tipping back a bottle of Wild Turkey and telling himself he didn't have any friends. He drank too much. She cared too much. She had read once somewhere that love wasn't always convenient, but she had never wanted to believe it could be hopeless. Jack swore he didn't want emotional entanglements. With tensions pulling her in all directions, she didn't feel strong enough to convince him otherwise.

She didn't feel strong enough to face Aunt Caroline tonight, either, but circumstances weren't offering any options. She had put it off as long as she could. Now she was going to have to sit down with her aunt and give voice to all the facts and fears about her sister.

Dread lying like a lead weight in her stomach, she put the car in gear and headed toward Belle Rivière, never aware of the eyes that watched her with vicious intent from cover of darkness.

The house was dark. Laurel let herself in the front door, feeling a guilty sense of relief. As necessary as it was to talk to Caroline about Savannah, she couldn't help being glad for a reprieve. The day had been long enough, trying enough.

The note on the hall table said Caroline had gone to New Iberia to spend the evening with friends. Mama Pearl would still be down at Prejean's, on kitchen duty until the last of the wake crowd had drunk the last of the coffee.

Laurel leaned against the hall table for a moment, trying to absorb the quiet. The old house stood around her, solid, substantial, safe, giving the odd creak and groan, sounds that were familiar and usually comforting. But tonight they only magnified the hollow feeling of loneliness that yawned inside her.

She felt alone. Abandoned. Guilty for having let her sister slip away toward madness.

Struggling with the feelings, she let herself out the hall door and went into the courtyard. Restlessly she walked the brick paths, staying near the gallery. After a few moments she settled on a bench and curled herself into the corner, tossing her purse onto the seat beside her.

The garden was mysterious by moonlight. Dark shapes that crouched and huddled, long shadows and hushed rustlings. By day it was growing lush and beautiful and in need of a weeding. That was what she had come to Belle Rivière for – quiet days of gardening, Mama Pearl's gruff fussing and fattening meals, Aunt Caroline's unflagging strength and pragmatism, Savannah's support.

Don't cry, Baby. Daddy's gone, but we'll always have each other.

How selfish she had been. Always taking Savannah's comfort, Savannah's protection. Too afraid of losing her mother's love to fight on Savannah's behalf. Burying herself in school, college, law school, work, while Savannah was left with bitter memories and her self-esteem in tatters.

Rise above your past. Put it behind you. Forget. She claimed she had, and it had always angered her that Savannah couldn't, *wouldn't.* Maybe all her sister had needed was someone to lean on, to help her, to support instead of ridicule, but Laurel had been off fighting other people's battles.

'I'm sorry, Sister,' she whispered, tears slipping down her cheeks. 'I'm so sorry. Please come home so I can tell you that in person.'

Her only answer was the call of a barred owl from the woods beyond L'Amour. Then stillness. Absolute stillness. The back of her neck tingled, and she sat up straighter, straining her eyes to see into the night, holding her breath and trying to hear beyond the rushing of her pulse in her ears. She imagined she could feel eyes on her, staring in through the back gate, but she could see nothing beyond the iron bars. She thought of her sister running through the night, wild with anger, full of pain.

'Savannah?'

Crickets sang, frogs answered back from the bayou, where a heavy mist crept over the bank.

Malevolence crawled over her skin like worms.

Eyes on the gate, she bent over her purse and fumbled for her gun.

'If you wanna shoot me, you're gonna have to turn around, *'tite chatte.'*

Laurel shrieked and whirled around to find Jack standing not three feet from her. Her heart went into warp drive. 'How the hell did you get in here?'

'The front door was open,' he said with a shrug. 'You really oughta be more careful, sugar. There's all kinds of lunatics running around these days.'

'Yes,' Laurel said, ignoring his wry tone. She was too damned spooked for banter. 'I thought I heard one on the other side of the gate.'

Frowning, Jack stepped past her and went to look. He came back, shaking his head. 'Nothing. What did you think it was? Someone in the bushes?'

Savannah, she thought, sick that it might have been, relieved that it hadn't been. 'What are you doing here?'

Good question. Jack stuffed his hands in the pockets of his jeans and wandered along the edge of the gallery and back. He had spent the evening walking along the bayou, trying to put as much distance as he could between himself and Prejean's Funeral Home. He couldn't bear the thought of a wake, and yet his thoughts had been filled with all of it – the coffin, the choking perfume of flowers, the intoning of the rosary. He could as well have been there for as raw as he felt now.

'I don' know,' he whispered, turning back toward Laurel. Lie. He knew too well. He needed her, wanted the feel of her in his arms because she was real and alive and he loved her. *Dieu*, how stupid, how cruel that he should fall in love with someone so good. He couldn't even tell her, because he knew it couldn't last. Nothing good ever did once he touched it.

'I saw your car,' he said, his voice strained and hoarse. 'Saw the light . . .'

His broad shoulders rose and fell. He turned to pace, but her small hand settled on his arm, holding him in place as effectively as an anchor. He looked down into her angel's face, and the air fisted in his lungs. She had left her glasses on the hall table, and she looked up at him with night blue eyes that mirrored the need that ached in his soul.

'I don't really care,' she said softly.

It didn't matter they had fought or that she had no hope for their future. This was just one night, and she felt so alone and so afraid. She looked up into his shadowed face, taking in the hard angles, the scarred chin, the eyes that had seen too much pain. It wasn't the face of the kind, safe lover she always envisioned for herself, but love him she did, and as they both stood there hurting, she needed him so badly, she thought she might die of it.

'Just tell me you'll stay,' she whispered. 'Just tonight.'

He should have said no. He should have walked away. He should never have come to her in the first place, but then he'd never been very good at doing what was right. And he couldn't look into her eyes and say no.

'You shouldn't want me,' he murmured, amazed that she did.

Laurel raised a hand and pressed her fingers to his lips. 'Don't tell me how bad you are, Jack. Show me how good you can be.'

He closed his eyes against a wave of pain, leaned down and brushed his lips against her cheek. It was as much of an answer as Laurel needed. Taking him by the hand, she led him up the back stairs and into her moonlit room.

They undressed each other quietly, patiently. They made love the same way, immersing themselves in the desire, steeping themselves in the experience, savoring the tenderness. Gentle touches. Soft, deep kisses. Caresses as sensuous as silk. A joining of bodies and two scarred souls. Straining to reach together for a kind of ecstasy that would banish shadows. A brilliant golden burst of pleasure. Trying desperately to hold on as it slipped away like stardust through their fingers.

And when it was over and Laurel lay asleep in his arms, Jack stared into the dark and wished with all that was left of his heart that he wouldn't have to let her go.

23

Chad Garrett tipped his battered Saints cap back on his head and let the sunrise hit him flush in the face. Above the Atchafalaya the sky was aglow with soft stripes of color. Orange the shade of a ripe peach, warm and estival. Pink as vibrant and silken as the underside of a conch shell. Deep, velvet blue, the last of the night, set with a diamond that was the morning star.

He grinned to himself at the image he had painted with his thoughts. He had a natural gift for words. He figured he would write down the description as part of his makeup work for playing hooky from school. Mrs. Cromwell would give him a thundering lecture for missing English class again, but she would melt like butter when he handed in his short story about dawn in the swamp and the peace a man could find on the water. She'd do handsprings over his new word – 'estival' – and that was an image that nearly made him chuckle. Mrs. Cromwell was fifty-eight and wore support hose and dresses that had enough fabric in them to clothe a family of four.

She was a good old girl, though, and Chad liked her as well as he liked any of his teachers. He was a good student, bright, capable. Hardly knew what a B was. But he didn't really care much for school, and, to the dismay of his teachers and the heartbreak of his mother, had no immediate plans to further his education once he graduated in June. This was where he wanted to be. In the swamp, observing nature, absorbing the beauty, the peace. He supposed he would relent after a year or two, go up to USL and study to become a naturalist or an environmental scientist of some kind or another. But for a while all he wanted to do was just be. He figured he would only be eighteen once. Might as well enjoy it.

He was his father's son in more respects than his big, raw-boned frame and square, good-looking face. Hap Garrett knew the value of contentment. He usually just smiled and turned a blind eye on those mornings when Chad didn't quite make it out of the boat shed without getting caught. As his dad liked to remind him, he'd been young once, too, and hadn't had much use for advanced algebra himself.

Chad steered his bass boat toward the shallows along a shaded bank, where a bit of yellow plastic ribbon marked one of his nets. The catch was good. He would make a couple hundred dollars today if his luck held down the line. The economics would appeal to Mr. Dinkle, whose class at ten he would miss.

He dumped the crawfish into an onion sack, sorting out the contorted body of a drowned water snake, which he tossed onto the bank. Some hungry scavenger would make a meal of it. Nothing went to waste in the swamp. Chad figured, if he was real lucky, he would witness nature's recycling, and that would appease Mr. Loop, fourth-period biology. He didn't figure he would have much of a wait. There was something up on the bank creating a powerful stink, the gagging, curiously sweet stench of death. The scent would act as a beacon.

Curious, he waded ashore and tied off his boat on a hackberry sapling. While he might not have given a fig how the balance of world power worked or how to find the square root of a negative, Chad wanted to know every detail about the life of the swamp.

It looked to him as if something had been dragged up on the bank. The weeds were bent and stained with blood. Might have been a deer that had gotten itself in trouble with a gator while drinking from the stream. It could have pulled itself back up onto the shore only to die of blood loss and shock. Or it could have been that a bobcat had caught himself a coon or a possum or a nutria, ate his fill, and left the rest. There were a dozen possibilities he could think of.

He pushed aside a tangle of branches and stopped cold in his tracks. Of the dozen possibilities he had considered, he hadn't included this. For the rest of his life he would see that face in his nightmares – beauty distorted grotesquely by death and the plain, hard realities of nature, blue eyes forever frozen in a shocked stare that made him think she had witnessed her own terrible fate and had seen beyond it to a terrible afterlife.

A woman lay dead at his feet. Horribly dead. Hideously dead. Naked and mutilated, with a white silk scarf knotted around her throat and a scrap of paper clutched in her stiff, lifeless hand.

Laurel woke alone. She wasn't surprised, so she told herself she couldn't be disappointed. But she was. Her brain told her she was foolish, that it wasn't practical or smart to want a future with Jack Boudreaux. He had too many ghosts, too much emotional baggage. But her brain couldn't do anything to banish her memories of the night – Jack's tenderness, the longing in his eyes, the pounding of his heart beneath her hand. Her heart was determined to hold on to those memories and the slim hope that went with them. Foolish, foolish heart.

He had gone at first light, she knew. Just as she had done before. She swept her arm across the vacant space beside her, finding nothing but a tangled sheet and a twisted spread. Not even his warmth lingered, just the scent of man and loving.

What would she do about him? What *could* she do? She couldn't change his image of himself. She had enough on her hands as it was.

That reminder brought thoughts of Savannah, and Laurel's stomach tensed like a fist at the thought of the conversation she would have with Aunt Caroline this morning. Restless, anxious, she climbed out of bed, pulled on a T-shirt and panties, and went in search of her pocketbook and the roll of Maalox tablets therein. It lay on the bench in the courtyard, where she had left it, the fine calfskin coated with thick, velvety dew. She wiped it off with the tail of her oversize T-shirt and went back upstairs to sit on the bed.

Careless, Laurel thought, reaching into the bag in search of her antacid tablets. She knew better than to leave a purse lying around, especially one with a semiautomatic handgun in it. Instead of the roll of tablets, she came up with the gaudy heart-shaped earring that had no mate and no explanation. The earwire had caught the chain of the little gold necklace, and she fished that out as well to untangle the mess and to work at untangling the mystery. It would give her mind something to do besides worry about her sister for a few moments. It would delay her conversation with Caroline.

The chain was twisted and knotted, and there seemed to be too many dangling ends. Strange, she thought, noting dimly that her heart was beating a little faster and her fingers fumbled at their task. She plucked at the gold butterfly and tugged a little harder at the chain, her breath coming in shorter bursts. Tears brimmed up in her eyes, not from frustration, not for any discernible reason. Silly, she thought, scratching at the tangle with the stub of a fingernail.

The butterfly and its necklace came free of the snag and fluttered to Laurel's lap, forgotten as cold, hard fingers of terror gripped her throat and squeezed. Hanging down from her trembling fist was a fine gold chain, and from the chain, swaying gently, a diamond chip winking as it caught the morning light, hung a small gold heart.

Savannah's.

'Oh, God. Oh, my God.'

The words barely broke the silence of the room. She sat there, shaking, icy rivulets of sweat running down her spine. Her lungs seemed to have turned to concrete, crushing her heart, incapable of expanding to draw breath. She stared at the pendant until her eyes were burning, fragmented thoughts shooting across her mind like shrapnel – Daddy standing behind Savannah at twelve, fastening the chain, smiling, kissing her cheek; Savannah at twenty, at thirty, still wearing it. She never took it off. Never.

It swung from Laurel's fist, the tiny diamond bright and mocking, and dread crept through her like disease, weakening her, breaking her down. Tears blurred the image of the heart as she thought back to the night she

684

had gone into Savannah's room. The feeling of stillness, of loss, of an absence that would never be filled.

'Oh, God,' she said, choking on the fear, doubling over. She pressed her fist and the necklace against her cheek as scalding tears squeezed out from between her lashes.

She couldn't deal with this, couldn't face what she knew in her heart must be true. God, she couldn't go to Aunt Caroline and Mama Pearl – She couldn't go to Vivian – She didn't want to be here – should never have come back. She wanted Jack, wanted his arms around her, wanted him to be the kind of man she could lean on—

Selfish, weak, coward.

The recriminations came hard, as sharp as the crack of a whip. She had to do something. She couldn't just huddle here on her bed, half naked and sobbing, wishing someone else would be strong for her. There had to be something she could do. It couldn't be too late.

'No. No. No,' she chanted, stumbling away from the bed.

She repeated the word over and over like a mantra as she tore open her wardrobe and drawers and grabbed a wrinkled pair of jeans, never letting go of the necklace. It wasn't too late. It couldn't be too late. She would go to Kenner and make him see. She would call in the damn FBI. They would find Savannah. It couldn't be too late.

Wild urgency drove her as she tugged on the jeans. At the heart of the feeling was futility, but she refused to recognize it or accept it. The situation couldn't be futile. She couldn't lose her sister. She wouldn't let it happen. There had to be something she could do. Dammit, she would *not* let it happen!

Frantic, she flung the bedroom door back and ran down the hall and down the stairs, the railing skimming through one hand, Savannah's necklace gripped tight in the other. Her sneakers pounded on the treads, her pulse pounded in her ears. She didn't register the pounding at the front door.

Caroline came into the hall from the dining room, already dressed for the day in stark black and white. She glanced up at Laurel, concern knitting her brows, her hand reaching out automatically for the brass knob.

As if in a dream, time became strangely elastic, stretching, slowing. Laurel's perceptions became almost painfully sharp. The blocks of white in Caroline's dress hurt her eyes, the smell of Chanel filled her head, the creak of door hinges shrieked in her ears. She tightened her fist, and the golden heart burned into her palm.

Kenner stepped into the hall, lean and grim, eyes shaded. The shadow of death. His hat in his hands. His lips moved, but Laurel couldn't hear his words above the suddenly amplified roaring of her pulse. She saw the color drain from Caroline's face, the stricken look in her eyes. Together

Kenner and Caroline turned and looked up at Laurel, and the knowledge pierced her heart like a knife.

'NO!!!' The denial tore from her throat like a scream. 'NO!!!' she screamed, stumbling down the last few stairs.

She hurled herself at Kenner, striking his chest with her fists.

Surreal, she thought dimly, a part of her feeling strangely detached from the turmoil of the moment. This couldn't be happening. She couldn't be yelling or lashing out at Kenner. This couldn't be the real world, because everything in her field of vision had become suddenly magnified, as if she were shrinking and shrinking. And the sound of Caroline's voice came to her as if through a fog.

'Laurel, no! She's gone. She's gone. Oh, dear God! She's dead!'

Another cry of anguish and shock reverberated against the high ceiling of the hall. In her peripheral vision, Laurel could see Mama Pearl, her face contorted, reaching for Caroline with one hand, the other groping along the wall as if she had gone blind.

'God have mercy, I love dat chil'. I love dat chil' like my own!'

'Mama doesn't love me,' Savannah said, her voice hollow and sad, breaking the stillness of the cool fall night.

They lay in bed together, wide awake, way past Laurel's bedtime. She cuddled against her sister, knowing she was supposed to be too old for it but afraid to move away. Not a week had passed since Daddy's funeral, and she was too aware of the precious, precarious state of life.

It was a knowledge no child should ever have to grasp. The weight of it was terrible. The fear it inspired had been with her day and night – that the world could be tipped upside down in a heartbeat. Everything she knew, everything she loved could be snatched away from her without warning.

Knowing that made her want to hang on with both hands to everything that was dear to her – her dolls, the kittens old mama cat had hidden in the boat house, Daddy's tie pin, Savannah. Most especially she wanted to hang on to Savannah – the person who loved her most after Daddy, the person who kept her from being alone.

'I love you, Sister,' she said, quivering inside at the desperation in her voice. 'I'll always love you.'

'I know, Baby,' Savannah murmured, kissing the top of her head. 'We'll always have each other. That's all that matters.'

Laurel sat down on the bottom step, dazed and weak, her stunned gaze locked on the small pendant that dangled from her fist. And the feeling she had feared so badly all those years ago crept over her and into her, spreading through her like ink, opening her heart like a chasm that grew wider by the second.

The sister who had loved her, protected her, defined her world, was gone. And it didn't matter that she was thirty, or that there were other people in her life now who mattered. In that moment, as she sat there on the step, she was ten years old all over again, and she was alone. Her world had turned upside down, and the most precious thing in it had been snatched away, leaving nothing behind but a small heart of gold.

'I want to see her.'

They sat in the parlor at Belle Rivière, Kenner, Danjermond, Laurel, and Caroline. An incongruous scene. The parlor with its soft pink walls and quietly elegant furnishings, a place of serenity and comfort, filled with brittle tension and people who had gathered to talk of a brutal, heinous crime. Men for whom this death was a part of their business, and family who couldn't reconcile the idea of one of their own being torn from their lives.

The sound of Mama Pearl weeping drifted in from the kitchen, breaking the silence that hung as Kenner and Danjermond exchanged a look. Laurel set her jaw and rose from the camelback sofa to pace.

Caroline sat at the other end of the sofa. Her aura of power and control had been snuffed out, doused by a tidal wave of shock and grief, leaving her powerless. A queen who had suddenly been stripped of her potency. For the first time since her brother had died she seemed completely at a loss, so stunned by the news that she wasn't even sure this was really happening. But of course it was. Savannah had been found murdered. That was the terrible reality.

Lifting a crumpled tissue to her eyes, Caroline looked up at Laurel, who paced the width of the Brussels carpet like a soldier, shoulders back, chin up. She had been this way when her daddy had died, as well, full of stubborn denial and anger. Ten years old, demanding she be taken to him, insisting that he wasn't dead.

She could remember too clearly the rage, the fear, the heartbreak, Vivian telling the girls to cry softly into their hankies like little ladies. Caroline had gone up to Savannah's room with them, and they had all lain on the bed and sobbed their hearts out together.

'I want to see her,' Laurel said again.

Caroline caught her eye and shook her head sadly, reproachfully. 'Laurel, darlin', don't . . .'

Laurel jerked away, clinging to her stubbornness like a life preserver. After her initial reaction to the news Kenner had brought, she had slammed the door on her grief, bottling it up, saving it for later. For now, she had to hang tough, she had to keep her head . . . or lose her mind altogether.

Kenner rose from the armchair, restless, unnerved by what he'd seen this morning out on Pony Bayou. If he lived to be a hundred, his sleep would forever be plagued by Annie Gerrard and Savannah Chandler, their bodies carved up like biology experiments, rotted and bloated by the effects of death and the merciless southern sun.

'I don't think that would be a very good idea,' he murmured.

Laurel wheeled on him, ears pinned, eyes flashing fire. 'You didn't think she was in any danger, either. You didn't think she would be anyplace but in bed with one of a hundred men,' she said bitterly, stalking him across the carpet. Toe to toe with him, she glared up into his lean, hard face and narrow eyes. 'Pardon me if I don't have a whole helluva lot of faith in what you think, Sheriff.'

He glanced away from her, unable to meet the accusation in her eyes. His gaze landed on a graceful side table that held framed photographs of the Chandler girls, Savannah's senior year high school picture catching his eye. He had a daughter nearly that age.

'Next of kin has to make a positive ID,' Laurel said, grasping hold of practicality for an excuse. She wasn't feeling practical. Desperation was like a wild thing inside her. She had to see her sister now, sooner than now. Maybe someone had made a mistake. Maybe it wasn't really her. Maybe Savannah wasn't really dead. God, she couldn't be dead. They had parted so angrily, left so many things unsaid. It just couldn't be true—

'We already have an ID, Laurel,' Danjermond said, his smooth, low voice penetrating her thoughts. He sat in Caroline's throne, his masculine grace perfectly at home draped over rose damask. He met her gaze evenly. 'Your stepfather came down to the funeral parlor.'

He could just as well have slapped her. The idea of Ross Leighton's being the first of them to see Savannah appalled her. The bastard had dealt Savannah enough degradation in her life. He shouldn't have been allowed anywhere near her in her death. Fresh hot tears welled in Laurel's eyes, and she turned her back on the district attorney.

'Sheriff Kenner and I realize the grief you've been dealt, Laurel,' he said, 'but time is of the essence here if we're to catch your sister's murderer. We need to talk about this necklace you found. You were a prosecutor. You understand, don't you, Laurel?'

Yes, she understood. Business. Danjermond and Kenner would take her sister's death and boil it down to facts and figures. It was their job. It had been her job once too.

'The necklace was Savannah's,' she said flatly. 'She never took it off. This morning it was in my pocketbook.'

'Do you have any idea how it might have gotten there?'

'I expect someone put it in there, but I didn't see it happen.'

'You think the killer put it there?'

Killer. Her stomach churned at the word, sending sour bile up the back of her throat. She choked it down and snatched a quick, hard breath, rubbing a hand at the base of her throat. 'No one else would have gotten it off Savannah. It meant the world to her. She would never have willingly taken it off.'

Danjermond rose and came around to face her, his hands in the pockets of his gray trousers. His expression was one she had seen in the courtroom a hundred times, a look she had honed to perfection herself – subtle disbelief, designed to rattle a witness. 'You think the murderer

688

took it off her and somehow slipped it into your handbag without your knowledge – for what purpose?'

The rush of anger was welcome. It distracted her, focused her attention on something she could affect the outcome of – an argument. She went to the Sheraton table and with jerky, angry movements, dug through the purse she had left there, tossing out Kleenex, Life Savers, a tampon. In one handful she scooped out the heart-shaped earring and the butterfly necklace and dumped them on a silver tray, then swung around to face Danjermond again. 'For the same reason he made certain I found these.'

The idea shook her to the core. A murderer, a psychopath had singled her out to send his trophies to. Why? To taunt, to challenge? She didn't want the challenge. She hadn't come here to be sucked into something twisted and sinister. The thought that someone was trying to do that made her want to cut and run as far as she could go, as fast as she could get there.

Danjermond pulled a slim gold pen out of his jacket pocket and poked at the items like a scientist, frowning. Kenner's eyes caught on the butterfly necklace, and he swore long and colorfully.

He shouldered Danjermond aside and bent to stare at the evidence Laurel Chandler had been carrying around in her handbag. 'That was Annie Gerrard's. Tony gave it to her. He asked about it when he picked up her personal effects.' Hard and sharp, his gaze cut to Laurel. 'Goddammit, why didn't you bring this to me?'

'Why would I?' Laurel snapped back. 'I found it in an envelope on the seat of my car. Why would I have assumed a serial killer had sent it to me? Why would I think you would do anything about it but laugh in my face?'

'Where'd you find the earring?' he demanded, knowing in his gut it belonged to another victim. The killer had kept a souvenir from each.

'I found it on the hall table. Savannah told me she brought it in from my car.' She felt violated as she thought of it. The animal who had killed her sister, who had killed at least half a dozen women, had let himself into her car, touched things she touched, left behind mementos of his crimes. A shudder passed through her at the idea, chilling her to the marrow.

Kenner straightened, still swearing half under his breath. He couldn't believe this was happening in his parish. He ruled with an iron fist and an eagle eye. How could this have happened? He felt like a cleanliness fanatic who had turned a light on only to find roaches in his kitchen.

'I'm impounding the car,' he declared, stalking across the room in search of a telephone. 'We'll dust it for prints, have the lab boys from New Iberia go over it for trace evidence. And I'll take the handbag too.'

Laurel nodded.

He snarled and turned to Caroline. 'I need to use a phone, and I need to bag this jewelry as evidence. Have you got any Ziploc bags?'

'I don't know,' she murmured, rising, shaken anew by this bizarre turn of events. She fussed with the black beads she wore, trying without success to think clearly. 'They would be in the kitchen, I suppose,' she mumbled, her gaze darting nervously to Laurel, to Kenner, to Danjermond, and back, as if one of them might have the answer. 'Pearl would know. We'll ask Pearl.'

They went out and down the hall. As the parlor door swung open then shut, the sound of Mama Pearl's wailing rose and fell. Laurel stood staring down at the cheap, gaudy earring with its chips of colored glass. Some woman had thought it was pretty, had worn it to feel special, had died wearing it. Had she died a brutal death, as Savannah had, suffering horribly, alone with her tormentor, begging for death? Tears rose in her eyes, in her throat. She held them at bay with sheer willpower.

'Why you, Laurel?' Danjermond's voice flowed over her like silk, the question burned like acid.

'I don't know,' she whispered.

'Why would he single you out? Is he someone you know? Are you someone he wants?'

She flinched at the thought, struggled to hang on to her logic. 'I – I d-don't fit the pattern.'

'No, you don't.' He hooked a finger beneath her chin and lifted her face, as if he thought he might see the answers in her eyes. 'Does he want you to catch him, Laurel? Or does he want to show you he can't be caught?'

She met his steady green gaze, felt it probing, felt its power. She backed away from it, from him, shaking her head, feeling too raw for this kind of cross examination. 'I don't know. I don't want to know.'

He arched a brow. 'You don't want to see him caught?'

'Of course I do,' she said vehemently. She paced away from him again, raking a hand back through the hair she hadn't even combed yet today. 'I want him caught,' she said, her voice trembling with the need for it. 'I want him tried and convicted and sentenced to a death worse than anything the courts would allow.' She stopped and glared up at him, hating him for his calm control. 'If I could, I'd be the one to drive the stake through his heart with my own two hands.'

'You have to catch him first.'

'That's Kenner's job, your job,' Laurel said, backing down again mentally and physically. 'Not mine.'

Danjermond lifted the earring on the end of his fine gold pen, watching as it twisted in the air and caught the light like a Christmas ornament. 'I don't think he would agree, Laurel.'

24

News of the murder cut through Bayou Breaux like a hurricane that left emotional devastation and uprooted fears in its wake. By noon there wasn't anyone in town who hadn't heard a telling and a retelling of Chad Garrett's story. It was the hot topic over comb-outs and manicures at Yvette's House of Style, where Savannah had had her nails done by Suzette Fourcade only days before. Suzette was near to inconsolable with hysterical grief over the loss of a friend and the idea of having touched someone who had since been killed. Yvette waited for the call to come from Prejean's asking her to do the grim honors of fixing Savannah's hair and makeup for her final public appearance before being laid to rest.

The story was served up with coffee and *beignets* at Madame Collette's, where Ruby Jeffcoat pontificated on the evils that awaited girls who wore skirts cut up to their fannies and no underwear, and Marvella Whatley refilled cups absently as her mind wandered back over the years she had served the Chandler girls rhubarb pie and Coca-Cola.

The old men on their bench in front of the hardware store shook their heads over the state of the world and watched the street with rheumy eyes that held anger and fear, and frustration that they were too old to protect their loved ones or to avenge them. And down at Collins Feed and Seed the boys all patted a dazed Ronnie Peltier on the shoulder and gathered in the break room without him to retell the tales of his and others' sexual exploits with Savannah. She was a legend among the male population of Partout Parish. If it hadn't been so gruesome, her sensational death would have seemed almost fitting.

All over town the details of the crime were broken down, scrutinized, analyzed, compared to the details of Annie Gerrard's death. Both women had been strangled. Both had been raped – or so everyone figured; the sheriff was keeping mum on that particular topic. Both had been subjected to the kind of horrors folks in Bayou Breaux had never dreamed one human being could put another through. But someone had dreamed it. Someone had done it. And rumor had it Savannah Chandler had been found with a page from a book clutched in her hand. A book called *Evil Illusions* by Jack Boudreaux.

'No one ever did know what to make of him,' Clem Haskell said, stirring a third packet of sugar into his coffee. Doc Broussard was after him to cut calories and reduce the size of the spare tire around his middle, but he was a cane grower and hell would freeze over before anyone got him to put chemical sweetener in his coffee or anyplace else. The stuff caused cancer and who knew what all, he was certain. His spoon rattled against his saucer, and he took hold of the cup and raised it to his lips, wishing he had something stronger to fortify his nerves. Too bad Reverend Baldwin frowned on strong drink.

March Branford forked up a chunk of cherry pie and stared down at it, his appetite in revolt as images of dead women flashed behind his sunken eyes like scenes from a movie. 'What kind of twisted mind writes trash the like of that? No normal God-fearing man,' he ventured, putting the fork down to tug on one long earlobe. 'The Lord never intended for man to profit from evil. That's the work of the devil, that's what that is.'

'That it is, Deacon Branford.'

Jimmy Lee nodded sagely, sadly, looking out on the audience of eavesdroppers in Madame Collette's as he ran his tongue along the jagged edges of two chipped caps. There wasn't a soul in the place who didn't look edgy. They'd had two murders in a matter of days. Annie Gerrard wasn't even in her tomb, and now poor Savannah Chandler was dead. People wanted an explanation. They wanted someone to be guilty. They wanted to be able to point a finger and say, 'He did it,' so they would be able to sleep nights. Jack Boudreaux seemed a prime candidate.

'Didn't I say the very same to y'all when last we met to pray?' he said, struggling to keep from lisping through the cracks in his dental work. 'Those books are the product of an evil mind. The poisonous spewings of Satan.'

Ken Powers knew all about poisonous spewings. His stepson Rick listened to rock groups with names like Megadeth and Slayer. Bunch of long-haired drug freaks who screamed out nothing but Satanic messages. And the kid was rotten to the core because of it. No respect for God or man. Sneaking pornographic magazines into the house and doing who-knew-what with that crowd of hoodlums he hung out with. They probably all read Jack Boudreaux's books and acted out the sex and violence with rock music blasting in the background.

'I knew the minute he bought that whore's house there was something strange about him,' Ken said, planting his elbows on the table and leaning toward the reverend, his round, pink face shining with conviction. He was himself a good Christian man, and wanted everyone to know it. By God, him and Nan and the rest of their kids would show the whole town what upstanding people they were. Never mind the bad seed son Nan had spawned from her first husband.

'He bought the house of a harlot who died a violent death. He writes of evil and vileness and sin. Now one of our own fallen daughters is found dead with a page from one of his books. It's a sign, as sure as the sign of Lucifer himself.'

Jimmy Lee bowed his head and folded his hands on the Formica tabletop. 'Amen, Deacon Powers. If only our good Sheriff Kenner could be made to see the light.'

While his deacons grumbled among themselves over who would have the honor of representing them with the sheriff, Jimmy Lee rubbed his tongue over his ruined teeth and wished Jack Boudreaux a nice trip to hell via Angola Penitentiary.

At that same moment Jack stood on the balcony at L'Amour, staring out at the bayou, suffering through a kind of hell Jimmy Lee Baldwin had never known – the hell of conscience. He had wandered the empty streets of town after leaving Laurel, trying to clear his head, and had ended up at Madame Collette's for a cup of coffee just as the breakfast crowd was coming in. Ruby Jeffcoat had wasted no time telling him the news, her eyes gleaming with malicious relish. Her sister Louise was a dispatcher in the sheriff's office and had it all firsthand. Some maniac had up and killed Savannah Chandler and left a page from one of Jack's books in her hand – stuck right under her thumb, so as not to blow away.

The rest of her juicy details had glanced off Jack. He didn't hear a word about how Chad Garrett had gotten sick and started a chain reaction with the deputies at the scene. He didn't hear Ruby's first sermon of the day on how women who behaved as whores were just asking for the kind of end Savannah Chandler had met. He didn't hear the clatter of coffee cups or the ring of flatware on china. He sat there at the counter, feeling as if he were having an out-of-body experience, and fragments of something Jimmy Lee Baldwin had said flashed in his head like lightning. '. . . *unstable minds . . . commit unspeakable acts . . .*'

Savannah was dead. All that wild, tormented spirit gone, wrung out and discarded like a rag. She had been so vibrant, so full of need and hate. He could hardly imagine all of that energy simply ceasing to exist.

No, not simply. There had been nothing simple about her death. It had been prolonged and hideous. '. . . *unstable minds . . . unspeakable acts . . .*' And she'd been found with a scrap of one of his books in her hand.

Stupidly, he wondered which book, which page, calling to mind a hundred scenes of death that had been telegraphed from his imagination down through his fingers and onto the pages of a book. Which one had Savannah been forced to endure?

Furious with himself, he stalked back into his bedroom and went to his desk. He didn't write to inspire; he wrote to entertain. He wrote to exorcise his own inner demons, not to lure others' out of hiding. He couldn't be held responsible because someone had used him as an excuse to commit murder. If it hadn't been his book, it would have been a song on the radio or a voice on television or a telepathic message from God. Blame could always be placed elsewhere.

Christ, he knew that, didn't he? He wasn't responsible; it was someone else's fault.

His writer's mind too easily conjured up an image of Savannah lying dead along the bayou, sightless eyes staring up at an unmerciful heaven. Swearing viciously, he swept an arm across his desk, sending debris flying – manuscript pages, scribbled notes, a royalty statement, pens, paper clips. He snatched up a stack of copies of *Evil Illusions* and hurled them one by one across the room as hard as he could throw them, knocking a water glass off his dresser and sending an etched glass lamp crashing to the cypress floor.

He didn't want Savannah Chandler in his head. He didn't want Laurel Chandler in his heart. He didn't want responsibility, couldn't handle it. He'd proven himself time and again. He was his father's son, the product of his mother's weakness and his old man's hate.

And he had another corpse on his conscience.

Clutching his hands over his head, he howled his rage and his pain up at the plaster medallion on the ceiling.

Why? When he wanted nothing from anyone, when he had given up all hope of having the kind of life he had always dreamed of – why did he still get pulled in? He'd done his best to avoid emotional entanglements. He'd made it clear to everyone that he shouldn't be relied upon. Yet here he was, in it up to his ears. The frustration of it hardened and trembled inside him. Eyes wild, chest heaving, he swung around in search of something else to vent it on.

Laurel stood in the doorway.

Everything inside Jack went instantly still and soft at the sight of her. The anger that had cloaked him vaporized, leaving him feeling naked and vulnerable, his heart pumping too hard in his chest. She looked like a waif in her baggy jeans and rumpled T-shirt. Her eyes, so warm and blue, dominated her small, pale face.

'Savannah is dead,' she whispered.

'I heard.'

She crossed her arms and kicked herself for wishing he would come to her and wrap her up in his embrace. That was what she had come here for: comfort and to escape the sound of sobbing and the incessant ringing of the telephone. Reporters calling in search of a story, friends calling to express genuine sympathy, townspeople calling on the pretense of compassion to appease their morbid curiosity. She had come to escape the ghoulish bustle of cops searching her sister's room and hauling her car away and asking redundant questions until she wanted to scream. She had come in search of a moment's peace, but as her gaze scanned over the wreckage from Jack's rage, she had the sinking feeling she wasn't going to find any.

'I'm going down to Prejean's to see her.'

'Jesus, Laurel . . .'

'I have to. She's—' She blinked hard and swallowed back the present tense, grimacing at the bitter taste. 'She was my sister. I can't just let her go . . . alone . . .'

Tears glossed across her vision, blurring her image of Jack. She didn't want to let them fall, not yet. Not in front of anyone. Later, when night had come and she'd seen to all the duties she needed to, when she was alone. All alone . . . She had to be strong now, just like when Daddy had died. Only when Daddy had died, she had had Savannah to lean on.

Don't cry, Baby. Daddy's gone, but we'll always have each other.

She gulped a breath of air and tried to distract herself from the memory by making a mental list of the things she needed to do. See Savannah, see that the arrangements were being made, and that Mr. Prejean had the right clothes to put her in, and that pink roses were ordered. Pink roses were Savannah's favorite. She would want lots of them, with baby's breath and white satin ribbons.

The grief hit her broadside, like a battering ram, and staggered her, shattering the strength that had somehow managed to hold her up during the endless interview with Kenner and Danjermond. She fell to her knees amid the debris from Jack's desk and put her face in her hands, sobbing as it tore through her with talons like daggers.

'Oh, God, she's dead!'

Jack didn't give himself time to think about his own pain, his own needs, the distance he had meant to put between himself and Laurel. He couldn't stand by and watch her fall apart. He didn't have it in him to walk away. The love he never should have allowed to take root bound him there, drew him to her.

He knelt beside her and gathered her close, squeezing his eyes shut at the sound of her weeping. The sobs racked her body, making him acutely aware of how small she was, how fragile. He cradled her against him as if she were made of crystal, and stroked her hair and kissed her temple, and rocked her, crooning to her softly in a language he wasn't even sure she understood.

'I miss her so much!' Laurel choked the words out, a fist of regret and remorse lodged in her throat.

The feelings filled her, ached in her bones, in her muscles, like a virus. Loss. Such a terrible sense of loss, an emptiness as hard as steel inside her. It had been only a matter of hours, and yet the sense of loneliness was crushing.

Why? That one question arose again and again. Savannah's death seemed so senseless, so sadistic. What kind of God could allow such cruelty? *Why?* It was the same question she had asked twenty years ago, when her father had been taken away from her. No one had had an answer for it then, either.

695

That was perhaps the worst of it. She was a person with a logical, practical mind. If a thing made sense, had a reason behind it, she could understand at least. But things that struck from out of the blue defied logic. There was no reason, no explanation she might find some comfort in. That left her with nothing, nothing to cling to, not even hope, because in a world where anything might happen at any time, unpredictability shoved hope aside and left fear in its place.

'I hate this!' she whispered, her face pressed into Jack's shoulder. 'I hate these feelings. God, I wish I'd never come back here!'

Jack rocked her, tightening his arms around her. 'It wouldn't have mattered, angel. It wouldn't have changed anything.'

Laurel thought of the trinkets the killer had left for her and wondered. Would he have sent them to someone else? Would he have killed some other woman's only sister?

Regardless of the answer, she was caught with the burden of guilt; someone died either way. Responsibility pressed down on her, just as it had in Scott County. She thought she would have given anything for the chance to get out, but she knew she wouldn't take the chance if it were offered. She was trapped by her own sense of duty and honor, stuck here in yet another nightmare.

'I'd undo it for you if I could,' Jack said softly.

Jack, who claimed to be nobody's hero, would have gone back and changed history for her. Laurel slipped her arms around him and held on, knowing he wasn't the man to anchor her life to. But the need and the knowledge clashed inside her, and need won out for the moment.

'We can go away for a few days,' he whispered. 'Get away from it. I know a cabin over on Bayou Noir—'

'I can't.' Laurel sat back a little, blinking up at him through her tears. She swiped a hand under her eyes and combed her hair back with her fingers. 'I – I can't go anywhere. There are things to do – arrangements—' She swallowed hard and let the real reason come to the fore. 'I have to find out who did this. Someone has to pay.'

'And you have to be the one to catch him?' Jack said sharply, her sense of responsibility rubbing against the grain of his selfishness. He wanted her safe and all to himself, if not forever, then for a little while. 'We've got a sheriff for that.'

'The killer isn't sending the sheriff trophies from his conquests,' she said bleakly. 'He's sent me three.'

The news hit Jack with the force of a baseball bat, leaving him incredulous, a little dizzy, a little sick. A murderer had singled her out. He sat back on his heels, his jaw slack, his fingers tight as he held her at arm's length. 'He's sent you what?'

'An earring. I don't know whose. And Annie Gerrard's necklace. This morning I found a necklace of Savannah's in my pocketbook.'

'Jesus Christ, Laurel! That's all the more reason to get the hell out!'

'That's what you'd do, Jack?' She arched a brow, studying him hard enough that he dropped his hands and glanced away. 'Cut and run? I don't think so. For all you like to play it that way, I don't think you would. I know I can't.'

'You'd rather end up with a silk scarf knotted around your throat?' he said brutally, his hands shaking at the idea of anyone's hurting her. The concern set everything inside him shaking. He never should have gotten involved with her. Of all the women he could have had, he'd fallen for the one who carried the weight of the world on her shoulders.

'I don't fit the pattern,' she said. 'I'm not promiscuous.'

'You been sleeping with me, haven't you, *'tite chatte*?'

Laurel scowled at the sardonic edge in his voice. 'That's different.'

He gave an exaggerated shrug. 'How is that different? You hardly know me, we go to bed together, we have sex. How is that different? You think this killer is gonna split hairs?'

'Stop it!' she snapped, hating him for belittling what they had had together. Even if he didn't want to call it love, it was more than sex. It certainly wasn't in the same category as what Savannah had shared with the likes of Ronnie Peltier and Jimmy Lee Baldwin. Her fingers curled over some of the papers he had swept off his desk in his rage, and she snatched them up and threw them at him, a gesture that was more symbolic of futility than fury.

'You amaze me,' Jack said, grabbing hold of his anger with both hands. Better to be angry than afraid. Better to push her away than to cling to her when he knew he'd lose her in the end anyway. 'You think you're Wonder Woman or something. Every bad thing that happens, you think you could have stopped it, you think you have to solve it, win the day for justice.'

'Oh, excuse me for being a responsible person!'

'That's not responsibility, that's arrogance.'

Laurel gasped as the jab stuck deep. 'How dare you say that to me!' she said, her voice a trembling whisper that rose in pitch and volume with each word. 'You sit up here in this private prison you bought yourself, drinking your liver into a knot, taking the blame for someone else ending their own life! Everything that happened was *your* fault – but, no, it's not really *your* fault because your father was a son of a bitch. Let's get him up here and we can have us a real finger-pointing session.'

'We can't,' he shouted, leaning over her.

'Why not?' she yelled, meeting his glare.

'Because I killed him!'

Like a marionette whose strings had been cut, Laurel plopped down on the floor amid the drift of manuscript pages and scribbled notes, stunned speechless.

'With my own two hands,' Jack whispered, lifting his hands for examination, the long, elegant fingers spread wide as he turned them this way and that.

He rose slowly to his feet, a strange calm settling inside him. He had wanted to be rid of her. Wasn't that what he had told himself as he walked the deserted streets of town in the gray mist before dawn? Loving her hurt too much, and the end, which was inevitable, would be excruciating. This was his chance to make the break, his chance to show her once and for all just what he was. Then *she* could walk away from him.

'He hit Maman one time too many. He knocked me aside too many times without ever thinking one day I wouldn't be puny and weak.'

He stared right through her, into his past, seeing it all once more – the shabby kitchen that smelled of grease, his mother cowering by the stained sink, Blackie going after her with his arm raised.

'I grabbed an iron skillet off the stove – it was the first thing that came to hand – and I hit him, smashed his skull in like an eggshell,' he said flatly, as if he needed to unplug all emotion to be able to tell the story. 'I don't think I meant to kill him,' he said, though after all these years he still wasn't sure. Christ knew he had wished Blackie dead often enough, to put an end to the fear and the shame. 'I just wanted him to stop hitting Maman. I was finally big enough to make him stop. That's all I wanted – for him to stop, for him to leave us alone.'

He sniffed and held his breath a moment, fighting the rise of childhood feelings and gathering the old bitterness as fuel to go on. 'And while my mother sat on the floor with blood running out of her broken nose, crying over this man who had abused her and her children for seventeen years, I dragged his body out to our *bâteau*. I took ol' Blackie for a ride into the swamp, tied an anchor around his middle, and dumped him in the deepest, darkest water I could find. No need for a decent burial when he was going straight to hell anyway. No need to drag the sheriff into it. We all just pretended he went out on a bender and never came back.

'That's the kind of man you think you fell in love with, sugar,' he said, his voice low and rough. 'You think you know me? You think you've got me pegged? You think mebbe there's something worth loving under all the scars? Think again. I killed my own father, drove my wife to suicide. I went from a profession where I got paid to lie and cheat to one that inspires twisted minds to commit murder.' A bitter smile twisted his mouth. 'Yeah, I'm a helluva guy, *chère*. You oughta fall in love with the like of me.'

She didn't say a word, just sat there staring up at him with those wide eyes, and he knew he would have given anything to be the kind of man she needed. A bitter thought. A foolish thought. He was the last man she needed. Laurel deserved a champion, a knight in shining armor, not a jaded mercenary, not a man with ghosts. He was nothing but the worst kind of bastard. What he was doing to her now was absolute proof of that. *Dieu*, she'd just lost her sister, and here he was breaking her heart just to save what was left of his own.

One of the papers on the floor caught his eye, and he bent and grabbed it up, a sad parody of a smile pulling at his lips as he read his own handwriting. He had forgotten all about his ulterior motive for getting to know her. Such a poor ruse, he hadn't made more than a token effort to convince himself. But here it was in black and white, just in time to finish the job of cutting his own throat.

'Here,' he murmured, handing it to her. 'Here's the kind of man you come to in your hour of grief, angel. I'm sorry you didn' believe me the first time I told you.'

Laurel didn't look at the piece of notebook paper she held in her hand. She stood up slowly on rubbery legs and watched Jack walk away from her. He went out onto the balcony without looking back, and she felt as though he had taken her heart out there with him. When she finally dropped her gaze to the carelessly scrawled notes, she knew he had pitched it off the balcony and into the murky waters of the bayou.

Laurel – obsessed with justice. A burden of guilt from past sins, real or imagined. Subdues femininity (unsuccessfully) with baggy clothes, etc. Represses sexuality (perfect conflict with prospective hero). A fascinating dichotomy of strength and fragility. Strong ties to dead father.

Need to get details on case that sent her over the edge. Were the accused guilty? Did she just want them to be? Why? Could write abuse into background.

A character profile. He'd been studying her, making notes for future reference. Her gaze fell to the floor, picking out the odd newspaper clippings among the sheets of typing paper and lined paper. The headlines jumped up at her as if they were three-dimensional: *Scott County Prosecutor Cries Wolf. Charges Dismissed, Chandler Resigns.*

She wouldn't have believed it was possible to hurt more than she already did. She would have been wrong. A new spring of pain bubbled up inside her. It was on a different level than the pain of losing Savannah, but it was no less sharp, no less acidic.

It wasn't as if he hadn't warned her, she thought, lashes beating back a fresh sheen of tears. It wasn't as if she hadn't warned herself. He wasn't the man for her. This wasn't the time. Too bad she had never gotten her heart to listen.

'Was it all grist for the mill, Jack?' she asked, going slowly, shakily to the open French doors. 'The way we made love? The way you cried when you told me about Evie? The way Annie died, and Savannah – is that all plot for the next best-seller?' The thought sickened her. 'Everything we did together, everything we – I – felt . . .' The words trailed off, the prospects too cruel to consider aloud.

'You missed your calling, Jack,' she said bitterly. 'You should have been an actor.'

He said nothing in his own defense. He just stood with his hands braced on the balcony railing, broad shoulders hunched, gaze fixed on the bayou. His expression was hard, closed, remote, as if he had taken himself to some dark place of solitude – or torment – within himself. Laurel wanted to hit him. She wanted to pound a confession out of him, a confession that refuted the damning evidence he had handed her himself. But she didn't hit him, and he didn't recant a word of his testimony. There wasn't a judge in the country who wouldn't have convicted him – for crimes of the heart, at the very least.

'I guess you proved your point,' she whispered. 'You're a bastard and a user. Bad for me.'

She stepped out onto the balcony, appalled that the day could be so beautiful, that the birds could be singing. Below them, the bayou moved, a sluggish stream of chocolate. Huey lay sleeping on the bank.

'I know that you can't help the things that shaped you,' she said, looking up at him through a watery haze that made him seem more dream than real. 'None of us can. Savannah couldn't change the fact that our stepfather used her as his private whore. I can't change the fact that I knew and never did anything about it,' she admitted, her voice choked with pain. 'But you know something, Jack? I'll be damned if I'll believe we don't have the power within us to get past all that and be something better.

'You put that in your book, Jack.' Chin up, tears streaming down her cheeks, she slipped the folded note-paper in his hip pocket. 'And at least be decent enough to write me a happy ending.'

Standing on pride alone, she turned and left him . . . left L'Amour . . . left her heart in pieces.

25

The summons to Beauvoir came before Laurel could leave the house for Prejean's. Vivian was on the brink of one of her spells, distraught over the news of Savannah's death. Dr. Broussard and Reverend Stipple had been sent for, but what she *really* needed was the comfort of having her only remaining child nearby.

Laurel's strongest urge was to say no. Vivian had disowned Savannah in life, had long ago ceased to love her. She couldn't keep from thinking that this was a ploy to gain attention, not a plea for sympathy or support. Vivian and Savannah had been rivals since the day of Savannah's birth. Why would that change after her death?

But the burden of guilt and family duty won out in the end. Laurel found herself in Caroline's burgundy BMW, turning up the tree-lined drive of her childhood home, cursing herself for being weak. She could almost envision Savannah looking down on her with disapproval. *Still scrambling for Mama's love, Baby? Aren't you pathetic.*

She cut the engine and lay her forehead against the steering wheel for a moment, shutting her eyes against the exhaustion that pulled at her. She couldn't have felt more battered if someone had taken a club to her. Every part of her felt bruised, every cell of her body ached – her skin, her hair, her teeth, her muscles, her heart. Most especially her heart.

Images of Jack kept rising before her mind's eye, and her besieged brain struggled to rationalize in the name of self-preservation. He had pushed her away because he was afraid of hurting her. He had pushed her away because he was afraid of being hurt. But nothing she came up with could refute the evidence she had held in her hands.

God, he'd been studying her, jotting down notes, formulating theories as if she were nothing more than a fictitious character. The pain of that was incredible.

And still she wanted him to love her. The shame of that was absolute. She wanted him to come to her and tell her it was all a mistake, that he loved her, that he would be there for her as she struggled with the grief of loss. What a fool she was. She'd known from the start he wasn't the kind of man to depend on.

She sucked in a jerky breath, fighting the tears. She would get through this. She would get over it. She would get over him. She would find some way to be strong for Savannah.

Olive answered the door, looking appropriately dolorous, her skin as gray as her uniform, her eyes bleak. The maid led the way up the grand staircase and down the hall, and Laurel followed automatically, her mind on other times spent here.

Like ghosts, she heard the voices of her childhood – Savannah's wild laugh, her own shy giggle, Daddy promising he would come find them and tickle them silly. The memories bombarded her – good and bad. She remembered walking down this same hall to her mother's room the day of Daddy's funeral, and watching while Vivian applied her makeup artfully around her puffy red eyes.

You must endeavor to be a little lady, Laurel. You're a Chandler, and that's what's expected.

Then Vivian had loaded up on Valium and sat through the funeral in a daze, while her daughters struggled to weep gracefully into their handkerchiefs.

Vivian's spell of depression after Jefferson's death had lasted two months. Then Ross Leighton had begun worming his way into their lives.

Vivian's rooms comprised a spacious suite that saw a decorator from Lafayette once a year. The latest incarnation was a festival of floral chintz in shades of teal and peach. Olive escorted Laurel through the sitting room with its clutter of English antiques, knocked on the door to the bedroom, and opened it an inch when the muffled invitation came from within. Eyes downcast like a whipped dog, the maid slunk away as Laurel went in.

Her mother stood by the French doors, wrapped in teal silk, one arm banded across her middle, the other hand rubbing absently at the base of her throat. Opals glowed warmly on her earlobes. A ring with a stone the size of a sparrow's egg drew the eye to the hand pressed against her chest. She turned as Laurel entered the room, her features drawn tight, eyes looking dramatically sunken beneath the camouflage of dark eye shadow.

'Oh, Laurel, thank God you've come,' she said, her voice reedy and strained. 'I had to see you for myself.'

'I'm here, Mama.'

Vivian shook her head in disbelief and paced listlessly. 'Savannah. I just can't accept what the sheriff had to say. That she was murdered. Like those other women, she was murdered. Strangled.' She whispered the word as if it were profane, her right hand still rubbing at her throat. 'Right here in our own backyard, practically. I swear, I can't bear the thought of it. The instant he told us, I nearly fainted. My throat constricted so, I could barely breathe. Ross had to bring my medication to the parlor, and I could hardly swallow it. He brought me straight to bed, but I couldn't rest until I'd seen you.'

'I was on my way to the funeral home,' Laurel said, toying with an arrangement of tiger lilies that filled a Dresden pitcher. 'Would you like to come?'

Vivian gasped and sank down on the edge of the bed, careful to keep her knees together and tilted properly, one hand expertly seeing that her robe was tucked just so. 'Heavens, no! I just couldn't bear it. Not now. I'm simply not up to it. I – I'm just weak with shock from it all, and filled with such emotions—'

She broke off as her beautiful aquamarine eyes filled, plucked a lace-edged hankie out of her breast pocket, and blotted at the moisture.

Anger built inside Laurel as she watched from beneath her lashes. Her sister was dead, and their mother sat here doing a one-woman show for sympathy. Poor Vivian lost the daughter she never loved. Poor Vivian, so fragile, so sensitive, like something out of Tennessee Williams.

'I haven't had a spell in so long,' she went on, twisting her handkerchief in her fingers. 'But I can feel it coming on, stealing over me like a shadow of doom. You can't know how I dread it. It's a terrible thing.'

'So is your daughter's murder,' Laurel said tightly.

Her mother's eyes went wide. Her hands stilled in her lap. 'Well, of course it is. It's horrible!'

Laurel turned and gave her a hard look of accusation. 'But the most important thing is how it affects you. Right?'

'Laurel! How can you say such a thing to me?'

She shouldn't have. She knew she shouldn't have. Good girls didn't sass back. Ladies kept their opinions to themselves. But all the dictates from her upbringing couldn't hold back the rage she had stored inside her all these years. In her mind she could see Savannah lying dead, could hardly allow herself to imagine the way her sister had suffered. And here was Vivian, playing Blanche DuBois. Always the center of attention. Never mind who else might be in pain.

'It was just the same when Daddy was killed,' she said, her voice trembling with the power of her emotions. 'It wasn't a matter of all of us losing him. You had to turn it around so the focus was on *you*, so people flocked out here to check on *you*, so they all went around town saying "Poor Vivian. She's in such a state."'

'I *was* in such a state!' Vivian exclaimed, pushing to her feet. 'I had lost my husband!'

'Well, it didn't take you long to find another one, did it?' Laurel snapped, the pains of childhood flowing through her like fresh, hot blood.

Her mother's eyes narrowed. 'You still resent my marrying Ross. All the sacrifices I made for you and your sister, and all I get in return is bitterness and criticism.'

'Daddy was barely cold in the ground!'

'He was dead,' she said harshly. 'He was gone and never coming back. I had to do something.'

'You didn't have to bring *him* into this house, into Daddy's room, into our lives.'

Into Savannah's bed. God, if it hadn't been for Ross Leighton, Savannah might still be alive. She might have grown up to fulfill all the potential he had crushed out from inside her.

'Ross was a fine catch,' Vivian said defensively, fussing with the lace at the throat of her nightgown. 'From a good family. Respected. Handsome. Wealthy in his own right. And willing to take on the children of another man. Not every man is willing to do that, you know. I can tell you, I was very grateful to have him come calling. I couldn't manage the plantation by myself. I was in such a weakened state after Jefferson died, I just didn't know if I'd ever function again.'

And along came Ross Leighton. Like a vulture. Like a wolf scenting lambs. Willing to take on another man's children? Willing to take their innocence. Vivian had no idea just how willing Ross had been.

Because Laurel had never told her.

'Don't tell Mama. . . . No one will ever believe you. . . .'

She wheeled toward her mother to let the terrible secret loose at long last, but the words turned to concrete in her mouth. What good would it do now? Would it bring Savannah back? Would it give them back their childhood? Or would it only prolong the pain and mire them all more deeply in the muck of the past?

'I did what was best for all of us,' Vivian said imperiously. 'Not that you or your sister ever showed a moment's appreciation. Your father spoiled you both so.

'And Savannah was always jealous of any attention I might have garnered for myself from Jefferson. She was no different with Ross. I swear, I don't know where that girl got her wildness, her stubbornness. I'd say from Jefferson's side; Caroline is just that way, you know. But Caroline never had an interest in men—'

'Stop it!' Laurel shouted, her voice ripping across the quiet, elegant room. Her mother gaped at her, mouth working soundlessly, like a bass out of water. 'It's none of your business who Aunt Caroline sleeps with. At least she's happy. At least she's not deluding herself into believing she needs to have a relationship with a man no matter what kind of slime he is.'

'No, she's not like Savannah that way, is she?' Vivian said archly. Her own anger simmering, she resumed her pacing along the length of the half-tester bed. 'I don't know how many times I told her to be a lady. All the hours of training, of showing by example how a lady should comport herself, and none of it doing any good at all. She lived like a tramp – dressing like a slut, going off to bed with any man who crooked his finger. God, the shame of it was almost too much to bear!' she said bitterly. 'And now she's killed because of it.'

She shook her head, wrapping her arms around herself as if trying to physically hold herself together. A fresh sheen of tears glistened in her eyes as she resumed her pacing. 'I don't know how I'll be able to hold my head up in town.'

'That's all you care about?' Laurel demanded, stunned. 'You think Savannah embarrassed you by falling prey to a psychopath?'

Vivian wheeled on her, eyes flashing. 'That's not what I said!'

'Yes, it is! That's exactly what you said. Christ, she was your daughter!'

'Yes, she was my daughter,' Vivian snapped, her face turning a mottled red as long-held feelings surfaced inside her. 'And I will *never* understand how that could be, how God could give me a child like her – so beautiful on the outside and rotten to the core. I will never understand—'

'Because we kept it from you!' Laurel cried.

She clamped her hands on top of her head and turned around, everything within her in turmoil. She had tried to tamp the truth down inside her again, to bury it for all time, but it ripped loose and clawed its way free. Savannah was dead indirectly because of what Ross had made her into. *And because I kept the silence.*

The guilt was like a vise, twisting and twisting, crushing her. She couldn't change the past, but someone had to pay. Vivian couldn't go on living in her watercolor fantasies. Ross couldn't be allowed to escape the consequences of his actions. Justice had to be served somehow, some way.

Vivian watched her with wary eyes. She swiped a strand of ash blond hair back behind her ear in an impatient gesture. 'What do you mean, "kept it from me"? Kept what from me?'

'That Ross, the wonderful, well-bred, charitable knight in shining armor who swept in and rescued you, molested your daughter.' She met her mother's shocked stare evenly, unblinking. 'He used her, in the carnal sense, night after night, week after week, year after year.'

'You're lying!' Vivian said on a gasp. She clutched a hand to her throat and swallowed twice, as if the words Laurel had spoken were gagging her. 'That's a horrid lie! Why would you say such a thing?'

'Because it's the truth and because I'm sick to death of keeping it a secret!' Laurel advanced on her mother, her hands balled into tight, white-knuckled fists at her side. 'Everything Savannah became is because of Ross Leighton. Now she's dead, and the one person who should be inconsolable is more concerned about her own image than her daughter's murder. I can't stand it!'

The slap connected solidly with her cheek and snapped her head to the side. She didn't try to block it or the second blow Vivian glanced off her shoulder. She deserved worse – not for what she had said to her mother, but for what she hadn't said all those years ago. Vivian shoved her, then backed away, her eyes wild, her lips twitching and trembling.

'You ungrateful little bitch!' she spat, her silky hair falling across her forehead and into her eyes. 'Lies. That's all you have in you is lies! You lied to those people in Georgia, now you're lying to me! You hated Ross from day one. You'd do anything to hurt him!'

'Yes, I hate him. I hate him for taking my father's place, but I hate him more for taking my sister.' The incredulity she had known during those years came back in a violent rush. How could their mother not have realized? How could that have gone on in her house without her suspecting? 'Didn't you ever wonder where he was all those nights, Mama? Or were you just thankful he wasn't coming to your bed?'

Vivian's face washed white, and she brought a trembling hand up to press against her mouth, to press back the cry, to hold back the bile that rose in her throat. She'd never cared for sex. It was messy and revolting, all that grunting and sweating. She'd never questioned Ross's calm acceptance of her disinclination to share her bed. She'd never thought once of where he might be relieving his manly urges – as long as he was discreet, she didn't care. But with her own daughter?

No. It couldn't be. Things like that didn't happen in good families.

'No,' she said softly, rejecting the possibility with her mind, with her body. She flung her hands out as if to push the idea away.

'Yes,' Laurel insisted. 'He came to her room two or three nights a week and had his way with her, whatever way he happened to be in a mood for – intercourse, oral sex—'

'Shut up! Shut up! I won't listen to this!' Vivian planted her hands over her ears to try to block out the ugly accusations. Laurel grabbed her wrists and jerked them down, shouting in her face.

'You *will* listen! You should have listened twenty years ago! If you had given a damn about anyone but yourself, you would have seen, you would have known,' she said, the realization bringing tears of bitterness to cloud her vision. 'I wouldn't have been afraid to tell you. I wouldn't have been afraid of losing your love. I was too young to know you weren't capable of giving any.'

Her mother pulled back from her, reeling as if she had been struck full in the face. 'I *always* loved you!'

'When it was convenient. When we were good little girls and no trouble. That's not love, Mama,' Laurel murmured, despair choking her. 'If you had loved us, you would have seen that Savannah needed help, that something was wrong, that Ross was a child molester.'

'He wasn't!' He couldn't be. She couldn't bear the thought of it.

'Ross Leighton treated your daughter like a whore until she believed that was all she could ever be.'

The red had crept back into Vivian's face, and her eyes bulged out like T-Grace Delahoussaye's. 'I don't believe you. You're a vicious little liar. Get out. Get out of my house!' she screamed. 'You're not my daughter! I don't have any daughters!'

Laurel gave her a long, hard stare. The hurt was sharp and deep, the disillusionment absolute. 'You know something,' she said quietly, the fury spent. 'I wish to God that were true.'

She left the room without looking back, without acknowledging the maid who had been eavesdropping in the hall. The more people who knew the truth, the better. Now that it was out of that terrible little black box of secrets inside her, Laurel had every intention of making Ross Leighton's perversity common knowledge in Partout Parish. He would never face the charges in court, but he could damn well face them every time he walked down a street or walked into a store or a restaurant. He would never do time inside the walls of a penitentiary; a sentence of public disgrace would have to suffice.

The front door swung open as Laurel came down the grand staircase, and her stepfather ushered in Reverend Stipple.

'Laurel,' Ross said, beaming one of his bland smiles up at her. 'I'm so glad you could come for your mother's sake.'

'You won't be.' Laurel stepped down onto the polished tile and cut a glance at the minister, whose small eyes widened as he scented trouble like a mouse scenting the approach of cats. He took an instinctive step back, his bony hands fumbling to straighten his limp seersucker jacket. Laurel wondered what he would think of Ross Leighton now; if he would condemn, or in his weak and ineffectual way find some excuse to make it all right.

'I told her,' she said, turning back to her stepfather.

Understanding dawned like shock in his eyes, but he pretended not to know, as he had pretended innocence all these years. 'Told her what, darlin'?'

'The truth about the way you used my sister when she was too young to stop you. The truth about the way you turned her into a whore for your own personal enjoyment.'

Reverend Stipple gasped at the words and their implications. Color crept up Ross's thick neck and into his face. He opened his mouth to protest, but Laurel cut him off with a sharp motion of her hand.

'Don't bother denying it while I'm standing here, you son of a bitch. I know what happened. I knew all along. I know what you turned her into. I know that she's dead because of it. I kept the silence all this time, kept that terrible secret inside me, let you get off scot-free. Not anymore,' she promised, her voice trembling as badly as the rest of her.

'I told Vivian,' she said, glaring up at him − hale and hearty with his suntan and his swept-back hair, the man of wealth and leisure in his green country club shirt and khaki slacks. He should have been the one cut up and left for dead. 'I told Vivian, and I sincerely hope that she kills you.'

Ross caught her arm as she started toward the door. 'Laurel, wait—'

She jerked away from him with a violent move, her eyes burning hate into his. 'No. I waited long enough.'

Hatred boiling inside her like a poison, she left the house and left the grounds, the tires of the car flinging crushed shell up in its wake.

And Ross Leighton stood at the door of the mansion he had taken from another man, and watched her go, panic writhing like a snake in his gut.

'Jesus Christ, I hate religious fanatics.' Kenner stretched back in his chair, trying to work out the kink between his shoulder blades. His gaze trailed the followers of The True Path out of the outer office and into the hall. He especially hated that they were men who lived around Bayou Breaux and were of an age to vote. That meant he had to give at least some token credence to what they had to say.

He turned his narrowed eyes on their ringleader, who still sat in the visitor's chair on the other side of the desk. Slick. That was the way he would describe Jimmy Lee Baldwin. He hated slick. Slick was damn near always trouble.

'So you think Jack Boudreaux strangled all them girls and cut 'em up for kicks?'

Jimmy Lee steepled his fingers and looked concerned, his tawny brows drawing into a little tent above his eyes, his tongue worrying over his chipped teeth. 'You've heard the testimony of my deacons, Sheriff. I'm not alone in my suspicions.'

'No. Well, other people have other suspicions.' Kenner shook a cigarette out of the crumpled pack on his desk and searched in vain for his matches. Danjermond, who was standing against the row of file cabinets, came forward and offered him a light from a slim wand of twenty-four karat gold. The sheriff inhaled deeply and blew a stream of blue at the grimy ceiling, never taking his eyes off Baldwin. 'What would you say if I told you someone came to me with a little story about you and Savannah Chandler?'

The preacher closed his eyes and shook his head as if he were in deep emotional pain. 'Laurel,' he murmured, privately cursing her to hell and gone. 'She came to me with the same story. Apparently the workings of Savannah's sadly twisted mind. Heaven only knows where she might have come up with such tales of depravity. I fear she walked a dark path,' he said with a dramatic sigh.

Kenner sniffed in derision and cleared his throat nosily. 'I don't give a rat's ass what path she walked. Why would she have it in for you?'

Jimmy Lee cut the theatrics in half. The sheriff was not a patient man. 'She was a regular at Frenchie's Landing. I would see that den of iniquity shut down.'

'You ever tie a woman up to have sex with her?' Kenner asked bluntly.

'Sheriff! I am a man of God!'

'Plenty of shit gets done in the name of God. Did you ever?'

Jimmy Lee looked him square in the eye, as innocent as an altar boy. 'I wouldn't dream of it.'

But he was dreaming of it when he left the sheriff's office five minutes later. And the face of the woman bound beneath him was Laurel Chandler's.

Kenner stubbed his cigarette out in the overflowing ashtray and swung his chair around to face Danjermond, privately wondering how the district attorney could manage to stay looking like some cover boy from

GQ while he looked and felt and smelled like a survivor of a jungle campaign. They had all been putting in hellish hours since the discovery of Annie Gerrard's body. The stress, the fatigue rolled off Danjermond like oil off Teflon.

'What do you think, Steve?' Kenner asked. 'Is the preacher a pervert, or is Jack Boudreaux our man?'

Danjermond tightened his jaw at the nickname, but made no comment. Twisting his signet ring on his finger, he wandered to the window, noticing with irritation that the blind had been hung crooked. 'I can't think that Annie Gerrard would have had anything to do with Baldwin, considering he was trying to shut down her parents' bar. He denies involvement with Savannah Chandler. No one has actually seen them together. As to Savannah's accusations – well, we know she was a woman who might say or do anything. She may well have had a grudge against him. We'll never know.'

'And Boudreaux?'

'Certainly has the kind of imagination it would take. If his books are anything to go by, he has a taste for violence. He knew both women. He has a reputation as a ladies' man.'

'But no stories floating around about him tying them up or getting rough.'

Danjermond turned from the window, pinning the sheriff with a penetrating stare. 'He may have killed his wife back in Houston, Sheriff Kenner,' he said darkly. 'Is that rough enough for you?'

Frowning hard in thought, Kenner reached for the pack of Camels on his desk, shook out the last one, and dangled it from his lip, 'Maybe we'd better have us a little chat with Mr. Jack Boudreaux.'

It was late afternoon by the time Laurel made it to Prejean's Funeral Home. Aunt Caroline had tried to talk her out of it. Hadn't the day been terrible enough? Wouldn't it be better to wait until after the autopsy and after Mr. Prejean had done his part? Wouldn't she rather remember her sister as something other than the victim of a brutal crime?

Yes, but she *was* the victim of a brutal crime, a crime she had suffered through alone. Laurel couldn't bear the thought of it. They had always had each other. Even when Ross was making his secret visits to Savannah's room, they had still shared the pain afterward. The idea that her sister had faced her killer all alone, in the swamp, where there was no one to hear her cries for help, where there was no such thing as forgiveness, no mercy . . .

Blinking back the tears, she pulled open the front door and stepped into the hall, then gagged at the heavy perfume of carnations and Lemon Pledge. A vacuum cleaner was droning in the Serenity room. Mantovani seeped out of the speaker system – syrupy violins and twittering flutes.

Lawrence Prejean stepped out of his office and walked right to her, as if he had sensed her presence. He was a small man, not much taller than Laurel, spare and wiry with an elegance that had long made her think of him as a Cajun Fred Astaire. He had a thin layer of neatly combed dark hair and big, liquid brown eyes that were perpetually sympathetic.

'*Chérie*, I'm so sorry for your loss,' he said softly, sliding an arm around her shoulders.

Laurel wondered dimly how, after so many losses, so many tragedies, he could still dispense such genuine feeling to the bereaved.

'Your Tante Caroline called to tell me you were coming down,' he said, taking her by the hand. 'Are you sure you want to do this, *chère*?'

'Yes.'

'You know we are transporting her to Lafayette tonight?'

'Yes, I know. I just want to sit with her for a while. I need to see her.'

She almost choked on the words, and shook her head, annoyed with herself. She had gone back to Belle Rivière from Beauvoir, taken a long shower, followed the dictates of Mama Pearl and lay down for a time, thinking all the while that she was composing herself, that she would be able to do this without breaking down. '*Comport yourself as a lady, Laurel. You're a Chandler; it's expected.*'

Prejean paused at the door to the embalming room and patted her hand consolingly, his big dark eyes as warm and deep as an ancient soul's. 'She was your sister,' he murmured. 'Of course you need to see her. Of course you will cry. You need to grieve. Grieve deeply, *chérie*. There is no shame in that you loved your sister.'

Her eyes glossed over, and she dug a hand into the pocketbook she'd borrowed from Caroline to pull out a crumpled pink tissue.

He ushered her into the room with a gentle hand on her shoulder. The aromas of flowers and dust spray were replaced by medicinal and strongly antiseptic scents, reminiscent of a high school biology lab. And beneath the overpowering smell of formaldehyde and ammonia, the fetid stench of death lingered. The room was as neat as any operating room, as cold and sterile. The linoleum shone under the glare of fluorescent lights. In the center of the floor stood the table.

Laurel stood beside the draped figure, still managing to find some fragment of hope that it wouldn't be her sister. Prejean pulled a chrome-and-plastic chair over and situated it in a way that suggested he thought she might pass out.

'You're ready, *chère*?' he whispered. After all his years in this business, he seldom tried to contradict the wishes of those who were left behind. Death stirred up many needs, both bright and dark. Only the one experiencing the loss could know what those needs were and how they had to be met.

At Laurel's nod he slowly folded down the drape, uncovering only the dead woman's face and carefully arranging the sheet so that it covered the horrible discoloration on her throat.

Laurel took one long, painful look at her sister's face, swollen and distorted, and that small, irrational part of her mind tried to tell her that her most desperate hope was a reality. This wasn't Savannah. It couldn't be. Savannah was beautiful. Savannah had always been the pretty one, and she had always been the little mouse. This couldn't be Savannah's wild, silken mane, this dull, matted tangle of hair. This couldn't be Savannah's elegant, patrician face, this flat-featured, gray mask.

But another part of her brain, the logical, practical part, overruled with a harsh voice. *That's your sister. Your sister is dead. Dead. Dead. Dead . . .* Her gaze seemed to zoom in on the grotesquely distorted features, on the single gold earring still pinned to the right ear – a loop of brightly polished, hammered gold that hung from a smaller loop of braided gold wire. Savannah had had a pair made in New Orleans. A present to herself for her last birthday. *This is your sister, this ugly corpse. She's dead.* The truth filled her mind, the putrid smell of it filled her nostrils and throat.

With a weak, piteous sound mewing in her throat, she sank down into the plastic chair and bent over her knees, torn between the need to cry and the need to vomit. Prejean had anticipated the possibility and sat a stainless steel bucket beside the chair. He squatted down beside her and brushed cool, soft fingers against her cheek.

'Are you all right, *chérie*? Should I call someone to take you home?'

'No,' she whispered, swallowing hard and willing her stomach to settle. 'No, I just want to sit here for a while, if that's all right.'

He patted the hand that gripped the arm of the chair. She was a brave little thing. 'Stay as long as you need, *petite*. The sheriff will be coming later. If you need anything, there's a buzzer near the door.'

Laurel nodded, knowing the procedure. She had always stood on the other side of it, where it looked logical and necessary. From where she sat now, her perceptions distorted by emotion, it seemed unbelievably cruel. Her sister had been taken from her, killed, and now the authorities would put her through the indignity of dissecting her body. The ME might find some crucial evidence that could solve the case and condemn the killer, she knew. But in that moment when grief threatened to swamp all else, she had a hard time accepting.

Questions from childhood drifted up through the layers of memory. Questions she had asked Savannah about death. '*Where did Daddy go, Sister? Do you think he's with the angels?*' They had been raised to believe in heaven and hell. But doubts had edged in on those beliefs from time to time, as they did for every child, for everyone. What if it wasn't true? What if life was all we had? Where would Savannah go? Savannah, so lost, so tormented. *Oh, please, God, let her find peace.*

Time slipped away as she sat there wondering, remembering, hurting, grieving. She let go of all the tears she had tried to hold on to, of all the pain she had been so afraid to feel. It all came pouring out in a torrent, in a storm that shook her and drained her. She knew Prejean checked on her once, but he left her alone, wise enough to realize she had to weather the onslaught of her grief alone. Alone, the way her sister had died.

She thought of that when the tears had all been cried. The way Savannah had died, the way Annie had died, the way their killer had chosen her to play games with.

'Does he want you to catch him, Laurel? Or does he want to show you he can't be caught?'

'I'll catch you, you bastard,' she whispered, staring hard at the shrouded body on the table. 'I'll catch you before you can put anyone else through this hell.'

The 'how' of that question eluded her for the moment. She had no jurisdiction here. Kenner wouldn't let her interfere. But the 'how' was unimportant just now. The vow was important. She had come home to hide from the shame and the failure of Scott County, where justice had not prevailed. She had wanted to turn away from the challenge here. She had watched Danjermond poke through the pieces of jewelry with his slim gold pen and listened to him ask her questions in his smooth, calm voice, and she had wanted nothing more than to turn and run. But she couldn't.

Justice would win this time. It had to. If there was no justice, then all the suffering was for nothing. Senseless. Meaningless. There had to be justice. Even now, even too late, she wanted justice for Savannah.

'What are you trying to atone for, Laurel?' Dr. Pritchard asked, tapping his pencil against his lips.

For my silence. For my cowardice. For the past.

Justice was the way.

She couldn't just put the past behind her. It would never be forgotten. But there could be justice, and she would do everything in her power to get it, she vowed as old fears and old guilts settled inside her and melded and solidified into a new strength. She would fight for justice, and she would win it . . . or die trying.

They came for the body at seven-thirty. Kenner and a deputy. They would escort the hearse to Lafayette and witness the autopsy, which would be performed by a team of pathologists. Partout Parish had neither the budget nor the need for the kind of equipment necessary for detailed forensic work. Laurel went out into the hall and stood there, not able to watch them zip her sister into a body bag. But she stayed until she heard the cars drive away and Prejean came back out of the room.

'I'll bring some clothes for her tomorrow,' she said, her heart like a weight in her chest. 'And there's a necklace – something our father gave her. I'll have to get it back from the sheriff. She wouldn't want to go anywhere without it.'

'I understand.'

But would Kenner? she wondered as she walked out into an evening that smelled of fresh-mowed grass and approaching rain. The necklace was evidence.

How had it gotten into her pocketbook? When? These were questions she had gone over with the sheriff half the morning. She turned them over and over again as she leaned on the roof of the BMW and watched the thin stream of traffic pass on Huey Long Boulevard. She either had to have been separated from the bag when it happened or had to have been in a crowd. Someone could have come into the house, into her room, but that seemed far too risky for a killer as smart as this one.

If not for the fact that she was now on her way to an appointment with a coroner, Laurel knew she once might have suspected Savannah, and the shame of that curled inside her. She hadn't wanted to think about it, but her mind had sorted all the information into logical rows and columns, and, God help her, the theory had begun to take shape. Savannah – unstable, jealous, filled with hate for the image she had of herself as a whore, a violent temper simmering just beneath the surface. Savannah – her big sister, her protector, the one person in the world she loved above all.

'I'm sorry, Sister,' she whispered, squeezing her raw, burning eyes shut against a fresh wave of guilt.

Think. She had to think. Savannah was gone; it wouldn't do any good to be sorry now.

The necklace could easily have been planted while she was in a crowded room. It would have been a simple matter of stepping close, making the drop, walking away. Easier than picking a pocket.

A crowd. Annie's wake. The thought that the killer might have come to his victim's wake was almost too ghoulish to contemplate. He might have stood in that room, as a hundred people had stood in that room, witnessed the kind of pain he had caused T-Grace and Ovide and their family, and felt what? Triumph? Amusement? It turned her stomach to think of it.

Half the town had crowded into the Serenity room to pay their respects to the Delahoussayes. She had wound her way through them, taking little notice of whom she passed or brushed up against. It literally could have been anyone.

A gleaming black, late-seventies Monte Carlo wheeled into Prejean's drive and pulled in behind the BMW. The tinted window on the driver's side slid down to reveal Leonce and a red leather interior. Beausoleil was playing on the tape deck, Michael Doucet's frenzied fiddle unmistakable. Leonce turned it down to a whine, then leaned out the window.

'Hey, *chère*, I heard about Savannah,' he said, frowning beneath the brim of his Panama hat. 'I'm really sorry.'

'Thank you, Leonce.'

'She was kinda wild, dat one, but me, I always liked her.' He shrugged. On the leather-wrapped steering wheel his fingers absently drummed time to the music. 'She just liked to pass a good time.'

Laurel couldn't find a suitable comment. Savannah had been far too complex to be described in one light sentence.

'Look,' he said. 'Why you don' come with me out to Frenchie's, *chère*? The bar's still closed, but there's a few of us gettin' together to talk and lift a few in Savannah's name. It might make you feel better. You can ride out with me.'

She was standing beside a perfectly good car with the keys in her hand. Why would she want to ride with him?

Her mind was working like a prosecutor's. She started to chide herself for it, but stopped short. She had every reason to be cautious and suspicious. Six women were dead. A killer had singled her out. Leonce had known both Annie and Savannah. . . .

She looked at him, at the scar that slashed across his face, at the tilt of his dark eyebrows and the neatly trimmed Vandyke, scrambling to say something before the silence became strained. 'Oh, I don't think so, Leonce. . . .'

'Come on,' he cajoled, motioning her closer with a flick of his wrist. 'It's good to talk through grief with friends.'

'I appreciate the thought, but I'm really not up to it. It's been a very long, very trying day.' That was the truth. She couldn't remember ever feeling as drained in quite the same way.

Leonce frowned and gunned the engine of the Monte Carlo. 'Suit yourself.'

'I should get home to Aunt Caroline. Thanks anyway.'

Without another word, he pulled back into the car, buzzed the window up, and wheeled out of Prejean's circular drive. The Monte Carlo hit the street and pulled away with an impressive show of horsepower and what Laurel imagined was a small show of temper.

The wheels of her mind began to turn again. Leonce. Jack's friend. Ovide and T-Grace treated him like a son. He took care of the bar in their absence and dispensed beer, shots, taproom wisdom . . . and milk. He had guessed at her stomach problems and given her a glass of milk the night they found Annie. Not the attitude of a homicidal misogynist.

Yes, he had known Annie and Savannah, but did she have any reason to suspect he killed them? Or was it only his appearance that made her see him in a sinister light? The scar that cut across his face both fascinated and repulsed her, but it wasn't proof of guilt. And she knew only too well that looks could be deceiving.

She was too exhausted to think straight; her beleaguered brain kept dropping the ball. Shaking loose the key to the car's door, she blew out a breath and tried to think of only one thing instead of ten – Belle Rivière. She would be in bed within the hour. If she was very, very lucky, she wouldn't dream.

26

Laurel almost cried when she saw the Jaguar parked in Caroline's drive. Danjermond. He was the last thing she needed to cap off the evening.

No, she amended, as Vivian's white Mercedes pulled in behind her at a drunken angle to the curb. *This* was the last thing she needed.

Ross bolted from the car, leaving the door wide open, and hurried toward her as she climbed out of the BMW. He looked a mess for the first time in the twenty years she had known him. His steel gray pompadour had been dismantled by numerous finger-combings. His expression, usually bland and smugly satisfied, was taut, thinned by stress, and his eyes seemed wider and darker – desperate.

'Laurel, for God's sake, you've got to talk to Vivian,' he said, grabbing for her arm.

She twisted away and took a step back. 'I don't have anything more to say to my mother, and I certainly don't have anything to say to you.'

'Jesus Christ,' he mumbled, rubbing a hand across his mouth. He glanced away from her, toward the sunset that bled over the western horizon. In that light, with a stubble of evening beard shadowing his cheeks and that haunted look in his eyes, he appeared like a drunk in dire need of a bottle. In fact, the aroma of whiskey clung to him like cologne, and he was weaving a little on his feet. 'You don't know what you've done.'

'No,' she said, taking another step back. 'This is about what *you* did, Ross. All I did was tell the truth. I should have told it twenty years ago.'

'I can handle Stipple,' he muttered, still not looking at her. 'The man is spineless. Besides, why should anyone believe you?' He turned his head and glared at her, hatred flaring bright in his eyes for one frightening moment. Laurel wished to hell Kenner hadn't confiscated her pocketbook with the handgun in it.

'Everyone knows you've got a screw loose,' he said. 'Look what happened up in Georgia. It's Vivian I'm not sure about. She won't let me in her room.'

'What difference should that make to you?' Laurel jeered, her temper overtaking her common sense. 'Pervert that you are, you've probably got some little fifteen-year-old on the side.'

He scowled at her, the thin, weak line of his mouth twisting. 'It's not the sex, you stupid little bitch. I haven't slept with Vivian in years. Why would I? She's colder than a witch's tit. She never wanted it.'

'And why would you care, when you could rape her daughter instead?'

His fleshy face turned scarlet, the color creeping up from his neck like a tide that pooled in his narrowed bloodshot eyes. 'I never raped anybody. Savannah was a little prick-teaser—'

'She was thirteen!' Laurel shouted, not caring if her voice carried through every screen in the neighborhood.

Ross waved it off, making an impatient face. 'It's in the past—'

'I'll say. Savannah is dead. You don't get more past tense than that.'

'Well, I didn't kill her!'

'You as good as did, you snake! If you think for a minute I'm going to make this easy on you—'

'Just talk to your mother, for chrissake!' he bellowed, weaving toward her.

'Why?' Laurel demanded. 'What do you need her for? She's all fresh out of teenage daughters for you to molest!'

'It's the money,' he snapped, admitting in his drunken rage what had been a secret all these years. He stalked her up the walk toward the house. 'It was always the money. Jefferson left everything in trust, that bastard. I can't touch a goddamn nickel without Vivian knowing.'

Laurel wanted to laugh. She doubted Vivian would end up believing her in the end. Her mother had an amazing capacity for rationalization and denial. But in the meantime, at least, Ross was suffering. And he would suffer every time he wondered who else she might have told and whether or not they had believed her even a little bit. Cowards died a thousand deaths. Not one too many for Ross Leighton, as far as she was concerned.

He shook his head, his face contorting in disgust. 'You're all the same. Whores and bitches to the end. That's what your sister was, you know,' he said tauntingly, poking a finger at her, his upper body listing heavily to the right. 'Hot-tailed little whore. She used to beg me for it.'

If she had had her gun, she would have killed him. Without hesitation. Without remorse. Screw 'a thousand deaths' – one bloody, agonizing death would have suited her fine. But she didn't have her gun. She could only stand on the walk in front of Belle Rivière, shaking with rage and hate.

'You son of a bitch!' she spat. 'She was a child!'

Ross sneered at her. 'Not when she was in bed with me.'

Laurel didn't know what she might do. The idea of clawing his eyes out was dawning in her brain when the front door opened and Danjermond's voice cut through the tension.

'Is there a problem here, Laurel? Ross?'

'The problem *is* Ross,' Laurel said tightly. She turned and brushed past the district attorney and went into the hall.

Caroline came out of the parlor wearing copper silk lounging pajamas, no jewelry, no makeup. She looked tiny and fragile – a word Laurel had never associated with her aunt.

'Is everything all right, darlin'?' she murmured. 'I thought I heard you drive up.'

Laurel heaved a sigh and snagged a hand back through her hair. 'I'm as all right as I'm going to be.'

'Did I hear Ross's voice?' she asked, puzzled.

'Yes, but don't worry about it, Aunt Caroline. He won't be staying.'

Shades of her usual spunk glowed in Caroline's cheeks as she lifted her chin. 'He certainly won't be. I haven't let that man in this house in twenty years. I'm not about to start tonight.'

'What's Danjermond doing here?'

'He wanted to speak with you about—' She broke off, pressing a small hand to her mouth as she struggled to search her brain for a word that seemed less threatening than 'murder.' 'The situation. He thought perhaps you'd be more relaxed without Sheriff Kenner present.'

'Mmmm.'

Needing something mundane to focus on, Laurel set her purse aside and shuffled through the mail that had been left for her on the hall table. It seemed wrong that she should have gotten mail on a day like this, but the post office didn't close down for personal tragedies. There was a letter from her attorney in Atlanta. A bill from the Ashland Heights Clinic. An ivory vellum envelope addressed in her mother's precise, elegant cursive. She tore it open carelessly and extracted an invitation.

The Partout Parish League of Women Voters
cordially invites you to a dinner with guest of honor
District Attorney Stephen Danjermond
Saturday evening, May the twenty-third
The Wisteria Golf and Country Club
Cocktails from 7 until 8
RSVP

The man himself came in from the lawn, looking mildly bemused. 'I can't say that I've ever seen Ross in such a state,' he said, his gaze falling squarely on Laurel. 'Were he and Savannah close?'

'In a manner of speaking,' Laurel grumbled, tossing the invitation back onto the table.

'Deputy Lawson is seeing him home. A stroke of luck that he was driving by.'

'You wanted to speak to me, Mr. Danjermond?' she asked, too

exhausted to suffer small talk. 'I don't mean to be rude, but can we get on with it? I'd really like to see an end to this day.'

He tipped his head like a prince granting her an audience and motioned for her to precede him into Caroline's office. He assumed the throne of command behind the feminine French desk. Somehow, it only made him look more masculine. In the amber light from the desk lamp his sexuality glowed around him like a holy aura.

Laurel wandered from bookshelf to bookshelf, too exhausted to be on her feet, too restless to sit. She felt his gaze follow her, but didn't turn to meet it.

'You had questions?' she prompted.

'How are you, Laurel?'

That one stopped her cold. She looked at him sideways. 'How am I supposed to be? My sister is dead. Her killer is playing cat-and-mouse games with me. That's not my idea of a good time.'

He studied her more intently than she would have cared for in the best of circumstances. As always, he made her feel underdressed and underfed, and she resisted the urge to reach up and check her hair, pushing her glasses up on her nose instead. Sitting behind the desk, he looked like the handsome, trustworthy anchor of a nightly news program, straight and tall, jacket cut to emphasize his shoulders, lighting set to show off his perfectly even features.

'You appear to be bearing up well, all things considered.'

She gave a short, cynical laugh and walked from behind one green velvet wing chair to the other, wishing she smoked so she could at least have the comfort of something to do with her hands. 'Don't be afraid to sound incredulous,' she said dryly. 'I am.'

'I think you're stronger than you give yourself credit for,' he murmured.

Laurel thought the strength was an illusion, that she was being held together by pressure and fear, but she didn't tell Danjermond that.

'What does this have to do with the case?' she asked.

'Strength is essential if you're going to help catch your sister's killer.'

'I'll do whatever I have to do.'

He hummed a note of approval as he toyed with his signet ring. 'Have you come up with any theories as to how or when your sister's necklace was deposited in your pocketbook?'

Tugging methodically on her earlobe, she called up what possibilities she had come up with earlier and sorted through them to pick and choose which she would give to Danjermond. 'I think it may have happened at Annie Gerrard's wake. Could have been anyone in the room.'

Leonce came vividly to mind, but she wasn't ready to say his name. No evidence. She couldn't get a conviction without evidence. Danjermond wouldn't like to hear about hunches.

'What about earlier that day?' he said, rising. Sliding his hands into the pockets of his trousers, he rounded the desk and squared off with her across the cherrywood butler's table. 'Who did you see that day?'

'Caroline, Mama Pearl, you, Kenner, Conroy Cooper. Jimmy Lee Baldwin – has Kenner spoken with him?'

'Yes, and he denies he's into kinky sex.'

She gave a sniff. 'What did you expect him to do – show you snapshots?'

'He denied the charges.'

'He's lying,' she said flatly.

Danjermond's broad shoulders lifted in an almost imperceptible shrug. 'Perhaps Savannah was lying.'

'No,' Laurel insisted stubbornly.

'You can be that certain?'

'I saw the marks on her wrists.' She dropped her gaze from his and did her best to concentrate on the polished surface of the table instead of the memory. 'She told me the Revver liked to play whip-me, whip-me games.'

'Did you see anyone else that day, that evening?' He let a pause hang in the air, then struck with precision, his gaze on her like radar. 'Jack Boudreaux, for instance?'

Laurel held herself steady, called on old skills, played her cards close to her vest. 'Why?'

He pursed his lips and contemplated word choices for a moment, almost seeming to relish the hint of the game in their conversation. 'He was . . . well acquainted . . . with Annie Gerrard,' he said carefully. 'Who knows how well he knew your sister? He's a man with a dark mind and a violent past.'

'Jack's no killer,' Laurel stated unequivocally.

One dark brow sketched upward. 'How can you be so sure of that, Laurel? You've known him how long? A week?' His logic was as cold as ice. When she didn't answer, his gaze narrowed, his voice softened. 'Or is it that you think you know him so well? Intimately, perhaps?'

Laurel backed away from him, away from the heat of his body and the chill of his peridot eyes. 'That's none of your damn business.'

She retreated, he pursued – physically, verbally, psychologically. 'Your sister was found with a page from one of his books in her hand.'

'A plant,' she said, putting a wing chair between them. 'Only a fool would incriminate himself that way.'

Danjermond ignored her supposition and pressed on. 'He had a wife, you know—'

With one sharp slash of her hand, Laurel tried to end the discussion. 'That's it,' she snapped, pushing past him and striding toward the door. She let him see the anger, but not the hurt. She didn't want to think of his knowing about Jack's tragedy. It was a violation, somehow. It was playing out of bounds. He fought slick and dirty. She would remember that if she ever had to face him in a courtroom. 'I've had all I can stand for one day. This conversation is over. You know your way out.'

She started out of the room, but his voice pulled on her like the strings of a puppet master as she neared the door. 'Kenner wants to talk to him, but he didn't seem to be anywhere around today,' he said softly. 'I wonder why that is.'

There could have been a hundred reasons for Jack's absence, Laurel thought as she stood with one hand gripping the door frame. He had certainly been around this morning – long enough to break her heart.

'Not everyone is what they seem, Laurel,' Danjermond murmured. 'You should know that. You should think about that.'

'I do know,' she said, staring straight ahead as his gaze bore into her back. 'I also know that I lost my only sister today. I'd like to mourn in private, thank you.'

She walked out on him and down the hall, but she had the feeling that his eyes followed her all the way upstairs.

Sleep came in fits and starts. The dreams were dark and relentless. Faces floated through her mind – Savannah's, Jack's, Jimmy Lee Baldwin's, and Leonce Comeau's. Danjermond's voice and visions of jewelry. The sick dread that came with thoughts of Ross and her mother and childhood nightmares.

At one-thirty Laurel gave up and switched on the bedside lamp, remembering the night Savannah had come in to check on her and had teased her about her poor taste in nightwear. She got up and changed from one baggy T-shirt to another, and came back to bed with a notepad and pen. Methodically she began making lists and notes, considering suspects and possibilities.

She was exhausted, body and soul, but she forced her mind to work. Like an athlete who had been away from the game with an injury, she felt every move was an effort, but the skills were still there. If she could hang on to the emotion, control her feelings, think clearly, the thoughts would flow easier and answers would come.

Baldwin. His name was a slash of capital letters at the top of the page. He was a liar and a con man. He had a temper. It wasn't difficult to imagine him getting rough with a woman. He had known Savannah, but what about Annie? Why would she have had anything to do with him? She might have gone to him on her parents' behalf. Might even have thought to discredit him with sex.

What about the other women? What about the jewelry? Could Baldwin have gotten Savannah's necklace into her purse without her knowledge? She would never have allowed him near enough when she had the bag with her, but Laurel remembered too clearly the feeling of being watched the night of Annie's wake, when she had come home and gone into the courtyard. The pocketbook had lain on a bench all night. Anyone might have crept into the garden . . .

. . . like Jack.

No. She wouldn't even consider it. Jack was no killer.

Did she think that because it was a fact, or because she loved him?

Loved. Past tense.

The thought triggered another memory. Conroy Cooper packing his bags. '. . . *I loved Savannah as best I could . . .' Loved.* Past tense. She scribbled the words down and lifted the pen to chew thoughtfully on the end of it. It was difficult to picture Cooper as a killer with his warm blue eyes and his warm molasses voice.

'*Not everyone is what they seem, Laurel. . . .*'

She sketched a question mark beside Cooper's name and went on.

Leonce made her uncomfortable, but not through any effort to do so. She felt vaguely guilty suspecting him. He had helped out the Delahoussayes all he could. He'd done his best to be a friend to her. Did she have any real reason to question him?

He had known Annie and Savannah. The others? He traveled some to sing with bands in other towns. That gave him opportunity, but short of questioning him herself, she had no way of knowing the when or where of his schedule. He liked to flirt, but the scar had to turn more women off than on. What kind of resentment would build inside a man from that constant rejection? Enough to make him hate women? Enough to make him kill?

The thought of resentment brought thoughts of Ross, and she added his name to the list, but knew that had less to do with fact than feeling. Still, look what he'd gotten away with for twenty years with no one suspecting.

Laurel blew a breath of frustration up into her bangs as she contemplated the list. Six women were dead. There had to be something that linked someone to all the murders.

Then why hadn't anyone caught him?

A chill crept over her flesh as she stared out the French doors into the dark of the night.

Eyes shine in the night along the bayou. The creatures of the night stalk and prowl. In the shadows the predator waits, watches, savors thoughts of victory. Above, an adversary sits in the glow of a lamp and wonders. An answer may come, but none will believe the truth. Too clever, too cunning, instincts too sharp to make a mistake. Mistakes are made by the weak, by the desperate, by the victim. The predator's mind is clear and sharp. No clouds of grief. No distractions of conscience. Only thoughts of ultimate victory and the taste of blood.

Jack rose from his desk to wander through the halls and rooms of L'Amour, trying not to think, trying not to feel, not at all surprised when he found himself on the balcony, staring across at the light in Laurel's room. She wasn't sleeping. Again.

He couldn't blame her. He knew what it was to lose someone. He knew the automatic questions and recriminations. *Could I have done anything to stop it? How could I have let it happen?* He still asked himself those questions of Evie's death. Laurel would ask them in regard to Savannah. She would take the burden on her small shoulders. He had accused her of arrogance, but that wasn't it. Responsibility. In a world that seemed increasingly out of anyone's control, Laurel chose to take responsibility – not only for herself, but for everyone around her.

And he wanted responsibility for no one.

But he wanted her love.

Selfish through and through, Jack.

He wasn't meant for love. Had never been. The comforts and warmth of it were for other men, better men.

Even as he thought it, he heard Laurel's voice, trembling with pain and pride. ' . . . *I'll be damned if we don't have the power to get past all that and be something better.*'

He had thought so, too, once. He'd been wrong. He wouldn't risk being wrong again. The pain was too much, too cruel, for a heart that had been broken too many times.

For another long moment he stood on the balcony and listened to thunder rumble in the distance and watched the light across the way. The air was heavy with the scent of rain and the feel of something dark and restless, like eyes in the night. For a second he thought he was being watched, but the restlessness was within him. A need for something he could never have, regret for things he couldn't change. Slowly, he turned and went back in to his bottle and his work with the idea of immersing himself in both.

And in the dark shadows along the bayou, a predator's eyes shine.

27

Laurel woke with a start and headache. Her breath came in pants as the residual uneasiness of a dream hung around her. Eyes. She'd felt eyes on her, staring from the dark. But she hadn't been able to see the face, had only known somehow that it was familiar.

It was only a dream, but the uneasiness lingered as she sat up slowly and took stock of herself and the room around her. It had rained. The glass of the French doors was spattered with windblown droplets. The weather system had moved on, but gray still clung to the sky where dawn should have been.

She rubbed a hand over her face, groaning a bit as the headache kicked the backs of her eyeballs. She didn't know how long she had slept. An hour, maybe two. The state of the bedclothes was a testimony to how badly she had slept. The sheets were torn loose from the foot of the bed, the spread was rumpled. The notes she had made were scattered.

Grimacing at the taste of bitter dreams in her mouth, she forced herself to get up and gather the papers and the pen. She snatched them up, one by one, following a trail of them across the floor. She dug her glasses out of the folds of the bedspread, slipped them on, and combed her bangs back with her fingers. The gears of her brain strained into motion with much creaking and grinding, slipping and catching.

Baldwin, Cooper, Leonce, Ross. Names and question marks filled the pages. Notes, hunches, feelings. Hunches and feelings weren't admissible in a court of law. She knew that better than most people.

She walked to the French doors, shuffling the pages, brow furrowed as she retraced the ramblings of her mind. *Not Jack*. The bold declaration caught her eye, and her heart gave a traitorous thump. Bits of evidence tried to surface in her mind – his duality, the way he could seemingly appear and disappear at will, his past, his profession. And she beat every one of them back down.

Through the windowpanes she could see a bit of L'Amour – mysterious, shabby, standing alone on the bank of the bayou – and she let herself wonder for just a second what he was doing, whether he regretted the things he'd said to her, whether he wished as strongly as she did for the feel of familiar arms around him.

'You've known him how long? A week?'

God, was it only that? It seemed so much longer. The minutes and hours of the past week had somehow been elongated, magnified, and packed densely with experience and needs and fears. It seemed like forever, and at the same time, it could never be enough.

Not productive thinking. He didn't want her, didn't want any chance at a relationship. He wanted his solitude and his self-inflicted pain. He wanted to play the party animal, then go home to his empty prison. And when she was thinking straight, she knew it was just as well that she leave him to it. She needed time to heal – the old wounds and the new. She needed to get her world back on its axis and find her own place in it. A fresh start was what she needed, not a man with a past haunting him.

Craving a breath of fresh, rain-washed morning air to clear her muzzy head, Laurel set the notes aside on a table, unlocked and swung open the doors, as she had done hundreds of times in her life.

A scream tore from her throat and she shot back across the room before her conscious mind could even register what she had seen. Hand clutched to a heart that was racing out of control, she forced her eyes to focus, forced her brain to accept the information sent to it.

Wound around the outside door handle was the limp, dead body of a cottonmouth snake.

'Goddamn it, I thought you were watching her, Deputy Pruitt!' Kenner bellowed.

The thin, pasty-faced young man stood on the balcony outside Laurel's room looking as if he were contemplating the advantages of jumping off.

'Yessir, I was, sir,' he said, trying unsuccessfully to swallow the knot in his throat. His Adam's apple bobbed as his eyes darted to the body of the snake. Christ Almighty, he hated snakes. Everyone knew he hated snakes. Dollars to doughnuts, Kenner would make him unwrap this one from that handle and bag it as evidence. It looked to be a good four feet long. 'I came on at four A.M., sir, and I swear I didn't see nothin'. I watched this house like a hawk.'

Kenner swaggered to the door, reached down, and flicked a finger under the head of the snake. It flipped up, exposing the patches of cream color on the underside of the throat, and flopped back down, hitting the wood with a dull thud. Deputy Pruitt turned a little grayer. Kenner scowled. Goddamn prissy kid.

'You came on at four. Myers left. How long did the two of you stand around chewing the fat out by the cars?'

Despite his pallor, a hint of red managed to creep into the deputy's cheeks. 'Just a while, sir. There wasn't nothin' goin' on. We'da heard.'

Snarling, Kenner stepped up to his underling and jabbed the kid's sternum hard with a forefinger. 'There sure as hell was *somethin'* going on, and the hell if you heard it,' he growled.

Pruitt clenched his jaw against the need to wince. 'Yessir,' he mumbled, miserable.

'Bag that snake as evidence, and don't touch one other goddamn thing. If you so much as smudge a fingerprint, I'll cram that cottonmouth down your throat. Do you understand me, Deputy Pruitt?'

'Yessir.' Too well. The image had him on the brink of gagging.

Kenner jerked away and turned back toward Laurel.

She sat on the bed in jeans and the T-shirt she had slept in. Caroline stood beside her, wrapped in a white silk robe, her expression the fierce look of a tiger whose cub had been threatened. Mama Pearl, a vision in red chenille, had planted her enormous bulk on a vanity stool that all but disappeared beneath her.

'Y'all didn't hear anything, didn't see anything?' Kenner asked.

Laurel answered, pushing herself to her feet. 'For the fourth time, no.'

She hadn't seen anything, hadn't heard anything. She had awakened haunted by the feeling of eyes on her. Her skin crawled.

Caroline crossed her arms and started pacing beside the bed, her lips pressed into a thin line of disapproval. She cut a dark, sharp look at Kenner. 'This is intolerable, Sheriff. My niece is being tormented by a psychopath, and your office can't manage to do so much as to keep her safe inside a locked house?'

'The house was under surveillance, Miz Chandler.'

'It would seem it was under better surveillance by the killer than by your deputies.'

Kenner shot a look at Pruitt, who was damn near green as he fumbled with the long, rubbery body of the dead snake, then his gaze moved beyond. Beyond the balcony, beyond the courtyard, to the house Jack Boudreaux had taken. The house of a dead whore. It would have been a simple matter to watch for the change of shifts, slip into the garden, and climb the stairs. Wrap a dead cottonmouth around the door handle – just as the killer had done in *Blood Will Tell*.

He'd been scanning the collective works of Jack Boudreaux last night. After seeing the kind of stuff that rotted in the man's imagination, the sheriff had no difficulty picturing him as a killer.

'It won't happen again, ma'am,' he growled. He dismissed Caroline and swung around to Deputy Wilson, a kid who had been built for the NFL but not blessed with speed. 'Go see if Boudreaux is home. I want to have me a little talk with him downtown.'

'Why?'

Laurel's question drew a narrow stare from the sheriff. 'Why not?'

Because I know him. Because I've slept with him. The answers weren't going to dissuade Kenner.

He strode from the room with his linebacker at his heels, leaving the unhappy Pruitt to wrestle with the snake and the contents of his own stomach.

Mama Pearl rocked herself up from the little vanity chair and reached out to pat Laurel's arm. 'You come on down to my kitchen, *chère*. I fix you tea and biscuits with honey.'

'I'm sorry, Mama Pearl,' she said, moving to the wardrobe to hunt for clothes. 'I have to get down to the courthouse.'

Caroline's brows snapped down over her dark eyes. 'Laurel, you can't mean it! You've had no rest and one terrible shock after another! Stay here,' she insisted, wrapping an arm around her niece's shoulders, keeping her from reaching for a blouse. She hugged Laurel hard, emotion suddenly clogging her throat. 'Stay here with me, sweetheart,' she whispered. 'Please. I don't want you getting involved in this. I don't want to lose you, too.'

Laurel looked from her aunt to the door, where the snake hung in a single loop and Deputy Pruitt leaned over the balcony disgracing himself all over the clematis vine. 'I'm already in it, Aunt Caroline,' she said softly. 'And there's only one way out.'

Jack woke with a pounding in his head and pounding on the front door of the house. He wished he could manage to ignore both. The banging in his head was the farewell gong of a substantial amount of Wild Turkey. The banging on the door turned out to be a very large deputy named Wilson, a man without sympathy or humor, who hauled him downtown to 'have a little talk' with Sheriff Kenner.

Now he was sitting in a straight chair that had to be an antique from the Inquisition, staring across a scarred table at Kenner's ugly mug.

'Do you want a lawyer?'

'Do I need one?' Jack returned, arching a brow. 'Am I being charged with something?'

'No. Should I be charging you?'

Depends, he thought. Heaven knew he was guilty of plenty. He dug a cigarette out of the breast pocket of his chambray shirt and dangled it from his lip. 'You catch a lot of idiots with that question?'

'A few.'

He struck a match and sucked crud deep into his lungs with the kind of greed known only to an ex-smoker fallen off the wagon.

'What do you call two thousand lawyers at the bottom of Lake Pontchartrain?' He left the appropriate pause for an answer, even though Kenner just sat there glaring at him. Jack flashed him a wry grin and blew twin streams of smoke out his nose. 'A good start.'

Kenner didn't so much as blink. 'Where were you this morning about four o'clock?'

'In my bed, dead sound asleep.'

'Interesting choice of words.'

Jack shrugged expansively. '*C'est vrai.* Words are my life.'

'Yeah,' Kenner sniffed. 'I've been reading some of your best-sellers, Jack. *Blood Will Tell. Evil Illusions.* You've got a sick mind.'

'I'm just doing my job,' Jack said glibly. He rubbed the ruby stud in his earlobe between thumb and forefinger and gave Kenner a wry look. 'You're the one plunked down six bucks for the pleasure of reading it.'

'I got them from the library.'

'Ouch.' He winced. 'No royalties from you.'

Again Kenner ignored him, sticking to his own agenda. 'Pretty reckless of you to steal ideas from your own work.'

Dread hit Jack in the belly like a boot. *Mon Dieu*, not again, not another dead girl. He sat up straighter and abandoned his cigarette in the tin ashtray on the table. 'What are you talkin' about?'

Kenner planted his elbows on the table and leaned forward, as well, jaw set, eyes narrowed. 'I'm talking about slipping over to Belle Rivière while the deputies were changing shifts and wrapping a dead cotton-mouth around the handle to Laurel Chandler's bedroom door.'

A potent combination of rage and fear swirled through Jack, and he surged to his feet, sending the chair screeching back on the linoleum. A killer had been playing games with her. Apparently the game was not over. And on the heels of those feelings came the guilt that a truly twisted mind had borrowed from his imagination.

He stalked the cheerless box of the interrogation room with his shoulders braced and his hands jammed at the waist of his jeans, doing his best to fight it all off. What he really needed, he told himself, was to get the hell out of town for a while. Until the killer was behind bars. Until Laurel had packed up and moved on with her life.

He stopped his pacing in front of what had to be a two-way glass and stared hard at the reflection of himself, wondering who might be on the other side.

Kenner watched him with hard, cold eyes, trying to read every nuance of expression and movement. 'You didn't happen to have anybody in bed with you can vouch for your whereabouts?'

Jack swung around to face him, brows pulling low over his eyes. 'I wouldn't do anything to hurt Laurel.'

The word 'liar' rang like a gong in his head, but he ignored it. He had pushed her out of his life for her own good, not to hurt her. And damn but he missed her already. The thought of her finding that snake, especially after everything else she had gone through, made him want to go to her to protect her. But he couldn't do that. Wouldn't. He was nobody's white knight.

Something thumped against the door, breaking his train of thought, then came the sound of an argument loud enough to be heard quite clearly.

'I don't give a damn what Sheriff Kenner had to say. Mr. Boudreaux has a right to counsel.'

'But, ma'am—'

'Don't you "But, ma'am" me, Deputy. I know my way around a police station, and I know my way around the law. Now open that door.'

The door cracked open, and the massive Wilson stuck his head in, looking browbeaten and sheepish. 'Excuse me, Sheriff Kenner?'

Kenner was out of his seat and fuming. He went to the door, grumbling under his breath, and grabbed the knob, just barely resisting the urge to slam it shut on Wilson's head.

'What's the problem here, Deputy?' He ground the whisper between his teeth like dust. 'You can't keep one goddamn little slip of a woman out of my hair for five minutes?'

Laurel's voice sliced through the crack in the door like a knife. 'Denying people their rights is serious business, Sheriff. I suggest you open that door at the risk of having me really tear through your hair – what's left of it.'

Jack rubbed a hand across his mouth to hide his smile. She was a spitfire – no two ways about it. Most women in her situation would have been home, hiding. They certainly wouldn't have come to his rescue after the things he'd said and the way he'd behaved, he thought, the smile dying abruptly.

'I don't need a lawyer, angel,' he said as Kenner stepped back and let her into the room.

She shot him a look that had turned better men to ashes. 'A man who represents himself has a fool for a client.'

'Miz Chandler,' Kenner began on a long, bone-weary sigh, 'I'm speaking with Mr. Boudreaux about the case you're involved in. This is a conflict of interest.'

'Not if I don't believe he did it,' Laurel said. 'Besides, this is a noncustodial interview, is it not?' She arched a brow above the rim of her oversize glasses, waiting for Kenner to refute the statement. 'No charges are being filed. In the event it becomes a conflict of interest, I will recommend Mr. Boudreaux seek other representation.'

Not giving a damn if either man wanted her there, Laurel marched across the room to the table and took the only seat that looked remotely comfortable – Kenner's. In her heart, she knew she wanted to be here for Jack, but she told herself she was really doing it for Savannah. The more she could find out about what was going on, the better her chance of helping crack the case, and the sooner it could all be laid to rest inside her.

Kenner scowled at her, then at Boudreaux, wishing fleetingly that he had listened to his old man way back when and gone into insurance. He pulled another straight chair out from the wall, set it at the end of the table, and planted one booted foot on the seat.

Jack slid lazily back down on the chair he had vacated and took up the smoldering butt of his cigarette between thumb and forefinger. He met Laurel's gaze for an instant and tried to read what she was thinking. She didn't flinch, didn't blink, didn't smile. There were delicate purple shadows beneath her eyes and a vulnerability around her mouth he was certain she didn't realize was there, but she didn't give him anything – except the impression that he'd hurt her badly and she was too damn proud to bend beneath the weight of it.

Kenner sniffed and cleared his throat rudely, digging a finger into the breast pocket of his uniform to pull a cigarette out from behind his badge. 'So, you don't have an alibi for this morning.'

Crushing out the stub of his smoke, Jack shot the sheriff a look. 'Innocent people don't need alibis.'

'You got an alibi for Wednesday night, ten 'til two A.M.?'

The question struck Laurel harder than it did Jack. Wednesday night. That had to be Savannah's time of death. Sometime between the hours of ten and two. Midnight. The dead of night. She felt chilled.

Wednesday night between ten and two. She had come home from dinner with Vivian around nine and gone to bed early because Aunt Caroline had been out with friends and Mama Pearl had been engrossed in a television movie. And something had jerked her from sleep in the middle of the night.

Oh, God, had she somehow known? Had she somehow sensed the moment her sister had passed from this world?

The thought left her feeling dizzy and weak.

Kenner deliberately ignored the sudden pallor of Laurel Chandler's skin. If she couldn't stand heat, she shouldn't have come into the kitchen. He kept his eyes on Jack and repeated the question.

Howling at the moon, Jack thought. Wandering the banks of the bayou, as he had done most of the day yesterday. Thinking, remembering, punishing himself. Alone.

'Where were you?' Kenner asked again.

'He was with me,' Laurel said softly, her heart pounding in her breast. She'd seen the light come on in his window. It had to have been two or after, but he wasn't answering, and she wasn't going to let Kenner pin Savannah's murder on him. Jack couldn't have killed Savannah. He couldn't have brutally murdered a woman and then been moved to tears at the thought of the wife and child he had lost. He couldn't have killed Savannah and then come home and made love with her sister until dawn.

She glanced up at him. His face was a blank, unreadable mask, the scar on his chin looking almost silver under the harsh fluorescent light. 'He was with me. We were together. All night.'

Swell. Kenner ground his teeth as he ground out his cigarette. The lady lawyer was the alibi. Wasn't that neat? He regarded her for long, silent moments, trying to read a lie in the delicate pink tint of her cheeks. She had loved her sister. He couldn't imagine her lying to cover the murderer's ass. He turned back to Boudreaux. 'Is that a fact?'

'Ah, me,' Jack drawled, forcing the corners of his mouth up into a smug, cat-in-the-cream smile as he splayed his hands across his chest. 'I'm not the kind of man to kiss and tell.'

'You're a smartass, that's what you are,' Kenner barked, his temper snapping. He leaned down in Boudreaux's face, his forefinger pointed like a pistol. 'There's nothing I hate like a smartass. Poor little Cajun kid got himself a scholarship and went off to college. You think that makes you a big shot now? You think 'cause some bunch of New York dickheads pay you money to write trash, that makes you better than ever'body? I say you're still a smartass little swamp rat.'

Laurel watched Jack's jaw tighten at the insult and knew Kenner had managed to strike a nerve more sensitive than most. 'Does this character assassination have anything to do with the case, Sheriff?' she asked sharply. 'Or are you just getting your jollies for the day?'

Kenner didn't take his eyes off Jack. 'I'll tell you what it has to do with the case. I've got me a dead woman found with a page from one of ol' Jack's books in her stiff little hand. I've got a dead snake wrapped around a door handle – just like in one of Jack's books. What does that add up to, counselor?'

'It adds up to shit,' Laurel declared. 'He'd be a fool to implicate himself that way.'

'Or a genius. What do you say, Jack? You think you're a genius?'

Jack lit another Marlboro and rolled his eyes, slouching back in his chair. 'Jesus, Kenner, you've been watching too many Clint Eastwood movies.'

'You ever tie a woman up to have sex with her?'

He held his gaze on Kenner's, avoiding even a glance at Laurel. 'I don't have to force women to go to bed with me.'

'No, but maybe you like it that way. Some men do.'

'Speak for yourself,' Jack said, tapping the ashtray. 'You're the one wearing handcuffs on your belt. I'm only into violence on paper. Ask anyone who knows me.'

Kenner's eyes glittered. 'I'd ask your wife, but it so happens she's dead too.'

'You son of a bitch.'

In one move, Jack came up out of the chair and flung his cigarette down on the floor to singe a hole in the linoleum. Fury built and burned inside him like steam, searing his skin from the inside out. He would have given anything for the chance to tear Kenner's head off without running the risk of prosecution. His hands balled into tight, white-knuckled fists at his sides.

Kenner smiled coldly, careful to move back a step or two, just in case. 'That's a nasty temper you have there, Jack,' he drawled.

Jack's mouth twisted into a sneer. 'Fuck you, Kenner. I'm outta here.' Without a backward glance, he stormed from the interrogation room.

'You have a real way with people, Sheriff,' Laurel said, brushing past Kenner on her way to the door.

'So does the killer,' he growled as she walked out.

Laurel followed Jack through a side door that got them out of the building without being seen by any of the reporters hanging around inside the courthouse. She caught up with him on the sidewalk that cut through the park north of the courthouse, where the moss-draped canopy of live oak offered token protection from the choking heat. The sun had finally emerged to boil the humidity left over from the rain. As a result, the park was empty, air-conditioning being favored way above perspiration. As she hurried down the sidewalk, sweat pearled between her breasts and shoulder blades.

Jack stopped and wheeled on her suddenly, and she brought herself up short, eyes wide at the fierce expression on his face.

'What the hell did you do that for?' he demanded.

Laurel brought her chin up defiantly. 'I knew Kenner was questioning you. I couldn't envision you calling an attorney for anything other than to ask him if he had Prince Albert in a can,' she said sarcastically.

'That's not what I'm talkin' about, sugar,' he said, wagging a finger under her nose. 'But while we're on the subject, I can damn well take care of myself.'

'Yeah, that's what I like,' Laurel drawled, rolling her eyes. 'A show of gratitude.'

'I'd be grateful if you'd keep that pretty little nose out of my business.'

'Oh, never mind that you follow me all over creation, butting in whenever you damn well feel like it! Besides, this is my business, too, Jack,' she said, jabbing her chest with a forefinger. 'It's my sister who's dead. Her killer is going to pay if I have to catch him with my own two hands!'

'And what if *I* killed her? You just gave me an alibi!'

'You didn't,' she declared stubbornly, blinking back the tears of frustration and fury that swam in her eyes.

'How do you know that?' Jack demanded. 'You don' know shit about where I was that night!'

'I know where *I* was half that night, and I wasn't with a killer!'

'Because we had sex—'

She hauled back a fist and slugged him on the arm as hard as she could. 'We made love, and don't you dare call it anything else. We made love, and you know it.'

He *did* know it. She had given herself to him without reserve, and he had taken and cherished every minute of it. He had known that night she was everything he'd ever wanted, and the knowledge scared him bone-deep.

'Why'd you lie to Kenner?' he demanded.

'Because you weren't giving an answer—'

'Why?'

'—and Kenner and Danjermond are more than willing to pin this whole Strangler case on you if they can—'

'Why'd you lie, Laurel?' he taunted, driven by a need that terrified him, knowing damn well he shouldn't want to hear the answer. 'Miss Law and Order,' he sneered. 'Miss Justice For All. Why'd you lie?'

'Because I love you!' she shouted, toe to toe with him.

'Oh, shit!' He jammed his hands on his waist, then planted them on top of his head and turned around in a circle. Panic snapped inside. Love. *Dieu*, the one thing he secretly always wanted, never deserved. The thing that held the most potential for pain. And Laurel was offering it to him – No. She was throwing it in his face, like a challenge, daring him to take it.

'Yeah, well I'm real happy about it, too, Jack,' Laurel shot back, his reaction stinging like a slap in the face. She sniffed and wiped a hand under her nose. 'I really need to fall in love right now. I really need to be in love with a man who's dedicated his life to self-torment.'

'Then just drop it,' Jack said cruelly. 'I never meant to give you more than a good time.'

'Oh, yeah, it's been a riot,' Laurel sneered, fighting the tears so hard, her head was pounding like a triphammer. 'It's been a regular Dr. Jekyll – Mr. Hyde laugh a minute!'

'Fair exchange for a little research,' he said, driving the knife a little deeper and hating himself for it.

'I don't believe you,' Laurel declared, grabbing onto that disbelief and clinging to it desperately, swinging it at him like a club. 'I don't believe that's the only reason you've been with me.'

'You can't dismiss evidence just because it doesn't suit you, counselor,' he said coldly.

'Tell me there's a book,' she demanded, glaring at him through her tears. She grabbed his arm and tried in vain to turn him toward her. 'You look me in the eye, Jack Boudreaux, and tell me there's a book with me in it. You couldn't be that cruel and be so tender with me at the same time.'

Jack had thought once that she would be a lousy poker player because he could see everything she felt in her eyes, but she was calling his bluff now with more guts than any man he'd ever faced across a table. And damned if he could do it. He couldn't look down into that earnest, beautiful face and tell her he'd never done anything but use her.

'I don't need this,' he grumbled, waving her off.

'No, you don't, do you, Jack?' Laurel said, advancing as he backed away across the thin grass. 'You'll be happy to sit in that dump of a house, beating on yourself for the next fifty years or until your liver gives out, whichever comes first. That's a helluva lot easier than taking a chance on finding something better.'

'I don't deserve anything better.'

'And what do I deserve?' she demanded. 'You called me arrogant. How dare you presume to know what's best for me? And what a fool you are to take the blame for someone else's weakness. Evie needed help. She could have gotten it for herself. Other people could have tried to help her. It wasn't all on your shoulders, Jack. You're not the keeper of the world.'

'Oh, Christ, that's rich! The pot calls the kettle black! You take everything on as if God Himself appointed you! You take the responsibility, you take the blame. Well, I've got news for you, sugar: I don' wanna be one of your great causes. Butt outta my life!'

Laurel stood there and watched him stalk away, so filled with pain and impotent fury that she couldn't seem to do anything but clench her muscles until she was trembling with it. 'Damn,' she muttered as a pair of tears slipped over her lashes and rolled down her cheeks. The wall of restraint cracked a little, and another drop of anger leaked out.

'Damn, damn, damn you, Jack Boudreaux!' she snarled under her breath.

Without a thought to the consequences, she turned and slammed her fist against the rough bark of a persimmon tree, scraping the thin skin on her knuckles and sending pain singing up her arm. Good. It was at least a better kind of pain than the one burning in her chest.

She loved him.

'Damn you, Jack,' she whispered.

Blinking against the tears, she lifted her hand and sucked on her knuckles, trying to think of what to do next. She had more important things to think of than her broken heart. She would go home and regroup. Spend some time with Aunt Caroline while her brain turned over clues and theories, trying to come up with a picture of a killer. Not because she didn't believe anyone else could do it, but because she was bound by duty and love for a sister who had sheltered and cared for her.

Danjermond was waiting for her beside Caroline's BMW. His coffee brown jacket hung open, the sides pushed back. His hands were in his trouser pockets. But if his stance was casual, his mood was not. Laurel sensed a tension about him, humming around him like electricity in the air.

'I'm surprised at you, Laurel,' he murmured, his gaze as sharp and steady as the beam of a laser.

The word 'surprised' translated to 'disappointed,' but Laurel wasn't particularly interested in what Stephen Danjermond thought of her, one way or the other. He was Vivian's choice for her, not her own, and she was through trying to please her mother. Without a word of comment, she dug a hand into her bag to fish out the keys.

'You lied,' he said flatly.

She didn't bother asking him how he knew any of what had happened in the interrogation room; she had been a prosecutor, had stood on the other side of two-way mirrors herself. Poker-faced, she looked up at him. 'I was with Jack the night Savannah died.'

'But not all night,' he insisted. 'I could hear the hesitation in your voice. Slight, but there. And Boudreaux's reaction – good, but guarded. He was surprised you would lie for him. So am I. I thought you were a purist. Justice by the book.'

'Jack didn't kill Savannah,' she said, sorting out the proper key and resisting the urge to back away from him.

'How do you know?' he queried softly. 'Instinct? Would you know the killer if you looked him in the eye, Laurel?'

She stared up at him, remembering the feel of a gaze in her dreams. Eyes without a face. Memory stirred uneasily. 'Perhaps.'

'The way you knew the defendants in Scott County were guilty? Instinct, but no evidence. You need evidence, Laurel,' he persisted. 'No one will believe you without evidence.'

'The charges are being dismissed, Ms. Chandler . . . lack of sufficient evidence . . . You didn't do your job, Ms. Chandler . . . You blew it. . . .' The voices echoed in her head, bringing with them shadows of the stress, the desperation. The combination threatened to shake her, but she held firm against them.

'You're the one who'll try this case if Kenner can make an arrest, Mr. Danjermond,' she said evenly. 'Maybe you should be more concerned about finding some evidence yourself instead of worrying about what I'm doing or not doing.'

He said nothing while she unlocked the door to the BMW and pulled it open. She stepped around it on the pretense of tossing her handbag on the seat, but was just as glad to put the distance and the steel between them.

'Isn't that right?' she said, turning toward him once again.

He smiled slightly, a smile that for its strange perfection made the nerves tingle along the back of her neck.

'Oh, I am working on it, Laurel,' he said softly, his green eyes shining as if he had sole possession of a wonderful secret. 'Rest assured, I will have enough evidence to get a conviction. More than enough.'

He let that promise ring in the air for a moment, then changed directions so smoothly and quickly, Laurel thought it was a wonder she didn't lose her balance. 'Are you coming to the dinner tonight?'

'No,' she said, appalled that he might think she would even consider it. 'After all that's happened recently, I'm sure you understand that I'm not feeling up to it.'

'Of course,' he murmured, reaching into an inside jacket pocket to extract a long, slim cigar. He trimmed the end with a pocket-size device, snipping it cleanly and efficiently. 'I understand completely. You've lost your sister. The best suspect we have is your lover—'

'What about Baldwin?' Laurel snapped, an odd, niggling feeling of panic fluttering in her stomach. 'What about—'

'He isn't intelligent enough,' Danjermond said sharply, cutting her off with his look as much as his words. His eyes were as bright and fervid as gemstones beneath the dark slash of his brows. 'He's a petty con man with delusions of grandeur. Do you really believe he could have committed crime after crime without implicating himself?'

'I think there's enough evidence to suspect him—'

'Then you haven't been paying attention, Laurel.' He shook his head almost imperceptibly, his eyes never letting go of hers. 'You disappoint me,' he whispered.

Slowly, almost sensuously, he slipped the tip of the cigar between his lips. Laurel watched, feeling oddly mesmerized, vaguely nervous. He dipped a hand into his pants pocket and came out not with the wafer-thin gold lighter, but with a book of matches.

A blood red book of matches.

Laurel caught only glimpses of black lacework script beneath his meticulously manicured fingers as he went about the ritual of lighting the cigar, but somehow, she didn't really need to see the name of the bar. Her heart pounded in her throat, in her head. Nausea swirled through her, and she curled her fingers tighter over the edge of the car door.

'This killer is brilliant, Laurel,' he said softly, smoothly. 'Brilliant, careful, strong. Strength is essential for success in his avocation. Strength of mind, strength of will.'

Laurel said nothing. Her eyes were glued to the matchbook. Already her brain had hit the denial stage. It couldn't be. There was an explanation. He'd taken it from the purse Kenner had confiscated.

Or he was a killer and he wanted her to know it.

Danjermond puffed absently on his cigar, turning the folder of matches over in his fingers like a magician warming up for a sleight of hand routine.

'Le Mascarade,' he murmured. 'Where no one is quite what they seem. We all wear masks, don't we, Laurel?' he asked, lifting a brow. 'The trick is finding out what lies behind them.'

He slipped the matchbook back into his pocket and strolled away, cherry-scented smoke curling in his wake like mystical ribbons.

28

Laurel sank down sideways on the seat of the BMW, her feet still on the concrete of the parking lot. All the questions, all the fears, swirled in her brain like a dirty, foaming whirlpool. Fragments of conversations, of feelings, of thoughts, bobbed and floated on the rest, one rising above the others – *'You believe in evil, don't you, Laurel?'*

'Oh, God. Oh, God,' she murmured as she sat there shaking, remembering the flash of lightning, the rumble of thunder, those clear green eyes on hers across the dinner table at Beauvoir. Tears flooded her eyes, and she raised her trembling hands to press them over her face.

It couldn't be. Stephen Danjermond was the district attorney. The League of Women Voters was giving him a dinner. He was sworn to uphold the law.

'Not everyone is what they seem, Laurel. You should know that. You should think about that.'

'Oh, Jesus.'

He was a man above suspicion. Above reproach. From one of the finest families in New Orleans. She had to be wrong. She had to be. The matchbook was a coincidence.

'Le Mascarade . . . We all wear masks, don't we, Laurel? The trick is finding out what lies behind them.'

'Le Mascarade . . . It's the kind of place you don' wanna go, sugar. Unless you like leather and you're into S&M.'

S&M. Bondage. Annie had been tied up. Savannah had been—

She clamped a hand over her mouth as her stomach heaved. She bent over, putting her head between her knees, and gagged as terrible images flashed behind her eyes. Blood. Pain. Screams. Delicate wrists straining against their bonds. Blood, so much blood. There was nothing in her stomach to come up, leaving her choking, coughing, as her body did its best to reject the possibilities that continued to bombard her.

Stephen Danjermond. District Attorney Danjermond. The golden boy. The favorite son. Destined for great things. What if he really was the killer?

And she was the only person who knew.

Laurel Chandler. The prosecutor who cried wolf.

No one would believe her. Not in a million years.

And he damn well knew it.

Cold sweat slicked over her face and her body, sour with the scent of fear. She dragged a hand across her forehead and into the damp tendrils of her bangs as she sat up and leaned heavily against the back of the seat. Funny, she thought, without the least trace of humor, she had actually been holding up pretty well in spite of everything. Savannah's death had devastated her heart, but mentally she had hung tough. Dr. Pritchard would have been proud. Until now. Stephen Danjermond had stood back and watched her fight, watched her hang on to her strength, then with no more effort than he would use to swat a fly, he stepped out of the shadows and knocked her legs completely out from under her.

'*Right and strength don't always coincide.*'

Was that what this was all about? A contest between justice and the laws of nature? A game? '*Does he want you to catch him, Laurel? Or does he want to show you he can't be caught?*' Was this what he had been alluding to when he had spoken of the two of them working together?

Or was she imagining things?

He had made her uncomfortable from the moment they had first met, but that wasn't a crime. She'd been under a terrible strain lately, hadn't eaten, hadn't slept. As she sat there panting for breath in the stagnant heat, the sounds of traffic rumbled in the background like the murmur of a distant ocean, someone stepped out of Bentley's Small Engine Shop across the street and hollered for Sonny. An indigo bunting fluttered down from the branches of a magnolia tree to poke its tiny head in an abandoned McDonald's bag in hopeful search of crumbs.

Beautiful little bird, she mused, her thoughts breaking into desultory chunks. It was decorated with gaudy, bright colors – yellow-green, violet-blue, red – that made it look as if an artist had flung paint at it with verve and abandon. How could anything that pretty just happen along for her to see if she had just been confronted by a murderer?

'*You haven't been paying attention, Laurel. . . .*'

'*This killer is brilliant. . . .*'

'*What do you think of sharks, Laurel?*'

Sharks moved silently, swiftly, cutting through the deep water, disturbing nothing until they struck. When they killed, they killed brutally, efficiently, completely without mercy or remorse.

'*Serial killers are the sharks of our society. . . .*'

Nerves trilled at the base of her neck. Memory stirred. The feel of a gaze in the dark. Eyes without a face. As her skin crawled and pebbled with goose bumps, she turned and looked out through the windshield at the courthouse. From a second-story window he looked down at her, knowing she saw him, knowing she could do nothing to stop him. She had no evidence he was a killer.

'*You need evidence to get a conviction, Laurel. . . .*'

The matchbook was all she had that could link him in any way. There was no law against having a red book of matches. At any rate, he could throw them away, say he'd never had them. It would be her word against his. No question who would win that contest. Besides, she couldn't prove who had left the matches in her car. There was no doubt there would be many prints – her own, Savannah's, Jack's.

Jack's.

'*The best suspect we have is your lover . . . Rest assured, I will have enough evidence to get a conviction. More than enough.*'

'Oh, God,' she whispered, her throat nearly closing on the words. 'He's building a case against Jack.'

The notion hit her like a sledgehammer, literally knocking her back in her seat. No one would have better access to hard evidence than the real killer. No one would be more adept at building a case than Stephen Danjermond. The politically ambitious Stephen Danjermond.

The sense of dread and disgust seeped deep into her bones as she considered the implications. What better feather in his cap than successfully convicting a man for crimes that had terrorized South Louisiana for a year and a half? A sensational crime. A sensational trial. A defendant whose name was known across America as the Master of the Macabre.

The press would have a field day. Danjermond would be hailed as a hero. Lifted up on the shoulders of the people of Acadiana without their ever suspecting there was blood on his hands. The case could take him anywhere he wanted to go.

Unless someone stopped him.

He'd thrown the gauntlet at her feet. He had chosen her as his adversary, then turned his back on her and sauntered away as if he didn't have a care in the world, as if he knew she didn't have a chance in hell of besting him. He was bigger, stronger, his mental skills honed to a razor's edge. He was admired and adored. And she was the woman who cried wolf, small and weak, her credibility in tatters, her battle skills rusted and atrophied. The only line of defense between Stephen Danjermond and his future.

If it would have done any good, she would have broken down and cried.

There was enough food in the house to feed an army platoon for a week. The rich, spicy aromas of gumbo and *etouffée* blended with the milder scents of sundry casseroles with a cream of mushroom soup base and the sweet perfumes of fresh fruit pies and spice cakes. Offerings from neighbors and friends who knew it wouldn't assuage the grief, but brought it anyway to show that they cared.

As she set her purse aside on the hall table, Laurel wondered absently if anyone had taken gumbo or spice cake out to Beauvoir. She supposed someone had. Not these same, salt-of-the-earth folk who had come to comfort Mama Pearl or Caroline's eclectic group of friends, but the women from the Junior League and the Hospital Auxiliary. They would have gone out to deliver their deviled eggs and chicken salad with a thin dose of sympathy. Pained smiles and sugarcoated apologies. Poor Vivian, how terrible to lose a daughter (but at least it was the tacky one). Poor Vivian, you must be beside yourself (it was such a scandalous death). And Vivian would nod and dab at her tears while casting glances askance to see if Ridilia Montrose had put dark meat in her chicken salad.

'Laurel?'

It was all Laurel could do to keep from jumping out of her skin, her nerves were strung so tight. She had hoped to slip upstairs unnoticed. Irrational as the thought was, she was sure her suspicions were written all over her face, that anyone who glanced at her would know what she was thinking and shake their heads sadly over her mental state.

Trying to compose herself, she bent her head and fussed with her glasses as Caroline stepped out of the parlor and came toward her with hands outstretched. Laurel caught her aunt's fingertips and squeezed, but her gaze moved past Caroline to the tall, striking redhead in the dark yellow dress, who came only as far as the doorway.

'Laurel, this is Margaret Ascott,' Caroline said, glancing between them. 'Margaret is a friend of mine from Lafayette.'

Margaret sent her a look of genuine sympathy from big dark eyes. 'I'm so sorry about your sister, Laurel,' she said in a low voice.

'Thank you,' Laurel murmured, too distracted to care just what kind of friend Margaret could be. All she could think was that she envied Caroline her friend. She would have dearly loved to have someone she could spill her heart out to.

Caroline's brow furrowed in concern. 'Darlin', you're as pale as milk. You must be exhausted. Come sit down.'

She couldn't. There was no way she could sit down and pretend she didn't have knowledge of her sister's killer, nor could she tell them – or anyone – yet. No one would believe her, she thought, her heart thudding wildly. Caroline would say she was under too much stress. Others would point to Scott County and say this was just another wild conclusion of an unbalanced mind.

She needed a plan. She needed to make her brain work until all the rust had flaked off and the gears turned swiftly and smoothly.

'Actually, I was thinking I might just go upstairs and lie down,' she said, amazed that she could sound so calm. It was as if her voice and her brain had detached from one another. Her gaze turned to the statuesque Ms. Ascott. 'I don't mean to be rude—'

'Not at all,' the woman assured her. 'I came to offer support and a shoulder, not to be entertained.'

'Do try to get some rest, sweetheart,' Caroline said, stroking a hand down Laurel's cheek. 'And have Pearl fix you a plate to take up with you. You need the nourishment, and she needs to fuss.'

'I'll do that.'

The afternoon passed like a year in prison. Laurel lay on the bed, her body begging for rest, her mind too overloaded and too exhausted to handle all the information it was trying to process. She forced herself to eat and struggled to keep the meal down as her thoughts dwelled on murder and broken trust. Every time she closed her eyes, she saw Danjermond. Too handsome, his features too perfect, his smile too symmetrical. Green eyes glowing into hers in a way that seemed not quite human.

But then, if he was what she thought he was, the word 'human' didn't really apply. If he had done the things she suspected he had done, then he had no soul, no conscience, and that made him an animal. The most cunning, the most dangerous predator in nature's chain.

Needing facts, she paged through back issues of the Lafayette *Daily Advertiser* she had dug out of the recycling stacks in the garage, and read and reread everything she could find on the Bayou Strangler case. But the stories were thin compared with the police reports she was accustomed to poring over, and she knew that critical information would have been withheld for official reasons – to weed out real suspects from the poor crazies who confessed to every crime that came down the pike, to allow genuine perps the opportunity to trip themselves up by revealing information that wasn't known to the general public. While the accounts of the killings were gruesome enough, Laurel knew that details had been toned down and left out. The reality of a murder scene, the horror of a corpse that had been abandoned—

God, an abandoned corpse. She closed her eyes against the sting of fresh tears. That was what her vibrant, beautiful, complex sister had been reduced to by Stephen Danjermond.

He had to be stopped, and she had to be the one to do it.

She thought longingly of her Lady Smith languishing in the evidence room of the sheriff's office, thought fleetingly of simply planting it between Danjermond's eyes and pulling the trigger. But she knew it couldn't happen that way.

Proof. Evidence. Her brain hammered on the words, and she got up from the bed to pace and chew the ragged edge of her thumbnail. He would know better than to keep things around that might implicate him. But might his arrogance outstrip his common sense?

He thought he was invincible. She had seen it in his eyes and had read it in profiles of other serial killers. He had run unchecked long enough to make him believe no one could catch him. That kind of power, that feeling of omnipotence, could ultimately be his downfall.

Keeping souvenirs from victims was a common practice among serial killers. She knew he had kept pieces of jewelry because he had given them to her, drawing her into his web without her even knowing it. Did that mean there were more pieces hidden somewhere?

No one knew where the women had been killed, only that their bodies had been transported and dumped. The bodies had been found in five parishes. Most of the victims had been from a parish other than the one where their bodies were found. Clever. He would know that involving multiple jurisdictions would complicate the investigations.

But the most important question was where had the murders taken place. All in one spot, a lair where he felt safe to practice his depravity? If that was the case, she didn't have a prayer of finding it. The area involved encompassed thousands of acres, much of it the wildest, most remote swampland in the United States. It would be easier to find the proverbial needle.

He would never have risked killing in his own home. He would never have risked being seen entertaining any of the women he had killed. They weren't the kind of women a man of Stephen Danjermond's position and breeding would associate with. But he was the sort of man women would trust – handsome, well dressed, well educated. Everyone expected homicide to come wild-eyed and ugly, poor and desperate and ill bred.

'*One never really knows what might hide behind ugliness or lurk in the heart of beauty.*'

His words rang in Laurel's head as she paced the confines of the room. To distract herself from the emotion that threatened to intrude on her thought processes, she did a mental inventory of the furniture and appointments. Then her gaze homed in on the invitation she had carried up with her from the hall table.

'*The Partout Parish League of Women Voters cordially invites you to a dinner . . .*'

With special guest the honorable Stephen Danjermond.

He probably hadn't killed anyone in his home, but he may well have brought his trophies there. And he would be out all evening, charming the people who would pave his way to greatness.

'What you're suggesting is against the law,' she murmured, pulling methodically on her earlobe.

She had never broken a law in her life.

She had never lost a sister, either.

She stood there for a long while, chewing contemplatively on her thumbnail, waiting for some solid reason to dissuade her. Some overriding sense of right and wrong. None came, only the memory of Danjermond slipping that matchbook into his pocket and strolling away as if he hadn't a care in the world. He thought he was invincible. He believed he could literally get away with murder. If he succeeded, then there was no justice. No law could overrule that simple truth.

'You believe in evil, don't you, Laurel. . . . And good must triumph over evil. . . .'

'Yes, Mr. Danjermond,' she whispered. 'It must.'

The sun was just setting when she finally slipped from the house. The dinner had begun at eight, but Laurel had been to enough functions of the same ilk to know that, while the baked Alaska would be served by nine, no one would get out of the Wisteria Club before ten-thirty. Then whoever would be usurping Vivian's role for the evening would whisk Danjermond off for drinks and inane small talk with the power elite of the group.

She calculated she would have a solid ninety minutes to search the house and get out safely. Provided she could escape from Belle Rivière without being caught.

Kenner had a deputy watching the house. The massive Wilson, who strolled the grounds like an overprotective Rottweiler. Laurel changed into dark jeans and a navy blue T-shirt, and prowled the balcony, waiting. In the end, Mama Pearl unwittingly came to her aid, coaxing the deputy into her kitchen for coffee and a piece of chocolate stack cake.

With Wilson out of the way, it was a simple matter of creeping down the outer staircase and slipping out a side gate.

Simple . . . except for the pair of eyes that followed her out of the courtyard and away from Belle Rivière.

29

Danjermond lived in a gracious old brick house three doors down from Conroy Cooper. Once part of a row of town houses, the building was three stories high and very narrow. The rest of the town houses had long ago fallen to the wrecking ball, leaving this one tall, elegant reminder of more genteel times. The front yard was graced with a pair of live oak heavily festooned with Spanish moss. The interlaced branches of the trees created a bower above the walk to a front entrance that boasted a black lacquered front door with a fanlight above. The only light that glowed in the gathering darkness came from the brass carriage lamp beside the door.

Laurel cut through Cooper's lawn and approached Danjermond's house from the rear, where the properties gradually backed down to the bayou. The neighborhood was quiet, populated primarily by older couples whose families had long since grown up and moved on. There were a few lights in windows up and down the block, but no one was outside to see her slip through a break in the tall hedge that surrounded Danjermond's backyard.

As at Belle Rivière, the small backyard had been paved with bricks more than a century ago and turned into a private courtyard where a small stone fountain gurgled and bougainvillea climbed what was left of the original brick wall. But there the similarities ended. There was no jungle of plant life here, no clutter of tables and chairs. The area had a very spare, austere, almost vacant feel to it. A single black wrought-iron bench sat dead center, directly behind the house, facing the fountain.

Laurel envisioned Danjermond sitting there, staring, contemplating, saying nothing, and a chill crawled over her despite the heat of the night. She had the strangest feeling she could sense his presence here, even though she knew he was away, and the idea of going into his home brought a sense of dread that lay in her stomach like a stone. Her skin was clammy with sweat, making her T-shirt stick to her in spots, drawing mosquitoes that she waved away impatiently as she forced herself to take one step and then another toward the house. She didn't have a choice and didn't have much time. There was no sense in dawdling just because she was spooked.

Even as she thought it, something rustled in the shrubbery at the back of the courtyard, and she whirled, wide-eyed to find – Nothing. A bird. A squirrel. Her imagination. Heart thumping at the base of her throat, she turned back to the house.

The last of the day had faded to black. Stars were winking on in the sky above, but their pinpoints of light did nothing to illuminate the courtyard. The hedge, a thicket well over six feet high, blocked out the surrounding world so completely that Laurel had to remind herself there were people in their living rooms watching television on either side.

The back door was locked. There had been a time when no one in Bayou Breaux would have dreamed of locking a door. Then crime had seeped out from the cities. Then Stephen Danjermond had come.

Nibbling on her thumbnail, she descended the stairs, trying to think of an alternate way in. The front would be locked, as well, not that she could risk going in that way. He might have a spare key hidden somewhere, but she didn't want to take time to search for it. The first-floor windows were way out of her reach – but the ground-floor windows weren't.

Like many old homes in south Louisiana, this one had been built with a ground floor used for storage; the living areas were above, high enough to thwart the inevitable floodwaters from the bayou. Laurel checked the nearest window, finding it jammed shut and stuck with age and old paint. Quickly she moved around the other side of the stairs and found a door that led beneath the stoop and presumably into the storage space.

She closed her fingers around the knob and tried to turn it, her hand slipping, slick with sweat, and her fingers weak with nerves. She wiped her palm on the leg of her jeans and tried again, holding her breath as the hardware caught, stuck, then, with an extra twist, released, and the door creaked open, revealing a space that was thick with cobwebs and dust. And who knew what else, Laurel thought as she pulled a flashlight from the hip pocket of her jeans. Shaded, undisturbed space close to the bayou. There wouldn't be anything unusual in finding a copperhead or two . . . or more. The famous scene from *Raiders of the Lost Ark* slithered up from the depths of her memory and crawled over her skin.

Shuddering, she steeled herself, drew a deep breath, pushed the door open – and a hand clamped over her mouth from behind. An arm banded around her middle, as strong as steel, and hauled her back against a body that was lean, rock-solid, and indisputably male.

Panic exploded in Laurel, shooting adrenaline through her veins, pumping strength into her arms and legs. She tried to bolt, tried to kick, tried to jab back with her elbows all at once, twisting violently in her captor's grasp. He grunted as her heel connected with his shin, but her satisfaction was small and short-lived as he tightened his hold around her middle.

'Dammit, *'tite chatte*, be still!'

As quick as a heartbeat, all the fight in her froze into paralyzing

744

disbelief. Jack. She went limp with relief, and he loosened his hold in response. Jack had come. Jack had followed her. Jack had scared the living hell out of her.

She twisted around in his embrace and smacked his arm as hard as she could with the barrel of the flashlight. 'You jackass!' she hissed under her breath. 'You scared me near to death!'

Jack jumped back to avoid a second thumping. He scowled at her while he rubbed at the rising welt on his arm. 'What the hell are you doin' here?' he demanded in a low, graveled voice.

Laurel gaped at him. 'What the hell are *you* doing here?'

'I followed you,' he admitted grudgingly, still cursing himself for it. If he hadn't been standing on the balcony when she had crept down the back steps of Belle Rivière . . . If he hadn't wondered why and let his imagination loose on the possibilities . . . If he had a lick of sense and the brains God gave a goat, he would have gone back in and sat down to work.

'Why?' she demanded, glaring up at him with fire in her eyes and a smudge of dirt on the tip of her upturned nose.

''Cause even money said you were gettin' into trouble.'

'So what do you care if I am?' Laurel snapped. 'You looked me in the face this morning and told me in no uncertain terms you didn't want me in your life. Make up your mind, Jack. You want me or you don't. You're in this or you're out.'

He set his jaw and looked past her into the dark of the storage space beneath the house. He wanted her. That wasn't the question, had never been the question. The question was whether he deserved her, whether he dared take the chance to find out. The answers eluded him still, lay inside him beneath a dark cloak he hadn't worked up the courage to look beneath. It was easier not to, simpler to let her walk out of his life.

'Why are you here?' he asked again, bringing his gaze back to her.

'Because I think I know who killed my sister.' Fingers tightening around the flashlight, eyes locked hard on his face, she took the plunge. 'Stephen Danjermond.'

Laurel held her breath, waiting for his reaction, praying he would believe her, certain he would not. Needing him to believe her.

Jack blew out a breath, tunneled his fingers back through his hair, feeling as if she had knocked him upside the head with a lead pipe. 'Danjermond!' he murmured, incredulous. 'He's the goddamn district attorney!'

Laurel's jaw tightened against the first wave of hurt. 'I know what he is. I know exactly what he is.'

He swore long and fluently. 'Why? Why do you think he's the one?'

'Because he all but told me he was,' she said, turning her back to him to shine her light under the stairs and to hide the disappointment. 'I don't have time to explain. You either believe me or you don't. Either way, I'm going into this house to look for some kind of proof.'

Jack took in the rigid set of her shoulders – so slim, so delicate, too often carrying a burden that would have crushed a lesser person. He thought of the burden that had broken her. She had lost everything – her career, her credibility, her husband – because she had believed justice had to win at all cost. And she would fight this fight, too, alone if she had to, because she believed.

Dieu, he couldn't remember if he had ever believed in anything except looking out for his own hide.

Laurel suffered through the silence, refusing to let her heart break. She didn't have the time for it now. Later, after she had figured out a way to nail Danjermond, then she would let herself deal with this. Now she had a job to do, and if she had to do it alone, so be it.

She choked down the knot in her throat and took a step into the space beneath the house. Jack clamped a hand over her shoulder and held her back.

'Hey, gimme that light, sugar. There might be snakes under here.'

They emerged on the first floor of the house, through a door tucked under the main staircase. Laurel toed her sneakers off to avoid tracking in sand and dirt. Jack, in boots, opted to dust them off on the legs of his jeans.

The house was dark, all looming shapes and sinister shadows. The smells of lemon polish and cherry-tinted tobacco hung in the air. A grandfather clock marked time in the hall, ticking the seconds away, chiming the half hour. Nine-thirty.

'What are we looking for?' Jack whispered, keeping a hand on Laurel's shoulder in deference to the protective instincts rising up in him.

'Trophies,' she answered, shining the narrow beam of the flashlight on the floor. Her breath hitched in her throat as something tall caught her eye near the front door, then seeped back out as she recognized the lines of a coat tree. 'We know the killer kept jewelry as souvenirs because he sent some to me. I'm betting he kept some for himself, as well, as keepsakes.'

'Jesus.'

She shone the light into the front room – a parlor – backed out of the doorway, and continued down the hall, past a small, elegant dining room, past a bathroom. A blocky ginger cat bolted out of the next room and streaked past them, growling, making a beeline for the stairs. Laurel paused to get her heartbeat down from warp speed, then ducked into the room the cat had dashed out of.

Bookcases covered the walls from the twelve-foot-high ceiling to the polished pine floor. Here the scent of Danjermond's expensive tobacco was strongest, the furniture polish an undertone to leather chairs and the faintly musty-sweet aroma of old books. A handsome cherrywood partners desk dominated the floor space. Behind it, an entertainment center held shelves of sophisticated stereo equipment.

Laurel skirted around a wing chair and took a look at the desktop. She was afraid they would have to go upstairs to find what they were looking for. Her instincts told her a killer would keep items that secret, that meaningful, in his most private lair – his bedroom. But a study was a close second, and Danjermond obviously spent a good deal of time in his.

Slipping around behind the desk, she cast the light over a humidor, a tray of correspondence, an immaculate blotter. She slipped two fingers into a brass pull and tried the slim center drawer.

'Damn, it's locked.'

Jack scanned the bookshelves by the thin, silvery light from the window, looking for a title that might strike a spark. People often hid things in books. Hollowed them out and filled them with treasures and secrets. He assumed there wasn't time to look through all of them, and searched for a likely candidate instead, but there were no titles like *The Naked and the Damned*, or *The Quick and the Dead*, or anything else that might appeal to a twisted sense of humor, just tomes on law and order, classics, poetry.

'Where's Danjermond?' he asked, pulling out a Conan Doyle first edition.

Laurel tried the drawers on the file cabinet with no luck. 'Being toasted by the royal order of pearls and girdles as a man they can all look up to and entrust with the chastity of their debutante daughters.'

She checked her watch and swore. They needed to find something soon, before the window of opportunity slid closed and locked them inside.

'What happens if we find something?' Jack asked as they climbed to the next floor. 'We don' exactly have a warrant, angel. No judge in the country would allow evidence obtained this illegally.'

'All I need is one piece,' Laurel said as she crept past a small guest room and a linen closet. 'Just one damning piece I can take to Kenner and hit him over the head with. He's probably turning your place upside down as we speak. Danjermond is trying to build a case against you.'

The news stopped Jack in his tracks. He had thought Kenner was grasping at straws, not that anyone in the courthouse had a plan. 'He really thinks he can pin Savannah's murder on me? And Annie's?'

'And four others. And don't think he won't figure out a way to do it. The man has a mind a Celtic knot would envy.'

And she was going to stop him. Jack thought, watching as she shone the beam of the flashlight into another bedroom. She was risking what was left of her reputation in part to protect him.

'Bingo,' she muttered, and pushed open the door.

The bed gave the room away as Danjermond's – a massive mahogany tester with ornately carved posts and a black velvet spread trimmed in gold. The underside of the canopy was decorated with shirred white silk. Jack reached up and pushed a section of fabric aside to reveal a mirror. Laurel said nothing to his arched brow. She didn't allow her mind to form any kind of scenario. She didn't want to imagine where Danjermond's sexual tastes ran, because one thought would lead to the next and on to delicate wrists bound and screams for mercy and—

'You okay, sugar?' Jack whispered. He didn't even try to stop himself from slipping his arms around her and pulling her back against him. She had gone pale too suddenly, her eyes were too wide. He bent his head and pressed a kiss to her temple. 'Come on. We'll take a look and get the hell outta here.'

Like every other room they had seen, this one was immaculate, impeccably decorated, strangely cold-feeling, as if no one lived here – or the one who did was not human. Not a thing was out of place. Every piece of furniture looked to be worth a fortune. Nothing appeared to have sentimental value. There were no photos of family, no small mementos of his youth. A barrister's bookcase between the windows held another collection of antique books – first editions of erotica that dated back to Renaissance Europe. But there was nothing else, no jewelry, no weapons, no photographs.

Disappointment pressed down on Laurel. She should have known better than to think Danjermond would make it easy on her, but she had hoped just the same. Now that hope slipped through her grasp like sand. If the evidence she needed wasn't here, then it could be anywhere in the Atchafalaya.

And with the disappointment came self-doubt. What if she was wrong? What if the killer was Baldwin or Leonce? Or Cooper. Or some nameless, faceless stranger.

No. She closed the last drawer on the dresser and straightened, rubbing her fingers against her temples. She wasn't wrong. She hadn't been wrong in Scott County; she wasn't wrong now. Stephen Danjermond was a killer. She knew it, could feel it, had always felt something like wariness around him. He was a killer, and he thought he was going to get away with murder.

If she couldn't find one way to implicate him, Laurel knew she would have to find another. And the longer it took her, the more women would die, and the more time Danjermond would have to build a case to frame Jack. The longer he would play his game with her, destroying her credibility, her confidence, her belief in a higher law than survival of the fittest.

'Let's go,' she whispered, hooking a finger through a belt loop on Jack's Levi's and pulling him away from the bookcase. 'I doubt he'll be back from the dinner for another hour, but we can't take chances.'

'Wait.'

It hit Jack like an epiphany as the flashlight beam swept across the collection of books. A trio bound in faded red leather sitting side by side by side on the upper lefthand shelf. *Le Petite Mort*, volumes one, two, and three. *The Little Death*. His eyes had scanned past them when he'd first realized that this collection was erotica. Erotica – the little death – orgasm. The title hadn't seemed out of place, but as he guided the beam of the light across the bindings, a sixth sense tensed in his gut like a fist.

Gently, he lifted the glass panel on the front of the case and slid it back out of the way. The three volumes came off the shelf as one.

Emotion lodged like a rock in Laurel's throat as she shone the light across a tangle of earrings and necklaces. More than six pieces. Many more. Tears swimming in her eyes, she reached in with a tweezers she'd pulled from her pocket and lifted out a heavy gold earring. A large circle of hammered gold hanging from a smaller loop of finely braided strands of antiqued gold.

'This is—' The present tense stuck to the roof of her mouth. She swallowed it back and tried again. 'This was Savannah's. She had a pair made in New Orleans. A present to herself for her birthday. She was wearing the other one when they found her.'

Jack kept his silence as they watched the gold hoop turn and catch the light. There were no words adequate to assuage the kind of pain he heard in Laurel's voice. Gently he closed the box and returned it to its spot in the bookcase. Laurel just stood there, her gaze locked on the earring, her eyes bleak. Jack slid an arm around her shoulders and bent his head down close to hers.

'You got him, sugar,' he whispered. 'That's the best you can do.'

'I wish it were enough,' Laurel murmured. She handed him the flashlight and dropped the earring into a Ziploc bag.

They took a final, quick glance around the room to make certain they had left everything as they had found it, then Laurel led the way into the hall, flashlight scanning the floor ahead of them – until the beam fell on a pair of polished black dress shoes.

Her first instinct was to run, but there was nowhere to run to. He stood between them and the head of the stairs. Behind her, Jack swore under his breath.

Slowly, she raised the flashlight, up the sharp, flawless crease of his black tuxedo trousers and higher, until the beam spotlighted the barrel of a silencer on the nine-millimeter gun he held in one hand and the pair of small canvas sneakers he held in the other.

'I believe these are yours, Laurel,' he said in that same even tone of voice he used for all occasions. 'How considerate of you to take them off.'

'What happened with the League of Women Voters?' she asked, a small, detached part of her mind wondering how she could be so calm. Her pulse rate had gone off the chart. Her blood pounded so in her ears, it was a wonder she could hear herself think. And she asked him about his dinner as if this were the most normal of circumstances.

Danjermond frowned in the pale wash of light that reached his face. 'In view of all the recent tragedies, I thought it inappropriate to allow the festivities to go on as they would have ordinarily.'

'A selfless gesture.'

A small, feline smile tucked up the corners of his mouth. 'I can be a very generous man, when I so choose.'

'Did you "so choose" with my sister?' Laurel asked bitterly, her voice trembling with rage, her left hand trembling badly enough to rattle the small plastic bag holding Savannah's earring.

He tipped his head in reproach, but his gaze went directly to the evidence, and anger rolled off him like steam. 'Now, Laurel, you don't really expect me to answer that, do you?'

'You might as well,' Jack said, easing out from behind Laurel. He took a step and then another to Danjermond's left, forcing him to split his attention between them. 'You're gonna kill us now, too – right?'

Danjermond contemplated the question for a moment, finally deciding to be magnanimous and gift them with an answer. 'C'est vrai, Jack, as you might say yourself. It isn't quite according to my plan, but adjustments must sometimes be made.'

'Sorry to inconvenience you,' Jack drawled sarcastically, moving a little forward, enough to draw Danjermond's full concern. The barrel of the gun swung even with his chest.

'That's near enough, Jack. Don't come any closer.'

'Or what?' Jack taunted. 'You'll shoot? You're gonna shoot anyway. Dead is dead.'

'No, no, mon ami,' Danjermond purred. 'There is most definitely a difference between instant death and being made to beg for death. Your cooperation could make all the difference for Miss Chandler.'

Jack weighed the odds, not liking them. Danjermond was going to kill them. Heaven only knew what kind of hell he planned to put them through. He had murdered at least six women, brutally, horribly. Jack had long ago ceased to care what happened to himself, but the idea of anything like that happening to Laurel was intolerable. He couldn't just stand helpless and let it happen. Damned if he was going to play into the hands of a madman.

Never looking away from Danjermond, he grabbed Laurel's arm and jerked it up, shining the beam of the flashlight in Danjermond's face, at the same time, twisting his body to shield Laurel and push her off to the side.

Danjermond swore and flung an arm up to block the blinding light. The gun bucked once in his hand, the explosion reduced to a soft thump by the silencer. A fat Chinese vase on a stand along the wall shattered, sending shards of porcelain flying in all directions. Water cascaded to the floor, and delphinium stems fell like pickup sticks.

Propelled by Jack's weight, Laurel stumbled sideways and fell to her knees. The flashlight sailed out of her grip and crashed to the floor, rolling out of her reach, sending bands of bright amber light tumbling across the wall. She tried to scramble after it, but Jack was in front of her and Danjermond beyond him, and it was clear the battle between them was far from over.

Head down, Jack lunged for Danjermond, planting a shoulder hard in the man's chest. The two of them landed on the polished wood floor, inches from the head of the stairs, and began wrestling for control of the gun. Jack grabbed hold of Danjermond's arm and slammed it hard against the floor, but before he could shake the pistol loose, a white-hot pain sliced into his right side, momentarily shorting out all thought and all strength.

Howling in pain and rage, he twisted around to find the source. A jagged shard of white porcelain protruded from his side with Danjermond's hand closed around it, as if around the hilt of a knife, blood oozing from between his fingers. As Jack reached to dislodge the impromptu knife, Danjermond swung the gun up and slammed it into his temple.

In the blink of an eye, the balance of power shifted. Jack struggled to stay on top as his consciousness dimmed, but the world dipped and tilted beneath him. Then suddenly they were rolling, through the water, over the broken vase, pain biting, muscles burning, heart pumping.

He managed to get a hand on Danjermond's throat and started to squeeze, but the district attorney was on top of him and pulling back, pulling away. Bringing the gun up. Laurel might have screamed, but all Jack was certain of was the sharp *thunk!* of a bullet splintering the floor millimeters from his head as he let go of Danjermond's windpipe and knocked his gun hand to the side.

Jack surged up, twisting to reverse their positions. Pain sliced through his side, pounded in his head. He blocked it out and fought on adrenaline, groping, pushing, turning. Danjermond's back slammed into the delicately turned white balusters that guarded the second-story landing, cracking one and shaking the whole balustrade, and the gun came out of his hand and skidded across the floor, toward the stairs.

Laurel jumped back as they wrestled, wanting to do something, but the gun was on the other side of the hall and the flashlight was somewhere on the floor beneath the tangle of grunting, straining male bodies. She glanced around for something, anything, she might use as a weapon, finding nothing, but she wasn't about to settle for prayer.

Do something, do something, she chanted mentally, turning and running back into Danjermond's bedroom. She had to find a weapon, something she could hit him with, stab him with, anything.

751

Jack slammed a left into Danjermond's face, then lunged up and forward, scrambling for the gun that was just out of his reach. His fingertips hit the silencer, and it spun away, sliding through the pool of water and broken glass. Focused, intent, he grabbed for it again and closed his fingers around the rubber grip on the handle.

At the same time, Danjermond found the flashlight. As Jack came up and started to swing around with the gun, Danjermond came to his knees and swung the flashlight like a club. It caught Jack a vicious blow on the side of his head, snapping his head around and clouding his vision to a gray blur. Brain synapses shorted out. The gun fell from his hand and tumbled down the steps, firing a useless shot into the wall.

He tried to stand, tried to block the second strike, but the messages never connected with the appropriate muscles. The blow landed, and everything faded to black.

Laurel burst out of the bedroom with a heavy ginger jar lamp in her hands, brandishing it like a club to swing at Danjermond's head. But he grabbed her arm as she stepped into the hall and her gaze went to Jack, and the lamp crashed to the floor.

'Jack!' Laurel screamed as he lay limp at the top of the stairs, the side of his face running with blood. Thoughts flashed fast-forward through her mind in that one elongated moment she stood there staring at his still body in the dark hall – he was dead, she'd lost him, she was alone with a killer.

She started to move forward, but Danjermond held her.

'Careful, Laurel,' he said quietly, his breath whistling in and out of his lungs. She could smell his sweat and his expensive cologne. She could smell blood and could only hope it was his. 'You don't want to step on glass,' he murmured.

'You're insane,' she charged, her voice a sharp, trembling whisper. She twisted around to glare up at him, her breath catching at the sinister cast his features took on in the orange-shadowed glow of the flashlight.

'No,' he said in return, smiling ever so faintly, his cool green eyes on hers, unblinking. 'I'm not.'

30

'I dislike compromise as a rule,' Danjermond said as he worked at binding Jack's hands and feet. 'But one has to be flexible in times of emergency.'

Laurel sat on an elegant Hepplewhite shield-back chair in the front hall, her wrists bound to the arms with straps of white silk, her ankles bound to the front legs. She wanted to scream, but silk clogged her mouth, leeching away the moisture and literally making her gag.

She watched Danjermond with a sick sense of dread pushing at the base of her throat and a strange, lethargic numbness dragging down on her. Dreamlike. No, nightmarish. If she could believe this was a nightmare, then it wouldn't be real. A trick of the mind. She couldn't decide what would be better – to be alert and terrified with the reality of the situation, or to be stunned senseless and believe it was all a bad dream.

Danjermond looked up at her, as if he had expected some response to his statement. He had taken the time to change out of his tuxedo and neatly bandage the hand he had cut during the fight. He was now in black jeans, boots, and a loose-fitting black shirt, an outfit that made him look like a modern-day warlock.

He had spread a blanket out on the floor so as not to get Jack's blood on the Oriental hall runner, and he checked and double-checked the bindings on his unconscious prisoner to make certain they were tight enough to hold but not so tight as to make impressions beneath the padding he had used first. The Bayou Strangler's victims were the ones who were to have bruises on their wrists, not the Strangler himself.

Laurel's gaze kept slipping down to Jack. She wasn't certain he was breathing. He had been unconscious nearly half an hour. Utterly motionless. Blood, sticky and brilliant red, matted his hair and glazed his temple and cheek like candy on an apple, but she couldn't tell whether or not he was still bleeding. *Dead men don't bleed*. She stared at his chest, willed it to move.

'I would rather have brought him to trial,' Danjermond went on. He rose gracefully and picked up a glass of burgundy from the hall table, sipping at it thoughtfully, savoring the wine. 'That was my intent all along. A murderer on a spree in Acadiana, running unchecked, no one able to stop him – until he reached Partout Parish. That was why I left the bodies where they could be found. There are, of course, many ways of disposing of bodies so as not to leave a trace. A man can get away with murder again and again if he is intelligent, careful, coolheaded.'

He finished his drink. The grandfather clock chimed the hour. Eleven. Jack still didn't move.

With a sigh, Danjermond hauled him up off the blanket and maneuvered him into a fireman's lift. Without a word to Laurel, he went down the hall, toward the kitchen. She heard the back door open and close, then silence.

Oh, God, Jack, please be alive, please come around. I don't want to die alone.

Alone. As Savannah had been, as Annie had been, as all those other women had been. God knew how many. He had left six bodies to be found because that suited his plans. There could have been dozens more, all of them gone without a trace, swallowed up by the Atchafalaya, never to be seen again, the victims' cries for pity heard only by the swamp.

The numbness began to fade, and fear took its place. Tears rose to burn the backs of her eyes.

A vision of Savannah's face floated through her mind. The scents of formaldehyde and ammonia with death lingering, cloyingly sweet, beneath it all. The stainless steel table. The draped figure. Prejean murmuring something apologetic. Savannah's face – not as it had been in life, but as death and its aftermath had distorted it.

The back door opened and closed again. Footsteps sounded in the kitchen, in the hall. She bit down hard on the gag and tried to beat back the tears with her lashes. *Don't show fear. He feeds on fear. It gives him power.*

'All right, Laurel,' Danjermond said, kneeling down to untie her feet. 'We're going to go for a little drive.' He looked up at her and smiled like a snake. 'To my little place in the country.'

Laurel knew the action was both futile and foolish, but she kicked him anyway, as hard as she could with her bare foot, catching him square in the diaphragm. He fell back, wheezing as the air punched out of his lungs, the look on his face worth whatever price he would make her pay.

Coughing, he rolled onto his knees and forced himself to his feet with one arm banded across his belly. He leaned against the hall table, sending her a sideways glare of pure, cold hate.

'You'll pay for that, Laurel,' he ground out between short, painful gasps.

She met his glare evenly. *Don't show fear. It gives him power.*

'Defiant little bitch,' he said, straightening slowly. A fire lit in his clear green eyes, glowing bright as he came toward her. 'Just as your sister was,' he said, smiling. 'Right up to the end. She defied me. Dared me. I think she quite liked being tortured. There was a certain . . . exultant quality to her screams.

'And she laughed,' he said softly, bending over her, careful to stay to the side. He brought his face down even with hers so she could see the wicked pleasure on his features as he spoke. 'She laughed as I took my blade and cut her breasts.'

Slowly, he reached out and cupped her breast with his long, elegant hand, testing its weight, molding its shape. He rubbed his thumb over the hard nub of her nipple, around and around, his gaze locked on hers, then began to tighten his fingers, squeezing and squeezing until she could no longer hold back the whimper of pain.

'She was completely insane by the end,' he whispered.

Laurel shuddered, trembling with revulsion as much as fear. She had expected him to strike back at her physically, but this was much worse. Psychological torment, giving her the intimate details of her sister's murder. She would rather have been beaten. And he knew it.

'She wanted the sex,' he said, untying her wrists from the arm of the chair. 'Even when she knew I was going to kill her, she had an orgasm. Even as I tightened the scarf around her throat, she had an orgasm as powerful as any I've ever experienced.' He met her eyes once again, that slight smile curling the corners of his wide, sensual mouth. 'But then they say death is the ultimate aphrodisiac. Perhaps you'll experience that kind of ecstasy, as well, Laurel.'

She was shaking uncontrollably as he hauled her up out of the chair and tied her hands behind her back. Thoughts of Savannah flashed through her mind. Thoughts of the two of them as children, before Ross had entered their lives and twisted the paths they would take. In that moment she hated him as much as she hated Stephen Danjermond. More. But it wasn't going to do any good to dwell on the past. The present held a clear and imminent danger. She was going to need all her energy, all her strength – physical and mental – directed to getting out of this alive.

Danjermond guided her out of the house the back way and took her around the side to an old carriage house that now served as a garage. They bypassed the Jaguar in favor of an old brown Chevy Blazer. He stuffed Laurel in the passenger's side and closed the door.

While he walked around the hood, she twisted around awkwardly to see Jack facedown on the seat behind her. He lay motionless, body bent at an awkward angle, feet on the floor behind the driver's seat. The dark blanket had been tossed carelessly over him and covered him from chin to boots.

In minutes they were driving out of town without having passed a car or a pedestrian who might have taken notice of them. When they were well beyond the town limits, alone on the bayou road, Danjermond pulled over and untied the gag.

Laurel spat the wad of cloth out of her mouth, glaring at him in the gloom of the cab. 'You won't get away with this,' she charged hoarsely, her throat and mouth parched.

Danjermond flicked a brow upward as he slid the Blazer into gear and started them on their journey once again. 'What a trite line, Laurel. And ridiculous. Of course I'll get away with it. I've been getting away with it since I was nineteen.'

He chuckled at her involuntary gasp of horror, like an indulgent adult amused at the naivete of a child. 'I was a college student,' he began, leaning over to push a cassette into the tape player. Mozart whispered out of the speakers, orderly and serene. 'I was an excellent student, naturally, with a great future ahead of me. But I had certain sexual appetites that required discretion.

'My father introduced me to the pleasures of the darker side of sex – indirectly. As a boy I once followed him on a visit to his mistress, and watched them through a window, fascinated and aroused by the games they played. I followed him many times after that before I realized he knew. When I was fourteen, he allowed me to visit her myself. To be properly initiated.

'I learned the privileges of wealth and the wisdom of discretion early on. So I knew better than to appease myself with a coed. Whores are much better at pleasing a man, anyway, and so much more expendable. I got carried away with one. Strangled her while we were in the throes of passion.

'No one ever suspected me. Why would they? I was the handsome, talented son of a prominent family, and she was just another whore who fell victim to a professional hazard.'

Laurel listened, shocked and repulsed at the lack of feeling in his voice. He was completely without remorse, completely devoid of conscience. Emotionless, soulless; he had said so himself that day at Beauvoir. There would be no appealing to his sense of mercy or humanity, because he didn't have any. Escape was their only hope, and that hope was so slim as to be nearly nonexistent. She couldn't leave Jack, couldn't take him with her even if she could somehow get away. And what chance did she have out here, barefoot with her hands tied behind her back? None. If Danjermond didn't get her, something else would.

They turned off the bayou road and onto a narrow dirt track that led deeper into the swamp. Branches slapped at the sides of the truck as it crept down the path. The growth was so thick, the headlights barely penetrated. Laurel felt cocooned within the dark confines of the Blazer, cocooned in a bizarre world where Mozart played while a murderer calmly told her his life story.

She tried to memorize the turns they took, tried to gauge how far they had gone, but everything seemed distorted – time, distance, reality. Her arms ached abominably from being held in such an unnatural position. Every lurch of the truck sent pain shooting between her shoulder blades.

She glanced into the backseat at Jack, and her heart flipped over as his left eye blinked open for a moment. He was alive. Though not much, it was something to hang on to.

'You surprised me, Laurel,' Danjermond said. He slowed the Blazer to a crawl as he piloted it through a shallow stream. As they climbed back onto what passed for solid ground out here, he stared at her across the cab, his lean face lit by the glow of the dashboard instruments. 'I really didn't think you would break into my home. Even after you lied to Kenner, I believed you were too "by the book" for that.'

'I don't give a damn about the book,' she said. 'I believe in justice. I'll take it whatever way I can get it.'

He smiled at that, truly pleased, and faced forward again as the path turned and ran along a bank. 'I was right. You're much stronger than you thought, Laurel. It's really too bad I had to catch you with evidence that could incriminate me. I would have enjoyed a longer game.'

He would have put her through Scott County all over again – the accusations, the disbelief, the desperation, all of it – for his own amusement. Laurel wanted to berate him for calling life and death a game. She wanted to rail at him for playing with the system he had sworn to uphold, but there seemed no point in it. He believed he was above it all – the law, the rules of society. And to date he had no reason to think otherwise. He had fooled everyone, had gotten away with the ultimate crime again and again.

'What will you do with us?' she asked flatly, deciding it was better to know than to imagine.

'I will lead the sheriff out to the site of a grisly murder-suicide I heard about through an anonymous tip. Poor Jack went over the edge at last. Couldn't deal with what he'd done to you. Took a gun and shot himself in the head.'

Thereby obliterating the head wound Danjermond had already dealt him. And she would die exactly as the others had died, tying Jack firmly to the series of murders. Danjermond would see to every detail. No one would question the outcome.

'Not quite the glamour of a trial,' she muttered.

'No. I do regret that. But still, there will be a good deal of regional and national news coverage, and as district attorney I will, naturally, act as spokesman for the parish.'

'Naturally.'

'Don't take it too hard, Laurel,' he said, as he piloted the Blazer into a ramshackle shed that was tucked between trees and nearly obscured by vines. He cut the engine and turned to face her. 'You couldn't have won. You couldn't have stopped me.'

Laurel said nothing. She stared at him across the narrow space of the cab, remembering clearly the way he had looked over the dinner table in the house she had grown up in. *'You believe in evil, don't you, Laurel?'*

Yes, she did believe in evil, and she knew without a doubt that she was looking into the face of it.

He hauled Jack out of the truck first, carrying him out of the shed and

757

out of her sight. Laurel struggled against the cloth that bound her hands, while her gaze scanned the cab for some kind of weapon – both acts useless. Danjermond was back for her quickly, and guided her ahead of him by her bound hands, down the muddy bank to an old *bâteau* that bobbed among the reeds.

At his prodding, she climbed in and sat on a black tarp on the flat bottom of the boat, with Jack lying in a heap behind her. Laurel leaned back and brushed her fingertips along the scuffed leather of his boots, trying to take some comfort in his nearness, and then her fingers stumbled over the lump of a knot.

Danjermond's attention was on the outboard motor. With a snap of his wrist, it roared to life and the boat eased away from the shore.

The black water gleamed like glass under the light of a partial moon. Bald cypress and tupelo trees jutted up from the smooth surface, straight and dark, looming above the swamp. In the near distance, thunder rolled and lightning flashed pink behind a bank of clouds. South, Laurel thought automatically, fingers picking awkwardly at the knot behind her. A storm moving up from the Gulf.

A storm, Jack thought dimly. Or was the rumbling in his head? *Dieu*, his head felt like an overripe melon that had met abruptly with the business end of a hammer. He forced his eyelids open – a monumental effort – and tried to take stock of his surroundings. A boat. He could hear the weak whine of a small outboard, feel the buoyancy of water beneath him, smell the rank aromas of damp and decomposing vegetation that was the bayou.

Fighting against the urge to cry out, he turned his head a scant inch and tried to make out the image above him. Women. Two. One. The shape blurred and multiplied, came together, then divided. Trying to clear his vision drained his strength, and he slipped back toward oblivion.

'I find the swamp a fascinating place, don't you, Laurel?'

Laurel. He struggled into full consciousness again, the strain making him dizzy. Laurel. Danger. Danjermond. The fight came back to him in broken snatches, just the memory intensifying the pain in his head. Danjermond had clubbed him. He had a concussion at the very least. At worst, what he was lapsing in and out of was not consciousness but existence. He forced a message down from his battered brain to his fingers, flexing them slowly, slightly. They moved – he thought.

He rested then, and conversation came to him in bits, fading in and out like a radio with poor reception.

'. . . a perfect world in many ways,' Danjermond said, his voice hollow and distant, as if it were coming down a long tunnel.

'. . . for predators . . . senseless killing . . .'

'. . . thrill of the hunt . . .'

'. . . sadistic son of a bitch . . .'

He almost smiled at that. Laurel. She would stand up to a tiger and spit in its eye before it had her for lunch. Her courage never ceased to amaze him. She wouldn't back down from Danjermond. But Danjermond would kill her just the same.

While I lie here and let it happen.

Blackie's face loomed up behind his eyelids, snarling, taunting. '*Good for nothin', T-Jack. Always were, always will be.*'

The boat seemed to spin beneath him, and nausea crawled up the back of his throat. An old hand at hangovers, he fought off the sensations, opened his eyes, and focused them hard on Laurel's back until the pounding in his head was so loud and relentless, he thought it a wonder no one else heard it. Gathering his strength, he made one effort to push himself up, but at that moment the motor cut and the *bâteau* bumped gently against a dock. Knocked off balance, he slumped back down, groaning as his head hit the bottom of the boat.

Laurel fought against the overwhelming urge to turn toward the faint moan. It was best not to react. If Jack was coming around, she didn't want Danjermond to know. They needed whatever slight edge they could get. She groaned, twisting her head to the side, as if trying to alleviate a cramp in her neck. Danjermond flicked a glance at her as he tied the boat off.

They had moved toward the storm as the storm had been moving toward them. It was overhead now. The sky was rumbling and crackling. The first flurry of fat raindrops hurled down on them, as Danjermond grabbed her by the arm and hauled her up on the rickety dock beside him. The boards groaned and dipped, elastic with rot, but they held as he turned and herded her onto shore and toward a tarpaper shack that teetered on stilts a few yards back from the dock.

The rain came harder. Lightning shattered the black of the sky, and the clouds ripped open, drenching them. Gasping, Laurel ducked her head as the water sluiced down her face. Danjermond hustled her up the steps and produced a key to the padlock that held the door shut.

The cabin was pitch-black inside, but the scent of blood assaulted her nostrils and balled in her throat. Human blood. Her sister's blood. Laurel squeezed her eyes closed as fear surged through her in a flood tide and bile rose up the back of her throat. Beneath the noise of rain on the tin roof, she could hear Danjermond shuffling around, striking a match.

'It isn't much, but it's dry,' he said, playing the humble host. Amusement tinted his voice as he reached out a hand and cupped her chin. 'Now, Laurel, you're not the sort to hide. Open your eyes and face your destiny head-on.'

He had lit candles, half a dozen or more. Tall tapers with flames that flickered and danced, their light waving sinuously over the meager contents of the ten-by-twelve room. A small dresser stood along the wall to her left with a cluster of candle stands on its scarred surface. A straight chair sat directly in front of her. Beyond it stood two more small, spindle-legged stands, one on either side of the bed, both of them crowned with a flickering candle.

All this Laurel took in through her peripheral vision, the facts filing themselves away in her brain while her attention was riveted on the bed. It was iron. Black iron. Slender pieces curved into graceful shapes to form the headboard and footboard. The four posts were low, entwined with pencil-slim iron vines and topped with polished brass finials in the shape of a spade. It was beautiful. Sinister. White silk ties hung from the headboard. A drape of sheer, pristine white silk covered the mattress, but dark stains showed through like shadows. Bloodstains.

Savannah had lain on that bed and had the life bled out of her, choked out of her. And Annie. And women whose names she would never know. Their screams filled her head like the echoes of ghosts. Their pain clawed at her. Their panic rose in her throat.

The thunder rolled. Lightning flashed through the window as bright as a spotlight. The rain poured down, pounding like nails on the roof.

Beyond the cabin stretched miles of wilderness. No one to help her. No one to hear her cries. No mercy. No justice. She thought of Jack and what might have been if fate had taken a kinder path for them both. Wondered dimly if any of it had ever been within their power.

Then Danjermond's hand closed on her arm and he led her toward the bed.

The rain came down as hard as hailstones, pelting exposed skin, slicing and pounding. A real frog strangler. Frogs, hell, Jack thought, coughing as the water pooled in the bottom of the boat and drifted into his mouth. *Strangler.*

The word slapped him into consciousness, and he jerked his head up, grunting hard at the pain, the dizziness. *Laurel.* She was gone. Danjermond was gone. Danjermond would kill her. *And you're lying in a goddamn boat in the rain. Worthless, good for nothing, son of a son of a bitch.*

Gritting his teeth against the agony, he tried to right himself, confused at first that he couldn't seem to move his arms. Pain came in staccato bursts as he rolled partway onto his back and took the pounding rain full in the face. His hands were tied behind him. His feet were tied.

But he had moved his feet. He thought. He tried now with some success. They were bound but not tightly. Loose enough to struggle against. Loose enough that he could work his boots off, and the binding with them.

The task sapped his energy, left him gasping for breath and choking on the rain, but he managed to get his feet free. Slowly he rolled over onto his knees and tried to bring his head up an inch at a time. The pain beat relentlessly, like a mallet inside his skull, the rhythm syncopated with a driving urgency.

Laurel. He had to get to Laurel. He would die in the process or in the aftermath, of that he had no doubt, but he had to try. For her . . . to make her proud . . . to show her he loved her . . . he hadn't told her . . . should have told her . . . wished he could have made it work . . .

The thoughts swirled around his brain as he struggled to stand in the boat, and the blackness swirled with them. Flecked with stars . . . promising relief . . . beckoning . . . sweeping in . . .

Fighting him was futile, but she fought him just the same. There was a principle involved. Honor. She would not go meekly to her death like a sheep to the proverbial slaughter. She wouldn't make it easy for him, would do her utmost to spoil his enjoyment.

The instant Danjermond's hand settled on her arm, Laurel jerked away from him and bolted for the door. He lunged after her, catching hold of her ponytail and jerking her back hard enough to make her teeth snap together. Laurel shrieked, in anger and pain, and twisted toward him, lashing out with her feet, kicking at his knees, his shins, any part of him she could hit.

His lips pulled back against his teeth in a feral snarl, and the back of his hand exploded against the side of her face, snapping her head to the side, bringing a burst of stars behind her eyes and the taste of blood to her mouth. The room seemed to swirl once around her, and unable to use her arms for balance, she staggered sideways and fell. On her knees, she tried to scramble for the door, never taking her eyes off it, willing herself to stand, to run, to get away. Adrenaline pumped through her like a drug, driving her forward even when Danjermond caught hold of her bound wrists and hauled her up and back, wrenching her arms in the sockets.

But her struggles stilled automatically as the blade of a dagger glinted in the candlelight.

Laurel's heart drummed, impossibly hard, impossibly loud, as the blade came nearer and nearer her face. It was slim and elegant, like the hand that curled around its golden hilt. The blade was polished steel that had been ornately engraved from the guard to the tip. Beautiful, deadly, like the man who held it.

'I would prefer if you would cooperate, Laurel,' he said, stepping in close behind her, his left hand sliding along her jaw, fingers pressing into her flesh. The knife inched nearer.

The pitch of his voice was the same even tone that had always somehow managed to strike a nerve in her, but no longer was it devoid of emotion. Anger strummed through every carefully enunciated word as he brought the dagger closer and closer. Her breath caught hard in her lungs as he touched the point of it to the very tip of her nose.

'Be a good girl, Laurel,' he murmured, sliding the dagger lightly downward. Over her upper lip to her lower lip. He let it linger in the valley between as if he were contemplating sliding it into her mouth. 'I know Vivian raised you to be a good girl.'

'*Be a good girl, Laurel. Don't make trouble, Laurel. Keep your mouth closed and your legs crossed, Laurel.*' Somehow, she didn't think this was a situation that had come to her mother's mind during those lectures on comportment.

Laurel said nothing, afraid to speak, afraid to breathe as the blade point traced down her chin, down the center of her throat to the vulnerable hollow at its base. If she struggled now, would he slice her throat and be done with her? That seemed preferable, but there were no guarantees. If she waited, bought time – even a minute or two – might she find another chance to break away?

Outside, the storm had rolled past and gone on its way toward Lafayette, but the rain continued, pelting the roof, tapping at the single, small window like bony fingertips. What kind of chance at survival would she have in the swamp? What kind of chance would she have here?

The dagger rested in the V of her collarbone, the point tickling the delicate flesh above. The sensation made her want to gag. She swallowed back the need, felt the tip bite into her skin. Every cell of her body was quivering. She felt as fragile as a twig, poised to snap in Danjermond's grasp. Her eyes filled, but she held back the tears, held back the hysteria, grabbed her sanity with both mental hands, and hung on as Danjermond's words about Savannah echoed in her head – '*She was completely insane by the end.*'

She wouldn't give him the satisfaction. He had killed her sister for sport, meant to climb on the bodies of his victims to fame in a profession he mocked with every breath he took.

'Damn you,' she whispered, seizing her anger and hate and using them as shields to beat back the terror. 'Damn you to hell.'

Danjermond leaned close, bringing his face down next to hers, rubbing his cheek against hers. 'I don't believe in an afterlife, Laurel,' he murmured, dragging the dagger down between her breasts, where her heart pounded beneath the thin fabric of her T-shirt. With a slight motion of his wrist the point nipped into the cotton and nudged her breast. 'I'd say, if there's a hell, it's here and now, and you're in it with me.'

A scream tore from her throat as Danjermond sliced violently downward with the blade, opening her T-shirt from neck band to hem. Instinctively, she bolted back, colliding with his long, lean body, her hands pressing against his engorged sex. His left arm snaked around her middle and held her there as he eased his pelvis forward and raised the dagger slowly to her left breast.

Razor-sharp, the blade kissed along the plump swell beneath her nipple, and her blood beaded, bright red, along the knife edge, rolling across it like pearls to splash down on the floor. The pain came seconds later, throbbing with her heartbeat. And finally the tears spilled over her lashes and rolled down her cheeks, pale counterpoints to the drops of blood sliding down her rib cage.

'Be a good girl, Laurel,' he purred, rubbing himself rhythmically against her. She shuddered in disgust as he traced his tongue up the line of her throat to her ear and caught the lobe between his teeth. 'There's no justice out here for you to find, Laurel,' he whispered. 'The only law is my law.'

He dragged her back to the bed, ignoring her resistance. With the dagger, he sliced the ties that bound her hands and quickly shoved her down on the bed, planting a knee in the middle of her chest to pin her down with his weight. Using the ties that had tethered other victims to this deathbed, he lashed her to the headboard.

'Too bad it's raining so,' he said conversationally as he sat on the bed beside her, admiring the sight of her glaring up at him. Taking up the dagger, he dipped it in her navel and drew it lightly up the quivering flesh of her belly, between her breasts. 'I would have brought Jack in and tried to rouse him for the performance. He should witness what his imagination only hints at, see for himself the power of it, the seduction. He has the darkness within him. Before he dies, he should witness the glory of it unleashed.'

The blade hooked under the neck band of her T-shirt and, with a practiced move, he sliced it open. With the tip of the dagger he peeled back the ruined garment on either side, baring her to his gaze.

'Dainty,' he whispered, rubbing the flat of the knife against her uninjured breast. 'Exquisitely feminine.'

'What happened to make you hate women so?' she asked, choking with revulsion as he dipped a thumb in the blood from the wound he had inflicted and painted it across first one nipple then the other.

Danjermond raised a brow. 'I don't hate women,' he said, sounding amused. 'This is my hobby. It's nothing personal.'

'I consider being murdered highly personal.'

He rose with a sigh and rounded the foot of the bed to sit on the straight chair. He dropped the dagger on the floor at his feet and casually began to unbutton his shirt. 'Well, yes, I suppose you would, all things considered. But then, that's been a longtime problem of yours, hasn't it, Laurel? You tend to personalize everything. That's what got you into such trouble in Georgia. You were too personally involved. You couldn't see the forest for the trees. We both know how important perspective is in building a case. A prosecuting attorney must be cold, thorough, detached. Emotionalism only leaves the door open for surprises from the opposition. As you've discovered for yourself, Laurel, I am a very thorough man. I don't tolerate surprises.'

Without warning, the cabin door exploded inward, the rotted frame splintering, rain and wind sweeping in, and Jack with it. His momentum carried him forward, and he bowled into a stunned Danjermond before the district attorney could do more than turn and gape at him. The wooden chair disintegrated into kindling beneath their combined weight and the two men crashed to the floor.

Laurel screamed Jack's name and struggled to sit up, trying to see. She could hear the struggle – the scuff of boots on the floor, the grunts and curses. She knew in her heart what the outcome would be. Jack was fighting literally with both hands tied behind his back, and he had to be barely conscious. Danjermond would kill him, just as surely as he would kill her – unless she could somehow manage to get herself free.

She wriggled up toward the headboard, inches at a time, trying not to strain against the ties that held her by her wrists, trying to move into a position that would give her some slack. Gritting her teeth, she concentrated on shutting out the sounds of the fight and tried to focus her mind on her bonds. Silk. Smooth, strong, slick, slippery. Her hands were small, fine-boned, her wrists delicate. If she concentrated, moved just right, didn't tighten them by struggling . . .

Jack struggled to keep Danjermond pinned beneath him, but his strength ebbed and flowed in erratic bursts, and his faulty sense of balance made it difficult to determine which way was up. He fought as best he could with his knees and his feet, jabbing, kicking when he could, ignoring the pain that screamed through his head and bit into his side.

Danjermond writhed beneath him, twisting, heaving upward. He reached for the dagger that had skittered across the floor, and Jack threw his weight hard against him, sending them both crashing into a table along the wall, and sending the table crashing to the floor.

Candles rolled like tenpins, their flames licking at anything in their path, catching hungrily at the old tarpaper that lined the walls of the shack.

The men rolled away from the fire, still struggling for supremacy. Jack managed to catch his adversary in the belly with his knee, but Danjermond struck back viciously, slamming his fist into the side of Jack's head. The pain sent Jack rolling, plummeting toward unconsciousness like a diver shooting toward the bottom of a black, black ocean.

He fought against it, held his breath, and fought to claw his way back up through the dark, up through the fireflies that swarmed in his brain. His vision cleared enough for him to make out flames licking greedily up the wall and three wavering versions of Danjermond silhouetted in front of the glow. Three devils from hell. Three Danjermonds raising an arm, three daggers gleaming, slashing toward him.

He dove for the man in the center, his shoulder hitting solid mass at the same instant the dagger plunged into his back. He felt a rib break, then a strange vacuum sensation in his chest. What little strength he had left sucked out of him, and he fell heavily to the floor, mouthing Laurel's name.

'Jack! Jack!' Laurel shouted his name to be heard above the roar of the fire that was devouring the wall of the shack. She shouted a third time, frantic to hear him answer, knowing that he wouldn't.

She had seen Danjermond rise, had seen the dagger slash down. Jack was dead. She was alone. It wouldn't matter that she had managed to work one hand free. She wouldn't have time to untie the other. Danjermond was on his feet already. Coming toward her. The dagger dripping blood. Jack's blood. Danjermond smiled like Lucifer himself against the backdrop of flame.

Don't look at him, work the knot, work the knot. Crying, coughing against the black smoke that was beginning to press down from the ceiling, she scrambled across the bed, fumbling to free her left hand.

Jack raised his head a fraction of an inch. All he could see were Danjermond's feet. Moving toward Laurel. From some deep inner well he drew the last drops of will and courage he had and swung his legs. He hit Danjermond in the backs of the knees, and the district attorney's legs buckled beneath him, sending him sprawling headlong into the flames.

The screams were terrible. Inhuman. Engulfed in flame, he managed to stand and tried frantically to run, stumbling and falling across the bed. Laurel screamed and flung herself off the other side as the silk spread ignited in a flash.

She staggered back from the ghoulish scene, choking on the smoke, eyes stinging so badly, she could barely hold them open. There was nothing to be done for Danjermond. And in that terrible, fire-bright moment, she didn't know whether she would have tried. All she knew with any certainty was that the cabin was going up like a tinderbox, and if they didn't get out quickly, she and Jack would share Danjermond's fate.

Crouching low to escape the worst of the smoke, she ran around the foot of the bed and dropped to her knees beside Jack's sprawled form.

'Jack!' she screamed, the sound almost consumed by the roar of the fire. 'Damn you, Jack, don't die on me now!'

She pulled at him, gritted her teeth, and threw all her strength into dragging him toward the door, shouting every inch of the way. Her curses and pleas penetrated the fog of Jack's consciousness. Her determination made him move his legs when he wasn't sure he could remember how. He latched onto the sound of her voice and the feel of her hand and the incredible power of her will, and used it all to propel himself forward. At the door, he caught hold of the splintered frame and got his feet under himself.

'Hurry!' Laurel shouted, wrapping an arm around his waist and trying to take his weight against her as they stumbled down the steps and started toward the bayou.

The rain was still falling, but it was no match for the old dried wood of the shack. The cabin lit up the night sky like a torch. The fire devoured it as if hell had opened up to consume all evidence of the atrocities that had been practiced there, devouring the perpetrator, as well, condemning him to a justice that was absolute.

Weak, choking from the smoke, staggering under Jack's weight, Laurel fell to her knees on the muddy bank, and Jack went down like a ton of bricks beside her.

'Oh, God, Jack! Don't die!' she demanded, bending over him. 'Don't be dead! Please don't be dead!'

She bent over him, bawling, her tears combining with the rain to splash down onto his face. With hands shaking violently, she touched his soot-covered cheek, his lips – trying to feel his breath, fumbled to find a pulse in his throat. Was it weak and thready, or was that her own?

His lashes fluttered upward, and he looked at her. Tried to smile. Tried to catch more than a teaspoon of air. 'Hey, angel,' he whispered, then had to try to breathe again. 'Mebbe I'm one of the good guys after all.'

Then darkness swept over him like a velvet blanket, and he surrendered to the pain.

31

He remembered in dreamlike bits and pieces. A force of will pushing, prodding, begging, swearing, goading him to move his feet. Take a step and another. The pain was blocked out, but not the weakness or the sense of disconnection between his mind and his body. He remembered feeling as if the essence of him were floating free, connected to his physical shell by the finest of threads. He remembered the powerful temptation to sever that tie and just drift away, but Laurel kept yanking him back. He remembered wondering vaguely how she could be so little and be so strong.

There was a boat in the fragments of memory. And rain. Rain and tears. Laurel crying over him. He wanted to tell her not to. He couldn't stand the thought of making her cry, even though he knew he had done it more than once, bastard that he was. There were many things he wanted to tell her, but he couldn't gather more than the urgency. The words bounced around in his head like bubbles. He had forgotten how to use his voice. The frustration exhausted him.

Darkness, light. The murmured voices of men and women in white clothes. Couldn't be heaven; he never would have gotten in the gate. Had to be a hospital.

Cool hands touching his arm, his cheek. Soft lips and whispers of love. Laurel.

Laurel had stayed with him, Nurse Washington had told him as she shuffled around his room, fussing and checking things. She was a short, squat, cube of a woman with mahogany skin and little sausage fingers that read his pulse with the feather-light touch of expertise. Miz Chandler had visited during the days he had spent in deep, drugged sleep. But didn't she have a lot on her plate, the poor little thing, what with her sister being killed and the sheriff's investigation and all? And weren't they lucky to have escaped with their lives? Mr. Danjermond a killer – Lord have mercy!

Jack tuned out the memory of her chatter now as he stood on his front step and watched Leonce drive away. As the Monte Carlo rolled out of sight, his gaze was drawn inexorably to Belle Rivière. At the core of his pounding head were thoughts of Laurel. She had sat with him, kissed his cheek, whispered that she loved him. He didn't deserve her love, but he knew without a doubt it was what had made him hang on to life when he could have easily let go. Laurel's voice coming to him through the mists, begging him to live, bribing him with her love.

Huey crawled out from under a tangle of long-neglected azalea bushes and climbed up in the step to give Jack's hand a sniff and a lick of welcome. Jack stared down at the hound, meeting the pair of weirdly mismatched eyes, and grudgingly scratched the dog's ear. Huey groaned and thumped his tail against the bricks.

'You're all the welcome I get, eh, Huey? That's what I get for breaking out.'

He pushed the door open and wandered into the house, letting the dog trail after him. Huey abandoned him to nose around the old draped furniture in search of mice. Jack took as deep a breath as he could manage and climbed the stairs one excruciating step at a time.

Somehow, he had expected to feel at home once he made it to his bedroom, but as he looked around, he realized this wasn't his home at all. It was still Madame Deveraux's boudoir. He was just marking time here. He hadn't done much more than change the sheets on the bed. He hadn't made this house his home, he admitted as he sank down on the mattress, wincing at the bite of his broken rib and the stab wound that sliced the tissue around it. It was his prison, the place where he turned on himself and endlessly cracked the whips of self-flagellation. The one thing he had done to make the place his own was hanging all his neckties in the live oak out front, and that had been more a sign of shame than of freedom. Like a flag on the door of a plague victim, it was a warning to those who would venture near that he couldn't handle a life that required ties of any kind.

That life had blown up in his face, and he had had to live with the fact that he'd been the one to lay the powder and light the fuse. What he had rebuilt for himself in the aftermath of the debacle was simple and safe for all concerned, he reminded himself as he stared up at the intricate plaster medallion on the ceiling. He had his writing, his pals at Frenchie's, enough willing lady friends to warm his bed when he wanted.

He had an empty house and an empty heart and no one to share them with save the ghosts of his past and a dog that wasn't his.

Jack shoved the thought away with an effort that had him squinting against the pain. His life swung on a pendulum between penance and parties, and it suited him fine. He was accountable to no one, responsible for nothing.

And still Laurel Chandler had managed to fall in love with him. The irony of it was too much – Laurel, the champion for justice, upholder of the law, in love with a man who had broken so many so carelessly, a man for whom justice was a sentence to emotional exile. She offered him everything he had ever wanted, everything he'd told himself he could never have.

If he had a shred of honor, he would walk away and leave her to fall in love with a better man than he could ever be.

The service was private. A blessing and a curse, Laurel thought. The pain went too deep for her to share it with people she hardly knew, but some of the deepest wounds had been inflicted by the only people present.

She sat with Caroline and Mama Pearl on one side of the chapel. Vivian and Ross sat on the other side, in the same pew but not together. Separated by an invisible wall of hate, together only out of Vivian's automatic attempt to put a 'normal' face on ugly family secrets. She would never confirm or deny the rumors once they began to spread – a lady didn't lower herself to airing the dirty laundry in public. She would most likely divorce Ross quietly and go on with her life as if he had never been a part of it, leaving him hanging alone on the gallows of public opinion.

Ross stared dully at the casket with its blanket of pink tea roses and baby's breath. Laurel wondered if he felt remorse or just regret for being exposed after all this time. She wouldn't have allowed him to come, regardless, but the choice hadn't been hers to make.

She wondered how he would weather the storm of accusation and condemnation once the story of the abuse became common knowledge – and she would damn well make certain it became common knowledge. Caroline had told her once that Ross was a weak man. If there was a God in heaven, the shame of the truth would crush him.

Reverend Stipple had pitifully little to say in the way of a eulogy. Laurel would have preferred he say nothing, but it was his church, this church where she and Savannah had been christened, where their father had pledged to love their mother until death. Where death had brought them all and half the parish to see Jefferson Chandler off to the next world.

She looked down at the lace-edged handkerchief she held and remembered too well how Savannah had sat beside her and taken her hand and whispered to her, '*Daddy's gone, but we'll always have each other, Baby.*'

Always.

Now death had brought them here again, these people whose lives were tied together in a painful knot of common experience.

Toward the end of the ceremony, Conroy Cooper slipped in the back and took a seat by himself. Laurel met his somber, soul-deep blue gaze as she walked out of the church, and saw the regret there, and the love, and she ached at the irony that of all the men her sister had known, she would love the one whose nobility put him out of her reach.

When everyone else had gone out, Laurel lingered in the shadows of the vestibule and watched Cooper lay a single white rose on the casket. For a long while he just stood there, head bent, one hand on the polished wood, saying good-bye in his low, smooth voice.

Laurel had labeled him an adulterer and condemned him for not being able to give Savannah the kind of commitment she wanted. But he had loved her as best he could, he said, while trying to keep a vow to a wife who no longer knew him. He had given Savannah all he could. It wasn't his fault she had needed so much more.

There was no coffee served after the burial. No time for normalcy to dilute the grief with talk of crops and babies and everyday things. Caroline drove them home to Belle Rivière in silence.

Mama Pearl went into her kitchen to take solace in the familiar ritual of brewing a pot of *café noir*. Caroline laid her keys on the hall table, turned and took Laurel's hands in hers. 'I'm going upstairs to lie down for a while,' she said, her strong voice softened by strain to a whisper. 'You should do the same, darlin'. It's been a terrible few days.'

Laurel struggled for a game smile and shook her head. 'I'm too restless to sleep. I was thinking I'd go into the courtyard for a while.'

Dark eyes shining with the kind of love and wisdom a mother should possess, Caroline nodded and squeezed Laurel's fingers. 'You've got it so pretty out there. It's a good place to look for a little peace.'

Laurel didn't expect to find any, but it was true she was going to look, to hope.

She strolled the pathways slowly, with her hands tucked deep in the pockets of her flowered skirt. A fitful breeze swirled the hem around her calves and brushed the ends of her hair across her shoulders. The day was warm and muggy with a sky that couldn't decide whether it should be a clear blue bowl or a tumble of angry gray clouds.

Despite the moods of the weather and the aura of sadness that hung on Laurel like a shroud, the garden offered what it always did. The rich scents of green growth, the soft, sweet perfumes of flowers bathed her senses, trying to soothe, offering comfort. Even the weeds tried to distract her, reminding her they needed pulling. Tomorrow, she promised, moving on down the path, searching for something she couldn't hope to find today.

She felt as if a crucial, turbulent chapter of her life had been abruptly closed. Savannah was gone. The secret they had shared all these years had been unlocked. Danjermond was dead, and while the investigation continued into the dark shadows of his past, and the headlines were still selling papers, the bottom line had been drawn. Between her testimony and the evidence in his home, and at the scene, Stephen Danjermond, Partout Parish district attorney, son of the Garden District Danjermonds of New Orleans, had been established as a serial killer.

She should have felt a sense of closure, she thought as she took a seat on the corner bench. But she felt more as if something had started to unravel and had been discarded with loose threads trailing all around. Savannah was gone. They would never have the chance to repair the cracks in their relationship; it would remain forever broken. The secret had been revealed, but she would go on being Vivian's daughter; Ross Leighton would forever be a part of her past, if not her future. Danjermond was dead, but every life he had touched would be indelibly marked by his betrayal.

And then there was Jack. The man who was bent on paying with his life for the sins of his past.

If she had a brain in her head, she would walk away, make a clean break, start over somewhere new. What had happened between her and Jack had happened too quickly, too intensely. A relationship had been the last thing she'd come home looking for, and Jack was far from the kind of man she had pictured herself with. He had used, abused, and derided the profession they once had in common. She didn't respect him because of it – but she respected the way he had turned himself around in the end, even if he claimed his motives were selfish. He lived a life built on shirking responsibility, another trait that irritated her strong sense of duty, but she had seen him defy that role time and again.

She kept seeing him in her mind's eye – not the rogue male with the wicked grin and the ruby in his earlobe, but the lonely, haunted man whose hidden needs reached deep into a loveless boyhood. She kept feeling the ache inside him that had touched her own heart, the ache of longing for things he thought he shouldn't have.

Jack painted himself as a user and a cad, good for nothing but a good time, but the fact of the matter was he had saved her life and shown a heroism that was exceedingly rare in this world.

He was so distinctly two different people. The trouble was convincing the 'bad' Jack that the 'good' Jack existed and deserved to have a chance at something better than a half life filled with pain.

Laurel closed her eyes and let her head fall back, turning her face up to the sky as the sun played hide-and-seek with the clouds. For a moment she let herself picture a life where they could truly start over, where people really did rise above their pasts and lived beyond the shadows, where she and Jack could simply have happiness without all the baggage attached.

'Dreamin' about me, sugar?'

It took a moment for Laurel to realize the voice had not come from inside her mind. Her eyes flew open, and she swung around on the bench to see him standing there leaning against one of Aunt Caroline's armless goddess statues in faded jeans and a chambray shirt hanging open down the front. He was pale beneath his tan, and there were lines of strain etched deep beside his dark eyes that combined with the shadow of his beard to make him look tough and dangerous. He smiled his pirate's grin, but there was too much pain in his eyes for him to quite pull it off.

'What the devil are you doing here?' Laurel exclaimed, shooting up off the bench. 'Don't you even try to tell me Dr. Broussard released you!'

He winced a little as the volume of her voice set off hammers in his head. *'Mais non,'* he drawled. 'Me, I sorta escaped.'

'Why does that not surprise me?'

'It's no big deal, *'tite chatte,'* he grumbled, rubbing a thumb against the goddess's forehead. 'All's I got is a boomer of a headache and a busted rib.'

Laurel scowled at him, jamming her hands on her hips. 'Your lung collapsed! You've got a concussion and stab wounds and—'

'Bon Dieu!' he gasped in mock surprise, black hair tumbling across his forehead as he looked up at her with wide eyes. 'Then mebbe I oughta sit down.'

He caught an arm around her waist and pulled her down with him, his actions stiff and slightly awkward, but effective enough to land her on his lap as he took his seat on the bench. She immediately scooted off him, but swung her legs around and remained on the bench beside him.

Jack frowned, shooting her a sideways look. 'I must be losin' my touch.'

Laurel sniffed. 'Losing your mind is more like it. You belong in a hospital. My God, you weren't even conscious the last time I saw you!'

'I'll live.'

Dismissing the topic, he looked down at her, taking in the deep shadows beneath her eyes. She couldn't have looked more exquisitely feminine or fragile, like a priceless piece of porcelain. That fragility had frightened him once, before he had discovered the strength that ran through it like threads of steel. But he had a feeling the strength was flagging today.

'How about you, sugar? How you doin'?'

'Savannah's funeral was today,' she said quietly.

Jack slipped an arm around her shoulders and eased her against him, pressing a kiss to the top of her head. It was all he needed to do. Laurel splayed her hand against his warm bare chest, above the pristine white bandage that bound his ribs, and simply cherished the way his heartbeat felt beneath her hand.

'I would have been there for you if I could have.'

She looked up at him, her face carefully blank as she tried to assess the shift of feelings in him and between them. 'You don't do funerals.'

'Yeah, well . . .' He sighed, fixing his gaze on the roses that climbed the brick wall beside them. 'That doesn't stop me from losin' friends, does it? It only stops me from being one.'

'Is that what we are?' Laurel asked quietly. 'Friends?'

'You saved my life.'

'And you saved mine,' she returned, rising to pace in front of the

772

bench with her arms crossed tight against her. 'What does that make us? Even?'

'What do you want it to make us?' Jack asked, hearing the edge in his voice and cursing himself for it. He hadn't come here to fight with her. He had come for – what? And why? Because he couldn't stay away? Because he thought he had to end what had taken root and twined around his heart like the ivy that curled around the foot of the bench? *You can't have it both ways, Jack.*

'I want more,' Laurel admitted. If that made her a fool, then she was a fool. If it made her weak, then she was weak. It was the truth. Too much of her life had been tied up in lies. She stopped her pacing and looked him in the eye, as sober as a judge. 'I love you, Jack. I keep telling myself I shouldn't, but I do.'

'You're right, angel.' Gritting his teeth against the pain, he rose slowly. 'You shouldn't,' he murmured and moved toward the gate, avoiding looking at her. If he looked at her, he would never be able to walk away.

'Not because you don't deserve it, Jack,' Laurel said, catching hold of his arm. 'Because it would be easier not to. But I had an easy relationship once, and it might have been safe, but it wasn't fair to either of us.

'I can't take the easy way out, Jack,' she murmured, already trembling inside in anticipation of his answer. 'Will you?'

'Sure,' he said, his voice little more than rough smoke, his eyes trained on some indistinguishable point in the middle distance. 'Haven't you figured it out by now, sugar? I'm a coward and a cad—'

'You're neither,' Laurel said strongly. 'If you were a coward, they would have buried me beside my sister today. If you were a cad, you wouldn't be trying so damn hard to do the noble thing and walk away from this.'

Tears rose effortlessly in her eyes, riding on the crest of her emotions. She tightened her grip on the solid muscle of his biceps, her small fingers barely making a dent. 'In a lot of ways you're as good a man as I've ever known, Jack Boudreaux,' she said hoarsely. 'I'd like a chance to make you believe that.'

And he wanted to believe it. God in heaven, how he wanted to believe it. The need was an ache within him he had spent a lifetime trying to bury. The need to be worth something, the need to be important to somebody.

He closed his eyes against it now, terrified the need would swallow him whole, terrified this moment was just a dream, a cruel joke, as every small hope of his childhood had been a cruel joke. It didn't make sense that she should love him. It didn't follow the plot line of his life that he should have this chance at happiness. There had to be a catch. The other shoe would drop on his head any minute now.

He just stood there, waiting, staring past her. His chin was quivering as he pressed his lips into a thin line. He blinked to clear his vision.

'Haven't you paid enough, Jack?' Laurel whispered. 'Haven't we both?'

'I dunno.' He tried to shrug, winced at the pain. 'You want a husband? You want babies?'

More than anything, she thought. The idea of giving him a second chance at those dreams, the idea of giving him a child, of the two of them creating a brand new life that would begin with no mistakes and no regrets was a wish she had scarcely let herself imagine.

'I want a future,' she said simply, the wish too precious, too fragile to voice. 'I want to go beyond the past. I want you to go with me.'

A life beyond the past. A life he had told himself he could have only in his dreams. He stepped back from her, slicking a hand back through his hair to rub the back of his neck.

Laurel watched him, holding her breath while her heart raced.

Jack turned and faced her, seeing all her hope, her fear, her pure, sweet beauty.

'I told myself if I had a drop of honor in me, I'd walk away from you,' he said softly. His lips twisted at the corners into a crooked, ironic smile. 'Lucky me, I never had much to start with.'

Laurel went into his arms, her heart overflowing. She pressed her cheek against his chest. 'You've got more than you know,' she whispered.

'I've got all I need if I've got you,' he said, and he lowered his mouth to hers for a kiss that was both bonding and beginning, promise and fulfillment . . . and love.

Epilogue

The pirogue *slices through the bayou, as silent as a blade. The sun melts down in the west, as rich and warm as molten gold. All around, the swamp is dim and hushed. Waiting, peaceful. The frogs sing among the lilies. An egret glides down to join its mate in their nest of sticks on the trunk of a fallen cypress.*

I look down at the woman in the boat. She smiles as if I own the moon. The courage of a tiger. The gentleness of a dove. My wife. I was nothing without her.

I pole the boat forward, toward home, and know contentment for the first time in my life.

Glossary of Cajun French Words and Phrases Used in This Book

allée	avenue, path
allons danser	let's dance
allons jouer la music, pas les femmes	let's go play music, not women
arrête sa	stop it
baire	mosquito netting
bâteau	boat
beau-père	stepfather
bébé	baby
bon à rien, tu, 'tit souris	good for nothing, you, little mouse
bon Dieu	good God
bon Dieu avoir pitié	good God have mercy
bonjour	good day
c'est assez	that is enough
c'est la vie	that is life
c'est vrai	that is true
c'est la guerre	that is war
catin	doll
cher/chère/chérie	term of endearment
coonass	slang term for Cajun, often derogatory
dépêche-toi	hurry up
espèces de tête dure	you hardheaded thing

etalon	stud, stallion
grand rond	literally 'big circle,' traditionally called at the start of a fight
grand-mère	grand-mother
gris-gris	spell, charm (as with voodoo)
joie de vie	joy of life
jolie fille	pretty lady
laissez le bon temps rouler	let the good times roll
Le Mascarade	The Masquerade
ma belle	my beautiful
ma douce amie	my sweet love
ma bon pichouette	my good little girl
mais oui/mais yeah	but yes
mais sa c'est fou	that's crazy
ma jolie fille	my pretty girl
'Ma Petite Fille Est Gone'	My Little Girl Is Gone
merci/merci boucoup	thanks/many thanks
mon ami	my friend
mon coeur	my heart
oui	yes
pas de bétises	no joking
pas du tout	not at all
petite fleur.	little flower
pirogue	canoelike craft
restaurant et salle de danse	restaurant and dance hall
roux	flour browned in fat, used for thickening gravy etc.
s'il vous plait	please
sa c'est de la couyonade	that is foolishness
sa me fait de le pain	I'm sorry
sa c'est honteu	that's a shame
son pine	his penis
tcheue poule	chicken ass

777

'tit boule	little balls
'tite ange	little angel
'tite chatte	little cat
traiteur	folk healer
tu menti	you lie
une belle femme	the pretty woman
va-te'n	go away
'Valse de Grand Mèche'	The Big Marsh Waltz
viens ici	come here